SEVEN DREAMS

SEVEN DREAMS

A BOOK OF NORTH AMERICAN LANDSCAPES

by

William T. Vollmann

VIKING

SEVEN DREAMS

ABOUT OUR CONTINENT
IN THE DAYS OF
INDIAN SERVICE

**Whose Scouts and Cavalrymen
(Commanded by Generals Howard, Gibbon, Sturgis and Miles)
Gave the *Nez Perces, Umatillas, Flatheads & Bannocks*
No LESS than
the ***OREGON DREAMERS*****

(Protected by the Government of our United States)
Determined that

They Deserved
**and no MORE than
I Feed My
DEAD BUFFALO
Because You Can't AMERICANIZE**

sweet
WALLOWA
nor throw down the plank at

* Big Hole *
**without
TEACHING INDIANS**

*** the Constitution ***
**by means of wholesome compulsion.
Someday they'll learn that**

THE AMERICANS ARE THEIR FRIENDS!

As Inferred From
CAMPAIGN MEMOIRS,
then Bowdlerized for All Sensibilities

b y

WILLIAM T. VOLLMANN

*(Nicknamed by Better Shots
"WILLIAM THE BLIND")*

VIKING

An imprint of Penguin Random House LLC

375 Hudson Street

New York, New York 10014

penguin.com

Maps and illustrations by the author

ISBN 978-0-670-01598-6

Printed in the United States of America

1   3   5   7   9   10   8   6   4   2

FIFTH DREAM

THE DYING GRASS

For Teresa

*F*or the most part, a civilized white man can discover but very few points of sympathy between his own nature and that of an Indian. With every disposition to do justice to their good qualities, he must be conscious that an impassable gulf lies between him and his red brethren of the prairie. Nay, so alien to himself do they appear, that having breathed for a few months or a few weeks the air of this region, he begins to look upon them as a troublesome and dangerous species of wild beast, and if expedient, he could shoot them with as little compunction as they themselves would experience after performing the same office upon him.

PARKMAN, *The Oregon Trail* (1849)

CONTENTS

The reader is encouraged to use the Chronology and Glossaries only as needed while reading *Seven Dreams*. The first gives context to characters and events in the text. The second define and sometimes give the origin of words which might be unfamiliar. Glossary 1 summarizes how and why specific characters have been fictionalized. In Glossary 2, the table of brevet ranks might help readers who wonder why Captain Perry is addressed as "colonel." As for the Source-Notes, they can be ignored or skimmed; their function is to record my starting points, which may interest travellers in other directions.

LIST OF MAPS

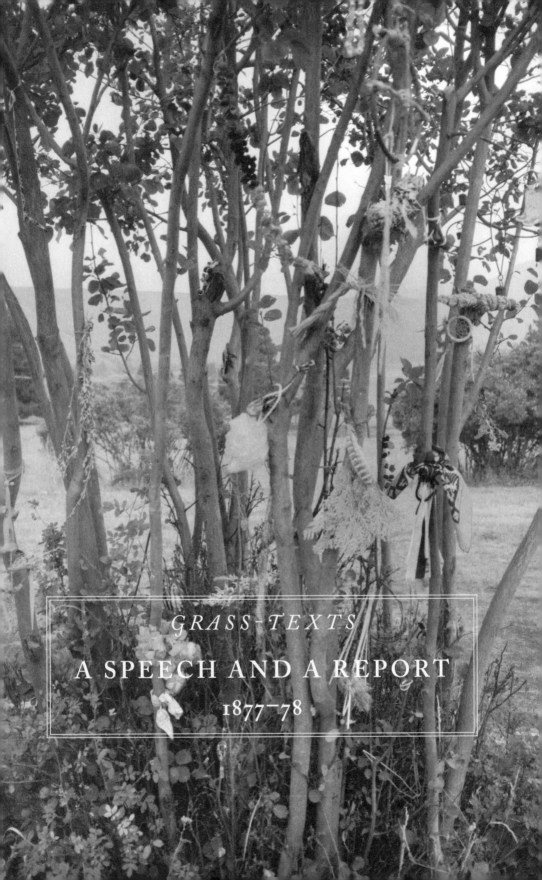

GRASS-TEXTS

A SPEECH AND A REPORT

1877-78

GRASS-TEXT I

AN INAUGURAL SPEECH

1877

*T*he President-elect advances into the Senate chamber and delivers his inaugural address (a saddlebag full of salt pork): *The permanent pacification of the country upon such principles and by such measures as will secure the complete protection of all its citizens in the free enjoyment of all their constitutional rights is now the one subject in our public affairs, which all thoughtful and patriotic citizens regard as of supreme importance.*

LORDY LORD, what could have transpired in our Republic, to render her citizens so unprotected?—Indian troubles, Mexican perils, our vast ocean front, the Silver Panic?—Well, I happened by Walt Whitman voting last November, and he'd thought it through; he wrote his ballot for free enjoyment, all right. They call him original, unusual, unsound, SATANIC, a true American. That means he's fixing to die. He's still revising his poem "Old War-Dreams." If you've ever seen him scribbling away with his superannuated hands, you'll know our nineteenth century's nearly gone. The twentieth's going to be twice as good. That's why I wish Walt could wake up from his war-dreams, which are grey and disappointingly dark, like so much Wyoming jade: *Long have they pass'd, faces and trenches and fields,* but no more of that, *where through the carnage I moved with a callous composure, or away from the fallen;* no more, a solid dozen years after we've saved our Union, why not keep facing forward? Let us comb away the relics from Walt's fields, fill in his trenches with marble monuments, and enshroud those faces (skeleton-visages all) with the thick white juice of Indian hemp. *Long have they pass'd;* so let them. Walt's sadness may have grown as long as his white beard, but he fights it; he votes straight Optimism ticket; as for me, I'd wish all sadness away, because our Republic's now superior to a hundred years old! In the next generation we'll annex Canada, I'll bet.

The retired colonel beside me would rather finish the job in Mexico first. Also, he's mortified about Little Big Horn. That's why he wants to enlarge the Army.—So sorry; it's going the other way.— I can see myself in each of the metal buttons of his drab-hued vest. And before us all the President-elect shines white-linened at wrist, neck and breast! His long narrow white face, eminently suited for being printed on paper money, his tapering beard, sunken eyes, bushy brows, distinguished temples and cliff-like forehead make of him such a statesman of the drum-corps that I cannot begrudge him either of his inaugurations (the first took place secretly just last Sunday). Up behind him broods his majestic wife—Lemonade Lucy, they call her; her dream is to outlaw booze and cleavage at the White House. She's as shiny, solid, heavy and comforting as a Colt Model 1873. O, and who could miss Dan Sickles? He's the one-legged general with the scowl and the moustache whose telegrams to four Southern states gained our candidate the victory even after he'd conceded. May the best trickster win! *Long have they pass'd,* so why can't we finally count ourselves permanently pacified? They say he's going to pull our troops out of the South. *I* say a standing army's un-American. The colonel's old enough to believe anything; I won't pick on him—but let the fools out West take care of themselves. We took care of *our* own Indians. We did what we had to and went home.— Howbeit, our President-elect, who's ever more grandly put together by the instant, I do confess, swore so sweetly upon his Bible just now that I fell in love with Government all over again! He's a walking compromise, by GOD; he won two days ago by a single electoral vote.

It might have been the most American campaign ever. *The dark horse from Ohio came in at an easy canter on the homestretch, beating the favorite of the field by a full length and a half.* I read that in the *Louisville Courier-Journal* last June. And now that dark horse is President! Praise the LORD and Dan Sickles. I'll never forget how the dark horse (a dark brown hackney, let's say) glared warily above his long beard, while William Wheeler, his Vice President, looked ever so sad, sulky and handsome. As for the opponents, Tilden was a chubby-cheeked, glib smiler, and his Vice President, Hendricks, appeared to be a Puritan with a secret. Even though Tilden's machine harvested two hundred and fifty-one thousand more votes than ours, *long have they pass'd,* because after the dark horse cantered sadly back to his paddock where Lemonade Lucy waited with the currying-brush, Dan Sickles, expert in gelding thoroughbreds, sent a basketful of late-night telegrams, with horse-racing tips attached. Republicans in South Carolina kept out the Democrats by force and refused to tally the returns of two counties. Hurrah! Louisiana would have gone for Hayes anyhow, I hear. Florida would have gone for Tilden. Had Oregon recognized her one Democratic elector, Tilden would have nibbled up that vote. But then I guess we might have annexed more Indians and turned *them* Republican! If this is too complicated for you, just remember a dark horse from Ohio, then the Electoral Commission's decision to let sleeping dogs lie, followed by the Democratic filibuster, the recess, Stevens's midnight call upon Bradley, who then decided not to count the Democratic votes, although Stevens might never have visited Bradley, who likewise might not have sold his influence, since some events do occur purely as a result of prayer; and we all lived happily ever after, thanks to the equivocal "Wormley Agreements." Land of the Pilgrims' pride, land where wet greenbacks dried; from every mountain side let freedom ring.

And don't say freedom comes free. The Texas & Pacific Railroad expects a handout now. Tennessee had better get the Postmaster Generalship. The South will endure another Republican administration, but no more Northern despotism, if you please! That's why they made the dark horse whinny out a promise to bring our soldiers home from Louisiana and South Carolina; you can wager your last dollar he won't stop there. And you know what, brother? It's all the same to me how they do things in Louisiana. We won the war and now let's go home.*

---

*In 1866 our Army mustered fifty-four thousand men. Now it's twenty-five thousand; *long have they pass'd.* Companies, regiments, brigades deflate like last year's wild grapes wrinkling on the vine. Maybe by 1886 we won't need an Army at all! The faster it shrinks, the better reconciled grow all those stoically retired slaveholders to our Government—not that I care about politics.

Our President-elect surely is a treat. Last year he was as green as a soldier's coffee beans. Now I can almost remember his name: Rutherford B. Hayes.— Another wounded war hero!— He's going to be a one-termer, because compromisers can't please anybody. How could he ever approach Dan Sickles, who's so famous that he once granted himself the privilege of donating a bone from his amputated leg to a museum? All the same, I enjoy him. He makes sad allusion to *the two distinct races whose peculiar relations to each other have brought upon us the deplorable complications and perplexities which exist in these States.* The retired colonel shakes his weary head at that, and I throw him a wink, for we both know exactly what complications and which perplexities. Now he and I have something in common! For what do we care about that other race? Didn't we bleed enough for them? I lost my son at Chancellorsville. Yes, sir. I keep his tintype right here in my pocket. That's Elias when he was sixteen. His chin takes after mine, but his eyes favor his mother's. He's one of thousands who paid for General Howard's negligence. My wife's never been the same. Some folks blame Hooker, but I say Howard should have done more than send out a handful of GOD——d pickets. And now the man's a brigadier general. I used to get apopletic on the subject of Howard, but, you know, *long have they pass'd,* so let 'em rot alone in their unmarked graves. Actually, I guess they mean to give them decent monuments now, or so I've heard. I rode out there in '67, just to try to understand that battle with my eyes, and a one-legged fellow said to me: Here's where the Secceshes came bursting through. We had no warning until dozens of deer rushed out from the trees. Our boys were stretched out along the Plank Road and the Orange Turnpike, down there . . .— Well, then we got friendly. I showed him Elias's tintype and he showed me his stump. We agreed: Nobody could have held that line. Stonewall Jackson took his fatal wound just past that ruined chimney, they say. I wish I could have seen *that* villain go down! And Howard's tent was up *there,* and him with his nose in a hymnal most likely. He faced most of our guns south—as if the enemy couldn't go around! That wasn't enough; he also gave away a brigade to Dan Sickles. They should have court-martialed him. I understand he retreated to that cemetery on the hill. Nobody can say where Elias fell, of course. I couldn't find any of his comrades. He kept to himself, that boy; he didn't make friends easily, not that people had anything against him, either. He was two days short of his nineteenth birthday. I guarantee that he didn't have much use for our *Christian General.* In one letter he wrote us, he put down that in Howard's hearing you couldn't say a word against the niggers. The way I look at it, when the Government calls on you to shed your blood, you've earned the right to speak your mind. And when you're forbidden to call a man *tyrant,* doesn't that make him one? Elias saw an officer drummed right out of the Army just for disagreeing with the idea of Emancipation. Don't mistake me; I wouldn't oppose it myself; I just don't trouble my appetite about it. Let the President-elect take care of his *two distinct races;* niggers are citizens now in all thirty-eight states of this Union; well, that's hardly my lookout; I don't see many niggers in Connecticut. (Just the other day, that old Walt Whitman remarked to me: *I can myself almost remember negro slaves in New York State, as my grandfather and great-grandfather own'd a number.*) Well, that General Howard's just crazy for darkies, apparently. Now it's come out that he embezzled Government funds on their behalf. And there's the real reason I'm in favor of shrinking down the Army: I want Howard cashiered. That won't bring Elias back, but perhaps it'll give me satisfaction. And Rutherford B. Hayes stands (if he stands for anything) for *convivial contraction.* To hell with war-dreams new and old; out with Howard! Just as in the Buffalo Country, so I hear, Crows will pull Dakota corpses off their tree-platforms and explode their guns right up against them, so I aim to blow up all my old sadnesses if I can, and live forever free from corpses. Therefore, my fellow Americans, even though I was a Tilden man, and Tilden got robbed, I'll sit here grinning and clapping all the way to the evening adjournment, the Congressmen flashing away on their dark horses, the dome of the Capitol shining overhead like a half-moon.

WILLIAM THE BLIND.
Washington, D.C., 1877.

GRASS-TEXT II

A REPORT

1878

---

*A*nd so the President-elect strides into the Senate chamber to say: *The permanent pacification,* as sharp and straight as a train's shadow, *of the country,* just as a brave man goes ahead to mark quicksand with sharpened poles so that Posterity can safely ford the river, *upon such principles and by such measures as will secure the complete protection of all its citizens,* even the ones at the Old Market in Saint Louis, *in the free enjoyment of all their constitutional rights,* O, don't remind me, *is now the one subject in our public affairs, which all thoughtful and patriotic citizens regard as of supreme importance.* What these principles are I don't remember (the colonel ought to, since he's a distinguished Indian fighter); as for the measures, let's call them simply *continual and energetic.* Hurrah for seven American dreams!

So let us fall asleep (ain't our President sominiferous?) and dream to death the golden-grassed camas prairies out West, so that we can pacify them, permanently, and upon such principles, & c, & c. Can we get the job done before the railroads strike? Quickly, reader, flitter westward with me, crossing the Little Missouri and then riding up along Crazy Woman's Fork of the Powder River; speed west through the Indian Territory, where we're already tightening the noose; ride super-westerly to the Arizona Territory, where we plant our corn with crowbars and (until General Howard's proudest peacemaking triumph) hunker down against Apache raids; thence to California, where we've just now whipped the Modocs; and so to good old Oregon, where pacification continues its progress, one case being explained by General Howard himself in terms as smooth as the mouth of a worn-out mare:

The "Report of Civil and Military Commission to Washington Territory and the Northwest" will be found published in the "Eighth Annual Report, Board of Indian Commisioners, 1876," commencing page 43. It will be seen by this report that the Commission failed to settle the difficulties with the non-treaty Nez Perces but made certain definite recommendations.

WILLIAM THE BLIND.
Portland, Oregon,
Department of the Columbia, 1878.

FIFTH DREAM

THE DYING GRASS

I

INDIAN SERVICE

1805‒77

The Indian service now devolving upon our army is necessarily arduous and unpopular. It involves a work that our peace-loving people think might be avoided. But fair-minded Americans cannot ignore, or fail to commend, the ability, industry, and perpetual sacrifices of their soldiers.

BRIGADIER GENERAL OLIVER OTIS HOWARD, U.S.A., 1881

And the Water and the Grass

and the water
and the grass
and the white ripples on grey water, and white clouds among grey clouds
and the wrinkled young silver skin of the water
and life-bright lichens on black branches

    and on the still, bright river, a man and woman slowly poling their
    log canoe

and the spiderweb (golden-green seed-wings already growing above the
darker leaves of maples this early in August)

and the smell of evergreens
and the living grass,
then the dying grass, brighter than an Indian basket

Nespelem

2009

and at the foot of Chief Joseph's grave, in the crotch of another tree, a
wilting feather, rags, and a twisted white stick dangling

PLENTY OF INDIANS ALL OVER
THE COUNTRY
1876–2009

. . . and then a pencilled manuscript on crumbling sheets in a beige folder, Blurick 1876, from between two of whose pages a yellow photograph sidled out like a flat-bellied cockroach. That was how I met the gaze of a fine half-breed girl who is dirt and bones now, with maybe a hank of grey or black hair to keep her company, or even a shred of moldy buckskin like a crumbling sheet in a beige folder, never mind a shard of bone breastplate trampled and lost like our memory of Blurick, on earth as it is in Heaven; come to me, girl, I'll be d——d if you won't do as I say! Don't look at me like that, or I'll . . .— I beg you, sir! No, please don't. I swear my heart is very good; there is not a bit of bad in it.— But none of that was written anywhere. Yellow locusts danced between the rocks. Even though the grass is dying we will do our best to find you a good reservation. But first we will do very well to establish ourselves. Nobody can be expected to put savages ahead of people. Get away from here or I'll put a bullet in you, I say! Why won't she look at me now? By GOD, she puts me in mind of White Bird hiding his face behind an eagle's wing! And then there's Joseph, whose eyes absorb my vision without giving me anything . . . In the Grande Ronde Valley (aspen leaves shimmering like coins, and distant cloud-shadowed pines blue like water) and then farther down that snaking creek-cañon of reddish-brown rock cutting deep into the yellow grass, way down in Wallowa, there used to be friendly or at least equivocal Nez Perce families some of whom spoke a kind of primitive English, called Chinook, and even helped us, more or less, back in 1853 or thereabouts, in the days when we read Horn's Guide and shop foremen still wore silk coats; Blurick's first wife lived above the grass, and even our tramps and socialists hesitated to go on strike—good years, one might suppose, but the cholera and the malaria were playing hide-and-seek in our American river towns. Poor Mrs. Blurick! Had her constitution possessed a trifle more "sand," she'd be a hundred and eighty-one years old to-day, in which case her husband might never have left home. He'd already disinterested himself in Nez Perces once he learned that they weren't really Pierced-Noses; don't ask me how they got their name. They were fine riders; I'll give them that. Some made fair Army scouts against other Indians. They were confiding, interesting, bewildering, intractable, ungrateful. Roaming Indians, we called them. In the end they declined to avail themselves of the advantages offered for their improvement. I'll grant that they themselves requested the Good Book—or, as they named it, *the Book of Light.* Reverend Spalding's log house, and the fruit trees of Lapwai, and all those Nez Perce farms of vegetables and corn made for a pretty picture, which might as well have been painted on the stage curtain of an opera house; presently it would split down the middle and withdraw into the walls, revealing the real entertainment. When we found gold in their country, Chief Joseph's father, who I am sorry to say had turned apostate, throwing down the Book of Light, tearing up the treaty that dispossessed him, then erecting a Dead Line of poles around Wallowa; and Old White Bird, who always waited before he spoke, both tried to keep us out (Old Looking-Glass was more politic), but we proved that it would profit them to oblige us. Old Joseph demanded: *What is your law?* We replied that he'd figure it out! We'd already dragged a previous treaty out of them, after the Cayuse War and before the final Rogue River War. Generally speaking, the first treaty with any nation of Indians goes down pretty easy, before we bind them to their promises and get out of ours. They still held a good piece of Northwest, as explained by the Indian Superintendent: *The Nez Perces Reservation is an immense tract of six thousand square miles, a territory far larger than the States of California and Rhode Island united.* But just then, as I was saying, we saw color in the quartz—bright yellow like a buffalo calf!—after which how could a just (and justly undermanned) Government exclude the miners? As for the rest of us, the railroad promised: *Your prairie farm will be a savings bank.* The Nez Perces accommodated themselves, or not. The descendants of those who signed the treaty and obediently Christianized themselves still dwell around Lapwai, even in this twenty-first century of ours. As for the others, such as Old Joseph, Old White Bird and the other malcontents, we could rely on their presence there in and out of the remnants of their allotment, right up until the summer of 1877; they made good neighbors throughout those seventy-two American years from when Captains Lewis and Clark first discovered their existence; right on through and beyond George Catlin's map of 1833, which is as elegant after its fashion as the crosses, diamonds and angular hourglasses of Sioux horse-beadwork; for across its wide white latitudes, horses and buffalo still run nearly wild across the golden grass through which the Columbia winds west by southwest to the Pacific, meeting Chinook Indians at its end, and before them, the Chilts; and in the upriver direction, after a blankness extending considerably east by northeast our voyage, the Flatheads, whom we'll soon pull in, because (as General Howard once explained to me) the partner of the player winning the first trick gathers the tricks for that deal. Futurity grins like the grass-skinned gape of a Nez Perce sweathouse, whose ears are interlaced poles—but from *here* to *there* will be awhile yet; as long as we camp *here*, the trail to *there* remains as long as the mummy-wrapped braids of that Brule Sioux chief Spotted Tail, as far as General Howard's pursuit of Joseph, as high as the Americans' GOD and as dark as an Indian's eyes. Hence why not leave the future to itself? Catlin closes his eyes to it; the Nez Perces can scarcely see it, being dazzled, no doubt, by the ever-rising luminosity of our cause: twenty-two years remain before the railroad treaty at Walla-Walla (here comes another long snake of Nez Perce riders with feathers in their streaming hair, waving an

American flag, ready to trade horses with us), eight more until the transaction they'll call the *thief treaty* and *we'll* name Necessity, then the last fourteen up to the war. Chief Joseph is unborn and General Howard three years old; don't imagine we're not on guard. In the vast triangle between the Columbia, the Multinomah and the Rocky Mountains, our mapmaker interrupts his whiteness with a discreet indication of the Snake Indians, to whom, they being enemies of our soon-to-be enemies the Blackfeet, we'll do the kindness of dealing with later, our oxen grazing for the night, and then our line of pale-tented wagons creeping forward. Southeast of that interesting tribe, not quite on the Multinomah, Catlin engraves our Nez Perces, rich in horse herds. So you see, getting at them is as convenient as palming the cards at euchre. Rush on to the seven-section map of Charles Preuss, published in the happy year 1846—thirty-one years of neighborliness left to go—and suggestively entitled TOPOGRAPHICAL MAP OF THE ROAD FROM MISSOURI TO OREGON. Congress prints ten thousand copies, so just maybe someone desires us to take that road (on which I will soon spy the torn beige canvas top of Blurick's wagon and its squeaking left front wheel): through the Buffalo Country and into the desert, until we come out into the bright river-breath at Farewell Bend, fording and ferrying west into Oregon, ascending the military road into orange grass swales and grey-green sagebrush (on the ridges the same dark green-grey cloud-shadows as at Little Big Horn), riding north-northwest past white outcroppings in the orange hills, crossing over a yellow-splashed ridge of orange grass and grey-lavender hills, approaching the bright yellow-green marsh-grass and yellow hill-horizons of the Grande Ronde country where Chief Joseph winters his horses along that high river resembling a late blue afternoon sky.— Old Joseph is dead by now; he has left tall poles to mark the boundaries of his country; Young Joseph has sworn never to sell his grave. But in Montana our steamboats now ascend through the Crow, Blackfoot and Flathead zones all the way to Fort Benton. In season we'll ring them all in. Sherman to Grant, 1868: *The chief use of the Peace Commission is to kill time which will do more to settle the Indians than anything we can do.* Why do these tribes hide from us whatever they have, like a squaw covering up her camas baking-pit? Just as here in America we play whist for a triple stake—this much a trick, that much a game, and this much a rubber—so in our Indian wars we venture such and such upon a battle, then whatever upon the inevitable outcome, and finally GOD knows what upon our secrets in Washington. *It will be seen by this report that the Commission failed to settle the difficulties with the non-treaty Nez Perces but made certain definite recommendations.—* Anyhow, why fight the Nez Perces? Haven't they been good Indians?— Yes, but they're now in the way of our stock animals. Besides, it's not merely Wallowa they claim. To hear them tell it, they're lords of a million acres! (Certainly no right to the soil can be obtained before confirmation by the Senate.)

Section VII, the best Preuss ever drew, stretches leftward, westward, from the Snake River or Lewis Fork of the Columbia (Blurick's party was now but two days eastward of here, having obtained the latest Indian news at Fort Hall, where our

California-bound gold-seekers passed the hat to tip Captain Travis and the scouts, said farewell to the caravan, and took the lefthand road, some few of the ladies waving their handkerchiefs good-bye), flowing away from the kindness of Latter-day Saints, above a blankness entitled S N A K E   I N D I A N S, then leftward along a curving flap of landscape which resembles meat bisected by veins and arteries and ending in dangling flaps of furry skin, westward and westward to the Powder River and **GRAND FORD**, across the narrow whiteness of **BLUE MOUNTAINS**—from whose vantages our aspiring ranchers may find it pleasant to dream northeast, watching how those silver-blue Wallowa peaks draw the storm-clouds in—then down the narrowing meat-flap around the Wallah-Wallah River to Fort Wallah-Wallah, above which, north of Longitude 118° and west of Latitude 46°, lies a kidney-shaped blankness entitled N E Z   P E R C É   I N D I A N S, where the journey ends, so it must by definition be the goal. And these Nez Perces swore that their hearts were good; they swore it three times. Hence we were still their loving neighbors, treating them as befits allies of Americans. Underground germinated order #016026, a beige-orange cross-reference card in a wooden drawer in the Oregon Historical Society: *Nez Perces, date unknown, location Idaho.* A Nez Perce woman and a boy in pretty white man's clothes crouch by a rock wall, in stereo view, their faces foggily peering off into an alternate past, the woman long-braided, and . . . Don't glare at me with those Indian eyes! I don't know you or your child. Where have your horses grazed now? Where's the frontier? And where could they have gone, our medals from Oregon's several Indian Wars? *There was plenty of Indians all over the Country,* says Blurick, so mustn't there have been plenty of wars? Now in hot attics and institutional vaults of decidely sub-archival womblike moistness our campaign ribbons have turned the colors of cattails and yellow grass. Our gratefully recognized services to Oregon have bro-ken into brittle bits in acidic folders. And our forced marches in the State of Mon-tana, our vigilance, courage and intelligence; the battles we lost in Idaho and the natural advantages we improved in Washington, all of which places used to be Territories, and before that Indian forests and golden grass, no, please don't. The treaty of 1855 and the Nez Perce War of 1877, the hazy grey ridge to the south and black birds on the lake, well, the way I look at it, we will have done very well to save any scraps of those whatsoever. Blurick 1876, there's a shard of Oregon peacetime! And then that's as old fashioned as a plug hat. *And at that time,* runs Blurick's manuscript, *we had 105 men able to handle a rifle. So with 105 of the old rimfire rifles and 32 wagons with families and men on horseback we left Kansas city with a man by the name of* Travis *or Captain Travis with 6 Scouts on Horseback that Sure Could Shoot.* And on the front porch of his two-storey house, *date 2002, lo-cation Portland, Oregon,* former headquarters of the Department of the Columbia (Brigadier General O. O. Howard commanding), where streetcars, steel bridges and raspberries fight against the golden grass, tall, lean Mr. Thomas Robinson lights another fluent cigarette. The street is hot and the grass is brown. Tom squints. He enjoys his tobacco slowly. Then it's darkroom time again. The safelight is already active, its housing closed down to bloodshot near-blindness; and the tray siphon runs as quiet as the voice of the Crow squaw Kills-Good. Tom closes the door behind him. Beside the paper safe, instants of Indian war, fixed on slices of silvered glass, await replication. That's how they survive a trifle longer—and reveal their tones to us. Once Tom printed a plate that appeared to be solid black; he left it under his cold light for a day and a half, until the silver halides on the paper found out what hid there: Kwakiutls in canoes, paddling across some coastal bay. Back then, so I've heard, there were plenty of Indians all over the country, Comanches launching their final raids out of Mexico, Crows fighting Sioux and hunting buffalo, Cheyennes riding the high and low plains, Apaches defying us in the desert mountains (pour him another drink, and Doc will describe to you from head to toe the corpse of a white woman he once found violated in the dirt and bristling with their arrows, back when he served in Crook's army); Modocs pleading to be left alone on their lava beds (now they'll rise up), Flatheads even yet asserting that our shadows are our souls, Umatillas and Cayuses running loose, Nez Perces not entirely reduced to reason. Well, Tom can print several tribes at once; for don't think he's a mere one-enlarger man! A trifle sallow, like a first-stage fixing solution tinted with stop bath, he can expose near about as well as Doc could shoot. He guards the whites of Blurick's eyes, to keep them white. That's the mark of a fine art print. (Never mind if they're actually bloodshot.) He sights his grain focus magnifier on the many shining buttons on Colonel Miles's bearskin coat. He hunts shadows around Joseph's out-of-focus daughter—her name was Sound Of Running Feet—preserving tonal variation no matter what else has gone. He burns and dodges with both hands, all the while footpedaling his enlarger on and off like a one-man band; I have never seen as acrobatic a darkroom artist as Tom. When the wand whirls in his left hand and the hole-cut card shimmies in his right, Chief Joseph's face shines wanly greenish-grey on the easel at f/5.6, all tones reversed—and the timer beeps, Tom steps on the pedal, and Joseph goes dark. Now Tom repositions his tools, having nothing to go on but his miraculous positional memory, then toe-taps the pedal, so that the sad chief comes pallidly back, while the dodging wand now holds back the light from the gorget at his throat. Meanwhile Tom darkens the fringed edge of the Pendleton blanket in the dead photographer's studio. For years he has bought up the relics of deceased lensmen: their half-blind dusty old bellows cameras, their trays, tongs, enlargers, contact printers, and above all their negatives, some of which are glass plates whose scratched silver-black memories have begun to frill at the edges. Talk about dust and time! He blasts away dust with an isothetical air compressor. He keeps his fading color slides in freezers. Sheet film and roll film lurk in their private archival cabinets. Here's a daguerreotype of General Howard when he was young, clenching his brows, which are near about as low as General Sherman's, and in the background, Lincoln faces General McClellan in the stifling shade of a Sibley tent, both their foreheads branded with stripes of sun-glare.— Tom, my friend, you'd better hoard that image beneath a marble slab.— The timer chirps like a prairie dog, and another picture of Kills-Good practically prints itself; she's kneeling in the grass by her kettle, boiling buffalo bones for soup, while the Crow Agent poses behind her with his left fist on his hip. Howard's bunch never met her when they were chasing Joseph through Yellow Stone, but Looking-Glass must have been a friend of hers. Now for a glass plate portrait of Colonel Perry, whom our Nez Perces whipped at the Battle of White Bird Cañon. In his latest rubberbanded bundle of scratched tintypes, for which he paid bottom dollar at a Pendleton estate sale, Tom possesses, maybe, a likeness of Lieutenant Wilkinson, Howard's wily aide-de-camp, although I'm actually more curious to lay eyes on the late Lieutenant Theller. The sulphurous fumes of fixer, less sweet in the nostrils but sweeter on the tongue than the powder-cloud from a Sharps carbine, prevent the landscapes of this old war-dream from darkening away; *long have they pass'd, hurrah, hurah, hurrah!* When Tom dies, his treasures will be inherited by that ungrateful university whose darkroom became first a larder of janitorial supplies, banker's boxes and adding machine tapes, and then, once the plumbing leaked, a room used by nobody—for Tom's out of style now, like a buffalo hunter. He owns more silver halide glimpses, glances and stares than any one soul could ever take in, but he has catalogued them by the tens of thousands and he has printed thousands and there are some he knows very well. Had he time enough to live, he would print up the Nez Perce War as lovingly as Peopeo Tholekt drew his horses on the pages of old Boston ledgers, making the animals blue, yellow, grey or vermilion, carefully shading them every which way, and sometimes braiding their tails—but photochemicals are getting expensive, and Tom's collection is as mortal as all of us. When old negatives begin to perish, they sometimes give off a vinegar smell. Tom has to print those fast. In a year or two, the contrast will go; they may turn pink; then they fade away, like the ambrotype of the second Mrs. Blurick, who like her predecessor died young. A certain war haunts me like a certain creek, scarlet with alkali, which bleeds into the Powder River; and what if its glass plates deteriorate to nothing before Tom prints them? General Howard is its hero, Chief Joseph its villain; and Blurick figures in it only by way of Doc, who may be our greatest American ever. Just as we refrain from shooting buffalo when we are creeping up on Indians, so I won't nail Doc just yet in this book about the Nez Perces. Tom has already shown me a dozen portraits of Joseph, and I am hoping that he possesses at least one plate depicting Shooting Thunder, who was accomplished at whistling for elk through an elderberry stalk and who while spying out good horses to steal helped his war-friends murder a music teacher named Richard Dietrich in Mammoth, Wyoming, as the day dimmed and the summer of 1877 approached the end of its pale yellow straining. To the Nez Perce remained nearly a month of flight until Colonel Miles trapped them at Bear's Paw. (This Miles is likewise a great American. That's why he died a general.)— First to spy the victim was White Thunder, better known by his nickname *Yellow Wolf* on account of a certain WYAKIN vision which he won as an adolescent in the Wallowa Mountains; his white necklace and long black locks had not yet been tonally reversed by any silver halide process; *long have they pass'd.* His mother Swan Woman was Joseph's first cousin; she dwelled on Looking-Glass's allotment until one dawn when the Bluecoats attacked it; as for his father Horse Blanket, he had aided the previous generation of Bluecoats in battle against Chief Kamiakun at Walla-Walla, and, when they looked to be overwhelmed, led them onto safe paths by night. Call them as grateful as leeches. Although his fury at Cut Arm* had by now refined itself such that whenever the Bostons saw his expression they were pretty sure that he must be a bad Indian, perhaps White Thunder would have let Richard Dietrich live, at least until all the Bostons' horses were stampeded off; but Shooting Thunder and Naked-Footed Bull, having shot some other Bostons so that the rest were hiding in the bushes, now converged in the hollow where the shadows were as dark as a smoked hide, and noticed this man standing in the doorway of the hotel as if he owned the right to exist exactly here, in considerable advance of the prairie schooners with their heavy freight, so that Naked-Footed Bull (whose hair was handsomely fixed with bone) therefore reminded White Thunder: My youngest brothers and my next-younger brother were not warriors. They and my sister were killed at Ground Squirrel Place

      (now Big Hole, formerly Ross's Hole—not marked on Colton's map),
  where dawn fog rises thicker and thicker
  from rocks as half-indistinct as buffalo dozing on their knees in mist:
      Bancroft Library, University of California, Berkeley.
      p E83.877.G1 1988 RESTRICTED.
      Gibbon, John (1827–1896).
      From where the sun now stands: a ms. of the Nez Percé war:
        Concealed by the thick timber of the mountains we succeeded in
        getting to the vicinity of Joseph's camp without being discovered,
            playing my high cards,
                while back on the Idaho side of Lo Lo, General
                Howard is still considering ladies' seal sets, muff
                and boa, reduced from eight to four dollars; once
                this campaign gets wound up he may order some
                for Lizzie, Bessie and Grace.
     Hold your fire when you see Joseph, because he may be keeping Mrs. Manuel—
        Gonna whap that steel on down, o, LORD.
        Gonna whap that steel on down
            for the sake of our unborn children and for all our
            ladies in their dark bell skirts:
                See that tipi down there? Get it well ablaze.

---

*General Howard.

Montana Historical Society Archives.
PAM 3339.
A Vision of the "Big Hole," by John Gibbon, Colonel, 7th Infantry:

> *By noon we top the main divide of all,*
> *The trail being fresh and plainly marked before,*
> *And march along through glades which gently fall*
> *Toward that spot we soon will dye with gore.*

Well, sir, I should say they'll show some fight.

Although Richard Dietrich had taken no part in the Nez Perce War, he certainly proved convenient, neither wondering nor being wondered about, as if he, like our Indians themselves, had been created solely for the purpose of target practice; never mind that Heinmot Tooyalakekt (he who was called *Joseph*) would have said, *this is not how to show bravery;* to Naked-Foot Bull he represented the object once seen which taints the memory forever, like Lieutenant Bradley's glimpse of that Sioux pony running free with a white man's blond scalp knotted to the bridle, or Mrs. Cowan's eternal Yellow Stone instant which comprises the cruelly grinning face of Strong Eagle, last of the Three Red Blankets, whose gun-barrel now spins with the magic levity of a compass needle toward her husband's forehead while another Indian yanks her back by her hair (she is screaming *Kill me, kill me first!*)—or Perry's first sight of the fallen Theller; or whatever it is that Major Shearer, Confederate States of America, might have discovered in the eyes of Mr. Squire's runaway nigger who now, in a Union tunic somewhat too large for him, comes charging straight this way with his bayonet out front, and even though he explodes that coon's head off his shoulders, Shearer will never now forget that even the lowest vilest darky can turn on you, just as if any worm could grow copperhead-fangs, which is why he hopes to club down lower races for the rest of his days, no matter how he disguises his hatred once the Lost Cause has terminated

> (but hallelujah! Rutherford B. Hayes has reeled in his nigger-loving
> Federal troops!);

or Sturgis after Joseph made a fool of him in the mountains of Yellow Stone, or Howard after Chancellorsville, Randall after Red Spy's bunch began galloping toward him at Cottonwood

> (this savage who will kill me now seeing into my skeleton with a
> Dreamer's SATANIC stare, as I wait for Colonel Perry to save me),

White Thunder after the young men ran away from Cut Arm in Red Owl's country, so that White Thunder's war-dream was lost

> (afterward there will be apple trees around this battlefield, but the
> fruit will be poor, remaining hard almost up to the moment it rots),

Trimble after Camas Meadows, Good Woman after Bear's Paw, Mason after the Modoc delegation assassinated General Canby, Wood after Red Heart's so-called trial

—o, my heart and the way it sinks, almost softly, not unlike the
fashion in the Big Hole Valley, where sagebrush prairies descend
into bushy rivers and yellow-green grass—
or Lizzie at home in Portland with her mouth open and her hands over
her eyes as she reads the first headline about White Bird Cañon, composing herself before Gracie leads the children in, dear GOD, O dear GOD,
don't let them murder Otis!—
or Naked-Footed Bull taking aim from behind
> (better than hunting for an eagle's nest
> and bluish-white constellations of juniper berries on the
> splintered old tree, whose abyss-outstretched bough is thick
> with yellow moss):
too late to save my sister
> > (White Thunder running to fight with but one shell in
> > his rifle, Rainbow already dead);
my little brothers unable to die in battle like men—
these four I will never see again:
Goose Maiden, Charcoal, Claw Necklace, Lone Crane,
> all wrapped in buffalo robes by my mother,
> buried by my mother and my uncle while we drove the
> Bluecoats up the hill,
Goose Maiden, Charcoal, Claw Necklace, Lone Crane,
> left alone when we fled to the camp called *Willows*
> > (we could not give them the song of Toohhool-
> > hoolsote's hand bell, but we returned them to
> > OUR MOTHER):
Goose Maiden, Charcoal, Claw Necklace, Lone Crane,
> dug up, robbed, and dishonored by Cut Arm's scouts,
> the Lice-Eaters,* the Enemies
> > who scalped them and sold their buffalo robes
> > and my brothers' beautiful necklaces,
> > all their brass bracelets and
> > my sister's beaded pouch
> > *(they have scalped my sister):*
> > > We shall paint ourselves with blood;
that is how it happens, and one cannot by any means avoid it:
> *Liyayaya!*
and Two Moons thinking to ride away with his woman to
White Bird Cañon and stay out of trouble,
> Chief Joseph meaning all the time to go on the reservation,

---

*Nez Perce name for the Bannocks.

Ad Chapman (whom the People call *Tsépmin*) interpreting everything to suit the general:

Hurrah! Hurrah!

which was why Naked-Footed Bull, who ever since the raids along the Chinook
Salmon Water wore feathers and red flannel in his long hair, and who ever since
the *thief treaty* (a child he was then) garnered hatreds as various as the colors of
bead-pulls on his hempen pouch's strings, now said: It is exactly as if this man
killed my brothers and sister.

He is no Bluecoat, only a Boston.

He is a white man, and will be a Bluecoat later to kill us. White Thunder, I am
telling you three times! Shooting Thunder, what do you say?

He wears good clothes—

I am a man; I am going to shoot him,

at which they all happily angered themselves, made drunk by the POWER
of their WYAKINS and their longings for the dead,

flying up, their hearts spattering sparks:

Brother, there are two of them in there.

When you hear me shoot the other one, shoot this one.

Watching their victim, then slowly turning his head in order to see farther into
this war-friend's heart, Shooting Thunder remained still, neither listening nor
looking for anything else and therefore evidently declining rather than merely
waiting to raise his 1866 Winchester repeater, with which he was extremely accurate at killing animals; then Naked-Footed Bull, seeking not to make noise even
with his breath, crawled forward alone through the dying grass, while the tall
Boston whom he meant to kill,

never imagining that he could be in the wrong by having embarked on
this touristic jaunt to Yellow Stone,

and thinking perhaps to-morrow to wander away from the hot
springs into the winding cañon, then down through the silver-
saged golden grass to the Gardiner River, which is striped with
shallow whitewater (anytime forever he could explore these high
shallow arroyos packed with scree),

squinted straight at him, not seeing him, wiping the sweat out of his eyes with a
fine blue bandana

(I am repaying them all—avenging my brothers and comforting my sister,
my sister Goose Maiden in her white dress of antelope skin),

and when Naked-Footed Bull had taken good aim,

his WYAKIN standing behind him, wearing the pale fangs and dark talons of
an angry bear,

he fired, winging Richard Dietrich in the arm, the red wound opening its mouth
and the yellow-white bone smiling; before he could scream twice, Shooting Thunder blasted him in the belly,

spilling his life all over, *áhaha!*

—his intestines generous as if with ripening berries,
 his lips parting as if to vomit
  (we shall tell Red Spy how he sobbed like a baby: *shlak, shlak!*)
—although it actually might have been White Thunder who killed him; for the story's tellers alter the deeds of its principals. In that final oval portrait, Dietrich stares palely and sadly away, as if he already foresees his murder; his collar is white and high, and his arms have been folded across his chest, with a bedroll tucked up under them.— He fell on his face, *shláyayaya!* Shooting Thunder sent a bullet longitudinally through his body. Then they murdered his friend Charles Kenck. Two other Bostons got away, running off the trail toward the beaver ponds, panting up the creek's cañon, gasping in the smell of tall grass while crows argued far above their little perils and their prayers which now flittered over the smoking white mineral deposits; giving up on the Army, these two Bostons finally froze in the shadows of the forest, in the place where the waterfall waves like the manes of many white horses, while White Thunder, Shooting Thunder and Naked-Footed Bull ran laughing into that house and carried away many wonderful clothes. When Lieutenant Doane's detachment found Dietrich's corpse, it was still warm.

PLENTY OF INDIANS ALL OVER THE COUNTRY (CONTINUED)
1876–2009

*N*ow that we have won the Nez Perce War (history has come to Oregon through Hellgate Toll), I can put by my dread throughout these hot summer Oregon river-days, and my woman rides with me between summerhouses along the river, showing me greenish-brown water, cattails, crows passing over the water; I show her ringnecked ducks; our days resemble white water from the necks of swans. *There was plenty of Indians all over the Country,* says Blurick, as indeed I would have expected, *as 76 was the Year of the* Custer Massacre—ten years now since the Comanches lassooed our soldiers and dragged them off to be hacked to death; four years since we drove out the Modocs (General Canby having explained: *Listen to me, you Indians have got to come under the white man's laws*); one year remaining for our Nez Perces.— Indian peacetime, Indian summer! My heart is very good. *Nez Perces, date unknown, location Oregon.* Indian territory has narrowed into a long needle of broken paper like a hair of yellow grass; the railroad's reached past Cheyenne. But Tom will keep the negatives safe. Richard Dietrich preserves himself in a freezer, even as the Nez Perce War fades forever:

Oregon State Archives.

Records of military departments, accession number 89A-12 (1847–1968),

each Indian zone contracting, more or less as the wilting leaves of
buffaloberries draw down against the stalk,

fewer Dreamer women in their basket hats

and another dark-and-tan cavalcade creaks up toward the Rockies,
dreaming wearily, bravely, avidly or desperately about Oregon:

The bold dragoon he has no care
As he rides along with his uncombed hair.

A flattish deep blue disk all rich with white clouds; that's Oregon, *the Garden
of the West.* Colorado may be the newest but Oregon remains the most glamorous
of our thirty-eight states: farthest from hideous old war-dreams. Blurick, well
recollecting how the Union Pacific Railroad tried to sell him on the thriving fruit
orchards of eastern Nebraska, has steeled himself against the persuasions of subsequent well-wishers; to his fellow citizens he remains a nullity, which is to say
that he's dreamed his own Seven Dreams, thank you very much, and so he'll pick
out his own d——d eighty acres. Oregon's clouds are so white, and they move so
fast! Some clouds resemble the snowy mountains whose edges cut through them.
Two thousand miles runs our Oregon Trail, with plenty of Indians all over the
country. Thanks to the Silver Panic, Congress can't underwrite but half an Army
nowadays, so every traveller must now perform his own Indian service. Doc says
once we get to Farewell Bend we ought to be all right. Texas Pete nags the whole
bunch to stay on the *qui vive,* but our celebrated Captain Travis, long may he ride,
declines to lose time on another Indian scare. It's plain that the reds are withering;
another generation and Progress will be safe. Over Blurick steals that gentle tipsi-
ness of hope which animates even the canniest of our emigrants. One finds it, for
instance, in those Northern schoolmarms who roll up their sleeves and head
South in dark bell skirts, meaning to uplift new-freed negro children. Emigrants
will do most anything to save their dreams. If you have ever observed the way
that desperately thirsty horses will slide down a bluff on their haunches in order
to reach water, you may achieve some comprehension of our American need
for success, which certainly beats settling for the broken-down ordinariness
between wars.

Of all the Americans in this book, Blurick remains the most opaque. Few remember him; none think him horrible. Good-natured almost to General Howard's extent, dull (if never to himself), inoffensively avoiding intimacy with other
travellers, for fear they might seek to talk him out of his course; no borrower,
but an occasional watchful lender, he inhales the incense of splendor, which to
more hardened souls manifests itself as the Big Dust. His war-dreams rarely return, and when they do, he consoles himself with Oregon. Custer's fall—the oc-
cupational hazard of detached columns—did buy us a troop increase, even if not
right here, not to-day; and the buffalo industry is still booming almost as phos-
phorescently as the Presidential campaign of Rutherford B. Hayes. You can get a

dollar fifteen for a fine-tanned bullskin, guaranteed Texas price. Blurick, who prior to now, in spite of dissatisfactions both invented and bequeathed and either way spreading as inevitably as cholera, never felt able to pass West or scarcely even to step out through his front door although he was getting older and older (his secret friend Mrs. Mack called him a born storekeeper), did study that industry and once halfway thought to become a hide man—but gave it up, on account of the murderous Indians. (One thing he learned in the war is giving things up.— Is there another?) As for prospecting, McLaughlin and his bunch have now struck it rich on the Empire State, while Kean and Hall keep their hydraulic claim in full blast over on Gold Hill; but how many shining-eyed miners clear five cents a day and less in honor of their delusions—and what about claim-jumpers? The future of even a half-spent fellow such as Blurick appears (at least to Blurick) as wide open as the faro table at the Bella Union down in Cheyenne—although Blurick has never enjoyed gambling. One might ask just why in that case he bound himself to Captain Travis's bunch. The answer: He's not enjoying it. Anyhow, inability to feel pleasure is no excuse for not taking chances. California, for instance, remains a placer miner's favorite risk. But that miner won't have fun, except maybe by burning down a Chinese laundry. Blurick, even when he gets to feeling near as hopeful as all those emigrants bound for the Black Hills now that Sitting Bull has been driven off, won't have fun either. If family still defined him, he'd be one of those unemployed factory men with hungry children; they don't care about gold; they'll settle for a good ranch. The railroads have cut wages by another ten cents, and likewise the collieries, so let's ride West! Preferring modest returns to the likelihood of getting infringed on, several sad speculators more or less of Blurick's stripe have begun trolling the soda lakes round about Laramie, for what they will not say, trying to buy on credit, railing against Tildenopathy; these men pray for the Presidency of Rutherford B. Hayes. Young men with broad shoulders contemplate the silver mines of Nevada, no matter that they'll be toiling for others. As for Blurick, he buys a roll of flannel at the outfitting shop. What's *he* about? The short answer: Nothing but getting away from the fevers of Missouri. Every last lounger condescends to advise him where to go and whom to vote for. Since widowerhood and Secession, all he wishes—setting aside his desire to farm easy, or else succeed at business—is to smoke cigars and play cards (never for money) with his one-legged comrades. But presently he (who by DIVINE peculiarity preserved all his limbs) determines not to drag useless through life, unlike his younger brother Jesse, who actually appears a good five years older, having never been himself since Chancellorsville, and who, the last person on whom GOD should have called to deliver them, rode up on his bay mare one Tuesday morning in '74, with the tidings that their speculator Daddy's heart had failed deep in a boarded-up ribcage in a locked and darkened stateroom of the steamer for New Orleans, thereby producing an intestate condition, as so frequently occurs—for how many children even in this wicked generation grow up so monstrous as to nag faltering parents to sign their wills? That was miserable enough. Within the year, Jesse, whose most tenderly hoarded memento was the following lavender ticket:

> U. S. SENATE
>
> Impeachment of the President
>
> ADMIT THE BEARER
>
> *APRIL 11TH 1868*

had become haunted by a monomania about the latest Presidential comedy, which you and I know better than to get exercised about

>   (Charles Nordhoff to Rutherford B. Hayes: *The darkies you'll have any how; the white Whigs are what you want to capture*),

but Jesse, a Tilden man, could not relinquish the stolen election; he barely realized that he had lost his "dash" although the looking-glass should have informed him that he now resembled exactly what he was: a panting, used-up old officer with his sackcloth jacket cinched too tight; in '75 he'd thought to enrich himself by becoming an Indian Agent, but he never even learned not to write the Office of Indian Affairs upon a sheet of foolscap, and certainly not to use pale ink; so the primary issue over which his affectionate elder sibling had to worry was how to guard him safe before he broke to pieces, which was why he received the whole farm, two years and thirty-one days short of the happy morning when both brothers could have burned the mortgage papers—a morning put off, I am afraid, by Jesse's failure to take note of falling sorghum prices, as a result of which the stronger heir, Wittfield, who was nearly as charitable as he imagined but who closed his eyes to the other reason why he yearned to divest himself—the very impulse against which General Sherman had warned them all when the Army disbanded—soldiered on, so to speak, in the house built so long ago on his late mother-in-law's property, but now commenced to dream that Progress called him out West into the dreamy garden-lands of Oregon; he had to make sure of himself or else; and so it came to pass, although he appeared to have been careful all his years, especially in his marriage, that like LORD knows how many thousand others, finding himself obliged to walk away from a

>   SHERIFF'S SALE. By virtue and authority of a special execution, issued from the office of the Clerk and of the Circuit Court of Saint Louis county, and to me directed, in favor of John R. Cunningham, and against Wittfield Blurick, I have levied upon and seized the following described real estate, to wit: Lots (3) and (4) of Indian Hill, and I will on WEDNESDAY, JANUARY 5th, 1876, between the hours of nine o'clock in the forenoon and five o'clock in the afternoon, at the East front of the Court-house, sell at public auction, for cash, to the highest bidder,

he wandered, bitter and grieved, to be sure—in part because neither Jesse nor

Jesse's children had troubled to appear—but also excited, past D. Crawford & Co. as if perhaps to purchase for Mrs. Mack, who would now either cut him off or demand an elopement, the best of their ladies' Siberian squirrel sets, reduced from eight dollars to four dollars fifty; and if in truth he might have been progressing toward the barroom, it was less to get drunk than to admire the chromos of Chinamen, Indians, Mexicans, negroes and other natives who posed so picturesquely all the way along the wall; when out from the doorway of the new "American Imperial" hotel strolled one of those bright new *business men,* probably en route to the barber shop to get shaved, who said to Blurick: Out of my way, d——d tramp!

Blurick had never been called a tramp before. Thanks to this greeting (although he had received worse at the courthouse), he recommenced to consider CHEAP LANDS, first in the Great Southwest, which is to say, Little Rock, Arkansas, guaranteed no grasshoppers—but what if there were grasshoppers all the same?

Jesse, as usual, purposed that he wait, this time on the grounds that within a couple of years one might be able to ride all the way West by railroad. Jesse's sons and daughters meanwhile moved away.

Some bankrupts go North where sleety winds drive down prices, and fools go East into the spent lands where nothing happens, while adventurers with "sand" in them dare to become business men; as for Blurick, he for his part calculated that because it costs five hundred dollars to build a workingman's cottage in Chicago, or three dollars to make a dugout in Nebraska (half of that going for the window), the frugal man proceeds to Oregon, saving the price of the window (which might easily shatter on the trail).

So he voted for Oregon:

> *And though they may be poor, not a man shall be a slave,*
> *Shouting the battle-cry of freedom,*

and with slow deliberation (in time Doc would chaff him that he couldn't even pack near as good as a squaw) assembled his outfit—boxes of bran-packed bacon, coffee beans of course, the molasses jug filled right to the cork, flour in hundred-pound double-sacks, Gail Borden's evaporated milk, a single India rubber sack of sugar, just in case he ever received company—skimping on mules and buying four oxen instead, figuring that he could always eat one if need be. Captain Travis explained that at Grande Ronde the Nez Perces would trade fresh horses for our jaded animals—at no loss to themselves, you may be sure. Blurick preferred to stick to his oxen. I admit that he did carry (well pampered by straw in a wooden crate) a glass jug of acqua-regia, just in case he found occasion to try gold nuggets, but somehow he knew that he'd never be rich. Therein as I believe lay his strength; he never dreamed too far ahead. For armament he strapped on a bright new Colt pistol, of course, and Jesse, wishing to have done more, presented him with Daddy's Sharps 1859, the one with the all-brass furniture. After that he never saw Jesse again. There remained the handful of gold dollars in his secret sack, never mind how much they came to; had he not engaged himself in that Western dream, in

order to find out what he truly expected of himself, he might have gone on believing, as do so many broken down citizens, that the history of America is the tallying of what we all once had in cash.

He proceeded to Kansas City, then
to the river and the grass,

> where Captain Travis, slow moving, high-collared, slender, bald and
> bearded, with shiny sad little eyes, teaches us how to caulk our wagon
> boxes with pitch and axle grease until they're as good as boats for the
> Platte crossing—which goes so easy that even Mrs. Graves's flour
> keeps dry,

and we come up the other side into Indian country, and roll on,
our ragged triple column of Bain wagons (all thirty-two of them) waxing five-
wide, then waning to single file just like the tides
with the Big Dust behind us, O my LORD,
Americans on the move, seizing a peace which resembles war,
and the calves bawling, half-dragged behind the wagons, our children quarrelling, playing Indian, reciting their lessons for Mother, following Doc whenever
he allows them, gathering twigs or buffalo chips for to-night's fire; mountains
unseen ahead, eleven more miles until camp, GOD willing; Brown and Baker,
who sure didn't serve in the cavalry, for they can't ride with any "dash," reliving
yesterday's round of whist; as our cavalcade swings rightward across the golden
grass at Captain Travis's signal, the Ridge family falling out to save a wheel from
working off their wagon,

> Doc to the right of me, galloping for fun, singing so proud—sunny side-
> whiskered man!

Ten more miles—

> > We ought to have a commissary wagon, just like the
> > Army.
> > Yeah? Who'd pay for it?
> > > And if you look at my map to-night you'll see
> > > it, due west of the West Fork of the Wallowa
> > > River . . .
> > > Why should gold be right there? Ain't no gold
> > > there.
> > > Well, Doc says . . .

> Even some of the oldest wells have been assayed at five to twelve
> hundred dollars a ton.
> Don't jawbone me, Travis.
> I'm not kidding you; *we can get out of this.*
> Forever?

—Mrs. Johnson near about the size of a church, in her eighth month I should
reckon, and her other young ones wearing her down:

> Jennie, Adaline, Oroville, George and Inka

> (I had that influenza near about three weeks ago and I just
> can't get rid of the headache right *here,* even after a teaspoon
> of calomel. But I feel fine. It's just that blessed headache, and
> when my little angels keep screeching—)

and our fan-shaped advance guard of scouts lost somewhere ahead in their
own dust,

Brown and Baker recalling the amusements attendant to making officers give
duplicate receipts during the Secession War,

and the way we used to march by night with General Crook and take Pi-Utes
by surprise, killing whomever we liked,

the two Texes meanwhile discounting, although not utterly, the riches supposed to sleep in dull yellow crystals beneath the Black Hills,

Doc cantering back to tease the cornhaired widow again,

> Blurick pulling his hat lower down his sunburned forehead,

>> thinking on maybe to-morrow greasing his front wheels with
>> pine tar

>> and grateful that Captain Travis has not confined our ox-wagons to
>> the rear

>>> (for it gets tedious to eat the neighbors' dust),

and the ladies already praying hard over Mrs. Graves.

Now this Blurick, so I discovered in the archives, keeps a barrel of whiskey in
his wagon, and he's wise enough to keep it a more exclusive secret than the true
mercy of GOD the Fountainhead. That's why Texas Red and Texas Pete (who may
best be distinguished by the fact that Red is or was, depending on whether the
Silver Panic will ever end, a master mechanic, while Pete, like Doc, is everything)
both act like bellboys circling round a rich gent's valise. Could that barrel likewise
pertain to the fact that our cornhaired widow, yes, the young, young widow from
Missouri, will not meet his eye? Although temperance was not exactly unyielding
in the late Mrs. Blurick, her bereaved spouse stands willing to wed a lady who
leaves a man's booze alone. But must she leave *him* alone? This evening as she
kneels in the golden grass, nourishing the fire beneath her bullet-shaped kettle
hanging from its tripod, he walks over, just to stretch his legs and pass the time
(better than playing "Pedro" for eggs with Pete), but the back of her neck flushes,
and she gazes down into the fire, and now her mother-in-law returns from the
creek with a fresh-rinsed piss bucket, so it's time to make tracks. Never mind
those temperance hags anyhow; better to be friends with men who sure can shoot!
Of these, Doc looks out for him most of all. Doc's a wise one, with the sunken eyes,
matted hair and flowing beard of a Secession War graduate. He's already near to
being a prominent citizen. Oregon's his meat; any day he's going to remove there
and farm until he dies. Blurick, who believes in freedom without having seen it,
considers investing a pinch of faith in Doc, who sure can shoot, knows the country, sings sweeter than a cricket and could tell any white man a thing or two about
horses.— Now, a fine Appaloosa that's broke in, Mr. Blurick, like one of them Nez

Perce ponies, that's a treat to ride. And you know what? I'm a-tellin' you this because I've took a shine to you. What you got to know about an Appaloosa is . . .
—Blurick, a pretty fair horseman himself, at least formerly, not that he ever galloped much, patiently attends, because it can't hurt to listen to any d——d thing
no matter how much it cloys him. And to enter another traveller's protection,
however rhetorical, is another kind of treat. Doc's got him a real Sharps buffalo
rifle with double set triggers, whereas poor Blurick, what's he got but that old box-
lock of his Daddy's? *Long have they pass'd.* Blurick needs education. Fortunately,
Doc will teach him the easy way to skin a buffalo, if they ever find one. Even now
it's not too late to become a hide man! The great herds linger out here in Indian
country; even nowadays one may still gather buffalo bones for souvenirs just beyond the railroad platforms of Nebraska; there must be live critters in Montana at
least. Furthermore, Doc now promises to show him the greatest d——d homestead in the State of Oregon. In fact Blurick has already been dreaming of a piece
of Hood River, inaugurating orchards of pear, apple and peach, cheering himself
with sunflowers, tall corn and maybe even a vineyard, not that he can afford all
that, but beyond the pines and aspens he can nearly see Mount Hood's blue-grey
pyramid shining with irregular polygons of snow to refresh him—O, if he had
only done with this stinking desert! The drinking water's gone foul in every cask,
and the river tastes of silt and sulphur. Mrs. Graves is septic, most likely dying and
won't stop groaning. And at night out here, O GOD! But Captain Travis invites
him for Prussian whist with the two Texes at a penny a point. Here's Brown and
no Baker. The whole bunch sit by the fire, with other fellows looking on (each
man's dream as heavy as the cartridge of a buffalo rifle), and there's Baker after all,
balling up his fist against his hip, like a boy playing at Army heroes. Blurick loses
and loses. Brown's for Tildenopathy, while Baker canvasses their hearts for Rutherford B. Hayes. Brown's against letting more foreigners in; how terrible it's getting with those German-language signs in Omaha! As for Baker, who's more
middle of the road, he likes Germans all right, but not Irishmen, who steal away
our jobs just like niggers. He used to work in a sugar refinery at Saint Louis; the
wages descended until Americans couldn't afford to stay on; then they brought in
the Germans. Hearing that, Blurick withdraws from politics, smiling shyly at the
ground. Preserving himself from reciprocity's awful rule, he declines a tipple of
Blackfoot rum under the young stars. Doc's shot an antelope, which sure relishes
pretty good over the fire, not that it goes far for so many hungry souls. Baker offers
to cut Blurick in on a section of the Umatilla country, at which Blurick gazes patiently at Brown. Captain Travis (no relation to the Travis at the Alamo) lets fly
that the Trail's a cakewalk now—nothing like twentythirty years ago when you
passed folks burying their friends near about every day. Blurick agrees it's not bad.
In his wagon, Doc presently counter-explains that Travis was *never* anything
more than a runaway *squaw man* from Hogeye, Texas, and the worst of it is the
d——d sonofabitch left his three little half-breeds behind!—O my word, says Blurick.— Then comes morning, and another tedious stretch of the Trail, Mrs. Graves

fixing to pass on anytime now, poor lady; when will she kindly shut up and die? Captain Travis calls a halt. Now the sun turns as red as a Sioux blanket. Declining the pleasures of accordion-singing around the campfire,

> *The men will cheer and the boys will shout,*
> *The ladies they will all turn out,*

> > like Mrs. Graves twitching her wrinkled cheeks as she cradles
> > her traveller's Bible,

> and if they don't, boys, why, you can always diddle some squaw
> until she—

> Cut it out. There's ladies present!

> I ain't seen none of *those* this entire trip.

> > And that's why I say the Black Hills are bogus. Fool's gold!

> > But east of the Willamette meridian, right here on this map—
> > What makes you so sure?

> > Heard it from a man in Lewiston. A real true man, name of—

Blurick ties the canvas shut in order to drink in peace and withdraw from within his barrel of dried pinto beans that marriage guide on the mysteries of the sexual system, as incarnated in the blue-eyed cornhaired widow in her linsey dress with the grimy calico apron always over it and a whole universe inside it; but right then, just as if the whiskey had shouted out, here comes Doc. Thank the LORD that gives me time to re-secrete my marriage guide (O for that orphan girl at Hood River!), not that Doc would serve me with any morality warrant. His guest has come on purpose to talk him out of the selfsame Hood River, because he can see that Blurick's a man in a million.— In the northeast section, boy, you won't believe it. I seen you unrolling Horn's map on your knee. Now listen. You can't trust Horn's map. That eastern section I'm talking about won't take second place to nothing, not for a d——d long time. They got great dirt. Throw a seed in, jump back and watch out! You can bank on that, Mr. Blurick. And some of the best summer growing climate I ever did see. The winter's not near as bad as they say. Any man who's got two balls can get by. They call it Wallowa up there, on account of there's a lot of buffalo wallows. When I was there, well, in point of fact I ain't never been quite there, but I know one who has, a fellow you can trust. You'll be close to the sky. Why, thank you, Mr. Blurick. Sure I'll drink that and an inch more. Say, do you carry any calomel? My hip is tormenting me. Never mind; just gimme more whiskey. Thank you; thank you. I always did love the open country. When I was a boy, Laramie was a hundred tents and you wouldn't believe how many horses. Up on the blockhouse wall they used to have a galloping horse, painted in Indian red. We'd see it every time we come through that gate. You have no GOD——d idea, Mr. Blurick, none at all. I get tears in my eyes when I recollect my little Pawnee pony. His name was Star. Those was fine times we had in those days. I had me some sweet years when I was a boy in Laramie. Now it's so wide a city you practically can't spit without them calling the law on you. There's nothing for me there. When I get rich, I'm going to plant me an orchard by a creek in Oregon. (Not at

Hood River, though. I hope you heard me. That section's practically closed.) Ripe pears, O my LORD, and every morning the sound of water! No Big Dust, never again, Amen. And as many horses as any man can keep. Some hay acres, watered green and fenced off good. Pretty fine grazing there in Wallowa. Easy trails to winter pasture. Cows'll fatten fast. There's a big lake, too, as blue as a jewel. And up in them mountains back of the lake they got quartz with color in it. Silver and gold, gold and silver! What about you, Mr. Blurick? You want me to tell you more about the country out thataway? Because before all them Jews and jackasses hear about it, we got to seal it up good for ourselves. That rich green valley with all them mountains around it, *I want it.* Now listen: Even Travis don't know much about the place. He'll talk you to death about gold mines, but he ain't never been far off the trail from Grande Ronde. Just ask him straight out if he's ever laid eyes on Florence, where they even got Chinamen now. And Lewiston's got the river, sure, but all that country gets hotter than hell. That's why I prefer that high green old Wallowa Valley! Travis is speculatin' on lots around Lewiston when so far as I know that land ain't even been rightly platted. Them Nez Perces is still squatting on it. Who knows what our next President will do? Tilden's a Copperhead; Hayes sweeps up votes from niggers. And Travis, he calls hisself captain but he ain't got no better right than me. I don't intend to go on scouting for him much longer. What call does that *squaw man* got telling me what to do?

An hour past dawn they are rolling toward Oregon. Five weeks yet, says Travis, who in the morning sunlight appears older than usual as he closes one eye in the saddle, nodding his head and mouthing the words of a hymn. Blurick worries about his axletree. Then the cornhaired widow casts her smile, which Blurick catches, thinking to himself: I sure ought to be thankful. Brown implies to Baker that the daily deeds of Captain Travis's six scouts, Doc's especially, compare in some sense to the Indian service of our dedicated cavalry and infantry. Mrs. Graves is screaming in Mrs. Johnson's wagon. Why didn't she take the railroad? Doc explains to Blackie about the bullet trick with horses. Blurick scratches himself through his woolen Army shirt: My LORD, what's biting me? I need more patience. Mrs. Barton must have more money than Mrs. Wilcox, since she is carrying cooking spices ordered all the way from the A&P in New York. Blurick offers to tune up her harness gear to-night. As for her pustulent dray, well, Blurick used to know more about matters equestrian, but after the Great Horse Plague of '71, when a quarter of those animals died throughout our United States, he decided to know less, and in this has succeeded pretty well, so Doc's the one to call on. Doc paints the sores with good white lead and says: No, ma'am, you don't owe me nothin.'— In the hottest time of the afternoon they halt to relieve the horses, and the two Texes stretch out in the dirt with ankles crossed, pillowing their heads on their saddles not unlike real cavalrymen; while Blurick (his eyes stinging with alkali) ducks behind his flap to admire the illustrations in the marriage guide, O my LORD. In Hood River he'll snake out some logs to build himself a cabin; he'll leave room to squeeze a woman and children inside. My neck's getting sore. Where's our bivouac to-night? He prays for Jesse and all the other folks back home in the States. He eats a spoonful of molasses. Then Travis sounds the move out, our scouts fanning ahead. Up on a butte a mounted Indian sits watching. Is that supposed to be a wonder of nature? At dusk when the wagons pull in and our two Texes ride out with four lucky men on flank watch (the sage-hills as grey as a Government blanket), Doc invites himself inside Blurick's wagon: Just a tipple, shaded by double canvas. Disinclined to play cards for money with any three sharpers in the grass, Blurick has accordingly sunk in the esteem of others (GOD-fearers excepted), for which reason he watches his own affairs ever more craftily; is or is not Doc my friend? What a wonder Mrs. Graves won't die! She reminds me of Mama; I don't know why. Just now he is spooning to-morrow's provisions from opened sacks into the various compartments of his mess chest, as Doc should have remembered—poor manners to inspect a man's food without his leave—actually, I'll wager he remembers pretty well; for Doc knows character just as he knows booze,

> which is why he advocates for the Presidency of Rutherford B. Hayes, who for all his manifest failings does at least promise to stand out of the way, so that our American business men (for instance, Brown and Baker) can accomplish what GOD set them down on earth for,

and therefore knowing that gold can unite even with lead, although it then tends toward brittleness, Doc, watching Blurick drive his wagon, or when he needs to trudge powerfully yet uncomplainingly along, balding and broadshouldered, enormous in his mediocrity and therefore alluring in the utility he seems to promise, thinks to alloy his dream of Wallowa, into which no other soul has entered (although Blackie prays for admittance), with the careful strength of Blurick, in order to lighten the strain which has been galling him since last summer among the ponderous cotton-woods of Farewell Bend when the dream swooped down upon him, more shining than all the gold of Oro Fino

(which I admit is nearly played out)

and Florence,

> where J. M. Miller washed out a hundred dollars' worth of color in one afternoon:

no, that rich green valley with mountains all around it, *that's* what I want:

> *Wallowa,*
>> and the water and the grass
>>> (gold for sure in the Wallowa River, and if not, there's bound to be something worth getting)
>> and the lake
>>> (I never cared about nothing before)
>> and the sparkle on the lake, the end of the dark turquoise of it, with its evergreens sloping up away from it into the sky
>>> (that Dead Line of ten-foot lodgepoles all peeled by

squaws and anchored in heaps of stone, to mark the
boundary of Joseph's country);

for gold in and of itself Doc cares nothing; it's pretty but useless, like a
gangue mineral—good only for what it commands. But Blurick's the type
for whom gold is an end as much as a means.— Well, Blurick? gold will
say, and Blurick must surely answer. The ghastly humidity of Farewell
Bend, its midges, mosquitoes and fevers affect Doc no more than a mix of
colors. Blurick's the sort (thinks Doc) who likewise won't be bothered by
little impediments. Back in Laramie when there came floods, snows and
scalpings, people used to say admiringly: *Doc don't care!* which while inaccurate was pragmatically true;

and this, as Doc knew right away, is prime barefoot whiskey, which means *undiluted.* A man who keeps a barrel of that is a man in a million, a man who will take
a chance on Wallowa.

Yeah.

Mighty refreshing in here, Mr. Blurick,

Shouting the battle-cry of freedom,

some ladies cooking frybread,

Mr. Johnson jawboning with Captain Travis
about Shoshonis

(we'll soon be coming into their
country):

No, sir! They're near about as treacherous
and cruel as them Confederate Bushwackers who shot my brother in the back—

Mrs. Johnson near her time,

Blurick not yet quite as ragged as a fron-
tiersman,

the widow quizzing her daughter out of a blue-
backed speller,

Well, you just lay down four logs and post your claim in the center.
That's good enough for Sioux country.

And for Wallowa!

—Travis holding the high hand at a penny a point
(no, sir, that's not why Travis's business is
down. Fact is, some families have took the
train to Ogden, for fear of them wicked
Indians),

two long benches running down the sides, one to sleep on when Blurick
feels like it and the other his dining-table and workbench, the floor in
between heaped with sacks of varying emptinesses, horse-bells hanging
from the hoops overhead, in case someone tries to make off with the
whole outfit some dark night, as has happened before to others

(but you're wrong, Pete; what the Modocs
had was Spencer carbines),

because the reason that J. C. Hearan suicided by taking chloroform
and morphine in his boardinghouse on Christy Avenue was that
some grifter ghosted away with his sack of dollars, preventing him
from setting out for *the Garden of the West;* this story echoed and
wobbled through every crooked distillery in Saint Louis, but since
Blurick (already a widower) was as I will kindly say *personally acquainted* with the landlady Mrs. Mack, he knew what was true and
even dreamed it just like Doc dreamed Wallowa; therefore he will
guard his possessions forever

—but why Wallowa? One might as well ask why the last note
of "Assembly" is blown four times!—

and after ridin' around all day keepin' watch for you all, I'm feelin' poorly.—
Blurick, who had been fixing to dream about the cornhaired widow from Missouri, refuses to argue it out.— If everybody hit me up for a drink, *then* where
would I be?— Don't you worry about that, Mr. Blurick; I'll keep them others off. I
know how to protect what's mine—at which point Doc rests his booted ankle on
that special sack of sugar, in a manner dislikable to Blurick, whose dislikes matter
less than he might imagine.— And I'll tell you what! I'll make sure you get special
treatment if them stinkin' reds attack. Who knows what them Blackfeet are up to?
Or maybe Sitting Bull's broken out. Never mind; I'm gonna be right here, looking
out for you! Mr. Blurick, do you get what I'm telling you? There's plenty of Indians
all over this country, more than you can know. *Never stop watching out.* You
remember that draw we passed by kind of quick this afternoon, that low holler
with all the thick yellow grass growin' high as sin? That's one nasty place! I seen it
a-crawlin' with 'em. They're real good at hidin' and sneakin'. They keep quiet; they
play dead. Even when you shoot one, he don't hardly moan. He just lays there,
fixin' on you and hopin' to get you. Last year we was campin' over there where that
burned patch is almost growed over. I told Travis he was a fool, but he said the
ladies was tired. Well, when the moon got low, sure enough, d——d reds come
sneakin' out and tried for our horses—

Plenty of Indians, and now Blurick, looking up between his wagon-ribs, spies
shadows dancing behind the cloth! Just crows, he reckons. Or big old fat wicked
vultures, or eagles. Ain't there plenty of eagles out here?

Oregon blows cool and sweet in Blurick's mind:

I sure got the Western Fever!

He hates Doc, but needs him: Praise GOD the greedy bastard's off hunting! Could
I whip him? If put in that position, I'd have to try. But I know his kind: He fights
ugly, probably carries a spikeneedle like some treacherous Injun, and I'll bet he
bites like a dog. If I have to whip him I'd better kill him. Can't manage *that* but by
shooting him in the back, which I'll never do. So, dear LORD, help us stay friends
at least until the Columbia.— Unlocking the bench again to get at his whiskey,

wondering whether the ladies have kept enough shortening to bake more pies on our next lay-by day, mulling over the cornhaired widow's allurements, positively disinterested in the conditions of the Wallowa section; longing to arrive at Farewell Bend, where his dream-Territory commences, he now unsheaths the future, hoping his money will hold out better than J. C. Hearan's, so that he can buy *his* sweet years in Oregon, maybe marry some grateful hardworking orphan girl

(since the cornhaired Missouri widow's deportment is commencing to remind him of the way his kerchiefed mother used to hold his youngest brother, the dead one whom she always favored, on the taut lap of her long brownish-black skirt, supporting the child's heavy head with both hands while he gazed up into her eyes, clutching her hair or playing with her earrings until she swung his hand away)

and a livid haze of green between the straight and slender tree trunks

and a vast shard of golden light amidst the evergreens of Oregon

fixin' on you and hopin' to get you

and the clean still mirror of the wide river

(but behind Oregon's wall of trees, plenty of Indians in the country, O, you bet)

and an orphan girl in neatly patched petticoats, an uncomplaining, hardworking sort who'd do anything to—

a sun-bleached quilt, a clean chamberpot under the bed and her yellow braids tied with calico ribbons

—and although Doc means to get me excited to think about the way a squaw folds in her blanketed arms across her breast when a white man gazes at her, them reds will never do it for me—

and her eyes closed but her lashes trembling when he

and her hope chest

but even an orphan girl might be expensive.

Now what you do, Blackie, when you get to the diggings and you make your strike, you make your amalgam of gold and quicksilver, and you hollow out a potato and bake it in your campfire all night. That draws the mercury out. In the morning you got yourself a bunch of pretty gold beads.

All rightie, Doc. I can do that.

'Course you can.

And Mr. Blurick's coming, too?

For sure he is.

I like him.

Why?

I don't know.

And I can bring Fidelia?

Why not?

And we three, we'll be the first three white men?

Nope.

Have you ever been there in Wallowa? You must have been.

Nope.

Then who's there?

Well, the Tulley brothers, they come into Wallowa soon as the Grande Ronde country dried up. Stockmen, Blackie, that's who they are. Don't know a thing about gold. Then Ward and McCormack, I don't know if they come in that same year or later on, maybe in '72. And Old Joseph said, boys, if a few hundred acres is all you want—

Doc?

What is it now?

Doc, am I gonna get rich?

Depends on you, boy. Don't have nothin' to do with me.

But it may well depend on where a fellow goes (not to mention when his war-dreams leave him alone). No matter what the Texes put forth, men are still striking color in the Black Hills. Wallowa's far more problematical; otherwise we would have taken it away from the reds before. Lewiston continues to be whorehouse and depot—as vice-ridden as Cheyenne—but so are San Francisco and any other number of cities unredeemed by Lemonade Lucy. The miners have rolled out; the grocers and bankers have moved in. On the bright side (says Blurick to himself), expenses are down. Not long since, a hundred pounds of flour cost ten dollars at Big Sandy and twenty-five at Fall River. Now an enterprising man can always jew the storekeepers down. The Trail's cheaper now, more civilized as Captain Travis likes to say and say again. But then why does Travis keep that Colt Navy pistol swinging between hip and thigh? Besides, shouldn't I save wherever I can? The Silver Panic may be GOD's punishment. Doc believes in gold. I never did. I can spend it but I can't dig it up. Nobody's going to do squat for a poor man. I could lose it all to-night, just like poor J. C. Hearan,

accordingly unlocking the bench to get at his whiskey before it too runs away (besides, there's a mealy taste in my mouth)

—and wishing Texas Pete and that pompous Mr. Donovan would shut up:

. . . collapse of the Northern Pacific . . .

Well, he tried to make a go of it selling Zell's Encyclopedia door to door.

Where?

Where the Wallowa meets the Grande Ronde.

Likely that child died of diphtheria.

And that d——d Blurick just sitting in there with both flaps down, drinking barefoot whiskey and doing nothing—

Yeah, that fool should be taught his manners—
After we ford the Snake—
If we can exchange some horses—
And Jay Cooke oughter be shot like an old horse.
My sister-in-law's stock certificates—
while Captain Travis, whose quarter horse is not near
as spirited as Doc's but considerably handsomer, now
raises his round tanned face, grips the crupper, frowns
out across the hills, then rides over to the other Tex.
They watch something through their field-glasses.

Well, then, when I saw them three purty squaws
crossing that long coulee, I rode forward—
So then he stole a swingletree right off the d——d
wagon and tried to sell it right back to Uncle Sam!
Who wouldn't?
And that's why he had to run away from the
Army.

No, Donovan, that was when Fiske & Hatch defaulted in New
York . . .—

I mislike the way that darkness seems to be moving over there. If I don't get myself
to sleep I'll be no good to-morrow, but right now I fairly dread to sleep! Why do
Tex and Travis keep shifting round and round? There do seem to be plenty of
Indians in this country. We'd all better keep our brightest lookout. Doc says he
will but *I* will.— And darkness swelters down. The wagons circle in. All around
shine Indian fires on the grass-hills. Travis says the reds could attack to-night, or
maybe to-morrow when we're strung out along the trail. When you hear them
singing, you'd d——d well better get ready.

So we do. And in the Blurick manuscript I, William the Blind, read: . . . *we went
through this battle without a scratch only the wagon shafts wore Hundreds of Arrows sticking in them* . . . Captain Travis runs a real bright outfit.

Prints from Compartment Four
1876–2009

*T*here were still buffalo-hunting Indians in those days, and sometimes,
although rarely, the Nez Perces traded with the Sioux, whom they would rather
fight

(Doc in Blurick's prairie schooner detailing the way that some Sioux warriors wear bone gorgets as elaborate as accordions—not that Blurick cares because anyhow there's plenty of Indians all over the country);
and there were more buffalo than even Doc could count
and Indians all over the country, if not quite so many as last year
and yellow grass, and thousands of wagons rolling through
(Doc calling the square dance while Baker played the violin);
soon the tall narrow pyramid of black girders would ascend into being, with the metal shed halfway up it, and the wheel shaft rotating on the stamping mill; never mind the Ice-Burg Drive-In and Tony's Dutch Lunch; to get to that stage, we couldn't wait on President Hayes! Yessir, no, ma'am; we cleaned out that country. *A scout named Doc on a fine Kentucky thoroughbred promised to kill the first Indian he saw and shot a squaw sitting on a log,* but what happened next to Blurick's party I cannot say, nor do I even know where most of them settled, I hope in prime Oregon bottom land, so that the new Mrs. Blurick (so what if she ain't yellowhaired?) could go out on a morning and fill two flour sacks full of blackberries—but Blurick might for commercial reasons have chosen or been chosen by some other Western venue far from Hood River, way away from Wallowa, never mind Portland or Pendleton: I mean someplace where the hot dirt streets of narrow-peaked white houses dead-ended in cliff-walls hot and grey with scree, and nothing but evergreens served for handholds, *Blurick, date unknown, location unknown;* for I had to leave his manuscript, it being now nearly closing hour at the Historical Society, where Tom stood ready to inspect and explain some Indian photographs I had served myself out of varnish-perfumed archive drawers straight from the Country of Dying Grass. Once upon a time there were so many buffalo along the Oregon Trail that you might see them stampede by for two hours. And Indians, too, I have read that there were quite a number of those.

Umatilla chief, Tom said. Not very good. Soft focus. Likely a dupe.

From the next yellow print, Indian eyes looked into me.— That starlike stamp on the reverse—W.A., you see—is Wesley Andrews. Wesley Andrews probably wasn't even alive when this picture was taken. You can tell by the flattened tonal scale that values are not really where they need to be.

Oregon State Archives.
Umatilla Indian War Claims Register, 1877–78.
Locator 2/11/01/07, one volume,
General Sheridan gently smoking his cigar,
Captain Pollock, all spruced up, staring ahead with Sara and the children, pretending they have all been digging gold,
although that should have been filed under
Oregon State Archives.
Nez Perce Indian War, 1877.
No locator.

Wood and Nanny,
Wood and Theller's squaw,
Wood and Sitka Khwan,
Wood and Mrs. Ehrgott,
silhouetted soldiers drawing up for inspection before General
Howard's Sibley tent, dawn-gazing straight ahead, as wilderness
breathes on them an inch beyond the picket-rope;
Wilkinson in his Salvation Army uniform,
Colonel and Mrs. Perry seated on their porch at Fort Lapwai, he in
his parade attire, she in a long dark skirt, trying to smile through
that little black dotted veil she was always wearing

and then another print. Tom said: I recognize this. Bannock Indians. Azo paper
is of course long discontinued now. You can still get it in grades one and four, but
only if you order an enormous quantity. The fact that there are already three sig-
natures stacked up means that it was old at the time it was printed. And here we
have more exposures. This was already a thirty- or forty-year-old neg at the time.

Again! he said sadly. Another copy. Blacks piled up, whites blocked out. Now,
this has been here a long time. Compartment Four refers to a filing that was used
from the 1890s to the 1930s. **Overland journeys, Todd,** that's fine. And this, I
would be very skeptical. I would be doubtful that it's a Bannock Indian village as
labeled. And of course! Look at **W. Andrews, Washington**! He stole the picture
from someone somehow, and he just captioned it *Bannock* because he thought it
would sell.

When the Nez Perce War broke out, the Bannocks stayed loyally on our side,
sitting with their children in the golden grass, before the dark cones
of their grass-skinned tipis, their heads hanging down, out of sun- or
camera-shyness,
copyright Wesley Andrews,
and then helping us hunt down Chief Joseph:

in the next orange print, copyright registered in the name of that cunning time
traveller Major Moorhouse, we see young braves in a line, safely mustered into the
United States Army. One of General Howard's white scouts, dawn-addicted young
Redington, canters up to the recently abandoned Nez Perce camp at Squaw Lake
and finds *a poor helpless old squaw* lying on ratty robes. She shuts her eyes *as if
expecting a bullet but not wanting to see it come. She seemed rather disappointed
when instead of shooting her I refilled her water-bottle . . . from a couple of shots I
heard ten minutes later as I followed the trail down the creek, one of our wild Bannock scouts acceded to her wishes . . .*

Oregon State Archives.
Bannock Indian War, 1878.
No locator.

Indian chief, yes, I recognize this picture, said Tom. I have seen a receipt dated
1936, five cents on wholesale, Benjamin Markham, who was one of Andrews's

printers. The muddy shadows are not going to lend themselves to pictorial excellence.

Wagon train scout, called "Doc." I can't exactly place him, but he looks familiar. Now, if you put the loupe right down on his breast pocket, you can make out that medallion he's wearing: **DEMOCRATIC PARTY DIED OF TILDENOPATHY, 1876, IN THE 60TH YEAR OF ITS AGE. SHAMMY TILDEN, LET IT R.I.P.** That dates this negative at right around the Centennial, so it should really be in Compartment Six. This Doc of yours, who looks like a mean bastard, was obviously a Hayes loyalist. Hayes or Tilden, what a choice!

Here came a postcard of an Indian at a county fair. The way the Indian looked at me, I felt the same sad thrill as that summer night when the locomotive whistled in Lewiston, Idaho. And the summer clouds of Oregon rushed along in the window like the ghosts of wagon trains.

Wallowa Lake, 1873. Copyright Major Moorhouse.

Nez Perces, 1877, location Wyoming.

Nez Perces, circa 1877, location Montana. They covered much ground that summer.

More dupes, said Tom. The flattened tonal scale is the dead giveaway here. There are no whites.

A platinotype presented us with a long slope of feather, then a bronze, faux-Roman Indian profile. That warrior knew the way to ford waterfalls. Tom said, still looking at the previous photograph: In the middle 1850s, an Army soldier had a camera and made salt prints. Let's see, *Grand conseil, Composé de dix Chefs nez-percé* . . . And this so-called "platinotype" uses corn starch emulsion to make the matte look. But Moorhouse shouldn't be in here. That's *vault* material.

Oregon State Archives.

Nez Perce Indian War, 1877.

No locator.

From what must have been an albumen print—for its tones were red and its highlights had yellowed to the hue of late afternoon summer strawfields in Umatilla, so brightly pale a gold as to be almost green (and it was foxed and speckled as if with tiny towns in the dips of the grassy land)—Chief Joseph stared out, his mouth clenched, his forehead steeply sloping back into the feather and the wave of frozen hair, his eyes squinting narrowly as he held his calumet high and steady for the lens of Major Moorhouse in 1901. Can you believe that he still hoped to go home to the paleness of the summer morning sky over Wallowa? His throat was encircled in bead-strings, and more beads made necklace-waves upon his chest. A plaid blanket hung from his waist.

Dupe, said Tom. And this is Moorhouse's famous picture of the Cayuse Twins. As you see, things keep getting worse and worse. *Nez Perce warriors. Wesley Andrews photo number* . . . That's right. Now, pictures from The Dalles with the typewriter label stapled to the raw board, that's the May Collection. Almost all the good pictures were stolen. The negs don't exist.

Corpse of Nez Perce squaw, 1877, location Big Hole, Montana Territory, signed by Major Moorhouse. *Nez Perce prisoners, 1877, Tongue River Cantonment, Montana Territory. Nez Perce prisoners, 1878, Indian Territory.*

Nez Perces, 1877, location Idaho Territory. And right there in Idaho, tucked in among the high plains of orange grass, the grain silos like fat rockets of dull metal, the train tracks and farms, not far from that crazy old red barn with a cylindrical hay bale sticking out the window, stands William Foster's grave:

Killed by Indians
July 4, 1877
Aged 24 Years

which is to say, slain by Nez Perces.

From time to time Cayuse portraits get misfiled under Nez Perce, said Tom.

Oregon State Archives.

Cayuse Indian War, 1847–50.

Boxes 47–50. Locator 2/21/01/07, twenty-five cubic feet,

> and proper reverence and regard for our patriotic memories
> > in the dry grass and sagebrush that chatters underfoot as my thoughts run toward Henry's Lake, faster than Sherman's telegraphed commands,
> and for crowds of mounted hunters, with their lances, bows and rifles projecting upward like masts at various tilts,
> > and the triangular and quadrilateral zones of green, red, yellow and white on Crow Indian parfleche bags
> and glory, lustre and
> everything for Wallowa.

As for this image of Walla Walla warriors, said Tom, I'm skeptical. The caption's been erased. In fact, I do recognize this image. This is a Nez Perce portrait, photographer unknown, stolen by Moorhouse:

Oregon State Archives.

Rogue River Indian War, 1855–56,

> when Ben Wright made Chetcoe Jennie strip naked while he horse-whipped her through the mud-streets of Port Orford: *Take it off, d——n you! now your drawers, you stinking redskinned bitch-whore fucking filthy pig, I'll show you who you are, you savage, fucking stinking, fucking fucking* GOD——*d animal whore . . .*—for which she arranged his murder, cut out his heart and ate a piece, and then the Rogue River War started,

No locator,

> while O. O. Howard, not yet a general, takes part in Seminole removal down in Florida.

Oregon State Archives.
Modoc Indian War campaign journal, 1873.
Locator 2/21/07/04, one cubic foot,
including the records of Perry, Theller, Trimble, Pollock and Mason, who will all fight Chief Joseph.

Blurick was right; there were plenty of Indians all over the country. You might even say they were as plentiful as tobacco in Missouri.— Now the Nez Perces, Captain Travis explained to Blurick,

who just now, observing the stern fashion in which the widow's ten-year-old daughter parts her hair, finds good breeding and prudence in her squinting appraisal of him in the moment when, striding soberly back from the creek with the cooking pail clean and full, she catches her smooth-armed cornhaired mother (who's a considerably better looker than his foxy former landlady Mrs. Mack, not to mention the half-breed woman he used to meet behind the slaughter-house) slowing to cock a smile at him,

yes, *him*, Mr. Wittfield Blurick,

one time about thirty years back they come to us on the Powder River to warn about unfriendly Indians,

but what the shit do I care about Indians thirty years gone when the widow's smiling at me?

And the daughter, O my LORD!

Anyhow, there's still quartz of all colors all over the country,
but the color of her hair, O GOD:
sweet black loam at the mouth of Oro Fino creek! So them tents at Lewiston—
And thousand-dollar claims on Rhodes Creek—
Sure, dreamer, back when Honest Abe was President.
Well, Doc says—
Then why's he still riding for Travis like some hired greaser?
How long before you found it out?
About Doc?
Who else?
and that quartz lode six miles below the Clearwater Forks—picked over going on sixteen years now, but still not entirely played out—
and Florence
(O, we always have a good time there!)
and LORD knows where else, up in the Bitter Root country, where we've cleaned up nearly all the Flatheads.
Doc's just talking out his ass. Ain't no gold in Wallowa.

Nobody can stop us, either. Joseph'll do as he's bid—
And Blurick—
Now Preacher's paying her his addresses, GoDd——n him for a tinhearted
sonofabitch. And Brown's not interested but Baker might be. But I'll get
her solid to myself. Bring her to my bosom. At least I hope I will. LORD,
but this journey's wearing on me now! I'll sure never forget all this.
My uncle was there, and just as you say, he never forgot it. You sure you don't want
no tipple? I heard you call it *Blackfoot rum*. Well, it ain't that; it's the good stuff,
the cornhaired widow hastening into the tall grass with something
wrapped up in her basket; well, there she goes, and I'd better act like one
of the boys if I don't want Travis against me because now he's frowning
with his hand on his hip, expressing his best General Grant, as if that
could impress me:
Listen up, Blurick, you sly temperance dog: I smell *yours* on your breath! And you
don't share, except with Doc. I'll stand you a taste and you stand me one, all right?
All right. Now, the bad Indians up there, they call 'em *Walla Wallas*. And when
Doctor Whitman had to hold the Walla Walla chief at gunpoint to keep the rest
of those devils from murdering everybody, well, that night went on longer than
ten GoDd——d years, but finally our Nez Perces come riding in and turned the
tables! I have to say *they* was all right, especially for Indians. Looking-Glass's
Daddy was there, and so were Joseph's and White Bird's. All big chiefs. Now their
sons got the same names. Crazy about blue beads even to-day, so that's what we
give 'em. And gold in their country, maybe even as much as in the Black Hills.
Time for them to stop roaming and settle down. Not many at all around the Hood
River where you're fixin' to go, but when we roll into Grande Ronde you're bound
to see some, mixing in with them Dreamers and river renegades. *Nez Perces*
means *pierced noses*, but most of 'em, I would say, they leave their noses alone.
When you see Nez Perces riding toward you, you can more or less trust 'em, so
you don't want to shoot. I already told Doc, he shoots a Nez Perce and I'll knock
his teeth out. But what I myself would do in Hood River, Mr. Blurick . . .
I showed Tom a reddish-brown scene from a Pendleton Roundup, a horseback
rider horned like a Viking chieftain, a line of Indians with beaver-fur mantles and
feathers in their hands.
This picture, I recognize the backdrop, said Tom. This is off the original neg.
You can see the emulsion flaking off, all the troubles of being a first-class neg.
Here's where you want to be,
near Pendleton,
the lovely low golden-grassed hills and
gold mines somewhere (but they've shut Florence and Oro Fino
down almost before Blurick got convinced)
the sky as cloudless as new bluing on a Remington's rolling block (real
fine weather in this section) and then, far away, a pale stripe of low grass
bearing zones of blue-grey trees where even last year we could do pretty

well cutting down poles from Indian scaffold burials for our campfires;
then down into the valley of golden grass

    (my heart is good)

where three yellow locomotives and many red container cars creep over
the Umatilla River and into Pendleton,

an amputated string of grainers by the white cylindrical towers of the
Pendleton Flour Mill,

creosote fumes rising up from the hot black railroad ballast, the single track
running black and true along the base of a wide round hill of yellowish-white
grass whose mostly deciduous trees, olive-green and dark reddish-green,
shade the steep-roofed antique houses, tall and narrow, which look down
across the gulley toward the grassy dirt-hills of the north,

then inside the Pendleton Woolen Mills the following testimonial, illustrated with a portrait ostensibly taken by the camera of Major Moorhouse:

    The Story of the
Wild Indian's Overcoat

The Historic Chief Joseph of the Nez Perces	**Arrayed in a Pendleton Indian Robe**

Now there's a valley I heard tell of, said Doc; they call it *Wallowa.* And I ain't
never been there, Mr. Blurick, but it's Heaven, is what they do say. They opened it
up to settlement just lately. See, looky down here on this map. Due east of the
southeast corner of Township Number One, then right here where the Wallowa
flows into the Grande Ronde. It's only Nez Perces up that way. Tame Indians. The
cavalry'll round 'em up next summer, probably.

Multiple years of erasures, said Tom. What a mess this is, what a mess.

I always ask for my prints to be full fine crop, he remarked then. Sometimes
you recognize little details that might be on the edge of the plate. That's just what
you need.

So I looked through the loupe, focusing on July 1876, and followed Blurick up
to the Snake River,

    and were I to more precisely delineate his insignificant trajectory in rela-
    tion to those of the actual moving principals in our American story, I'd

note that Colonel Miles, already called *general,* and advocate of flares, carrier pigeons and other modern methods of communication, is just now leading his column out of Fort Leavenworth in high hopes of liquidating Sitting Bull, subsequent to a stop at Fort Lincoln to re-condole with Mrs. Custer, who has not yet departed the ravening infancy of her widowhood;

while General Terry (the hero of everything) and Colonel Gibbon (the hero of Big Hole) respectively take the Fifth Cavalry and the Twenty-second Infantry;

so that General Sheridan, having demanded good news, sits smoking his cigar as tenderly as Rutherford B. Hayes handles Lemonade Lucy, and Miles's enemy, especially loathed for having made, unlike Miles, brigadier general, even attainted as he is

(captured by the Secceshes)

—I mean of course General Crook

(who unfortunately has the President's ear)—

advances with the Fifth and the Fourth

(and Crook merely despises Miles for a blustering bumpkin, whereas he outright hates Terry)

and Chief Joseph, who is called Heinmot Tooyalakekt, flitters in and out of Wallowa, which is his home, but not his only home (each summer, we find him more in the way)

while General O. O. Howard, this Dream's hero,

with whom Crook shares the habit of abstinence from spirituous drink and whom Crook scorns for what he, a cynical humorist, prefers to interpret as pious humbuggery

(for instance, standing before his opened Sibley tent, with a stick-cross high behind him, reading aloud from his Bible, with the soldiers keeping their slouch hats on until the prayer: his face seemed longer and almost delicate when he was younger),

having commanded the Department of the Columbia for two years now, since the Modocs murdered Canby, stays in with Lizzie and the children at present, organizing Indian removal on paper:

The twenty-fifth will mark Harry's seventh birthday already; he's behaving very well; Lizzie wishes him to receive a new pair of shoes. He's very fond of those lemon crackers which folks bring on the Oregon Trail; I wonder where I could find him some? Grace will doubtless bake some sweet or other to mark the occasion. Such an acomplished young woman she's become; it brings a lump to my throat! But why can't she keep her beaux? (Bessie will be delighted; she'll probably believe the party's for her.) And on his

leave days Guy is always keen to keep up with Miles's movements
on my map. I must admit to entertaining the highest hopes of
that son. Chauncey and John are the ones I hardly know, LORD
help me—

and then through the loupe I followed the Columbia all the way to the emulsion's
flaking edge, up to Nespelem, where the hills are as soft as a moleskin shirt:

WHERE YOU WANT TO BE
2009

and coming out of the wet forest of Elk Heights:
CHERRIES
EXIT 93
PERFECT PEACHES
EXIT 93
then down into the golden grass
and sagebrush
a long green field between a dark ridge and the Valley Christian School
THORP FRUIT AND ANTIQUES
Nectarines $7.50 a box
     (and singing hymns on the prairie),
haybales stacked in semicircular tents at
RYEGRASS
ELEV. 2555
then down the long yellow slope of desert, across the Columbia
whose water-speech resembles the breath of one who speaks as she
weeps
and back up into the green and yellow fields which decorate themselves
with high sprinklers
CHERRIES FOR SALE
CORN
WATERMELONS
MELONS
nearly the same as what Looking-Glass's People used to grow,
        a mid-green potato field, the paler yellow-green of corn,
     as Doc says: See them deer running thataway? Must be water
     someways up that cañon,
past stone walls
to a high plain of yellow grass with rocks bursting through:

ENTERING EUPHRATA
>   (formerly called Indian Graves
>   and before that known as *Haupt Pah,* which means
>   *Cottonwood Place*)

Oasis Park

Golf

Fishing Derby

We Buy Aluminum Cans

Super Sweet Corn

Supermatic Superwash

WELCOME TO SOAP LAKE

Shopping

Art Museum

To-day's Your Lucky Day!

ROCKS FOR 2 MI
>   (yes, two miles' worth of boulders ascending into the clouds)

PUBLIC FISHING

ROCKS FOR 5 1/2 MI

MOTEL

Pioneer Cemetery

high plains, low clouds, islands in the long river
>   (grass as long as Custer's blond hair),

water and reeds running up to the edge of the scree
long and sky-blue like Banks Lake,
then on the edge of a desert lake a rich huddle of trees on the blocky cliff-
steps, some with caves behind them:

ENTERING ELECTRIC CITY

ROCKS FOR SALE

Coulee Playland on Banks Lake

City Hall Grand Coulee

Wild Life Parking

and the steep clean sweep of the Grand Coulee Dam, which after seventy-
five years continues as fresh as the latest industrial site
then down to lost houses and trees in the midst of the desert:

COLVILLE INDIAN RESERVATION

1.3 MILLION ACRES

and coming down into the rain by the grey river with its brown rocks to
pale golden grass with silver sagebrush bursting out of it:

ENTERING ELMER CITY

NESPELEM 12

and looking way down through the loupe into the silver and blue of the
river and across the golden grass into the bushes,
rickety black fences in the golden grass, then steep rock

(what a mess this is, what a mess),
and inscribed on a big rock:
Shaw Fruit & Produce
—I'm skeptical. The caption's been erased:
sunflowers around a pickup truck, tiny houses painted different faded colors,
then up into the rainclouds a black-topped jumble of grassy butte,
a rock-tumulus shabby with scrub
(whose lush seclusion reminds me of the cave in which Joseph
might have been born)
then entering Colville Indian Agency:
Here's where you want to be—
lots of metal sheds, a trading post, a soccer field
because
THE CHURCHES OF NESPELEM WELCOME YOU
and all of them assuredly stand ready to save us all from
FIRE DANGER TODAY
and from brush and bushy trees along the river's edge and possibly even
from the
Nespelem Tribal Longhouse
where the end of the golden grass comes visible;
and if one were to continue north into those thicker and lusher meadows beyond
the glass plate's edge, one would start to see pines again; but then the cemetery
would be diminishing in the auto's rearview mirror, so I reverse my gaze in order
to search for Chief Joseph and find

MY PRECIOUS LITTLE GIRL
HAYLEE ROXANNE
JUNE 5 2004
OCT 6 2004

—my heart is good;
my heart is grass;
graves in the gravel and golden grass,
multiple years of erasures
and a worn and weathered pipe in the shape of a
corseted female torso (Burial 52), a doll's head (Burial
93), a bifacial ovate knife from Burial 20 and
a cowboy hat and glasses on a wooden cross from which a belt hangs,
then the headstones of ever so many dead Indian Army and Navy men:
There was plenty of Indians all over the Country,
and on a hill of gravel, two stones in a metal cup, four pictures of James
Dean, baskets, toy cars, dolls, plastic flowers, flags and pinwheels

and a locust-serenaded solitary white cement monument, large and
crumbling, unmarked
> (That's right. Almost all the good pictures were stolen. The negs
> don't exist.)

and looking up through the sagebrush and into the clouds
and looking down into the town spread sparsely out a long narrow valley
of grass
and turning away from the graves with their many tiny American flags
and returning south into the arid grasslands
> (red shack in the grass, tan house in the pines
> **HERITAGE MARKER AHEAD**
> **BELIEVE ON THE LORD**
> (the Ketch Pen Tavern, gang signs),

then down into the cool river shrubs,
up into log cabin style homes
in the sagebrush, a fence and a lawn,
I meet a man with long flowing black hair, who kindly explains:
> Left, and right, and left, and left again

to the other cemetery:
> Here's where you want to be,

where at the head of a long and narrow bed of white gravel framed by greyly
weathered wood, surrounded by kindred silver-brown wooden crosses and kept
company by stones, I see it:
> a white marble column with his profile
> (made after a photo by Major Moorhouse, they say),

a beaded gorget or bracelet hanging from an antler
and the words
> CHIEF JOSEPH
>> —he had that Cayuse blood, remember? The blood of those
>> who murdered the missionaries,
>>> dark-suited Spalding standing beneath a tree, calling
>>> down his GOD upon them as they sit quietly upon the
>>> grass; they must work, submit to Christian punish-
>>> ment, and

pennies ringed round on the plinth for him whom his People called
> HIN-MAH-TOO-YAH-LAT-KET
> Thunder Rolling in Mountain
> Erected June 20, 1905
> by the Washington
> State Historical
> Society

beyond which the ground curves down to the A-frame houses in the grass

and the river,
then the mountains and clouds looking back toward Wallowa,
Wallowa:
> My heart is good—
Wallowa:
> There is no badness in it;
> here's where you want to be.

WALLOWA
1906–1876

1

*F*irst there was a monument to HIN-MAH-TOO-YAH-LAT-KET, which the sculptor unchiseled into rough blankness; then he returned the borrowed photograph to Major Moorhouse, who (if it was he) passed the glass plate from right to left in half a dozen ruby-lit chemical baths, slid it into the film holder, loaded it in his camera, opened and closed the shutter, unfocused the lens, and turned away from Chief Joseph, whose gravelled hummock had slowly risen far away in Colville, Washington, in the place called Nespelem. And in Lewiston, Idaho, near the southwest corner of the Carnegie Library in Pioneer Park, the green grass was dimpled; only one part of the rim still stood. Once upon a time this had been a rifle pit. During the Nez Perce War, the terrified settlers tried to make themselves ready for anything. In later life their Indian nightmares would return as simple mortality; their younger children never understood even when Daddy told them three times. The general did not return, the volunteers kept quiet and the latest Americans made themselves ready for the World War. Now beneath a silver dollar moon the freight train bridge on the river below unmade itself, while the pit deepened because this other concavity in the gravel (too dry there even for yellow grass) began to rise. Beneath it, anti-time's gravity drew dust into mucky and bony coherence, returned what worms had stolen, rushed rotting flesh back onto the bone-frame (an owl crying out, the moon as pale as a new soldier marching into his first battle), then freshened dirt back into an old man's cold corpse, rebuilding the coffin around him until all was as good as new, and the gravediggers unspaded earth, raised Joseph on ropes while white men in cowboy hats sat all around, unhammered the Christmas box, laid him back in bed and stood round him, because the Americans were his friends! His eyes opened; his heart grew good. And how can I not wish the same for everyone in Colville? From glass plate negatives I have seen the way the Colville Indians used to trap salmon, naked, clubbing the shining fish, facing Kettle Falls. May they too breathe again. Joseph breathed, got well, his pigtails still as grey as the cones of a lodgepole pine but beginning to enrich themselves with black, renewed the smooth conceal-ments of his angry grief even as blind old Wottolen won back his sight and forgot every badness bit by bit. Joseph hunted out his first winter with Lieutenant Wood's son Erskine, rejoined the Lapwai exiles (Welweyas the half-woman throwing off her man's clothes in joyous relief), inhaled again the lovely scent of Springtime's braids, returned to Good Woman's arms, reëntrained for the Indian Territory, gathering up reborn children there, reëmbarked for Leavenworth so that Spring-time could disinter their baby, rode back to Bismarck, Tongue River and Bear's Paw where he unuttered the speech of surrender (which Lieutenant Wood and Ad Chapman accordingly unembellished), rejoined White Bird, welcomed Looking-Glass, Toohhoolhoolsote and Ollokot to life, helped them fight the Bluecoats who now unringed themselves; and with his wives, daughters and other ever-augmenting People rode backwards to Shallow Place, Camas Meadows, then Ground Squirrel Place, where Welweyas's mother came alive because Gibbon no longer surprised them (another happy negative), since Burning Coals agreed to lend his swift horses to our best men, and so back to Weippe, Cliff Place and then the Enemy River where Welweyas the half-woman flirted with Rainbow, back in total eleven or fifteen hundred miles, depending on how we count, to the Wallowa Valley, from which Joseph's enemies disappeared, unstitching the black goods employed at Lieutenant Theller's funeral, unloading Chapman's gun, rapidly filling in their gold mines, giving back fish to streams and treasures to graves, unbuilding towns, pulling up surveyors' stakes, while Looking-Glass returned to his country with all his trust in Bostons proved right, and Toohhoolhoolsote's People went roaming, even as Springtime, Fair Land, Cloudburst, Good Woman and Sound Of Running Feet planted camas bulbs for the People's impending past convenience, and shell-earrings shone in their long black hair. (The People had a word for the sound of sizzling hair, and another for the sound of broken bones falling down.) Told in this order, Joseph's story becomes happy. From bone-gravel and worm-grass I sought to assemble it, in the cool rich night, Labor Day night, now seventy-five degrees according to the neon clock-thermometer over First Bank; before dark the tem-perature had been nearly a hundred. On the moon, which a moment ago had of-fered a dark continent upon its yellow disk, a furry yellow ring disguised its own origins, like a story growing out of the ground. And I, William the Blind, who must myself soon go underground, have begun several stories in this way, ashes to ashes and dust to life; here I am still doing it with the same stubbornness exemplified by the flagpole in the rock before the courthouse (Anno Domini MCMIX), the four-faced clock above the bench on the courthouse lawn, the concrete arch in commemoration of WALLOWA COUNTY PIONEERS, and inside this arch, in case one might not understand, an arch of words reads: IN MEMORY OF THE FIRST SETTLERS, who drove the Nez Perce off this property.

> GENERAL O. O. HOWARD TO COMMANDING OFFICER, FORT WALLA WALLA, FEBRUARY 5, 1877: The Department Commander purposes, as early in the coming spring as practicable, to send a suitable force into the valley for a summer encampment, to remain until Joseph and his band leave in the autumn.

Yes, sir.

> HEADQUARTERS, DEPARTMENT OF THE COLUMBIA. PORTLAND, OREGON, MARCH 1, 1877. Please correct impression in Walla Walla newspapers that campaign against Joseph has been ordered. Indians so informed may begin to strike scattered families. General O. O. Howard.

Yes, sir.

I walked the empty sidewalk past a *FOR SALE* sign. On West North Street, the dingy collars and pipes of Wade Rain Sprinkler Irrigation were not made any more appealing by the yellow-lit window that exposed them. Crossed American flags and an orange declaration of **VACANCY** at the Wilderness Inn Motel persuaded me of the settled ownership of this place.— Multiple years of erasures, said Tom.

On South River Street, I peered in through the white blinds of Valley Barber, and saw the two barber chairs, two brooms in the corner, the long counter, the whisks and brushes, and the mirror.

Summary Report Blank 1962–1964
Community Improvement Program
Club name(s): . . . Wallowa County Junior Women's Club.

> Long years of neglect had left the Indian National Cemetery an unkempt area of tall grass and weeds. A landscaping of the area was undertaken by our club.

Inspired by these junior women, I too wish to landscape the Indian cemetery called Wallowa. So permit me, please, to reanimate General Howard, who is bearded, one-armed, sweaty-haired, sunken-eyed, a reliable Civil War man like Doc, almost pre-Raphaelite in appearance, a dreamer like me. Once time goes rightly he will become ever snowier of beard, face, hair and hand, with the right sleeve empty in his dark suit. In 1877 he is forty-nine. GOD bless you, general:

> **George J. Mitchell Department of Special Collections and Archives, Bowdoin College Library.**
> **O. O. Howard papers:**
>> and your neat and almost childishly rounded script

(General Sherman's resembles loops of wire)
and the graceful twirls of your capital letter $\mathcal{P}$, which resembles a
smallish capital "J" whose top intersects the innermost loop of a
spiral figure:
Ever so many cubic feet
and then
Oregon State Archives.
General Orders, 1847–1959,
yellow now like autumn thistles.
Locator 2/21/09/04, five cubic feet.
Joseph's already envaulted here, I see, and likewise Toohhoolhoolsote.

The land has always belonged to us, said Toohhoolhoolsote, who was renowned
among the Dreamers
like the smell of water at dusk in Wallowa
and the golden grass
and the shadows of the grass
and his shadow lengthening on the rocks.

I will not be afraid of Toohhoolhoolsote's shadow. He is dead and I am alive. He
is dead. He is dead.

2

Come on and be a man, Mr. Blurick, says Doc. Take a chance on Wallowa.

But Blurick still dreams of the Hood River, and someday a vineyard; licking his
forefinger clean, then wiping it on his shirt,
while Texas Pete winds a strip of rawhide around a mule's cracked hoof
and the red sun oversees all our dark-skirted women kneeling down in
the rushes to get water
(no, that was back before Terry's nomination for major-general
was confirmed. You forget that we'd already captured Fort
Fisher.
—Quit fighting the war, Travis!)
and digging their cooking-trench two feet long,
as Blurick remembers how three weeks ago, when the level was
higher in his whiskey barrel and he felt less weary of Doc,
who come to think of it resembles General Grant still more
than Travis, doing up the hard, bearded look to perfection,
although less sorrowfully than his model,
who never got arrested for trading on a reservation without a
license
(neither did Doc, who rode out of Quapaw before the
Modoc Agent served him any trouble),
he used to drink and drink with that man until they both loved

each other, because Doc for all his faults is one to learn from and a
fine defender of any true friend; hence:

Doc, where are you actually from?

Laramie, I done told you. Can't you listen? A man don't like
to be asked that question twice. So I'm telling you again,
Laramie, and I expect you to hear me. O my good LORD, the
horse I used to have there, Blurick! His name was Star. Tears
in my eyes. Yep, I was right there in Laramie when Red Cloud
walked right out of the council, after all we'd done for him,
and I said to that Commissioner Taylor, who was never
nothin' but a fawner, I said to him, mark my words, I said, you
ain't heard the last of them Sioux, I said—and *before the year
was out,* that red-dyed villain staged the Fetterman Massacre,
and what I said to Commissioner Taylor, I said it again to
General William Tecumseh fucking Sherman in '68, I said it
straight to his face, because I'm telling you, Blurick, when
Sherman and Terry rode into Laramie in '68—

I guess you've had enough.

No. You gimme another drink right now.

If I don't, what'll you do about it?

You stay around me long enough and maybe you'll find out—
and while the cornhaired widow darns up a rent in Travis's spare shirt,
that so-called Reverend Farris, whom for tolerance we call Preacher,
prays in a shout, as he does each dawn and dusk, for the death of Sitting
Bull, and the deliverance of our present and prospective United States
from all SATANIC reds,

Blurick passes Brown's wagon, whose flap is open, and glimpsing the man bowed
over something, hiding it and himself equally well beneath his slouch hat (what
secret does he treasure there?), then forgetting Brown, leading his oxen round to
the feed box in the back of the wagon, then picketing them to get what joy they
can of dust and weeds, smiling vaguely round to remember his late wife Eliza Bell,
whom he used to call Pet, and hopping onto his own spring seat, sipping his barefoot whiskey, his tongue as numbly metallic as if he has tasted an Oregon grape,
wishes to reach some fort or tent city so that he can post off a two-center letter to
his brother Jesse, who might be in trouble or dying; for Wittfield Blurick sure
means to be good,

and just like a mule turning a well-windlass, he pulls full wearily within the
apparatus of hope, drawing up his burden bit by bit, bracing his legs, knowing
that once this bucket comes up, somebody will empty it and cast it back down
the hole for him to draw up again, again; such is life, Mama used to say, and
she was right, but every mule on the wild side of half-broken years thirsts to
pull free from that sort of life, running, fornicating, chewing low-hanging
fruit, you name it; such is our fallen nature, O my LORD. Why on earth this

inoffensive grifter (who never even got to Wallowa) should now become a life-long mania of Doc's is a question comparable to the one I'd like to ask Colonel Perry, who hates his wife for no reason I ever saw, or Wood, who unaccountably tilts against the Army, Larry Ott, who just can't abide leaving Nez Perces aboveground, or Theller's vengeful widow—for he's neither hating nor hateful, this oldish half-ruined man sometimes dreaming of women and always calculating money and costs

as he retraces his dreams upon Horn's map all the way past Fort Walla Walla down the Columbia to The Dalles, where the Indians must now be smoking salmon, and then **OREGON CITY**, Portland and the coast (as if he were going home to Mrs. Mack); his aunt's people will meet him in Oregon City, where the bosomy cornhaired young widow from Missouri evidently means to settle, not that it matters since she d——n never looks his way anymore! In Portland, Blurick might pick up something lucrative, in the buying and selling line; after all, Government dollars must be flowing there; it's the headquarters of the District of Columbia! Then he'll hotfoot it for Hood River. If Portland doesn't work out, it's Hood River for Blurick just the same, but maybe a smaller home without picture windows. Interrupting these projects, Doc, who knows the secret reason why Lincoln was killed (Wilkes Booth was a puppet of the niggers), now informs him gratis of the fashion in which certain loving Indian couples comb each other's hair

>and come early evening in Hood River, while I'm smoking a pipe on our front porch, she sets herself down so gentle in my lap, and I start combing her long blonde locks with an ivory comb while she's running her sweet fingers through my hair,

>D——d if I ain't seen it, Blurick! The way they touch each other's an abomination!

because Doc, loving him like a true comrade, means to hold him back *here* where the **NEZ PERCES** or **SAPTINS** occupy an indefinite white grandness above the Salmon River Mountains, east of W A L L A W A L L A and west of N O R T H - W E S T T E R R I T O R Y. Adventure through Range No. 46 east; now you're coming into Wallowa. What in blazes do I care? Doc's sure wearing on me. I'd rather get shut of that fellow and plant my vineyard

>where Mount Hood crowns its blue-green forest ridge over the meadows, and below me my neighbors' farms

>>(I'm not afraid of Doc),

>wrapped in golden grass and cherry trees

>and fronting the Hood River fast and dark:

>>*The LORD your GOD is bringing you into a good land, a land of brooks of water, of fountains and springs, flowing forth in valleys and hills, a land of wheat and barley,*

so that Blurick, who now sits high, watching the other wagons roll on ahead of him, with Mrs. Graves's various traps upheaped behind him like the jetsam of a wrecked ship, will walk up the trail eating pears, all the way to the sweet tall purple lupines humming with bees all summer,

the crisp shadow of a spruce branch-tip with every needle in place projected on a bleached white stump,

and a cabin in sight of Mount Hood

and (to hell & blazes with that haughty widow!) an orphan girl now already pregnant,

blue mountains and green mountains below, where

Doc, how many more miles to Farewell Bend?

Doc?

Soon's you get to Pendleton, Jerry Despain will board your horse on good hay and grain for fifty cents cash. *Remember* that name.

What are you, his brother-in-law?

Doc, why won't you answer me?

He's set on that Hood River. Even though I tole him and tole him that all the best sections have been claimed and growed up tight—

Let him alone, Doc.

Doc?

There's a nigger in every woodpile. What's *your* nigger's name?

Cut it out, Doc. I ain't scared of you. Blurick, if I was you I'd show him the business end of your Sharps—

Tell me what you got against Wallowa, Mr. Blurick. Tell me why you won't take a chance. I got this here dip compass that can find copper and nickel, and I'll teach you how to use it.

You keep it. I aim to raise an orchard.

Ain't I told you about the *gold* up there? Wallowa gold, Blurick! That's no lie. Richer than Alder Gulch. Wallowa's got everything.

I s'pose it might.

And blood-red salmon in Wallowa Lake, so many you can kill 'em by the dozen with clubs.

Kill 'em yourself.

Might be more gold in Wallowa than they've took out of even the Black Hills. Just dig up your color and buy your farm—

On Horn's map—

I already warned you against Horn's map, but you won't listen.

I'll think on it.

No. Say your piece against Wallowa right now.

Plenty of Indians up that way. The map says **NEZ PERCES**. That's what it says. So it ain't easy till they get driven out. And you know mining is way down in north Idaho. Whenever Chinamen come in, it's all over. And I ain't seen no pictures of that country, neither, but I *have* seen a steel engraving, plain as the dickens, of a Hood River farm, and that's what I aim to get. And I read in a reliable Christian newspaper published down in Bethany, Virginia, that this same Hood River country flows with milk and honey. That's exactly the words they used and no mistake.

You hear that, Captain Travis? This man's yellow. He's no better than a coward.

Lay off him. CHRIST, why pick on an American when there's more'n enough Indians to fight?

What's Indians got to do with it? When we reach Farewell Bend we'll need to—

Any man want to bet there ain't good Indians?

You turning preacher in your old age?

Let's not get off the track. Doc and Blurick are squaring up to fight, and there ain't no other fun around here.

When we get to our nooning place—

Hell, Blurick won't fight.

Then there won't be no quarrel.

We'll see. When Doc says something, he don't never go back on it.

Your oxen are holding up pretty good, Blurick. I see you know how to pamper them animals.

Yeah.

Now, Blurick, be a man and stand up to Doc if you don't want him pestering you.

Blurick, you watch out for him. One time I seen him brain a man with the edge of a tin plate.

Getting back on the subject of Indians—

Cut it out. We ain't interested. Didn't your Mama never tell you you're simple?

    The first time I saw an Indian out here—

    First time you heard a horse piss you thought it was Niagara Falls.

        But Tilden stands for keeping down canal tolls.

        Well, but Hayes says right here—

        But Baker says to Brown—

            Good syrup and sugar at Walla-Walla.

                Then he says to me, *can't you picture Blurick in his granny's come-hither dress, riding sidesaddle like a girl?*

And Tilden has come out against building palaces for the insane. He'll keep Government out of our pockets.

Quit it now. Doc's getting mean again.

He's *been* mean ever since

        . . . ever since the Oro Fino route got opened as a wagon road—

        But they got all the gold out.

        Not quite. Chief Joseph stands in the way.

Because this d——d Jew Government—

And there's other rich strikes they tell about, between Florence and White Bird Creek.

Now, when you find you an Indian to canoe you across the
Columbia, you got to set him straight. Whatever he wants,
you offer *half.*

You told me. Now for Pete's sake shut up.

Who's playing to-night?

Not me. I seen you stock a bower and an ace.

No, it's Doc that done that. I ain't no cardsharp, honest Injun, and if you say
anything different I'll—

We're not supposed to sell weapons or powder to Indians no more,
I don't care how kind they be—

What about knives?

Sure. You can sell anybody a knife, I guess.

Blurick, you'll stand up to him?

I aim to mind my own business,

turning his back upon these croakers and idlers who don't much care for
his health. Last night when he was tallying his sacks of beans and cornmeal (some of which he might afford to sell in Hood River), Doc came in
without asking. He's not scared of Doc, not quite.

Blurick, if you don't put your foot down, Doc's gonna keep on teasin' you every
day a little more nasty and violent.

I'll take care of myself.

What's the hangup back there?

Mrs. Graves finally passed.

Just now? Poor lady. Who's gonna bury her?

She's no relation of mine.

Travis, I seen how your eyes wigwagged when them kids said *typhoid.*

Weren't no typhoid.

Then let's see you bury her.

In the first place—

Aw, hell.

It's too hot right now. You could fry an egg on my wagon-rims.

Is Preacher in there?

Sure. He's been prayin' over her two days straight, so you think he'd miss this?
This is his meat.

He must be related to that *Christian General.*

Which one?

Howard. He played the dunce at Chancellorsville—

Don't *you* have a long memory!

Wasn't so long ago,

while Blurick, sober as a cart horse, ducks inside his double-covered wagon to dream about the *Wonder Orchards* of Oregon while relishing that private drink of reinvigoration, from which he ordinarily refrains until near about four-or five-o'-clock, when we herd our oxen, mules and horses inside the wagon circle; and the widow comes back from the river without looking his way, GoDd——n her and hello to a new dream:

> **WANTED:** Girl of good references, and who is represented to be of good character. Must be inclined to matrimony,

. . . under the influence of whiskey, Pete . . .

and pretty, and

Just then he smells Doc coming. Drawing his Colt, he lays it down between his legs and drops his slouch hat over it.

Pete, wasn't you at Chancellorsville?

Don't get me started.

I heard tell Bode's division was way down east by southeast on the Plank Road, and then that d——d Uh-Oh Howard—

Now, Travis allows this is a real fine place to camp. Well, Blurick, I shit on this GoDd——d place! I call this place *Camp Cholery*. You see that marsh down there? That's where the cholery comes from. I've seen a dozen folks buried thanks to those vapors. Come nightfall you'll see.

I don't care about that. I got quinine, genuine pharmaceutical grade.

Quinine don't mean *nothing*. You don't know *nothing* about cholery.

Maybe I do.

Like what?

My wife died from it.

Goes to show she didn't know nothing about it, either. Gimme a drink.

Nope.

Why not?

On account of what you said about my wife.

Just now?

Yeah.

Is that her picture in that locket?

Might be.

Sure it is. I recollect when you showed it to Travis. A fine looking gal, she was. Near about as tiny as a Snake squaw. Now what was her name?

None of your business.

Undoing two brass eagle buttons of his shortcoat, Doc draws out a buckskin neck-pouch:

Now, Blurick,

> with the sightless stare of a badly wounded man who lies on the battlefield hoping for the doctor,

this'll be the convincer. I want you to realize that I mean you good. Where do you s'pose this color hails from?

From inside your stinkin' jacket. Listen up, Doc—

You ever hear of Oro Fino?

Well, according to what I been reading—

That's why I said you don't know *nothing*. It's a ways between Wallowa and Kamiah. Been booming for more than fifteen years now, and they ain't hardly gotten started. Gonna make the Comstock Lode look like squaw trash. They already drug in Chinamen to work them mines up around there. In Florence they got Chinks d——n near everywhere. Yellow niggers diggin' up yellow color,

> snow-fine gold dust in a buckskin bag for me to dream of
>> (he's fixing to *make* me dream!)
> but I'll be dreaming of a longhaired yellowhaired orphan girl beside me in Hood River,

so you better think it over.

Sure.

You got acqua-regia in here, don't you?

What if I do?

I can smell it. I smelled that chlorine sting of it the first time I ever come in here. Your jug-bung's cracked, Blurick. Know what I'm saying?

O, shut your d——d mouth.

I'll prove it's genuine gold. Get out your acqua-regia and try it.

Nope.

Blurick, are you a hard money man? I'm talkin' to *you*.

Way I look at it, a man's politics is his own business.

I said yellow niggers, yellow color. Don't be a GoDd——d *yellow man*.

> That fool Doc's still wishin' on Oro Fino. Heard him puttin' the bite on Blurick just now.
> O, come on, Pete! Even Doc can't actually believe—

Travis, them ladies asked me can we halt for—

Tell 'em no.

It don't rightly signify till they hear it from you.

All right.

Hey, you, Brown! If you don't watch out, your horse might choke on that weed.

> You done made your point already, Doc. I said I'll think it over. Now, in here's *my* place. Why don't you let me be?
> You gimme that Horn's map.

For what?

To wipe my ass.

Blurick, are you gonna fight him like a man?

Is something moving down that cañon?

Doc, you better come out now and—

> Blurick, you can't get away from me.

> So long for now then,

>> both of them glaring down at Blurick's slouch hat, and then
>> Doc goes.

That's just a doe an' her fawn. Ain't that a doe, Doc?

I'm callin' in my wages soon's we reach The Dalles.

But you signed your obligation to Captain Travis.

I said I'm done soon's we roll into The Dalles. Guess you won't hardly need me then.

We sure won't. What I like about you, Doc, you always do exactly as you aim to—

Hey, Travis! Doc means to leave this outfit—

So I heard.

And he—

Far as I'm concerned, Doc, you can cash out at Farewell Bend. Take your d——d traps and ride for Wallowa—

No.

You, Red, come ride ahead up here . . .

> You hear that? Travis must be getting yellow. Doc said he was quitting, and that Travis only—

> He's more partial to that Texas Pete. They been together since Bloody Angle.

> What about him and Doc?

> Well, I myself have known Doc since before the Bank of California went under, and he's always been mean—

> Heard Doc say that Blurick's on the run from his wife. What do you think about that?

> Secretive types like Blurick might pull anything. What the hell do you care? Are you one of our foremost citizens or something? Maybe she's a hell-and-brimstone bitch—

>> . . . played out like Oro Fino . . .

>>> . . . nothing but winter wheat in Wallowa . . .

>>>> . . . a good talk over the situation . . .

>>>> . . . the White Man's Party in Charleston . . .

>>>> . . . Rutherfraud B. Hayes, the fraud of the century! *He* won't win.

Doc, why do you want to jump ship?

That's my business.

Not at The Dalles!

Why not?

Cheaper goods in Portland. Fine Clatsop squaws—

I aim to make some history up Wallowa way, and none of you d——d yellow-bellies will get drib nor drab of my glory. I'll be somebody you'll take off your hat to.

You keep right on pumpin' your lizard lips like that, Doc, we'll take off your hat for you. Only glory you got goin' for you is your meanness—

Tell you what. Some night you're gonna get your throat slit open and your cold blue balls tucked right up there—

Blurick, don't give him no more whiskey.

I won't.

I don't want his yellow whiskey. Got me my own supply now.

We can all see that. Listen, Doc, you're acting like a fool. Why don't you snooze it off?

So you consider that I'm too drunk to shoot straight? Then I'll show you something to make you think twice. The very next Injun we see, buck or squaw, I don't give two shits if it's a GODd——d papoose, you just watch me—

EXTRACTS, *OR*, HOW THE NEZ PERCE GOT CIVILIZED AND IMPROVED
1805–77

1

Those people treated us well gave us to eat roots dried roots made in bread, roots boiled, one Sammon, berries of red haws some dried . . .

> WILLIAM CLARK, describing the first encounter of Lewis and Clark with the Nez Perce, 1805

I think we can justly affirm to the honor of these people that they are the most hospitable, honest, and sincere people that we have met with in our voyage.

> MERIWETHER LEWIS, summing up the Nez Perce, 1806

The Nez Perces . . . make many promises to work & listen to instruction . . . Say they do not have difficulty with the white men as the Cayouses do, & that we shall find it so.

> NARCISSA PRENTISS WHITMAN, 1836

The Nez Perces & Waiilatpu Indians have a great number of horses, many cattle & some sheep, which if our Government had possession of the country would be a pledge for their good conduct inasmuch as they would not like to jeopardize their property.

MARCUS WHITMAN, 1844

In one day the Americans became as numerous as the grass.

PEOPEO MOXMOX, Walla-Walla Indian, 1855

When the [Yakima] Indians hesitated, the Governor said to tell the chief, "if they don't sign this treaty, they will walk in blood knee-deep."

WILLIAM CAMERON MCKAY, interpreter's son at Walla Walla, 1855

The Nez Percés received a reservation of approximately 7,694,270 acres in present-day Oregon and Idaho, which was later reduced to about 756,968 acres.

ROBERT H. RUBY AND JOHN A. BROWN, events at Walla-Walla, 1855

I have just received your note of 25th inst., informing me that a party of miners are on the Nez Perce Reservation in violation of law.

MAJOR ENOCH STEEN, to Indian Agent Andrew J. Cain, 1860

I am of the opinion that there is gold in the Bitter Root Mts, and that it is in the interest of the government, as well as these Indians . . . to throw the gold region out of the reservation . . . I have exercised all the authority I possess as the civil authority here, and to make any effort that would betray my utter helplessness, would only excite the minds of the Indians to a state of desperation, feeling they were entirely deserted.

AGENT CAIN, to Edward R. Geary, Superintendent of Indian Affairs, 1860

Before the end of this century . . . the Africans among us in a subordinate position will amount to 11 million persons. What shall be done with them? We must expand or perish. We are constrained by an inexorable necessity to accept expansion or extermination.

ROBERT TOOMBS, calling for Georgia to secede from the Union, 1860

A single empire embracing the entire world, and controlling, without extinguishing, local organizations and nationalities, has been not only the dream of conquerors but the ideal of speculative philanthropists. Our own dominion is of such extent and power that it may, so far as this continent is concerned, be looked upon as something like an approach to the realization of such an ideal.

JAMES RUSSELL LOWELL, arguing against seccession, 1861

The Nez Perces are the most intelligent and exemplary Indians on the North Pacific Coast, and they boast of never having murdered a white man.

DOCTOR G. A. NOBLE, *ca.* 1861

The truth is, the close of the war with our resources unimpaired gives an elevation, a scope to the ideas of leading capitalists far higher than anything ever undertaken in this country before. They talk of millions as confidently as formerly of thousands.

GENERAL WILLIAM T. SHERMAN'S BROTHER JOHN, to General Sherman, 1865

Surely our Government would not allow law-abiding, loyal citizens to be driven from their homes. The white man only asks a quarter section on which to support his family. The Indian is welcome to the hills for pasturage.

Letter in the *Lewiston Radiator,* 25 February 1865, from "K."

I do not apprehend a Genl Indian War, but for years we will have a kind of unpleasant state of hostilities that can only be terminated with the destruction of hostile bands.

GENERAL WILLIAM T. SHERMAN, to President Grant, 1866

This valley [Wallowa] should be surveyed as soon as practicable, for the wigwam of the savage will soon give way to the whites. Instead of the hunting and fishing grounds of the red men, the valley will teem with a thriving and busy population.

ORIGINAL FIELD NOTES, WALLOWA COUNTY CLERK'S OFFICE, 1866

Congress have the exclusive right of pre-emption to all Indian lands lying within the territories of the United States . . . and the Indians have only a right of occupancy, and the United States possess the legal title, subject to that occupancy, but with an absolute and exclusive right to extinguish the Indian title of occupancy, either by conquest or purchase.

KENT'S *AMERICAN LAW,* 1867

All who cling to their old hunting grounds are hostile and will remain so until killed off.

GENERAL WILLIAM T. SHERMAN, to John Sherman, 1868

I told him [Joseph] that it was useless for them to talk about sending the whites away, that they were there by higher authority than I and I could not remove them . . . It is a great pity that the valley was ever opened for settlement.

JOHN B. MONTEITH, U.S. Indian Agent, 1872

The American cannot keep his arms folded. He must embark on something, and once embarked he must go on and on forever; for if he stops, those who follow him would crush him under their feet. His life is one long campaign . . .

JOSEPH ALEXANDER, GRAF VON HÜBNER, 1873

Custer, of course, was delighted to be once more upon the plains . . . The Southwest having been conquered, it now became necessary to turn attention to the Northwest.

A CORPS OF COMPETENT WRITERS AND ARTISTS, events of 1873

The great barrier to the settlement of the Wallowa, one of the finest agricultural and stock raising countries on the Pacific slope, has at last been overcome, the bridge across the great Wallowa river was completed and thrown open to travel . . . thousands of men . . . are heading in that direction . . .

A. C. SMITH, 1873

It is hereby ordered that the tract of land above described be withheld from entry and settlement as public lands, and that the same be set apart as a reservation for the roaming Nez Perce Indians . . .

PRESIDENT U. S. GRANT, 1873

READ WHITE MEN . . . THE WALLOWA GONE . . . DIRTY, GREASY INDIANS TO HOLD THE VALLEY.

Editorial in the *Mountain Sentinel*, 1873

Should Government decide against locating the Indian reservation there [in Wallowa], and order the Indians to leave or remain away, I respectfully suggest that timely and deliberate preparation should be made to enforce that order, and protect the white inhabitants from the rage which probably might inspire the Indians under disappointment of being deprived of what they highly value and apparently consider as justly theirs.

CAPTAIN STEPHEN G. WHIPPLE, First Cavalry, Company "L," 1874

It is hereby ordered that the order, dated June 16, 1873, withdrawing from sale and settlement and setting apart the Wallowa Valley in Oregon . . . as an Indian reservation, is hereby revoked and annulled; and the aforesaid tract of country is hereby restored to the public domain.

PRESIDENT U. S. GRANT, 1875

I think it a great mistake to take from Joseph and his band of Nez Perces that valley.

GENERAL O. O. HOWARD, 1876

2

Special orders from Brigadier-General O. O. Howard, Brevet Major-General U.S. Army, commanding Department of the Columbia, to Captain Stephen G. Whipple, First Cavalry "L." March 14, 1877. Two companies to encamp on the west side of Wallowa river, near its junction with the Grande Ronde, for the mutual protection of the citizens and Indians in that vicinity.

Your camp location will be about twenty-five miles from Summerville. Put up log shelters, captain. The pine woods will be convenient.

I'm sure they will, sir.

You'll set out as soon as the season permits you to cross the Blue-ridge with wheeled vehicles.

Yessir.

And remember, Whipple: No violent measures are authorized without more definite instructions.

THEIR HEARTS HAVE CHANGED
MARCH–MAY 1877

1

*T*his Chief Joseph is quite the debater, so they say. He makes a remarkable impression at first. Unfortunately, he's not even as civilized as his late apostate father;

and ascending the Columbia River Gorge, with Portland
> (latitude 45° 30', longitude 122° 27' 30")

now left in care of Lizzie,

they make a brave array of men, ready to follow commands and dreams wherever those might lead:

> **Oregon State Archives.**
> **General Orders, 1847–1959.**
> **Locator 2/21/09/04, five cubic feet.**

most of them citizens who have exchanged the falling wages back East for Indian troubles

—and here and there an Army man on his Indian service.

I mean, Blackie, we were walkin' up green, green trails. We went around the bend and the first thing we saw was a big trout jumpin'. That's when I says, I got to get my piece of Wallowa. I'm gonna take my piece right on the edge of the lake, where I saw that fish

and a fish jumps in the river while a horseman eyes them from the Oregon side.

> The day will come, sir, when this property will be very valuable.

> Right you are, Fletch. Unfortunately, we'll still be toiling away at our Indian service!

> But, general, if we're likely to remain in this Department we might as well begin thinking about property.

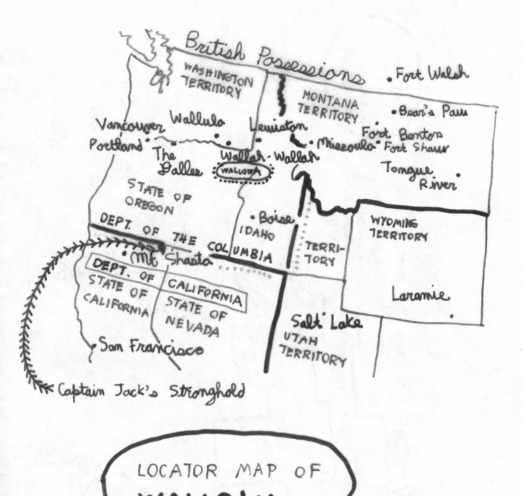

LOCATOR MAP OF
WALLOWA

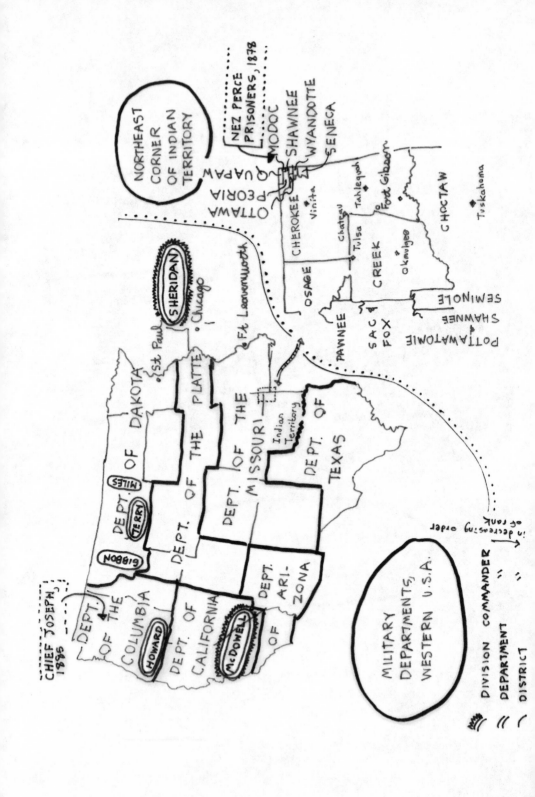

NEZ PERCE PRISONERS, 1878

NORTHEAST CORNER OF INDIAN TERRITORY

MODOC
SHAWNEE
WYANDOTTE
SENECA

QUAPAW
PEORIA
OTTAWA

CHEROKEE
Vinita
Tahlequah
Chelsea
Tulsa
Okmulgee
Fort Gibson

CHOCTAW
Tuskahoma

OSAGE

CREEK

SEMINOLE
SHAWNEE
POTTAWATOMIE

PAWNEE
SAC &
FOX

SHERIDAN
St. Paul
Chicago
Ft. Leavenworth

DEPT. OF DAKOTA
MILES
TERRY
GIBBON

DEPT. OF THE PLATTE

DEPT. OF THE MISSOURI
Indian Territory

DEPT. OF TEXAS

CHIEF JOSEPH, 1895

DEPT. OF THE COLUMBIA
HOWARD

DEPT. OF CALIFORNIA

DEPT. OF ARI- ZONA
McDOWELL

MILITARY DEPARTMENTS, WESTERN U.S.A.

in decreasing order of rank

DIVISION COMMANDER
" DEPARTMENT "
" DISTRICT "

He has had the reputation of being a notorious Dreamer
for as long as we've heard of him. The same goes for his
brother.

What about the other Indians?

GOD disposes, Fletch.

We'll see. Looking-Glass and White Bird may be more
flexible.

See here, boy, you can't establish your suit until you can take every
trick in it.

I know that,

carrion-birds darkening the scaffold atop that tall cliff-island
of that ancient Indian graveyard.

Lizzie will be ordering Vick's flower seeds from Roch-
ester, New York. Out here it's not too late to plant—

You don't know nothing. See how I just swept up this whole hand?
That's not fair!

Of course it ain't. Cards ain't supposed to be fair.

You're out of luck. Nobody takes shinplasters at The
Dalles. It's near about impossible even to cash a greenback.

How about Lewiston?

O, if you can hold out until then! Always some good
Samaritan up there who'll take your d——d money.

You may not know this, general, but I recently
met your son in the Sportsmen's Emporium. He
was buying gunmetal-polish on your behalf.

On Front Street?

Yessir. A likely young officer.

Thank you. That would be Guy, my eldest. No,
Fletch, everything has already been gone over.
Enjoy yourself . . .

Wallowa? Is that where we're goin,' Doc?

Don't you even remember?

I'm just trusting you. You said we could be volunteers.

Only if we need to.

I want to.

Then go sign up with that d——d general over there by the paddlewheel. I don't
care shit about glory.

How come Blurick ran away?

He'll get his.

Don't he have an aunt or something in Hood River?

He's dead to me.

No, he was near the bottom of his class at West Point.

No danger in this section.

Fine spot for a saw-mill.

> We've got no warrant to settle on wild lands beyond the latest boundaries until they have been ceded in an orderly way.
>
> What are you, some kind of Jew lawyer?

> > Well, the truth is, Lizzie is mad about that rock soap washing powder you can send away for in San Francisco. So when she thought to do Mrs. Perry a kindness and give her a pound of it, I couldn't refuse.
> >
> > Of course not, sir. As soon as we arrive at Lapwai I'll hand it off.
> >
> > A relief to get rid of it. Thank you, Fletch, for troubling yourself—

So I'm workin' with you, Doc. I swear I'll do just what you say.

You'll do fine.

Doc, you said you'd seen them Nez Perces.

That's right. Been to Wallowa scores of times.

What're they like?

Just Injuns.

And you can speak Injun, right?

Ain't nothin' to it.

Why won't you say more about Wallowa?

Them green lands in Wallowa, why should Injuns get the benefit? And that lake, we'll call it Lake Heaven. Wait till you see it. Honest Injun, you can see the fins of speckled trout forty foot down! And salmon red as blood. That's how it is—

You swear?

Sure. And right there I seen gold inside of a hill, with that genuine yellow color. Travis already struck it rich, and he's nothin' but a *squaw man* wolfer. And *them,* they ain't hardly better than animals. You know what I spied them doin' one time? Well, they—

Good morning to you, General Howard. Good morning, lieutenant.

Good morning, Captain Wolf. What's for breakfast to-day?

Salmon, coffee, steak and potatoes.

This scenery is unsurpassed. These wild cascades!

Well, general, one gets used to it. And how are Mrs. Howard and the children?

Now the sun goes as wide as Blurick's wagon-wheels, and they see

> dark green and light green late summer forest walling the river in
> and the morning's white gloss on alder leaves

> > and two more woodhawks felling trees to vend to boilermen as white breath speeds from our tall dark smokestack, Old Glory seething upon its forward-canted flagpole, passengers gripping the railings

and the shadow of Rooster Rock reflected in a stagnant marsh.

He's a nigger lover.

Who is?

Him:

> tall, whitebearded now, immaculately medalled, tricked out in double button-rows and epaulettes, the empty sleeve stiff and straight.

Shut your mouth. He's looking at us.

No he ain't.

He turned tail at Chancellorsville.

That's not so. He exercised the functions of a commanding officer against overwhelming—

He's a—

Now the cliffs descend (the ship's white flank briefly exploding into sunny dazzlement) and the golden grass becomes a sort of sky inhabited by blue-grey clouds of trees

> and striated basalt cliffs where a dark pine droops down its needles like a weeping willow, dark rock snickering irregularly through the orange grass,
>
> the world brown and gold,
>
> silver and blue,
>
> and the pale yellow of the hill grass at noon,
>
> the wettish, blondish-green fleece on steep and windy slopes along the Columbia at The Dalles:
>
>> Fast and shipshape, captain!
>>
>> Throw down the plank.
>>
>> Aye, aye.
>>
>> Well, General Howard, welcome to The Dalles,

city of tents, formerly bazaar of Indians

> (even the Modocs used to trade here),

where at present the serviceberries remain far from ripe, and three young ladies stand giggling and waving by the floating dock. Cordwood and plumped out oat-sacks, trodden dirt; thus The Dalles—not yet as wide and busy as the railroad terminal at Council Bluffs, Nebraska, but Progress is coming. The pilot lets fall the mail sack; citizens swarm around it. A pair of honeymooners make their *pic-nic* on a blanket beneath an aspen, beaming at each other. An off-duty cavalryman waters his horse. Starting, he salutes the general, who smilingly nods in return. Indians sit in the dirt streets, quietly drinking whiskey because it's too early for them to cure salmon. One of them shows each passerby a letter signed by some unknown person and reading: *This is a good Indian.* Soon we will get them onto some reservation. General Howard lays down his head at Umatilla House, among the many who seek sleep with their boots on. Fletch is already snoring heartily. How young he is! Reminds me of Guy, who I'm sure is doing well. In which establishment will that young couple I saw under the aspen find peace to-night? Not here, I hope. Lizzie and I were about that age when we were married. I'll not forget how tenderly she used to smile at me. She seems wonderfully discouraged nowadays. LORD, may I soon discover how to cheer her! Now I lay me—but already he can feel between himself and sleep his mind's weary hand sorting through that faded saddlebag of hemp and cornstalks in which our dreams are kept, and finding, inevitably, Edisto, of which he would rather never dream. No, I shall not. Accordingly, the nightmares arrive, like thin dark streams of Illinois regiments wisping down the raw Allatoona hillside to reënforce our Union fort. First the flower-scented porches of Beaufort rise up about him, and he begins once more to see the elderly negresses standing in the dirt outside the Fuller House (now in moderate disrepair since the dismissal of General Saxton), with that pencil-shaped sentry-box tall and white beside them, and shade trees behind the fence. Against all desire he perceives himself approaching John Seabrook's white plantation mansion on Edisto Island, with a single cloud centered over the roof and confiscated cotton drying on the lawn—but no, the lawn has returned to its immaculate state, and the Seabrooks control their cotton as before. A negro crowd gazes upon him in a silence not yet hopeless even now; somehow he will save them. *General: You will acknowledge the receipt and obedience of these instructions*—which he must now read to them who wait upon him here at Edisto. No, I decline. He sits up. The lantern being merely half-shuttered—sufficient light to work—on the table he unrolls Colton's map, weighting the corners with four bullets:

The Dalles right here, then east to Celilo (must ask about that Spanish Hole up inland):

Our general never quits, GOD bless him!

and Wallula on the Columbia where it narrows, right north of Old Fort Walla-Walla, then east-southeast to Walla Walla:

A credit to the service.

Are you fixing to rejoin?

and Lewiston,

which the reds once called *Riverfork*,

and the pre-American blankness, already gridded, of the Nez Perce Indian Reservation into whose northwestern part Lewiston and consequently Fort Lapwai have insinuated themselves:

Not enough excitement anymore,

Lapwai now metonymized in his mind by Colonel Perry's smooth bearded spadeshaped face, which in former years appeared gentle

and Mrs. Perry's, poor lady,

and going down the south-southeasterly snaggle of the Salmon River, we come first to White Bird Creek, then John Day's Creek, then the two easterly branches of Slate Creek, along which restless Americans have already begun to settle; and in the blank map-country eastward of those tributaries we find Nevada, Florence (whose gold mines are petering out) and Millersburg,

then, of greatest present significance, the northern half of Joseph's valley, which on Colton's map is still called **WALLOWA IND. RESERVN.**— mistakenly now that it has been withdrawn again from the Indians. Whipple's bunch are keeping that country buttoned down, I trust.

And the Roseburg citizens aim to put in an oil mill.

Well, once we build up Wallowa—

The air grows as thick as Pittsburgh factory-smoke. Sitting on the corner bed, two miners play cards all night. One of them keeps saying: Hardly better than animals.— Men are marching loudly out to piss. A fat grocer fans himself, then vomits in a chamberpot. An old rancher and his son are murmuring sadly over the news from Cleveland: the Standard Oil coopers have gone on strike. Why should it trouble them? Perhaps their relations live out there. A loathsome fly drones round and round his ear; he cannot catch it. Perhaps if I still had my right hand . . . A Spaniard of some sort lies on his back, masticating pilot biscuit. A stockman entertains three comrades with loud declamations from *Fox's Ethiopian Comicalities.* None of this is how it ought to be, but who am I to insist on special treatment? The Army holds no sway here. I'm not so old yet, nor so proud. So he lights a candle and reads Cicero, on whom they began last month at the Officers' Club in Portland. To be sure, I enjoyed Dumas's adventure-entertainments with less reserve. Does that mean I'm worn out? I must keep my Latin up—it cost me so much labor to con it in the first place! O, me! The thing is to remain unaffected by those evil-mouthed citizens over there. LORD preserve me from hating them! May they be less corrupt than they seem. Refugees from justice, familiars of some livery stable, Indian haters, claim hunters, what are they? Deliver me from evil; their indiscretions are not my business. O, but like this fly they *are* hateful beyond description. Hardly better than animals. And the water, and the grass, and Edisto, and Lizzie's thin trembling mouth, and this journey, and those profane men over there, although it's not for me to call them bad, when will they all swim away? I must confess, Latin is more difficult than the *parlez-vous* we used to play at back at Bowdoin College. And Lizzie's eyes, is it merely the change of life or do I fail her worse and worse? I pray that Joseph will come in as easily as Cochise and his Apaches did. No doubt he will, if I reason with him. The Apache case testifies to the power of goodness. O, how unpleasant General Crook became once I prevented him from putting them out of the way! (That manner he has of turning his face infinitesimally to one side when he stares at one with his blue-grey eyes—quite inhuman, for a fact.) And as I get older I worry more, of course; last week Lizzie said: Dearest, you never used to see such difficulties in anything.— Well, the anniversary of Father's death is coming round: thirty-seven years. That never fails to unman me. And I've told her, but she doesn't realize:

Crook's influence truly waxes against me in Washington. Is that why Sherman has grown cold? He's been less available since Edisto. It didn't help that I lost two years of military service. But surely he won't replace me, so long as this business goes smoothly at Lapwai. Monteith is awfully strong against Joseph, I believe (must learn what Sladen thinks). Nearly every settler dislikes Indians and would wipe them out. How can I help the Nez Perces to know their own interest? Sherman hates them all worse than negroes. If I resigned the service, Lizzie wouldn't know what to do with me. But if I were to be ordained . . . The stink of their boots! When will this night end? Sherman used to advise me to write a book. I should, actually. I'll pay off the lawyers this year, and if Congress would give me relief . . . But my salary's in depreciated greenbacks. Grace's tuition is paid up through Christmas; praise GOD. That pledge of ten thousand dollars to the university, was I crazy? Lizzie never complains. After seven children, the skin of her face remains fair, delicate and taut . . . It must please her, to look so much younger than her age. If I have disappointed her, I pray that she will forgive me. I have tried many things with her now, and . . . But those men in the corner don't care how foul they are. Their low type has brought about most of our Indian problems. They're worse than *squaw men*, whose licentiousness may at least improve into marital love. Their crimes cry out to Heaven. And so, for the Indians' own sake . . . Lizzie never asks me anything anymore. She has forgotten everything but unhappiness. When Harry and Bessie are older I'll bring her here to see the country. Perhaps Grace will find time to accompany us, but I suppose she'll have married one of her beaux. Someday, when the Indians are finally ripe for education, I hope to endow them their own college. Have those men no consideration for the sensibilities of others? They goad me like flies on a mule's open sores! But nobody else is troubled, so I must bear it. No, they are uttering obscenities now. That's too much.

Rising, he says: Gentlemen, you're offending this house. Go out or be quiet.

You can't discipline us, general. We're not in the Army.

This place is under Army jurisdiction. Now keep the peace at once, or I'll have you arrested.

Ain't you the general who—

Sir,

> his empty sleeve swishing angrily like a whip,
>> as Fletch now leaps up, longing to defend him,

I don't know who *you* are, but since you're asking who I am, I am a soldier who has never turned a corner to avoid a bullet. Now will you do as I say? I won't warn you again.

They glare at him, one man actually gnashing his teeth, but so far govern themselves as to converse in ugly whispers.— So he wishes Fletch a second good night, rolls up Colton's map and returns to Cicero. He cannot approve that writer's vanity, nor, worse yet, his inability to make up his mind, nor, worst of all, his cowardice. A slaveholder, moreover, and a rented rhetorician! At least Cicero can be called happy in his friend Atticus. Who would not desire such a companion, who never fails to advise, console and flatter upon request? To-night General Howard has almost reached the end of the year 50 B.C. Caesar determines to cross the Rubicon. Once he does, the Civil War will commence; and the statues of the Roman gods will sweat blood. *Long have they pass'd.* Pompey, who disdained when he should have flattered, now too late begins to fear his rival. As for Cicero, he has obligated himself to both dictators. Pompey represents the legitimate authority of the Republic, so Cicero feels bound to serve him, but the man's many errors repel him—yet he dreads his own fate should Caesar be victorious. He writes another desperate letter to Atticus. *"Depugna," inquis, "potius quom servias."* Which is to say: *"Fight," you tell me, "rather than be slaves." The result will be proscription if one is vanquished and slavery even if one wins. "What shall I do then?" What the cattle do, who when scattered follow flocks of their own kind. As an ox follows the herd, so shall I follow the "right party," or whoever are said to be the "right party," even if they rush to destruction.* First the general considers this question; then it seems to him that he continues to consider it, until the clerk knocks shockingly at each door, announcing: *Four-o'-clock!* so that no one will miss the train to Celilo,

  which unseeingly passes Toohhoolhoolzote and seven other Dreamers watching from the rocks there where the river is bifurcated by the reflection of Cape
  Horn as the shining tracks run on along the base of that basalt cliff and curve
  round into the yellow morning sky, running on to Celilo:
  the birds fall silent; then comes the train, roaring, smoking and hooting,
  making itself gone
    (it is warped, says Toohhoolhoolzote),
  gone to Celilo
where the steamer waits to convey Fletch and the general upriver, because
I pledge allegiance to the flag
    and to this green-gold and brown-cliffed land,
    all things soft and low,
        and my Lizzie
    mirror-river, rock columns in frozen explosions, bursting out of grass-slopes,
    bursting out of clouds
of the United States of America
    such dappling, such slopes of green and gold
(America),
    the hills like soft prisms because they show so many cañons, so many
    facets
of America. The land has always belonged to us.

  More coffee, general?

  Yes, please. I must say, it'll be extremely pleasant to be sitting ourselves down again on Colonel Perry's porch! And that gracious wife of his!

  Yessir.

Tell me, Fletch, *entre nous*, which of our ladies at Lapwai is the favorite of the younger officers?

Well, general, I should have to say Mrs. Theller—

Of course. A regular belle! Are you tired?

Not at all, sir.

Take a snooze if you wish; I won't need you at all this morning . . .

> I voted for Tilden because he's a hard money man. Hayes has been bewitched by easy money.
>
> We all voted for Tilden. Therefore, he won. Well, look who moved into the White House—
>
>> Excuse me, general, but I'd like your autograph to give to my mother.
>
> Hayes made no mistake on the national debt.
>
>> All right. Here you are, sir.
>
>> Thanks, general; it'll be a real feather in her cap. She's a collector. All you Government men have been real kind to her. Tilden's the only one who ever turned her down.
>
> This here state would have gone for Tilden. Well, they nullified the Democratic vote

of America. In America, where the slanting gorge-walls go grey, a Umatilla woman is smoke-tanning a buckskin.

And what about the Boxer cartridge, general?

It's not the best, but since it is so widely used by the English Government, that fact alone recommends it.

My Daddy sure swore by it.

Well, captain, it was pretty good for his day. My father kept a case or two on the farm. As you know, it's not reloadable. Moreover, it's made of iron, which is a serious defect,

> and the blue of the John Day River meets the grey of the Columbia
>
> and the blue-treed yellow horizon, soft as a Pendleton blanket, high on the rolling ridges of this world of yellow grass
>
>> and then a sodden meadow of purple camas flowers
>
>>> (near about as good as the land along our Dead River back home)

where beside a blind and ancient Umatilla who leans on his stick, with his dark face low and his grey-riddled black hair loose around his neck, a wide-faced Indian girl whose black braids run all the way down to her waist and who wears huge pale disk-earrings of bone stands on a rock overlooking the steamer, her breasts and shoulders yoked in many stripes of dark trade beads and yellowish-white bearteeth; she gazes upon the ship with placid sadness, her dark hands barely touching each other on the lap of her dead white buckskin dress,

> and the gaze of that Indian girl—

They ain't hardly better than animals.

           Some armed Injuns hereabout kicking up a dust!

You swore you'd learn me that Chinook jargon—

I reckon she wouldn't even scream.

Doc, you suppose them beads on her is worth anything?

Not as much as gold. We'll get a Chinaman to wash our gold. Them kind work for next to nothing.

Sometimes they got coppers on 'em, or even silver dollars, I swear. They don't understand the value of money, or

        her breasts and white buckskin dress.

One time I got one of them squaws alone. She didn't even—

So what, hero? They're easier to catch than mosquitoes.

Mosquitoes is what they are.

But they'll give a man venereal.

They all talk Chinook. Most can even—

Some are real loyal. I knowed a trapper who, every time he come home to his squaw, he brung her ribbons and beads, and she—

I hate all them stinking *squaw men,*

       and her hands.

Are you a *squaw man*? I said are you?

Don't let the general hear.

You know what they say about *him*?

That's him, all right. Our motherlovin' *Christian Soldier.*

That's Nigger Lover Howard over there.

       And so when we tried to settle our section, they says to us—

       Well, we come out here by ox team like the rest of them, and when we

       filed on our acres, they—

Look at all them Injuns setting on the rocks.

Plenty of Indians all over this country.

Not for long.

Another fine squaw.

Cayuse.

No she ain't.

I'd trade her for her horse.

They used to sell one good horse for a squaw-axe or a few blue beads. Don't know what they want for their horses now.

That's not truly General Howard, is it?

O yes it is. Don't you con that empty sleeve?

I saw him give a dollar to Whiskey Jack one time. He—

That nigger college got named after him.

They say he—

Be d——d to whatever *they* say!

What a bright, intelligent face that woman has! Umatilla, wouldn't you guess?
Each man to his own taste, general. You certainly know your Indians.
That's my job, captain.
Do you suppose Joseph will make any trouble?
      and now the rolling cañons of sagebrush, and the river so blue,
        the sky pallid with summer's dust,
        and the olive-green secrecy of Three Mile cañon shining dark and humid
        in the hot grass
of Boardman, Oregon, which has always belonged to
        cattails, marshes, wet grey shrubs
        and meadows
            of America
where there will someday be the great town of Irrigon
and the Umatilla Army Depot
        and the dirty lavender of the smoke far away over the yellow grass
of Oregon,
Washington,
Idaho,
Montana
        and her dress,
        the lap of her dress,
        her dress, her white buckskin dress
        and her eyes
    (I want to meet her in Irrigon)
        and—
            Did she have a pass?
            I reckon so.
How quiet is the river nowadays?
Well, if you leave the Dreamers out of it—
How many Dreamers do you notice as a rule?
I can't rightly say. They lurk back in the cañons.
Who are those loud, profane men over there?
Never saw them before. I'm sure you meet a lot of them in the Army, general.
Yes. Pretty grand country here, all right,
        tawny and blue, soft hills made of hard triangles
            and the faded triangles painted on her Umatilla cornhusk purse,
        everything shaded
        the sky strictly sunny, strictly clouded
            (and a century and a quarter later I rode toward La Grande late on
            a sunny November afternoon, with gold and brown rectangles in-
            scribed on the rising and falling grassscape)
when they arrive in Wallula, the head of navigation, at 5:00 p.m.

General Howard, an Indian wants to see you.

All right. Send him in.

You are General Howard?

That's right.

I come from Smohalla, from across the river. You know his name?

One of the Dreamers. Wilkinson, please seal this letter.

Yessir.

Smohalla will speak with you.

I have no communication for him from Washington. He must obey his Indian Agent, and go on some reservation.

Maybe he does not like to hear you speak in such a way, General Howard.

What's your name?

Smohalla sends me.

Well, tell your Smohallie that his deleterious influence has produced much suffering among you Indians.

You will not meet with him?

If he likes, I'll visit him on my return. Wilkinson, please bring me two sheets of paper.

Where do you go now, General Howard?

That's my business. Good day to you.

The railroad conveys him to Fort Walla-Walla.

Good evening, general.

Good evening to you, colonel. Very kind of you to meet me here—

A pleasure, sir. Would you care for a hot cup of tea?

Upon my soul, but this is GOD-given hospitality! Thank you. Any news?

Chief Joseph's brother Ollicut will come at six. Chief Joseph will come at ten to-morrow morning.

Very good. Have you prepared a meeting place?

The band-room will do, sir. There are benches which the Indians can use, and chairs for us.

All right. And now, if you don't mind, I've been itching to try your new Gatlings.

Fine sport! If you like, sir, we'll try them at two, three, five and eight hundred yards. You're not too tired?

By no means. So this is the mechanism. And how quickly do they load? My word! And you sight them like this? At those white blankets? Let loose!

Would you like to do the honors, sir?

Well . . . why not? Three—two—one—*fire!*

Good shooting, sir.

So that's that. Now I believe Mr. Gatling: two discharges per second! Those poor blankets look like they've caught the measles . . .

Well, sir, what's your opinion?

I think that warfare is coming to its best and quickest results.

He meets with Joseph and Ollicut—very clever young Indians he thinks them, and prepared to listen to reason. They agree upon a more formal conference at Fort Lapwai so that more Nez Perce bucks can be there.

Now, Ollicut, do you know a Dreamer named Skimiah?

General, he admits that he does.

Look, then—there he is in the guardhouse! That will be the future of any other Dreamer who declines to comply with Government instructions. Do you understand?

Sir, he replies: *General Howard, I understand very well.*

Good. Please inform all your braves.

General, Smohallie sends for you again.

Tell him he must come to me. I care not whether or not I see him.

He comes.

Then please get me that interpreter again. I suppose those are his Indians across the river

> where the tents and tipis nearly recall the Union outer lines in '63 or '64 when our uniforms were grime-stained and our sentries' rifles, leaning against tripods of rickety sticks, aimed straight up at Heaven; our pale tents wandered on and on toward a Confederate horizon of trodden mud—
>
>> *long have they pass'd,* thank GOD!— And surely the merest interval of Indian service in Walla Walla,
>>
>>> where fields, tree-walls and even a few white houses and churches have begun to sprout out of the blank plats—
>>>
>>>> although they remain vulnerable should these Dreamers rise up—don't the Indian Agents see it?—
>>
>> will get me on to Lapwai, and after wrapping up that business with Joseph it will be back to Lizzie, who

That's right, general. The Columbia River renegades.

Who's that character standing in my light?

That's just Doc. He's—

Fletch, would you mind having the colonel look over this estimate before we telegraph it to Portland?

Yes, sir.

General, Mr. Pambrum speaks the Walla-Walla language.

How did he learn it?

He's a half-breed and a *squaw man.*

All right. Send for him. Smohallie can wait in the band-room.

He may not like that, general.

All the better. Well, Fletch, they're certainly making all the ceremonial show they can. Quite a lot of blankets and feathers!

I should say so, sir.

Do you think we'll have trouble with them?

To me, sir, they have an ugly look.

I suppose they've learned of Skimiah's arrest.

I should think so, sir.

General, this is Mr. Pambrum.

Good evening, Mr. Pambrum. Ask Smohallie what I can do for him.

I'll do my best. General, he wishes to say that he wants peace, but he reserves the right to roam wherever he pleases, because the land has always belonged to the Indians.

So he denies the jurisdiction of the United States?

Just a moment. He answers that he does.

How many other Dreamers does he associate with, and where are they concentrated?

He refuses to say.

Tell him that the land has been opened up. I earnestly advise him to run to the shelter of the reservation.

Smohalla repeats he wants peace.

As do I. So let us part on good terms, in spite of that cross-grained scowl of his. Shall we shake hands? Very good. What's next?

General Howard, the Indian Agent at Yakima has sent us an insubordinate Indian.

Confine him at Fort Vancouver. Anything else?

No, sir.

All right. When do we leave for Lewiston?

And so for two days more they ascend first the Columbia and then the Snake, crossing the Idaho line and thus arriving at the aforesaid tent city, where he despatches Fletch to buy kerosene at the livery stable (and, although Wilkinson would have been more adept at this, to discreetly smell out prohibited liquor sales to the Army), then proceeding on posthaste to Fort Lapwai,

> established: 1862
>> (one year before the Idaho Territory itself)
> extent: twelve hundred and twenty-six acres
> situation: within Nez Perce Indian reservation, twelve miles from Lewiston

just before six-o'-clock in the evening,

> both companies forming up before longbearded Major Mason (who used to be much thinner in his Modoc days) on the main parade,
> the band playing "Yankee Doodle"
>> (known to be the general's favorite tune),
> and that Army smell, so similar everywhere,
> and the line of cavalry troops, most of them on white geldings, the general reviewing them at the side, elegantly horsed, saluting with his left arm, the infantry drawn up in dark squares of blueness variegated with greasy greys of elder issue
> as our good Indians look shyly on—

O my LORD, the broad, deep-cracked faces of those interesting old
squaws!—

and there's Trimble in that famous sack coat of his, and poor Miller's still
a captain, I see! What hope can he own in this peacetime Army?

General Howard? I'm Lieutenant Theller, if you remember—

Of course. Our bold Appaloosa rider! And

(remembering her smile as clean as Lizzie's white lace collar)

how is your elegant wife?

Very well, thank you, sir, and Colonel Perry sends his compliments; he's
on duty just now. The FitzGeralds have readied their house for you. Welcome to
Lapwai.

Pleased to know you again, lieutenant.

Good evening, general.

And you as well, Agent Monteith. Let me read you my instructions from
General Sherman of the War Department. There's also this document from
the commanding general of the Military Division of the Pacific. We all know
that the military will play a necessary part in placing the Indians on their reservations.

Yes, sir.

The land has always belonged to us.

Well, general, how do you find Fort Lapwai nowadays?

A very pleasant place, and in fine order. Whose farm is that?

James Reuben's, sir. One of our best Indians. Shall I fetch him?

I hear that Reverend Spalding grew thirty-pound melons in this soil.

Yessir.

What news from Chief Joseph?

We expect him to arrive with about fifty other Indians.

You've informed him what the Government has ruled?

I sent Mr. Reuben out to Wallowa to tell them to come on the reservation, so
they understand there is no getting out of it. If you'd like, I can call him to—

Well, good evening, Colonel Perry! This post does credit to its commander.

You're too kind, general. How is Mrs. Howard?

She's well, thank you. And Mrs. Perry?

No complaints, sir.

I hear that she and Mrs. FitzGerald have established a Sunday school.

Yessir, with Mrs. Theller's help. We have about ten white children here.

Good. Now, if I remember, that's the route to Mount Idaho yonder.

Yessir.

I'd like to establish a more visible presence on that road for the benefit of
Joseph's Indians. Send mail riders out to Cottonwood every day.

We're all itching to ride, sir. I'll despatch a trooper instantly.

Thank you, colonel. Now, Mr. Monteith, I've read your reports.

I appreciate it, general. And General Sherman has suggested—

As you've just been told, I'm in touch with General Sherman myself.

Right. Now, general, I am as fond of these Nez Perces as I would be of my own children. I hope you'll be free to hear them sing hymns this Sunday—

That will be my sincere pleasure. And what about Joseph?

His band hasn't yet seen the light. But that's what you're here for, I believe.

You well know that we cannot take the offensive at all until further instructions from Washington.

Well, general—

I'm glad indeed that you did not fix any time for the ultimatum of Joseph's coming.

General Howard, might we discuss this in private?

All right. Now, colonel, we'll want to pitch a long hospital tent for our visitors. Leave one side open for the sentry's inspection. Keep the garrison on alert in the barracks.

Yes, sir. I propose we host them in the parade ground, where we can—

Exactly. Just a moment. Now, Mr. Monteith,

> who towers tall and thin, his pallid face projecting a very false impression
> of timidity as he lowers his forehead confidentially, his gaze shining like
> his watch-chain—how many such intriguers haven't I met?

> (LORD, but this fellow needs to organize his beard!)

what can I do for you?

General, all of us here at Fort Lapwai feel concern about the Columbia River renegades.

More so than about Joseph?

Well, but if we can keep him and Smohallie apart . . . I understand you laid down the law to Smohallie.

Yes, he met me, with great parade and tragic manner . . .

I trust my reports didn't alarm you, general.

Soldiers never fear, Mr. Monteith, but they do prepare.

My word, but that was well spoken—

You have an interpreter, I'm sure.

Whitman always serves me well.

And is there a minister in the vicinity?

Not since my father's death, although Father Cataldo at the Catholic mission has learned Nez Perce, not that my Indians are as grateful as they might be. He took the choicest land for his Indians yonder, on Mission Creek—

How many Indians go to church hereabouts?

About two hundred, general.

I'm informed that Reverend Spalding enrolled more than four hundred at Kamiah before his death.

Well, after all, he became a full time missionary in his last years, while I have my duties as Indian Agent, unfortunately. Without me, these people might starve to death, so I can't simply—

Come now, Mr. Monteith. I intended no offense.

Well, the position here is no sinecure, I assure you. Moreover, as you probably know, Chief Lawyer hails from Kamiah, where people are more thrifty and wide-awake than here. In spite of all I can do, my Indians maintain connections with Joseph and his renegades. Family ties, you know. That subchief Jacob is the worst. I'm working on getting him removed. You'll soon learn how the land lies, general, and you can count on me to bring you the most up to date information.

O, I can see that. Who gives it to you?

What do you mean, sir?

Which Indians can you rely on to inform you?

Well, James Reuben, for one. A real good Indian. Captain John and Old George do what they're told, but Reuben reports to me every day—

Anything else I should know about Father Cataldo?

Confidentially, general, he opposes the importation of non-treaty Nez Perces into his domain. You know how Catholics can be, general. Spalding used to blame them for his failure here, when in fact the Cayuses—

I'll speak with the father. Anything else?

I guess not—

Then let him open the meeting with a prayer. With luck, they'll take it to heart.

As you say, general. I think they're coming now.

Colonel, is everything in order?

Yes, sir.

Why, they're as thick as June bugs!

No, they can't be Cayuses, because these here are Nez Perces.

Well, I say they're Cayuses.

Their papooses sure are cute.

I've diddled younger squaws than that. They're all side meat.

Look there! D'you see that little boy trying so bravely to ride that wild horse? I surely love to see that.

Bet you anything he'll get throwed before you count five.

No, he's *tough*. He's a little Philadelphia prize fighter.

One—two—

Stand straight. Captain's looking.

Three—

And that's Joseph over there? He don't look like much.

That's Ollicut.

How the fuck do you know?

I'd like to give him one between the eyes.

Fine horse he's got.

And skates only seventy-five cents a pair at Barney & Berry's
Club, but my husband swore she'd outgrow them before win-
ter, so we refrained.
He was right, you know.
I must say, Joseph's Indians turn my stomach.
Especially the squaws.
And what do *you* think, Mrs. Theller?
O, they're striking enough in their way. My husband says—
Did you ever light on anything as ugly as that old squaw over there? Less
personality than a tree stump—
I'd say the same about you. Anyways, what in blazes do you mean to
study squaws for? You one of them perverted *squaw men*?
Straighten up. General's coming.
No he ain't. That's just the major and—
O, *that* sport.
Now *there's* Goody-Goody Howard on the march—
    Lord Jesusnim *hishaiyahokinisha—*
And Theller with his twice-waxed moustache and his—
I tried to talk business to that pretty little squaw in the red blanket and
got stone nowhere. Sure is hard to make 'em understand.
    Kaih kaih ka kush makea
    Kaih kaih ka kush makea
    Hissapakaisha ka kush kaih kaih kaih makea.
Why, I know that tune! That's "Whiter Than Snow."
Sure is.
Always liked that hymn. They sing it real nice.
Strangest dialect I ever did hear. Is it a speech impediment?
I don't reckon so.
Well, then it must be a brogue. I hear tell they're Welsh Indians.
But that Sergeant Parnell, he's a genuine Paddy and he can't make out a
word when they—
Gimme a smoke.
Help yourself.
Pretty yaller dress she's got on.
I meant the one in the red.
O, that one's always hanging around,
        and with those sweet Injun eyes of hers I'll bet she'd prove full
        gentle like a ringdove in a cage, but I couldn't never say a word to
        the boys or they'd tilt against me.
They talk Chinook when they fancy to.
Less talk and more shooting is my prescription.
Perry's glaring at us! We'd better—

Well, Joseph, I have come to hear whatever you have to say. No, Fletch, I'll need you over there. Stenographer, please begin now.

White Bird and his band are on their way, replies his interlocutor, gazing sidelong at him from beneath an immense feather headdress, with an expression almost of slyness. They will arrive to-morrow.

Mr. Whitman, tell Joseph that we have our instructions from Washington, and that if he decides at once to comply with the wishes of the Government, he can take his pick of vacant land. White Bird will have his own turn.

General, Smohalla wishes to speak first.

Yes, I recognize his friendly face. He may go ahead.

He warns me to interpret correctly, for their children's and grandchildren's sake. I've assured him that I would. Now this other Dreamer is saying: We want to talk a long time, many days, about the earth, about our land.

And who's he?

He won't introduce himself.

Have you seen him before?

I don't remember him, general.

He reminds me of a woman I used to know back at Watervliet who couldn't bear to be beaten at euchre. Mrs. Symington, her name was. Well, what saucy old fellows they both are! And see how the rest follow their words. Tell them that we wish to hear whatever they have to say, however long it takes them to say it, even many days, I suppose, but in the end the Indians must obey the order of the Government of the United States.

Ollicut replies to you: We have respect for the whites, but for their part they treat me as a dog, and I sometimes think my friends are different from what I supposed.

Tell him that Joseph, Agent Monteith and I are all under the same Government. Tell them that whatever it commands us to do, we must do.

The Dreamers are objecting again, general. Shall I translate?

Is it more of the same?

It seems so.

Tell them that they must give good advice, or I shall be obliged to arrest and punish them. What do they say now?

Now they change their tone.

All right. Don't translate for a moment, please, Mr. Whitman. Mr. Monteith, Joseph seems to me to wear a very sour, noncommittal appearance.

I agree. And James Reuben, that good Indian I told you about, he's informed me—

We'd best let them consider their situation. Mr. Whitman, kindly begin again. We invite them to continue this conference to-morrow.

They say they're willing.

Well, then, colonel, would you care to show me the river scenery? It's a lovely evening for a walk.

2

Ask Joseph how he is.

He says he is very happy this morning, general.

I like to hear that. Now what?

This chief is introducing himself, general. His name is White Bird, and his Indians roam down by the Salmon River. He's telling you about his father and grandfather and so forth. Shall I summarize?

Does it relate to our business?

Not directly.

He's been loyal so far, I understand.

I believe so.— I'm sorry; I didn't catch what Joseph said to him just now. And White Bird says he has ridden far to meet with us. Now Joseph is presenting him to us.

A demure-looking Indian! What does he have to hide with that eagle's wing in front of his eyes and nose? Don't translate that, Mr. Whitman.

And this is Toohhoolhoolzote.

A Caucasian-hater, I see. Tell them both that I also have travelled a long way, and I hope that we can get down to business.

Toohhoolhoolzote says: *There are always two parties to a dispute. The right one will come out ahead.*

An optimist.

Toohhoolhoolzote says that he belongs to the earth, and that she is his mother.

He can say whatever he likes, but he must obey the Government and move to the reservation.

He declines to grant the Government in Washington the right to think for the Indians.

Mr. Whitman, don't translate for a moment. Colonel, how long will it take to bring troops here from Grande Ronde?

We can do it by Monday, sir.

Mr. Whitman, tell the Indians that the conference is adjourned until Monday.

General, Chief Joseph informs us that he is very satisfied, and wishes to shake your hand.

And I would like to shake his. And Ollicut's, and White Bird's, and even this *Toohulhusote*'s if he wishes it.

I think he doesn't.

All right. Well, I admire the physiques of these Nez Perces. Do you see how naturally they ride? Superior skirmishers, no doubt! What do you think of 'em, Mr. Monteith?

General, a hardy race! In my opinion they bear cold as well as even the Mandans—

We'd better drill this skeleton garrison of ours, and let off the howitzer this afternoon, to keep our guests good-mannered. Do we have provisions enough to feed them all through Tuesday or Wednesday?

Yes, sir.

There's nothing like letting an Indian eat his fill to keep him satisfied. Negroes are the same. After all, in their state of life how often can they count on a good dinner?

Yes, sir.

Although it strikes me that Indians as a class tend to be less grateful than negroes.

Yes, sir.

Can we get any Gatlings by Monday?

I think not, sir.

And we'll celebrate the Sabbath together, of course. That may prove beneficial. And when they attend divine services they'll certainly be picturesque in their costumes.

Excellent idea, general. Shall we get Father Cataldo again?

Well, at least he believes in GOD.

Sir, if you prefer, Archie Lawyer will preach in Nez Perce. What do you think of him?

An extremely spiritual fellow. But I see that our young Joseph holds himself aloof.

I suspect the Dreamers have gotten to him, sir.

3

Evening (not yet "Tattoo"):

    Colonel Perry's shady front porch, and Mrs. Perry serving coffee all around,

        Mrs. Theller laying out her famous buttermilk cake,

    cicadas singing on the main parade.

Welcome back, Captain Whipple.

Thanks, general. Fine to see you again—

Well, and how was it out there at Grande Ronde?

Quiet as usual, sir.

Ideal panoramas, I'd suppose.

Well, general, it's up high, you know, real close to the sky . . .

No trouble from our Indians?

They pretty much kept their distance, sir. Turns out they roam widely, as you know—

Looking for food?

Yessir. In spring they eat the inner bark of pine trees—

Poor creatures! They'll be better off on the reservation.

No doubt, sir.

How soon do they intend on moving their tipis to Wallowa?

Imminently, now the grass grows high.

And did the warriors behave themselves?

The bad ones stayed clear, sir. Some came to play cards with the boys.

Without whiskey, I trust.

Well, sir, some bad white men sell it to 'em at Lewiston, right behind the livery stable. One of my privates won a pony off a sorry old buck who would have gambled away his wife, but I put a stop to it. That red got passing disappointed, and then I—

No threats offered, no violence toward your men?

None, sir.

Who are the most influential Indians?

Joseph and Ollicut, of course, then White Bird, Looking-Glass, Hushush Cute—

What about that Medicine man Toohhoolhoolzote?

Well, sir, they sure listen to him, but he commands just a handful of warriors. He never did stay long when he rode in. Seems to prefer it up in his mountains.

How would you compare these people with the Modoc prisoners you escorted to the Indian Territory* last year?

There's no comparison at all, sir. The Nez Perces are the most compliant Indians I've ever seen. They keep trying to get along—

I'm glad to hear it. And what did you do for fun?

Well, one fellow brought along a volume of *Black Wit and Darky Conversations*. So at least we had us some laughs—

You know, Whipple, I rather admire Joseph and his Indians.

Yessir.

I suspect that if we use them kindly they could become quite attached to us.

Yessir.

How do you imagine they're taking this?

Well, sir, I'm no Indian, but if it were me, I don't suppose I'd like to be turned out from my home. Good grazing land along the Grande Ronde even in winter, and, well, Wallowa's an awfully beautiful valley, sir.

How is the situation in Wallowa?

Filling up with white men—

Did you fellows find any more gold?

Not really, sir.

None at all?

To tell you the truth, sir, we were all searching for it like the dickens! One sample showed color, but the private who found it has a reputation for card sharping. He could have salted it with gold dust.

Well, well.

So nobody's guessing the place will be anywhere near as rich as Florence. But I may say, sir, that a man could carve out a fine homestead up there by Wallowa Lake, if the winter's not too cold—

So I hear. After this is over, perhaps I'll bring Mrs. Howard there for a holiday.

---

*The approximate precursor of Oklahoma.

I'm sure she'll like it, sir.

At any rate, there's no sense in feeling sorry for the Indians.

Heavens, no, sir.

We Army officers can't expect to be our own masters.

Captain Whipple inspects the brass eagle button of his sleeve. He inquires: Then who can, general?

The general's eyes shine.— The *citizens.*

4

Come Monday morning, more Indians than ever appear to be riding round and round Fort Lapwai. Most (excepting of course our good Indians, who in any event keep their distance) have painted their faces red; and Toohhoolhoolzote has risen up among the Dreamers like a black bear on his hind legs. Ollokot shakes hands with Perry's bugler. Looking-Glass has not yet arrived; White Bird studies the soldiers from behind his fan. Two baffled little Cayuse girl-children, dressed in their blanket-coats, beaded necklaces and shell earrings, stare out at the general between the corral's fence-slats, and he smiles at them, wondering whether they might be related to Joseph on his mother's side—best to ask James Reuben, since Mr. Whitman cannot clear up this question. But Mr. Whitman now reports that one of them just said: *We are riding in a circle to count their rifles.* To tell the truth, many of these Nez Perces, especially the ragged old bucks, compare unfavorably to the idlers who infest certain stagecoach stations. The squaws sit watchful in their striped blanket-coats. What would Lizzie think of them? Most are as brightly kerchiefed as colored women. Mrs. FitzGerald and Mrs. Perry cannot approve of their ideas of fashion: yellow skirts with blue dresses, red dresses under green aprons. He smiles at them, but their eyes flash unpleasantly; again he remembers the disappointed negroes of Edisto. And this lovely young one with the lush black hair and the beadwork in blue and white animal patterns across the breast and shoulders of her buckskin dress, he remembers her from church yesterday. His young friend Lieutenant Wood (currently on detached service in Alaska) might have made a poem out of her. What a remarkable beauty she is! (Lizzie of course would be disgusted.) He greets her with his heartiest *how;* she hangs her head. Wilkinson, who is always keen to unearth relationships, conjectures that she might be one of Joseph's nieces, although that appears unlikely. It borders on shameful how little we've discovered concerning the entourage of this ambiguous Indian. Whipple ought to know; when he comes the matter will be cleared up. Now, where's Trimble? He should be at the head of his company just now. Is he getting slack? Perry's got something against him. Mrs. Theller has turned out for the show, and likewise Mrs. Perry in her buff-colored Sunday bonnet, then behind them the doctor's wife, the company laundresses with all their children, the Monteith women and a couple of strong-jawed lady missionary types from Kamiah.

Still more warriors arrive, their hair well greased with bear oil, and although they have laid down or concealed their rifles, he declines to trust them. And the Dreamers' salutations to him are obviously twined with their false embroideries. As for Chief Joseph, he makes a fine picture on his Cayuse stallion. Needless to say, yesterday he failed to put in an appearance at church. The sunlight shines bright and flat on his face. For an instant the general cannot look away from the black peak of hair above his pale forehead.

What's your opinion, Mason?

Could turn nasty, sir.

Sladen?

General, we'd better be ready for anything.

Perry?

Sir, I propose to put this post on alert.

I see.

Sir, the Modocs behaved in a similar way at the peace conference.

Circling like this?

Not exactly, general. Just acted shifty. But I'm told that the Walla-Wallas and Cayuses rode circles round the treaty ground, just before they rose up.

You're referring back to '55, I believe.

Yessir.

Out of curiosity, were the Modocs ever as friendly as Joseph's Indians?

No, sir.

> And Mrs. Sanford in Pendleton carries ladies' Centennial combs, from what I hear. I should like to get one for Black Jennie; her hair is always such an ugly tangle. Ned has promised me—
> But, o, her prices!
> Mrs. Perry, just now your husband appears rather—

Thank you, Perry.

Yessir.

To make a point, he permits Perry to form up the garrison. At this a grim horseman cries loudly: *Kaa náko haamankhnáawyanikh kaakíne hilkilíinenikh?*

Mr. Whitman, what did that Indian say just now?

Begging your pardon, general, he said, *why are they acting brave and milling around here?*

I was just wondering the same about them. Look how they grin at his speech! The Dreamers have done their work well. Where's Smohallie?

Over there, sir.

O, so he is. Keep an eye on him. Where's the other one?

Perhaps we gave him a fright the other day.

Even so, were I a betting man I'd risk a silver dollar that Toohhoolhoolzote's remained faithful to *his* principles. And how does Joseph appear to you, colonel?

Guarded, sir.

Doesn't he always?

Yes, sir.

He rides gracefully.

Doesn't he, though?

                    Best lookin' Injun I ever come across.

You know, Whipple, before the war, when I was stationed in Maine, I used to train horses. I had a pure white Arabian named Mallach. Rather tall, but slender-legged. I used to gallop all over the country on his back.

Yes, sir.

Did I tell you this before?

Well, yes, sir.

But Joseph's horse looks ideal.

I should say so, sir.

He's watching us.

Yes, sir. Perhaps that skinny red's coming too near . . .

And the other chiefs? You know them better than I, Mr. Monteith.

General, just now they grate unpleasantly on my mind. These Dreamers are notorious.

And that old fellow with the angry eyes, who's he?

Never saw him before, sir.

What's he saying?

Thief treaty.

No, Wilkinson. This note goes to Walla-Walla and that one to Portland. Now, Perry, who's that one with the mirror around his neck?

They call him Looking-Glass, which was his father's name for the same reason. A good Indian. He's always signed everything.

I thought his father declined to sign the treaty.

So he did, sir, but the son is never saucy.

Why didn't he introduce himself before?

Perhaps he's a shy Indian, sir.

Thank you for that speculation, colonel. And what was the name of Joseph's father?

Also Joseph.

Very dynastic, these Nez Perces. Mr. Whitman, I assume that with them property also descends through the male line?

I once asked them about it, and they answered: *All our father's uncles are our grandfathers and our mother's aunts are our grandmothers.*

That's more than enough detail, I should say. Is it true that Old Joseph was present when the missionaries got murdered at Spalding?

I don't think so, sir. But his wife was a Cayuse—

All right, let's come to order. Stenographer, are you ready? Mr. Whitman, would you like some water? Tell them that we are ready to hear their decision.

What does Joseph say?

He declines to speak just yet. Toohhoolhoolzote wishes to have his say.

By all means. No doubt he'll take a leaf from Smohallie's book.

He says, *the land has always belonged to us. We came from the earth; she is our mother; our bodies must go back to her. The land must not be sold.*

Mr. Monteith, tally their faces. How many would you say agree with him?

I would say all of them, general.

Then firmness will be needed. Mr. Whitman, ask Toohhoolhoolzote whether he has anything new to say.

He's repeating himself, general. He's going back to the beginning with the business about the earth.

Toohhoolhoolzote, you Nez Perces made an agreement with the United States Government. Your group might have been in opposition to the Indians who signed the treaty, but you are in the minority and so you will have to follow the majority.

We have never made any trade. Part of the Indians gave up their land. I never did. The earth is part of my body and I never gave up the earth.

I do not want to hear you say anything more like that. You have thirty days to move to the reservation. I am telling you.

You ask me to talk, then tell me to say no more. I am a chief! I ask no man to come and tell me what I must do.

Yes, you are a chief. All the same, I am telling you! You have thirty days.

Go back to your own country, General Howard. Tell them you are chief there. I am chief here,

> the Indian's eyes shining like the cinders which flitter from a steamboat's stacks.

What person pretends to divide the land and put me on it?

I am the man. I had hoped that you Indians were sensible enough to make me your friend and not your enemy.

General, now even White Bird says that he would be ruled by white men if he had been taught to be ruled by white men, but as it is, he is ruled by the earth.

And when these other Indians say *Aa, aaa,* that signifies agreement with his words?

Correct.

Colonel Perry,

> recollecting that time at Fort Sill when Stumbling Bear and Lone Wolf tried to murder General Sherman while he was arresting the Kiowas,

how do you read Looking-Glass's face?

Well, sir, I suspect he feels as White Bird does.

And Joseph?

Closed in upon himself, sir.

I see how it is. Tell Toohhoolhoolzote the following: White Bird and Joseph appear to have good hearts, but yours is bad. You must go to the Indian Territory. I will send you there if it takes years and years. Chief Joseph and White Bird may come with me to choose reservation lands which suit them. But you will have to stay with Colonel Perry. Now, colonel, lead this dangerous Indian out of the council and put him in confinement. Mr. Whitman, what do these other Indians say now?

Now their hearts have changed, general, and they stand ready to obey the Government.

5

What should they have done, after all? What the cattle do. Or, in Cicero's Latin, *idem quod pecudes.*

He feels for them, of course. He disapproves not only of our national Indian policy, but also of Wallowa's heedless seizure. But Washington has given instructions, and there must be an end.

Once when he was a boy, two men murdered another. One of the killers was hanged and the other went to prison. Troubled by the discrepancy, he said: Father, it seems unfair.

The law's not about fairness, Otis.

Then what's it about?

His father smiled kindly. *Finality*, he said.

He has never forgotten this. Fairness would have been best, to be sure. But at least we can achieve finality. Once the Indians are safely settled, and the remaining lands opened for settlement, then—

Sir, Joseph and Looking-Glass wish to see you.

Send them in. Where's Mr. Whitman?

Here, sir.

The door opens,

> illustrating the way that on Joseph's red-ochered cheekbones lamplight can give way to shadow along an almost horizontal slanting boundary as distinct as a hand's edge
>
> and his narrow-lidded eyes, whose dark caution is peculiarly reminiscent of Lizzie's
>
> and I smell Lieutenant Theller's pomade.

Shall I invite them to sit down, sir?

Tell them that General Howard is listening.

They beseech you to release Toohhoolhoolzote. They will stand surety for his behavior with their own lives.

All right. Let him go. Anything else, Mr. Whitman?

They thank you with all their hearts, general. They say that they can see now that you are a kind man,

> the old Dreamer shambling out, grimacing, staring quickly and crook-

edly down at the ground, clasping his blanket tight around his waist
(with GOD's help, *he* won't be so saucy in future!),
Looking-Glass wooden-faced beneath that peculiar hat of his,
and then Joseph, whose dark neck shines white from that gorget of bearteeth he so often wears,
and Joseph

> (Looking-Glass is a better known quantity, awed and loyal,
> like White Bird who hides behind his eagle feather, unable to
> meet my gaze)—

Tell them that I am a sincere friend of all Indians who obey the Government.
I told them, sir.
And what did they say?
They're ready to ride with you and select their reservations, general.
Tell them that I have been praying for this result with all my heart, and that
this is one of the happiest days of my life. Tell them that I mean only their good—
They say they know, sir.
Gentlemen, what do you think of this?
Congratulations, general! It's going to be smooth sailing now!
I concur with that, sir.
Wilkinson, I'll need my horse at once.
Yes, sir.
Mr. Monteith, Mr. Whitman, will you join us?
Of course, general.
Tell them that we'll ride together in a quarter-hour to look at the land.
They're joyful to ride with you, sir. They want to know if you'll race with them.
By GOD, I will! Will you look at that interesting horse-hobble! Just a rock with
a hole in it—
Our native basalt, general.
I wonder what those other Nez Perces are up to over there by the river?
I'd say they're holding some kind of powwow.
They're Looking-Glass's Indians?
Joseph's, sir, and I think that buck there is one of Toohhoolhoolzote's.
I've never looked upon a livelier scene. Gentlemen, this should be an adven-
ture. May I see Joseph's saddle?
He offers to present it to you.
Well, that's kind! Too kind. No, I can't accept. Colonel, are our horses ready?
Yes, sir.
What's their word for horse?
Ah, general, that's not so simple. There is one word for a palomino, and an-
other for a roan. There is a word for a horse with a black streak running down the
middle of its face—
Never mind. Let's all gallop together across this inviting plain of golden
grass . . .

6

And in a cut between the goldenhaired hills, a flock of starlings like living shadows passes over the riders, their darkness frosting the grass into deeper pallor to the very horizon of this wide, wide land.

AND THE WORLD KEEPS GETTING WIDER
AND WIDER
MAY 31–JUNE 9

1

*I*n the dying dark, Springtime rolls away, she who once slept so sweetly in his arms. The dogs are barking: Good Woman and Sound Of Running Feet have gone down to the creek. Once he awoke before others, but since the council at Butterfly Place* some rain has darkened his way, even to that kind of sleep which is clotted red like birds' eyes. Like Springtime, he feels heavy, but for the only other cause: He sees death coming.

Flying out of dreams that resemble skulls in a circle in an old tale, he lays his hand on her buttock; while she, the widening one who remains as delicious as a sego lily's root, wearily begins to sit up. She is pulling her bleached buckskin dress down over her belly, she who used to be lonely for him even when she was menstruating; he can hear the hissing of the deerhide across her skin, and the faintest rattle of the beads. Very slowly she breathes. He is still lying on his back. Clasping his hands, he watches the last stars through the smokehole, thankful that she has suppressed her weeping in order to make herself brave:

It is on the verge of ending,
    now when cous season is nearly over:
        two moons too early to net salmon at Wallowa Lake,
and Springtime is decorating herself for the day. Now she is painting her face red.

Remembering how she used to sing when she bathed in the Enemy River, and what she sometimes whispers in his arms, he smiles at her, but she does not see. He sits up. She turns toward him. He pulls on his deerskin shirt,
    Black Mane-Stripe, Brown One and Spotted Head whickering outside
    (Good Woman must now be riding Ocher One)

---

*The meaning of "Lapwai."

and the bad dreams go.

Someone is cooking outside. He smells smoke and soup.

Now he is listening to Springtime's belly, while she caresses his head. The baby makes a noise inside: *shlal, shlal.*

He hears Ollokot's wives going to the river with the little boy, and just down the meadow from their lodge, Welweyas the half-woman is untying the flap of the tipi she shares with her mother, old Agate Woman, whose husband was killed by Lice-Eaters two winters since. White Thunder must have already gone hunting. Someone coughs. The last stars have set.

2

Springtime begins to braid his hair, although Good Woman will certainly be jealous. She rolls up their buffalo robe. Now she is blowing on the fire. Soon the women will be pounding roots, and the reckless young men will recommence to beat their untanned elkskin, singing songs of killing. He cannot decide how to straighten their hearts.

He longs to keep listening to the baby. Springtime's hair is showering him as if she were shaking apart a cluster of berries. Her lap smells like smoke, sweat and bunchgrass.

3

She should be sleeping in the women's house. White Thunder and Good Woman are making themselves angry; exactly now she ought not to be too much near men. But she has told him in terror: My dear husband, I have Dreamed that some good Helper of mine is turning away!

—by which she meant that her WYAKIN will abandon her!—

an evil Dream indeed;

and since all things are ending in any case, he will not drive away his youngest wife whose heart sometimes gets scared like a child's.

4

Must we certainly go?

Síikstiwaa, * I am speaking to you from the root of my heart. Shall our People be killed?

No, husband, but you told me we have never sold our country . . .

So I have said, and I spoke straight. But, *síikstiwaa,* now we are becoming tame. We must keep ourselves quiet forever.

And never come back here?

---

*Darling.

Cut Arm has said that we may ask for a paper whenever we wish to come out from our painted land.* But we must not bring too many horses, in case the Bostons dislike it.

He will never let us out!

No. We leave here forever,
> as dawn comes suddenly, spraying golden rays as if a SKY PALOMINO had
> swished his tail, the long bright hairs of it fanning out:
>> lightning more slender than cracks in a rock
>> and mosquitoes on the lake, and their reflections;
>> curtain of orange in the sky,
>> then two rainbows,
>> the river high, puddles in the grass
>>> (thunder again),
>> the world cool and wet, rapidly brightening
>> and frog songs at dawn there north of the lake
> when she says: The land has always belonged to us.

—Be silent now. I shall not unsay my words to Cut Arm,
> although in everyone's hearing I promised my father never to sell our country.

5

Springtime, whom some falsely say he loves the most, was once a woman who liked to speak at night. Since the council at Butterfly Place
> (where we once had a village)
she has become quiet.

But now, knowing that he will never beat her, she begins showing her heart too much, crying out (her cheeks shimmering with tears): The Bostons unsay everything!
> —or unsing what we once knew
>> (Cut Arm glaring, the Bostons cheering as at a Scalp Dance,
>> our doom as faithful as the gleam of Looking-Glass's mirror),
> for just as in old tales a man who urinates in the same spot where a
> woman did can make her pregnant, so this *thief treaty* to which we never
> put our mark has magically conveyed away the remnants of our country:
>> Wallowa,
>> and Eel Place, where Looking-Glass's People used to live,
>> Sunflower Place, which we lost long ago,
>> Sparse-Snowed† Place: White Bird's country,
>> Chinook Salmon Mountains: Toohhoolhoolsote's place,
>> Shale-Rock Mountain,
>> Split Rock: the camas meadow where we now ride to meet our

---

*Reservation.
†White Bird Cañon.

relations for the last time,
Imnaha
and all our pretty rivers of beaver and salmon,
wintering places, horse prairies, pitch-gathering groves;
the places where we used to cut lodgepoles,
and the hills, forests, caves, ridges and bunchgrass of our
home:

> *Thief treaty!*

Now she has finished decorating his hair, so, thanking her, he rises, putting on his brass bracelets, affixing his collar of otterskin, and wrapping himself in the King George blanket which Looking-Glass gave him last fall at Eel Place. The morning brightens further. Outside the tipi, Good Woman has begun to spread blankets on the dewy grass, laying out cous-roots to dry a little more before she pounds them.

Springtime goes to the sweathouse. Then she will bathe in the cold river, to make her baby strong.

6

Again she murmurs: *Thief treaty!*

Smiling carefully, hoping to spare her from understanding why he has obeyed Cut Arm,

old Cut Arm, mangier than a buffalo in spring,
who humiliated us by showing the rifle, shrilling like the mother in the
stories who becomes so angry that she gains the Power to fly away,
Cut Arm, who handled Toohhoolhoolsote like an animal,

he remarks: Each time, they become less human than before. Now we shall see how it ends.

Then he paints his face red and yellow.

7

Ollokot and White Thunder are speaking outside. He hears Ollokot say: Then tell the young men . . .

8

He goes out. Some young men speak of punishing the Bostons. He replies: Let this talk be finished.

9

Good Woman goes in. He follows her. Presently she says: Could this have been different?

Some Places Where the People Lived...

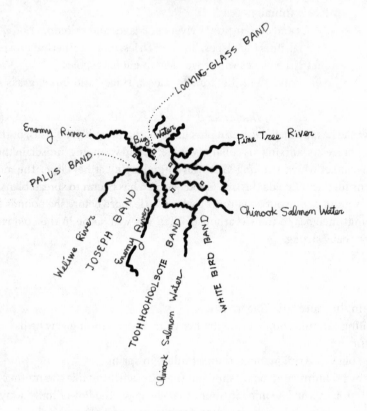

LOOKING-GLASS BAND

Enemy River

Big Water

Pine Tree River

PALUS BAND

Chinook Salmon Water

Weliwe River

JOSEPH BAND

Enemy River

TOOHHOOHOOLSOTE BAND

WHITE BIRD BAND

Chinook Salmon Water

... And How the Bostons Mapped Them

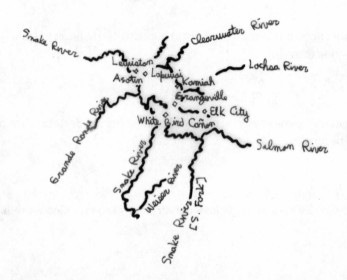

Snake River

Clearwater River

Lewiston

Lochsa River

Asotin

Lapwai

Kamiah

Grangeville

Elk City

Grande Ronde River

White Bird Cañon

Snake River

Salmon River

Weiser River

Snake River [S. Fork]

↑N

No, *síikstiwaa*. You know that my father told me to stop my ears whenever the Bostons sought to buy our country. They did not buy it; they stole it.

10

Springtime is lying down again; but her pains must not have begun, or she would have departed for the women's lodge.

Now Good Woman is boiling tea; he wonders what she foresees, and the fire says *taqaqaq*. A branch of balsam fir hangs over where she sleeps, to frighten away her bad dreams. Even this calm elder wife of his has now been visited by nightmares of a thunder-noisy CREATURE with nine pairs of wings. A gun speaks and a bugle sings from the Bluecoats' camp. Ollokot has studied these noises at Butterfly Place; he explains that through them the Bluecoats are commanded like slaves. Good Woman pours tea for him and for Springtime; perhaps at Split Rock there will be coffee. Black-eyed like an antelope, Springtime sets their last chokecherry cakes before him, and he strokes her face, but she repeats: You never sold our country.

Good Woman resumes plaiting a berry basket. (Springtime must not do such work; any knotting or interlacing would hinder the baby from coming out.)

He says: You remember that I told Cut Arm: These Bostons who came here were the cause of all our trouble.

To please them both he eats a little. Good Woman strokes Springtime's belly. Rising, he slings his .44 Winchester carbine over his shoulder; once his father carried this weapon. Again he goes out.

He trims the mane of Black Mane-Stripe, his favorite horse.

When he returns, the morning is hot and dry. Fair Land, Cloudburst, Good Woman, Sound Of Running Feet and Springtime sit pounding cous-root: *kíw! kíw! kíw!*

11

Sound Of Running Feet asks him: Father, where did you go to meet your WYAKIN?

Faraway Mountain.

Is that on our painted land?

No.

Then where shall I go? Next summer I'll be old enough—

I cannot tell you. Perhaps that is all finished now.

12

Already the People have begun decorating their favorite horses to please their friends and relations at Split Rock, decorating themselves with bells and buttons.

The women are painting their faces in joy, and the young men try to keep quiet, remembering what he has told them,

   but now Geese Three Times Alighting On Water insults Cut Arm again, our young men riding round and round, laughing to remember Cut Arm's angry face when Toohhoolhoolsote asked him in the council just who or what this *Washington* was

      (at least they have not yet begun to beat the untanned elkskin).

   Going to them, he sadly says: You cannot have what you wish. Whether you fight the Bostons or not, they are too many; in the end you must obey them. My heart tells me that it is better to go on painted land and keep quiet, even though they will make us poor. At least we shall still be alive with our families.

   They listen. Then he goes away.

   White Thunder returns with four ducks tied to his saddle; his eyes are shining at the songs of the young men.

   Good Woman says that Springtime's baby will not be born before we ride to Split Rock. She begins pounding cous with Cloudburst and Fair Land

      and the Bostons' chimney-smoke flies up

      as the horses say: *Hinimí.*

13

   He has ridden to his father's grave, and slaughtered a last horse there in that place more dear to him than any other. Down by the lake he has visited his baby son. Perhaps the Bostons will dig them up. They might do anything.

14

   As Toohhoolhoolsote truly said, we came from the EARTH;
      this EARTH here
      with Her jettings and leapings of white water
      from the high creeks that become waterfalls
      above our lake
         (the lake a deeper blue from above yet still lucent),
      the valley hidden as if to test our memory of Her;
She is OUR MOTHER; our bodies must go back to Her. This land,
      tongue of lake,
      great gorge of scree and evergreen down which water roars
must not be sold. But indeed it has been,
      our lake and golden grass,
      camas just coming into blue flower,
      and our fathers' graves,
so now nears time to gather in the herds and go.

15

His People come with angry faces. As before, certain Bostons who took land in our country have entered our hills and branded our calves with their brands. The young men call on him, saying: Let us take the Bostons' cattle, one for one.

He says: No. We must not trouble them. Some may be innocent.

16

Ollokot says: My dear brother, some young men refuse to leave our home.

Do not tell me their names. Go to them and say that if they do this reckless thing, for the People's sake I must hunt after them with my rifle.

17

Siikstiwaa, I am telling you three times: He will kill us if we make his heart angry.

Is he married?

He has a wife and children.

They must be a family of killers.

18

Ollokot rides to the lake, returning with a string of seven ducks
> as the women and the old ones dig up caches of beads and bullets, bulg-
> ing camas bags, silver plates from Lewis and Clark . . .

The red salmon have not yet come. How may we depart without them?

Springtime goes to the sweathouse; she is feeling unwell. Good Woman follows after her. Springtime has no mother anymore, so Good Woman must help to bring her baby out.

Ollokot paints his face with the fine red earth that Fair Land always gathers for him from a hill high above the lake. He smokes the pipe with his brother. Then he too kills a horse upon their father's grave.

19

Good Woman's mother died in Looking-Glass's country. Good Woman will never again visit her grave. She says: Now I am hating Cut Arm.

Siikstiwaa, he is nothing. It is after the Bluecoats go away that we shall have more trouble, from other Bostons who keep coming.

Let us go far away from all of them:
> from our lake,
> our valley of many horses,
> our father's grave
>> —just before he passed into the Country of Brightness he asked of
>> me never to sell OUR MOTHER—
> from all our graves and caches,
> but where shall we go?

They devour us everywhere:

Thief treaty!

20

Springtime asks: If we dislike our painted land, can we go away?

No.

Never?

Only if we ride all the way to the Buffalo Country, *síikstiwaa*. The Crows are our friends.

You found it a good place . . .

But so many enemies there, I am telling you three times! The Crows are brave, but they can never rest in their own land. Cutthroats,* Walking Cutthroats† and Arapaho devour them.

Does that country please your heart?

It's good for hunting, horses and war:
> this Crow Country with its dragonflies and buffaloberries, the many
> milkweed pods like green testicles on proud stalks, and the pyramid-
> faced river bluffs, prairies dotted with buffalo in place of trees, buffalo
> skulls encircled by flowers, fatty meat sizzling over feast-fires, enemies to
> kill without pity, and the Big Horn River greyish-brownish-green.

21

You say that we must stay forever on painted land.

Síikstiwaa, that is so.

Never to go out?

Perhaps our Agent will be gentle.

Tell us about our new country. What is it like?

You know that I rode all day with Cut Arm and there was no good land left.

---

*Lakota.
†Cheyennes.

22

Síikstiwaa, you're not eating.

It presses on my belly.

Any day . . .

It moves again now—

A strong child, like its mother, he whispers, stroking her hair.

Good Woman turns back to the fire, and he says: After the council we'll give a feast.

Thank you, husband.

Roasted shoulder meat—

He is grateful for Ollokot's wives; they will show her how to make herself brave.

The young boys are making bridles out of grass. The last women have returned from separate winter camps where they cached more packloads of cous, hoping the Bostons will not find them once we ride to Split Rock

where all the headmen will be gathered together;

Split Rock, where we shall learn each other's hearts to no purpose:

we are pleasing Cut Arm by riding away from our country forever.

23

Toohhoolhoolsote has departed to his country and will meet us with his People, who ride more quickly than ours. (He came here to excite our young men; we invited him to be gone.) Looking-Glass will meet us on his black horse, with all his People ready. Perhaps Red Owl will come. White Bird, Húsishúsis Kute and Hahtalekin will be at Split Rock, where everything must be decided.

And so their white tipis which have risen and tapered high over the golden grass, each point crowned by the outspread fingers of its lodgepoles, these come down to fold themselves. Lassoos hiss like rain. The women are tying cowhide bags to the breastbands of their horses. No one speaks of Cut Arm, that bad one who offended our feelings. Of Heinmot Tooyalakekt they say: This matter is troubling his heart.

Overwatched by yawning Bluecoats who should not have entered this country within the one moon Cut Arm allowed (this too hurts their hearts), they mount and ride, their rivers of horses following and preceding them,

Thief treaty!

yes, their horses laden with lodgepoles, mats, blankets and young children lashed high and safe, gripping the reins in imitation of their parents, happy up high;

shining brown horses with lowered heads,

Appaloosa horses, Pawnee ponies, spotted Kilickitat horses and even some Kentucky thoroughbreds bought from the Bostons or their enemies,

horse-treasures to shine through the golden grass

as they ride in a wide line out of Wallowa with the mountains behind them

(my heart is good; I am telling you three times);

and looking down on the river which widens far below, shining darkly in the
white cañon, with similarly trees around and along it, the cañon widening
into golden mounds, angled brown darknesses and occasional bands of basalt,
with steep bands of blackberry bushes and trees running down the cliffsides

(it is plainer and plainer),

the world swelling before them like the vulva of one who gives birth,

they leave their home, only for awhile:

White Thunder cantering ahead, where he likes to be, longing to ride drunk and
singing, shooting a rifle into some mean Boston's window;

then Heinmot Tooyalakekt and Ollokot, their best horses' bridles glowing with
disks of German silver like frozen mist from Wallowa Lake,

dogs barking all around the huge-eyed horses, men wearing deerskins, blankets,
rifles and brass bracelets, babies in the cradleboards strapped to the backs of
women who ride with their pigtails tied up in handkerchiefs or else sometimes
sport beargrass caps, lovely women in red dresses:

Cloudburst and Fair Land,

Springtime, so round in her dress of snowy buckskin, which she has decorated
with many beaded stripes along the shoulders;

now she is riding Brown One

(saving White Belly-Spot, her handsomest horse, for when she rides
in to the other People at Split Rock),

Good Woman on White Stripe,

Sound Of Running Feet riding Little One (a present from her Uncle Ollokot)

and leading Spotted Head, who is but half broken

(this girl is beautiful and nearly marriage-ready, although she has
not yet been to the women's house nor found her WYAKIN; her
elkskin dress is tricked out with porcupine quills and elk teeth; her
black braids are greased so that they shine like obsidian; her feet
are in beaded elkhide moccasins, and she wears an otterskin neck-
piece decorated with hordes of little shells);

and women in long yellow skirts to the ankle and blue scarves, grandmothers
in beaded buffalo robes, anxious wives (already thinking about drying salmon),

with the long cous breads swaying from their saddles;

old men, young men,

then their great hoards of horses;

and the world keeps getting wider and wider, shining like the white
feather in HUMMINGBIRD's heart,

the chokecherry blossoms also white,

the buttes on the far side almost a hazy horizon,

the far down trees as grey-green as Toohhoolhoolsote's pipe-bowl,

a single squat yet fluffy cloud like a buffalo cow,
hollow clatterings of many horses' hooves,
whips falling lightly,
warriors to right and left,
some from Wallowa, others from our other lands:
Grey Eagle, Shooting Thunder,
Geese Three Times Alighting On Water,
riding out into the world
of dark deer droppings in the poison oak,
our grey river sluggishly winding through the green grass in irregular
wide gut-loops at the bottom of the cañon:
briskly rides his *síikstiwaa* Good Woman, beside his *síikstiwaa* Springtime,
who does not yet have a cradleboard;
and Springtime looks back:
here we have lived; here we lived;
but Sound Of Running Feet, his beautiful daughter, looks only ahead into the
world,
the river hissing over smooth pale grey pebbles,
lush water and tall cool stands of trees with golden grass in their shade
and a rock overhanging with a tree on it,
and the peeled lodgepoles my father once set in stone to mark off the
borders of our country from the Bostons,
who treat us like dogs.
So they drive their horses and cattle down the river, wondering how it will be
once they have entered their painted land, perhaps never to go out:
Thief treaty!
Our country is growing virulent.

24

Now the sage hens have already finished dancing in the Buffalo Country
where my father rode with me,
where my brother's wife Cloudburst was born;
soon the berries there will be turning red. I long to ride away there with
the People. But I promised my father not to sell his bones. We must all
decide together.
Two Moons calls us women—
He has no sense.

25

Their hair is rich with feathers, bones and beads. At the ford they will make
rafts of buffalo robes to carry the women and children across

and down from the shoulder of golden-yellow grass into green-brown
and blue-brown hollows of space descending banded and twisted into the
hazy cañon whose far wall is the end of the world
which has come already for the Walking Cutthroats,
> and the Modocs
>> whose boys once shot frogs with bows and arrows which their
>> fathers had made them; now the boys and their fathers are
>> gone,
>> in the Indian Territory or underground;
> and the Cayuse, our cousins,
>> who dared to kill the Whitmans, and, moreover, once lived
>> on good lands;
> the Klatsop,
and now arrives for the Cutthroats themselves:
> even Crazy Horse rode onto a reservation, they say (but perhaps it
> is not so),
> and Sitting Bull has fled
>> (but surely he will return to kill more Bluecoats)
and so it comes for us,
> our life in Wallowa to be buried in the ground like an afterbirth
> because Cut Arm showed the rifle
>> (like leeches the Bostons are clinging to our country with
>> their mouths)
as we ride away toward distant dark green forked trees,
> we People, COYOTE's children,
our cañon immense and misty,
yellow-and-dark rolls of the earth's grassy belly-fat going down and down
> into Gorge Place,
>> Imnaha,
down
to the first smell of sagebrush

Thief treaty!

then the first tree,
glad glint of evening water, our dogs rushing to drink
the Enemy River in the evening: chocolate and silver and the brown flat
rocks beneath brown water,
> high water,
the far side still within our country
> (Springtime, feeling nauseous, fears the deep part of the river,
> which we call *green water*);
now we build boats of buffalo skin, entering the bluish-silver eddy,
> the river shouting and bubbling *mululululu.*

Many calves drown in the high spring water. This too the People will remember in their anger.

26

Making boats of buffalo hides, we ferry across our People,
      horses and warriors swimming diligently, bearing our treasures,
      dogs swimming free,
and then, before we have swum all the herd, some Bostons come galloping with guns to stampede some hundred horses away
         —another robbery about which Cut Arm is indifferent,
            but if we kill these Bostons, Cut Arm will choke us in rope.
So again they have robbed us.

AND BLACK BIRDS ON THE LAKE
JUNE 10–13

1

*S*itting amidst pocked reddish-grey rocks, weary of playing the Bone Game, trapped as if they have swallowed magic stones, those three, of whom two must be called doomed, gaze out across the pale blue lake, which dwells in haze at the margin of golden grass in this place called Split Rock, where Red Bear's People so often pass the time; then Swan Necklace says: *It is plainer and plainer,*
      as a fish splashes: *mokh!*
Still Shore Crossing will not speak, although he has ears to hear them, and him that pair would convince, because he is their friend and has Power,
      if by no means comparable to Toohhoolhoolsote's
         (but Cut Arm's soldiers now line up so long and straight that even
            Toohhoolhoolsote's WYAKIN magic cannot bend them into a circle)
      nor yet like White Bird's
         (that quiet chief is gracious to these young men even as he would
            smile upon a child's fishing spear):
indeed he now begins to have Power of his own
      Shore Crossing, he who can run down nearly any man or horse
         (he will soon be foremost of the Three Red Blankets),
      dead chief's son but not yet chief,

he who has breasted the Chinook Salmon Water each day for five winters
(and swimming the Enemy River when his wife nets eels at Eel Place, he
has seen old-painted GRASSHOPPER PEOPLE swarming up the boulder-
cliffs like poison oak,
yes, rushing over wide sandbars and poison oak, with the Enemy River fast and wide,
WYAKINS watching him much as he does his woman
whenever that pain departs his heart,
and hot hazy hills of rock and yellow grass;
and on the dark rocks painted LIZARD PEOPLE, some of them dancing upon dots,

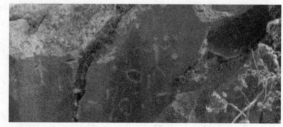

and herds of painted ELK with backcurved horns
from the time before our People were here);
he can tame wild horses
—but not even he can drive our cattle through this high water,
and now his pain settles back upon him, beginning to speak straight within his
bones.

2

Bear-hearted Toohhoolhoolsote from Salmon Place,
who can remember when old men still hung wampum-shells from their
pierced noses
and the Bostons kept out of his country,
sits well turned out in goatskin leggings and a long-fringed deerskin shirt. He has
decorated himself with loop necklaces of the best bone beads; he has painted his
face red and yellow. His ancient wives bake camas under smoking hillocks of dirt.
To-night before the council they will help him roach his hair.
White Bird, head-chief of Sparse-Snowed Place,
who from behind his feather-fan has watched the Bostons at Butterfly Place, learning why their bugle blows and how they pitch
their tents to resemble profiles of white horses grazing,
has arrived, bitter and careful, dressed in a robe of white buckskin decorated with
white seashells. He comes ahead of *Kate* his wife,
who carries his little son, the one who will be White Bird after him;
beside her ride cousins, nieces and old women;

with him his nephew Young White Bird has ridden,
    and Shore Crossing alongside Red Moccasin Tops—first cousins, promising
    young killers, Red Blankets—
    and Strong Eagle in his elkhide shirt with porcupine quills at the shoulders
        (he will live to be last of the Three Red Blankets),
    well-braided Loon, who is loud for war, since he has not yet won a name for
    himself,
    Swan Necklace and Red Spy, agile and ready men
        —all warriors of White Bird:
more than others his People hate the Bostons, who have grown up in their country
like poisonous mushrooms.
    Five Wounds and Rainbow, both fated to greatness against the Bluecoats, have
not yet ridden home from the Buffalo Country; while Wounded Head
        (whose name in these days is still Last Time On Earth)
sits between the opened flaps of his lodge, rocking his febrile little boy. His wife,
too anxious to go dig camas, whisks away flies from the man and child, longing
for her child not yet to die
as Toohhoolhoolsote smokes the pipe with White Bird
right here at Split Rock,
    where the bunchgrass goes so high that our horses scarcely need to lower
    their heads when they graze
    and we sit awaiting Looking-Glass,
        settling in a circle,
    discussing our troubles round and round while only the pain speaks
    straight,
        Good Woman and Cloudburst boiling soup
            (their sister-wives and husbands have not yet arrived),
        the first locusts singing *tekh-tekh-tekh!*
our young men speaking quickly:
        We have never killed the Bostons, even when they kill us! We kill
        only meat with our bullets.
        And sometimes Lice-Eaters and Cutthroats—
our old men talking and talking, *pokát, pokát,* like MAGPIE pecking out
the fat from COYOTE's eyes,
speaking in pain,
        while Swan Necklace invites Shore Crossing to tear down some
        Boston's fence, to frighten white women
            (or else to shoot Cut Arm while he is opening and shutting
            his mouth; that will cool us all!)
        and Red Moccasin Tops urges Shore Crossing to put on the shirt
        which a man wears;
    while we gamble again at the Stick Game,
        spending sunset, moon and dawn,

wondering if our best men will ride home in time from the Buffalo Country,

camas fading out of flower, blue blossoms and white both falling away.

3

Looking-Glass rides in on his favorite black horse, singing,
and behind him, first among women, his proud elder wife Blackberry Person
(once a girl most difficult to meet, and yet he obtained her; she has long since become his;
they grow old)
and his younger wife Asking Maiden, who wears a new brass medal around her neck,
her lovely round face shining in the sun
(we hear that Blackberry Person has begun to make herself jealous);
then their two daughters ride in, both husband-ready;
their faces are painted yellow, white and red, and they are smiling from side to side as they drive in their many horses.
After Looking-Glass comes Chief Red Heart, moderate, even-hearted,
with his wife, his daughter (who in captivity will enchant Lieutenant Wood) and his four sons:
Over The Point, most battle-famed,
then Allutakanin, whose heart means to follow him to war
and the two younger brothers who must still obey their father
then, on his favorite yellow horse, Peopeo Tholekt, well trusted by his chief
(steady-eyed, double-tressed, brave and careful):
he wants no war; his wife will soon give birth at Butterfly Place;
and White Thunder's old mother, Swan Woman, whom Peopeo looks after,
his war-friend Wottolen, *he who remembers;*
now he is arriving here with his half-grown boy Black Eagle
—all these our hearts joyfully remember,
but first among them is certainly Chief Looking-Glass,
whom the Crows call *Arrowhead:*
brave and lucky, tall, staring unsmiling from beneath his beaded hat, with the long dark-tipped white chain of eagle-feathers riding down his shoulder and all the way to his horse's belly, his feathered lance high, his eyes in shadow,
and now come Hahtalekin, Húsishúsis Kute and all the other Palouse from Eel Place:
Looking-Glass's kin-friends,

and miserly old Burning Coals whipping in his great herd
—all the People who have not sold OUR MOTHER now gathering here,
    the cañon darkened by our wealth of horses.

4

Looking-Glass unrolls his cloud-white buckskin, which a certain Crow woman
tanned for him. The mirror shines upon his throat, and his wives and daughters
wear many bracelets of German silver which he stripped from a Lakota woman
after his great battle in the Buffalo Country,
    back in the days when ravens were still white,
and he half-smiles to hear the old men say *pokát, pokát,* telling our chiefs what
the chiefs already know,
        and Húsishúsis Kute trades pipes with White Bird,
          Fair Land gathering bedding-grass for her husband's lodge,
        Looking-Glass now explaining how the young Crow boys play the
        arrow-throwing game,
            our best men listening with all their hearts to hear what he
            has spoken
            (even Bostons follow his words),
    and Strong Eagle races horses with Burning Coals
    while, sitting in the rocks, Red Moccasin Tops and Swan Necklace invite
    Shore Crossing to do what men must do.

5

In rides Ollokot,
    of all braves most handsome,
        with his hair roached back just so
        and red ribbons streaming from his many-beaded collar of otterskin,
    he who leads the young men of Wallowa,
and leaps off his cream-colored horse
        (he has just given his elder wife Fair Land a necklace of two dozen bear
        claws),
while his brother, Heinmot Tooyalakekt, the tender one, who can distinguish the
hair-partings of his two wives even in darkness, by smell or by touch,
    he whom the Bostons call *Joseph,*
brings in the old, the sick, the widows and orphans, caring for everyone:
helping Springtime from her horse, he says: Toohhoolhoolsote, Looking-Glass,
Hahtalekin, White Bird, all my chiefs; People, my heart is glad to look upon you
again!

6

Looking-Glass's wives and daughters raise up his tipi, which they have painted blue and green,
>even as Fair Land and Cloudburst establish Ollokot's lodge,
>>then help Good Woman with hers (since Springtime is now of no use);
>>and they all now make a women's house for the menstruants and especially for Springtime, a quiet dark place for her to rest .
>>>—when Swan Necklace says: Shore Crossing, it was a shame on you to let your father die unavenged. What befell you in the Cayuse country, that you forgot your father's blood?

7

In the grass, bending down with their digging sticks, our buckskin-clothed women harvest camas bulbs, breaking off the unripe ones and replanting them for next summer, murmuring Dreamer songs, making pits, straightening, rubbing their backs with their fists as they gaze upon the sober-eyed horses and beautiful-eyed warriors who ride round and round. Some young children are swimming, hunting for frogs and fish. Now comes midday, and the women rest. Then all of them,
>Cloudburst and Niktseewhy,
>Heyoom Telebinmi and Tuk'not,
>Welweyas the half-woman, her mother Agate Woman
>>(she Dreams not how soon she will be dead),
>Wounded Head's sister Wetwhowees
>>(who has just now married Red Sun)
>and his wife Helping Another,
>>along with old Towhee, her mother,
>>all filling one pit with what they have gathered
>—while Swan Necklace's sister Where Ducks Are Around,
>>she who should soon be married,
>Toohhoolhoolsote's wrinkled wives, who work quickly and by themselves,
>White Thunder's mother Swan Woman,
>Grey Eagle's daughter White Feather,
>>whose WYAKIN declines to warn her that before summer's end she will be called Broken Tooth,
>>and Good Woman, first wife of Heinmot Tooyalakekt
they are now covering up camas in other pits of hot stones and steaming wet ryegrass.

Springtime helps as she can, then wearily sits down inside the women's lodge. Now she is weaving cattail mats for the roof of a tipi. Fair Land hopes to bring her smoked salmon from the Downstream People; that will make her strong. Good

Woman begins digging baneberry roots, so that Springtime will have tea to help her milk come in,

> as Feathers Around The Neck, whose Power is so famous for curing, circles the lake by himself, searching for secret herbs,
>
>> while as soon as his sister leaves the lodge to help roast camas, Sun Tied begins to massage his wife's seven-month belly; she has made herself sore from riding.

Burning Coals (he who is old) trims the manes of his herd; while the young men race horses; they lust for wives whose nipples will be as hard as early August rosehips. Just as grebes perform the Weed Dance to allure their females, so White Bird's warriors ride round and round, proclaiming deeds of fame. The Wallowa men try to keep quiet, remembering the words of their two brother-chiefs. But why not gamble and ride? So they hurl themselves from their stallions' backs, hiding on one side or the other, then spring up again. It is almost as it always was, but the future glares in on them like bear eyes shining in the dark:

> no more fishing for dog salmon with Smohalla's People at Little Stacked Hills,
> and never again to the Buffalo Country.

The Bostons are stealing and ruining our land! Our young men are restless. They play the Bone Game. John Dog shoots his carbine into the air. Red Cloud and Red Earth, Ela-a-ta-hat and Im-nie-wah-yon, Speaking Water and White Hawk, Kills Himself and Subject to Death, Loon and No Swan, White Bull and Black Elk, No Tail Grizzly, Bad Young Grizzly Bear and Rattle Blanket, now they have all arrived. Fire Body challenges Red Spy to an arrow-shooting match. Some say that even yet matters might turn out well, as when COYOTE cunningly entreated the MONSTER: *You have already swallowed all the People, so swallow Me likewise, so that I won't get lonely.*— They pass hands across each other's horses to feel which seems strongest. Then they wager pelts against blankets, flinging them down. Some bet the rings from their wives' ears. They quarrel with one another, because Cut Arm's commands have a disgusting taste. They detest to go forever into one small place.

8

Overlooking our river of many-colored horses roaring amidst the creepers and trees of Split Rock, Toohhoolhoolsote says: These painted lands are too small. Our horses will starve.

9

Laying out a deerskin on the grass, Swan Necklace's wife says: Come eat with us.— Shore Crossing thanks her, smiling at this lovely one whom his brother-friend has won. His own wife, pregnant and alone, is digging hill-roots across the Salmon, up at Horseshoe Bend,

and since Cut Arm showed the rifle, even she, his own *síikstiwaa*, demands to know why he would imprison her and their child in a narrow
place, never again to ride where they please, nor meet the People all together; only to sit in darkness and be the Bostons' slaves, while our horses
starve to death;

    she has warned that should he himself prefer to go there, why, then per-
haps she will go away from him,

> not thinking how the Bostons will punish us all,

> or even kill us as they did his father,

    but at least Swan Necklace's wife will now clothe the anger of his heart:

> I am not my father.

10

Now as he decorates his horse, Heinmot Tooyalakekt,

> who demanded this young man's father's murderer from the Bostons
> > (they refused),

approaches him in all discretion to say: Shore Crossing, you have done well to
obey your father's dying words, and keep your hands unstained.

    The young man lowers his head, proud and shy from the Wallowa chief's praise.

11

The chiefs have incensed themselves with sweetgrass. Now they pass the pipe,
watching the ducks swim away when our children try to catch them. A very young
boy shoots. He wastes an arrow. The chiefs are sorry for him.

    They have considered this matter each in his own way:

    We have always lived here.

> We have become soiled.

> > We must stir up war for Cut Arm.

> > No, you are wrong. Who can make a fight against
> > big guns?

> *Thief treaty!*

They treat us like slaves—

And soon they will wipe their buttocks on our heads!

    We need a wide country, so that we can always find meat . . .

    Sitting Bull has ridden across the Medicine Line—forever, they say. The Blue-
coats dare not follow. And there are many buffalo over there.

    Would you ride to *him*, our enemy?

    Cut Arm is worse.

    No, he has not killed us. Sitting Bull has slain our friends and relations
forever—death to him!

    Cut Arm showed the rifle.

And those Butterfly Place People who signed the *thief treaty*—
> remembering Lawyer's face seemingly at peace with itself, although
> he sold our MOTHER's body:
>> *Thief treaty!*

Four chiefs went to *Washington* and three came back—
> Tsams Lúpin* and his lying Book of Light†—
>> And then that Boston said to my mother's
>> brother: This is *my* land.
>> But your mother's brother kept quiet.
>> Here is how I would have acted—

Death to all of them,
> while Hoof Necklace and Little Man Chief ride around implacably
> on fast horses,
> Red Moccasin Tops murmurs to his father Yellow Bull
>> —a fearless old killer who has befriended both Wallowa
>> chiefs—
> who will not answer: *Keep quiet until we ride onto our meagre
> painted land,*
>> and Good Woman brews a special tea to calm Spring-
>> time's belly
> while Toohhoolhoolsote turtles in his head:
> he who can speak in the ancient language which we barely
> understand now says nothing.

12

How can we kill them all? There are too many.
If we go on painted land, what will we have to eat?
Cut Arm has no heart,
> while Looking-Glass, who in his youth was glad to have old men talk,
> now grows old himself, and expects to be followed.

When I gave my hand to Cut Arm, and told him to hold it forever, this was his
answer.
>> *Thief treaty!*

I told Cut Arm, *the line is drawn;* then he showed us the rifle!
How can he give what is already ours?
He would pen us up forever,
> never to make our names and live for ourselves,
>> chasing buffalo herds like stormclouds on the golden grass, proving
>> ourselves at the Sun Dance, while Crow maidens encourage us,

---

*James Reuben.
†The Bible.

nor to capture a silver-bridled Lakota horse and kill his many-feathered
rider, wresting away his German silver bangles to give to my woman.
We *must* go in to the reservation. Do you wish to be hanged?
Must we obey the Book of Light like those People at Butterfly Place?
No!
We have always helped the Bostons, from their weakest days. They promised
to be our friends forever.
I am telling you three times: *They have decided,*

> Cut Arm's words crackling like flames eating little sticks, while we sat
> silent there at Butterfly Place,

>> our young men staring, frowning, lowering their eyelids,

>>> desiring that Heinmot Tooyalakekt would speak out

>>> or else that Rainbow and the other great men should come

>>>> (disappointed in his uncle, White Thunder has begun

>>>> to fix his dream on them)

>>> while the Bluecoats laid hands on Toohhoolhoolsote, as if he were
>>> a slave!

13

They mean to put us in a small place.
Yes, to corral us like their horses!

> to make us nevermore Dream

>> (Smohalla kneeling in the front row of the Dreamers, wearing a
>> pale robe, with his left hand on his heart and his right hand on his
>> thigh, and his many delicate snowy braids caressing his gaunt
>> cheeks, parting his lips as if to gasp for breath:

>>> *We are flying up,*

>> Dreamers with their dark braids and shell earrings shaking and
>> their eyes shining, Dreaming where they please
>> as Toohhoolhoolsote rings the bell
>> and Smohalla's wide dark pupils enlarge

>>> never again

>> for us to wait on WOWSHUXLUH to tell us everything:

>>> *Now is the time to dance here;*

>>> *now is the time for huckleberries to grow,*

> so that we ride across the golden grass to Dream).

They showed the rifle!
—withdrawing his own rifle from its beaded scabbard.

>>>> No better than when a girl is forced to
>>>> marry—

Toohhoolhoolsote's women still pounding cous which they must have
hastily gathered just before departing their home

and Loon shouting: *Kill all the Bostons!*

—the mold-white Bostons, who sprout up everywhere, even on our best camas meadows.

14

Looking-Glass, so friend-rich everywhere, now takes the pipe to say: Hear my words! My grandfather took care of the Bostons* like a brother. He changed shirts and horses with them. Their hearts have grown crooked, but ours remain straight. White Bird, it has been three summers since you called me into council. I told you: *Brothers, I do not care to fight the Bostons.* My heart has not changed.

Again White Bird hides his face behind his fan; he remains as reclusive as a black-crowned night heron. Finally he takes the pipe: Toohhoolhoolsote, Cut Arm has insulted you above us other chiefs. What do you say?

White Bird, I shall answer. We cannot deny that Bostons mean to remove us from OUR MOTHER; they are settling on Her like buffalo gnats and wounding Her flesh. But what would you? If you desire to fight them and die, that is all right. If not, let us go quietly onto our painted land and become women. And this I would say to Heinmot Tooyalakekt: My brother, we are all waiting upon your words; we now open our ears. It is you whom these Bostons love above all others. After Cut Arm put me away, you spoke for all the People.— Heinmot Tooyalakekt, you have sold our country!

My brother, I would not wish to contradict you, but you have not spoken straight. My father warned never to take any presents from white men. Ollokot was there; you may ask him if it was not so. Hear me, my chiefs: I have sold nothing, I am telling you three times! But that made no difference, for the Bostons have told lies and robbed us of OUR MOTHER. Looking-Glass, I call on you to answer this council as you answered me. You are a war-chief! Looking-Glass, can we by any means turn these Bostons aside?

Since I have been asked, so I shall now speak. When the gold miners came into my country, my father warned them away, but one Boston said: *For every white man you kill, a thousand will take his place.* Unless we ride away forever to the Buffalo Country, we can do nothing but keep quiet on painted land.

Then Moss Beard† will be our chief! He means to steal our horses and punish us for Dreaming!

Strong Eagle, says Heinmot Tooyalakekt, that may well be so. Now that Cut Arm has showed the rifle, we must all complete our hearts. I shall save my Wallowa People's blood if I can. Should your People wish to fight, it is not my place to say no. But as for me, I shall give up my country. For my women, children and old ones I go against my promise to him who was my father and chief. I shall now live

---

*In this case, the Lewis and Clark expedition.
†Agent Monteith.

and die on painted land, never to go out. Even my father's grave I have left forever.
   Then the old men talk *pokát, pokát,* while the young men begin to beat the untanned elkhide. When they call once more on Heinmot Tooyalakekt to show his heart (since he has nearly become Cut Arm's grandson, perhaps he can save us), he gives them these words: My father used to say: *Talking slowly is good.*

15

   Even again they call upon him, in suspicion and fear, ready to make themselves angry
            (for was it not he who bowed to Cut Arm like some womanish slave?),
so that he says:
   My People, you ask me to show my heart. I hope the young men will listen. Do not avenge your wrongs. Follow our promise to Cut Arm. We who spoke for you have warned him three times at Butterfly Place that we shall never sell the bones of our fathers, nor part with the flesh of OUR MOTHER. He has closed his ears. We must now ride onto painted land and become poor. Otherwise his Bluecoats will shoot us. My chiefs, and all you young men, I know very well you are strong and fearless, while the Bostons are weak like children. They can hardly shoot or ride horses. Even so, they number too many; we cannot keep them out of our country. Hear me: It is finished.

16

   Now Springtime must return to the women's house; she is getting ready to give birth, and so her husband goes to kill beef for her feast,
       riding away over Buzzard Mountain with Ollokot and others,
          as the old men keep saying *pokát, pokát:*
               Wait until camas season comes to Weippe; then we shall ride there
               and decide this with Charlot's People*—
               No! By then we shall be penned up on painted land. Cut Arm will
               never let us come out again.
               Why not fight? War will come to us. No matter how well we mind
               Cut Arm, the Bostons will break their promises,
          while White Thunder rides round and round with his dear war-brother
          Wottolen, longing to dream some great dream through which the People
          will not lose everything
               (to which Wottolen replies: *Soon we shall be flying up*
                  —for he lacks fear: no bullet can kill him);
                     and grasshoppers sing our lake into darkness,
          while Yellow Bull and his son come to Toohhoolhoolsote to smoke the pipe,

---

*A Flathead band from the Bitter Root Valley.

staring at the fire, insulting Cut Arm and making their hearts angry
  as the bear-hearted chief's pair of ancient wives sit silent and
  seemly within the lodge,
   listening,
and when Swan Necklace and Strong Eagle ask White Bird to judge the words of
Looking-Glass and Heinmot Tooyalakekt, he says from behind his fan: Whatever
they have decided must be right for them
—after which Red Moccasin Tops,
  he whose Cayuse grandfather was hanged by the Bostons
once more urges Shore Crossing to put on the shirt which a man wears.

17

Red Moccasin Tops says: Hear me now! That crooked-hearted Boston keeps
living here in our country! My brother, has your heart forgotten how he asked
your father for land, and your father was kind and gave it to him? Shore Crossing,
I am telling you three times! You do not answer.

I speak now as my father ordered.

But this Boston fenced out your father from his own garden, I am telling you!
When your father came to speak with him, this Boston killed him—your own
father, Chief Eagle Robe! And now they pen us up forever . . .

Shore Crossing, sick as if from a bad smell, his thoughts wavering and shapeless, keeps silence,
  for we should be instructed by old people, not by men of our own age,
   not this cousin of mine, nor even Swan Necklace, my war-friend
   and sister's son, my father's grandson, who has killed Kalispels and
   Lice-Eaters with my help,
  so that Shore Crossing's heart resembles an unhorsed hunter's face licked
  raw by a buffalo; because Swan Necklace, watching him, exemplifies a
  lizard still mostly in its cliff-cave, perfectly motionless to avoid the attentions of dangerous birds
   such as Looking-Glass, *the Bostons' friend,*
  but already rigidly elongated in the direction of the young leaf it pretends
  not to desire:
You know as well as we where he lives. Brother, ride with us, just for awhile.
Soon we shall ride no more.
Always doing nothing in a narrow place—
Stirring ashes like old women—
Never at Split Rock again, nor to visit the Wallowa People—
No more camas unless the Agent is feeling kind—
Hungry, sick, doing nothing—
And never to the Buffalo Country—
  Brother, let us hear your heart now!

Shore Crossing, he who can shoot everything, even golden eagles, keeps silent
—but to never once see dawn in the Buffalo Country,
>(Looking-Glass always says: Buffalo meat is the best.
>Only buffalo meat will do),
nor steal war ponies from the Cutthroats and Walking Cutthroats
>(because Cut Arm would pen us up:
>*Thief treaty!*),
never even to share salmon with the Downriver People,
just to leave our country forever
>(I am almost ready,
>>walking into something),
>*it is warped*
—but I shall remain quiet.
>When the Painted Arrows count coup against any of us, we
>avenge it.

And here is Swan Necklace, his pale round face raised proud, his dark eyes deep and steady, a feather in his hair and white nutshaped rings upon his pigtails, white necklaces concentric about his throat and chest, sitting still. When a breeze begins to blow from the lake, robe-fringe stirs at his ankles. His young hands shine. In a voice as sharp-edged as beargrass he says: The Bluecoats will send us to a small place, I am telling you three times! Even in the peace council, Cut Arm spoke the rifle! And he made Toohhoolhoolsote prisoner. *They have trampled us into the ground.*

>*Thief treaty.*

Red Moccasin Tops now says: Brother, let us kill the white man who killed Eagle Robe. Or would you rather go to a small place to pass the time with hungry old women?

He is not here. This I have heard from Red Heart: he has fled to the gold mines in Florence. We can never get at him there.

Then let us kill another one. Why not him who likes to set his dogs on us?

Shore Crossing will not speak; he is wrapping himself in his blanket, but Swan Necklace says: That one owns a fine horse and a rifle. Perhaps he has *getting-drunk liquid.** He dwells alone. *Why not him?*

Brothers, my eyes are rolling around,
>the Sun as red as the nostril of a galloping horse,
>and now the wind is blowing.

18

His hounds bark, and the old man sits up, reaching under the pillow for the revolver

---

*Whiskey.

but Swan Necklace's plump young face rises in the window like a
moon:
Get him, Butch! Get him, Jupiter!
but even as the face gloats at him he hears his squealing brutes
clubbed down.
Why, you no good Indian bastard! I'll pay you back for that! And after I get you,
I'll pin down your squaws—
but that proud mouth almost seems to smile even though its corners turn
down:
by GOD I should have knowed better than to leave the shutter
ajar no matter how hot it was! Holy JESUS, help me now! If I
can just
because although the revolver is charged, the instant it
flashes into sight they'll
sweet summer evening sky, yellowgold, and the
river singing
two seconds is all I need
of sky and
this house whose beams I hewed out with hope
and sweat, for Thine is the Kingdom
and if I try for my buffalo gun—not even a foot away,
right there leaning up against the wall—that's two seconds, maybe three, but if I miss
the sky
it'll have to be the revolver: one into his face and then
but I can buy them off, that's it, I know,
I *knew;* I always knew the evil of them Indians. There must be one
more of them outside at least because they're such GODD——n
cowards—
and in the intruder's pale brown hands a Sharps now gleams dark, rising
I got to do it, *right now*—
Hey, you Indians, I didn't do nothing—
so if I stare right into his cruel eyes
and at his forehead which sweat-shines like his many, many necklaces as
the rifle speaks.
My GOD, you've *shot* me, you d—— d Indian! *Help!* These Injuns are murdering me—
and then the rifle speaks again, into his face.

19

So he who killed Dakoopin is dead, just as we would have it
(my heart flies up to the SUN),

bloody and silverhaired on his bearskin pillow, a fly circling round his open mouth

here in this place called Tipsusleimah which the Bostons have stolen for themselves along with so many others, gashing OUR MOTHER, uprooting Her hair,

> shooting Dakoopin, a crippled woman* without harm in her; thus we have punished him; we are laughing and making ourselves brave, we who are from Sparse-Snowed Place and Wallowa:
> so we give ourselves his guns, tear apart his Bible, rend the silver dollars from his pockets, scalp him, take his bullets, powder, sugar, coffee and *getting-drunk liquid*
>> (discussing our troubles round and round)
> because Cut Arm showed the rifle, and these Bostons mean to suck the marrow from our bones! Hear me, *these* Bostons here on this land they have painted away from us, exactly these are the ones who signed the paper to the Grandfather† in *Washington* to get us removed.
> If I am to speak, I shall now speak from my heart. (Dakoopin's spirit may then be gladdened.) Let us ride to tell Toohhoolhoolsote, whom Cut Arm has shamed; no, brother, this has been no more glorious than washing the ashes off sweathouse rocks; that old man showed no fight! Let us continue straightforwardly in the way we used to live (Looking-Glass and White Bird acted thus before they got old): we shall be praised! Let us ride quickly to some other place, and kill more Bostons; completing our hearts we shall kill them; like grizzly bears we shall rush toward their blood,

and staking their horses in another bad Boston's wheat field, in order to lure him out

> (because last year in this place a certain tall Boston for his own amusement took up his blacksnake whip and lashed two of our young men whom he had never seen before, and when Ollokot complained at Butterfly Place, the Bostons called a council to judge who was in the wrong, and this very man, who now plants wheat in our country, wounding the flesh of OUR MOTHER, sat on the council and decided: *the tall Boston was in the right,*
> and he, this one here, he was also the one who when his friend murdered Shore Crossing's father said: *He should not be prosecuted for killing a dog*),

they hide on the field's edge, in the growing yellow grass,

> over them the yellow and crimson emblem of a redwing blackbird;

---

*Her name means "Broken."
†President.

until two Bostons come running to curse them,
>   the SUN falling
as the one who judged against the People now sees a rifle rising up out of
the grass, shouts, strikes his brother's arm, and back they run
but Swan Necklace stands up smiling with his WYAKIN riding him
>   to full dusk
and Red Moccasin Tops leaps out singing
while Shore Crossing takes aim
>   (this is nothing: far less trouble than running down a wild mustang)
so that they kill those two dogs: *Áhaha!*
>   —the moon as yellow-white as an old horse's tongue
>   and
blood darker than Salish* cherries.

THE TIME HAS PASSED
JUNE 14

1

*S*wan Woman, older than anyone knows, slowly twining her pigtails while camas bakes underground; ancient Tzi-kal-tza who has tied stones to his braids; Fair Land, more than thirty springs old (the beads rattling and jingling across her breasts), who now suckles her little boy; Good Woman, who is gathering more grass and moss for Springtime's baby; and Toohhoolhoolsote, who this morning as every other has stiffened his hair with clay in order to Dream this EARTH
>   of yellow locusts dancing between the rocks,
>   cattails and yellow grass,
they all raise their heads when Two Moons comes running to the chiefs, crying out: Here comes Swan Necklace on a white man's horse—

2

And Toohhoolhoolsote, rising, turns away, wrapping himself in his buffalo robe, hunching in his head, drawing in his arms, until he has almost become stone.

---

*Flathead.

3

Swan Necklace, Red Moccasin Tops and Shore Crossing encamp at Round
Willow Stream, waiting for other warriors to come;
　　and now Big Morning is riding Swan Necklace's new horse round and round:
　　　　a pretty roan stallion
　　　　　　　(the two who were humiliated with the blacksnake whip know this
　　　　　　　horse very well)
　　　　　　　　　and Toohhoolhoolsote speaks into White Bird's ear
　　as Shore Crossing's wife, who has not yet given birth, rides in from Round Willow Stream, joyously singing the war-song, with Red Moccasin Tops riding
ahead, likewise singing,
　　while before him, Shore Crossing rides in singing at last, red flannel in his
feathered hair, bearing a great Sharps buffalo rifle: his trophy of the Bostons
he has killed
　　　　　　　—but Red Owl, Húsishúsis Kute and Yellow Grizzly Bear (he
　　　　　　　who first insulted Shore Crossing) run to Looking-Glass,
　　　　　　　　　who has always known what must befall should our
　　　　　　　　　People kill any Bostons—
　　　　　　　while three longhaired men with red-painted faces and ecstatic
　　　　　　　eyes sell Wounded Head an almost-new black Winchester in ex-
　　　　　　　change for the horse he is riding, and when his wife points angrily
　　　　　　　to their sick baby, crying: Bad man, how can you go to war and leave
　　　　　　　your son?, he replies: The rifle will be mine but not for war, I prom-
　　　　　　　ise you! Now we can ride away to the mountains for deer and sheep,
　　　　　　　escaping the war of these other people
　　as Red Moccasin Tops cries out: We have killed four! Shore Crossing is a man
after all—
　　so that his proud father Yellow Bull begins singing the war-song
　　　　because now we shall never be penned up here anymore; we shall ride away,
　　　　away, all the way to the Buffalo Country to be *lucky men* like Looking-
　　　　Glass; Swan Necklace has promised me that Crow women make good
　　　　sweethearts; I shall find one; I shall find two; I shall eat cottonwood jelly
　　　　with them in the spring
　　　　　　　(my horse flies like thunder, faster than daybreak)
　　　　while Two Moons cries: Warriors, let us ride out and kill more Bostons!
　　　　　　　at which Toohhoolhoolsote looks up, his eyes half-closed
　　　　　　　and his mouth curving down; no one knows what lives
　　　　　　　in his heart; sunlight glares like tears upon his leathery
　　　　　　　cheeks; he says: Now I am glad,
　　　　　　　　　then leaps onto one of his buffalo horses, a wise one

named Brown Head, cantering away with his fiercest
young men;
for many, o so many, of our proud and tortured People *must* rise up in joy,
knowing in their hearts that few things can be more beautiful than this
smoothly moonfaced young warrior Shore Crossing with his two long waves
of hair shining down past his armpits and his many white loops of necklace
enriching him like all this summer's worth of bright days, while a cartridge
belt sashes tight the plaid blanket-coat whose fringes fall past his ankles
    (he will now become foremost of our daring ones, the Three Red Blankets);
his wife's heart has grown proud; at last he has acted like a man;
    but Looking-Glass's People cast against these young men voices both
deep and shrill,
        Red Heart's wife crying out: The Bostons never did anything to
        hurt me! You have killed them, Shore Crossing! Swan Necklace and
        Red Moccasin Tops, you have killed them! You have bad hearts.
        Now they will be killing us,
the women tearing down their lodges, even abandoning their camas
bulbs so tediously gathered and now cooking underground
    (White Bird and *Kate* withdrawing silently into their lodge)
as Looking-Glass says,
        staring the killers down:
You have acted like children in murdering these Bostons. My hands are
not stained with their blood; nor shall they be. If you desire war, then
fight, but not with my help. I ride now into my country, which Cut Arm
has painted out for me. Do not visit me there! The Bluecoats will swoop
on you like bluejays on dead meat. My heart is sad for you. Now I am going away, for I wish to remain at peace,
        and even before his wives and daughters have finished taking down
        his lodge he has leapt onto his black buffalo pony,
        who advances with lowered head, his mane standing upright like
        his ears,
            at which Red Moccasin Tops,
                who will become the second of the Three Red Blankets,
            says: Shore Crossing, my brother, here is one chief who yearns
            to stir up ashes forever like an old woman!
                    as White Thunder, whose place is with the Wallowa
                    People, hastens to his dear mother Swan Woman
                        (perhaps he will see her no more),
                    and gives her his rifle, so that she will never fall
                    hungry;
                    he bids good-bye to Peopeo Tholekt, who leaps
                    onto his longnecked yellow horse

—but Wottolen and Black Eagle have completed
their hearts: they will stay here, just for awhile,
while Chief Red Heart is now persuading all his sons to come
and lie quiet with him and Looking-Glass on painted land:
the good place called *Kamnaka,* which Cut Arm has
promised us,
although Over The Point desires to fight, and likewise his
brother Allutakanin;
just now they choose to take care of their mother and sister,
thereby comforting their father's heart,
for who knows how Cut Arm will revenge himself?
—and gathering in their horses, Looking-Glass's People begin riding
quickly away
(perhaps we are parting forever),
riding hard toward Kamnaka,
Looking-Glass and his brother presently turning aside
from the others to warn the white man Tsépmin, with
whom they once traded horses, to get out of there before White Bird's warriors think to visit his ranch,
Tsépmin first disbelieving, then stubborn, then
owl-eyed,
and Looking-Glass rides away beside his brother, the
bells and beads singing on their horses' martingales;
now they are all cantering north through the sweet green swales
until the horses tire,
our children silent with terror
(now they will kill our relatives),
willows and cottonwoods along our streams—
thief treaty!—
avoiding Riverfork,* where we once had a cemetery
(the Bostons dug it up),
and the green becomes yellow, the cottonwoods dark-leaved in opposition to TRAVELLER the SUN
as we ride down into the rabbitbrush, another bend, and then the drier
rolls of land greet us with grasses green and yellow, lavender-grey
country ahead
as the smooth land opens out and coarsens into sagebrush, and
dark rock-teeth begin to gnaw out of the golden grass,
cottonwoods like silvergreen clouds in the sky of yellow grass,
sweep of yellow meadows, lodgepole pine forests, all forest ahead

*Lewiston.

(a family of deer, the fawns bounding like rabbits: we leave
them, in order to ride more quickly to the place where Cut
Arm promised we'll be safe),
upcurving and downdrooping parallels of pine branches
—and then Kamnaka, our reservation, this scrap of flesh which Cut
Arm has left us,
where we shall forgo camas, surely for this summer only, baking
eels on sticks;
—and likewise even Húsishúsis Kute,
who spoke for the Palouses at Butterfly Place,
spurning Cut Arm's safe-conduct pass, smilingly explaining to the
Bostons *because I might get it dirty*
(Cut Arm frowning horribly, speaking hard to his tallest
Bluecoat and writing marks on a snow-white paper),
yes, even Húsishúsis Kute now rides away with his chief, Hahtalekin, and
all the Palouses
(thus we who remain say they are as women to dread the punishments of Cut Arm
while we ourselves hope that Cut Arm will learn to be
sorry for what we are now beginning to accomplish);
we shall abide here where we have always been;
or perhaps ride east to the Buffalo Country for awhile, to meet our friends
the Crows and kill Cutthroats and Shinbones* (and perhaps Lice-Eaters on
the way); and we shall certainly kill buffalo, as many as we wish:
Ride with me, brothers! Let us kill more Bostons; I say it three times.
Shore Crossing has spoken. I shall follow him—
This will bring bad luck.
No,
warriors with their hair down, raising their feathered lances, riding red-
blanketed on their lovely horses,
Toohhoolhoolsote singing over them as an-
other trout leaps out of the lake,
riding, riding,
away on their decorated horses, joyous for cruelty
and Springtime keeps asking for her husband.
Tell Fair Land—
Look! Red Owl's wife gave me her puppy—
Now we shall give Cut Arm his war.
It was not we who stirred this up, but Cut Arm.
I mean to capture many horses.

---

*Blackfeet.

And I also:
> *Pim.*
>> *Pim.*
>>> *Pim.*

We have made ourselves new.

SOME KIND OF PEACE
JUNE 14–16

1

*R*eady to hear the purport of their visitor's heart, he stands beside Ollokot, there on the far side of Buzzard Mountain where the wind blows cool, as Two Moons, that good warrior well known, canters up on his mouse-colored horse,
>the women squinting anxiously through the smoke of the roasting meat—
>>his dear daughter Sound Of Running Feet
>>>(a modest girl who makes few errors),
>>Ollokot's younger wife Cloudburst
>>and the half-woman Welweyas
>>>(Fair Land, who is Ollokot's other wife, having stayed with Good Woman at Split Rock to help Springtime give birth)—
>all turning their darkening ribbons of beef on green sticks;
>and John Wilson and Half Moon, they who are fishing-skilled, have just run up from the creek when Two Moons leaps down, caressing the horse's neck, and says:
>>Some young men have gone to war,
>at which Heinmot Tooyalakekt (he who is called *Joseph*) smiles painfully,
>>his heart screaming *qoh! qoh! qoh! qoh!* like a raven
>>as Welweyas's hand goes to her throat
>and Two Moons, whose blanket has been folded over his left arm, now draws it in tightly around his waist, left hand separated from right by a single thickness of woolcloth,
>standing large-eyed, waiting to hear what the brother chiefs will say:

Heinmot Tooyalakekt hides his heart
while Ollokot seems nearly glad.

2

They leave most of the hides to rot, the men and Welweyas slinging their rifles over their shoulders, as the daughter and the brother's younger wife finish cinching bags of meat upon their twelve packhorses, with carrion-birds already blackly clouded on the cow-guts,

and now the men are riding ahead

(John Wilson, carrying smoked trout for his sister, murmuring a secret prayer to his WYAKIN:

I am flying up),

Two Moons cantering beside Ollokot, wondering how it is going to be,

Half Moon watching the horizon for something bad,

Heinmot Tooyalakekt already half-bewitched by Cut Arm's angry face, which floats before him in the air

(as for Ollokot, he hates Cut Arm worse than Sitting Bull),

but Welweyas canters singing and laughing, as if she does not understand; perhaps she is making herself brave.

3

So again they cross the roaring Chinook Salmon Water, raising their rifles high while their fine horses swim them from bank to bank; unspeaking they ride

(their hearts as various as those of gamblers playing the Stick Game),

back to Split Rock, from where so many People have already fled,

panicked women whipping their horses' heads,

leaving dog dung, dead circles of grass, opened pits, steaming hillocks within which camas sweats for nothing,

but White Thunder, this excellent young man soon to become great, is waiting on his uncles (he has painted his face)

and our buffalo hunters are beginning to ride in from the Lo Lo Trail,

while White Bird sings one of the oldest Dreamer songs:

All People, all animals! OUR MOTHER will die! The buffalo will perish, our liberty broken!

the SUN glaring down the white-gorgeted chests of our warriors who dance by the lake's edge, each knot in their dark braids picked out with its own white jewel of light, light on their round shell-disk earrings, the stripes of their blankets and the rectangles and diamonds of their leggings glowing whiter than the whites of their well-shaded eyes;

to them Heinmot Tooyalakekt says: I am weary of your conduct; soon you will be sorry for what you have done; there is no remedy now, while Toohhoolhoolsote's wives, obeying their master, keep on digging, steaming, pounding and smoking camas, and his nephews dry arrow-shafts,

some young men ecstatically beating an untanned elkskin, singing war-songs,

as Fair Land makes soup for everyone.

4

White Bird rides his horse round and round, saying: Now we shall not go on the reservation.

5

Where is Looking-Glass?
He took his people away; they have been gone two days—
To their reservation?
—at which Toohhoolhoolsote snarls: If they conclude to become slaves of Cut Arm and the Bostons forever, I cannot help it.

6

Good Woman crawls out from the tipi, wearing many beads.
Is it well with Springtime?
Very well, and you have another daughter. They are sleeping in the women's house—
Good, and my thanks to you and Fair Land. Soon we must be riding away.

7

White Thunder waits to come to him.
They sit down together to smoke kinnikinnick,
watching black birds on the lake,
the locusts singing *tekh-tekh-tekh!*,
until he says: Now tell me. Did you ride with those young men?
No! Uncle, you know that I have always opened my ears to your words!
I am glad. Who were they?
Only one from our band.
Shall I guess?
Geese Three Times Alighting On Water.
So I supposed. My dear nephew, he has done wrong.
What will you say to him?
Nothing now. Who gave him a rifle?

My dear uncle, his heart had grown angered, so he rode to that place with only bow and arrow!

      —and then White Thunder begins to relate who went killing and which Bostons died; how it began and what the three first killers,

          Swan Necklace, Shore Crossing and Red Moccasin Tops,

have said, when Looking-Glass rode away, and what rose up in People's hearts when Toohhoolhoolsote then set out alongside his fiercest men and White Bird's best killers

      and Geese Three Times Alighting On Water

          (they have now raped women and attacked children);

so that he well perceives that this nephew of his has grown thirsty to kill Bostons

      —but to think on our young men

          (even Geese Three Times Alighting On Water, who is bad and un-
          deserving,

          and these meanly grinning warriors of White Bird's and Toohhool-
          hoolsote's who have now gotten even with the Bostons:

              Shore Crossing proud that all the People now know what we
              have done)

raising their lances, riding necklaced and braided, bearing quivers and a few old Henry rifles against the great wheeled guns of the Bluecoats

      —how could they not see what will happen?—

to consider the Bluecoats revenging themselves on our women and children,

this wounds his heart:

      Cut Arm will be killing us all;

          such is Cut Arm, who pretends to be as kind as a grandfather.

8

Sound Of Running Feet rides into camp, leading the packhorses, Cloudburst coming up wearily behind

          (some women say she does not work hard enough),

and Fair Land, *Kate*, Welweyas, Good Woman and Toohhoolhoolsote's wives help them unload the animals, so that there is beef for Springtime and everyone

      —but Welweyas's heart grows sad, for she has left her skinning
      knife behind at Buzzard Mountain—

while a half-drunk young man from White Bird's band rides round and round, screaming: *Wounded Head gave me this horse for the rifle I gave him. Now Wounded Head will ride to war!*

and Helping Another, Wounded Head's dear wife, sits by the doorway of her lodge, rocking her sick little boy, angry and sad.

9

Toohhoolhoolsote lifts his head,
>   and now comes dusk as black as his horse's tail.

10

So Heinmot Tooyalakekt meets his baby girl,
>   his three women looking up at him:
>>   Good Woman, picking nits from Springtime's hair, believing that
>>   he will act rightly,
>>   Sound Of Running Feet so pleased with her new sister that she
>>   wishes she herself could have made her,
>>   Springtime sitting straight and still, hoping to bring him joy by
>>   doing other brave things.

He gives them each a fine copper bracelet.

Taking the baby in his arms, he says: My youngest one, you are strong; soon
you will be as high as spring grass.

11

Walking apart with his brother, still desiring in his heart that we may lay down
some fine thing at Cut Arm's feet and ride quietly to the reservation, he asks what
must happen, and Ollokot replies: You and I heard for ourselves that all the chiefs
spoke for peace; not even Toohhoolhoolsote wished to kill Cut Arm. We talked
peace; now there is no talk about that.

12

White Thunder goes to Old Yellow Wolf, his uncle, whose name he carries.*
He says: Heinmot Tooyalakekt's heart is angry.

My dear nephew, his own father used to warn us about these Bostons, saying:
*In their hearts, we and they are not equal; they intend to starve us all and make us
slaves; they will run us off our own country.*

Then you are for war?

In any event, now you young men can get your taste of it—

---

*His true (WYAKIN) name was White Thunder, but this was intimate; everyone addressed him as Yellow Wolf.

13

White Bird's wife, smallfaced and perfect (why do the Bostons call her *Kate*?),
who wears crossed sashes of trade beads over her shoulders, in our
grandmothers' style,
stares childishly upon the men, then withdraws to help Fair Land, whom she loves
more than those brother-chiefs' other wives; and so they sit in the grass, pounding
baked camas between stones
while the horses say: *Hinimí!*
and Cloudburst, who has enriched the beds with fresh grass in her husband's
lodge, now comes to them,
the warriors singing,
and Fair Land, standing behind Cloudburst, rests a hand on her shoulder, coldly half-smiling at the young men who have done bad things
as their husband begins to smoke the pipe with the other chiefs:
Again they talk over which young men have gone killing among the Bostons,
and what they did,
speaking *pokát, pokát,*
(thus it has been done, without telling us:
we are as eels caught against something in the water),
and down at the lake's edge, Strong Eagle, who would have
wished to be one of the three first killers, is pounding the
elkhide with them
and Shot In The Belly says to Wounded Head: They are fighting near Mount Idaho. Let us go see—
pokát, pokát, pokát, pokát,
until Heinmot Tooyalakekt, seeking to complete his heart, passes the pipe and
asks: What should *now* be done?
to which Toohhoolhoolsote,
he who is easily angered,
replies: I am a man, and I shall die,
so that they know his heart remains turned toward war; to him blood will taste
as delicious as fat.
(He is already old; how could it harm him to be killed?)
Next White Bird shows his heart: If I am to speak, I must say this: Since our
hands have become stained, we can stay at home no more,
Kate looking out at him from her sitting-place, even as Fair Land goes on
pounding the soft-baked camas,
Toohhoolhoolsote staring into the fire like some Power in a story Who is about
to close the door very quickly,
and Cloudburst begins carrying bedding-grass into Ollokot's tipi,
the fire flaring up, the dogs whining for more meat.

Pitying the People
>(Fair Land still expecting to go to her favorite gathering-place once the huckleberries ripen
>
>—while Two Moons, hopeful man, thinks to ride with his woman to Sparse-Snowed Place and stay out of trouble!—
>
>and even Ollokot forgets that we may never again ride to Weippe in mid-summer
>>to meet our friends and relatives among the other peoples, dig camas and Dream;
>
>>while Good Woman, so wise about human beings, cannot understand what we must soon suffer)

and perceiving that the young men
>(among them Geese Three Times Alighting On Water)

keep watching him and Ollokot,
Heinmot Tooyalakekt takes the pipe to say: Hear me now! Let us show Cut Arm that our hearts are good. If we stay right here in this place until the Bluecoats come, we might make some kind of peace with them,
to which Ollokot says: Heinmot Tooyalakekt is my brother and my chief. What he has said is right.

>Toohhoolhoolsote growls: Again and again you turn to Cut Arm—you, who told us: *We shall never yield up our fathers' graves,*
>>Ollokot biting his lip with rage,
>>
>>his brother almost smiling, in order not to divide the People any deeper,
>>as Toohhoolhoolsote speaks on:

To me it makes no difference. Let us go our own way. We shall give Cut Arm his war, and you Wallowa People can try once more to sell your country. My brothers, I am opening my ears: How much coffee or molasses will they pay you for your father's bones? Will they give you a lick of sugar once they have wiped their buttocks on your heads?
>>*Thief treaty!*

>Pointing his finger at the old chief, Ollokot answers: Before the young men became murderers, even you Chinook Salmon Water People chose to leave your home! Toohhoolhoolsote, we are not as women, to change our hearts with everything that happens—

>White Bird smokes the pipe: My chiefs, perhaps we shall fight Cut Arm, or maybe we shall ride away somewhere else, just for awhile. That is all I have to say,
>>at which Heinmot Tooyalakekt,
>>>whose heart screams *qoh! qoh! qoh! qoh!,*

says: My chiefs, you have all spoken well. For this I am grateful. We must do whatever we find best. This night I'll Dream on what to do.

Good Woman has sweetened her breath with columbine; presently he goes in to her.

14

In his ear she whispers: *Kate* has shown me her husband's heart.
What is it, *síikstiwa*?
      (Springtime sits up listening.)
Some have told White Bird that you and Ollokot mean to run away and save
yourselves. You will ride to Butterfly Place to become Cut Arm's slaves. Then you
will help him kill us.
Síikstiwaa, if you weep you'll bring me bad luck.

15

In the darkness he remembers Cut Arm's hair, the color of a mudfish, and the
Bostons talking like dogs lapping up water,
sitting high, while we must seat ourselves on the ground before them
      (Cut Arm murmuring with Moss Beard, the Bluecoats showing the rifle
      always, and those Bostons from Mount Idaho,
            which we used to call Rawhide Place,
      and from Chinook Salmon Water, all watching us with triumphant
      hatred)
as the baby begins to cry,
      Springtime sleepily lifting her out of the cradleboard,
            which has not yet been decorated,
      and White Thunder snoring uneasily by the doorway,
            through which the breeze comes, smelling of lake and horses,
            far away coyotes singing,
      the baby suckling loudly,
      Sound Of Running Feet sleeping on her side,
            the moon shining silver in the smokehole.
Heinmot Tooyalakekt begins to sleep, wondering into which dark place his
dreams will pull him,
      sick in his heart, which will not stop crying *qoh! qoh! qoh! qoh!*,
      asking himself why Sound Of Running Feet no longer asks him anything,
            turning his heart to wondering whether anything can be undone
            even now that our worst young men have decided for us what we
            shall do:
                  I must show anger to no one, not even them
                        (since I saved myself from doing so to the worst of
                        Bostons);
      stretching out his legs, then unwrapping the blanket from his shoulders:
            Now we have set ourselves against them:
            against their rifles and bugles

and the staring eyes of the Bluecoats whenever Cut Arm opens and
closes his mouth
    (I am telling you three times),
and Cut Arm showing the rifle, while the Bostons' women sing
túmm like katydids.

Now from the lake comes the cry of a marten: *paq! paq!*
so that he remembers Wallowa Lake,
beginning to swim out into the crystalline heart of its dreaminess, and then
    pim,
        pim!
a bullet passes through the lodge, *zzzzzzz!*
and White Thunder leaps up, shouting: People, enemies are shooting in here!
as the baby begins to scream.

His blood is on fire! Longing to kill these Bostons, he comforts his women
while his brave nephew runs out with his rifle:
    pim!
and the Bostons gallop away, their horses crying: *Hinimí.*

16

At dawn, Two Moons and some other People are riding away in fear to Weir Place,[*]
while he sits watching them go, with his head in his hands: The Bostons will kill us now
    while Good Woman, Cloudburst and Sound Of Running Feet strike the
    lodgepoles,
then catch the horses, expecting to pack and ride away,
    for most other People have already ridden to Sparse-Snowed Place
    in White Bird's country; even Three Feathers and Metal-Eyed
    Crane now pack up their lodges,
        although Geese Three Times Alighting On Water is already
        getting drunk with the Three Red Blankets; since they are
        from White Bird's band he says nothing to them, but to Geese
        Three Times Alighting On Water he says slowly:
            You are not chief. I am chief. If Cut Arm takes you, he
            will choke you in rope. Perhaps he will kill us all. You
            have brought evil upon all your People,
    then turns away
        (Geese Three Times Alighting On Water unable to reply, be-
        cause he is nearly drunk),
as Fair Land finishes taking down her husband's lodge;
    Welweyas and Agate Woman, whose task was smaller since they
    own fewer things, are already tying lodgepoles to their horses

---

[*]On the Clearwater, near the town of Stites.

while Ollokot speaks with the young men; again and again he is speaking
>   (they promise that they have made themselves brave forever);
as *Kate*, who has now packed White Bird's tipi onto her horses, sits doing
nothing, not even pounding camas,
>   unlike Toohhoolhoolsote's wrinkled old wives in their smoke-
>   blackened deerskin shirts adorned with tarnished brass buttons,
>   who must always be working:
>>   loudly pounding cous, which they wished to do at home
>>>   (Cut Arm prevented that; they hope someone will
>>>   pound him to death):
and White Thunder is riding round and round, singing his Wyakin song
>   (war is a mirror for him to see himself)
>   —but his uncle Old Yellow Wolf warns: If you ride to war and get shot,
>   no weeping!—
while Heinmot Tooyalakekt sits beside his .44 Winchester carbine, staring at the
lake;
>   and little Kalkalshuatash, whom the Bostons call *Jason,* in a feathered
>   otterskin cap which his wife made too large for his head, stands before him in
>   the dirty old robes of a poor man, clutching the eagle's wing whose Power he
>   scarcely knows, waiting patiently for this one who is his chief to restore him
>   to safety, wealth and joy.
>   Heinmot Tooyalakekt sits awhile, just for awhile, hoping to be advised by his
own heart,
>>   the locusts singing *tekh-tekh-tekh!*
then finishes decorating the cradleboard for his new child,
>>   carving snowberries, camas and salmon,
>   listening silently to the songs of the young men,
>>   some of whom nearly taunt him for sitting there like a woman,
then rises, trimming and retrimming the manes of his favorite horses
—until White Bird comes to see the bullet hole in his lodge.
>   Now again they are all talking, *pokát, pokát*
>>   (if there is going to be a war, then when it is over we can still talk with the
>>   Bluecoats),
and presently he says to Ollokot: Our father would not have sold our country!

17

Since the others have eaten, Fair Land is now roasting meat on sticks for
Springtime
>>   (who has not entirely stopped bleeding),
>   and the young men are still beating the untanned elkskin, singing war-
>   songs
as Ollokot replies: Elder brother, I know not what to say.

18

Pitying him, he now says: Let us withdraw into our mountains until the Bostons have forgotten us
—but Heinmot Tooyalakekt reminds him: In that case we would be hiding forever.
We would lose our horses. Then we would become nothing.

19

Gazing into his heart, his women wait for him to say where we must go.

JUST FOR AWHILE
JUNE 15–16

1

*W*e shall remove ourselves to Sparse-Snowed Place, which White Bird's
People know so well;

> his women and Ollokot's now opening up smoldering dirt camas-ovens
> and packing whatever they can in bags and baskets
>> (as Springtime, whispering a secret song, ties fast to the cradle-
>> board that buckskin pouch within which dwells her baby's dried
>> umbilical cord);

we shall round up our last cows and horses,
then ride away, just for awhile.

To the young men beating the elkskin, he says: Why are you making yourselves
brave for *this?*

They know not what to say, for our best killers have already departed for
Sparse-Snowed Place,

> but White Thunder (who does not say so) begins to feel that his uncle is
> speaking wrong: War has begun now! It is not the time to discourage
> those who must fight! Still, I must keep quiet; for my uncle is my chief.
> —He asks his Uncle Ollokot what should be done about Cut Arm, and is
> told: My dear nephew, if Cut Arm troubles me, I shall fight him at once!

They keep talking, *pokát, pokát,*

> so that Sound Of Running Feet begins almost laughing to remember the
> tale of how the five Musselshell Sisters sang to COYOTE *Tse-pe pip-ya,*

tse-pe-pip-ya; then COYOTE tricked them into dancing until dawn, so
that they dried up:

> exactly so have the young men tricked the old men, who went on
> talking until we began to kill Bostons; now they too have dried
> away into nothing!

> > —and Sound Of Running Feet begins flying up, flying up:

> > > even though my father has made himself angry, still my
> > > heart is thrilled that new things are now beginning to
> > > happen exactly here where nothing has ever happened.

Now we are striking camp, the women cinching baskets, bags and blankets
most tightly on the horses and whipping them into speed; we are all departing,

> Ollokot's wives in their fine elkskin dresses,
> Fair Land and Springtime equally proud and beautiful,
> and our copper bracelets glittering as we ride

> > (her husband smiling at Springtime, pretending that his heart is
> > not sorry as he says: The Bluecoats will soon be coming for us);

through our country we keep riding toward Sparse-Snowed Place,

> with the hay-colored slopes of Split Rock going grey in their rise on either side
> > and the bunchgrass as high as our horses' bellies
> until to the northwest the cañon splits:
> we take the lefthand fork, the west fork

to Driving-In Cave:

> crumbling rock lip overhanging the cliff with many shards and facets, with
> blackberries thickly screening its mouth
> and the happy splash of the creek in this bright and humid forest
> here where the Ancient People lived
> and where our best grandfathers corralled a large party of Snake warriors,
> then built a fire and smoked them to death.

> > Now Cut Arm will see if we cannot treat him the same or worse,
> > we Nimiipu, we People
> > who until now never killed any Boston no matter how many of us they
> > did to death. Now we shall teach them how to be killers!

> > > as Shore Crossing's wife tries to lead a few shy women in the war-
> > > song
> > > and Star Doctor, Kapoochas and Toohhoolhoolsote sit drumming
> > > within that cool cave with its tar drippings shining on the ceiling
> > > and its generations of soot

—My chiefs, why did you not ride on to Sparse-Snowed Place?
Here we wait to hear your heart.—

Here indeed wait the People in their robes and leggings of many colors, and as
they now sit in a circle, Heinmot Tooyalakekt walks around them three times;
there is a leaded black pipe of peace, but he smokes the furred and eagle-feathered
red pipe of war, saying: Soon we must fight the Bostons, who steal and kill all the

time. My heart is sad. Young men who have thirsted for war, I ask you: Will we act like small children and be chased back and back? They will cut down all trees and plow all the ground; there will be no place left even for our dead bodies,

  so that the warriors' hearts joy to hear that he will not go against them and ride
  to Cut Arm after they have disobeyed his advice,
but then he says: Now we shall have to fight. But I shall not tolerate any more harming of women and children. The Bostons are like grizzly bears. Let us be People. I did not tell you to commence this war. If you dislike what I am telling you now, go away.

  Then Toohhoolhoolsote prays to OUR MOTHER: May it be well. May we nevermore be interfered with. May we kill them and drive them away, the Bluecoats, Cut Arm and all the Bostons.

2

 So they move to Sparse-Snowed Place
   where in olden days the WYAKIN-named warrior-chief Red Grizzly Bear
   lived
   and after him his son Koolkooltom dwelled with many cattle;
   here within the highest of the two Cemetery Buttes lie Chief Pah Wyan
   and his two wives, all killed by the Lice-Eaters
    (these graves belong to us; we shall never give them up):
here so many war parties have gathered and returned,
and here we have many horses not yet gathered up;
   and here Toohhoolhoolsote and White Bird, who know this country better than others, will soon be riding together over the hills with the bravest young men, planning how best to trap the Bluecoats in case they
   should come
   as Sound Of Running Feet trims the mane of Spotted Head, then decorates Little One with a beaded collar she has made
    (he is her favorite, because whenever she comes near, he licks her
    face like a dog);
   and Ollokot, he who so often leads the young men, speaks many times
   with White Bird, who for a handful of days and nights stayed outside Cut
   Arm's house at Butterfly Place, to watch the Bluecoats' war-games, and
   overhear their tricks
    (I am telling you three times, they speak through their bugles!);
and now Shore Crossing, Strong Eagle and Red Moccasin Tops take off their shirts
 of salmon-hued deerskin; they put on blood-red war-blankets,
  becoming the Three Red Blankets
   (and sewing this story to the previous one
   and sewing the next story to this one,
   I, William the Blind, who cannot even tell you why Swan Necklace, who

was one of the first three killers, was not then counted among the Three
Red Blankets:

> Perhaps the tale is as others have told it,
>> that Swan Necklace was merely a young boy, a horse-holder;
>> or perhaps after killing the old Boston he lost his courage
>> or took pity on the terrors of his old mother and promised not
>> to leave her during this war,
>> or gracefully yielded his place to the aspirations of Strong
>> Eagle, the newest of the Three Red Blankets)

as old ones and children and women settle in a circle
and the young men beat the untanned elkskin:

> now they are lashing war-bells around their ankles
> and dancing the War Dance

and White Bird tells them: Now, my People, you must do the best that you can.
No one told you to kill those Bostons. In peacetime you cannot kill them, either
by night or by day. Now we have war, so you may kill any Bostons you wish, day
or night, except that you must not kill their women. And what becomes of us we
shall see.

WELL, COLONEL, THIS MEANS BUSINESS
JUNE 15

*W*ell, colonel, this means business.
Yes, sir.
Are your men in readiness?
Yes, sir, except for some transportation that must come from Lewiston.
Wilkinson, get ready to go to Walla-Walla at once.
Yes, sir.
And send in the half-breed. I understand he speaks English quite freely?
Yes, sir.
What's his name?
Mr. West.
Colonel, how well do you know Mr. Brown?
A reliable man, general. Never told us anything untrue—
And he vouches for this half-breed. Are you acquainted with his character?
Well, he's a half-breed, sir.
By your order, sir, Mr. West is waiting for you.

Send him in.

Yes, sir.

Good afternoon, Mr. West.

Good afternoon, General Howard. Good afternoon, Colonel Perry.

Mr. West is short, his hair long, loose and black. He possesses in common with his in-law Chief Joseph the following quality: Whether that smile or grimace of his expresses pain will never be betrayed. The general memorizes his face, picks up a pen and commences writing as neatly as a lady.

So you come from Mr. Brown?

Sure.

Have you read these letters which you brought?

No. They were sealed.

That's right. Now tell us in your own words what you have seen at Mount Idaho.

Cottonwood House white people killed in the night time.

How many?

Mr. Day, he is dying. Maybe dead now. Mr. Norton dead in the road. And Mrs. Norton, she get a bullet through both legs. Mr. Moore, I didn't see his wound, but they say he get a bullet in the hip. Chamberlain family, they almost all dead. Mr. Chamberlain shot. One child, they cut out his tongue and cut his neck. A very good boy; I like him. Maybe he is dying, maybe not. The other one, they crush his face between their knees, crush him like a louse! He is dead in the road, with his brains squeezed out. I saw him, general, I am telling you three times! Mrs. Chamberlain in bad shape. Very bad Indians. They rape her, take turns, and—

That's enough.

They say seven more white people dead on the Salmon River, but I don't know.

Who did it?

Maybe Salmon River Indians.

Nez Perces?

I think so.

Were Chief Joseph and his confederates involved?

Maybe,

> gazing down through the window into the silverleaved cottonwoods along the river.

But I don't know.

Thank you, Mr. West. If you would kindly wait outside, I'll prepare a letter to Mr. Brown.

Without a word, Mr. West turns his back, opens the door, passes through, and gently shuts it behind him. The general writes for another moment, signs his name, and lays down his pen.

Well, colonel?

Sir, since the Salmon is White Bird's hunting grounds—

I'm aware of that. When will your transportation arrive?

Within the hour, general.

So your men are prepared to move out to-night?

They sure are, general.

Fletch, send for Captain Trimble and come straight back here. Colonel Perry, bide here an instant. Is Wilkinson back yet?

Waiting outside, sir.

Send him in.

Yes, sir.

Wilkinson, are you ready?

Yes, sir.

Lieutenant Bomus will accompany you. I think the best plan would be to ride to Lewiston, and then requisition a stagecoach.

Yes, sir.

It's a hundred and ten miles to Walla-Walla—

Yes, sir. We can be there by to-morrow morning.

Early morning, if possible.

Yes, sir. We'll ride like blazes.

I know you will! Bomus, is your buggy ready?

Yes, sir.

Here's a despatch to Colonel Wood in Portland. Is it legible?

Yes, sir.

Seal it then. Fletch, come in. And I've drawn up this other despatch to General McDowell in San Francisco just now after examining Mr. West. Gentlemen, although I bear the responsibility, I do invite your opinions. Fletch, would you kindly read it back to us before it's sealed?

Yes, sir. *Indians began by murdering a white man in revenge for a murder of his. Since then they have begun war upon the people near Mount Idaho.*

Stop an instant. You understand that General Sherman himself will see this. Can we offer him more than a theory regarding the identity of these murderers?

Toohhoolhoolzote, sir? All the Dreamers could be behind it, but—

Looking-Glass?

I think he's loyal, sir. When that half-breed rode in just now—

You mean Mr. West?

Yes, sir. When he came here, Looking-Glass's brother accompanied him without fear. A good Indian—

Then could Joseph have done this?

But, general, he seemed quite reconciled. Remember how we raced horses with him and he was laughing like a child?

What about White Bird? You heard Colonel Perry's opinion.

Sir, he kept hiding behind his fan—

Personally, sir, I'd suspect Ollicut, who dominates his brother—

All right. We don't know. We'll leave it at *Indians.* You know, gentlemen, I would have done anything to prevent this.

Yes, sir.

Colonel, the next chapter depends on you. By the way, has Mrs. Perry reached The Dalles safely?

Yes, sir. Thank you for asking.

What a stainless wife! My beau ideal of an Army woman! All the same, she's better off downriver. Yes, Trimble, come in. As I've informed Colonel Perry, we'll need both companies to march for Mount Idaho by dusk at the latest. What is it now, Fletch?

Yes, sir, the half-breed—

Here's his letter to take back to Mr. Brown. But he's to wait. Seal it up.

Yessir.

Colonel Perry, Captain Trimble, you'd better galvanize your troops. No delay will be accepted. I'll inspect both companies shortly. That's all.

Yessir.

Lieutenant Bomus, give me back that paper for a moment. Now I've added the bit about Colonel Perry's command. As you see, it should be inserted here. Can you read it?

Yes, sir. It's very clear.

Now read back the rest.

Other troops are being brought forward as fast as possible. Give me authority for twenty-five scouts. Think we will make short work of it.

That's right. Now here's one more despatch for San Francisco; don't read it back; just seal it. And here's a private letter for Portland. Wilkinson, Bomus, are you ready to set out?

Yes, sir.

After the telegraph goes through, please have someone inform Mrs. Trimble and Mrs. Parnell that their husbands have marched on duty with Colonel Perry. I'll visit Mrs. Theller myself and see how she's getting along. Wait in Walla-Walla until an answer comes through from Portland. Colonel Wood will inform you when we can expect the troops and supplies to arrive in Lewiston.

Yes, sir.

After you hear from Portland, if no reply has come in from San Francisco, ride back to Lewiston and show Colonel Wood's reply to Colonel Watkins. Agent Monteith should be present in case he can supply any new information; I believe he's riding out to-morrow. And while you're in Lewiston, use your eyes, both of you, because I need to know what mood Smohallie's Indians are in.

Yes, sir.

Then good-bye and good luck to both of you, he says, beginning to write something else.

Good-bye, sir, they reply.

Fletch, prepare a clean copy of this other letter to Mr. Brown as quickly as you can. Mr. West will ride in company with the troops. Where's Looking-Glass's brother?

Gone, sir, back to his reservation.

All right.

What news of Perry's wagons?

Another half-hour, general.

I'll hold Colonel Watkins responsible if they're not in time.

Yes, sir. General, I was supposed to remind you—

What?

Your son's birthday—

Yes. Ten years old to-day. Kind of you, Fletch—

He rises and thankfully departs this stifling little cabin, which is dark, cracked and resinous. All his life he has loved the outdoors. He breathes deep. The afternoon is nearly over; the pack mules have finally arrived from Lewiston. Striding across the parade ground to the cavalry corral, he finds Perry's bunch stowing their three days' rations in their saddlebags and patching their trousers. They are eager to ride, their hopes as blue as the Clearwater River. Some of them helped Crook clean up the Pi-Utes ten years ago; several fought the Secceshes. As for Perry, who thinks nothing of marching through knee-deep snow just to capture a couple of squaws, he certainly has "sand" enough, praise GOD. And Perry's men, how happy they appear, to see a little more action in their Indian service! The canny ones rub soap or tallow inside their shoes. Two very young shavetails sit reënforcing the seats and knees of their breeches with white canvas patches. The post trader is making the rounds, offering cocaine at a dollar twenty-five a bottle, although only one tall, nervous soldier pulls out his money; from the way he keeps blinking in the sun, he probably wishes to get some medicine for his eyes. A swarm of Germans reënters the long barracks at a trot, then rushes out again, several of them with bundles for the laundresses. Anyhow, they have a half-hour yet. He likes Germans; they remind him of his old Eleventh Corps. Glancing north, he sees the sentry striding imperturbably back and forth before the guard-house. He nearly expects to glimpse Mrs. Perry peeking out the window of her pleasant home, but of course she is absent. The FitzGerald children remain out of the way, thank goodness. LORD, how warm Lapwai can be! The arid hill across the river seems to reflect the sunshine back upon the parade ground, which of course must be an illusion. His forehead glows as if he were helping Lizzie pull the soup-pot out of the fireplace. Anyhow he is long past caring about sunburn. He approaches quietly, not wishing to spook Perry's bunch. Mr. West, man of the hour, draws a map in the dirt, marking the known locations of dead white people with little sticks. The infantry are especially interested. Perceiving the general, they leap to their feet and salute; at which he smiles silently. The horses dance about, flirting their heads and shaking their tails against the flies; and the mule drivers keep packing food, powder and bullets into even loads on the *aparejos*.

Perry, I'll ensure that you get credit for Joseph's capture.

Thank you, general. And if Theller—

We'll see. How long have you known him?

O, a good long while! Since before the Modocs—

He looks grand in his trial blues. Good hunting to both of you.

Thanks, general.

Now, Perry, do you need anything?

No, sir.

On the other side of the parade ground, Company "H" is in a slightly more advanced state of preparedness, nobody rushing in and out of barracks, the mules nearly all packed, Trimble beaming and bustling in his old slouch hat, which must be left over from the Modoc War.

Well, captain, everything in order?

Couldn't be better, general.

Where did you get that cartridge belt?

Made it myself, sir.

A neat job. Are your recruits ready to fight?

They're as pleased as children to get out into the field.

How's Lieutenant Parnell?

A great right hand to me, sir.

Good. By the way, Trimble, I'm sure you know that I hold you in equal regard with Colonel Perry. He's in command simply because he has the brevet. Otherwise I'd hardly know how to choose between you—

Thanks for saying so, sir. I'm proud to follow his orders—

Carry on.

Mrs. FitzGerald's children stare at him from Perry's front porch.

The leather perfume of the harness shop he has always liked. All trim appears in good to excellent condition. He passes by, impatient to hear the bugle blow "Assembly," and arrives at the Thellers' residence. Mrs. Theller, white-bonneted, is currying her husband's stallion.— Good afternoon, General Howard, she says.

Good afternoon, madam. You women have the harder part, staying home and waiting. I pray that Lieutenant Theller won't be away from us long.

Thank you, General Howard. I'll be all right.

A spirited Appaloosa! Your husband rides fearlessly—

He's always loved fast horses—

Please come to me if you need anything.

The woman nods and tries to smile, brushing pale brown horsehairs off her dark skirt.

He draws Perry aside to say: We both know that ninety-odd men may not suffice for the work ahead, but if we wait for reënforcements, these renegades will keep on murdering.

I understand, sir. We'll do our best.

I know you will! The Congressional penny-pinchers can't begin to understand the requirements of our Indian service—

No, sir.

Form up!

Have I ever told you how General Sherman refers to the situation? He calls it *the Quaker policy.*

That's sure how it is, general—

Remember, colonel, these Indians aren't Modocs. Show firmness, and they'll come right around.

Company "H," present!

Yessir.

Well, Captain Trimble, your men make a brave show.

Thanks, general.

Company "F," present!

And yours also, colonel.

We mean well anyhow, sir—

And I expect you to *do* well.

Thank you, sir.

A beautiful afternoon.

Yessir.

What is it, Perry?

Sir, do you suppose Joseph is actually behind this?

We did forget, I think, that even in the veins of Joseph there runs some of the Cayuse blood on his mother's side. And it was the Cayuses who massacred the Whitman couple who labored so devotedly to bring them to GOD. *Blood tells!* Why lose sight of that?

Yes, sir.

How soon will you be ready?

In a quarter-hour, sir. We're just watering the mules. The horses have drunk their fill.

Very good. When Mrs. Perry arrives in Portland, my wife will look after her.

I sure appreciate it, general. What now, Theller?

Beg to report, colonel, the men can march out at once.

Well, sound "Boots and Saddles."

"Boots and Saddles!"

Who's your bugler?

John Jones, general.

He blows with verve . . .

I'll tell him, sir.

Where's Mr. West?

He's fixing to ride ahead, sir. I gave him a fresh horse—

Don't let him out of your sight until Grangeville.

Yessir.

All right, Perry. Fletch, come over here.

Yessir.

They look slouchy.

Well, our postwar Army—

What's your impression?

Trimble's all right, general. A brick. After all, he's the one who captured Captain Jack. Parnell I don't know so well, but he seems solid. Sure helped Crook whip the Pi-Utes! And Perry and Theller are like brothers.

Do go on.

Sir, Wilkinson always says that the difference between Theller and Perry is the difference between local time and railroad time.

Don't get tricky on me. Anyhow, the responsibility's mine. Send for Theller.

Yessir.

Lieutenant Theller, a private word.

Yes, sir.

It's natural that your wife's alarmed.

General, it's just that she and Mrs. Osborne used to attend the same church. But Delia's got plenty of "sand" in her, actually. When Colonel Perry and I were chasing the Modocs she even—

Of course she does. And I promise to look after her.

> GOD bless her, but she adores him almost too much for an Army wife! To
> me she resembles a nurse holding a wounded soldier's hand
>> like that pretty, gentle young widow at Mount Pleasant Hospital, as
>> modest as Lizzie (who always buttons her collar right up to the
>> throat); her name escapes me; she sat with our boys when they were
>> dying, and I remember one handsome lieutenant from Connecticut
>> who had never been engaged and asked most respectfully if he
>> could kiss her on the lips. She held him while he bled to death.

Thank you kindly, sir. I appreciate it.

That will be all, lieutenant. Now, where's Perry?

Sir, we're all in order. A hundred and three effectives.

Well, they make a very fine appearance, and so do you, my boys. Go and show these Indians their mistake.

So we will. Good-bye, general!

Good-bye, colonel. You must not get whipped.

No danger of that, sir! Sound the move out.

Yes, sir.

Forward!

Forward—

> to the bugles' two long notes of walking-music,
> the line of cavalry troops as if on parade
>> a fine dust of desiccated horse manure now powdering everyone's
>> lips
> and the regimental band drawn up, serenading Perry
> and the jingle of blue-clad men and the smell of horses in the golden grass
>> of what will be the United States of America

as Mrs. Theller, Mrs. FitzGerald and all the laundresses wave their handkerchiefs so proudly

                (Perry a particularly brave sight in his high-colored
                tunic,
                      Trimble more down to earth in his altered
                      sack coat)
        . . . and Father Cataldo finds it politic to bless them, I see
           —when will Monteith let me alone?—
                      I'd better write John straightaway they're out of
                      sight (would have missed his birthday anyway,
                      but Lizzie will make it right) . . .
     Perry will be too good a soldier to look back!

as, swaying easily in their saddles, their pistoled hips steady and still,
their burnished Springfield carbines taut-slung, they depart the parade
ground, passing four abreast, tangent to the circle of Christian Nez Perce
tipis which in their conical pallor resemble the skirts of corseted giant-
esses, the Indians waving to them anxiously, James Reuben leading a
hymn:

       Wakesh nun pakilauitin
       Jehovan'm yiyauki
           (Lewiston's organizing sixty men)—
     and that glance of my favorite squaw in the beaded dress, the long
     braids, the dark eyebrows, the half-smile of her—
         Three cheers for Perry!
         Hurrah!
           Hurrah!
           Hurrah!

and ahead, the brown hills with basalt eyebrows
and behind, the five hundred and eighty-six blue-green acres of our hay
reserve
     (the sparkles of the Clearwater alongside)
and a wide-spreading cottonwood,
then a little cornfield
     below the place where not long ago the People had a village called
     Ridge Crossing
as the way meets lower, greener hills.

    And they leave the low narrow valley where Lapwai is, following the Mount
Idaho road.

SHOULD BE A PLEASURABLE FIGHT
JUNE 15–17

1

*S*kirmishers and flankers, fan out.
All right, colonel. Men, let's go,
> transecting the silence in each hot side-cañon crowded with scrub, in the
> cottonwood forest around the creek (not that they expect to find Joseph's
> Indians anywhere near)—
Soldier, did you miss that sign over there?
No, sir. It's all dried up,
> but where once this war has been won we will grow trees heavy with apples,
>> on earth as it is in Idaho,
>> give us this day our daily fruit
>> and deliver us from the
> pines and red rock by Lapwai Creek, whose shiny trickle hides itself
> (the thirsty cottonwoods gone yellow)
> and the hot hills now forested into outright darkness,
>> our tame Indian scouts ahead (what if they too prove treacherous?),
> the cañons ever more evergreen than what will be farmlands, even our
> mules descending in good order toward the emerald walls of Lawyer Creek
> and the recapitulation of green American fields:
> *The bold dragoon he has no care*
> *As he rides along with his uncombed hair,*
soil as rich as chocolate cake,
and then
> night and
>> —because it's in a circular from Headquarters.
>> Yessir—
camp, "Tattoo," "Taps" (the night as black as a soldier's pipe) and
the first gun, "Reveille" and
> dawn,
>> Perry halfheartedly rinsing out his filthy frying pan with
>> old coffee and Theller whistling his favorite song, "The Bold
>> Dragoon."
>> Well, sir, how would you rate this mission?
>> Same as you, Theller. Just another GoDD——d Indian hunt.
>> Yessir,

currying Flash again, embracing the horse round the
neck, caressing his ears, while Perry, who certainly
loves his own mount, Diamond, yet perhaps not quite
so extravagantly, stands by half-smiling.
Whipple spent the winter with 'em, and you'd think he would
have doped out more. According to what he told the old man,
they were already acting whipped. However . . .
Well, sir, I'm looking forward to setting them straight.
Fine to get out of close quarters, anyhow. And, Theller, you
know how much pleasure I get out of riding with you.
It's mutual, sir.

   Move out!

   (Johnnie Jonesey, sober for once, blowing the call with
   verve just as our general said),
and the squeaking of the ammunition train, and our horses'
dark tails sparkling up and down, and
our cavalrymen in their dark blue flannel shirts each with its
three sun-bright brass buttons and
our other cavalrymen in old grey blouses and
our patient sunburned infantry in greasy trousers, marching
at a hundred ten paces to the minute.

Looks like smoke ahead.

Is that Cottonwood?

That's the Old Mill.

No it ain't.

My back is killing me.

Then them Injuns won't have to.

They must've set some haystacks on fire.

Now you see that over there?

Ain't nothing to see.

No, that's Mount Idaho.

How do you know? You ain't never been there.

I know because I know. Anyhow, Captain Trimble he said—

That's not Mount Idaho at all.

You was never there neither.

Well, I know because you say it *is* Mount Idaho, and everything you say turns
out wrong.

Mr. West, is that Mount Idaho?

No.

Boy, he ain't none too respectful, considering that he's a half-breed.

Mr. West, is that Mr. Norton's wagon up there?

Yes, colonel.

Them dead horses sure do stink.

We're gonna make some dead Injuns stink worse, ain't we, Doc?

Keep in good order there.

Yes, sir.

Where's that dead Indian at?

Mr. West, didn't you mention we got one of yours?

That's right.

Where's he at?

I can't rightly say.

Well, thank the LORD we got one. Mr. West, ain't you grateful we got one?

Sure.

Well, was he under Joseph's orders or not?

He was nothing but a lame old man.

Mr. West, how many buck Injuns does Joseph command?

His sons and nephews listen to him.

What about Ollicut and *his* bucks?

The same.

Then who's in charge?

Hey, Mr. West, was your Daddy a *squaw man* or was your Mama an Indian-chasing whore?

Soldier, you respect Mr. West or I'll punch your teeth out.

Yessir.

I didn't hear you.

Yessir, Lieutenant Theller, sir!

Doc says Joseph'll be hard to kill.

Why's that, Doc?

Why should I tell you?

You're a cold one. Anyhow, you all get Joseph and I'll get me White Bird. I hanker after those feathers of his.

For what?

Where's Mr. West?

He took a powder. That's him way down the column.

Well, you teased him too hard.

Looks like sign over there.

That ain't nothing. Just squaw trash.

Pack train's falling behind, colonel.

I can see that. Call a halt.

Halt.

None too soon, either. Right, Doc?

I'm not tired.

Then carry my rifle for me if you still have so much snap.

Shut up.

Doc, you're a caution. Where'd you ever get that field-glass at?

Wouldn't you like to know?

No, that's not what I heard. You see, ever since the money kings demonetized the silver dollar . . .

And then that d——d mountain howitzer ran down three of Captain Pollock's company at Wallula!

They've killed up to twelve men sure.

I heard twenty-nine. No wonder them Mount Idaho people are forted up.

Forward!

Forward!

> *Now the captain said to John Henry:*
> *Gonna bring that steam drill round.*

Where's that d——d Joseph at?

> Theller, you've supervised your lot for a long spell now. In confidence, what do you think?
>
> They don't drill as well as they should, sir, and that's a fact. A lot of raw shavetails and stupid grinning Germans. But Mr. Joe won't know that.
>
> You're a caution! What about Company "F"?
>
> Sir, I believe Captain Trimble's jealous.
>
> Of us?
>
> Of you, sir.
>
> He's got reason. Slack with his men—
>
> Yessir. But Parnell's got a pretty fine way with them. They'll be up to snuff against a few drunken Indians.
>
> Good leadership, eh? Well, they won't beat us out!
>
> Not a chance, sir.
>
> Anyhow, Theller, you must be in the clover to-day. I know how you crave excitement.
>
> That's a fact, sir—

Gonna bring that steam drill round.

> Excuse me, Colonel Perry, sir, but some men have fallen out behind the ammunition train.
>
> D——n the yellow bastards! Theller, you ride the line and whip 'em back into shape—

Gonna bring that steam drill out on the job,
Gonna whap that steel on down, O, LORD.

> Right away, sir.

Hey you, Blackie, you remember that time in Saint Joseph when them Injuns crossed over to threaten people?

Gonna whap that steel on down.

They was Sioux.

That's right. They was Injuns. Two of their squaws stole a hog and drug him over the ice by his hind legs. And we was too yellow to go get him back! That's when I learned never to give way to Injuns.

Those Injuns got nothing to do with—

No, sir, lieutenant. We didn't find any sign of them down there.

Keep a bright lookout, boys!

Yes, sir.

Is it true what they say?

What who says?

I'll trade you a—

No you won't.

Wonder if Jenny's writing me a letter about now.

What does she write?

O, always the same thing. Tells me to be careful.

Yes, sir, we checked the mouth of that cañon and all we found was this horn spoon

> and the sharp glitter of scree,
> snow-white flowers still on the higher branches of the chokecherry trees.

So which plant is that *camas* that the squaws pick? I'm near ready to eat some.

You'd eat anything.

Well, which is it?

Ask Mr. West.

I'm not askin' him *nothing.*

Doc knows.

No, I was standing there when the general spoke to the captain. He said—

> What do you think, Theller?
> They're in fine form, sir! Ready for the fight—

So which one is that *camas*?

Well, it's no good until the stalk is dead. That's why them Modocs—

But which one is it?

If you give that half-breed a slug of whiskey he can tell it real good.

I said I ain't givin' him nothin'.

He tells it so you can almost see it. You want to know how a dozen Injuns have their way with a white woman? They grab her by the hair and—

Well, my horse never once got saddle-sores. It's all to do with the blanket.

No it don't. If you stick with a plain Mexican saddle—

And he says when you see the bruises on her face, and half her hair torn right out of her head—

Is that a fact?

And when she bit one of 'em, he took a rock and knocked her front teeth out.

How should that breed know? Must've been right there helpin' 'em.

And here's the most interesting part. He says that when they get a woman who never did it that way—

Be a relief when that sun goes down.

Well, I wouldn't live in this here valley. Soil's indifferent over most of it.

What the hell d'you mean? Look down into all them bottoms so nicely timbered with cottonwood. There's gonna be nice farms here, real nice, once the
United States come in.

Then why are so many folks in Lewiston hitting the trail? It's poor country,
actually. Bad hot summers—

They're leaving because they don't have *guts.* That's all.

Did he find sign over there?

That breed's not lifting a finger to get us any d——d sign.

Doc says—

I don't care if you got the same silk sheets the King of England sleeps on, if you
don't take care of your horse—

That's not what I said.

O, yes it is.

Should be a pleasurable fight.

And then what they did to Mrs. Manuel, they—

    That horse ain't no good.

Joseph's a coward. Otherwise he would have faced justice.

Anyhow, he can't go far with all his papooses and squaws.

What we should have done, the very first second we rode into Wallowa, was . . .

That *Christian Soldier* they stuck us with wouldn't never allow that.

He ought to do missionary work, not hinder us. Captain Whipple said—

    I said, he ain't no good. And you don't know how to ride him, either.

    Cut it out.

        . . . Injuns wandering around like tramps and criminal bummers,
        never letting our private property alone . . .

How much longer to Grangeville?

    and then Grangeville:

    some hot fields orange, some russet,

    stained tents,

    with the Grange Hill jackassically stockaded, and worried ladies peeping
    out through the gate (once upon a time they congratulated themselves on
    getting away from the Louisiana cholera and the Missouri malaria belt),

        and dear little American children one shade less precious than
        Heaven,

    sparse-whiskered citizens:

            Hell, we can lick them Indians. They ain't one of 'em
            Sitting Bull.

            And you ain't General Sherman, neither!

    and a pale-complected resolute young lady with her hair parted so
    as to form a snowy forehead-triangle,

    a skinny, sunburned, tearless old woman in her grandmother's
    bonnet,

not to mention the ever-renowned Mr. Croaesdale,

and Major Shearer with his old needle gun from the Secession War
>(he hates President Hayes for waving the bloody shirt and
>badmouthing the South),

and watching our cavalry with near-hysterical excitement, spitting
dark juice, a certain settler in Umatilla-beaded buckskins, fidgeting
in the golden grass as if he could dance there all day and night, with
his coffee steaming on the fire, his piebald dog beside him in the
dirt, and behind him his or someone's tools scattered in front of a
covered wagon, perhaps the lumberman's, from which the horse
has long been unhitched, and beside the wagon a pallid pole parting the darkness of this man's grubby-pale tent

>(Who's that lunatic?

>O, that's Ad Chapman the horse-breeder. One of them *squaw
>men!*)

and all the other forlorn and furious people whose grip on this country
now threatens to devolve into the mere dream it used to be:

Halt,

planting the swallowtailed American flag of our guidon
>across the road from Elias Darr's blacksmith shop,

and the tired soldiers jingle to a stop, the mules pissing loudly.

Fall in, roll call.

Right face!

Break ranks!

Dismissed!

You mean this is all there is?

Now Mount Idaho's right up there. A much more imposing situation.

I'd say.

Boy, them people sure do hang back.

I'll bet it's your face that makes 'em want to scream.

What's the matter with them people?

All right, men. We'll bivouac in that grass there,
>their bones as grateful as if they were already home again:

>Pickets *out!*

and the horses jerking down their heads, smelling grass, the cavalrymen
unsaddling, leading their mounts to the stream, caressing them like sweethearts, crushing horseflies, cleaning hooves, balming saddle-sores with good
white lead, breaking out the curry combs, drivers unpacking the mules, kicking and getting kicked, half-tents rising and rubber blankets unrolling:

>Captain Trimble, sir, ain't there more admiring damsels than
>this?

>Wouldn't *you* like to know, soldier?

>Yessir,

. . . and if the reds come creeping through the grass . . .

that *squaw man* still staring like a yokel.

Parnell, inspect that man.

Yessir, Captain Trimble.

Now put out your pickets, Theller. I don't care if we're in town.

Yessir. Form up the line. Pickets *out*!

Yessir.

I don't see any action. Now where's my GODD——d support line?

We're ready, lieutenant.

Then move out. *Now.*

Yessir.

So now they count twenty-nine murdered by Joseph's reds.

And ever since the Republicans stole them two states, the Democrats—

Wakesh nun pakilauitin

JEHOVAN'M *yiyauki*—

You there in the old shortcoat.

Yessir.

Where've I seen you before?

Well, colonel, remember that chloride strike that started Silver City? You was right alongside General Crook—

I was with him, but not there. What's your name, soldier, and how do you know me?

Name's Doc, colonel. I just seen you around—

All right, asshole, get back to digging that sink. JESUS *CHRIST*.

And detail three men over there.

Yessir.

No, Trimble, I have it on authority that the only reason Pollock got his commission in the Secession War was his Indian service in Utah.

No, they discharged me from the Ohio and Mississippi Railroad and that's the sole reason I signed up with this GODD——d outfit.

Well, boy, ain't this better than laying track?

Either way they work us like niggers.

But this place must have a shorter growing season than Lewiston, being up so high.

Well, that Mr. Brown from Brown's Hotel, he swears you can get a good hundred and fifty days.

He would.

Once we've built railheads to the good
farmlands north of the Clearwater—

Excuse me, colonel, are you in command?

That's right. Where are the Indians?

They rode across the prairie thataway, toward the Salmon country—

Fine. What's your name?

Shearer, colonel. We've raised some volunteers. That's Wilmot and Randall
over there. And you know our Mr. Chapman—

Theller, ain't that the one who's always badmouthing Mr. Pambrun?

Yessir. Monteith hired him once—

Chapman, what the hell are you doing here?

Fact is, colonel, I live down in White Bird Cañon, and I been waiting for you
all to help me whip them cowardly Indians. I got me the best racing-horse—

Sure. And you, Mr. Shearer, what do you want of us? The troops are tired.

You see, colonel, Mr. Croaesdale, whose farm is right up there—

Pleased to know you, colonel. Now, my strategy—

And Mr. Brown here—

Because if they shoot into our houses—

We'll talk more in a minute. Theller, find out how our bunch are managing.

Yessir:

> Well, soldier, how are you keeping?
>
> Like good salt pork, lieutenant.
>
> You aim to own a piece of this valley?
>
> Yessir, Lieutenant Theller, sir!
>
> All right. Then let's carry out our Indian service.
>
> Yessir, me and the boys, and them volunteers, we all—

> > Captain Trimble, sir, this man disobeyed my direct order—

> > > Looking-Glass is evidently the leader of the malcontents in
> > > his country.

> > Then punish him.

> > Yessir.

No, sir. Mr. West just went in there, but that little Manuel girl's still a-weeping
too hard to—

All right, Curran. Bring him here. Mr. Shearer, have the other victims stated
anything new?

No, colonel. Mrs. Chamberlain said the ringleader was a tall, evil-smelling
Indian with his hair in a roach and—

Fucking CHRIST. Could have been any of them.

Yessir.

> > > . . . and you, you're the firewood detail. Get to it
> > > now. Did you think we packed a Chinaman along
> > > to do it for you?

Right away, sir.

Dutch Flat is nearly all taken up now, and more immigrants coming in.

June 16th 1877

My Dear Wife:

I am camped with my detachment near Mount Idaho. I have marched at least 60 miles on scarcely any sleep, so it sure is pleasant to stop

Hey, you, boy, come over here!

for dinner & forage,

the brilliant yellow comet-trail of horse piss shooting down between dark brown legs.

The colonel anticipates encountering our Nez Perces within the next day or two,

You, boy!

as Joseph must be much encumbered with his squaws and children. We all agree it will not prove a very long campaign, so I should soon be back at the fort. Darling, I hope it's not true what I heard that the cholery has come to Lewiston. If, so, don't take the washing to John Chinaman, since you know it's those Celestials that spread disease. Also, every penny we can save will

You the one that got away from the Indians?

Yeah.

All by your lonesome?

Well, Lynn Bowers she took off her skirt to run faster, and then we both sneaked away toward Grange Hill here, through the high bunchgrass, and they never did spy us.

Where's this Lynn Bowers?

Resting, because she—

How old is she?

I don't know. Maybe eighteen—

How old are you?

Nine.

What's your name?

Hill.

Hill what?

Norton.

They killed your Daddy?

Yeah . . .

Where's your Mama?

Leave the boy be.

Hill, you want to be a soldier when you grow up? A genuine Indian killer?

Sure.

We're gonna take care of all those Indians who hurt your Mama and killed your Daddy.

I thank you—

Was that Lynn Bowers a ladylove of yours?

Was she a handsome sight when she showed you her titties?

Excuse me. I need to go.

Well, was she?

Soldiers, we're right grateful to see you! I've been praying all day for your safe arrival. I run the boardinghouse here—

Ma'am, do you have anything to eat?

> Will somebody take the bell off that GoDD——d white mare?

>> No, it's perfectly practical. I knew a private with a pet owl, and that d——d bird learned not to mind artillery, even at Gettysburg.

>> You're a caution! Maybe one of our tame Injuns can catch you a crow.

>>> Well, the cost of maintaining voluntary armies of European strength would bleed the Government.

>>> No matter. We've got enough men to whip anybody.

Mrs. Benedict asked me where I was going and when I told her I was on my way home, she said, you'd better not go any further because the Indians have broken out at last and they shot my husband.

Ma'am, don't you worry no more. We're gonna make you a heap of good Indians.

> They're recuperating up there at Brown's Hotel. The child won't never talk, since they cut the tongue right out of its head.

> That ain't what Mr. Croaesdale said. He said—

> Well, when the Modocs murdered Mrs. Boddy's sons, she said to us, and I'll never forget it:

>> Doc, can I borrow your needle and thread? I'd be obliged—

>> And then,

>>> smoothing out his dark blue saddle blanket on the grass,

>>> soon as I got to Lewiston, first thing I see's Lieutenant Theller, and you know what he was up to? You know that place at the river's edge—

>>> I don't believe it.

>>>> One of those times when we don't need no GoDD——d inquest.

They've barricaded Mount Idaho.

Thirty-eight killed.

Well, I heard twenty-four.

And half a dozen ladies outraged.

The blacksmith's in there casting bullets—

And a dentist in Corvallis got throwed from a horse last week. Stone dead.

This here's a pretty decent bivouac. Better than last night.

He maketh me to lie down in green pastures; He leadeth me beside the—

In other words, a pretty decent bivouac. Now be a good bunky and smash up a hunk of that pilot bread—

They shot Mrs. Chamberlain in the breast with an arrow, and raped her *over and over.*

How many times exactly?

    No, I'll kindle the fire. Just you bring me more of them little sticks.

    All right,

        kettled tripods bubbling away over campfires, coffee improved by Borden's evaporated milk, and the setting sun glittering like a brass eagle button.

      I'm sure tiring of that grin on Blackie's face—

      Well, he got engaged.

      To whom?

      To Miss Fidelia Wallace.

      From Lewiston?

      That's right.

      Didn't know she was sweet on him.

      He promised her picture windows, he says.

      Picture windows! Ain't he worried about stones?

        Just all of a sudden we seen them Secceshes and they shot Wilbur in his guts.

        Where was that, Doc?

        Gettysburg. But Wilbur, he—

Why didn't General Howard ride here himself?

Shut your mouth.

Colonel Perry, we didn't mean to insult your general.

Good. Now what about these Indians of yours?

O, colonel, you can easily whip the scoundrels.

And what they did to Mrs. Manuel—

    Mr. Brown, do you see that Mr. West?

    No, captain. He must've sneaked off.

Excuse me, Colonel Perry. May we have a word with you now?

All right.

We're concerned citizens of Grangeville—

    Yeah, they sure do look concerned, all right.

What's your name, sir?

I'm Mr. Ayers.

    a self-important old fellow, as plump and neck-less as a .50-calibre 1866 service cartridge; it's on account of pushy fools like you that we Army men have to keep performing Indian service when

what are you GODd——n *citizens* good for?

All right, Mr. Ayers. We've come to your defense and we've had a d——d long march. What else can we do for you?

Colonel, if they cross the Salmon River . . .

So what if they do?

Well, it's just that it'll be considerably easier to execute justice on those Indians beforehand. The Salmon is quite some river. You'll believe it when you see it.

I've seen it. Theller, could you get Captain Trimble over here?

Mr. Ayers is right, colonel. We appreciate that you're tired, but we only want to help. We'll ride with you—

I know you.

Of course you do. I'm Arthur Chapman, colonel. They call me Ad.

O yes, I've sure seen you around. The world-famous *squaw man.*

Looky here, colonel, I'm volunteering my services. And many's the time I been paid good hard cash money to interpret down at Lapwai, because I speak Nez Perce better than Whitman or Pambrun or anyone—

Colonel, he lives down where the bad Indians have—

Hey, *squaw man,* whose side is your wife on?

Excuse me, colonel, but that's none of your d——d business. And you keep teasing me, you better watch out. And I been out here among Indians for twenty-two years, and my experience proves for a fact—

Then I take it you do at least know the red country hereabouts.

Sure. Like they told you just now, I ranch in White Bird Cañon. All of us here, we've got to keep track of our livestock—

Quite a fiery horse you got there, Chapman.

He don't never quit!

We'll see about that. How many hours to the Snake?

With your mules and guns and all, maybe four.

Theller, where's the map?

Here, sir:

> the Salmon River flowing more or less east-west, and Rocky Cañon winding northeast from it into the wide oval of the Camas Prairie where Tolo Lake shines blankly, as if seeking to make itself innocuous under threat of Perry's deepset gaze; then east of that comes White Bird Creek, winding northeast and losing itself in the hills
>
>> (Theller meanwhile dreaming on a certain handsome Blackfoot squaw he sometimes likes to visit in Lewiston);
>
> while east of that flows Springs Creek, then Cañon Creek and Ned Gidding's Creek; then we're in the gold mines of Florence by Pioneer and Meadow Creeks all along the north side of the Salmon. The miners are shitting their pants, I guess.

All right, Mr. Ayers. Lay out your proposal.

If we go thisaway, then down through that White Bird Creek—

That's where Chief White Bird lives?

Yessir,

> Shearer folding his arms and sucking at something, perhaps an
> abscessed tooth, and Ad Chapman fidgeting back and forth.

Where's Tolo Lake? We'll have to check that out.

Over here, sir.

And here's where White Bird Crick meets the Snake—

Sixteen miles to the cañon.

Trimble, what do you think?

Maybe he's right, colonel—

Theller?

I agree—

Gentlemen, you can withdraw while we discuss this among ourselves. Just step across the road there. Trimble, you're sold on this?

I guess so. If Joseph gets away, our names'll be mud all through this country. But too bad for the troops—

Go organize your bunch before they get too comfortable. Now, Theller, take a stroll with me. You don't look happy.

Colonel, it's like this. I don't cotton to those citizens dictating to us.

Well, well! That's not the Fighting Theller I know—

D——nit, sir, I'm no coward, and I'll—

Never mind my teasing. Are the men up to it?

They're pretty soft, sir. Kind of tuckered out. Better than Trimble's company anyhow. Maybe a night march would toughen them up. I don't care; you give the word and I'll drive 'em twice as hard as Georgia niggers!

I'll tell you what I'm thinking. You know as well as I that the first blow against Indians is decisive. After that, they're on the alert, and these Nez Perces have got d——d good horses. If we march to-night, we can maybe wipe this up to-morrow. Once they cross the river it could drag on.

Sir, I could scout ahead and—

Theller, you have my word that I'll place you in the vanguard. How about it?

I'm your man, sir!

And leave those volunteers to me. I'll keep them in their GoDd——d places.

Thank you, sir. I sure despise pushy civilians like them.

Same here. But you inform the mule drivers and I'll go deal with our heroes across the road.

Yessir.

I guess we'd better let the boys eat.

Thirty minutes enough, sir?

> Them mules is worn down.
>
> And bandage up your feet.

We'll move out at ten-o'-clock.

All right, colonel.

I want that commissary wagon to hand out all the coffee they can drink.

Yessir.

　I sure am ready to sack out. D——d Theller was riding my ass all day.

　　No, but when Rodes halted to keep unentangled from Colston's division, that gave Howard a chance to regroup, and that was the *only* reason we—

　　You're forgetting about Stonewall Jackson. Without him killed, the Rebs would have—

　　Yeah, but them halfwit Germans in Eleventh Corps—

　　　Who's on guard?

So I asked Colonel Perry,

　　sizzling up Army beef in a number four frypan,

　　　with that excited *squaw man* Chapman now on his prancing grey racehorse, patrolling round and round,

　　　Blackie unrolling his rubber blanket, yearning for the longish melody of "Tattoo," when a soldier can finally think about laying down his head,

　　　and the *concerned citizen* Mr. Ayers sitting against a hitching post, cleaning the octagonal barrel of his superannuated .45-60 Winchester,

　　　while Captain Trimble prowls the line,

　　　　accompanied by Lieutenant Parnell, who sure knows what it's like to charge Pi-Utes in the Infernal Caverns and see his men shot down from behind the rocks,

if I could purpose it to the general when we get back to Lapwai, and he flat out refused.

He did?

Cursed me out like I was some stinking nigger!

He's eloquent that way.

Well, I don't see no harm in singing songs together, especially if some of them was hymns. I'll bet our Christian General won't never say no to that. But that Colonel Perry, he just told me to—

He's a hard one,

　　scrubbing out the frying pan with sand,

and I admire him for that.

Well, I still say there wouldn't be no harm.

Don't tell me you're writing your Jenny another GoDd——d letter when ain't nothing's hardly happened.

That's why I say any reservation's too good for 'em.

Tell you what I did one time. I was draggin' a bunch of scraggly-ass cowards over the Oregon Trail, and this here Blurick was the worst: so yellow that he could hardly sleep for fear of Indians! Used to drink himself to sleep. Wouldn't never even share. So I says to him, see here, I says, I'm gonna show you how easy it is. Just watch me. I'll shoot the first Injun I see. And right upon two hours later we happened upon this squaw just settin' there on a log like she owned it, so I shot her between the eyes. She sure pissed herself! There was other Injuns in the scrub, but they just turned tail. They didn't want no part of what that squaw got. That's what we got to do, unless we want to lie awake in fear.

And then what, Doc? What did that Blurick do then?

There was no helping him. As d——d yellow as a Chinaman.

    See them officers? Everything's tending toward a march.

    No it ain't.

Jonesey, sound "the General."

Yes, sir

    (blowing like a regular chanticleer: Theller and I both sure admire his
    spirit!)

Well, d——d if they're not going to make us night march again!

Fuck them. Fuck this Army. Fuck Colonel Perry for a slavedriving Irishman.

After sixty-two fucking miles!

What do you care? You bought yourself a brand new three-dollar bridle.

Them citizens is so scared—

    Better fill our canteens.

    All right, boys, let's pull up pins and *move*

        as Perry cinches Diamond's bellyband.

Let's see how *they* ride.

You s'pose they've got whiskey?

If that Lynn Bowers would come—

You mean Linda Bowers.

Lynn.

No it ain't,

    Doc tying up his coffee and bacon in the blanket again, wrapping it round
    his shoulder, crunching coffee beans between his yellow teeth so that he
    can go all night, and memorizing Ad Chapman's face, wondering where
    this sonofabitch got the gall to work that shiteating colonel to jew us out of
    another night's sleep when Mr. Joe's going to skedaddle or not regardless,
    although we'll sure finish this one way or another, however long it takes;
        what the hell:

Trumpeter, let's have "Boots and Saddles." *Now.*

Lucky is what they are, that we've come to help 'em out. A few marauding In-juns and they're all in a tizzy. Can't they keep down their own reds?

No one asked you,

    the troops already leading into line,

        and our volunteers passing proud to come to the relief of Idaho.

Jonesey, blow "To Horse."

I heard they'll have us swim across some river—

Can you swim?

Prepare to mount. Mount.

Well, howdy-do *and* so long.

        Never did see that Lynn Bowers with her skirt off.

              Forward!

        Bare-breasted like an Apache squaw . . .

Forward!

    . . . Perry, tall and almost serene, riding lightly

    and Theller straightening out our column

        (Trimble and Parnell unseen behind Company "H," driving it
        along)

    and the crickets in the dark

        (our vigor and happy spirit):

Not a very lively parade.

No, sir.

Skirmishers and flankers *out.*

Right, colonel. Let's go, men:

    to cast down the Dreamers' mandate

    and improve the miseries Joseph has caused.

Sure wish the moon would rise.

They raped Mrs. Walsh and Mrs. Osborne. And—

You told us that before,

    and another mile and

Colonel Perry, sir, some men are already falling out.

Round 'em up and keep 'em on the go.

Yessir.

They should have drunk more coffee.

Yessir,

    and the sound of men breathing

    and the moon as huge as a horse's eye

    and the grass, the silverwhite grass.

Theller, you're going to patrol around the lake for Indians. I'm guessing that they're gone. Take twenty men, a scout and some of these volunteers. Engage anything that moves.

Yes, sir. Corporal Curran, get me nineteen good men and Cutmouth Sam. You're number twenty, corporal. We'll leave in ten minutes. Now, which of you Grangeville fellows wants to come along?

I will.

You're a sport, Chapman,

    more grim than furious.

Who else?

Lieutenant, I want in.

And you are?

I already introduced myself.

Well, do it again.

Shearer. George Shearer, formerly a major in the Confederate States.

A Seccesh! Well, have you seen the light yet?

Lieutenant Theller, I'm a loyal American.

Starting now, *Mr.* Shearer, you're under my command. No more of that *major* shit. You don't shoot without my say-so, all right?

All right, lieutenant.

Where's Sam?

Here I am, lieutenant.

You found sign?

There's sure sign all over the place, sir, but the freshest tracks go down into White Bird Cañon. They must have struck their lodges in a GoDd——d hurry.

Guilty consciences, no doubt.

Yessir.

Hey, you, put out that pipe! You want an Indian arrow in your teeth? Put it out, sonofabitch. *Now.*

Yessir.

Is that an arrowhead? I collect those.

So do them Lewiston men. You can sell to them men, although they'll jew you down.

Something just moved between those rocks.

Mr. Shearer, how's the catfish in this lake?

Not bad.

Over here, Sam!

No, that ain't fresher than my dead grandmother.

I say it's plenty fresh.

Sam, what do you think?

Sam's off hiding somewhere. Probably warning his friends—

That ain't right. Sam's on the square. Why, one time he—

All them campfires is nothing but *dead, dead* ashes.

Here's a stash of camas bulbs, fresh-roasted!

Break it open, boys, and help yourselves.

And a worn out mockersin.

Then you've gone and found your wages, Blackie boy!

Any more of them ovens?

This one's cleaned out.

If this here was my place, I'd plant an acre of buckwheat.

Your place is in the sinks behind the whorehouse tent.

Looky here, some Injun must've stolen this sheep bell. Maybe to keep track of his squaw—

Ready, men? All right. Move out, and keep each other in sight. No talking, now,

> the moon, still low, as round as a woman's hatbox
> and Tolo Lake,
>> as a fish splashes: *mokh!*

Corporal, sir, far as we can tell in this dark they cleared out.

All right. No fresh sign, lieutenant.

Good job, corporal. Let's ride back. At your ease, men. *Mr.* Shearer, how was your brief career in the army of the winning side?

Lieutenant, we're all Americans.

Right about that, *mister,*
> and the brightening moon, moonlight on their bayonets:

Lake's clear of Indians, colonel,
> the men now refilling their canteens.

All right, Theller. Which way do their tracks run?

Sir, a few go north, and Ad Chapman believes those are Looking-Glass and his Indians skedaddling to the reservation to keep their noses clean. White Bird's lot might have gone with 'em, but I doubt it, since the main sign points straight ahead toward his home cañon. Must be a good five hundred horses heading thataway—

Joseph—

And more.

How about that Chapman?

Well, sir, he's gung-ho enough. He's got "sand."

I appreciate your trouble, lieutenant. All right, prepare the men to move out.

Yes, sir.

>> as the moon ascends over the camas prairie whose swales are
>> dotted with trees.
>> Not a healthful place for us to charge, because they—
> O, cut it out.

Mr. Shearer, is this country still familiar to you?

To be honest, colonel, Mr. Chapman knows this section better than I. He's had more truck with the Injuns here on account of his wife is one of them.

Takes all kinds, don't it? Where's Mr. Chapman?

Right here.

Mr. Chapman, what's in it for you?

What do you mean?

Since you're one of those *squaw men* . . .

Those are fighting words, colonel.

All the same, there's no reason for you and me to fight, as long as you're on the side of the United States.

I said I am. Now have you picked on me enough?

Is your Mrs. Chapman a fullblood?

She's Umatilla, without any Nez Perce in her. And I won't see her insulted by you. And furthermore, these Nez Perces causing all the trouble, I can whip 'em singlehanded, because they're nothing but yellowbellied cowards.

You put her away, didn't you?

What's it to you?

Got tired of being a *squaw man.*

Now I'll get you.

Mr. Chapman, is this the rise you were talking about?

Sure is. That's White Bird Cañon down there. *Lahmotta,* they call it. Now, where my ranch is, you can't see it on account of the buttes—

I don't give two shits about your ranch. Where are the reds?

Colonel, they're sure to be along the creek, thataway—

Good. The men can stand down now. Three hours' sleep until dawn

> in the cool dark,
> the dark, the dark
> (as dark and tightly twined as an Indian berry basket).

Yes, sir,

>> and the blue night sky

>>> beneath which Blackie dreams of Fidelia
>>> while Cash, that refugee from a sheet-metal factory in Cleveland, dreams about Lynn Bowers, empress of his fancy; to-night she is barebreasted like an Apache squaw because once upon a time he had to do with the sharpened bone plug set just beneath the lower lip of a married Apache woman, a harlot who showed him no dislike, and, O, the straight bangs of her, my adorable Apache gal! I'd have to say she was kind, even if she did give me the lues. Now for Lynn Bowers, with her straightcut chestnut hair, and her blue eyes, and the bone plug under her lip—

>> and picture windows for Fidelia (there's Blackie's dream)

> and a bush silhouetted against the ridgetop, then three more to the south,
> the stars surprisingly white in the hazy night.

Then all the trees are overhead and against and around the men like the night itself. Perry and Theller sit mostly silent together against a boulder, with their carbines beside them. Theller begins to snore, then starts awake.

How long did I sleep, colonel?

O, less than five minutes. Want a smoke?

Sure—and thank you, sir! Well, another adventure . . . !

Theller, you know what I think?

What's that, sir? By the way, that's a fine draw of tobacco you gave me—

Toohhoolhoolzote's the bad one. Joseph's just a girlie young Injun; once we nab him, he'll do whatever we say. Ollicut's a villain, but we can take care of him anytime. We've got Looking-Glass, White Bird and those others good and beaten down. But Toohhoolhoolzote, JESUS GOD! Did you see the look in his eye when me and the general laid hands on him at Lapwai?

I sure did, colonel.

And after we locked him up, you know what the general said to me? Something about his evil, glittering gaze, or some such . . .

Yessir; our general's full of fancies—

Well, what was your impression?

Of Toohhoolhoolzote, sir? Nowhere near as fearsome as a Modoc.

That was some campaign, wasn't it?

You remember the party we had after Captain Jack was finally hanged? How those ranchers' daughters could dance!

Not as well as Captain Jack—

Now *there*, sir, was one of the worst Indian monsters that ever haunted this earth—

O, those lava beds and that cursed creeping fog! And that Lieutenant Colonel Wheaton was a d——n fucking—

A real heroic expedition, sir. Every now and then I entertain myself by telling it over to Delia until she gets the shivers—

After which you comfort her, I'll bet!

Well, sir, I do my best.

Anyhow, Theller, that's how it seems to me. Toohhoolhoolzote's the root of all this trouble. Joseph's just his pawn. We need to get that old growler.

And *fix* him. Right, colonel?

Just don't let the general hear about it. He's squeamish.

That's for sure. Sir, if you want to shut your eyes for a bit, I'll keep a watch—

Thanks, Theller, but you know I never can sleep before action. Get a bit sick to my stomach, as you may remember. You were always cool as ice—

I'm just a fool for excitement, colonel. Delia always says—

Colonel, sir, the volunteers are drinking.

So what?

They're drinking a lot.

Tell Chapman to come here. Not Shearer.

Yessir.

Mr. Chapman, are you and your men such GODd——d fools as to get drunk a couple of hours before a battle?

We can hold our liquor, colonel. I know these boys just like—

O, fuck off. Crawl away under that sissy hat of yours. Go diddle your redskin wife. What the hell did you come here for?

Colonel, I'll put in a complaint against you. Don't think I won't.

Go to blazes. D——d *squaw man!*

Colonel, sir, the scouts are raring to go. They say—

You hear that, Theller?

Yessir.

Better ride out.

Yessir,

> the eastern horizon as white as the parting of a Nez Perce woman's black, black hair,

>> Theller exultant, loving his horse, proud of his command, knowing his Springfield right down to worm and tompion:

vanished ahead now with his squad of six,
and dawn,
the men counting off their hundred rounds from the saddlebags, filling
their belt-loops and pockets, swinging out the cylinders of their Colt .45s:
Load with cartridges; load!
and
Double columns now. Company "F," move out. Injuns and volunteers on flank.
Yessir. All right, boys . . .
and a pale cloud in the saddle of the dark ridge behind White Bird Creek,
the crickets loud in the cool bushes, the water deeper than shadow, more
invisible than the night itself, but one can smell it above and below the
stink of cavalry sweat.
Company "H," move out.
Yessir. *Move out!*
Just as Umatillas will make American coins into pendants, blankets into
dresses, so our cavalry must now change these outlaws into good Indians,
and from far away rise the little-drum-sounds of their coming: *pim, pim,
pim—*
and the door of the morning is almost opened:
White Bird Cañon,
and down that stony wagon road:
Help me—
You hear that?
Help me, please—
Companies, halt. Ma'am, who the hell are you?
A pale little body, ain't she?
Mrs. Isabella Benedict is my name. These are my two youngest children. The
Indians killed my husband
(having first shot him through both legs, an injury which their neighbor
Hurdy Gurdy Brown pronounced susceptible to the cold water cure, and
then while they waited for the Nez Perces to come back, Isabella, scrubbing the floor, which had kept splintering the youngest's feet, heard a
noise, and staring out into the bright green summer rectangle of hot
humid light, saw nothing, but here came the sound of footsteps in dry
grass: *shlokh, shlokh.* He never did them any harm! All he was doing, I
swear, was making sure the cows were all right. I'll never throughout my
days forget those first three gunshots, but first we kept waiting and praying, hoping the other miners would return in time with their weapons,
and then when I went to pick onions from our garden I saw them for real
and Samuel told us to run for it and GOD bless us because he couldn't run
no more, and we couldn't hardly bear to leave him but Mr. Bacon promised to stand by him and Samuel said to me, Bella, think on our little
ones, and may the LORD protect you, so I took the girls by the hand and

we started running out by the back gate but the Nez Perces were already homing in on us, so we had to come creeping back, and Samuel had already crawled away out the window, leaving a trail of blood like a dying deer, and we never saw him anymore. Then came those three shots, and Mr. Bacon falling down on his back, and the faces in the window, O my GOD, those hateful Indian eyes . . .)

Give them some rations.

Yessir.

Poor lady!

Mr. Chapman, do you know these individuals?

Sure do, captain. My neighbors—

Now, Mrs. Benedict, ma'am, where did those Indians go?

Down there, toward the crick. And Mr. Bacon and Mr. Baker, they're all lying dead, O JESUS, O JESUS. I witnessed what they did to Mr. Devine. And the Indians, their faces rose up in the window, and then the baby—

What about Mrs. Manuel? Have you seen her?

O JESUS—

How many Indians, Mrs. Benedict?

Hundreds and hundreds, o, dear JESUS—

Who's in charge? Is it Joseph?

I don't know. My GOD, my GOD, they're all on the warpath! And when I pled for my children's life, they—

They let you go, looks like. Was it Joseph?

They—

You knew them?

They—

Here's a blanket, ma'am. Your troubles are finished. You just set there and wait. We'll be back to take care of you just as soon as we've whupped them.

Don't go down there, I pray you—

You just wait on us.

No!

All right now. Just take a rest here, ma'am.

Don't go; O, dear JESUS!

Companies, move out. Volunteers on flank.

Our Father Which art in Heaven, hallowed be Thy name. Thy Kingdom come; Thy will be—

Yessir.

O, that sad lady and them poor little children—

It would make your heart ache to see the little children hereabouts that never cry except when you say the word *Indians*.

Well, all them bad times are coming to an end to-day.

Stand up for these, the wrong'd, the aggriev'd,

They carried off Jack Manuel's wife. Never did hear from her again.

In deepest pits of darkness found,
Tell us anything we haven't heard, sport.
Of Heav'n's most sacred gifts bereaved,
O you fucking—
The task'd—the scourg'd—in fetters bound.
For all we know she's safe at Slate Creek.
You never met Jack Manuel. Much less his wife—
Mr. Joe shot her in cold blood and then burned her in her house. That's what
the little Manuel girl said, and she—
Then why didn't that Mrs. Benedict know nothing about it?
I'd rather hear from Lynn Bowers.
It was *Linda* Bowers.
Lynn.
And they mutilated that other fellow. They—
You told us that a dozen times.
That's White Bird Creek way down there and the Salmon's way past it,
    the gorge softer than Hell's Cañon, but still wide and deep enough to give
    birth to any story
    and a smell of water from the darkness:
I can't see nothing.
Mr. Chapman, what sort of country lies down yonder?
Well, lieutenant, the Indians call it *hik'íseyce*, which means *a wrinkled country.*
        I'd wager his red bitch taught him that word.
        Careful! Lieutenant warned us not to—
        To hell with the lieutenant *and* his mother.
So you're saying it's rough.
Got that right. It's—
D——n! What's that noise?
A coyote.
Never heard no coyote go on quite like that—
Bring me a scout. I don't know why those scouts never report—
Sir, *I* know.
Getting good and bright now.
Yes it is,
    like our lust for Indian horses.
They're in a fix now, boys! We'll have fine plunging fire, because this here's
what they call a key position—
O, fuck you and your education.
                And look before you shoot, in case we can save
                Mrs. Manuel.
                Chapman says her place is down about there.
                He ought to know. I'd say he loves women, all
                right.

Lieutenant Theller.

Yes, sir.

What did you find on your scout?

All quiet, sir.

You have the best eyes of any officer. What can you see beyond the river?

Well, sir, a succession of steeps, with pointed or rounded tops . . .

Take your time. Use the field glass.

Snowy peaks far away, and

          (the Salmon River hiding beyond the horizon)—

What's all that down there?

Horses, sir. More than I can count.

Then where are the hostiles?

Is that smoke down there?

Where the hell are them scouts?

That must be their camp, maybe four miles down,

      gazing down into the green trees along the creek where the many pallid
      tipis glow like dawn clouds
      and to the east, too bright in the morning sun, side-cañons like parallel green
      chevrons in the yellow-green and yellow-grey slope above the creek, and

               Doc?

               Shut up.

               To-day's Sunday.

               So what?

               That's why our *Christian Soldier* ain't here.

               He's—

Can we run off their horses? That's the finest herd I ever did see.

Ready, men! Here they come.

Where's Trimble?

Well, sir, he's back with—

Theller, I'll tell you this. If he could, he'd quit the Army and be off somewhere
stripping out gold with a bunch of Chinamen.

D——d right, sir.

Theller, take your squad a hundred yards ahead.

All right, colonel. *Forward!*

Company "F," dismount.

Yessir.

Company "H," to my right. Close order now. Keep to your saddles.

Yessir.

Aw, that ain't but half a dozen, and they're flyin' the white flag—

Shit on their white flag! Godd——n killers!

Sir, the squaws are rounding up their horses down there.

Send the volunteers to that outcropping where they can't do mischief.

Yessir.

Colonel Perry, sir, them Indians is—

Lower arms.

Sir, Mr. Chapman's out there and won't come back.

He's a fool to ride around in that big white hat. What a target.

Well, he's an in-law of Mr. Joe himself—

Sir, should I go turn him around?

Sir, he's—

          Pim.

He's done it now. D——d jackassical sonofabitch disobeyed a direct order.

          Pim,

                white powder-smoke arising purer than a summer cloud.

          Pim.

He did it again, sir.

I do have eyes and ears, corporal.

He—

          Did he get one?

          They're all riding away—

          No they ain't,

                dogs howling, and then the frail note of a birdbone whistle sounding five times from far down the cañon.

Colonel Perry?

          Crazy thing about that Chapman is he's a *squaw man.* Gets it every night he can stand it from a scrawny Umatilla bitch. The ugliest little cunt I ever did see. So why he and Joseph's Indians ain't better friends sure beats me.

          No, he sent her away—

             Now what?

          Maybe Joseph took a turn with his wife—

          Well, I guess I would have shot at them devils myself.

             D——d sun in my eyes—

Trimble.

Yessir?

                  Colonel's in a rage.

                  How do you know?

                  Look at how he bites his lip—

                  He's not even a colonel.

                  Watch out.

What the fuck's wrong with your company?

It's the Indian mares down there, sir; they're exciting our horses—

Form in order *right now.*

Yessir. Trumpeter—

Trimble, I want your company over there on right flank.

Yessir. Along the ridgeline?

Right. Move out now.

Yessir! Company "H," *move out!*

Jonesey, sound the advance.

 Yessir!

  Advance!

   Go! Go! Go!

    O, the girl I left behind me . . .

Company "F," we'll deploy between Trimble and Theller. Trumpeter, blow! *Prepare to mount,*

   John Jones trumpeting away so cheerfully.

You heard him, men.

Mount.

Form up by fours! Speed it up, cocksuckers!

Company "F," prepare to forward

    to clean out the Nez Perce nation.

Yessir, colonel! Now we're going to get us some revenge. Remember what those devils did. You heard more just now from Mrs. Benedict. They need to be put down.

  Trumpeter—

  Advance!

Let's go. *Let's go! Hurrah,*

    my blood as loud as White Bird Creek,

  hurrah,

   hurrah!

 but the line of Nez Perce warriors explodes from the defile, galloping through the golden grass, the horses tricked out in silver, blue and scarlet, saddle-blankets brilliant,

 sheltered in the glare of the rising sun.

2

Parnell, can you see what's happening down there?

Too much dust, colonel. The enemy horses are sure kicking it up.

Tell Mr. Chapman to come here. I aim to kick his squaw-loving teeth in—

Yessir, he's—

What the hell are his rabble doing now?

Colonel, they're leaving the column—

Fuck, sir, it's that no-account Shearer—

On the contrary, sir, it's Chapman who's to blame—

Sir, the Indians are attacking!

How many?

Sir, I estimate fifty hostiles on our right—

Sir, I disagree with that. Not more'n just a dozen bushwackers—

Then shoot them down. Now get me a scout.

      Is that Joseph over there?

      How the hell should I know? D——d sun in my face—

Captain Trimble, sir, they're coming up the west cañon.

That Joseph is a clever sonofabitch.

Guess so, captain. You want me to send a scout down there?

Captain, sir, Colonel Perry wants Company "H" to—

      Now, men, let them have it!

      Fire!

      You're shooting high.

      Yessir. The sun—

      What's the fucking matter with you? Let's see you get an Indian.

      Yessir.

Lieutenant, go get those volunteers back on flank.

      Volunteers back to that swale, you GoDd——d cowards! Hurry it

      up! Mr. Chapman, you sack of shit—

          One of 'em's got a fat-ass buffalo gun! That's what's booming—

Sir, I see more of 'em over there!

On our left now—

Is Theller holding that swale?

Yessir.

Steady now. Wait till they come farther up the cañon.

Number fours, hold the horses.

Brace yourselves,

                and

We're taking fire, sir.

GoDd——nit, they're shooting my boys right out of their saddles!

Dismount. *All cavalry dismount and—*

Trumpeter, sound the—

Pick some men to take the horses out of danger. Down there, I guess, where

that yellow grass—

Yessir.

Skirmish formation. Return fire now.

Yessir,

      each trooper flipping up his front sight so that the Christmas-tree-shaped

      window clicks into vertical.

         If I only had me my old Sharps, I'd drop down those bucks!

Aim for those three in the red blankets. They must be the leaders.

Yessir.

     Pim. Pim. Pim. Pim. Pim.

     You're shooting low—

     They—

Why, they're taunting us! That's the purpose of their outfit.

Yessir,

the three in red

(Shore Crossing, Strong Eagle and Red Moccasin Tops)

dancing amidst our bullets like colts around lazy bumblebees.

Pim.

—in that yaller grass—

Pim.

No, over there.

Pim.

Watch out! They're

Pim.

Pim.

—since them Injuns keep ducking down behind the ridge—

Bring me a scout.

Yessir.

O, it's Umatilla Jim, is it?

Yes, captain.

We need to reconnoiter that enemy village down there

in the thin pubic-hairy greenness of the gulch of White Bird Creek, between two rolling yellow hills like breasts, rich trees and blackeyed susans sprouting up out of the long wet slit

to see if we can burn it.

I'll try, captain.

Jim, you've got to do better than that.

I'll get as close as I can—

Go.

One volunteer wounded over there, sir. Sure is hollering like a—

Why can't we get the range? Where the fuck are they firing from?

Down there, sir, in White Bird Creek—

That's an awfully long way.

Yessir. And then from behind that yellow ridge there—

Colonel Perry, sir, the trumpeter's dead.

Jonesey? He—

Shot out of the saddle before we even—

Colonel, sir, we're taking fire all along the line.

Where's my other trumpeter?

Sir, he says he's lost his trumpet, sir.

He *what?*

JESUS, that buffalo rifle just got Sergeant Gunn! Took his head off—

Sir, our handlers can't control the horses—

D——nit, kill me some GODd——ned Indians!

We're doing our best, sir,

volunteers falling blackly on the soft ridge on our left, the mounted Indians in the gulley below taking rapid aim, then ducking behind the golden grass, our horses shying and screaming like stormclouds across the yellow sky

(so hot),

stink of sweat, powder and horseflesh.

Soldier, the reason your gun won't fire is that the barrel's fouled up. You'd better ram it out right now.

Yessir, lieutenant.

Didn't your Daddy ever teach you how to clean a gun? JESUS CHRIST.

Sir, these Indians seem more stubborn than usual. They've got breechloaders and—

So we need to develop our cavalry more aggressively. Get ready to ride down and around there . . .

Our left is caving in, colonel, sir.

I can see that. Let's pull it in.

Yes, sir. Men, fall back! Colonel says fall back!

Colonel, the volunteers are running away.

Good riddance.

Yessir.

Fall back on the right. Easy now. Steady. Form a line right here, three yards apart, left and right. Doubletime, now,

a right compact body of Indians, but hid behind their powder-smoke.

Colonel, a message from Captain Trimble—

Why's Theller the only one I can count on?

Colonel, the horses are running away—

A steely rattle as Perry turns in the saddle, his spurs flashing in the sun, to say: Let's have some discipline now. Where's that scout?

He never came back.

Your breech is fouled.

Yessir.

Pick out the empty shell with your fucking knife.

Yessir.

Sir, the horses are stampeding—

Sir?

What is it now, sergeant?

Joseph's turning our left. He's run the volunteers right off the butte.

Fucking JESUS, even running away they can't fucking manage, so *fuck* them!

Yessir. They're enfilading us—

Hold the line, d——n you!

Yessir. The volunteers—

To hell with them. Sergeant McCarthy, pick half a dozen men and retain that bluff there until I relieve you. On the double now.

Yes, sir. Squad, form up! Werner, Gunn, Nielson, you hold the horses.

Right away, sir—

> They're as thick as fucking prairie chickens! They—
> Got near about as many feathers—
>> *Pim.*

> And they're getting around us,
>> the Indians swinging around in the rear of our left flank, rid-
>> ing, running, leaping and ducking through the grass, and from
>> their rifle-barrels blossom flames even yellower than the grass.

Commence firing.

You heard the sergeant! Do your best endeavor, men.

Sergeant, sir, we can't get the range yet. It's half a mile or more to where those Indians—

> Where are they?
> Shut up,
>> their hot rifle-barrels swelling now so that they miss more widely.
>> Well, well, this sure is a pretty outlook.

If I only had me my old Sharps—

> Popping up their heads right there—

Don't you see them sneaking by on our right? *Drill them,* you GODD——d fuckers!

>> but all these Indians, leaping onto the backs of their cantering horses to
>> fire, then quickly ducking down again, their faces calmly alert, the feath-
>> ers glowing in their hair
>>> and white gunsmoke amidst the dust of many horses coming to-
>>> gether in a fight,
>>> Perry now down on one knee, sighting his Remington across the
>>> golden grass to remind them all how it's done, the men behind him
>>> now regaining heart, raising their own rifles
>>> and then that unseen monster buffalo rifle roaring, shocking this
>>> echoing mist of white sulphur-smoke so that for an instant no one
>>> can hear,
>> and the smell of the grass
>> and the trembling flowers
>> conspire so that we lose sight of our places on the line, Companies "H"
>> and "F" now accordingly mingling:
>>> Where's Theller, sir?
>>> He—
>>>> *Rally on the right! Come on, GODD——n you!*

Soldier, ride to Captain Trimble and tell him we're being attacked from the rear. Request permission to fall back.

Yes, sir.

> Fall back, fall back!
> Perry's falling back!

No he ain't. Now you just stand right here and

And on a cream-hued horse rides Ollokot himself, smoothfaced, longnecked and almost feminine, his eyes and forehead painted red, with many white necklaces upon his throat and his hair-peak streaked with sunshine and a triangle of white cloth widening out from an oval ring placed high up on one of his pigtails, calmly enlarging himself upon our eyes, aiming at the buttons and golden ribstripes across the blue-blackness of a militia officer's coat, galloping toward us through the grass which is pale tan like elk teeth.

That devil's the one!

Get him!

> but Shore Crossing with the great buffalo gun, laughing, swings round
> and fires at full gallop:

>> *Pim!*

>>> (a jolly whist party, ace high and cut for trump)

—and another private flies back bloody into the golden grass.

Is it Joseph's brother?

That's Joseph!

No it ain't.

How the hell should I know?

>> *Pim.*

A roar of agony, not from an Indian

> and smoke-puffs tinier than marbles flash amidst the dark green trees of
> White Bird Creek, beyond which our binoculars cannot see

Get that Indian!

He's—

Sir, that man over there needs a doctor.

Can't nobody kill one shitty little Injun?

Colonel, they're sneaking through that yellow grass up there.

Getting bolder, aren't they?

Sir, they're—

Keep yourselves covered.

Sir, there's no cover—

Shut your teeth or I'll kick them for you. Shoot, d——n you, shoot!

> . . . in our rear.

>> *Pim,*

>>> the Springfield's action hardly moving, solid,
>>> reliable, all in a block,
>>> smoke widening on either side of the barrel,
>>> smell of sweet sulphur, bitter taste of charcoal.

3

Permission to fall back granted, sir.

Thank GOD! Tell the men to fall back toward Lieutenant Parnell.

Yes, sir. I heard Lieutenant Theller's lost his horse—

      Can't go on to Salmon River, Trimble.

        No, sir, that's annihilation. I'll command Parnell to withdraw—

Now, sergeant, we have to make a stand here. You'll lead the right advance squad.

Yes, sir.

        Doc, why do you keep grinning like that? Are you crazy or what?

Get ready to charge.

What?

Bugler's fucking dead. Now horse yourself and—

Captain's changed his mind, boys, I don't know why. Unhorse yourselves and hold this bluff until—

They're in the rear now.

Lieutenant, I've been shot—

Do your best endeavor now. That's all you can do.

Yessir.

Lieutenant, we—

      Pim. Pim. Pim. Pim. Pim. Pim. Pim.

Lieutenant? Lieutenant Parnell?

That's my name.

Morrisey's stopped one, lieutenant, sir. He's—

All right, men. You make a stand here. I'm going to get help from Captain Trimble. Until I get back, Sergeant McCarthy's in charge. *I will not leave you,* I swear by the ALMIGHTY GOD.

    Where's Lieutenant Theller?

Yessir. Good luck, lieutenant—

You men, be heroes and help our wounded move along.

Yessir.

Sergeant McCarthy, sir, I—

Not that one. He's a goner.

Morrisey, hold on! You've got to fight!

    Pim.

Sergeant, Murphy's been—

Get that Indian!

Shooting low—

Sarge, don't leave me

    here in the breath-sucking heat of the wind where tumbleweeds sway

        his head hanging down,

ramming the barrel until the cartridge seats,
aiming,
carefully, vainly firing,
spitting out frothy sulphur-saliva,
nor up between the mounds where a locust rattles darkly
down in the dust of war
where the pile of dead troopers still bleeds, their arms and legs dangling
down like a forest of old tack in a carriagehouse.

4

Ollokot, watch me shoot him as he moves away.
Pim.
You shot well.
Now this one.
Why did he stand still?
He did not know how to fight.
He's weeping for the very last time.
Look! Four or five of them, hiding in those rocks—
Shoot them,
the locusts singing *tekh-tekh-tekh!*
and riding up easily among the Bluecoats, who fall dead before they can finish
loading their rifles, our warriors prove their hearts. As easily as a good knife
swims through a crimson glob of buffalo flesh, parting it into two grinning
lips, so the People have sliced right through their milling enemy. Cut Arm
showed us the rifle. We shall be herded no more; I am telling you three times!
Now I'll jump down on this one—
like an owl into a prairie dog town.
He's dead now. Give me his ammunition.
I'll give his pistol to a pretty woman.
That's right, brother. Pistols are too weak for men.
That one's still alive.
Watch me fix him.
That rock's too small.
You'll see.
No, that took care of him.
I want his rifle.
What else does he have?
(slicing away the shiny brass eagle buttons which our People have always
longed to possess).
Cut Arm will be feeling brilliant and brave to-morrow.
I want to kill Cut Arm,
riding to kill: I shall taste it.

5

All right, men. We're going to retreat up the cañon—
Yessir, lieutenant.
Get back from here! Keep shooting at them, you idiots! Aim lower,
    looking down south into a grass defile,
        the warriors' club-arms and rifle-arms flying upward like wings as
        they come riding fast
    with the three mounds to the west and east, in ascending stages to the west:
                    Pim. Pim—
    and the ridgeline behind which Company "F" has fled, dancing the broken dance,
    then the golden tumbleweeds,
    a single dark and leathery tree down in the hollow
(I don't want to die to-day),
    my rifle nearly too hot to hold
    and from an oval hollow of grass parallel to the creek an Indian springs
    up shooting
        at me
    Pim.
Another Indian behind the rock! I keep shooting high—
    at that snarling old bear who's wearing a wolf's head
    and the brightness of their eagle feather headdresses
    in the tumult of the dancing grass:
        Pim.
                Pim.
If I could shoot their women and children,
    in the long narrow line of trees down White Bird Creek, where they must
    be hiding and waiting
        down there
then they'd
    Lieutenant Theller, sir, this cañon's a dead end.
        Pim.
    and the rock by his ankle explodes.
And those asswipe volunteers who got us into this—
Form a circle, men. Drag the dead horses in.
Yessir.
They're crawling up close.
Lieutenant, sir—
Make your bullets count. All we can do is wait on Colonel Perry.
They're slaughtering us!
    Pim. Pim. Pim. Pim. Pim. Pim.

6

Corporal John L. Thompson, First Cavalry, Company "F," looks
  down the golden hollow and over the golden mound and down into
  White Bird Creek with its serpent of trees and up the immense slanting
  shelf of golden grass, which is fractured by tree-filled S-shaped cañons
    (they have forgotten me)
  and from that stunted tree at the very edge of the tallest rocky knoll, with
  the hollow deep below the hot wind blowing at my back
    and a heartbeatbeatbeatbeatbeatbeat,
    chambering the big round with his forefinger, then flipping back
    the curved, angled, grooved, flat, infinitely-sided block of metal
    over the cylindrical trench so that it falls in and rests on its
    corner, and then with two blackened fingers pushing against
    spring pressure until the far side of the assembly strikes the rear
    of the chamber, and finally pushing still harder until the lever
    rises and
      LORD be mine help, and if only they hadn't taken away my
      Sharps; I've practically never missed with a Sharps
  flipping up the front sight and aiming at this Indian:
    Pim!
  and thumbing back the serpent, then thumbing up the trapdoor so
  that the spent brass leaps out into the grass and
    now if I but pay this shot better mind, sight low, hold my
    breath and draw the trigger back real slow
      and then withdraw even just to Johnson's ranch,
    chambering the next round:
It's *me* he's coming for. He's aiming to
    now all goes slow
      Colonel Perry swears a Sharps will penetrate seasoned white
      pine seven inches and more at a distance of thirty yards
    and a heartbeat
      whereas a Springfield
  Pim,
  and all those bearteeth laid out in rows on the Indian's buckskin yoke
  remind him of the rows of horseshoes neatly straddling the beam of his
  uncle's blacksmithing establishment back in Walla-Walla where he
That's my horse he's got! He stole my horse.
    and a heartbeat
    and the sky
This is not real and could never be true, because
    the Indian's arm rising

(each of his terrifying eyeballs resembling the black spot on a
poisonous white baneberry)
my mouth is dry
and the horseshoes glitter in his uncle's shop as if they
What's he hissing at me?
and a heartbeat
will penetrate seasoned white pine
Pim.
the pain as dazzling as the sun in the brown river where Mary first said to me
my saber down there on the grass
the golden grass
(they don't have no lines to turn, so what the hell were we supposed
to do?)
blood on the back of my hand
and cracking of breastbone just as when at Thanksgiving Daddy used to
penetrate seasoned white pine for seven inches
and a heartbeat
my heart hurts
heartbeatbeatbeatbeatbeat
the pain settling in his heart; it was always there; *there is nothing but this
pain* and can never be anything else; he would pay any price to be free of
it; nothing else matters
this evil pain is screaming but I cannot scream
Maureen's too small to remember me
and a heartbeat like the great clang of the blacksmith's hammer
to never see Mary again
and those black savage eyes shining with hate
Thief treaty!
and the smell of his breath as he
those hateful Indian eyes
rusty steel
No, not into my
and his
and a heartbeat
if I bite the tip off when
it comes in as smoothly as the worn whitestone grinding wheel of
smoothly into me with
pain beyond pain beyond horror beyond sadness
O, my GOD, O, Mary and my own Maureen
seasoned white pine, seasoned white pine, because a man will
never show fear, you d——d Indian.
I'm choking on my blood while he laughs at me:
getting cold

the world is white
    and a heartbeat
the world is gold with dying grass and
    he skewered me so I can't even
Are those flies or is that the sun?
      and
    his hate; his *hateful Indian eyes* on me; that gruesome smile;
If I must die then please GOD my MAKER allow me to die hating the Indian:
    I hate—
And he went tumbling, *tsálalal.*

7

Get me another scout.
Yessir.
Where did Captain Trimble get to?
He was galloping straight toward that ridge when they—
Now what's this here?
Well, sir, he raised up and was hit and—
All right, but don't leave his GOD——d rifle for Joseph! Is that Colonel Perry's
horse right there? Sun's in my eyes—
      Gonna be hot to-day.
Yes, lieutenant. And Colonel Perry's still—
Fine. Try and gather the men in. We'll retreat up the ravine,
    running up the steep yellow hills, chasing the wind up to the hazy sky
    and the Indians before and behind, shooting
      (dead soldiers and no dead Indians)
until we can make a stand.
      Yessir. Men, let's move.
      Them devils in the red blankets—
    Trumpeter—
    Don't you know he's dead?
Lieutenant, lieutenant! You said you'd bring help!
I could not bring you help, sergeant. You see how everything is going. Now let's
go. That ascent's a good four hundred feet,
    and up the bluff: the chimney rock dropping off to the south, straight down
    Don't leave the line!
    up that cañon waveringly grooved with trees
    Shlokh-shlokh. Shlokh-shlokh. Shlokh-shlokh.
Now I am aiming at this one.
    Shlokh-shlokh.
My arrow sings. He has fallen down. My arrow sticks in his eye.
    and

the grasses looking gentler when they are bent
a blackeyed susan nodding eagerly at the dying man
Pim. Pim. Pim. Pim.

Trumpeter—

What the hell is McCarthy doing? Has he abandoned his position?

Sure looks like it, captain.

Well, ride out there and order him back
to his rock: a twisted tree overhanging the void
and golden grass dancing at the edge,
a far drop down into the winding green line where a few of our troops
still hide until they are killed.

Doublequick, now—we need to make a stand . . .

Gazing up the hollow at the eastern yellow breast and western rock breast,
where a single grassy tree makes do for a navel, Lieutenant Parnell finally spies a
few of Colonel Perry's men.

Company report. *That's all?* Lieutenant, it's a pleasure to see you alive.

Thank you, captain, sir.

Are you wounded?

No, sir. A man died next to me and—
The volunteers are behind us. One just got shot in the hip; there's
an Indian behind that boulder there—

Sir, they're trying to stampede us again.

Then fire a volley.

Ready, aim—aim *well—fire!*

How many did you kill?

Looks like they're running away, sir.

I said how many hostiles down?

None, sir.

D——nit, are none of you fit men?

I think I got one, sir.

Then what's that, the holy resurrection?
Where's Lieutenant Theller?
Colonel told him to take charge of the men, so he told off a squad and—

Sir, there's more of them behind that knoll.

Can we storm that position? Speak up, shithead!

Unlikely, sir. They're too—

Get back!

Men, you can't fall out now. Anybody who wants to stay alive has got to reach
Mount Idaho. Fire another volley.

Ready, aim—*fire!* Soldier, you heard me. Why didn't you fire?

My gun's choked up, lieutenant.

Sir, I think they mean to drive us into the cañon.

Godd——nit, colonel, they have shot me in the—

Somebody see to that soldier over there.

Yessir.

That buffalo gun—

What the fuck is Trimble doing?

He's running up that plateau, colonel—

You shut your fucking mouth or I'll kick your teeth in. Talking like that about your commanding officer—

Yessir.

Parnell, report!

Twenty men left, sir.

All right. O, hell, they've shot my horse—

Take mine, colonel.

Those shiteating red devils—

Colonel Perry, sir, I—

You call that a skirmish line? Lieutenant, can't you form them up? Listen, men. Joseph's fixing to drive us into that deep cañon there. If he succeeds, we're dead. Now, all of you, clear your pistols; clear your rifles. Ram them out; move, move, *move!* Every man who has ammunition better load his Colt, *now.* Now load your Springfields. We're going to give those brutes a volley, right between their fucking Indian eyes. Ready? Here they come, riding up through that tall grass. On the count of three, we'll give 'em what they deserve. Here we go, now: *one, two, three—*

> *Pim.*

Sir, they're falling back!

All right, move out. CHRIST, we still haven't killed a single GODD——d Indian.

Colonel, sir, please take my horse.

Fuck that. Men, we scared 'em off for the moment. Now let's ride for that knoll there—

Yessir. He says Lieutenant Theller's got another horse; he's riding bareback—

Fine. Now let's go. When we reach that tree we're going to give them another volley,

> looking down from the reddish volcanic rocks, golden grass and dry
> pines at White Bird Summit, down into a pale and hazy cañon.

Lieutenant, did you see Sergeant McCarthy?

If he's still alive, sir, I'd guess he's down about there,

> gazing out into the air where we must go once we die
>> or inside the sun,
>>> or beneath black beetles and caterpillars in the cracked earth—
... says we'll make another stand at Johnson's ranch—

Sir, I can't go no more.

What the fuck do you want me to do about it, soldier? Now put one foot in front of the other—

Sir, I—

I'll shoot you right here. Now *move*. That's right. I'll be *watching* you.

Ride for it!

This is Little Big Horn all over again.

Cut it out.

Sure could use a drink of water.

Four more miles.

Take it cool, now, boys. We'll get out.

Where's Lieutenant Theller?

I saw him on that wagon road, sir—

How long ago?

I—

Where's Trimble?

Last I saw him, colonel, he was riding thataway.

I see. And is that more fucking Indians up ahead?

Looks like citizens from Mount Idaho, sir.

Well, I'm glad to see they could get their thumbs out of their precious assholes.

CHRIST, it's only nine-o'-clock in the morning.

Yessir. Enemy riding away, sir.

Lieutenant Parnell.

Yessir.

What's your estimate of our casualties?

If Captain Trimble's made it in, sir—

Then he'd be here with these citizens.

Could be all the way to Grangeville, sir.

Enough.

Colonel Perry, sir, these men from Mount Idaho are requesting permission to pursue the Indians.

Tell them they've done enough damage.

Yessir. Sir, they want to talk to you.

I don't want to talk to them just yet. They can wait their turn.

Yessir.

Well, lieutenant?

I'd guess we lost fifty men.

We'll call the roll when the stragglers come in, but I wouldn't be surprised if you were right.

Yessir. Colonel Perry, sir, may I ask a question?

Go ahead.

Sir, what exactly happened?

NEWS
JUNE 18

Once more, while they wait outside the door, he demands himself to believe that all is GOD's will. On this very hot morning, the pitch oozes out of the raw pinewood walls.

Theller failed to verify my confidence—as I should have known; Boyle warned me he kept unfit associations in Lewiston. Did he acquire some vicious habit there? Whatever else could explain it? By GOD, it wasn't as if he was fighting Americans!

No, the general's still in there.

I must never let anyone see my disappointment, the widow most of all. LORD JESUS, please take her by the hand and lead her to OUR FATHER. Dear GOD, will you hold your afflicted daughter in your loving arms to-day, to-morrow and for ever?

I thought I knew him: a steady Vermonter—

and Wilkinson's usually so adept at sniffing out bad character. Did he not wish to peach on a brother officer?

How will Monteith use this opportunity?

And foul George Crook, the Indian-murderer—I'm aware he's hated me ever since I prevented him from wiping out Cochise's tribe—my GOD, my GOD! The President was his subordinate at Cloyd's Mountain— and even Sherman thinks the world of Crook—

and Colonel Sully will naturally strive for advantage; and

I certainly underestimated these Nez Perces! Now I must ruin Joseph quickly, or the other tribes will take up arms.

O, what a tragedy for the Indians! When they could have won safe haven, however provisional—and I thought I had helped them!

—remembering how the negroes down on Edisto Island and in New Orleans and in Fernandina, Florida, and everywhere else in the South kept telling him that only *land* would save them, even the merest acre apiece, something on which they could live and grow food, and in this he finally could not assist them; but in the case of the Nez Perces he had been given precisely that power; he aimed to give the Indians a decent amount of land, and even select it for them, or permit them (within limits) to select it

(but Joseph made a fool of me).

He remembers the way that Sherman could offer a man half a dozen brilliant plans at every conference.— And what shall my plan be? I have studied the map again, haunted by Sturgis's division at Antietam, and that terrible *sunken road,* truly

a Valley of the Shadow, where the Confederates hid. White Bird Cañon must
have resembled that place. But the fact is that Sturgis *took* the hostile battery . . .
and it will not be trivial to encircle Joseph. (LORD, bow down Thine ear, and hear.)
Above all I must isolate him from Smohallie's renegades. He is master of this
country, and can withdraw from my cavalry in nearly any direction. Wallowa's a
true fortress, I understand. Therefore—

If I'd only kept Toohhoolhoolzote in irons! *We came from the earth,* with never
any letup; *she is our mother; our bodies must go back to her*

> —glaring at me like a wounded buffalo when I seized him, Mrs.
> FitzGerald shrinking against her husband, Monteith playing with
> his beard most knowingly, and Joseph,
>> Joseph—

And I won't forget how White Bird disguised his face from me behind his eagle
feathers when he began to meditate resistance against our Government.

> When Ollicut appeared so afraid to promise anything,
> was that simply because he must defer to his brother or
> because he was aready plotting? Such a well behaved
> young man I thought him—

Sherman will say I'm soft.

> Lizzie won't be sleeping.

If I'm not quick, Crook will seize Sherman's ear,
> or even the President's.

I must be gentle with Perry.

They lacked the added discipline which is required in retreat. I learned that
lesson back at the second Battle of Bull Run. I assumed that Perry understood. He
should have! After all, he put down the Modocs in fine style, so Mason tells me.

And Wilkinson's mournful obedience, as if he too is coming to despise me . . .

Did I fail to carry out every needful task in support of Perry's march? *No.*

> Lizzie and Grace will find out to-morrow,
> most likely.

> Thank GOD Mrs. Trimble and Mrs. Parnell
> are at Walla Walla.

Anyhow, who'd ever have imagined they'd retreat? Perry and Theller of all people!

> (Which black goods should I offer for Theller's funeral?)

They must have done their best, even with

> Monteith everlastingly at my shoulder
> (fading tall and pale into the corner as if he were helpless
> instead of Machiavellian, picking at his frayed beard:
> LORD forgive him)

Thus my chastisement.

And I *trusted* Joseph almost like my own son! He smiled so innocently into my eyes—

He opens the door. Soon their horror will alter into pity, anger and scorn, with
him the object of all of these. He gazes calmly outward. This too I take upon myself.

Sir, Father Cataldo said—

Easy, Fletch. Mrs. Theller will send for him if she needs him. Do any of the men want leave to pray?

I'll ask around, sir.

Please tell the father I'll call on him later. Come to think of it, is he nearby?

Sure is, general. I'll fetch him.

> They pursued Perry's men all the way to J. M. Crook's lane, I heard—
>> Threw out their horse herd to cover their movements and then—
>>> Digging rifle pits to-day in Lewiston—
> Five hundred Indians on Hangman Creek . . .
>> When Joseph deployed his skirmishers—
>>> Burned Mrs. Manuel alive.
>> The settlers at Palouse are all running away—
> I sure hope them Grangeville people are forted up.
> The general must be—o.

Father Cataldo, please come in.

Thank you, general. I wanted to—

Father, I must be brief. Agent Monteith informs me that you consistently discouraged the non-treaties from settling with you on Mission Creek.

General, I assure you that I've been neutral in this matter.

Sometimes neutrality is equivalent to positive opposition. Perhaps you ought to speak to your flock.

With all respect, general, isn't it too late now to settle those renegades anywhere but the stockade?

In fact, there should be every incentive for the wiser Indians to turn over Joseph and the other ringleaders.

What happens then?

That's not your concern, Father. But please do inform your Indians of my expectations. Thank you; that will be all. Lieutenant Wilkinson!

Yessir.

Has Major Mason returned?

Not yet, general; the steamer—

Do you have a final tally of the victims on John Day Creek?

Four, general,

>> the "Fatigue" call blaring out, notes ascending and descending, troopers wearily forming up in work squads.
>>> Extra good peaches this year in Hood River—

What word about Sergeant McCarthy?

Still missing, sir.

GOD protect him! That would be thirty-five of ours fallen at this White Bird Cañon.

Yessir.

In a quarter-hour I'll need a fair copy of the despatch to General Sherman.

Yessir.

Who's commander of the guard to-night?

Captain Trimble, sir.

Remind him from me that his men may be prone to panic at present. Any exaggerated demonstrations on their part must not be tolerated. No shooting at shadows—

Yessir.

How are you holding up?

I'll get through this, sir—

I know you will. You're a soldier—one of the bravest.

Thank you, sir. I—

And now, general, if you could make the time—

Not just now, Mr. Monteith. I'll send for you when I need you.

General, my Indians are saying—

That's all, Mr. Monteith. Wilkinson, is Lieutenant Fletcher still under the weather?

Afraid so, sir. A mild case of fever—

Systemic infection. Are you infected?

I'm holding up, sir. There's a fellow from the newspaper who wants to speak with you. He's been—

Tell him to wait. And I'd like Colonel Perry to report to me in fifteen minutes.

Yessir. He's coming directly—

Call in Mr. West and all the loyal scouts. Has Mr. West returned to Mount Idaho?

Haven't seen him at the fort to-day, sir.

Well, who's brave enough to ride up there and get him?

I'll do it, general.

Thank you, Wilkinson. I'll remember that. Take two mounted men with you. With luck, some of our missing may have turned up there. And while you're in that neighborhood, I'd like you to assess the morale of the volunteers. Get back as quickly as you can.

Shouldn't be a problem, sir.

Fletch, would you get Lieutenant Bomus's tally of ordnance?

Right away, sir.

It needs to be completely up to date.

Yessir. General, this just came from Lewiston.

From Colonel McConville, I see. All right. He's forming a company of citizens. Let's hope he'll teach them better military discipline than Chapman's lot. Now send this to Fort Walla-Walla. Any news from Portland?

Not yet, general. But Captain Randall up at Mount Idaho—

Please assemble the officers at nine-o'-clock. Has Mrs. Theller made her appearance this morning?

Not yet, sir. I don't believe she knows—

I'll be back in a quarter of an hour.

His ears sing as he strides across the dusty grass toward the cabin,

past the multitudes of silent "A" tents
>   (in the wavering arc of tipis along the creek our good Indians,
>   not daring to show themselves, softly singing:
>   *Wakesh nun pakilauitin*
>   *JEHOVAN'M yiyauki . . .*),

Mrs. FitzGerald and the children watching him from the second-storey windows of their grand house,
>   and through the tiny white blossoms of bindweed in the golden grass, the locusts buzzing as if to perforate the sweltering sun-breath of the ground.

The Theller residence stands upon the far side of the parade ground. No children, and she's young; I pray that some good man takes her in marriage if she's . . .

Blessed be GOD, the FATHER of mercies and the GOD of all comfort.

High overhead, our flag snaps angrily in the hot wind. If Joseph gets me, who will be the one to do as I am doing now? And Lizzie will open the door and—

He places his right foot on the first step. Before he can ascend, the door opens.

Please come in, General Howard.

To delay for an instant the horror of revealing his gaze to this beautiful young woman freshly arisen from her honey-colored spinning wheel, whose wood glistens with sweat, oil and wax, he stares down at his boots while he scrapes them against the threshold, then raises his eyes to see just ahead of him the creamy oval of the braided rug which his boots must now defile, and on it, facing the door side by side, the two chairs which her husband once improvised from ammunition crates and she covered in cretonne with the frill fully pleated on (the doily on the lefthand head-rest greased with the man's pomade); the faded chromo of President Lincoln on the wall and
>   her eyelids red and swollen, but she has not yet clad herself in black—
>   hope and faith unto the end; Lizzie would do the same
>>   (I remember when Lizzie was this pretty—O, so long ago)
>>   Monteith's sister-in-law would know better what to say
>>   (on her brown hand, work-roughened like a man's, the wedding ring)

and

He's dead?
>   the familiar scent of castille soap

My dear Mrs. Theller, he's with OUR SAVIOR now—

He's dead!

And died a hero—
>   the packing-trunk gaping open
>>   (only imitation leather),
>   exposing a grey plaid winter blanket and two of her husband's red flannel shirts, each as neatly folded as a square of hardtack.

Tell me everything.
>   —the worst thing she could have said.

II

Edisto

1862–74

God has limited the power of man, and though in the kindness of your heart you would alleviate all the ills of humanity it is not in your power. Nor is it in your power to fulfill one-tenth part of the expectations of those who framed the bureau for freedmen, refugees, and abandoned estates.

General William T. Sherman, to General Howard, 1865

My good mother . . . always leaned to the idea that kindness, shown even to enemies, would win in time. It may, if not misunderstood, but how often kindness is imputed to want of courage.

Brigadier General Oliver Otis Howard, U.S.A., 1907

A Good Man in a High Place
1862–74

1

*A*lthough the stump of his right arm, septic again, tired him nearly unto death, goading and draining him as unceasingly as the drizzle on Cheraw while he ordered his pontoon bridge laid across the Pedee, he consoled himself with waking dreams of vanishing entirely into the secret world of Lizzie's love. There came fever-instants when the waterfalling march-rhythm of his troops hovered as still to him as the half-woven striped scarf stretched out on Lizzie's loom—finished years ago, no doubt, for he had last seen that during his convalescence after Fair Oaks. Again the arm-stump disturbed his sleep, screeching like a grindstone, grating and clacking like a troop train in that hot slow filthy rain, a nigger rain he heard his men call it; from this he turned away. Generals Sherman and Blair arrived later, requisitioning a blockade-runner's house. His own house lay farther downtown. His patient Seventeenth Corps were drenched, so he felt halfway ashamed of his situation, but had he renounced it, he would have forfeited due respect and confidence—and the differential was tolerable, the majority of the command being on furlough from what we used to call the Dark Valley; for there would be battle neither to-day nor to-morrow, no more slow dying to-night in unstaffed filthy hospitals in order to help the slave owners lose the Lost Cause. Something tugged at him like an orphaned foal. At those miscellaneous instants when he could exist unseen, his eyes refreshed themselves with tears. General Sherman had ordered him to rest, saying: Howard, you're too important to my Army!— The doctor gave him calomel, which although he ordinarily declined it now refreshed him somewhat by veiling him to himself, so that he could continue naked in his own eyes: namely, bearded, slender, his arms folded across his breast, his long sword curving brightly down from elbow to ankle, staring ahead. Pitying every foundering horse, he seemed to see Lizzie's eyes whenever he closed his own; we name that fever. Justice now compelled him to punish a soldier at Cheraw for robbing a lady's ring from her finger; others had invaded ladies' bureaux, so on them too he laid the penalty.— But, general, they're the enemy, and Sherman told us to live off the country!— No one liked him. At his camp near Cassaville, General Wood had cried out: What's the use, Howard, of your being so singular? Come along and have a good time with the rest of us. Why not?— Fortunately, Sherman called that fellow to account, saying: Wood, let Howard alone! I want one officer who don't drink.— So they remanded him to his Bible, his Lizzie thoughts and his brother Charley; but he knew they were laughing at him or worse. To think that Wood was one of his own division commanders! Sherman at least he could rely on, always. And Lizzie—

> my Lizzie:
> your pale, narrow face,
> thin lips and dark, alert eyes,
> your scanty, delicate curls,
>> and the children you've given me, Guy especially, but Grace, o yes, and Bessie and
> and the way that when we find ourselves alone and I stroke your temples, your tense mouth begins to smile,
>> Lizzie O Lizzie

is the second of my two sweet secrets.

General Sherman visited him in his fever there at Cheraw and said: Well, friend Howard, there's no further great impediment between us and Cape Fear!— and he would have set out for Cape Fear right then if Sherman had wished it.

(Sherman to Howard, Savannah, January 16th, 1865: *General: I have read your reports of Saturday and yesterday and was glad you got the position of Pocotaligo so cheaply. It is of great value to us, and I wish you to have it thoroughly strengthened.*)

Two days previously, entreated by the Mayor of Columbia for any help or advice respecting the citizens, who had just lost two-thirds of their city in various fires accomplished by accident, malice, recklessness and military necessity, not to mention whiskey, Sherman, crushing out his cigar on a broken dinnerplate, glared with angry mocking desperation or worse at this Southern gentleman, then grinned and said: Go to Howard; he runs the religion of this Army!— And to their suppliant enemy Howard turned over half of his commissary just gathered in.

General Howard, what should we do when these supplies are exhausted?

Sir, I recommend that you send out foraging parties just as we do. Pay for what you take with official chits, and make good with real money as soon as you can. I'll pray for you all—

The mayor stared.

GOD bless you, sir. I'll pray for you and all your citizens.

GOD bless you, general—

The earth shook when they blew up the powder magazine. They smashed train-wheels and smokestacks, burned Confederate stationery, helped themselves to all the small arms they could use and destroyed the rest. As they continued their march to the sea, he looked back on the ruins and shook his head, thinking: What a wild desert. If Lizzie could see this, she'd probably—

Dear JESUS, please let me be a good man in a high place.

Meanwhile, Sherman commanded: *If any of your foragers are murdered, take life for life.*

He horrifies me, but I love him. In his heart he is good. He will put this rebellion down, and then there will be peace.

As they passed through South Carolina, each corps overlined its march with black smoke.

2

Just as upon the pale tan potentialities of a root storage bag a Nez Perce woman sometimes weaves representations of feathers, each comprising a strict stern parallelogram joined across the quills to its mirror image; and over these feathers she may craft her V-shaped bands of light and darkness, so upon the faded attenuation of this life, General O. O. Howard would impose the exact geometries of a loving spirit, no matter how scornfully his designs might be condemned. At the Secession War's end he came into a high place indeed; his Philadelphia lectures were popular amusements! Why shouldn't he move the world? His heart was good. Before the war, when he first came forward, at Mr. Lynde's Methodist church in Tampa (Mr. Lynde weeping for joy, his hand on Howard's head, the altar glowing and flickering through Howard's own tears), several of his brother officers denounced him for disgracing the uniform, and some even called for his promotion to a madhouse; but he accepted this mortification, trusting himself to our GOOD SHEPHERD. After Gettysburg, with the stars in the long thick-bordered rectangles on his dark shoulders, other soldiers became acquiescent to our Christian General with his double column of buttons and his pale left hand, his pale face widening a trifle, a few white threads flawing his beard, his hair beginning to thin, a faraway attitude in his gaze. Often he'd sing a hymn at a religious service at the corps field hospital, after which the chaplain preached to the wounded: *Make your bodies and spirits a living sacrifice.*— Frequently the trembling, out of tune chorus in which he led them (his own voice never anything but steady) would be parted, as is a pond's skin by a falling stone, by a dying soldier's groans, or the explosion of an enemy shell in the trees; but the hymn would re-form, rippling back into quavering approximations of smoothness even as the medical officers and their attendants tiptoed about, soaked and caked in blood from their faces to their knees, dripping with it from their rolled up sleeves; sometimes, as in that tiny church at Cassaville which our medical corps had taken over, he'd kneel to pray with or for bleeding men while the doctors operated by the flickering light of pine knots, while rain, thunder and shelling strove their devilish best to ban the possibility of speech.

It had likewise been in Tampa (he had been posted there to assist in removing the Seminole tribe) that he was compelled to see Colonel Munroe of the Fourth Artillery whipping his slave *just to make him a good boy.* Howard was in the colonel's office. The child had to come when called, of course. He must have been about twelve. He danced about while Munroe was switching him, screwing up his eyes, laughing and crying.— There, William! Whip you in the morning before you have done anything, and then you'll be a good boy all day.— And the boy, very black, huge-eyed, perhaps a trifle sly, whirled and leaped and capered almost drolly, dreading each stroke of his master's cane but fearing beyond imagination what would happen should he fail to submit.

Lieutenant Howard, I dislike the way you're studying me. What would you say if I ordered you to cane my nigger for me?

I'd reply, sir, that that would not pertain to my military duties.

Get out. You're too soft for this Army.

Quietly closing the door behind him, he strode away from the child's rhythmic shrieks.

That night the young man, slender, stalking nervously in his quarters, with his arms folded across his breast, considered what JESUS CHRIST would have told the colonel. Surely it would have been something brave. Or would it? When is mildness best? Moreover, for those of us who, not being CHRIST, cherish obligations to our wives and skepticism regarding our powers, not to mention respect for the harmony of society, what are we called on to do? Whenever he tried to do something good and failed, Charley boy always said, as a good brother ought: O, do try again!— And he would. But the fact that this earth and everything on it rushes along at a significant tilt in relation to the celestial ecliptic of reason and righteousness; and the additional datum that it intersects this invisible line no more than a couple of times a year, at equinoxes of sweetness, merely renders the rest of our existence all the more bewildering, or, if you like, offensive. Most people, even the best—General Sherman, for instance, or Lizzie, for whom it was a matter of course that babies soil their clothes—managed to remain at ease off the ecliptic. Hence Sherman simply chose not to involve himself in the negroes' problems (or the ruined Southern citizens'), while Lizzie, trying to comfort him, opined that since colored people had survived slavery, not to mention dark and horrid old Africa, they were surely coming into better days now; he didn't need to feel so terribly about the present confusion! Surely by the end of our lives it would get sorted out. Didn't he have faith in America, in PROGRESS? Had he lost his arm and so many comrades for nothing? Darling, please be more optimistic. (Or, if you like: Do try again!) It would have relieved him exceedingly to be able to subscribe to either position. Although he had nearly emancipated himself from fear, he remained vulnerable to *shame.* He disliked going against the quotidian grain. Since his heart called on him to do so nonetheless, he strove to annoy his fellow citizens (and humiliate Lizzie and the children) no more than necessary.

Even at West Point he'd yearned to be an Abolitionist; so he later told himself. In any event, he preserved himself undisclosed until a Southern classmate demanded his views. He would not lie then, naturally. After that his fellow cadets formed a clique against him. Since he had also dared, in contravention to the traditions of the service, to visit a friend who was an enlisted man, most of them cut him completely. There were months when no one spoke to him except in classes and drills. Well, he was constituted to bear loneliness! Over the years he persuaded himself that he had been braver in that situation than was actually the case; but I cannot condemn this fiction, since it encouraged his resolution for

the future. Other graduates gained decades-long friendships and expeditious connections. He won something sadder and stranger. They thought of him as *poor old
Howard.*

At the very first Battle of Bull Run, when he was still unmaimed, this matter
was already tormenting him, in the person of a beautiful, terrified woman who
came to his tent, carrying her darker-complected child in her arms and not even
knowing how to address him by rank: Sir, I'm a slave woman and this here's my
child. Let me and my child go free!

Lincoln had not proclaimed Emancipation, nor even threatened it. Wherein
lay the right course?

Thereupon a poorish white woman announced herself, scolding him pertly:
That there woman's my slave! Now, sir, you must send her straight back to me, for
she and the boy, they're my property.

His soldiers were all grinning, wondering how this would come off. Only his
aide-de-camp, who happened to be Charley boy, stood on his side. He refrained
from glancing at the slave woman's tear-soaked face.

To the mistress he curtly said: There's your property; take it.

FATHER, should I say more or less than this?

But, Colonel Howard, I *can't.* She's stronger than I. You must give me a guard!

Madam, I will not. I will never use bayonets to drive a poor girl and child into
bondage.

His star declined in that instant; his men grew disgusted with their nigger-
loving commander. Charley boy, proud beneath the skin (in time he would take
part in raising up freedmen's schools in Florida, Georgia and South Carolina),
contented himself with a grin, so as not to inflame further indignation against his
brother. The mistress, after tearfully accusing him of ruining her—her nigger and
the little one were practically all she had in the world—advanced with practised
fluency into vituperation. He allotted that performance fifteen seconds. After he
had called a lieutenant and two enlisted men to escort her out of camp, he sincerely pitied her. Meanwhile, without his active connivance, which would have
been illegal, the negress just happened to escape that night with her son to Washington, and he did not feel ashamed.

3

Whenever for recreation and instruction he read old accounts of our Revolutionary War, one of his most absorbing pursuits was the study of how the negroes
had been handled. When he wished to discuss what he had learned, only his
brothers were at all interested.

One sleepless night in Florida he had copied out this sentence from a British
officer's journal, September 1776: *Their army is the strangest that ever was collected: Old men of 60, Boys of 14, and Blacks of all ages, and ragged for the most
part, compose the motley Crew, who are to give the law to G. Britain and tyrannize*

over His Majesty's Subjects in America. It was all he could do not to recite this to Colonel Munroe. The Tree of Liberty had been fertilized in part with negro blood! Shouldn't the negroes share fully in our national blessings?

But at the beginning of the Secession War, while waiting for his volunteer commission to come through, he tried to encourage himself by reading about Paul Revere's ride, about Lexington and Concord and Bunker Hill, and suchlike inspiriting incidents of valor; when by accident he found himself browsing over Lord Dunmore's proclamation, which promised to free any negroes who deserted their American masters and fought for the King; and subjoined to this he found a fire-eating patriot reply in the *Virginia Gazette,* dated November 1775: *Should there be any amongst the negroes weak enough to believe that lord Dunmore intends to do them a kindness, and wicked enough to provoke the fury of the Americans against their defenceless fathers and mothers, their wives, their women and children, let them only consider the difficulty of effecting their escape, and what they must expect to suffer if they fall into the hands of the Americans.*

As he knew well enough, in 1861 any number of Virginians still thought much the same.

4

In 1862, when the confiscation measure came before Congress, a member warned: Sir, pass these acts, emancipate their negroes, place arms in the hands of these human gorillas to murder their masters and violate their wives and daughters, and you will have a war such as was never witnessed in the worst days of the French Revolution.

The Army mostly agreed.

When he court-martialed a young officer for speaking offensively against Abolition and the President, many stopped laughing at him and commenced hating him.

He was sorry and almost shamed. But Lincoln's Emancipation Proclamation had been nothing less to him than Elisha's call on Mount Carmel: *Choose ye this day whom ye will serve!*

5

He had chosen. Among Abolitionist missionaries he grew famous. Henry Ward Beecher praised him as *a christian minister and soldier, doing a kind of military work, but who is so performing it that it is as an iron candlestick carrying a wax candle lighted and signifying the word of* GOD *and the* SPIRIT OF LOVE. I now see him among the Methodists in Baltimore. To them he reports that even in Florida, where he was once stationed, local Christians believe that negroes have souls. The audience gazes worshipfully at his empty sleeve. He cries out: THE ALMIGHTY has been leading us step by step through the war . . .

Amen!

Shall we sacrifice the Republic that we have saved? The church must stand up and tell the truth!

Amen! Amen!

And they fling themselves into universally adopted resolutions.

6

It was at the beginning of the war's last year that he first saw colored schools, at Saint Helena, Beaufort and other Carolina islands. Here came a line of black women in grubby ankle-length skirts of whatever fabric and pattern, rounding a great field's corner, bearing cotton bales on their heads, while the men bore their own burdens on their shoulders—but then there were the children at desks, reading and reciting from blue-backed spellers. He who would that very August share the commencement platform at Bowdoin with General Grant conceived himself to be a man in a high place, whose best endeavor had hope of raising up the negroes into the rights and privileges they certainly deserved.

General Rufus Saxton and his wife escorted him through all these establishments. He was astonished to find the negro pupils to be as far along in their studies as would be any white children of their age. It was then that he realized that these people were more than deserving objects of compassion. They were capable of becoming *Americans.*

Lighting another cigar, Sherman said: I like niggers well enough as niggers, but when fools and idiots try to make niggers better than ourselves, I have an opinion.

Then Sherman issued Special Field Order No. 15. The plantations of these Sea Islands were now to be given over to negro planters, with General Saxton in charge of the redistribution. Sherman was good—

And so once Lee had surrendered, and he who wished with all his heart to do good was informed that the murdered President had wished him to preside over the Freedmen's Bureau, although his doubts grew as eerie as hostile Indians lurking in a thicket of quaking aspens, he knew that he would take up this burden.— Sherman earnestly advised him to forgo the honor. It would harm his career and cause him much suffering. Nor was poor Lizzie enthusiastic. No matter. He did not even consult his brothers— who, of course, approved. He was a man in a high place at last—and with so much to accomplish! His observers and statisticians estimated that there were now *four million negro ex-slaves,* wandering the roads from Maryland to Mexico.

7

I see him at the podium of the grand hall in Springfield, Massachusetts, calmly telling his audience: The Southern man lets go of slavery inch by inch, piece by piece, but he really does not do so, and I do not think he will till he is constrained to it by the power and needs of freedom itself.

From the audience a man shouts out: *Amen!*

Smiling graciously, our speaker continues: You should read the systems proposed from so many different quarters. Every plan has in it the very gist of slavery . . .

Hear, hear!

Punish the rebels!

On the other hand, let me say that there is a large class of our fellow-citizens in the North who reason in this way: *Slavery is a great crime; therefore all slaveholders are conscious criminals.* No kindness is shown them, no sympathy felt them.

The hall is silent.

Southern men are generally outspoken, he tells them steadily. What is the truth? It is that a large body of them are sincere. Strange as it may seem, they heartily disbelieve in freedom for the negro—

Murderers!

No, sir. They are not. They even now reason upon Emancipation as a curse of GOD cast upon them . . .

8

At first giving the negroes lands of their own, schools, hospitals and perhaps even the franchise all seemed not only possible but likely. People often said to him: General, may GOD preserve you long in the service of your country!— This brought him close to tears, although he tried not to show it. He'd attained the pleasure of hearing his name published *happily*. Chancellorsville was forgotten, and the jealous officers who'd become his enemies when General Sherman promoted him over their heads to lead the Army of the Tennessee grew appeased, pitying him all over again to hear of his unglamorous appointment to help the negroes. Brigadier General Hunt, I do admit, let fly the following sentiments: *As to the "Christian Soldier," I have no great opinion of him either as soldier or as head of the Freedmen's Bureau or as a man.* And General Sherman warned him yet again: If you don't watch out, you'll be blackballed, general!—to which he replied: General, they blackballed me at West Point, and I'm still walking this earth.

At the center of his conviction, like the coral in the paperweight, lived Edisto. That former Tory Stronghold, like its negroes, meant less to most Americans than to him. Here the Golden Rule shone enacted. All the Sea Islands had been renewed, turned over in some measure to their former slaves, ever since the days back in '62 when we had to quarter negroes from Fernandina in the public library at Beaufort. And now among great magnolia trees, tiny white-roofed houses sprang up for the benefit of the newly freed families. He used to close his eyes and pray to be as happy as the negro children on Ladies Island:

JESUS *make the blind to see*

JESUS *make the cripple to walk.*

Brigadier General Hunt remarked: O, Howard's going places, all right. Just like a heifer tied to a wagon tongue—

9

He meets with Mr. Frederick Douglass and other delegates from the colored people. They have made an appointment with him in the opinion that he opposes giving them the vote.

No, gentlemen. My conviction is that, first, all citizens should be equal before the law, and then, as in a military generalship, one position should be carried at a time, and then the next tenable position, each of which I would fortify and defend for the right . . .

Would fortify, General Howard? Or *will* fortify? When do you suppose that negro suffrage will come into being, if not now, while the South is still weak?

Mr. Douglass, I assure you that I was all along in favor of eventual suffrage for the negroes, but hoped it might be limited at least by an educational qualification—

Why, sir? *Why,* when the most illiterate bandit of the Ku Klux Klan enjoys the right to vote?

Mr. Douglass, would you have us throw ourselves at a position which is not yet tenable to our force? The only result will be a revulsion of opinion against your race. Do you not agree?

General Howard, no one can deny that you mean us well. But it might be that you're overcautious here—

My dear brother, sometimes it's best to make haste slowly. Now, will you all kindly pray with me?

10

He writes the new President, in whose goodness he strives to believe to the very end, since each of our Presidents must be the personification of Government, selected by the people and for the people, even this fox with the thinning hair, sharp nose and chiseled cheeks: *From the course pursued by the Inspectors, I suspect the object of the inspection, as they understood it, was to bring the Freedmen's Bureau into contempt before the country, and to do this, they have endeavored to prove maladministration.*

In GOD's name, Otis, what reply can you expect?

Never mind that, dearest. Have the children behaved well to-day?

Gracie was adorable. She keeps calling for her Papa! Guy keeps getting into your things and trying to put them in his mouth—

A compliment, no doubt! Lizzie, do you know how greatly I love you?

O, dearest—

Come here.

Tell me everything.

Mr. Johnson is giving up the law pretty fast and I begin to tremble with anxiety for the freedman. This is *entre nous*.

I promise. (Gracie dear, go entertain your brother.)

Yet he's cordial to me and so are his household officials.

You don't call him *Mr. Johnson* to his face?

Never, Lizzie. He's our President!

> as I was certainly made to feel long before I'd even passed the bronze ornaments of the immense East Room; thank GOD Lizzie didn't have to come along; she would have been extremely

And how do you suppose it will turn out?

I have to believe that all the blood and devastated cities bought something good. Lizzie darling, please kneel down with me and

> help me put out of mind the glance he gave me from beneath his low dark brows and

pray that the negroes will get justice:

HEAVENLY FATHER, please hear our supplication unto You, which we make not for ourselves—

11

The faces at Edisto, the golden shine of sunlight on the throat of a buxom negro girl, and the way she pursed her coral lips over her hymnal, these improved his hopes until he glowed whenever he came home to Lizzie, as never before or after, and she was happy and proud.— General Butler has got a bill through Congress, he informed her. The Bureau will have all leftover uniforms . . .

Dearest, I'm so glad.

> Did they beat the negro when they pulled him out of jail?
>
> Well, general, I don't know that from personal observation. And speaking as one white man to another—

Well, General Howard, we didn't mean the United States no harm. All we ever aspired to was to own a nigger, and now we can't even hope for that.

Sir, I extend my hand to you—my left hand, it has to be, for we've all lost something in the war. I pray there will never be another battle, now that we're all reconciled. Accept Emancipation, sir! Put by your resentments. The negroes are now your fellow citizens, and neither of you can enslave the other.

What the hell are you talking about, general? A nigger will never be my equal, let alone anything better.

Sir, I won't have profanity in my office. And I don't care to hear the negroes run down. If there is some help I can give you, ask me for it. Otherwise get out and let me carry out my business

> among the dreams and Cherokee roses of the Sea Islands
> and the wisterias and yellow jasmines,

the negroes happy in the Government's promise that the fields they work belong to them.

He resolves (and Charley boy agrees) to treat everyone, white or colored, Union man, Copperhead or virulent ex-Seccesh, as a friend, and to trust the Agents of his Bureau—for why would they have taken on this work, were it not to do good? Help me to take and fortify the next position for the negroes, O JESUS. Samuel Fullerton was his assistant adjutant general in the Fourth Corps; why not hire him, and other reliable Army men? Whenever compelled by the Bureau's expanding range to go beyond this class of individuals, he selects those whom he knows for men of integrity and with Christian hearts.

He looks up his old comrade General Rufus Saxton in the Sea Islands, whom some call incompetent, although that cannot be so—for see what great things he has done for the negroes!— General, he says, you have my confidence.— I treasure that, general.

WON AND FORTIFIED
1865–1907

1

*J*ust as in the course of punishing a Sioux village we naturally burn their tipis, jerked meat, buffalo robes, dried roots, beaded headdresses, etcetera, so, one would think, when we have the secessionists dead to rights, we might as well at least strip the richest ones of a few acres here and there, on which to establish their former slaves. But in fact we don't *choose* to punish them! In place of General Crook in his reeking deerskins, or our on-again-off-again best boy Custer, or firm, bluff Colonel Miles, who proved so loyal when General Howard's arm got amputated at Fair Oaks, we follow President Johnson, who compassionates his fellow landowners; O yes, he's the finest Christian I ever did see.

Lizzie's bread has just risen. President Johnson whistles up his dogs.

When them night riders shot Joe Bell for refusing to resign his office to a white man, shot him an' burned him and then shot him again, and his widow was a-cryin' out: *O LORD GOD OF HOSTS, help us to escape this country and get somewheres where we can live—*

Now, sir, people have suffered on both sides of this fight. Let's look forward. Your people are free, and the Government has sent me here to help you.

Well, General Howard, sir, here in Alabama they're saying you exert a dangerous effect upon our negroes—

Never mind. In Edisto, at least, the position has been won and fortifed by Special Field Order Number Fifteen, January 1865:

> the line of Africans in dirty, dusty faded calico dresses and knee-torn trousers, standing still as he approaches across the mud:
> LORD bless you, General Howard!
> GOD bless you all. And how are you managing nowadays?
> Well, better than in them slave times. O, general, and bye and bye we's gonna get rid of *all* our afflictions, if the good LORD wills—

Shaking General Saxton's hand, he withdraws into his office to write Lizzie: *The negroes must be employed & instructed, clothed, and fed, borne with and kindly treated as well as emancipated. Praise GOD, we are doing all this, and no wonder! For He in His wise Providence is holding us to it, North and South—and how could He fail to be a GOOD GENERAL, and support us in what He commands? O, my sweet Lizzie, if you could only hear the laughter of the little negro children, and view the assiduity with which they vie to answer their kind teacher when she calls upon them at school! I wish I could prevail upon Mr. Johnson to come down from Washington in order to observe*

> a certain negro boy whose rags were in so advanced a state of decay as nearly to resemble a fishing-net, and this little brown boy raised his eyes, coolly and fearlessly; I nearly smiled at his audacity; and

the benefits already conferred. How is Guy's whooping cough? I often worry over that brave little man, who will, I hope, grow up to be soldier like his father—altho' if he finds within himself some less sanguinary capacity I will be all approval— especially now that everything has been settled fairly & generously, so that perhaps there may never need to be another war in the United States. Mrs. Saxton sends you her greetings & adieux, and

why am I happier in Edisto than practically anywhere else?

The Bureau grows. It appoints negroes to labor arbitration boards, issues pensions, prizes and back pay, opens schools. Mr. Robert Scott, known for his skill with arithmetic, enumerates the destitute colored population of South Carolina.

2

By June of 1865, the negroes of Richmond are already calling upon General Howard to protect them; the white city fathers mean to make it lawful to whip them again.

3

The President begins to restore land to the slaveholders. After all, isn't he a well-heeled Southern gent?

Lizzie begs her husband to leave the negroes alone before he gets dragged down to ruin. Smiling pleasantly, he advises the President that whenever any Confederate worth more than twenty thousand dollars should be pardoned, such a one ought to be compelled to deed over five acres or even ten to his former slaves. Let the land be given to the paterfamilias, and let him succeed or fail with it in American style.— Lizzie falls to her knees, praying that OUR FATHER will protect her husband.

4

The President no longer receives him. The Bureau's Agents request instructions as to the confiscated lands. He answers: We will make use of them until compelled to give them up.

His old Army comrade Fullerton, whom he installed in a high position at the Bureau, turns out to be the President's tool and spy.

Refusing to be led into discouragement, never mind that of late SATAN has commenced whispering into his ear that the business which he has been given to complete for others is as mucky as the smell of the Snake River at Farewell Bend, he accepts General Saxton's resignation when the time comes (for the general will not hold his nose and compromise with the original white landowners of Edisto) and defends his Agents as best he can.

He establishes a savings bank and even a university for the negroes, which in due course will be named after him.

He pledges ten thousand dollars of his own money to this Howard University. He donates eight hundred and sixty dollars to the church and the YMCA. The immortal A. P. Ketchum calls him *the most successful man in the world in the securing of money for educational and religious purposes.*

5

After meeting the leading negroes of New Orleans at the Bureau des Affranchis, he sends them away happy and convinced that he will save them from the new forms of slavery; needless to say, it has also become his task to placate the negroes' employers, their former owners. But GOD and the Golden Rule may accomplish many unforeseen results.

6

The President rescinds Special Field Order Number Fifteen. Accordingly, the head of the Freedmen's Bureau must journey to Edisto, to inform the negroes of their altered situation. No more negresses will be drying their cotton on John Seabrook's lawn. It is October, a pleasant travelling-month in the South, and the hours too quickly spend themselves; he would rather never go there to see that very dark man, lined of forehead, staring at him, hands on knees; and that wide negro woman with a great wide apron which will later rebound to mind when he first sees the great white rectangle (composed of many bone-pipes) of a Nez Perce warrior's breastplate; she sits gazing into his face when he informs the assembly that they must restore their lands to the planters; and on her lap is an infant of unknown sex, dressed in a calico sack.

7

They follow him to his office in Beaufort, a dozen of them, coming up around the turn of his steep front porch steps, passing through the portico and into his sitting-room, shuttered nowadays so that the returning white neighbors can't break the pane simply by throwing stones. General Saxton has already sailed away. He invites them in. They stink of muck and sweat, like soldiers. He sends the orderly over to the three brick storeys of the Beaufort Hotel, to fetch five gallons of lemonade. The man returns in terror of the Jayhawkers who grinningly tap the butts of their holstered pistols right there outside the pale-planked clothing-shop on Bay Street. And the negroes wait to see what he will do—as if *his* conscience should be as itchy as an old Indian blanket!

The faint breeze smells of flowers and horse manure. They demand to know whether he has done everything he can. He prays with them; he leads them in a hymn.

8

After that sad convocation, certain freedmen from Edisto somehow meet the cost of travelling all the way to his office in Charleston. He receives them well; the white neighbors are disgusted. After praying with his guests he says: You are right in wanting homesteads and will surely be defended in the possession of every one which you shall purchase or have already purchased.

But, General Howard, we worked them lands because you *promised* them was *ours.*

Not wishing to give way to tears, he grows stern while he explains: The Government does not wish to befriend its enemies and injure its friends, but

> O, Lizzie, in fact the Government *has* betrayed them!—and so I too, being but an Agent of this selfsame Government without which my life lacks justification because I love the United States of America as much as you, the children, Miles and redbearded Sherman, and near as much as Jesus, must now compel them who have suffered so much to drink the bitter cup, because *this President*

considers a forgiven man in the light of a citizen restored to the rights of property excepting as to slaves.

But, general, what are we to do now?

Return home, pray for those who have persecuted you, and work patiently. I will do my utmost to ensure that the Government helps you to get land—

With congratulations and a prayer, he issues a marriage certificate to a negro couple with eight children; the parents have been cohabiting since 1842. And then they all depart, still halfway hoping.

9

In section three of Senate Bill Sixty, he purposes that the Government purchase lands for resale to negroes at cost. The President vetoes the bill. In the galleries, negroes roar with rage.

10

Anti-negro riots break out in Memphis and New Orleans. Colored people are raped, tortured, robbed and murdered. The Freedmen's Bureau cannot protect them.

11

The Government begins to employ the Bureau's Agents as strikebreakers.

12

On the passbooks of the bank he has established and supported (it comes to possess thirty-four branches), appear the following words: *I consider the Freedman's Savings and Trust Company to be greatly needed by the colored people, and have welcomed it as an auxiliary to the Freedman's Bureau. signed Maj. Gen'l O. O. Howard.*

The bank will fail in 1874. More than sixty-one thousand negroes will lose their deposits.

13

Agents serve him with various papers the like of which he could never have imagined, and presently issue a command to the Sergeant-at-arms of the Senate to summon General O. O. Howard of Washington D. C. to appear before the Committee of the House of Representatives at ten-o'-clock a.m., the first day of June, 1867, not to depart without leave of said Committee. Herein fail not, and make certain of this summons. He fails not, although Lizzie can't sleep for weeping. Poor woman, such is a Christian's life . . .

You'll get through this, general.

O, don't concern yourself on my account. It can't be as eerie as my entrance examination at Bowdoin College, when I got *quizzed* by Professor Boody in a chamber of articulated skeletons, although Hancock's against me because I asserted my seniority rights over him at Gettysburg. The President hates me even more now, and the negro-hating Democrats will get me if they can. Hooker has loathed me ever since Chancellorsville. But since General Sherman has promoted me over him, I—

Smiling, he wishes good morning to Mr. Hiram Barber, the hostile witness who seeks to ruin him. Mr. Barber turns away.

14

Although their purpose is as diseased as the purple-speckled red berries of false Solomon's seal, how can it be for him to contest them in anger? This is the shrine of America, the temple of Government.

. . . to order.

. . . the charges against General O. O. Howard . . .

and the nauseating curves of the Senate Chamber

as he dreams back upon the colonnaded entrance atop the steep stairs of John Seabrook's plantation at Edisto (the house slaves' quarters below)

and the sundial in Seabrook's garden, and a little negro boy beside it,

negresses bending in the lovely cotton, while the overseer sits high on his horse.

In the gallery sits his brother Rowland, smiling at him. He wishes Charley boy were also here. And Lizzie—

No, I perforce agree with the honorable member from Alabama. Here's a so-called Christian who has played thimble-rig with the law.

Pious hypocrite! We ought to ride him out on a rail—

The nigger-loving *Coward of Chancellorsville!*

Get this: My cousin-in-law heard him say that *a nigro wench is as good as a white lady.*

And the second charge, the selling of lands for the supposed benefit of the Howard University but actually to the profit of himself, his family, friends and staff—

I wonder if I'll be in jail for Gracie's tenth birthday? Three more weeks exactly. She's an understanding child; she'll comfort her mother. I suppose these proceedings will grind on for a couple of years—

Sherman was right. I never should have accepted this office.

If only Sherman could be here!

But if I can do good, even now . . .

And the seventh charge, that he resold Government lumber to his employees:

Nigger lover! Probably gets it every Saturday night from some old black mammy at his coon university.

That's right, that's right! Did you hear the joke about how he lost his arm?

Therefore, I desire an investigation at the earliest possible instant! It is widely believed that General Howard employed public funds for bribery and other immoral purposes—

Hear, hear!

Then let them come forward with a bill of indictment.

LORD, there's Lizzie in the gallery! Doesn't Rowland see her? How pale she is! But she won't cry; she'd never give them the satisfaction of—

—a ten-minute recess.

General . . . ?

I'm sorry. Woolgathering—

I just wanted to say that that man who keeps passing notes to the Senators is a Jayhawker. General Saxton has seen him at Edisto, tormenting the negroes by night.

15

Otis, I'm praying for you.

Thanks, Rowland; I—

Are you afraid?

Ashamed, I admit, to be disgraced like this, even without cause. But not afraid, my prospects as pallid as a bale of cotton on a negress's head.

I believe in you, brother! When these wicked men slander you, I—

No, GOD *knows my heart and my life!* Better to go to prison than to deceive Him—

Whatever befalls, I'll look after Lizzie and the children—

Anyhow, GOD wills this.

16

The tenth charge, that from Bureau funds he paid forty thousand dollars to construct the First Congregational Church . . .

GOD wills this. He does.

The thirteenth, that he diverted public funds to build a Lunatic Asylum . . .

And at the next recess, as he seeks Lizzie, who must have gone to the convenience, an ancient negress in the gallery says to him, as if he were her beloved little boy: I see you been lashed with trouble, Ginnel Howard . . .

17

And there he stands, year after year, long after the end of the Freedmen's Bureau, laughed at, half-ruined, enslaved by legal fees and his own subordinates' crookedness and negligence; and even during the Nez Perce War he remains chained in his high place:

cancelled like those dark green ten-cent prairie wagon postage stamps ("**HARDSHIPS OF EMIGRATION**") in Grace Howard's scrapbook.

18

President Grant rescues him, altering the court-martial into a Court of Inquiry presided over by General Sherman. One of its members is his dear friend Colonel Miles, who was beside him when he lost his arm at Fair Oaks. This is worse. He stands white-bearded in the ornate maw and between the pillared teeth of the House of Representatives.

Mr. Townsend resolves to acquit him, calling him deserving of the gratitude of the American people, and Lizzie weeps silently in the gallery.

Mr. Pierce says slowly: Mr. Speaker, I purpose to consider the charges against General O. O. Howard in the order they are preferred,

o, my GOD, take from me this cup of mud and tears,

and sustain him in regard to the first charge, his donations to the Howard University,

the third, the ambiguous bonds issued in aid of the First Congregational Church,

the eighth, that he pays rent from Bureau funds to the Trustees of the Howard University,

the ninth, that he draws three salaries—gentlemen, his salary from the Howard University is a dollar a year!—

the twelfth, that he perpetrated land fraud upon both the freedmen and the Government,

the fifteenth, that he made of the Bureau a ring of corrupt linkage with the Southern political machine.

In conclusion, fellow members, permit me to remind you that the gentleman from New York, who has proferred these charges against the general, is a leader in the most corrupt political organization known to American history, an apologist for treason, the friend of the enemies of his country . . .

Lizzie continues to weep. Thank GOD she didn't bring the children.

Grant, Sherman and Miles render everything nearly as perfect as the lever action of a Winchester 1866. By then there are grey stripes in his dark whiskers.

After his acquittal, Miles writes him a letter: *I think you must realize that "the* LORD *reigns."*

And so our hero receives a do-gooder's customary accolades. The Secretary of the Navy opines: *Howard, at the beginning of the War, was a religious man of small calibre, but had become a pious fraud.* General Crook writes: *I was at loss to make out whether it was his vanity or his cheek that enabled him to hold up his head in this lofty manner.* He saves the Apaches, fights Joseph, wins the Bannock Indian War. By then it is 1878. The War Department lodges three civil suits against him.

19

In his autobiography, published in 1907, he seems to have come round to a sunnier view of it all, as proven by this passage: *After years of thinking and observation I am inclined to think that the restoration of their lands to the planters proved for all their future better for the negroes.*

GENERAL CROOK'S ASSESSMENT
1872

*C*rook, to whom he was generous and gracious, and who despised him not only because he interfered with the business of killing Apaches, but also because we Americans scorn failure of any sort, had this to say of the hero of Edisto: *He told me he thought the* CREATOR *had placed him on earth to be a Moses to the Negro. Having accomplished that mission, he thought his next mission was with the Indian.*

WASHINGTON, D.C.
1871

I am glad you troubled to see me, says the Commissioner. Not many military men would even think of coming here. Tell me, what is your opinion of our Indian policy?

In a word, unfortunate.

How so, general?

We're creating a large class of beggars and gypsies.

Correct. And they'll inevitably become a sore upon the body politic unless we confine them on the reservations. I suppose you think we're in the wrong to pauperize them.

Mr. Walker, it would seem more fair to reward the good Indians, or at least leave them alone.

I have no objection to that. Let them alone as long as we can. Time is our ally. You know as well as I that there are innumerable little rifts of agricultural or mining settlements all over our Western country which if unmolested will in a very few years become self-protecting communities, but which in the event of a general Indian war occurring at the present time, would utterly and instantly disappear, either by abandonment or by massacre. The Army's task is to stall the Indians, through enticement and obfuscation if possible, by force if not, until those little towns can take care of their own expansion. After that, we won't need you.

Every night I pray about this matter. If we can only get the whites to do the Indians justice—

Walker removes his almost iridescently luminous oval spectacles. He stares at the general. His right eye appears to be a trifle lower than his left. Grey hairs creep sparsely across the crown of his wrinkled skull. His moustache remains thick and young; sideburns grow out in wild patches but have already taken the grey blight. From within the dark suit the creases of his white sleeves and collar peep out impressively enough, for a civilian. Robbed of them, he might almost pass for one of the many sad drunks we find throughout this imperfect Republic, especially since he shares with most slaves of Demon Gin that propensity to gaze with a vampire's lust into our eyes, his white claylike face animated by whichever eldritch motive enthralls him; otherwise he could sleep, in the gutter, in the grave. Walker's pallid melancholy, of course, derives from no more discreditable a cause than a defect of sunlight and exercise. Here sits a man who courts apoplexy; so Howard pities him. But what can it signify when the pitier finds himself pitied?

My dear general, he now says, I am familiar with your efforts in the Freedmen's Bureau, and I commend your sentiments of Christian charity to the negroes. Be assured that you have my deepest respect.

Thank you.

Someday your labors will bear wonderful fruits—

As they are now doing, sir—

No doubt. And I can assure you that our national charity to the Indian, once the need for it becomes apparent at all levels of Government, will produce equally happy results.

But why Indians of a superior sort, who have always helped us and shown receptivity to our schools and missionaries, must be reduced from enjoying some decent fraction of their own lands to living on charity, that, Mr. Walker, is beyond me. Surely the Army could be deployed at need to protect the reservations from white encroachment.

I see that General Sherman spoke truly when he referred to you as a *Christian Soldier.* Would you agree with him that the Army is under strength?

I'm afraid so.

Well, then, if the penny-pinchers in Congress ever build our battalions back up again, you, Sherman and I must have another talk about all this. Now, when do you set off for the Territories?

Mr. Walker, I ask you upon your faith as a Christian, are we doing right by our Indians?

No. And since we are both speaking frankly to one another, did you succeed in doing right by your negroes?

Why speak in the past tense? I'll keep doing my utmost.

Naturally. But the Freedmen's Bureau is no more. We both know the reason: The negroes were becoming dangerous to the planters' interests. Your Bureau had expropriated their lands. Worse yet, by attempting to make the negroes self-sufficient you threatened the labor supply. That's why you got squelched.

I disagree. The Bureau failed simply on account of ignorant race prejudice. It may take a generation or two before the negroes achieve an utter equality of rights. But consider how much better off they have become within this single decade! With the Indians, unfortunately, matters appear to be going in the other direction.

General Howard, the negroes, poor as they were, possessed something of value, and so our system of industry did what self-preservation demanded. Now, the Indians are not yet poor, not all of them, and so our system is even more interested in them at the moment. Consider this: Had the settlements of our United States not been extended beyond the frontier of 1867, all the Indians of the continent would to the end of time have found upon the plains an inexhaustible supply of food and clothing. Were the westward course of population to be stayed at the barriers of to-day, the Indians would still have hope of life. But another such five years will see the Indians of Dakota and Montana as poor as the Indians of Nevada and Southern California; that is, reduced to a habitual condition of suffering from want of food.

You put it cruelly, Mr. Walker. Once more I urge you to consult your conscience.

The freedom of expansion which is working these results is to us of incalculable value. To the Indian it is of incalculable cost. But this growth is bringing imperial greatness to the nation. Would you reject that?

How could anyone reject our national destiny?

Ringingly said! And I understand as well as you that our expansion requires us to make good to the original owners of the soil the loss by which we so greatly gain. This is your department, General Howard. Everyone looks up to you, the man of mercy, the soldier of charity. We will endow each tribe and capitalize the money in eternal trust. Surely you have confidence in me?

I promise to believe in your good heart.

Thank you. And I most earnestly solicit your good efforts in the administration of these portions. We need men of practical humanity, men of justice, GODly men to shelter the Indians within their paternal care, until every Indian in the United States has realized civilization.

Yes, I see—

I know you do. I also know you understand that very possibly not all of our hopes will be vindicated. However that may be . . .

However that may be, Commissioner, of course we must conform to the law. As a soldier I recognize that—

I never doubted that you did. I assure you, general, that as soon as you come into the West you will find no variance whatsoever between law, policy, philanthropy and common sense.

III

The Burial of
Lieutenant Theller

June 1877

Many officers fail with large commands, and the reason is traceable to their encumbering their minds with the detail.

GENERAL O. O. HOWARD, 1907

WE HAVE NOW SEEN HIS DEEDS
JUNE 18

*S*it down, Perry. There's something I want to say to you. There is always a theory of war which will forestall the imputation of blame to those who do not deserve it. Do you know how that theory runs?

No, sir.

It is to impute the credit of one's great defeat to his enemy,
> a single locust stridulating as the younger man strains to preserve him-
> self unmoving and then
>> (through the window I see Agent Monteith striding long-legged to
>> haunt me with pale and paler insinuations—
>>> he *can't* already have Sherman's ear!—
>> and at his heels that handsome fellow with quadroonlike features:
>> his favorite *good Indian,* James Reuben, who may or may not talk
>> straight, although he carries a fine hymn-tune; Wilkinson had bet-
>> ter suss him out).

Perry, Joseph has shown impressive generalship. Console yourself with the fact that this war will be remembered in history: *we* will be remembered.

Yes, sir.

And if there is any Court of Inquiry, I will speak in your defense. You have my word.

Thank you, sir.

What troubles you the most?

General, I—

Perry, you're a fine officer, and I care for you as a father for his son. Kindly let me help you.

Sir, when do we move out? We—

You and Theller were comrades. I know. We all bear those scars.

Yessir. You're aware, general, that aside from last year's Custer debacle, this is the most crushing defeat ever inflicted upon us by the Indians. *Ever.*

Indeed, indeed, a sad roll call . . .

Theller plus thirty-three enlisted—

By the way, I understand that Mrs. Theller was previously married to a Mr. Butler, when the Twenty-first was out at Fort McDermitt. Can you tell me any-thing about her situation?

No idea, sir.

I suppose not. Now how did it happen, Perry?

We were outnumbered, sir,

> and as we rode down, the wide yellow bowl closed up, the knolls hemmed
> us in—

And outgeneraled.

If you say so, sir.

And you lost control of your volunteers?

They disobeyed my orders, sir, and that Ad Chapman was the worst.

But he didn't lead them, did he?

No, sir. They were commanded by Mr. Shearer, the so-called major from the Confederate States, and *he* turned tail right away once Jonesey was killed, but Chapman was already galloping for his life—

I see. And your scouts?

General, those no-good Indians—

Perry, I've heard it said that Captain Trimble refused to assist you in making your stand, and even fled the field.

Sir, he did seem in a hurry to get away. But what with no trumpet left to carry my command—

So you don't care to prefer charges against him.

No, sir.

That's magnanimous of you, and I'm sure it's for the best. Now, Perry, what led you to think that the Indians could be attacked as you did?

Sir, that Chapman—

Did Mr. Chapman say anything with reference to Joseph's strength?

No, sir; he just went ahead and—

How well do you know him?

I might have seen him around the fort once or twice—

And his wife?

General, I never saw her. From what that Mr. Ayers remarked to me, most all the white people are pretty disgusted at her.

For what?

For being—what she is. Anyhow, I hear he sent her back to her reservation.

All right. Now, once the battle started, why didn't you kill more Nez Perces?

Sir, they—

Did you kill any?

We must have done, sir.

I understand that some breechblocks failed to close during the Custer fight.

Yessir, so I've heard . . .

Did you observe any such problem with your Springfields?

No, sir, although perhaps the dust—

Did the breechblocks close or not?

Yes they did, sir. But the men kind of froze up—

Perry, a few more may yet come in from that cañon. Sergeant McCarthy for example is a miracle of resourceful survival. But even if we're lucky enough to deduct, let's say, three from those thirty-four, we must still add the more than twenty civilians on Camas Prairie, White Bird Creek and vicinity.

Murdered, sir. By that—

Yes. Speaking of Mr. Joe, did you see him at the battle?

No, sir. Theller and I had intended to bag him for you—

Then whom did you see?

Well, that Ollicut was fiendishly active, sir; he must have done for half a dozen of our boys. I didn't lay eyes on Toohhoolhoolzote. My GOD, the reds were just everywhere! And every buck had a squaw waiting on him with three fresh horses—

What about Looking-Glass?

Frankly, sir, I kept watching for the glint of the sun on that tin mirror of his, but I never discovered him or any of his bucks. My guess is that he's lying low on his reservation. If Whipple had been there he might have recognized more of 'em. But as for Chief Joseph, whatever Chapman will tell you's a lie. And Joseph's a—

He must be their mastermind.

Yessir.

Isn't he?

I—

At the council he demeaned himself well, for the most part.

Yessir, once we got Toohhoolhoolzote out of the way.

That's right, Perry. He appeared suggestible. And now the newspapers begin to call him *The Red Napoleon.*

I'd say a red devil, sir.

You know, it's strangely difficult to believe there was so much evil in Joseph's heart, but we have now seen his deeds. Don't worry, Perry. They may have won a battle; they may win one or two others; but do you seriously entertain the idea that a tribe of Indians can whip the United States?

No, sir.

Stay a moment. Wilkinson!

Here I am, general.

Are you prepared to take dictation? No, not the one to General Sherman. This is for Portland. Page two. That's correct. Now write: *Unfortunately, the assault was not successful. The Indians turned the left flank of the command. I have only high commendation for the conduct of Colonel Perry and his officers for an effort that deserved better results.*

Sir, I—

That's all, Perry. Wilkinson, here's a private letter, also to Portland.

All right, general.

Any news of my son?

The Twenty-first will release him to you imminently, sir.

And did you see Mrs. Theller to-day?

No, sir.

Get the boys to carry a barrel of water over there, so she's not obliged to come out until she wishes.

Yessir.

Has Major Mason arrived?

Yessir.

Send him in. O, good morning, Mason. Please sit down. How are you to-day?

Fit and ready to fight, sir.

Good. Now, Mason, you're an experienced Indian fighter. In confidence, did you expect Perry to fail?

Not at all, sir. He showed tremendous zeal against the Modocs—

What about Trimble?

The same, general. He personally took Captain Jack prisoner. Considerable initiative—

Then why were they unable to subdue Joseph's Indians?

Incoherent strategy, sir! Fatigue, bad marksmanship, unauthorized movements by the volunteers. I understand that the Mount Idaho bunch persuaded Perry to hold back our Nez Perce scouts, because—

What's the lesson to be learned?

General, I believe that to fight savages successfully, one of two things must be done—either the savages must be divided into hostile bands and made to fight each other, or the civilized soldier must be trained down as closely as possible to the level of the savage. We don't have time to train down our troops, so we'll need Indians.

As usual! Have you finished raising your scouts?

Yessir. James Reuben's lined up his best Nez Perce bucks, all good Christians with families here on the reservation.

He's Joseph's nephew or something.

Well, yessir; he's married to Joseph's sister. But Mr. Monteith guarantees his loyalty.

I want some Bannocks. They despise all Nez Perces, I understand.

Yessir. And for Umatillas I can—

Can you sum up Ad Chapman?

Well, general, Perry's seen him around—

Perry called him a liar.

General, I don't know what to—

Thanks, Mason. Be reminded that the press will be observing us. Don't be surprised to find yourself mentioned, perhaps unfavorably. Furthermore, I'll have you know in confidence that General Sherman himself will be overseeing this campaign. You may inform Sladen, but nobody else for now.

Yessir. So whenever General Sheridan—

He'll bear me a grudge, of course. He thinks I've gone over his head.

General, you can count on my loyalty in this.

Thanks. That's it.

Good-bye then, general.

> *Wakesh nun pakilauitin*
> JEHOVAN'M *yiyauki*—

Wilkinson, have you seen Mrs. Theller yet?

No, sir. Her curtains are still down.

I promised to give her husband a hero's grave—

SO THIS WAS JOSEPH'S PLAN
JUNE 18–22

1

*S*o this was Joseph's plan, gentlemen—to start the war through a series of outrages, in the usual style, and thereby call out our troops from Lapwai before we could reënforce them from distant points, and finally to prepare his ambuscade. The most vital thing now is to contain him before he can stir up his friends. All of us in this service have experience with Indian rages. The Nez Perces still refuse to believe their hour's over. It's our task to prove the fact to them. Questions?

Sir, if we have a clean shot—

Not Joseph, certainly. Nor Ollicut. At present we need them to persuade their people to surrender. Any man who kills wantonly will be court-martialed. Prisoners will receive a fair trial, just as the Modoc murderers did. Colonel Perry was there, and so was Major Mason. They can tell you how it's done.

What about Toohhoolhoolzote, general?

A large, thick-necked, obstinate old savage of the worst type,
    and a meteor destined to fall and fail into obscurest darkness, GOD have
    mercy even upon *him*.

He violated his parole.

Yes, sir.

But if he gives himself up, he's a prisoner of war, and you know that quite well. The same goes for all of them, and especially the chiefs. Enough of this.

General?

Yes, Trimble, what is it?

With respect, sir, we ought to be chasing Joseph right now! I'll more than gladly ride—

And be ambushed all over again? By Friday, GOD willing, Companies "L" and

"E" will be here. Remember, that's a march of more than two hundred miles in six days! We can't ask more of them. We'll have five companies of the Twenty-first, and a company of the Fourth Artillery—Lieutenant Wilkinson, isn't that Miller's?

Right, sir. Company "E," armed as infantry—

Thank you. That ought to raise our effective strength above two hundred. Moreover, the friendly Indians have proposed to drive in their pony-herds, so that we can all ride. What is it now, Pollock?

General, the ponies are Indian trained, and will always go to their friends.

That may be so, but at last, using the ponies, we will wear Joseph out.

Yes, sir.

Gentlemen, I'm taking the field in person. Major Mason here will be my chief of staff. And Captain Whipple has wintered with Joseph's Indians, so he'll be well acquainted with their tricks. As for Captain Winters, I've heard the greatest reports of him. Their companies will be a blessing to us. Believe me, we'll sally as soon as it's convenient. Now, from the direction that Joseph's Indians have chosen, I see the necessity of interposing some forces at once between them and the Weisser Indians. Major Green will organize a force at Boise City and deploy it on the Weisser River. I'll bring Bendire's First Cavalry from Harney . . .

and

Gentlemen, there's no occasion for panic. Bull Run was worse than this.

2

You over there from Mount Idaho—Mr. Randall, I believe?

That's right, general. I'm actually captain of these volunteers. Now, me and Lew Wilmot have made ourselves a plan—

Are you a captain in the United States Army?

I wouldn't say that.

Then what kind of captain are you?

A captain by acclamation.

Mr. Randall, I expect you and all the volunteers to put yourselves under Army discipline for the duration of this campaign. No more outrages against peaceful Indians.

Now, looky here, General Howard, it's actually *the Indians* who—

I'm not hearing respect in your tone. You know as well as I that the conduct of your settlers has irritated the Indians. If you'd behaved like Christians, we could have gotten them onto the reservation without any violence—

So let's take care of 'em now.

Be silent. Since my earlier remarks seem to have been lost on you, I'll restate them: Now that Joseph has begun his foray, Indians all along the Columbia may give him sympathy and help. To prevent this, Mr. Randall, I have given and will give certain orders. You will follow *all* my orders or I will put you under arrest. Now sit down and be quiet. Colonel Perry, keep an eye on this man for the rest of this conference.

Yes, sir,

the appeal in Perry's eyes reflecting what I saw in that young, young private at Chancellorsville who hoped *I* could save him—shot through both lungs, and panicking as he suffocated—

Now he's recovering himself, thank GOD,

while in fact Perry, palpably expressionless, contrasts his present commander with General Crook, who never would have debased himself with any such council of war:

When old Crook is doping out what to do, he strides past the camp perimeter, sets down his rife, crosses his knees, wraps his arms about his legs, and rubs his nose; then he leaps onto his horse and we follow. *He'd* tell us how it's done, O yes by fucking JESUS!

Furthermore, gentlemen, I call to your attention that Joseph's worst outrages against the Salmon River people were stimulated, in part, by ardent spirits. Anyone who makes an Indian drunk sows the whirlwind. Moreover, I've been told that some volunteers were intoxicated at White Bird Cañon. Can everyone draw that lesson?

But, general—

No? Then here it is: *There will be no liquor whatsoever on this campaign.* Do you all understand me now?

Yessir.

Good. As I was saying, we will soon be in charge of an undetermined number of Kamiah people. Chief Lawyer's bringing in the missionaries, sub-agents and other civilians. I'll expect you to be on your good behavior when they arrive. There may be Indians in their train, because at present our friendly Nez Perces at Kamiah are a little inclined to panic. No matter what your feelings toward Indians may be, I'll tolerate absolutely no highhandedness toward those people. Gentlemen, do I have your assent?

Yessir.

Don't you all understand that once we move out on Joseph's trail, it would substantially annoy us if the Indians around Lapwai should rise up?

Yessir.

Father Cataldo says his Injuns are all quiet up on Hangman Creek—

Colonel Sully, you'll remain in charge here.

Yessir.

Why that look, colonel?

General, I'm a proven Indian fighter—

And a soldier under orders. Now, Captain Pollock, what's your question?

Well, general, I believe we ought to ask Mr. West, Mr. Chapman and men of that stripe what they've heard. From them being half-breeds and *squaw men* and running with Indians all the time, they ought to know whether the other Indians mean devilment or not.

All right. Where's Mr. West?

                Probably playin' kiss-and-tell with his d——d Indians—

Anybody know where he might be? All right, Mr. Randall, be useful and bring him in.

Right away, general.

Now, Mr. Chapman as I understood it actually fired on our Indians under flag of truce at White Bird. Is that so?

No, sir! Chapman's on our side. Joseph's bucks attacked us first. And if anybody's told you different, general, why, that's a GODD——d lie.

Excuse me, gentlemen. Captain Jocelyn, would you please step outside with me for a moment?

Sure will, general.

Now, captain, this is the first such language I've heard since arriving here, and I do not care to hear more.

All right, sir.

                Fuck this shiteating niggerloving general and the
                whole GODD——d fucking brass-mounted Army
                and all these sourmouthed Christian monkeys.

Were you present at White Bird Cañon?

No, sir,

                and you weren't either, you one-armed holy roller.
                And you sure weren't where you were supposed to
                be at Chancellorsville.

So you're defending Mr. Chapman by hearsay.

But, general, I know for a fact—

Thank you, captain. Let's get back to it. Now, Lieutenant Fletcher, could you unroll the map over here?

Yes, sir.

Thank you.

We will run them down until they die or go on the reservation. That is all I need to tell you.

GRACE'S BIRTHDAY
JUNE 22

*W*ell, well; to-morrow always *does* come.

That's right, general.

Lieutenant Wood will be catching up with us any day now. Although his leave came through, he decided not to stay in Alaska.

That's no surprise to me, sir. Once he heard about Mr. Joe's doings, he wouldn't abandon us.

You're right about that. He's a loyal young man, and he'll distinguish himself, GOD willing.

Yes, sir.

As you have, my friend.

Thanks, general. I aim to do my best.

How sick do you suppose Fletch is?

O, he's better, sir. Says he can hardly wait to ride out—

Does he still pray?

Absolutely, sir, in his own fashion, even if he's not a perfect churchgoer. I respect him very much.

Wilkinson, what's your opinion of Father Cataldo?

I'd call him effective in his sphere, sir.

Well put. It will be tragic if he fails to persuade his flock to remain on the right side of Uncle Sam.

If they forget themselves, sir, we can sure take care of them.

Day and night I've been asking OUR LORD for a speedy and humane victory over our enemies.

Yessir.

In your opinion, what's the mood in this fort?

I'd say we're all eager to bring Joseph down, sir.

Yes. How long has Agent Monteith been standing out there?

A good quarter-hour, sir.

Who's with him?

An Indian, sir. I don't believe I've laid eyes on him before—

Well, I guess we'd better ask them in, don't you think?

Right away, sir.

Ah, good evening, general! We're all of us very, very eager to cheer you on.

Is that a compliment, sir?

General, please don't take it any other way! It's only that I do suspect that

General Sherman would prefer—

Mr. Monteith, I'll thank you to leave the matter of General Sherman's preferences to General Sherman.— Just a moment. Wagons and teams in running order, Sladen?

Yessir. I checked every muleteer—

That's all. Now, Mr. Monteith, who is this with you?

If you remember, general, you requested my guidance in the matter of Indian scouts. This is Umatilla Jim, and he comes very, very highly recommended. I mean, our Nez Perces may act on conflicted interests—

Have a seat, Mr. Monteith. Wilkinson, would you be so kind as to bring a chair for our Indian?

Right away, sir.

Well?

Thanks, general. Now, I imagine you'll be needing to know about Jim's antecedents—

I believe I'd asked you to furnish me with treaty Nez Perces, not with Indians of other tribes. And really you should have conducted this business with Major Mason; he's in charge of personnel. Thanks, Wilkinson. Do sit down, Jim.

Thanks, general.

Jim, how do you feel about this war?

I don't have much of an opinion.

Sir, excuse me but I see Colonel Perry arriving together with Captain Randall. Looks like they're disagreeing.

Could you detain them for an instant?

Absolutely, sir.

Now, general, getting back to Jim—

Mr. Monteith, I have five minutes. Please do remain seated, and let me chat with Jim,

> Monteith staring pale and unkempt at me like a moth-eaten revenant, the brightest thing about him being the chain of his pocket-watch, which loops down from his breast-pocket, his shoulders slumping as steeply as the dark gables of an old New England roof. To undercut his own favorite, James Reuben—what on earth is he about?

So, Jim, from your nickname I take it you're a Umatilla.

That's right, general.

Why do you want to be a scout?

They said there'd be good wages—

Good wages, *sir.*

That's all right, Monteith. He's not yet mustered in. Now, Jim, you do know that you'll need to prove yourself to Major Mason, and if you're acceptable to him, you can take the oath—

I understand, general.

Jim, are you a Christian?

If you want me to be, general.

Pretty good answer! In fact it would please me to see you in church. Now, how familiar are you with Joseph?

I know him a bit. Not too good, general, but a little bit. You see, my wife is related to his cousin.

He certainly stole a march on us this time! Is there anything about him it would help me to know?

I'll hunt him down the best I can for you, general. And I can ride without no saddle—

All right. I assume you've been to Wallowa?

I sure have, general.

A pretty valley, don't you think?

It's all right. Plenty of bunchgrass there around Imnaha. Feed a lot of cows and horses . . .

And a lake.

Real good water, general.

You know, back where I hail from we also have a very fine clear lake. White perch, black bass, pickerel—a rewarding locale for angling . . .

Yessir.

Well, well, Jim. So you like it there at Wallowa?

Chief Joseph sure does.

But he wasn't born there, so it's beyond me why he's hung onto it so obstinately.

Maybe since Old Joseph is buried by the lake—

Well, we certainly could have removed his father's remains to the reservation. It's a fairly common practice in the United States.

I don't know about that.

But wasn't Joseph born right here at Lapwai, before Old Joseph turned apostate?

Answer the general, Jim.

I think he wasn't.

Where was he born, then? inquires Cut Arm more sharply, ignorant that beyond Wallowa the world ends in seven blue knives, with rivers between them

and that after Joseph's defeat there will be a road, and cows on that road

(Hell's Cañon sickening us at the edge of our sight);

there will be a straight fence along the ridgetop, with the cañon off the edge.

Umatilla Jim's soul, conveyed to Wallowa by the general's question, now speeds north, beyond where the world ends:

the wide yellow hills charred in patches by forest fires, solitary trees remaining here and there

and as he sadly gazes into the general's face (Agent Monteith frowning as if in wonder), Jim's neckerchief tightens around his throat, his mouth curves gently down, his greying, greasy braids shine upon his breast, half hiding the Centennial medal which Tsépmin told him was money, his eyes commence to close a trifle and his mind rushes through

a forested cañon whose sides are grey with dying grass; the forest snakes green along the river bottom; this cañon opens up into a valley of yellow grass and green trees, with rocks bursting out
and finds again (for a good scout finds everything he's ever seen before)
the bush-topped, grasshaired chimney of rock:

a dark phallus rising out of its pubis of bushes; where it widens, it hides, amidst saplings, raspberries, golden grass and poison oak; and below all this, the Grande Ronde runs brown between grey stones, vanishing into the darkness between trees.

In a cave, general. That's what they say.

Have you seen it?

Sure.

Jim, you can step outside now.

All right, general.

Mr. Monteith, do you trust this fellow not to pick fights with my Nez Perce scouts?

I do, general—*honest Injun!*

Ha—ha—ha! You're a droll one. All right. Thanks for your trouble. Please walk him over to Major Mason to get mustered in. Lieutenant Wilkinson and I have more business ahead of us, so is there anything else?

General, I'd advise you to—

Generals rarely take advice from civilians, Agent Monteith. And now, a very tranquil night to you. Would you show him out, Wilkinson?

Well, then, general, good night.

Now what about Perry and Randall?

Just a personal difference between them, sir. They're on the square now.

You're a considerate friend to me, Wilkinson, and I'll never forget it. O, and here's a private letter to Portland.

I'll make sure it goes out before we ride away, sir.

You see, Wilkinson, it's Grace's birthday. Can you believe it? She was born exactly twenty years ago to-day. At that time I was in Florida, removing the Seminoles. Mrs. Howard wrote me from Leeds—

Miss Howard is a fine young lady, general. Many happy returns to her!

Wood used to stop by. He's almost a brother to her.

Yessir, I know he admires her talent for piano . . .

He's talented himself. Have you seen his sketches?

Yessir.

Entre nous, my son Guy may be a trifle jealous of him, I fear.

Yessir.

Some suitor will propose any day now. Her youth's flying by, it seems—

She's a belle, sir,

> remembering how the last time that the Howards invited him for
> dinner—

> > certainly an agreeable fireside:

> > > Sherman's visiting card uppermost in that brass receiver from
> > > Eugene Jaccard's: genuine quality! Someday I'll own one of
> > > sterling silver!

> > > > (frankly, I would rather pass an evening with these peo-
> > > > ple than in the household of my own intended whose
> > > > mother gives me the screaming willies)—

Grace was present with Chauncey,

> who is everything I could have wished for in my own younger
> brother,

while Guy was away on duty with the Twelfth, and the innocuous James
likewise absent; John G. said prayers very prettily (a lively, likely child!),
and then they all toasted the United States, raising their glasses of root
beer, *the national temperance drink.* The general told the same joke as
always, the one about the three horses and the two little sheep; on the
mantlepiece, in a barely tarnished brass frame, he remained young,
moody and handsome in his Brady studio portrait, glowering palely
away, with his arms folded on his breast—yes, he still had both of them—
and his sword riding at his hip. Harry and Bessie sat up straight and
continued on their good behavior, while Grace, to tell the truth, appeared
formidable in her stiff wide petticoats, with her hair twisted up tight,
thanks to goodness knows how many pins. She kept smiling brighteyed,
with a pearl necklace taut around her long white neck; until Wilkinson,
who of course must be counted the best observer in and of the general's
circle, stared away from her. He had always felt more at his ease with Mrs.
Howard than with this immaculately cared for young lady, politely bred
though she was—and this might have constituted the very stress point;
he kept battling off a hovering perverse notion, which he naturally concealed, although perhaps not utterly, at least not from Mrs. Howard's
mild eyes, to reach out and with his forefinger simply *touch* Grace's black
velvet throat-band, where her little cross was fastened,

> although she in no way tempted me and never would, even if I
> didn't have Sallie's promise

> > (for Wilkinson admits, if only to himself, that he has made
> > certain mistakes with Grace, not least in openly smiling at

her ludicrous pretension to understand her father's affairs, never mind that he is happy to grant her, at least at first sight, the appearance of a GODfearing heart),

and her mouth is domineering, although she is certainly an extremely accomplished young lady.

Thank you for saying so. I wish I'd had more leisure to enjoy her childhood. O, such a pretty little sprite she used to be when she ran about in a nightdress and her hair unpinned! When you have children of your own, you'll see . . .

Yessir. Not many men have sacrificed as much as you and still continued on in the service—

Kindly said, if exaggerated. There's Sladen, for instance. And during the war there were so many who—am I getting maudlin, Wilkinson?

Of course not, general.

I got her a copy of Martine's *Sensible Letter-Writer.* A real standby!

I'm sure she'll be grateful, sir.

Well, Lizzie must have wrapped it for her—

Of course Miss Howard understands—

O, I don't know how much she understands.

Sir, I wouldn't take it to heart—

No,

recollecting how Wood used to sing along when she played the piano. That young man had been an exceptionally graceful dancer ever since West Point, they said, and at Camp Bidwell he used to attend every ball with the ranchers' daughters

(Wilkinson informs me he dances *the German* most gracefully

although how would *he* know?)—

o, is it "Tattoo" already? I'd better send for Mason . . .

and little Bessie clapping her hands in time, Lizzie knitting by the fire, smiling over her daughter and that young man and possibly half wishing that he would fall out with his Nanny Smith

while behind the residence of Agent Monteith our good treaty Indians keep singing:

Wakesh nun pakilauitin

JEHOVAN'M yiyauki—

but what on Earth has Lizzie got against Wilkinson? Well, I confess he can appear a trifle sour, but he's brave and honest, not to mention a true Christian, whereas Wood . . .

I don't suppose that Gracie was ever interested in him, not that it matters now.

Does Wood lie to me about his faith or lack of it?

Wilkinson informs me that he declined to sing hymns at last year's jamboree.

Someday I should take her at least as far as The Dalles. She's so innocent of realities. But her mother isn't, not anymore. Poor Lizzie—

If Joseph gets me, what will become of my family? Lizzie insists she will never remarry. But Grace has good metal in her, and JEHOVAH will provide. Guy's got force of character. Too bad he judges so harshly. If he gets promoted a pay grade or two, then

Wakesh nun pakilauitin
JEHOVAN'M yiyauki,

and if General Sherman wished it, or for that matter the President, Congress could issue an appropriation for my outstanding lawyer fees; otherwise the estate will be eaten up. Well, the children will surely save Lizzie from the poorhouse.

Come to think of it, why shouldn't Joseph be plotting to assassinate me at this very instant? His Cayuse relations planned their murder of the Whitmans with the farsighted treachery of Judases! But who among Lapwai's good Indians would carry it out?— This Umatilla Jim, for all I know . . . although I must confess I like him.— Well, it's in the LORD's hands (and might be a relief). Moreover, for all Joseph's now proven dissimulating ingenuity,

O, those brilliantly noncommittal eyes of his!

—evil's fearful power—

and his Dreamer's peak of hair, his shoulder-length braids, and those eight necklaces around his handsome throat (might each strand bear its own meaning? I should ask),

I consider him incompetent to execute any such deed from afar. In battle, of course, all is possible:

Gettysburg

Chancellorsville

Antietam

(where Wilkinson got his wound)

Fair Oaks

(where I got mine)

Bull Run

and Little Big Horn: Mrs. Custer folding her hands in her lap at the memorial service, gazing down and away from us, her dark duster fastened up to her throat, her high cheekbones and dark eyes almost squawlike—implacable woman!—but shouldn't that be a virtue of sorts in an Army wife?

She never replied to Lizzie's letter of condolence. Disdain or prostration? LORD, I must push away such thoughts! She received too many letters and too much grief.

But I do feel sad on Lizzie's account.

Sheridan informed me that she longs to be at Sitting Bull's hanging. Should Joseph kill me and should she seek to console Lizzie by saying: Dearie, we'll sit together in the front row when Joseph dances at a rope's end . . .

I'd almost like to see that myself!

Poor Custer! But I must pray for his murderers—and for his widow

and Mrs. Theller, who I fear will not soon submit to her loss

(I wouldn't like to be the next Indian she meets!)

and Mrs. FitzGerald, who's now terrified I'll send her husband into the field, as of course I must

(I'd better look in on her this evening)

and Lizzie,

who can take care of herself no matter how blue she feels.

Anyhow, all that's up to Him *Who knoweth all things.* To think that Marcus Gilbert closed his eyes but last year, eighty-five years old, having served in the War of 1812!— and meanwhile the Gilbert family, so Rowland tells me, has nearly died out in Leeds, although they were prominent among the original settlers; why that should be passeth understanding; praised be His Mysteries, *Amen.* Leeds! I don't suppose I'll ever again live there

where the light comes through the clouds to strike Androscoggin Lake

(how I remember the long golden streaks on the lake

and then the light of the ice

and the fields rich and creamy with snow!).

And shall I too live to eighty-five, or shall I die of arrow or bullet next week in some Idaho cañon?

But the children, especially Chauncey—no, actually, Gracie's the one who

rides so elegantly. I wonder if she ever forgave me for not buying that brown hackney? I didn't want her to worry about my debts, so she must have thought me simply *mean.* For a fact, she deserves a better horse than the bay.

Guy will look after her, if he's spared, and so will

OUR FATHER Who
and Joseph's perpetually downturned mouth—
why does he make that expression?
—strangely like Custer: coarse-faced, big-nosed, staring
out from under his big dark slouch hat, stubble on his lip
and chin, shadows on his chin; long curly hair down the
back of his neck; he could almost be a Mexican miner.—
Dearest, he's had a very hard life, Lizzie whispered in my
ear.— And a hard death! But he died gloriously for Government and country; he's surely in Heaven—
art in Heaven
Libbie Custer with her hands in her lap
hallowed be Thy Name
and Lizzie: Dearest, if you died I don't know what I'd do.
Please don't ever. Promise me.
Thy Kingdom come:
She can care for herself.
Wilkinson behaves well, as if he weren't afraid. A stellar
product of the artillery branch! He has good hope of
Heaven.
I should have written a letter to Gracie.
There's still time.
If I could take Lizzie back to Saratoga Springs and sit on the hotel porch
drinking a tumbler of Congress water, she'd
Wilkinson looks tired! Why do the young so often ex-
perience more difficulties in that department? Well, it
can't be helped.
He's not afraid, is he?
Wakesh nun pakilauitin
JEHOVAN'M yiyauki—
Saratoga can't compare to Niagara Falls.
And Lizzie in her bathing-dress at Atlantic City, a long time
ago (I don't suppose we'll ever again
)
Now. Has Lieutenant Bomus completed his report?
Yessir. All the trousers were already distributed. And it's just as you thought;
the 1876-issue overcoats never came in, not that we'll require them in this weather!
Anyhow, the usual holdup at Leavenworth—
Have you seen them?
No, sir.
Well, the cape is longer, and there are fewer buttons. Sherman is enamored.
Not very different from previous issue, actually. If you'd like one, I'll bring it up
the next time I steam up from Portland.

Thanks, general; you're very thoughtful.

What's our current strength?

A total force of two hundred and twenty-seven effectives, sir, verified by Major Mason. And when we pick up Perry's survivors at Grangeville—

Well, it'll have to do.

Thy will be done

Sir, we'll have Joseph whipped in two weeks at the outside.

No doubt.

Sir, why can't we strike him with more troops?

I *cannot* safely diminish Fort Lapwai as long as Joseph threatens Kamiah. You ought to see that, Wilkinson! We'll raise two additional companies to occupy him until we can concentrate our forces. General Sherman has agreed to transship us a contingent of troops from the South . . .

General—

You realize, Wilkinson, what this means—the defeat of Emancipation. Once the Government has withdrawn to completion, the former masters will be able to disenfranchise the freedmen—

I'm very sorry, sir.

Well, such is necessity. Is your question answered?

Yessir. The negroes will be in my prayers—

Good. And perhaps even our glowering Mr. Randall will be of help against Joseph, if he's not confined in the guardhouse by then.

Let's hope he isn't, sir.

What's your opinion of him?

Nothing but a bruiser, sir.

And this Umatilla Jim?

Seems all right to me, sir.

I'll bet Monteith would call him *a straight arrow*—

You slay me, sir.

Before you retire to-night, will you please confirm that he's on the recruiting return?

Absolutely, sir.

You see, Wilkinson, since the Indians of Malheur Agency are the least civilized of any, we can't reduce Harney's strength below two companies. Captain Paige has begun to organize more volunteers at Walla-Walla—

That's all right, then, sir.

You know Harney, don't you?

A real American, sir. He won't let you down.

And Paige is a friend of Ad Chapman's.

Well, sir, that may be so, but unlike him, Captain Paige is no *squaw man*.

Are you intimating that Mr. Chapman bears watching?

It's hard to know what to make of him, sir. Mighty fine horses he breeds—

Is it his choice of spouse which troubles you?

Sir, if I may ask, what do *you* think about it?

What would you have me think, Wilkinson?

Sir, you have a bigger heart than most men. The way it seems to several of us, a man who loves an Indian must be an Indian lover, so who's he going to love when an Indian war breaks out?

JESUS said, *love thy neighbor as thyself.*

Yessir.

I know you're with me on that, Wilkinson, although it may sound ludicrous to our less religious soldiers. At any rate . . .

Yessir.

Naturally, a civilized white man is lowered in many respects by marrying an uncivilized Indian woman; still, many an Indian woman married to a white man has borne him worthy children.

Yessir. Mr. West for example is certainly a decent enough half-breed—

Enough on this. You distrust Mr. Chapman,
> who for what it's worth (good instincts, Wilkinson!) reminds me of one of those Wayne people who sell cattle and sheep to Boston; Father always used to say there was something sharp about them; Chapman's got that sort of face—
>> although not exactly, for the Wayne people guard themselves, hoping to be mistaken for boulders, while he wallows in his enjoyment: a galloping case of that Western disease, *the "thrills."*

Perry insists that he definitely fired the first shot at White Bird Cañon.

Then he must have done, sir.

So Captain Jocelyn lied to me.

Yessir.

Why?

He's afraid we might be soft on the Indians.

And what's your feeling about that?

I feel you'll be fair and generous as always, sir.

Thank you.

And blot this rebellion out—

Of course.

Sir, if that bit about Chapman appears in Perry's report, will the Government take it out on us?

It won't be in the report. I've spoken with Major Mason.

I'm glad of that on Perry's account, sir,
> and still believe the general—poor haunted old one-armed man!—has been far too lenient with Perry and should have sent him to be court-martialed. If only I could have been in charge at White Bird Cañon! Perry does not comprehend how to deploy his men and should probably be removed from command. When will he stop lying to protect himself? To think he will be leading a share of the column to-morrow! All the same—

Yes. Have you written to your parents?

Well, sir, I've made the time, but—

Your father's health is failing, I believe.

My sisters are keeping him comfortable, sir.

Is he using laudanum?

Yessir. The doctor says it's rallied him wonderfully.

A miraculous medicine! I took it after my amputation. Every night at bedtime, four or five drops, depending on the pain, and then I'd drift straight off! But Mrs. Howard said it made me snore, so I gave it up.

Yessir. Some people say it's hard to stop.

I didn't find it so.

> Is he getting ill? He looks pale. Perhaps it's merely the excitement. But he's been on Indian service before. I should let him rest—

Now, Wilkinson, what about your Sallie with the dark curls?

I did write her, sir. Thanks for asking.

Don't forget your parents to-night.

Sir, I promise.

That procedure's always wisest for a soldier. Then he can meet Fate without any clutter in his heart—

Yessir.

Come to think of it, I wish I could find time to drop a line to my brother Charley.

Shall I take dictation now, sir?

No, no. You wouldn't believe how brave he was in the Secession War! We were both wounded on the same day. He was hit first. Seeing him laughing and joking all covered in blood, well, I felt proud to be his brother. Then he was wounded again at Fredericksburg—

I've heard that you were pretty tough yourself, sir.

Why don't you go lie down, Wilkinson? You look unwell.

Not at all, sir.

Getting late . . . We should all turn in. O, but how pleasant it is here
> (the murmurs of officers enjoying one last cool evening on Perry's front porch, although of course the occasion must be duller without Mrs. Perry and Mrs. Theller) . . .

How are your brothers?

Very well indeed, sir.

I suspect you'd like Charley boy, not that he'll ever come West. He's got "sand" in him—a real man! Wonder what he's about nowadays. And it's actually been some months since we've heard from Rowland. Well, well. Probably Mrs. Howard is keeping his letter for me right now in Portland.

She's an iron lady, sir—

Thank you. Truehearted—

Yessir.

Let's step out a moment, shall we? Look at Mars!

Yessir. And there's Arcturus, I believe—

> whose sight suddenly and inexplicably fills the general with an almost ruthless lust to ken the unknown mountains and rivers of what Mr. Chapman has called *this wrinkled country*—as if we, not Joseph, sought escape! If so, from what or whom? Our hearts are good:

We've seen a lot of country together, Wilkinson.

Yessir. Sometimes I think back on Pasqual's camp at Yuma—

Has it already been five years?

Yes, sir. And all his Indians giving their whoop when we sat down on those funny three-legged stools!

Soon we'll gain our opportunity to compare Pasqual's operatic skills with Joseph's.

Yessir. I don't know whose Indians can yell the loudest, but when it comes to fashion, Mr. Joe wins. Quite the dapper villain! And what a dirty, raggedy old shirt Pasqual had—

But he certainly put on the airs of a king, didn't he?

That he did, sir.

I must admit that he behaved nobly in defeat. I wonder if those Yumas will ever give trouble again . . .

But Wilkinson (who ordinarily prefers judgments to fancies) has begun just this once, as if he intuits the possibility of a longish campaign, to sink into himself, remembering from that mission of his general's into the pale red and tan borderlands a certain handsome young squaw who squatted over a sagebrush fire, boiling roots in an old pot. General Crook having ejected him from the council proceeding for proselytizing, Wilkinson strode away, low in spirits (especially on the poor general's account), seeking a tranquil spot to peruse his pocket Testament, or write a letter to Sallie, or, if nothing better could be done, eavesdrop on the Indians for his commander's sake, when this surprisingly agreeable distraction supervened. (As a rule, Wilkinson was invulnerable to enticements.) Seeing how he gazed upon her, she rose apprehensively, nicely decked out in silver earrings, beaded moccasins and a dirty cotton dress—well, it was her face that allured him most of all. In her Indian way she appeared nearly perfect in his sight, so that, having already been thrown off his game by the unexpected holiday, he halfway imagined that customary rules relaxed themselves, not that he of all people ever intended anything more vicious than a flirtation. Perhaps it was merely that she wasn't Sallie, although it could have been something about her Indian eyes. He sought to introduce himself, but she pulled her shawl over her face, gazing down at the red dirt between her feet. It was hot, and he began to sweat as he squinted out beneath his hat-brim at the damsel of his ever so uncharacteristic desire, the mountains half erased by the dusty brown air. She walked away. An elderly squaw was chuckling. He remembered two small boys, heavy-featured like negroes, throwing pebbles into the Colorado River . . .

On earth as it is in Heaven.

Good night, Wilkinson. GOD bless you!

And you, general. I predict that Pasqual's war-whoop will prove more impressive than Joseph's—

ALASKA SOUNDS FINE AND COOL
JUNE 22–23

1

*L*ooks like fine ranching land, general.

Joseph called it a good country, didn't he?

Guess he was right about that, sir. When do you think we'll reach the front?

LORD knows where it is, Fletch. But Joseph must be drunk with blood. It may be simpler than we imagine to catch him—

I hope so, sir.

And after you've checked out Slate Creek, Mr. Reuben, then ride on back as soon as you can. Here's a pass, valid two days, but you'd d——n well better be back by to-morrow morning.

All right, captain.

Take Jim with you. Old George and Captain John will stay with us.

Umatilla Jim, sir?

Yep. General's orders. Now, you two ride for the Salmon River doublequick.

But the longest-range rifles they must have—

How do you know?

Because I asked Mr. West, and because Captain Trimble told me about that monster buffalo gun they were murdering our boys with at White Bird Cañon, although I do remember that last year at Little Big Horn they had no better than—

Well, that was last year. Who the hell knows what Injuns have this year?

They sure won't have Gatlings.

That would be a sight. Anyhow, your Mr. West is nothing better than a breed, so whatever he says about rifles is—

—stationed in Wallowa.

Yessir, I should think so.

Lieutenant Wood, welcome back to the Twenty-first!
Thanks, captain. It's been awhile—
How's your fever?
I don't mind it, sir.
Don't neglect it. It'll be a disappointment to all of us if you're too ill to play a significant part.
No fear of that, general!
I just saw Doctor Alexander yonder. Why don't you ask for a dose of quinine?
Yessir.
Wilkinson's looking more run down to-day. Is he all right?
Can't speak for him, sir.
All right. How's Wood managing?
Shall I fetch him, sir?
Please do.
Right away, sir.

Doc, you ever ride the Old Chisholm Trail?
Well, laddie, of *course* I did.
You've been practically everywhere, is that so?
Something like that.
Where do you think we're off to now?
Why, to give Mr. Joe a hole in the ground!

Their entire forces can't exceed two hundred bucks, unless Smohallie . . .
But those three devils in the red blankets must have done for twenty good men!
We'll pay 'em back for sure!

Wood, it's fine to see you back. No time to greet you at Lapwai. How was Sitka?
Very exotic, general. And three days ago I looked in on Mrs. Howard—
Goodhearted of you. She's well?
Yessir.
Was Mrs. Perry in evidence?
Yessir; she gave me a letter for her husband. Very sad and nervous, I should say. And here's a note to you from Mrs. Howard.
Thanks. How was Grace?
Anticipating her party—
All right. Now, I think you know how bad this is.
I do, general. What a tragedy at White Bird Cañon—
The general pats his shoulder, smiling

more or less as I must have done the first time I gazed on my arm-stump—since Charley and the men were there I knew to smile and make light of it, after Charley's fashion—what practice I've gained smiling at bad news!

Fifty volunteers have arrived from the Columbia country.

> Says who?
>
> Blackie read it in the paper.
>
> Then where are they?

as Chapman canters up the line on his racing-horse, sweating and chewing, smirking like a whist fiend punching his extra tricks on the tally card

> (the general on a stolid brown gelding named Elmo)

—while Wood, wiping his forehead, cocks his handsome face, his eyes only partially shaded by the campaign cap. To-morrow he'll be sunburned like us.

We'll stop there and lay them to rest.

Yessir.

You weren't close pals with Theller, were you?

> which unearths that evening behind Lynch's blacksmith shop in Walla Walla, and then that tent in Lewiston—dear GOD, please don't ever let the general, never,
>
> or Nanny—especially not her! But how could she?

I knew him somewhat, general. But since I don't play cards—

That's right. How's civilian morale on the coast?

Well, sir, in Astoria they were all cheering us from the wharf and crying out: *Go in and kill 'em all, boys. Don't spare the bloody savages.* Pretty much the same all the way upriver. Even the Celilo Indians wanted us to wipe out Mr. Joe and his lot—

So our Indian service has grown popular again, hasn't it, Wood?

I guess so, general.

Even among the Indians! General Sherman will be amused.— Have you heard from your brother?

Still at the Navy Department, sir.

Of course. Now tell me about Alaska. Did you write up some pretty sketches of forests and Esquimaux and whatnot?

I did my best, sir.

Once we wind down this campaign I'd like to read them. Or sooner, if time permits.

Thank you, sir.

You have the gift of tongues, Wood.

Yessir.

The Pentecost. The sacred fire.

Yessir.

So. It's an exceedingly rich country up there, I understand.

Well, sir, once we dug up lead intermixed with silver. The Indians around Sitka tell great yarns about gold and copper, but even the traders are so ignorant that you can hardly believe—

Captain Jocelyn, what is it?

Three men have fallen out already, general. And Ad Chapman says—

What's their trouble?

Heatstroke, sir.

Tie them onto mules if you have to, but punish any malingerers. Nobody stops.

I'll take charge of it, sir.

Wood, you can tell me more at another date. I must confess, at the moment Alaska sounds fine and cool!

> —and, rising up in the stirrups to gaze forward at our fan-shaped advance guard, then back along his army's great sweaty curve, heroes without ghosts, instruments of hope, young men who love war and old men who can be elsewhere even as they march, all ready for a fight, their bandoliers shining like diagonal blades of grass, the four-columned cavalry in blue, beige, grubby brown or once-white as they feel the necessity, the black tar-paint softening and oozing on their backpacks, the long line of stinking mule-wagons creaking and squeaking, the muleteers cursing under stained canvas (soon they will learn to fear punishment for this), the Gatlings rolling along shinily and almost comically on their massive carriages, the old howitzer teetering and creaking, sixty axes, five shovels and three hand axes in the tool wagon, our captains riding up and down the column to prowl for stragglers, the marchers darkening with distance into a narrow column interrupted intermittently by the cottonwoods in this narrow Lapwai Valley, then farther away by the great white rectangular clouds of the wagons,

> > *The men will cheer and the boys will shout,*
> > *The ladies they will all turn out;*

> > we'll see about that.

> > O, I need a horse doctor!

> More than he needs you, jackass.

> > > And then she died of a humidity fever at Farewell Bend. That's the only GODd——d reason he ever became a *squaw man.*

> > That's not reason enough.

> > > And then he turned Perry's flank.

> > If you want a fight I can sure give it to you.

> > > And Perry sure didn't give him no fight. Then when the volunteers broke from the line—

> > > *No.* That wasn't how it happened.

> > You know what, bruiser? You threaten me, you just might not make it back,

back across the raketeeth of our upraised procreant guns, beyond the thunder of our mule-whackers' whips, back toward the vanished beginning, whose houses, storehouses, barracks, etcetera (now restored to Monteith, who whenever he must share sovereignty becomes as resentful and vicious as an Indian pony), comprise a square letter P from whose enclosure our tall flag flies, the good Indians sadly singing

Wakesh nun pakilauitin
Jehovan'm *yiyauki,*
the Stars and Stripes flying over the center of our column
and Blackie dreaming to himself: picture windows for
Fidelia,
and Captain Pollock says that feller was killed
about eight days ago and his wife shot through
both legs.
Poor lady! Where's she now?
At Mount Idaho,
the veterans of Company "D" entertained by that *young*
look in Wood's eyes and his absurdly curly hair,
the general (moderately annoyed by an urge to urinate) permits his fondness to rush back much farther westward, all the way to the winding plats
of Portland on her bald-shaved river frontage, the Willamette River
swaying through her center; and here, at Tenth and Morrison, Lizzie
must have pretended not to be worrying about him while Wood shyly
declaimed the pentameters of his briefest Alaskan verse, whose secret
theme must have been as rare to everyone as a blue buffalo skin: —Harry
and Bessie would have applauded along with the grownups, after which
Lizzie and Mrs. Perry hastily penned their letters, Grace blew out the
candles and
And we'll all feel gay when
Johnny comes marching home.
Yes, sir.
That's fine, Wood. Glad you're back. Captain Trimble, what have your flankers
found?
No fresh sign, sir.
All right.
How's Company "H"?
Real fine, sir.
Ride up here with me. A remarkable view.
Yessir.
We've both seen plenty of action in our time, wouldn't you say?
Yessir, and I'm praying for action to-day.
A worthy prayer. Now, Trimble, do you blame the volunteers for the disaster
at White Bird Cañon?
No, sir.
Chapman fired on Joseph's envoys, I understand.
Well, general, but volunteers are all the same. Do you remember when the
Oregonians murdered our Modoc prisoners? It's incumbent on us to take those
kinds of tricks into account and—
Then who's to blame?

Colonel Perry, sir, as I'm prepared to testify.

You'd better be very sure of your facts, captain.

I am, sir.

Have you and Colonel Perry developed any personal contention?

No, sir.

That will be all. Captain Jocelyn, what is it?

General Howard, sir, the citizens—

Tell them to wait until called for. O, there you are, Lieutenant Bomus. Your pack train is a thing of beauty.

Thank you, sir.

A treat to be on the march at last, don't you think? Near serious fun,
> this sweet brown creek on its bed of white stones,
> the clovery smell of the locust-tree leaves,
>> cartridges at my left hip,
> the lovely hills curving and rolling, the sky pressing down closer
>> as we wonder how to figure out what Chief Joseph is planning for us.

Yessir.

Did you leave the miners satisfied about their compensation?

I practically had to turn the artillery on them, sir! What ingrates! That one old man from Florence was the worst. He threatened that if his mules didn't come back he would—

Everybody hopes to swindle Uncle Sam.

Yessir.

Anything else on your mind, lieutenant?

Well, the greenhorns keep falling out, sir.

That's a captain's department, not yours.

Yessir. The latest shoes from Fort Leavenworth—

Why didn't you inform me at Lapwai? There's nothing to be done now.

General, I did write a report.

All right. They'll have to march, shoes or no shoes. What else?

General, I'd feel easier if I could ride up and down the column throughout the day, until the new service animals have proven themselves . . .

Good man! And let's elongate our train a trifle. Lieutenant Fletcher, ride to the rear and inform Captain Pollock. I've learned that to Indians a stretched-out string of troops can be mighty impressive. Joseph's spies might think we're a thousand strong.

Yessir.

But no more than necessary, Fletch. Twenty percent, let's say.

All right, sir.

Keep your eye on the mule drivers.

Yessir. I've smelled no liquor yet.

You will. And that teamster in the third wagon yonder, I've seen him whipping his animals. Try to catch him at it.

Yessir.

Captain Miller, the horses seem full of spirit.

Yessir.

You can take pride in this column.

Thank you, general.

How many of these drivers are smuggling whiskey?

Probably all of them, sir.

I hope not. Well, keep your brightest lookout. We have to prevent this.

Yessir.

Now what time do you expect us to reach Junction Trail?

I should say by six if we don't elongate too much, sir.

What word from our scouts?

James Reuben called on me less than an hour ago, sir, and at that time there'd been no contact with Joseph.

Now who are those other two Indians?

Captain John and Old George. Very loyal, sir.

Very good, captain. Carry on.

All right, general,

> coming up into the pines and aspens, the pines clasping sky in their arms,
>
> illuminated by that unremitting heat which cures tobacco into a profitable color
>
> as we bold dragoons ride up into the grassy, rocky pine forest
>
>> (better this than bein' a jack up in Wisconsin, sawing trees day and night like some nigger),
>
> and then up into the first rise, pine gulleys dominate in the grass right until the deep shady winds of Lawyer Cañon.

By the way, do you have any idea where Lieutenant Wilkinson went off to?

I saw him puking at the side just now, sir. He didn't stop or cause any delay, just kept right on and—

How bad did he look?

Not very, I'd say, sir. Just the heat—

I see. You there, private, what's your name?

Schmidt, general.

What's the matter?

General, sir, my shirttails—

Then cut them off, but not until camp. If you hold up the column you'll be punished.

Yessir.

Fletch, would you hunt up Major Mason and find out how he purposes to establish our reserves to-night? And tell Captain Sladen I need him.

Right away, general.

O, and mention that I think it permissible for them to build fires at pleasure.

Yessir.

All of them except the pickets, of course—

Does your arm trouble you, general?

I'm fine. That will be all, Fletch.

2

Planting the guidon in a stubble field at Junction Trail (by which time it has commenced raining), they break ranks, detail their picket line, water the animals, cook and shelter according to their capacities (the officers all in one tent), burnish their arms and rest early, rising at "Reveille" just past four in the morning, as Bugler Brooks fires the morning gun and the sky improves itself from black to grey, like the dozenth wad of cleaning rag rammed through the barrel of a powder-fouled Springfield. The general, wearing his one blue overall suit which will fade month by month in the course of this campaign, is already cross-verifying reports with Major Mason. Our new Bannock scouts have been out all night, each one dreaming of getting a Nez Perce scalp lock. Between them and the tame Nez Perces whom we have hired on in the cause of liberty—Old George, Captain Jack, James Reuben—stretch scant webs of affection. As for Umatilla Jim, who knows how *he'll* jump? The tired troopers remain likewise word-niggardly, their discomforts, fears, hopes (mostly of deserting) and rages as luridly various as the painted faces of an Indian cavalcade. With aching eyes and stinking hands they curry the horses. Doc, excited and pleased, explains to Blackie: *Now, back when I was a scout on my own hook,* while Wood,

> whose character will most conveniently reveal itself upon my telling you that the first time he saw those two lines of dark-clad cadets at perpendiculars to the long white sweep of the Academy hall thrilled him much less than observing the petticoated ladies being escorted by their top-hatted soldier-men across the plain of West Point and foreseeing certain possibilities,

finishes likewise early, stealing a moment from the Army to bring his diary closer to the present: *Left Portland 5 A.M. Captain Wolf promised to post my letter to Nanny. Whether he will is "as GOD disposes." Excited to see the general; less so the rest of the bunch. Smiles of the colored laundresses. Fletch's prediction: A week to whip Joseph, but a month to catch that old stinker Toohhoolhoolzote. Through the mountain cliffs, clouds and mists of the Cascade Range to Dalles. The gates of the river lurid with sultry clouds.* Then comes breakfast and the move out at six, with sun-glare tautening their cheeks against their skulls. After an hour of march one begins to know in truth that one is working his legs, while after three hours one might as well have been walking all one's life, and thus it will be until one's shoes wear out; thus the only lesson of this Nez Perce War. *Lurid with sultry clouds,* or should I have written *lurid with sultry cloud*? And why does Wilkinson dislike me although he pretends not to? Or is it merely his manner of late? By midmorning the basalt clouds in the sky-hill of golden grass have gone lavender. The general's dear friend Sladen, who was his aide-de-camp when he persuaded Cochise's Apaches to come in on the reservation, canters pleasantly up and down the line, no matter that for a year and a half now he's lacked a left foot: skittish pony, shattered ankle, gangrene. And the march goes forward—shavetailing in the Indian country, O yes, yes, yes; *left, left, LEFT:*

This rifle sure enough feels as heavy as a nigger hoe.

How would you know?

Now tell us all about Alaska, Wood. Did you see gold nuggets and such?

Not really. As I told the general—

O yes. Do bring *him* up.

What's your implication?

Some of us here are closer to him than you.

Excuse me, Wilkinson,

and by the way, when I consider this Sallie of yours, I wonder: How could any woman whose heart vibrates with the slightest feeling ever endure the prospect of living with you?

but since answering requires me to recapitulate what I told the general, and since some of you were there, I didn't want to be a bore, that's all.

All right, Wood, no offense. Just don't act unique before your brother officers.

Mrs. Norton was slightly shot through her calves.

And that Colonel Perry, they should—

He'll be acquitted. If Reno and Benteen could walk away after Little Big Horn—

Well, Chapman,

whose grey horse is near about as good as the general's and whose hair is greasier than Indian pemmican,

you must be feeling mighty fine to-day. You got your war on—

What the hell are you talking about?

Ain't you the one that fired the first shot?

No, the honor's all yours, Larry. Chief Joseph shot first at White Bird Cañon. Nearly creased my horse. I saw his wicked Injun eyes, and I sure did shoot back.

That's not what Shearer told me.

Well, he's just an ex-Seccesh, and one day I'll fix him. And don't tell me it wasn't you that gunned down Chief Tipyahlanah the other year—

What a d——d redskinned sonofabitch *he* was! Tried to prevent me from plowing—

He was a good Injun, the kind a man can work with. Me, I would have let him stick around until we got Wallowa nice and easy.

You don't know nothing. You remember what Elfers said when they acquitted me? *Can't punish a man just for shooting a dog,* he said. Tipyahlanah should have been underground long before I done what I done.

Looking-Glass said it was *you* the Injuns wanted to kill when they went on their rampage. And you so scared you dressed up like a Chinaman and ran all the way to Florence to hide in the diggings!

That's right. You was on the inside track with Looking-Glass. What does that say about you?

What does it say, Larry?

Who else warned you? Heard tell from your *wife,* didn't you, Chapman? Someday a decent white man's going to cut her throat. So quit it, you d——d *squaw man.*

You'd better watch yourself, Larry.

They arrive at Norton's at one-thirty in the afternoon, perfumed by the stink of their sweating saddle-horses.

3

At Norton's ranch that evening, forty-three miles out of Lapwai, Wood, seated on a corral's gate with his knees wide apart, his hands and forehead sunburned, the wrinkles of his cavalry boots as dazzling to his tender eyes as the Clearwater's ripples, withdraws the pistol from his hip and finds it, though uncomfortably hot to the touch, still clean beyond the most distant peril of any demerit. He slides it back home, reads two more pages of *The Old-Fashioned Girl* by Mrs. Alcott, which there had never been reason for him not to finish on the voyage home from Sitka, remembers his Alaskan copper bracelet, which he now clasps around his left wrist for the duration of the campaign, then, since the enlisted men of Company "D" can manage without him for another quarter-hour, opens his notebook and essays to compose a poem on the subject of his fiancee's chestnut hair, which she keeps at near about ankle length, but (reader, don't tell!) bores himself. So doesn't he love her? I know *I* do, and all I've ever seen of her is her photograph. As for Wood, even while proudly granting the tendency of this or any Indian war to harden him into a manly rage, he's far from averse to Nanny's smooth fair face, which constitutes poetry itself, in part because it has half-consistently neglected him; hence he prefers Shelley's idealizations to Byron's cynicisms, for where and how can an American live without ideals? In fact he has promised to love this nation above all else, save only GOD. But it's so hot, especially after Alaska! And White Bird Cañon won't be pleasant—almost ten days they've been lying there. Fletch informs me that some officers are exercised against our general on account of Perry's failure. Well, they'll see otherwise! But I

> You may call this a picket line, but I don't. I'm coming back in ten minutes, and I'd better see a GODd——d picket line.
> Yessir,

the sun as great and round as a wagonwheel,

Craig's Mountain behind us,
Wilkinson scarlet with sunburn,
our tame Nez Perce scouts watching me, their many
pallid necklace-beads soon to shine in the campfire-
light.

No. Admit that the rich men could destroy all the
greenback circulation if we don't watch out.
That's why Tilden—
Tilden's a *socialist.*
What's that exactly?
Now he's putting out his reserves and supports where
he should, you see, after it's too late, when Mr. Joe has
already—
Quite a yaller jacket's nest.
Lieutenant Fletcher, how high did we climb?
From Lapwai? About two and a half thousand feet.
Thank you, sir. You see? It's like Grangeville. You see, Blackie? I'll bet you
twenty dollars there's but half as many growing days here as in Lewiston—
Fletch, why don't you have a sweetheart?
O, I'll get one when I feel the urge.

Well, he's sure laid hisself liable.
O no. It's us who'll get the blame and him the credit.
That's the way of the Army.
Then why the DEVIL did you join, you coward?
Shut up.
If General Crook was here he'd sure have this cleaned
up fast. He don't coddle no noble red man.

You're hard on him, since his father's a drunkard.
You deny that that bears watching?
No. I say that in America we don't hold a man's
origins against him. Thomas Jefferson used to re-
ceive European potentates in his nightshirt—
Wood's hardly a dead President.
Fine. Lay off him, Wilkinson. You don't have to
like him.
Do you?
He's unformed and conceited. We don't know if
he'll funk it when the fight comes. But we
shouldn't prejudge a brother officer. And since he
has the general's ear, why do yourself a mischief?
I suppose I'm jealous.
That he got to see Alaska while we were drilling
at Lapwai?

Fletch, you've never understood—

Looky here. They even left their milk pails on the fence.

You fixing to steal one?

keep thinking about immortality. That's the question that screams through everything to-night. If those savages murder me, will I see anything after I close my eyes, or will it just be

Them chickens and flowers is all thirsted to death. What a shame; what a shame.

They tore up all their clothes—

Sugar and salt and trash all in a mess—

Not a bad little roadhouse, at least before them Injuns wrecked it.

Well, you should see what they did to the Manuel place.

Ad Chapman used to own that property. The way I heard it, he sold it to Manuel because he—

And then Mrs. Manuel got burned alive by Joseph. Her little girl had to stand there and watch it—

For two bits I'd shoot 'em all.

I suppose they intend to operate on the settlements in the Wallowa. I mean, that's Joseph's beef, ain't it? It was Wallowa he showed mad about.

That's right. That means they won't go far. We'll finish 'em off in two weeks.

I wanted to see that place anyhow. Captain Whipple's bunch are saying it's mighty fine grassland, especially where Bear Creek meets the Wallowa River.

Forget it. The big boys must have that section sewed up.

No, this horse needs a full dozen quarts.

But an Injun horse—

I got me a gold pan in my outfit.

Just like Captain Pollock! Why, he's crazy for—

I'm gonna be rich. You'll see. When the officers aren't snooping I'll check out every stream—

Now, when is the king the proper lead?

Don't you even know that?

Doc, if I did I wouldn't be asking you!

All rightie, let's see your cards. Now, what's the five GODD——d laws of euchre? Quote them back to me.

Well . . .

night without stars? Unpractised as I am, I do dread this expedition, although I'm sure it won't be as bad as leaping the hurdles at cavalry exercises at West Point; how I longed then to avert my eyes! After my first battle, or my first wound, it won't be so bad. And I think my love for America stands beyond fear. We'll see. Anyhow, Fletch is right; we'll finish Joseph pretty soon. And Nanny will be proud I went to war. Truth to tell, the only reason I didn't stay in Alaska was money. It takes cash to marry her. No, that's not true. I would have regretted missing this excitement, and of course I'd be ashamed if my brother officers were to develop a bad opinion of me. But now, when we're drawing so near that dismal cañon, I wish I could

How did Norton get away?

He didn't, jackass! Mr. Joe shot him down—

I tried to ask Chapman, but he—

And Colonel Perry lost fourteen horses at White Bird Cañon.

If they'd only remained in the Cottonwood House—

Don't you know nothing? *This* is the Cottonwood House.

That must be Norton over there. They say his wife got it but *good.* Now, what they did to her, you see, first they—

What's the password?

Stars and Stripes.

All right. O, it's you, Jim. Where you been?

Around.

Seen any bad Injuns?

Well, I caught my reflection in the stream.

You're a caution! Most hilarious Injun I ever knew.

Thanks.

General wants you.

All right. Where's he?

Over thataway.

Well, Doc said to me, the way you can tell gold from pyrite, you get you some mercury and—

So they took her to Brown's Hotel. But she'll recover, they say. Joseph shot her through both legs—

No, Custer didn't show cowardice. None whatsoever, and that's an iron fact. It was Reno who—

Joseph himself took a gun and shot her?

Custer could of whipped them Sioux, but he was drunk.

What he did, he put White Bird up to it. I heard from Ad Chapman, who sure knows Indians—

He was as sober as you are now.

Sober as your stinking grandmother—

at least throw off this mood, perhaps by recounting Grace Howard's eighteen hairpins; O how tightly her hair is tucked up! I'll bet she'd love to dance. But I'll never find out. Besides, she'd tell Nanny. And now I'm confined among these loud buffoons who *never shut up*—

like the drunks shouting from the windows of the Eureka Saloon in Portland; actually I long to drink some booze right now, if the general wouldn't find out. Fletch would go shares with me, *maybe,* on a very dark night, but Wilkinson would tell the general. That mean-looking Chapman might be carrying some. Can't ask him. That lady at the Eureka showed me her

> a thousand times better than anything Nanny ever
> Once we're married I'll teach her, gently but firmly. To make me happy she'll
> But what if she she won't?

That ain't Norton. Don't you know nothing? He got killed by Mr. Joe personal. And that Lew Wilmot with the volunteers, they say he turned tail and left 'em in the lurch here at Norton's, because—

How do you know Mr. Joe pulled the trigger and not some other Injun? You talk like you was there. Well, was you there?

He's the chief, see. How could it happen without the chief gave his say-so? Well, then who's that feller?

That's Chapman the *squaw man*.

If that's what he is then where's his squaw at?

Probably keeps her tied up in the barn, with her legs wide open.

Each man of us believes he'll stay alive. Even I, nauseous with anxiety, can't imagine not coming back.

I must strive better to remember my CREATOR before death should overtake me. If I ask Wilkinson for guidance he might like me better. What makes the general so brave? Or is he just shamming it as I am? It must be different for old men. After this is over I must ask him frankly—what am I thinking? How could I ever ask him? He'd count me yellow—

O, he ain't bad. He showed Joseph the rifle at the very start—

Evening, lieutenant.

Good evening, Jim. You looking for the general?

That's right.

Well, he's in that tent.

Then I guess I'd better go there.

What is it about that Indian I don't like? But now I'll imagine Nanny, just to show myself I can do it. I'm stroking her smooth white cheek, which always reminds me of porcelain. I take her face in my hands and

and

> Sometimes when I'm with her I'm so bored I can't stand it! When the fellows gave it out that Theller felt ennui with his wife, I could hardly believe it—peach of a lady!—but there he was in that Lewiston tent—
>> (last time I saw him alive)
> and Wilkinson's sure not as fond of his Sallie as he claims
>> (to tell the truth, she sounds about as simple as an Aetna Centennial sewing machine)
> and even the general has been known to allude unenthusiastically to the marital state; so does that mean that whichever bride I end up with will disappoint me? That cannot be true.

I'd better go peg out my blanket with the officers pretty soon or they'll call me peculiar. But, dear LORD, don't let me end up like them! Trimble will tell us all over again how many of the Modoc horses were no bigger than dogs, and I'll have to ask after Pollock's brood; his wife must be in the family way again. Well, he's been good to me. But I dislike applauding his nigger songs. Although Parnell must have recollections of being a British Lancer. Will he tell me anything? That would pass the time. GOD help me to outstretch myself

and attach Nanny to me so she can't

Sing us a fine song.

Nope.

The general's right: Wilkinson and Fletch do both look run down. I wonder if it's typhoid?

Trimble's mad against Perry. He spoke of testifying.

That Umatilla Jim bears watching, I fear. Better tell Fletch when I—

So there you are, Wood! Are you correcting your memoirs?

No, Wilkinson, I'm writing yours. Did you enjoy the march?

Well, it's fine to breathe a different atmosphere from Lapwai, anyway . . .

Wood, are you settled now back at home?

Sure am, Captain Pollock. You're looking fit—

By GOD, my boy, we loved it at Wallula! Every man jack except that melancholic major was tanned and healthy. Plenty of fishing, and sometimes we even got to play "base ball." Not that we had your opportunities, of course.

Well, sir, I didn't exactly find any gold!

You didn't? D——mnit if I didn't count on you to make us rich! What's the matter with you?

All they talked about was copper.

To hell with copper! Did you buy that new hat up in Alaska?

In The Dalles.

And then that Lynn Bowers lifted up her petticoats—

Should have figured.

Wood, tell us again about that Chilcat chief.

All right. Well, when Sitka Jack, who's a "character" on his own account, took me to his lodge, or palace as I should say, I knew right off that here was a true potentate of the red men! Imagine grand totem poles on either side of him, carved to resemble grotesque heads stacked on top of each other. He looked me over like a man who wouldn't be imposed on. I told him about the fearsome one-armed chief who had sent me, and he pretended not to be impressed. The squaws brought out baskets of smoked salmon and blueberries. When he gave me permission to go upriver—

And did you find Alaskan gold? Tell us honestly—

No, tell us about the squaws!

Fine-figured, and very piquant.

Piquant, he says! By the way, Wood, Sladen was asking about your people. He's wondering if you're connected to Ralph Erskine, whom I gather was a friend or something of his family.

Well, I do know that Elizabeth Erskine, daughter of Ralph Erskine, is one of my ancestors and I can prove it once I bring Nanny out West, because my mother has a silver spoon engraved $\mathcal{E}\cdot\mathcal{E}\cdot$,

by which time Wilkinson is already passing round his Sallie's ambrotype:
             What a belle she is, and how she can smile!
so that Fletch pores dreamily over the portrait, until Wilkinson's eyes commence to flash. What Fletch is particularly curious to know (for no good reason) is whether a lock of Sallie's hair lives coiled within this romantic object, but he's too polite to open it without leave,

> which reminds me of Nanny, staring slightly downward, smiling, with her hair coiled elegantly upon her head, and her earrings as colorful as peacock's tails. Somehow I can almost imagine Fletch killed and in his grave. But Wilkinson's impervious to bullets, and I'm simply going to be careful

but *brave*, of course—better brave than careful even if I

> > how much would Nanny miss me? Maybe she's still exchanging letters with Mr. Tracy Gould, d——n him, or that other smart rich bastard whom her father thinks the world of.

I'd wager he's got his heart fixed on this here place if Norton don't come back. See him gazin' slyly about?

You got your heart fixed on this place, don't you?

Now you quit shitting on Mr. Chapman. I don't care if he's a *squaw man*. He's a true metal-hearted American—

What's your dream?

My dream about what?

Every American's got a dream.

I'd marry a nice white gal and we'd find ourselves a walnut-shaded ranch house in a grassy draw by a creek—the right kind of creek, you see, not wide enough to flood or thin enough to go dry in August . . .

Well, I aim to be up higher. Maybe someplace like Wallowa, if the winter's not too bad.

Now that his brother officers have momentarily finished with him, Wood commences to consider all over what he often did in Alaska (with certain intermissions): namely, the way that Nanny's reddish-brown hair flows to her knees—a sight of awe-potent abundance now conscientiously represented by:

~~cataract of chestnut locks~~
~~secrets of her~~
her—o, GoDd——nit! Never seek to compel the Muse. All the same:
~~the blue ribbon in Nanny's hair~~

> and that passionate pride in herself which I quickly learned to feel about her

and hope someday to feel about myself, although her pride derives half from her studied performance of herself as a woman and half from the form whose perfection manifests itself in the eyes and attentions of men, whereas I for my part have not yet relinquished the hope of becoming myself in some true and simple yet worthy way which will not require self-consciousness. Can there be a woman of this type? Perhaps squaws are this way.

> Doc?
> What is it now?
> How big is a scalp?
> Just about the size of a silver dollar.
> Is that really how big mine is?
> Sure.
> And an—
> You'll find out, probably to-morrow. Now let me be.

If I had my Shelley here I'd borrow just two lines. Nanny would never

> > Will I be the one to get Joseph to-morrow? To be the hero of the hour and also
> > > see him bleed! Pollock told me he burns women alive.
> > > > What's the password? Stop or I'll shoot!
> > > > *Stars and Stripes.*
> > > > O, it's Jim.
> > > > Now let me come into the shade; it's hot out here.

~~the kiss of her hair~~
~~of her~~
~~her little you-know-what~~
~~as she o'ersees my romantic vigil~~

> > Then where's Norton at?
> > What?
> > I said where's Norton at?
> > > How can I think when they
> > Took his folks to Grangeville.
> > Left the dirty work to us, did he?

General, Umatilla Jim is here.

Do come in. Jim, have a seat. How are you enjoying military life?

Pretty good, general.

Joseph's in the bag, don't you think?

Yessir.

Teach me an Indian word, Jim. My wife has advised me to write a book about Indians.

> *Wapato.*

And what's that?

Duck potato. Sometimes they call it arrowweed. There's some in the pond down there. Our squaws wade in and pull it up with their toes—

Wapato.

That's right.

Thank you, Jim. I like that medallion of yours. So you're a Rutherford Hayes man, I see.

Very funny, general.

Well, then where did you get it?

Mr. Tsépmin paid me this, when I took his wife back to the reservation. He said it's worth money. Is it, general?

Is Mrs. Chapman a loose woman?

O no, general, just old. Worn out teeth. Five children now. Tsépmin he got tired of her, said to me, *Jim, take her away quick!*— But what he gave me, it's not worth money?

My LORD! Do you suppose Colonel Perry is getting close?

Well, general, he left Grangeville two hours ago, riding fast—

What sign of Joseph?

Nothing fresh. I guess they're across the Salmon, digging camas and arguing out their next move—

He's a very dangerous Indian.

Yessir.

Jim, what do you suppose he's thinking right now?

BATTLE WITHOUT MUSIC
JUNE 24

1

*W*e're ready to move out, general.

It's Sunday.

Well, yes it is, sir.

You'd surely like to hear that move out bugle, wouldn't you, Captain Jocelyn?

You're right about that, general.

Your zeal reminds me of a little story. You see, the regimental band was playing in order to urge us on at Fredericksburg. Were you at that battle, captain?

No, sir.

I didn't think so. Well, it was an impressive engagement. The enemy had deployed every battery they could. Some of our men were nervous. So the band played, to give us heart and impel us forward. It was very rousing music, captain.

Yessir.

And then a Confederate shell struck it, and all its members were killed. We went into battle without music, captain. That will be all. Fletch, who's officer of the day?

Captain Whipple, general.

Is he aware that to-day as on every other Sunday there's to be a dress inspection?

Of course, sir.

All right. Evidently it slipped Captain Jocelyn's mind.

2

But I should have begun my accounting of this Sunday right at dawn, when the morning gun has said what it could, and Colonel Perry, his pipe lost or stolen back in Lapwai in the days when Theller still lived, rolls himself a smoke in a scrap of letterhead which advertises B. F. Field's patent for compressed board of any thickness, manufactured at Lyons, Iowa. Every man in Company "F" had better answer roll call, and to hell with the others. Soon they will be smashing their pilot bread or boiling it in coffee; pork-steam will perfume the officers' commissary; but not yet. Perry has always favored this early hour for watchful thinking, and he imagines that he is happy. The letter which Wood delivered from Mrs. Perry in Portland was satisfactory in its sentiments of loyalty, worry and hinted desire, although it left her husband as bleak as usual. He wishes he could have drawn a new uniform for this campaign, which may well drag on like the Modoc War. As soon as Wilkinson appears, he will ask to study Colton's map. The general's tent remains shut, but Perry knows that unless his superior officer expired during the night, he must be poring over the small square leather-bound Gospels which his brother Charles gave him in some darkly remote year before the Secession War was ever heard of.— GODd——d one-armed General Prayer Book!— And where are the reds? Perry, like his general, would rather go over and over the country in his head, with the aim of predicting the movements of the arch-enemy, Mr. Joe. Since that villain loves Wallowa so much, why wouldn't he sweep back through there with his braves, wiping out all the Americans he can? According to our scouts, the valley continues quiet, but so was White Bird Cañon until we heard that screech owl's cry. High time to clean out Wallowa, and burn the contents of every hide dump and camas pit! Captain Whipple will have mapped those sites if he's worth anything. Settlers and volunteers can do the rest—or will they also fuck that up? GODd——n this, and d——n Mr. Joe. Anger and grief for the fallen Theller come curving in an almost shocking white flash like the twin stabbers of a longhorn bull. This time I'm not intending to bring a single live Indian home from the field, except maybe some pretty little Nez Perce squaw who doesn't scream. I'll make her promise that her heart's good forever, and then if she does what I say, I'll let her go in Lewiston. Anyhow I'd never get away with it, not while old Prayer Book's in charge. He don't know a thing. Does he even realize how to starve Mr. Joe? We ought to set the camas prairie on fire. Once his roots are all burned up, then we have to keep him away from his hunting grounds. Better ask James Reuben how to destroy that *cous* they eat. And I'll shoot and keep shooting; I won't take squaw prisoners—although I won't shoot down their children on purpose, no matter in hell what they've done to ours.

All this he thinks between the first and second notes of "Reveille," just after the morning gun.

At the third note (5:30 a.m.), the tent opens,

> the men rustling, yawning, rising, buckling on their pistol belts, Perry, already immaculately ready, with his hands on his hips:

>> If General Crook were in charge of this outfit, he'd be over the ridgetop hunting mountain sheep, and all the same we'd be a d——d sight better organized.

Is Lieutenant Wilkinson still abed at this hour?

Seems a bit feverish, general. Should I fetch him?

Has he reported sick?

No, sir.

Then I expect to see him in five minutes, in full trim and with a good excuse.

Yessir.

>> Captain Randall, Lieutenant Bomus needs to verify that your requisition is correct. Just because your volunteers showed up unprepared—

>> Lieutenant, I'll tell you what you can do with your d——d bullshit. And you can tell the general—

>> O can I?

> *Roll call!*

Wilkinson, I thought you knew how important it is to set an example at the beginning of a campaign.

I apologize, general—

Are you sick?

I'm all right, sir.

Look at me, Wilkinson,

> and, dear LORD, preserve this fine young man from the whitish fur on the tongue, the morning and evening fevers, the vomiting, flux and thirst of *typhoid.*

Yessir.

Report to Doctor Alexander at once, and I hope you feel better. Go now. Perry, will Joseph have crossed the Salmon?

I expect so, general. A mighty inconvenient stream for us—

Isn't that Toohhoolhoolzote's territory yonder?

Sure is. Pretty rough country in that direction, if they withdraw into the mountains—

Could the River Renegades have linked up with them over there?

Well, general, you know how easily Indians can move.

Yes. Have you doped out the nearest ford to White Bird Cañon?

No, sir. On Colton's map—

I'm disappointed in you. Then send me Chapman; he knows the country. Are you ready to set out for Grangeville?

Sure am, general.

Go then, and GOD bless you. Fletch, who was officer of the day?

Captain Jocelyn, sir.

Can you fetch him? O, good morning, captain. A pleasure to see you. What happened on your line?

It's dead quiet, sir. The pickets report no contact.

Naturally. Indians don't give way step by step. They gallop away.

Yessir.

What news from your scouts?

Well, general, I'm expecting two of our Bannocks to ride in from Slate Creek any minute now. The other scouts have reported in, and they believe that most or all the hostiles have skedaddled to the Salmon River.

Is Looking-Glass still quiet on his reservation?

Sure is, general.

Good. I expect that Colonel Perry will confirm their report once he rides in.

Yessir.

From now on, we'll verify and double-verify, so that Joseph and his confederates can't surprise us again.

Absolutely, sir. And the men are eagerly awaiting the move out call—

Well, but we must give Colonel Green time to get in position from Boise. If Joseph makes a junction with the Weisser Indians, we'll be that much farther from victory.

Yessir.

And you heard my point about Colonel Perry. He may not arrive for some hours. Who knows what he might encounter en route?

Yessir.

As for Joseph's Indians, if they're still there once we've finished our business at White Bird Cañon, we'll drive them into the water.

I should certainly hope so, sir.

All right, captain;

> FATHER IN HEAVEN, help me continue impartial to this hostile blockhead whose shiny desperation to repeat Perry's folly fatuously supposes itself twin to Lowe's tears—sincere, I have no doubt—when Custer refused to take the two Gatlings to Little Big Horn; GOD help me to

carry on. Now, Fletch, I need Captains Trimble, Miller and Whipple.

Right away, sir.

Captain Trimble, how are you this morning?

Ready for action, sir.

I'm glad. But, Fletch, I don't smell coffee. Go see if there's some failure at the commissary wagon.

Yessir.

Now, Trimble, some citizen families on Slate Creek have barricaded themselves against the Indians. I need you to reënforce them.

All right, general.

Show yourself as actively as you can. Try to fix Joseph's attention on you while we get in position.

I'll do my best, sir. Should be a mite easier than Gettysburg!

No doubt. O, good morning, gentlemen. Excellent coffee, don't you think? Brew us another pot, would you, Fletch?

Right away, general.

Captain Miller, once Colonel Perry has delivered his report, you'll lead the infantry to Johnson's ranch.

Yessir.

In the meantime, of course, we'll hold our usual inspection.

Yessir.

Everything had better shine like a silver dollar.

Yessir.

Before you go, Trimble, what's your opinion of our Indian allies?

You mean James Reuben's bunch, sir?

Yes.

Well, Parnell always says to me—

Lieutenant Parnell, what exactly do you always say?

Well, general, I often like to say: *That's Indian character for you.* The instant we whipped the Pi-Utes, Crook asked for ten bucks to volunteer against the Pit River Indians, and ten of the finest stepped forward, ready to heal their wounded spirits by attacking a weaker foe. So these tame Nez Perces—

I see. Wilkinson, what did Doctor Alexander tell you?

Fit for duty, sir.

All right. O, good morning, Captain Pollock. How are you getting along?

Very well indeed, sir.

Discover any gold nuggets?

Now, general, if you mean to tease me—

I'm sure you've been helping Lieutenant Wood find his feet again.

O yes—

That's fine. Now, Captain Whipple, we'll take the cavalry to Grangeville. Who knows? The citizens there might even be grateful.

With citizens one never knows, sir.

A man of experience! In the meantime, gentlemen, I urge you to profit by the Sabbath. Fletch, where's Lieutenant Bomus?

3

And now I see Boyle, Wilkinson, Fletch, Wood,
> who thanks to his mother's praying frenzies has aways despised Sundays,
Pollock, Trimble, Ad Chapman and ever so many others, including our good Nez
Perces and the agreeable Umatilla Jim, opening their mouths wide to sing the
praises appropriate to Divine service, led by their *Christian Soldier*. It is the anniversary of Little Big Horn. They pray for Lieutenant-Colonel Custer.

4

Then James Reuben and the other scouts are singing:
> *Au namotihu Saviourna, kapisin'o,*
> *Hinak naktatasha, hina-woino.*

Jim, that tune rings familiar, but they've transposed the key. What are they
singing?

O, they sing that at Lapwai all the time, general. That's "Yield Not to Temptation."

Capital! I must say, Mr. Monteith and his father have done well.

Yessir.

And what might be tempting our Indians nowadays? That's the question of the
hour.

Can't rightly say, general,
> his medallion glittering like something almost valuable,
> and Wood, whose copper bracelet (a precautionary measure against dis-
> ease) is already unpleasantly hot around his wrist, although it's not yet
> eight-o'-clock a.m., draws picket duty with a squad of Germans from
> Company "D,"
> > who have just finished polishing their bayonets for inspection,

and so goes the day:
> Well, I should say with that d——d Blurick is where our troubles started.
> Doc used to be just so bright and friendly! And then, because Blurick
> wouldn't take his advice, Doc got sore. If Blurick had just shut up and
> done what Doc told him to do—
> > Then she says to me: I don't want no more children. We can't hardly
> > afford to keep our four alive as it is. So I tells her, I says, then if you
> > won't give me my marital rights, I'm off to the Army and to hell
> > with you!
> > > No, Pollock, that was actually before Perry got wounded
> > > in the dawn attack. The Modocs came out of the mist—
> > > Naturally Sundays have got to be sacred for good old Howard.
> > > Well, guess what? Chief Joseph don't never stop on Sundays,

as the general calls Captain John and Old George to the doorway of his Sibley
tent, smiling on them, treating them as would a father,

> while some of those who had the wherewithal to buy cocaine at Lapwai
> now swallow just a drop or two of that medicine, which recruits them
> marvelously,

>> the nearest mule driver dozing in his spring seat, with flies settling
>> on his shoulders,

and Captain Pollock, perspiring like a miner, curses those members of Company "D" who failed inspection, after which he assigns moderate punishments

> (Companies "F" and "H" receiving comparable edifications),

after which a few Nimrods go out hoping to kill some dinner for their messmates

> while Umatilla Jim glides around our camp with something like a horse's
> permanent tiptoe stance

and one or two professors explore the Indian question:

Well, if it ain't Jimmy Reuben. With that shiny gun of yours and your
Lapwai education, you might believe you're as good as a white man.

What do you want, Tsépmin?

Just respect. McConville's bunch are watching you. Blood will out,
Jimmy.

Tsépmin, you want to make trouble, make trouble. I can't prevent you.

D——d right.

Chapman, are you harassing this Indian?

Why don't you ask him, lieutenant?

Thank you, Lieutenant Wilkinson. This man and I were just talking.

All right then.

That's right, Jimmy. Don't you never go against me, or I'll get you.

Tsépmin, I have to ride out now.

You watch and see what I'll do,

> but all he does is curry his grey horse and then drop down out of
> sight to drink Blackfoot whiskey, enjoying to think through this
> campaign, and in particular how best to put before the general his
> comrade Major Shearer,

>> who until his death-day will secrete within his breast-pocket
>> a Confederate hundred-dollar bill which depicts the South
>> striking down the North, and who now sits at Idaho hoping
>> to convince himself that he is not in trouble over White Bird
>> Cañon: The climax of misfortune . . . ! How can I bear up beneath the load of it all? If Chapman sees me through on this,
>> I sure won't forget it!

and some write letters

> (Pollock, for instance, advising his dear Sara: *I do hope Johnny and Ella
> keep the flower beds clear of weeds*)

or essay the Stick Game with our Bannock scouts,

these dark men in their stovepipe hats and smoke-colored shirts or old Army uniforms, who frown patiently downward when we look at them, the sun-lines thick and white across their dark foreheads and down the bridges of their wide dark noses and under their dark cheeks as they roll their kinninnick cigarettes,

as Captain Randall's bunch jawbones with Larry Ott, the slayer of Shore Crossing's father

(the jury let him off, saying: *he should not be prosecuted for killing a dog*), while others touch up the lovely deep bluing on every screw and fitting of their trapdoor Springfields, as if that could improve their luck, then sound out the *East Oregonian:*

Two boys killed a cougar in Lane County the other day. Says so right here, as Wood, having seen his Germans through their picket duty without having to write any of them up, takes a quarter-hour for a certain private pursuit:

~~Her rain of chestnut tresses enamors my repose~~

Lieutenant Wood, are you one of them Sunday school bunch?

Mr. Randall, what can I do for you?

I'm *Captain* Randall. Captain of these volunteers.

So I've heard.

What are you writing? It entertains me to see a grown man write in a notebook.

Something to my girl.

A letter?

Something like that.

That's good. If you're going to that much trouble you'd better marry her.

Thanks for the advice, Mr. Randall. And now I'll return to my business—

until Perry, to whom these swales are so familiar that he might as well be a passenger on the New York to Philadelphia train, passing all those barns painted in honor of Doctor Drake's Plantation Bitters, finally rides in from Grangeville.

Wood, is it true that your father once got you an interview with President Grant?

Well, general, that's so, although I never asked to have one. I was at Baltimore City College—

And what did the President do?

He said pleasant things about my father. That's about it. Lit one cigar with the end of another. Never said he would nominate me for West Point, nor did I have any idea about it—

while Captain Jocelyn keeps yearning for the move out.

A Happy Recollection of the "East Woods"
June 25

1

*T*he next day he rises with his customary earliness, zealous to reëstablish his command at Johnson's ranch, or what remains of it. Right at the morning gun the men are already swarming upright to groom their horses. Wilkinson insists on feeling recovered, so he despatches him at the head of a mounted detachment to capture two deserters. For every man, pilot bread and coffee straight from the saddlebag. He writes a greeting to General Sherman; the morning sizzles; now they've finished fitting up the wagons. Since Perry reports that the hostile Nez Perces remain in the vicinity of White Bird Cañon, we'll approach that neighborhood with extreme deliberation. Really, Perry's failure has put me in a highly awkward position! *Common sense: the state of mind the result of careful observation.* So Professor Mahan used to say at West Point. Now I understand, but the rest of them don't. For most men, careless observation suffices. LORD knows I won't let that Joseph out-general me again.

All right now, prepare to mount,

> and as the bugler sounds that call, the cavalrymen are already standing at their horses' heads, grasping the swan-necked pommels of their saddles, and

Mount!

> as they mount all together and

Move out.

Move out!

> —Bugler Brooks blowing the advance; but there is no band to play "The Girl I Left Behind Me":

Trimble to Slate Creek (his advance guard fanning out a trifle too exactly, but they'll loosen up, I reckon):

> *Left,*
> > *left,*
> > > *left!*

Miller rightward to Johnson's (merely four miles from there to White Bird Cañon),

> Doctor Alexander riding rearward to treat another rattlesnake case with ammonia and whiskey,

Whipple and I to Grangeville,

well, we made a pretty brisk start,

our good Indians all painted up,

Chapman galloping idiotically up and down the line

(must admit that's a fabulous stallion he's got

—and they give me old Elmer the gelding; how symbolic! Well, if he can't keep up I'll take another horse. So far he seems capable enough, wide in the chest, no sores . . .),

Whipple leading the sunburned column with the regulation twenty-eight-inch step, a hundred ten paces to the minute, *Left—left—left:*

drums and bugles, bugles and drums,

good Christians of Wilkinson's stripe, and unrequited votaries of corn whiskey whose names are presently concealed,

marching four abreast through the golden grass, top hats darkly shining, fists clenched and swinging

up over the swales to where our soldiers raggedly await:

Good morning, men. Are you ready to fight again?

We sure are, general. You reached us sooner than we thought possible—

Well, then, why such hangdog faces? Where are my brisk and hearty troopers? Would Lieutenant Theller wish to see you like this? Now that's better. We're back in business, with more cavalry, infantry and artillery than Joseph can stomach. In short, reënforcements! Is that clear?

Yessir.

Now show Captain Whipple's men good courtesy, and help them refresh themselves after their march. I'm riding to Mount Idaho to reassure the citizens. That won't take long. We'll move out this afternoon. That's all. Jim, did you have a pleasant ride?

Not bad, general.

Did you see any of your relatives?

They left pretty quick. A lot of lodgepoles still in Rocky Cañon—

How far is that?

Maybe four miles. Not a real good place.

How many Indians were camping there?

I'd say six hundred.

All right. Sir, you must be Mr. Croaesdale.

That's my name, yes.

How do you do? I am General Howard of the United States Army.

Tickled to meet you! I've improvised some field-works—

Very creditable. Did you ever study military science? Now guide me straightaway to Mount Idaho.

Yessir.

Excuse me, general, but my name's Mr. Ayers, and I've got important information for you. It's being said that there's a dozen strange Indians hanging around

Celilo, and they held a powwow with the Injuns across the river. Some of the Ya-
kimas are fixing to join Joseph.

It's being said by whom?

Well, general, I read it in the paper.

We'll look into it. That will be all. Yes?

General Howard, sir, are you aware—

And you are?

Major Shearer, sir.

O yes, of the former Confederate States.

Yessir. I'm in charge of these volunteers—

If you and they were regulars I'd drum you all out of the service.

General, I—

Yes,

> no doubt a cool officer under proper command
>> (for Shearer's heavy-eyebrowed, skeptical-looking face awards him
>> easy *gravitas*,
>>> although his expression brings back to mind the year before
>>> last when Lizzie and Grace were killing four chickens to bring
>>> to the church supper, and when I came home from Vancouver
>>> Barracks, Harry, who must have been just six, was sitting on
>>> a fencepost, watching with extreme delight, no matter that
>>> his mother had warned him that he would get whipped if he
>>> got any blood on his clothes—truly it was comical to see the
>>> play of caution and avidity on the little boy's face! That's how
>>> this poor citizen is, longing to be in charge and fearing he's in
>>> trouble);
> and he means well with his old needle gun.

Major, I'll speak to Captain Whipple about you and then we'll see. For the time
being, you're still in command.

Thank you, general. I'll—

Mr. Croaesdale, you must be very fond of the country out here. What fine
views you people possess:

> weeping willows,
> the pallor of young apples on the tree
> and hayfields slanting down to Grangeville,
>> not to mention Mrs. Croaesdale:
>>> darkhaired and gracefully large, like our new First Lady.

Well, it suits us. By the way, I want you to know, general, that I shall be filing a
depredation claim against the Indians. They looted a cabin of mine out at Cottonwood and—

Mr. Croaesdale, please allow me to catch the Indians first.

One item may be of concern to your troops. Joseph is now in possession of all
my explosive bullets.

How many cases?

O, half a dozen at least, and in my depredation claim—

Thank you for informing me. That's unfortunate, but we faced worse in the Secession War. Now please excuse me; I must interview two more of Joseph's victims,

> and dusk,

> > our sentry chanting *All's well* throughout the night.

2

Well, Perry, this march calls up bad memories for you, doesn't it?

You could say that, sir. I'm ready to fight—

I never doubted it. You and Whipple will lead us down to the head of the cañon.

Yessir.

What's your opinion of Mr. Reuben's Indians?

General, Captain John has been working with the Army for twenty-two years, off and on. Colonel Wright didn't hang him, so he must have been pretty good.

Very funny. And the other one? He has an Indian look, but at least his hair's short . . .

That's Old George, sir. I don't know him so well. They say he's real good-natured.

We'll find out. How are your horses, by the way?

Excellent, thank you, sir. The scouts have already rounded up another half-dozen of Mr. Joe's ponies—

Well, see to it that they really do belong to Joseph and not to some good Indian.

You can count on us, general.

> > Well, he expired not making any sound, some instants after he was shot, so I didn't know at first; I said something to him, and when he didn't answer I saw his eye blown out and then them reds—
> >
> > That's enough.
> >
> > Give the DEVIL his due. Mr. Joe ain't no meaner than a road agent.
> >
> > O *fuck* you.

Now, Perry, you'll show me the transverse ravine where your men escaped.

Yessir.

Mr. Chapman,

> > whatever you and your volunteers might have done to bring about Perry's defeat, how can I not give you the benefit of the doubt, when we're all tainted by old Adam and his sin, and when our adversaries had, after all, just committed murder after breaking their promises to me? In your blithe self-promotion you would prefer me to credit your absurd excuses as if they were printed on the leaves of this tiny

Bible, but since you are the same as I (and Joseph), you bear watching, unfortunately.

I want you to guide Captain Paige's volunteers through those hills over there. Don't stray from the ridgeline.

Sure thing, general.

Quite a fine horse you have.

Thanks, general. See, I raise 'em myself, and, the main trick to it—

You and Mr. Shearer are friends, I understand.

Yessir, and the way to manage him is to call him *major;* he likes that.

Chapman, I'll manage him as I choose.

Yessir. He's real good. Already caught one of them hostile reds and bashed his head in. They respect him. He'll make sure everything's slick.

Enough. How well would you say you know Joseph?

Better than any other white man, for sure. Real good. I'd say I know him cold.

And White Bird, you must have seen him often. Could you define his habits?

Hides his cards, general. Even the other bucks wonder what he's thinking. Anyhow they're all villains.

No doubt. Did they pillage your ranch?

Haven't been down there since I got my thoroughbreds away. Pretty likely.

Yes.— O, what a vast, charming expanse!

Yessir. And I got all my thoroughbreds safe away, so Mr. Joe can't—

I believe those mountains yonder, don't they lie between the Salmon and the Snake?

Right you are, general.

Then that must be Toohhoolhoolzote's country

> and where the slanting walls of golden grass finally meet the green
> grass there will soon be horses:
>> horses black on the grass
>> and far away the river dark and cool.
>>> *The men they will cheer and the boys they will shout—*

Yessir. You've got a real good eye—

Thanks. Now, Captain Miller and Captain Winters,

> drinking bad water from canvas-covered flat bottles,

you'll lead your infantry and cavalry straight ahead down the main cañon trail. Keep your best flankers and skirmishers out.

Yessir.

A burial detail will follow each column. Colonel Perry, you know the lay of the land. How quickly can the job be done? We don't want to leave any of ours uncovered.

Depends on the heat, sir. If we ride out early—

We'll start at six-thirty to-morrow morning.

Plenty of light then, sir.

Yes—

remembering the September dawning in the "East Woods" of Antietam when he awoke to find that the soldiers he'd slept among were all *dead;* soon his division was given the task of burying them. *Dead!*

Not enough blankets to cover them all, and heads, hands and feet impaled in trees, and

(the dead horses stinking still worse)

after the war and the Grand Review, when I tried to tell Lizzie, she was hanging up a cheesecloth to dry.

Where's Doctor Alexander? O, there you are. You'll make an examination of each body recovered: wounds and mutilations.

Yessir.

I'll instruct Major Mason's detail to assist you as required.

Thank you, sir. Given the lapse of time since they were killed—

I know you'll do your best, doctor.

Of course, sir.

We'll all feel relieved when they're decently in the ground.

Yessir.

Now take this paper to Captain Sladen. And would you tell Major Mason I need him for a moment?

Yessir.

Major, as you know, one requirement of your rank is to inventory the property of deceased soldiers. I'll count on you to identify the effects of each body and tabulate it in your report within twenty-four hours after the last burial at White Bird Cañon. Do you see any difficulty in carrying out this duty?

None at all, sir.

Thank you, major. O, good evening, Wilkinson. It stays light so late nowadays.

Yessir. The coyotes are already out—

O, can you hear them?

Yessir, down in the cañon—

My hearing begins to fail. Too much noise during the Secession War.

Yessir.

Well, there will be less matter to bury. Now what is it?

Beg to report, sir, we secured both deserters, and they're being held at Mount Idaho.

Very efficient of you! In your opinion, how shall we dispose of them?

Well, general, it would deduct from the strength of our command to escort them all the way to jail at Lapwai, and at Mount Idaho some drunken volunteer would soon cut them loose. They made no resistance when I arrested them. I wouldn't call them vicious—

All right. Shave their heads and return them to duty, on your responsibility.

Yessir.

Whose are they?

Captain Trimble's, sir.

They're to forfeit a month's pay. Ensure that Major Mason is informed. And Captain Trimble will send me a report.

Yessir. He usually flogs them—

Now, Wilkinson, what's your opinion of this so-called Major Shearer?

O, well, sir, I'd say he's all right. Brave and active. Less impulsive than Chapman—

A GoDfearing man?

Technically, general, a communicant of the Episcopal Church, but—

I don't suppose he ever came to General Eaton's notice.

Likely not, sir.

On a related subject, Wilkinson, why weren't you at Sallie Eaton's wedding?

Don't you remember, sir? My mother—

O, forgive me! Sorry to touch on a sad subject. I think I mentioned that it took place at Trinity Church.

Then was it Bishop Morris?

Exactly. And Grace was a bridesmaid. She wore some blue silk thing. Very impressive. Now she's all agog to have her own Episcopal wedding. Has to find a husband first, of course.

Ha, ha! Well, sir, Shearer's in politics, they say, so he surely goes to church. Chapman will know.

All right. Find out whatever tales they tell about him, because I want a useful man in charge of Mount Idaho. If Joseph gets behind us—

And counting off their scores of men, they leave at six-thirty in the morning.

BURIAL
JUNE 26

1

*A*round his face Wood winds his silk scarf, woven by his fiancee Nanny. The smell comes through.

His copper bracelet burns. Dear GoD, may it preserve me from sickness even here!

> There's two more over here.
> All right, let's get 'em into the ground.
> Where's the doctor?
> Anybody found Theller? The general wanted to be told,
> > not by the roar of flies, nor by these buzzards like
> > low slow clouds,

the sky cracked violet-grey like cottonwood
bark,

poison oak living between the yellow grass and
the leaden dirt.

Lieutenant Wood, sir, it's just a boot up there, and Captain Pollock said—

Good enough, private. Just bring it in to the detail and they'll take care of it.
Have you covered that coulee?

No, sir.

Well, you know what to do.

Get the job done, Company "D"! You! Don't stand there puking,
shitfaces! Or are you fixing to leave the job to others? Who the fuck
do you think you are? Up, up, *up!*

Yessir.

Wood, are you getting pooped out?

Not at all, captain.

I didn't think so. You're doing fine. Pretty hardboiled.

Thanks, Captain Pollock. Those Germans down there need oversight. They
keep stopping to pray.

Well, keep them on their feet.

I sure will, captain. What do you think about all this?

A short campaign. All that has got to be done is to catch the leaders and hang
them. Back to work now.

Yessir.

So Joseph kept his line retired down there in that
woods—

But Perry had a real straight shot down through here,
and he—

Shut up. If he hears you—

Doctor, there's another one for you just down the coulee.

And never a single d——d dead Indian!

Is the hole dug?

Yessir. We got him covered just like you said.

And five more for the doctor, down thataway just across the stage road,

like all them tumbleweeds heaped up
against the wall at Farewell Bend,
when Fidelia was weeping and

These ones are lacking their—

Just rotted off, or else it was coyotes.

O yeah? What about that poor devil up there in the
thorn tree with his balls cut off and crammed into his
mouth? What about him, GoDd——nit?

Them savages had better expect the same.

A sad disaster, I should say. Mr. Joe seized the favorable ground—

And take note, boys: Them trueblue volunteers turned tail—

Don't fill it in yet. I found another piece.

Good GOD!

This entrenching bayonet's a true convenience, I must say, especially in this rocky soil.

Well, then, dig away. Don't leave his boots sticking out.

And here's where Ollicut came a-charging—

How the hell do *you* know?

Because Sergeant McCarthy—

Unidentified. Two bullet holes in skull, both arms missing, torso partly consumed by animals.

Yessir.

No, that won't keep the flies off you.

But when they swarm on a fellow's face, after crawling all over *them*—

And none of 'em made a stand! Not one. They're scattered all across this country, and every man alone! No one stopped to help his comrade, or nobody was in command, because—

Unidentified. Arrow wound in neck, lips removed, possibly by birds. Head possibly scalped. Actually, I don't know about that.

Doctor, I should say he's been scalped.

Leave it as I dictated it. *Unidentified. Deep gashes in arms and legs. Head missing.*

Well, looky here. I just found me a silver dollar.

You going to steal a dead man's money? Throw it in the hole or give it to the major for his d——d inventory.

Ain't *you* tenderhearted? Why don't you gallop into bed with our Christian General—

GOD, it stinks—

I've long since learned not to show my head twice when an Indian's watching.

Ain't you the educated one.

Seriously, I'm afraid Mr. Joe's got the whip over us.

O, cut it out.

Unidentified. Throat cut, three bullet holes in lower abdomen, left leg missing (possibly cut off), right arm broken.

Yessir. But, doctor, his—

Colonel Perry, sir, this man here's getting the shakes. Says he can't—

All right, sergeant, I'll talk to him: *You!* Why, you GoDd——d freak.
If we were at Lapwai I'd hang you up by your thumbs. You're not
man enough to be in this Army. Would you walk away and leave
your comrades unburied? These brave, brave men who died here!
You're not even the same species. *I'd like to kick you in your d——d*
teeth. Now get to work; I don't care if you drown in your own
puke.— Sergeant, if he slacks off again, shave his head and throw
him in irons. Christ, what a yellow-bellied slacker—

Spencer and Henry rifle shells found near the remains.

Yessir.

And this one got done in with a buffalo rifle, doctor. See the slug?

Thank you, soldier. I'll get to that presently.

2

Why must there be horror in the world? Ravishing and burning women! (Is
that what our Southern brethren would term a *barbeque?*) How can I understand
GoD? But surely Progress

> (forty pounds of gear burning his hips and shoulders, the copper bracelet
> guarding him from evil:
>> This must be Jonesey. They sure messed him up good.
>> Took his trumpet, too)

and the maggots,

> maggots and Progress

and Nanny's letter about the Centennial: she disliked riding through
Fairmount Park:

> O, to see Mr. Joe hang, and shiny flies enshrouding *him!*
> Did he truly burn women? Whenever I start feeling faint, all I need
> to do is imagine Nanny in his clutches,
>> maggots spewing out of a headless, farting corpse swollen up
>> in death's pregnancy as two choking young soldiers lift it up,
>>> no worse than green salt hides at the tannery although I
>>> must say I feel hot and sickish, with bile down in my throat
>>>> and cottonwoods grey amidst the greenness of
>>>> the creek's other trees,
>> maggots raining, raining so pure and white down onto the
>> golden grass
>>> of America,
>>>> our burial party advancing down the swales to-
>>>> ward the creek, hoping for Indian relics since Mr.
>>>> Joe must have decamped in haste (why shouldn't
>>>> we discover something pleasanter than the car-
>>>> casses of our friends?)

and a bloodstained pocket diary in the grass, most
pages ripped out, I suppose by the savages; on the last
leaf it runs: and alsoe Tobacao the wead that a soldier
likes eaven better than he does Whiskey.

How's your lot doing, Fletch?

O, they've found half a dozen. A worm's eye view, so to speak. Thank GOD it's
clouding up.

Might mean rain.

At least it'll wash the stench away,

and Colonel McConville's volunteer company creeping up the draw (I'll
bet they're wishing they'd rested in Lewiston!):

Be a man, Wilson. Ain't you seen dead folks before?

I sure have, sir.

O my JESUS—

Then control yourself.

Colonel, I—

We're all mad as hell about this. Now, Wilson, don't you worry:
Them Indians'll pay before we're through.

Is that Theller? See, he's got a—

No it ain't.

Well, who is it then?

How in blazes should I know? They all smell the same.

You're not acquainted with McConville, are you, Wood?

No.

A hard-charging man. Once we were both at Fort Vancouver.

Fletch, if I get killed, will you write to Nanny?

You can bank on it. I'll tell her a handsome young squaw kissed you
to death.

What call did the squaws have to mutilate them, sir?

What do you mean?

And that's also what them squaws did at Little Big Horn. They
should be exterminated.

Stay cool. You never went to Little Big Horn, so you don't
know about it. And keep digging that hole, *doublequick*,
GODd——n you!

But look how the cheeks are torn right off the faces!

That's simply how they rot, Wilson. Does your Mama know
you're simple? When a dead man bloats, he busts open, and that's
how it is. Didn't your fucking GODd——d Mama teach you that?

Then how the hell did their arms go missing, colonel?

Coyotes. Keep digging and you can keep entertaining me.
You're the most hilarious clown of a performing animal that's
stood before me on his hind legs all this stinking day.

Yessir.

What is it now?

Begging your pardon, colonel, but I'm dead sure the squaws did it.

Wilson, you're a fucking caution. Exactly why are you so sure?

Because that's how Indians are, sir.

Well, you just keep right on digging while you formulate your Indian theories,

> the grey sky sucking at the high grass-breasts, carrion birds hopping in the rain and Wilson's theories fading down into a bleached lump of race prejudice until
>> O joy!
> he's called upon to inter that corpse with its privates crammed in its mouth, thereby proving that this mocking Colonel McConville is a Godd——d Indian lover like Uh-Oh Howard

as the flies' brassy buzzing directs them up into another thorn gulch: Theller.

Send a message to the general.

Yessir. And Colonel Perry wants to pay his respects—

That's right. They fought the Modocs together, didn't they?

—our wrists and foreheads sunburned after the first half hour in the lava beds

and no matter whatever happens to me now, I will

> *Stand up for JESUS! Tell me where,*
>> *My SAVIOR, Thou wouldst have me stand?*
> *What work, what burden bear,*
>> *What cause to plead, what foe withstand?*

O Godd——n Mr. Joe to hell

and that yellow Trimble, who jewed his way out of riding down here and Godd——n all this and everything.

3

The first time we ever rode to Lewiston together, in September it must have been, he pulled us a drink and commenced to tell me about Delia; he couldn't stop, and I, amazed not so much out of pity (although I felt that later, and also shame on his account) as from the strangeness that he had looked into my heart and trusted me unlike any other man or woman before or since.

And then the very next time when he and I were out on the Mount Idaho road, cantering our horses into the shade of the high grassy bluffs:

> *The bold dragoon he has no care*
> *As he rides along with his uncombed hair,*

and he telling me still more about Delia and that Blackfoot squaw he was so crazy for (that's what made him ashamed, and therefore sometimes hard toward his fellow men), I said: Show her to me. So he did. Right away, in spite of my better instincts, I liked the look of that whore, who was half gone although from the color of her liquor I could see they'd watered it down near about to nothing; give an Indian a white man's drink and you can blow him over! GOD, we both could have done anything we wanted to her.

He never complained about anything, except about Delia, and that was hardly complaining. The only thing I held against him was the idiot way he pomaded his hair.

He always rode near as easy as an Indian in the saddle.

How could anyone not love Delia? But he didn't, and I'm not sure she ever cared for him, and I

> remember willows and young cottonwoods on the sandbar, the Clearwater deeper here than in Kamiah where all those white stones shine half-dry, and us picketing our horse on the edge of the cottonwoods while we tippled a bottle of that Red O'Donnell's barefoot whiskey and then he asked me
>
> and that lousy general instructing me: *Perry, you must not get whipped!* as if I ever planned to do anything but my GOD——d best
>
> and poor Jonesey blowing the trumpet so smooth and grand you'd never know he was the resident guardhouse drunk
>
> and on that sandbar improved with shady cottonwoods, I will always remember Theller gambling with Indians; he was even pretty good at that stick game of theirs (maybe his squaw taught him; I never thought of that before)
>
> and I certainly never thought to find him here

in this dead-end cañon, where Joseph evidently encircled them; I sure see how the ground lies! The savages must have been just peeping over that slanting ridgeline like rocks, and the sun in our men's faces, and then out of ammunition, and then

> seven bodies, doctor, and then two more up there, dismounted men it seems;
>> as thick as the wool bales lying around Lee and Company's establishment in Barnard:
>> slouch caps, underdrawers, trousers, belts and blouses,
>> bellies pregnant with gas, swollen greenish hands grappling emptiness, boots and rifles lifted by the enemy
>>> (nothing compared to Gettysburg),
>> all seven naked, robbed and rotten. Well, so what? Everything stinks in the end.
>>> Could that really be him? Not easy to know him now. That's Flash's bridle all right. And there's his hat. I guess that's him.

That's him.

All right, soldier. *Unidentified. Arrow penetrating from left eye into brainpan. Multiple blunt trauma. Teeth knocked out, evidently with rock.*

Well, I guess in their excitement they didn't cinch up their horses, or else—

Shut up, soldier.

Weren't there but six in his squad?

Yessir, but I'm supposing that when they all fell back—

Colonel, can you help us there?

He told off six men,

and I've seen him naked before but I never saw him dead, his halfnaked ribcage shining like the white canvas of a covered wagon.

Thanks, colonel.

Can't even tell where the bullet went in.

Doctor Alexander, have you found what did for him?

Well, colonel, he was shot in the brain, I'd say with a Sharps. Here's the ball: .50 calibre. He must have died instantly

Thanks. Let's get him in the ground—

Yessir. A friend of yours, I know.

That's right.

O, he's got the shakes!

No he don't.

It'll be another few moments yet, because—

The general's right. Nothing stinks like a dead horse.

That breastpin on his undershirt; it unlatches to show her photo-graph; O, they stole it, those GoDd——d reds; well, of *course* they would.

Them Injuns sure took all the souvenirs.

Shut up, d——n you!

Sorry, colonel.

We could dig a nice grave for him up thisaway, colonel, on top of the hill—

—and Perry, balling up his fists as if to strike the private who will direct him, strides straight off to that place, and expressing nothing but wrath, he touches Theller's corrupted hand.

4

Well, Major Mason?

General, I've examined Lieutenant Theller's remains under the observation of Colonel Perry—

Was the doctor present?

Yessir. He's still with the body.

"Stand up for JESUS." Thus in death . . .

Go on.

The sainted son address'd his sire—

It appears that after they murdered Theller, Joseph's Indians looted his gold watch, gold chain, gold buttons and several other less valuable items, such as a breastpin of sentimental value to his wife.

I'm sorry to hear that, major.

And, as he spake with failing breath,

Sir, many of the other bodies seem likewise to have been stripped of their accoutrements,

Rose heaven-ward on his car of fire,

black flies roaring out of an olive-green hollow in the high bluff, a stench, no blue cloth, only naked black-and-yellow carcasses, faces like nutshells

and picture windows for Fidelia. I won't tell her much about this. Wonder how her folks would feel about a Christmas wedding? Because my enlistment's up in December, and I sure don't care to lose more of my life. Although I hate to let down Doc—

Go on, major.

Yessir. In the case of the enlisted men, of course, it's more difficult to know just what property they possessed before death. But I would hazard that the Nez Perces robbed them of rings, gold dust, money and the like.

I'm sure this will be detailed beyond doubt in your report. Anything else?

Colonel Perry has been especially helpful, sir, especially on the subject of Lieutenant Theller's belongings. He knew most of these men quite well by sight, although postmortem changes—

Of course he did. All right, Wilkinson, let's step over here for an instant. Did you check on Doctor Alexander?

Yessir, and he seems to be keeping up with each new discovery. A good man. He did ask me to inform you that due to the lapse of time—

He mentioned that yesterday. Do you have my letter to Mrs. Theller?

Yessir.

Then add: *Your husband's remains have been located and respectfully committed to earth by the men who loved him. I regret to inform you that his valuables cannot be returned to you at this time as the hostiles must have taken them. We may well discover them in the course of the campaign.* O, and please ask Colonel Perry to verify the doctor's list with Major Mason. Golden sleeve-buttons, I understand.

Yessir, and his pistol.

Of course. Well, *all of us here hope you are bearing up under your great affliction. If I can serve you in any way, please command me at any time. Your sincere friend,* that's right. And I'll want you to visit each captain discreetly, to ask that any signs of corpse-robbing among our own be reported to Major Mason.

Yessir.

Don't act so shocked! They'd do it to the enemy. They probably did it at Little Big Horn and blamed the Indians. Human ghouls!

Yessir.

I want this operation to finish within another hour. We need to camp and throw out our skirmish line. When you discover him, please send Captain Sladen over here.

Yessir.

Lieutenant Wood, what are you about?

General, Captain Pollock asked me to—

All right. He relies on you to prepare his reports, I understand.

Well, general, I do my best. For Colonel Perry's casualty return, he—

Come aside with me. Now how are you managing?

Very well, thank you, sir,

   feet itching fiercely in the sweltering boots and stomach qualmish,

      hot wind-breath of putrefying carrion and a fly walking on my ear.

Do you want to ask me something?

General, what's your opinion of this battlefield, I mean from a professional point of view?

I'd say Joseph's ground could not have been better selected.

Thank you, sir.

Are you going to vomit, Wood?

Of course not, sir.

Good. To-day you've gained knowledge, haven't you?

Yessir.

How would you characterize what you've learned?

Well, sir, it feels, I'd say, *poisonous.*

We burned five thousand dead service animals at Gettysburg. You can imagine the rest.

Yessir.

Remember, you must never show weakness before the men.

Thanks for the advice, general. I'll remember,

   and I wonder who's going to be promoted to Theller's position?

You cannot be a soldier and turn away from death. Do you see that corpse in the grass?

Yessir—

Get those two privates to carry it down for the doctor. That's right. I don't think the limbs will come off. Now what do you fear?

I don't fear it at all. I dislike the way it's grinning at me—

And the odor, of course.

That, too—

Wood, very soon you'll find that these manifestations cannot move you. Then you'll almost be a soldier. You'll need to master only two more things. Can you guess what they are?

Fear of pain, general?

Correct for one. Now for the other.

Belief, it must be. Belief in—

Now carry on. Have you satisfied your other obligations to Captain Pollock?

Yessir.

Good. The Dayton volunteers have just arrived. A Captain Hunter is in command. Go see what you can do for him and his company. Then return to your duties. That's all. No, Fletch, give that inventory to Lieutenant Bomus. That's right. Captain Miller, send out your cavalry to scout, and then corral the train. We've got to wrap this up here,

   the yellow grass going green in the rain.

Yessir.

Well?

No sign of any hostiles, general.

      Think they're watching us?

      Sure.

All right. Form the camp. And strengthen your pickets to-night. Remember, gentlemen: All told, we're fewer than a single regiment of the Secession War.

Yes, sir. I'll give the men permission to wash in the creek—

Fine, but keep a lookout.

And so they plant the guidon on Camp Theller on the Salmon, turning out the animals under the shade trees:

 Roll call,

  right face,

   dismissed!

   pickets out, terrified and on their bellies with their Springfields
   cocked

while the others blow the Funeral March,

angry, anxious, disgusted, hoping for victory and souvenirs,

   spreading out their saddle blankets in order on the company street,
   then overlaying their rubber blankets (their saddles will be their
   pillows),

    our infantry making do with less,

and white blossoms wilting on the chokecherry trees.

5

Then comes rain,

 rain all night,

  Bugler Brooks blowing "Stable Call,"

the horses halfheartedly curried

 (But that Mrs. Benedict, she didn't never get violated. Joseph took pity on her little ones.

 Mrs. Bacon got shot down right in front of 'em, but that husband of hers . . .

 I hear she married at fifteen.

 Is that right? Pretty red hair she's got. A real eligible widow),

Wilkinson singing hymns along with a few interested fellows:

 One, two, three—

 "Stand up for Jesus." Thus in death

 The sainted son address'd his sire,

 And, as he spake with failing breath,

 Rose heaven-ward on his car of fire.

 That's real nice. I never knew that song before,

and uncooked salt pork on pilot bread so stale they must crush it between stones,

 detesting these Indians whose presence curses the earth,

 turning up their collars against the rain

  (the luckier men roofing themselves under oilcloth and blankets),

 all hating their cruel general who has ordered: *no campfires, no visiting*

  (wisely, no doubt, for what if those cricket-songs were Nez Perce signals, and Joseph were preparing even now to murder us in the dark, perhaps assisted by Smohallie's devils?),

 their no-account general, Uh-Oh Howard, who, being in charge of operations, must bear the blame for Perry's defeat.

6

Rain, rain, and Blackie fetches coffee-water from the creek; rain, and his corpse-perfumed hand brushes moisture from his nose: I found me this little Indian bag. It sure would be handy to keep our sugar in.

Throw it in the fire. You heard me. No messmate of mine is keeping any squaw trash.

Both of you shut up.

We're entertaining you.

No you ain't. I'd rather be playing a game of "base ball" back at Lapwai.

7

Soldier, your blanket is a Godd——n lousy rag.

Yessir.

Why can't you take care of it?

Well, colonel, they gave me a rotten one.

And you couldn't be bothered to check it out at Lapwai? Sleep in the rain then.

Yessir.

Run up to Lieutenant Bomus and see if you can wheedle a spare. Don't let Lieutenant Wilkinson see you *visiting.* You can say I gave you permission.

I thank you, Colonel Perry.

GODD——ned Leavenworth contractors should be *shot—*

Yessir.

Men, keep on the lookout.

Yessir,

> men coughing and quietly cursing, Blackie's belly, wrists and shoulder-blades clammy with rain and old sweat, his thighs getting cold:
>> When will this end? This is not my life; and what if I'll never be alive anymore? I hate these stinking instants and sodden hours—which I lay before Chief Joseph, our enemy,
> Doc sitting on a boulder sewing rawhide bindings on the bottoms of his trousers,

and men sleeping in the wet grass.

8

Wood, staring up at the night sky, listens to a falling branch. He pulls his rubber blanket away from his head, then down again. Rain runs down his forehead. Someone is coughing. In Captain Pollock's tent the other young officers are all singing nigger songs to raise each other's spirits. Wood likes these men well enough, but it is crowded in there and he would rather be in the rain, which he certainly learned to endure in Alaska. His copper armband feels pleasantly cool. He prays: *Dear LORD, I thank You for preserving me from the Battle of White Bird Cañon.*

9

Wilkinson, how are you bearing up?

Very well indeed, thanks, general.

Not quite as pleasant as our stroll beneath Arcturus the other night.

Not quite, sir. Just a moment, sir; let me trim the wick—

Much better. Now can you see to take more dictation?

Yessir. To Portland or San Francisco?

Portland, to be telegraphed onward. *Please ask General Sherman to send one (1) regiment of infantry for duty in this Department. This force will be needed for permanent occupation.*

Yessir.

The Indians throughout the northern and eastern parts of the Department are very restless and uneasy.

Yessir.

Now tell Captain Whipple to come here. I need to quiz him about this country.

Right away, general. And what about Ad Chapman?

O, let him not buzz around me before I'm a carcass! We met enough flies to-day!

10

Having flittered and hovered over Colton's map with Whipple, until he knows the terrain well enough for to-morrow, and so now waiting Mason's report on coör-dinations achieved, the general sits in his tent, on a stool made out of a packing-box overlaid with one of Lizzie's old curtain-covers which she has fitted to the occasion (the cloth folds up to almost nothing on the march, and it makes him happy to look upon the work of her hands), with Colton's map from this year outspread before him on another packing-case as he listens to the roar of the Salmon River, remembering GOD's promise against all heathens: *They were as the grass of the field, and as the green herb, as the grass on the housetops, and as corn blasted before it be grown up.*

Having overseen his files strike down into the cañon this morning, most of them unflinching, and remembering the expectations of Captain Joceyln, the anxiety of Mr. Croaesdale, and that sad crazed woman whom Joseph violated,

> and Joseph's eyes, not to mention the lightning-blasted streak of grey in Looking-Glass's hair

> > (Lizzie must be suffering nightmares),

> and the time not long ago when I considered Joseph and Ollicut to be good Indians,

he broods perplexed:

> Should I wait upon my second force collecting at Lapwai

> > —Throckmorton's, Rodney's and Morris's companies of Fourth Artillery, and Burton's company from Twenty-first Infantry

> > > (our effectives hence practically doubled to four hundred men)—

or immediately pursue Joseph across the Salmon before he can commit more murders? Should I underestimate him a second time, McDowell will write to Sherman—

> > When should I make a junction with Trimble's command?

> > I must say, I like Captain Pollock even better than I remembered. An energetic, straightforward officer. A fine father for Wood, I trust.

> LORD, I'm tired!

Dismissing Theller's specter with no desperate gesture, for he is familiar with many such, he shuts the doorflap, refreshes his arm-stump with carbolic acid, deepens his study of the way that the Little Salmon and the South Fork wriggle down south by southeast into the green and beige and pink blanknesses at the heart of Colton's map, which was printed just this year

> > (that's where Joseph will withdraw, no doubt: precisely into the place we do not know),

opens the flap again, and pleases himself remembering the spring leaves beginning to clothe the skeletal tree-fingers upon the natural dyke of the "Indian carry"
where our bygone red men portaged their canoes, Mr. Stinchfield's rowboat, tied
to a pine, swaying across those trees' reflections; and at the far side of the carry,
Androscoggin Lake glows with liquid mist-light. His father, who died when the
boy was ten, is smiling at him; just this once they will go fishing.

I wonder if Mother ever got a single holiday with him? O, in their time it was
work, work, work! I'm practically ashamed to be so lucky—

What is it now, Mr. Chapman?

I think you got the wrong idea about me, general.

Don't irritate me.

General, if I didn't know how to deal with Injuns, I wouldn't have taken one
unto my bosom just like the Good Book says. And maybe you're not aware of my
capabilities. One thing I sure can do—

You sent her back to the reservation, I hear.

Her mother's passing sick, general—

No doubt.

And, you know, general, I could easily have kept out of this affair, but I *volunteered.*

That you did. And fired on Joseph when he raised the white flag.

That wasn't Joseph anyway. It was Wettiwetti Houlis and his no-good bucks—

Not to the point.

I can tell you keep right on suspecting me, general. That ain't fair.

Mr. Chapman, you can go now.

Yessir.

Wilkinson, what news?

Sir, I have Major Mason's report—

Thanks. First thing in the morning, you and the major are to detail an escort
of twenty men and ride back up toward Norton's to fetch the artillery wagons. I
know you'll be on guard; Joseph could strike anywhere. Return by the thirtieth at
the latest. The citizens are getting frazzled.

Yessir.

Any despatch yet from Captain Trimble?

No, sir.

Now can you take dictation, please?

I'm ready, sir.

*On the twenty-sixth we successfully accomplished a reconnaissance into the
cañon while Captain Paige with twenty volunteers from Walla Walla traversed the
ridgeline, and altho' the captain has not yet reported in person I am informed by
scouts that he has located the hostiles' position on the far side of the Salmon. After
burying our dead, we went into camp—*

Yessir.

How's Perry holding up?

Very stoic, sir.

Good. Where's James Reuben?

Well, sir, he and Jim are trolling the timber over there, just in case there's more unburied—

That goes beyond duty, especially for red men! I'll remember them in my prayers to-night.

And I also, sir.

Before we complete this despatch I need to see Doctor Alexander.

I'll bring him straightaway, general.

Good evening, doctor. You've had some unpleasant work.

Did my best, sir . . .

You surely did, and it won't go unrecalled. Now, I need to ask you something.

Yessir.

Were the bodies mutilated?

General, at this stage there's no proof either way. The coyotes—

Were any of them scalped?

Again, no proof, because when the head begins to—

All right. In your best judgment, did Joseph outrage these bodies or not?

In a court of law, applying the rule of innocent until proven guilty, I'd need to acquit Joseph. As for my own personal feelings—

So no proof.

No, general.

Next matter: Did you find anything pertaining to the missing woman, Mrs. Manuel?

I'm sorry, sir—

Thank you, Doctor Alexander. Get some rest now. If our scouts discover any more bodies you'll be informed in the morning. You're a very steady officer, and I'm grateful to have you in my command.

Thank you, sir.

Ready, Wilkinson? *After burying our dead, we went into camp, having failed to establish the whereabouts of Mrs. Manuel.* Shall I mention that there is no proof of mutilations?

General, I'd hold off. There was that one soldier found with his—

Fine. *We anticipate bringing Chief Joseph to submission within the next several days. Morale is high.* Closing salutation. Take that and the other despatches to Norton's and find a message rider to carry it on from there. Rest now.

Good night, general.

Good night, and GOD bless you.

11

Umatilla Jim and Tsams Lúpin are sitting in a thicket, with their sodden blankets pulled tight around themselves and their slouch hats down over their eyes. Lifting his head from his chest, Tsams Lúpin

(he who was once called by another name)
says in his own language
    (which Tsépmin could have spoken to him had he chosen):
My brother, I shall now save you from the dark fire, and teach you from the Book
of Light. Will you pray with me to JESUS?
to which Jim
    (who has kept his true name,
        which no Boston knows except for Tsépmin)
replies in the same tongue: I shall not trouble my heart with Him. Perhaps He has
helped you, but only for awhile, *brother.* When the Bostons have finished devouring the other People, they will finish eating you.
    No, my brother,
        pointing with his long smooth finger,
you speak wrongly! Now take JESUS into your heart. He is your only protection,
        the rain running down his cheeks like tears
           as the thunder says: *Timm!*
and Umatilla Jim says: Tell me, *brother.* Was it you who told Moss Beard to
get Bluecoats to drive in your People? So I have heard from White Bird's
young men.
    Áhaha! So they are your friends! Now I am beginning to see into your heart.
    Speak straight, *brother.*
    I told Cut Arm that if he wished to move our former relations the Dreamer
People onto painted land that cannot feed their horses, he had better get Bluecoats, because otherwise they will not go. That is all I told him.
    So your heart pities them.
    Of course, for when they die they will suffer forever in the dark fire—as will
you. But regarding to this war they have acted wickedly. I am praying as we ride:
JESUS, may they soon be cast down, in order to lead them to repentance. Now for
the last time, will you pray with me?
    Dear *brother,* I have not the same heart as you. But I am not against you; to me
it is all the same.

12

    Wood, luxuriously oilskinned, again shakes the rubber blanket, pulls off his
cap in hopes of cooling his sweaty curls, his flesh cold and wet, his face roasting
with sunburn, his mouth dry as old leather, and the cavalry trousers sticking to
his knees, writing by feel in the dripping dark:
    Dearest Nanny,
    ~~*You wouldn't believe the sights and smells of*~~
        Pollock's bunch still brightly singing nigger songs,
    ~~*To-day the scarf you made me was a comfort, because*~~
    I have come to believe in the existence of absolute evil. ~~*To-day I When I*~~

~~saw the remains of Lieutenant Theller, who led his squad in a hopeless~~
~~stand against the red savages, I~~
Had I been capable of predicting his fate, I would have
    (LORD help me)
done nothing

> because, not comprehending the cause (and there might have been
> none), but registering no less certainly than he did the Idaho sun
> on the parade ground and presently, after several unreceived essays
> in ingratiation, returning Theller's dislike for him, he cut the man's
> acquaintance as thoroughly as possible, not that the Army respects
> such aspirations, particularly out on the frontier; indeed, he once
> at the Vancouver barracks overheard the general explaining to a
> terrified young shavetail, for what reason he never knew, that it is
> not only necessary but pleasing to learn to rule and be ruled by men
> one detests—but not by Theller, Wood insisted to himself, desiring
> and accordingly justifying the utter expungement from this earth
> of his brother officer, whom PROVIDENCE accordingly doomed him
> to encounter in Lewiston, the steamboat to Walla-Walla, the first
> stage to Alaska, being delayed due to a leak in the boiler; so on that
> bright hot afternoon last summer (two months after Custer's fall,
>
> > while Doc, Blackie and Blurick rode in Captain Travis's
> > thirty-two-wagon caravan toward Farewell Bend),
>
> Wood, remembering a certain establishment in San Francisco
> where he had once spent a twenty-dollar goldpiece and change on
> a certain lady who
>
> > actually it was not her at all, but the transaction, which
> > made him feel ashamed, fulfilled and hilarious—
> >
> > > joy blossoming up around the piano-player's ironwood hands,
> > > the bartender pacing softly in his black and white vest behind
> > > the L-shaped granite counter where a flock of gorgeously
> > > feathered soiled doves sat crossing and uncrossing their
> > > thighs, smiling at the miners who had just steamed in from
> > > Sacramento or perhaps the Klamath country and so re-
> > > mained both rich and desperate (but not for long); while mul-
> > > titudes of worthy old sports in clean shirts laughed in
> > > company at discreet tables between the wooden pillars of this
> > > establishment, temporary couples swirling wine glasses at
> > > one another, and the waiter twisted himself into a letter C as
> > > he loaded up his left arm with a mountain of dishes, convinc-
> > > ingly pretending not to see what the diners might be up to:
> > >
> > > > Would you care to come upstairs with me, lieutenant?
> > > > No, ma'am. I'd love to, but I've gotten engaged.
> > > > What a sweet boy! Is that her daguerreotype?

Yes, ma'am.

And she's promised to marry you?

Well, she—

Then here's a kiss to remember me by—

he thought to recapitulate the triumph in a certain tent overlooking the Snake,

Smooth whiskey and good company, lieutenant! *Guaranteed,* because voyaging to Alaska would be daring, so he longed to do something a trifle evil (if not so much as to become unworthy of Nanny); and therefore, having outgrown the kettles and buckets hanging from the ceiling-hooks at the sutler's store, he sought out that tent (which he must have marked out last time), found it, ducked his head when the smiling, red-faced man in gumboots raised the canvas flap, and passed in to the secret world:

two drunken woodhawks, their timber well sold to Captain Wolf and already ten percent pissed away, and

a boy flourishing cards in his slender fingers, as delicately as a musician, and

Theller, purple-faced, lolling like a worn out cavalryman asleep in the saddle, his hand down the bosom of a plump Blackfoot squaw in a muslin dress painted with red and yellow horses

(now what seems strangest of all is not what he was doing or even that I spied him with her, but that she hadn't yet learned to stop decorating herself with horses, as if she were still some sort of virgin in regard to higher civilization; usually they seek to imitate our white women, in order to
)

Nanny, if you could only imagine the round of the soldier's life! ~~If I could only tell you~~

and he opened his eyes, saw me and *cursed.*

Sometimes I do slip into reveries about that squaw! She wasn't beautiful, but something about her dress,

the lovely horses cantering across her breasts and belly as if she were their world

and her knees apart and her bare feet in the pale stirrups of a tan saddle as we go riding through the golden grass:

She leads and I follow. At the bank of an unknown river, she sits me down. Then I commence to kiss each horse on her dress

but here's Theller with his arm across them and

his hand rooting under them, calling me the
worst oath I ever knew,
the squaw hanging her head, although not for
shame—
unaffected in all her ways: neither powdered
cheeks nor pencilled eyebrows for her!
And I myself would have treated her kindly, and
someday she and I would have journeyed to her
Country of Horses.
*There is a Country of Horses, Nanny, and someday, once the Army's made
it safe, I will take you there, and I will show you*
Theller black, yellow and stinking, veiled in flies:
I can't get his smell off my hands!
And what if she doesn't care to go there?
O, to lie down now with that Blackfoot squaw, and work my hand
up her dress,
kissing her red and yellow horses,
yellow like Theller's flesh.

13

Peculiar to say, he feels that by getting acquainted with these dead men he now
knows Nanny better than before.

14

Rising at two a.m. in case Mr. Joe should strike, they form a line and lie on
their rifles, awaiting daylight.
Well, this sure is swell.
Quit it.
All pickets in position, Captain Pollock.
You check them every half hour.
Yessir.
Almost the Fourth of July. I suppose we'll still be in the field,
wriggling their greasy stinking toes in their boots as the grass prickles
their sweaty necks.
Anyhow, it's better than patrolling the sinks back at Lapwai
as more rain drifts and drifts,
the coyotes singing, perhaps already rooting up the dead,
and it almost seems as if they can hear blood dripping underground.

Salmon Crossing
June 28–July 1

1

*H*ey, you scout. Where have I seen you before?

Lewiston, colonel.

What's your name?

Jim.

O yes. Umatilla Jim.

That's right, colonel.

Now I remember. Didn't you track Palouses one time for Colonel Wright?

I sure did, sir. And I got me some.

And then you deserted.

Colonel Píli,* it wasn't like that.

Well, what the fuck was it like then? Answer me right now, and if I'm not satisfied I'll have you punished.

                       Fresh sign over thataway—

                       Well, I should say!

I did my job, colonel, and after them Palouses got whipped I asked my wages and the colonel didn't pay me. Told me to clear the hell out or he'd hang me like the others—

Which others?

Heyoom Tookaitat for one, and then—

That's a GoDd——d Nez Perce name.

That's right, colonel. One of the boat packers. He liked to drink sometimes. You were there.

I was where?

Well, I saw you standing by that big cottonwood tree on the south side of the Clearwater. The colonel hanged Heyoom Tookaitat for losing a bag of flour. Said he'd stolen it, but Heyoom Tookaitat said it fell in the river. When the wagon drove off and left him kicking in the air, most of the white folks clapped—

I don't have time to shoot the shit with you, Jim. Go do whatever you're supposed to be doing.

All right, colonel.

Jim, aren't you married to Mr. Joe's sister or something like that?

My wife's the niece of his cousin.

So you're fighting your own squaw's relatives.

---

*Perry.

Well, colonel, I ride where I ride—

What's her name?

Annie, colonel. She stays home.

And she's Nez Perce, right?

Sure.

Then you're a Dreamer. Because *she* must be a Dreamer.

My heart is good, colonel. I been to church—

Skedaddle,

> recollecting pretty fucking well now how that hanging had gone
> and how immediately afterward Jim, who had actually been
> drummed out for running off his mouth at the colonel, rode away
> into the high yellow hills north of Lewiston across the Clearwater,
> where Theller and I used to gallop our horses up in the green grass:
>> I ought to tell the general, but he's already against me.

2

Captain Paige, what news?

General, we marched along the ridgecrest as you ordered, and when we could see down into the Salmon country we discovered a large force of hostiles.

Good:

> *Hear, O Israel: you are to pass over the Jordan this day, to go in to dispossess na-*
> *tions greater and mightier than yourselves, cities great and fortified up to Heaven.*
>> *Thief treaty!*

Did they leave anything behind?

Nothing of value, sir. The reds have removed their plunder, loose stock and squaws across the river to a well fortified place on the divide.

Thank you, captain. Lieutenant Fletcher, take his report. Captain Winters, detail four more scouts and sweep our back trail up to the Nez Perce village at White Bird Cañon, then ride straight back here as quickly as you can. If Joseph has divided his forces, there may be fresh sign over there.

Yessir.

> Yep, that there's a regular lodgepole trail. Must be hundreds of wild
> Nez Perces on the other side. Maybe all of 'em.
> Not for much longer.
> You got balls right now. I'm curious to see if they'll drop off come
> fighting time.
>> And should Joseph threaten Lewiston—

What is it, Wood?

General, Captain Hunter's men have scouted upstream. They found and buried the remains of three settlers murdered by Joseph. Apparently the bodies were pretty much all burned up except their feet in the boots.

Names?

Captain Hunter deduces they were Mason, Osborne and some Frenchman who wasn't known in the country but—

Write up a report. Well, Captain Trimble, how was your ride in?

Tell you the truth, some of the shavetails are still pretty shaken up, general.

They'll have to get over it.

Yessir. They never saw Gettysburg—

I first met you there, right before it got bad. Do you remember?

Of course, general. You'd already lost your arm—

So I had. Perry, your detail did mark Theller's grave? The widow plans to move his remains.

Yessir.

> Now with the blowing of the trumpet hearts are about to meet.

General, I can see those horsemen but I can't tell who they are. Here's my field-glass—

I don't need it, Whipple. They're Joseph's Indians. You of anyone ought to recognize them. You lived with them all winter.

Now, general, I—

One can tell them at great distances by the ease and grace of the arms. See how smoothly their whips go up and down? The way we use our reins is jerky and angular in comparison.

Yessir. They're making a real threatening demonstration—

Sir, I count eighty-seven blanket-waving warriors.

In that case we have to . . .

. . . Impractical for a pontoon train . . .

But the general promised us . . .

(the sun smoking their separate wearinesses out through their eyeballs).

Deploy a hundred sharpshooters on the ridge, doublequick.

Yessir.

Do they hope to turn my flank at Rocky Cañon?

But, general, they're savages!

Where's that James Reuben? I'd like to know what they're shouting at us.

General, sir, he's out on picket. But Ad Chapman—

All right, fetch Mr. Chapman here.

Howdy do, general.

Chapman, I'm putting you to the test. What are the hostiles crying out?

Well, general, they're taunting our good Indians—you know, Reuben and his bunch. They're calling on them to come over and fight.

What else?

That's all, sir.

Can you recognize any voices? What about Joseph's?

O, now I hear him for sure, general. He's yelling out real bloodcurdling things, calling on SATAN—

As I expected.

Yessir.

How much were you paid to interpret at Lapwai?

Well, I used to get a dollar a day and more, hard cash money—

Are you aware of the circular from the Indian Office, dated the thirty-first?

Of when, sir?

Of last month, of course.

No, sir.

Indian interpreters must now be paid at the rate of eighty-one and a half cents per day.

General, I can tell you for a fact that Agent Monteith gave Pambrun more than that when you was telling Joseph his business, which was just this month. And the thing about Pambrun is, he's a—

Where's James Reuben?

Down at the river. Yellow Wolf and that bunch are daring him to swim across and fight. I'll get him straightaway, general. But Whitman, who don't speak Injun near about as well even as Pambrun, he—

Bring Reuben, doublequick. And when you get back here, and whenever I summon you, shut your face until I ask you a question. When I ask you a question, answer the question and then shut your face. Now get out of here. You there, corporal.

Yessir.

Climb that ridge as quickly as you can and find out for me why we're not dropping any Indians.

Right away, general.

Someone bring me Lieutenant Miller.

Yessir.

Good morning, lieutenant. How's life in the First Cavalry?

Very good indeed, sir. The boys are thrilled to escape from barracks—

I like to hear that. Quite a picturesque chase our Joseph is leading us. Have you ever been out here before?

No, sir.

Miller, you're to get the pack trains safely back to Lapwai for a refit. You may catch up to Major Mason, but I doubt it. Go see Lieutenant Bomus; he'll inform you what supplies we need. Colonel Perry's company will escort you. Are Paige's volunteers quitting already?

Seems like it, general.

No loss. Since they're returning home, they might as well keep you company. How soon can you move out?

In an hour, general.

Good man! I'll hold you to it. That's all. Now, Fletch, why haven't I received a completed report on that false alarm last night?

General, the picket whom they fired on was only wounded in the shoulder, but in the dark they thought—

Who's meant by *they?*

Well, sir—

Are you involved in concealing somebody's negligence?

No, sir.

Very well. I need all available commanders at once.

Yessir.

Well, gentlemen, let's fix our point of attack. Lieutenant Otis?

General, right behind you I've located a height where we can sweep Joseph's camp with our fieldpieces—

That will panic the Indians, without a doubt, but then we'll merely be chasing them again. We must cross that river and finish this. Back already, corporal? Good man! Now what news from the ridge?

Our sharpshooters can't get the reds in range, sir, because they—

Can't get them in range. I see. Lieutenant Parnell, you're an old veteran. What wisdom-pearls would you cast before us swine?

Well, general, this is exactly what these Indians do: They scatter to the four winds at the approach of troops. Nothing to do now but scout the whole country . . .

No, lieutenant. We're going to whip Joseph right here. What is it, Captain Jocelyn?

I suspect that Joseph's aim is to humiliate us, sir. He's insulting the U.S. Army. Therefore—

Therefore we must cross the river,

    this wide grey-and-silver river with its sandy beaches, and then the steep yellow, green and orange hill concealing where it cuts into the earth; thus the Salmon in its deep cañon

        (Wood, unable even to properly describe the way that some clouds resemble pale blue flower-cups, has satisfied himself by writing in his diary *a foaming torrent rushing through desolation:*

            He longs to kill an Indian).

        An ugly river to cross, boys! Hope it don't rain again.

Perry, can you propose a ford?

Yessir, a mile and a half above the mouth of White Bird Creek.

Engineers, do you concur?

He's right, general, because we—

I expect you to finish your bridge within three hours.

Yessir.

Plant your batteries.

Right away, general.

Colonel Perry, prepare your company to move out. Miller's nearly ready, I believe.

Yessir.

Rodney's to bivouac at Camp Theller. Get my artillery in position. Lieutenant Fletcher, stir up those engineers!

General, sir, Joseph's scouts are coming down firing!

How many?

Sir, I—

To horse. Colonel Perry, despatch an advance rider to notify Major Mason.

At once, sir. And we're pulling out of here in fifteen minutes.

GODspeed. Lieutenant Otis, why aren't your Gatlings firing?

The thing is, general, they—

 Why, look at all them Indians,

  jeering and shouting, flaunting their blankets

   (weren't there but three Red Blankets at White Bird
    Cañon?),

  shooting rifles and arrows

  —and here comes the thunder of a buffalo gun!

   Well, for the love of Moses! Where did they get that?

   Who knows where they get anything?

  Fire at will!

   —But how are we to get even with stony-souled Mr. Joe?

   Maybe by

 Constructing a ferry—

I expected better and more rapid results.

General, they're working like niggers, but the river—

  Captain Pollock, sir, the general's mad against our whole company—

 Artillery nearly in position—

  As busy as a saloon on Hanging Day!

3

Lieutenant Fletcher, where are they now?

General, Chapman says—

All right. Send me Chapman.

Howdy, general. You see, soon as we got across the river, Mr. Joe crossed back again. It's easier for Indians, because they—

Thanks. Is that Wilkinson coming in?

Yessir.

Get him something to eat and then bring him straight here. Now where's James Reuben?

Here I am, general.

Mr. Reuben, how can we prevent Joseph's Indians from crossing the river at will?

I'm sorry I don't know, General Howard. I'll pray on it—

  Well, this is rich. Maybe we'll still be doing this come Independence Day.

What do you care? Won't be no ice-cream out here anyways.

Well, in Baltimore you can't even get an ice-cream on Sunday.

What the hell do I care about Baltimore?

What's on your mind now, Chapman?

My wife had a dream, general, before this all started. Dreamed Mr. Joe'd sneak back across the Grande Ronde and—

Wilkinson, get this man out of my sight. And make him understand that if he annoys me again to-day, he'll be punished.

Yessir. Come away *now*, Mr. Chapman.

Did you overhear that, Fletch?

I did, sir.

His wife must be a Dreamer.

General, I'm not aware—

Bring James Reuben back here.

Right away, sir.

Unnerved by Chapman

    (who ought to act more like a white man—what is he, anyway? He wears
    pointed-toe mule-eared boots like some cowboy);

and therefore despatching two of James Reuben's Indians with safe conduct passes to scout the rapids of the Grande Ronde by the reddish-tan rocks (the same hue as the cover of Wood's account book) where some Devil Cave is or may be (Reuben has never heard of it, but smilingly remarks that Mrs. Chapman, more accurately known as the former Mrs. Chapman, may indeed know something about devils), the general allows himself to dream of Lizzie for an eyeblink, until a courier rides up with the daily report from Lapwai: No news of a coördinated red uprising, nor any sign of Smohallie's river renegades, but our good Indians remain in a panic. He remembers marching through Maryland when after all their war-cries the Secessionists lay low and we began to hope they might after all be persuaded home. This time I will refrain from entertaining any such expectations.

Well, Fletch,

    his deductions about Chief Joseph's movements unpredictably variable
    in clarity

        in much the same way that some swales in Umatilla country gleam
        golden with their own light while others remain a dull yellow-green
        or yellow-grey,

nothing to do now but wait once more upon our engineers.

Yessir,

    and where's his GODd——d hymn-book?— O, I shouldn't think that!

Despatch this to Captain Whipple.

Right away, general.

How are we doing for rations?

Running low, sir.

I want to test Lieutenant Wood. Send him out tonight to meet the pack train.

I'll tell him, sir.

Fine snowy mountains yonder.

Yessir. They're called the "Seven Devils"—

Isn't to-day Colonel Miles's wedding anniversary?

General, I'll check at my first opportunity.

No, I'm certain of it. He married Sherman's niece, you know.

Yessir. Was it more than a year he served with you?

Six months. Partway through Fair Oaks. He was also wounded there, as I must have told you. A very fine officer and a friend. Here's a note to him. Post it at the next opportunity.

I'll make sure of it, sir. Sir, the volunteers wish to report to you.

Good afternoon, Mr. Wilmot.

Afternoon, general. We digged up Mr. Joe's caches on Deer Creek, and burned everything unusable, just like you said. Must have been ten thousand pounds of flour and two thousand pounds of camas, and brass kettles, axes, buffalo robes, you name it. Quite a bonfire—

Where's James Reuben? O, there you are. Whose supplies would those have been?

General, Toohhoolhoolzote's People used to winter there.

Good. Yes, Mr. Wilmot.

See, general, if he heads toward the Snake country—

What about horses?

We drove in a hundred and forty-seven head, general.

Fine. Thank you.

   And Mr. Joe's swept around us again. When's our general going to
   do something?

Grimacing, he summons Wilkinson's ear, hand and notepad in order to telegraph the facts of the matter straight to General Sherman.

CLEANING OUT WALLOWA
SOMETIME IN JULY, 1877

I'd sure say it's high time we got the go-ahead.

Well, you know General Day-After-To-morrow. Pretty d——d good we ever heard back,

   as they complete the circumnavigation of Wallowa Lake,

     knocking down that tripod of crooked sticks which rose over the
     converging stone lanes of the fish-weir,

then kicking the stones apart
to make this country beautifully blank;
and riding up to the site of Mr. Joe's last camp
where that Indian expert, Mr. A. C. Smith, shows them how to
probe the ground for camas pits:
all cleaned out right here;
after which they begin to sweep the country eastward toward Imnaha
where certain reds used to winter their horses until our stockmen
took possession
(no stockmen at present: too hot and dangerous,
but nothing's too dangerous for trueblue American
volunteers!)
—spreading out in a skirmish line just as they remember from their old war
dreams.
Now they are coming out into the golden grass and sagebrush,
over the lip of the valley, then down,
seeking caches to burn,
their way still sheltered by overhanging chandeliers of elderberries in the
shadows
as the creek goes blue and braids.
And that's why I keep saying this is prime country for a white man. With a
crick like that, you could do anything. Nobody could boss you around.
I might try me some apple trees over there.
I'd rather graze my stock. Gonna breed me the biggest herd you ever saw, and
fence out simpletons like you. Apple trees! You don't know nothing.
Ostrander saw fresh spoor down there—
What about it? Anybody can't follow a herd of Injuns and their horses tram-
pling their way along don't deserve to live.
How dangerous you think them reds could be?
O, they've cleared out—
What do you say, Mr. Smith?
They could sure double back.
Captain Booth said—
He's yellow. Won't crawl out of Grande Ronde. Tried to get us under his com-
mand—
If I were an Indian I'd fight for this valley to the last ditch.
You're a card, Captain Cullen!
Apparently them two Frenchies they shot on John Day Creek—
Mr. Smith, how long have you known Joseph?
Well, quite awhile. Several years. Ever since I took my section here in Wallowa.
When did he start giving you trouble?
O, he took his time.
I guess they've skedaddled.

They're magic on a horse, believe me. And if they split up, they can hide good; any Injun can! 'Course if they split up we'll get the squaws and their brood.

You reckon a squaw is good for anything?

You'll surely find out.

What about the papooses?

What about 'em, greenhorn? You want 'em to grow up so they can come snea-kin' back here some night and cut your throat?

A man down Pendleton way swore to me they've got some kind of treasure hid somewhere in these hills. So when we catch Joseph or Looking-Glass—

You're a dreamer.

But the placer mines where Doc and that bunch—

All played out, ten years ago and more. No gold around here. Nothing in this for us but saddle-sores and sleepless nights. Maybe a bag of camas if you relish that. I'd feed it to my pigs.

If we just catch one Indian, we'll make him tell us—

Mr. Smith, what's this here?

Just an old Indian trail.

I don't see why we can't go by the levelest way.

Well, Captain Booth said—

I don't give two shits what he said. Look who he reports to. That *Christian Sol-dier*. Can't even whip a handful of yellowbellied reds. You know he's a nigger lover,

> riding past a stately elderberry tree, a lone pine on the edge of the golden
> grass,
>> knocking down every marker in Old Joseph's Dead Line,
>> ready to burn camas and shoot horses,
> and sunflowers here and there,
>> as golden-yellow as Major Shearer's orders
>>> (to hell with those, and to hell with Captain Booth's, and
>>> Godd——n the "sand"-less fool who lost Chancellorsville),
> followed by a deep gorge of basalt and brown grass,
> the river shining and snaking far below.

Could be we'll dig up some good things down there.

You never lose hope, do you?

Anyhow, so far this Hell's Cañon don't look so bad.

You don't know nothing. We're not half there yet,

> the river vanishing at the lip of the next precipice
> and lovely shady places along the hill-edge where water-threads weave
> themselves down from rock crevices and across darkly olive moss as
> slimy as slaughtered hog's guts,
> then small pools,
> shadow-stripes already shrinking as morning wears on,
> rosehips everywhere
> and the sound of water luxuriant and safe.

Now this here, you could nearly raise a family if you fenced it off. Enough water to—

Yeah, what do you know about it?

What do you say, Mr. Smith? You're from here.

It fits the bill for grazing stock. That's what it's good for,

> hot rock hurting our horses' hooves,
> golden grass pimpled with rock
> and down on the right a grassy hollow of pines, rosehips and water which
> if a man lived there could become an entire beautiful world.

Mr. Smith, what do you say about Indian treasures?

I told you.

But if there was any—

I say look for any hill with horse bones on it. That'll be a Nez Perce graveyard.
I say dig up everything and burn it.

Captain Cullen, why do we have to keep ridin' up here?

We got to keep the high ground until we know where they are.

Well, that's a puddle of old donkey-piss!

You can't talk like that. Don't you remember you're a *territorial volunteer*?

If it hadn't've been for you, it would have slipped my mind.

What're them fellers wavin' at us for?

Ostrander's found another cache.

Let him burn it. He don't need us.

Getting to be poorer country hereabouts.

What do you know about it? For all you know, the mother lode is waitin' to be
dug up right down there

> past that clump of juniper on the bluff's rounded corner
> or somewhere on the wide, slanting plateau of golden grass like a hand
> with cut off fingers
> after which come the dark cliffs, and far below, the wide blue river.

Now what do you say? And we still ain't lockin' eyeballs with Hell's Cañon.

This ain't so bad,

> neither the horridly leaning walls, striped with hot black rock
> nor the gulf
> and then Hell's Cañon.

Mr. Smith, what do you say about this?

I been down there. Mr. Joe used to call it *Gorge Place*. A good place for reds
to hide.

This ain't nothin'. I seen deeper holes than this.

Like your grandma's whatever. I bet you seen that.

You watch yourself or I'll shoot your teeth out,

> after which comes Hell's Cañon
> and then Hell's Cañon:

>> They fall quiet. Nobody wants to go down there.

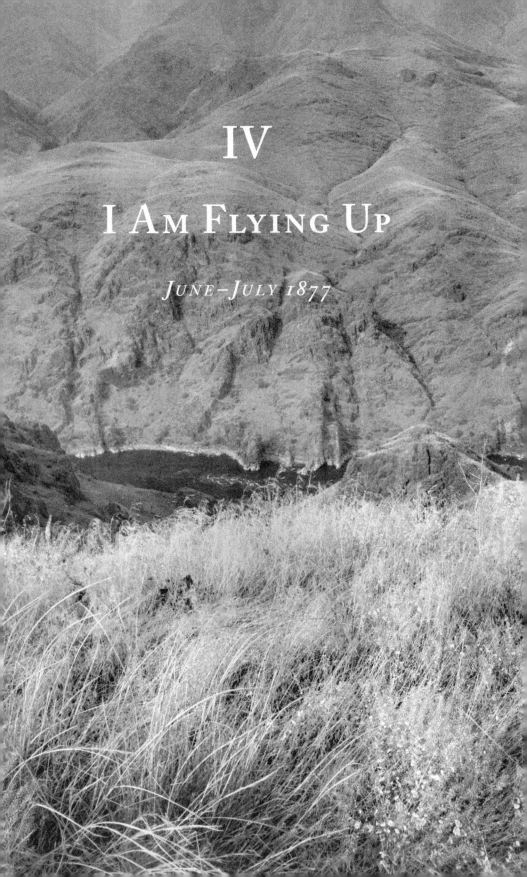

IV

I Am Flying Up

June–July 1877

It was those Christian Nez Perces who made with the Government a *thief treaty.* Sold to the Government all this land. Sold what did not belong to them. We got nothing for our country. None of *our* chiefs signed that land-stealing treaty.

WHITE THUNDER (known as Yellow Wolf), probably before 1935

It was always hard to love a Government which, theoretically, was a mere machine and which could extend no sympathy to people in disaster, nor kindness to the impoverished.

GENERAL O. O. HOWARD, 1907

HERE AT THIS DANCE
JUNE 18–25

1

*O*nce our old women have finished crawling all over the battlefield, snatching up spent cartridges with which to decorate themselves
(Bluecoats like puddles of dark death in the bright grass),
the rest of the People have long since gleaned what they wished:
weapons and ammunition above all, then gold buttons, hardbread, canteens, canvas pouches, cartridges, belts, boots, dark blue blouses, and sometimes tiny bags of sugar or gold dust plucked from within the undershirts of these dead enemies
(pinning the corpses down with sticks when they are too ugly to touch),
slitting strips of leather from the saddles, harvesting bridles from the mouths of dead horses (what shall we do with them?),
and gloating over the bulbous ring of a bayonet clasp, the figure eight of a spring cover, guard plates and band swivels and beating the thickets to be sure none are left alive.
The chiefs have said: Do not scalp,
and Heinmot Tooyalakekt, who fought alongside others but was not war-chief, takes nothing from the dead, except ammunition for his .44 Winchester carbine,
but when Sound Of Running Feet claps her hands to see so many shining war-toys all together, her Uncle Ollokot smilingly gives her one: a pistol in a bloodstained leather belt; and the girl's heart grows so happy that she nearly shouts,
but Good Woman goes on boiling camas soup.

2

Camping down by the creek, setting brave young men to watch exactly here at Sparse-Snowed Place
(soon we must be hiding),
singing the victory song,
we are dancing, swimming like salmon,
Toohhoolhoolsote laughing, his shame avenged:
Hasten; evening shadows be!
Now we have seen their blood flow out.

So we are singing WYAKIN songs:

> Our young men did right to *speak the arrow!* Far better this than to steal a Boston's cow in punishment for all our cows which we have lost.

We shall never be afraid anymore.

3

Ollokot,

> that quick-smiling chief who treasures up his many horses,
> he who leads the young men of Wallowa,

has killed a Bluecoat who wore pretty shoulder-stripes

> (the man fought bravely but childishly, bleeding from three wounds, shooting blindly from within a circle of dead horses);

from his corpse

> (the flies on him already as blackly clustered as chokecherries)

Ollokot strips first a breastpin, which he gives to Cloudburst

> (within it lurks a picture of a pretty Boston woman, which she spits on, then drops into the fire),

then a gold chain, which he gives Fair Land, so that she may buy whatever she desires from Bostons along the trail; and a handful of gold buttons which he gives out to the young men (his heart is good); and finally, best of all, a wristwatch of fine golden metal like the iris of an owl's eye, and this he offers to his elder brother,

> who says: Brother, I must not keep your present, for if I am ever called on to speak with Cut Arm and he finds this thing, he will choke me in rope!

so Ollokot gives it to White Bird, he who has watched the Bostons dig up so much gold out of his country.

4

Shore Crossing has become renowned—a true chief's son. Now he can hardly imagine that he would have ever gone the other way. His WYAKIN is great, his joy translucent like pine bark. Soon he will shoot more Bluecoats; he will cut them into pieces until they are dust; he has completed his heart,

> shaking for joy his buffalo rifle,
> > the big old one, the thundering one which terrifies;
> proud to hear his wife singing the war-song:
> > indeed our Three Red Blankets have become great men, who whenever they like can surely each get themselves a Crow woman who has decorated her dress with nine hundred elk teeth,
> > > although some craven People still insist that the Three Red Blankets behaved immorally when they commenced this war which in truth Cut Arm began.

Shore Crossing is flying up,
> our women laughing to hear him tell over how childishly the Blue-
> coats fought;

in the camp-smell of horses and dust Strong Eagle is flying up
>> (let us go home to our reservation! If we ride there
>> and lay down our rifles, will the Bostons continue to be
>> angry?
>> Strong Eagle, I shall not lie; I shall tell the truth. They
>> will choke you in rope);

Red Moccasin Tops,
> on whom two snows ago a certain Boston storekeeper renowned for
> never giving change to us People drew a bead and let drive, the bullet
> grazing the back of his head
>> (now this bad Boston lies dead in the river, while Red Moccasin
>> Tops is alive forever:
>> no one can kill him),

is flying up and Dreaming;
likewise his father Yellow Bull,
> he who has killed Cutthroats alongside Looking-Glass and the Crows
>> (and who joined us in tasting those two loosehaired Boston bitches
>> in their cabin by the Chinook Salmon Water after we shot their
>> husbands:
>>> *Áhaha!*);

while Swan Necklace gloats to embrace the reddish-brown gleam of a well-
handled rifle-stock of seasoned walnut, as sunlight commences silvering that
long, long barrel of blued steel,
and Loon, who believes he has made himself brave, decorates himself with two
Springfields and seven cartridge belts
> (perhaps he will stake one gun at the Bone Game, or trade it for a box of
> exploding bullets from Cottonwood Place);

White Thunder, Shooting Thunder and Red Spy are beating the green elkhide
with Wottolen and his young son Black Eagle, all singing their WYAKIN songs,
> flying up exactly here where so many miners' wagons have gashed OUR
> MOTHER.

Going Alone, who shot a Bluecoat right off his horse, then shot him again as
he lay struggling and bleeding in the dying grass, finds many young boys to hear
his tale
—so many are now flying up!—
> unmarried women enjoying the dance of our brave men, exalting their
> hearts with drum-booms
>> (even the half-woman Welweyas dreaming of laughingly stabbing
>> wounded Bluecoats with her belt knife),
>>> Springtime suckling the baby, wrapping up camas

cakes, wishing that Cut Arm will now forget us and his
disgrace,
while Fair Land is making fringe for her husband's shirt
(now she will have buttons on her dress like those
that the soldiers wear),
the sunset as red as raw buffalo meat,
as Heinmot Tooyalakekt sits smoking kinnikinnick with White Thunder and Ollokot,
lacking Looking-Glass, the *lucky man* who fled to his painted land
(his People alone will now be safe);
looking upstream into the cleft between darkening green hills
(whitecaps lazily elongating; a beaver dam, snags of sticks),
listening to his heart cry: *qoh, qoh, qoh!* even though there is nothing to decide
anymore:
from to-day we shall be running and fighting, hiding and creeping like
snakes, riding away and away from our home;
as Ollokot says: My dear brother, I am glad we shall not be going on painted land.

5

We have been keeping some of Cut Arm's scouts:
Butterfly Place People with whom we sometimes played the Ball
Game,
and formerly in our family—
no more, not these bad and feeble ones who abandoned their Dreams and
WYAKINS.
Old Tzi-kal-tza says: Lead them before the chiefs. What they say will be done.
These creatures are weeping; their JESUS has turned them into women! The
Three Red Blankets shout: *Áhaha!*
but here is Yuwishalaikt, who was our cousin
(we pity him)
and this silly fellow here who is now called *Lopinson Mínton**
—while Animal In A Hole, who only last summer played our game with
us at Weippe, catching the ball filled with deer-hair,
he has become *Tso Alpít*†
but his father remains one of us, and pleads for him, saying: The Bluecoats could not harm us, while we have killed so many of them! Please let
my son run away now,
although White Bird's braves demand to hear what we shall do in
case these Butterfly Place men become more perfidious; already
they have been disappointing us, helping Cut Arm's killers

---

*Robinson Minthon.
†Joe Albert.

(indeed it is in certain hearts to ride to Butterfly Place and cut
open Moss Beard's throat);

while White Thunder, who has fought well, says to the council: My heart
sorrows for these prisoners here who are not men. Since they are weeping, let them run back home!

and Heinmot Tooyalakekt shows his heart: Even now they remain our
relatives,

so that the other chiefs take pity, warning these wretched Butterfly Place
ones: Open your ears! If you help the Bluecoats again, and if we catch you,
we shall surely whip you with hazel switches,

and then we allow them to run away: *Áhaha!*

6

The chiefs call another council, to which we must bring our new rifles. They
tell old Tzi-kal-tza to count them, which he does: sixty-three. The pistols, women's
toys, no one counts,

and White Thunder, wishing to make himself similar to Uncle Ollokot
(who has made Sound Of Running Feet so glad),

nearly gives his own six-shooter to his Aunt Good Woman, but Wottolen,
wise at foreseeing, says: Brother, why scorn what you have found? It weighs
nothing. Be ready; some day or night you may need to crawl like a snake when
you fight,

and presently these words will prove good;

but now we sleep.

7

Not long after the rising of TRAVELLER THE SUN we hear the ravens' wing-
beats, *shlap, shlap!* and clans of dark birds settle down on the battlefield:

Qoh! Qoh! Qoh!

and in that time just before morning has ended, our brave hunters come riding
home from the Buffalo Country: Rainbow and Five Wounds, exactly those whom
we have awaited; our scouts were watching out for them on the trail; now they
have arrived, the ones so wise in war, whom even Sitting Bull must fear.

Hearing of our trouble, they have ridden quickly. Now they are arriving; they
come on lovely horses, singing.

To tall Rainbow,

he who can never be killed after sunrise,

we give a trapdoor Springfield from a dead Bluecoat; and he rejoices in his heart
(then gives his old musket to Five Fogs, a young man who thinks the old way,
but even a musket is too new for Five Fogs, so he gambles it into Loon's
hands, preferring his arrows).

To Five Wounds we offer a fine Sharps, but he already has a Henry repeater which he won in trade from the Crows.

These two, the cunning ones, advise us to cross the Chinook Salmon Water, and then, if Bluecoats come shooting and galloping

(we know they will),

then let them try to meet us

(they swim like children!);

and if they finally reach our side, we can cross back again.

Thus on the third day the chiefs say: Let us quickly cross to somewhere further, following the rivers and the country between them, seeking the place which now fails to exist, as if each tree had become a lake or a crystal of ice,

so we lassoo our horses

and White Bird's People begin uncaching their own sacks of gold dust, some gathered from creek-places before the miners found them, some stolen from the Bostons in other summers (for although our hearts cannot believe it, we may perhaps never return here);

our women tying bundles of river-reeds together,

packing up tipis, food, dogs, horses and children,

all the warriors in their striped and plaided blanket-coats—not one yet killed—

we are riding down to the high-flowing river, the angry river:

six hundred People, fifteen hundred horses

(the Enemy River was worse than this);

and now the women are plaiting serviceberry vines into ropes;

making boats of dressed buffalo hides lashed to frames of green willow, we pass over the Chinook Salmon Water easily, with each boat pulled by swimming horses and guided by swimming men.

We cross without error

(even horse-rich old Burning Coals gets his entire herd over, with his quiet daughter's help);

then ride through the yellow grass to Deer Creek,

with Heinmot Tooyalakekt (he who is called *Joseph*) helping the weaker ones,

especially his dear wife Springtime,

whose heart is now less burdened than when at Butterfly Place, on the day called *Sapalwit*, the People were commanded to come into council with Cut Arm next morning, to be threatened and shown the rifle, and her husband could not sleep

(now her heart flies up, because we have escaped being penned up on painted land, and because her husband remains joyful over the baby whom she has given him);

and Sound Of Running Feet can now drive horses as well as her mother,
    so that as he rides past on his cream-colored war stallion, her Uncle
    Ollokot smiles, remembering when she was a little longhaired girl
    running in the grass, with a string of beads in her teeth;
        this summer or next it will be time for her to seek her
        WYAKIN;
    and once the People have arrayed themselves in a circle, Ollokot tells the
    Wallowa warriors what they must do,
    while thirty brave men watch behind at Split Rock, in case the Bluecoats
    should come;
the breeze now singing through the line of white tipis at the edge of the willow'd
creek in the slit between golden-grassed hills,
    while we sing the Dreamer song:
        Bell-song, heart-song,
        O my brothers, my sisters,
        now I am meeting you;
        now I am meeting you;
        now I am meeting you here at this dance,
            longing to shoot Cut Arm, who would choke us all with rope.

8

Fair Land has nearly decorated Springtime's baby's dress with porcupine quills
when the warriors ride up to the butte by Deer Creek waving a blanket: *Bluecoats
are coming. Cut Arm himself is coming.*
    How many horses?
    We cannot see them all.
    Here comes the horde of Walking Soldiers, filing down the ridge, and then
guns riding on wagons,
and so, to calm our children, we bring our camp up to the Country of the Medicine
Tree
    (which perfumes our homes and scares away moths from our buffalo robes);
        the sky now as lavender as evening primrose,
            horses neighing, lodgepoles outspreading against the pale
            sky;
        Ollokot canters up to comfort his wives and take his baby son in his
        arms
            (some People say that he loves Fair Land too much, as if she
            has bewitched him with beaver-musk and camomile);
        and Heinmot Tooyalakekt also sees to his family;
here among the Medicine Trees we rest,
    Good Woman singing, rocking Springtime's baby girl in the cradleboard
    which their husband has made

and Wottolen shows Black Eagle how to lock down the breechblock
with the cam latch
the old ones gambling at the Stick Game, betting buffalo robes against
the dead Bluecoats' shirts and cartridge belts;
while Rainbow, Five Wounds and our other best men watch the river all night,
softly singing their WYAKIN songs as they did when the Bluecoats
rode down into sight at that sunrise at Sparse-Snowed Place,
and the Bluecoats do nothing.
White Thunder and Shooting Thunder have already unwrapped their Medicine bundles; they long to tie them to their arms and kill more Bluecoats:
since Ollokot and Rainbow are not afraid, these two feel likewise at peace within
their hearts.

9

Next morning, we ride slowly up and down the riverbank, shooting at Bluecoats for fun (but saving our explosive bullets),
laughing at Cut Arm, whose killers shoot at us from the hills, badly, then
stay on their side, fearing the river's deep part, the *green water:*
slowly, like children, they rope themselves so that they may come fight
us . . . and their rope breaks:
Áhaha, they are contemptible.
We are laughing as we shoot,
at which Tsams Lúpin (Cut Arm's slave) now shouts at us: *You are frightened old women!*
to which Rattle Blanket shouts back: *Then come over the water. We shall
scalp you!*
and Shore Crossing, laughing, cups his hands around his mouth to shout:
*You from Butterfly Place are the scared women, not us! You are becoming
fat, eating Government food!*
and we laugh to see Tsams Lúpin make himself angry.
Now at last our enemies have again begun to cross this river,
whose water is bluish-green like death camas leaves,
and we enjoy to watch them, laughing at the threats of these Butterfly Place slaves
who sold their country and ours
(thief treaty!)
but: Give them room to arrive, poor fellows!
—so we ride away down the river,
and when Rainbow and Shore Crossing come to tell us that they have finally
reached our side, we do as Rainbow and Five Wounds advised, and cross back
again:
Áhaha.

WHERE THE ENEMY RIVER GOES
JUNE 26

1

*T*he People say: Let us quickly go upstream to somewhere further,
    although nothing will catch us,
        not moldy old Cut Arm,
but Toohhoolhoolsote is angering himself now,
    flying up,
      singing them into anger against Bluecoats and Bostons,
and White Bird's young men have begun singing:
Loathsome old man,
I'll scoop him up with fire!
        as the women gather fire-sticks as if to burn up Cut Arm (whose prom-
        ises are bad red berries pretending to be chokecherries)
        and brave Wottolen,
           he who remembers and whom no bullet can kill,
        changes presents with his war-friend White Thunder, Dreams awhile
        with Star Doctor, smokes the pipe with Heinmot Tooyalakekt, summons
        his son Black Eagle and rides home to Looking-Glass's country, where
        there will be no war:
           for White Thunder's dear mother he brings a sack of Bluecoat
           coffee,
           and a gold Bluecoat button for his wife
—as Toohhoolhoolsote sings, and his song is as sweet as the greyish-
white breast-feathers of a downy woodpecker:
        We are spinning.
        We are spinning as we go.
           Welweyas is flirting with Rainbow,
                who, never having tasted a half-woman, finds this mo-
                ment as alluring and dangerous as when BUTTERFLY
                opened and closed Herself;
Heinmot Tooyalakekt is decorating Black Mane-Stripe,
    his strongest gentle one, who never bites the other stallions but simply backs
    into them until they fall aside,
and Ollokot smiles when Cloudburst begins to sing
so that Fair Land, worrying that their husband prefers his younger wife, throws a
twig on the women's pile, then turns away,

beginning to remember a dream which once befell her high up in the cedars, spruces and pines where it gets cool and grassy and the cous grows; it happened before she married Ollokot, when she rode her pony up from shade to hot and resinous-smelling sunlight to pick cous with her mother and sisters,

> green lichens growing downward on the trees like upside-down tufts of grass,
>
> then the clumps of yellow grass in the grey dirt at the edge of the trees where the world drops down, down toward the pale green-grey and pale green-blue knife-ridge cañon where the Enemy River goes,

and that night in her mother's lodge she dreamed of falling; she could not cry out to her WYAKIN; and down below were red flames like bad red berries

> or like the eyes of SOMETHING
>
> > —an unlucky dream—

and Fair Land fears that to-night she may dream this dream again.

2

White Thunder has killed another deer, giving the meat to others, and now his aunt Good Woman and his mother Swan Woman are scraping the skin;

> to-morrow they will stain the deerskin with the smoke of rotted pine wood;

while Toohhoolhoolsote is beating the drum, to make the Bluecoats concave. The People are no more to be penned up out of sight forever in a narrow place. I am flying up. I am leaping up. I am worshipping,

> going up into the sunshaped silhouette of lodgepoles to find Power, meeting our WYAKINS in the sun of a smokehole,
>
> > perhaps to kill more Bostons, and make our People live again.

V

THE REST OF MY DAYS

JULY–AUGUST 1877

Emma was kneeling with her arm around [her husband George] Cowan's neck, when an Indian came up, and catching her by the hand, tried to pull her away. He pulled one of her arms from his neck, and then another Indian, seeing that Cowan's head was exposed, put a pistol to his face and shot him in the forehead. Emma fainted, then, and I jumped and screamed . . .

IDA CARPENTER, sister of Emma Cowan, 1877

. . . my desire for life returned, and it seems the spirit of revenge took complete possession of me . . . I took a solemn vow that I would devote the rest of my days to killing Indians, especially Nez Perces.

GEORGE COWAN, 1877

WE GAVE LOOKING-GLASS AN OPPORTUNITY
JUNE 29–JULY 1

1

I'm glad to hear that Looking-Glass remains at home. If the others who gave me promises had kept them, there would have been peace and prosperity, not war.

Yes, sir.

General, sir, Mr. West just rode in from Mount Idaho.

Send him over here.

Yes, sir. Here he comes now, sir.

A pleasure to meet you again, Mr. West.

Good afternoon, General Howard.

What news?

Mr. Silverwood and Mr. Dempster, their houses got burned by bad Indians.

My word. Joseph's bucks ride fast.

When we rode to ask Looking-Glass for information, some Indians made us go away.

Looking-Glass's Indians?

Yes.

Perhaps they were afraid.

General, I don't know their reasons.

Thank you, Mr. West. Why don't you rest your horse and take a meal? Tell the cook I said it was all right. I'll send for you soon.

Good,

      and Mr. West strides away,

            the general looking after him, shaking his head.

General, sir, there's that Injun scout again. Wants to whisper some nonsense to you personal.

What's his name?

Umatilla Jim, he's called. I don't like his look, sir.

Why not?

He watches us all the time out of the corner of his eye.

Send him to me.

Yes, sir. If you'll allow me, I'd as soon stay right behind him in case he tries to knife you.

Thank you, soldier. I'm sure I can handle him. Now send him along.

Here he is now, sir. I'll be watching him.

Good afternoon, Jim. What do you have to tell me?

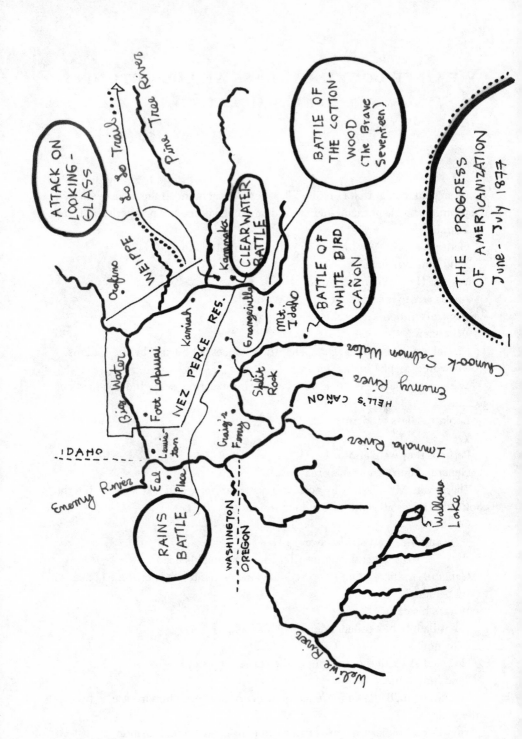

THE PROGRESS OF AMERICANIZATION
June – July 1877

ATTACK ON LOOKING-GLASS

BATTLE OF THE COTTONWOOD (The Brave Seventeen)

CLEARWATER BATTLE

BATTLE OF WHITE BIRD CAÑON

RAINS BATTLE

Pine Tree River

To go Trail

WEIPPE

Orofino

Big Water

Fort Lapwai

NEZ PERCE RES.

Kamiah

Kamiaka

Grangeville

Mt. Idaho

Lewiston

Craig's Ferry

Split Rock

HELL'S CAÑON

Chinook Salmon Water

Enemy River

Imnaha River

Wallowa Lake

Wallowa River

Eel Place

IDAHO

WASHINGTON
OREGON

Enemy River

General Howard, I think soon Chief Looking-Glass will make trouble. Already forty warriors from him go to help Joseph—

How do you know?

My uncle listened in Looking-Glass's camp. Everybody's talking about it.

Did he see any stock belonging to Mr. Silverwood or Mr. Dempster?

I don't know their brands.

Soldier, see if you can muster up that information.

That's easy, sir. We was just asking Mr. West about that. He knows for a fact Mr. Silverwood's brand is an S inside a circle, and Mr. Dempster uses two X's.

You're sure?

Yessir.

I commend you, soldier. You have the makings of an officer.

Thank you, sir.

You're with Captain Trimble's bunch.

Yessir.

What's your name?

Well, sir, they call me Blackie.

I'll remember you. Well, Jim?

I didn't see those brands down there, general.

Did your uncle hear anything from Looking-Glass himself?

No, sir. He couldn't get that close.

So what exactly did he hear?

Bad things. They think Joseph is correct in everything. They say whites break all their promises.

What do *you* say?

I just try to get along in life, general.

In your opinion, are most of Looking-Glass's Indians Dreamers?

Sure they are, general. Otherwise they'd live at Lapwai.

How many tipis in their camp?

I'd say eleven, sir. Maybe to-day there are more or less.

Thank you, Jim. I'll remember your loyalty. You may return to your duties. Wilkinson, is James Reuben around?

I'll fetch him, general.

Good morning, Mr. Reuben.

Morning, general.

Is Looking-Glass a good Indian?

No, sir. He don't believe in the LORD.

Is he helping Joseph?

I don't think so, general. When those Indians took the warpath, Looking-Glass rode away.

Are the bad Indians visiting him?

Could be, general. They're his relatives, so maybe they ride into camp to do their DEVIL worship dance or trade horses—

What do you mean by DEVIL worship?

General, you know that the Book of Light says: *Thou shalt have no GODS before Me.* Well, that bunch, they pray to the RED SALMON, kill horses to worship dead people, sing evil sings about MOTHER EARTH.

GOD bless you, Mr. Reuben! You have learned what's right. But tell me: Did Looking-Glass's Indians burn the white men's houses?

I don't know, sir.

Mr. Reuben, thank you for your candor. Please believe that I'll do whatever is best for your people. That's all. Wilkinson, I need Mr. Chapman.

Right away, sir.

Sit down, Chapman.

Don't mind if I do. General, I was just thinking. You and me, well, we could go into business. I could sell horses to the Army, and what you'd do, see, is you'd—

Chapman, I understand that when Joseph launched his outbreak, Looking-Glass rode over to your ranch to warn you away from Salmon River.

That's just it. He came and threatened me. Told me to get out or the reds would kill me.

So he wasn't trying to save your life?

No, sir. What he wanted was what they all want: to run us out. And that's why we got to run *them* out.

Speak to the purpose. Did Looking-Glass visit you out of neighborly concern, or for some other reason?

To scare me out of my rights, general. He knew I had outstanding horses, and he thought I'd up and leave 'em. Then he could gather in my herd, so his most vicious bucks could swoop like lightning on them Slate Creek people, and maybe wipe out Grangeville and Mount Idaho—

Would you swear to that on a Bible?

Sure, general. I'd swear on anything.

That's all, Chapman. Go now. Fletch, where's Captain Whipple?

Sir, he and Captain Perry are up there with the volunteers.

Bring him here.

Yes, sir.

Good afternoon, Whipple. How are your men?

Ready to kill some Indians, sir.

That's the spirit! Now, captain, can you vouch for Umatilla Jim?

He's all right, sir, for an Indian. So far everything he says has turned out true.

He told me in confidence that Looking-Glass is turning treacherous.

Then I'd believe it, sir. Most of them do go treacherous, in my opinion.

Mr. Reuben's not firm against Looking-Glass.

Then it's one Indian's word against another's, ain't it, sir?

Captain, how well do you understand Looking-Glass?

Not well, sir.

But last winter, when you sojurned with Joseph—

Yessir. Looking-Glass was generally out roaming around. That one is a real hunter. I'll give him that.

Is Looking-Glass well disposed toward you?

I'd say indifferent, sir. Perhaps a trifle arrogant. He sure likes to jawbone about Lewis and Clark. His grandfather gave them a horse or something. We never heard the end of it.

And you're familiar with his new reservation.

Yessir, I know the map.

We need to take care of him. He could attack our rear. Captain Whipple, go with your cavalry and your Gatling guns, arrest Looking-Glass and all the other Indians encamped with or near him, and turn them over to the volunteers at Mount Idaho.

Turn them over for what, sir?

For safekeeping, captain.

Yessir. I reckon they'll keep those Indians safe. They remember what Indians did around Mount Idaho.

Make sure your men don't harm Looking-Glass. You've familiarized your-selves with him before. Remember, he wears a mirror at his throat.

I'll tell them, sir. Let's pray for the best.

I'll hold you responsible if Looking-Glass is killed.

Yes, sir.

By the way, Whipple, you knew Lieutenant Theller pretty well, didn't you?

I suppose so, sir. Not as well as Colonel Perry.

Naturally. Was he a drinking man? I'm aware that many of you are, but you never let me catch you.

That's right, general. No drinking in your army.

Well, was he?

You could say that. He wasn't excessive in his habits.

And Colonel Perry?

I don't know about him, sir.

All right. Go now and carry out your orders. You'll want to be in position be-fore dawn.

Right away, sir.— Lieutenant Shelton, Company "L" moves out to-night!

Yessir, Captain Whipple, sir! The men have been longing for a fight.

Hitch up the Gatlings and hand out three days' rations. We'll leave at nine-o'-clock.

Yes, sir,

> and so they ride all night with Mr. West. Arriving at Mount Idaho, where that so-called Major Shearer pretends to be in charge, and the patriotic blacksmith is still forming bullets by the pailful, they rest their men and horses, recruit Captain-by-acclamation Randall and nineteen other vol-unteers from Brown's Hotel, from which establishment they try and fail to requisition some canned oysters, verify that no entertainment may be

had at the Chinese laundry, then ride off in the hot pine-scent of late afternoon, singing "Turn Back Pharaoh's Army,"
>   tar bubbling in the seams of their sunstruck rucksacks and
>   the trees and rocks thickly lichened, the brown water fast but
>   shallow,
making poor progress due to their heavy Gatlings, so that not until considerably past dawn do they see from their hidden hill
the river shining through the humid green grass,
the white gravel boundary of that water and
sunshine on the lodgepoles rising like spread fingers from the narrow
pale tipis in the tall grass
of this place called Kamnaka where fat cows graze and women boil tea
>   (among them a goodlooking girl in a deerskin dress),
as children point up at us;
Kamnaka, reserve of pines, aspens, clean water,
>   squash, corn, beans, melons, camas,
with the pale softgrassed hills behind the river sometimes widening, the
white stones of the far shore shining in the sun
and we smell trees and hear many horses.
Load with cartridges; load!
>   and
How many bucks do you count, lieutenant?
Hardly any, sir. Maybe they've all deserted to Joseph.
Where's Umatilla Jim?
I'll find him, sir.
When the scout rises silently up at his side, a crawling shadow in his long black
wool cape with beads and bearteeth sewn in adjacent verticals to make long hor-
izontal stripes across the breast and shoulders, Captain Whipple loves him sud-
denly and meaninglessly, at that moment believing him best and most faithful
among all who know the green turns of this Clearwater Cañon, and whispers: Jim,
where do you think the warriors have gone to?
Can I look through your field-glass, captain?
Be careful with it,
>   the forks of whitewater around boulders now crisp in his vision,
>   and then
>   the rich horse herd and
Captain, I can't say for sure, but I wouldn't reckon more than twenty here can
fight. The rest are old. Maybe they went to Kamiah to be Dreamers, because I
heard Smohallie's headed there. Maybe they're already with Joseph. Some may be
inside those lodges right now. But, captain, these people don't look afraid—
Then we'll surprise them. Can you spy Looking-Glass?
No, sir.
That's fine, Jim. Lieutenant Shelton, prepare for battle.

Yes, sir. Just a moment, sir. They must have seen us. Here comes an Indian on a horse.

Mount the men, lieutenant. No bugle calls.

Yes, sir.

I want a scout to watch our rear in case they're planning something like they did at White Bird Cañon.

Yes, sir. I've detailed James Reuben.

Yeah, he can go. Jim, you stay with me.

Whatever you say, captain. I'm ready.

Do you know that Indian?

Sure, captain. Do you want me to kill him?

We'll see.

All men on horse and ready, sir!

Ride to the crest and show yourselves. No bugle.

Yes, sir. Company "L," move out to the crest. You too, volunteers. Hold your fire.

Company "L" moving out!,

> frozen in their saddles, overwatching
> old Nez Perce women, whose wrinkled foreheads are lowered like those
> of butting heifers, the whites of their eyes glaring in their dark faces
> and the young mothers in their sun-bleached blanket-coats, standing in
> the grass, staring up at us, with babies on their backs.

All right, Jim, walk on down the hill with me. Let's go now, not doublequick, not holding back, just natural, yeah, that's fine, Jim, that's fine,

> as Jim reaches inside his shirt and pulls out that prized Centennial
> medal he's so crazy about
>> (all the boys love to josh him, saying: Hey, Jim, what do you
>> care? You reds can't even vote!—to which he answers: O, I'm
>> just passing the time):
> that fine brass medal for Rutherford Hayes, with sunlight glaring
> from our President's sunken brass eyes, sunlight silvering his
> puffed-out beard, and then the glorious deep-cut words **CENTEN-
> NIAL AMERICA,**
>> so that Captain Whipple wonders whether Jim believes that
>> this thing makes him lucky, or just helps him look big in front
>> of the other Indians; who knows what goes through a red's
>> mind?
> as they descend the hill.

Ask that Indian who he is and what he wants.

He says, his name is Peopeo Tholekt. I met him before, many times catching eels. He's like a nephew to Looking-Glass.

Then we're in luck. Tell him to bring Looking-Glass here.

He says, Looking-Glass's heart is good, real good. He don't want trouble. He says, we kept our promise to General Howard, so you soldiers should go away, and this Indian who stares out liquid-eyed at me from above his white gorget, his skin verdigrised like the brass barrel of our twelve-pounder and his stare burning deeper as he invades my eyes while denying me his, why does he glare so brazenly at me?

> (big round eyes in a little round face—O yes, he's just a little fellow—prettied up with a feather headdress, white shell earrings, a gorget of long white bone-beads, and then many, many necklace-loops spilling down his chest, some of them pendanted with shell-beads
>
> > and that feathered whistle round his neck: does Jim know what that means?)

yes, him on his fine yellow horse—

he'd better not reach for anything or I'll

Captain, this one's a good Indian for sure.

That's fine, Jim. Lieutenant, tell the men to unhorse and fan out across the hilltop.

Yes, sir.

Jim, tell your friend Peo Peo that he's got to bring Looking-Glass over here, and that's how it is.

He says, he rides now to Looking-Glass.

Jim, here's my field-glass. Watch where he goes. I'm counting on you to discover which tipi Looking-Glass is in.

I'll try my best, captain.

They wait, Whipple slowly wiping his palms on the hem of his filthy canvas frock, and down across the river are only cows and horses now, and that Nez Perce warrior (whom he must certainly have spied last winter) slowly fording the brown river, which is dark and white between the grassed hills which dwindle to the east. To the west, the river seems blue with leaping lines of light.

D——n me if he doesn't take his time! I'd like to send a lead reminder up his ass.

If he rides quick, we might say he's afraid. That's the reason, captain.

Shut up unless I ask you something, Jim. Did you hear?

Sure, captain.

Lieutenant, you stay here with Jim while I see how the men are doing. As soon as that Indian comes back, you let me know.

I sure will, sir. Jim, don't mind what the captain said to you just now. He's always edgy before a battle.

Don't worry, lieutenant, I didn't pay it no mind,

> watching the brown river,
>
> closed-up tipis
>
> and a brass kettle boiling in deserted ashes
>
> > (Jim touching his weasel-skin bracelet),
>
> golden grass going greyish-white in the rising sun,
>
> > as a horse gnaws at his hobble
> >
> > and

Here they come, lieutenant. Two reds.

Sergeant, go tell the captain.

Yes, sir.

Who's that with him? Is that Looking-Glass?

                 (—as slow as the schoolhouse clock on a summer day—)

I don't believe so, lieutenant. That other man holds a white pole. Looking-Glass wouldn't do that himself.

Well, boys, looks like he's in the bag!

Yes, sir, but Jim believes it's not Looking-Glass.

Lieutenant Shelton, Jim, mount your horses. Lieutenant Rains, assume command. Keep the men ready. If we cross the river, wait thirty minutes. If there's no signal from us by that time, commence the attack.

Yes, sir.

Synchronize watches. I don't want you shooting us in fifteen minutes.

Seven-forty.

Seven-forty.

Good luck, lieutenant. Lieutenant Shelton, let's go. Just down into the swale. This is far enough. Let them come the rest of the way to us. Who's that other Indian, Jim?

Don't know, sir.

Is he an important chief, at least?

Nope.

Ask him why he didn't bring Looking-Glass.

Peopeo Tholekt says, *Looking-Glass is my chief! I bear you his words. He comes here to escape the war. Do not cross to our side of the river. We want no trouble with you at all.* Peopeo Tholekt says—

Cut it short, you villain. Jim, tell him to take us to Looking-Glass

    and the wet green leaves

    and our horses mincing across the shallow cool water

        (Umatilla Jim's horse wants to drink, but he reins up its head),

    the tipis enlarging,

    Nez Perces emerging,

        unsmiling,

    and the sun hot on our necks

    and

        a shot (whose echoes resemble ripples):

        Pim,

               pimpimpim,

cunning, well aimed, premeditated, hence almost certainly from one of the Mount Idaho volunteers, takes off an old woman's head: lightning-flash of skull as white as the waterline of the Snake River, then currants crushed in an invisible hand—

GODd——nit! Back across the creek! Ride, ride; gallop like the DEVIL!

... women screaming (the braver squaws now running for the horses)
and the first return shot,
   which brings about the chittering of the Gatlings down through the tipis
   and the Indians running into the trees:
Hurrah, hurrah, hurrah!
I couldn't control them, captain—
So I see. Cease firing! *Cease firing!* Company "L," you shitheads, if Looking-
Glass gets away, you're for it. And you GODD——d motherfucking mulesucking
volunteer assholes! Lieutenant Rains, I'm disappointed. And Captain Randall, you
lousy niggerbrained excuse for an ape, I'm reporting you to the general. No, shut
the fuck up. Men, form up, form up! Skirmish foundation. Prepare to follow up the
attack. Lieutenant Shelton, lead the volunteers to that high hill over there. The rest
of you follow me. Sound bugle.
   Forward!
   Forward!
      toward the woman wrapped in a wolfskin who runs at them and then
      away
      and the woman with the baby on her back, riding desperately into the
      Clearwater on a stumbling horse:
         Pim!
            (drowned)
      and Indians rushing into the trees.
   All right. Lieutenant Forse, Lieutenant Shelton, pick twenty men and drive in
all the Indians' horses.
   Yes, sir. Boys, we'll have to run the Indians off those rocks. Then let's circle in
over there . . .
   We're on the job, lieutenant.
   Jim, do you see Looking-Glass?
   Afraid not, captain. But I sure do see some volunteers down there. They must
have set the tipis on fire—
      the burning falling lodgepoles for an instant as lovely as the maze of nest-
      ing black and white stripes on an Indian basket
         and
      a broken string of elk teeth, scattered in the grass like cloves of garlic.
   Captain, sir, reporting for the volunteers, sir! We did our best to catch Looking-
Glass, but he—
   Shut the fuck up, shit-heel! Lieutenant Rains, how many enemy dead?
   Three, sir. Several wounded.
   Any sign of Looking-Glass?
   Guess he went running off to Joseph.
      And I winged that Injun on the yellow horse—
   Nice country down here. Good for a horse ranch.
   And I got me this genuine silk buffalo hide.

They raped Helen Walsh. Every time she hears the word *Indian* she gets to weeping—

Hey, John, what did you find in that buckskin bag?

How many casualties on our side?

John, give me some of those.

No sign of him, sir.

Don't make that face, John.

Sir, the volunteers have organized a foraging party. Looks like we're all going to have some fresh beef!

2

Captain Whipple, report.

Well, general, we gave Looking-Glass an opportunity to surrender, but he wouldn't have any of it. The result was that a couple of Indians got killed. We destroyed the camp and most of their supplies.

What about their horses?

We caught seven hundred and twenty-five ponies, sir, and drove them all to Mount Idaho, just as you ordered.

Good work, captain, but what about Looking-Glass?

He and his confederates escaped, sir. Probably went straight to Joseph, just like that Umatilla Jim warned us—

I'm sorry you failed to capture the band. Why did you delay your operation until after dawn?

The volunteers led us out of our way, sir, so we arrived late—

Perhaps I expected too much of your tired horses . . .

3

And that evening, looking across the whitestone beach at their ruined camp, they decide to be enemies with Cut Arm's people forever. Now we shall all be hunting Bostons side by side

(our men striping their faces with widespread warpainted fingers, our women wailing):

Far Mountain and her baby have drowned;

Black Raven bleeds from three bullet wounds;

Big Old Woman is dead,

as a fish splashes: *mokh!*

Cut Arm is crooked indeed;

he has become one who loves the smell of blood.

He has stolen twelve hundred horses!

Until now Looking-Glass,

he whose Grandfather Looking-Glass, sometimes called Bighorn because

that is what he wore lashed to his left arm, became brothers with the first
Bostons who ever came to us,

and whose father, Old Looking-Glass, signed the first treaty with the
Bostons, giving away most of our country, for which we were never paid
(twenty-two snows ago, he rode onto the treaty ground, with a
Shinbone's scalp hanging from his saddle, to warn us against trust-
ing the Bostons, who wished to make him a war-chief next to
Lawyer),

has always obeyed Cut Arm and this *thief treaty;*
indeed, Looking-Glass,

whose heart assures him that he has unfailingly valued the Bostons' friendship
at its actual questionable worth,

has been nearly as successful as SOMEONE who can turn into a raven. Even now
(being unable to change himself like the golden grass that bows in the wind), he
cannot close his heart against astonishment: why have the Bostons behaved in
this way?

I rode to Tsépmin with my brother and warned him! Surely it was
not he who told the Bluecoats to break our friendship with the Bostons. Or is it now true what White Bird's young men have said, that
Tsépmin is a Boston and therefore a liar?

Or is Cut Arm the liar? Or has he no power over these Bluecoats
who perhaps rode here just to steal our horses?

Who are these Bostons?

Since Cut Arm has now stolen his white horse, Looking-Glass sits on his favorite black one, with his tall beaded hat pulled down almost to his eyes, while his
wives keen over their bayonet-pierced kettles.

The Bluecoats have urinated on the place where we held our WYAKIN dances.

Looking-Glass says bitterly: *Hasten; evening shadows be!*

Swan Woman, White Thunder's mother, waves her son's rifle, cursing the
Bostons—how she longs to shoot their faces!

Peopeo Tholekt rides wounded; some Boston has shot him in the leg;

Cut Arm is crooked; but his own chief, Looking-Glass, has scarcely
acted a man's part, to send him twice to meet those Bostons.

Sliding painfully off his yellow stallion, limping across the grass, he digs in the
smoldering hole where his lodge used to be. Although the Bluecoats have taken
everything, even the bag of vermilion pigment, he has kept with him his MEDI-
CINE bag

with the half-mummified woodpecker head
and the bird-bone whistle which can save him from bullets.

Wottolen says: Hear me, all of you People! Now I begin to understand that
White Bird's young men have acted in the straight way, I am telling you three
times!

Looking-Glass then says: My People, I shall never make peace with the Bostons. My People, so long as I live I shall fight them, these treacherous *Americans.*

Wrapping Big Old Woman, Far Mountain and the baby in blankets, since all the buffalo robes have been stolen and burned, they bury them within the riverbank, ringing the small bell while the warriors keep watch. Far Mountain's husband is named Rifle; he has seen but does not yet understand.

The best men decide that we shall go to Red Owl's country.

Then they mount their horses, bluffs and cañon-walls going greenish-grey now, and to throw Cut Arm off their trail they ride awhile through the brownish-green water. They are fleeing upstream,

> up the Big Water,
>> the yellow-green and silver-green needles of young junipers:
>
> Looking-Glass with his wives and daughters,
>> and that round mirror weakly reflecting twilight in his hair;
>
> and that brave woman Arrowhead on her white horse
> (she carries the same name as Looking-Glass, but perhaps her heart has more sense, for it was she who stopped to tie up Peopeo Tholekt's leg even as the other People galloped away in terror),
>
> Chief Three Feathers and his People,
>
> Chief Red Heart with his wife and children
>> (his eldest son, Over The Point, saying: Soon we shall revenge ourselves),
>
> and all the other People, angry and sad,
>
> horse-poor, robbed of winter food, hoping to eat berries from the branches as they go,
>> the cañon getting greener, rockier, narrower, the river twisting over sharp brown rocks;
>
> they are riding all night,
>> hunting eels and creeksuckers to eat,
>>> riding away from the place called Kamnaka
>>>> (now we have done this for the last time),

as in the darkness rises the Redfaced Talking Star.*

At Bear Claw Place, Wottolen kills a doe just before dawn comes; here they rest, the women trimming meat from the bones,

> and Looking-Glass's wives make him little balls of deer fat spiced with balsamroot seeds,

but many children are too scared to sleep.

Black Raven dies. Ringing the hand bell, they decorate him, wrap him in a buffalo robe, bury him, then depart silently. Hunts No More opens and closes his big hands.

Looking-Glass and Red Owl have decided; they explain what must now be done. Wottolen is satisfied; they will follow his counsel at last. Peopeo Tholekt

---

*Jupiter.

begins remembering everything, in order to make pictures when the time comes. In the lowest scree the last purple flowers of the wild onion are already withering.

They ride for the country of Red Owl, who is of their People,

> he whose grandfather killed a Crow warrior most bravely, in the days before we had peace with that nation
>
>> although War Singer first counted coup on the dead man, and therefore got to keep his scalp;
>
> Red Owl, who is rich in food and horses;

there they will send word to White Bird, Toohhoolhoolsote, Heinmot Tooyalakekt and the others.

THE BLACK ARABIAN
JULY 2

1

*W*hipple, you're to march to Norton's ranch and await the arrival of Captain Perry's company. Your objective is to keep Joseph from recrossing the Salmon and turning my communications.

Very good, sir.

I'm still disappointed that you failed to capture Looking-Glass.

I'm sorry, sir. The volunteers—

Where *are* the volunteers?

Captain Randall led them back to Mount Idaho, sir.

Bendire's in position to the south. My troops will secure the front. Trimble at Slate Creek will hold the left. It's crucial not to let Joseph pass. Will you do your best endeavor this time?

My very best, sir.

Leave no stone unturned, Captain Whipple.

Yes, sir.

I expect of the cavalry tremendous vigor and activity even if it should kill a few horses.

We'll do our utmost, sir.

Whipple, if you get in trouble, don't hesitate to pray. GOD always listens.

Thanks for the advice, sir,

> and if you hadn't left Colonel Sully with his thumb up his ass back at Lapwai, we might actually have killed some reds by now; two or three squaws don't signify. Our men sleeping in the rain with no blankets be-

cause you thought to skedaddle into the field before Sherman got General Crook to replace you, and all of us cursing you, in low and secret whispers, of course, because you won't permit cursing in your GODD——d Army of fucking penwiping Bible-kissing cock-twiddlers! To the DEVIL with you, general! And now you've got it in for me because Looking-Glass ran away. After marching through the night and rubbing out their shitty little village just as I was supposed to do—

That's all. Yes, Wilkinson, what is it?

A rider just brought these despatches for you, sir.

Make sure he gets a meal.

Yessir.

Well, well. Fletch, cast your eye on *this*. Every white man in the country wants to tell me what to do, from the look of it.

I'll sell them tickets, general. You and I'll get rich—

Very funny. At least Smohallie's quiet for the moment. No other bad news anywhere. I hear from Mr. Cornoyer that his Indians are more scared than any white man could be.

There's Indians for you. Any trouble up there, sir?

From citizens? Not yet.

Well, general, I expect they'll bide their time until we've whipped Joseph and then kill a few of Mr. Cornoyer's Indians.

The old story. Let's pray it goes otherwise.

Yessir.

I don't hear any bugle calls. Go straightaway to Captain Whipple and inform him that he'd better move out within a half-hour. Then see if you can find out what's delaying Wilkinson.

Yessir.

2

Wilkinson, what is it now?

General, that Ad Chapman approached me just now—

Well?

He feared that if he went directly to you, you wouldn't accept, so he fetched his stablekeeper here to me, with a racing-horse for you—

No.

All right, sir. I'll return the animal. A mighty beautiful black Arabian, and, if I may say so, better suited to a general than that gelding they gave you at Lapwai.

Wilkinson, it's extremely bad policy to be obligated to someone like Chapman.

Yessir, but we're clearing his property of hostile Indians, and a real charger might come in handy for operations. You know, sir, that storekeeper Mr. Rudolph outfitted Sergeant McCarthy with new boots and gloves and wouldn't take one copper cent—

McCarthy's a different case. A pity to take it out of his pay after his ordeal, even in this postwar Army.

Yessir.

What is it?

Well, general, you know how I look up to you, and expect others to do so. You'd look mighty dashing on that Arabian. Chapman can sure spare him; he's got three hundred more. And if any newspapermen get out here, sir, a spot of glamour couldn't hurt this campaign, especially since that bunch of scribblers can't understand strategy—

Bless you, Wilkinson, but you may be right. Let's see this famous horse . . .

TAKING THE SHORTEST LINE
(A TRIUMPH OF EMPIRICAL GEOMETRY)
JULY 2–4

1

Fletch, I need Captain Babitt at once.

Yessir.

Well, captain, how's the life of an ordnance man?

Sir, Lieutenant Otis and I were just saying—

Captain, I need you to ride to Mount Idaho and find Captain Whipple. I've instructed him to proceed to Norton's, *doublequick*, then link up with Colonel Perry, who will escort the pack train.

Yessir. So Mr. Joe has—

Yes, he's leading us in circles! If you can believe it, James Reuben's Indians have sighted his tipis right back on that very camas prairie by Rocky Cañon where he plotted his war! General Sherman will be disappointed in us, I fear.

Yessir.

It's urgent that we discover whether Joseph means to double across the Salmon yet again. Whipple has got to scout the country.

General, I can ride out in ten minutes.

Thank you, captain. Energetic officers like you will see us through this campaign. GOD bless you! Now, Wilkinson, we'd better draft another despatch to Colonel Perry. Has he embarked the resupply?

Yessir; Captain Miller's column is halfway back to Norton's. Shall I carry the message?

I can't spare you, unfortunately. You're too valuable.

THE REST OF MY DAYS 341

Thank you, general.

Entre nous, in your opinion whose was the failure in the Looking-Glass affair? Whipple blames the volunteers.

So did Colonel Perry, sir.

Wilkinson, what are you insinuating?

General, I never insinuate.

Forgive me . . .

I merely meant to indicate that the citizens are more to blame than the Army for any lack of progress in this campaign. And Captain Randall was sullen and rude to you at Lapwai; I won't forget that.

Why do you suppose he's always spoiling for a fight?

Well, general, he did help himself to fifty acres of the reservation.

And settled on it?

Yessir.

Who told you that?

O, general, I just asked around.

All right. To-day we need to move the entire command up to Craig's Ferry.

Yessir.

A fatiguing march.

Yessir, but once Joseph's between us and Perry—

So I pray, Wilkinson. We need the shortest possible line, since Joseph's so much better mounted than any of us in this postwar Army.

Yessir. Excepting you and that Ad Chapman!

Entre nous, I'm extremely gratified with my black charger. You steered me right.

Thank you, sir. If you wish, I could ride ahead and—

Besides, you're still unwell. Take good care of yourself, my boy.

Yessir.

Is your pad ready? *Colonel: Joseph has swung north, in order to make a junction with Hushush Cute and Looking-Glass. They may commit further depredations on Slate Creek. Guard the pack train with the utmost vigilance. I expect you and Captain Whipple to protect the settlers around Norton's until our return. Try to fix the enemy's attention until we have returned to Grangeville. Please assure your men of my gratitude for their exertions. GOD willing, Joseph will be destroyed as soon as we can force him to give battle.* That's all. And have you sent my message to Colonel Sully?

Yessir.

Wilkinson.

Yessir.

Are Sully and Monteith intriguing against me?

About the colonel I can't say, general, although he seems to be of an honorable stripe.

Thank you. And I note what you declined to say.

Yessir.

What about James Reuben? Mr. Chapman keeps tilting against him.

General, before we rode out of Lapwai I persuaded Agent Monteith to show me Mr. Reuben's ration check, and I verified that all the dependents listed on it were good Indians.

Very energetic of you! All right. What's the name of his wife?

E-la-wee-naomey, general.

Not a very Christian name, I'm afraid. And she's Joseph's sister.

Yessir.

Have we heard from Major Mason to-day?

Not yet, sir.

Come here. Just as I supposed. Your forehead is hot.

Not at all, general.

Lie down here. Just for a quarter-hour. That fever is persistent, isn't it? No, close your eyes and rest. I'll call when I need you.— O, hello, Fletch. Have you curried that stallion of mine?

Yessir. That's one fine hot-blooded riding breed!

I'm going to call him Arrow.

Why not, sir?

> What we need is a good running fight with them reds, and I mean to tell the general—

>> ... to strike them at Craig's Ferry, if they don't cross back again ...

>> What about Wood?

>> O, he's got "sand" enough! Rains saw him break his collarbone riding bareback on an untamed horse.

>> If it had been me I wouldn't have been thrown.

>> That James Reuben is kind of haughty. You'd think he'd realize his position as a relative of Mr. Joe,

> as Captain Trimble inspects his boys:

>> Doc just this side of passable

>> while Blackie, stiff, shy, young and proud, stares straight ahead, angling his rifle to perfection, with his hair banged neatly below his cap and his Dad's old horse pistol stuck in his waistband,

> and so-called Colonel McConville, whose stern bony face and high collar gives him a preacher look, re-explains to a re-markably unimpressed Major Mason just what his volunteers expect from the Army

> while Wood, correcting Captain Pollock's latest Morning Report—a task at which he excels—is telling himself, never

supposing that no one cares: They imagine the reason I refused the residue of my leave was to fight with *them!* That fiction's made me popular, for the moment. What if it's even so? Who am I to know what the true reason was? It might have been
. . . *To cut off Joseph from his hunting grounds.* Have you got that, Fletch?

The man for that is Red O'Donnell, but if the general ever—

Sure have, sir. Then the usual salutation?

Yes,

when perhaps the truth is merely that Wood needs to do something dramatic and active, like most young people and therefore like most Americans: Just think what Nanny would say if I got Joseph! It would be in the newspaper. I need to be a success here. I can get along with Wilkinson. I'll make myself do it. Even he can't be as strictly religious as my own mother!

Now go inform Lieutenant Otis that the artillery must make better progress to-day. If need be, they're to march all night.

Right away, general.

Are you also getting ill?

No, sir.

Wilkinson, my boy, you'd better drink more coffee now.

Wilkinson? He's as cold-blooded as a draught horse.

Sir, I'm all right now

(closing his eyes, he can see how the plains flatten out southeast of Cottonwood: no place there to bottle up Joseph! But if I remind the general about Rocky Cañon . . .)

Good. Where's Sladen? There you are, old friend! Well, well, who would have thought we'd be crossing and recrossing the Salmon like this! And Joseph can do it so easily! Sometimes it must be exhilarating to be an Indian.

Yessir.

How would you rate McConville's volunteers?

A liability, general.

I agree. Where's Fletch?

Here, sir.

Get me McConville. Yes, good morning, sir. Your orders are to cross the Salmon at or near Horse Shoe Bend and proceed across Brown's Mountain toward the Snake—

Yes, sir. With Randall's bunch?

That's right. All of you, beat the country for Joseph! We need to make him give battle. When you find him, despatch a rider to me immediately. Enough said.

General, we'll move out now.

Yes, good-bye, sir. Now, Sladen, look over the map with me. Do you see Deer Creek Cañon?

Sure do, sir. Concerned about ambushes, I take it?

You're a genius. Now if we send our flankers *here* . . .

Yessir. Too bad Colonel Perry's not with us; he knows the country almost like an Indian.

I'll give Jocelyn the opportunity. Thanks, Sladen. How's the leg?

About the same as your arm, general.

Ha, ha! That's all.

> Here you are, Captain Pollock. If you sign at the end, I'll take it to the general.

> Wood, you're a GODsend. LORD, but this paperwork gives me blue balls!

Good morning, Captain Jocelyn. How are your bunch?

Ready for some hunting, general!

Then bag me Joseph, if you please! You'll lead the column. How will you deploy your flankers?

Like this, general, *here* and *here*, although the map—

Report to me just before we enter Deer Creek Cañon. Move out in fifteen minutes.

Yessir.

> Bugler, sound "Boots and Saddles," and keep it up.

> Let's go, boys!

>> —buckling on their carbine-belts and strapping tight their hats.

>> Can't Brooks stop spitting in his bugle?

>> Ever since Jonesey punched him in the teeth—

>> Lay off Jonesey. He's dead.

> Now, just as soon as Pollock's bunch pulls out, that's when you duck into Red O'Donnell's wagon. Don't let them officers see you—

2

Sound the forward.

> *Forward!*

>> our blue-overalled general grinning like a little boy as he gallops

>> Arrow.

They're marching briskly, gentlemen.

Well, sir, we all want blood!

> . . . since Mr. Joe's pulled our tails again!

So his machine progresses

> *left—left—LEFT,*

Captain Trimble in his patched sack coat,

Sladen on his chocolate-brown horse,

James Reuben, submissive and boyish, with surprisingly delicate hands, then our second-best Indians: Old George, Captain John and Umatilla Jim, whom the general considers near about as broadfaced as an Apache, Fletch and Wilkinson,

    the former in his Navy blue flannel blouse
    and the latter,

        who secretly admires the Swiss "dash" of the 1872 plaited Army blouse, which every officer of his acquaintance despises for its pompous unmanliness,

    indefinably more elegant than anyone,

the general in his blue overalls, riding easy, jawboning with one of the citizen volunteers,

Doc marching wide-eyed and singing in his baggy trousers, his boots sagged and cracked, his fat knife hanging down off his cartridge belt, the rifle downpointed from its shoulder sling, his tin cup swaying at his hip, his hat warped down into some greasy part of his skin

and Blackie right behind him,

then Larry Ott, who shot Shore Crossing's father, smoking a pipe as he rides, with his tangle of red hair swinging back and forth against his neck, touching his shoulders,

and Red O'Donnell, the most obliging muleteer a man could meet, likewise smoking his pipe, unwearyingly flicking his long whip as he sits there in the spring seat, with his hidden cargo of reddish-crusted chains, drills, pincers and hammers rattling on the wagon's shelves, and horseshoes upside down on their rack

as we leave the Salmon River, creeping up Deer Creek Cañon,

    which is so thick with shrubs that we cannot see the water beneath us,

    although our horses bend down to drink whenever we permit them,

        all of us unknowingly beginning to surrender to the darkening pines, with the lost meadows behind us still brilliantly yellow in our memories

            —but just as the golden infinite below us dulls down by stages into blue waves, so what is past likewise loses life and light, except for the yellow grass itself,

            yellow swellings of earth, which now—they too!—go green and blue in their hollows, while the deeper grass-walled gorges alter into red and purple,

            the sky clouding over above us

                (when we were children, we imagined that this world was a brighter place, whose wicked Indians couldn't ever get out of fairytales, painted land and old soldiers' self-aggrandizements),

            and each raincloud bearing the dark polish of a well-used Indian pipe

as we follow our general in what may well prove to be another circle,
riding forward, dreading Chief Joseph where the pine forest runnels greenness
down into the golden grass:

Mr. Chapman, have you been up Brown's Mountain?

Yes indeedy.

And Craig's Mountain?

You bet I have, general. Mr. Joe's bunch call it *Faraway Mountain.* When
their papooses get big enough to be Dreamers, they go up there one by
one to give themselves to SATAN.

SATAN! You're sure of this?

As sure as death, general.

Well, well! Now what are the chances that Joseph would hide out up
there?

If he did, we'd find his trail. He's not about to leave us all them fifteen
hundred pretty horses—

All right. Where is he?

General, he and his stinking reds could have crossed the Salmon another
six times by now.

And you purpose?

Well, now, if we keep on toward Craig's Ferry, and Colonel Perry keeps
an eye out thataway—

That's all,

   except for the moist dusk of Deer Creek, not far from the future's
   apple trees and fences

and now Biblical rain,

   rain and mud and rain as we flounder up the steep trail

     (our general gripping the pommel since Arrow keeps slip-
     ping, leaving him without a hand to wipe the rain off his face:

      why won't he wear a slouch hat like the rest of us?)

     What a hogback!

      Table-lands—

     Call this Dead Mule Trail—

     Another mule gone.

     How many now?

     Four.

       I'll remind you officers of what Captain Sladen always
       says: *What a mule has done is known. What he is doing
       may be seen, but what he will do the next minute the
       mind of a philosopher cannot fathom.*

       That's a good one, general. I'll tell it to Red O'Donnell;
       he's got the best funnybone of all our muleteers.

         Yeah, sure is hilarious when a mule suicides along
         with all our coffee—

General's no complainer; I'll say that for him.

You look jolly, Chapman.

I always did enjoy a good rain. Once this country is settled, that's what we're all a-gonna be doing every Sunday. Just praying for rain.

Retracing every GODD——n step, and in worse country—

And no sign of Mr. Joe—

He's probably laughing half a mile *behind* us!

as that night we lie down in mud and water in the place we call *Camp Misery.*

Doc?

Shut up.

Doc, how do you stay dry?

You don't.

Right now the folks will be haying back home.

Blackie, leave me be.

By "Tattoo," Red O'Donnell has sold out of stock,

for on nights like these there's only one way to keep warm.

3

Marching up the cañon to Brown's Mountain on another showery day, shivering that night up on Camp Howard Ridge

(as many disappointments in sight as the half-dead cigars which always lie around General Sherman)

—good forage for the horses, at least—

some of us discover that our boots have already begun to rot,

as the general, having been apprised by James Reuben that Joseph is moving toward a probable junction with Looking-Glass, says to Wilkinson that night inside the Sibley tent: Our shortest line may be to turn back via White Bird Cañon.

FOURTH OF JULY

1

*H*e's allowed Mr. Joe to make fools of us on at least three occasions now, and I for one—

Captain Jocelyn, you're slandering him, and I won't allow it.

You aiming to *report* me, Sladen?

Not this time. But you'd better cut it out.

Whatever you say. But tell me—

Tell you what?

You served with him in Apache country. Isn't that so?

That's right.

General Crook said—

Now you listen, captain. Crook's got no use for reservations. He wants all the Indians underground, and you know it. Maybe you think the same way, in which case you don't deserve the name of Christian. Now, from the way you're glaring at me, I'll bet you imagine that Christianity's a disease, and the general's got a bad case of it. You think that because he's patient with your insulting, insubordinate slurs, and because he's missing one arm, he's not man enough to raise the other one against you. Well, by GOD, you should have seen him shaking it in James Bullard's face the time he threatened to murder our Apache guide,

> our general reddening with rage as he slowly said: I accosted you, sir, as a gentleman, and you reply by trying to insult me. I am a soldier, sir, and not to be intimidated by threats—

> Bullard cringing back, too yellow to go for his gun,

O, why waste my breath? This time I won't report you, captain, but do watch your GODd——d dirty mouth unless you're craving court-martial. And if you suppose that since I'm also partly crippled you don't need to fear me, well, captain, I'll meet you to-night and we'll see who's the better man, GODd——n you.

Is something the matter, Sladen?

No, sir,

> loosening the bellyband of his weary horse here where our Nez Perce and Umatilla scouts have already encamped per orders, the curving, wavering column making the Big Dust far behind, the teamsters' white-topped wagons long since gone dirty brown, our Gatlings invisible.

Did I hear profanity just now?

Well, not exactly, sir.

Captain Jocelyn, is there anything you want to say?

No, sir.

All right. Plant the guidon,

> the flag as welcome as the sound of water in the Apache country,
>> Mount Idaho up there above us (I wonder if Mr. Croaesdale has added to his field-works?), John's Creek running beside us fast and clear,
>>> as cool as the light on our Springfield carbines,
>> the two star-circlets on our American flag lovely one within the other:

We'll call this Camp Rains.

Yessir. *Halt.*

Halt! Fall in—roll call,

their arms and legs stinging almost pleasantly with sunburn.

And there'll be ice cream and Arctic soda on First Street.

Well, general, a creditable march.

And a prize shooting match at Willamette Grove, I'll bet.

I suppose so, Wilkinson. Fifteen miles . . .

Well, shut up, because we're not gonna be there,

gazing back down across the no longer white tops of his supply wagons, the company street springing up, his teamsters already arguing over their mess accounts.

Happy to be off Brown's Mountain, sir—

Yes, the men look tired. Time to blow "Stables."

D——n you, soldier, your horse is sweating! Don't you know enough not to throw a blanket over him?

as Red O'Donnell spits calomel into his mule's sores,

Perry currying Diamond, then slowly, sweetly stroking the U S brand on the horse's left shoulder,

Wood telling off four men from "D" Company to dig the sinks,

Mason despatching a rider to discover for all of us on earth why Lieutenant Otis's artillery remains so far behind that not even their dust has yet risen up,

Wilkinson demanding of the shyly grinning German at the cook wagon to hurry up with our general's coffee,

Doc cutting a deerskin patch for the blister on Blackie's heel.

And this month Congress has stopped paying the Army.

Where do you read that?

Right here. Happy Fourth of July to you.

Now that was one determined and successful campaign! By the time Crook was finished, every Pi-Ute within a hundred miles was making a beeline for the reservation.

Parnell, this operation will be even better. I'd still lay money on fucking old General Prayer Book.

Wilkinson, could you curry Arrow? Can't have him so dusty—

Right away, general. Has he pulled any tricks?

A marvelous horse. Much more interesting than Elmo. He and I are becoming good friends . . .

> You present him as one of those officers who travel from post to post with their greyhounds, never cleaning up reds—
>
> That's just about how he is.
>
> Shut up, Jocelyn,
>
>> as coffee-steam begins its rise, summoning us to the commissary-wagon.
>>
>>> Whipple
>>>
>>>> of whose abilities the general continues to cherish the greatest possible opinion,
>>>>
>>>> or else Perry must have made contact with them by this morning at the latest, because the way the Salmon flows on Colton's map—
>>>>
>>>> No, Fletch. Joseph's situation is such that he will try to withdraw—
>>>>
>>>> If they take the Mount Idaho Road, sir, the volunteers—
>>>>
>>>> I wouldn't count on that bunch.

Before kneeling down in Mr. Lynde's Methodist church in Tampa, when he still sought a dream to live out—namely, the as yet unthought of repudiation of that quality which in Perry, Sherman and so many other men must be something more innate than outrage—he cherished the honor-pride which his father and then West Point (his monthly blue slip from the Engineer Department listing, nearly always, zero demerits) had bred in him, so he imagined; in retrospect it was sourceless. Boys who sneak out at night to dig for phantom treasure show a kind of business ambition, to be sure, but we who believe only in the narrow double doors and single window of the miner's cage must smile at it; and Cut Arm, who delves up toward JESUS, not down toward yellow nuggets, may find occasion to smile upon the rest of us—one reason that the contempt of others so often approaches him, blocky and lowbellied like a Hereford bull. He insists to himself: Those who are really the servants of the LORD should work together.— Alas, on this basis it can be tricky to mobilize volunteers! (I've heard them mocking at the shrillness of my voice. Well, Caesar was also shrill.)

I do hope Perry isn't getting into trouble again.

2

Captain Pollock, can your company spare you an instant?

Of course, general. They're practically bivouacked—

Captain, you've had Lieutenant Wood in your service ever since Camp Bidwell. Isn't that so?

It sure is, general.

How do you grade him?

First-rate, sir. He broke in his recruits right away, and when I gave him some recordkeeping to do, he didn't let me down. I'd almost say he enjoys writing our reports, if you can imagine—

What about his morals?

He don't drink, if that's what you mean, sir. He don't swear—

Anything else, Pollock?

A ladies' man, sir, but in a harmless way.

Is he still engaged?

I haven't asked him lately. He writes a lot of letters, sir. Sometimes he gets a kind of desperate look on his face—

Is he popular?

A few in the company have complained he's too well-travelled, sir. But the truth is, he never looks down on any man who pulls his weight.

How does he stand on the Indian question?

Well, sir, he likes Indians more than some. But I have no doubt he can shoot them when he needs to.

Thanks for your candor, Pollock, and a happy Fourth to you! That will be all. Lieutenant Fletcher, where's Lieutenant Wilkinson?

Still sick, sir.

Should Wilkinson grow unable to carry out his duties—

O, general!

No, that probably won't happen. Even so, how would you like to see Wood as your colleague?

A fine officer and a friend—

And your rival in the decorative arts!

3

A very fine horse you have, Chapman.

And you, too, general!

Well, thank you for Arrow. He's a remarkable animal. Are all your horses like him?

Pretty much, if I do say so. Guess who taught me the best way to geld my colts? Looking-Glass! He was a pretty good Indian at one time, until White Bird and Mr. Joe put a bug up his ear.

Yes. Go have a rest now. You've ridden hard.

O, I ain't tired, general. You know, that James Reuben sure is one stuck-up red. He looks us right in the eye—

Why shouldn't he?

Because of what he is.

Chapman, you talk almost like a pro-slavery man. Have you no sympathy for the Indians?

Now see here, general! I was *never* with the Secceshes, which is more than that so-called Major Shearer can say—

Enough. I didn't mean to insult you. Do you have anything against Mr. Reuben other than the way he looks at you?

General, he's Joseph's brother-in-law!

Is that all?

Yessir,

> the man's cheerful race hatred as evident as the bulge of a Navy revolver in a sack coat. At least he's honest.

Chapman, go catch Joseph for me and let me get back to my business.

The thing is—

Get out. Fletch, bring me one of the reports that Wood's written for Captain Pollock. I need to verify that his handwriting's easy on the eye.

Yessir.

Wilkinson, how's the fever?

Just fine, sir, and happy Fourth!

Same to you, old friend! Do you still trust James Reuben?

Frankly, sir, I prefer Old George and Captain John. They're just good old simple Indians. Educated reds such as Mr. Reuben may be capable of dishonesty, and I consider it significant when he hesitated to come out strong against Looking-Glass. Do you remember how he equivocated?

Well, well! . . . But you know, he's very up on his Bible.

Yessir. I do credit him there.

4

Trimble, holding his ideals above his head, much like an Indian walking bare-footed through snow to keep his moccasins dry, still hopes for a speedy termination of the Nez Perce campaign

> —our absolute duty to extend the United States—
>
> —an indignant public sentiment—
>
> > *Wakesh nun pakilauitin*
> >
> > JEHOVAN'M *yiyauki*—
> >
> > > the general sitting on a cottonwood root, while Wilkinson stands before him:
> > >
> > > > And, sir, Frank Parker says it was a real jaw-dropper to watch them ford the Salmon, yelling, swimming thousands of horses across with all their papooses, and then—
> > > >
> > > > Wilkinson, you're excited. The main thing is this: We have Joseph on the run.
> > > >
> > > > Yessir,
> > >
> > > as we read out newspapers ten days old,

drinking tins of ebony coffee,
> our Bannock scouts wrapping themselves
> in their long trade blankets as they listen:
>> the Damon Lodge No. 4 met as usual
>> in the Castle Hall at Pendleton last
>> Wednesday evening
>> while John McGuinesss and some
>> treacherous Chinaman or other killed
>> each other in a gunfight at Idaho City
>> and

This GoDd——d dirt is harder than pilot bread!
> Believe me, Blackie, Wallowa's gonna be superior to the
> Black Hills. All them Germans, Irishmen and other
> trash blowin' their dollars on the stagecoach out there,
> they'll crawl back with nothin.'
> 'Course I believe you. I always believe you.
> And don't never stop believing,

but between Trimble, Perry and Mason, like a hairy fly from the sinks, flits the Modoc episode, annoying them even on this Fourth of July with stale fears, deaths, embitterments mostly against Colonel Gillem (not Captain Jack's bunch, who fought, surrendered and were punished nearly as intended), so that sometimes the three officers dislike one another for the sake of that weary mild vileness which each to the other two exemplifies; at the same time, Mason feels fond of both these subordinates, who got Jack, and therefore didn't let down the command; while they for their part perceive that fondness and the protection which it may supply; so that it is actually round Trimble and Perry's bearded heads that the loathsome fly most generally rushes, irritating them much as would the news of some new outbreak of Indians already driven onto the reservation; and these disconcerting botherations keep Trimble sufficiently out of joint that were he asked, which nobody would ever do, he might find himself unable to formulate what he would wish of Perry, except, of course, the other's removal by death, demotion or transfer; neither man can imagine being anything but a soldier, unlike Wood, or for that matter Wood's superior Captain Pollock, whose gold-hopes, far from perishing (he has tried his luck in the gold fields of El Dorado County and once even made five hundred dollars a day but mis-invested it), have been magnified by the keenings of his brood; anyhow, what can a fellow do, but sweat through life while avoiding the trickeries of dreams? There are worse things than drilling and killing. So Trimble oversees the dismounting, roll call, then dismissal of Company "H,"
> recollecting how a few days before he clambered up the rock face to take
> the rifle from Captain Jack and lead him down to imprisonment with
> iron fetters, followed by a speedy trial, hanging, pickling, decapitation
> and delivery to a museum, Perry's bunch (which of course included

Trimble's own company) were sitting with their bunch one day by the
eastern shore of Tule Lake, eating their lunches on the ground with their
backs against a swallow-ridden sandstone cliff which the Modocs had
pecked out with depictions of setting suns, full suns, peculiar insects
which might have been moths if moths could skeletonize and if their
wings had ribs; then there were armbones descending into triple-taloned
claws, parallel wave-forms, squares pecked out to enclose right-angled
groove-labyrinths, snake-grooves crowned with spreading fingers like
the lodgepoles atop an Indian tipi, buglike schematic humanoids, mushrooms or perhaps phalli, nested double circles, Y-shaped incisions and
lines of short vertical markings like tallyings, and there was something
resembling a heart above a long vertical groove, while a birdlike figure
spread her downcurving arms, and from a certain oval rose a long hooked
neck as to represent an egret bending down toward the water to troll for
fat insects; then there was a vertical slash topped with nested inverted
V's; had there been only one of those latter, the vertical stroke might have

been an arrow, but the way it was made, Trimble supposed that it must
be a grasshead; after all, so much of this tall greenish-yellow grass grew
about; and then here was grooved something like the inverted or falling
seedhead of a stalk of what must have been dying grass, which made him
inexplicably sad—why even consider dying grass?—but Mount Shasta,
broad, purple and heavenly white against the greyer clouds of midmorning, improved his melancholy into something like his customary resolution, and the wall of slanting strata remained capable of projecting a
bracingly chilly shadow, so that the troops of Companies "F" and "H"
could refresh and recruit themselves while they waited for the Warm
Springs Indian scouts to find the spoor of Captain Jack: moccasin-prints
hid in the sparsest boulder-sand; striding up to Colonel Perry with a
smile (for in those days they were still friends), Trimble discovered him
engaged in nothing less innocuous than a smoke with Lieutenant Theller,
yet somehow felt unwanted; and when he captured Captain Jack, it
seemed to him, incorrectly perhaps, that his commander would have preferred for Theller to get the credit. Sad, indifferent, disgusted, Trimble
asked himself why he and Lieutenant Parnell, whom he admired, were
not as Perry and Theller; and, unable to answer this, now turned to remembering his days at Fort McDermitt, Winemecca, where Theller had

also been on duty—a reliable officer, with a charming wife who evidently cherished him; Delia or Dellia had been her name; he had heard it pronounced but never seen it spelled,

and Parnell directs "Stable Call":

currycombs click

> as Wilkinson, yawning now (not long since he has ridden hard to Mount Idaho and back with three despatches from the general), his face crazy with hair and stubble, folds his arms in his lap, with his stinking hat low over his eyes, and leans forward, offering Wood the soles of his parted boots,
>
> Wood offering himself what he conceives to be the bravely natural days of the soldier,

while Bomus initials his tally of mules killed in the ascent of Brown's Mountain and Fletch kinnikinnicks his pipe, moderately interested as he watches the sweating, uncomplaining pickets disappear around the camp

as the rest of the bunch goes into bivouac,

gossiping about Lewiston and Looking-Glass,

> dreaming about the shaded porches of Mount Idaho, and Mr. Croaesdale's pretty English wife (does she willingly celebrate the Fourth?),

showing mad at Mr. Joe:

> No, that poor little Hattie Chamberlain was already dead when we got there. A-layin' in the dirt by her Daddy. And the other girl, the reds shot her in the neck and cut off her tongue, but she ...
>
> > (never speaking of Joseph as we used to of Burnside (much less Lee), or even a brigand such as Nathan Bedford Forrest, who tied up so many Union troops that Sherman advocated his assassination—LORD, no!— for the way we refer to Joseph is as an escaped prisoner);

and, truth to tell, feeling lonesome away from their folks on this holiday:

> They must be out on the green by now, eating corn and listening to speeches—
>
> And a picnic at East Portland Park!
>
> Not just a picnic, but a *national picnic.*
>
> You're too d——d much.
>
> And Daddy with his Rutherford B. Hayes medal shining.
>
> > Mr. Joe has already played his strongest cards ...

—and worse than lonesome whenever Lieutenant Parnell gets to talking about the time he took Company "H" through Skull Creek Cañon and saw weird arched windows in the basalt (right as they came into view of safety at Camp Warner, the Pi-Utes attacked)

> —almost like a ghost story!—

but mostly they are footsore, jealous and admiring of Ad Chapman, who never
gets weary (the general is the same, but he's in a more peculiar category),
 yearning for coffee and maybe canned oysters
   (I wish the general would make a speech.
   Not me. I've heard enough from him),
  waiting to hear whether Captain Whipple has found the enemy,
 and what treats Colonel Perry's supply train might be hauling in:
   Once we get to Norton's—
   And then we'll whip Mr. Joe—
  teasing Blackie about Fidelia,
   as Eltonhead and Duncan get punished for fighting,
our guidon streaming in the wind like the braids of an Apache squaw on
a galloping horse:
our sweet and lovely flag, which cannot be defiled:
  red stripes as dearly sad as soldiers' blood
   (Theller in the coffin with eyes which cannot close, because
   his eyes are holes)
and our bright starlilies in the blue American sky:
  thirty-eight stars!— Stars precisely as numerous as the bullet-
  holes in the skull of Little Bear's squaw, which you can see for
  yourself at the Army Medical Museum in Washington, D.C.
   But to-day's the day we add the thirty-ninth; new states
   always come in on July Fourth. To-day it's Colorado. Or
   was Colorado the thirty-eighth? Who can keep track,
   except maybe Wilkinson?
Perry feels sorry for his wife, hoping that Mrs. Howard is looking after her,
while Mrs. Howard stares glassily down at Colton's map, drinking coffee and wiping flies from her face,
as her husband remembers the Fourth of July in Maine:
  the "spread eagle" speeches and the militiamen's white and red pompoms
   (what a sad, spent bunch I have here to-day!)
  and their officers' lovely white plumes, and then the governor and his
  staff;
   but now I forget who used to fire the cannon-salute. Very small-
   calibre cannon they were.
    Shall I give Lieutenant Otis something to do? He'd love to fire
    off a volley. But we might need every last round for Joseph.
LORD, how weary I am! How many more years can I keep this up? Sometimes
I think those who fell in the war were lucky. Must never tell Lizzie how I
  at the very instant that Wood is postulating that *the realization of*
  death grows out of America's bloody earth,
which is why he now says:
Captain Trimble, were you at Five Forks?

Sure was. Not to mention Gettysburg and Cold Harbor.

Tell us, sir, what was the worst?

O, for me Gettysburg, and maybe the general would agree with me, although he had a time of it at Chancellorsville, as you know. Bad intelligence, Wood. Could have happened to anyone. You're passing fond of him, aren't you?

Very much, captain. He's been good to me,

> but somehow

>> (perhaps merely on account of the general's partiality for Perry) these words bring out in Captain Trimble something akin to that famous grimness of General Grant in awkward civilian situations.

5

Fletch lights his pipe, while Wilkinson begins to prowl around the sinks.

Were you at the Centennial, Wood?

No, I couldn't get away.

They have a new machine called a *typewriter*. Looks like a sewing machine. You press a key and—

> Before you know it we'll be getting a pint of booze at Theodore's cigar shop in Umatilla.

> O, I do *love* that place! On the glorious Fourth, my word, to be drinking whiskey, even barefoot whiskey, and watching the ladies on the other side of the street, even if they never cast a glance your way . . .

>> My brother-in-law has served in Charleston, South Carolina, and he wrote me that down there in those parts, at least from what he could see, only the niggers turn out for Independence Day.

>> Why ain't he there no more?

>> President sent his unit home.

>> Betcha them niggers has been keeping themselves real cool and quiet ever since.

>> Good thing, since the Government has done enough for them.

6

Remember when we celebrated this day at Gettysburg?

O yes.

Then I lined up what infantry I could find along with Berry's troops.

Yessir.

But the difficulty, you see, was that famous stone wall on Marye's Heights behind which all those Secceshes were eventually killed.

> Let's have an eagle-scream for American independence!
> *Hurrah, hurrah, hooray!,*
>> the joy of our America rising like the sun,

Wood worrying about our poor weak Government, which resembles the GOD of a Kabbalist in its shining need, wavering over a continent which teems with Indians who hate us; while Wilkinson, who thinks less about extramilitary politics, simply associates with America a goodness as brilliantly indefinable as the HOLY SPIRIT itself.

(He joined in '62, with the Twenty-third New York Volunteers. Even then he started each morning by singing a hymn.)

When I was a cadet, our muskets were still loaded in ten motions.

Hard to believe, general . . .

Hurrah, hurrah, hooray!

No, Wilkinson, you ask him.

General, we officers were hoping you might say something to us to commemorate this Fourth.

All right. Well, that's very flattering, actually. I hope I can think of something to please them . . . Are they assembled, Wilkinson? At ease, all of you. Gentlemen, my good grandfather used to put me on his knee and tell me about his father, who was an officer in the Continental Army. I don't think he was at Lexington, but he might have been at Bunker Hill. You know, those stories of the Revolution were almost as sacred to us children as the stories of the Bible . . .

7

Then a despatch rider comes galloping in.

Sad news, gentlemen. Two of Captain Whipple's scouts were fired on, and at least one was killed. It seems Whipple sent out a relief party under Lieutenant Rains, and Joseph wiped them out to the last man.

8

And so now it has become a desolate Fourth of July, really as mournful as Doc's long white hair—

sad for the general, who'd thought Rains a likely young fellow,

sadder still for Wilkinson, who had felt certain obscure attachments,

saddest of all for Wood:

because Rains was his classmate at West Point, he now achieves his apotheosis of hatred for Mr. Joe.

9

This must have occurred in the vicinity of Rocky Cañon.

Yes, sir.

What's this, another rider? What is it now?

General, just as you predicted, Looking-Glass has joined the enemy, and they've doubled back on the Salmon—

Then they must already have crossed my communications beyond Norton's ranch.

I can't say for sure, general.

Sir, Captain Whipple sent out Lieutenant Rains with ten men, and the Indians killed them all!

That's already been announced, Fletch. We'll be taking Mr. Joe behind the woodshed pretty soon.

Yessir.

Are Randall's bunch back at Mount Idaho?

As far as we know, sir. Those volunteers . . .

Bring me Hunter and McConville.

Yessir.

Gentlemen, you've probably heard what happened to Lieutenant Rains's detachment.

We sure have, general, and we'd like to tell you—

Lead your volunteers immediately by way of Rocky Cañon to reënforce Perry's command. Go now. That's all. Fletch, where's my horse?

Sir, should our main body ride through Rocky Cañon?

I think Joseph is only making a raid. His women, children and plunder must be near the Snake River. We'll seek him there.

Yessir.

Wilkinson, take dictation. This is to Colonel Perry . . .

He Could Have Made Money Anywhere
July 2–5

1

No, Miller, that's not so. You see, I ran First Cavalry and Madigan ran a company of the Twenty-third. When I charged eastward, Madigan charged the south. It was nowhere near as dangerous for him as for me, but he was the one who got killed. You don't know anything about it.

All right, Perry—

No. You weren't there. You never served under General Crook. You never saw what fiends those Pi-Utes were. When we took their position, we found one of their little papooses strangled with a forked stick, so it couldn't give 'em away. Meanwhile they were all creeping out like cowards. Miller, you ain't seen nothing until you've gone down sixty feet into the Hell Caves, waiting and waiting for a Pi-Ute to spring at you. Worse than the Modoc Stronghold! That's how you get a case of nerves, and that's what Madigan got. When my wife read about us in the newspapers, she sure kicked up a scream. And in those days, you see, Crook made us winter in holes three feet deep, with a fire hole and a tent on top, to . . .

> but in the course of saying this, Perry finds himself overcome by something as unlikely as the *creaking* sound of Mormon crickets squashed beneath our wagon wheels around Glenns Ferry when we all first rode out West ever so long ago and there were still buffalo in Omaha, while Old Joseph, believe it or not, lived like a Christian: He can't stop thinking of Theller.— So he hears himself saying (Miller presumes he is speaking of General Crook):

He could have made money anywhere.

2

Captain Whipple, why are you all the way out here?

Colonel, Mr. Joe's just wiped out Lieutenant Rains with all his men. The enemy's thataway—

I'm taking command.

Yessir. We brought the mountain howitzer in case your pack train—

I sure appreciate it. We would have fallen into their trap.

Colonel Perry, I—

You know, Whipple, you're the best of the bunch. If you'd have been with me at White Bird Cañon—

Thank you, sir. It would have been an honor.

Another thing. If General Howard runs you down about Looking-Glass's escape, don't take it to heart. I've heard what happened. Those volunteers fucked you over. They can't hold their fire. Was Ad Chapman there?

No, sir.

Well, he's the worst. He ruined us at White Bird Cañon. Should be shot.

Dutch Holmes fired first, and then that Osterhout—

I've seen them both around Lapwai, and that's what they are: *volunteers.* Believe me, Whipple, I know how it is. All right, get me a rider. Yes, you. Can you write? Then here goes, to Colonel Sully: *Indians around us all day in force and very demonstrative. Rains, ten soldiers and two scouts killed. Had not Whipple come to our rescue, we would have been taken in . . .*

Thanks, colonel; that's real white of you.

I mean every word. You, rider, read it back to me. Yeah, fine. Now take it to Lapwai, doublequick, and watch yourself. Make sure they send on a copy to the general.

Yessir.

Now, Whipple, tell me what happened.

Colonel, I sent out two citizens to reconnoiter the country just as the general ordered: Foster and that little Blewett. Their instructions were to discover if the reds were still around Craig's Ferry . . .

3

We are going down toward Split Rock,
    or perhaps to Wallowa
        (or even to Weippe if our best men so decide,
           for now it has just begun to be Eel Season, when our hearts turn
           toward riding into that camas ground, driving our horses as we
           wish, camping here and there along the Big Water whenever we
           desire crawling food,
                Old Looking-Glass's favorite)
    or else, if our hearts tell us so, we shall visit Red Owl's country
    or Toohhoolhoolsote's home,
           lowering our buffalo horns on strings as we ride, dipping them into
           the creeks,
passing across the grass and down into the grey-hazed mounds of trees,
down into the blueness between blue hills and mountains
    (Steep Forever Place),
hugging the steep slopes, pines and grass and sky, descending the cañon-edge
where cliffs nearly touch the trees;
so down we go, and down, until walled in by golden grass:
    grassed mountains in an immense golden cañon;
balancing lodgepoles on each side of our ponies, driving a thousand horses and
more,
    dogs running all around us, our women whipping the pack animals,
        Burning Coals and his daughter worrying about their horses,
we are riding down our cañon, as grassy and flowery forest begins to rise up in
the middle,
    Ollokot with his little son and roundfaced, smoothfaced young wives,
    Heinmot Tooyalakekt sitting easy on Black Mane-Stripe, teasing his
    wives and children; he has decorated himself in one of his many blanket-
    coats studded with brass;
    Wounded Head beside his small boy who is just now old enough to ride
    by himself,
        while his mother-in-law, little old Towhee, and his dear wife
          Helping Another are ahead of them driving in horses,
    our old ones chuckling or complaining, watching everything as they ride,
    our long-braided young women showing off their elkteeth-studded
    blouses and abalone earrings,

and Welweyas in her striped blanket-dress, with brass buttons in
her pierced ears,
    she who rides a horse so tall and easy,
longs to dance the Rabbit Dance again to-night;
        now she is telling Sound Of Running Feet the girl's favorite
        tale, about the time when COYOTE and FOX got hungry, so
        that They decided to dress up as women and marry men who
        would feed Them, thereby receiving delicious courtship meat,
        just for awhile; and just before the moment of nuptial truth,
        COYOTE raped His husband's sister; then He and FOX ran
        safely away forever:
        Sound Of Running Feet begins laughing; then asks: Whom
        would you marry? and Welweyas, kneeing One-Eye forward,
        shouts back: *You!*,
            cantering up to help her mother beat a half-broken stal-
            lion,
    our best men wearing feathers, war-bonnets, weasel-skins and wolf's-heads
in their hair,
    while some of us wave tall Dreamer sticks
and rippled dark water twists around between immense steep brownish cliffs,
then vanishes: the Chinook Salmon Water
—then finally the cañon's pink rock drops away into grass-hills
and we ride out through the trees into camas prairie,
    laughing at Cut Arm and decorating our faces
        while some of us roam Meadow Place* so that our women may dig
        late-blooming camas,
            and Springtime sings over her baby, who has now com-
            menced to thrive,
            as Good Woman poultices a mare's eye;
            Cloudburst, the hardworking one
                (it is said that their husband's heart loves Fair Land bet-
                ter),
            lies down early
                (her back is sore from grubbing up roots)
            and opens the breastpin which Ollokot gave her, wondering
            if she should keep anything inside it;
    and John Dog, tired of sitting in camp, rides hunting in the hazy
cañons between here and the Enemy River
    and our chiefs quarrel about riding back to Split Rock or not:
        pokát, pokát
—but Red Spy,

---

*The Joseph Plains between the Snake and Salmon rivers.

one of our most rapid scouts
>   (so small and light that he could almost be a boy)
—his heart is thirsting for more war, longing to fly up and venture out onto the
edge of its own beat—
sets out stalking;
thus it is he who first sees on the rock-horizon two mounted Bostons,
>   angry enemies who shoot at him, hoping to steal his life:
>>   *Pim-pim-pim! . . . Pim!*
>   —their bullets singing against boulders:
>   They are nothing, not even mice-eaters!
>>   (For what do they come riding into our country?)
>   Now he has begun to sing his WYAKIN song,
>>   praising the HAIL that falls suddenly,
as he pretends to ride away, then hides his pony in a coulee, creeping snakewise
between boulders until he can fire a good first shot, holding his breath:
>>>   *Pim!*
—and at once they are galloping away like enemy women trying not to get raped!
I shall now be driving them like deer; let the HAIL now fall suddenly:
>   and indeed the shorter Boston's horse stumbles, throwing him
>>   (he cannot even ride; he is worthless like rotten bones)
down into the golden grass
>   (he cries out: *Shlak!*),
and the taller Boston flees on, unable to make himself brave. It then becomes easy
>   (any man could do it)
to approach this little one, shoot him in the head as he cowers against a hillside:
>   *taq!*
then sing the *scalp haloo,*
>   the tall Boston therefore galloping away in terror
>>   (now I have begun to teach him something).
>   So Red Spy skips up to his twitching enemy to see what good things there may be
>>   (remembering that our chiefs have said: *You must not scalp*):
to him comes a Winchester rifle, a half-empty cartridge belt, brass buttons, variously decorated greenbacks
>   (these I shall trade to the Bostons for whatever pleases my heart)
a canteen, a needle and thread, and even a magic *eye necklace** through which he
can see far
>   —as the *scalp haloo* travels and echoes,
>>   travelling like the AIR BIRD,
>>>   and so arrives exactly here in the flat place where we have now
>>>   settled in a circle,
>>>>   the chiefs still smoking the pipe for nothing,

---

*Field-glasses.

so that Shooting Thunder, White Thunder and Twice Alighting On Water therefore catch horses and come galloping to see what sport remains,
> with them tall young Rainbow, our greatest buffalo hunter but for Looking-
> Glass
> > —he has painted himself red and crowned himself with feathers of all
> > colors; he wears a single necklace around his slender throat and little
> > silver conchos jingle in his braids—
all of them now chasing the last Boston, just in fun
> (there is no badness in our hearts),
> Red Spy giggling, even White Thunder laughing
> > (I must not tell my Uncle Heinmot Tooyalakekt),
> and upraising that dead Boston's Sharps he got at Sparse-Snowed Place
> > (a Springfield would shoot better)
> as the tall Boston gallops foolishly on his tiring horse, arrow-straight across
> the prairie:
> > I shall now shoot him between his shoulderblades!
—but Rainbow says: *No.* Brothers, let him lead us to the others and get them before they send scouts to Butterfly Place,
so that White Thunder says: Now I have opened my ears,
and we chase that tall Boston all the way to Cottonwood Place.
> Here stand their tents in a hole. Now they will be making themselves angry.
They must soon ride out—*áhahaha!*
> Now indeed they are coming, just as we foretold:
> eleven Bluecoats, one of them an officer
> > (Wood's old classmate Lieutenant Rains, who, disappointed not to
> > be the one to bag Looking-Glass, hopes now to do good execution
> > on little Blewett's killer),
> and leading them, the tall Boston whom we allowed to get away:
> > they are furious as they ride,
> cantering up the road, with their rifles upward,
> > coming into the country where yellow hills are falling to the east and
> > rising to the west,
> becoming doomed,
> > as more warriors ride out in need of prey:
> Red Spy, White Thunder, Strong Eagle, Five Wounds, Shore Crossing, Rain-
> bow, Two Moons and even White Bird are now lying low,
> > > their hearts hoping to discover Tsépmin or Cut Arm among these
> > > others,
> > > or even Píli the tall one (we have killed his brother at Sparse-
> > > Snowed Place).
> Now let us ambush them!— They wheel around,
> > shouting in terror, whipping their horses,
galloping up the yellow hills to die, like salmon swimming upriver at Celilo Falls.

So we are chasing them down,
      reminding these Bostons that our country will never belong to them,
Rainbow on the left, Five Wounds on the right:
shooting their horses as they go;
we are driving them like buffalo.
      Some try to break away, but Strong Eagle,
      he who will live to be last of the Three Red Blankets,
pretends to be hiding behind a dead pine, inviting the Bluecoats to shoot at him
(they get distracted like children):
          just as a killdeer lures away enemies from his nest by pretending that his
          wing is broken, so little by little he coaxes these bad men into danger,
             singing his WYAKIN song, so that their bullets all go wide;
                they keep on hoping and forgetting, raising themselves up so
                that we may choose which one to kill
until we are all exactly where we prefer to be
      —led by Shore Crossing, whose war-hope has grown as vast and never-
      alighting as the AIR BIRD—
and then we gallop out from the trees, swarming down (we are pleasing our
hearts),
driving them in together
      through the low lichened rocks on the slanting meadow of yellow grass, with
      yellow plains and blue-black walls of trees down in the hot haze:
      they are crying, weeping like women
          (truly they are laughable; we should never have helped their grand-
          fathers!),
huddling among low boulders
      (as did those others when we began to surround and kill them at Sparse-
      Snowed Place: this is how they die),
shooting *pim! pim!* (always missing),
and White Thunder crawls slowly down the hill, aiming his Sharps as sweetly as
if he were asking his mother to come and pick lice from his hair:
      pim!
—and now has come the turn of that tall Boston whom we used to bring them
here:
          Pim!
          —Tsalalal!
—while from between two boulders which these enemies keep missing with their
guns, Rainbow, loving the long easy trigger pull of the trapdoor Springfield, sights
on a fat Bluecoat
      who has now lost his cap (his hair is reddish-brown like the head of a
      male cowbird),
holds a breath, and drops him,
      guts exploding from the man's belly,

and clearing the action, he loads another cartridge into the breech,
his war-brothers now tightening the circle,
> Five Moons and Shore Crossing laughing as they shoot
>> (no need to spend explosive bullets),
> the Bluecoats dying, soiling themselves;
now we are happy, and go to see:
> They are all killed,
>> those Bluecoats who have pierced our country and shaken it up into
>> ever so many bloody pieces,
> except for one whom we shot in the forehead and the breast; blood runs down
> his face, and he tries to speak, *kek, kek,* so we shoot him again in the breast,
>> just to help him
>>> (he is sweating like a broken-in horse),
> but he will not be helped in that way,
so to save him from feeling troubled, we club him to death:
> *Qáw! Qáw! Qáw! Qáw! Qáw!*

Qáw!

then take all their horses and rifles, with whatever cartridges can be found,
> but remembering what we promised our chiefs, we leave the gloves on
> the officer's hand, the ring on his finger.
Meanwhile our People ride on safely toward Red Owl's country,
> singing the victory song
>> (Welweyas the half-woman sings the loudest; her mother
>> moves away),
> and we are feeling dazzling and brave.

4

All right, Whipple; we'd better fort up before the reds get here.
Yessir,
> our boys ripping planks out of Norton's place, throwing up a stockade
>> (Perry stalking through the camp, feeling slightly sickish as he al-
>> ways does before close action),
> deepening rifle pits
>> and digging in the Gatlings, sighting them along the road in case
>> the hostiles should come that way
>>> as a volunteer despatch rider rides out like mad for Mount
>>> Idaho,
and that very evening
> (the night as thick and hot as the last great buffalo herd),
the Indians besiege us
> (from their quickness to find us out, Perry and Whipple determine that
> they must be in communication with sympathizers at Lapwai:

Monteith had better scrub out his reservation!):
Go‌ᴅᴅ——n you, you Go‌ᴅᴅ——n white men, and Go‌ᴅᴅ——n Go‌ᴅᴅ——n General Howard!
—Pim!... pim!
—but praise Go‌ᴅ the Gatlings keep them off!

Well, colonel, the general should be pleased. We know where the hostiles are.

Perry feels happy that Whipple is with him. It feels almost like having Theller
back.

5

At eight-o'clock next morning the Brave Seventeen,
their saddlebags filled up with coffee and hardbread, thanks to the landlady of Brown's Hotel
(her hair parted almost like a man's, her wrinkles both vertical and horizontal)
—a true American patriot—
set out from Mount Idaho, led by Captain-by-acclamation Randall and a couple
of his bruisers,
thinking to save the despatch rider from getting murdered by reds on his
return
and prove that citizens are just as good as Army men
and give the lie to the so-called command of that Copperhead grifter
George Shearer, who has already galloped thataway as if he were still the
bantam rooster of some two-cent Confederate piss-hole;
anyhow poor Perry, the Dunce of White Bird Cañon, could use a hand
—for on whom can he call but Uh-Oh Howard's army of new-
imported foreigners and European sweepings?—
besides, just maybe we feel like making trouble
(being unable to forget the way we had to run Mrs. Chamberlain
down and surround her before she would believe we were her
friends: this tale alone explains why all reds need to be rubbed out):
Colonel Perry's been attacked at Cottonwood House!
By Joseph?
Who else?
I heard firing last night—
Remember, they've got fixed ammunition.
And then Whipple's command formed a solid line of battle
on the east edge of the ravine, but Mr. Joe—
Volunteers, ride at once,
and the Brave Seventeen, bravely fitted out, depart to show what real Americans
can do,
deploying strictly according to order,

spiritually reënforced by the double-domed immensity of the Corliss Steam
Engine high on its platform above the throng at last year's Centennial Exhibition:

> like two Assyrian helmets upon the headless necks of metal sphinxes
> whose spinal columns are ladders:

>> one thousand five hundred horsepower!

>>> Well, this will sure be memorable in the annals of Injun warfare,

but soon they are all alone out on the prairie

> (in the yellow grass, dark boulders resemble a huddle of Bannock warriors with
> their blankets pulled tight);

then even more alone:

My horse smells Indians!

Well, you'd better control him,

but both fellows should have listened to that one horse, because even though most
warriors have now returned to guarding People and horses in their journey toward Red Owl's country,

> while Shore Crossing rides singing round and round, happy to consider more
> fighting on the trail,

the chiefs, necklaced and blanket-wrapped, have sent Twice Alighting On Water
and seven others to watch the Bluecoats in their holes

> (if they come out again we must fight them),

>> so that Geese Three Times Alighting On Water,

>>> he whose heart felt sad when he shot his arrow into that little Boston child's arm along the Chinook Salmon Water,

>> rides with fewer than two hands' worth of warriors to watch the Mount
>> Idaho road

>> and presently discovers Bostons on the horizon, riding exactly here:

>>> giving the young boys their horses to hold, they lie down by the
>>> roadside, ready to shoot Bostons from ambush

>>> but the Bostons do not come;

>> so we must follow them,

>> and *now* the Bostons get off their horses,

>>> because mounted these worthless ones can scarcely fight;

>> and then we see behind them three hands and more of other enemies
>> galloping forward:

the Brave Seventeen.

> So we hide again, this time instructing only one boy, our youngest, to be horse-
holder;

>> while White Thunder,

>>> he who knows how to chase the buffalo and what the LIGHTNING
>>> says,

>> is throwing off his deerskin shirt, rolling down his leggings,

and now we are waiting for the enemies, but when they turn east instead, we
mount and pursue them

> (Ollokot tells us what to do),

>> hoping to chase them round and round the rocks as we did to those Blue-
>> coats the other day,

because they are riding toward our column of People!

> —our women watching open-mouthed from the Red Rock Spring as we
> drive our prey like rabbits;

now they see us:

>> *Áhaha!*

and dismount to shoot better: easier for us;

we shoot them; they shoot us,

> expecting to punish Mr. Joe and all his stinking reds

>> until Charles Chase's horse takes an Indian bullet through the
>> nose:

>>> my GOD, my GOD!;

then Wounded Mouth, the oldest of us here

and father of that traitor Animal In A Hole

> *(Tso Alpít),*

> whom we caught scouting for Cut Arm at Sparse-Snowed Place,

gets a bullet in the belly—the first of us to be badly hurt in this war, as Wottolen, *he who remembers,* will later say;

Wounded Mouth never groans; we make him comfortable in rock-shade

> (to-night White Bird will sing over him, and Feathers Around The Neck

>> —so strong comes his Power that he was a sorcerer even in his
>> childhood—

> will burn sweetgrass from the Buffalo Country,

>> cleansing the badness with that perfume which is milder than
>> sage's, almost honeyed, but partaking of tobacco also;

all the same, Wounded Mouth will die;

> to-morrow morning we shall paint his face red and bury him; then
> we must try not to say his name)

>> —*No!* says White Thunder. It was certainly I who found Jy-
>> eloo's body all bloody in the grass, I am telling you three
>> times! *He* was first to die in this fight . . .—

and now, White Cloud, the half-brother of Two Moons, gets shot in the
thigh:

> his horse falls on him; we pull him out and help him ride away

>> (that horse's skeleton will be lying here long after this war)—

and Ollokot's horse becomes tired, so the boy About Asleep rides to Red
Rock Spring,

> and Cloudburst, his brave younger wife, comes galloping to the
> battle with a fresh stallion in tow

(as she sings to her WYAKIN, Power begins to come, with a
raven's near-silent passage through the air),
and now our joy grows as rich as organ-fat because we are killing these
Bostons,
Ben Evans screaming four times, each scream distinct
(his end as shocking as a Pittsburgh striker's brick smashing
into a soldier's face)
Randall desperately feeding in each golden cartridge with his hot
powder–blackened forefinger,
bracing the rifle tight against cheek and shoulder,
the long black barrel heating fast:
nearer, my GOD, to Thee.

6

At Norton's we hear those gunshots and then a rider comes galloping:
Colonel Perry, we need help! The reds are murdering us!
—and although it has frequently been said that upon gazing into the eyes
of a dangerous violent man one sees *nothing*, the case of Perry is otherwise, for deep within his sight-holes, something cool, aware and certain
of itself, never wondering who it is, pulses almost idly, entertaining itself
with the possibility of emergence:
I remember pretty d——d well when the general had to shut that
Randall up, and directed me to keep an eye on him:
just another miserable citizen, like the ones who betrayed me
at White Bird Cañon:
They always get themselves in trouble, then drag us into it.
The general's right. Without them, there wouldn't
be any Nez Perce War.
And now we're expected to bleed for them.
Major Shearer, already affronted by the cool treatment he has received from
Colonel Perry,
and longing (an addiction our general recognizes quite well) to once
more be able to utter that prideful phrase *an officer of the command*
—for I was with the Army of the Tennessee at Chickamauga
when we whipped Lincoln's niggers!—
begins wondering whose collar to shake, for *Chief Joseph is murdering the Brave
Seventeen!* I shall not stand quiet. By heaven, my path is clear:
Colonel Perry, those men out there require immediate relief!
Yes, but the reds are hoping to draw us out.
In JESUS's name, colonel!
Climbing to the highest point of his defensive works, Perry,

whose nightmares resemble hostile reds swaying and circling on their
horses,
gazes through his field-glass to discover the blond head of Lew Wilmot
and then White Thunder, clutching a smooth-knobbed war club,
standing tall, his face brightly painted, his mouth clenched, singing
his WYAKIN song
(I've seen that red around)
then Randall, bleeding, falling:
well, it's sure no ruse, but we can't render any help—
good riddance, actually!
and Mr. Joe's devils galloping around the others, tighter and tighter:
Help us, colonel! They're butchering us!
They got themselves into this. Joseph wants to lure me out so he can
destroy me in detail.
Colonel, why aren't you answering me? You going to let the boys be killed out there?
It's true that if I do nothing they'll call me yellow. Can hardly bear to see
those reds kill Americans, even if they're nothing but a gaggle of fucking
volunteers . . .
Mr. Shearer, just what do you want me to do? Remember what you said to me
last time? *O, come on, colonel, you can easily whip the scoundrels.* We thought you
knew something,
glaring redly, his eyes sticky and inflamed with dust,
and then you sons of bitches stampeded us right into Mr. Joe's clutches, turned
tail and left us to bleed—
Are you saying you'll just watch our bunch get murdered? Is that what you're
saying?
Listen up, asshole. If I send out my troops to save you—
Colonel, what's the excitement down the hill?
Hello, Whipple. Some citizens on the Mount Idaho road are getting cut to
pieces by Indians, and nothing can be done to help them.
Why the hell not?
We're too late. That's all.
Did you hear that, men? It's Randall's bunch fighting it out with
Joseph, and our colonel says it's *just too late.*
Well, it ain't! We got to speak to the colonel, right now—
Colonel Perry, the man who goes down there is a d——d fool, but he's a d——d
coward if he don't.
Shut your mouth, Shearer.
I deny your authority—
Go eat cornbread, Johnny Reb! One more word from you and you're in chains.
If Shearer won't go, *I'll go,* orders or no orders! Americans are dying out there!
Twenty-five volunteers, step forward—

Sergeant Simpson, you're under arrest. After this is over, you'll be court-martialed for insubordination. Yes, Whipple, what do you have to say?

For the love of GOD, colonel, let me go—!

You too? All right then. Since it's you. Go, and good luck. Remember, we can't reënforce you. If Joseph gets in here he'll have our Gatlings—

Thanks, colonel. Hurry up, men!

> —saddling up, cramming extra cartridges in both pockets of their can-
> tenisses, pulling themselves up onto their horses—

Blow forward bugle.

Forward!

>> into the nippled grass-mounds and furry-grassed gorges, farther
>> and farther into danger, while Perry stands upon his breastworks
>> listening:
>>> *Charge!*

and so they rescue fifteen of the Brave Seventeen (two survivors badly wounded), while Perry is branded a coward.

7

Sir, I'll thank you to use more respectful language toward one of my bravest and most energetic officers.

But, general, he just stood there and—

Gentlemen, I will say that reasonable caution in the presence of superior forces should be commended.

They wasn't superior forces, General Howard. They was just Indians.

If they were *just Indians,* then *just Indians* did a pretty good job killing your captain and his men. If they were *just Indians,* why can't you clean them up without the assistance of the United States? Now get out.

We should have known, boys. General's always gonna—

Sure is a shame.

General, I—

Never mind, Perry. Now go stir up your company. In forty-five minutes we'll be on the march.

> When all them soldiers run us down and tell us what to do—
>> And Captain Randall's dead, thanks to *Yellow Perry,*
>> after which he cannot help but resemble the man who stays
>> mounted all night to keep a lookout for Indians:
>> the *yellow man*
>>> (while Randall, His Royal Dead Excellency, will be buried
>>> with full Masonic honors);

and on the march that day, finding and losing *the Red Napoleon's* trail, Perry, trying not to think about a certain soldier's widow whom he's sweet on (her name begins with D), calls up in his skull's magic lantern show a lively Pi-Ute squaw well

painted with yellow dots over her cheekbones and three black lines on her
forehead,
then overhears Miller's sneering gibe flashing up the column: *He could have made
money anywhere.*

MISERY HILL
JULY 8–10

1

*N*ow the volunteers realize that they will have to clean up the reds themselves, since the Army is run by characters such as Uh-Oh Howard and Yellow
Perry, so they set out to find Mr. Joe
    even as the general's troops are dismantling Luke Billy's cabin to make a
    raft:
        O, Uncle Sam will pay you. Just send him a letter,
    and the rope breaks, the raft is lost and Luke Billy never gets paid
        (after all, he's just an Indian),
so our troops must detour again
        (on Colton's map it is not much more than a finger's breadth from
        White Bird Creek to the Clearwater, with Mount Idaho in between
        them, but even Cut Arm can now begin to appreciate the logistical
        difficulties of deploying troops in that country:
            what this country offers most of all is space; how could any-
            one subjugate it?
            We'll do our best, sir);
as our brave volunteers, undiscouraged by their previous adventures, saddle up
some of those mighty fine stallions we confiscated from Looking-Glass
and start following the Indian trail across the prairie:
    Mr. Joe's about reached his zenith, I'd say.
    O, he can get even more famous if he does to other women what he—
riding down the rolling sweep of hill, across camas prairie russet, yellow, grey
and green
and watching for ambush in the forested side-hollows,
    Shearer still sizzling over his last exchange with Colonel Perry:
    Shearer, were you at Missionary Ridge?
    So what if I was?
    Remember when you Johnny Rebs got panicked and routed? An

ugly sight even for some of us who chased you. That's how it was
with all your volunteers at White Bird Cañon, and *you weren't even
there.* You're the yellow one, my boy! Call me yellow one more time
and I'll shoot you in your corn dodger's face—

as he leads his troop on, envious of Ad Chapman, who's gotten in good
with the general

and determined to put a spider in Perry's dumpling forever;
so they keep hunting for reds, hoping to get Mr. Joe *and* his horses,
riding through the sky on a cloud made of prairie grass:

He could be holed up in Cottonwood Cañon, because last summer when
I skimmed off a few of his yearlings . . .

Therefore they ride down thataway, still pretty sure that what happened to
Rains, the Brave Seventeen and that bunch at White Bird Cañon should never
have happened and therefore cannot happen to them,

chasing greeds and dreads through the sharp narrow bends of the cañon

(evergreens on one side only),

down into the cañon's haze, the trees in irregular formation, the grass paler on
the ridges, browner and greyer on the steeps whose shadows hang down from
them at midday:

our *Red Napoleon* must be lurking somewhere within this horizon of
smoke-blue mountains

(probably torturing little children again in his typically savage
fashion

or renting out Mrs. Manuel for two brass buttons a go);
then the grass grows more camel-colored and hay-colored, beset with steep
green side-cañons

(someday there will be apple trees down here),

and they come up into alders and aspens

(grass as grey as wilted spiderwebs dangling from basalt boulders)

and poison oak and tall pines,
until they find the trouble they were looking for.

2

That great buffalo rifle roars monstrously, exploding a boulder so that the
horses scream,
then roars again:

the shooter being a grim tall muscular savage who flaunts a red blanket
at them

(if Captain Randall were still alive, he'd know who it is).

O for a breeze down there in the cottonwood shade,
and water to drink!

I'd say we're as good as gone.

How many shots you have left?
Eleven for the revolver and eight for the carbine. You?
Still got my full twelve and twenty-five.
Gonna call this place Misery Hill—
Camp Misery. We'll be here day and night unless the Army comes,
  his tongue like a stone in his desperately dry mouth;
    their lives will go in much the way that urine sinks almost instantly
    between the rocks, leaving foam for an instant or two.
Besieged up here in shallow rifle-pits upon the low green rise of Misery Hill
  (a few trees, fields' stony sides, a cool breeze,
  hill-grooves fringed with dying shrubs
  the top hardpacked with blackstone),
looking down on the prairie's ubiquitous undulations:
    Where the hell is Uh-Oh Howard?
    Dig in and shut up,
  pale blue ridge on the left
  the slope of yellow grass
  and Indians shooting up from the bewildering rolls of grass-flesh,
the heat working at every man
  (all them Injuns need to do is keep us from water);
here indeed comes a night without water, as the warriors attack twice.
Then what?
In the end our volunteers are saved by Mr. Joe's unfathomable withdrawal:
  late morning:
    clouds part way over the curving ridge-horizon to the west,
and the reds stole all our decent horses.

3

So they bring the People down safe into Red Owl's country,
  whose jewel is that lovely brown river scaled with light:
    the Big Water,*
  deep brown river floored and edged with white stones,
  where they find Looking-Glass's People
  (from far away they recognize them)
comforting them for Cut Arm's treachery by returning to them full forty of their
horses;
    and Looking-Glass smiles, believing that he has become once more the
    lucky man,
    as White Thunder leads to him his favorite black stallion, whose name
    will now be *Home From Capture.*

---

*Clearwater River.

WHEN HE HEARS THE WHISPER
JULY 11

1

*S*ound Of Running Feet is bewitched, but only a little; Toohhoolhoolsote pulls out a bloody worm from her belly, and before dawn she has become well; so her father gives the old *tiwét* three horses, and Good Woman smiles, then lies down to sleep, just for awhile

until TRAVELLER THE SUN says: *I shall rise,*

as Ollokot comes out of his lodge yawning, wrapping his striped blanket around him,

Cloudburst still giggling within

(hoping she is now pregnant),

while Fair Land, having suckled the baby boy, places him in the cradleboard, carries him outside, sets him down beside her, then begins to unpack half-dried camas from her fine cornhusk bags with the geometric patterns

(some bulbs have mildewed, for lately the People lack time to preserve their food);

and Peopeo Tholekt is telling White Thunder how after the Blue-coats shot him in the leg at Kamnaka there was no pain but then the world began to turn yellow

(hoping to trade something for a new skinning knife, Wel-weyas the half-woman is smiling toward Toohhoolhoolsote's young men, who unfortunately dislike her);

Wounded Head's dear wife Helping Another is cleaning their little boy's shirt with white clay;

now Cloudburst has dressed and comes to help her sister-wife, doing as she is told,

while Springtime scrapes a dry hide (the baby still asleep)

and Looking-Glass's wives are tying his hair,

and our oldest women, some of whom still wear white beads and brass as did their grandmothers, crawl slowly over the ground, searching for roots and herbs,

the girls dipping up fish with their nets,

Hahtalekin's women drying meat

while *Kate* is boiling White Bird's leggings to clean them of lice and dirt,

No Swan, Stripe Turned In, Five Snows and Loon already playing the Stick Game,

and Toohhoolhoolsote, joying in his new horses, trims their manes to his liking, then enters his lodge to rest
 (to-morrow he will paint them red and yellow, then decorate them
 with ribbons and feathers)
as White Thunder begins carefully trading away his new Sharps for a
horse from Looking-Glass
 (although it has now killed white men at Cottonwood Place, he prefers his old 1866 Winchester repeater),
Red Spy untying the buckskin pouch of assorted screws for his Springfield and
the other chiefs and best men now smoking the pipe together
here in Cañon's Mouth Place where the river is making riffles:
 White Bird, that expert in discretion, speaking last,
 while Ollokot and Heinmot Tooyalakekt, being inexperienced, also say
 less than might be,
 and Hahtalekin prefers to wait and listen, since his band is small;
 —but Rainbow in his deerskin shirt of many-hued embroideries, and
 Swan Necklace and the Three Red Blankets, their hearts beat ready for
 more war!—
and although this is Red Owl's country
 —indeed, precisely here is his reservation which the Bostons have
 left to him—
he knows not what to do, since the Bostons attacked Looking-Glass's
People at Kamnaka
 (nor should he chatter first like a squirrel, for Looking-Glass, his
 chief, is the true war-chief);
thus it happens that Looking-Glass, the acclaimed one,
 now recommencing to be rich in horses,
who first opens his heart, saying
 as he has already said three times:
Since Cut Arm attacked me, I have lost all confidence in the Bluecoats,
 but what should next be done remains dark.

Toohhoolhoolsote has returned to the fire. He smokes awhile, then says: The
Bostons will never leave us alone. Why not fight them here? Soon they will come.
We shall fight them and die; then all will be straight.

Red Owl now says: It is not for me to contradict this chief. However, my heart
feels sad for our women and children who cannot fight well when they are being
killed. Here begins the South Trail to the Buffalo Country. Shall we not ride there?
That place has everything! Looking-Glass, do I not speak straight? Whose heart
could hate that beautiful land? Even if we lose our own countries, and the People
grow sad or tired on the way, still we can stay awhile with the Crows.

Heinmot Tooyalakekt says: Later perhaps we shall return to our country,
 at which White Bird covers his face with his fan.

2

The baby has a speckled rash on her thighs, so Springtime strips her, dips sumac leaves in the river,

> which runs wider and faster than our river back home which descends through Imnaha to the Enemy River,

> the pale red reflection of white shore-gravel blending into dark brown,

and places them on her skin. She looks surprised, but does not cry. Her mother ties her back into the cradleboard, raises her up and returns to help Good Woman and Sound Of Running Feet dry camas

> as the horses say: *Hinimí,*

>> the locusts singing *tekh-tekh-tekh!,*

>>> two young girls working with porcupine quills

>>> and Shore Crossing's pregnant wife cleaning the fishing lines with river sage;

and Elder Deer invites White Thunder to go and see a certain Bluecoat whom the People have killed

> (we caught him alone, so he must have been running away from Cut Arm)

while White Bird,

> knowing that Looking-Glass blames him for what could not be prevented

>> —that Shore Crossing and those others rode out to kill those Bostons on Salmon Creek—

comes to make everything straight by helping that chief to break a palomino,

> Toohhoolhoolsote's wives boiling venison broth,

>>> Burning Coals, most horse-wealthy of us all, mending a rope, half-smiling to watch Long Ears, his favorite stallion, turn round to nuzzle Lucky One's flank

>>>> (Strong Eagle wishes to make a trade, one for one, but the stingy old man replies: You are making me tired by talking!)

>>> —as Red Spy, as smooth and delicate as a snake, laughingly explains to the old men

>>> (our women and children admiring from behind)

>>> how he crawled forward boulder by boulder at Cottonwood Place, until he could shoot that sniveling little Boston in the head: *taq!*

—and Peopeo Tholekt repeats to White Thunder: We were sitting quiet at Kamnaka, I am telling you three times! When the Bluecoats called for Looking-Glass, I rode up to see what they wanted, and some ugly Boston hit me with his rifle. I shall tell you this: They have caused this fight!

> as Heinmot Tooyalakekt sits murmuring with Ollokot.

3

Now it has become afternoon. Some elegant young men, mostly not tattooed, with their hair loose and shining on their shoulders, are gambling at the Stick Game, while other men and boys race horses at the water's edge
　　and at the end of camp the young boys are still playing the Bone Game, gambling for dead Bluecoats' treasures,
　　　　rushing the bone from hand to hand
as Fair Land pounds dried meat and Ollokot withdraws into his lodge again with Cloudburst,
　　who presently comes out to bathe in the river,
　　　　learning her reflection, which wavers over the whorled rocks: indeed her heart worries for nothing: she can still be beautiful for him;
　　　　　while Looking-Glass says aside to Wottolen: Heinmot Tooyalakekt is nothing compared to his father,
　　and White Thunder's mother boils yarrow for Peopeo Tholekt, who after poulticing his leg goes riding with Many Coyotes and some other warriors, just for awhile, just to look around:
　　　　across Big Water and up to where Cliff Place rears, steep, hard and gnarled, from beneath a threadbare arch of yellow grass which drops down horribly
　　　　and up one of the side-cañons there, hoping to surprise deer among the sweet-smelling firs, ponderosa pines, ripening elderberries on the bush,
　　while down here at Cañon's Mouth, Looking-Glass's other People go on sleeping, cooking or happily decorating their horses, which the warriors have restored to them,
and Toohhoolhoolsote begins to trim a horse's tail.

4

Looking-Glass, the excellent one,
　　who so much resembles his late father both in his face and his speaking, will never sorrow like a woman merely because he has lost his country and his wealth has been devoured:
　　　　I have always said, *Bluecoat, you are my elder brother; Boston, you are my elder brother. I would never kill your children!* And I stood against White Bird's and Toohhoolhoolsote's bad young men when they began to kill. All the same, Cut Arm has stolen my country! My heart is sick. But I am still a *lucky man,* and
he can still shoot and ride a horse;

his hopes of the Buffalo Country have already begun comforting him like
sweetgrass perfume: not strong but enduring, faintly sour-sweet like a
root vegetable's;

in that place it is as Red Owl said: there will be everything;

and the Three Red Blankets smoke with Red Owl, Shore Crossing calling out: Now that you have come here with us, Looking-Glass, I am
very glad. Together we shall kill Bostons, as many of them as we can get!

—at which Peopeo Tholekt remarks to White Thunder: Had
the Bluecoats found Looking-Glass, he would have been killed.
But had he been a man, he would have gone and met them,
so that White Thunder understands that this war-friend of
his is ashamed for his chief;

therefore, the Three Red Blankets acted straight to start this
war, and the ones who spoke against it, even his own Uncle
Heinmot Tooyalakekt, were not telling us true things.

And yet his uncle is brave and good.

Wishing to speak with him about this war, White Thunder approaches Heinmot Tooyalakekt's lodge, but perceives that he is troubled about some matter, so
he leaves him alone to listen to his heart,

wondering what it would be like to try a Boston woman
(Yellow Bull has told him that the bitches whom he tasted after
killing their husbands were made exactly like ours, but their butterflies were hairy),

longing to steal horses from the Mount Idaho people,
unceasingly wishing to shoot Tsépmin and Cut Arm

—above all, Cut Arm, who threatened us at Butterfly Place—

visiting his mother Swan Woman (Red Owl's sisters have given her food),

mounting his good brown horse to see the races better,

when he hears the whisper of the first artillery shell.

I DON'T EXPECT THIS TO DRAG ON

JULY 10–12

1

*D*oc, why do you always carry two knives? You afraid of losing one?
Don't you know *nothing?* This is a skinning-knife and this here's a ripping-knife.
All right, but what do you need both of 'em for?

Good LORD, you sure don't know nothing.

Can I have one?

What'll you give me for it?

What do you want?

What do you have?

Don't have nothing.

Then get out of my face. I'm sick of you.

Whatcha going to do, poke me with one of them knives?

You can bank on it.

You just made a lifelong enemy out of me. I won't forget you.

Lifelong, he said. Well, boys, let's find out how long his yellow life lasts—

Cut it out, both of you.

What's it to you?

> When are we finally going to fight and finish it?
>
> Well, James Reuben says the hostiles are in the timber south of the Clearwater.
>
> What does Jim say?
>
> Umatilla Jim? He don't say nothing.
>
> That's why I like him.

>> Have you heard of Elk City? That's Elk City up there.
>>
>> Long gone. Degenerated into a Chinese camp and then—

>>> Then how come they're building a blockhouse against
>>> the reds? I read it in this newspaper right here.
>>>
>>> And Mr. Joe leading us round and round—
>>>
>>> D——d *Praying General* don't know nothing—
>>>
>>> But that sure is a fine black charger he rides.
>>>
>>> Ad Chapman gave him that horse, I heard.
>>>
>>> Well, that ain't so.
>>>
>>> And picture windows for Fidelia. I promised her. She said to
>>> me: Nobody else ever offered me that. She said—

> There's still gold up thataway.
>
> Not anymore there ain't. Ghost town.
>
> But Slick Rogers in Lewiston, he up and swore hisself blue—
>
> To put you off the *track.*
>
> He ain't that kind.
>
> Then why's he rich?
>
> They say White Bird pays in gold. Keeps a sack of gold dust, and
> that's why he didn't want no miners . . .

>> as they march into the smell of the creek
>> and tall grass stands green and cool in the creek defile, which
>> is thick with wild roses.

So this is Elk City.

No it ain't.

Doc? Hey you, Doc!

What is it now?

Is this Elk City?

Nope.

What about picture windows?

Sure, boy. You can get your Fidelia a solid half-dozen of those if you play your high card—

> And then Perry lost his nerve again at Cottonwood. He oughtn't lead us no more.

> Shut up. You know what'll happen if he hears?

Well, that was Magruder's ranch down by the crick; he owned the first store. And Squaw Hill up there where the Injuns always camp—

Which Injuns?

Halt!

  Dismount!

where grey grass glares out on a bleached hillside which curves like the flank of a giant horse

  (the chokecherries beginning to fruit),

> Fletch and Wilkinson still both looking sick,

> Pollock, pretending that he needs to shit, permitting his company to look after itself while he squeezes between snowberry bushes to inspect a likely ledge:

>> well, no gold, by GOD, but some small promise of getting galena or carbonates out of this;

> Perry (who prefers to curry the horse himself) smiling to watch Diamond rolling on his side as if epileptic, then rising easy, snorting, trotting off into the grass:

>> I like to give him some freedom before I picket him;

and around the ruins of Thelbert Wall's homestead they plant the guidon at last, O my LORD; I sure long to desert this Army.

2

Where's our *Christian Soldier* at?

Back in his big fat Sibley tent, kissing the Bible or something with his favorite pet—

Lieutenant Wilkinson ain't bad. He's straight with us. He's always—

I mean Lieutenant Wood from Company "D." This morning I heard Doc telling Blackie: You just watch; the general will make him aide-de-camp.

Why are you against him?

On account of he's always writing down our mistakes in that little book of his—

That's nothing. That's just his memoirs.

And Colonel Perry swears he rushed his front line down the hill
right away, but from what I heard Captain Whipple say—
Captain Trimble, sir, could you please tell the fellows again how you took
Captain Jack's gun?
Well, he was here on the rock ledge, just looking down at me, and I figured if I did nothing he'd either shoot me or himself, so I climbed up and
took it from his hands. A real nasty-looking red he was. Then he said to
me, he said:
Chokecherries ain't ripe.
Where's Mr. Joe at, anyway?
Plenty of Indians all around the country.
Not for much longer, by GOD,
as they gather wild plums with big seeds in them,
and fill their caps with soft white snowberries (edible, but nearly taste-
less),
greasing up their blisters and boiling pilot biscuits in coffee to soften
them.
What did you find?
Nothing.
Then why'd you wrap it up? It's potatoes, ain't it?
Burned potatoes.
Well, how can they not be? The whole GODd——d ranch is burned.
Pretty soon old Mr. Joe's gonna learn how that feels.
He won't feel nothing when we're through.
But Mrs. Joe's gonna feel plenty when I get ahold of *her*.
Which Mrs. Joe?
All of 'em,
as Wood, having represented to Lieutenant Bomus the current needs of
Company "D" (more coffee beans per capita), pulls taut each leather strap
of his boots through its ankle-buckle, wishing that his stockings were
dry. Nanny couldn't be bothered to knit me any more even though she
knew in plenty of time that I was going West. Still flirting, no doubt, with
that Mr. Tracy Gould,
the commissary wagon steaming (*that* coffee smells strong
enough),
while his general looks up from the map:
Mr. Reuben, are you sure of this?
General, since I've been here with you I didn't see for myself, but my Kamiah
people say the bad Indians are dancing the war dance down there—
Can you read a map?
Yessir.
Then show me.

Down about there, general.

Thank you, Mr. Reuben. You may return to your duties. Wilkinson, who's commander of the guard to-night?

Colonel Winters, general.

Fine. Now, Wilkinson, between you and me, I don't expect that Joseph will try any mischief here. But since he knows we're on his tail . . .

Right, general. His drunken bucks might stampede him into some foolishness.

Yes. Please advise Colonel Winters to arrange for an extra inspection of his pickets during the small hours.

Sure will, sir.

Now when's Lieutenant Howard expected?

According to the Twelfth, he's already been released to us, but since we're out in the field—

Write another despatch to Lapwai.

Straightaway, general. It'll be a treat to campaign with your son.

He's monstrous fond of you. You'll show him what to do.

Yessir.

Where's Colonel Perry?

Well, general, I saw him just a quarter-hour ago with the scouts. Some misunderstanding with James Reuben. Shall I run down and—

I'll have to speak with him about his performance at Cottonwood, although to-night may not be the time.

Yessir.

I'm not sure he shouldn't have come far sooner to the aid of those volunteers.

Yessir. Here he comes now.

Thank you, Wilkinson.

Perry, have you got a moment?

Yessir.

You are

> a soul-wounded man, and I will not increase your suffering now since you
> need to be keeping up with your Morning Report Book.

Sure am, general.

Good. What's the name of that teamster yonder?

O'Malley, general,

> and I won't inform you that Crook knew every packer by name—
> but why am I so angry at this kind, brave, one-armed man who never
> complains and means me only good, especially when we both share Get-
> tysburg
>> (fifty thousand half dead or worse),
>> the northeast-southwest oval of Cemetery Hill, the two barns, then
>> General Meade's headquarters on the eminence overlooking the
>> schoolhouse, and due east of that Powers's Hill, our defenses drawn
>> in like an elongated north-south pincer claw closing on nothing,

then to the west the much longer Secessionist line running north-
northeast, and this selfsame one-armed general ready to ride forward into the bullets on that first of July

and the second, and the third, and then when it ended and we celebrated the Fourth, we

. . . but this Fourth of July, Mr. Joe was giving me another
whipping, and the general—

Have you seen how he treats his mules?

Yessir. A real ignorant brute of a Paddy.

All right. You warn him, and then if we catch him at it to-morrow, he can be
punished.

Yessir.

That's all. Sladen, a word with you.

Yessir.

Now, about our dispositions back at Lapwai . . .

Chapman, you d——d yellowbelly.

I resent that, *Captain* Perry. Especially coming
from you.

Shut up, squaw trash.

Wilkinson, there have been far too many stragglers so far on this march. After
you see Colonel Winters, ask the company commanders what ideas for improvement they might purpose. I'll expect your report in thirty minutes. Meanwhile
send Major Mason to me.

Right away, sir.

The press is publishing ugly insinuations about us, Wilkinson.

Yessir.

Very unfair.

That's how civilians are, general! As soon as we whip Mr. Joe, they'll turn right
around.

I hope so. Has Lieutenant Fletcher been pulling his weight?

Fletch is a brick, sir! A true officer and a friend.

Pleased to hear it. That'll be all,

truly pleased and exactly all,

although after "Tattoo" he sits out on a boulder beneath the stars,
feeling a trifle low about those personal insults recently published—

All's well!

What do you say, boys? Does Joseph still have
Mrs. Manuel?

O how I pity those poor women in the hands of
fiends.

Carry on—

I hope Lizzie has finally found a shop where she can buy a better grade of whalebone for her dress. How is she holding up? Well, this is nothing compared to real war. No doubt she is anxious anyhow; it seems to get worse for Army wives the longer they live. Which of our neighbors will be so cruel as to show her the latest newspaper? I would bet on every one! Praise GOD I don't have to read them,

consoling himself with the memory of that bright December night in 1864 when he asked to accompany General Sherman in the requisitioned oyster-skiff down the crooked river and past the sunken steamer to Fort McAllister, where the oarsmen tied up at a drift-log and then General Hazen

(who in '68, a few days subsequent to that darkly icy dawn which saw in the ambiguous Battle of the Washita, would accuse Custer of trying to butcher the Kiowas on their reservation, since Custer had denounced Hazen for protecting a renegade tribe from punishment)—

Dear FATHER, deliver me from my perplexities so that I may perform the right!

(they all despise me for a milksop of Hazen's sort)—

invited them for dinner, kindly including his prisoner, Major Anderson, after which they continued on toward the gunboat, stepping prudently and sometimes gingerly since the battlefield was still mined with torpedoes, one of which now blew up a soldier searching for his dead comrade:

General Howard, we'll make those murdering Secceshes *feel* their murders! I'll laugh to watch our prisoners dance on de-mining duty, GODd——n them! What do you say?

Yessir.

General, you're *soft.*

I am, general.

But you've got "sand," so I *love* you, general!

And I you, general—

as the two of them boarded a yawl and proceeded downstream to the *Dandelion,* where after exchanging news with Colonel Williamson they returned to the fort, once again successfully avoiding the torpedoes, and lay down to sleep on the floor beside General Hazen and his men, but General Sherman was almost immediately summoned to see General Foster; for in those days one went without sleep, and now it's no different except that I'm older and the enemy's less noble

and, come to think of it, I *will* sleep

(but upon closing his eyes he seems once again to see Joseph's face, which not long since he found quite personable and which he now considers as wicked as any of the skeleton-pictures which Sitting Bull drew in the roster-book of his crimes).

3

Morning gun and "Reveille," dawn, roll call and coffee:
Gonna be a fine hot morning,
> but still nearly chilly, shaded nearly everywhere, the faint breeze stinking of men and horses.
You share them potatoes.
All right.
I'll give some hardbread.
I don't want it.
Let's see them potatoes. No, I mean it. You mean that's all you got?
Them artillery's looking awfully fagged out for riding up here in wagons just like royalty.
Well, I sure don't envy them all the same.
Why not?
I said you share them potatoes.
Might be gold hidden somewhere hereabouts like under the smokehouse chimney. Stands to reason that Mr. Wall would have—
Doc says—
Why do you care what Doc says?
He's the only one who never tells a lie about anything.

4

General, Colonel McConville's riding in with his volunteers.
Get me Colonel Perry at once. O, good morning, Mr. McConville. This is Colonel Perry, the man you charged with cowardice.
McConville, you've lied about me to the general. Told black lies—
Is that a fact? Well, Colonel Perry, you're a d——d fucking yellow-livered, ass-licking—
Arrest that man.
There he goes!
Catch him!
Ha! Got him for you, general!
Thanks, Wilkinson. Unload his weapons. Mr. McConville, it makes my blood boil to hear any man blaspheme an officer.
General Howard, you told me to make out all the charges in writing and get my

survivors to sign them, and then you would have Colonel Perry court-martialed. I told you that we volunteers rode to Colonel Perry's relief, and you know how he rewarded us! We met the Indians before noon and it was nearly four before Captain Winters came down, which wasn't by Colonel Perry's orders, and all the time we could plainly see the colonel with his command, just looking on at Cottonwood! And—

Colonel Perry, any comments?

General, I'd just like to point out that he calls me a coward and then tries to run away.

Point taken. Well, Mr. McConville, I'm very sorry the way it turned out at Cottonwood. Colonel Perry acted for the good of the entire command. Get some breakfast, and then guide us to where Joseph is camped.

General, please return my ammunition. I'll do nothing of the kind. I'm going home.

Go, then, *coward*. I'm disgusted. Get out. Yes. Colonel Perry, you handled him perfectly.

Thanks, general, I—

You'd best see to your company now.

Yessir. Thank you.

Wilkinson, we won't discuss this. Not now. Colonel Perry has just suffered a public insult, and we don't need to make him feel any worse.

Of course not, general.

By the way, what are the men saying about that affair?

Well, sir, of course they dislike it when Shearer and Wilmot and those other civilians criticize the Army, although it must have been hard on them to watch Randall's bunch getting killed in plain sight.

I detect your implication. You'd better pray for guidance and forbearance.

Yessir.

That's all.

5

Down there on the river bottom, sir, a large force of them, Umatilla Jim says, which verifies what those volunteers—

All right, Fletch. Why didn't James Reuben spot them?

I don't know, general, but he did say—

Consider his allegiances. Then you'll be a better staff officer.

Yessir.

Did Jim enumerate them?

He counted fifteen hundred head of stock, maybe more.

Then that's Joseph, for a fact. Now, where's Lieutenant Otis?

I'll get him straightaway, sir—

Don't take it to heart, Fletch. You're a fine officer already and I'm proud of you.

Thanks, general, I—

O, good morning, lieutenant. How's life in the Fourth?

We're all loving it, sir.

Well, what redblooded American wouldn't? Magnificent country—and a truly interesting adventure Joseph's providing us.

You could say that, sir.

Lieutenant Otis, did I ever tell you that before the War of the Rebellion I served in Ordnance?

No, sir.

A very interesting field, with many new developments.

Yessir.

Are you keeping up with progress?

I do my best, sir.

Good. Good. You see, lieutenant, when I graduated from West Point, they gave me my choice of any arm of service. The reason I settled on the Ordnance Department was that in those days, each powder station was allotted a house for the convenience of a married officer.

Yessir.

Are you married?

No, sir.

Those were fine days, lieutenant. Are you enjoying *your* fine days?

Well, I hope so, sir.

Good. Now, is there anything you need? I'm counting on you to teach Joseph what a Gatling can do, and I want him to learn that lesson so well that he'll be convinced for all time. Am I clear?

Yessir.

Remember: With the current ordnance capabilities of this Army, I don't expect this to drag on.

Yessir.

That's all. On your way out, kindly visit Lieutenant Bomus. He has some inventories to go over with you. Good luck to-day. Now, Fletch, could you find Captain Sladen, please?

Doublequick!

And good morning to you, Wood. Hello, Captain Pollock. How's Company "D"?

All prepared, general.

A splendid chance to strike the hostiles.

Sure is, sir!

By the bye, Wood, is it true that your father knows General Sherman?

O yes; I'd call them great friends—

You don't say! And all this time you never told me.

Well, sir, of course it's no credit on me—

That will be all. Captain Miller, I'm counting on you to keep a fatherly eye on Lieutenant Otis. He seems unseasoned.

I'll do what I can, sir.

Thank you. Colonel Winters, how's "E" troop?
Ready to march, general.
Then you'll head the column. GOD bless you.
Thank you, sir—
> Bugler, sound "The General."
> Yessir.
>> *To horse—*
>> All right, boys, let's go put Mr. Joe in the ground—

6

Passing in review before their general, who seems considerably pleased, they move out in their bluecoats, ragshirts, Secession War blouses and once-white knee-long canvas frocks, *left—left—left!*—a hundred ten paces to the minute, these rectiform identities of men, down through the cool ridge-forest, toward their future, that fast dark river in what will be late afternoon, the Clearwater clean and deep in its cañon, some of them just tired, some indifferent, and a good few frantic to whip Mr. Joe and his reds, their hopes as infinitely reusable as quicksilver; because although Indian service may not be the easiest job in the world, breaking sod in order to plant oats bought on credit is best left to the victims of the men in alligator boots who troll the railroad platform at Omaha, so why not march on awhile with the fellows in this command?

7

Trimble's flankers have already glimpsed two of Joseph's horse-herders riding down from the bluff, and Perry rides ready, his heart pounding, listening for birdcalls which might in fact be the signals of Indians, watching for uprising silhouettes, favorably comparing these wooded cañons to Captain Jack's country—already four years now!— five since the reds murdered Canby—recollecting how two dawns prior to the final assault on the Stronghold he had knelt at the edge of a certain prominence of bitter black angles, gripping two boulders as if to wrench them apart while he cautiously presented his face to peer down the slit between them at the Lava Beds, and some near-forgotten milksop of a private cowered in a hollow behind them when Theller, his waist ringed round with fifty pounds and more of ammo pouches, stood up tall, cheerfully smoking his pipe of kinnikinnick as if he were proof against any Modoc; the rock-knives cutting into his knees, Perry, who had always taken pride in his eyes, studied and studied, but couldn't make out any living thing except for some shivering tufts of bleached grass, and then Theller whispered happily: Well, colonel, do you see what I see?

8

Riding along his column (tormented as always nowadays by the urge to urinate), he reins in Arrow and listens:

Must be excessively mortifying to him, I should say.

Without a doubt!

and wonders if they are referring to him, the march slowing for some reason (what's Mason's excuse?),

after which they cross the Jackson Bridge, hoping to see Indians,

Chapman pausing beside Umatilla Jim on a little rise, that pair laughing nearly soundlessly, Chapman crossing his ankles, wagging a forefinger, with his hat pulled low, while Jim, cocking his head, his left hand resting easy on the receiver of his shoulder-slung Remington, which points off nearly horizontal, stares off somewhere which no one except perhaps Chapman can see, leather boots squeaking:

And Susie writes me that they're calling it a very grave offense.

Well, he must have taken up with bad companions.

Private family matters, evidently. He rides on, joying in Arrow's spirited sensitivity: the gentlest stroking of his neck, or a knee-squeeze, and this horse instantaneously understands!

—the low horizon as wide-faced around our troops as cherubic Mason, whom Wilkinson, ever eavesdropping for his general's greater good, now catches muttering with Perry about the evil days of '64 when all the reds joined in attacking the Oregon Stage Road—a twelve-hundred-mile front—at which Wilkinson, who up till now has remained unimpressed by Joseph, momentarily half-believes (such is blocky Mason's credibility) in a general Indian uprising coördinated between Joseph, Smohallie and perhaps even the Crows or Sitting Bull, although surely not both; and perhaps those degenerate Cayuses and Umatillas might play the jackals' part; not unimpressed by these fancies, Wilkinson says to himself: Well, we may be up against it, all right!—but then, perceiving that Mason and Perry speak of '64 merely in order to improve the time, he almost smiles, then rides off (refusing to let his fever annoy him), in order to verify the smooth movement of the column, and, if duty permits, to seek his friend Fletch, whom he will likewise now entertain with the specters of '64,

Wood longing for this last decisive meeting with our enemies,

Wilkinson wishing our general's blue overall suit were newer
(it would enhance his authority),

the small drums hissing like snakes, bugles singing as we march
outward, because to be an American means never to halt,

Chapman now prancing back up to me

(is it worth reprimanding this civilian fool for his holiday?):

No sign thataway, general. Jim and me, we wanted to check out that cañon there, because Mr. Joe could use it to double back and strike Lewiston—

You're showing initiative, Chapman, and I like that. And Jim's a very interesting Indian—*mighty interesting* as men say in these parts—

Well, general, he ain't half bad.

He escorted your family to the reservation, I hear.

That's about the size of it, general. I paid her more ponies than she's worth—

But why?

O, to keep the family safe from Mr. Joe. He's like to do to her what he did to Mrs. Manuel—

Well, very prudent of you! But you must go back to your wife after this. GOD is not mocked.

No, sirree. No, He sure ain't.

Now, Chapman, what on earth's the use of that forty-pound saddle?

Well, general, it suits me, I guess.

In this country it encumbers your horse for no good reason.

General, you can whip me fair if you ever catch me straggling—

You've got a point. Straggling isn't one of your vices. Wilkinson, what is it?

Sir, I caught a man drinking whiskey.

Who is it?

A volunteer from Lewiston. He's so drunk I can't make out which company he's in.

Find his commander and bring him straight to me. An example must be made.

　　　Halt!

　　This time we won't allow Joseph to take the offensive.

　　Give 'em that old-time religion!

　　Gonna bring that steam drill out on the job,

　　Gonna whap that steel on down, o, LORD.

　　Gonna whap that steel on down.

Now, boys, when we see Joseph, let's paunch that redskinned sonofabitch,

　　and the noon sun as white as a war-bonnet and

Who's that?

Looks like Lieutenant Fletcher.

He's sure lathered up about something.

Probably smelled booze on Doc's breath—

Beg to report, general, sir.

Yes, lieutenant; what is it?

They're in that deep ravine down near the mouth of the Cottonwood and—

How many?

Sir, I saw mostly horses. Didn't stop to count the tipis—

Back in their old home ground, are they? Well done, Fletch! Now, catch your breath and water your horse.

Yessir.

O, I'm highly delighted!

Yessir.

How's your fever?

Much better, thank you, sir.

All right, gentlemen. I expect us to be in position within a half-hour. We'll break them up with sweeping fire. Captain Trimble.

Yessir.

Establish your troops forward and right, doublequick. Wilkinson, you'll ride with them.

Yessir. Brooks, sound the move out.

Hurrah, hurrah! Down with the saucy curs!

> *Mine eyes have seen the glory of the coming of the LORD;*

and the sudden rising of our horses' ears:

Lieutenant Otis, is your artillery ready?

You can count on us, general.

> *He is trampling out the vintage where the grapes of wrath are stored;*

Sir, they've—

> *loosed the fateful lightning of his terrible swift sword—*

Them squaws are taking down their tipis real fast.

Well, they're gonna get whipped this time.

Riding to the bluff (sweating freely and very refreshed therefrom), he spies the hostiles, who suddenly see him and begin to run about in a frenzy. The women are indeed rushing to ingather their animals. He raises his field-glasses—a tricky move for a one-armed rider drawing Indian fire—and through them seems to recognize Joseph's horse, and Joseph, although, strange to say, his arch-enemy appears to be keeping back with the women and children. Well, for all I know he delegates his murders to be carried out by confederates and pawns.

It's almost one-o'-clock, lieutenant. I expect you to start firing by one.

Yessir.

My word, what crowds and masses of Indians down there! Is that our treacherous Looking-Glass who rides the ocher-brown Appaloosa?

Sorry, general, I can't make him out from here—

white flash of sunlight on a horse's hindquarters and

Sir, I see the mirror on his forehead! It's Looking-Glass and no mistake.

Where?

Down there at about eleven-o'-clock, where the—

I don't see any mirror, Fletch. You're overheated—

No, it's . . . Must have only been the sun. Sorry, general.

What a lovely animal anyhow! Smallheaded like an Irish draught horse. Where's Mr. Chapman?

Right here, general. This is sure gonna be good!

Now they've seen us. Look at 'em getting their horses in.

So what? This won't last long.

Not unless they—

Now, Chapman, if the volunteers disobey orders this time I'll have them all in irons.

Have your boys been telling tall tales on me again, sir?

It's not for you to ask the questions. But if you possess the slightest influence over these citizens, you'd best keep them under control.

Anything for GOD, America and the Army!

And at that, at fifty-eight minutes past noon, Lieutenant Otis's howitzer, accompanied by the two Gatlings, begins to fire into the Indians down below—as loud as a steam organ in a floating circus!—so that the ripples, waves and rapids on the Clearwater, which an instant before rather resembled the general's brother Charles's careful slender right-tilted cursive in greenish-brown ink, now leap and heave, as will the Big Hole Valley's watercourses in afternoons of late summer hailstones. And in those first easy, happy instants of the engagement, praise the LORD, it seems that all our enemies in that cañon are surely being drilled into brown and crimson pulp.

Sir, they're running their horses up the south fork.

Keep shooting at their stock.

> A shame about them horses
>> as the wild deer go running like greyhounds.
>> Even our general hankers after Mr. Joe's Appaloosies! Before this started,
>> Mr. Joe proposed to switch horses with the general, but he—

Getting awful dusty down there.

>>> Injuns call it the Big Dust, when many rifles shoot into the
>>> same place.
>>> I can't hear you; the Gatlings are too d——d loud—
>>> And *hurrah* for our howitzer!

Sight higher. That's right. *Now* you're drilling them,

>>> shooting into the Big Dust, roaring light funneling out of the
>>> guns.
>> Actually, he offered to give him his Appaloosa free and clear. But the
>> general was too *Christian* to take him up on it. And now he's

Out of range now, sir.

Well, Mr. Chapman?

That cañon on your left is their only way out, general.

You're certain?

Yessir.

Where does it go?

Behind us.

Then set up the guns on the next bluff as fast as you can, lieutenant. Colonel Winters, gather up your cavalry and escort him. Don't let them out!

Yessir.

Looks to be about a mile—

General, Mr. Joe's waiting for us over there!

Good. Let's give him his battle. Forward, men.

> Looks to be a sharp engagement, Captain Whipple.
> I'd say, sir.
>> Well, so there they are again. Those tramplin' Injun hosts—
>>> and yes, this is the ground where we shall fight, the place we
>>> must make bloody.

Men, there's going to be a fight. This time you'd better kill me some Indians.

O yessir, we're all going to be Godd——d generals at the end.

Load with cartridges; load!

—their Indian service now becoming precisely as weighty as twenty of these, which is to say two rows of ten, the bullets ready to fly out, the primers shining up like silver pupils in golden-ringed birds' eyes.

Sound the move out.

Move out!

Hurrah, hurrah, hurrah, hurrah, hurrah—

Enemy's already dismounted and in position, general. Even some primitive fortifications—

Well, he had less distance to cover than we did. Firing's getting brisk now, isn't it?

Yessir. We're holding the line.

Of course you are, soldier.

They're flanking our right—

Then halt them, jackass! Where's that d——d Gatling?

Did you see Joseph?

No, sir, but Toohhoolhoolzote—

. . . already pinked two of our boys—

How many Indians?

About forty, sir:

grim braves who have doffed their salmon-hued deerskin shirts and leap about almost naked, shooting at us from stump to stump

(Whipple, who ought to know, informs me that he has glimpsed Toohhoolhoolzote clinging spiderlike to that underlip of rocks),

firing on the right and the left,

one of our German soldiers, nearly cleanshaven, grimacing shyly at me like a recruit at Chancellorsville—

Captain, they're swarming up out of both ravines—

That's all Joseph has? Fletch, bring your horse up alongside. Come on, men! There they are!

Watch yourself, general; that's—

Pim!

All right. Fire at will. Winters, mind your left. Burton, fix your infantry on the right—quickly, now!

Hurrah!

Pim,

pim,

pim,

pim-pim-pim!

That was close.

Well, Fletch, we've stirred them up.

Yessir; they're enveloping the bluff. But look there, general, down on the road! The reds—

Tell the general they're killing our packers!

You're shooting low, soldier.

Ride to Colonel Perry at once. He *must* save the pack train. Go now,

at which Fletch vaults into the saddle nearly as lightly as an Indian, galloping unscathed through a pattering of bullets, wondering whether he will live another five minutes:

Colonel Perry, General Howard desires that you mount your men and drive back those Indians.

Why not, lieutenant? Brooks, blow "To Horse." Captain Whipple, ready Company "L." Company "F," let's go give Mr. Joe one between the eyes. General Howard's counting on us to bring in our boys safe.

Prepare to mount!

Mount!

Listen now: "L" on the left and "F" on the right. Fan out as we sweep around the train. Move, GODd——n you!

Advance!

Charge!

and the general, observing through his field-glass how Perry and Whipple, riding into action with lightning perfection, swoop down upon Joseph's flankers, driving them off at the last instant

(two muleteers dead, apparently),

experiences less joy than mere relief that Perry has not funked it, praise GOD, praise GOD:

Perry riding ahead of his troop; no one can deny he's brave

(if I meet that McConville again, I'll demand a retraction),

and that he rides Diamond in masterful style,

but Joseph is also, I must admit, a daring, agile, intelligent and obstinate adversary; and should he capture the other pack train—

as through his field-glass he sees the mule driver widening his eyes at him from beneath a fifty-cent hat just before an Indian bullet penetrates the wagon.

General, they got one mule in the belly and the other in—

Then shoot those mules and carry the howitzer rounds to Lieutenant Otis, on your backs if you have to.

But, general, they—

Shut up. What is it now, Fletch?

Sir, Colonel Perry says that the main pack train—

Don't worry; it's nearly within our lines.

But, general, the reds are coming up that ravine!

Where?

> Chapman says—
>
> *Pim,*
>
>> *pim!*

Back down there, sir—

That Injun's got the cannon!

Fletch, we need one of Rodney's howitzers on the plateau right away.

Yessir; I'll ride there now.

> A pretty good cross-fire from Mr. Joe. Did he go to West Point or what?
>
> Yeah, we're in for it now.

>> Who's that Indian with the wolf's head over his scalp?
>>
>> Toohhoolhoolzote, sir. And that's Joseph howling threats—

>>> Colonel Winters, the general asks you to shell the Indians.
>>>
>>> I'll do that, lieutenant. Boys, you heard him. Lay down some eggs!

>>>> *Timm! Timm! Timm!*

General, Chief Joseph is making another demonstration over there.

All right.

>>> Major Mason, sir, Colonel Winters requests support.
>>>
>>> Send Burton's company.
>>>
>>> Yessir.

General, Lieutenant Otis is practically out of shells.

Fetch him some.

General, sir, the Indians have taken the spring.

I'm disappointed to hear that. Whose fault is it?

Sir, I—

General, Doctor Alexander needs two more stretcher-bearers.

Excuse me, general, but the pack train—

Yes, Joseph's closing in on it, all right. Ah, Wilkinson, there you are. Ride out at once to bring the train in safe, and GOD bless you.

> Right away, sir,
>
>> kneeing his horse, spurring forward
>>
>>> (LORD! The general failed to protect the train! Better to never re-mind him of this; he must feel mortified . . .)
>>
>> and galloping out to the edge of the bluff, expecting to be killed,
>>
>>> then down into the Big Dust.

Where's our covering fire? Fletch, wake up Captain Rodney right now. He'd better lay down some lead before Wilkinson is killed.

> Yessir,

and the howitzer, positioned among the trees, fires at the officer's word, its crew bracing their legs as the roar shakes their bones and the great smoke stalks across the ground:

>   *Timm!*

>   Wilkinson's already down *there?*

>   He just missed another one!

>   No, that went wide.

>   Cover him, you apes!

Well, men, there rides an outstanding young officer.

Yessir,

>   *pim, pim, pim, pim!*

>   They almost got him!

Chapman, could Joseph's Indians have repeaters?

They sure could, general,

>   Wilkinson galloping, drawing fire even while swerving and veering, the small train coming in after him, and Trimble's best now boiling out of their rifle-pits to discourage Joseph's marauders:

>   *Pim!*

Bomus, don't worry. If anyone can save our powder and supplies, it's Wilkinson.

Yessir.

Captain Pollock, do you see that Indian flaunting a red blanket?

By golly, I sure do, general, and I recognize him from the Salmon River. I hate that savage! He means to insult us—

And two more of them Red Blankets a-taunting us—

Is that Joseph out there?

You recognize him, do you? How I wish my eyes were younger!

Yessir; we've been trying to get him, but he's out of range.

>   Train's almost on high ground—

Mason,

>   a trifle mortified at the success of Joseph's assault,

we'd better pull in our defenses. All service animals in the center. As soon as the train comes in . . .

Yessir.

Chapman, where can we water our animals?

Ain't no crick or nothing, general, exceptin' that spring controlled by the reds.

Bomus, how's our water supply?

Low, sir.

Where's Lieutenant Wood?

He's making "D" Company dig rifle-pits over there,

>   worm-crawling through the dying grass, licking their cracked lips, expecting

an Indian bullet in the back.

Look, general, Wilkinson's galloping in! And Trimble's—

Them reds—

All right. The pack train's safe again. I'm very fond of Lieutenant Wilkinson.
Yessir.

    Injuns in the woods up there!

        Pim, pim!

           —heat and noise and blood,

           the Nez Perces galloping up onto the bluff, firing guns and
           arrows, some standing on their horses' backs, others clinging
           to the animals' flanks as they must have done at White Bird
           Cañon; now I begin to see how Perry must have felt.

    The way they dart from rock to rock sure is—

Trimble and Rodney, dismount your cavalry and dig in along our rear. Joseph's
assaulting us in fine style.

Yessir.

He really shows considerable skill, wouldn't you say?

Well, general—

Now, gentlemen, what do you purpose to do about Chief Joseph?

9

Now perhaps we shall die and visit the Sky Country for awhile:

    Toohhoolhoolsote is making himself angry, preparing to challenge Cut Arm.
As cruel and furious as a grizzly bear, he strips for war,

        red-painted Ollokot meanwhile calling out to his war-friends,

           these rapid young men with shell-disks like epaulettes on
           their shoulders and many loops of shell-beads around their
           smooth brown necks, their hair braided like white girls', or
           long and loose down their shoulders, with magic ovals at their
           throats, in striped blanket-coats and striped blanket-leggings,
           their eyes alert yet remote;

        and Shore Crossing, the great man who began this war, cries out:
        Let us kill these Bostons who have stolen our country! Let us die
        fighting them, and let some other people take our country!

—white smoke coming from the mountains, followed by the explosion down here
at the river's edge:

    Timm!

        Shore Crossing throwing on his red blanket, tying on his Medicine
        bag,

           loudly chanting his WYAKIN song

             (he has painted his face red and black),

while Many Coyotes comes galloping down from Cliff Place, shouting: A thousand Bluecoats are nearing!

        —women screaming,

the babies sobbing, *shlak, shlak!,*

Heinmot Tooyalakekt sending boys and women to gather in our horses, holding back some warriors in case the camp should need them (we have less than a hundred),

Cloudburst, half-dressed, running back from the river to Ollokot's lodge,

Bluecoats shooting down exploding balls near but not yet into our camp:

a noise like buffalo thunder:

Timm!

White Bird calling to his best men: You wished for this war and you began it. Now it is here. I expect you to fight until you are shot in the breast, not in the back!

after which he shows his other People where they will be safest from the rifles and Gatlings

(not for nothing did he watch the Bluecoats playing war at Butterfly Place, blowing their bugles, aiming badly:

he's learned how far their guns can shoot;

a little back, just a little, and we can laugh at them);

while twenty brave young men and boys throw off their leggings and lovely deerskin shirts, leaping onto buffalo ponies, following Toohhoolhoolsote to war:

We shall shake the red blanket over this country; we shall shake the blanket at Cut Arm!

—riding upstream

—deerprints in the mud

and constellations of pale orange rocks all the way across the shallow rapid brownness of the river which now goes blue just before it vanishes around the bend:

first White Thunder, happy with all his heart to fight back against the Bostons again

—my uncle cannot blame me!—

and to match himself against the Three Red Blankets

(perhaps I myself will kill Cut Arm

and take the star he wears);

seizing his Winchester, leaving his six-shooter with his dear mother Swan Woman in case danger should come to her (she takes it without a word),

throwing off leggings and deerskin shirt,

full quickly he leaps onto his wise brown horse

(he carries his ceremonial club, which is beaded light and dark blue, pink, orange, green and white;

now its head is stained with the blood and brains of that Boston at Cottonwood Place who kept crying: *kek, kek, kek!*)

and with him rides his war-brother Wottolen, whose WYAKIN has prom-

ised him immunity from bullets
>(Black Eagle is too young; he stays down here at Big Water, driving
>in horses)

—then Red Spy, our far-seeing, agile young killer, whose WYAKIN, although kin to HAIL, is as smooth-maned as a mustang,
and Hair Cut Upward riding beside Hair Cut Short,
the boys ready to hold the warriors' horses,
and the Three Red Blankets joyous to kill again
>(Shore Crossing still rich in cartridges for his magic buffalo gun),
all singing their WYAKIN songs
and now fording the river to the narrow side of the cañon, galloping up
to Cliff Place
>>which might have once been a ROCK PERSON frowning down, Her
>>skirts of scree trailing almost all the way to the river;
>>on either side of Her, a forest gorge runs up toward the ridge where
>>Cut Arm is assembling his killers
and we take the lefthand gorge,
>quickly emerging from the trees, our way now underscored by grey dirt
>and greenish-lichened rock, poison oak clambering up the dry rocks:
>>we are flying up
>>>(White Thunder's heart commencing to feel fear—never to be
>>>afraid!),
and now Toohhoolhoolsote sends White Thunder ahead to spy out the Bluecoats, Cut Arm's slaves,
>>who, squatting like frogs, firing their guns, prepare to overrun our
>>village, unless we prevent them.

White Thunder shouts over his shoulder: *Can you not see their actions?*
at which Toohhoolhoolsote leads them in a gallop down across the ravine,
>calling Cut Arm in anger: *Come fight, you moldy one!*
>and: *Cut Arm, come here and die!*
then up its side, picketing their horses just below the ridge, the young boys
guarding them,
Toohhoolhoolsote roaring: Dig rifle-pits!
>as the warriors pile up stones in the warm dry grass, placing themselves
>invisibly,
>>Bluecoats shooting wildly down: *pim!* and *pim!* and *timm!*
>>the sky pale blue.

10

Toohhoolhoolsote, ready to die, creeps uphill like a snake, pointing his rifle
ahead, shooting:
>*Pim! . . . Pim!*

so that two Bluecoats fall dead,
           their eyes open,
           their beard-bristles as blue as Douglas fir needles,
and the Bluecoats shoot back, *pim pim pim pim,* killing nothing.

11

Gentlemen, who will lead an infantry charge?
I will, general.
Thank you, Captain Miles. I count on you to clear that ravine.
Yessir.
                Where's Joseph? I mean to get him between his Indian eyes.
                General says he saw him—
           Now you see that big rock shaped sort of like the pommel of a
           squaw saddle?
           You mean that chimney there?
           That's right.
                We'll be exposed for a good hundred yards.
                Can't be helped.
Move out,
                our bugles echoing down the cañon:
           All right, you Baltimore bruisers! Let's see you beat them Injuns down.
Charge!
                The LORD is my shepherd; I shall not, shall not—
                and the terrifying boom of what must be a buffalo gun
                     (I think Perry mentioned this when I debriefed him about
                     White Bird Cañon):
                Captain Bancroft *flying* off the saddle, falling on his bleeding face.
                My praise shall be of Thee,
                     sun on the Indian ponies' heads:
                I shall not want.
                     D——d Indians!
                          Glory, glory, hallelujah,
the hissing of the rifles almost like lassoos
and Indians screeching in triumph
     (some nearby savage threatening James Reuben):
                          Glory, glory, hallelujah—
And if you gaze over thataway, general, you can see that Lieutenant Forse has
ridden over the bluffs with the right flank of the troop attached to Captain Miles's
battalion . . .
Is this Lieutenant Forse a friend of yours?
Not at all, sir,

a wave of Indians boiling out of the ravine, halting our charge:

pim, pim, pim!

as they dart from rock to rock, ducking down before we can kill them, their guns flickering faster than Lizzie's darning needle:

They got Lieutenant Williams!

But Doc finally got him a red.

Quite a galling fire down there—

Watch out, boys!

Pim!

—shot him through the brain—

Pim!

Pim!

General, it's turning a trifle dangerous right here.

Control yourself, Wilkinson—

Sir, I was simply worried about you. You lead our army—

Give 'em another volley!

You know, Wilkinson, I remember standing with Sherman and various staff officers on high ground near Adairsville, surveying the lines through our field-glasses:

O, JESUS! I'm shot! O, JESUS, o, JESUS!

Well, them *fucking* savages. Look how they—

Then aim for his horse. Can't you even cripple an Injun's horse? You're shooting high. Still shooting high. You're flinching. Cut out that flinching and you'll get you one.

Glory, glory, hallelujah—

Now they're caving in!

Forse has silenced that enfilading fire—

Who's he?

Guess I pinked that fat squaw—

That's a shame, because she's only a—

Pinked her *good.* Trying to bring her buck a fresh horse.

Then shoot the horse:

Pim!

when the enemy shelled us. We weren't expecting *that,* Wilkinson, I can tell you!

JESUS, o, JESUS!

That's one solid line of Injuns.

Well, they killed and crippled a few horses, and they wounded Colonels Jackson and Bliss—have I told you about Colonel Bliss?

O, JESUS, o, JESUS! O, JESUS, o JESUS, o, JESUS, o, JESUS, o, o—

No, sir.

A Confederate bullet came humming by and clipped his insignia right off his shoulder! We all had a laugh! And General Sherman said

JESUS, O, JESUS GODD——n!

Lieutenant Parnell, that man out there needs a doctor.

Yessir. Men, you heard the general. Any volunteers?

I'll get him.

We need two more. All right. You and you. Go now.

> I shall not want; I shall not want. The LORD is my shepherd, I shall not want, yea, though I, shall not, shall not, and
>
> a Nez Perce horseman in a pillbox hat whose dark hair spills in two streams to his waist comes galloping and firing
>
> through the Valley of the Shadow of

JESUS, O, JESUS!

> I sure hope they can etherize that wound in Lewiston.

He's—

Here they come, boys!

General, there's a gap in our lines.

So I see, Captain Jocelyn. Mr. Chapman, what are those hostiles shouting at us now?

Sounds like *thief treaty*.

12

Wilkinson, get me Captain Miller.

Yessir.

Captain, you're to charge Joseph's center. I hope you can make a junction with Colonel Winters. Meanwhile, Wilkinson, commence a sham advance on the right. Gather every last orderly and muleteer, fire your guns, blow your trumpets, bang pots and pans if need be—anything to turn Joseph's attention away from Captain Miller! Is that clear?

Yessir.

General, I can man a howitzer if that will free up a—

Good for you, Fletch!

More Indians on our left, sir!

> —and hostiles creeping up the bluff, nodding their heads between boulders as they shoot and duck,
>
> > exploding an infantryman's canteen right as he is drinking from it—

Well, Perry and Whipple had better stop them.

Yessir.

> Savages ain't supposed to entrench themselves!
>
> *Pim!*
>
> O, they got me, boys! Tell my Emily back home; tell her I—

Now, Captain Miller, we're depending on you.

That's fine, general,

> lighting his pipe, his blue eyes exploding with mirth.

> *To horse!*

>> —our halfnaked enemies, reddish-brown and indeed almost smoky-hued, glistening with oil and sweat, springing up again and again to shoot at us, or flaunting those GODD——d red blankets just out of range, baring their teeth as they peer around the pine-trunks to aim their Springfields—*our* guns, taken from our dead at White Bird Cañon—

> *Mount!*

>> then comes the roar, the flash and white gunsmoke wriggling voluptuously in the hot air, the whine and smack of the bullet in dirt or flesh:

>>> *O, o JESUS! Captain, sir, I'm—o, captain, captain—*

>>> Get him off his horse, doublequick.

>>> *GODD——n you, you GODD——n Bostons! What you mean, stealing our country?*

Are you ready, captain?

Yessir.

Then move out.

> *Move out!*

>> Indians rising up all around like trees, their bullets hissing and chuckling.

Our turn, general.

Good luck, Wilkinson.

> *Move out,*

>> the gravel on the far bank going grey in the late afternoon shadow.

Well, Mason, what do you think?

Looks like the boys are shooting too high, sir. A common defect of the Springfields—

Or the boys are rattled.

Maybe so, sir.

Frankly, I'm disappointed.

Yessir.

General, Miller's almost there—

> And looky, boys, old Miller's smoking his pipe as he rides! He don't give two shits about them reds—

So I see. What's Perry about?

Defending Lieutenant Otis—

Who's hardly creased a single tipi down in that village. What's his excuse?

General, the range—

I was once an ordnance officer, and I know all about range. It's not the range.

Sir, I—

          . . . and a red sharpshooter behind that stump!

Tell me, Mason, who controls the spring just now?

The Indians, sir.

Can Perry or Whipple retake it?

General, in my opinion our line won't hold if either detachment—

Someone get me Colonel Perry.

Right away, sir.

Colonel, your company and Captain Whipple's are to charge on the left. Capture that spring.

General, for that I need artillery.

Take Morris's bunch.

All right,

      feeling sickish as ever before a charge: maybe I'll get Joseph—

Company "F," over here, doublequick! Well, men, this is it. General wants us to move out.

        Move out,

        but the Nez Perces countercharge.

          Pour lead into 'em, boys!

            striking at the root of the evil:

              Pim! Pim! Pim! Pim! Timm!

They're dug in. We're not doing great execution.

No, sir.

Wilkinson, what do you think?

General, Colonel Perry's looking tired down there, and the Indians—

So I see. It's no use. Cancel the assault.

Yessir,

      Perry riding slowly in, his grief now as familiar as the black droop of Diamond's lower lip.

        Look how that turned out.

        Simply because the artillery can't—

Tell every man on the line to dig in. It's getting dark.

General, the reds are attacking Wilkinson, but he's—

        O, no, o, no—

Yessir. Captain Miller's made the junction,

      the hostiles withdrawing back across the cañon, where the far side of the world has hazed itself greyish-green.

        O, no, o, no—

        Private McNally's dead.

We heard.

They got Lieutenant Williams.

Old news.

Captain Bancroft's been killed!

We know all that.

Welcome back, Wilkinson. You made a fine diversion.

> *O, no, o, no—*
> Someone help that wounded man,
>   as the sky goes pinkish-orange.
> He can't be helped till Lewiston.
> Why can't he have calomel?
> Well, he can't.

Thanks, general,

> but hurrah for Miller is what I'd rather hear you say! That was one of the bravest charges I ever saw. All we have to do is keep pushing them back. And praise GOD the men all remain firm and steady, excepting only those cowardly teamsters. For Thine is the Kingdom, and the glory, forever and ever, Amen. I must admit Wood is showing pluck, although I still can't like him, and frankly think the less of Fletch for feeding Wood's greenhorn conceit. A fine thing to be doing something for our country at last— and much better than enduring the cannonades of the Secession War! How contemptible these Nez Perces are! *An eye for an eye;* let that be our law until we've overthrown them . . . but shouldn't we close up our line? At any point the reds might get through! How can they be so cunning in hiding themselves? This steep country sure hinders our fire! Toohhoolhoolzote is the most horrible of them; I'd like to get him myself! If he comes charging and gnashing his teeth at me, I pray I won't flinch. The general's sure excited now. He ought to have more confidence in us. We'll pull through; I know we shall. But the reds—

I won't forget your courage. Well, well. A pity Perry failed. It'll be a thirsty night.

13

When Toohhoolhoolsote signals them to pull back, only White Thunder, too angry to believe in his own death, dares to recover his horse,

> all of them fleeing each after his own nature:
> Loon,
>
>> who until exactly now has been thinking once we have killed and driven off all these Bluecoats to paint his face with clay and dress himself in fine buckskin, so that Looking-Glass's daughters will say: *How handsome and brave is this young man!,*
>
> losing his way, beginning to fear that even the chiefs and WYAKINS cannot save us,

so that the Bluecoats, storming and charging downhill, seize the warriors' white-footed horses,

wheeled guns shooting as loudly as many women pounding cous
together, and with almost that same dry thumping sound:
　　　　death is working; death is beating roots; soon death will eat,
but no one has yet been killed; so they run away, farther and farther down the
steep side-cañons, until it is safe to laugh at Cut Arm,
　　　　waiting for the chiefs to say what must now be done.
　　White Bird's advice has given the People confidence: the bullets cannot hurt
them here; only the howitzer shells are dangerous.
　　Peopeo Tholekt blows his eagle-bone whistle five times; now the Bluecoats'
bullets cannot see him;
　　　　and Looking-Glass, running from his lodge, withdraws his 1866 Win-
　　　　chester from its long-fringed elkhide case which one of his Crow wom-
　　　　enfriends has beadworked with a white-outlined, black-and-yellow-striped
　　　　hourglass running down the center of a blue rectangle; even now when
　　　　there should be time to feel only hungry rage, the old chief's heart cannot
　　　　help but be gladdened by a lightning-flash of loveliness; then the rifle is
　　　　out, the first cartridge chambered in; and, throwing down guncase and
　　　　deerskin shirt for his wives to collect, he slings the Winchester over his
　　　　naked shoulder, leaps up onto Home From Capture, to whom he has
　　　　given a German silver necklace, and gallops across the river, longing most
　　　　of all to kill and terrify Cut Arm's Bostons,
while Heinmot Tooyalakekt, whose face is already wasted and thin, has been for-
tifying the camp, still holding back some young men in case Toohhoolhoolsote
should fail: Cut Arm must not get here!
　　　　Timm!
Toohhoolhoolsote is running away!
No, he only changes his place . . .
Is Cut Arm coming? He wears a blue suit and a star on his hat—
Not him! He is scared. Weeping like a woman, afraid to ride down and die—
　　　　Áhaha!
Now Rainbow,
　　　　the cunning one, who made Cut Arm cross the Chinook Salmon Water
　　　　twice for nothing,
　　　　undefeated, for his Power endures like JUNIPER, which remains green
　　　　even in winter
　　　　(he can never be killed after sunrise),
gallops up the ravine on his bay war horse, leading another party of brave men
to aid Toohhoolhoolsote,
　　　　our bearish one who always speaks sharply without fear;
　　　　　　then the half-woman Welweyas, irresolute but longing to help her
　　　　　　People, straps on her six-shooter (which has three rounds in it),
　　　　　　jumps on her horse . . .
　　　　　　. . . but Heinmot Tooyalakekt,

he who is her chief,

calls her kindly, setting her to helping the old women pack their saddlebags, in case Cut Arm should come;

and Rainbow, casting his steady almost mild Dreamer's glance upon the enemy, now swings up the barrel of his new Springfield and fires as he rides, so that a Boston shouts: *O—o—o!*

while Five Wounds, who yesterday was Four Wounds, leads more warriors:

Five Snows, Stripes Turned In, Red Spy, No Swan and Loon,

ascending the gorge on the other side of Cliff Place,

bringing fresh horses to Toohhoolhoolsote,

while Shore Crossing, who never misses, keeps firing that monstrous roaring Sharps buffalo rifle:

Timm!

—wounding and killing Bluecoats

(so that envy rises up in the heart of Red Spy,

who won two packages of .50 explosive bullets when we first attacked Cottonwood Place,

so he now thumbs the first such cartridge into his trapdoor Springfield and aims at a Bluecoat officer:

Pim!... taq!...

—he has missed him!)

and Ollokot, setting his mouth in brave rage, leads the best young men of Wallowa into the fight:

they are still shouting their WYAKIN songs;

White Thunder now galloping downhill, his mind clear, his heart happy to be fighting well among all who refuse to be penned up on painted land;

he is believing in Toohhoolhoolsote, whose WYAKIN is almost as strong as WOWSHUXLUH (which only Smohalla may touch),

the white gravel on the far side of the river glowing in the sun, the near side cliff-shadowed

—then Wottolen, *he who remembers,* rides to tell him: Going Across is dead!

(perhaps we cannot paint his face red; we must try to mention him no more)

as four women carry to camp a wounded warrior:

for Grizzly Bear Blanket, he whom we acclaim for his killing of Big Bellies,* has been shot also;

he is whiter than a salmon which has spawned

(to-night Feathers Around The Neck will sing over him);

then White Thunder, Wottolen, Black Eagle and Peopeo Tholekt go riding after Toohhoolhoolsote, to Cliff Place, around which the grass is greyed and dead, and up the piney side-cañon,

---

*Gros Ventres.

giving their horses to Red Feather Of The Wing and the other young boys,
creeping on their bellies through the Indian pipes,
digging rifle-pits all along the timber-line, then aiming,

Ollokot's eyes round and hard, his smooth face set, his high forehead pitiless, his narrow lips tightly closed, his roached hair rising
up into a back-curved knife as he swings up his .44 Remington,
which he prefers to any of our new Springfield carbines,

White Thunder hoping to kill the bugler, without whom Bluecoats lose
all understanding (so White Bird proved in the previous battle); he aims
his 1866 Winchester as

About Asleep, fourteen years old

(still he has not even heard every tale about the SHADOW
PEOPLE, HUMMINGBIRD and MUSSELSHELL WOMAN),

rides up on a grey Cayuse horse to bring canteens and buffalo
horns full of water

(his little brother is jealous):

Tumm!

and Heinmot Tooyalakekt shooting sadly and carefully with his .44 Winchester carbine

(he is a good hunter, but not like Rainbow or Swan Necklace;
whether he has now killed a Bluecoat we cannot tell:

he can shoot a bear nearly as accurately as Shore Crossing,
but his desires have now become as hidden as buckskin ponies in the high golden grass);

and Peopeo Tholekt keeps shouting at Cut Arm: Come and fight in a man's way,
General Day-After-To-morrow! Don't play like a little boy! You big moldy Boston,
I'm not afraid!

14

Look! Animal In A Hole has broken his word!
The chiefs behaved wrongly not to kill him—
Traitor!
Call him!
Tso Alpít, we shall wipe our buttocks on your head!
Crooked-hearted one, GODd——n you, *Tso!* We let you run away from Sparse-
Snowed Place, and now what do you mean by breaking your promise to us?
If you keep shouting at me, I shall shoot—
Why are you fighting us? The Bostons have killed your father at Cottonwood
Place, and still you go on being Cut Arm's slave!
My father is dead?
Wounded Mouth is dead! Your father is dead!

—at which Animal In A Hole runs in Bluecoat uniform across the field, down that hot horrible open field, both the Bostons and the People shooting at him

(for even Heinmot Tooyalakekt has now commenced to scare or kill these Butterfly Place enemies who were once our kin),

and so he has returned to us; indeed we shall accept him back. Never more will he be called *Tso Alpít*. Stripping off his Boston clothes forever, he takes a horse, rides into the fight, and by nightfall the Bostons have shot him in the thigh.

15

But Buck Antlers now runs away to the Bostons.

16

White Thunder is shooting Bostons from a rifle-pit,

longing for water,

and sand and gravel keep cutting his face whenever the bullets strike near,

his happiness bleeding away as this battle goes on

—his war-friend Wottolen fighting somewhere alone (but for his WYAKIN—

Lightning-Struck, Mean Man and Fire Body dug in behind boulders—all men who will kill and die without hesitation; but when their courage cannot be seen, and the Bluecoats keep shooting, when we must count our bullets, and Cut Arm never shows himself (how then can we kill him to end this war?), then something terrible begins to be felt, not yet strong enough to drive us downhill, but growing in Power up behind the pines where the Bluecoats lie shooting down:

We cannot drive them away!

Last time we killed them—but this time they do not go—and what if even our chiefs cannot decide what to do? To kill and die as Toohhoolhoolsote says, must there be only this?

Now they are bringing him water, these good young boys with eagle-feathered hair who stare up into his face, longing to be warriors like him, their bone necklaces immaculately looped, hornpipe beads marching down their deerskinned chests as elegantly as if they were wearing their own skeletons, and the abalone shells in their ears looking up into the sky like sunflowers.

Smiling, he says: Younger brothers, how you have decorated yourselves! But when you wish to fight, you must strip for war.

Calling upon his WYAKIN, he forces his happiness to rise up once more from his belly into his heart; he is shooting; he is silently singing as he thumbs each cartridge into the Winchester and shoots; again he is growing thirsty,

lonelier and lonelier,
only his WYAKIN and his Uncle Old Yellow Wolf now beside him,
bullets humming *túmm!* like many katydids,
(every man alone)
and a bullet strikes his uncle's head: —Old Yellow Wolf tumbles down,
tsálalal!
Making himself furious, White Thunder most silently sings his WYAKIN song
of WOLF Power, shooting at the Bostons,
carefully watching for Cut Arm, hoping to vengefully explode his
forehead—
but Cut Arm, never brave, hides behind his slaves—
and presently Old Yellow Wolf wakes up to fight again; his WYAKIN has saved
him;
with war they keep refreshing themselves
—but no boys come with water anymore, and our best men must fight on,
the Three Red Blankets hunkered farther up the hill, singing songs
against Cut Arm as they shoot
and his uncle-chief Heinmot Tooyalakekt has now taken up the rifle
(so White Thunder has heard, but this may or may not be so);
while Looking-Glass, they say, sits bewildered in camp:
(perhaps even now he hesitates to cut away his friendship with the Bostons),
but here for certain lies Toohhoolhoolsote, growling as he aims.

17

The young boys About Asleep and Red Feather Of The Wing crawl up with
more water,
and Red Feather Of The Wing, who carries a dead Bluecoat's revolver,
would now make himself brave:
creeping to the ridgetop, he aims at a Bluecoat, fires and misses,
our warriors laughing at him, but kindly,
the Bluecoats replying *pim pim pim pim,* until we are all deafened,
death pounding bones up there behind the pines, getting ready
to eat,
TRAVELLER THE SUN troubling our eyes
White Thunder nauseously thirsty, longing for the end of this painful
light,
laying down his head, just for awhile,
his WYAKIN flying away:
now he finds himself dreaming that he is creeping uphill; he begins
to see Cut Arm, whose eyes are as feeble as a buffalo's,
but as he prepares to shoot that hateful moldy one,

Wottolen, rising up from nowhere, strikes him with a whip to make him brave:
Hear me, brother! Bluecoats are coming right here!

So they fight until dark.

18

No campfires, men. If you want to keep warm, dig yourselves deep.
Yessir.
Bomus, I want ammunition and a fresh hot pancake for every soldier on the line.
Yessir; I'll see to it.
Where's Captain Miller?
Over here, sir—
A fine charge you made.
It was nothing, general. These Indians are no match for Modocs—
And no match for you! Well, well. Getting pretty dark, Captain Trimble.
Sure is, general.
In your opinion, what's the circumference of Joseph's zone?
Maybe twenty miles, general.
I suppose you're right,
> as rocks scratch and clatter around us in the night: the Nez Perces are
> enlarging their fortifications,
> to which sounds of trowel bayonets reply as our bunch finishes digging in
> (better too deep than the other way around, even if it's your own grave);
>> and Whipple, scraping dry tongue across chapped lips, lies on his
>> back, longing to kill Toohhoolhoolzote, whose neck is as thick as
>> the pipe of a Sibley stove,
>>> and smash Looking-Glass's head in for escaping arrest
>> as an owl hoots (or maybe it's an Indian):
>>> *O, no, o, no—*
Listen to them drumming and screaming down there. Do you suppose they're
mourning their dead?
Wouldn't put it past them, sir.
How are you and Colonel Perry managing together?
O, just fine, sir.
Trimble, if you ever feel discouraged, please come to me.
Thank you, sir,
> you sanctimonious sonofabitch.
Carry on. Now where's Umatilla Jim?
Here I am, general.
How are you doing, soldier?
Real good.
> *O, no, o, no—*
Jim, what's that *hum, hum, hum* they're singing down there?

Well, sir, that's the Scalp Dance.
I should have known,
> as Joseph's camp-smoke occludes the stars, squaws wail over their dead and Dreamers drum
> and we lurk low here at Headquarters, whose fortifications are pack-saddles and boulders
>> (smell of sweat and tarry rucksacks),
> Captain Jocelyn praying: May I become one of those who love our neighbors as ourselves, *Amen.*

19

Doc, are you still on night watch?
Can't you see I am, Blackie? What's the matter with you?
Let me keep you company. I'm not sleepy.
Suit yourself.
Doc?
What?
Doc, are we going to to whip Joseph?
To-morrow he'll cut and run. You'll see.
How do you know?
I always know. Now shut up.

20

Sitting in a hole, resting his head on a grizzled rock, Wood wonders whether Chief Joseph will kill or be killed to-morrow
> (his right heel itching in his boot)
and when Captain Jackson will get here with the resupply
>> (All right, Perry, what's going on along your front?
>> Not much, general. Just listening for reds—)
and why he feels awkward toward Wilkinson, to whom for some reason he had missed saying good-bye when departing for Alaska
> (when called upon, will I be as brave as he was to-day?),
the heel-itch worsening, phantasms of Nanny as cool and wet as the copper band on his wrist:
>> several brother officers have remarked on Nanny's moderate (which is to say, not at all imaginary) resemblance to Mrs. FitzGerald back at Lapwai, at least when Nanny's hair is up as in the locket-portrait which her intended wears about his neck; to be sure, Mrs. FitzGerald (shall I call her Emily?) has borne children and shows it; all the same, both ladies offer their beholders the round-cheeked angelic delicacy of porcelain dolls;

o, how I could cherish and protect a woman like that
—or any woman!
A repeat of Camp Misery.
O, no, JESUS, o, no—
and indeed, now that most of them (Doc the gallant exception) have forgotten
Mrs. Manuel, Wood has been dwelling on her the more, longing to save her.
Lieutenant Forse is still out there on the skirmish line.
Who's he?
The general has explained that in addition to being subjected to what for our
American women is worse than death itself—and even the most loving husband
must quail to take back into his bosom the wretch who might poison her family
with syphilis—an Indian captive is compelled to bear on her back, year after year,
such heaps of peltries, lodgepoles, & c, as might tire a mule; and at his pleasure
her so-called husband can sell her to another and another, whose squaws entertain themselves in pricking her with needles and knives, pulling her hair out,
clubbing her unconscious. And then her rations, foul and meagre
—but above all *the fate worse than death,* and
pulling off his boot, scratching that itch, then writing in his diary
(feeling rather than seeing the letters he makes): *Squandered lives
of men that meet lonely and awful deaths,* and
Mr. Joe's feeding the graveyard again,
Nez Perces shifting rocks ever so quietly in that dark woods no
more than a hundred feet away as I should reckon, which makes me
wonder if they have already murdered our pickets and are creeping
forward and
Chief Joseph and
that Blackfoot squaw of Theller's, alertly unsmiling into my
face as if she were as ready as I to go riding palominos side by
side and forever (shall I close my eyes just for a quarter-hour?)
O, no, o, no—
not when the general endures the night within his
house of boulders, the trembling lantern-flame
nearly invisible as he bends over the map, perhaps
praying,
and her nipples as reddish-purple as the wild plums back at
Wall Creek and
General Custer's essays in *The Galaxy,* whose every installment Wood
used to follow (his father saved each number for him during his cadet-
ship at West Point): little white children murdered by Indian fiends, and
liberty and deliverance!
after which Mrs. Manuel (*Jeanette* or *Jenett* they say her name is; and she has long
yellow hair) will throw her arms around me and say:
The men need water. Does any officer have enough "sand" in him to try?

I'll do my best, Captain Pollock.

Be as quiet as a thief, Wood! By GOD, we don't want to lose you!

—and so, shouldering two buckets, he goes forward, instantaneously forgetting the dryness in his mouth, straining his eyes for any movement as he belly-crawls over the lip of the position, knowing that the Indians are far better creepers than he, so that as he inches farther into the night and his sense of his comrades behind him stretches, then severs,

blackness leaching down upon him from the sky,

feeding the graveyard again,

he tries to pretend that this is merely some exercise just past the white camp tents tucked neatly beneath the trees at the edge of West Point's lawn; all the same, he begins to burn and tingle between his shoulderblades, as if his murderer were nearly upon him:

and why should the whole world feel so menacing, just because I might get killed? Why should that matter?

He consoles himself by attending to what he has already begun to call *that current which is the stream of the universe.*

Something hovers over his neck, perhaps a moth.

That time when I stood up to that drunken stagecoach driver who d——d me and my Government to hell was no worse than this. Am I afraid? Sure. Was I then? Even so I dug my revolver into his right side to make him carry us on to Bidwell. And if Chief Joseph leaps up right now I'll shoot him in the face.

If I get killed right now, I guess the general will write my mother.

Nanny will hear about it from her, then forget me.

Shivering in his breeze-raked sweat-clammed uniform, he who until now used to dream of fighting the Modocs' evil genius, Scarface Charley

(as if that monster could come up from his grave in the moonlight, gripping a muzzle-loader!)

continues forward, with the two empty buckets carried one inside the other in his left hand,

trying to see a sweet mind-picture of Nanny putting up her hair and grinning at him, but her face is all faded like an incompletely fixed albumen print

(for some unknown reason he remembers that poor old draught horse named Floy who broke a leg; Father had me put him down)

as White Thunder, who lay here until now and would certainly have killed him, drops below the ridge in search of Wottolen, to share with him the water which one of the young boys brought to him in a dead Bluecoat's canteen from Sparse-Snowed Place;

and Wood, believing in a *dark wind,* longing to find rescue in some understanding
of the night noises (which one signifies death?) and hearing far away some other
breeze unless it could be the hissing of the Clearwater itself, finally reaches the
spring, shocked to find no death there, drinks until he get nauseous, fills the buckets and spends a half-hour on the return:

> I must not spill, nor make any noise
>> (night clotted on the ceiling of his skull, dripping down through
>> his eyes);

so that he brings both buckets back full, and our whole command praises him.

21

> In the smoking lodge we have built for the old men
>> (half-circle of boulders up against the little cliff where the pine trees end
>> not far from Spring Place),
>>> the REDFACED TALKING STAR now high and bright,

the warriors talk and talk just as at Split Rock, blaming one another for this war
and for not fighting better

>> (they say that Looking-Glass, who has lifted his rifle at last, is fighting
>> poorly, as if Cut Arm has bewitched him,
>> and that Rainbow should be killing more Bluecoats
>> while Heinmot Tooyalakekt,
>>> he who supposes that he can calm us by talking,
>> prefers to be a chief only of women and children—
>>> although they never utter such words where Ollokot may hear);

no two of us are of one heart.

>>> Down in camp, Cloudburst has Dreamed that Ollokot will die at
>>> dawn; she is weeping in the arms of her sister-wife
>>>> whose little son now wakes to whimper
>>> while in the neighboring tipi Heinmot Tooyalakekt's women, trust-
>>> ing in their husband-chief, calmly simmer soup for our best men
>>> who defend us, waiting for About Asleep and the other young boys
>>> to carry it uphill
>>>> (Springtime's child sleeps easily, filled with milk,
>>>> and Sound Of Running Feet has already made herself brave
>>>>> —but it is she whose peril most troubles her father's
>>>>> heart:
>>>>> he knows his wives, and Springtime's baby can be car-
>>>>> ried everywhere, but this half-grown daughter of his,
>>>>> who can help her best?
>>>>>> Five winters previous, in the lodge at Walla Walla
>>>>>> where before the Bostons burned it down, the
>>>>>> Dreamers used to dance, men facing women,

Smohalla ringing the bell, Toohhoolhoolsote drumming, Heinmot Tooyalakekt chanting beside his brother, Good Woman chanting very sweetly with her eyes closed, smiling, and Springtime chanting with her breast heaving, there stood between them his dear daughter, who opened her eyes and peeped at him to see whether he remembered her.

He must now clear his mind of this.)

And in the smoking lodge they pass the pipe, *pokát, pokát.*

(About Asleep has not been killed; he crawls up here with more water from the river.)

It is well that Húsishúsis Kute, Two Moons and other old men are here. But now certain young men begin to avoid the fighting, hiding here,

crouching in a circle.

Since Buck Antlers ran away to the Bostons, Hair Cut Short has become timid. He lies smoking with the old men, and they do not scold him, for he is no child; he may do what he likes. Before dawn he too runs away to the Bluecoats.

22

By moonlight the Three Red Blankets are creeping up Cliff Place; even now the scree is hot enough to burn their hands; even now they are hoping to kill Cut Arm as he sleeps,

but never find him (he has failed to make himself brave!);

while White Thunder, hunting lesser prey, embraces the perimeter of the Bluecoats' camp

(just so I shall magnify my Power),

slowly, slowly raising his head: close by he can hear Tsépmin's rapid unevenly whining voice, waxing and waning like a mosquito's, *wá-wa;* but cannot see to shoot; so he saves his bullets:

shall I then kill Píli the tall one? He is a chief. That would grieve Cut Arm's heart—

áhaha!

—while down below the women begin to weep for Going Across and Grizzly Bear Blanket

as Heinmot Tooyalakekt calls upon some of our best men, saying: Since you have spoken so bravely against Looking-Glass and me, enlighten our ears: Just what do you intend in this fight?

—but although they pretend to respect him, for his People's sake (and not least for Ollokot's),

their hearts never cease whispering: Who is this young chief who never led anyone in war, and begged us not to kill Bostons? Could

he be the favored little boy whom someone has sent for a coal to
light our council pipe?
—and there in the smoking lodge our old men and cowards keep crouching, listening to the Bluecoats murmuring.

23

Shivering under the failing stars, Wilkinson,
who has no doubt that the general will prevail, no matter what
DEVILS Joseph and his Dreamers may call on,
and hoping the general will call upon *him*—momentarily,
anticipates the dawn:
Pim,
while on his back, feeling with each nauseous heartbeat not only the
spread cloud-wings across the moon as if some monstrous bat were outlined there, but, worse yet, the Indians wailing and drumming, the coyotes singing far away, Wood, unable to sleep, waits for dawn to dirty the
sky so that they can fight again until the fighting is over, after which they
will once again go hunting corpses by smell, dig graves, then march, hot,
sleepless, thirsty, stinking, disgusted and hate-sick, again, again, this being our Indian service, which designs to roll up our Nez Perces now
chanting murder and black magic down there by the river whose music
we accordingly cannot hear; and the mystery of dawn, which since White
Bird Cañon moves him less, now settles upon his breast incarnated as
dread; O LORD, deliver me from this day.
And day comes, blue-grey, then suddenly peach-colored,
the Clearwater mirror-still below,
o, no, o, no—
and light-lines on the dark water resembling cracks in the ice.
Gazing down over the flats into the blue-grey cañon hills, the river and Indians
momentarily out of sight, Wood awaits his general's order:
Is every man on the line?
Yessir.
Colonel Perry, you're to take that spring at any cost. Miller, Rodney, you'll be
under the colonel's command. I expect a charge in fifteen minutes exactly. Lieutenant Otis, soften up the Indians with your battery, *now.*
Yessir. Commence firing:
Pim
pim
pim
pim pim pim!
Timm!
Tumm!

Now, men, when we charge let's head between those two boulders—
Yessir.

    O, no, o, no—

        o—

Timm!

We'll be able to get Looking-Glass as soon as he signals with his
mirror; when it catches the sun—

Timm!

Cease firing.

Lieutenant Otis, you'll lay down covering fire as needed. Colonel, are you
ready?

Ready, general!

Ready—

    move out:

        Right—

            forward—

                fours—

    (Lieutenant Otis's battery firing merrily)—

                charge!

All right, men, tickle the reds as fast as you can! Take some pressure off
the assault!

    Fire!

        Go, go, go!

I see Joseph's bunch are still in fine condition.

Yessir.

Well?

General, they've secured the spring!

Good. Dig in some artillery over there.

Yessir.

Another bloody day.

Yessir.

What report from our front?

The enemy is engaged in active reconnaissance; we just shot one who came
galloping out of the woods—

Now bring water and hot coffee to the front. No man's to remain thirsty anymore.

Yessir,

    sun on their slouch hats

    —and how gratefully they carry bucket-pairs from the spring back to
    their comrades!

        Jim says don't peer over the edge. He says Mr. Joe's waiting—

        There's a red right there!

        Soon as you raise your rifle he'll—

D——n, he ducked down!

See, Jim's wise to that. He's a knowing Indian.

To me he looks more treacherous than Mr. West.

And to me you look like a d——d double-dyed nigger.

General, Lieutenant Forse has been on the skirmish line day and night. He's gone in every charge. This man deserves to be noticed.

Thanks, Wilkinson; I'll note him down. Captain Pollock, how's Company "D"?

Real fine, general. Lieutenant Wood made the crawl for water last night.

O, he did? Tell him I'm extremely pleased. Doctor Alexander, how many casualties so far?

Seven killed, twenty-one moderately to severely wounded, and—

All right. Do you need anything?

No, sir.

Keep at it, doctor. Well, Perry, what do you say?

A tough little skirmish, general.

I'm going forward now. What is it, Mr. Reuben?

General, the bad Indians want to kill you. They call you *the Indian herder*. If you show yourself, you'll be throwing away your life.

I don't care about that.

General, he's right. You have nothing to prove. Without you, who will lead this campaign?

Enough, Wilkinson. Colonel Perry, pull back the artillery and form a reserve. Captain Miller, I'm counting on your battalion to break through Joseph's center left, turn right and then charge his positions from the rear. Do you understand?

Perfectly, general.

You did well yesterday.

Thank you, sir.

Now go prepare your men. I expect your advance at two-thirty sharp.

Yessir.

Lieutenant Otis, I want some decisive plunging fire.

Yessir.

We'll punish these reds and then go home.

24

Aiming at the wicked Bluecoats, firing from behind rocks, White Thunder gets shot in the arm, then just below the eye (his sight half-darkened there forever:
blood in his mouth:
as bitter as the taste of buffaloberries before the first frost),
in neither case hearing the bullet's voice
—while Five Wounds is shot in the right hand, *pim!*—
Wottolen unceasingly singing his WYAKIN song,

brave Rainbow shooting everywhere
> (even in the night he kept fighting although his WYAKIN cannot
> protect him before sunrise),

our women leading new horses to the battlefield,
and About Asleep crawling up and down the steep rock-groove bringing
soup and water

as Shore Crossing, who can shoot golden eagles from the sky, takes aim with his buffalo gun: *timm!*—wounding another Bluecoat;
> (White Thunder is consoled to hear the wailings of this injured one:
> like the man who howls in the Wolf Dance)

but now a howitzer shell strikes Mean Man, grazing his arm,

while Heinmot Tooyalakekt (he who is called *Joseph*) crawls into the smoking lodge, where even more weak young men have secluded themselves in order to pass the pipe with the old men;
then Rainbow comes in; likewise Five Wounds, White Thunder, Over The Point and Strong Eagle,
> he who is third of the Three Red Blankets,
>> bullets drumming on the boulders all around them

as Heinmot Tooyalakekt takes the pipe: You desired to kill Bostons. Now what would you do? Cut Arm took us by surprise here. We cannot defeat him,
> the shooting dying down,
>> White Thunder carefully cleaning his fouled Winchester with sin-
>> gle stalks of bunchgrass
> and the locusts singing *tekh-tekh-tekh!*—

so that they can hear Swan Necklace singing songs against Cut Arm, and Shore Crossing is shouting: GODD——*n you, Cut Arm!*— at which Loon,
> he who was among the loudest for war when we all met together at Split
> Rock but has done nothing,

takes the pipe to say: There he goes, acting brave; but it is his fault that we have lost so much wealth,
to which Rainbow, always calm in war, says: Listen! You have spoken in a way which approaches evil,
so that the young men fall silent,
until another coward named No Swan, who has spent the night in camp with women
> (his heart is as shallow as a bison horn spoon),

takes the pipe to say: We have fought Cut Arm, I am telling you three times! Our hearts are straight. He cannot come down to the river, so we have defeated him. My chiefs and brothers, let us now ride away.
> Strong Eagle says: Peopeo Tholekt is wounded; still he keeps fighting. Why do
> you sit here like a woman?

and Toohhoolhoolsote cries out: What are you? I myself am a man—
> Loon says: If you desire it, go and fight; I say nothing against it,

to which No Swan adds: Why fight when the Bluecoats have not attacked our lodges?
    But Over The Point,
        he with the necklace of grizzly bearteeth
           (all from bears he has killed),
        and best son of Chief Red Heart,
        whose country is up on the ridge now infested by the Bluecoats:
           (he never dreamed of learning that however we may act is solely for
           death),
points his finger in No Swan's face, shouting: Speak straight! You started this war,
and now you hide from it,
    and just exactly now, when he sees that these vapid young men lack the cour-
    age to continue down their own bloody path, his last least hopeful hope gets
    pared down to nothing, so that he completes his heart, saying (what he does
    not yet believe that he means):
If you will not stay to fight Cut Arm, then let us move away,
    at which the young men grow insulted,
        so that hope creeps back into his heart, but for nothing.
           This is the bad thing here, exactly this: that the resolution of these
           who began by killing Bostons now bends like grass.
    Rainbow,
        he who never fears even this darkness of Bluecoats rising up behind the
        pines, grinding bones, preparing to overwhelm us,
now speaks: Over The Point is right. Hear me! Even now, if we make ourselves
brave, we can kill many Bluecoats and maybe drive them off. They cannot shoot.
Anyhow, every man must die.
        Looking-Glass is moving his camp. He wishes to save his People.
        He may do as he likes.
    Once more Heinmot Tooyalakekt opens his heart: Why are all you men sitting
around here? What keeps you from the fight? You who have talked the rifle, now
is the time to use it!
    Stripping off his elkskin shirt, Over The Point shouts: Get ready! Now let the
young men mount their horses! We shall go fight the soldiers to the end!
    And Five Wounds says: Young men, you ride often, too often to the women!
You came here to fight. I shall now loose your horses.
    No Swan cries out: You have no right to do so!
    —loneliness screaming from his eyes—
        as Loon explains: If they kill us to-day, we cannot kill them to-morrow,
so that Over The Point,
    his dream of killing Cut Arm having come to resemble a turtle glittering un-
    derwater before it dives,
says, only to Rainbow and the other best men: Then let us quit the fight,
and to the others: You cowards, I shall die soon, but you will live to be slaves,
    turning away, throwing on his shirt, leaping down among bullets to the grove

where the young boys keep the horses, and then riding sadly downhill with his brother Allutakanin.

25

And then, just as in youth we each go alone, climbing a mountain to meet our WYAKIN, so now we turn away from war,
no longer hearing our WYAKINS, nor seeing anything but death,
walking, then suddenly running away as the Bluecoats come after
(our wisest ones have saved their horses exactly here: they go galloping down the the steep hill),
Shore Crossing,
who can mount a wild horse in the middle of a river,
riding easily down with the other two Red Blankets,
never dreaming we will not stop to fight;
Toohhoolhoolsote,
strongest of the Chinook Salmon Water People,
lowering his head like an angry buffalo bull pawing the dirt
—just now he hates our young men worse than Cut Arm!—
and Rainbow on his bay war horse, never gazing back;
Peopeo Tholekt, riding his longnecked yellow stallion, ashamed that these whom he has called war-friends have forgotten how to make themselves brave,
Ollokot leading the young men of Wallowa back toward camp,
Heinmot Tooyalakekt
(he who is called *Joseph*)
rushing after them, gripping the barrel of his shoulder-slung .44 Winchester in his left hand as he shouts: *Stay; hear me; we must prevent Cut Arm from opening the way!*
—but their hearts cannot listen—
and Loon begins running and running in the pain of fear, which pretends to save him from the anguish of death, only now, just for awhile
as he looks back, discovering Bluecoats coming down,
carrying death, shooting as they run (they will be perfect killers),
their bugle still far away:
I could shoot one or two more.
No. We must help our families run away!
So Ollokot comes galloping home to find the elder wife of his heart standing before the blanket-sewn doorway of the tipi, long-braided, with a plaid blanket hanging neatly down from her shoulders, its fringe licking below her waist, her hands unmoving upon the beaded camas bag she has made, her little son watching with his head forward, the whites of his eyes catching the light—and some-

one's tiny daughter, barely old enough to walk, wrapped in a grubby scrap of
blanket, watches because the others do:

he is shouting: *Pack up and ride! Hurry, hurry, hurry!*

and her mouth opens, then she and Cloudburst are running for the
horses

while up on Battle Ridge, About Asleep's near-brother Rosebush tells
him to run, so he leaps on his grey Cayuse stallion and gallops down the
ravine,

Not Swan's headfeathers coming off on a tree branch as he runs:
bad luck,

so that only White Thunder remains, fighting all alone, his thoughts as heavy
as a bone breastplate, until his war-friend Wottolen comes at his own great
peril to warn him that the People have already begun going away, all of them!

How could they so forsake themselves?

Those last two now begin to flee,

as if Cut Arm were not laughable, but someone to fear:

so horrible to look at—so pale and angry!

(I am telling you three times: He is eerie like a white-
and-blue-beaded horse mask),

while Heinmot Tooyalakekt comes galloping down on Black Mane-
Stripe: People, pack your horses and ride!

guns saying *pim! pim! pim!* just as a bad child cracks
bones—

here come the Bostons, crawling everywhere like the
vermin on a buffalo robe!—

children wailing, women stripping the tipis as quickly as they can,

Looking-Glass's People already out of sight.

Even as Wottolen runs on toward the horses, White Thunder drops down
behind a rock,

no longer hoping to kill Cut Arm, who never makes himself brave, but calling upon his WYAKIN for the Power to shoot Tsépmin as he comes galloping:

Tsépmin, who would both kill us and taste our women,

who fired the first shot at Sparse-Snowed Place

—he used to call us brother and eat our meat (watching me but
pretending not to, his face like a hibernating suckerfish's)—

to destroy him I would pay my life!

but Tsépmin has galloped down the other side of Cliff Place; my rifle cannot touch him.

Even now White Thunder would lurk here to kill Bluecoats as they pass—no
matter if he must die for doing so!—

for he remembers how easily he and Rainbow and merely a few others
divided the line of charging Bluecoats at Cottonwood Place and then
encircled those two herds, shooting into them:

Will my WYAKIN help me now?

No!— White Thunder must flee with all the cowards,
  believing finally that his Uncle Heinmot Tooyalakekt spoke straight at
  Split Rock Place: the young men made themselves brave for nothing . . .
Now the Bluecoats' Horse People have almost arrived at Big Water
  (which they luckily hesitate to cross)
    and Good Woman, Cloudburst, Springtime and Fair Land rush to
    catch horses with their hemp-spun ropes,
    packing bags of camas and cous, screaming, buckling on dead Blue-
    coats' pistols,
      but Springtime was far down by the river, bathing the
      baby's rash; now she is just beginning to run back to
      camp, but the cradleboard is heavy
    (Good Woman does not wish to leave without her husband,
    who may be killed while caring for everybody; she says: Ride
    ahead of me, just for a little while . . .)
Toohhoolhoolsote now riding grimly into camp,
  sending his panicked wives forward with as many of his horses as
  they can catch,
  pulling on his goatskin leggings,
   timm!
  throwing on his deerskin shirt,
pim-pim-pim-pim!
    tying on his otterskin collar so that the tail hangs down his throat
    as Heinmot Tooyalakekt helps the old ones toward the cañon,
    and Good Woman begins to ride after,
      appearing brave enough in her pale tan buckskin dress
      with the strings of blue beadwork
        (fearing above all things that Sound Of Running
        Feet will be killed);
and then Toohhoolhoolsote spies several of his horses far away across the
river; his wives could not catch them. Now the Bluecoats are almost here; leaving his wealth, he must ride away
  ahead of Wottolen, White Thunder's war-friend, now so tired from fighting that he can hardly run;
    howitzer-smoke like the steam which rises from a sweathouse,
  he can find no animal to ride:
  but his cousin Weeahweoktpoo comes on a white horse to save him;
and now almost all the People have fled; only About Asleep remains, waiting for
his father to ride down
  (his mother has already lifted up his younger brother onto her speediest
  horse; now they are galloping, galloping fast and far);
and the boy's brother-in-law Elm Limb calls to him, then rides away:
  Timm! Timm!

About Asleep, my son, why are you here?
Father, I am waiting for you!
The old warrior smiles. They begin to ride away together, and then
        —*pim!*—
the boy's grey stallion is shot in the right shoulder,
    Elm Limb galloping back to give him the horse he is leading,
        shooting out at the Bluecoats from beneath his horse's neck;
but the saddle, too loose, twists sideways, and About Asleep falls off,
    the Bluecoats aleady down on the flats, their Horse People now riding close,
so Elm Limb leaps down to cinch it for him,
and then those three ride away—

26

Feeling himself to be the last one, White Thunder completes his spring back
into the part-stripped camp, hoping that his mother or his uncles' women will
have gathered in his horses:
on a pole outside Heinmot Tooyalakekt's lodge he finds his leggings and deerskin
shirt;
now the Bluecoats are almost here; they have begun shooting at him,
    but there by the river is Aunt Springtime,
        she who hoped so greatly and expected so much,
      clinging to her bucking horse,
      weeping and whipping him to make him listen as he prances in
    terror at the artillery shells:
        White Belly-spot, who was always so easy to ride—
Timm! ... *Timm!*
      she cannot mount him with her baby, who weeps *shlak! shlak!* in
    her cradleboard on the ground—
        Pim!
Timm!
      —so White Thunder hands her up the cradleboard
      and she is laughing with relief,
      galloping away now with her lovely daughter in the cradleboard she
      and her husband have decorated
        as White Thunder rides behind her, the Bostons missing ev-
        ery shot.

27

Ready to move out?
Yessir—
Excuse me, general, but I see the Big Dust coming from the south—

From the south? I doubt it's the River Renegades—

But, general, the Weisser Indians—

General, it's our new supply train.

Fine. Captain Miller, it's two-thirty-one.

Yessir. Move out!

>Move out:

>>along the meadow ridge,

>>to the edge of the grass-world

>>and then into range of Chief Joseph's sharpshooters:

>>>*Pim!*

>>>>Who's that man who was killed?

>>>>O, just another Pennsylvania Dutchman from German-town. Pretty good soldier, though. Never complained; once I saw him carry some weakling's ammo and canteen—

>>>*Pim!*

That's Joseph over there!

Can you actually tell him from Ollicut?

Sir, they got one of ours—

There he goes! Now he's broken through—

>Toohhoolhoolzote, thick and blocky like a Piedmont bull, rearing up to fire, the shot not even heard in the battle's midst but the red flame in his rifle's eye and the white smoke twisting up from it solid evidence of his hateful Indian malice, so we pour on lead but his head ducks instantly down, and now his victim is screaming:

>>Gut-shot, looks like; I'd like to see Doctor Alexander patch *that* up!

General, Joseph's trying to—

All right. Good; we've rolled up Joseph's flank. Rodney, send your reserve forward.

Right away, sir.

O, good afternoon, Major Keeler. How's everything at Lapwai?

Pretty good, general. What's going on here?

We're dislodging Joseph from his barricades, so I hope. Would you care to watch the battle?

Thank you, sir.

Look yonder. Major, I'll confess I'm very proud of Captain Miller. What a charge! And now Rodney's almost through the breach. Wilkinson, is every man ready on the line?

Yessir.

I expect a general attack in five minutes.

Yessir,

>Blackie praying

>and Perry tightening Diamond's bellyband.

   Mount!
General, this is most impressive. Chief Joseph's giving way—
That he is.
      Sir, the reds are falling back—
         ... into the cañon ...
      Advance!
      Bugler Brooks blowing like heaven
      as from our left, Perry,
               who believes, like all good cavalrymen, that mobility
               and courage lend such advantage to an attack that even
               the new guns being invented will be overwhelmed by us
               in our charges—so never mind Mr. Joe and his murder-
               ing savages!
         now, calmly immobile upon his galloping horse, untouched
         by the wind which strains at his sleeves and moustache,
      leads his company down into the cañon:
               Pim,
                     pim,
               flying so freely out of this murderous misery of dying grass
               and lurking reds, down toward the coolness of the river,
                     pim!
 Timm!
            and watching for White Bird's Dreamer's peak of hair:
               how I'd like to make him eat lead!
      —nobody unready to die
            (Wilkinson positively longing to lay down his life, if only un-
            der the general's eye),
      Perry's bunch galloping ahead, raising their rifles to shoot at what
      might have been near point-blank range if the parties would only
      be gracious enough to hold still
      and with Trimble's company right behind him, Lieutenant Parnell
      rising up in the stirrups and laughing:
                     Pim!
      Chapman charging downhill in that buckskin jacket so prettily
      beaded by the squaw wife he put away
            —for all his faults, he sure is a brave man—
      and Blackie,
            having dreamed of an Injun's gaze fixed on him and sucking
            something out of him, now follows Doc,
                  his cheekbones sooted up and protruding and his pu-
                  pils huge, staring up after him like a small boy
      as Wood,

who has mastered what it pleases him to call the trick of the
thing (not considering how much his handsome youthfulness
might assist his so-called methods),
charges happily at Captain Pollock's side:

Dear LORD, thank You for preserving me last night and for
helping me to show bravery before the general, and if I die
now, may it be instantaneous.

Pim! Pim!

Surround the ponies!

. . . and now Perry, whose eyes are nearly as far-seeing as field-
glasses, can already spy the crowds of squaws boiling around their
conelike tipis, hoping to collect their stinking Indian trash and
scuttle off—LORD, help me hit them hard!

Fletch, ride to Lieutenant Otis and tell him to bring the howitzers forward,
escorted by Trimble's company. This Gatling's to go ahead.

Sure thing, general!

I want you to pour lead into the Indians.

Yessir:

Pim-pim-pim-pim-pim-pim-pim-pim-pim-pim-pim!

and Joseph's Indians screeching up the cañon.

Wilkinson, what's the delay?

Sir, the infantry can't ford the river to get at Joseph—

Ride down there at once and galvanize the cavalry.

Yessir.

General, if I may say so, your cavalry is perfectly—

Major Keeler,

as in the field-glass, Ad Chapman, rapidly diminishing, turtles down his
head, raises his long pistol nearly vertical, and fires

(the Indians writhing about on their galloping horses, swinging
themselves down out of sight to take aim from behind their Appaloosas' necks),

you're my guest. I'm delighted to offer you this vantage of our battle. But you're
not one of my staff officers, and I haven't solicited your commentaries or appreciations.

Forgive me, general—

Say no more. Now where's Wilkinson?

Sir, he's a quarter of the way down—

I'm getting disappointed in Perry.

General, the cavalry's crossing the river—

Now he'd better pursue Joseph up the bluff. *What on earth is he doing?* Well,
Fletch, is Otis on the move yet?

He sure is, general, and doublequick—

Where's Wilkinson?

Halfway to the river, sir—

Fletch, gallop over the river to Perry. He's assaulting the village instead of chasing Joseph. If the wicked bucks get away—

Yessir—

When you overtake Wilkinson, send him straight to me. Go now.

Yessir.

> You see that? Perry got licked at White Bird Cañon, and he dithered at Norton's when Mr. Joe was killing them volunteers; now he's yellow. Even the general said—

Major, shall we ride down and visit Joseph?

By all means, general. Quite a fine racing-horse you've got there—

Thanks.

> Two tipis already in flames—
>
> And all them squaws screaming—
>
> Tickle 'em with lead!
>
> General's riding down like thunder—
>
> *Onward, Christian Soldiers!*

—cantering down a fissure which resembles a sergeant's chevron, the river jerking in and out of sight on the steep cañon trail and the first Gatling chittering like a grasshopper

> (most of the Indians already gone, unfortunately,
>
>> but here's a dead warrior at last, flat on his back in the rifle-pit by that lone pine; is he the only "good" Indian we've made during this battle?),

then our howitzers beginning to cough and scream:

spherical case opening like seedpods to let their bullets out,

> and our Springfields kicking up dust two and four hundred yards downhill,
>
>> Joseph's ponies stampeding up the side-cañons
>>
>>> (nothing on earth's as pretty as a white-and-ocher paint horse! I pray I can bring one home to Grace before she marries),

and swinging up the breechblock to eject the dead casing, Perry fires at a gallop, just missing one of the Three Red Blankets.

> They're scattering to the north.
>
> Then Perry had better keep at them.

Halt a moment, major. My field-glass shows new Indians.

Yessir, approaching their tipis from the—

We must have surprised them. Hello, Wilkinson. What word from Colonel Perry?

General, the Nez Perce village is almost secured—

I'm turning you round again. Do you see those warriors riding up the river?

Just an instant, sir . . . Yessir, a strong contingent, and not yet visible from below.

Warn Colonel Perry without delay. He's to ferry the infantry across on his horses. We don't need another White Bird Cañon.

That's a fact, sir—

Doubletime, Wilkinson!

Right away, general—

All right, major,

> discovering in his field-glass the last contingent of enemy squaws: huge-eyed, braided women with round faces, some darker than others, whipping their heads halfway round their necks to stare up at us as they gallop away up into that far side-cañon
>
> > —out of range of our Gatlings, unfortunately.

Shall we finish our ride?

Yessir. Getting dark—

Well, well. Perhaps Perry did right. The village is in our hands

> and with it the corpse of a squaw whom he could have sworn was actually Comanche or some Mexican breed.

> > Looky there. We must all be safe now. Here come the souvenir hunters from Lewiston.

> > > *O, no, o, no,*

> > > > Trumpeter Brooks blowing the "Watering" call.

> > Snagged me this beaded saddlebag full of camas! Who's hungry? Blackie, you hungry?

> > > *O, no, o, o, o, no—*

> > Hey, you, what's your trouble?

> > *O, no, o, no—*

> > Where's Doctor Alexander?

> > Well, that awning down there must be the field hospital. What else could it be?

> > Then for CHRIST's sake help me carry this devil down there—

> > Can't you see he's already about to choke? So long to him.

> > > *O, no, o, no—*

Pretty fine looking trout stream,

> its mane of light-stripes perfectly in order, another Indian puppy dead and bleeding on the bank,

> > our tired troopers already raising up the company street, delighted to fill their canteens from this river that deserves its name,

> > > coyotes howling on the bluff, perhaps digging up Joseph's dead,

> and the smell of pines,

> > rosehips and yarrow,

the smell of water strengthening as coolness comes,
the river bottom very brown.
What are you shooting their dogs for?

28

Well, Mason?

General, Joseph is running from the Clearwater country; the volunteers report him to have between five hundred and a thousand Indians of both sexes with him.

That's not what James Reuben says.

After all, general, Mr. Reuben isn't a white man.

How does that bear on the question?

Excuse me, general; I forgot—

You forgot my peculiarities, didn't you? That will be all. Wilkinson, make the rounds and find out who saw Joseph. Captain Pollock, you're officer of the day, I believe.

Yessir.

Are your pickets out?

Of course, general.

Good man! I don't suppose Joseph will annoy us to-night.

Well, sir, you never do know about a red.

To-morrow your bunch will bury our dead and then carry the wounded to Grangeville. Inform Doctor Alexander.

All right, general. Should we bury any who die on the way?

No. Hurry along, in case the hostiles should strike you. Expect a despatch from me on your arrival. Now where's Chapman?

Right here, general.

The Indians are defeated.

Well, now, general—

Are you tired?

No, sir.

I didn't think you would be. Rest an hour, then set out after Joseph with your volunteers. We don't want him assaulting Kamiah.

Yessir. The scouts tell me—

Shut up. Fletch, did you have time to make any sketches of the battle?

I'm sorry, sir—

Never mind.

Bring Perry and Miller here.

Right away, general.

Colonel Perry, Captain Miller, I want to thank you for your brave accomplishments to-day. This morning as I watched you lead the charge to retake the spring, I said to myself: I can never hope for two finer officers.

General, we—

Great is the Truth, and must prevail. Yes, Miller, what is it?

Sir, Lieutenant Otis's barrage was invaluable to us—

Very commendable to praise a brother officer. Thanks again, gentlemen; you may return to your business. Wilkinson, what do you have for me?

General, the men are pillaging Joseph's camp.

Let them. That's just what we did on the March to the Sea. Whatever we don't want, we'll burn,

> our boys ranging over the battlefield, in high glee to taste Mr. Joe's camas bread, not that it relishes all that well (Doc warns that eating too much will bring on a spell of the shits),
>
> Perry on Diamond, gliding moodily across the trampled grass, frowning but keeping silent as three privates from Company "F" bend to the earth, listening and tapping it in hopes of hunting out secret pits, behind him a great orange tree of flame blossoming with smoke (the destruction of unwanted buffalo hides, dip nets, saddles, beadworked root bags):
>
>> the camas bread smelling delicious at first, nearly like a housewife's molasses cake rising in the Dutch oven;
>>
>> then it begins to burn
>
> as even Mason and Sladen stride curiously about, as if they too hoped to win souvenirs
>
>> (Chapman and Umatilla Jim merrily gleaning beads together from a pile of squaw trash: they really do manage without rest!),
>>
>>> the last Indians now out of sight in the far hills:
>>>
>>> I don't care what General Howard calls it. *I* call it a drawn battle.
>>>
>>> Watch your mouth, Jocelyn,
>
> Blackie looking open-mouthed at everything, then turning to stare at that beetling cliff which rises as high and vertical as Sherman's pale forehead between the two cañons through which we came charging down,
>
>> and for all he is worth he now studies that gradually slanting cañon, screened by tall pines, creeping almost parallel to the rock (the Indians went thataway)
>>
>> and listens to the rattling of the cottonwood leaves and the river water—
>
> only for an instant, until Colonel Perry sets him and three others to digging the company sink;
>
> as Wilkinson, not in the least interested in heathen plunder, silently oversees the burnings, his hands in his pockets:
>
>> Unfortunately I must blame Perry once again for letting Joseph get away, although this Lieutenant Otis as I can see is the one who's most heartily displeased the general; the point is that we've failed to close the campaign;
>
> and Wood, who to Wilkinson really does appear kindhearted, is helping

a wounded private down from the hospital wagon so that the man can ease himself.

Any hint of Mrs. Manuel?

No, sir,

> although the enemy has left behind many brass and copper bracelets, some of them finer than Wood's
>
> and even silver plate (where on earth did they get that?);

as the general rides through the Indian camp, surprised to find the destruction so unimpressive—unlike, for instance, Columbia, where there was more to destroy, and the town mostly burned

> (the palmetto tree by the State House still standing after two fires: strange to say, our troops, who were not exactly patient-hearted by then, respected its pride as an emblem of South Carolina
>
> and I was younger and stronger, expecting to retire from the Army and become a minister or mathematics teacher; Lizzie claims she would have been happier)—

> > Mr. Joe's whipped for sure!

> > > That's another thing I like about Wood. He eschews card games.

> > > > Yessir.

Lieutenant Otis made inadequate use of his artillery! I cannot recommend that officer for anything.

> > Grab yourself an Injun blanket before we set fire.

> > Thanks, Doc. Got me this fine beaded robe—

> > You'll never carry it even ten miles. Sell it to them Lewiston grubbers.

> > > Doc, why do you keeping taking a chance on me?

> > > Because you're one in a million. You're gonna make me proud.

> > > You're real good and kind . . .

> > > Not many would say so, Blackie. Now you hush up and get to work. Dig them sinks the way they like it. Blackie, you're makin' good now. Just keep on.

General, we've captured nearly thirty of Joseph's horses.

Shoot the worn out animals and turn the rest over to Lieutenant Bomus. He knows who has a use for them.

Yessir. What about the scouts?

Lieutenant Fletcher, that's at your discretion, but no one is to slow down this march, including especially Mr. Chapman. All horses not in service by to-morrow are to be shot. The rest had better be branded and inventoried. That's all.

Yessir.

Well, Lieutenant Bomus?

Eighty-three tipis, general.

Burn them all.

Yessir. My word, all the primitive trash they've left . . . !

Well, Bomus, they must not have expected to lose.

No, sir,

 as Trimble,

   who agrees with Lieutenant Parnell that if that stinking yellow-
   bellied ditherer Perry had stuck to business, Mr. Joe would have
   eaten lead to-night

    (one thing I'll say for Perry: He's as hard as hell.

     You'd be, too, with that hysterical bitch he married. You
     should have heard her when he got his Modoc wound!),

pulls his old slouch hat low, puts his hands on his hips and watches Company "H" with a gaze like unto fondness,

   the flames now roaring out of that heap of Indian trash, rising up
   like walls of flowers;

   and just as the Clearwater sometimes reflects red rock in its brownness, so this fire occasionally gives rise, among our veterans, at
   least, to fine and dramatic detached pictures of burning Atlanta;

while Lieutenant Bomus's bunch get about lassooing the best Indian ponies by their front legs, throwing them down, one man holding their
heads, the second raising their forefeet high and tight together in the
lassoo's bite, and a third branding them U S .

29

Exciting operations, Wood.

That's for sure, general.

The troops showed great *éclat*.

Yessir.

Because he remembers the long train of horse-drawn wagons, sometimes
thirty or even more in a caravan, bringing the wounded to Mount Pleasant Hospital, he cannot be overwhelmed by the groans, screams and prayers of those
fifty-odd soldiers who now await transportation to Lewiston.

During the Rebellion, when we made do with an old ginger pop wagon for our
ambulance . . .

Yessir,

  but the general closes his eyes, recalling from Gettysburg an exhausted
  young private taking his first step on the crutches his messmates had
  carved for him.

We Rode Away Exactly When We Wished
July 12

1

*A*nd now it is exactly like this:
Our meat is spoiled, and Red Owl has lost his country,
but we defeated Cut Arm
    —since we killed many of his slaves and fought him for awhile, then tired
    of him and rode away exactly when we wished,
        grieving for the beaded shirts, gold dust, flour, camas and other fine
        things now seized by the Bostons
            and for Red Thunder, Going Across, Grizzly Bear Blanket,
            and Whittling—all shot dead by Cut Arm
            as Red Owl's women wail for their home;
and we are riding away
    (Cut Arm has burned eighty lodges);
with our blankets tight about us we are riding away:
    Chief Red Owl and Chief Three Feathers,
    Swan Necklace, he who started this war
        (now he is helping his dear sister Where Ducks Are Around; her
        horse cannot stop being afraid)
    and Burning Coals
        (that cunning old man has saved nearly all his horses),
    wise old White Bird beside *Kate,* his clever wife, who rescued his Medi-
    cine treasures
        (her Wyakin is Spring Ice);
    then the half-breed Bunched Lightning, who did not fight much but
    amused our hearts by yelling Godd——n you! at the Bostons,
    Sun Tied, that quiet young man who always helps his sister and his preg-
    nant wife,
    Roaring Eagle, who nearly captured Cut Arm's pack train;
        (Shore Crossing murmuring to his wife: I am ashamed because
        Swan Necklace urged me into doing bad things,
            dreading that Swan Necklace may overhear);
    Hahtalekin, Húsishúsis Kute, Star Doctor and all the other Palouses:
    Wounded Breast, who just now has won his fine good name:
        desiring to make himself brave, he rode up into range of the Blue-
        coats, received the wound of his desiring:

pim:

turned his horse around, and as he was cantering away, a bullet entered his back

—*pim!*—

and departed his chest,

so that he lay down in the river, sang his WYAKIN song, purged himself and returned to the fight;

Red Heart with his family;

while beside his dear wife Helping Another, his mother-in-law Towhee and his strong sister Wetwhowees,

who will soon show her Power in the fight at Ground Squirrel Place, rides Wounded Head, leading another pony by the halter, with their tiny son tied on it (the boy is just now out of the cradleboard),

followed by Looking-Glass, who rides straight and tall on Home From Capture, with his hat low over his eyes and his Winchester slung over his shoulder in its beadworked case; his heart is perfect; he can do everything; he is leading and protecting his wives:

Blackberry Person, quiet and sad (their tipi is burning; the kettle is lost),

Asking Maiden

(whom Good Woman suspects is pregnant)

imperious in her Boston shirt of Navy blue broadcloth, decorated with elkteeth and brass buttons, her cuffs cut from a blood-red King George blanket

(no holes yet in her goatskin leggings);

behind them come both daughters, and then

brave Rainbow, who has saved his bay war horse,

Rattle Blanket, Five Snows, Stripes Turned In, Coyote With Flints,

Heinmot Tooyalakekt,

recognizing from far away the red, black and beige triangles upon Springtime's woven hat and the many bead-stripes on her leggings, his heart screaming *qoh-qoh-qoh!* to learn that she and the baby have not been safe

—to-day he has lost many blanket-coats and buffalo robes—

he turns round his horse, riding back to her . . .

and then Going Alone, a brave one who killed a Horse Person at Sparse-Snowed Place,

Animal In A Hole, he who has finally given up betraying his People

(riding carefully, in pain, his thigh wrapped up and yarrowed against the wound the Bostons gave him),

Peopeo Tholekt riding easily on that yellow horse, his leg beginning to heal, eagle feathers curving back away from his head,

Ollokot in a checked Boston shirt, with his hair roached high and shining

and a nine-looped necklace of white beads around his throat, a wide ribbon knotted at his sidelock, the two ends, exactly even, sweat-soaked and
clinging to his neck, his eyes shocked and weary but not yet defeated,
     and then Cloudburst leading seven packhorses,
     Fair Land with her son tied to her, and a saddlebag filled with pre-
     cious things;
and now again Heinmot Tooyalakekt, who can foresee the end but never
expected this, riding back silent among his braves with their long
Dreamer hair and their plaid or striped blanket-coats,
     and behind them Good Woman, bareback on White Stripe,
        leading Short-Tailed One and Ocher One
           (she has saved more things than most women);
Sound Of Running Feet, who has lost all her horses but the one she
rides:
        her favorite, Little One,
     and Springtime riding White Belly-Spot, with her braids flowing
loose (she has lost her beargrass cap),
        with her baby girl sleeping in the cradleboard, safely looped
        over the high pommel,
then cowardly Loon, hiding among the old ones and
Welweyas the half-woman, she who can rub a penis until it shines
        (all she now owns are her horse, her clothes and a bag of cous
        flour);
and beside her, her old mother, Agate Woman, weeping because she too
has lost most everything,
Red Moccasin Tops's father Yellow Bull,
White Bird with all his People from Sparse-Snowed Place
        and dogs darting between their stallions' legs, hoping to steal meat
        somewhere, even a loose leather strap;
Old Yellow Wolf
        —he who once lived in the same house as Tsépmin—
he is silently grimacing, riding beside his dear sister Swan Woman, who
has now poulticed his head-wound with the roots of Oregon grape; with
them rides her son, his nephew White Thunder,
        whose griefs, thronging in like buffalo on a dusty hazy day, cannot
        yet be distinguished one from the other, although at least he knows
        in his heart that the face of DEATH Who watched him from behind
        the pines on that ridgetop, pounding bones as a woman does cous,
        never did penetrate past his shell of mere amazement; he showed
        no fear;
and Shooting Thunder
with his war-friend Naked-Footed Bull, who is ready to kill all Bluecoats
but not yet to murder any Boston, for his sister Goose Maiden in her white

dress of antelope skin still lives to ride a horse; his three young brothers
Charcoal, Claw Necklace and Lone Crane have not yet been killed;
and Toohhoolhoolsote, robbed of nearly twenty of his horses
> (his anger and grief resembling something known by smell),
raging at our crooked young men, his loop necklace of bone beads rattling like the skeleton they came from
> (both old wives riding behind, afraid of him),
Going Across's mother weeping
>> (once Cut Arm has passed on to Kamiah, she will ride back to bury
>> her son beneath the tree where he died),
> our lives now as steep as Cliff Place;
indeed we are riding away; this is easy for our People, who have already gazed so
many times into the greenish-brown mirror of the Big Water at sunrise and
moonset and evening. Cut Arm can never catch us.

2

Wottolen, Over The Point and the Three Red Blankets scout behind us, safely
shadowed by ridgetop stones, in order to inform their hearts of Cut Arm's laughable creepings:
> First comes Tsépmin,
>> he whom we once helped,
> riding his lovely grey horse,
>> crooked Tsépmin, whom Looking-Glass pitied and warned away so
>> that our young men would not kill him along with the Bostons,
>> he to whom we taught our language
>>> (now he would kill us),
>> galloping so bravely up here
>>> —if he comes closer perhaps we shall kill him—
>>> —but his wicked Boston friends begin to appear behind him, the
>>> tall grass swaying in time with their horses' manes,
>>>> enough of them to trouble us,
> and we withdraw to warn our chiefs.

3

Riding like ghosts through our old home, we camp in High Rock Place,
>> settling in a circle,
> young boys making new bridles out of grass, to replace the ones which
> fell into the Bluecoats' hands,
> babies weeping, *shlak, shlak!*
>> as White Thunder washes his wounded eye in spring water,
>>> because water is Medicine for everything,

while yet again Looking-Glass tells Ollokot (who smiles meaning-lessly): All their promises to me about my reservation have been no good; the Bostons were lying to me! Cut Arm wanted me to keep still while he herded the rest of you People. I kept quiet but it has done no good. Now I begin to hate these white people . . . !
—women laying out food to see how much was saved
and boiling yarrow for the injured men,
    making that dark greenish-brown tea which smells sweeter than spearmint,
        and while Heinmot Tooyalakekt and Ollokot are opening the horses' blisters with serviceberry twigs,
        Wottolen comforts his brave son and his wife
            (their tipi has been burned, and likewise all their camas bags):
        thirsting for the pinkish-orange evening light over the far side of the river in the Buffalo Country, *he who remembers* promises to bring them to a rich hunting-ground without Bostons
        as wolfskin-caped Arrowhead, who has saved her white stallion, comes to see how Peopeo Tholekt's bullet wound is healing
        and the Three Red Blankets whisper together with Swan Necklace
            (after which Strong Eagle cries out: It has always been so! I shall not lie down and keep quiet!);
    and no one calls out: *Hasten; evening shadows be!*
    but Cloudburst is singing to some children the old song about the girls of the FIR PEOPLE.
Looking-Glass says: You People are like women. How can you defeat Cut Arm? That is exactly why I moved my lodges.

4

White Bird's young men, and Toohhoolhoolsote's—it is their warriors who be-gan this war—keep quiet, listening to Looking-Glass with disgust in their hearts
    —for just as COYOTE once died and then transformed Himself into a Sal-ish brave so that He could come back and marry His own desirable daughter, so Looking-Glass, having died to us by fleeing to his painted land, has now returned to take up a place that should not be his.

5

Five Snows and Stripes Turned In approach our chiefs, saying: What shall we do now? Our women have nothing to eat!

—but Heinmot Tooyalakekt tells these young men: Since you would not open your ears to my words, now you may feed your bellies with war!

    (he is making them ashamed by speaking),

after which Fair Land gives them soup.

6

Sound Of Running Feet is fondling her favorite puppy. She says: My father, when shall we come back?

My dear daughter, we shall be gone for awhile.

7

Certain Wallowa People come to him wailing: women and old ones. They sorrow because Cut Arm burned their lodges. To them he says: The young men could not endure to enter painted land. This day we have seen that they will not fight, either. What is left to us but riding away?

8

Now the chiefs and warriors have a smoke:

Even though he disappointed our young men back there at Big Water

        (for his fighting was no more distinguished than that Wallowa camp-chief Heinmot Tooyalakekt's),

Looking-Glass, the excellently-travelled,

        he who once paid twenty horses for a bride when other men offered five,

will be head-chief as we go

        so that his heart-hurt begins to be eased

            (although Toohhoolhoolsote has said: Looking-Glass, you were a fool to enslave yourself to some hardtack and a trifle of sugar and coffee. You trusted Cut Arm, and he devoured your country. Looking-Glass, hear me! I want no child for my head-chief!);

and to-morrow we shall make bullboats to cross the river near Kamiah,

        maybe at Fish Trap Place,

by the grass-grown fossilized Heart of the MONSTER from whose blood COYOTE made the people

        (exactly there where our People once helped Lewis and Clark from one bank to the other)

where the thickets are already shining orange with rosehips;

then perhaps we shall return to White Bird's country to dig camas

or even to Wallowa,
   Wallowa,
or ride to the Buffalo Country for awhile, just for awhile.

9

Toohhoolhoolsote, as sunlight glows in the wrinkles of his dark cheeks, takes the pipe to say: I know it is not right to run away from our home. We are exactly at this place. We want to remain exactly at this place. How many times must they wipe their buttocks on our heads? Hear me, my chiefs! Let us ambush the Blue-coats at MONSTER-Udder Place. We should kill them and die.

Over The Point replies: Too many young men did not show bravery. I am tell-ing you three times! They will not fight,

> and Wottolen, *he who remembers*, looks and listens, so that our children's children will know.

10

Then Heinmot Tooyalakekt smokes and says: Here is my heart. Listen! I shall ride to Cut Arm for a talk. Perhaps he will even let me ride out again . . .
   —at which White Bird,
      whose best men we now begin to blame for this war,
swipes away the pipe: My chiefs, great men, this heart of mine means no evil against Heinmot Tooyalakekt, who is our brother. But if he goes to the Bluecoats, some People may fear that he will desert us to act in the enemy way.

Ollokot speaks angrily: Surely my elder brother must be trusted to do the right, —to which Looking-Glass answers: I did everything for the Bostons and they at-tacked me! Heinmot Tooyalakekt, how can you trust Cut Arm now?

All of you know my heart. Looking-Glass, you are as my brother—

Looking-Glass being silent, the Wallowa chief continues: I have warned you that we cannot win this war. The Bluecoats and Bostons keep hunting us. Shall we flee and flee forever until we starve in the mountains? Perhaps we can still knot some kind of peace.

Snatching the pipe, Toohhoolhoolsote shouts: Would you have Cut Arm choke us in rope? I shall not die that way, not with your peace-knot about my neck—

No. I would ride alone to Butterfly Place, and speak to Cut Arm about what is now best both for our People and the Bostons.

My dear brother, the Bostons' hearts are not so. And what if they turn your heart away from us?

They can never do that.

White Bird says: Toohhoolhoolsote speaks straight. The People from Butterfly Place, they who were once our relatives, have become our enemies forever.

Heinmot Tooyalakekt says: Then I shall not go.

11

He lies down with his family on buffalo robes; they have no tipi anymore, since Cut Arm burned it.

Springtime and Cloudburst have already gathered a basket of snowberries, from which Fair Land is making tea; her kettle bubbles *mulululu.* Good Woman has likewise saved her kettle, together with some pounded roots, so there is soup. When White Thunder comes to eat, he offers her his pistol which his mother Swan Woman gave back to him, but she smiles, points to her daughter's Colt, and says: Sound Of Running Feet will protect me.

Although Fair Land has lost her pestle for pounding meat, Ollokot can make her another. Cloudburst is gathering grass for bedding. Ollokot visits his brother to say: You would make a better head-chief than Looking-Glass.

What would be the use? The People's hearts are apart on everything. I shall be camp-chief; that is all,
> suddenly unable not to see his dead father, who tore up the *thief treaty:*
>> his round frail face grew almost womanly in old age; his braids hung thinly down to his breast.

Smiling quickly, Ollokot returns to his wives and son.

12

Sound Of Running Feet will not eat. Perhaps she is sorrowing for her horses. She sits with her hair down and her knees drawn up, gazing at the ground.

Springtime, suckling the baby, turns away from him
> (Cut Arm has swallowed up the cattail mats she wove at Split Rock; now she must make new ones for when the rain comes),

so he goes to Good Woman,
> remembering when he first laid fine cloth over Springtime's head, showing his heart to marry her,
> trusting in the loving patience of Good Woman, his loyal elder wife,

who now murmurs: Husband, hear her! Had it not been for our nephew, Cut Arm would have devoured her!
> Ashamed for all of them, White Thunder wraps himself in his blanket.

Heinmot Tooyalakekt sits still, calming his heart. Springtime should not have insulted him, but he pities her. Taking one of her braids in his hand, he tells her: *Síikstiwaa,* I am chief, and must take care of everyone. The young men were not of one heart. In their weakness they let Cut Arm enter our camp. Then what could I do but help all the People?

Since she will not answer, he says: And why did my women not ride together?

Now Good Woman grows angry, while Springtime regards him with wondering doubt. He remembers the night he first began to know her body, when she lay in his arms very softly singing the song that the magic bride sings when she wishes the trees to bend down to her.

13

As for Looking-Glass,
      he who is also called *Black Swan* and *Wind-Wrapped,*
he has already begun explaining to the young boys how many sleeps it will be until we reach the Salish Country.

KAMIAH
JULY 13–14

1

*H*ow about a game of chess?
Did I tell you I saw Morphy play?
You've told us half a dozen times. Now, how about it?
For money or not?
I don't care,
      as another boatload returns from the battlefield, blowing her whistle in high glee, the relic-hunters waving horse ornaments, buffalo hides and war bonnets.
Ain't they the lucky-hearts! After we run all the danger—
I thought we burned all that.
They dug it up. You get me?
Look at them bastards getting drunk. No chance for us.
Not in Howard's GoDD——d army.
If we was with Gibbon, Miles or Crook—
Not Crook, O sweet JESUS—
Guess what I heard from Captain Halstead. Well, it seems that our *Christian Soldier* claimed all them Secceshes at Chancellorsville was nothing more'n fences! Halstead requested him, as polite as you please, just to look through his field-glasses, but of course that was hard work for a one-armed ignoramus—
    Cut it out.

And Colonel Perry insists that the attack on the Brave Seventeen was diversionary, so that Mr. Joe could get his squaws and ponies past us—

Wakesh nun pakilauitin

JEHOVAN'M *yiyauki*—

Sure wish Reuben and his reds would shut up—

O, it's a pretty good hymn.

Listen, boys. Chapman can get you whiskey.

So can Red O'Donnell. Chapman ain't got but Blackfoot rum, and he charges by the swallow. What you do is, you ask him for quinine, and he—

Where was *that* fucker when we were burying the boys at White Bird Cañon?

Why, that's easy. Getting his squaw wife to piss out something he can sell for booze—

But if the general—

GoDd——n him! For two cents I'd—

On the topic of two cents, will you play for money or no?

Nope.

You afraid you won't live to spend it?

I can outshoot any Indian who ever lived.

How about any ten Indians?

Trimble says there was nothing extraordinary about Joseph's defense. Remember, he had the advantage of the river—

I thought you were asking me about chess.

Then what's your reply?

Sure.

Praise GOD it's cooling down!

It smells like water:

the smell of the river at night and
of horse blankets and
the undulating black walls of earth around everything and
this purple sky, too humid to be starless.

2

Men, your conduct has given me great satisfaction, and I'm sure we'll soon bring Joseph to justice. Fix your minds on the campaign ahead, and do remember that to-day is the Sabbath. I'll pray for our success. That's all.

General, what's your best opinion?

I'd say Joseph is nearly played out. What would you say?

Yessir. I wish the reds hadn't crossed the river—

A fine hot day, isn't it, Sladen?

Yessir,

near as enervating as a high summer afternoon at Farewell Bend, O my LORD (but Arizona was worse),

and Lieutenant Bomus's detail is shooting seven more of Joseph's
played out horses.

> Doc?

Is your Morning Report Book already in order?

> Doc?

Sure is, general.

That's the spirit! When you have a moment, could you bring me the Descriptive Book? And I'd like Lieutenant Bomus to come here. Fletch, will you take some dictation, please?

Yessir.

How's Wilkinson?

A bit worse, general. Sure thing he's caught intermittent fever. He won't lie down.

I'll pray for him. Now, Sergeant Workman was unmarried, I see.

Yessir. My records indicate the father—

Dear Mr. Workman, my sincere condolences on the death in battle of your brave son James. He was in Company "A," correct?

Yessir.

Your son James, yes, *who will be greatly missed by the men of Company "A." He died at the Clearwater River on July 12th, 1877, defending Americans from a cruel and treacherous foe. Your family can be assured of my prayers for all of you and of my personal gratitude for Sergeant Workman's sacrifice. If there is anything I can do for you, please do not hesitate to command me. Yours sincerely.*

Yessir.

You have beautiful penmanship, Fletch.

Thank you, sir,

> wondering if the enemy might be watching from the dense green coolnesses of the cascara buckthorn trees.

I used to write a rather neat hand myself, back in the day. Now for Corporal Marquardt. Also of Company "A," I believe.

Yessir.

Did you know him?

Hardly at all, sir.

Who's next of kin?

His wife, I believe . . . Yessir.

Does she reside in Lewiston?

Walla-Walla, sir.

Dear Mrs. Marquardt, my heartfelt condolences on the death of your husband Charles, who fell at the Clearwater River on July 12th, 1877, protecting Americans from hostile Nez Perce Indians. As the Scriptures say—

Excuse me, general. One of our Indians is here with a messenger from Joseph!

Well, well! Perhaps our Gatlings impressed him more than we supposed. Is that the fellow yonder?

Yessir.

He looks ill at ease, for a fact. Fletch, we'll finish our business later. Who's the best interpreter in camp?

James Reuben, sir, without a doubt.

Better than Mr. Chapman?

Sir, seeing as how Reuben and this emissary are both Indians—

I take your meaning. Then fetch Mr. Reuben, show him to this Indian and then bring them both to me along with Major Mason.

Yessir.

O, good morning, gentlemen. Mr. Reuben, this man seems familiar to my eyes.

That's right, general. He was at our council—

When Joseph promised to come in to the reservation. O yes. What's his name?

Kulkulsuitim.

And he comes officially from Joseph?

He claims so, general.

And what do you say?

Since his family's all Dreamers—

Naturally. Fetch him coffee and a piece of bread. Now, what does Joseph wish to tell me?

Kulkulsuitim says, Joseph wants to see General Howard.

Then he should come.

Kulkulsuitim asks: Will Joseph be safe here?

He must surrender.

He says: As for Joseph, his heart is good and he always meant to go on the reservation, but he cannot speak for the others.

Is this to the point?

Sorry, general. I don't understand.

Mr. Reuben, Joseph can come in and surrender his band if he likes. We shall then treat them as prisoners of war. If the others want to keep fighting, we'll hunt them down.

General, Kulkulsuitim asks again: If Joseph comes in to camp, will you allow him to go out again?

Not if he comes in to surrender. And if he comes in for any other purpose, he'll gain nothing.

General, he says, maybe Joseph can persuade the others.

The others already know everything I would tell Joseph. They must surrender without conditions. The murderers of our people will be tried and punished. The other Indians will be sent to their reservations.

Kulkulsuitim says: Joseph feels afraid, because Looking-Glass was quiet on his reservation, but soldiers attacked him anyway.

Tell Kulkulsuitim that Joseph will have enough to worry about in consideration of his own situation. What happens to Looking-Glass is my responsibility, not Joseph's. Major Mason, something's not right about this. Who's officer of the day?

Captain Pollock, sir.

Fletch, find the captain straightaway and have him put the guard on alert.

Yessir.

Now, Mr. Reuben, if Joseph means to come in, he'd better do so without delay. Kindly inform Kulkulsuitim—

General, Kulkulsuitim means to say—

Ask him: Will he bring in Joseph or not?

He says he will ride to Joseph now.

We'll wait two hours. What's your thought on that, Major Mason?

Generous of you, sir.

Overgenerous?

I don't know, sir.

Surely Joseph should be given one last opportunity to keep his word. Fletch, go find out the meaning of those gunshots yonder.

Right away, sir.

Mr. Reuben, did you convey my words?

Yes, general. Kulkulsuitim says: Joseph stays a little bit far, and his women and children cannot come quickly. Joseph can be here when the sun comes *there*.

That's east. Does he mean to-morrow?

I believe so, general.

All right. Well, Fletch?

Somebody's taking potshots from the north bank, sir. Seems to be just one or two individuals. We can't see to return fire.

Send Umatilla Jim across and bring me his report. And I still need Lieutenant Bomus.

Yessir.

Excuse me, general, but I can go there—

Thank you, Mr. Reuben, but you're needed here

and I suspect you'd ride straight off with this Kulkulsuitim to the place where Joseph sits straight and still with a hatchet across his lap, hoping to entrap you in some murderous collusion.

Were I only a surer shot, Joseph's Indians might more highly esteem me.

Major Mason, why does that frown disfigure your usually sunny face?

Sir, I worry about them ambushing us.

Mr. Reuben, does your Indian know anything about these gunshots?

He says they're a surprise to him, sir.

Ask him again: Will Joseph come to-morrow morning?

He hopes so, and he'll do his best.

Then tell him to bring Joseph quickly. Fletch, Colonel Miller will receive his arms. We'll want our troops in place at the ferry as of sunrise.

I'll tell him right now, sir.

Mr. Reuben, tell this Indian that we'll wait until nine-o'-clock a.m., and no longer.

Kulkulsuitim says

> (the gaze of this Indian delicate, almost stately, high-chinned and deco-
> rated, over-wealthy in its painted pride, hence conditional in its friendli-
> ness—nearly provoking me to ignore the maxims of war, and seize him
> whose tribe has in truth violated its parole):

Our hearts have turned good. And he says—

Tell him to go instantly.

And Kulkulsuitim goes. His roach of greased black hair glitters in the sunlight like the lens of a field-glass. His horse vanishes before he does. The last they see of him is his buckskinned shoulder, which shines between the cottonwoods like a muted second sun, and then he disappears utterly in a place of purple elderber-ries packed together like clusters of grapeshot.

Mr. Reuben, what's your judgment?

I'll pray that Joseph comes in, general.

A pleasing answer! Come back straightaway when the Indians appear. By the way, how would you rate Umatilla Jim?

Neither good nor bad. He will not follow the Book of Light. But he avoids evil people.

All right; return to your duties. Now, Fletch, before we finish with Mrs. Mar-quardt, let's draft a despatch to Headquarters.

San Francisco, sir?

That's right.

I'm ready, sir.

Joseph has promised to break away from White Bird and give himself up to-morrow. He says he was forced to move to-day. I see evidence of the band's breaking up. Splendid news, don't you think?

Yessir.

> Excepting Sladen, they all distrust me more than ever now, even Fletch,
> never mind Wilkinson who despite his illness ought to show greater
> faith, for the men no less than for his own sake.
>
> No, forgive me, LORD: Wilkinson's loyal.

>> When I released that Seminole woman Mattie at Lake Okeechobee,
>> she led her child away and promised to establish communication
>> with the renegade chief Billy-Bowlegs, but that was the last we ever
>> saw of her. Being merely Chief of Ordnance, I had much ado to get
>> my comrades to agree, and after that, how they laughed and con-
>> demned me, some in the filthiest words—

>>> But no matter how often we break our promises to GOD, He
>>> holds out His hand to us again. Should I do less?

Is Umatilla Jim back yet?

No, sir.

Colonel Perry, you wear a hangdog face just now. Is anything wrong?

No, sir.

What is it?

General, I wish we'd kept that Indian here and squeezed him a little.

O yes. Those are General Crook's methods, Perry. Did you enjoy serving under him?

A great Indian fighter, sir.

And a very energetic officer, a real credit to our service.

Yessir.

Even he admits there's another side to the Indian character. It simply needs to be cultivated.

Yessir.

We need to win over the chiefs.

Yessir.

For instance, Washakie has been praised by the Indian Department for his ability to keep his Indians together. That facilitates the task of our service, wouldn't you say?

O, yessir, without a doubt.

You know, Perry, it's possible to be both kind and brave. Colonel Miles, for instance, was one of the most courageous officers I ever commanded during the Secession War. And yet he intervened on Grey Beard's behalf to keep him from getting sent to Florida with the other Cheyennes.

I heard about that, sir.

Anything else?

No, sir,

> remembering how the week before Christmas of 1866 it was stormy and cold at Fort Boise and I told off forty-five men of Company "F," then nabbed my ten Indians and two citizens to follow General Crook up the Owyhee River, and by dawn we were in position in sight of the hostile rancheria. Crook
>
>> (six feet high, bright-eyed and wide-faced, most often in a private's greatcoat)
>>
>>> —of course I was young and might have been happy: all of us out of the Secession War, and I possessed of some honor, miles and miles of virgin country to define and interesting Indians to fight, Crook our latest hero—and we weren't easy to impress—
>>
>> the strands of his greying beard wisping around his throat in all directions like a frayed rope, right down to his topmost glowing button)
>
> rode forward and we galloped after, punishing so many Indians that hardly any got away, our only loss being Sergeant O'Toole, who strange to say was as cautious as a man can be and not mar his good name.
>
> Crook sure wouldn't be pussyfooting around like this. I wonder what the *Christian Soldier* would say if I told him that Crook always refuses to shake hands with any surrendering chief? He glares, rubs his nose, then

puts it straight to them: *I'm sorry you want to surrender because other-wise we could kill you in the field and save trouble for the Government.* But our *Christian Soldier* declines to fight the DEVIL with fire, because he's too d——d good for this world! How his goodness chills me!

And now comes night as black and sticky as an infantryman's backpack, then "Reveille," dawn, and the morning gun as Colonel Miller forms up his troops on the so-called parade ground:

smell of coffee from the commissary wagon,

rubber blankets airing on the bushes,

Wood, given a half-hour's holiday by Captain Pollock, fondling his first-ever war trophy—a horn spoon from the Clearwater

(if I set it on a silver chain, will Nanny wear it around her neck?)—

then returns it to his pocket, yawning over last week's paper, which Red O'Donnell "snagged" for him in town:

General Meiggs wishes to terminate the Washington Monument with a me-tallic spire, and

The South Cleared of Troops

and fine 4-4 bleached muslin for nine cents a yard,

Sladen, Wilkinson and the general, waiting on Joseph, sitting side by side on a log and quietly singing *"Stand up for JESUS"* until:

All right, very harmonious. Now, Sladen, bring Captain Trimble over here,

while Perry and Trimble, silently asserting each other's invisibility, take roll calls closer to the river, and Jocelyn's men struggle to *fall in*—a joke, ha, ha.

Still the danger of an Indian raid on Lewiston . . .

So Wood distinguished himself at the Clearwater.

So I heard.

Come on, Fletch. Admit you were surprised.

Well, sir, he's sure sucking up to Joseph.

We're all flattered by a bit of unction now and then, aren't we, soldier? If the general can sweet talk Joseph into our clutches, what's the harm?

Yessir,

the Oregon grapes in their fat pale bunches more vivid than elderberries,

and the yellow-green and silver-green needles of young junipers

and a swollen horse carcass floating down the river, evidently another souvenir from our late battle on the Clearwater.

Well, he's finessing quite a bit. Must have trumps in strength.

Ah, he's changed his suit. Well, the command must be against him. I'll—

Now you're eldest hand.

Here comes a horseman! Must be from Joseph—

Nope. I know that horse. That's one of our tame Indians. A courier from Lewiston, most likely.

No it ain't.

Yes it is. Now do you admit I'm right?

Sure.

Courier riding in, Lieutenant Fletcher!

Thank you. I'll take that. Stand down and have a rest.

Well, Fletch, what's this? Any news from Joseph?

No, sir. General Sherman has sent the Second Infantry in answer to your telegraphed request of June twenty-seventh—

Direct it to Lewiston to be placed under Colonel Sully's command.

Yessir.

Mr. Chapman, what is it now?

General, I've lived in Indian country for, well, must be gettin' on twenty-two odd years, and I'd say I know these Indians. And what I can tell you, and I'm telling you straight—

That's enough. Wilkinson, what word from the scouts?

Nothing yet, sir.

Now what?

Pretty ugly country hereabouts.

Poor land, for a fact. Only two crops out of five seasons, they say.

Then why didn't they leave it to the d——d Injuns and save us all this fucking misery?

Trimble, how's your company?

All in order, general.

Perry, are the volunteers shaping up?

Well, sir, they're learning to obey orders. I'll give them that much—

In savage warfare, the personal qualities of the voluntary soldier count for more than does the skill of his officers.

Yessir.

You don't think much of Major Shearer and his kind, do you?

No, sir.

So keep leading the noncomissioned volunteers by example. They did good execution at the Battle of the Clearwater.

Yessir.

Colonel Perry, that will be all. Have the scouts seen any Indians approaching?

No, sir.

Stay on the *qui vive*, Mason.

Yessir. We'll keep our best lookout—

And so they wait as patiently and gently as Christians, but the Nez Perces never do ride in.

Why, look at that! Our god——d old Christian General has let Joseph fool us again! They've skedaddled.

IT NOW BECOMES MY DUTY TO CHANGE THE DIRECTION OF MY OPERATIONS
JULY 15

*F*letch, how is Wood's handwriting?

Very passable, sir.

Well, his reports are consistent. So are his letters to me. Have you seen his drawings?

Haven't had the pleasure, sir. He used to doodle in the old days, but was passing shy—

All right. This will be to Major Shearer. By the way, how many volunteers does he command?

Sixteen officers and a hundred and twenty-one privates, general.

You certainly keep well abreast! Ready now?

Yessir.

Major: It now becomes my duty to change the direction of my operations,
> for just as mineral-bearing waters may dissolve away certain of the rocks through which they travel, replacing, say, calcite by quartz, or lime carbonate by lime silicate, so Lizzie's torch travels slowly up the stairs at Tenth and Morrison to alter Bessie's nightmares of Indians hurting Papa, inducing a sweeter sleep without the child knowing or remembering why; and I, William the Blind, cannot see why this metallurgical phenomenon, which is called metasomatism, might not likewise apply to Bessie's Papa, whose self-schooled bravery (achieved out of many silent agonies) and natural love of the right, for which he has been punished

since boyhood, may finally have begun a transmutation, thanks to the seeping operation of Joseph's latest treachery. O, his *hateful Indian eyes!* His rapes and murders are for a court, not me, to judge. But didn't he make me a promise at Lapwai? And now again at Kamiah he's made a fool of me! I know what they all say:

> Red Cloud spurning us at Fort Laramie, then murdering Fetterman's entire detachment;
>
> Captain Jack shooting Canby under flag of truce
>> (Lieutenant Bomus, if you pay me this bill at Lapwai I'll give you back a dollar hard money right now.
>> *No!*);
>
> Santana sneering at Agent Tatum, drawing rations even while raiding in Texas;
>
> Sitting Bull resisting our Government's just demands and entrapping Custer—

All the same, I will go on offering kindness whenever circumstances allow. This effort must make me better, if it accomplishes nothing else.

I leave a force of one company of artillery, one of infantry, and one of cavalry, strongly posted opposite against Kamiah, rationed for twenty days. I wish you to guard Grangeville and Mount Idaho until the arrival of Major Green.

Is that it, sir?

I pray we can rely on him, Fletch.

I've heard great reports of him, sir.

We'd better catch Joseph before he flees all the way into General Terry's Department.

Yessir.

If I entrain troops on the Northern Pacific Railroad as far as Spokane Falls, then march them east up through the Bitter Roots . . .

Yessir,

> my poor general, your gaze like that of some sad little child who's been carried West on an orphan train!

No, just thinking aloud. Message continues: *Six hundred and twenty-two Indian horses were receipted for by the Mount Idaho Company. Please have the members of the companies cull out such horses as are necessary for mounting the men, or other military purposes, and drive the balance into Rocky Cañon and kill them, reporting the number killed to me. Thank the officers and men for all their coöperation and sacrifice, and assure the community at Grangeville and Mount Idaho that I shall not rest until every house is safe.*

Got it, sir.

Thank you. Now could you please bring Major Mason here?

Yessir.

O, hello, major. How soon will this outfit be ready to move out?

Not before the thirtieth, general, I'm sorry to say. Our resupply—

Major, you know full well that with every day we wait, Joseph rides farther ahead.

Yessir,

staring down at an evening primrose.

We'll start at dawn on the twenty-sixth.

Yessir.

What have your scouts dug up?

Well, general, the Nez Perces are still in the area, it seems. They lost significant mobility after the Clearwater battle. James Reuben opines that if he can speak with Joseph—

No. Do you trust Mr. Reuben?

I do, sir. An honest Christian Indian.

Where's Umatilla Jim?

In the field just now, sir, chasing the trail. But he told Fletch that since we've destroyed so much of their food the other day, they'll almost surely stop to dig camas at Weippe—

And then it's the Buffalo Country, I suppose.

Yessir. That's where I'd go in Joseph's shoes.

Not if the Army can prevent it. Mason, you're to lead McConville's volunteers and—since you trust them—James Reuben's bunch. Chapman can interpret. Your task is to confirm his intentions.

Sure, general. I could follow Hangman Creek—

Ask Chapman, but use your judgment. Perform a reconnaissance in detail, but take no risks. You don't need to trail him past Musselshell Creek. The Indians assure me, and the map confirms, that the forest rapidly becomes almost impassable in the Rockies. Once Joseph's committed to the Lo Lo Trail, he can't turn off it.

So I'm to verify that he's definitely gone east—

That's right. How soon can you move out?

Within half an hour, general. Sooner, if our citizens bestir themselves.

GOD bless you, Mason! Report every day. Fletch, seal up those despatches.

Yessir.

Major Mason is a mighty fine soldier.

Yessir.

And draft something to Captain Rawn in Missoula. He'll need to form a line to stop Joseph from linking up with the Flatheads. I don't know what forces are available in that Department. See what you can find out.

Yessir.

Rawn's a cipher, but he's the senior captain out there. Make sure you mention the glorious record of the Seventh Infantry. I've heard his wife is ill; inquire after her. I'll inspect your work in five minutes. Now, Wilkinson, get me Lieutenant Otis.

Right away, sir.

Lieutenant, I'm disappointed that your artillery failed to accomplish greater execution on the Clearwater. I had expected you to destroy or subjugate those

Indians in short order.

Yessir.

Well, lieutenant?

Sir, Joseph seemed to understand the range of our guns
> which you most unfairly demand to be as reliable as Aetna Centennial
> sewing machines; maybe in ten or twenty years, when everything will be
> more beautiful and automatic, sure, then you'll have the right to jawbone
> me, but you can't estimate my difficulties right now—all the more galling,
> d——nit, since you used to be an ordnance man yourself—you expect me
> to hit the bull's eye

almost by instinct, and he deployed his bucks exactly as close to us as was safe. Secondly—

He showed great boldness, didn't he?

Yessir.

Lieutenant, do you understand that your Gatlings may have a rough road ahead of them?

I do, general.

Well, if I were you, I'd be giving that matter my utmost attention. Because next time I'll expect, shall we say, a more sweeping performance. We're rolling out within the week.

Yessir.

You can go. Fletch, recopy the despatch to Captain Rawn as amended, and then bring me James Reuben.

Yessir. General, here he is.

Come in, Mr. Reuben. How are you getting along?

Pretty good, general. We were just fixing to ride out with the major—

In your opinion, is Joseph going home?

Do you mean Wallowa, sir?

Where else would I mean?

Yessir.

Where else would I mean, Mr. Reuben?

Well, general, Joseph would say, all this country is his, because the last treaty—

Enough. Is he returning to Wallowa?

Sir, I'm praying about this every night—

Commendable.

General, I think Joseph's Indians are hungry for camas root. His squaws were digging camas at Tepahlewam* when the war started. Then people were afraid, and ran away. Not much camas up high in Wallowa, general. Anyhow, around this time, Joseph's Indians, they like to go to Weippe. Good camas there, very good! Meet Flatheads, take a rest, I think that's Joseph's plan. Maybe then some young men ride to the Buffalo Country—

---

*Nimiputumít for "Split Rock."

How many days to reach the Flathead country?

From here, six days. I remember well. Pretty blue camas flowers, so pretty! Before I went on the reservation—

Thank you, Mr. Reuben. Do you like the Flatheads?

Yessir. Very good Indians, except for Chief Charlot.

And what's his defect?

He won't go on the reservation.

We'd better induce the Flatheads not to panic and thereby swell Joseph's host. Do you understand?

Yessir. I can ride ahead—

And run into Joseph?

General, if we go by Hangman Creek, Joseph won't—

How you go is Major Mason's affair. Now tell me this: Do you like Joseph?

No, general. No more.

He's your uncle-in-law.

That's right, general.

Are your scouts satisfied with Army life?

Yessir. They sure enjoy riding through their old places—

All right. Go see Lieutenant Bomus. He has extra rations for you. Then hit the trail. I expect you to mind Major Mason as you would your own father.

Thank you, general.

Wilkinson, as soon as Umatilla Jim rides in, verify Mr. Reuben's assertions.

Yessir.

Your boots are a disgrace.

Sorry, general, I'll—

Who's the Flathead Agent?

Peter Ronan, sir. He's said to be popular with his Indians—

That's a marvel! Perhaps he doesn't steal. Draft a despatch to him. I want his Flatheads on full alert. And he's to coördinate with Rawn, to prepare for any incursion.

I'll take care of it, sir.

Now, do Nez Perces intermarry with Flatheads?

Unfortunately they do, sir. Several of Joseph's bunch are part Flathead, so their relatives over there may want to—

Rawn will isolate them. *Entre nous,* how bad is the press?

Unpleasant, general. In New York they're alleging that you—

Yes. Read this wire:

> See *Associated Press* despatches which state General Howard's
> removal under consideration by cabinet.

Sir, I'm truly sorry . . .

What do you purpose?

Well, sir, we could correct the story.

You know very well what happens to an Army officer who communicates with newspapers.

Yessir. Wood's a clever officer, and he owes everything to you. Why not commission him to send out his sketches and whatnot, anonymously?

Thanks, Wilkinson. You're a true friend. Bring me Captain Pollock.

Right away, sir.

Well, captain, how are you keeping?

Good as gold, general.

That's the spirit! Now, what's your impression of Wood?

A very intellectual young officer, sir. He's good at writing reports.

And did he win your men over?

He drilled the recruits to my satisfaction at Camp Bidwell. And he has a knack with civilians, so thanks to him we got invited to an extra dance or two—

Nothing against him?

No, sir.

Thanks, Pollock. That's all. Fletch, assemble all the company heads immediately.

Yessir.

Are you recovered from your fever?

Yessir.

Who's more ill—you or Wilkinson?

Neither of us, general.

Don't lie to me, Fletch. I'll be demanding even more of you for awhile now, and I need you not to funk.

General, I won't funk, I promise.

You showed great initiative at Clearwater.

Thank you, sir.

And then bring me the four most energetic mule drivers.

Yessir. Company heads are all here, sir.

Men, we've defeated Joseph's treacherous allies under Looking-Glass, and driven them off.

Yessir.

We have freed the Department of the Columbia of their presence.

Yessir,

> you lying incompetent Christian gasbag; they should have hanged you after Chancellorsville. Can't even round up half-dead squaws encumbered by papooses—

The campaign has been a brilliant success thus far. We will continue as we have begun until Joseph is destroyed. Within the hour, each of you will furnish a written report on your companies' strength and readiness. That's all.

THE BERRIES WILL NOW BE TURNING RED
JULY 15

1

*T*he berries will now be turning red in the Buffalo Country, where perhaps
we shall go
  by way of the Lice-Eaters' lands,
    leaving Kamiah, where some of us once lived,
    riding farther from Wallowa, where something once was,
  past the hot springs,
  to stay awhile, just awhile, with our relatives the Salish,
    with whom we once hunted buffalo and fought the Shinbones,
  then with our friends the Crows:
    Chief Blackfoot, the *lucky man,*
    Curly and even Horse Rider
    and all the warriors whose hair touches the ground:
      brothers to Looking-Glass, who has given away so many
      horses,
      Looking-Glass, who knows the way,
    and thence to the infinite fat meat of the Buffalo Country
  —or shall we ride home
    to Wallowa, the Chinook Salmon Water, Red Owl's country, Looking-
    Glass's reservation?
Now that Cut Arm has been punished, perhaps he will tire and sail away down
the Enemy River,
    although no matter how many times we defeat the Bostons, they
    come after us again, again, like evil POWERS which never fail to rise
    up and return to life, seeking to suck marrow from our bones.

2

So we fill our pipes here by the river at Weippe,
    where our People first met Lewis and Clark and saved them from
    starving,
      and afternoon's last coolness, such as it is, shelters behind the
      thickety branches, leaves and young green hips of cluster roses;
smoking tobacco mixed with kinnikinnick, our old and young men consider what
to do,

even as the bluejays say: *Chá-á, chá-á!*
and our horses say: *Hinimí*
in this place of cluster rose's close-gathered ovoid leaves, soft, green and moist,
this place of camas and bunchgrass,
the young women drying serviceberries
while Shooting Thunder, Loon, Stripes Turned In, Toohhoolhoolsote and the Three Red
Blankets burn down every ranch that the Bostons have inflicted here upon our home
(before this summer there were none);
then we kill their cattle, revenging ourselves on Cut Arm while feeding the People;
but Sun Tied leads his wife into a shady place to massage her sore
belly
(she has now reached her eighth month)
as his sister Crystal makes grass beds for their lodge;
and in the forest Ollokot shoots twice and finally kills a
deer—Looking-Glass laughs at him for wasting a bullet—
but White Thunder sits quiet with his war-brother Wottolen; now their
griefs are visible: they have lost their dream for the other young men who
could not make themselves brave;
yet still they would ride on to the Buffalo Country if our best men agree,
for Wottolen wishes to give the People two buffalo robes for
each one that Cut Arm has burned
(Wottolen cannot fear; his WYAKIN is strong),
while White Thunder's heart lusts to steal a Cutthroat pony
whose bridle shines with German silver,
even as our hunger-fearing old women and our women whose treasures
Cut Arm devoured and who can scarcely believe in this new wealth of
meat now dig camas, although the season is late:
flowers have fallen, blue and white alike, so that death camas cannot be distinguished from what is good to eat; all the same, the
bulbs have grown larger
(time once more to Dream of WOWSHUXLUH with His shining metal eye, His squat beak and worn feathertail; watching
high on His single round leg, He knows when summer's
camas must begin to die);
Good Woman sends her daughter to help Toohhoolhoolsote's wives
—Wolf Old Woman and Place Of Arrival, scrawny grandmothers
who understand the ground—
now they are teaching her how to know death camas without its flower,
and she is grubbing up deep roots for them with all her young strength,
while Wolf Old Woman makes her laugh by telling the story of how
it was back in the days when GOPHERS used to bake camas, and
COYOTE married five GOPHER sisters, who dug Him a long tunnel
so that He could creep secretly all the way to TRAVELLER THE SUN;

then Place Of Arrival shows her how in one more MOON-waning the wild
onions and wild carrots will have ripened underground exactly here—not yet—
and presently she runs back to show Welweyas what root-lore she has
learned

> (for the half-woman, who is actually much older and should not
> now be forsaking her own mother, behaves toward Sound Of Run-
> ning Feet like a grateful younger sister)

even as Toohhoolhoolsote's wives boil up a soup of the Bostons' beef, thick-
ening it with well-cracked marrowbones, fresh camas and a little cous bread

> while fat bubbles nicely out of well-roasted cow intestines

as Toohhoolhoolsote races horses with Burning Coals, who wins and
wins with Lucky One,
and Heinmot Tooyalakekt wonders with Ollokot what kind of luck
Looking-Glass carries in his heart.

Springtime, leaving the baby to sleep in her cradleboard near Good Woman,
creeps down to the creek in hopes of killing something new for soup,

> catching a shoveler duck with her husband's dip-net:
>> —so beautiful, that bird! red belly, blue wings and orange eyes—

so that she returns singing with happiness, and boils the meat with Fair
Land and Cloudburst

> since this creature is the WYAKIN of Good Woman, who may not
> eat of it.

>> Ollokot, laughing at his brother with seeming cheerfulness
>> only, says: So it happens! First she refrains from the women's
>> lodge; then she plays with what only a man should use,
>> to which the elder chief replies: My dear brother, since we
>> have lost our country, let us at least keep our wives' affec-
>> tions. If she uses my net, this cannot harm me.
>> About that we shall see, replies Ollokot

as Good Woman, having trimmed the purple-red strips of beef and hung them
over the fire to smoke, now begins to make her sister-wife a new cap of beargrass,
since the People may be riding far, and the nights will be getting cold;

> and we await our scouts, to learn whether they will come galloping in,
> shouting that Cut Arm follows us even now;
> but still it is quiet to the west

and once the best men have sat in a circle (their copper bracelets shining in the
sun), Toohhoolhoolsote offers his smoke to AHKUNKENEKOO, then draws three
times upon the pipe.

3

White Bird says: I am grateful to the other chiefs for showing their minds. This
is good, and I hope that we can all be of one heart, now when the Bostons are

hunting us. Perhaps we can still make friends with the Cutthroats. Sitting Bull has dwelled in the Old Woman's Country since last winter, and likes the Redcoats, I have heard,

> to which Heinmot Tooyalakekt listens pleasantly, letting the pipe pass by, with his narrow dark pigtails wrapped in many loops of narrow rawhide whose irregularity makes it resemble strings of white shell-beads
>> (his dark gaze flicking everywhere, his peak of hair recently trimmed by Good Woman):
> supple in body and mind, alive, aware, almost seeming to smile but in fact merely masked in pleasantry

as Looking-Glass, flicking down his eyes, meaningfully or not, at the necklace of bear claws that he wears, seizes the pipe: Now I shall tell you my heart. Hear me, my chiefs. The Cutthroats are all crooked! You do not know them as I do,

> seeing before him the enemy whose horse is masked halfway down the neck, the mask white-beaded with red-, blue- and black-beaded overpatterning rectangled, diamonded and triangled like Navajo sandpaintings:
> Cutthroats, enemies, Lakota! They will kill us all.

Taking the pipe, Heinmot Tooyalakekt then says: My chiefs, do we fight to keep our lives? No. Hear me: We fight for this place where our fathers' bones lie buried. I would not lead my women among strangers to die in a strange land. Those who once named me a Boston-fearing coward, to them I now say: Stay here and fight beside me. We shall hide our women behind us in these mountains and die fighting for them. Better that than ride away to some unknown country.

Tossing back his round head, Toohhoolhoolsote watches them through narrowed eyes.

4

Looking-Glass says: Heinmot Tooyalakekt, my dear brother, we cannot go back home. I, Looking-Glass, am telling you! Moreover, the Cutthroats long to wipe their buttocks on our heads. Listen! I am opening my heart. Where now can we live but in the Buffalo Country? Even Cut Arm will not follow us there!

White Bird hides behind his fan of feathers. Toohhoolhoolsote is silent.

> Heinmot Tooyalakekt, whose face is dark and smooth, shining clean with light like an otter's just out of water, nearly begins to smile, perhaps, or even to agree—but Looking-Glass knows his heart:
>> This young chief, the merest camp-chief, lacks experience and cares for nothing, save only that the People do not quarrel.

So Looking-Glass,

he whom the Crows call *Arrowhead*,

cries out, waving mosquitoes away: Would you People die hungry? Buffalo meat is the best. Only buffalo meat will do,

> as smoke blows delicious from the Bostons' sizzling beef.

5

Then White Bird,
> who knows Bluecoats (if not the Bostons) better than Looking-Glass
>> —has he not watched them march day after day like slaves to their
>> bugle at Butterfly Place, and shoot their rifles badly, like children?
> and who always behaves even-temperedly
>> (to him Two Moons, Wottolen and other great men have already
>> come without Looking-Glass's knowledge, for their hearts distrust
>> the Crows
>>> whom our grandfathers fought alongside the Snakes
>>> whenever we were not fighting the Snakes),

says: My young men hungered to fight, and already they have lost heart! They have failed us and shamed themselves. Young men, listen! Young men, it is on your account that we lost our wealth at Big Water. Whatever you now say, I have small confidence in you,
> at which Loon stares sullenly ahead, his roached hair rising perfectly, his
> nineteen white necklace-loops arrayed across his breast.

My People, from here to the Crow Country we must ride for many suns. From here straight north to the Old Woman's Country is not far. Since we have quit the fight, let us ride quickly to a safe place before more of you become cowards.

Growing angry, Looking-Glass takes the pipe: White Bird, hear me. I thank you for opening your heart, and I would never contradict you. But have you forgotten when Eagle That Shakes Himself
> (he who was a chief among the Crows)

called on us to stop eating the Bostons' sugar? White Bird, you were there! He said to us: *You People are cowards. Kill the Bostons who murder you!* Had we agreed, he too would have risen up against the Bostons and joined hands with Sitting Bull. But when he rode to those Cutthroats to make peace, Sitting Bull took his life! The Cutthroats are more dangerous than the Bostons, I am telling you!

Toohhoolhoolsote the grizzly-tempered,
> who remembers from the Butterfly Place council how Cut Arm kept grin-
> ning at him with the long teeth of an old horse,
> and who now hates our young men forever
>> (through them Cut Arm lives to haunt us again),

smokes the pipe, then says: My heart does not care where we go. Let us ride where we please. This war will surely follow us. If our buffalo hunters say that the Crows will act straight, then I am satisfied. Five Wounds and Rainbow, what happened at Big Water was not your fault! Now open your hearts to us.

Yes, we both agree with Looking-Glass,
> and the Three Red Blankets are of the same heart,

while Swan Necklace yearns likewise for the Buffalo Country; he is
longing to steal enemy horses of all colors;

    although Wottolen believes that White Bird speaks straight
and White Thunder keeps quiet because Old Yellow
Wolf says nothing, while Heinmot Tooyalakekt, White
Bird and Looking-Glass all differ

and Over The Point, like Toohhoolhoolsote, has been hurt in his
heart by our woman-hearted young men who would not fight at Big
Water; he cares not where we now go

and Wounded Head would seek any quiet place to live with his
little son and his dear wife Helping Another.

Enough talking! Let us ride to the Buffalo Country.

White Bird says: Whatever you decide is good.

So Looking-Glass takes the pipe once more to say: Hear me, my chiefs! The Crows
are my own brothers. With them our People will be safe, I am telling you three times!

And Hahtalekin, who has not yet opened his mouth, draws in a long smoke and says:
Very well, Looking-Glass; you are head-chief now; take us to the Crow Country . . .

6

But Chief Red Heart, who was at Kamnaka with Looking-Glass and Three
Feathers when the Bostons attacked, now takes the pipe to say: We shall not go.
We shall ride to Kamiah and go on the reservation.

7

So it will be:

Looking-Glass, he whose dreams are as lovely as horses, will teach the young
men how to hunt buffalo in exactly the way we have always done it until now;

thus our People will become rich again,

    while Heinmot Tooyalakekt, saying nothing, knowing that their course
is uncertain,

        wondering whether Red Heart's way is the best

        (although Looking-Glass has warned him three times:
Brother, you are reckless! No matter what you tell them, those
crooked-hearted Bostons will treat your People like enemies),

cannot help Dreaming back along the trail, only for awhile:

    swimming the Enemy River on Black Mane-Stripe,

        who is stronger and more intelligent than any of Tsépmin's
horses,

        then riding up along OUR MOTHER's backbone, past Eel Place

        (where our People sometimes used to stay, just for awhile,

catching eels or digging cous),
south down the lightning-crooked evergreen cañon, where the blue
mountain-horizon lives in its jaws,
down its steep, steep gorge which is shagged with grass and split by
faraway cañon-grooves,
to the river called *Welíwe*,*
where we once had a village of that name,
and its forest, which we follow up and out of the watershed, into the
next cañon
(which snakes south across the Bostons' line into *Oregon*),
mountains widening ahead;
and now the world is meadow, with mountains on the horizon
and the smooth greenness of the grass,
the sky-bowl of grass:
Wallowa, our valley once dark with horses.
I am turning; I am turning; I am turning back;
I shall circle back.

8

And so Heinmot Tooyalakekt,
knowing better than to interpose himself between quarrelling chiefs,
tells his women,
who have been turning the beef-strips which hang in greenwood smoke,
doctoring horses,
gathering berries,
all the while sweating and steaming the white camas roots in underground pits, pouring water on the mounds, cooking them until they
blacken, then pounding them, steaming them again, smoking them over
the lodge-fire so that they will keep as well as the Bostons' hardbread
(as Welweyas looks up shyly from behind the others, anxious to
hear what will be spoken):
My lovely ones, now we have completed our hearts,
promising Springtime a buffalo liver as soon as he can make a kill
(Good Woman needs nothing,
nor Sound Of Running Feet, who—clever girl!— has already packed
a horseload of roots
—we can pound or bake them once we reach the Salish);
and Ollokot tells his wives: We shall not go to Sitting Bull,
at which Fair Land smiles in delight

---

*The Grande Ronde River. The meaning of this word is unknown to me.

because her fear was exactly this: to have her face smashed open
with a brass-studded Lakota quirt.

Yes, now it has happened that even our women wish to ride to the Buffalo
Country, where we shall eat berries from the branches without being afraid
and make ourselves new buffalo robes,

Looking-Glass's wives longing for new earrings of German silver:
the Buffalo Country is where such treasures come from—
Toohhoolhoolsote's wives delighted to learn they will soon be
gumming sweet red flesh, which is better than beef

and *Kate* pounding camas without a word, Welweyas helping her
(but when they go together to care for their horses' hooves, Heinmot Tooyalakekt murmurs to Ollokot: Brother, if I am killed, remember this: Whenever
you go into council with Looking-Glass, take care for the People! He is a good
man, but Cut Arm's treachery has addled his heart. You know that he has always been quickly angered; now he is rash. We have comforted him for the loss
of his country by making him our head-chief; perhaps indeed he will be best,
especially in the Bostons' country where he is known; but he greatly hungers
to get his own way)
as the chiefs call for five brave men to stay here for three suns more, watching out
for Cut Arm:

White Cloud, Shore Crossing
(he who can leap off a wild horse without falling),
Red Moccasin Tops, Red Spy and Rainbow—
leaving them a side of roasted beef

—while Red Heart and Chief Three Feathers depart with their
People for Kamiah

(Looking-Glass saying: My brother, on account of what Cut
Arm has done to me, I fear for you.

And I for you, brother! You are determined to wander like
wolves. You have no home; what will become of you?);

and then, gathering their horses, the People ride east, commencing that hard trail
of roots, rocks, sky, muck and fallen timbers.

As they depart their home, Toohhoolhoolsote says to his young men: I wonder
if this ground has anything to say?

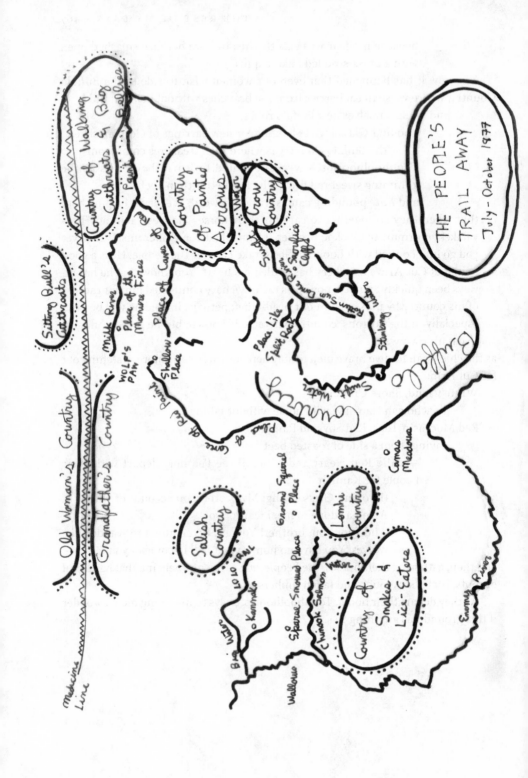

THE PEOPLE'S
TRAIL AWAY
July – October 1877

Country of Walking Cutthroats & Big Bellies

Sitting Bull's Cutthroats

Country of Painted Arrows

Crow Country

Old Woman's Country

Grandfather's Country

Medicine Line

Milk River

Place of the Manure Fires

Place of Caves

Shallow Place

Wolf's Paw

Place of Red Point

Place Like Split Rock

Small River

Sacrifice Camp

Redish Sun Dance River

Stinking Water

Smelly Water

Buffalo Country

Buffalo

Place of Ground Squirrel

Camas Meadows

Salish Country

Lo Lo Trail

o Kamiah

Sparse-Snowed Place

Lemhi Country

Country of Snakes & Lice-Eaters

Chinook Salmon Water

Big Water

Wallowa

Enemy River

HOW CUT ARM
SAW IT
July–October 1877

BRITISH POSSESSIONS

UNITED STATES

ASSINIBOINES & GROS VENTRES

SIOUX

Missouri River

Milk River

BEARS PAW MTS.

Mile's Field

MILES'S DISTRICT

CROWS

Stone River

Yellow River

Tongue River Cantonment

Custer

Massacre

Powder River

Tongue River

Little Big Horn River

Big Horn River

Missouri River

Rosebud Fork

BIG SNOWY MTS

Musselshell River

LITTLE SNOWY MTS.

Judith River

Coulson

Cañon Creek

Clark's Fork

MONTANA TERRITORY

WYOMING TERRITORY

Clearwater

YELLOW-STONE NAT'L PARK

WYOMING TERR.

IDAHO TERRITORY

Fort Benton

Fort Shaw

GIBBON'S DISTRICT

Deer Lodge

Missouri River

FLATHEAD RES.

ROCKY MTS.

Missoula

Lo Lo

Stevensville

Fort Corvallis

Big Hole

Virginia City

Bannock City

Camas Meadows

Lemhi Pass

BANNOCKS & LEMHI RES.

SALMON RIVER

SNAKE MTS.

MONTANA TERRITORY

BITTER ROOT MTS.

Clearwater

Oro Fino

Kamiah

Stranggville

Mt. Idaho

White Bird Cañon

Lapwai

Salmon River

Boise

Snake River

Whipple

WASHINGTON TERRITORY

IDAHO TERRITORY

STATE OF OREGON (1859)

Walla Walla

OREGON

HOWARD'S DEPARTMENT

IDAHO TERRITORY

49° LAT.

FAMILY REUNION
JULY 17

1

*U*ntil now all they have heard is a towhee digging through dead leaves in hopes of finding some delicious insect;
but White Cloud,

> who has fought in every battle
>> (his horse killed under him at Cottonwood, falling down,
>> half-crushing his thigh, which he healed with his WYAKIN Power),

is first to hear voices coming up from Weippe. We strip off our leggings and deer-skin shirts, and he whispers: No more red blankets! Let us not be warning them anymore when they come,

> as far away sounds the bugle.

Now we can hear their horses, and we see the Big Dust. They are speaking in our language, following our trail, so they must be the crooked Butterfly Place People

>> (their WYAKINS have forsaken them, lunging away, bunching front
>> legs like fleeing deer):

> first *Tsams Lúpin*, Cut Arm's greedy, crooked slave, who has become an
> enemy to our religion; he is devouring us as he goes;
> then Jokais and Meopkowit, who now call themselves *Kaptín Tsan* and
> *Ol Tsolts*[*] (each one has a daughter riding away with our People),
> White Thunder's badhearted half-brother Horse Blanket,
> Sheared Wolf, who now calls himself *Tsan Lavih*,[†]
> *Aplaham Pluks*[‡]
> and eight or nine other traitors,

>> those whom we set free after they fought against us at Sparse-
>> Snowed Place.

Now we see them all at once,
> carefully inviting them
>> as we lurk behind ferns in evergreen shade

and Tsépmin, whom we once called brother, comes grinningly galloping up on his grey horse. Shall we finally please our hearts by killing him?

> As they come riding up the trail we commence to aim
>> (they are as indiscreet of speech as common nighthawks).

---

[*]Captain John and Old George.
[†]John Levi.
[‡]Abraham Brooks.

2

Shore Crossing shoots *Tsams Lúpin* in the arm
>because Cut Arm has laid hands on Toohhoolhoolsote, who spoke for us
>>(I am unsteadying myself);

while at the same time Red Spy (saving his explosive bullets) shoots *Aplaham Pluks,*
>who now begins bleeding and crying:
>>—we are smiling to see the other Crooked People tie him to a
>>horse!—

and now White Cloud, holding his Winchester steady, carefully shoots
Sheared Wolf
>who falls into a thicket of wild rose. Bending low, Red Spy runs quickly
>there. From his belt he withdraws a dead Bluecoat's Colt
>>(more and more of us warriors have been realizing the worth
>>of these women's toys)
>>—at which Sheared Wolf,
>>>he who was already warned,
>>whispers: Wait, brother, I have news for the People!
>>>reaching out his bloody hands toward Red Spy,
>>>>who giggles, saying: Tell us your news when you reach
>>>>your *Heaven,*
>>>>>and shoots him in the lungs until all the bullets
>>>>>have gone:
>>>>>>*Áhaha!*
>>—Tsépmin, open-mouthed, yanks his stallion's head around, gal-
>>loping back down the trail just as he did at Sparse-Snowed Place
>>>where he began this war:
>>he has always been too crooked to make himself brave.

The bugle is blowing; the Bluecoats prepare their wheeled gun,
so we slip back into the bitter cherries and white maples where the boys hold our
horses,
leap up and ride away to tell the People, asking our hearts as we go:
>>How can we make the Bluecoats raise their arms in terror? They
>>will not turn back.

ADVICE FROM A MILITARY GENIUS
JULY 19

*V*ery good, Mason; you discovered Joseph's track. Now, how many Indians would you estimate were laying for you in this ambush?

At least fifty, general. Our vanguard was lucky to escape.

Thank you, colonel. That will be all. Chapman, what do you want now?

General, when I got near that thicket I seen Mr. Joe glaring at me, plain as daylight! And I'm pretty sure I saw White Bird—

Well, well!

I can guarantee you this, general: Them Nez Perces are so yellow, they wouldn't dare waylay us like that unless they kept an entire war party at Weippe! Now when we ride in there, general, if we can grab us some of Mr. Joe's squaws and children—

So you believe that the hostiles have not in fact embarked on the Lo Lo Trail.

I don't know about that. But in my experience, sir, them Dreamers stick like glue to their friends. So maybe while the squaws are riding forward, Mr. Joe's got the River Renegades to help him.

Is this inference, or did you in fact see Smohallie?

I don't even know what an inference is, general. With all respect, I never grew up with your advantages. My point is, Smohallie may have brought his renegades there, but don't you worry; I know 'em real good, near about as good as Mr. Joe—

You can go.

Sure thing, general.

Fletch, what do you make of that?

I have no opinion, sir.

Chapman wouldn't intentionally mislead me. He's brutal, but not vicious. And he certainly does know his Indians.

Yessir.

Fletch, wouldn't it be fine if we could bag them all in one swoop?

AMERICAN SECRETS
JULY 20

1

*W*here's Joseph now?

About thirty miles ahead now, sir. Just about at Weippe.

Thanks, Mr. Reuben. By the way, what do you think about Umatilla Jim?

No good, general.

Tell me why.

Umatillas are real crooked Indians, General Howard! Many of them Dreamers—

Is Jim a Dreamer?

I don't know, sir.

Excuse me, general—

Yes, Fletch, what is it?

Some Indians are riding in to surrender.

2

Get me Umatilla Jim.

Right away, sir.

Who are these people?

Red Heart is their chief, general. He's cousin to Looking-Glass. The other big man is Three Feathers. Red Heart says, they were hunting in the Buffalo Country, just for awhile, and when they got back to Weippe, Chief Joseph told them about the war. They didn't know nothing about that. They're good Indians, never killed anybody. They want to ride straight to their reservation and keep quiet.

Well, we don't have any reservations left. They were absent when those were being given out.

That's right, general. They say—

They're all Dreamers, aren't they? Look at their hair!

That's so,

> the squaws smiling at us as if we ought to like them,
> several braves bearing the silver medal-likenesses of bygone Presidents
> in hopes of being allowed to ride back to their hunting grounds
> (they're just like little children).

Jim, if we sent them to Kamiah, how would they get along?

Their Agent over there, he's pretty darn strict, I know. He'd make 'em be good. Cut their hair, make 'em go to church,

as Red Heart

> (canted eagle feather in his topknot, loose hair down to his blanket-wrapped breast, downpointing bearclaws circling his throat)

narrows his eyes, staring at us almost unwinkingly, one side of his mouth curving down and the other up, as if he might be ready for either extremity of fortune:

> most likely this man has lived through an apoplectic fit; his mouth reminds me of Uncle Stillman's.

Ask them if they were present when Captain Whipple tried to arrest Looking-Glass.

General, he says: Yes, they were there. He don't understand why soldiers started shooting—

Well, you know why, don't you, Jim?

I sure do, general.

How do you feel about it?

I don't feel much of anything, general.

They said before that they were in the Buffalo Country.

Yessir.

Fletch, get me Captain Throckmorton.

Right away, sir.

Good afternoon, captain. You're to convene a military commission at once. Try these Indians for the Salmon Creek murders.

Yessir. Shall I pull James Reuben from scout duty to be my interpreter?

No. Unfortunately, we can't expect the Indians to be unbiased in a matter which concerns their kin. The only white man of use is Ad Chapman, apparently. *Entre nous*, he bears watching.

So I've heard, sir.

Come to think of it, send him here.

Yessir.

Hello, Chapman.

Hello, general; I ain't seen you since yesterday.

Yes. Are you acquainted with Red Heart?

Sure am, sir. He and his bunch are real bad Indians.

How so?

Well, general, I interpreted for 'em one time at Lapwai, last year it must have been, and they kept asking me why the white people were taking their land. *Stealing* was what they called it.

And you set them straight.

General, they had their minds made up hard! Couldn't care less about the facts.

So what did they want?

O, they meant that Agent Monteith should defraud the Government, and I'll tell you frankly, general, sometimes things run pretty loose at Lapwai.

This is not to the purpose,

> but might be useful in case Monteith seeks to turn General Sherman
> against me, although I should not descend to such intrigues no matter
> what my enemies may do.

Cross my heart, general, but one time Agent Monteith paid me five dollars
cash money to sign a paper saying he'd delivered beef and blankets to the Indians,
and he never did it.

Mr. Chapman, are you familiar with this circular from the year before last? I
happen to carry it with me. Wilkinson, you know which paper I want. Yes, thank
you. Now listen, Mr. Chapman: *Clause sixteen. Agents, or others, making* authorized presents *to Indians, should have the bills witnessed by the Interpreter, with
certificate that he saw the article delivered.*

Never saw that one, general, but I guess I've signed a few blank papers in
my day—

Blank papers! My word! I'd better read to you from clause nineteen of the same
circular: *Signing or certifying vouchers or receipts, IN BLANK, is fraught with evil,
and is strictly prohibited.*

Well, general, now I know.

That's right. Can I count on you to interpret fairly for the commission?

Sure, general.

Swear on this Bible.

I swear I'll tell folks how it is, so help me GOD.

Captain Throckmorton, I expect you to reveal the true doings of these Indians.

I'll get started right away, sir.

3

Well?

General, we adjourned for want of witnesses.

And Chapman couldn't dig up anything to exonerate or convict them?

Frankly, general, he sometimes—

Well, he's the only reliable interpreter we have!

Yessir. We could get Mr. Pambrun from Lapwai.

Captain, I'm disappointed. Did you fail to reach any judgment?

Not at all, general. Red Heart confesses that his two elder sons have gone with
Looking-Glass.

More to the point, was Red Heart on Looking-Glass's reservation this month,
or was he in the Buffalo Country? He told me two stories.

I think he was on the reservation, sir.

Keep them under guard. Captain Throckmorton, come with me.

Yessir.

Captain, whether or not we can obtain witnesses to their acts, these Indians
must be held as prisoners of war for the duration of this campaign. They were with

Looking-Glass, a known confederate of Joseph's. Keep them to-night, and march them to-morrow to Fort Vancouver.

You bet I will, general! Shall I clap irons on the bucks?

That's your responsibility.

Yessir. Glad to finally clean up a few reds.

4

Who's officer of the day?

Lieutenant Wood, sir.

Bring him here.

Well, Wood, how does it feel to be in charge?

Pretty good, general.

Then you have the makings of high-grade officer. Now, Wood, until to-morrow these prisoners are your responsibility. If they escape, I'll have to punish you.

I understand, sir.

Any questions?

None at all, sir.

Wood, they cannot be permitted to roam about as they used to do. You've seen how Looking-Glass turned evil.

Yessir.

And the fact is that given the current temper of the white people, Red Heart's band will not be safe on their reservation.

I certainly see your point, general.

Finally, we need to reassure the doubters back East. They will expect us to have captured prisoners after all our exertions. Do you understand?

Yessir.

Wood, don't look at me like that! If we had infinite dedicated troopers to protect Red Heart forever, and keep him out of mischief, then we could ring him round on his reservation, and all the best to him. But *I will not have their blood on my conscience.*

5

Not a very pleasant thing, confining these redskins, who appear sincerely in-nocent:

> seventeen warriors, counting Red Heart and this Three Feathers; twenty-three squaws and children: all accounted for
>> while some old soldier slowly, carefully fashions three buffalo-skin hats from what must have been one of Mr. Joe's tipis.
>> Fletch, who grew up riding a chestnut Arab horse, an elegant animal with the typical curving neck of that breed, finds little

to praise in these confiscated Nez Perce horses. Which one
was Red Heart's? No, he's definitely not as straightbacked as
an Arabian.
Captain Pollock,
    who served quite happily on this trial commission and agreed
    with Captain Throckmorton on Red Heart's guilt,
acts proud that I am carrying out this duty with what I hope comes
off as easy imperturbability:
By GOD, Wood, someday you'll be Inspector-General of Prisons!
—laughing at me, only because he likes me
    (how lucky I have been in my superiors!)
        And now the can-makers have gone on strike in
        Baltimore.
        That city was half Seccesh anyhow. Why even
        read the paper? It's never good news.
        If you don't want it, I'll take it to Wood. He looks
        pretty bored over there.
I'm ashamed when they look at me. Red Heart offers me a smoke of his pipe;
his daughter reddens when I try to give her hardbread. Her brothers are cool to
me; well, how can I blame them? But of course the general is correct; the very fact
that they rode in here (and surely passed Joseph at Weippe) is suspicious. If we
don't confine them, they'll give him aid and comfort as they're able.
    Besides, I yearn to be promoted
        (closing his weary burning eyes, and instantly seeing again projected
    upon his eyelids the court-martial's officers sitting behind two tables:
        C. E. S. Wood, officer of the day, frankly proud of the sheen of his
        brass buttons):
            Wood showed a lot of heart at Clearwater. The
            way he crawled to that spring all by himself, well,
            all I can say is he's a credit to the Army.
            He's as crazy for excitement as that Ad Chapman,
and had I argued with the general, Red Heart's band would be no better off, while
I'd be worse off. And Joseph did burn Mrs. Manuel alive; her daughter has sworn
an oath to that effect, and Chapman asserts the same.
    Red Heart keeps gazing at me. What is he thinking? He wears a copper band
as I do, but high up on his biceps,
        as an owl hoots far away,
            the locusts singing *tekh-tekh-tekh!*
    and the moon rises.
    What's on Red Heart's mind? If I could but hear the whispering thoughts of
these Indians—
    As I have leisure perhaps I will ask Jim to teach me some Chinook, or at least

the Indian sign language, which must be a valuable accomplishment for any officer out here in the West.

What interesting faces those Nez Perce women have! I respect squaws' hard
hands, scarred in the battles of digging and flensing and pounding and dragging
and shall I say life? So why do I so rarely seek their contact but turn to the velvety
touch of idle hands? O, their lovely texture, and the cream and rose tints and
graceful movement when Nanny lays her hand upon my arm,

> and now for some reason the necklaces on Red Heart's daughter
>> (whose name delicacy forbids him to ask Umatilla Jim:
>>> the two sons, however, are called Nenetsukusten and Teme-
>>> mah Ilppilp)
> remind him of the cross on the black velvet band around Grace Howard's
> neck, and the way her throat pulses so sweetly when I compliment her
> piano playing;
> the instant he laid eyes on this fetching young squaw he knew what he
> would be doing to-morrow night on his return to "D" Company
>> ("Taps" and the evening gun and then when we all lie down
>> in the dark on our rubber blankets . . .),
> because three years ago, when he wrote away to Doctor Jacques of
> the Central Medical Institute on Chestnut Street, who can treat
> spermatorrhea, or sexual weakness, especially when caused by se-
> cret habits of youth
> and also longstanding cases of gonorrhea, syphilis, orchitis
>> (he even offers adult male visitors a private tour of his Mu-
>> seum of Anatomy),
> Wood,
>> who when he was a cadet used to cut off the cylindrical brass
>> button over his heart to give to his lady of the minute at Flir-
>> tation Wall,
> read the circular and took the medicine, but it turned out there was
> no help for cravings as bestial as his.

6

In the morning, the prisoners are despatched to Kamiah en route to Fort Vancouver,

> the general in private conference in his tent:
>> And a copy to General McDowell, with the usual salutation.
>> Have you got that, Wilkinson? All right. Now this will be a tele-
>> gram to General Sherman. Are you ready? *Majority of hostile
>> Indians have fled by Lo Lo Trail eastward to Buffalo Country.
>> Thirty-five men, women and children have voluntarily surren-
>> dered themselves. Gen. Howard is in pursuit in a direct line . . .*

and Jocelyn's four-man detail now shoveling earth over the sinks:

> And then, right before the outbreak, one of White Bird's Indians came by Chapman's place and offered him double for an old Navy pistol.
>
> So what did Chapman do?
>
>> ... called out the Maryland National Guard.
>
> Whipped him out of there, so he says.
>
>> That's chickenshit. I say the National Guard is chickenshit.
>
> What do *you* say?
>
> Well, he ran away at White Bird Cañon, he turned tail at this little ambuscado of Mr. Joe's, but you and I saw him flying down the hill at Clearwater, as brave as George Washington. He's a puzzler,

the squaws, who evidently had expected different treatment, weeping pitifully as the guards form them up into a convoy,

> and Wood, although now relieved by Parnell, stands watching,
>
>> hoping that Captain Pollock will not call him imminently
>
>>> (really I should lie down for an hour),
>
>> writing in his diary: *Musings on the unhappy people. Thoughts on the Indian as a man and a brother. Inability to fuse with the white man. Similarity of some of these men to the Roman type,*

as one of the younger women, sobbing, removes her beaded ornaments and gives them to Umatilla Jim, asking him to find her little daughter somewhere about Kamiah and present them to her

(I'll bet that villain will sell them to a souvenir hunter!)

and an old man cuts bead ornaments off his moccasins as a remembrance for his wife:

> significant that neither of them will trust Chapman or James Reuben! And I lacked the brass (except on my buttons) to offer myself!

Now the men are paired off, the women and children allowed to straggle along any old how,

no need for irons until Lapwai:

> a hundred degrees to-day and sixty miles to walk; I wonder if white children would fall out of the column and die?
>
> But let me restore to mind that picture of Joseph's squaws squatting down in the grass at White Bird Cañon, stripping and scalping our dead boys and very occasionally clubbing a dying trooper in the face:
>
>> Chapman swears that's what they do.
>
>> I must ask the general.

No, boys, this is serious. Now the railroad
men have struck in Pittsburgh.
It's them Irish Catholics that done it.
I'd sure rather be out here.

Just as any significant quantity of silver can bleach the gold with which it has
been alloyed, so horror and shame now begin, but only begin

—for like Red Heart's squaws, he cannot yet entirely dislodge himself
from a thicket of mere astonishment—

to dull down Wood's lustrous notions

(I suspect that after the campaign the general will never speak of this:
—what if every campaign *must* comprise such operations?
Anyhow, we didn't kill them),
although I never imagined that we would be setting out
on our endless soldier-trails to become keepers of innocent Indian convicts.

There are American secrets which I must now begin to gather like snowberries
in pale half-dozens. If my brother officers only possessed the courage and kindness to withstand my own questioning and explain to me why this is right, I would
be grateful. Perhaps I'll approach Fletch,

after I get promoted

—Wood not at all wishing to resemble that forty-nine-year-old major about whom Captain Pollock regularly soliloquizes:
married to some pretty little Clarabelle, the "Belle of the Em-
barcadero," who has espoused herself six times now and
sounds ready for a seventh, probably with the quartermaster;
so the major came down with a case of melancholy and got confined to the hospital,
staring and staring as if waiting for the cottonwood leaves to
turn yellow,
and Pollock first swore at him, then told him (rightly as it seems to
me) to flux himself of that Godd——n whore
as I must flux myself of sentimentality,
not that I care to be like Perry or Umatilla Jim
(although who knows what Jim thinks?)

In the strengthening sun-glare our soldiers lead them steadily down through
the cottonwoods to the wide river,

which is wide and dark grey-brown with a narrow shore of white stones,
and just before the column loses itself in roses and thistles, Wood sees that old man,
exemplar of the Roman type,
who cut the beadwork off his moccasins now glancing over his shoulder at Kamiah,
or perhaps past Kamiah at the dome of yellow-grassed hill between forest ridges
(do we march that way to Weippe? I should ask somebody in Mason's
bunch

or wait until the general permits me to examine Colton's map);
then they disappear and reappear:
    another old squaw is evidently weeping now, her head as heavy as a branch of
    elderberries
        —unpleasant to see, so he turns away, sickish from lack of sleep, peering
        (just to see something other than the prisoners) at the slanting red hills,
            the nauseating scree-threatened trees always hiding his view:
            Where are the enemy? It's so hot;
                    he feels bewildered by the chokecherries and birds; the sun is
                    burning his back; his eyes sting with sleeplessness
and Pollock's batman, Wally Scanlon, strolls up with a black eye from
fighting, laughingly wheedling him: Please, lieutenant, would you do me
a kindness and plead my case with the captain so I don't have stable duty
forever?

Pertaining to Mrs. Theller's Bonnet
July 21

—and that d——d Trimble, just because he's a brevet major, always tried to
lord it over me; Theller saw through *him!* And because he abandoned from the
command at White Bird Cañon and I never said a word, he can't stand me. I would
have let him alone: Jesus; nearly everyone else funked! But he means to bring me
down. Well, that don't scare me. I ought to call him out some night when we get
back to Lapwai. We can settle it with fists. But if he wants to be a shit and testify
against me, I'll show him daylight. I'm watching him. He'd better not go courting
Chapman. Chapman's the one that fired on Joseph before I gave the order. Then
he turned tail. He was yellow at White Bird, yellow at the Clearwater, and from
what Mason tells me he was no d——d different out there by Weippe. No wonder
I saw him with Trimble. They're the same kind. Actually, Chapman's worse. He
ought to be gelded and locked up at Leavenworth. He's influencing the general
against me. He's poisoning this campaign. He killed Theller, and he knows it. If I
told the general about that Blackfoot squaw he knocked up right here in Kamiah
who miscarried, maybe on purpose when he went back to his Umatilla bitch, that
would sure make his nigger-loving Christian eyes pop out! Soon as we get back to
Lapwai I'm going to look up Mr. Pambrun, because he's seen her come whining to
Chapman, wanting money. He'll be my witness. Maggie, that's her name. Why any
white man would fuck her is beyond me. She stinks, like all reds and niggers. And

that other Umatilla cunt that pooped out five of his brats—JESUS CHRIST!—if I lined her and Maggie right up before the general, that would be one hilarious day, especially once my wife got wind, GODD——n *her* because she's the reason I'll never see Delia untying her snow-white bonnet.

Hey, you, Chapman.

What do you want, colonel?

How's Maggie? You going to show her off to the general? I'll bet he'd enjoy learning why two squaws are better than one.

I'll get you, colonel.

Why don't you?

   —his vision of vengeance as fine as a young Nez Perce woman leading a decorated horse.

THEY CALLED ME *DREAMER*
JULY 22

1

*W*ood, can you take dictation on horseback?

I'll do my best, sir.

Then you're promoted to aide-de-camp.

Well, thank you, general. I—

All right. Captain Pollock will give you what you need.

Yessir.

Your handling of Red Heart's bunch was on the money. Wilkinson informs me that you were kind but firm. The worst thing one can do with Indians is give them false hopes.— No, Fletch, I'm busy just now.

Yessir.

I once made that mistake with negroes. It caused them great disappointment. Of course, I believed everything I was saying. What do you think about negroes?

I think the negro is the most genial being on earth.

Well said, Wood! Well said—

When we were at the head of the Column of Triumph for President Grant, there were so many loving black mammies with pots of hot coffee . . .

And biscuits? Nobody can make biscuits like an old negro woman!

O, yes, general, those were lifesavers, I should say, for it was frostbite weather; all we had were our white silk gloves . . .

Fine. You're to take sketches of the battlefields and Indians as you have leisure,

Wood. Those will be valuable to historians someday. Your draughtsmanship comes highly praised. A pupil of Robert Weir, were you?

That's right, general.

Why did you never show us your sketches when you visited? Mrs. Howard would have been extremely interested.

Well, sir, you're always so kind, and I, I, it's embarrassing to impose myself, especially since you encourage my literary efforts as it is—

And commendable efforts they are, Wood! I wish I had your facility—

Thank you, sir.

Did I tell you that

      some quality in your sudden smile reminds me of who I might have been

      had my father not died so early? I hope not. Shall I merely mention that a cousin of Mrs. Howard's happens to be acquainted with your father? We discovered that by accident, while you were in Alaska.

      Must never give you any hint—

No, sir, you didn't tell me . . .

A GODfearing man, and in his day a credit to the Navy, from what I've heard.

Thank you, sir.

In the year we've known each other, you've mentioned him less than half a dozen times.

General, he drinks.

I'm proud that you've defeated that temptation, Wood.

I've been warned by his example—

Good. Now I do need to ask you something else. This never needed discussion in the earlier course of our friendship, but as you ascend the ranks, you get more frequently surveilled by the public. You'll soon find, Wood, that fame is not identical with approbation.

I understand, sir.

So. Your West Point record is extraordinarily profuse in demerits, isn't it?

I'm afraid that's true, sir.

In your class you were fourth from rock bottom, in fact. Soiled collar, swinging your arms after drill, that sort of thing?

Yessir, just like that—

Did any cadets make a vendetta against you?

Well, sir, not exactly—

I know what that can be like, Wood. Feel free to confide in me.

General, they always used to tease me—not maliciously, you understand—and sometimes they called me *Dreamer:*

      a heart-thud impelling his general to remember Smohallie: surely fo-

      menting the Columbia River renegades *at this moment*

          with his SATANically glittering eyes:

              the land has always belonged to us

          (can't Wood imagine what *Dreamer* connotes to me?)

—and even that slyly craven Homili, who hates his reservation but pretends to play the clown; even *he* owns Smohallie for a friend and so-called priest and what Joseph did to Mrs. Manuel, incited by Dreams—to think I trusted in his honor!—

If they haven't bashed her skull in yet, she must remain the concubine and burden-chattel of some foul brute and ever under Joseph's hatefully magnetic eyes.

All right, Wood. I understand. Mrs. Howard and I are perfectly fond of you as you are. But you're to be a well turned out soldier now. No more dreams, except off duty. Do I have your word?

That you do, general, and I thank you sincerely for this opportunity.

Now go see Captain Pollock. I think he has a first-class saddle for you—

2

Wood undoes the burning hot buckle of his cavalry belt and pisses, remembering Nanny's dark upturned glance. To-night if the general doesn't need me I'll write her that I've been promoted and

her brown hair down to her knees: If I could run my hand through it right now and her not wearing a stitch:

my toothmarks all over her buttocks, her tongue in my mouth, her wedding dress crumpled on the floor—

but *no*, she'll say:

Pickets out!

Honestly, Wilkinson, I don't care about those railroad strikes.

Our wedding night: Nanny, uplift your face and kiss me:

Yessir:

O, Erskine, I am yours and you're my darling *dreamer*—

but what if a woman can perceive when her husband is already *experienced?*

Perry, you rode to Weippe last year. Show me how we ought to forward our supplies.

Frankly, general, there's not much of a road—

But if we assault Joseph *here*—

Maybe Nanny won't mind.

O, but she will.

Yessir.

And when I saw Theller's Blackfoot squaw in her muslin dress decorated with red and yellow horses, I would have given everything to

Dearest Nanny: ~~This afternoon General Howard informed me that I~~

(. . . my future prospects now even wider than Grace Howard's bell skirts! O, if Nanny ever dressed up as quaintly as that, I'd undertake to tell her:

Yessir.)

~~I almost hesitate to inform you of the following, for fear that you'll think me~~ ~~conceited. To-day I~~

What if Sitka Khwan gave me the venereal? But I don't suppose she had anything, because she didn't behave like a prostitute at all. Three months now with no symptoms, so aren't I safe? I intend to keep

my portrait in the locket around Nanny's neck

(do they truly cauterize it with mercury?)

and that rancher's widow whose hair was yellow like balsamroot flowers in early July

(but that was harmless, she being a widow, and lonely, even grateful; we parted friends and gleeful accomplices:

they'll never catch us out):

Summing up, I feel *pure*

—which is to say Wood feels hopeful (as so many young men can be in every general and specific way) that continued indulgence with himself, the general and this campaign, will produce some quasi-magnetic alignment of convenience and true principle—because life (I mean Progress) has never yet repudiated his desires—especially now that he has been raised up (Wilkinson was the first to congratulate him), but

Mrs. Howard's smile would freeze so hard and ugly if she were apprised of my adventures; I've seen it happen when the general disappoints her. What is a love that will not forgive? When she turns that face on the general, I've felt afraid of her. Hard old woman! To me she's never said an unkind word, perhaps because I didn't marry her.

After Nanny becomes my wife, I'll make a resolution never to think about Sitka Khwan again. But if I'd stayed in Alaska I would have married that squaw.

Mrs. Howard would step backward, into the kitchen, or rush to the bedroom to shut the door. The general would say: Get out, Wood. We'll never be at home to you anymore.— And sisterly Grace, I can't even bear to

Sitka Khwan peers round-eyed and round-faced at me over her naked shoulder, her black hair flowing like smoke down her throat, her cheeks smudged with smoke. Suddenly she smiles. Has the

Hoonah chief given her to me forever or for one night only? They were all sitting at my side when the chief said something and they laughed and their

with mercury.

Theller's squaw smells of whiskey, buckskin and sweat

and Sitka Khwan smells of salmon, smoke, cedar and sweat

(once upon a time, Wood appeared to please her in his uniform with the two columns of glowing buttons. Hiding his
face in her lustrous fishy hair, he began frantically to lick her
throat).

3

Where's Ad Chapman?

Here I am, general.

Can you vouch for Jack Carlton?

Yessir. A right good lumberman—

Fletch, send this Mr. Carlton to Lewiston at once. You'd better ride to-night and return before our move out. He's to engage fifty men to precede us on the Lo Lo Trail and cut timber so that our wagons can get through. Will he need a voucher from Lieutenant Bomus?

I'll get him one, general.

Chapman, that's all. Mason, what did you wish to say?

General, it'll be no joke to supply ourselves all the way to Lo Lo—

Well, GOD disposes—which reminds me, Fletch: Fetch Lieutenant Bomus. Mason, don't forget to verify your Morning Report. Wilkinson, send a rider to The Dalles, for some Warm Springs scouts; bring them to Colonel Wheaton, double-quick. And, Fletch, I want some fierce, angry, Nez Perce–hating Bannocks from Fort Hall. Draw up a despatch at once. All right, Wood. This will be for Major Shearer.

Yessir. I'm ready,

as Sitka Khwan squats to piss, giggling. Nanny would *die*. Enough about that.

Do you know how to dateline our despatches?

Yessir. All from here will say *Headquarters, Department of the Columbia, Camp Alfred Sully, Idaho Territory.*

From now on I'll expect you to insert all such information on your own initiative.

I'll remember, sir.

I don't doubt it. So. *Major: In a few days after Major Green's arrival, I propose to have the country hereabouts thoroughly scouted.* Wood, are you keeping up?

Yessir.

Meanwhile if you can cross the Salmon with about thirty men, chosen from your two companies, and search the country beyond the river, picking up small parties of Indians or their families . . .

Got it, sir.

And, I said *of Indians or their families,* yes, *and procure information taking the same to Captain Whipple commanding the reserve at the Croaesdale farm . . .*

Yessir. Is the arm troubling you?

No. The trouble, Wood, is *this:*

> Lo Lo's utter absence from Colton's most up to date map, which offers nothing between Clearwater and the Montana line but green or pink blanknesses.

4

What is it now, Mason?

It's private, sir.

Fletch, Wilkinson, go improve yourselves somehow. Major Mason will fetch you back. All right, Mason, you have my ear.

General, that so-called Major Shearer—

Get to the point.

He wrote me this letter, sir, complaining about Colonel Perry at Cottonwood. Shall I summarize?

Since you must talk about it . . .

Well, general, he claims that Perry funked it. Lost his head, put Shearer in charge of thirty-eight men down in two rifle-pits and abdicated all defense. Shearer eventually demanded a Gatling from him and got it. On the next day Perry suppposedly expressed helplessness when Joseph's Indians were cutting the volunteers to pieces, and refused to do anything. Shearer also holds a grudge against Captain Whipple—

You did well to show discretion toward the two officers concerned. Tell me, is there anybody whom Major Shearer approves of?

Well, sir, Mr. Chapman, whom of course he calls *Captain* Chapman—

But Chapman disapproves of *him.*

Now there's a backbiter, sir. Turns on anyone who exposes his lies—

I've asked you this before: Was Perry over-cautious during the Modoc campaign?

No, sir. After that patrol got ambushed, and a third of the men were wiped out—

When Gillem got relieved of command—

Exactly, sir. It was dangerous, all right. Just about like now. And Perry never exactly hung back—

Mason, tell me straight. After the Lava Beds, White Bird Cañon and now Cottonwood, do you retain full confidence in Colonel Perry?

Yessir. That Shearer's a conceited spite-monger who shouldn't be allowed to impugn the Army—

And in your view Chapman's equally unreliable—

General, you *know* he's the worst! If he hadn't fired on Joseph's white flag, those reds might all be on the reservation now, and the ringleaders hanged—

Thank you, Mason. That will be all. O, hello, Wood. Let me borrow your note-pad, please. And then go collect Bomus's readiness report

while I write wearily lefthanded, in penmanship whose loops I've learned to render so eerily neat that they'll never seem like mine:

Major: Regarding your communication of the 26th instant to Major Mason, I'll do you the one-time courtesy of disregarding it. No citizen, no matter what may be his situation, should lower himself to disparage conscientious officers who endanger themselves and their troops in order to relieve him from Indian outrages. Very truly yours, O. O. Howard, Brig. Gen., U. S. Army.

Now seal this up and address it, Wilkinson. It's to Major Shearer. O, there you are, Bomus.

Forgive me, general; I was down there at the wagon park, because Lieutenant Otis's wagon—

Bomus, do you have enough salt?

For what, general?

To issue as extra rations. The boys might be eating dead mules before we're through.

An interesting thought. Well, yessir. Do you expect us to go far?

We shall see. Now can I do anything for you?

Everything's pretty bright so far, sir.

Thanks for saying that. You're one of my finest officers. Don't hesitate to ask for help. Trimble, Perry, your men stink; make them to bathe in the river while there's an opportunity.

5

Then Chapman comes prancing up without permission, drooling tobacco juice:

a nasty fellow; I ought to tell him off more strictly

—although he's one of GOD's creatures, lost and ugly as I am—but to abandon his squaw and children!—and then if he and Shearer are seriously intriguing against my command . . . !

—but have his allies been found out?

All right, Lieutenant Howard, there's your Daddy, and I have to say—

Lieutenant Howard reporting, father.

Thank you, Chapman; leave us alone now. Well, Guy . . .

How was your ride in?

Excellent, father, and I met so many great characters I wish I could have sketched them. They all asked me how soon we'll whip Joseph. This one old miner, what a face! If I'd had that special drawing-pen of Wood's—

How's Mother?

She baked you some honey biscuits, which I brought, but Mrs. Perry's a real cross to bear; she won't stop weeping. Mother's near about sick of her. And Grace finished knitting your socks; I have them here—

Well, well, my son. Glad to have you with me . . .

Where's Joseph, father?

Halfway to the United States! Should be a picturesque campaign, in those high forests. You'll be my aide-de-camp. Speaking of Wood, I've just appointed him to the same post, so you'll be working at close quarters with him, Fletch and Wilkinson.

O, Wilkie! Has he done well?

He has, Guy, but you're not to quiz me like that. Now, do you need to refresh yourself or are you ready to work?

I'm ready, father.

That's my son! Ready for anything!— You know I'll treat you more strictly than the others.

I understand, father. When do we set out?

As soon as Mr. Chapman's friend has rounded up fifty lumbermen from Lewiston.

Mr. Chapman thinks the world of you, father—

O, he does? Watch out for him. Now, Guy, it's Harry's eighth birthday.

I remember, father.

I hope you'll send a thought his way to-night.

Of course I will, father.

A relief he never quarrels with Bessie—

They adore each other! You should see him carrying her around the house—

Yes. Well, we can't miss *her* birthday at least.

What a joker you are, father! Imagine chasing that silly Joseph for another two months! Between us, how long do you give him?

Entre nous, I suspect he'll cross into Gibbon's Department. But when he comes down the Lo Lo Trail, Captain Rawn will be waiting for him. I've already telegraphed ahead. This should be over in two weeks, with GOD's help.

I won't tell anyone, father.

Of course you won't. Now go find Major Sladen and bring him to me . . .

ACCIDENTS DO HAPPEN, SIR
JULY 29–31

1

*H*ere's Lewis and Clark's map. At Weippe there's a large meadow of this *quamash* or *camas* that their squaws like to dig. Chapman believes we'll find Indians. We'll try to trap them there.

Yes, sir.

Have you sampled it?

It's not bad, sir. A white root . . .

Lewis and Clark also ate prairie dog at Weippe and found it quite delicious, just as good as squirrel.

Yes, sir.

It's mid-July when they start to dig up their camas, so this should be more or less the season when they'll be following that habit, wouldn't you think?

I should imagine so, sir.

Send me a scout. Ah, it's Jim. At your ease, soldier. How's life?

Very good, general.

What's the country like around Weippe?

Camas marsh inside forest.

What sort of forest?

Hackmatack, Ponderosa pine, spruce, fir—big trees, general! Sometimes it's very wild. Good chokecherries there. Serviceberries . . .

Can we ambush the bad Indians there?

No-good poison ivy. Sometimes the wild rose has thorns—

Draft me a map of the place, Jim. O, I see. Right. You draw very well. Now show me where you'd ambush people who are digging camas.

Squaws.

That's right.

You want to kill their squaws, all right, we kill 'em.

No. I want them to surrender. Then I'll put them on a good reservation.

Whatever you say, general.

You can go. Sladen, I'd like your opinion of Jim's map.

Looks true to me. He's behaved real clever and honest.

Anything else?

Not much detail in this part, sir.

Very observant. In fact the marsh extends all the way down *here*.

Sir, it's a wonder the way you can remember the lay of a land you've never seen—

O, me! No man could equal Sherman at that study. As faithful as a daguerro-type! Well, Bomus?

Jack Carlton has thirty-nine lumbermen on the go, general, and I've got them all vouchered.

Good. Officers, inform your men that we'll sound "Reveille" at four a.m.

They'll be ready, sir.

And make sure Company "D" looks to their horses this time. Very shabby yesterday—

Yessir.

I'd thought better of Captain Pollock.

Yessir.

Captain Jocelyn.

Yessir.

Did you hear what Jim said just now?

I did, sir.

He thinks we're going to murder their squaws.

Accidents do happen, sir.

You're officer of the day to-morrow. I'm holding you responsible to make sure they don't. Not to-morrow.

Yessir. Plenty of Indians all over the country, sir.

Right. You get your boys ready. Major Mason, is everything on the square with you?

O yes, general.

Thank you, major. Lieutenant Fletcher, take Lieutenants Wood and Howard to the perimeter and show them how we arrange our pickets. You two newer officers had better pay attention. We're entering real Indian country to-morrow.

Yessir.

Now, Wilkinson, before we turn in, I need you to prepare this despatch to Colonel Wood* in Portland.

Yessir. That won't take but a quarter-hour, and then if you like I can—

Tell me, how's your spot of fever?

O, not bad, sir. How about you? Does your arm want cleaning out?

It's all right. Now what were you proposing?

If it would spare you trouble to dictate a letter to Mrs. Howard—

Yes, it's been some weeks now since we set out from Lapwai, hasn't it? Poor lady—

That's right, general. Thirty-eight days.

I hope we can wrap this up before Joseph crosses into Gibbon's Department.

That would be most convenient, sir.

We may be needed to put down these railroad strikes.

Yessir.

---

*No relation to Lieutenant Wood.

Sterling antagonists, these Nez Perces! Sometimes I nearly feel the old thrill—

Yessir. They certainly do know how to murder and run.

Well, you finish copying that despatch and I'll write Mrs. Howard myself. After all these years she's learned that it's no good complaining about my lefthanded penmanship!

I'll have it ready momentarily, sir.

Thank you, Wilkinson. And keep an eye on that fever. The Army needs you.

Yessir.

Swivelling his attention to Portland, he permits himself to remember the house on Tenth and Morrison where to-morrow come late morning, with John, Harry and Bessie off at school, Chauncey long at his clerkship, Lizzie will be sitting at her high-castled loom in the sunniest corner, overseen from the mantel by the oval drinking-water-basket (now put to merely ornamental use) which one of our good Christian Indians wove for her out of beargrass. I pray that James is writing home faithfully, because that makes Lizzie so contented. (He's "cramming" to become an engineer.) And in the rocking chair Grace will be darning socks, trying to keep her mother from worrying about this campaign. After we get Joseph (so it appears from certain intimations of Major Wood) it may be necessary to reëstablish our household by the Vancouver Barracks. Lizzie will not be happy.

2

Truth to tell (Wilkinson having educated himself into being a close reader of his commander's miseries), the arm-stump does annoy, thanks to a certain smoky dawn years away from victory, the foe fusillading us as they have been doing since 5:00 a.m., and our side sadly singing:

John Brown's body lies a-molderin' in the grave—

Who was John Brown? Nobody ever knew—not even that bedraggled widow, so they say. He must have been unspeakably grim, mad and wicked—but he sacrificed himself for our African brethren. I have not done this (not yet). I perceive the right and must stand up for it no matter what my enemies say—but am I brave enough? I think so. How I long to show OUR LORD (and Lizzie, Charley, all of them) the deepmost color of my courage! All the same, who would have imagined that difficulty would be my ease, drudging my bread, my own tears my wine, sorrow my happiness? Did my father's early death make me so, or was it always in my blood? And did old John Brown calcify entirely to mercilessness in the performance of his duty, or was he sometimes touched with private tears? Please, FATHER, don't let them see mine. O dear JESUS, Whose Cross I kiss, take my hand now; let me be Your younger brother as together we ascend this hill toward death. And You, FATHER, I thank You that bravery has proved my best and most sacred joy. Don't let them see, *Amen.* Let me be the first to follow every order wise or reckless, so long only as it is just.

I wish to-day I could look upon James in his mother's arms, and Guy and Gracie dressed up for church. And Lizzie

(whose baby will come very soon now, more easily than James did, I pray),
yes, and Lizzie—

> Now, see, they got their rifle-pits there and there
> and there, and then felled trees—
> All right, colonel.
> So we're gonna punch on through down this-
> away—

Whoah, Nathaniel! That cannonball sure did skip like the
DEVIL!
General enjoys to kick 'em when they're—

Well, boys, we're going to reënforce the first line. General French has called for
help, apparently.

We'll give it our best, sir.

That's the spirit! Now, once we cross the railroad track, we'd better look out.
They're—

> and a still heavier rolling fire of muskets as Miles curries Excelsior, whis-
> pering to the nervous horse, while Charley salves Lightning's saddle-
> sores with good white lead and

General, they're all coming at us!

Without skirmishers, I see,

> training his field-glass on that dark stand of timber around which they
> must ride

> (Charley's thoughts corked up tighter than a bottle of new matches).

That shows commendable knowledge, but after all, it's their terrain. All right,
now; form your line—

> *Ready on the line.*

Fire at will.

That's a fresh regiment, isn't it? Perhaps one of the Mississippi—

Fire!

A smart "Reveille," Charley! But what a pity to fight on the Sabbath! Miles, are
the boys ready to go?

Thirsty for blood, sir!

All right.

Sound "Boots and Saddles."

Yessir.

General, the enemy's falling back.

I can see that. Send Colonel Miller's regiment forward. Cross should return
into reserve.

Yessir.

> Sound the move out.
> Let's beat 'em down, boys!

His brown horse shot through the shoulder at once, he leaps off and mounts
the grey, his brother following on his last reserve animal, the "zebra."

John Brown's body lies a-molderin' in the grave—
> Got him in the belly.
> > Look out; they'll see the sun on your field-glass—
John Brown's body lies a-molderin' in the grave—
But his soul goes marching on.
Charley, you'll lead the Sixty-first as well as any man.
> > *To arms!*
I'll do my best. GOD be with you, Otis!
> > > *To arms! To arms!*
Praise His name. Good luck, brother—
> > > > *To arms! To arms! To arms, in Dixie!*
He himself rides ahead of the Sixty-fourth, crying: *Forward!*
Forward!
To Richmond!
> shells screeching and whispering, pines and oaks crashing together, feel-
ing rather than hearing the army at his back, Charley long vanished into
the smoke, and Miles cantering almost at his shoulder:
John Brown's body lies a-molderin' in the grave—
> > *To arms! To arms! To arms, in Dixie!*
> Watch out!
> > *Advance, the flag of Dixie!*
> > *Hurrah! Hurrah!*
and the sizzling rifle-balls and
March!
> *Lies a-molderin' in the grave—*
> > *HURRAH! HURRAH!*
and moving forward finely toward French's line, the grey as intelligent
and ready to please as a thoroughbred,
> *Hurrah! Hurrah!*
> *Hurrah! Hurrah!*
a Mississippi rifle-ball strikes him warmly in the forearm.
Forward!
He rides on, Miles now well en route with the despatch to Cross, rides on, the
pain commencing to grapple at him, its skeleton fingers digging maliciously into
his wound, the grey shuddering oddly, and he rides on, rides on, toward the enlarging bearded mouths of the Confederates who sorrowfully scream:
> > *Advance, the flag of Dixie!*
> > *Hurrah! Hurrah!*
> rides on toward Richmond, may it please GOD:
Hurrah!
Otis, Otis, the zebra's killed, so I— You're hurt!
Yes. Would you kindly bind up my arm? Thank you, brother.
How bad is it?

—so hot this morning, and the fair oaks of Fair Oaks uprooted—what a crime! Isn't it enough for men to kill men? I feel sickish, I suppose because

John Brown's body lies a-molderin' in the grave,
John Brown's body lies a-molderin' in the grave,
John Brown's body lies a-molderin' in the grave,
  But his soul goes marching on.
    Hurrah! Hurrah!

Not bad.

Otis? GOD bless you, Otis!

    To arms! To arms! To arms, in Dixie!

Don't worry, Charley boy. Now run back to the Sixty-first, quickly. *Go now.*

Forward!

Forward!

  His soul goes marching on,
    one glove white, one red, and Lizzie, Lizzie:
    To arms! To arms! To arms, in Dixie!

Tell Brooke's regiment to lie down.

Yes, sir.

  and a shell whispers overhead while another smashes down to the left, ruining a fine grove of pines, and

Good work, gentlemen! We're breaking their line. Isn't that the Seven Pines crossroads over there?

To arms, in Dixie!

Yes, sir. How's the wound, sir?

Fine. So those must be our tents from yesterday. A shame the men left them . . .

Watch out, general! They're kneeling and firing at us—

  and a storm of musket-balls:

To arms, in Dixie! Dixie! Dixie!

Forward!

Forward!

Halt them here. Down on your bellies and return fire.

Dixie!

Halt! Get down! Fire at will!

  and the hideous chuckling of a cannonball rolling between the trees; sometimes when a ball strikes the road and comes whirling toward him he likes to jocularly kick it, if it is not coming on so rapidly as to do him an injury and

    Dixie! Dixie! Dixie!

  and

What's going on in the rear? Are they falling back?

I got me one!

Lieutenant, sir, can you get us covering fire over here?

Fire!
General, are you—
Where's Miles?
  Dixie Dixie Dixie Dixie Dixie Dixie
General—
Yes. Find me another horse. I'm afraid you may have to shoot the grey—
   Dixie Dixie Dixie Dixie Dixie Dixie Dixie
    Dixie Dixie Dixie Dixie Dixie
     Dixie
      Dixie

General, your arm—
O, so they shot me again. Well, they haven't shot it off.
General, you shall not be killed.
Please take your hands off me, lieutenant.
Yes, sir.
       Dixie
Now help me up, if you would. I appreciate your—
    O! O—o—
Is he dead?
Yes, general.
He gave his life for mine. Said I should not be killed . . .
Yessir.
What was his name?
Lieutenant McIntyre, sir.
All right. Is that Colonel Barlow over there?
That's right, general.
  Dixie Dixie Dixie Dixie Dixie Dixie
General—
Bring him to me.
General, your arm looks pretty bad. How are you holding up?
A trifle faint. Take command, colonel.
       Dixie
       Dixie

Of the whole brigade, sir?
Of course not; Cross has the seniority. Just this part . . .
Yes, sir.
Colonel Barlow, stand your ground and . . .
    How the South's great heart rejoices
     At your cannons' ringing voices!
Yes, sir! Major, escort General Howard to the rear.
Right away, sir.
Looks like the enemy's giving way.
   His . . . soul . . . goes . . . mar-ching . . . on.

That's so, general. Lean on my shoulder if you want to.

Where's Cross?

Dixie

Dixie

I don't know, sir. I think the surgeon's over this way.

I wonder how bad this is? This major's so solemn, I may need to convalesce for a day or two, but bloody effusions never do signify one way or the other. For instance, a scalp wound—

—managing, sir? Because if you—

Cross is in the clover now; he's always longed for this. Lizzie would surely take my hand and

Lizzie, Lizzie! Your shining throat's as sweet as Jersey milk.

Quite a number of wounded men.

Business as usual, sir.

Right you are!

Advance, the flag of Dixie!

Hurrah! Hurrah!

Where's Barlow? I don't see him now—

Just keep on, general. Don't worry about a thing. We're nearly there.

And tell Barlow—

Otis!

And Miles must find out from Cross—

Well, well, Charley. You, too!

—your handsome, narrow, sloping face (the mark of a Howard), blue and sweating; I pray the LORD: Spare him as You see fit, for Mother's sake; but if she is meant to be left with only one son out of us three, then may Rowland become her perfect friend. I know Lizzie will do for her whatever any daughter can.—

Where is it?

In the thigh; a moderate wound—

You look like a comical old grandpa, using your scabbard for a cane like that! And that foxskin robe over your arm, what a thespian touch—

Please, Otis; please lie down—

Let me bind up your arm, general. Good. Good. Ah, I see. Orderly, get the general into a stretcher.

and then

Good afternoon, Doctor Hammond. How's Charley?

I'll examine him next. Now would you like a nip of anesthetic? At times like this, even a temperance man—

No, thank you. Kindly get on with it.

Hold his arm to the plank. This will be painful for a moment. There. Good. Again. You're a very brave man, sir. Most fellows flinch at least. Just a bit more. O, I see. I'll have to cut it out. Sir, take a deep breath. Here it comes. This may smart.

Good. One more little pinch now. And one more. (Clamp that, orderly.) Well, general, the collection of metal in your arm is positively eclectic! The first wound was caused by this pretty little round Mississippi bullet. And here's the other one, quite an elongated leaden projectile—

Shaped like a minnie, I should say—

Quite right, general.

I suppose future warfare will . . .

Why don't you lie down again, please, general?

Everything will get more automatic, and . . .

Yessir.

Once we standardize our calibres, wars won't drag on the way they do now.

Yessir.

Beautiful and automatic . . .

General, your arm is broken. You need to rest. Please lie down here at once and I'll bring Doctor Palmer.

All right . . .

> *Dixie*
>
> and flies descending brassily: bravery without prudence or mercy—
> shiny, gruesome, hateful—tickling me, drinking my blood. Has it been
> definitely proved that they carry typhoid? Charley must be very
>
> > General?

General?

O, good afternoon, gentlemen. Or is it still morning?

> Your arm had better come off, sir.

All right, go ahead . . . Happy to lose only my arm . . .

Not before five p.m., general.

Why not?

Reaction must set in.

Perfect. For every action, so he was taught at Bowdoin College, there's an equal and opposite

> agony,
>
> > corrected first by the tourniquet, biting whiter and whiter, then another
> > stretcher, and the amputating room with its corner-mound of hands, legs
> > and bloody bandages humming with flies, Miles, bless him, now me-
> > thodically cleaning the teeth of the doctor's saw with that silly handker-
> > chief of his, being like all dandies a great believer in hygiene, as if he, as
> > if, and Charley praying at my side, I hope for poor Lizzie,
> >
> > > Guy being already a tough little man, aged six, who will surely suc-
> > > ceed in life, whereas Gracie
> > >
> > > > —if only Lizzie could be softer with her!—
> > > >
> > > > *but what if* God *takes Lizzie?* In that darkened bedchamber
> > > > where she's now lying in, with no chloroform for her when the
> > > > baby comes, what if the Angel of Death has already

Dixie

but Gracie came easily. Dear JESUS, if it be Your will, please
spare Lizzie awhile, for the children's sake. Visit Your will on
me as it pleases You, but

Charley and Rowland will

Lizzie my Lizzie my Lizzie my

Gracie

Dear LORD, how it stinks in here!

. . . a-molderin' in the grave . . .

while little James will never know me. I wonder what he'll become
(he's near about as quiet as they say I was)

and the new one still nameless—I pray for an easy birth—and
Lizzie,

Charley's lips moving rapidly, Lizzie my Lizzie (did we beat back John-
ston's attack?), and then my HEAVENLY FATHER, help me to bear this—
how fine that I am not afraid!—

Miles gripping my arm fast to the blood-rotted greasy plank—unforgettable friend!—and forgive us *now* this day, *this day,* the other patients
screaming as always O GOD, but I will not, O, no, o, not me, *no* and O *my*
JESUS.

Breathe this chloroform now, general.

3

Rather a sullen rain, general.

True enough. Well, let's get about it.

All right, sir. *Let's go; headquarters across the river!*

Forward.

Forward!

Major Mason, I expect the entire column to be in motion before five.

We'll make sure of that, sir.

and

between trees and stumps the pallid half-tents tenuously announce
themselves, in one of which Captain Trimble, his temples clenched with
fatigue or something worse (may this pass from me, O LORD), his breakfast completed and his company in Lieutenant Parnell's practiced hands,
should for a fact be initialing the muster roll, or, better yet, he ought to
be strolling indefatigably through the drizzle this very minute, terrifying any stragglers whose oilcloth awnings and soaked bedrolls remain
unpacked, but instead he takes a bitter swig of quinine, courtesy of everyone's friend Ad Chapman, who lent him this round black bottle after
"Reveille," then takes a five-minute vacation first to worry in a civic-minded
spirit about the railroad strikes and then reread the new-formed Grand

Army of the Republic's circular calling on our soldiers and veterans to hold every Congressman's feet to the fire until we get the appropriations we deserve, Perry's defeat (inferior numbers, undertrained) being a case in point:

> *Wakesh nun pakilauitin*
> Jehovan'm *yiyauki—*

And Lieutenant Ferguson has been pooped out after since he was grazed by Joseph's bullet. We ought to return him to Vancouver,

but the Godd——d Copperhead Democrats *wanted* to spread us thin so that we'd pull out of the South and they could reënslave their niggers as they are in fact doing, not that I care,

> Blackie rolling up his rubber blanket as the rain runs into his collar
>
> > (he cannot shake last night's bad dream of his Fidelia with that hard look on her face when she is squinting into the sun, and her skirt so straight and narrow down to her ankles, and those half-dozen brass buttons leading my eyes down from her throat to her bosom as she stands there with her hands behind her back, acting so cross even though I sure haven't done nothing)

as Captain Pollock explains to the intellectuals of Company "D": Well, boys, ever since Joseph fooled away our time just like those Modocs did, I for one have been contemplating execution of his stinking savage ass!

while

> Doc, warping his hat down, waxes an arm's length of thread, humming "Yankee Doodle."

Would you care to come under this awning, sir? There's still a good half-hour.

Thanks, Fletch. Wood, have you produced any sketches for me?

Yessir. Here's the first one: "U.S. Troops Crossing the Salmon."

My word, how atmospheric! It brings me straight back to those grim hills down by Camp Theller, and I almost seem to see that golden grass! And there go our men, very small in that vast country—excuse me, what did Chapman call it? *The wrinkled land,* or some such . . .

Yessir.

What's your opinion, Fletch?

Wood's caught it exactly, general.

Thank you both.

And those pine-guarded stony bluffs remind me of my home in Maine. Very impressive, Wood! Now, the thing is, during that operation we were badly misunderstood, especially back East. The press didn't realize what we accomplished. So

I'd like to see something with more victorious associations. Keep at it, Wood, and when you get it right, I'm sure we can get it published. It'll do a world of good for the Army.

Yessir.

Meanwhile, go over the Morning Report Book, because Captain Jocelyn has made two errors. See if you can find them. Now, Fletch, where's the chart?

I'll unroll it, sir:

> Colton's older map showing better than the new, in beige and pink and
> green, the approximate haunts of our Bannocks, Snakes and Nez Perces,
> although perhaps these ranges have been a trifle indrawn, for the conve-
> nience of future settlement.

Thanks. You see, Fletch, at this rate we can't stop Joseph before he enters Gibbon's Department.

Yessir. Shall I prepare another despatch to remind them?

It had better go direct to Sherman. Are you ready?

Now I am, general.

The Indians are reported reënforced by Smohallie's River Renegades since our victory of the eleventh and twelfth at Clearwater. In another month I shall be able to make clean work of the entire field.

Very good, general. Another month?

We've disappointed him already.

I take your point, sir.

It would be ridiculous if Joseph got past the Army again.

Yessir. Have you had dealings with Colonel Gibbon?

An enthusiastic officer, and quite a sportsman, too, almost like General Crook. Well, I don't suppose the map will help us with to-day's snail's inch. Roll it up. Now are you tired? Take a rest if you like. I may as well answer some letters.

Sound "The General."

Yessir,

as Captain John and Old George sit watching us, smoking kinnikinnick with James Reuben,

who because *blood will tell* may be our best hope for the Nez Perces:

Captain John's father cleaned up pretty well as a ferryman when the Gold Rush came to Lewiston, and the other seems equally enterprising, so far as I can judge,

while Umatilla Jim rides silently into the rain, hunting Joseph again. I must say he shows more pep than our Nez Perce scouts, even including Reuben; Monteith did well for once

(he's probably writing Sherman, earnest

toward discrediting me, but I must not judge him without cause).

But we need to get this scouting on a more organized footing. Some officer subordinate to Mason—

Do you need me for anything, sir?

I'm fine,

which is to say past fresh, thanks to that arm of mine, not to mention more nightmares of hateful Indian eyes (at my age one must expect decline), all the same, I know that I can go on and *on*, unlike this nearly unblooded, fresh-faced young Fletch, well-meaning though he is, whose canvas suit remains still nearly white and who therefore should

Take a rest while you can.

Thank you, general, but I don't mind a little secretary duty.

All right then, and thank you! Ready? *Dear sir, your kind letter is received*—yes, Wilkinson, what is it?

A volunteer and one of ours came to blows over a woman, sir. The soldier pulled a knife—

What sort of woman?

Well, sir, you know.

When was this?

Just now, general.

Was she injured?

She ran off screeching hearty as an opera singer, so I'd say not—

Who's at fault?

Sir, I'm afraid the volunteer was drunk—

One of Captain McConville's?

Yessir.

Drum him out. Trace the source of the liquor and report to me.

Yessir.

Now, the other man, whose is he?

Belongs to Captain Winters, sir. He was at our prayer meeting yesterday—

All the worse. Keep him in irons until Mason decides his case. Wood, you're to instigate the court-martial when we bivouac to-night. I'll expect your report to-morrow by breakfast, countersigned by Captain Winters, and also by Captain McConville, assuming that McConville can write his own name. And on the march I'll quiz you to see if you found both faults in Captain Jocelyn's Morning Report. Wilkinson, oversee the teamsters and rank the companies in order of readiness; report before "Boots and Saddles." Lieutenant Howard, go now and take James Reuben's verbal report. Insist on it; he's not to start without permission. Now, Fletch, just finish that letter in the usual manner, and I'll sign it later. This next one goes to General Smith at Washington: *Dear General: Please see if you cannot give* D. J. Richardson, *the bearer, something to do . . .*

and the stink of wet wool, flaps down on the commissary wagon, raindrops as thick and black as Mormon crickets as the muleteers tie canvas covers over the wagon bows, and

> *Dearest Nanny*
>
>> (writing secretly like a naughty schoolboy, his project hidden from the general and Fletch by the immense covers of the Morning Report Book, which he already comprehends perfectly):
>
> *I have never done anything unkind to you* ~~*or even done anything you told me not to do*~~*. If in a time of strain & weakness I told you things which you never should have known (altho' I think that you are intelligent enough to have surmised them already, whether or not you admitted to yourself that you did), still, you ought not to judge me so harshly for speaking words which, it surely seems, will not be acted upon.* Do I sincerely mean that? Whoever I truly am I hope to discover through my actions. That must be why I'm fighting Joseph. But I do feel something like remorse about Red Heart
>
>> although the following passage (long since memorized) from his Kent's *American Law* once again succeeds in consoling him:
>>
>>> *Every man is, in judgment of law, a party to the acts of his own government, and a war between the governments of two nations is a war between all the individuals of one and all the individuals of which the other nation is composed.*
>>
>> I suppose we would have done the same thing to Looking-Glass if he hadn't gotten away. And rightly, too.
>>
>> Anyhow I didn't have the power to stop it.

That's right, Fletch. O, hello, Mason.

General, Chief Black Otter just rode into Kamiah with half a dozen bucks and their families. They claim to be good Indians.

Who's their head-chief?

Looking-Glass, sir.

Arrest them all. Thank you, Mason. Fletch, are you ready? *Endorsement:* <u>*Francis Mills*</u> *was a good soldier and deserves your consideration.* That's the best I can honestly say of him. Perhaps slightly better than I ought . . .

> *Do you truly believe that people can help their feelings? If I was culpable in revealing them to you, still, I made the best amends I could.*
> ~~*I kept the promise I made to you and*~~
> ~~*I would have kept my promise to you, but, as you know*~~
> Will it go on raining forever?
>
> Is Fletch looking at me? Thank GOD that lynx-eyed Wilkinson's momentarily away!
>
> I could surely use a swallow of whiskey. Wonder if Ad Chapman

has some? Better not ask. Well, in a week or two, when we're back
and I get leave to ride to Lewiston—
>Sound "Boots and Saddles."
>Yessir.

~~I have never~~
~~I have always~~
~~I am still doing my best endeavor to keep my promise~~
I

>>long not to count for anything, to be nothing but a good sol-
>>dier, expending myself in the service of this general, so that
>>I'll never be called on to
>>>uproot the guidon or

Do as you think best, dear girl. My feelings ~~remain the same~~
~~will never change are entirely different and must remain so until you~~
>>>Shoulder arms,
>>>the sky growing as pallid as a snake's belly
>>>and Perry stroking the hard sloping shelf of Diamond's
>>>forehead:
>>>>You're the best GODD——d horse I ever—

>>Although sometimes I simply hate her! LORD forgive me—
have scarcely altered, you cheating bitch! *I am proud of them because you are so pure & good, but you are not in any way responsible
for my welfare or future actions.* ~~Should you continue in your present course with Mr. Tracy Gould I shall kill you and him.~~ *You will
always have my*
>>>drizzly dawn, as dark as a sweaty buffalo's back,
>>>and

The LORD *hath opened His armoury, and hath brought forth the weapons
of His indignation: for this is the work of the* LORD GOD *of hosts in the
Land of the Chaldeans. Come against her from the utmost border,* and
>>>Sound the move out.

Move out!
—groaning of wheels,
glassy almost-echoes of hooves in mud
and the squeaking boot-treads of our slouch-hatted infrantrymen,
>*Left—left—left my wife and seven small children behind me.*
>*Now you've got it, d——n you, keep it—left—left—*LEFT!
weary ones:
>>steady men, blacklisted strikers, escapees from the Silver Panic,
>>careerists, Indian-haters, bugle-lovers, wife-beaters, would-be
>>*squaw men* of both the virginal and the syphilitic subspecies, for-
>>mer Secessionists, future deserters, superannuated firemen from
>>the Baltimore & Ohio Railroad

(salary: fifty-five dollars a month in 1873, thirty a month
in 1877)
            d——n you, keep it (don't let the general hear!),
unemployed tin millers from Pittsburgh,
officers who have cheerfully weathered snowstorms in Dakota dug-
outs on half-pay,
and rotund Major Mason, whose sad, bearded, longfaced look must
have once resembled our general's,
Pollock, then Perry and his new accuser Whipple,
Sladen, greasy-haired, disheveled, sweaty, stinking, his chin ringed
round with beard, his dark hair wet on his forehead, his trousers
ripped: the rain brightens up his chocolate horse but scarcely improves his disposition;
and Trimble, who actually is not so weary (ever since he was a boy,
and saw glory in the yellow stripe which descended a captain's grey
trouser-leg, he wanted to be a soldier),
            Jocelyn, of course, whose politics must have always been as
            easy to point from the shoulder as his good old breechloading
            Sharps;
then blue-eyed Captain Miller, the hero of Clearwater, as cool as a
stagecoach driver, smoking his pipe and faintly smiling as the rain
runs down his pale beard,
and stone-broke miners, immigrants, wanderlusting boys,
            Can't enjoy every minute of life.
            Not hardly, sir!
                (Maybe now we'll finally see some excite-
                ment),
whose pale canvas frocks, darkened by the rain, can get no wetter than
they have been all night; now at least these men will be warmed by sweat,
            the sky as dull as German silver,
a hundred ten paces to the minute,
beautiful and automatic:
            Glory, glory, hallelujah—
                picture windows for Fidelia,
                and the customary ingratitude of our Republic.
The happiest man by far is Ad Chapman, whose eyes are shining nearly as huge
and bright as the freightyard lanterns of Pittsburgh,
            next comes Guy, who means to show what he can do,
            although Wood is still pretty tickled about his promotion, longing all the
            better to act and believe.
            We won't catch them to-day and we won't catch them to-morrow.
            I'll wager we'll be chasing them a good month, 'cause I heard that
            Injun say to Captain Whipple—

Glory, glory, hallelujah—
    muffled sour walking-music from the bugle
and officers disheartened by their men's unfitness and jealous of
their own old brevet ranks.
    Yes, Mason, what is it?
    The advance guard can't fan out as ordered, general. The trail
gets so narrow ahead—
    All right. Send Lieutenant Fletcher forward with the appro-
priate instructions. No, Wood, about that you need to ask
Doctor Alexander. I'm surprised nobody told you. The casualty return originates with him.
    Glory, glory, hallelujah—
And all on account of our Christian General, who's more credulous
than a child!
        His truth goes marching on!
        Left—left—LEFT,
           northeast toward Weippe, losing ground
           against the enemy, half-sick with sleepless-
           ness, mud-heavy, fearing ambush, clammy
           in their half-motley uniforms:
           slow as a fucking covered wagon cavalcade
           of lazy know-nothing civilians and whining
           old women who never stop complaining
           about the stink of the Big Dust.
It must be here that the loneliness of the Indian country of which
we have merely commenced to take possession, and at that so nominally that nothing but violence will save our claims from being
laughed away, begins to march along with us, very quick and correct in its movements, although uncouth in the gaze and teeth it
turns upon us, proposing to nibble us up before we notice, our desire consequently being to ride away from here, but now as long as
we continue forward, everywhere we go will be again here in the
dying golden grass of what is not yet America even though it will
certainly become so, which is why we pursue Joseph as far as we
must, our Springfields ready with a round in the chamber and our
faces fixed as we seek earth stained by his sign, riding east now
toward our dear United States, the general watching us without
imparting anything but affable trivialities; we will carry Joseph to
the gallows, and if that isn't good enough, we will kick him down to
Hell. Wheaton, Trimble, Perry, Mason and other officers who took
part in the Modoc War know this loneliness all too well; for it took
the form of this or that comrade's desiccated carcass, tucked neatly
into some irregularity in the Lava Beds, and not only mutilated but

also thoroughly stripped, for the Modocs enjoy to wear U.S. Army shirts, while their squaws do well enough with dresses they've robbed from white women. As for Mr. Joe and his d——d reds,

They don't amount to much, now, do they, Doc?

Just shut up and march.

There you are, Wood. The soldier in trouble is a Private Johann Holzer. Apparently he brandished a dagger but didn't use it. Captain Winters informs me he's never been in trouble before.

Thanks, Wilkinson. How are you holding up?

Fine, of course,

brushing away raindrops as long as the buckskin strings on the sleeves of an Indian shirt.

Are you hinting it's not good to be Christian?

Naw.

If we're not better than the Indians, we wouldn't deserve to fight them.

Of course we're better than *reds,*

our chain of command angling down in a long, gentle diagonal, just like a horse trace,

Doc recruiting Blackie back to full effectiveness with a sip from his cocaine bottle,

and Colonel Perry always picking on me and Lieutenant Wilkinson trying to sniff out my whiskey and this mud no more solid than ten outhouse turds.

So after we whip these Nez Perces, we should get a holy Joe to come in and teach them right from wrong. That would be the Christian thing to do.

Let's sing a sweeter hymn now, boys! I'm itching for a happy tune—

No.

Why not?

'Cause this ain't no pleasure trip.

Back so soon, Jim?

Yessir.

Where's James Reuben?

Well, colonel, he's out thataway.

But not you.

No, sir.

You're in his detachment.

No, sir. I'm on right flank. And Captain Whipple, he told me—

What sign?

Couple dead dogs, not fresh, and some lodgepoles left in a hurry, like they was—

Where'd you get that pony?

Well, colonel, Mr. Joe must have lost it.

That's a thirty-five-dollar pony at least. Near as good as a racing-horse.

I don't know about that.

About that, *sir.*

Sorry, colonel.

Jim, someday I'm going to see you hanged.

Anything can happen, colonel.

Get about your d——d business. Anyhow, what *is* your business? No, don't tell me. Just get out of here. You make me want to puke,

> and until the end of my life,

>> d——d rain tickling the back of my neck, fat white drops dangling on the brim of my cap, then tumbling down onto Diamond's mane which sure is wet enough already—how I hate the clinging of these cold wet sleeves and this GoDd——d rain and sonofabitch Mr. Joe above all, for *I will remember,* O yes

>>> (and my d——d wife demanding to know why I can't make more of myself);

> I will remember the ride from Norton's at the general's side as we looked down into White Bird Cañon, the yellow and blue folds of that hateful land and Theller lying across his horse's neck, cloaked in flies and

> and now this Umatilla Jim (blurred in the rain) skulks, skylarks and pretends to look sorry

>> *(I will number the hairs of your head).*

Yessir.

> So if you want to keep your bones inside your skin and your scalp on your head, then listen to me. The way you are now, you won't kill no Indians. Now here's what you're gonna do.

> O, quit it, Doc. Leave the kid be.

> What's it gonna be, boy? Him or me?

> Tell me what I need to do, Doc.

> All right. First thing is, save your strength or you won't be no d——d good. Now the reason you feel so punk is you didn't get no sleep. And you didn't get no sleep because you didn't wrap yourself up right against the rain. Now, Blackie, the way you wrap yourself up, you prick two holes in your blanket and—

Anybody want a smoke?

All right.

Sure.

Thanks, Guy.

Why, this is hundred percent tobacco.

You bet it is, Fletch,

> and I know too well that all of you are awkward with me because no matter whether I act contrary to my father or imitate him, I express a false position, but then am I supposed to do nothing?

Guy, you're a wonder! But you'll be sorry when this is gone.

Come on. How long can it take to whip Joseph?

Let's bet.

I got a twenty-dollar goldpiece says it won't be till September.

O, cut it out. That's passing ridiculous.

What do you say, Wood?

> Watch out for Wood! His father was Surgeon General of the Navy!

Being so long away, I won't venture to—

Lieutenant Otis is a gambling man. He wagers we'll drive the reds into Gibbon's Department and be quits.

My father will never leave it like that.

All right then.

Well?

Two men have already fallen out, general.

Bring them to me,

> and he overglances them almost with pity.

Meanwhile his great double column rides and marches on, the wagons heavy with ammunition, our Gatlings screeching wheel-dirges on their too-wide caissons, sticking in and out of mud, all cargo boxes more or less steady on the mules' double-cushioned *aparejos.*

> *The bold dragoon he has no care*
> *As he rides along with his uncombed hair.*

4

> *The bold dragoon he has no care*
> *As he rides along with his uncombed hair.*
> *The bold dragoon he has no care*
> *As he rides along with his uncombed hair.*
> *The bold dragoon he has no care*
> *As he rides along with his uncombed hair.*
> *The bold dragoon he has no care*
> *As he rides along with his uncombed hair.*
> *The bold dragoon he has no care*
> *As he rides along with his uncombed hair.*
> *The bold dragoon he has no care*
> *As he rides along with his uncombed hair.*

The bold dragoon he has no care
As he rides along with his uncombed hair.

5

The bold dragoon he has no care
As he rides along with his uncombed hair.
The bold dragoon he has no care
As he rides along with his uncombed hair
   in America.
The bold dragoon he has no care
As he rides along with his uncombed hair.
                    Glory, glory, hallelujah—
Yessir. No, sir,
        left—left—LEFT,
            all but Chapman and the scouts now tiring
                (although Perry, for instance, never gives a d——n how
                he feels),
            their anxieties closely crowded in, like the ovoid foliage of the
            cascara buckthorn
                (for what if Mr. Joe were laying low right here with all his
                villains, and their rifles cocked and aimed at us?
                —although I have confidence in our reds; they're
                    the ones who'll get shot first if they miss the trick),
            and the weariest troopers outright jealous of the Mount Idaho
            volunteers who are not only exempted from this march but can
            even ride back to Looking-Glass's village whenever they feel like
            it (in between raids and harvests), burrowing for Indian treasures:
                Peter Minturn, that genuine character (and a hundred
                percent Tilden man), loves to tell how he set to digging
                up an old grave for souvenirs, the beads of an unstrung
                necklace curving around in a crazy arc within rotting
                deerskin so that at first he believed them to be teeth in
                a decaying human jaw, and then he blew the dirt off
                them and saw that some were fine old hornpipe and
                others were elktooth, obsidian, blue glass; for several he
                got a dollar apiece in Lewiston; Peter repeats this tale
                every afternoon when Ad Chapman rides in, because
                Ad's the greediest man alive; nothing's jollier than to
                spite him with news of money he might have made,
            and the leathern shoulder-slings of their carbines darkening in the rain.
The hope of final victory
Within my bosom burning,

Is mingling with sweet thoughts of thee
And of my fond returning . . .

—to Nanny, who will be trilling to herself while she waits, arranging white roses in a bowl. What is it that translates women into such foreign creatures? When I see a squaw naked, she grows more akin to me than any white woman, although how could she possibly, this member of an alien race?

        I wonder if I could make Theller's squaw feel good? I'm sure I did with Sitka Khwan,

                Wilkinson humming a hymn as the tar-bucket swings under Red O'Donnell's wagon and the general believes in me! I want to do whatever I can for his success, and be a shining part of his machine! So what if I never lie down in a dry bed? I'm stronger and stronger!

And when I take Nanny to be my wife at last, and on our wedding night she presents herself to me in bed with not a stitch on

        I fear she'll insist on blowing out the candle. Awfully hard to imagine, for instance, my mother's nakedness, while any squaw with whom I stand face to face becomes potentially undressable, because

        The bold dragoon he has no care
        As he rides along with his uncombed hair,

            following the off-key bugle calls to misery or death, hoping that Reuben will soon make contact with our reds, while Nanny turns away,

                although I'm so tired I'm near to forgetting her name, Nanny Nanny Nanny; I've so underslept that I might spew, Perry's glaring eyeballs keep glowing behind my eyelids like evening suns—I need to ride this off!—but I'd rather sit in the saddle and dream my way back to Nanny,

                    all the way back to the rear of our column, whose faint clashings resemble the sound of tin-cone janglers along the bottom edge of a Sioux squaw's strike-a-light pouch,

pulling her white dress over her head, because she is alone
        (except for Mr. Tracy Gould),
so if I could even rest my chin in my hand for an instant
and then close my eyes,

        for I long however selfishly to lie down under the wagon cover of the supply train, just for an hour, with my head on a flour sack, rocking, rocking down the trail, with the rain pelting canvas overhead, resting my back, closing my eyes, with Nanny somehow beside me,

and lie down with her, who now seems to be
showing me her white roses in a bowl, but never her white buttocks in the
strawberry leaves, because she won't, certainly not if I ask it of her incau-
tiously or too soon; she will turn away and go indignantly into the house,
left—left—LEFT.

6

The bold dragoon he has no care
As he rides along with his uncombed hair,

raising high our flag, scorning all hindrance to our American idea.
No, sir, at last report Mr. Joe's not returned to Weippe.
That must mean the Lo Lo Trail.
Afraid so, general. James Reuben's Injuns are on the case to
ensure they don't double back—
If they did, it would be through *here.*
That's right, sir, if the map can be trusted.
Next time that Umatilla Jim rides in, have him look it over.
Find out how well Chapman actually knows this country.
Pretty well, sir, so he claims.
What do you mean, Wilkinson?
Nothing, sir,

when in fact Wilkinson believes Chapman's attitude toward this campaign to be decidedly frivolous, his actions at the Battle of White Bird Cañon to have been
deleterious if not outright reprehensible (although
Wilkinson is far from denying Perry's responsibility for
that contretemps), and will henceforth make whatever
good faith effort he can to keep Chapman away from the
general, or, failing that, to weaken his ascending influence over the general, or at least to remind and warn the
general of the dangers of men of Chapman's type.

Now what about Jack Carlton?
He's widened the road about fifteen miles past Weippe.
That's all?
Afraid so, general. Apparently his bunch are terrified of am-
bushes. Shall I ride forward and stir them up?
Send Chapman. You write the note. Keep it short and stern.
He's to cut ten miles a day, or I'll advise the Government not
to pay him.
I like that, general!
And tell Fletch to prepare a despatch for Major Shearer; I
need to verify that his Indians are still quiet.

Right away, sir.

I'm guessing it's *stone* quiet at Mount Idaho with Joseph gone.

Yessir.

Afterward, ride back to Captain Spurgin and secure his opinion about cutting a road along *here* to ambush Smohallie if the Renegades come after us.

Yessir. Do you think the Gatlings could get through?

No. But under pressure Spurgin or even Otis might improvise something.

Yessir.

A steady rain.

Yessir.

Believe it or not, Wilkinson, the Renegades do remain a threat. We'd better remind the command at Lapwai . . .

The bold dragoon he has no care
As he rides along with his uncombed hair.

What's your name, soldier?

Well, general, they call me Doc.

How old are you?

Forty-nine, sir.

Where do you come from?

Laramie, sir. Or thereabouts—

All right, soldier. Keep it up,

disliking the man's brutal face

(Sladen, do you remember the way an Apache strikes a match on the sole of his bare foot? This man could have done so on his forehead! What a character. I'll point him out to you.

(Yessir.

(How are you holding up?

(Happy to be in the saddle again, sir.

(That's the spirit! By the way, Sladen, when would you say it was that that bold dragoon song became popular with the Army? It's quite a pleasing tune, really.)

The bold dragoon he has no care
As he rides along with his uncombed hair,

the arrested men shambling at the rear of our column, poor Fletch still a trifle green (he'd better visit Doctor Alexander again),

Captain Trimble jealous of Wood's former superior Captain Pollock (whom the general has always indulged to so remarkable an extent that many of us officers disdain him as a professional favorite), and yearning to punish Colonel Perry for the deaths of his men at White Bird Cañon, but longing still more to sight on those Indians in their salmon-hued deerskin shirts;

Wilkinson, who has heard, although he will not so far impugn the dead as to believe without proof, that Theller was a lifter of skirts, now wondering, as does his general, how the Battle of White Bird Cañon would have turned out had Theller not been substituted for Lieutenant Bomus, upon whom he now looks with a friendlier eye;

General Sherman's despatched and telegraphed presence overtowering us all like the flagpole in a lonely pairie fort,

and Joseph leading me a creditable chase, o, me—how will I catch him? When I do, I must write a note to Mrs. Theller

and Lizzie,

the sweet smell of sticky laurel,

Them Injuns burned women alive at Norton's ranch. I heard it myself from Mr. Chapman, who knows 'em as well as any white man—

And I seen what they done to our fellows at White Bird Cañon. They cut their heads off and their arms was torn off in pieces,

and will Mrs. Manuel still be alive, or have they taken turns with her and then knocked her over the head? GOD of our fathers, lay Your hand on the head of this captive, forsaken woman in her trouble, and should it befall me to set down my life for hers, as I would cheerfully do, comfort Lizzie in her affliction, and help Guy and the younger ones to bear it; O my GOD, permit me to show these Nez Perces reason before they commit more murders, *Amen.*

AND PERRY CONTEMPLATES THE MOUNTAINS
AUGUST 1

1

*G*eneral, sir, we found another cache of Indian supplies down thataway.

Burn it.

Very good, sir.

My word! Look at all those Indian trails.

Yes, sir.

You heard him, soldier. Dig up that trash and touch fire, doublequick.

Yessir.

Hard and dark like camas but it must be meat—

'Course it is. Lemme smell it. O LORD, ain't you ever seen dog meat?

How would you know?

How would I know? I was at the dog feast for Red Cloud we had back in Laramie. We could have poisoned a heap of savages then, except for that d——d Quaker policy.

Count on Doc to know it all. Looky, boys! He's eatin' it!

And you should, too. Gives you strength—

We'll get there exhausted, and then Mr. Joe'll be gone again.

They've gone to our right.

Yessir.

Mason, where were you ambushed?

Up thataway, general, right after the trees get high.

And your scout died on the spot?

No, sir, we carried him back a ways and buried him that night.

Commendable. Well, well, so this is Weippe:

bluebunch wheatgrass preening itself like a greenish-grey peacock, camas,

buffalograss flattened down by the Indians and grazed down by the horses.

Yessir. See, Joseph burned down that ranch—

When this is over, the owner had better file a claim with the Government.— O, it's Umatilla Jim! Well, soldier, what have you turned up?

General, I looked at that chart Lieutenant Wood showed me, and there's a place by Oro Fino where I've seen 'em camp; it's called *Timí-map.* I rode all the way out there. But no bad Indians in sight, not even Smohalla—

Timmy map. What is it?

General, in English it's—

General Howard, sir, the artillery's stuck.

How far back?

Only a quarter-mile, sir.

Jim, return to your duties. Now, Lieutenant Otis, what precisely do you mean by *stuck?*

Sir, the wagons—

Guy, see if you can extricate the lieutenant from his difficulties. That's all. Beautiful country, isn't it, Captain Whipple?

Yessir,

as some of our other good Indians,

James Reuben (his wrist-wound now bandaged in flannel), Old
George, Captain John and Umatilla Jim,

now beginning to ride forward on scout, turn back to gaze at him, evidently in hope or expectation of some modification to their orders, and
without knowing why he remembers two Edisto freedmen in faded,
stinking rags torn at the knee, wide-eyed, their lips parted with silences
coming out, their eyes fixed on him in hope and patience, asking for no
more than to keep the places they have earned;

then our flankers find another of Joseph's castoffs: the old horse's nostrils
pulsing feebly as if he understands

when one of Bomus's bunch takes aim, to deny the Indians any benefit:

pim!

and Red O'Donnell,

who reigns over a thorough-brace mule wagon with platform
springs,

sadly spits.

Perry, did you ever pass this way with General Crook?

No, general, but for all I know he's hunted this far out.

Someday I'd like to bring Mrs. Howard to see this.

Yessir.

When the Pacific railroads shall be completed, this camas prairie will not be
despised. These wicked Indians have loved these broad acres, which they have not
been wise enough to cultivate.

Yessir.

Gonna bring that steam drill out on the job,
Gonna whap that steel on down—

Best hog wallow I ever did see. Won't take long to root up all them camas
bulbs.

Doc, you said there'd be blue flowers just like a lake.

Well, they're all bloomed out.

Now they've shot down rioters in Reading. Sent
out the artillery . . .

Shut up. We've got enough trouble right here.

Captain Pollock's hoping we'll spy color on this march.

He's a hoper, all right.

Well, there's a contact-metamorphic deposit up thataway. I
can tell from the—

Well, does that mean gold or not?

Beats me.

Lieutenant Fletcher, sir, that Umatilla Jim has lassooed
one of Joseph's ponies. He wants to know, can he have
two horses?

Tell him to shoot one, general's orders.

Yessir.

Will he get sullen?

No, sir, he don't never make trouble.

What's going on, Fletch?

O, one of our scouts was getting greedy, general.

And you kept him in line, did you?

Yessir.

By the way, how do you rate Captain John?

O, he's just an old bummer, sir. Wants to fill his belly at Government expense and maybe kill other Indians for sport. I wouldn't be surprised if he has no daughter among Joseph's bunch.

Who's your favorite scout?

James Reuben, sir. A sincere Christian.

Good. Good. O, hello, Guy. Problem solved, I take it?

Well, father, Lieutenant Otis—

If it's not solved, go back again,

while the officers poke around the Indians' deserted camp, hoping for souvenirs:

ravens and bluejays rising up from a rotten charnel-hill of cow-guts and hides hacked wantonly, the uppermost of which reveals the Double T brand

and a dead dog thrown on top,

camas-baking pits left open like abandoned graves

—not even Doc finds anything good!—

then Wood gazes up the trail, wondering how far this war will call on us to ride, and who we will become once all this country belongs to us, and what camas tastes like:

I should have tried it at Clearwater. Red Heart's squaws would have given me a little.

2

Captain Whipple, take a walk with me.

Yessir.

I've heard that you were dissatisfied with Colonel Perry's actions at Cottonwood.

From whom, sir?

That's not to the point. You could be more charitable to a fellow officer.

Yessir.

Have you anything to say?

O, general, it was heartwrenching to see the reds massacring the Brave Seventeen and—

You thought him inactive, didn't you? Well, he hasn't complained about your failure to arrest Looking-Glass—

glancing at him with a cold sharpness which pierces Whipple's prospects of getting along tranquilly through this campaign.

3

Just as a good soldier descends through the roof of a Modoc wickiup, with his rifle pointed down into darkness, Perry now recommences to explore the death of Theller, confident of discovering some foul terror or else nothing. I pray the LORD that Delia never learns how he used to recreate in Lewiston. Meanwhile I can't help but wish I'd kept him better company there instead of worrying about what might have been beneath me or what my wife or the general could have found out. All the music in that one tent, and that Blackfoot squaw he was so crazy for . . . as soon as we've whipped Joseph and ride back to Lapwai, I aim to look her up and tell her, just to see if she flushes and how if at all her shining black eyes alter, when I tell her that he won't be coming back, not that she could have pinned her hopes on a white man not to mention married although for all I know he never told her fuck about himself. Besides, she's nothing but a GODd——d whore, probably clap-ripe and all that; it's a wonder he never gave Delia anything, although come to think of it why could she never have children? That one time at Red O'Donnell's he told me that she actually liked it a little too much, never satisfied, and it may be that that type of woman is the one that can't conceive. During the Modoc campaign she miscarried, he told me. Well, if I'd been in his shoes I would never have rolled away from her for a two-bit Injun harlot, especially a Blackfoot, who except any Sioux must be just about the worst of the worst. But it was as if he had such high spirits that no one woman could have been enough. That must have been why Delia chose him in the first place; she's a needing kind of woman, for a fact. How she adored him! Just brightened right up whenever he came riding home. He had that way with women and animals—always travelled with a lump of sugar for any contingency. Even Diamond liked him near about as well as me. My wife in spite of her come-hither hymn-singing voice was the only one never to cast a glance his way; she must have known something. Well, d——n her anyway. I should have known I'm not the marrying type. Last time after I had to take my belt to her, with my hand twisted good and tight in her hair so I could keep her face just deep enough in the pillow that she couldn't scream but not so deep as to smother her, Theller must have seen something in my face because he made that remark about vengeful women which if it had originated in any other man's mouth, even the general's, I would have made sure his teeth came out afterwards, whereas with Theller I knew he only meant me kindness in his joking temporizing way just as I knew without his telling me that that Blackfoot bitch meant something to him, and in retrospect I can't even name him any part of a fool. What should a man like him have done, and for that matter how's a man like me supposed to live? If I ever become a general, will I be better off? Not that any such thing can happen after White Bird Cañon. If Bugler Jones hadn't gotten himself killed and that other jackass had kept hold of his trumpet, I could have held control. And that shitty piss-ant Chapman, prancing around to-day so dandy on his grey, like he's running for President, he and those no good volunteers, I hope the Nez Perces stuff their balls in their mouths so I don't have to. In the Court of Inquiry I'll prove it was Chapman who destroyed us. I told that sonofabitch to hold fire while we parleyed; we weren't in any kind of skirmish line. He hasn't once expressed regret. I'm going to get him. I'm going to break him down. Not for me. I should offer up a prayer for Theller, just in case it would do any good. I can't see that it wouldn't. And he would take it kindly if I gave that Blackfoot squaw a dollar or two, saying it was from him. That couldn't hurt Delia, could it? I'll bet she's never going to marry again. Some folks would say that's a sign of loyalty and strength; for the general it's strength to say no to near about everything, but Theller said yes to Delia, yes to that whore and LORD knows how many others, yes to every fight and gambling game and daredevil ride not incompatible with honor and some other principle he never told me. The way his eyes were laughing with excitement when I ordered him forward, he, *no,* how could I have known it would be his death? When he rode ahead, it wouldn't have been irrevocable but for Chapman, and those d——d trumpeters, but before we knew it the battle was lost. He must have thought I'd come back for him. I would have, if I'd known. Well, how was I to, with no communications left? At least he had the satisfaction of making a stand. I retreated. I had to, to save what was left. But how am I supposed to live with that? The Court of Inquiry has got to fix the blame on somebody. The general's going to point to Joseph, which is d——d white of him and better than I deserve, but hardly to the point. And it's not even like there's anything I can say. Should I have sent those volunteers home when they started drinking that night on White Bird Hill? They're the ones who insisted we had to halt Joseph before he crossed the Salmon, and they were right about that, because look what a chase he's led us afterward; and moreover, those Mount Idaho men sure did know the country. So what should I have done? When Theller told off his squad and rode away, it still seemed all right even then,

down into the golden grass,

pim! pim! kíw!

his men reeling across their horses, groaning, bleeding, so that when we found them they were all wrecked up,

and that grin on his face when he waved to us made him look the way he did when he was up to some foolery in Lewiston, or the way he liked to talk like a gallant to my wife, just to tease her, while she wouldn't have any of it! And then in the Modoc War, when he pretended to be smitten with that ugly old squaw, just to make us laugh, what a caution! And that prank he played on Captain Boyle, with that fool's gold—

Better stop thinking about him. Here comes our *Christian Soldier* again. One thing I'll say for him: Even one-armed he sure can ride a horse.

Colonel, I'm afraid we have a climb ahead of us.

Sure looks like it, sir. But Carlton's bunch are making good progress up toward Lo Lo.

Who told you that?

I heard it from Chapman, general. And once Spurgin gets started—

Perry, Joseph is getting away.

Sir, we're all real sorry.

He may already have reached Montana Territory.

Yessir,

> looking up at the needles waving in the pine-crowns.

I expect more effort from our Indian scouts. Who's proved himself so far?

None of 'em, sir, except maybe James Reuben, who I'd be the first to admit is a real good Indian. Kept right on after he was shot.

What about Jim?

Jim who, sir?

Umatilla Jim.

O, there's a villain, general. One time Colonel Wright nearly hanged him.

For what?

He stole a sack of flour, sir.

O he did, did he?

Sure did, sir,

> and he unfailingly puts me in mind of some nigger hiding in the water cart of a livery stable.

How are you holding up?

Rock solid, general. I could ride a thousand miles.

You'd better not have to! The citizens are tiring of this campaign, Perry. We must quickly bring Joseph to justice.

I sure agree with you there, general.

4

Lieutenant Howard, walk with me.

Yessir.

Guy, there's something I would ask you.

Father, just say what you want me to do and it will be done.

I want you to try and be friends with Wood.

5

A fine excursion, Wood.

Sure is, general.

How does it compare with Alaska?

Not quite so grand as that, sir. But I admire this grand forest. It'll be a treat to cross the Rockies!

Ride up here with me. Did you ever hear disagreeable rumors about Lieutenant Theller's private life?

No, sir.

An appropriate reply for the comrade of a fallen officer! But you see, I mean to help Perry clear himself any way he can when he goes before the Court of Inquiry. And the Court will wish to find fault. If Theller happened to be, for instance, drunk, that would of course reflect badly on Perry, but perhaps not so badly as otherwise.

I know nothing about it, general.

Lieutenant Wood, return to your place in the column. I'll see you presently.—
He's very loyal, wouldn't you say, Wilkinson?

You could put it that way, sir,

> at which the general knees his horse and rides a little forward, grimacing,
> so that Wilkinson wonders whether his pert remark has offended; in fact,
> upon the general has lately descended that common affliction of old men,
> a frequent need to urinate, even though there are times when hardly any-
> thing comes out; and it now ever more often happens that even when he
> empties his bladder five minutes before the move out, almost as soon as he
> has swung himself into the saddle the need to relieve himself returns; and
> once they commence the march, Arrow rocking beneath and against him,
> the sensation grows rapidly intolerable, and there is but one thing to do
> about it, namely, nothing, for he will not show weakness before his soldiers;
> he has begun to drink less coffee in the morning, and as a rule to reduce
> his consumption of liquids until they have planted the guidon for the night,
> but in the hot conditions of this Nez Perce campaign such abstemiousness
> could backfire; so the best solution, as with the throbbings of his arm-
> stump, is patience, which, thank GOD, he possesses more of year by year;
> although he might not be what he was in his best days, in every significant
> respect he must be counted wealthy in blessings, which to maintain the
> Army's respect he must conceal, so he merely says:

Fletch, that mule yonder is staggering in the traces. Go find out how much weight he's hauling. It had better not be more than a hundred twenty-five pounds.

6

Mr. Chapman, you look mighty pleased with yourself.

General, I love this here country.

And why on earth is that?

Because this is the best timbered region left in the U.S. Just reckon up all them trees at three dollars and ten dollars each—

This isn't the U.S. yet.

Well, it will be general. You can bet on that.

I daresay you're right.

Now whereabouts is Leeds, general? Ain't that where your folks is from?

It's around twenty miles west of Augusta. Some of us feel proud to dwell so near the capital of our State.

I never been out that far east, general. I—

That's all, Chapman,

    and then gazing into the rolling eyes of a horse with the blind staggers:

Shoot that animal.

Right away, sir.

Joseph is extremely cruel to his horses.

Yessir.

Fletch, this time you be the one to ride up to Carlton. Tell him I'm gaining on him. If his roadcutters can't keep ahead of this army, they'll be fired.

Yessir. Good-bye, general!

GOD bless you! Well, Bomus, are you keeping the teamsters up to the mark?

O, sir, they've contracted so many bills on Uncle Sam! They even—

Practice saying the most beautiful word in the English language.

What's that, general?

No. That's all you need to tell them.— Lieutenant Howard, what's the matter with your horse? He's favoring his left front foot.

Sir, he—

Captain Winters, was the court-martial wrapped up?

Yessir. Private Holzer's to lose a week's pay and pull extra fatigue duty for a week. He was only—

You're certain that he wasn't drinking?

I am, sir.

All right. Lieutenant Howard, go see how the artillery wagons are managing, and on the way tell Major Mason that I need him again. Stay on the *qui vive;* you may find evidence of liquor. Bomus and I will hear your report. And where's Captain Jocelyn? O, there you are. It's fine and grand to see this original forest-line.

Yessir.

Inspect your flankers; Joseph must be as aware as I that this is ambush terrain. For that reason, be careful, and GOD bless you. Quickly now.

Right away, general!

    Soon's we've whipped Mr. Joe you're buying me a drink in Lewiston. Real GODd——d barefoot whiskey, too. Red O'Donnell's. You gonna remember?

Sure.

If you don't I'm gonna remind you.

Cut it out.

No, I made a little wager on Mr. Joe. I was betting he'd give our *Christian Soldier* the slip—

How much did you clear?

None of your business.

What do you say, kid? Is it my business?

    Yes, Wilkinson, what is it now? Two more stragglers?

    Just so, major,

        because

my continued scrutiny of malingerers and evildoers will comprise a valuable service to the Army and our general, no matter how sorely the miscreants may dislike me; such is my cross; I will not permit any further degradation of our purpose—especially with Perry and so many other officers unfit for their trusts.

Now back when Crook commanded the Department of Arizona, there was a blue-eyed little Polack laundress, and after her husband took sick she had to—

You already told us, and nobody believed it the first time.

7

Doctor Alexander, we'll ascend those mountains to-morrow.

Yessir.

I know that medical science has improved considerably. What's the lookout for Rocky Mountain fever?

No predicting it, general, hence no preventing it. And no cure but rest.

All right. Then I won't concern myself. If you discover any symptoms, be sure to inform me on the *qui vive*.

Yessir,

the wagons still groaning toward our long-planted guidon, hidden within their own Big Dust

(they could sure make better progress!);

and Buffalo Horn on his whiteheaded pony, shoulder to shoulder with Buffalo Jim, with their hair pulled back behind them

while Perry, grimacing, relieved that Company "F" is squared away, closes his trousers, turns away from the sinks, sweat dripping down his neck

—*Pickets out!*

and he plucks a rich hank of buffalograss, feeds it to Diamond

(who snatches it with his yellow teeth, rolls his eyes and says: *Hinimí*),

caresses the bell mare's head, strolls to the perimeter, taps kinnikinnick into his pipe

(no, general, they haven't yet reëstablished contact with the enemy)

but for a moment forbears to light it,

inhaling the evening breeze, which graces him with the bitter smell of ripening black chokecherries in their mazes of serrated leaves

(a few laggards still red);

then, with his hands on his hips and his feet wide apart, he squints ahead at the mountains, thinking: I wouldn't want to be anywhere else in the world!

Whenever a Child Slips

1

*H*aving hunted since first light in this country which he has begun to know nearly as well as home, Shooting Thunder, now riding up to Old Man Place, pickets Black Face-Stripe to graze, creeps over the ridge and into the thicket,
    calling upon his WYAKIN Power,
whistles through an elderberry stalk, so that a buck elk comes slowly into the meadow:
    pim!
at which Naked-Footed Bull rises up, and together they butcher the meat, washing it in the creek, packing it on their horses,
    the bluejays saying: *chá-á, chá-á!*, settling onto the purple guts.
They ride back down to the People,
    who are catching salmon as they go,
        the women picking berries along the river's edge;
    withdrawing from Cut Arm, their enemy, but slowly, since Cut Arm is slow.
        (Laughing as they ride, the People excite one another to
        laugh, telling tales of Cut Arm who is their bad friend.)

2

Now the Great River* grows greener than brown
    as Fair Land and Springtime bathe their babies by a powdery beach,
        then mount again, riding for awhile with White Bird's People,
            Dreaming of dancing and sizzling buffalo meat
all the way up to the rock ripples.
            They will soon be down there, marching on the edge of the river.
            Then let us rapidly and secretly go up these ridges to some-
            place further, and attack them again.
            But our women are weeping, and we cannot agree.

3

We are riding up,
    our old women clouting the packhorses' heads with big sticks and
    screaming at them,

---

*Middle fork of the Clearwater.

bloodying the branches they must leap over;
we are carrying our wealth quickly toward the top of the trail:
Toohhoolhoolsote, who used to swim underwater but will not say
whether he has ever practiced flying by night,
Shore Crossing,
he who has swum across the Chinook Salmon Water and back for
each day of the last five winters,
hoping to steal palomino horses in the Buffalo Country;
White Bird, who conceals about his neck that fishheaded Medicine whistle which can call coyotes and eagles,
Heinmot Tooyalakekt on Black Mane-Stripe, travelling this trail which
he once rode with his father, who many times rode it with White Bird
and with Looking-Glass's father in the days when the Bostons first began
digging gold out of our home:
his heart is smiling to know that soon he will be giving buffalo bone
beads to all his women:
lovely Springtime on White Belly-Spot, with the baby in the
cradleboard,
dark-eyed, staring as if she understands,
Good Woman, grey-braided, blowing her nose on the ground
as she rides Ocher One,
then Sound Of Running Feet, bareback on Little One, the
only horse still belonging to her;
she is silent as she rides, like some legendary woman
who longs for a greyish-blue cloud
(her father desires to get her a fancy Crow robe);
next rides Welweyas the half-woman, who cannot stop being jealous of
Looking-Glass's lovely daughters
(although they have begun to cast their gazes at our young men,
their father still believes each of them as pure as the Crow woman
who dares to eat buffalo tongue at the Sun Dance)
and of White Feather, Grey Eagle's daughter
(who has still not yet become Broken Tooth):
but mostly Welweyas likes to make herself womanly in Cloudburst's
fashion, or Good Woman's
—not her mother's:
Agate Woman acts too much like a man—
and now Looking-Glass's wives and daughters ride past, clouting their
recreant horses with sticks
(some stallions scream and show their teeth);
and Tzi-kal-tza, seventy-two winters old, leans forward on a pony he has
never named, in a blanket-coat so dirty that the stripes barely show, his
walnut-brown wrinkled round face set in a meaningless smile, his sunken

eyes nearly closed as he rides with his old musket slung across his shoulder, bobbing his head beneath the branches, the lightness of his streaming hair, which falls halfway down his biceps, the best clue that he has
Boston blood

    (because in 1805 William Clark used Red Grizzly Bear's sister as a
    wife);

our children swaying as they go through the muted red of huckleberry
stems:

    Grandmother, I grow tired.

    Be strong, my sweet little girl, and then I shall name you according
    to your habits.

    Grandfather, I feel so tired!

    Make yourself brave, my sweet little girl, and I shall sing you songs,
the boy named About Asleep,

    who still rides the brown horse that Elm Limb gave him at the Cliff
    Place Fight,

watching to learn where the river comes and goes

        as Helping Another's sorrel bites Agate Woman's bay,

        and our dogs lope alongside the horsewomen who have fed
        them in camp, never getting trampled,

White Thunder riding beside his uncle Old Yellow Wolf, whose head-
wound has scabbed over;

    and because the young men would not stay to kill and die, those
    two have no dreams anymore; what can they do but help the People
    ride away forever, into clouds as still as the rocks in this river?

Just ahead of Peopeo Tholekt rides Looking-Glass, his chief,

    with that round mirror flashing, dappling, darkening and dazzling
    in his hair, depending on the forest overhead;

he is happy to be leading all the People away from the Bostons
and trying to close his heart to his lost country, in much the same way
that we avoid dwelling on those who are dead,

    although just now he cannot stop remembering that spring day
    when he was almost young and his father, seizing a bearded miner's
    horse by the bridle, turned it around, at which the band of miners
    pushed on through, so Old Looking-Glass called his warriors to
    drive them back across the boundary of our country, but those
    wicked Bostons merely returned to Oro Fino to gather up some
    killers, who galloped through our line and fortified themselves
    upon the river, after which we left them alone to devour that place

        (those who say that Looking-Glass became weakminded be-
        cause Cut Arm broke his heart at Kamnaka should not set
        aside this occasion sixteen years earlier when Looking-Glass
        had to see the breaking of his father's heart,

to which Toohhoolhoolsote has said: this makes no difference, for we who are men were born in order to be
brave and then die)
while Five Wounds rides back along the trail to seek Red Spy, but finds only cool
clouds and the river: Cut Arm must still be far behind
so that our freedom is ripening
as we arrive at the fork with Pine Tree River:*
banks lush with grass and ferns, ravinesides erupting into miniature
crags crowned with trees
here where Sacajawea guided Lewis and Clark, leading those cold
and hungry Bostons to the People
(we should have pushed sticks up their anuses);
low basalt rocks spanning the water
(lowering our buffalo horns, we now fill them)
and rich wet flowers, yellow and lavender,
by the cave where White Thunder and Old Yellow Wolf once hid from the
Lice-Eaters on their way home from the Buffalo Country,
home to Wallowa,
Good Woman murmuring: Springtime, you must try to trust
in our husband's heart,
the sky clouding over;
then Looking-Glass, riding Home From Capture, leads us above these rocks and
rapids, up the bank and back along the Lo Lo Trail:
Hasten; evening shadows be!
—smell of campfire-smoke
and camas, elk-meat, fish and berries
and a few last marrowbones from the Bostons' beef at Weippe—
as Sound Of Running Feet curries Little One, who licks her face,
and Good Woman finishes plaiting Springtime's new cap of cedar bark and beargrass.

4

In the dark, Heinmot Tooyalakekt sits murmuring aside with Ollokot,
dreading the coming days when the pine needles will turn rusty and our
bullets will be gone; as
Springtime sleeps apart, her baby girl—now one moon old—in the cradleboard
with her mouth open, and
Toohhoolhoolsote's wives, alone beneath one blanket, silently gloat over the treasures their husband gave them in Sparse-Snowed Place:
three lovely gold cavalry-buttons like the tiny yellow blossoms of the
creeping Oregon grape;

---

*Conjectural meaning of *láqsa,* the Lochsa River.

and Looking-Glass, whose wives await him, stares into the fire, considering the country which Cut Arm stole from him,
     longing for the Buffalo Country, where he will again be rich,
the stars above him now nearly as huge as the shining elkteeth in their nested semicircles on his Crow sweetheart's red-hemmed dress of night-blue trade cloth
     (now he remembers the white borders on her beaded moccasins)
and far below, the river ripples *mululululu.*

5

Good Woman and Sound Of Running Feet sleep side by side beneath a buffalo robe. In their dreams they are pulling themselves up by the tree-branches. Whenever a child slips, white stones roar down the cañon.

6

Now ascending the mountains, which once used to be GIANTS
     (fearing our People because we were fashioned from a great OTTER's
     heart, They stood watch against us until They turned to stone),
we parallel Pine Tree River, scraping our heads against grey spruce-fingers,
riding farther out of our home,
toward the United States*
     where the Salish and Crows will greet us, and we shall hunt buffalo,
branches whipping our foreheads
     as White Thunder's stern mother Swan Woman clouts horses all day,
          and looking behind, Heinmot Tooyalakekt sees Springtime
          shrouded with mosquitoes as she rides, fanning the baby's swollen
          face,
     while Sound Of Running Feet, pressing her lips together, whips the pack-
     horses bloody, forcing them over deadfalls that they dread to cross),
winding around fallen trees, crossing creeks, scaring buffalo ponies, traversing
steep slippery rock
     (sometimes a horse will fall, and then we leave him for Cut Arm),
the hiss of a shale-slide ahead
     —now we must goad the horses over sharp loose rocks which clink be-
     neath them like hunks of Boston glass—
and whiteheaded hawks watching from the sky
     (Cut Arm, whom we like to call *Sleeveless,* still many days behind us:
          perhaps he will have gone home,
          the Bluecoats returning to be his slaves again at Butterfly Place)

---

*Apparently some of the Nez Perces mistakenly believed that the U.S.A. began in Montana, which in fact would not join the Union until 1889.

as Good Woman detours down a steep green side-cañon to gather strawberries
and a squirrel raises its tail.

Perhaps we shall ride back here when the huckleberries have finished ripening.

7

Here rides Wounded Head on Speckled One, leading another pony by the halter, with his tiny son riding on it, well necklaced and decked out;
    and then one of Toohhoolhoolsote's grandnieces,
        the child's brown hand on her thigh as she rides a pony bareback,
    followed by Heinmot Tooyalakekt,
        wishing to make of Springtime a silver-belted shell-dotted woman
        and to gladden Good Woman's heart with more horses,
    riding Black Mane-Stripe and leading the horse bearing Animal In A Hole,
        who grips the cantle of his saddle to ease the pain of his wounded leg,
            gazing down into a bowl of mountain forest
            and goldenrods dancing between the rocks,
        hating Cut Arm as he goes
            (and Ollokot and Toohhoolhoolsote must now call their young men
            to roll another great dead tree off the trail);
as Heinmot Tooyalakekt, carefully helping Animal In A Hole, all the while decorates his heart with a memory of Wallowa:
        south of the lake, riding up into the pines in the cool morning where the
        sphagnum moss grows thick and soft like the mane of green grass on
        each ridge's neck, he looks down from Black Mane-Stripe to see his fa-
        ther's grave, then pickets the horse to graze, climbing the high gorge's
        sunny wall
            on which a few saplings and grass-hanks cling in crevices,
                the dying ones drooping down toward the roaring water below,
        then coming out onto the deer trail to breathe the morning on the edge
        of a slanting strawberry meadow, gazing down across the grand gorge of
        pines which hides the river but not its loud voice, he strides up toward
        the evergreen-spotted grey crags
            (which from camp,
                where Good Woman and Springtime are pounding cous,
            appear turquoise like the earth paint which comes from the cinder
            cones to the west in the old Umatilla Country)
        where the lake cannot be seen;
        now he continues up the trail to his favorite wet shady rock between
        waterfalls, where sweet white foam goes over turtle-shaped rocks and
        knobby slippery rocks,
            the water galloping like white horses
            the herd soon dividing,

the righthand fork going bronzy-dark in the tree-shadows of the
edge,
while to the left, the white drops leap brightly up at the edge,
then down below:
he sees aspens, scree, pines and sunshine
and no water; the water has vanished into air:
and may this memory shine secretly forever.

8

Ascending dark green mountain-shoulders and riding over deadfalls across a
rapid creek
(not yet the buffaloberries fading into pink beads as they dry),
Looking-Glass rises back up into his best dreams, in much the same way that in
old stories dead meat can become a deer
while White Thunder now leads the horse on which Animal In A Hole
sits, leaning forward, white and grimacing, seeking not to cry out, wishing he had stayed with Cut Arm and lain safe in the golden grass;
and the People ride east, regretting their buffalo robes and other treasures
(although Toohhoolhoolsote's careful wives have most certainly saved those
three gold buttons from the dead Bluecoats),
looking across the deep valley at the blue-green indistinctness of the
other forest wall
whipping their horses over fallen logs
(one of Fair Land's horses has run away, for which she blames
Cloudburst,
who sulks)
Heinmot Tooyalakekt encouraging his women: Soon we shall reach Meadow
Camp, where there is good grass.

9

Early one evening they ride at last over Chipmunk Mountain,
the western sky going yellow like the fat on the edges of buffalo steaks;
indeed they are coming into Meadow Camp,
where a water-strider makes ripples on the inverted triangle of a spruce's
reflection,
a dragonfly hovering energetically against grass-tuft's tip
(and far away, a woodpecker-sound)
as a tawny striped chipmunk darts headfirst down white rocks.
Sun Tied's wife will soon give birth; his sister Crystal
helps her out of the saddle.
Happily the women turn out the tired horses,

settling in a circle,
picking leaves for tea
>> as the boy About Asleep steals into a thicket in hopes of
>> killing a porcupine,
Toohhoolhoolsote's wives winging their shoulders with great
long bundles of firewood which scrape against the trees on
either side as these old women creep forward, each one leaning on the straightest strongest stick she has destined for
burning,
pouring from woven bags the dark wizened ovals of baked camas
bulbs,
>> but Fair Land, whose WYAKIN always helps her to find roots,
>> quickly digs up fresh food with her camas hook
as fires keep hissing, the few remaining kettles boiling,
>> when Sound Of Running Feet, coming back with an armload of
>> twigs to burn, overhears her father murmur to her second mother:
>> *Síikstiwaa*, I am asking you to forgive me. Now I have spoken, and
>> I have tried sincerely to speak from my heart . . .
Heinmot Tooyalakekt races horses with the young men and loses; his heart is
not in any game; now he walks down among the trees until he has found Secret
Rock Place; here in the gloom of interlaced branches he sits considering the words
of his father,
>> he who is dead and so should not be thought of without great cause:
>> Wellammoutkin, *the Cropped-Forelock One*
>>> (one of his most important names, for only those with the
>>> utmost knowlege may cut their hair so and wind up their
>>> braids in a high coil):
>> my father, who tied back his hair
>>> just for awhile (now he is dead):
>>>> before the *thief treaty*, he told the Bostons at Weippe:
>>>> *There is where I live, and there is where I wish to leave
>>>> my body,*
>>>>> pointing to Wallowa.
Looking-Glass, White Bird, Hahtalekein and Toohhoolhoolsote can
do as they please. But what shall I now do and where shall I take my
People?
>> No help comes; the son's heart cries *qoh! qoh! qoh!*

10

Fair Land is making her family's bed with ferns and grass, laying buffalo robes
on top,
>> happy to prepare for lying down exactly here

because Ollokot knows how to please her vulva's tongue;*
   now before dark she is cutting beargrass for baskets,
      glimpsing a buck deer flee down the steep slope
as Heinmot Tooyalakekt sits working quills out of the nose of Agate Woman's
dog which has rashly attacked a porcupine
and Looking-Glass's wives lay out the worst of the King George blankets they
have saved,
   Blackberry Person despondent,
   Asking Maiden still a lovely oval-faced woman with a high smooth forehead and braids of shining black hair, who holds her head like the chief's
daughter she is, compressing her narrow lips;
      Looking-Glass's daughters thinking back on the wide white grav-
      elly sandbar on which they once liked to make a campfire, in the
      country that Cut Arm stole from them
         where the aspens, pines and spruces get sparser on the grassy
         hills of Red Owl's country,
         slanting morning tree-shadows down on the grey-grassed
         river-cliffs,
            fat-fingered leaves of yellow glacier lily along the bank
            and morning's green reflections of alders bent eastward in
            the Big Water.
      The two girls ask their father: Does your heart never grieve for our
      home?
      —to which he replies: I used to sorrow; now there is none of that
      left. Listen, my lovely ones: We shall find many good places in the
      Buffalo Country; I am telling you three times,
while White Bird's People camp apart from Looking-Glass,
   for just as Ollokot,
      who loves to breed the fastest racehorses,
   looks upon Cut Arm's mules,
   so Looking-Glass looks on White Bird's killers,
      who have ruined our home forever;
         even as White Bird's People are murmuring to one another:
         Looking-Glass is a coward who forsook us at Split Rock; he
         should not be head-chief!
         and some of them eat cous bread, while certain women boil
         their families a soup of Boston beef,
            likewise *Kate*, who has saved from Cut Arm her pem-
            mican well moistened with steelhead salmon oil, but
            keeps it hidden in a beadwork bag in case the trail
            should grow worse

---

*Clitoris.

and Toohhoolhoolsote's women boil up a soup of pounded cous:
    their favorite food; they've escaped with four saddlebags full,
        and we all still have dried beef from our good friends the Bostons.
Peopeo Tholekt's leg has well healed; he needs Arrowhead no more; so she
boils a tea for Old Yellow Wolf's wound, then relieves the horses' blisters
      and at the meadow's edge Toohhoolhoolsote waves an eagle's tail-
      feather in time with the Dreamer drum
    while Swan Necklace and the Three Red Blankets begin playing at the
    Stick Game with some of Looking-Glass's young men.
Sound Of Running Feet picks lice from both her mothers' hair
    and as silently as an old warrior smokes kinnikinnick, a cloud issues from
    the horizon.

11

Next day they cross the cloudy pass,
    Fair Land leaping off her horse to dig the white and yellow earth
    from a certain hillside beneath the evergreens, so that in a new way
    her husband can paint his face
        (Cut Arm has devoured most such treasures in his bonfires;
        to Ollokot only a small pouch of her red ocher from Wallowa
        remains)
    and coming down east with the tops of the evergreens going greyish-
    green beneath them in the lightning-fires of midsummer,
    winding down in yellow grass beneath the trees,
      the trail drying out, the country warming
        (of all the women, only Cloudburst has been here before; Ol-
        lokot bought her in the Salish Country);
    they pass an outcropping with two trees on its weird vertical rocks
        (here Rainbow's grandfather once killed a Crow chief by trickery,
        in the days when the Snakes were our friends),
    and lava piled glob on glob and the river winding down bright blackish-
    brown in the sun,
    grass on the south side of a fine ridge, and a fine camas meadow,
then reach the three hot springs, each warmer than the last, where the People may
happily sweat themselves
  but Wottolen and White Thunder now come cantering up the trail,
    Wottolen calling out: My chiefs! Many Bluecoats and Salish are waiting for us
    ahead at Narrow Place.

FAIRLY RELIABLE IS NOT GOOD ENOUGH
JULY 31–AUGUST 2

1

*Q*uite a plutonic night!

Now, what's the situation with our pickets?

All quiet and in position, sir.

Have you been reading your Edgar Poe again?

Spades are trumps.

What about Buffalo Horn? I don't like his look.

I didn't know you'd studied him, Fletch,

the darkness incensed with cedar logs, campfire sparks rushing up into the stars, which glitter like the pale beads on a Sioux squaw's awl-case as Perry wonders whether Joseph is even now moving into position, preparing to pick us off from the timber

and Guy sits on a rock, making for his sister Grace a pretty little pen-and-ink drawing (all by memory, and better than any of Wood's efforts) of three pines on a high mountain ridge, and crosshatched clouds behind.

Wakesh nun pakilauitin
JEHOVAN'M yiyauki—

Well, what can you expect of Injuns?

But our Jim, now, you have to admit he's solid gold. Red gold anyhow. Jollier than any of Reuben's bunch. He knows a lot of hilarious tricks.

Name me one.

I seen him throw his dagger and hit the bull's eye at twenty-five feet.

He's a Umatilla, like Chapman's wife.

Well, that's his name, so—

If them Umatillas don't keep quiet on their reservation, we'll take care of them next.

Jim swears to me all Umatillas are good Injuns, cross his double-dyed heart, because they

Holding a tenace, are you?

Quoth the raven, NEVERMORE. Isn't that how it goes?

That's right.

Well, well, he's underplayed us in our own suit! Better put up my best card.

Will you let me borrow your copy sometime?

I don't have any book but this little diary.

O. I'm sorry,

>brushing a spark off the shoulder of his stable frock as the coyotes sing far down and away.

I thought you must be reading something. You're always—

It's hard to believe Poe was a New Yorker. My uncle is a New Yorker, and I find him quite sane.

I've never visited New York.

A city with its own special ways. Drearier than before, of course, with so many business failures. When you go into a restaurant up there,

>remembering a certain Broadway lady in crimson velvet, and dreaming of being a natty gentleman in a pale green suit,

>while Fletch patches his trouser-knee with canvas

>and Wood reënters his diary,

>>because I'll keep trying to describe the way Nanny used to kiss me over and over: just one more kiss and then a hug, with her head on my breast and my hand in her ankle-length hair, and a sob, and then that one time she reached down into her cleavage and withdrew a golden locket, nicely warmed, containing her photograph and a strand of her golden-brown hair, O GOD, and there was always one more kiss and then a kiss when I finally went, so that I always had the feeling that if I simply asked her in the right way,

if you want codfish balls, make sure you tell your waiter *sleeve buttons*. Believe it or not, that's actually what they call them.

I think I heard that before.

Then it's doubly true.

Codfish balls would be a decent switch from these sad pancakes.

And if you want ham and beans, remember to order *stars and stripes*.

According to Jim, when we reach Lo Lo there'll be hot springs and a brook with plenty of trout.

Where *is* Jim, anyhow?

>What's wrong, Perry?

>I'm all right, sir.

>By the way, Mrs. Howard mentioned in her latest letter to me that Mrs. Perry is becoming a great favorite with our children. Bessie especially adores her, and she's shy, even for her age. Well, your wife won her over—

>Thank you, sir.

>How fit is your company?

>Fighting fit, sir. Ready to help Mr. Joe see daylight—

>This is tough country.

>Yessir.

>Are their boots holding up?

So-so, general. Some Leavenworth tailor jewed us all down—

We're not short of tallow.

Right, sir. And my boys know better than to fall out on account of a few blisters—

Yes. Are you remembering White Bird Cañon?

How did you know, sir?

O, I know

> (the young colonel's grief as heavy as a sweaty canvas greatcoat).

>> Then Black would have marched on his pawns to certain victory.

>> But the only way to save his knight—

Did I ever tell you about Captain Dessaur?

No, sir.

Well, he was a very likely officer. Somewhat like you, in fact. When his distraught young wife begged him to resign just before Chancellorsville, I disapproved his application, and he was killed.

>> All right, so what was the next move?

>> He castled, and then—

I understand, sir.

I believe she suffered from a hysterical condition.

>> O, like *this*.

>> Exactly. Very clever, don't you think?

>> That seems like a European sort of move. Who were the players?

>> The young Prince Ouroussoff *versus* Jaenisch.

Yessir.

And Dessaur was no coward; he simply worried about his wife—

Yessir.

Quite beautiful, as a matter of fact. Her daguerrotype was among his effects. A smart young lady, not unlike Jenny Lind. Who wouldn't want to come home to such a bride?

You're correct about that, sir—

>> Prince Ouroussoff's not so young. And I thought Jaenisch had dropped out of the game.

>> You're mistaken. Although this chronicle—

Perry, what you feel at this moment *will never leave you*. Give up expecting it to. All you can do is be brave.

Of course, sir.

>> Where did you get that old book anyway?

>> General Howard lent it to me. You see? Here's his signature. He used to study out of it.

>> O, from before the Rebellion! That's the first time I've seen something he signed with his right hand.

>> The advice is still actually informative, to my surprise—

Glory, glory, hallelujah—
Cut it out.

2

Father, there's something I was wondering.

What is it?

Well—

I hope it's not another dispute between you and a brother officer.

O, not at all! I was just . . . Father, tell me again what happened when you took the Apaches to meet President Grant.

Were you aware that Wood had a private interview with Grant?

No, sir.

Yes, his father pulled strings. Grant personally recommended him to West Point.

Yessir. And when the Apaches—

Why, they opened their hearts to him in set speeches, and he gave them pleasant rejoinders. But their richest enjoyment was our visit to the College of Deaf Mutes . . .

And they rode back happy to Arizona?

Of course.

Father, do you think that the Government can ever satisfy the Indians?

3

That night he dreams that Umatilla Jim has guided him—as if he required that!—to the little cemetery in Leeds where his parents are buried (and where in fact our pioneers used to keep a stockade in case of Indian attack), and Jim's eyes begin to glow like suns behind smoked glass, at which moment he understands that this Indian can see down under the earth to count all the wedding rings upon the skeleton hands of dead women; he understands further that Jim intends to steal these rings, including his mother's; now already the humid twilight of a Maine summer has greyed down the air, and as he stands behind and slightly to the right of Jim, he too learns to see the golden shinings of rings burning up through the glass like the sunshine at Lapwai, and as his uncanny companion turns slowly round, it develops that for the first time he is *smiling,*

while Wood dreams of the concentrically circular shelves of Wanamaker's department store like a great cattle show; he accompanies Nanny to the post which proclaims **LADIES FURNISHING GOODS**, after which she disappears;

and (strange to relate) Wilkinson dreams not of his very own Sallie, but of the soft plump beauties of Lemonade Lucy, the bustled skirts of Lemonade Lucy, whom he has seen only in the illustrated newspapers;

then together comes "Reveille," dawn and the morning gun, muster, move out,

> Spurgin's bunch in the vanguard, tirelessly wood-pecking with their axes,
>
> then the artillery, which can no longer be permitted to fall behind.

>> Well, Mason, how do you like Wood as A.D.C.?
>> Much better in camp than in garrison, sir. He has plenty of pluck.
>> Glad to hear it,

and Perry, riding high on Diamond as the trail permits, looking sharply at the fork of his saddle, as if something could be wrong with it, leading his column of time-servers, Indian haters, true Americans and youths ripe for the maiming,

Fletch, Wood and Wilkinson trying to out-general each other

> (their brass buttons less shiny than formerly, I am sorry to say);

then Trimble's bunch,

> leading their horses over fallen logs, crawling under branches, managing not to curse in the general's hearing,

shepherded by Lieutenant Parnell, who, not at all fatigued, remembers that October ten years since when Perry and Harris were sent away to Camp Harney and the rest of us had to march all the way into California with Crook to whip those GoDd——d Snakes; compared to that, this is easier than easy

> (and I was in the Charge of the Six Hundred at Balaclava, so whatever else life and death can shoot at me will be *nothing!*)
> —and Parnell's sentiment, which he likes to share with the world, might in part explain the fond smile of his commander, which is to say old Trimble himself, the soldier's soldier, who hates to wear his pattern blue overcoat, on the grounds that it makes him more visible to any sniping red, yet sentimentally adheres to the superseded cording on his blouse—

while Chapman keeps up his end of a thoroughly interesting conversation with our general, that pair riding the two best GoDd——d horses in the entire outfit

> (after this campaign I might strike a bargain with that snake and get me something decent to ride):

>> A pretty rough trail. All that horsehair and blood on the branches—
>> No man living can get as much out of a horse as an Indian can.
>> Right you are, Mr. Chapman,

followed by Company "D," whose commander, Captain Pollock, our loyalest family man excepting only the general, still hopes and at intervals even prays that upon reaching Missoula we'll immediately find ourselves able to hang Joseph and take up the line of march back to Vancouver,

by which time Wilkinson, having peeled off from his two comrades, is riding up and down the line, hunting down stragglers,

wishing to someday hear Dwight Moody in the Hippodrome:

We shall meet beyond the river by and by—

Ring the bells of Heaven! There is joy to-day—

while Fletch is now teaching Wood how to watch for ambushes

(but at least, thank GOD, no worries about a flank attack on these ridges)

and Red O'Donnell, foreseeing that his mule team will dig in its collective heels at the sight of this waist-high boulder over which the wagon must go, begins to persuade each animal in advance by means of skull-thumpings with his longhandled fry pan;

after him comes Major Mason, the round and tireless one who now rides forward along the right flank until he has met Perry

—because Mason, whose nature is more unbending than the general's, perhaps for the simple reason that as a midlevel officer he has never found this world open to modification, had sat with the commissioners in the peace parley tent back in '73 on that cold spring afternoon when Captain Jack told Canby: *I am a true Modoc. I am not afraid to die. I am not afraid of them brass buttons,* and accordingly distrusted that savage all the way to the bone-wells behind those sullen Indian eyes (although, to be sure, he was nearly as shocked as the others when the Modocs, deriding Jack for a fish-hearted squaw, threatened to unseat him as chief and so goaded him into killing Canby); on similar grounds he had suspected Chief Joseph at Lapwai, Joseph being if not derisive or threatening certainly unsubmissive; if to a smaller degree than Jack had ever been (Mason agreed with Perry and the general that Toohhoolhoolzote was a far more dangerous Indian); at home he used to tell his wife: It's like this, Mary; certain Indians are just our bad luck, and since he never continued, out loud at least, I find it unlikely that Mary understood that at such moments he was faulting his general, O. O. Howard, who made bad luck for the rest of us when he permitted himself to be gulled by Indians so that a rip-tide pulled us all back just when we expected to make landfall on the virgin shore of our American dream; remembering how Canby had misjudged

Jack for a rational creature, even troubling to explain to the Modoc chief, who proposed that if the Indian murderers were turned over to the Army to be hanged, then the settler men and Army men who had murdered Modoc children and squaws should be likewise turned over to him, Jack, to be punished in accordance with tribal law, that no such symmetry existed or could exist: *Why, Jack, you have no law. Only one law can live at a time,* which pronouncement had struck Mason, who was otherwise unimpressed with that general, as so true as to stand like certain Bible verses *beyond* truth; ever after, whenever any Indian chief, be he no matter how picturesque, eloquent or otherwise accomplished, sought to argue against the Government, Mason simply stared at him, knowing that Indians have no law, a realization which had come, if at all, far too late to our *Christian Soldier,* who pretended that parleys mattered and treaties could come to something. Nowadays, seeing any Indian off reservation, even one bearing a pass, Mason's impulse, which of course he refrains from acting on, is to halt him, search him and demand: What do you want?— Parleys do in fact have one purpose: to spin out time. Canby treated with Jack while our troops drew nearer to the Stronghold. Joseph treated with us to delay the inevitable. Mason knows that the most important business in his charge is moving and stopping. He led two companies of the Twenty-first down from Fort Vancouver; he shifted them to Hospital Rock; after Canby's assassination he received and disregarded Colonel Gillem's order to surround the Stronghold, knowing that any such a rash assault would use up his troops to no purpose. Therefore, Mason, like Perry, is in certain quarters considered a coward. And this makes the two men allies

as ferns, spruce and lodgepole pines choke the hills:

Well, Joseph sure can't escape by any side march.

Even taller than the cedars we used to find in Tennessee!

O, I sure do remember those days.

And gazing up at Colonel Perry

(the tallest one whom I have ever seen)

Umatilla Jim decides: If I become like him, frightening and silent, wearing the blue shirt, *then,* even small as I am, I shall never be penned up like the Wallowa People.

If I become like him, he can no longer hurt my pride. I shall now Dream how to be his brother.

What's the holdup back there?

Captain, sir, some men are getting sick.

Well, they will have to stand it.

Yessir.

You know, Chapman, back home in Leeds we also have tall pines—not like this, of course. We're quite proud of our forestry.

Yessir,

as they follow Chief Joseph, slowly chewing on hardtack as they walk or ride

(across a green gorge, over a spruce-skeleton)

behind Spurgin's bunch of road-cutters, whose formerly white canvas overalls were cut out of Secession War tents,

marching along the narrow winding ridgecrest, sometimes letting our howitzers down with ropes, ready at any instant to be ambushed by Joseph or that villain Looking-Glass, for Captain Rawn must have turned them back by now

(Barely enough grass to keep animals alive—

Tell that to the Christian Yokel who's driving us through here!

Sure would have been easier to hang Mr. Joe back at Lapwai),

the Lochsa River sometimes green where it is deep, silver-white with wrinkles of cloud-light on the near bank, then brown on the far side where it touches the white gravel, after which the evergreen forest rises all the way into distant blueness,

poor Lieutenant Otis maneuvering over and around tree-rooted boulders our Gatlings with their famous cannonlike guncarriages and their bulbous plugs from which the many barrels sprout,

the general trying not to smile in Guy's direction

(for this young man is so loyal and eager to give satisfaction),

Wood still hoping to capture Joseph and then make good sign-talk with some likely squaw,

and flat white rocks bursting out of the ferny hills, the creeks loud, the clover crawling with bees

(is Fidelia afraid of bees? I never asked her. We could raise honey, maybe even enough to sell. And then I'll buy her all the picture windows she wishes),

and a pinkish-grey oval of scree way up between the spruces, almost at the ridgetop,

—and Trimble's practically tired out.

That old veteran? You must be mistaken.

Yessir.

Thanks for informing me, Wilkinson. I'll keep an eye on him

as on the creamy yellow of elderberry blossoms

and the pale yellow of a spruce-hand's fingertips,

Diamond and all the other horses snatching side-meat from trees as they go,

black clouds of ripe elderberries in the sky of foliage:

You see, Dan Sickles commanded at Dowdall's Tavern—
Where else? He's a positive major-general of barefoot whiskey.
And then when our general turned over one of his brigades to
Sickles—
But don't forget: That was Hooker's orders.
I don't care. Uh-Oh Howard should have spoken up!
Things turned around once Dan Sickles was at Hazel Grove!
No, that GoDd——d Dan Sickles lost his GoDd——d leg when
he went too far ahead at Little Round Top. It wasn't at Chan-
cellorsville.
O, wake up from your sad old war-dreams, jackasses!

and looking back down the Clearwater on that late summer afternoon he
sees the bends of fern-spruce forest commence to draw into the naked
basalt and the golden grass where they have all ridden not long since, there
where the hills are lower and balder, and Chief Joseph was closer; now
comes the blinding whiteness of the evening sun on the dark Clearwater,

pine shadows striped sideways across the hills and the cañonsides
going grey,
Bugler Brooks happily planting the guidon and pinning the headquarters flag to a pine tree:

Camp Spurgin, the general names it
(Bomus already worrying about how to provide for our
six hundred animals)
our companies watering and currying, tying up for the night
(had better send Wilkinson to watch those lumbermen in
case of whiskey, and I don't trust Chapman, either):
Now that we've taken possession of the Wallowa—
Both shrapnel and spherical case—
Dead horses—
pickets out:
No, Jocelyn. Trimble might have taken Captain Jack's surrender, but all the same he arrived later than I did at the Lava Beds,
as Captain Pollock, having gotten his bunch on the
square, not that anything resembling a company street
is possible in this broken country, reaches almost shyly
into the frogmouth pocket of his trousers, brings out a
piece of quartz laced with promising yellow color, and
delays for another two shakes the pleasure of testing it
in acqua-regia,
Doc sharing his cocaine bottle with Umatilla Jim,
Mason badgering out a comfy hole in the hill, which he always likes to do first thing, so that he won't tumble off the
mountain in his sleep,

our Bannocks cheerfully setting rabbit-snares
around that thicket over there,
while Whipple, who platonically adores her, smilingly recalls
Mrs. FitzGerald's cooking to Trimble, who nods, his cheek
bulging with a flinty fragment of hardbread,

their topic of conversation overheard by Chapman, who
will never forget the time he was called into Lapwai to
interpret in a dispute between some miners and that
Indian who had the brass to say they'd raped his wife,
and Chapman, having done his duty to the full satisfaction of everybody but the Indian, and expecting to be
well treated, made the mistake, since he had been invited to drink a root beer with the officers on Colonel
Perry's porch, of greeting Mrs. FitzGerald en route,
solely because she was standing in her doorway and because he knew his courtesies—and she told him to go
away because he drank, stank and was a *squaw man.*
Why, you porcelain-faced bitch! I've had better side-
meat than you. If I could get away with it, I'd whip your
face until you was all cut to hell. And then just staring
down through me with your nasty half-smile like I was
some nobody! . . . I'll show her, or my name ain't Ad
Chapman. If I can't make her pay some other way, I'll
sure put a spider in her dumpling!

—while Sladen and the general, with their coffee cups on stones so
that nothing spills out, sit jawboning beneath a great pine, recollecting Chancellorsville and the Freedmen's Bureau, then congrat-
ulating each other all over again for saving Cochise's Apaches from
General Crook,

enjoying forgetting about Chief Joseph, just for awhile,
talking about the wide dark face and spreading shoulder-
length hair of the Apache chief Victorio, who looked out at
them with obsidian eyes
and that pair of Apache twins in calico dresses, who sat with
their dark hands in their laps

—but just as Umatilla Jim can tell what every broken
twig means, so Wilkinson knows exactly what significance each of us has or ought to bear in relation to the
general; and he now determines that Sladen should be
more dispensable

as Wood laughingly tells Fletch: When General
Sherman learned how many demerits I'd totted
up, he said: My GOD, Wood, you'll *never* get

through! So don't you look to me for any help,
young man; you buckle down and win for yourself!
—our Bannocks now refreshing themselves on acorn bread made
long ago by their squaws,
weary cavalrymen splayed and sprawled out on tree-roots and
boulder-stairs,
and then more bad dreams charging round and round like Indians.

4

Umatilla Jim,
who used to sing his TAKH* Song at the Winter Spirit Dance
but never fainted, which was how he learned that he could not become a shaman,
lies out on picket down by Pine Tree River,
listening to the darkness in case our enemies should double back like snakes
(Looking-Glass is cunningest, but Rainbow and the Three Red
Blankets are most dangerous: his heart yearns to kill them),
but hears only night birds;
his weaselskin bracelet gives him the Power to see everything, but he sees nothing:
the enemies are not here;
but Jim will stay here until dawn, to please Píli and the general,
making himself brave, wishing for money
and Dreaming of his TAKH, the SPIDER.

5

On the contrary, Wilkinson, the original Martin design, without the reëntrant
fold, is fairly reliable.
No, sir, I do think our Bannocks are reliable.
Fairly reliable is not good enough, and you might as well admit it. Now, your
Martin is nowhere near as fine a cartridge as the Berdan, which we make in Con-
necticut for the Russian Government.
Well, then what about our Nez Perces? Just because they act like
good Indians—
Just because it's good enough for illiterate Cossacks—
Whoopla! Are you still arguing over that?
What else is left to argue over?
Chin up, Wilkinson! Are you already tired of our company?
O, my chin's up, all right. Say, Fletch, have you ever even laid eyes on a Berdan?
I'll bet you haven't.

---

*The Umatilla version of a WYAKIN.

Guy, could you bring Lieutenant Bomus up here?

Right away, father.

Good evening, lieutenant. How are you holding up?

Very well, sir. Thanks for asking.

Now, what about the animals?

The mules are fine, sir. Some of the horses are wearing down. This nasty grey wiregrass can't sustain—

You know that we hope to whip Joseph in the Bitter Root Valley.

Yessir.

But man proposes, GOD disposes.

So I've heard, sir.

How many of Joseph's ponies are still in service?

Twenty-seven, sir.

Now that we're nearing Fort Missoula, you'll find your opportunity to requisition fresh transportation. I expect you to have an estimate for me by morning.

Here it is, sir; I brought it with me when Lieutenant Howard—

Lieutenant, you're quite a fine soldier. Did you know that?

You're very kind to me, general.

Under the circumstances, the citizens of Montana can hardly expect to be paid in ready money. And they ought to be aware that any note we issue to them may take that much longer to be honored by our Government, since they're not yet part of the United States. Wood, could you draft a recapitulation for Governor Potts?

Yessir. Shall I—

No, because we don't yet know the figures. Bomus, I'm going to inspect your estimate right now, with the help of Lieutenant Wood. Report back to me at assembly call to-morrow morning. At that time, if your estimate is satisfactory, as I'm sure it will be, I'll direct you to prepare a provisional Abstract "D."

Yessir.

That will be all, Bomus. I won't forget your efficiency. Wood, you look peaked. I'll see you at "Reveille." Now, Wilkinson, who's the field officer of the day?

It's Captain Trimble, sir.

Tell him to question the scouts about a suspicious Indian named Poker Joe. Lean Elk, they also call him. A half-breed, actually. I expect a report in the morning. His mother or father was French. Our Bannocks may have some personal grudge against him, or not. Buffalo Horn claims he's in league with Joseph, and apparently he's a familiar sight on the Lo Lo. If so, we could meet trouble any night.

Right away, general.

All right. Now, between you and me, how's Wood coming along?

Well enough, sir,

> thus establishing that he bears no animus against Wood, who, while his
> military experience, let alone his maturity, cannot pretend to excellence,

and whose mannerisms strike any observer as simultaneously aloof and ridiculous, nonetheless remains one of ours.

A very promising young officer. He looks up to you.

Yessir.

I'm turning in.

Good night, general!

Good night,

and he enters his tent, lights the lantern, and pores over Lewis and Clark's old map, followed by the last two of Colton's, all the better to lead his command up through the Lo Lo Pass, which looks to be as narrow as the clasp of his brother Charles's pocket Gospels, following which he prays to OUR FATHER

for Lizzie and all the children,

likewise for a rapid victory over Joseph and his wicked confederates and finally to become better:

I have not always done right. In many things I ought to have been more careful,

especially to Lizzie, my sweetest and my dearest, *Amen*—

who, bent over a chair with the mixing bowl on it, her tired hands in the dough, gazes sharply up at him as he enters the room, her long dress powdered here and there with flour, pinewood (all she could buy just then) crackling resinously in the tall-piped stove, the teapot steaming needlessly (she must have forgotten), her face hardened by unpleasant thoughts, and then her eyes suddenly liquid with love and perhaps pity as she straightens up, her hands gloved with white balls, and he, slowly approaching her, knows what he must do: he

wakes an instant before "Reveille."

The sleepless dawn begins to glow far, far down below them, as it did two months ago in White Bird Cañon; and from a perfect darkness begins to shine a crystal blue still more perfect:

full dawn,

the dawn horizon as white as the stripe on a polecat's back.

6

Yes, Wood, what is it now?

Our couriers have just—

The ones we sent to Missoula?

Yessir.

Bring them here at once. Good morning, gentlemen. Why the long faces?

General, Captain Rawn has let the Indians through!

What do you mean?

Sir, he made a deal with Looking-Glass. And Joseph was—

I don't believe it!

Not a shot was fired, sir! The volunteers turned tail! And the Nez Perces are stocking up on provisions in the Bitter Root Valley; no storekeeper dares refuse them what they ask, even ammunition—

Anything else?

No, sir.

Go recruit your horses and ask Lieutenant Wilkinson to find you a meal. Wood, Fletch, assemble all officers captain and above at once.

Right away, sir. They're all present—

> as Umatilla Jim, taking a pinch of kinnikinnick from the flower-beaded pouch that his mother, now blind, once made for him, sits discreetly on a rock, expecting to receive new orders.

Gentlemen, no doubt you've heard the news. I know how quickly information of whatever quality travels in the Army. Let's none of us think the worst of Captain Rawn until we learn all the facts. Now, we have just lost another round to Joseph. At this rate he'll be able to lead us all over the country and perhaps even re-install himself at Wallowa before winter. Since we cannot catch him as things are, I'm dividing this command. I'll lead the advance column, and you, Major Mason, will push this bunch along as expeditiously as possible.

Yessir.

The service animals are exhausted. Lay your mules over for a spell at Summit Prairies, then string out and drive as long as you can see.

We sure will, general—

Lieutenant Fletcher.

Yessir.

Ride to Missoula at once and get all the supplies you can. Then gallop south and rejoin me; I'll probably be around Stevensville . . .

Right away, general.

God bless you! Wood, fetch James Reuben here.

He's ahead on scout, sir. Shall I recall him?

No, get me Chapman. Wilkinson, did you feed those messengers?

Yessir, and now they're dead asleep—

Where's that map? All right, Mr. Chapman, since you know this country, if you were riding out of here in a hurry to-morrow at dawn, where would you stop for the night?

Now would you mean by myself, general, or with this heavy-riding gang of yours?

Don't insult the Army, or you'll see what I can do.

No offense, general, I . . . A small detachment on good horses could camp down here where the river forks, near about twenty-one miles—

All right.

> To horse,
>> drawing up the company line
>>> (Arrow snorting, evidently longing to chase
>>> Chapman's grey racer):
> Prepare to mount.
> Mount,
>> his tired troops flashing into their saddles like parallel-swinging
>> teeth of the same great machine.

PEACE TREATY
JULY 26–28

1

*F*irst of all comes Looking-Glass, whom some call *Flint Necklace,* he who has himself placed beautiful necklaces on so many People; he rides his favorite white horse. From a wristband beaded red, blue, orange and pink, he dangles a round mirror within a great star. His right hand holds a lance tied with the white handkerchief of truce. He is our head-chief, our war-chief. Behind ride White Bird and Heinmot Tooyalakekt, and then, on Elm Limb's brown horse, comes the boy named About Asleep, a smiling horse-holder whose presence cannot scare the Bostons.

Ollokot and Toohhoolhoolsote have stayed ready with our warriors in camp by the creek, should the Bostons turn treacherous yet again. Rainbow, Five Wounds, White Thunder and the Three Red Blankets keep on guard, riding round and round, or lurking in trailside thickets with their rifles pointed out; their carefulness will not fail.

Last night Looking-Glass was tortured by a bad dream of Cut Arm sucking the marrow from a bone. But Cut Arm merely creeps about in Idaho; perhaps he has already returned to Kamiah; he is General Day-After-To-morrow. And if you remember our People's tale in which a spring jets up from the parting of someone's hair, your heart will understand how grand and beautiful things may be born according to their own rules. Thus Looking-Glass, the successful man who invariably receives his due, decides that Cut Arm's attack upon his village must have been an error, that when Tsépmin fired at our truce flag at Sparse-Snowed Place, that was a private falseness for which Cut Arm cannot be blamed; even Cut Arm's showing of the rifle at Butterfly Place was no outcome foreknown; had Toohhoolhoolsote spoken less fiercely in that council, we would live safe within our painted lands. And now Cut Arm is far away, hence unreal; so it appears to Looking-Glass that all may yet be smoothed out. His wives have soothed him; his daughters have decorated his hair. Proudly now he rides, his confidence once more glowing like the white feather in HUMMINGBIRD's heart.

White Bird, whose young men caused this war, should have stayed in camp with Toohhoolhoolsote. They have made too much sadness for our People and the Bostons;
    likewise, Tsépmin, who was once my brother, caused much trouble by lying about me, as Animal In A Hole has certainly told me. Tsépmin infuriates my heart. He should be killed, although even this I can forgo to keep the peace,
        I, Looking-Glass, who am the People's best advantage here in *Montana*, where every Boston knows me.
        Had White Bird listened to me just now, he would be hiding himself from these Bluecoats.
As they ride forward, even Looking-Glass, the *lucky man*, cannot prevent his heart from crying *qoh, qoh, qoh!*

2

The soldier chief has tried to make some wall across the cañon. He builds like a child; his accomplishment is nothing. Here at the beginning of the United States (where the Salish used to have their country, just for awhile) he waits with his Bluecoats and Bostons, and of course there must be others who spy through the trees.

Looking-Glass dismounts. The Bluecoats stare greedily at his fine white stallion, whose name is Home From Capture, and on whose bridle live lovely-graved disks of German silver,
    as White Bird and Heinmot Tooyalakekt leap likewise off their horses and About Asleep, taking the chiefs' animals by the bridles, leads them aside to graze,
        standing ready to bring them quickly, should the Bostons reveal more crookedness;
            while far from the river, past woody-red and woodyorange mushrooms growing between the spread roots of decaying oaks, runs another brown creek whose turtle-shaped boulders glisten where water intermittently rills and bubbles over them; and here, screened by ferns and alders, Rainbow calls upon his WYAKIN, Who like White Thunder's is a WOLF, and once he has finished singing the WOLF song, Rainbow, gazing up ahead at the notch of grey sky where the pines and spruces pretend to end, leaps onto his bay horse and begins following after his chiefs, to protect them as may be needed

even as Heinmot Tooyalakekt,
> he whom the Bostons call *Joseph,*

sorrows to see the Salish,
> who have always been our friends,

now helping the Bostons, talking and watching for them, with white rags tied around their foreheads and arms, so that the Bostons will understand to kill us instead of them:
> How could I resent them? They too have sold their fathers' bones,
> or else lost them for no pay;

but White Bird, whose eyes begin to flash, thinks differently.

3

Surveying the breastworks, Looking-Glass says to these others
> (whose Salish slave, bewitched by the Book of Light, interprets both ways):

I shall now speak. We are riding to the Buffalo Country. We mean to pass through your settlements without trouble. I am telling you three times: We wish no harm to anyone.

The soldier chief acts stupefied, like someone who has eaten too much steelhead salmon. Presently he says: You cannot go around me.

Heinmot Tooyalakekt explains: We are going around you peacefully if you permit it. One way or another, we are going around you.

So you're Chief Joseph! You're becoming a real famous Indian. Why don't you surrender and go on the reservation? Make your bucks give up all these rifles and trust in fair treatment.

Captain Rawn, my People have endured enough fair treatment from the *Americans.* They wish only to ride away to the Buffalo Country and never come back here.

Joseph, they say that you are the greatest war-chief since Sitting Bull. Listen to me. Save your women and children. I cannot permit you to go around me unless you leave your weapons here.

I am no war-chief. It is Looking-Glass, White Bird, Toohhoolhoolsote and Ollokot who lead the young men. Looking-Glass, what do you say?

Captain, if you desire to build corrals for our People I shall not stop you, but hear me: We are not horses. You cannot hold us back,
> as White Bird, smiling, covers his face with his feather-fan.

Well, White Bird, what do you have to say? I know you pretty well; your picture sells for a solid silver quarter around here. Why not save yourself? Are you prepared to surrender your Indians to the Government?

Captain, we remember a big war that happened on the Distant River.* Your Bluecoats fought the Cayuses, Umatillas and other tribes; and we helped you. You promised to hang only the murderers, so the Indians surrendered, and then you

---

*The Columbia.

hanged many People whose hearts were good. Now how do we know that you will not hang us once we give you our rifles?

Well, that is up to the Government, not up to me.

Looking-Glass says: Now we go to speak with our People. Shall we come into council to-morrow?

Very well. You may have until to-morrow. But remember my stipulation. You must lay down your arms,

> at which Rainbow shouts from the forest: *Cut Arm showed the rifle, and we answered with the rifle, and that answer stands unto this very sun!*

4

Wishing to punish these Bostons, three Red Blankets ride round and round the camp, demanding: Young men, why are you not stirring up war here?

Looking-Glass shouts: Without you, we People would never have Boston blood on our hands! You caused me to lose my country. Now stop this talk or else ride away; I am head-chief—

5

Most People in camp agree with Looking-Glass that we must try to keep the Bostons as our friends, since there are so many of them

> (although not even Looking-Glass wishes to give up his rifle);

so that when Toohhoolhoolsote says: Hear me! The Bostons are bad ones who wear two faces!

> at which Sound Of Running Feet, listening with *Kate* and Welweyas the
> half-woman from behind the wide dark pyramid of a young lodgepole pine
>> (Fair Land meanwhile piercing an abscess on the shoulder of Ol-
>> lokot's buffalo pony, while Good Woman and Cloudburst sit drying
>> huckleberries on a blanket, fanning the flies away,
>>> while Springtime lies down; she feels unwell, and the baby is hungry),
> begins to pull the pistol from her belt, only a little, so that not even *Kate*
> will see
>> (Toohhoolhoolsote has spoken straight!—hence the girl pretends
>> she will shoot a Boston in the face:
>>> *pim!*
>> so that flies will thicken on him like chokecherries just as they did
>> on those dead Bluecoats in Sparse-Snowed Place),
> then
>> (as Welweyas listens with her mouth wide open to our best men
>> and chiefs
>> and *Kate* sits mending a camas bag)
> slides it back inside its sleeping-place, playing with it carefully and discreetly,

comforted by its lovely metal, which is silvery like the underside of a soap-
berry leaf,
the best men now reply: Toohhoolhoolsote, no one means to contradict you, but even
with Crooked Hearts one must try to make treaties. Our war was with Cut Arm in
Idaho. Now we find ourselves in another country. Looking-Glass knows these *Americans;* how can they harm us? They are feeble and foolish like little boys. But if we kill
them, then their relations will grow angry. Let us have peace, just for awhile . . .

Toohhoolhoolsote begins polishing an arrow shaft, wishing someday to return
home and shoot more of those Butterfly Place men whose hearts were so false. He
says: It is all the same. Let us kill, die or ride away.

White Bird, hiding his face behind his white-feathered fan, is now assailed by
the ghost of woman-lipped Lawyer, who sold our country twenty-two snows ago,
with his strangely sensual half-smile, his eyes round in knowing submission, his hair wriggling in wide twin waterfalls down to his breast, his
forehead shaded by the brim of his ornate cylindrical basket-cap,
but Looking-Glass is not like that!
yet that strangely shining smile of Lawyer returns as if to
warn White Bird:
a smile knowing without sadness, as if Lawyer gave utterly himself to what he did: selling OUR MOTHER
without the consent of Dreamers and chiefs
—he lived well for that, and died a happy slave,
unlike Looking-Glass, who is our chief;
therefore I shall say nothing.
Then Heinmot Tooyalakekt warns them all from his heart: They wish to trap
us here until other Bluecoats come! Let us continue on in the best way we can, by
peace or by war,
but at this Looking-Glass grows offended: —for so well does he know what to do
and where to lead us that our very next camp already rises from his heart
(many times has he rested here with the Crows and Salish; now his
memories of other summers are as the sounds of a horseman in the
stream, not quite echoing but sharper than they would be on to-
day's hard dirt:
I remember when the *Lucky Man* and I went against Sitting
Bull, and the Salish respected us because we married with
them
and because the Bostons were our friends);
he will bring us easily through Narrow Place and to this camping-place which he
can already see on the edge of the golden grass,
if the People only mind his words;
so he raises his voice: Did you not all make me head-chief? Heinmot Tooyalakekt,
do you mean to break your promise and fight, or will you leave this to me?

Very well, Looking-Glass; you are right. Go ahead and do the best.

6

And so once again Looking-Glass
>> admitting to himself that our long friendship with the Bostons is no lon-
>> ger what it should be—but surely the Bostons cannot all be liars!—
rides down to meet this soldier chief,
>> riding so tall on his white horse, whose collar is red and blue trade cloth
>> backed with canvas and embroidered by his younger wife Asking Maiden
>> in long narrow zigzags and diamonds of white pony beads;
pulls his hat lower down his forehead, upraises his chin
> and this Bluecoat, as curious as an antelope, stares at him unmoving,
>>> so that Looking-Glass, greeting his *American* friends whose names
>>> he knows from so many summers adventuring to the Buffalo Coun-
>>> try, now reminds their young men:
>>>> I have two good-looking daughters at camp. Ride up and see
>>>> them!
>>>> No, thank you,
> the soldier chief still staring,
after which indeed
>> (just as when a child goes into the forest alone to seek his WYAKIN he
>> never gets harmed)
all turns out exactly as Looking-Glass has said, for early next morning, as TRAV-
ELLER THE SUN strikes the crowns of the tall pines
>> (a flock of cedar waxwings already hunting berries),
the People ride out, sending women, children and old ones along the side way,
>> removing the brass bells from the trappings of their horses, to avoid
>> warning the Bostons,
while Looking-Glass, sitting on his horse, frowns down at our fighters and shouts:
Young men, listen! You have started one war. Do not begin another. Do as I say!
Even if these *Americans* ride toward you, do not shoot. You must not kill them
unless they begin to kill us. I, Looking-Glass, your head-chief, have now spoken,
>> the young men staring up at him with their Dreamer eyes, their hair all
>> roached back and their necklaces showing nested wide arcs of white
>> beads in the fringed darknesses between the lips of their open-gaping
>> beadwork vests or plaid Boston shirts, their braids ornamented with
>> rings of otter-fur, and great white shell-earrings shining against their
>> chins, pricked out with wheel-like patterns
>>> (they have now drunk war enough; they are no longer yearning to
>>> kill);
thus along the high rounded ridgetops to the north, amidst greyish-green grass
and evergreens, our warriors walk their horses very slowly past the Bluecoats and
terrified Bostons,

who rush into rifle-pits, gripping their guns
>(thirty-five Bluecoats, a hundred and fifty anxious Bostons,
>seven hundred People),
>>the soldier chief unmoving like a stick;
>and all too well these others perceive that our best men, riding so slowly
>along the ridge, could shoot down into those holes and kill them all,
>>Looking-Glass riding his dear white horse, Home From Capture,
>>with ever more scornful slowness,
>>>with that round mirror shining in his hair as he waves his hat
>>>down at the Bostons,
>>>who respond with submissive silence
>>>>—they are ones who do not understand how to fight!—
>>Ollokot sitting easy on his cream-colored horse, with that .44 Rem-
>>ington holstered at his side,
>>Heinmot Tooyalakekt on Black Mane-Stripe, with his .44 Winchester
>>carbine slung barrel up across his shoulder,
>>as Burning Coals on Long Ears, whose headpiece is beaded red and
>>yellow, sings to his many horses,
>>while Fire Body,
>>>he who killed the trumpeter with that long shot at Sparse-
>>>Snowed Place,
>>wonders what might happen if he shot this Captain Rawn;
>>Toohhoolhoolsote's young men jeering at the white enemies,
>>Red Spy, Shooting Thunder and White Thunder pleased in their
>>hearts that the Bluecoats fear us,
>>the Three Red Blankets hoping to taste blood again
>>—although Looking-Glass keeps shouting: *Don't shoot; don't shoot;*
>>*let the Bostons shoot first!*
>>>—which they do not:
>>>>he has convinced Shore Crossing not to fire his
>>>>magic rifle
>>>while Fair Land gazes back at the mountains where the Lo Lo
>>>Trail leads home
>>>>(we might return once the Bostons swear to kill us no
>>>>more)
and when three Bostons come ragefully galloping, our warriors halt them with
leveled rifles, disarm them, and then Looking-Glass says: Go home, my friends;
let there be a treaty between our People and yours; we shall harm no one!
—and so we ride out of Narrow Place, coming into this country so well known to us,
>>the sharp green teeth of the Bitter Root Mountains dwindling to
>>blue-grey in the south,
>exactly here where long ago the girl Wet-ka-weis was stolen from our
>People by Shoshonis, who first raped and then traded her; certain Bos-

tons were kind, and helped her run away; so she informed us upon her
dying return;
so we ride, then,
as Toohhoolhoolsote's leg-rattles hiss like snakes,
into the United States of America, safe and happy with Looking-Glass's new
treaty.

LOOKING-GLASS'S DREAM
JULY 28–CA. AUGUST 2

1

*L*ooking-Glass has dreamed of spying on a Cutthroat camp, then getting
caught:
now he is dead, and someone, perhaps his Crow friends, has wrapped
him up in buffalo robes,
dogs sniffing and grinning all around;
the scaffold has already been lashed and withed into four saplings; his
mourners are riding away;
this dream he used to dream many times, long ago, when he was young and helped
the Crows fight the Cutthroats. Now he never dreams it.

2

It is good to smoke with our friends and relations the Salish, if not as delicious
as it might have been had they not helped the Bostons at Narrow Place. Here there
is no war. The Bluecoats have gone home. The Bostons are quiet; the Salish hate
them less than they do the Shinbones, who have driven them west of the Divide.

So Looking-Glass, whom the Salish know as *Big Hawk*, leads his People into
camp by J. P. McClain's ranch, here in Chief Left Hand's country
(a month too late for wild roses and blue lupines),
and now we have decorated our faces
as our young men tell jokes about Cut Arm the Moldy (we shall wipe our
buttocks on his head)
and even White Thunder, ordinarily so modest, begins to inform
our Salish cousins of his doings:
And then, when he could not die by himself, we crushed that
Bluecoat's head, *taq!*

Looking-Glass knows everything here:

the Jocko River, where even a Boston could catch twenty or thirty trout in an
hour,

and the whitewashed Agency sheds and buildings within the picket fence:

> the Bostons are his friends, even Mr. Ronan the Indian Agent and his
> wife Mary with her knee-length hair
>> (once they allowed him to help himself to their apple orchard);
> and certain pretty Salish women who have become wives to the Agent's
> Bostons, just for awhile;

he has been present when the Salish Dog Soldiers ride through camp singing
and waving their rattles;

all this is well known to Looking-Glass's heart;

moreover, the Bostons have shown him inside F. L. Worden's mill at Missoula;

they have said: Looking-Glass, you're sure the most honest Indian we know!

—and now at Looking-Glass's word our women begin cutting bed-grass, unrolling
blankets and boiling soup,

> there at the river's edge, in the golden grass worn away by deer.

Chief Left Hand

> (Eagle Of The Light's brother)

leaps off his horse to meet us, with two circlets of bells strapped to his naked leg,
a blanket falling down from his hips, covering the other leg, ten necklace-ellipses
concentric on his naked chest, his throat choked snug in dentalia, his forehead
crowned with feathers, his face weathered and wary

> so that Looking-Glass,
>> he who must now lead the People,
> feels queasy in his heart about Left Hand,
>> who used to be our friend;

but the Salish women are happy to see our women,

> trading with them their last pretty white bitterroots for flinty hunks of smoked
> Boston beef from Weippe:

they make snowberry poultices for Peopeo Tholekt and Animal In A Hole, for
which we must thank them in our hearts

>> (and poor-hearted Loon, who wished most of all to be a brave and
>> longhaired man whose face would be handsomely painted, now be-
>> lieves in his heart that these Salish maidens are looking him over);

now Fair Land and Cloudburst have already begun boiling bitterroots into
white jelly for their son and their dear husband;

Springtime is softening dried Boston meat in boiling water until we can
eat it

>> (her husband caresses her neck and she smiles at him,
>>> her teeth as white as the tiny full moons of reflected glare which
>>> shine out from buffaloberries in the summer afternoons);

> Toohhoolhoolsote, almost silent, cants his head, closes his eyes,

unlike Looking-Glass's daughters, who, well decorated, watch their
Salish cousins with encouraging half-smiles
         (some People believe them to be as man-hungry as the GRIZZLY
        BEAR SISTERS)
and Left Hand greets us in words as long and straight as a courting flute
        (Heinmot Tooyalakekt now gives him a new blanket-coat with brass but-
        tons, receiving in return the well-fringed deerskin shirt that the Salish
        chief has been wearing)
while Stripes Turned In trades a dead Bluecoat's canteen for a woven bag of pemmican.
    When some Bostons ride in, evidently by mistake, Looking-Glass's young men
catch them. Toohhoolhoolsote's warriors are shouting and cursing, but Looking-
Glass remains our head-chief; and to these prisoners he says: We have made a
treaty. Go home to your women; we shall never harm you,
at which the Bostons leap on their horses, galloping away in terror
   (we cannot prevent ourselves from laughing).

3

Now we are dancing the Spirit Dance here in the dying grass:
    Toohhoolhoolsote has hypnotized himself
    and Heinmot Tooyalakekt and Ollokot are now Dreaming, with their
    blanket-stripes turning;
            the Three Red Blankets are flying up
                and for a long time, frowning as if blindly, Star Doctor droops
                his head, inhaling the scents of faraway salmon and camas,
                then rings the Dreamer's bell . . .
        and Sound Of Running Feet, who has not yet climbed Faraway
        Mountain to meet her WYAKIN, begins to Dream of SOMETHING
        elongated like a horse's head;
    White Bird is carried away in Dreams
        (while Looking-Glass dances but does not Dream
            and in a hollow tree, hunching its shoulders, a screech-owl
            gives us its yellow gaze)
so that the Salish say: Our Agent will not like this. We were almost forgetting how
to Dream.

4

   Calling a council, Heinmot Tooyalakekt and Toohhoolhoolsote ask what shall
be done
        exactly now when the Salish have withdrawn themselves to sleep
            and the People's lodges grow pallid, the pole-mounted disks of our
            war-shields resembling dim reflections of the moon.

We are smoking kinnikinnick, passing the pipe around the circle.

From the Buffalo Country three of our warriors have just this day arrived; their chief is Grizzly Bear Youth,

> who has been scouting for a Bluecoat named Bear Coat[*]
>
> > (which proves that the Bostons outside of *Idaho* are still our friends);

he says: I shall now show you my mind. Crow warriors are scouting for Bluecoats against the Painted Arrows[†] and Cutthroats! All Bluecoats are brothers, I am telling you three times! Since Cut Arm has no pity for you, neither will Bear Coat or these Crows he has bought for coffee and molasses. If you wish to stay free, ride quickly north, across the Salish painted lands,

> perhaps through War-Chief Arlee's country
>
> > (his mother was of the People),

and over the Medicine Line to the Old Woman's Country

> > —as a fish splashes: *mokh!*

Next speaks one whom we barely know: Lean Elk, gambler and breeder of stallions

> > —soon to be famous among us—

> who rode up on one of his many spotted racehorses, dressed in Salish style with a choker of black and white dentalium, with a feather waving over his head, and quillwork on his brass-buttoned trade vest;
>
> > he is of our People even though his father was a Boston[‡] and he lives here in the Salish country;
> >
> > > when he injured himself hunting on the Lo Lo Trail, the Bostons cast distrust upon him, saying: *You must have been fighting alongside Chief Joseph!*

—So he must now ride away with us. He tells the council: Grizzly Bear Youth speaks straight! Unless we cross the Medicine Line, the Bostons will surely hunt us.

Looking-Glass rears up, replying: Indeed this is something to consider in our hearts. But hear me, all you chiefs and best men: The Salish helped the Bluecoats just now at the Narrow Place. We can never trust them;

> and Rainbow
>
> > (craving a certain dark yellow horse of which he has Dreamed: surely in the Buffalo Counry he will find it)

> and his war-brother Five Wounds
>
> > —those two who some say fight bravest and wisest of us all
> >
> > > (although others prefer the Three Red Blankets)—

> both agree that Looking-Glass continues to be right: the Buffalo Country remains best;

---

[*]Howard's old comrade Colonel Nelson Miles.
[†]Cheyennes.
[‡]Probably a Frenchman.

there where to the east the grey-brown river speeds toward the
shrub-grizzled mountains in the shadow of cloud-strata, and the
farthest of the arrow-straight, blue-grey cloud-lines already mist
down widening rays of rain;
on the horizon the yellow grass is shadowed green; and above it
hang pure white and blue boulders made out of clouds;
then the horizon thickens, darkens,
and the world grows black with buffalo;
and where the buffalo are, there sweet Crow women will
come riding, with their hair-partings painted vermilion.
Taking the pipe one after the other, White Bird and Red Owl both assert that
we should ride straight to the Old Woman's Country regardless;
likewise Wottolen, Red Owl and Two Moons,
although they cannot tell us how it will be in the Old Woman's
Country, or whether we can ever come back again
(because as Red Owl says: They live so far off that perhaps my
heart will never reach them);
while Sound Of Running Feet, who is sitting by the fire
with her mothers and her new sister, mending the seam
of her father's moccasins, wonders why the men talk on
and on, *pokát, pokát,*
for in our legends, whenever COYOTE gets killed
and thrown into the river, He is soon awakened
by MAGPIE's pecking at His eye-fat, *pokát, pokát,*
at which He invariably complains that MAGPIE
has now interrupted Him just as He was helping
some women ford the river
and just then her dear mother Springtime, whose heart
is often happier or sadder than Good Woman's, murmurs to the others: *pokát, pokát!*
and they all giggle
while Owhi, Horn Hide Dresser and Ugly Grizzly Bear Boy,
just now returned from the Big Bellies and barely escaped from
roving Bostons,
speak likewise against Looking-Glass's long road to the Buffalo Country,
where the Bluecoats, having driven out Sitting Bull, might next
come hunting us;
hence they likewise cry out that White Bird has spoken what is true.
Then Heinmot Tooyalakekt,
he who has been called *Joseph,*
although the Bostons baptized him *Ephraim,*
takes the pipe, smokes and is silent, then finally begins to speak: Much has been
said. Our hearts are now divided. White Bird and Looking-Glass have the most

wisdom about this country; for many summers they have been riding through here to hunt buffalo. It is for them to agree with each other, and tell us what to do. Looking-Glass, you are head-chief. We must follow you. Carefully complete your heart! Consider what White Bird has to say. As for me, I have seen this country only once before, so I have no words.

Looking-Glass says: I have saved you all from shedding more Boston blood, and you ought to thank me. Heinmot Tooyalakekt, am I not right?

> but just as he has always taken care to decline the Bostons' presents, to prevent them from pretending that he sold them his country for a pair of blankets, so now Heinmot Tooyalakekt in silent carefulness smiles away the other chief's words, and

Toohhoolhoolsote, shaking himself so that his necklaces hiss and rattle, presently says: Take care, Looking-Glass, lest you become another of those men about whom you always complain, the ones who can be bought for a plug of tobacco!

> —at which Ollokot, suspecting that his brother is being referred to, sets his mouth in anger as the bear-hearted chief speaks on:

Looking-Glass, you have made yourself delighted with this new treaty. Well, we shall learn its price.

Like a screech-owl, ageing Looking-Glass,
> he who once had a country,
stares great-eyed at him
> —and the resinous branches are exploding in the fire: *tóq!*

as he says: Hear me now. It is your braves who caused this trouble, yours and White Bird's. Had you all stayed quiet on your painted lands as I did, there would have been no war.

5

Truth to tell, Looking-Glass has reason never to ride to Sitting-Bull,
for he has joyously slain many Cutthroats,
> not least the womanfaced lovely young enemy brave who held his eagle shield against me, who raised up his stone-ball club against me—I saw the teeth in his smile when I shot him off his pony—that Cutthroat enemy in the striped cloth shirt!

he has fought even against great Crazy Horse, who painted himself with white hailstones at Little Big Horn
> (I hear he has surrendered to Bear Coat);

he has faced off against Moving Robe Woman, who is more dangerous than two grizzlies:
> proudly does my heart remember her smooth oval face, red-painted, crinkled with rage, her braids flapping in the wind as she pulled the trigger of her Colt six-shooter, the shells of her eardrops rattling and their paddle-shaped endplates of abalone slapping against her high hard little breasts

(how I have yearned to kill her!)
—what welcome will these enemies offer Looking-Glass the *lucky man?*

6

So we have decided it: to leave Cut Arm far behind, turn our backs upon the
Salish, and go to Looking-Glass's friends the Crows,
          travelling together
               (for as White Bird has truly said: If we go to the Crows, we all
                must go)
       riding away from our fathers' graves, into the country where not so many
       names of places are known.
Soon we shall ascend new mountains, then come down into the Buffalo Coun-
try, where the forest must let us go, and singing flocks of lazuli buntings will bear
their many colors to the summer bushes and streams; then the EARTH OUR
MOTHER will widen before us.
Once more Fair Land dreams of the other side of some river.

7

At dawn Shore Crossing's wife is already rolling up their blanket
       (soon her baby will come);
       Shore Crossing has already swum in the river
as we begin to break camp,
       the shadows slowly drawing in from the banks of Montana's river-slits,
       night clinging a trifle longer beneath dead logs and weed-mounds right
       on the shore; then these too lose their Power, giving way to their comple-
       mentary aspects of brown-green reflection; and where those shallow
       streams flow fastest across the gravel, flocks of fingernail-shaped suns
       tremble in place; and wherever the gaze may speed, it finds a partially
       melted sun in the shallows, its whiteness capable of ruining the vision,
       afflicting any eye with swarming spots both white and black;
exchanging presents with our relations the Salish,
       whom the Shoshonis call *the Shaved-Head People;*
and since they fear the Bostons, their hearts grow happy when we ride away;
       we are lonely as we go,
          with clouds like long strands of white algae in the morning sky, and
          a cool wind coming off the river;
and now Looking-Glass's People set out on the trail,
       wondering about Red Heart's People, hoping they have come safe to the
       painted land, hemmed in without cruelty on Cut Arm's part
          (Burning Coals is still whispering to his horse herd and deco-
          rating Lucky One, whom he will ride to-day);

and Red Owl remembers late summer days in his lost country, all colors
sometimes clouded down at Cañon's Mouth,
>   where we once used to live, just for awhile,
and the reddish-brown handholds of Cliff Place, where we once climbed
after deer, then looked down at the cool brown water
>   (when the breeze was right we could smell the green grass),
and our decorated tipis which Cut Arm has now burned:
>>   as we were riding away from the battle, Red Owl committed the
>>   error of looking back; now he cannot vomit out of his heart the
>>   sight of Cut Arm's bonfire . . .
—second ride Toohhoolhoolsote's People (who can travel most quickly of us all,
but prefer to let Looking-Glass go ahead and meet whatever blame):
>   some of their young men go to watch from Rocky Ridge Mountain, in
>   case Cut Arm should be creeping here, but they find nothing bad;
after them, having turned his six best racehorses into our herd, rides Lean Elk
>   (Looking-Glass has said: Who is Lean Elk that he was not with us from
>   the beginning of our troubles? If you wish to follow him, I am satisfied; I
>   have shown you my heart. Let the trouble be yours);
and Wild Oat Moss, a warrior with many Salish relatives,
after whom ride White Bird's People,
>>   Swan Necklace and Strong Eagle adventuring off the trail; now they are
>>   draining the blood from a deer they have just shot; their women will be
>>   pleased;
>>   while Shore Crossing rides steadily with that heavy-barrelled buffalo rifle
>>   over his shoulder,
then Star Doctor, Húsishúsis Kute, Chief Hahtalekin and the other Palouses,
and Ollokot now leads our young men out of camp
as Springtime, Fair Land, Good Woman, Sound Of Running Feet, Cloudburst and
Welweyas the half-woman
>   (whose dearest love is helping other women)
finish packing their horses;
>>   and Welweyas's mother Agate Woman returns to the meadow with her
>>   camas hook, hoping to receive a certain secret root from her WYAKIN
>>   even as Heinmot Tooyalakekt goes down to a private place by the river,
>>   hearing the horses say: *Hinimí*
>>>   (farther and farther away)
>>   and watching as Good Woman spreads her thighs, beginning to wade across
>>   the river squatwise and rapidly, her bare feet as tough as her moccasins on
>>   the sharp rocks; and instead of shadow she casts a pool of coldly burning
>>   white sunlight around her at every step, as if when she weighs down the
>>   water she is squeezing light out of it; and when she stops, turning back to
>>   gaze at him, wriggling braids of light hang from her heels, seeming ready to
>>   swim away downstream at any instant; and then, gazing down at the water,

she returns to him in careful slowness, bearing the light with her as she goes. Squatting lower, with her silver-threaded black braids now grazing the water, she makes urine. She smiles up at him. The black bangs slant across her oval face, and she wears shell-disk earrings saved from Cut Arm. Then she wades back to a deeper place, never slipping on the furry green algae, squats low again as if to make more urine, and suddenly catches a trout.

8

Riding south through the Bitter Root Valley,
> our horse-wealth even now as thick and roiling and luminous as midges
> over a brown river on a late summer morning
>> (that stingy old Burning Coals owns more stallions than anyone),
the People allow themselves to be led by Looking-Glass,
> who believes that his life is still following the steady water-glide of a
> grebe with its bill aimed straight forward;
>> camas now long out of flower,
>>> Springtime missing Brown One, her favorite horse, whom
>>> Cut Arm stole after the fight at Big Water;
>>> Good Woman seeks late bitterroots for Springtime (they are good
>>> for breast milk); perhaps the Salish women in Charlot's country
>>> will help her;
and wherever we go, the Bostons shyly hide, which pleases our hearts.

White Thunder, who grew up hunting buffalo, begins to feel like singing—for soon we shall be riding and hunting forever!

But Heinmot Tooyalakekt feels sorrow: in our home the longtailed wild ginger's leaves must have begun to wilt just now.

Stopping at the Berry-Picking Place which the Salish once showed us, Swan Woman, Cloudburst, *Kate* and Good Woman pick six baskets of huckleberries
> (laughing at the Salish,
> who never pound meat together with berries)
> as Springtime and Fair Land hang up their cradleboards from an aspen
> tree and pick huckleberries together
>> (as naughty Cloudburst, seizing her chance, runs to tease Ollokot,
>> whispering in his ear: My darling husband, will you tell me that I
>> am your loveliest one?
>> —Enough! Now be silent),
> while Shore Crossing shoots a golden eagle from a tree, then gives away
> the feathers to his friends;
then we ride on,
> dipping our buffalo horns into the creek as we go.
>> White Bird is saying: Let them now decorate their faces for Char-
>> lot's People

>   (if we are good to them then they should give us good pres-
>   ents),

and Looking-Glass is painting himself red and yellow.

Heinmot Tooyalakekt, his heart rising into joy, begins gazing at his beautiful younger wife:

>   longing to play again with her butterfly,* whose pale pinkness reminds
>   him of buffaloberries picked from the stalk not long since,

and she turns around in the saddle, understands his eyes, flushes, looks away and then back again, smiling now

>   (in the cradleboard their baby stares at TRAVELLER THE
>   SUN),

then says: Husband, make your heart happy! All is now straight!

Indeed Looking-Glass has done well.

I cannot contradict you, since we go to the Buffalo Country, where Bostons are few and we shall always have meat. Is that not so?

Síikstiwaa, he answers, even now I would give my own life to undo what the young men have done.

9

First they ride into Charlot's camp across the river from the town of Stevensville,
>   tipis secluding themselves on the meadow which has decorated itself
>   with the pallid orange seedheads, almost like miniature cattails, of Or-
>   egon grape,
>>   and there are already so many silver-purple berries which the chil-
>>   dren are hoping to pick, but first we must smoke a pipe with the
>>   Salish

because White Bird is hoping to meet his dear uncle, Eagle of the Light, who re-mains chief of eleven lodges in this place
>   (once he lived with us at Sparse-Snowed Place, but the Bostons kept ruin-
>   ing us with *getting-drunk liquid,* so he rode away exactly here;
>>   nowadays they are tormenting him again, because he refuses to go
>>   onto painted land),

while Looking-Glass means to take counsel of Charlot,
>   who, however, tells him: Why shall I shake hands with men whose hands
>   are stained with blood? My hands are clean!
>>   —Rainbow hoping nonetheless to please the Salish maidens who
>>   enchant him with the wavy beadwork on their buckskin dresses
>>>   (they have perfumed themselves with balsam needles)
>>   as Good Woman trades some jerked Boston beef for a good
>>   wooden-handled berry pounder to give to Fair Land,

---

*Vulva.

who lost hers in Red Owl's country (Cut Arm devoured it);

and Charlot, with whom our best men have fought against the
Shinbones, rides round and round in a Boston's stovepipe hat,
proudly wearing the military cloak and striped belly-sash that Governor Stevens gave out twenty-two years ago, for the treaty before
the *thief treaty:*

pulling his hat low over his eyes, he frowns at Looking-Glass
even as Lone Bird, one of our bravest young men, rides
around calling out: We should keep riding, riding fast!
Death may now be following on our trail,

although Grizzly Bear Youth, whose WYAKIN is
the AIR BIRD, has Dreamed of nothing evil;

then Charlot says: Hear me, my dear brothers, friends and relations! My heart is sad
at this trouble you have brought upon yourselves. Now I must think upon the best
way for my People and yours. The Bostons here will hunt you down like angry bears;
between them and the Bostons where you came there is no difference; they are both
Americans. Rest to-night, then hasten east. If you have no care for your own women
and children, take pity on ours! The Bostons long to devour the last morsels of my
country. If you stay in this place, they will say that we both conspire against them.
Then we too shall lose our freedom.

Yes, says Toohhoolhoolsote, I well understand what your freedom is. Hear me,
Charlot! You have lost your courage. I shall no more call you chief, for you have
learned to live like a toothless old woman pounding meat which she cannot eat!
—at which Looking-Glass shouts: I who am head-chief dislike this talk! Charlot,
I say to you what I said to the Bluecoats: We shall pass on to the Buffalo Country,
with or without your friendship. Bid us welcome or not; it is all the same to me.
Have you forgotten my deeds?

Not at all, Looking-Glass, I welcome you; may your hearts all be at peace; only
I pray you not to stay too long . . .

so we settle in a circle:

Kate, not much listening to the chiefs, has spied ripe chokecherries,
so she and Welweyas, Agate Woman and Cloudburst, Helping Another and old Towhee now gather them, laying them out to dry on
elkhides before their lodges,
and the Salish women come to help

(Welweyas admires the smell of their hair),
giving them horsemint to crush up and sprinkle over the fruit so
that no flies will land on it,

although many do land regardless,
as the Salish men sigh sadly over Burning Coals's great herd of horses
(here it has proved impossible to keep so many).
Now some People go shopping in Stevensville,

although Charlot's People stay quiet in their lodges, fearing that the Bostons will punish them after we have gone

    —besides, they have ridden to Stevensville before—

and Fair Land will not go

    (Cloudburst, who longs just to look, and maybe to obtain some lovely thing, locks her mouth, unwilling to go against her elder sister-wife);

Sound Of Running Feet, whose heart despises Bostons, keeps her baby sister with her in camp, so that her mothers may please their hearts in Stevensville;

    although it should be confessed that even this obedient one, who has brass buttons, gold dust, needles and other treasures in a tiny flower-patterned beaded bag that her Aunt Fair Land made for her, would have liked to discover whatever newness she could—especially because in the Buffalo Country there may be no more Bostons forever, which was why she had quietly asked: Mother, may I ride in to buy Boston things?—to which Good Woman replied: My daughter, you have no sense! Stay here in camp and help. The Bostons sell nothing good! . . . and off she rode with Springtime to buy no-good things, leaving Sound Of Running Feet behind:

now she is asking Fair Land to tell again the tale of WATER WOMAN—the girl's favorite story—as they sit together fanning flies off the drying chokecherries,

    and for a moment Cloudburst turns away, resentfully opening and shutting the breastpin that Ollokot gave her)—

so we are riding up Main Street, our warriors well feathered and painted, with red flannel in their hair,

    Looking-Glass first, like a proud bird outspreading his tail,

    calling to his old Boston friends: Hear me, merchants! We need food, and we can pay. Open your doors, or we shall take without paying!

and the Bostons rush to unlock their shops,

  which the People enter happily

    (Looking-Glass truly knows how to speak to Bostons!):

our young women unwrapping five dollar bills from around their braids, happy to pay triple for hardbread and brown sugar,

    Good Woman and Springtime keeping close together, with their husband nearby them

    (his heart desires nothing here),

Wounded Head's wife beside About Asleep's mother, hoping for
flour,
Looking-Glass's wives and daughters knowing full well what to
bargain for,
even as Arrowhead, she who always rides with a wolfskin over her
shoulders, pays gold dust for a bottle of calomel
while Shore Crossing seeks cartridges for his great buffalo rifle
   —he has begun dreaming of his own death—
but the merchant laughs and shakes his head; that gun was for
great-grandfathers!
Espowyes, who is also called *Thunder-Eyes,* stands high in the stirrups
on a horse tricked out with a yoke of stripes and triangles; he is wearing
a war bonnet of eagle feathers, and as he now comes up Main Street he
upraises a Cutthroat tomahawk, just to tease the Bostons;
following him rides Peopeo Tholekt on his longnecked yellow horse,
and then Old Yellow Wolf, Wottolen and Black Eagle, those three all
leaping off their stallions together, and entering each retail establishment, just for awhile, until the Bostons lower their heads;
and Yellow Bull, who once killed certain Bostons in their homes back at
the Chinook Salmon Water,
while Grey Eagle leads his daughter White Feather into the apothecary's
shop, where they look without buying anything;
and old Tzi-kal-tza, happy to see Bostons again, tells each merchant: *Me
Clark!* although the merchants will not smile back;
Ollokot pays up-to-date greenbacks for bags of flour and coffee
   (as usual, the Bostons mark up the prices),
then chooses new blankets for his wives;
and White Thunder comes riding up Main Street with one cartridge belt
across the shoulder and the other around his waist:
   He walks into a store and lays down a gold button from the dead
   Bluecoat officer at Sparse-Snowed Place. He points to a plug of tobacco and the scared bearded Boston lays it on the counter,
   acrosss an opened spread of newspaper
      (*The Missoulian*)
   whose headline reads
      (White Thunder cannot read it):
   HELP! HELP! WHITE BIRD DEFIANT! COME RUNNING!
   He points to an opened crate of Winchester cartridges. The Boston
   shakes his head;
but Shooting Thunder meets no trouble in purchasing a two-bladed
screwdriver for a Springfield rifle (his), with an attached wrench for the
mainspring;

and Welweyas the half-woman, wishing to get something fine for Sound
Of Running Feet, is trying to sell a shield-shaped pin of silvered brass, with
an eagle on top and Rutherford B. Hayes handsomely, pallidly ferrotyped
within an oval window whose sash reads **OUR CENTENNIAL PRESIDENT**.
No, squaw. That ain't money. No good.
No good?
Where'd you get this, anyway?

10

As for Toohhoolhoolsote,
   whom we once appointed to speak for us before Cut Arm,
he declines to chaffer with Bostons,
      being one who has ridden three times to P'na, where Smohalla's tule
      lodge rises steep, narrow and unusually long—since that *lucky man* now
      has more than a dozen wives—not far from the rapids where the Sacred
      Island guards its rock-images, ready to drown all ignorant and impure;
      and within the lodge, our line of men now faces our line of women across
      the white sand of the dance floor as Smohalla rings the handbell; all this
      is good in Toohhoolhoolsote's heart, because Smohalla will never sell
      OUR MOTHER, remaking Her into a dead tree gnawed by ants;
let others meet those Bostons if they wish,
      the Bostons, who herd People and drive away animals everywhere.

11

A pair of Bostons sell *getting-drunk liquid,*
      so that Looking-Glass and White Bird must whip three crazy braves out
      of town, to avoid annoying any Bostons
while Toohhoolhoolsote says to Rainbow: I know the true worth of Bostons' talk;
      then his warriors pillage a Boston's house,
      loving the cool darkness, where a long spiderweb tapers as it descends
      from the smokehouse ceiling until it becomes nearly ropelike,
   playing with a tea set, a Bible and a birdcage,
   cutting a harness to pieces,
   then seizing bags of coffee and flour to feed their People
      and also laying hands on a few horses;
   but Looking-Glass, who always knows what to do,
makes them return the horses and even brand seven of their own horses with his
brand;
   because we must keep our treaty:
      the *Americans* are our friends; it is only Cut Arm and his Bluecoats and
      Bostons who hate us in their hearts.

12

A whiskey-vending Boston comes to camp and sells them ammunition; they pay with a brown mare. Indeed the *Americans* are their friends.

13

Again Looking-Glass complains (not to White Bird, whose chief the man is, but to Heinmot Tooyalakekt, who will listen) that Shore Crossing keeps causing trouble among the Bostons.— The Wallowa chief replies: What was he to do? When the Bostons killed his father, we told him that he should have made himself brave. Now that he has taken revenge, we must not blame him.

His women take pleasure in the coffee and flour they have bought,
> trading some with Salish women
>> (who dare not go to Stevensville)
> for serviceberry cakes;
and Welweyas now wears a leather-sheathed Wilson skinning knife around her neck
> (price: that goldpiece she gleaned from the battlefield at Sparse-Snowed Place).

Springtime feels happy-hearted in her new beargrass cap; she thanks her elder sister-wife. Now she has laid down fresh grass bedding; from a fine piece of deerskin she begins cutting out new moccasins for her husband,
> whose hair is now being roached anew by Good Woman,
while the young men are shouting, laughing and showing their hands as they play the Stick Game
> (the evening clouds as complex as the white fernlike intricacies of yarrow leaves),
>> as Sun Tied's wife sits quiet under a cottonwood; her birth-pangs are almost coming,
> and Lean Elk races horses with Ollokot, who loses three times;
> White Thunder smokes the pipe with Old Yellow Wolf and Wottolen,
>> whose heart remains clear of any evil Dream,
and Sound Of Running Feet, standing before the striped blanket hung out to air on a branch beside her father's lodge
> (Good Woman has given her a green hair-ribbon from Stevensville:
>> to-night she will cherish it; perhaps to-morrow she will wear it),
watches the gambling, wondering how it would be to get gambled away to some handsome brave, for it is the time of life when a girl begins to Dream for herself.

We dance the Rabbit Dance with the Salish
> (Burning Coals's daughter keeps acting husband-hungry),

and then Heinmot Tooyalakekt rings the handbell while his long braids
fall down his chest, barely swaying, at which Ollokot, Toohhoolhoolsote,
Looking Glass and Hahtalekin commence to beat the drums, and so the
People chant and dance with Charlot's People, who like Left Hand's People have forgotten much,
and Sound Of Running Feet suddenly begins to sing:

> Gun *will help.*
> Gun *will help.*
> Gun *will help.*

> Springtime weeps. Good Woman and Heinmot Tooyalakekt
> keep their eyes closed,
>> and Charlot rings the handbell.

For that one last time we camp in Charlot's country, and in the night time we
see the Three Sisters* shining in the sky.

14

We are going, following the river, departing from war,
> offering tobacco to the Medicine Tree,
> and far below us, the river ripples *mululululu.*
Soon we shall rest at Ground Squirrel Place
> where our women can cut new lodgepoles
>> (a few warriors can ride with them to watch for grizzly
>> bears);
> then Sun Tied's wife will surely give birth at last:
>> —to a girl, as both she and he have Dreamed—
and once we arrive in the Crow Country, we shall kill much meat
and sun-dry all the buffalo hides we wish; then we shall make new lodges, so
that Cut Arm will not have harmed us forever.
But Heinmot Tooyalakekt remembers Wallowa's dark clouds of horses and
then his father's grave
> and the lake, the sparkle on the lake,
>> which opens out like its own world of dark turquoise
> and evergreens sloping up away from it into the sky,
> and the mountains behind it growing smoky grey as Traveller the
> Sun begins to set,
>> the sky going white now
>>> but not as white as the fingernail moon rising over the ridge
>> while golden grass dulls to silver-white and grey
>> and the cool creek, already almost black, sings more powerfully in
>> the silence,

---

*Probably three stars in the handle of the Big Dipper.

the western sky orange now, bearing salmon-colored clouds
  (the mountains not yet as dark as the trees)
and things emerge from underneath:
    hissing black water down beneath the leaves,
    silver grass reaching for the MOON
    and shadows crawling up out of the snowberry thickets
        (whose flowers and berries remain white amidst their dark,
        dark leaves)
and in the black water I see my WYAKIN, the OTTER
and I almost see my father
and the water and the grass.

15

And now after all our riding we shall turn up into the Bitter Root Mountains;
we have come up against the ending-place of our ancient country
  (once all this land was for us and our brothers the Salish;
  it now begins to seem to our hearts that we rode around here long ago).
As we approach these mountains, they grow, wrapping around this world in a
dark blue embrace.
Riding up toward the cold stars, we pull tight our blankets, and even Swan
Woman puts on her beargrass cap.
We are riding up,
    our eager boys and old ones, best men and cradleboarded babies, our
    lovely women with their braids white-ringed with beads and their blan-
    kets perfectly striped and plaided by unknown Bostons,
        Sun Tied's wife holding her belly in her left hand while
        her right arm wards away branches,
        Cloudburst still regretful that Ollokot would not invite her to
        Stevensville,
        Wottolen and White Thunder following a game trail to a creek,
        hesitating whether to follow it up or down
as our horses say: *Hinimí*.
        Rocks roll down from under their hooves.
  We are crossing the divide;
    there are no more larch trees;
  we are eating the first sour chokecherries as we go;
and now we will be riding down toward the morning SUN where the country is
bleached like a buffalo robe.
  And on the fourth day since our peace treaty with the Bostons, we stop to cut
lodgepoles.

GIBBON AT MISSOULA
AUGUST 2–4

1

So this is the county seat—
my boys down on Front Street, getting drunk while they can and pissing into
the Hell Gate River,
> waiting for the infantry to march in
>> (we'll be a hundred and thirty-five effectives by to-night
>>> if you count a crapload of volunteers),

nice little white houses at the riverfront, O, boy, and the Kennedy House, not to mention that gristmill out there, then yellow-green field-squares of American Progress,
> here where our Flatheads, lolling almost naked on the knoll within a
> circular perimeter of tipis, used to watch two braves at a time go creeping
> on their knees, competing in the Ring Game,
>> back in the years and centuries before Indian service arrived;

harvesters at work
and even mountains. A d——d sight better than Tongue River, but not for long,
because after this business with Mr. Joe, I'll whip the Cheyennes (but how can
I prevent Miles from taking credit? GoDD——n his soul.). Wish I was out fishing. Never mind that new bank they're so proud of—how much demonetized
silver has it got? Oxen lying down in the streets—well, who wouldn't? What
two-cent pisser'd want to live here?

> Missoula, Montana, O, my GoDD——d back.

What do you think of our city, colonel?
Quite a promising burgh. You folks will make a first rate job of it, just as soon
as Mr. Joe's been cleared out. And the location seems very, you know, salubrious.
Thanks, colonel. I'll quote you on that. And I'm sure going to write some
mighty admiring words about you and your shining Seventh Infantry!
Fine. That's wonderful. Heard you was with the volunteers at Lo Lo.
Yessir.
Come on. Admit you got disappointed.
Sure. *Fort Fizzle*, they're calling it—
Well, Rawn done what he could with not enough men. Some of you Bitter
Rooters were cowards, and some of our boys also maybe might have done better;
don't print that. Anyhow, you saw Joseph and Looking-Glass and that bunch?
That's right, colonel. Real proud-looking Indians. Last of the breed, I guess. No,
I'm not blaming the Army. They outnumbered us three to one.

Got you some local color, did you? All right, Mr. Barbour. I hope to afford you better news before long. See you around. Lieutenant Bradley, take some dictation now. You're the best writer in this Army.

All right, general.*

Have you telegraphed to Fort Shaw?

Sure have, sir.

Well, then this is to Governor Potts. Usual salutation, and too bad he couldn't make it, not that I care.

Yes, sir.

Please give instructions to have no negotiations with the Indians, and the men should have no hesitancy in—you got that?

Yes, sir.

Or should it be *hesitation?* Guess it don't much signify.

No, sir.

In shooting down any armed Indian they meet not known to belong to one of the peaceful tribes.

Got it, sir.

What a disgrace, though, that Rawn! To chitterchat with Looking-Glass, and let the reds straight through!

Couldn't agree more, sir.

Is he still in a sulk?

Last I heard, sir, he was exhorting "I" Company.

Well, well. I s'pose it was *them* who was the cowards. Or the volunteers, at least. Orderly! O, it's you, Schlept. Find a courier and get this telegraphed at Deer Lodge.

Yessir.

Now, Bradley, where are my good Indians?

That Bannock chief Buffalo Horn has sent you some fine-looking bucks; they're dining with Woodruff's boys. Hounding them for firewater, apparently—

What else would Indians do?

On that subject, general, I've just heard back from the Agent at Jocko, and his Flatheads remain quiet.

Rawn said as much.

Yessir.

Mr. Barbour kept bending my ear about Flatheads. He called 'em as treacherous as rattlesnakes. Said they're fixing to join Mr. Joe.

Yessir, I heard him all right. But their Agent ought to know them better than he does.

I s'pose. Thank GOD for tame Indians! How long ago were they removed from here?

---

*This appellation was more generously used in the nineteenth century than now. Gibbon was in charge, so his men called him the general of the expedition (and the whole military district). Moreover, he had been a major general in 1864. Like his colleagues Miles and Sturgis, he was forced to live with the reduction in rank necessitated by the shrunken postwar army. See p. 1249.

Six years, general.

Charlot's bunch may turn out different. When Rawn gets back from Stevensville, we'll see. O, hello there, Jacobs! What have you got for us?

Well, sir, enough mules finally, I guess, but piss-poor rations—

Rustle up some more. We depend on you. Sanno, what sport?

"G" Company's ready, general. They want to drink. And there's another scout in. Some Indian. Mr. Joe's lot are still straggling out of this valley—

He showed you on the map? No, let him get drunk. I see; right *there*. That confirms the Bannock reports. Joseph has become pretty deliberate in his movements. Thinks we've forgotten him, evidently. Well, Sanno, have we?

Not by a d——d shot, general!

Ha, ha! You've sure got "sand"! Go ahead and let your boys off the leash, but I expect 'em fit to march to-morrow. And you and Woodruff had better finish getting our rations in shape, not that we should carry much. That's right. Sanno, you're a brick! "D" Company's already at the Blackfoot Bar, I hear. Tell Hardin I'd like to hear from him this evening. Well, Browning, how're your bunch?

Ready to puncture a few Indians, general. D'you remember Sergeant Frederick? He's caressing that twelve-pound baby of his.

Ha, ha! His *baby!* I'd sure hate to see the mother. Well, maybe we'll find you at the Blackfoot. Keep an eye on our volunteers. That's right, boys; go ahead; I don't need you. And now, Bradley, let's whip off a reply to General Howard's wire. That old fool should have been cashiered a century ago. You know what they called him after Chancellorsville? Called him *Uh-Oh Howard.*

I feel sorry for him, sir.

Well, Bradley, you've got a kind heart in that barrel chest of yours. If you can believe it, he's still on the wrong side of Lo Lo Pass! Singing hymns with niggers, I s'pose.

The President nearly sacked him, I heard—

Where did you hear that?— Not my business.— As you can imagine, Rawn's bitter against old Howard. Howard commanded him to hold back the reds, and gave him no means.

He sure didn't, sir.

No Godd——d means at all! Tell me, Bradley, do you blame Rawn?

General, if I'd been in his place I'd at least have fired a few shots.

That goes for me. Tell Howard we're on the case, and all that.

Yessir.

Where's Second Cavalry?

No news since they left the Yellow Stone, sir.

Pretty hilly country . . . Once the railroad reaches here, we'll have it cushy on our Indian service.

You said it, sir!— O, another despatch from the Flathead Agent. He says the Pend d'Oreilles have promised to behave themselves and will even fight Joseph if he comes on the reservation.

Indian promises . . .

Yessir.

Well, Browning's confident.

He sure is, general.

How's his company *really* making out?

All rested up, and ready to head out when we do.

Woodruff don't think so.

I trust Captain Browning, sir.

We'll see. Where's Hardin?

At the Blackfoot, sir.

Good. This new post ain't much, eh? Captain Rain still don't have a roof over himself—

No, sir. Life in the postwar Army!

You hit that nail on the head. D——d Congress! Spent our tax dollars on Black Sambo, looks like. At least that's over. Thank GOD for President Hayes!

General, none of the boys can make out why Grant didn't do more for us.

Politics. Don't you ever believe he forgot the Army! . . . Where's English right now?

Probably in Will Logan's tent. Shall I fetch him here, sir?

I guess it'll wait until the rest roll in.— O, hiya, Woodruff! What have you got?

Charlot's Flatheads have crawled off to French Gulch. They want nothing to do with Mr. Joe.

Seen the light, eh? Who questioned the chiefs?

Well, since Rawn warned 'em—

Our laughingstock. Do go on.

Father Van Gorp swore to their obedience.

That's good. This Nez Perce buck they call *Poker Joe,* or *Lean Elk* I guess is his other name—you know, the one who's flitting around—what about him?

With your permission, sir, we'll shoot him on sight.

For the best, I guess. Now, Woodruff, see if you can't help Sanno with our supply. Rations are still no good, apparently. Then you're a free man until "Tattoo."

All right, sir.

Now, Bradley, I think we're through.

That was easy, general.

You still play cards?

Sometimes, sir.

Uh-Oh Howard plays whist. I met a professional gambler once who looked down on that game. Said it was nothing more than a time killer.

Don't know about that, sir.

Or a lady killer.

Yessir.

A wonder I never played cards with you last year. Well, you're a hard man to pin down, Bradley. Always hunting Indians.

Thank you, general.

And thank *you* for not saying *I told you so.* Woodruff and I were dead wrong! We just *knew* those Nez Perces would head north, and you said south. Why they didn't cross the Medicine Line is beyond me. Well, I should have listened to you.

We'll get 'em eventually, sir.

I expect we will. O, yes. We take care of business out here in our Indian service! So have you heard from your wife?

Not yet, sir.

A lovely lady. And sweet little children she's given you. Wish I'd had your luck. A pleasure to see 'em again at that party, I must say.

Thanks, general.

Where are you stopping at to-night?

Coolidge's tent, sir. And cooking with Will Logan.

And English has dropped in, you said. All right. You like Missoula?

I'm indifferent, sir.

Well, I'm not. What a shithole. You'd think the citizens could *do more* for us. Just like President Grant—

I'd say the town compares favorably to Fort Benton, sir.

You would? All right. You need to do anything?

No, sir, I'm all caught up.

You got time to kill, Bradley? Is time weighing you down here in Missipissoula, Monfuckingtana?

Not at all, sir.

You can take a snooze or a snort if you'd rather.

I prefer your company, general.

Well, that's nice. How's your Custer book coming along?

I'm nearly ready to polish up the part where we found the general and his command.

Now that sure was a sad day, Bradley. A real sad day. I guess our boy wonder got ahead of himself.

He should have waited on us, sir.

Well, that's how he was. Wanted to overshadow General Crook. And all the time we waited on *him.* Terry and I tried to make him see reason, but he meant to win all the laurels. How many times have you and I hashed this over?

O, a fair number, sir.

Now tell me, son, just between us, did you actually give him your best six scouts, or did you keep 'em for yourself?

General, I sent him the only six who not only knew the country but could be counted on not to blast at buffalo when we were creeping up on a hundred lodges of Sioux. So for my part I don't feel guilty—

Told off half a dozen of the finest, eh? Mighty white of you! I always wondered.

Sir—

Did I ever ask you that before?

Yessir.

No offense, Bradley. And then off he went after that d——d Major Reno. Last we heard of him. Quite a shocker. I won't soon forget the look on Terry's face when you came riding up with the news—

Did you believe it first thing, general? I couldn't quite, myself. Not until I saw them lying naked all over the plain, after the squaws had been at them with knives and axes—

A pretty unforgettable campaign, all right! The things we see as we perform our Indian service, o, me!

Well, general, we'll clean up the Sioux one of these days.

I reckon so, if Miles don't steal a march on us. Pure poison, that fellow.

He thirsts for his star, they say.

Thirsts for it, eh? Is that how they put it? Well, they're right. Anyhow, one or the other of us'll get Sitting Bull, just like you said.

I'm looking forward to it, sir.

After these Nez Perces.

Right you are, sir. When I think on how they burned those Idaho women and children alive—

And such a nice long column, we could easily double 'em up. A mile from end to end, Rawn said. Now this report here says they was *five miles long* passing through Stevensville. Imagine that, Bradley! What would you do if you owned that many horses?

Sell them, sir.

Practical of you. Anyway, if we can just catch 'em in open country, it'll be over.

We will, sir. Once they cross the Divide, they'll spread out. Then we'll get them. And no worry about the Crows; we know how to manage *them.*

What's the latest press about Mr. Joe?

Well, sir, this is just in from the outhouse, right on top of the pile:

Indian Outbreak in Idaho—The Salmon River and Nez Perces Indians Doing Ugly Work on Camas Prairie. 500 Indians on Hangman Creek. In the hand to hand fighting Col. Perry fell, and about one half of the command are said to have been killed. Another phase of the matter is a warning to our Missoula neighbors to be on the alert.

Corn seven cents a pound.

That's one good ass-wiper and no mistake.

Right you are, general.

Now, listen, Bradley: We're not going to wait on Uh-Oh Howard for anything, and that's a fact. Why, that bleeding-hearted old fool! And we won't wait on the governor, either. The sooner we sound the move out, the faster we'll get Mr. Joe into the ground. He must be quite some Injun. What's the name of that white woman he's supposed to be carrying with him? I'll bet he knocked her over the head after the first hour of fun. But if he's kept her, son, and if we rescue her, our fortune's made forever. Did you hear how Miles adopted them three sisters he rescued from the Cheyennes? What was their name?

German, sir.

That's it. You remember everything. And he shoved a bill through Congress to sustain them gals, with his name printed on it. That's Nelson Miles! So that dame Mr. Joe took off with, you see . . .

I'll keep a bright lookout, sir. Mrs. Manuel's her name. She wears long yellow braids.

Was her husband a greaser? With a name like that . . .

I don't know, sir.

Say, do you remember the Rosebud punch we invented on the Sioux campaign? Do you know how to make it?

Equal parts champagne cider and whiskey, sir. Shall I see if I can wangle the ingredients?

Send Schlept over to that bar out there. He can bring some back. D——n me if I'm not dry! What about you, Bradley?

I'd enjoy the nostalgia, general.

Now, which card game you enjoy the best?

Well, poker.

I thought it was euchre.

No, sir.

Poker then,

> says his general, Colonel John Gibbon, Seventh United States Infantry: iron-white-bearded, frosty-moustached, but still blackhaired, with two columns of buttons on his chest (he looks far stricter than he is).

Here's a deck. You cut and I'll deal. No sense playing for money. That way we avoid bad feelings.

Fine by me, sir. And here's our exhilarating compound!

Thank you, Schlept. Are you a Communist?

No, sir.

I thought you Germans were Communists.

No, sir.

Go have a drink or a snooze.— Here's how, Bradley!

How!

Now that definitely wets the whistle, wouldn't you say?

I definitely would, sir.

Bradley, I like you. You're going to be commander of the scouts again.

Thanks, general, and I'm looking forward to this.

If it wasn't for those penny-pinching shit-heels in Congress, I'd be a real general by now, and so you'd be colonel at least.

Thank you, sir. That means a lot to me.

What's that bar out there anyway? I already forgot the name.

The Blackfoot. Sounds like our boys are getting lively in there.

Must be Browning's company. They shot out the lights yet?

You want me to check, sir?

Just cut the GoDd——n cards.

2

Say what you like about them Springfields, but I remember when I had me a fine-looking Sharps .44 with buckhorn sights—

Yeah, back when your granny was digging potatoes with a nigger hoe.

O, that put fire in his eye!

I'll get you for that.

I said to him, I said: *Rawn, from one Pennsylvanian to another, you were a hundred percent yellow to let Mr. Joe through.* But the way he explained it, he just looked me in the eye and said—

This is worse than barefoot whiskey.

And our general told the Governor to reënforce us so that we could flank Joseph, but *that* didn't happen.

Then Mr. Joe murdered a hundred and ninety-one whites in an ambush.

And my Cousin David wrote me from Pittsburgh; he says it's nearly a civil war

Well, I'll shoot Indians but I won't kill no starving railroad men.

If we ever make it into a fight with those reds, I'm going to get me a warrior's fancy jacket, with all them beads sewn on in rainbows. That's what I want for my souvenir.

What the DEVIL do you mean? They've got three thousand fine horses!

First she says to me, pay me a cup of firewater.

But all they gave me was this muzzle-loader.

And then Rawn up and skedaddled.

And then when I had sent in my calling card, she says to me, she says, *I wish I wasn't already engaged.*

And over there's Will Logan from Helena.
Runs the trading post here. Sometimes he'll
take credit if he likes your face.

Who the fuck are you, oldtimer? Says he'll *get me.* I oughta paunch you with
my Bowie knife—

And Henry Buck says they're all stretched out. Looking-Glass always
rides in front. It took an hour and more for their column to pass Fort
Owen.

Well, back in January of last year right before Benedict Brothers failed again in New
York, my Cousin Edward brought in his
mother-in-law's ring to be appraised, and he
never got it back. Of course the old bitch
said he'd pawned it for strong drink. The
wife wouldn't take his side, so he joined the
Army. And I had nothing better to do, so—

I actually love a fight.

Doc, we don't need to—

Shut up, Johnny. You there, I'd love to slit your belly open. *Then* I'd kill you.

What a hero! I'll bet your Mama was one of them squaw monsters that tortures people. You stink like a no-account redskin.

I'll show you red.

I said who the fuck are you?

A volunteer.

O, he won a treble.

Doc?

I said shut up.

And the Agent's keeping watch on Eagle Of The Light, because he may defect to Looking-Glass. A real sinister Indian.
So I said to the Agent, Mr. Ronan, I said:

Where's Nellie?

Ain't seen her.

And then Mrs. Ronan, she's the one with the long, long hair,
she said to me, she said:

Is somebody else behind the curtain?

No,

because most of the women and children in Missoula
are hiding in the courthouse now, to save themselves
from Mr. Joe,

And I said to Mr. Ronan:

Well, she promised me a turn.

She oughta be right back.

> If I find out you've lied to me I'll crack your head.

No, it won't compare.

> Coolidge has a seven months' leave coming to him—

He won't win this one.

He sure will,

> the same hard strange faces as everywhere.

> Now, Chagoo Hurpa (his name means *Broken Penis*), he's another of our good Sioux, who scouted for Custer last year, and one time we decided to get him drunk—

He's nothing like Sitting Bull.

My Indians claim it's not him but White Bird that runs their outfit.

> Sorry, soldier. This establishment don't take shinplasters. We only trust hard money.

> Well, how'm I supposed to get a drink?

> *The bold dragoon he has no care*

> *As he rides along with his uncombed hair.*

Howard broke their backs at Clearwater.

That's not what I heard. From what I heard, that Howard ain't done nothing. He's a coward; that was proved way back at Chancellorsville. That's why this has dragged on all the way to our Department. And I'll tell you another thing: He's a nigger lover.

How do you know?

Don't you remember that bureau in Washington that kept handing out our tax money to niggers? Well, he was the head of it.

> *The bold dragoon he has no care—*

You don't say.

What's a nigger need money for anyway?

> Hey you, darky!

> Yessir.

> Why d'you got holes in your shoes? *I* know! You must've put your money in Uh-Oh Howard's nigger bank!

> That's right, sir. I surely did.

On that subject, I once knew me a fellow who carried some gold leaf with him all the way from Saint Louis and he tarted up his silver dollars and he—

Me, I never got to Washington except right at the beginning and then the final review, of course—

Where's your people at?

I'm from Connecticut, originally.

They call you Wooden Nutmegs.

That's right.

Well, why'd you come all the way out here?

I was broke and lookin' for excitement.

I said, how am I supposed to get a drink?

If you're with the Seventh then how come I never saw you?

Our company's the one at Fort Ellis.

Well, why are you away from your company?

Wouldn't you like to know?

I sure as hell would. I came here to drink, and these shin-plasters are guaranteed by the United States Government.

Well, soldier, this ain't the United States. Don't you know nothin'?

Hey, you, barkeep, I'll buy him a whiskey.

Thanks, Jimmy.

Anyhow, I expect you think well of the general.

Gibbon's got a head on his shoulders. I'd follow him anywhere.

Thank GOD he's not a nigger lover like Howard.

Maybe he was just obeying orders. I mean, his wife's not a nigger. And he's a good Christian and all. I think to call a man a nigger lover's a pretty serious charge.

The bold dragoon he has no care
As he rides along with his uncombed hair.

Them two are fixin' to fight over there.

Shut your mouth and cut the cards.

Where's Nellie? I could use a piece of ass.

Where in blazes do you imagine she is, Paddy?

The bold dragoon he has no—

O, cut it out. You sing like a turkey.

Don't Paddy me. I'm as American as you.

You got balls enough to fight me?

All right now, Doc. That's fine. Don't you get exercised about nothing. It's all fine.

Here's how, Bradley!

How!

Nobody can say Indian service ain't dangerous.

3

General, something's a mystery.

What?

Well, I remember when I met Doctor Hunter's family last year at the Warm Springs of Yellow Stone. The Sioux had attacked their resort; they seemed to live in fear. And you'd think after all Mr. Joe's massacres, the folks hereabouts would feel the same. But they don't.

Well, Bradley, our Nez Perces are nothing in comparison to the Sioux. All they mean to do is get away.

I guess you're right, sir. They even pay for what they take.

With gold plundered from our dead boys at White Bird Cañon. Don't forget that.

Believe me, general, I won't.

SOON WE SHALL BE RIDING THROUGH THE GOLDEN GRASS

1

*C*oming over the Divide, into the former Salish Country,
where OUR MOTHER begins to spread Herself out,
   down into the draw which widens and greens into prairie,
and following the sweet brown stream down the winding glade,
   that brown creek suddenly boiling with hailstones,
      that creek brown-green and lush with algae, sunken into tall green
      grass and shrubs flanked by ghost-grey sage
         (here from time to time we have met our Crow friends,
         but sometimes the Shinbones ambush us),
the People arrive at Ground Squirrel Place,
   where we have always dug camas on our way to the Buffalo Country:
      smell of young leaves and clean powdery dirt,
      plains ahead and forest behind
         (steep dark forest of pines)—
here shall we rest, while our lodgepoles dry out.

2

Ollokot's stallions graze in the bunchgrass, their white dapplings shining in
the sun,
   as Rainbow pickets his tired bay war horse, thinking to make himself a head
   ornament of buffalo skin once we have come all the way into the Buffalo
   Country,
   and White Thunder cleans the hooves of his mother's ponies,
   Toohhoolhoolsote salves his horses' sores,
      his happy old wives digging camas right away

(they will erect his lodge between Whitefoot's and Chohnikia's),
while Looking-Glass's horses lunge down to graze,
the long naked lodgepoles drying fragrantly in the sun.
Now we can erect our homes for the first time since we escaped from Red
Owl's country:
Ollokot's tipi rising up beside Heinmot Tooyalakekt's,
Looking-Glass's next to Huapin's and facing east, like a Crow tipi,
and by the river a lodge apart for Sun Tied's wife to give birth,
while between Looking-Glass's and White Bird's lodges is a space
wide enough for our young boys to go creeping through, bird-
hunting their way from the flowering grass into the sparkling green
willows,
hailstones melting on the grass, swallows cheeping quietly across
the creek,
and beyond the river slants the meadow like a green buckskin
where our horses will graze to-night,
and above it the greenish-grey wall of lodgepole pines
where the mountains begin, grey clouds and white
clouds dropping their fingers down to touch each peak,
white lobes of cloud-reflections sinewed by ripples in the dark
stream with its nodding, shaking willows
here where our grandfathers used to kill all the buffalo calves
they ever wished for
as Lone Bird forgets his dream of death
and all our tipis now rise tall and narrow along the meadow-creek,
the beargrass in full flower now; summer in its prime,
and
Looking-Glass's Appaloosas grazing nearby for his delight,
Burning Coals greedily counting over his own horse-herd
as Ollokot's wives dig camas with Welweyas's mother,
Wounded Head's wife and Looking-Glass's daughters,
Shore Crossing helping his dear wife, shaping
lodgepoles with his axe,
looking forward to coming into the Buffalo
Country where there will be even more
game and we can get buffalo robes;
but Sound Of Running Feet says to her mother: And let
me become nicely dressed in buckskins all over, so that
I become a lovely girl,
and Good Woman begins to knit her a cornhusk bag.
We are settled in a circle in the low greenish-
yellow island of river-trees in the hot golden grass
around the tipis, in the place where the western

hills open out like a woman's legs. We are roast-
ing trout and baking camas, so that the grey-
green slope of trees silhouettes itself in smoke.
We are resting, making ourselves cool:
Heinmot Tooyalakekt's wives sweetening their skins with buffalo tallow,
White Feather doctoring her father's horses,
Looking-Glass's wives plucking out their pubic hairs,
Toohhoolhoolsote's women crawling through the grass, digging herbs
and roots because they have no more cous.

3

Soon we shall be riding through the golden grass, across the river and over the
gilded morning-horizon to the snow-rimmed amethyst mountains
where we shall be far away from Bostons forever:
the Buffalo Country.
Looking-Glass,
he who has given away so many horses,
promises us every good thing within his heart.
Our home is floating, floating down.

4

Lean Elk races horses with Burning Coals, Ollokot, Heinmot Tooyalakekt and
Looking-Glass:
Lean Elk's stallion is fastest, but all the horses are tired.
Ollokot has now killed a deer,
so Cloudburst, Fair Land, Good Woman and the half-woman Welweyas begin to
butcher it
(Welweyas feels very proud of the Wilson skinning knife she
bought from that tall bearded Boston at Stevensville),
after which they are preserving meat,
singing, trampling on robe-covered mounds of part-dried flesh to force
the blood out,
hanging up meat-strips to be smoked,
rubbing the deerhide with watered brains, then smoking it into yellowness
because Sound Of Running Feet hopes to make a new shirt for her father.
While Fair Land and Springtime bathe their babies together,
Toohhoolhoolsote's young men keep smiling as he repeats again
and again: I told Cut Arm, *are you trying to scare me? Are you trying
to tell me the day on which I shall die?*
(Wottolen tells him: I see Cut Arm coming in the night,
but Toohhoolhoolsote does not see it)

and Sound Of Running Feet helps Looking-Glass's daughters in picking the best
white lacy yarrow to salve our wounded and blistered ones,

> Rainbow, Stripe Turned In, Five Snows and Shooting Thunder gambling
> beads and cartridges in the Stick Game,
> betting tobacco against a whip,
> guessing which hand holds the black stick, which the white, and which
> hands are empty.

>> Mother, last night I felt SOMETHING in the trees, but there was
>> nothing there . . .

>>> looking back up west where the draw goes all green with wil-
>>> lows and brush and then narrows up into a green slit in the
>>> hazy blue mountains.

5

Having Dreamed of evil,

> although the AIR BIRD has not lately hovered over Grizzly Bear Youth
> (his sleep is now empty),

Red Spy and Red Moccasin Tops send their wives to Burning Coals to say: Uncle,
hear us! Bluecoats or Bostons may be on our trail. Our horses are tired. Your stallions are famous. Lend us a pair of them, so that our husbands may ride back over
the mountains to watch for the People.

I shall not, because my horses are precious to me and because Looking-Glass
forbids it.

Uncle, we know very well how much your heart loves Lucky One and Long
Ears. Our husbands would be satisfied with others—

Now I have closed my ears. Your husbands are reckless. They would lame my
stallions, or gamble them away. Go now; I have spoken.

So the women return to their lodges; perhaps they are pleased that their husbands will stay in camp with them.

> (Burning Coals's daughter feels ashamed.)

6

Whispering and giggling, Heinmot Tooyalakekt's wives and eldest daughter
go into the willows to bathe,

> perfuming their clothes with balsam fir needles they have picked on the trail
> and scenting their hair with fir needles pounded into deer grease, just as
> the Salish women did.

When they come home to their lodge, Springtime asks her husband: Are we
now different?

Who are these sweet-smelling ones? Could you be Charlot's lovely daughters
who have run away?

And he laughs a little with his three Salish women.

Now Welweyas approaches Sound Of Running Feet, admiring the girl and longing to be like her; soon she too has perfumed her hair.

7

In their tipi
          as the locusts begin to sing *tekh-tekh-tekh!*,
sit White Bird and *Kate*, his short braids and her long braids in front, their heads high, watching the People playing in the dying grass
          as the other boys tease About Asleep because he failed to catch a green-
          winged teal in the river
                    and in the women's lodge, Sun Tied's wife bites her lip because the
                    baby's head is coming out of her, but she makes herself brave, and
                    Crystal holds her hand
          while Springtime chars her new digging stick's point in the hearth-fire to
          harden it.
White Bird
          (who seems to hear that someone is approaching us)
comes out of his lodge. He says: Looking-Glass, how do we know that the Bostons will not attack? Let us leave our lodgepoles and quickly ride to the Buffalo Country—

My dear brother, why should they break our treaty? We have done them no harm. They have no war with us.

Even so, says White Bird, it is better to be ready.

Looking-Glass replies: Many lies have been uttered on this subject. Hear me now. I am head-chief, and I have made a treaty with all these *Americans*. Now I have spoken.

8

Heinmot Tooyalakekt,
          he who expects no evil,
is playing with his new baby daughter
as Good Woman threads her needle,
          the tall grass turning green and yellow in the shadow and peach-gold in
          a streak all the way to the bluff of willows and the sagebrush ridge,
          our camas pits steaming,
          mosquitoes rising from the creek,
while White Bird lies down in his lodge
          (now *Kate* is crushing vermin in the seams of his deerskin robe):
having learned which wood cuts easily, he can see no use in sawing at Looking-Glass's stubborn heart.

Just as White Feather will keep her name yet a little while (she has not yet become Broken Tooth), so Looking-Glass continues to be the *lucky man:*

some girls are attracted to him even though he has already made two
wives for himself;

laughingly he invites our young men to gamble with him at the Stick Game:

I am guessing in the middle; I shall win the stick pieces hidden in the inner
pair of hands; they are opening their fists now; they are opening, and I have
gambled away my blanket.

    To-morrow perhaps they will race their horses and gamble as they last
did in Red Owl's country

        (Looking-Glass has said that we need not ride away from this place
until we have made ourselves strong again).

            What would you have us do? Our lodgepoles are worn
out; we must stop somewhere.

Hasten; evening shadows be!

    —silhouettes of swallows flittering against the TRAVELLER THE SUN,

        the lodges' smoke-ears open, wisps coming out

            while in the women's lodge, Crystal finishes sing-
ing the baby out of Sun Tied's wife: a girl, just as
we have Dreamed

    as something glints and glares behind the greyish cones of lodge-
pole pines.

We are Dreaming, flying round and round; we shall become Flying People;
our young men and young women wish to dance the Rabbit Dance

        while Welweyas withdraws herself behind the willows, whis-
pering to SOMEONE:

            Since my WYAKIN cannot make me man or woman,
may I at least make myself over,
    decorating my heart;
may I die brave,

and Wottolen takes his dear son Black Eagle down along the creek so that
the boy can try a dead Bluecoat's trapdoor Springfield:

    pim!

Yes, my son; you have shot well. But exploding bullets must not be wasted;
they are for our dear friends the Bluecoats.

    Where's Cut Arm?

    He must be tired. Now he goes back to his own country.

    Looking-Glass named him General Day-After-To-morrow.

    If Cut Arm comes here—

    We'll stick something up his anus.

    Now he's crying! He wishes he never showed us the rifle.

    He's rushing down the river to his wife.

    Does he have one?

9

Springtime walks away to salve three bleeding packhorses, carrying her sleepy
baby, singing to her,
       evening SUNshine gilding the creek
          (she is scared by the high, high mountains to the south:
             flat like a cow's back, then down)
    while Good Woman squats by slow-boiling soup
       until her husband calls her into the lodge:
          he smiles at her
          as she drops down the blanket-door
          and unties the blanket around her waist;
before Springtime returns she is back to boiling soup
   as White Thunder's ancient mother Swan Woman bends over her tripodded
   kettle, stirs, looks over at Good Woman, and grins;
       while Sound Of Running Feet begins to wonder what it would be like to
       be married and feel a man's penis inside her
          in this sunset all across the marshy prairies whose rivers run
          brownish-blue, sporting flowers along the bank
             (hordes of swallows over the river),
          all within the shadowed greyish arms of descending sagebrush ridges,
               young boys playing their own Bone Game at camp's edge,
            Toohhoolhoolsote studying the thin basketwork of willow
            stalks, as if it could be lucky,
            and watching a pale doe the color of the grass loping away
            with her fawn; now they are gone behind the willows.
  The women have now tied up a few horses near their lodges, so that come dawn
they can ride them to catch the rest. Sound Of Running Feet calls Little One; he
licks her face and then she pickets him in the willows by her father's lodge;
          and although SOMETHING is watching through the paired and
          twisted needles of lodgepole pines,
   the young men dance the war-dance, louder and louder—
       but Looking-Glass, who expects to lead a deer-hunt to-morrow, with-
       draws into his lodge to taste his wives
          (closing his eyes, he seems to see SOMETHING like the punctuated
          circular figures on Ollokot's shirt);
             while in the women's lodge, mother, midwife and newborn
             baby are sleeping
    and Toohhoolhoolsote, his Power not as great as he supposes, has already
    lost himself in dreams of the Great River which begins the Lo Lo Trail
          while White Bird begins to Dream a lucky dream of a white calf
          sucking at its mother,

Welweyas's old mother Agate Woman snoring loudly in her lodge,
Red Owl meanwhile dreaming himself back down through the
pines and aspens and yellow-green bluffs of his stolen country, the
Big Water wider and bluer than ever before; and a flat white sand-
island sparkling with aspens is waiting for him;
and the new-married women all seclude themselves to taste their husbands and rest,
for to-morrow morning they mean to be digging roots while it is
still cool;
then Good Woman will go out to cut firewood and load it
onto one of her horses, in case someone needs it on the prairies ahead;
they are all dreaming down, dreaming down,
their skin lodges closing up against the cooling air, their war-
shields dulling down into darkness, stars passing through their
outspread lodgepole-fingers:
sleep flows around them all as soft as this creek's play within willows and
clover rich horse-grass.

10

Another nightmare creeps up on Springtime, but when she gasps and opens
her eyes, it executes the leaping retreat of a deer
as Sound Of Running Feet stares at her, afraid and angry
(on this ill-omened night the girl can hear even the faint tin-
kling of an old woman's bead necklace as she sits in her tipi
oiling her pigtails)
and Heinmot Tooyalakekt awakes, wishing for Springtime to be
lying on her back with her butterfly wide open as she sings little
songs to him
(so it used to be),
but seeing her GHOST-stricken face
—shining with sweat,
paler than a yarrow flower—
he rolls back up against his other wife,
whose dreams are as rich as the baskets she and Springtime
have filled with huckleberries;
while Springtime, dragging the back of her hand across her forehead, half sits up, looks at her baby and lies down again,
staring up into the tipi's conical skeleton, hoping to see stars
through the smoke-slit
and White Thunder, who has finished dancing the war-dance, now crawls into the
lodge and wraps himself in his blanket.

LIEUTENANT BRADLEY SCOUTS AHEAD
AUGUST 4–8

1

*G*oing up out of the Bitter Root Valley, *left—left—left!* from the silky yellow-green grass, where yellow-headed mulleins crane their sweetly furry necks, Gibbon's avengers (a hundred and forty-six fighting men, if we count our volunteers) gaze back on farmhouses and grainfields, leave a shining brown creek in the meadow, the horses angrily switching their tails, the unlucky mules huffing, screeching, blaring and groaning beneath the weight of the dissassembled Hotchkiss cannons on the steel-framed *aparejos*. Bradley is wishing for a couple of Gatlings like the ones we have been deploying against the strikers at Pittsburgh; the trail ahead may prevent heavier guns from furthering our ideals, which are:

> a dawn attack (the late Custer's speciality)
>> to disorganize the Nez Perces through pressure on their squaws and papooses
>>> and avenge our slight at Fort Fizzle,
>>>> not to mention the murder of our brave boys at White Bird Cañon:
> by golly, we'll nudge Mr. Joe to take a little think!
>> Well, he sent Pardee up the Lo Lo Trail to see if Uh-Oh Howard can send a hundred cavalry, doublequick—

A farmer's wife with her shy child stands in front of her barn to wave farewell to us, which we consider mighty sweet. The bold dragoon he has no care,

> although just as the Bitter Root Mountains get taller and more jagged to the south of Fort Corvallis, so the volunteers' apprehensions of Chief Joseph elongate even over the crowns of lodgepole pines, until some of them yearn to sneak home, but what would the neighbors say?
>> Every volunteer has a star-pointed soul
>> and although I crave to tell you all about Captain Caitlin the wise Indian fighter, and Myron Lockwood the experienced Indian hater (it was his house that Toohhoolhoolzote's bunch pillaged back in the Bitter Root Valley), not to mention the steadfast German privates who will soon get punctured, it behooves me not to interrupt our narrative mechanism (whose two main automata are General Howard and that SATANIC *Red Napoleon*, Mr. Joe) by dwelling on the accidental personalities of this other army which will shortly

perform its purpose and withdraw, leaving our protagonist and antagonist alone again; so please let me limit my gaze to

Gibbon on his old grey horse, plotting against Miles and Crook,
scorning Howard, continuing to judge Benteen unforgivable thanks
to his desertion of Custer, remembering the pleasant sight of those
Cheyenne squaws in their ribbon-hemmed dresses

and Bradley, defender of women.

At first the trail is smooth as an Indian treaty, well made for our howitzers'
creaking pomp. Between Custer—greasy-bearded and on top of the world, slouch-
ing on a stool before his tent, with Indians and dogs kneeling all around him—and
ramrod manqué Uh-Oh Howard; between the dead daredevil and the live incompetent, there goes Gibbon, into the forest coolness:

> *Stand up for these, the wrong'd, the aggriev'd,*
> *In deepest pits of darkness found,*
> *Of Heav'n's most sacred gifts bereaved,*
> *The task'd—the scourg'd—in fetters bound.*

Thinking on his lonely wife (and perhaps the sad hymn does its mite to drag
him down), Bradley, munching on a fragment of hardbread as he goes, finds his
spirits setting as does the sun between the legs of a scaffold grave, but reminds
himself that this will never do if he wishes to secure a decent result in the onrushing
campaign. Truth to tell, when his enlistment expires he may remove his family to
Tongue River, where he sees opportunities to make a farm. The general might even
permit him to remain on some kind of detached service. Now the advance guard
must draw in as the way forward narrows, and Bradley grows alert, remembering
all too well how the Sioux, for instance, sometimes lurk on ridgetops to ambuscade
us; according to Rawn, Chief Joseph essayed some version of this on the westward
reach of the Lo Lo Trail, killing a scout or two; and so (the accustomed nightmare),
what if Joseph should link up with Sitting Bull?

McClain was too chickenshit to shoot when they camped on
his property. Could have potted Looking-Glass fair and
square.

No, I knew McDonald. He was killed by Sioux back in '68. Left three little
children. His wife's a fine-spirited woman—

So what?

So they'll spread out after Big Hole, and then if we flank
'em—

Well, when Phil Kearny said to me, *Gibbon*, he said, *it's another Bull Run*, even then I couldn't have guessed—

Rawn had better kill a lot of Indians if he expects to live
this down.

You probably can't even guess how they calculate a miner's inch in
California.

Why should I care, you sonofabitch?

Right face—roll call—
the bad sun wearying at last, the moon glowing like the round shell hanging from
a Cheyenne woman's ear, bright and brighter against her blue-black braids.

 Emerging from the pines into a steep meadow
   (the thick hard stalks, almost bamboo-like, of the last beargrass growing
   in a clump like a blond Indian's topknot),
they traverse a steeply slanting hill of red pine needles, the horses' hooves slipping, the muleteers' hands sweating, the trail now as crooked as the Indian Bureau
as they approach the clouds.

2

 Fine grass for the horses.

 Yes, sir. But soon it'll get steep and gloomy. The mules can eat wire-grass. O,
there's another of those spavined Injun horses.

 We're wearing Joseph down, soldier.

 Yes, sir,
   pines and spruces with the bark stricken away in vertical orange stripes,
   poison oak green and crazy red, bark chips red and orange beneath the
   green grass and weeds, long stripes of sunny grass amidst the shadow
   and smoke,
     sun on their shoulders, sweat cooling on the backs of their hands:
     If Hell were one of these scree-walled sun-blasted spots where sad
     serviceberry leaves wilt on the twig, we might see the DEVIL any
     minute.

 Now shoot that stray horse.

 Right away, sir.

 Where's Blodgett?

 I'll get him, general.

 All right now, Mr. Blodgett, this trail's getting pretty rough. Are you positive
we won't need pack mules?

 Well, now, I told you I've brought light-loaded wagons all the way up from Bannock. Now, your wagons are heavy with lead. They're not light wagons, Colonel
Gibbon. Not at all. But if we sort of portage over the rough parts—

 How bad's it going to get?

 O, plenty worse until we cross the Divide.

 Thanks, Mr. Blodgett.

 Call me Joe if you want to, colonel.

 Why, that's right friendly of you, Joe. Now that'll be all,
   looking back toward the sky-blue buttes and peaks of the Bitter Root
   Range.

 No fresh sign thataway, sir.

 All right,

as they circumnavigate a threaded obelisk of a stump, perhaps twenty feet high, whose grooves whirl round, ascending counterclockwise through stripes of shadow,

still following Lewis and Clark's map more or less

(the Nez Perces were good guides here, back in the days before they became enemies of American freedom);

and the poison oak twitches in the smoky breeze as a woodpecker taps away.

You seen Doc?

Nope.

Now, when they raped Elizabeth Osborn, what they did was . . .

I heard Helen Walsh got it worse.

That ain't so.

What do you know about it?

Gonna bring that steel drill out on the job,
Gonna whap that steel on down, o, LORD.
Gonna whap that steel on down.

Killed Mrs. Manuel's little girl right in front of her. Then they outraged her. Nobody knows if she's dead or alive.

I know,

green moss fanning out from the silver claws of dead trees.

Round and round they go, switchbacking up the forty-five-degree slope, cutting trees for the ordnance wagons, longing for the other side,

the horses lunging down at weeds whenever they can, the pack mules wedging themselves between trees,

a pine's black fingers drooping down over the edge

(as a dark marmot slinks speedily across the trail, pulling its belly in),

creaking and creeping up toward the clouds, the horses nearly played out, naked sky above the last tree

(Bradley thinking about his Custer book, and so half dreaming of Sioux warriors waving buffalo robes at Little Big Horn,

while Johnny after all the interesting stories that Doc has told him now begins thinking about maybe after we have whipped Joseph taking the opportunity to grab a nice young roundheaded squaw by the braid and pulling her head back;

she may squint and grimace, but, ripping away the beads from her throat, Johnny will make her do as he wishes)

and we gaze over our shoulder back across the gulf of the Bitter Root Valley, the shoulders of the greyish-blue mountains from which Uh-Oh Howard's useless rifle-polishers still strain to be free.

Soldier, you look familiar.

Thanks, general. Me and Johnny here, we volunteered at Fort Corvallis.

Where have I seen you?

Back at Antietam, general. We was—

What's your name?

Doc.

Well, well. There's never enough war for some folks, I guess. Yours truly included . . .

We now approach the backbone of the Divide, which prickles out its pine trees as if it were an elongated porcupine,

> our column hugging the narrow slope and coming around to a place where the cañon walls draw in:

>> hot smell of pines and honey.

>>> the east side of the Divide gentle and green, many pines, much grass and white yarrow and brown meadow-ponds glitter as at Lo Lo Pass

>>> and cold black ashes of an expired Indian camp.

A dying pine bends into an arch, its crown nearly scraping the ground.

> I'm tired of getting whipped across the face by them twigs—

> O, wipe the gum off your lip.

This branch here is the headwaters of Jefferson's River. Now, that branch there—

Any sign?

Here's an eagle feather, sir, but maybe it don't mean nothing. Another dead pony where those bluejays are.

General, some of the boys was wondering why the Twenty-second ain't here to help now the Cheyennes have been cleaned up.

Reasons of state, son. The President sent 'em to Chicago to put down the strike.

Well, what about the Twenty-third?

Sent 'em to Saint Louis. Another strike out there. Now shut up, son,

> and then to the north, down into the gulch of piny wind and water, then a great nude ridge of golden grass like the flank of a palomino horse, softly curving into the sky, illuminated with lighter yellow markings and

> lodgepole pines fallen everywhere across the path, and

Dry camp, boys.

We didn't make even twenty-five miles to-day. GoDd——d crooked trail! That Blodgett is a—

> And Uh-Oh Howard's just now reached Fort Fizzle. He and his—

>> Gonna kill me some of them. And get me some Injun souvenirs.

>> D——d fool, you'd shoot your own leg off if you—

> Most of this horseshit here is two or three days old.

> What's down there?

> I'll go look.

We found sign over thisaway, lieutenant, sir!

But Second Lieutenant Woodruff, smoothfaced, his uniform studded with pips, stares slightly away.

3

Where's Lieutenant Bradley?

Right through them trees, general.

Bradley, I need you to mount a scouting party and find out if the hostiles are going toward Big Hole or back into Idaho. How soon can you head out?

In ten minutes, sir.

You come back alive.

Don't worry, sir! Do you remember how I took my Crows on that night scout last year, and you and Captain Clifford thought we'd never come back?

I sure do, son.

And we found the enemy—

Of course you did. Did you ever learn to howl like a wolf, the way those Crows do?

I'm not suited for that, sir.

I'm just teasing you. Now good luck.

Good-bye, general, and thanks for the adventure,

marching continuously down the mountain with a couple of scouts,

the country steepening into pine glens and rockpiles cached within ancient tree-roots:

Well, almost back in the Buffalo Country.

That's right, lieutenant,

and crawling across open ground, holding their breaths,

concealing themselves in a favorable screen of trees,

slowly creeping up to the crest of each ridge and peering over ever so cautiously, they begin to hear axes biting trees

(squaws cutting lodgepoles)

and swing around unseen until they can descend through another place, where they now hear the Indian dogs faintly yipping; then they climb a tree and through their field-glasses finally glimpse

(JESUS, there they are, and all bottled up so far as I can tell. No coulees hiding mounted bucks as at Little Big Horn, but how can I know that for a fact?)

a meadow-horde of horses with their necks lowered

(ready for slaughter),

and other horses browsing down by the creek, and

a rather small village, actually—maybe half the size of the one at Little Big Horn—but I'd sure better con those swales—or could Mr. Joe's best be hiding in the willows right now to get the last laugh?

They'd do anything. No, even they wouldn't stake out their children in camp like that. They can't be aware of us. This is it. Soon I'll be telling the general:

We seem to have made a discovery, sir,

for indeed Bradley, happily remembering the time last year when he and his Crows spied Sioux smoke over the Rosebud River, may be the one true soldier among this book of mine's pasteboard characters:

For just as this curious fellow,

James Bradley, First Lieutenant, Seventh Infantry,

once had his interpreter pull down a Sioux grave-scaffold, tear off the red blanket and rob the corpse, thereby discovering a soldier's hymn-book, accompanied by love letters from his wife—trophies from the American whom this Sioux, dead now near about two years, must have killed—so now, with equal wholesome eagerness, he strips the veil from hateful Mr. Joe, who, though he may not know it, must accordingly soon himself be *dead*,

Bradley now exhilarating himself to see down there in the Hole through his field-glass the smoke-columns of those many lodges, and the dark dots of Joseph's horses grazing freely all around, which proves that these Nez Perces suspect nothing,

and looking down into the still brown and blue and silver pools on the Big Hole River, with the plain of yellow grass creating the horizon behind, and then the mountains,

sun hot on the back of his neck, ground cold on his belly

and the tipis still far down on the river-green where it has become just a ribbon in the golden grass, a long grey horizon of fine smoke behind, which Bradley cannot smell because it is blowing away down east

and through the field-glasses he sees steam from the tipis' necks, and

a young yet already weatherbeaten squaw with white shell-earrings emerging into the golden grass, evidently to relieve herself, for after glancing in all directions, even seemingly at him, she squats down into a willow thicket

as Bradley remembers a certain shy, sad, dark Crow woman who could almost have been Mexican and whose shell-beads shone like stars upon her dark blue trade-cloth dress (he had noticed her in the incidentally lustful way of men, never acting on his urge, nor dismissing it from his fancy, either, because something about her narrow mouth pleasured him deep in his heart),

then arises, returns to the meadow and begins to dig roots. If all goes well they'll be neutralized to-morrow. LORD save us, I hope the dear old general will show some energy at last! Otherwise we'll be chasing Mr. Joe all the way back to Idaho or GOD knows where, and I won't be in my good girl's arms until Christmas or even Easter. Is she thinking about me? Is she praying for me as I told her to do? I ought to love her and the children the same, but I can't help loving her best. Just as soon as we wrap up Joseph, I'll be with her.

4

We should be able to destroy most of them, sir. They don't have any sentinels out.

I'm proud of you, Bradley. You're one of the best. Now give me a picture.

Well, general, Joseph's village is laid out on the far side of a creek, in a V-shape, with the apex toward us.

Then we'll strike the apex. Logan will advance on the right . . .

I'll take the left, sir, if you'll allow me.

Sure thing, son. Now, do our Bannocks bear watching as much as the Crows?

I should say they're more prudent and alert, sir. They won't betray us to Joseph—

Any more advice for your doddering old general? I made my New Year's resolution: Always listen to Jim Bradley.

Sir, I'll bet we could get up some cavalry and scare away their horses. Then we'd make short work of them.

Thanks. You deserve to take a snooze. Rest up now. Yes, that's all. Captain Humble, I need to talk to you.

What is it, colonel?

We're going to run off Joseph's herd. So we need all your volunteers mounted to ride with our nineteen men on horse.

Well, colonel, if my men feel like going forward in accordance with that order, that's their lookout, but I won't under any circumstances order them myself to do that, because if we get into a fight with Joseph with your infantry still way back there behind us, it'll be suicide, and—

That's enough. I'd rather have nobody than an unwilling soldier. Captain Caitlin's going to take command.

5

Laying down his carbine, Bradley, expanding and revising his Custer manuscript, now inserts our sweetest wish: *May the military operations that are now in progress result in so complete an overthrow of the hell-hounds called Sioux that never again shall poor women be made the victims of such barbarity at their hands!*

And, speaking of poor women: *I wish the campaign was over this blessed minute that I might be with you again.* I wonder if she—

> Sir, we caught two more Indian ponies, half-lame and—

>> Well, them redskins pillaged Mr. Landrum's house near about five dollars' worth. They broke open Mr. Lockwood's house and shot Mr. Stewart's cattle. They—

> Picket them with the others.

>> Kill 'em all!

Yessir.

>> But, Lockwood, didn't Chief White Bird make his bucks reimburse you in horses?

>> Why, those was just used-up, spavined Cayuse nags that couldn't hardly walk! They branded 'em with my brand just to mock me. They laid waste everything in my home excepting the stove. And them Cayuse nags just about trampled my field.

But since here I must be, ransacking among my most cautious phrases so that she'll know I miss her, *I make the best of it.* Could do with more of that Rosebud punch. *Harvest time will bring it around all right, and we'll all be marching home and be glad enough to get there,* especially now that they've learned to value my opinion. I guess we'll be in at the death, since Howard's so far behind. Mr. Joe seems pretty careless, I must admit. Hard for me to muster up the same hatred for him I feel toward Sitting Bull, but once he kills our first man I suppose I'll get on track. Would I truly rather stay at home? When the Custer book's published and she reads about the good times we sometimes had on the march,

>> and Bradley suddenly longs inexplicably for the Sioux plains, which are almost entirely in orange-brown shadow, with only here and there a few cloud-neglected places of brilliant yellow grass,

could be she'll wonder. I'll never forget what the general said to the Crows last year: *Men who want to sleep in their tipis every night don't want to go to war. Men that want to have their squaws in their tipis when they go to war, they can go hang! We don't go to war that way. We don't want anybody who goes to war that way.* LORD, when they heard that they all looked mightily impressed! I was, too. For a fact, I surely don't want my squaw in my tipi out here. GOD grant she never figures *that* out! *I hear that Benson has arrived, and that Burnett has given him one of the horses I left behind to come in with. I fear it is Paddy, and that after all you will miss your rides.* Poor darling, she has so few entertainments. I wonder if I should consider resigning the service? But the Custer book sure won't pay off my debts—

GENERAL G—— moves in a mysterious way His wonders to perform, but it's bound to be "homeward bound" at last, and till then, and always, be a good girl. Do nothing to your disadvantage or to make me unhappy, and don't forget or fail to pray for

Your Affectionate Husband,
James H. Bradley.

Good evening, general.

When it comes to genuine American English, you know what's what, don't you, Bradley?

O, I'm just a soldier, sir.

You're a good man, Bradley. Not stuck up like some.

General, I sure enjoy these adventures in the field.

> I wonder what you would say if I told you how much better I like you, general, when you are attired for the chase like this, than when I see you in your shoulder-braided double-buttoned dress uniform? With your hair combed and your beard trimmed, you diminish into a cadet, and your head grows a trifle small on your shoulders. As you are now, I feel moved to remember all the trout we've caught together, and the grief we've shared together at Little Big Horn, which makes you dear to me— no matter that I consider you tactically stupid, and at times lazy

>> (remembering when his commander wouldn't lift a finger against the Sioux last spring, perhaps because he'd been drawn into Custer and Terry's orbit of passivity, the lull before the Last Stand, as if they all knew it would happen and wished to save their energies for it).

Bradley, did I tell you I'm composing a verse about this campaign?

No, sir, I wasn't aware—

To be honest, I'm inspired by your literary doings. I'm going to read you a stanza, and then you say what you think. Tell me straight, now.

Let's hear it, sir.

> *And raising our guidon, it's onward we go,*
>> *Our bayonets polish'd, our strides in array,*
> *Preparing to cross swords with the heathenish foe*
>> *Until we've condemn'd them for murder to pay.*

I like it, sir. It's to the point.

WHAT ICICLES SAY
AUGUST 9–10

1

*D*usk, and the dying grass goes dark like a squaw's resined water-basket—
    cold rations (no fires),
    the grasshopers as squeaky as the wooden wheels of the twelve-pound howitzer, and every man soaping the insides of his shoes.

Here's the lay of Mr. Joe's camp—

Bradley says—

If we can stampede the women—

And then sweep right and left; that should panic the reds—

Tell your men to take a rest. We'll attack at dawn. Now I want to see Sergeant Frederick.

Here I am, general.

Why can't you detail a full five?

Well, sir—

They tell me that howitzer's your *baby*. Can't you take care of your own d——d baby?

General, I—

Who are your four?

Corporal Sale and two good privates, sir. And me—

Never mind. I know you're under strength. "D" Company can spare Sergeant Daly, and I'm going to give you Private Bennett from "B" Company. Now you take good care of that man.

Yessir. I know him.

Brave old John Bennett! Enlisted seven times . . .

Yes, sir.

Now, if we can't put down Mr. Joe right away, we'll all be depending on you. You start out at first light with your *baby* and plenty of shells, and don't take your time, either. You got me, Frederick?

Sure do, sir,

and the stars rush up like sparks.

Now, when we strike the creek . . .

Yessir.

With Sanno's bunch hitting them on the right—

Doc, is that too much grease in there?

Nope. You done right. Now break out your handkerchief and rub it in. But you don't want no grease on the trigger. Wipe that off.

I thank you, Doc.

All right. Now shut up,

cool moments agglutinating into night's rocks, a landscape on which one might clamber forward or backward

as they creep forward with all care, because even though no enemy sentries have been seen by the scouts (Indians are incapable of discipline), every American remembers White Bird Cañon. They indeed encounter no one, and form themselves on a convenient knoll, so that come dawn they'll be ready for work.

General says hold your fire when you see Joseph, because he may be keeping Mrs. Manuel for his concubine—

Yessir, I've told my boys, but—

But nothing. And get your d——d Bannocks to lie down until we give the orders.

Yessir,

and

Not much of a moon.

Moon enough.

> a flick of the moon across dark rocks and
>
> the night still as hard and dark as an old saddle and

Almost time, soldier.

Yes, sir.

> > Hoping and halfway expecting that the Nez Perce campaign will finish by noon, Bradley, guiltily galvanized by the lapse, promises himself to write his mother a letter,
> >
> > > the Bannocks more silent than trees.

Load with cartridges; load! Extras in your pockets. This is the finish. Now stick together and fight like heroes—

Down on the eastern horizon, a dark concretion of cloud and mountain clings, sediment fallen out of the grey pallor above. The sky is brighter still in the north, where the upcreeping sun finds scanter lurking-ground. The world is grey with fog; the Indian campfires bear pale yellow penumbras which thicken and mute themselves in the rising mist until no ray of enemy-light can be seen. Down steal our American soldiers, their sabres muffled, trying not to step on loud dry sticks, the scouts whistling ahead like owls. Mosquitoes sting their cold hands. Shaggy willows loom in the fog like buffalo. As yet the land cannot be said to possess any color; the river offers grey pools of light as instant by instant the grey sky goes bluish,

> > and gazing down and around at the great sky-jewel and the reddish-purplish-grey horizon of clouds below it, they taste futurity, listening for the dim sight and smell of nothingness, peering into every dark sound with the barrels of their rifles, hearing the odor of sweat and smelling the song of war,

the Indian horses raising their heads,

> > stream-bends now likewise going blue, and the top of the eastern horizon-wall commencing to fragment into cloud-fleece and pale greenish sky,
> >
> > the river in the blackish ground shining much more brightly than the sky, like quicksilver crawling and glowing across black rock,
> >
> > silhouetted tipis beginning to detach themselves from the darkness,
> >
> > > Sanno's killers crawling in from the right,
> >
> > the world still lavender-dark behind Gibbon's bunch in the slanting pine forest where their howitzer waits,

as their general, sensing that his grey is about to whinny, stuffs grass in its mouth,

the silhouettes of the mountains they crossed yesterday just beginning to show.

And now to the east a bluish scarf of mist unrolls slightly above the base of the mountains.

A dog barks; the horses say: *Hinimí.* The enemy do not awake.

In the grey grass, yarrow-flowers form white galaxies. Holding their breaths as they creep across the boggy grass (tautfaced Bradley in the lead), they spy reflections of willow-silhouettes in the pale blue river just ahead. The willow-leaves around them are pale grey, almost white with moonglow. Sometimes clusters of leaves in lone willows on the grass resemble chandeliers. Each leaf is a narrow miniature boat, with two tapering ends. And now each blade of grass in the wet meadow glows white.

A high planet gleams pure: Mars, no doubt. The dawn smells like water and mint.

Ducking down to be caressed by the limp wet fingers of willow-leaves, they peer through the branches, and discover white leaves speeding together down the black river, the eastern sky now peach-colored over the mountains

while on the enemy bank, the willows silhouetted, the tipis tall narrow triangles of pale grey,

the river becoming bluer and brighter, then slowly beginning to yellow into gold

(the moon as bright as ever, but less relevant),

an Indian dog barks once,

the sky yellow now, so that they scarcely dare to breathe in their cold-stiffened canvas frocks, pressing themselves against the many cool bone-white willow-trunks which radiate so crazily out of the ground (above these the reddish-dark branches and leaves, then a milky stripe of river interrupted by branch-silhouettes, then the earth-darkness of the enemy bank, the pale tipis whose lodgepoles meet up top and then fan out to claw against the sky, the mountains, the greenish-yellow heavens); and

faint scent of wild rose somewhere close in the grass and

stink-whiff of beaverskins tanning in the stream and

the moon's reflection broken up into a wriggling worm of white light and

as the first Indian, some old man, evidently a horse-herder, emerges from his tipi and approaches the river, the first shot sings:

Pim!

and he cries out quick and high like a hare, then

pim! pim! pim! pim!

falls into the river, as:

Send 'em to the happy hunting grounds, boys!

We'll try to get 'em all, sir.

Hurrah, hurrah, hurrah!

Joseph's dogs baying and barking at last, his horses screaming, Indians rushing from the tipis,

and our boys waist deep in glowing orange river, struggling numb-fingered up the other bank in an instant and

O, those hateful Indian eyes!

volleying low, pumping lead into those tipis before the reds can sit up, killing and killing,

but

They're running for the willows—

Watch out! Lieutenant—

My dear Mrs. Bradley:

to see the Sioux plains one more time, golden in the late afternoon and

Keep moving, boys!

We hope you will be able to bear up under your great affliction. How uncertain is life! Your dear husband wrote to me at the beginning of the campaign "that your separation would not again be so long."

Always your obt. servt. & friend,

I said move, you GODd——d cowards! Can't do nothing for him now—

My Dear Madam:

If the Herald people can at any time lift or lessen the burden of your great sorrow, will you not please to command us, that we may in some adequate form express the general sentiment of

Hurrah, hurrah, hurrah!

My Dear Child:

With a broken heart and grief unconsolable I can only say that the news of James's death reached me by telegram from Chicago, on Sunday evening at 9.0.c. p.m., 12th instant.

Since that moment I have been so prostrated that my life seems fast ebbing away. But this is a consolation as I am so anxious to join my dear boy in the better world. What disposition do you intend to have made of his remains? I am anxious if it does not conflict with your feelings to have him buried on his native soil. Affectionately,

Hurrah!

Hurrah!

Hurrah!

My Dear Daughter:
I received your letter and also the pictures of that dar-
ling little granddaughter of mine. When James fell I
hope he did not live long enough to look back and see
those dear ones he left behind. I cannot write more now
as I am absolutely

rushing down the lanes between close-growing tipis, horses screaming, morning stars exploding yellow from the barrels of carbines and pistols, a screeching Indian bending back his head, throwing wide his arms, his Sharps carbine
speeding down into the muck,

Stand up for these, the wrong'd, the aggriev'd,
In deepest pits of darkness found,

while behind and between two tipis an Indian draws an unwavering bead on
the mass of Bluecoats who fire straight in, then hack and slash with their sabres as they rush by, already in good order, eager to fulfill their instructions:

a dying Indian convulsing on all fours like a dog—proof of our
superiority
and Sanno's bunch volleying into the women's lodge:
Hurrah!
then give them another,
tear the door open, verify both squaws dead, and crush in the newborn baby's head with a rifle butt,

now rushing forward through the sulphur-sweet, bitter-tasting white fog
of gunsmoke
and the chestnut-smell of camas baking underground, bullets singing
through the tipis, and the sounds of splintering poles,

Company "K" now finally coming under fire from the willows.
Don't fire so fast.
But I want to get me one, Doc!
You got to cover your Injun before you draw the trigger. I seen you shooting
wild. You blow through all your cartridges an' then what?

2

Wounded Head awakes between volleys,
his wife and little boy gone away,
goes out to smoke still unknowing, lights his pipe, and a warrior shouts out: Lie
down or you will be shot!
as bullets come hissing and slapping through his lodge,
so that he takes up rifle and cartridges, with his Medicine bundle of striped wolfskin, then seeks out the fight, still not understanding what he will find,
and here sits his war-mate belly-shot
as all around come women's screams.

3

Prone beneath a willow-branch, with tall grass disguising him, Two Moons is already waiting,

> remembering how at Sparse-Snowed Place we were ready and looking up into the dawn when they showed themselves arrogant, foolish and silhouetted on the ridge just between the two yellow breasts; they began to ride down, while Shore Crossing and Swan Necklace laughed beside me, they who started this war:

> > Why does Cut Arm never stop hiding? How can he be killed?

Now here comes the first Bluecoat, apparently caged between the dark rake-leaves of angelica. Holding his breath, Two Moons draws the trigger inward, toward his heart, and red teeth explode from the soldier's face. Another one rushes toward him, his eyes pale blue like breadroot flowers, but Two Moons is invisible. His WY-AKIN (ring-eyed, crimson-nosed and feather-muzzled like a Northern Cheyenne horse mask) has promised that he will live to become frail. His wife will die before him, while his pigtails will freeze white; his face will shrink around his skull like forgotten brown nutmeat. A mounted enemy approaches! The horse's leg descends, approaching Two Moons's shoulder, the hoof angling delicately down, then clears him; perhaps the horse smells him as he does the horse, which hesitates, the rider unsuspecting, then minces on. Two Moons holds his fire. More Bluecoats now invest the place, all of them on foot. He remains still,

dreading that he should not have told his wife to lie still in the tipi:

> *my wife will die before me:*

> no, not yet; darling, lie still, for my WYAKIN to

Shláyayaya.

Hurrah!

> Now get up and run, darling—

because the *Americans* are shooting and shooting and among our women hiding in the water their bullets now find

> a child's life, as easily crushed out as the rattling buzzing of a dragonfly
> and the water
> and the grass
> and

> > a handsome young squaw in a fringed and beaded dress, staring at Johnny for an eyeblink so JESUS what the hell am I supposed to do, the reins gathered lightly in across her lap, then kicking the pony's belly and lunging away across the yellow grass

> > > (flames already bejewelling the spread dark pine-fingers atop the pallid Indian lodges, but the wet hides merely smoke):

> > flushing, he lowers the barrel of his Springfield (don't let Doc call me yellow) and

and

That Doc sure can shoot.

Right through her d——d heart, looks like—

D——d tipis won't catch fire—

How many buffalo robes did you find?

Don't tell me you're fixin' to cart one of those all the way to hell and gone.

Nothing like a buffalo robe to sleep in.

Well, I say you're a fool, but try that tipi over there.

General said—

Just don't let the general see, you woodhead.

No, I been in that tipi. Not much left in there.

Maybe you missed something.

Maybe I didn't. Set it on fire.

Where's the captain?

Who the fuck cares where that—

Hey, Blodgett found some of their camas cakes! Don't forget your friends—

But the packer guide leaps back onto his horse, stuffing his face, flashing his whip so happily in the air, trotting the tired bay round and round.

Watch out!

Hell, she ain't done nothin'. She's just a little Injun gal. She—

Pim.

Well, you sure killed yourself another one.

And Doc, his huge eyes sky-blue and beautiful, tears off the dead child's necklace: pale turquoise beads on a string of rawhide.

Now there's a waste of a squaw.

They're not called squaws until they're ripe.

Mighty ugly little monkey anyhow.

Is it true they don't have no—

Looky here. See for yourself.

Hell, there's plenty of Clatsop squaws back in Portland. Cost you a nickel or a cup of firewater.

Now you spy that one lurkin' in that thicket down there? Believes I can't see her! Watch me now. She'll never know a thing:

. . . Pim.

Did you see that, boy? Got her in the eye. When they pitch forward so rapid like that, they don't even realize they been killed, and that's a fact.

How do *you* know what they realize?

'Cause I fought in the Army of the Potomac, boy! Glory, hallelujah, yeah, yeah, yeah. I seen my comrades struck by rebel fire.

Over there—

Pim pim,

into the Land of Brightness.

Don't waste your—

They've posted themselves in the willows yonder. Could
be a whole brood of 'em.

I say smoke 'em out.

Watch out! That one's still—

Pim pim pim pim.

Pim pim pim.

He sure ain't movin' now.

All they that go down to the dust shall bow before Him.

Yessir, I seen 'em. You watch men die year after year, you figure out the result.
Now you see that papoose all grimaced up like it died hard? Take it from me, boy:
it didn't feel nothin.' That's just because the muscles go through their own changes
whenever a face dies.

Pim. Pim.

Pim.

and a longhaired brave lies bloody, a pipe clenched in his hand

(might sell that for a souvenir on the way back to Tongue
River)

—but Doc, near about ambushed by that Indian pipe, remembers
Wilbur at Gettysburg, shot in the belly, smoking *his* last pipe in the shade of
an oak tree, trying to smile, fixing to be brave, and then losing his breath:

Help me, Doc!

Ain't no help for you, Wilbur. Be brave now.

They shot me,

plucking at that ferrotype Abe Lincoln portrait badge he always
wore pinned over his heart.

Godd——n, Seccesh in the bushes, he—

I ain't much for writing, but I'll try an' write your folks if'n you got any.

Doc! Doc—

Don't go yellow on me now. You ain't the first that ever died.

Where are you, Doc? Doc, I can't see no more—

Glory, glory, halleluujah—

Doc, I'm *cold*, Doc—

Doc drags his bloody sleeve across his eyes and

So cold!

Doc, you ain't weepin' over no dead Injuns, are you now? What's the Godd——d
matter with you?

Ain't nothin' wrong with *me*.

Grinning to prove it, Doc kicks the dead Indian in the teeth, then spies

a new-dead half-grown squaw with her legs already apart, thanks to
Johnny, so

he shoves a stick up her just for a laugh, then leapfrogs up to
straddle her face,

slice off her elkteeth earrings for his collection, and
skip high in the sun!
What do you want that trash for, Doc?
That's my business.
Thought for a minute you was goin' *yellow* on us, Doc—
Pim.
Johnny, that wasn't nothin'. Just an Indian dog. What call you got shooting a
dog that never did nothin'?
Thought it might be something more serious
as Pahit Palikt, son of Yo-hoy-ta-m-sat, lies still as a
corpse beneath the buffalo robes in his father's lodge,
listening to his dog whimpering as it dies.
Gonna call you the Dog Catcher. Wasting your ammo on a—
Where's Captain Caitlin?
Boys, Doc kicked Ollicut in the teeth just now! I saw him do it.
That ain't Ollicut.
Well, who is it?
Just some old Indian.
Shoot him again then.
Pim.
This is chickenshit. I didn't come here to kill squaws and papooses. Where's
the bucks a-hidin' at?
And moving finely forward,
dead women's hair hanging down like the dark brown carcasses of lam-
preys which dangle together from the long sticks across the drying racks
—*the blood of* JESUS CHRIST *His Son cleanseth us from all sin,*—
and a sweeping volley to break up the enemy alignment:
That's for Helen Walsh. Now here's for Mrs. Osborne and that poor
little child that Joseph mutilated—
(the sky darkened by terrified birds),
they continue to destroy these hostile Indians, hoping to end this little war to-day,
with GOD's help, and thus be heroes and get ahead in life.
Now, where's the fighting at?
The Bluecoats having ridden on, Two Moons creeps forth and advances carefully along the creek, longing to kill more of them.
Well, keep it up, boys! We have 'em in confusion—
This ought to discourage those d——d reds!

4

White Bird has finally awoken from his lucky dream; he rushes out to rally his
warriors: *Stop now!* Why are we retreating? Since the world was made, brave men

defend their People. Shall we run up to the mountains so that Bluecoats may kill our women and children before our eyes? Better to die fighting! Now is the time; fight!

> as Peopeo Tholekt emerges wide-eyed, his face momentarily almost like a woman's

>> (while poor Loon tries to make himself brave, then hides in the willows until he hears our women packing the horses)

and Looking-Glass,

> our well-famed war-chief,

now shouts, shaking his Winchester in the air: Shore Crossing, Red Moccasin Tops, Swan Necklace! This is a battle! These men are not asleep as were those you murdered in *Idaho*. You sought to break my promise to the Bluecoats at Lo Lo. Now has come time to show whatever courage may be in your hearts. So kill on all sides! I would rather see you shot down than all the other warriors, for you began this war. Fight!

5

As soon as the Bluecoats, having volleyed once into his lodge, hasten on to kill more People, Shore Crossing, furious beyond words at Looking-Glass, takes up his massive buffalo rifle (that present from the first Boston we killed), then helps his wife crawl out:

> she is bleeding and silent

>> (has she been shot to die?);

>> perhaps he can Dream this away, or awaken from it

> as they run sideways;

> now she is stumbling; he leads her by the hand

>> (she is whispering her WYAKIN song)

to a willow thicket where they can throw themselves down

> (she lands on her pregnant belly; will the baby now die?);

while Rainbow, the best of us, has already positioned himself in some nearby darkness

> (but he lacks his Medicine bundle; perhaps his WOLF will not come);

and Shore Crossing, laying his gun across a log,

> he who can wrestle any man to the ground,

now listens to his wife's stifled panting, waiting for the soldiers to burst out of the willows.

Now indeed they are arriving,

> these killers who can never act straight.

Shore Crossing and Rainbow begin aiming at the line of Bluecoats,

> who charge toward them, tall and shouting;

>> while behind them Black Eagle runs back to his family's lodge to get

his rope of fine black horsehair, throwing himself down as bullets
sing through the walls:
>> *shláyayaya!*
and then Shore Crossing, he who never misses, uplifts his buffalo gun, holds his
breath and begins to draw back the trigger even as the barrel is still moving
upward:
the first Bluecoat's chest detonates with a great bloody roar,
> his heart-fire brighter than the rising sun,
but even as he crashes back among his comrades like a felled tree, the next Bluecoat
> (thin-faced like a minister, wide-eyed, with a long white beard)
shoots Shore Crossing in the head,
> which shines like lightning as the bullet destroys it
>> (he is the first of the Three Red Blankets to die);
and before he has even completed his fall, his widow,
> as vainly brave as the black tern who dives at a boy to defend her nest
>> (it was to please her heart that he first began this war),
chambers a round, taking up the gun, which she can barely lift,
> her WYAKIN pointing straight up like the tail of a flying grackle,
and kills the killer with that same horrific roar:
> his head flies off his neck in a stream of bloody fire—
but before she can shoot again, the third Bluecoat, who now stands over her like
a bear, shoots her in the throat
and she tumbles down twitching across her husband's corpse:
> *Tsálalal,*
and then Shore Crossing's gun falls forward with the chamber open
while Rainbow slips away through gunsmoke to shoot from a safer place.

6

And then Rainbow,
> our clear-hearted one who protects us
> and who once led Cut Arm across the Chinook Salmon Water and back
> again,
>> just for awhile,
now thumbs down the next cartridge into the breech of his trapdoor Springfield,
> taking aim (less trouble than shooting a running buffalo
>> —any boy could do it):
>> *pim!*
so that a Bluecoat cries out like a child and doubles over, pissing himself
>> as Lean Elk creeps snakelike down to inherit Shore Crossing's
>> magic gun
>>> (forty cartridges left);

and *pim!*
—another Bluecoat falls into the creek face down.

Now Rainbow's heart is laughing; his rifle keeps spitting out death, punishing these killers for what they have done,
but just before TRAVELLER THE SUN clears the mountains, a bullet flies
tsssss!
(his WYAKIN cannot protect him before sunrise;
his WOLF never came);
so that this bullet finds a home between his lungs.

7

But Toohhoolhoolsote has assumed his WYAKIN Power, the crown of claws furiously blossoming from his bear-heart.— Pack the horses! he commands his wives,

thrusting that dressed wolf's head down over his hair
and buckling on a dead Boston's belt of .44 calibre catridges, he rips
open the first box of exploding bullets from Cottonwood Place,
pours them into a deerskin pouch which he throws over his neck,
seizes his Sharps, first chambering a non-exploding round,
and bursts out of his lodge:
Áhahaha!
—he who has carried home two dead blacktail bucks, one in each hand—
seeking Cut Arm but discovering a running Boston who now drops to his knees,
beginning to sight on him with a Winchester,
but before this enemy can accomplish any death, Toohhoolhoolsote, snarling,
lunges forward, the Sharps protruding from his close-set hairy hands like some
monstrous proboscis,
and fires seemingly without aiming:
O O, *o, JESUS!* O God, O, help me, boys, I can't stand it, for that
d——d red has got me—

8

Heinmot Tooyalakekt awakes in dread, his heart exploding so painfully that for an instant he believes he has been shot;
then, when the bullets begin coming *kíw—kíw—kíw!* through the walls of his lodge, he claps a hand over Springtime's mouth
(she has already begun screaming)
and pushes her down hard against Good Woman and Sound Of Running Feet, hiding them under blankets and buffalo hide robes, groping for his rifle, cartridges, moccasins and Medicine bundle,
but the baby will not stop wailing, and a bullet hums in, certainly hunting her:

kíw!
　—killers will soon be arriving exactly here!—
so that Springtime, tearing herself free from Good Woman, sits up to save her
lovely one—
but even as she reaches out, the next bullet smashes her arm, *qáw!*
　(we see the bone showing)
　　—then enters the floor near Good Woman's head,
at which her husband, whose rifle is not by the door where it should be, rushes out
half-naked to kill this killer or die
　—but the Bluecoats have already passed, their rifles flashing ahead
　　(first they are volleying into every tipi; then they will come back to finish
　　us);
in desperate hurry he returns, whispering through the doorway to his women to
catch horses and quickly ride away:
Good Woman and Sound Of Running Feet spring out, fully dressed
　(and his heart is joyful to find the Colt at his daughter's hip;
　he gathers her in against him
　because she is staring through everything from behind part-closed eyes,
　　　her hair still fragrant with balsam fir jelly:
　　Little One, her dearest horse, lies screaming on his back, kicking with all
　　four legs;
　then her mother pulls her away and the instant has ended)
so that he now takes the baby from Springtime, as she creeps out
　(she has not yet dressed herself),
dragging the cradleboard behind her, eyes wide, biting her lip in agony
　　　(somewhere near, Looking-Glass's daughters will not stop scream-
　　　ing)
　　as Sound Of Running Feet and Good Woman begin to crawl like snakes
　　through the willows,
　　　the mother moving her lips, secretly singing her Wyakin song
　　　　(they cannot hear when he whispers: *Hurry!*)
—and Springtime cannot make her wounded arm go inside the buckskin dress;
　　—only the arm! Perhaps she will live!—
　as he hears Bluecoats roaring close by,
　　　　his horrified heart crying *qoh! qoh! qoh!*;
and when he begins to bends her arm, her eyes go wider and she tries to bite him;
now he has dressed her
　(she who has always decorated herself);
then he takes his knife
　　(pim! pim! pim-pim-pim-pim!),
cuts a strip from a fine white King George blanket
　　　—those killers will soon be coming back—
bandages her arm (the thick cloth already becoming red),

then whispers: *Síikstiwaa*, hear me! Wake up or you will be killed! Go—find a horse and go! With the baby I shall follow—
  My baby—
      who keeps screeching
          (perhaps she will cause our death)
      and wets him when he lifts her out of the cradleboard.
  Husband, I have been shot—
  Get down! Go now
      (kneeling, she falls on her arm, screams, then begins to creep away toward
      our horses;
          perhaps I shall see her no more);
then, considering the long trail ahead, he slides his daughter back into the cradle-board, at which she falls silent
      (suddenly she has begun sleeping)
—and the Bluecoats are arriving, so that rifleless he carries her into the willows.

9

As the Bluecoats come charging through the grass, Wounded Head and his war-friends take aim:
                  they are now setting our tipis on fire, while
          Wounded Head and a certain tall moustached Bluecoat miss each other,
          but Wounded Head's second shot kills the enemy: *shláyayaya!*
              just as White Bird's nephew, Young White Bird (nine snows old),
              begins running with his mother toward the river willows and a
              bullet shoots off his thumb and his mother's middle finger
after which the next Bluecoat shoots Wounded Head through his roached hair; the bullet creases the top of his head, and he falls unconscious. When he awakes, he ties the magic wolfskin in his hair, praising the WOLF WYAKIN Who has saved him.

10

Now Shore Crossing's long wide buffalo gun has come back to life, shooting down Bluecoats at intervals, each time from a different hidden place as Lean Elk creeps through the willows (for such is the great rifle's smoke and roar that when-ever it fires, the Bluecoats immediately volley back)
          and White Thunder, whose heart is now most furiously gladdened to
          have kept the pistol he won at at Sparse-Snowed Place, looking to be sure
          that all six cylinders have been loaded
              (in our burning tipis children begin screaming),
          takes up his war club
              (he has lent his 1866 Winchester to Wottolen),

then creeps through the willows with the pistol pointed forward, determined to be brave, ready to become a greater killer
as once again the noise of their rifles begins to remind him of many
women pounding roots together: *kíw, kíw, kíw!*
        (the sound I know from my dear mother Swan Woman—where is she?)
           as a woman keeps shouting: Men, why won't you defend us?
and a boy gives him an old rifle with one cartridge in it
             —but his heart shrinks hard in grief when an old man shouts:
             People, Rainbow has been killed!—
                  while Peopeo Tholekt (not wearing his hornpipe breast-
                  plate, lacking the eagle feather at his throat) runs for-
                  ward, saying in his heart, just as he did when the
                  Bluecoats attacked Looking-Glass's reservation: *Now I
                  am to die as a brave man!*
                  and Fire Body, the cunning shot who killed Cut Arm's
                  bugler at Sparse-Snowed Place, gets a Bluecoat officer in
                  the belly: *timm!*
           even as a kindhearted Bluecoat gives a quarter-dollar each to
two little boys he caught hiding behind their mother's corpse:
what does he mean to do here?
                  —and Grizzly Bear Youth, getting strangled by a mon-
                  strous Boston, is saved by Over The Point, Red Owl's
                  son,
                     who shoots the Boston in his side: *taq!*
                     —the needle-charge breaking Grizzly Bear
                     Youth's arm;
and Two Moons finds Heinmot Tooyalakekt with a cradleboard in his arms. This
chief now sadly says: Remember that I have no gun to defend myself—
   Skip for your life, uncle! Without the gun you can do nothing. Save your
daughter!
—at which Heinmot Tooyalakekt turns away, drawing the cradleboard tighter in
against his heart as he flees, the baby not dead after all, screaming herself purple.

11

Now he has almost reached the horses. Hearing clicking sounds, he finds Welweyas the half-woman down in the willows by her dead mother, loading a Bluecoat's six-shooter: How she longs to make herself brave! (She is no warrior; she will
rapidly be killed.)
   He says: Welweyas, my dear younger sister, help the People quickly! You
women must pack up our camp and set forth while the best men keep those Bluecoats in their holes. Take my baby to Good Woman. Will you come now with me?
Yes, that is good . . .

12

Two Moons joins some fighters in the willows. They are shooting at the Blue-coats. A warrior says: *Rainbow is dead.*

That cannot be so.

It happened before sunrise—

Where is he?

Down there.

Since my warmate has now been killed, I must see his body.

In the grass, with his face naked to the sky, lies Rainbow with a bullet in his heart; and just as Toohhoolhoolsote's eyes go musselshell-blind when he Dreams, so it is now with the eyes of Rainbow,

> our longhaired one who never forgot to carry an armload of sweetgrass into the sweat lodge.

> He killed five Bluecoats before they took his life.

Now here comes Five Wounds to see him, crying out: My brother has passed away. I too now shall go . . .

A warrior named Going Out brings a canteen of *getting-drunk liquid*—a dead Bluecoat's gift. He says: I captured this. Anyone who wishes may drink.

Five Wounds says: Give it to me.— He drinks,

> as a sizzling tipi falls over; the soldiers have lassooed it;
> and by the river a woman keeps screaming
> even as Well Behaved Maiden pleads with the shaman Kah-pots:
> Can you not save us?
> No, granddaughter, my Power cannot help! Run away down the creek—

already the ravens are settling.

> > Where is Wottolen?
> > > White Bird still lives, I am telling you three times!
> > Take the boy—
> Who saw my mother?

Five Wounds throws down the canteen, raises his rifle and says: Let us cross the water to the Bluecoats, then kill them all,

> but my heart longs to have painted myself red.

Where are they now?

Up there, digging themselves into holes. We shall follow them:

> > *Glory, glory, hallelujah—*

so that Two Moons skips from willow to willow with his rifle ready,

> fords the bloody creek, following Five Wounds, and
> > *Glory, glory, hallelujah:*

rifles sing and

he throws himself down at the willows' very edge, sighting with his Winchester, slowly, slowly drawing back the trigger:

Pim!

so that a Bluecoat leaps high, then falls;

and he runs ahead, flying up,

trees creaking in the wind, no bird singing:

Glory, glory, hallelujah—

Glory, glory, hallelujah,

and reaches the bluff's brow.

The soldiers fire:

Shláyayaya!

and

now Five Wounds has parted from us; we shall see him no more.

13

Knowing that as soon as it is safe to do so, others will rescue the rifle of that brave man and bear it away, Two Moons ducks down to the safety of the creek and follows it up through the trees to a place where his warmates have surrounded a trenchful of soldiers

even as White Thunder, still seeking Wottolen, finds the dead wife of Shore Crossing lying atop his corpse as if to shelter that brave one;

then he passes the corpse of his dear cousin No Heart,

who on that cold night between the two days when we fought Cut Arm at Big Water agreed to warm a shivering young woman in a rifle-pit;

this thing is not to be done in war, as our old ones have warned, and so even though that pretty woman

(now floating in the river, drained of blood)

would have liked to nestle between them, White Thunder arose and crept back into the darkness to hunt Bluecoats, while No Heart stayed with the girl until sunrise,

which must explain why his WYAKIN has now permitted him to be killed; and Wounded Head's sister Wetwhowees turns a Bluecoat's bayonet away from her breast, knocking him down

(Over The Point shoots him dead)

even as that one same kindly Bluecoat now plucks a baby from a dead woman's bloody grasp and hands it to another woman to care for

(will he now give her twenty-five cents?);

while as her mother finishes splinting her other mother's arm

(and Cloudburst, sobbing, snatches up two more cowskin bags, tying them to the horses' breastbands),

Sound Of Running Feet creeps back like a snake to see if her father still lives, and also to steal a bag of camas bread from their lodge, just one, so that her family will not go hungry, but when she ever so slowly peers over Little One's carcass (Ocher One lies belly up by the river) she finds that the tipi is now burning and three of Cut Arm's soldiers, slender and white like bitterroots, are pulling it down, so she retreats into the willows, crawling near the creek where a bloody woman and child are floating face down, and in terror she withdraws her Colt pistol, holds it out before her and cocks it—

at which a Bluecoat rises monstrously before her (he must have heard the click), and swivels his rifle toward her breast:

she fires: *pim!*

> a cloud of sulphur-sweet white smoke rushing out of her Colt, hanging in the air as concretely as a loop of intestine when we cut open a deer's belly,

and he falls dead with teeth exploding from his mouth:

> *Tsalalal!*

then she runs

but there are no more Bluecoats in her way.

14

Wounded Head seeks his wife and child. The little boy has been shot in the hip; he is screaming. Helping Another was shot in her lower back, as she tried to flee the Bluecoats; the bullet flew out through her breast, *shláyayaya!*

She says: Husband, when I was hiding in the willows, a small girl was there, so I laid my arm over her, but then a bullet came—

Now clear your heart and be silent, for I shall care for you both,

> and he secludes himself in the tipi, helping them while the battle goes on, as her old mother runs to pack the horses.

15

Kicking aside the smoldering lodgepoles, and with long sticks poking away singed hides, we discover what the Bluecoats have done:

> a cross-shaped bullet wound in a young girl's forehead,
> yellow fat and purple meat ripped open in a grandmother's heart,
> another dead boy, eyes shut and mouth open, and
> the small boy, open-eyed, almost smiling, his skull unlocked by a tumbling bullet; he lies in a puddle of his own brains
>> (the web of his hand tattooed with specks of burned powder where he grabbed at the barrel of the Bluecoat's rifle, struggling to turn it away)

—exactly here stands silent Wottolen, *he who remembers,* so
that our children's children will know this—

and

we are crying out

(the fat of dead children still sizzling like resinous wood);

now we shall tear the Bluecoats loose from their lives.

16

Still fearing for his mother Swan Woman,

who cannot now be helped,

White Thunder springs out of the willows, his heart hurting him like a wound;
John Dog has been shot in the forehead; all the same he will not trade his full gun
for White Thunder's empty one

(he means to die fighting, not to run away)

and in the river before them floats the dead boy with the hole in his skull

(one of Toohhoolhoolsote's People);

still he keeps hunting Bluecoats to kill
—until his Uncle Ollokot shouts: Yellow Wolf,* why are you crawling there? Here
is your rifle; Wottolen has sent it for you. Nephew, your heart is strong; we have
need of you; come help us wipe out these murderers!
so that White Thunder runs toward him, happy to be back among our best men
who will now try to drive Cut Arm's killers under the ground:

Chase them out!

Where is Cut Arm?

(Toohhoolhoolsote roaring like a grizzly bear,

but he can bewitch no one with his hand)

—and as White Thunder chants his WYAKIN song, he begins to feel in his heart
that he has been singing it since his birth; indeed it has become the very heartbeat
of his life,

his WYAKIN, the WOLF, helping him to hunt and drink the Bluecoats' blood,
and then Ollokot tells him who has been harmed, in order to better enrage his heart:

he sorrows for his lovely Aunt Springtime and his dear Aunt Fair Land,

she who almost surely cannot live

(about Swan Woman Ollokot has not heard):

it is as if all the blood in his heart has clotted into grief.

There! See him running away!

Raising the Winchester, he shoots while running: *pim!*

(Ollokot is smiling),

so that this Bluecoat leaps up eagerly to bleed from his heart; now he is dying with
the musical rattle of a crane.

---

*The name by which White Thunder was called by others.

During that Big Water battle one moon ago, after Fire Body crawled up to him at Cliff Place, encouraging him to die well and advising him to aim for officers, White Thunder raised his rifle and knocked down one officer, then a second, after which the Bluecoats boiled away in confusion! Thus exactly here at Ground Squirrel Place his heart hopes to kill officers,

Cut Arm most of all

(that maimed old moldy one with the star on his hat)

or Tsépmin who was our brother,

but it begins to seem that neither one can be killed.

17

Heinmot Tooyalakekt and No Heart have saved our horses,
> while Hahtalekin's People, who heard the Bluecoats whispering just before they attacked, drove them out of their part of camp, so that most of their lodges remain undestroyed;
> now they are helping others;

therefore Peopeo Tholekt,
> his eyes huge above his white gorget,

blows his eagle-bone whistle five times, then runs uphill, returning to the fight,
>> over him now his dark WYAKIN, like a cormorant raising up its wings to dry,
>>> and Bluecoats firing from behind the pines, two sprawled out dead, one staring at the blood gushing from his shoulder; a pallid Bluecoat kneels down, watching us wide-eyed as he fumbles another cartridge out of his belt, and the nodding golden grass kisses his boots

exactly here where Peopeo Tholekt meets the Two Red Blankets, against whom the People keep crying out: *You who began this trouble, go fight! Here is the work you thirsted for! Fight for us now—*
so that they run furiously down upon the soldiers, and Red Moccasin Tops destroys one most easily,
>> Strong Eagle and Peopeo Tholekt all the time shooting down into a Bluecoat trench,
>> until Strong Eagle has spent his cartridges, at which they quarrel, and he takes Peopeo's rifle and ammunition
>>> while somewhere nearby, Red Spy is yelling the *scalp halloo;*
and leaving Strong Eagle, Peopeo Tholekt sprints weaponless,
>> worrying about his favorite yellow horse,
>>> past Wottolen and Over The Point, who shoot while singing their WYAKIN songs

(clear in his heart because Heinmot Tooyalekekt has
saved his son Black Eagle),
down to the People to see how they are
(in that row of dead children, the black soiling of gunpowder
around an especially close-range forehead wound records the
mercy of instant death)
and finding Black One still alive, he leaps onto him bareback, riding
back up toward the voice of a big gun
where Temettiki and Stripes Turned Down are seeking to capture the Bluecoats' cannon,
looking down past the ankle-high green grass with the dead wood lying
in it and the dark wood showing through, shaded by lodgepole pines;
then the world drops off into the wide green light of Ground Squirrel
Place, going yellow at the horizon
(where is Cut Arm the Moldy?);
and Peopeo Tholekt,
who was wounded first in the arm by Cutthroats,
then in the thigh by Bluecoats,
feels ready to die without much fear
in the shade of his tall WYAKIN with the green eyes and the mouthful of
bear's teeth,
and then Stripes Turned Down kills the Bluecoat who has been loading the gun
as Temettiki shoots some mules and steals others,
our bullets saying *shláyayaya,* which is what icicles say when they strike together,
the last *Americans* running away uphill (they were never men).
Peopeo Tholekt says: Hear me, brothers; let us bring down this cannon and
make it kill!
But their hearts are all mule-greedy! Now they are driving their captured animals
down to the women, leaving him alone with the big gun, which he cannot move, so
he removes the wheels, rolls the gun downhill on its side, and sadly buries it
as Young White Bird's father, riding up to see what has been done,
finds a good Army rope, coils it up and carries it to be packed on
one of the horses
and others come for ammunition:
a fine present from Cut Arm!
—and then Peopeo Tholekt, still sorrowing with all his heart for the killing they
could have done,
looks down from there to see how Ground Squirrel Place grows greener and
greener the farther one's gaze goes, the river bends taking on a greenish cast, even
though the grass on the steep slope down has long since gone brownish-gold, and
the aspen leaves have already begun their dying,
some tipis still smoldering, pinecones lying in the grass.

18

Now Red Moccasin Tops,
    Chief Yellow Bull's son,
    and second of the Three Red Blankets
        (some call him the best of our best men, although others preferred
        Rainbow),
lifts up his head to shoot, and two bullets meet him,
so that only one Red Blanket remains: Strong Eagle, who gets shot in the hip as he
runs downhill; he will ride with the People to their last battle.

19

And we are covering them up; we are weeping as we dig,
    as a dark, dark crow watches them richly;
    although we cannot paint their faces red, we are wrapping them in our
    best buffalo robes, which we close tight:
        Sun Tied's sister, and his wife, and her newborn baby girl;
        About Asleep's mother,
            whom we found floating in the bloody river, with four
            other dead women beside her,
        Shore Crossing
            (his eyes and forehead gone)
        and Red Moccasin Tops
            (fist-size holes in his chest and arm, the face untouched,
            eyes and mouth wide open as if in expectation),
        Welweyas's mother Agate Woman
            (clubbed to death with a rifle butt; perhaps the Blue-
            coats caught her shooting)
        Ta Mah Utah Likt,
            killed with the same bullet that slew her baby as she ran
            with both sons toward the willows
                (the older boy is here to bury her),
        Hahtalekin, who was chief of the Palouses,
        and Rainbow,
            he who protected us,
        broken open,
        and
            sixty or ninety others
                (perhaps a hundred have been killed:
                    how are we to mention so many no more?—
                    how shall we avoid their teeming ghosts?);

but Five Wounds we cannot bury, for the Bluecoats
keep shooting whenever we approach his body:
stone and earth on top
(not daring to kill their favorite horses for fear that the Lice-
Eaters will find their graves);
shovelling the riverbank over them,
our children grubbing for sugar and hardbread in the pockets of dead
Bluecoats
(About Asleep turning over one dead Boston, then cutting at his
shirt, treasuring up his buttons as black as an antelope's eyes: payment for his mother
as Heinmot Tooyalakekt lifts up the boy's younger brother
onto the father's horse),
snatching up canteens, matches, trowel bayonets and silver dollars,
the women then running back to the tipis to save what they can, leaving their
lodgepoles, throwing down their digging-sticks,
holding horses, hoisting up their children, rolling up blankets,
some men keeping the Bluecoats under fire, the others helping their People to
make ready,
and Cloudburst, still weeping, lassoos and packs as many horses as she can
(Welweyas hoists the cradleboard up onto Springtime's horse:
the battle-deafened baby stares without moving)
while Fair Land, whom we have dragged out, lies groaning in the grass
(stripe of dark blood under her nose, and great foul bubble of pallid foam
between her parted lips:
Welweyas, almost screaming, rushes to pick yarrow for her)
and Good Woman,
that good woman indeed, who can dress a deerskin quick and clean,
helps Springtime onto her horse, saying: *Ride now!*
Cloudburst padding Fair Land's saddle with grass so that she will suffer
less on the trail
(she has put on the necklace of two dozen bearclaws which her
husband gave her at Split Rock);
old Swan Woman is whipping as many horses as she can,
and now Sound Of Running Feet has returned, swinging out the cylinder of her
Colt, plucking out the dead brass casing and inserting a new round
in silence, all in silence;
until she says: Mother, they have killed Ocher One
and her mother says: *Ride now,* my dearest daughter! Help Springtime—
and so the girl and the wounded woman ride away on Fair Land's horses, following the other People who are not warriors down the trail toward Willows Place,
Heinmot Tooyalakekt packing up racehorses for Lean Elk,
who is up there fighting,

Cloudburst and Good Woman now lifting Fair Land into the saddle, with Welweyas's man-strong help;

and Cloudburst, remembering how Ollokot warned her at Cottonwood Place not to bring a horse broadside to a line of shooting Bluecoats, looks over her shoulder at the hated ones,

and the smoldering hides,

the dead,

the grasslike flames around the Bluecoats' holes

—until a bullet comes: *kíw!*

so that Cloudburst must now make herself brave;

and like a common nighthawk opening his wings to show his white stripes, so her WYAKIN rises over her, comforting and encouraging her,

making her ever more herself.

20

Grey Eagle has been shot; he knows that he will soon die. His daughter White Feather has been shot in the arm, like Springtime; she can live. Splinting her arm and lashing it over her heart, he calls her brother and they lift her up onto a fast horse. He sends her away with her stepmother and the other women, old ones and children. Then Grey Eagle turns away. He will help the other wounded, until he dies.

21

Well, the bucks have rallied, boys,

and Gibbon upraises his field-glass, thereby discovering how in much the same fashion that those looting railroad-harridans of Pittsburgh lift up the hems of their skirts to scoop away loose flour, then run down the alleys, hoping to escape the clubs of our brave police, so Joseph's squaws are now dodging cunningly away, somehow loading whatever trash they can onto their ponies and hitting the trail to delay their encounter with justice,

withdrawing, shooting into the Big Dust,

but then a bullet knocks the glass out of his hand.

22

To the top of the hill, the top of the hill, or we're lost!

Corporal, shut up; you're not in command. Now dig trenches, men! We'll need to make a stand. Doublequick now!

as the Army members of this command (the volunteers are out of luck)

employ their experimental Rice bayonets, forting themselves into the dirt
of the lower slope,

    cursing, tearing off their shirttails with trembling fingers to wipe
    the fouled breeches of their Springfields,

    prying out spent shells with hunting knives,

never turning their backs on the brown-silver shine of water in the green
of Big Hole:

               Logan got a bullet in his brain!

          Woodruff's shot in both legs—

and hardly anybody still cares to watch through a field-glass the way that
Joseph's horses bunch up their backs when they run
because the red snipers keep shooting,

    Gibbon wishing he could plunge his wounded leg back into the cold
    river or drink a swig of cocaine,

        English convulsing in his final agony

soldiers dying in the low wet grass, seeing the pulsing golden grass all
around the edge of the world,

    but hearing a sound which resembles the way a mule groans when
    one tightens his cinch, Doc lets fly: must be a wounded red. The
    sound stops.

Our heroes hide in holes,

    lost to the smell of mint in the river-grass and to the dark shinings of
    smooth shallow water-windings in late afternoon, and the wavery green
    reflection of grass wriggling from each bank,

because now the Indians have fired the golden grass, and the sky is all silver
smoke.

23

Indeed we are setting fire; we are burning the dying grass; we shall kill these
Bluecoats as they have killed our People; we shall catch them all on fire

    even as Good Woman packs another six horses;

        and Welweyas comes back running, clutching to her flat
        chest many long cakes of dried serviceberries from the Salish
        country

        (they are still faintly fragrant with horsemint):

    Good Woman wraps them in a dead Bluecoat's shirt and ties
    them onto Agate Woman's bay horse

    while Springtime, who has ridden nearly out of sight, grips the
    cantle one-handed, biting her lips for pain, fearing most of all for
    her baby.

        Their chief wears a yellow coat and rides a grey horse; he is
        not Cut Arm—

Kill him!

Red Spy rushes low to fire the grass;

> and from behind a lodgepole pine Ollokot is watching, his dark round eyes alert and cautious as he squeezes the trigger of his .44 Remington— missing his kill—

Toohhoolhoolsote's best men are shooting and shouting: Cut Arm, come out and die!

—but our fire goes out.

24

White Cloud and Two Moons fight side by side, while Peopeo Tholekt kills another Bluecoat, shooting joyously down into a trench,

> as Ollokot incites the young men: Remember how you left the battle at Big Water, so that Cut Arm destroyed our camp! You have made us all fight, so fight!

and Over The Point now stands beside Yellow Bull, who has begun to avenge his slain son Red Moccasin Tops:

> *I am flying up, flying up to kill;*
> *My YELLOW BULL runs before me;*
> *I am spinning round;*
> *My WYAKIN will help,*

while Toohhoolhoolsote fights by himself,

> and just as a cornered grizzly rips open a dog's belly, so this grim wide old chief throws himself upon any of Cut Arm's killers who are not yet cowering in holes:
>> he gashes them to death, devouring the life within their hearts
>>> from which their blood comes out dark red like a prairie dog's nose

> even as Red Spy, thumbing the first explosive bullet into his trapdoor Springfield, sights on a young Bluecoat in a hole:
>> *Pim! . . . taq! . . .*
>> *Áhaha!* He has destroyed this soldier boy's face.

25

Johnny, boy, did you take my advice and save you some cartridges?

I surely did, Doc.

Good, 'cause now's when you'll truly value 'em. Keep one for you, boy. Then them Injuns can't never do you no harm.

But the boy groans and pales, shot through the guts.

Doc?

What is it now?

Doc, I'm hurting powerful bad.

Well, I knowed Howard Morton, who got blinded in one eye by an Indian bullet back in '68. Didn't never hear him cryin' about it.

Then I won't say no more.

That's the way. You just bear up as good as you can and be a man.

26

Now Traveller the Sun is departing Ground Squirrel Place, the many white loops of Ollokot's necklace catching twilight just a little as he overwatches the enemy, warning the young: My dear brothers, this time you must not turn away from the fight. Remember your People, who can no longer travel quickly. They are wounded and dying because we failed to keep watch. Looking-Glass, can you hear my words? Look down at the river, where so many of us now lie dead. This is a shame upon your leadership. Looking-Glass, what do you say?

But Looking-Glass is silent.

A Bluecoat's rifle shines up—and carefully, doing his best, White Thunder shoots down at that place until he hears a scream

as the Moon rises

and for a long time there is only silence from the trench; then a warrior hoots softly, and with great excellence Ollokot shoots down, killing another Bluecoat;

then it gets cold,

> our battle-stripped best men covering themselves with the shirts of the dead Bluecoats who lie hereabouts;
>
> and grim old Toohhoolhoolsote, with his pistol hand pinching the striped blanket tight across his crotch, frowns with faraway eyes, his hair roached but unbraided, his shining white necklace-loops so densely contiguous that they pretend to be armor;
>
> noiselessly he lets the blanket fall, swinging up his Winchester to instantly discharge a burst of flame:
>
>> *Pim!*
>
> so that from the trench-darkness a Bluecoat or Boston whom only he was able to see now roars in pain,
>
> at which he smiles, lowering the rifle and resuming his blanket, while Strong Eagle, he who can almost speak the Boston language, shouts happily down:
>
> *GoDd——n you, you d——n white man! Kill Indians sleeping, then cry like little boy!*

Listen! They are crying like women!

Fighting no more . . .

Shall we take pity on them?

Down there some young boy keeps sobbing for water.

Let's kill him.

There he is—
Ah, he's dying.
Kill him; kill him!

27

Fire slowly. Don't spend your bullets and not get Indians.
Now our predicament is perilous.
Our chances are pretty fair.
Keep yourself covered.
Let's stand them off. Don't any of you have "sand"?

> *No, no, no! O JESUS! Somebody shoot me, GODD——nit! I can't stand it!*
> *JESUS, JESUS,*

>> but Doctor Blalock could still fix me up, maybe,

>>> sweet Doctor Nelson G. Blalock at Fort Walla-Walla, with his
>>> white beard as clean and pretty as cotton candy, his round
>>> spectacles like jewels, will fill a bottle of elixir terpin hydrate*
>>> for any man with the means; he's done it for me before, so
>>> that must be why I can almost see that tall narrow bottle with
>>> its squared edges; just a sip of the stuff would set me straight,
>>> O LORD. Three swigs, and I'd share the rest around! Then I'd
>>> set myself in the soft leather chair while the barber ties a
>>> white cloth around my throat. I'd inhale the perfume of shav-
>>> ing soap and close my eyes. I'd sure enjoy a sleep—

Just before dawn, as the Bluecoats and the warriors who besiege them both
stay silent in order to hear each other, there comes the chortling bugle-call of a
sandhill crane.

28

They must of drawed off. Getting real quiet now.
Well, then *you* stick your head out.
General, we carried everything before us, but then Joseph—
Well, we might have been whipped, but we broke the back of the Nez Perce
nation.

29

Two Moons is already out of sight; he is helping the women, children and older
ones to get away,

> the babies weeping, *shlak, shlak!,*

---

*This contained codeine.

and Lean Elk leads them, riding quickly on one of his racehorses;
White Bird riding quiet with *Kate* because he is old,
as Heinmot Tooyalakekt,
>he who is called *Joseph,*
helps old ones, women, children
>>while Wounded Head, stunned by the deaths of Rainbow and so many
>>other best men, rides with his wife and their dying child, unable to im-
>>prove his heart,
>>>with his sister Wetwhowees
>>>>(she who has saved herself from a Bluecoat's bayonet through
>>>>great strength)
>>>riding ahead
>>and looking back, Yellow Bull sees the Cut Arm's Lice-Eaters shooting
>>Kah-pots the shaman:
>>>*pim!*
—Toohhoolhoolsote, Looking-Glass and the other warriors corralling the Bluecoats all night, until Ollokot urges them to go help the People
>(he stays awhile, just a little while, to watch over his good friends the *Ameri-*
>*cans*, while the People ride farther and farther away);
thus Looking-Glass the unexcelled,
>he who has given so many horses at the Sun Dance
>>(soon his hair will be as silver as river sand),
rides silently down the trail, with his uncased Winchester over his shoulder
>and the black horse's snout flaring against the grass
White Bird gallops up alongside him to shout: *Looking-Glass, what do you say*
now? Here is the peace treaty you made with your great friends the Bostons.

At Least Idaho and Oregon Are Safe
August 11

1

*B*ut the horse herd escaped nearly intact?
Afraid so, general. Those cunning squaws—
How many Indian ponies were captured?
Shall I inventory our Bannocks, sir? They—
My question might not have been to the point. Have we a surplus of service
animals?

In fact, general, we've got about all of Joseph's horses we can use.

Shoot the rest.

Right away, sir.

O, good morning, Wood.

Good morning, general. You're up early.

Well, but these are exciting times! Joseph's near the finish.

Certainly looks like it, sir.

Who's Gibbon's new adjutant-general?

I'll find out right away, sir.

He's to prepare me an abstract of Joseph's killed and wounded for despatch to General Sherman.

Yessir. I understand they hid most of their dead—

You meant to add that our Bannocks dug them up.

Yessir.

Wood, you're very sensitive. Believe me, I cherish that in you.

Yessir.

You were still en route from Alaska when I interviewed the survivors of Joseph's massacre. I don't believe you had the privilege of meeting Mrs. Chamberlain.

No, sir.

Women of her sort make me wonder whether hers might be the stronger sex. She endured quite a lot. The boy was murdered according to the mother's statement by having his head placed between the knees of a powerful Indian and so crushed to death. The other child was torn from its mother, a piece of its tongue cut out and a knife run clear through its neck. Mrs. Chamberlain was repeatedly outraged by the Indians and received severe injuries.

Yessir.

And when you're finished, ask the surgeon if Colonel Gibbon is well enough for a visit.

2

Good morning, colonel. I hear from our surgeon that you're recovering rapidly. A most powerful constitution you have!

Well, thank you, general. Guess I was luckier than my horse.

Are you taking Dover's powder?

Yessir. Quite the miracle drug—

Well, colonel, you certainly gave Mr. Joe something to think about.

I hope so, General Howard. I sure do hope so. You know, I can't help but admire the way he rallied his forces. And then to box us up like that! They fight near about as good as Americans!

Joseph's redoubtable, all right. And as slippery as they come—

That's a fact, general. That sure is a fact. He's a one-man band. "G" Company lost fourteen out of twenty-five—

Heroes. We won't forget them—

Yessir. Greatest Indian I ever came up against—

Now, colonel,

> seeking to emulate his old mentor at Bowdoin College, Professor Thomas
> C. Upham:
>> tall, sixty as all too soon I must be, his head drooping;
>> good at coaxing out confessions from erring boys, kindly at reason-
>> ing with them, a trifle shy as I once was and in truth will always be
>> even if in my position I must pretend otherwise,

the Eastern press sometimes fails to realize what our Indian service may require. And it's on their reports that Congress, unfortunately in my opinion, tends to rely. And it's Congress which keeps whittling away at our poor old Army.

Be d——d to the Eastern press, I say!

Colonel Gibbon, I don't in the least care for profanity.

Excuse me, general. I was just talking as one old soldier to another—

All right. Now, colonel, do you remember that business with the Third Colorado at Sand Creek? You know, with the Cheyennes . . .

O, general, do I ever! The glory days of '64. You was marching with Sherman to the sea, and I—

That's not quite to the purpose.

All right then, general, I did used to know that Colonel Chivington. The *Fighting Parson*, they called him! Kind of like you in that respect. O, but he hated Indians worse than Robert E. Lee hated niggers. Gave the whole cavalry a black eye, if I may say so. If he hadn't of massacred those Cheyennes, they never would have turned against us. They used to be very persuadable Indians, at least in my opinion, and now look at them! We'll probably need to wipe them out.

If so, colonel, that will be a matter of regret to any decent American. Black Kettle's band had shown absolute submission and friendship to the Government. Without a shadow of excuse, the Third shot them down. I've never understood that outlook.

On the bright side, though, our Custer sure took care of Black Kettle once those Indians went bad! Pretty audacious, general, a dawn raid in a blizzard! I had that in mind right here at Big Hole. Tell you the truth, I was thumbing over poor Custer's memoirs not long ago—

However the case turns out, what are the Cheyennes going to think of us in the future when we send missionaries for their instruction?

Now, that's a puzzler, general, and no mistake.

Moreover, Colonel Chivington's indiscretion tilted public opinion against the Army, and after '65 the Copperheads used that against us. Disagree with me if you like, colonel, but in my opinion every such incident incites our enemies in Congress to reduce military appropriations.

Well, General Howard, sir, I don't know about that. You're sure a deep thinker when it comes to politics—

Now tell me the truth, man to man. I promise not to use it against you. Was it absolutely necessary to shoot down Joseph's squaws?

General, upon my honor I assure you that they were as brave and quick with a gun as the bucks! And when a squaw notices her husband falling down dead with a big hole in his forehead, why, she can get right bloodthirsty. You should have seen 'em blasting away at us! A credit to their race. As for the papooses, we saved 'em where we could, but when you're shooting into a closed-up tipi at dawn, well, general, war is war and you can't refine it. Isn't that how General Sherman put it?

Colonel Gibbon, you need not quote General Sherman to me. I hope you'll think carefully about what I've just said, and in the future, please try to spare women and children whenever you can.

Yessir.

Well, the loss of life was unfortunate, but at all events, Joseph has been frustrated, and Idaho and Oregon are safe.

Now for Montana, sir!

Ha, ha, ha! I hardly think that even Lincoln could have put it better. You do have a way with words—

General, thanks for all you done for me and my men, and if my men got ahead of themselves and caused the Army any inconvenience, I sure do apologize.

Well, colonel, I suppose I should let you rest. But I'll look in on you later, if you like.

It would be an honor, general. And if you ever have a slow moment while I'm still on your hands, I could maybe challenge you to a game of whist—

Gladly! Do you have a second or should I round up two of my officers?

OBSEQUIES

*S*ome of our lumbermen feel sorry for Joseph's Indians. Pretending that it's only to prevent stinking up the country, they rebury the enemy dead whom our Bannocks have dishonored:

a truly Christian deed,

but the souvenir hunters are now riding in; they will dig up everything all over again.

Looking-Glass Is Silent
August 9–11

1

*B*y midafternoon, grass going russet under thunderheads where the land opens up to the east of Ground Squirrel Place—

the locusts singing *tekh-tekh-tekh!*—

Fair Land can go no more without groaning. Strapping her to a travois, the People go on riding, whipping their horses' heads,

> Sound Of Running Feet on one of her dying aunt's stallions, whom she now names Helper (she has lost her otterskin neckpiece in the half-burned lodge),

>> while her father, who has saved Black Mane-Stripe, rides up and down the line, learning who is most hurt and who lacks food and blankets,

> Young White Bird laughing at himself as he tries with a newly thumbless hand to guide his pony;

>> Wounded Head not far behind; his wife bleeds silently, but their little boy keeps screaming with pain;

as John Dog, shot in the forehead, embraces his horse's neck so that his dizziness cannot unseat him,

> while Burning Coals, stunned and terrified, keeps dreading that one of our best men will harm him for refusing to lend his horses

> (he has saved the whole herd).

No one remembers him, so his heart flies back into his ribs;

> then he sees to his wounded daughter

>> (surely she has not been shot to die)

> as Swan Woman, White Thunder's old mother, drives her horses in among his

>> (Wottolen led them safe, then brought her camas bags and lodge-skins, for his war-friend's sake).

Geese Three Times Alighting On Water grieves for Shore Crossing,

> who once gave him a Sharps rifle from some Boston named *Jack* who had been killed

>> (now he has a dead Bluecoat's Springfield);

> perhaps he should grieve for Red Moccasin Tops also, or even for Shore Crossing's wife; but only Shore Crossing,

he who could ride any unbroken stallion across the Chinook
Salmon Water,
showed him kindness. Geese Three Times Alighting On Water rides easily; he cannot understand in his heart what has happened.
And old Kapoochas the shaman never harmed anyone; the Bluecoats have shot
him in the hip,
while Burning Coals's daughter rides bleeding
(White Bird will sing over her to-night)
as the blanket tied around Fair Land's waist darkens with blood.

2

This is the time when our women should be gathering berries. The enemy have
a hold on us; we shall be dead.
Wottolen comes galloping from Ollokot to say that new Bluecoats are marching down from the mountains; soon they will be at Ground Squirrel Place. (No
one has yet seen Cut Arm.)
Looking back, we see smoke from the lodges they have burned;
they burned *Kate*'s pemmican camas bread, and the fine deerhides that
Fair Land once smoked into perfect yellowness
and they have burned our children.
Heinmot Tooyalakekt cannot keep from watching over his shoulder;
but Toohhoolhoolsote,
he who will not be enslaved,
declines to look back.

3

Ollokot has not yet ridden up with the brave rearguard.
Our warriors flank us right and left, glaring outward, for why should the worst
not swoop again exactly here? The *Americans* have excelled; they have killed us.
How can we kill them all?
Lean Elk rides behind, bearing Shore Crossing's buffalo gun. Black Eagle's
daughter has become one who cannot stop bleeding, and on her face the look of a
woman who has just spilled boiling water upon herself. Cloudburst gazes at the
trail, riding, riding,
through the wriggling grooves between swales where creeks hide themselves under long worms of willow-clumps,
then down into the sagebrush swales whose hearts are white sand,
while Fair Land's baby son whimpers in the jolting cradleboard,
drowning out the bubbling allurements of a male sage grouse.
Heinmot Tooyalakekt,
he who would carry anything uphill for his women,

now rides up alongside his sisters-in-law;

> from the elder one's drooping hand he takes the whip and beats the pack-
> horses for her,
>
> then approaches Springtime,
>
>> whispering: *Síikstiwaa*, this time I did not leave you behind,
>>
>> waits awhile,
>
> then rides bitterly silent to Sound Of Running Feet and strokes her hair
>> (she will not look up);

to his elder wife he murmurs:

> Will she live?
>
> Husband, she must surely die:
>
>> Fair Land, against whom no ill can be said, and who cranes
>> her head left and right as if she is counting horses. Her heart
>> must be hoping that Ollokot will arrive in time.

4

In the camp called *Willows* (where willow-islands twitch in golden grass, reek-ing of rain and dust), a good place remembered by our buffalo hunters, the war-riors dig rifle-pits from which to watch all night behind, and Cloudburst prepares fire and food just as she and Fair Land have always done together, while Sound Of Running Feet,

> who wishes to know why our shamans cannot send Cut Arm bad luck,

pickets the family's horses; and her father goes to speak to the young boy About Asleep,

> he who brought canteens up to our warriors at the Big Water fight, and
> who bravely awaited his father even as Cut Arm's killers were coming:
>
>> to-day he has seen his mother shot to death in the river
>>
>> (her wound as pink and petite as a wild rose);

to him Heinmot Tooyalakekt says: My dear nephew, if you go on making yourself brave you will surely become one of our best men,

> then returns to his family, almost in tears.
>
>> The boy's father goes alone into the trees.
>>
>> And Fair Land must die; Fair Land must die! Her face grows as white as
>> Crow-tanned buckskin.
>>
>> When will Ollokot ride in?

Longing for her father to caress her again, Sound Of Running Feet watches him as she sits on the far side of the fire mending a horsehair rope for some widow or orphan; then, when instead he whispers with her two mothers, she begins to touch the Colt at her hip, wondering if the song now rising up in her heart is one she might have Dreamed:

> *Gun is good;*
>
> *Gun will help;*

then carefully they lay Fair Land on silk buffalo robes;

   she who used to dream of the other side of the river is now arriving there, and Good Woman soothes her wounds with resin from the inner bark of the balsam fir

     as Feathers Around The Neck begins to sing over her, very softly

        (we dare not drum, for fear that Cut Arm's killers might hear);

      and Springtime, very pale, holds the baby in the crook of her left arm as she nurses

       (after which her husband whispers: *Be brave,*

        cutting the bullet out of her arm);

        Hasten; evening shadows be!

  Although White Bird, who owns great Medicine, tries to suck the evil from her, Fair Land is weeping silently for the small son she must soon leave,

        (Cloudburst rocks him in her arms);

    then Heinmot Tooyalakekt takes her hand, for his heart speaks thus: Now, my beloved sister, you are going away for the last time. You are leaving me for the last time. My sister, I shall see you no more;

and early next morning, just before Ollokot's warriors arrive from the battlefield, the coyotes fall silent and she dies:

   Fair Land, the kindly one,

     who always gave us the best to eat

      (Ollokot loved her best, they say).

Now she is dead; now she has gone away from us.

  Not daring to light a fire by the grave, their funeral cries muted, with paint, beads and copper bracelets they decorate her, and tie her snugly in her buffalo robe: Fair Land, who will never ride again. Tuk-le-kas rings the small bell. They wrap their faces in blankets. Disguising the pit as secretly as they can, in hopes that Cut Arm's Lice-Eaters will not molest her, they set out again, hanging wild rose twigs on the cradleboards as they travel, to keep away evil from their children. Now Cloudburst must be the small boy's only mother.

5

  When Looking-Glass rides in with the rearguard, Heinmot Tooyalakekt sits looking at him, tilting back his head, resting his hands on his knees, his sleeves long-fringed, his leggings hung with tassels, his hair loose at his shoulders, frowning, his eyes narrowing as if he is about to say *kill.* Then he turns away.

6

  Ollokot has saved his elder brother's .44 Winchester from the half-burned lodge. He hands it over, together with a Bluecoat's cartridge belt. He now says: Someday I must ride back here,

and Heinmot Tooyalakekt understands: Ollokot yearns to care for his elder wife's grave
as we once did for our mother's and our father's
in Wallowa,

> back home where at this season the oval lakes ripple brown and green in the morning wind; a fish jumps; a young fir tree trembles; two bluejays argue
> and exactly in this place, up high, there was a steep hill where Fair Land used to dig red earth paint
> and here my brother Ollokot
>> (now grating his hair short in her memory)
> used to come to her, so that when I saw him turning his horse in that direction, I used to leave him easily, in gladness for them both. May he someday return here to Willows, and kill a horse for her.

7

Looking-Glass says: People, now we must hurry!—and no one replies.
Blacktail Eagle's daughter sways bleeding;
> she is silently weeping; in her heart she is secretly chanting
>> even as cleverhanded Arrowhead, who poulticed up Peopeo Tholekt's leg on the day that Cut Arm stole Looking-Glass's country, presses her WYAKIN pouch against the dying woman's heart, frantically singing
> and Welweyas the half-woman, who adored Fair Land like her own mother,
>> whose name must likewise be mentioned no more,
> rides tall and rigid on some dead woman's spotted horse, her face as hard as flint leather, her big hands sunburned, her belt knife missing from its sheath, and grief cutting her flesh like a taut bowstring.
>> Some have said that stepping over the dead will make them alive again. Welweyas has found that this is not so.

8

Toohhoolhoolsote says: I did not ask Looking-Glass to be chief over us here. You listened to him, and so Cut Arm's killers have struck you. I shall follow Looking-Glass no more.— My People, shall we ride away?

Since his best men say nothing, Heinmot Tooyalekekt now replies: You People from Chinook Salmon Water may go wherever your hearts tell you. But if the Bluecoats find you, you will be few against many. Toohhoolhoolsote, my dear brother, let us call a council about what has happened. Then we shall decide together.

9

Passing through dry places, they snatch up the sticky yellow flowers of gum-weed, whose tea will make them feel stronger. The young boys fashion new bridles out of grass, to replace the ones that were lost. About Asleep rides quietly beside his father. Wottolen smiles to see his son Black Eagle. Toohhoolhoolsote is count-ing his remaining horses. Ollokot and Heinmot Tooyalakekt ride ahead, hoping to kill sage grouse for the women and children, but they catch nothing; perhaps their WYAKINS are against them. Springtime is feverish; her husband had to cut her arm open to the bone. Sound Of Running Feet carries the cradleboard as she rides. Cloudburst cannot stop weeping. Fair Land's child sleeps in the cradle-board, and Looking-Glass is silent; he is no longer one who is eager to speak.

On they ride, spying unceasingly for new horses to steal, each night calling out the names of the newly dead. The tired wounded warriors use willow sticks to make themselves vomit, so that they may become stronger.

10

Now the chiefs speak to Looking-Glass,
　　　　he who is called *Flint Necklace* and *Wind-Wrapped,*
telling him: You said that you have eyes to see. Your heart has no eyes. It cannot see anything.

Hear me! he shouts in anger. It was not I who lost the Bostons' friendship, nor sought to attack the Bluecoats in their childish fort at Lo Lo. Whatever evil has come to us must be blamed on your young men who went murdering along the Chinook Salmon River!

—but White Bird, whose warriors he has thus insulted, snatches away the pipe: You called us reckless. Even Red Heart you called foolish for going against you, and tak-ing his People away to surrender at Kamiah. Looking-Glass, you are getting old; you have lost your sense! Be grateful that we refrain from whipping you like a bad dog!

Heinmot Tooyalakekt, who is no war-chief, and would never wish to be head-chief, keeps silent,
　　　　　　deep creases running out from the wings of his nose to the corners of his
　　　　　　　grimly smiling mouth, then back in again and down almost to his chin
　　　　　　　　　(he is wondering when Cut Arm will come);
but Wottolen, Red Owl and Two Moons murmur against Looking-Glass, and Hahtalekin, who usually agrees with his brother chief, now says: Looking-Glass, open your ears! Rainbow and Five Wounds, who followed your heart, are dead. *You have killed them,*
　　　　at which Wottolen, *he who remembers,* looks silently from each to the other
　　　　　　(his heart encloses the names of all our dead)
—and then Strong Eagle, last of the Three Red Blankets, slowly takes the pipe:

Looking-Glass, since you are older than my father, and I am no chief, it should hardly be for me to speak to you in this way; yet, Looking-Glass, you were the reckless one. We never trusted your treaty with the Bostons. When we held our council in Chief Left Hand's country, you refused to listen to so many best men. Hear me, Looking-Glass! If not for you, we might now be safe in the Old Woman's Country. From the very first your heart has grown angered when People follow any course other than yours. Since you demanded to be head-chief, it was for you to protect us; yet you have not done so.

When the accused chief begins to reply, Ollokot stares through him, his eyes half-closed, with an eagle feather in his hair,
as White Bird says
(the first time he has ever interrupted another in council):
Looking-Glass, I understand you well! We never act right; it is only you who are perfect.
And so Lean Elk becomes head-chief. He must now straighten us out.

11

Now we are riding south toward the Lemhi People, with whom we used to hunt buffalo long ago,
for awhile, just for awhile,
and soon we shall learn how well they receive us. If they are unkind, we shall continue toward the Crows, or perhaps we shall quickly cross the Medicine Line.

Our horses grow tired; some old ones ask to be left on the trail for the Lice-Eaters; White Thunder has not stopped to tie his hair.

Springtime grows worse; Good Woman packs new mud into her wound.

Sun Tied rides silent, wifeless, sisterless, childless.

The sister of Swan Necklace weakens, for the Bluecoats shot her through the stomach. That is how they treat us. Blood and dirt stain her lovely red dress, her dress of King George cloth. How can she live? Stopping her wound with fresh green yarrow leaves, they lift her onto a lovely Appaloosa and ride east,
fleeing, fleeing, like the half-hairless buffalo herds plagued by June flies,
babies on their backs, dying packhorses trembling under the whip,
looking back into the dip in the prairie where the river of Ground Squirrel Place comes out of the mountains:
there our children, they who lately danced as brilliant as sunstruck midges over river-grass, lie buried within OUR MOTHER
and dug up by the Lice-Eaters to be dishonored and scalped:
our lovely girls, who will dig camas no more;
while the old men mourn Rainbow, who was nearly as great as they imagine that they once were;
and so they come into camp as if their hearts have all become singed:
twilight, and the dogs whining in weariness, the women loosing the horses to graze;

Sound Of Running Feet goes out to cut grass for her mothers, and
her father is afraid for her but says nothing,

as Toohhoolhoolsote gathers serviceberry twigs to make new
arrows

while Good Woman is emptying a bag of half-dried camas roots on
the grass, to see what has spoiled;

the warriors dig rifle-pits, and Lean Elk says: Rest now. To-morrow we must ride
longer and faster on the trail.

But Swan Necklace's sister,

she who is named Where Ducks Are Around,

lies on a buffalo robe, sighing like a silver-green froth of aspens in the wind. Now
her face has become nearly the color of a blue grouse. The medicine women are
singing over her. Soon they will decorate her; Heinmot Tooyalakekt will give her
a fine King George blanket. Her mother wipes her mouth; her brother,

he who was with Shore Crossing and Red Moccasin Tops when they
killed that first old Boston and launched the war

(now those two war-friends are dead; they have gone away forever),

stands not knowing what to do: Why was she harmed who harmed no one? Now
he commences to hate the Bostons' women, even though Heinmot Tooyalakekt has
said: We could have killed their women and children, but we would feel ashamed
to commit so cowardly an act.

The dying woman begins to choke. Swan Woman,

she who sang over Espowes when he was belly-wounded at Sparse-
Snowed Place and cured him,

cannot save her.

Now it is raining, the sagebrush seething greenish-silver in the evening breeze,
and all who are not watching for Cut Arm and Bluecoats lay out blankets or
canvases if they have them. In the morning she too has gone into the Land of
Brightness, so Tuk-le-kas rings the small bell, and they wrap her away in earth as
secretly as can be,

looking back west at Ground Squirrel Place from the sage-hills,

seeing some snow on southwestern peaks of the Bitter Roots,

Ground Squirrel Place greyish,

a family of piebald elk gliding over the sage

That night Swan Necklace must fumigate his sleeping-place with branches of
balsam fir, to deter her sad SPIRIT from haunting them.

12

Toohhoolhoolsote has been singing over many People's wounds, his heavy eyelids half-closed:

I am flying up.

I am leaping up.

I am worshipping,
and White Bird has also sung;
even so, Grey Eagle must now die,
he who knew he could not live,
fading painfully, without complaint,
less lucky than the ones who were quickly dead,
leaving his daughter In-Who-Lise,
who used to be called White Feather and now, thanks to a Bluecoat's rifle-butt, is called Broken Tooth;
her sister bled to death at Ground Squirrel Place.
She is still pretty with her slanting bangs and lush-patterned
blankets.
Tuk-le-kas rings the small bell, and we hide him as best we can from the cunning Lice-Eaters.

13

Ollokot sits against a tree, holding Fair Land's child. He has begun to grow old.

That night he dreams that he is bending over Fair Land, whispering in her ear: *Síikstiwaa*, you must not die . . .

When he awakes, he remembers his dream but keeps it secret. He goes to help his brother.

There is ice in the kettle. Cloudburst weeps as she packs the horses. Springtime is crazed with fever, although Good Woman boils snowberry twigs into brown tea; they tie her to a travois.

Lean Elk is shouting: *Hurry, hurry!*

14

The People say: When he should have been watching, Looking-Glass was tasting his wives!

But it is said that the Salish never could have killed the Blackfoot warrior-
woman Running Eagle had she not disobeyed the SUN's command and opened her
legs to a man; and so perhaps Looking-Glass would not have exposed them to the
Bluecoats' attack had he not failed to follow some secret rule which his WYAKIN
had laid down for him;
and Burning Coals was equally to blame for refusing to lend his horses;
likewise Heinmot Tooyalakekt, who longed not to worry.

We are all angry at Looking-Glass, and some young men speak of killing him,
but Heinmot Tooyalakekt makes us straight,
for the fault was all of ours
and to Looking-Glass he says: Shore Crossing is dead; now you must blame him
no more; he fought well,

as we ride through this summer which alters toward its end:

       the common nighthawks have already begun to fly away.

Heinmot Tooyalakekt begins to believe in his heart that perhaps the young men were correct to start this war, since we and the Bostons can never be made over again; we cannot understand them.

15

Looking-Glass, swaying in every way—held up only by his wives and daughters—cannot bear to be a nothing:

       he has lost his great friends the Bostons

       and his country;

       now his own People consider him as contemptible as someone reduced to eating mice

              (although Toohhoolhoolsote, he who is easily angered, now forbears to growl against him

                     —maybe because he himself failed to Dream that the Bluecoats were creeping down around us like snakes—

              and Heinmot Tooyalakekt is never unkind);

so Looking-Glass impels his hopes

       (Heinmot Tooyalakekt has none)

toward the far green country where the rainclouds are buffalo

and the river runs wide over white gravel as an arch of raincloud shades white thunderheads between its legs;

his plans grow as graceful as horses and clouds:

       In the Buffalo Country we shall all be happy again.

VI

VERY BEAUTIFUL AND ALMOST AUTOMATIC

AUGUST–SEPTEMBER 1877

The machinery for production of metallic ammunition, both in the Government and private factories, has been brought to a high degree of perfection, its very beautiful and almost automatic character and performance, uniform and accurate production, making it the admiration of the beholder.

Ordnance Memoranda [sic] *No. 14*, 1873

As I looked upon the battalion for the first time when in line of battle in two ranks, I thought I had never seen anything handsomer. There did not appear to be a motion throughout the line, and later, the movement in column presented an appearance even more beautiful. Though the motions were angular and stiff enough, the effect upon the beholder was that of a complete machine which could make no failure as long as it was in order.

Brigadier General Oliver Otis Howard, U.S.A., 1907

SKINNER MEADOWS
AUGUST 13

1

*W*e're in my country now, says Doc. This here's the Buffalo Country!
—as wide, yellow and open as White Bird Cañon when we first rode
down into it, Ad Chapman merry with excitement on his grey racing-
horse then as now, knowing that intrepidity is never wrong, since tactical
misjudgments can be set right by fusillades (we'll see how Joseph sweats
this one out!),

our advance guard blossoming fanward

and the column rolling along in a pretty d——d good line

     (Get the wagons back in order at once!

     Yessir!)

     in utter contradistinction to the way an orchestra can seem to be a
     collection of solitudes, the pianist bent over his instrument of toil,
     twitching like a war horse which has just taken an enemy bullet in
     mid-charge, the pretty violinists nervously jittering, the drummer
     standing aloof behind his instrument, thoughtfully tapping it like
     a doctor testing for knee-reflex, the only appearance of social orga-
     nization deriving from that bank of cellists who stand poised with
     upraised bows

          (until suddenly, when the piano soloist briskens up, all those
          bows commence to move together),

our Bannocks painted more luridly than our Nez Perces,

Wilkinson remarking to Fletch that Joseph's escapes thus far, to be sure,
are remarkable, but unlikely to be repeated much longer

          (*We shall meet beyond the river by and by—*

          and then, Mr. Joe, *and then . . .*),

Guy riding as excellently as his father

     (although of course his Army-issue gelding cannot compare to Ar-
     row),

and the young man now squints, gripping the reins in his left hand, flicking dust from his eyelashes and briefly, secretly fingering his Grant
medal: SERENE AMIDST ALARMS, INFLEXIBLE IN FAITH, INVINCIBLE IN ARMS

          (his Uncle Charley wears the same talisman—a gift from Father),

     and wondering what Red O'Donnell keeps in the bench box of his
wagon

as we gather in another half-dozen horses left behind by Joseph in his
flight

>(procedure: turn a few fresh ones over to Lieutenant Bomus and
>shoot the rest),

the general considering another forced march for to-morrow

>because if we follow up our victory thoroughly, Joseph will have to
>come in or be destroyed (I anticipate wrapping this up within a
>week),

the horizon ahead as straight as a beef cow's back, and on the horizon
behind, Big Hole contracting into the merest greenish-grey dip,

>Captain Whipple,

>>who arrived on the battlefield too late for any close action,
>>and is disappointed that Looking-Glass and Mr. Joe gave us
>>the slip again

>>>(we should have nailed them way back at Cottonwood,
>>>while they were setting Mr. McFinn's house afire),

>>daydreaming about Mrs. FitzGerald (a mighty elegant lady) and the
>>laundresses at Lapwai—jolly gals some of whom may have dimmed
>>within his mental gallery of detached pictures after that long win-
>>ter among Joseph's Indians, but he can still visualize their little
>>houses there between the barracks and Lapwai Creek; and he loves
>>to remember how they sing, flirt and brightly quarrel in the eve-
>>nings

>>>as our Bannocks dig up another Nez Perce squaw, scalp her,
>>>stab her, hack off her earrings and rob her of her buffalo robe

>>>>(when the Lice-Eaters unearth Fair Land, whom he rec-
>>>>ognizes, having eaten at her lodge-fire, Umatilla Jim
>>>>begins to smile; he is making himself remember the
>>>>way that his mother used to sing on the first morning
>>>>of digging roots; as long as his mother keeps singing,
>>>>his heart cannot be hurt)

>but what the fuck does Doc mean by the Buffalo Country? Ain't no
>buffalo in sight hereabouts; Injuns must've run 'em off unless our
>hide men have already gotten to it.

>>Will this d——d general never stop?

>>Well, once the Union Pacific puts in the railroad from Chey-
>>enne to Deadwood . . .

That Doc gets on my nerves. O, what the hell.

So why the DEVIL does this slanting ridge of golden grass make me want
to puke? Those black rocks peeking up over the top like niggerheads and
the sun in my eyes, nothing special here at all,

>Theller leaping up, his hat flying off and his Colt tumbling from
>his hand.

Were his six all dead by then? I'd wager not, for he was always the bravest; he would have exposed himself:

> thin black lines of Joseph's rifle-barrels zeroing in on him from the ridgeline, white smoke and then the savages creeping closer:

> > *Pim,*

> > > *pim,*

> > > > *pim—*

GoDd——n, how I loathe that Chapman for messing me up at White Bird Cañon. What's the general see in him anyway? Well, he's good with horses.

Then where's them buffalo at, Doc?

Right here? All killed.

> GoDd——n them forever; if I can, I'll kill them all:

> > a bullet in Joseph's wicked face, then I'll knock his squaws and papooses over the head

> > to be scalped by our Bannocks

> > > (fun to watch Ollokot hang—a limber type like him'll give a better show than Captain Jack)

> > and Looking-Glass, White Bird and Toohhoolhoolzote brought safely down, all their squaw trash shrivelling in the fire—

Theller, you were the best friend I ever had.

Then it's not your country no more, I reckon.

You'd better watch out or some night I'll just cut your throat.

Doc, ain't there still buffalo?

You can bank on it, boys! The Buffalo Country's just smaller than it was, that's all. But there's buffalo and to spare! Ain't this America? Well, ain't it?

Whatever you say.

Yes indeedy. Don't pay that grifter no mind. We're coming into the good place. Even Wallowa don't hold a candle to it. I was all through here with Captain Travis, one of the best d——d buffalo hunters who ever lived! He could shoot near about as good as an Injun. A real fine country. And so bright your eyes'll be achin' once you gaze east. You'll find out.

> No, sir. Only an abandoned camp with some Indian tobacco and a Chinaman's shirt—

> > Actually she's a perfect bitch at home, and that's why I enlisted.

> > Where'd you dig her up in the first place?

Down that cañon thataway, sir.

Well, keep up your best effort.

> > For six months I kept up my best effort and then she . . .

Sure, captain.

For sure them Sioux do ride this far west. That's why we'd better keep our brightest lookout . . .

Then you must have been at Bentonville.

Yessir.

When Hardee was Commandant of Cadets at West Point, I used to tutor his son, who joined the Texas Cavalry. He was killed pretty quickly at Bentonville. Always in the forefront, that boy. My classmate General S. D. Lee told me the news . . .

Yessir.

Fetch Mason here.

Rightaway, sir.

Well, Mason, what do you think?

All in order, general—

I mean Joseph.

Sir, he's been routed repeatedly. In his condition he can't make a fight. If we can only catch them—

There is that.

Tell you the truth, sir, I'll be glad when we get into the open country.

You speak for us all, Mason.

Because the men are starting to—

Fine. Now where's Captain Sladen?

Up thataway, general. Shall I call him here?

No, I'll ride in his direction, and I'd like to do something for Sladen after this. Wonder how much his leg pains him in the saddle to-day? I'll never find out. He and Mason both deserve a good supper. Bomus, too, now that I've got to know him. Solid metal in that man! Lizzie, bless her, will surely wish to entertain the Perrys once they're reunited (if Perry ever gets down to Portland, as he must for that Court of Inquiry), and we ought to invite all my aides-de-camp and maybe Doctor Alexander, who has served so cheerfully, but what about Trimble now that he and Perry have fallen out? Well, since he generally take his leave in Lewiston—

Now all of you listen up. The best place to kill you a buffalo, well, now, it's a circle the size of a cowboy hat, just back of the shoulderblade. You just aim for that

circle and you'll be all right. Then pale frothy blood blubbers out his nostrils, and
that's *it*, boys; that's it.

Sing us that song again, Doc!

All righty. I'll learn you this verse:

> Our meat it was of buffalo hump; like iron was our bread,
> An' all we got to sleep on was a buffalo for a bed—

Now there's a fine old-timey song.

What do you mean, old-timey? That's *now*.

Then where's the d——d buffalo chips?

Doc, how many buffalo have you killed in your time?

Could be hundreds, my boy, not that I'm up there with Buffalo Bill. That fella
makes a *job* out of it. But you see these two knives I got? Well . . .

Now they found sign over thataway after all
> where a hundred and thirty years later I, William the Blind, will ride
> south on the desert prairie where it gets olive green with round bales; I
> will look east past the haybales and black cows to a smoky horizon like a
> washed out, poorly fixed nineteenth-century photograph as I try to imag-
> ine how it would have been: General Howard doing his best endeavor
> even though the mailbag keeps chasing him, demanding precisely what
> he cannot furnish just now; for a good portion of his communications, as
> so often in July and August, originates from the Board of Commissioners
> for Foreign Missions—a worthy enough organization, but they ought to
> wait until I whip Joseph:

> *Halt.*
>> *Dismount.*
>>> *Roll call.*
>>>> *Right face.*
>>>>> *Dismissed,*

Chapman drooling tobacco juice
(he would like to buy a sugarloaf
sombrero hat next time he rides
into some big cattle town, because then he would stand taller),
Bomus detailing two privates to shoot
the latest bunch of Joseph's scrawny
Cayuse nags.

I hardly wish to open this one. Another begging letter, for certain.
*Tacoma, Washington Territory. Drinking whiskey has never been a
fault of mine, and* GOD *helping it never shall. I was married merely
three weeks ago, to a lady who is a member of the Episcopal Church.*
Was that truly written in March? Where is it postmarked? He
might be one of Wheaton's bunch. Maybe Grace knows him from

Sallie Eaton's wedding; how can I say? My arm pains me. It saps and shames me; meanwhile Joseph is getting away. What does this newlywed want? Money, no doubt. Well, say he's told the truth; I can send him five dollars with a sincere note from Wilkinson; may he have joy in his bride—

They'll be dragging along more slowly now that their squaws and little ones are bleeding.

In fact we have a pool going. I'm betting that Mr. Joe will be captured tomorrow or thereabouts. What do you think, general?

Quit it. Don't you know the general's not a betting man?

We've definitely gotten these Indians on the alert.

That's right. That's right. So what we want to do is . . .

Not wishing to sleep out under the stars with the men just now, he ducks down into the dark rectangular doorway of that Sibley tent, as maybe they would prefer a general to behave in any case. I am pretty convinced that most of these troopers are becoming my fast friends.

2

Guy, I have something to tell you about Gibbon's battlefield. However badly you feel about what we saw, you can be assured that it is the best that could have been done.

Don't worry, father; I didn't feel bad at all! It's only what Joseph deserved.

3

Sending away Wood, Fletch and Wilkinson, he writes with his own left hand (for the sake of discretion): *I cannot recommend this officer for promotion,*
         referring of course to Gibbon,
then seals the letter himself, bends over Colton's bullet-weighted map, wondering how best to cut off Joseph from the free ranges of the Buffalo Country

(James Reuben asserts that the hostiles will double back toward Wallowa), slouches in a chair outside his tent's rectangular doorway, thinking: When Chief Lawyer signed a promise, and then Reuben swore to obey the laws of CHRIST, Joseph for his part . . .

   and Looking-Glass

      and then above all Toohhoolhoolzote

—if I complete this thought, will it truly be of service? LORD help me to remedy my defects and carry on in good spirits (we need more boots and horses) before Perry funks again, or Wood does something dishonorable in obedience to what he idiotically imagines to be his angelic impulses; is the entire Army going rotten? All I can do is track Joseph to the end

   and try every day to elevate the character of this or that member of my command,

enlisted men throwing themselves down, cavalrymen scratching at their
calves through the long boots

(Blackie, who keeps hearing about the railroad strikes, asks a man
from Philadelphia what to think, and is informed that we need to
burn out all the monopolies),

Red O'Donnell sitting in the back of his wagon, swinging his
tired legs, offering Dandy Jim tobacco at a dollar an ounce
when it goes for a dollar a pound back at Lapwai

as some civilian kid comes riding in with some fresh
Bannocks, *Redington*, his name is, fresh and eager, with
the milk hardly dry on his upper lip

(he must be a runaway like us):

How old are you, son?

Almost seventeen, General Howard.

No doubt. Here for adventure, is it?

Yessir. Captain Fisher sent me—

Lieutenant Howard, get this young man a meal and find
out what he's good for. Wilkinson, go find out why the
ordnance wagons were to slow to-day. Wood, see how
our pickets are disposed and then report. Fletch, can't
you find anything to do? Why hasn't Brooks blown
"Stable Call"?

and then "Mess Call" and then an early moonrise,
Umatilla Jim dreaming of a certain lovely loosehaired young Bannock squaw in a stroud dress
decorated with concentric V's of cowrie shells

(the Agent would fine me twenty dollars
hard cash money if I brought her to the reservation, and my wife would hate her for
being a Lice-Eater:

better just to pay her or get her
drunk),

while Wood and Fletch now stretch out their blankets on the grass by the
general's feet. Fletch,

who actually comprehends Shelley's verse about the vale of Cashmire,

has traded a cartridge for a decorated pouch of kinnikinnick from some
Bannock scout. He fills Wood's pipe, then his own. They clink pipes together in pretense of toasting wineglasses, and the general smiles fondly.
Patching the heel of his sock, Wood now considers comparative mascu-
linities, beginning with the reeking rutting maleness of Ad Chapman,

whose dark hair is receding although his moustache is still
thick; he keeps his chin nearly bare of bristle, perhaps thinking

to please the general, although that's not likely given that his
sensitivities are as nearly arrowproof as the corral at Fort Laramie; his fingers are strangely delicate, and he likes to sit with
his hands open in his lap: thus Chapman,
who so far as I can tell would like nothing better than a good rape,
unless it's to shoot Indians in the back and make money. Out in
these Western parts he represents our dominant type: seething,
squalid Americanism. I used to think I knew what an American
was. I supposed I was one, or my father, never mind his drunken-
ness and cruelty. The general, now, he's a true American man, no
genius, maybe, but still one of the best. And Fletch, cheerful, brave,
suave, a trifle mercurial although he conceals it, I guess he's one of
my type, which is why we like each other and believe that Americans ought to be like us. We believe in fighting for the right, extending our empire, protecting women and children, and we're
willing to take chances to do so, not necessarily because we're good,
although we deserve due credit for that, but because to stay home
rotting on a little farm, with no prospect of remaking ourselves, is
worse than getting killed in battle, and I feel the same even after
White Bird Cañon and the Clearwater. What happened at Big Hole,
well, it wasn't me and I'm not going to think about it. At least I'll try
not to, because what's the use? I shall think of Nanny whenever I
please,
and if she were here I would gather for her these sweet pink
flowers of the wild rose, because
old Trimble here positively insists that when the reds
were singing their *hum, hum, hum* that night at Clearwater, he doped out every nuance, if you can believe it!
Isn't that so, Trimble?
Well, I should say that our bunch could pretty readily
discern the different phases of their emotional expressions—
and someday I'll take her to the Ladies' Parlor of Stewart's "Cast-
Iron" Palace in New York. I wonder if Mrs. Howard has ever purchased hosiery there? I'll bet she hasn't. I hereby forget Big Hole
(although Joseph for his part forfeited all humanity when he raped
and murdered those people on the Salmon). I want to be the best
man I can, which means to emulate Fletch, and learn what poise
and endurance I can from the general, and certainly to distinguish
myself from Wilkinson, whom I admit to be courageous but who
considers himself manly not only because he can lead a charge
without revealing the slightest uneasiness but also because it entertains him to describe to city ladies how our squaws collect enough

lice to make a mouthful—and yet he flatters the general more subtly than any woman, laying on sympathy and not much more; poor old Prayer-book never sees how he is being taken in! Does Wilkinson not perceive himself? Maybe I don't understand him, but to me he does seem the creeping climbing hypocrite—which may signify that he is suited for Indian service. The fact that he is against me, and Perry with him, ought to concern me more than it does. Perry of course can do nothing, unless he "snaps" and murders me. His fist is heavier than mine, for a fact; in any fight he could beat me down. I give myself credit for fearing him. But Wilkinson constitutes a greater peril. Must I cultivate that man, in order to preserve my standing with the general? Or am I supposed to start singing hymns? I won't, at least not for now. Maybe I'll do it to please the general, if I can be sure that pleasing him will please myself. *No.* Nor will I consider

So then, what we'll do when we catch 'em is—

Hell's bells. We don't have time for that. I'm just gonna shoot every Nez Perce who—

Did you never read Josh Billings? I'm wild for his brand of humor. Now, what we all know about Nez Perces is exactly what he used to say about mules: *Tha never hav no dissease that a good club wont heal.*

Right on, Uncle Josh! He's a caution—

All the same, it's plumb disgusting when our Bannocks scalp them dead squaws.

Well, I know for a fact Mr. Joe scalped Lieutenant Theller.

That's not so.

I was there at White Bird Cañon. What are you then, some kind of Indian lover?

I was on corpse detail same as you. I ought to know.

You're one of them *squaw men*, ain't you, boy? Why else would you stand up for red devils? That's a crime against nature, bringin' little Injuns into the world. Look at Mr. Joe, now, when he had him his pick of the reservation lands. A-raping and a-murdering. And the way all squaws stink like rancid meat—

Don't hurt Jim's feelings. He can hear us.

I don't care if he—

Cut it out. Jim, you know how to play poker?

Sure, corporal.

Before "Tattoo" we'll play a hand. You're invited.

All right.

What's your favorite kind of poker?

Any kind.

What's your favorite kind of gambling?

My favorite game is the Bone Game.

What the hell is that, Jim?

The general hasn't forgotten me in my trouble; I confess that

(something awful the way that d——d Trimble's swung against me!)
but what he told me meaning to comfort my heart even if he hadn't poisoned it with pious absurdities and offensive expectation of playing the
father to all his inferiors in rank even as he cringes before Sherman's
signature on a dirty document and poisonously pretends even to himself
to forgive Hunt, Crook and all the others against whom he must surely
hold himself in a position of the most desperate rivalry

(I know Crook's opinion of him, because I've heard it direct from
his lips)
is no good to me except that I do appreciate his intent, and pity him for
being an old man under a cloud, and need him to be on my side

(I'll tell the court that Joseph outnumbered me three to one
(and if I make peace with Chapman I bet he'll swear the same, to
let himself off)
because I hate the man who tries to know me
but not Theller, who knew without trying. Why was everything so easy
with him?

—and then "Taps,"

a few gunshots well past our picket line
(just our Bannocks cleaning up),

as Captain Pollock, who sleeps on his stomach,
resists his nightly yearning to shout wicked oaths
against the cast-iron buttons on his undershirt
and in Wood's nightmares an old woman on horseback raises
her breechloader against him, a blanket laid across her thighs
and many triangle-patterned bags dangling by her feet;
he shoots wide and then hears

"Reveille,"

Wilkinson

—who has not yet found an answer to the problem of
what to do with Sallie; were she considerably older,
which is to say (take the bull by the horns) a nonbleeder,
I might be less disgusted; but I must respect her readiness to be an Army wife, and her capacity for being
jolly, and remember what intriguers other women can
be, and O, how sweetly she recites the Gospels!—
up first to bring the general his coffee
even before our sergeants begin calling the roll

on this drier, pinier morning, more like autumn than
yesterday, as we gaze down through the pines whose

silhouetted cones resemble crazy Confederate ordnance, down to the still blue river-pools where our go-
getter Bannocks, GOD bless them, are already excavating
scalps and suchlike grave-loot,

a few of our boys likewise prospecting for
souvenirs:

Look at this:

another dead old man, shot in the chest, his
mouth open as if he still yearns to scream,
and in his bloody hand (he must have tried
to show it to his killer) a letter signed by
some illegible eminence informing us all:
This is a good Indian.

Remember when the Secceshes evacuated Richmond? All that loot they left behind?

All right, Brooks, let's hear "The General,"
then "Boots and Saddles" and
Move out!

—the August sun already high over the prairie, so that
our unfittest men resume complaining of headaches.

More sign up there, Colonel Perry, sir!

What is it?

Looks like some Injun's bloody mockersin. Like he was limpin' along, tryin' to
stay with the rest, when—

That's fine, soldier. Keep at it,

Wilkinson delighting in recollecting that hard ride with the general in pursuit of Gibbon and Mr. Joe,

the uneven teeth of Trapper Peak within the Bitter Root
Mountains, the Bitter Root River so brown and silver, with
brown rocks below:

As my uncle would say, *timber thick, grass poor.*

Bet I could sell that in town for a dollar.

A dollar, hell! Didn't you see them volunteers lighting out for Helena with
that squaw trash they dug up? They're gonna be *rich*, boys!

Then pick up that stinkin' mockersin and try to sell it. Captain Fisher might—

O, no. I ain't falling out of line to—

Just listen to that cold steel ring, good LORD;

Just—

Stop chanting that GODd——d nigger song.

What d'you mean?

John Henry was nothin' but a coal-black nigger from the shittiest hole in West
Virginia.

He was born in Texas, as good a white man as you or me.

You're not from Texas. *I'm* from Texas. Bet you never even heard of the White Leagues.

> No, sir. Just another grave our Bannocks found. One of Mr.
> Joe's. They're digging for scalps.
>
> They'd better not fall behind.
>
> I'll remind 'em, sir.

> > *The bold dragoon he has no care*
> > *As he rides along with his uncombed hair,*

riding down toward the Snake River Cañon with Theller, down into the pale blue horizon-wall, the two of us singing:

> *The bold dragoon he has no care*
> *As he rides along with his uncombed hair,*

en route to Lewiston to accept delivery on Delia's roll of carmined indigo

> > (now that he's dead I can stop calling her Mrs. Theller if she
> > GoDd——n);

and looking down beyond that into the dusty pastel cañon where the Snake and the Clearwater touch, blue trees obscuring the rivers, pale as the colors painted on parfleche, we used to hunt

> > (maybe it only happened twice and it couldn't have been for
> > long or we would have reported late at Lapwai)

for signs of gold even though the experts already turned everything over back in '59

> (gay sport out here, if they'd just leave us be):

O those filthy Indian sons of bitches, I'd like to cut their livers out.

4

How much farther does Montana go?

What do you mean, how far does it go?

Well, how far does it go?

Dumplinghead, this here's one of the most gigantic territories on earth!

Yeah, so what do you know about it?

I been all over here. I know John Taylor in Beaver Head Valley and Bolatoe Ross in New York Gulch and—

Bolatoe's not there no more.

Where's that Jim riding off to?

Doing his job, I reckon.

He sure comes and goes.

5

Well, Jim, how do you like Army food?

Well, corporal, at this time of year we like to eat dog salmon.

I heard you teaching the general to speak Indian. Teach me an Injun word.

Sure. I'll teach you a good one. You want to know how to say *fuck?*

Boys, let's hear it.

Pátskh.

Aw, come on, Jim. What white man can even say that?

Say it again.

Pátskh.

Pot-sick.

Pretty good.

Too much for me. Why the hell can't you Injuns make your lingo easy?

         No, sir. No sign of anyone but Mr. Joe's Indians,

            and our Bannocks have now pulled from some squaw's

            corpse a very fine necklace with two dozen bear claws;

                that new kid Redington is doing his best endeavor

                to jew them out of it; what a hilarious young card-

                sharp he is! How old is he, anyway? And now

                they're all digging for scalps—

        Well, make sure they look out for Sioux. Miles's boys are

        cleaning up the Powder River, so the enemy may run here.

        Yessir.

                Sure is well timbered country.

                That's a fact.

                Gonna be worth a hundred dollars an acre at

                least.

And to-night maybe we can get Jim to teach us the Bone Game.

To hell with that.

Watch yourself, boy! If the general hears you—

                Now, if you find a dead soldier in the Sioux country, if

                he's chopped in the face with a tomahawk or shot full of

                arrows, you know he must have still been alive, because

                they don't trouble themselves with a body that can't feel

                tortured. The squaws are the worst for that. They're

                fiends, I swear! Should all be exterminated—

                We'll take care of that part, won't we, boys?

Halt.

Dismount:

        flat enough to pitch the tents in two facing lines.

All right, gentlemen. Let's push Gibbon's success as far as possible. All Joseph can do now is hold on here and there until he withdraws.

Yes, sir.

Sladen, where's the large scale map?

Here, sir.

All right. As you know, gentlemen, Colonel Miles sent out the Seventh Cavalry on the eleventh. How soon can they be in position to stop Joseph's flight eastward? Major Mason, what would you say?

Assuming fifteen miles a day, general, that's more than two weeks from Tongue River to Yellow Stone. And we can't predict Joseph's course.

Get Mr. Chapman.

Right away, sir.

What can I do for you, general? I been meaning to tell you—

Now, Chapman, since you've married almost into Joseph's family, so to speak, we're hoping you'll share your expert knowledge with us. Where do you suppose the hostiles are going?

To the Crows, general. That's a real sure guess, because we got their supplies, and their squaws and papooses are getting worn out, especially the wounded. And Looking-Glass, you see, he's friends with—

I asked about Joseph, not Looking-Glass.

Well, I been out here in Indian country for twenty-two years, and I ain't never seen anything as fiendish as that Mr. Joe. A star candidate for the gallows, all right! Kind of like Captain Jack, I should say—

Thank you, Chapman. Did you ever meet Captain Jack?

Never had the opportunity, general.

All right; go. Gentlemen, he may well be correct about the Crows . . . Mason, what do you say?

He doesn't impress me, sir.

All right. Where's that new boy Redington?

Here, sir.

Do you know this country?

No, sir, but—

Enough. Captain Jocelyn, I can see you have something to say. Are you still chafing at the slowness of this march? Don't think I haven't spied those secret looks you like to share with Captain Pollock. Well?

Yes, sir, as a matter of fact I—

Shut up. Back to you, Mason. In any event, Sturgis will need to spread out his companies.

Yessir. But if we can squeeze the reds so they go right *here*—

An awfully sharp angle of battle, given the terrain.

Maybe so, sir.

And, as you've just admitted, we *don't* know that Joseph will even ride that way.

Yessir. But I should think that if the Seventh detaches some good fast riders down along *here*—

Thank you, Mason. We'll all expect the best from Sturgis, of course. Meanwhile, we might be compelled to drive our boys a trifle harder, unfortunately,

because Mrs. Manuel may still be alive,

violated and otherwise tortured by Joseph's bucks, perhaps by Joseph himself, over and over, haunted by her murdered children, suffering by contact with that pitch-dark withering curse, praying for us to save her, while we coddle drunken volunteers and unfit shavetails; O LORD, I shall not forsake her; LORD, I harken unto Your Scriptures:

Remember those that are in bonds as if bound with them.

Lieutenant Wood, why so silent?

General, I—

Are you unwell?

Not at all, sir.

I understand you've committed a lot of poetry to memory.

Yessir.

How about reciting something for us, to celebrate our victory at Big Hole?

Yessir. I—

Well?

And the widows of Ashur are loud in their wail,
And the idols are broke in the temple of BAAL;

Not half bad!

And the might of the Gentile, unsmote by the sword,
Hath melted like snow in the glance of the LORD!

Thank you, Wood. I'd say that's quite to the point. Who's your poet?

Lord Byron, sir.

Byron? I'm surprised. Mason, are those the casualty returns? Thank you. All right, gentlemen, carry on.

6

I'd say matters have shaped themselves fairly well, wouldn't you, Guy?

Yes, father; Mr. Joe's on the run now.

Good,

knowing how the rest regard his son; and knowing likewise that because they never knew Guy as a child they cannot see into the mysteries of his character, making allowances for his warps and twists: O, for a fact he *can* be a bully, but that's because he grew up getting taunted as the son of a nigger lover. If I'd washed my hands of the negroes as my cowardice inclined me to do, leaving President Lincoln's wishes to die after him, who knows if by now I wouldn't have had Sherman's position? And for Guy to be all the time overhearing their sneers, longing to be proud of me, seeing me disgraced, denounced for embezzlement and worse, perhaps he's suffered worse than I who lost my father so early.

Someday I must tell him about the time my two negro boys went riding into town to get my laundry:

Get off that horse, nigger.

We will welcome to our numbers the loyal, true and brave,
Shouting the battle-cry of freedom.

My errand is for General Howard, said the brave one who would not run away,

so they shot him.

When I visited him in the hospital, his arm had already been amputated; he was dying.— You're a good praying boy, I said to him, hoping that his death would be fast and easy. And I filled myself with tears, realizing that I could do nothing,

And though they may be poor, not a man shall be a slave,
Shouting the battle-cry of freedom,

the sun shining on their bayonets.

7

How are you managing?

Very well, thanks, father.

Would you like to turn in?

Whatever you think best.

O, I don't mind either way. It's scarcely past "Tattoo" . . .

By the way, father, I have a treat, courtesy of Colonel Gibbon's officers. Apparently that Lieutenant Bradley who got killed carried an Eastern newspaper in his kit. He'd already shared it with everyone interested, so they said I could have it, to give to you—

What is it?

The *New York Times,* father, pretty recent. July. Shall I read it to you?

Well, all right. But no politics. No need to hear them insult the Army. Is there an art or literature section? We ought to improve our minds . . .

Here's a review of some foreign novel. How would that be, father?

Go ahead.

Turgénieff has written a new book! it says. Do you know Turgénieff?

No.

The intense dreariness of the subjects, the melancholy conclusion to which they come, the dreadfully sad environment of each scene of Russian life . . .

What's the password?

Constitution.

All right; you can pass.

As a whole the novel is not as interesting as some earlier ones.

No, it certainly doesn't sound very interesting.

The impression one gets of Russia and the Russians is simply terrible... Father, would you like to go to Russia and see the Czar?

I don't think so, especially if it's as dreadfully sad there as they say. We're awfully lucky to be Americans, Guy.

8

Listening to the unseen river below the dark horizon, Wood lies on his back, watching the pale night sky.— What is my place in this? he wishes to ascertain,

> beside him, the pallor of a complex leaf, then a long pale stick in the dark dirt,
>> and Umatilla Jim far away, silently singing a song about bitterroot,
>> and the chlorine stench of acqua-regia from the direction of Company "D": Pollock must have been prospecting again,
> and O for that sweet nigger whore who laid me on her mattress covered with cretonne, riding on top of me happy and secret behind those cretonne curtains:
>> almost as good as Sitka Khwan.
>> If I fell in love with a nigger woman I would marry her forever; I don't care what they say.
>>> Way I see it, Captain Pollock, if you had a cabin here you could ride out winter real easy, probably shoot a moose right from your door.
>>> That may be so, but I want gold.
> And O for all sweet women,
> *all of them!*

so what have I to do with this life, war and Army? Where the trees go, up into the sky, is where I want to go, *alive,* for my adventure. I don't want to be chasing a tribe of Indians to death.

The general must never know how I feel.

Dear LORD, preserve me from becoming a killer and a murderer of women and children:

> for instance, those three little children I saw back there, dead and roasted
>> (if you have ever seen an accident at any of the seven white lead mills of Pittsburgh, you will know the smell and color of their flesh)

and all our bunch shaking Gibbon's hand.

I hope I'm putting on a competent performance.

He's turning against me.

I wish Wilkinson were more sympathetic.

O, why can't I sleep?

RED SALMON SEASON
AUGUST 11–15

1

*W*e are riding away, riding away, riding away to kill,
      the locusts singing *tekh-tekh-tekh!*,
  now when it is the season to catch red salmon at Wallowa Lake and in the
rivers of our home
      —and when Toohhoolhoolsote was young, we even used to canoe
      down the Enemy River and the Distant River to catch salmon,
          just for awhile:—
  we are pleasing Cut Arm by riding ever farther from our country,
      sorrowing and hating as we go.
They have killed our children;
they are a family of killers.

2

In the dark, Sound Of Running Feet awakens screaming, as if again she were
looking westward through grey-green walls of willow, the river hidden, darkness
within, moon-white willow leaves slowly, slowly dying into grey as Cut Arm's killers ford the stream, levelling their Springfields at our tipis
      (the blood we lie in as brilliant as the black and white feathers in our long
      hair):
her mother slaps her for troubling People's sleep, so that her heart is shamed;
she is ember-gazing,
     her other mother, Springtime, trying to smile at her;
        perhaps she has not slept much; her wound annoys her;
          at least the baby sleeps.
Her father comes running. Seeing that she has come to no harm, he strokes
her face. She looks away.
      He lost his Medicine bundle at Ground Squirrel Place. Now that she has
      discovered this secret
        (hearing him ask both her mothers if it had somehow been saved),
      sorrow and terror sicken her heart:
He has no Power anymore!
      Now he has returned to his council with Uncle Ollokot and the young men,
      making the People's way,

although he knows that their world is lost,
her mother opening woven bags, laying out what food there is
as Cloudburst leaves Ollokot's lodge, rubbing her weeping eyes (she who always rose early with Fair Land)
and Sound Of Running Feet slips on her moccasins,
dogs barking, injured People groaning,
strokes the nose of her new horse, Helper, and walks to the edge of camp,
where the orange moon, mottled and very bright, hangs over a dark wall of trees whose shadows are utterly black and whose dagger-shaped leaves are veined as if with white finger-bones; while the dying grass, each blade of which seems white, strives to caress her;
and at the beginning of the wall of trees lies a fallen log, and then she must part the white-veined-leaved branches to go in,
cocking the revolver which Uncle Ollokot gave her, fearing that someone will kill her;
now she is squatting here where the night is cold and moist with an infinity of dark byways and animals, and no killer comes
(only a skunk's banded white glow by the river
and the thuddings of birds in a river-cave);
so she wipes herself with wet grass, pulls up her leggings, unlatches the cylinder, tilting its cartridges into her hand, lets down the hammer, then reloads and seats the Colt in the holster (which is still crusted with its dead Bluecoat's blood),
and returns to camp,
helping other women lash the worst-wounded People onto horses and travoises:
these ones must travel slowly, starting early and coming in late;
her father and other kind men will lead them in short packstrings,
and so they depart first,
passing the eerie blue, green and yellow of a sagebrush hill on this foggy dawn
while Sound Of Running Feet cleans Springtime's wound, and the others begin to strike camp,
Lean Elk shouting: *Hurry, hurry!*
(Good Woman whispering to her sister-wife: It hurts my heart to see Ollokot's face),
and then the rest of the People set out,
dogs slinking, babies sobbing *shlak! shlak!*
(Springtime's child mostly quiet in the cradleboard, her eyes shining),
and now the sky becomes as blue as a turkey's head,
Wounded Head carrying his dying little boy in the saddle
and leading his wife's horse, which pulls her behind on a travois

(the dark hole in her breast resembles a hummingbird's head);
then comes old Tzi-kal-tza, who was not hurt,
About Asleep, who cannot stop remembering his mother
> (it is not good to mention her name, even though my sad father is thinking it),
and beside him White Bird,
> who now rides off the trail and blows his fishheaded Medicine whistle to summon eagles, so that our weary warriors may gain Power from their feathers,
>> but the eagles will not come;
then White Thunder's mother Swan Woman, busily clouting the horses along,
Two Moons and his wife Hat On The Side Of The Head,
tall Arrowhead on her white horse,
Húsishúsis Kute, whom Cut Arm imagined to be chief of the Palouses
> (perhaps he may yet become so, now that Hahtalekin has been killed)
and Loon (he who once considered himself brave), biting his lip, pulling at his white necklace-loops, bleeding from the forehead,
followed by old Kapoochas the shaman, whose hip-wound has swelled with stinking pus
> (Heinmot Tooyalakekt has comforted him with a new brass-studded blanket-coat),
and then Looking-Glass,
> the one who always used to say *I have spoken,*
now merely grimacing, leaning forward on his buffalo horse, the long fringes of his deerskin shirt breeze-trembling along with the stallion's mane, and around his neck (not in his hair to-day) that tin mirror shining like his shame,
> as his younger wife, Asking Maiden,
>> who wears around her neck a medal in honor of our savior, President Rutherford B. Hayes,
> watches him in shock and fright,
>> while Blackberry Person, who has been married to him longer, rides quietly between their two meek daughters
>>> (her heart feels more pity than surprise);
then comes stingy old Burning Coals, driving his great herd, ever watching behind, for fear of Cut Arm the Invisible
> (Lean Elk has made him unbell his richly jingling horses);
after him ride many old women, whipping and clouting our pack animals with all their might,

with tired old men following after
—but White Thunder buckles on his pistol and two cartridge belts, loop-
ing the rifle-case over his shoulder:
he and his war-friends must ride back to watch the west, in case the
Bluecoats and Lice-Eaters should appear out of blue foggy mountain-
shapes;
>   now these young men have drawn rearward enough to see the blue
>   claw-scratchings in the snowpeaks from which Cut Arm's killers
>   came sneaking down;
>   soon they will be overlooking Ground Squirrel Place,
>>   riding, riding (they will not camp with the People to-night),
>>>   those blue mountains rising up,
>>   and then the hoarse cry of a yellowheaded blackbird
>   as they recross that sky-blue stream in the yellow grass where Ol-
>   lokot's heart first understood that Fair Land was dying;
>   and dismount in a haven of willows at the edge of the evergreen
>   forest, hiding like river spiders,
>>   watching,
hoping to ambush a Lice-Eater or else some treacherous scout from the
Kamiah People
(our People no more):
now at last, squinting their sun-inflamed eyes, they spy Cut Arm again,
cantering at the head of his slaves, on that black stallion which Tsépmin
must have given him (so well do they recognize his precious hoard of
thoroughbreds):
>>>   and beside him exactly there jitters Tsépmin on his grey racer
>>>   (what a lean and wiry Boston he is!
>>>>   —light in the saddle, unable to keep still—
>>>   never can we shoot him!),
>>   and Píli the tall one, whose brother we so joyfully killed,
after which from left and right some Lice-Eaters,
>   they who have also wiped their buttocks on our heads,
>>   and led the Bluecoats here while Looking-Glass lay on his
>>   belly so that his wives could scratch between his shoulder-
>>   blades,
begin to come cantering:
>   and through the dead Bluecoat's field-glass White Thunder sees a
>   certain Lice-Eater (not yet Buffalo Horn) approaching beneath a
>   rectangular headdress of parfleche painted in diamonds and tri-
>   angles of earth pigment, with eagle feathers swaying behind, so
>   that he raises his Springfield
but more Lice-Eaters have come—too many to be attacked,
and White Thunder's spies withdraw up the trail, each in his own way,

our fine young men, our best men, for whom killing enemies is as
lovely as a woman squatting with her thighs spread,
hiding, guarding their People,
who keep following Lean Elk and the wounded toward Horse Prairie,
staying closer together than before, in case some enemy should appear,
our horses tired
    (and many of their decorations have been lost at Ground
    Squirrel Place and Big Water);
thinking of home or Cut Arm, we gaze back northwest at the snowy
mountains
    (the Big Hole Valley so rich and wide and green and wet when I,
    William the Blind, came thirteen decades later to view its brown
    pools, green alfalfa and green grass
        —a beautiful red barn, a wagon wheel,
            crisscross fences and black clouds of cows on the green sea—
    under cultivation this place reminded me of the Wallowa Valley);
White Bird now halting us, removing his Winchester from the case his
mother once beaded for him as he rides off the trail to discover just how
a certain slender old river-cut wends into the tall yellow grass:
    no ambush,
and so we ride on into late morning, turning out the horses to graze
    exactly here where the serviceberry leaves have already be-
    gun to go red,
    the women fetching water, cooking breakfast:
        camas porridge, hardbread from dead Bluecoats and willow
        bark tea with Boston sugar from Stevensville,
            Welweyas sharing out her mother's serviceberry cakes
            from the Salish country,
    Cloudburst, Good Woman and Arrowhead digging up roots of Or-
    egon grape: fever-simples,
        and that small girl whose name Sound Of Running Feet does
        not know, the one who got shot in the arm at Ground Squirrel
        Place, stands trying not to cry while her mother pours water
        through the bullet-hole,
    Ollokot's grief resembling the blackness within a bobolink's gaping
    beak,
    Heinmot Tooyalakekt remembering when Springtime's gaze was
    bright like the late noon sun in a river,
after which we must again be riding
    where the mint breeze blows and yellow lichen clings in filamented
    clouds around dead and dying branches and on the trunks of an-
    cient pines, almost glowing where the dark black shadows are,
    shining greenish-yellow like suns,

Strong Eagle and Over The Point riding ahead in case the
Bostons have made new ranches exactly here,

    followed by Yellow Bull, who seeks never again to men-
tion his slain son Red Moccasin Tops

    and Swan Necklace (whose WYAKIN is longnecked and
high-eared like an elk) craving to kill again

    and once more to rape Boston bitches as we did when
the war began at Chinook Salmon Water

        because as a young man he found himself nearly
daunted by Wolf Old Woman, Toohhoolhool-
sote's younger wife, with her grimly narrowed
eyes and her lower lip, which was very full, and
pressed frowningly against the upper, as if she
were unceasingly fighting some sadness, and the
wearisomeness of the struggle brought her anger;

           thus he will avenge his heart forever on
women,

              but only Boston women;

although just now we find only more yarrow, entering the smell of
mint and pines

    as Springtime sees the polka-dotted breast of a northern
flicker

—then we hear the sound of a creek whose name not even our buffalo hunters know,

    tall grass tickling our ponies' bellies,

and TRAVELLER THE SUN keeps shining through fat glistening orange
currants in clouds low on the branch

    (our women pick them while riding, for Lean Elk keeps cry-
ing: *Hurry, hurry!*

        —he may well say so, since he has not yet lost his race-
horses);

not one of us does not fear Cut Arm's killers; so we go on riding, riding,
until some can ride no more,

    dismounting, departing their relations, crawling into quiet thickets
where they will not be seen again,

        except by Lice-Eaters come to rob their corpses and harvest
their scalps.

3

Two women scream. A wind-shaken berry bush has tricked them.

White Bird says: Don't worry; if we see Bostons anywhere we shall fall upon
them in some way.

4

Camping in a place where they can watch down through the lodgepole pines into the lake,

      a place, like all places, with a name, although now they have come so far from home that only their buffalo-hunters know what it is called, and the others do not ask,

they turn out their horses, clean the wounds and burns of those whom the Blue-coats have harmed, bandaging them with grass

           (Springtime's arm is pustulent and fat; it is purple like the cone of a balsam fir),

     as Towhee cleans the hooves of her dying grandson's pony

          even as Burning Coals, furious, cuts the tendons of his first lame horse (may Cut Arm the Moldy now try to ride him!)

          and Sound Of Running Feet gets firewood,

      Shooting Thunder unfolding his two-bladed screwdriver (time to clean his Springfield carbine) and

White Bird singing over old Kapoochas the shaman, whose hip-wound is worsening,

      Helping Another, whose breast-wound pains her whenever she breathes, touching in wonder the reddish-brown wound-crust near her husband's scalp where that bullet merely glanced

          (whenever her mother tries to poultice her, she pushes the old woman away, whispering: *Save your grand-child!*)

Good Woman boiling soup, Cloudburst feeding Fair Land's child, then picking lice from his hair

     as Sound Of Running Feet hears her mother say to Aunt Spring-time: My sister, it is good for you and me to hear each other. I do not want my heart to separate from yours, or for your heart to be-come closed to our husband's. We must never stop caring for each other and our children,

   while Looking-Glass keeps sitting by himself

     (his wives and daughters poulticing their sore horses).

On the mare called Small Old One,

     Fair Land's favorite,

in a saddlebag which Fair Land once packed, rides a fringed-leather dress which Fair Land made. Cloudburst now unpacks this and gives it to her husband,

     who takes it silently,

        walking quickly uphill

to inhale in secret the scent of his dead wife,

after which he buries this lovely garment, hoping that the Lice-Eaters will not find it.

Now we are unrolling their buffalo robes on the still green clouds of pine needles, drumming, chanting and wailing,

lilypads superimposed on the shimmering upside-down mountains of a tree-ridge's reflection on the still brown water,

as Cloudburst trims Ollokot's hair in mourning for Fair Land, and he trims hers

and Springtime flinches at the crack of a pinecone upon the ground

(her heart wishes for Feathers Around The Neck to sing over her, so that her arm will heal, but SOMETHING covers her mouth whenever she would ask her husband to buy this ceremony);

then comes another noise, duller than a small-calibre gunshot;

mist ascends, until the squirrels running up the pine trees take on the same color as the branches;

and the burned children cannot stop weeping.

Now Wounded Head's small son grows feverish; the Bluecoat's bullet has poisoned him. White Bird's Power cannot suck the evil out. The child groans. Wounded Head keeps whispering to him the winter's tales of how the youngest MOUSE SISTER became a GOPHER's bride and why Fox's son-in-law hid the magic arrowhead, but the boy cannot listen; his face turns hot and yellow; he chatters his teeth and dies. When his mother tries to wrap him in a blanket for his burial, blood bursts from her breast-wound, and she creeps away to rest, struggling to keep silent, while Wounded Head and old Towhee carry him uphill, hiding him deep in the dirt, hoping that no Lice-Eaters will find him to-morrow;

and Toohhoolhoolsote, proceeding with a careful heart, begins to make a song for this dead child,

after which we must do our best never to mention him.

Lean Elk says: To-morrow we shall ride until night.

5

In the morning light

(Springtime is startled by the sudden low groan of a turkey vulture in a tree, and then she laughs),

once our best men have ridden ahead with the wounded,

Burning Coals whispering sorrowfully to the lame horse he must leave behind, the other People break camp,

looking down the steep drop of piney dirt into the pale green grass at the lake's edge, the lake almost entirely enclosed by trees, with glimpses of sagebrush ridge between them, and not many clumps of poison oak

as Arrowhead leaps onto her white stallion.

Ollokot stares palely forward, his hair-roach higher and brighter than his elder brother's.

Sound Of Running Feet's elkhide moccasins have worn almost through. The moccasins which Springtime was making for her husband have been lost at Ground Squirrel Place. Good Woman ranges up and down the trail, angrily whipping the horse herd.

Supporting her on her horse as she sways, caressing her back, Heinmot Tooyalakekt walks beside Springtime for awhile; and their baby sleeps in the cradleboard, well tied to the pommel of her saddle.

Towhee rides behind her son-in-law, who will not turn to look at her. Her daughter rides alone, kneeing her horse when anyone tries to speak with her.

As she rides away on Helper, Sound Of Running Feet watches the rocks shining at the bottom of the lake, and the brook flowing through the wet grass at the south shore;

we are fleeing, hating as we go:

high summer, so that the cowbirds are everywhere.

6

Next morning, Helping Another is ready to ride again even though her breastwound still hisses like a musselshell when she breathes, and Wounded Head whispers: *Síikstiwaa*, you are strong

as they come into the wide plateau of golden grass, mountains all around

(the sun glaring on Lean Elk's brass-buttoned trade vest),

air and yellow blossoms,

locusts singing *tekh-tekh-tekh-tekh-tekh!*

in the golden grass of Horse Prairie,

white with yarrow and purple with daisy fleabane,

where White Bird's father used to hunt buffalo

(long have they pass'd);

and Five Snows,

who is always longing for *getting-drunk liquid*,

begins singing his WYAKIN song, hoping to soon kill some Bostons.

Arriving at a pretty creek, Good Woman leaps off Short-Tailed One to gather sweetgrass for the wounded,

while Swan Woman, Cloudburst, Welweyas and Old Wolf Woman gather tarragon, to poultice the children's tired legs;

watching over them all, Peopeo Tholekt,

he whose left arm is crooked,

sits on a log, tapping kinnikinnick into the ancient pipe which

Looking-Glass gave him; now he is smoking with Wottolen, with
  their rifles beside them
  as his yellow horse says: *Hinimí,*
—but White Thunder, unable to forget
  (my heart should not remember him)
  that the final expression of Shore Crossing,
  he who won every long race,
  was *bewilderment,*
thirsts for something to kill:
  and a doe, glowing reddish in the sun, runs from the thicket, speeds
  across their gaze, rocking as she goes:
  he brings her down.
Good Woman lends her deerhide scraper to his mother,
  whose heart thirsts for a shiny new hide.
Hurry, hurry! Lean Elk warns us; we are nearly as helpless as buffalo swimming across a river; what if some band of killers awaits in the tall grass?
But the horses must graze, and the People are tired. So we follow his words,
but not too much.

7

Traversing the sagebrush bluff of golden grass, descending a shoulder of sagebrush through a few willows, they come into fine buffalo grass
and meadows whose summer flowers are now beginning to die,
  Looking-Glass silent:
    just now, although he does not wish it, his heart will not stop turn-
    ing toward Night-Fishing Place, which once lay in his country, just
    for awhile:
      here my father used to bring me, and after we had set our nets
      he would teach me all the SAYAK STARS
      and the STAR called BEAR SNEAKING UP and
  Lean Elk wondering where to lead these People,
  Helping Another longing to be lowered from her horse and be left to die
    (her husband Wounded Head will not do it; her mother Towhee
    promises that she will live),
  Heinmot Tooyalakekt turning his heart back toward home:
    now on the Lo Lo Trail the birds will be eating the scarlet berries
    of the mountain ash
    and it will be Salmon Spawning Season in all our rivers,
      yes, and in Wallowa,
  as they ride on through the Horse Prairie, hungering to hide among the Crows,
    our buffalo hunters remembering that in time they will reach a sagebrush

slope on the edge of an arroyo with a river in it, where pines will begin to
burst out of the sand and then they will look down a riverine draw, so
green, with a cloud of white aspens,

into a secret Medicine Place,

the others knowing nothing

as Only Half Grizzly Bear dies in the saddle.

8

At prairie's end the Bostons have now made a ranch
from which the People steal eighty-seven horses, the young men laughing
áhaha to have harmed the Bostons,

whom our grandfathers permitted to be our guests, giving them every
good thing:

the Boston way is crime!

(Burning Coals grows angry; we refuse to share with him because he would not lend two stallions.)

So we ride forever, killing as we go,

we who have been as war-thirsty as the Three Red Blankets, as greedy as
Burning Coals, as blind as Looking-Glass

(our copper bracelets tarnishing on our arms);

and now White Thunder, Shooting Thunder and Red Spy, riding ahead of the
People, hunt out another ranch, where food is cooking,

Looking-Glass riding hard behind them on Home From Capture, raising
a rifle in one hand,

Red Spy laughing: I had thought to meet some Bostons to-day, and
now I have met them! My heart tells me what to do with them,

after which White Bird says: Some of Cut Arm's killers dress like Bostons. Therefore, we shall now begin to kill Bostons,

and his brother chiefs answer nothing against this,

except that Heinmot Tooyalakekt calls out: Young men, listen! While he
lived, my father often said: *We should make up our minds before we talk,*
to which the young men reply: We know our minds,

so that Looking-Glass sits still upon his horse as his younger
wife Asking Maiden fans him with grass

and Heinmot Tooyalakekt, turning aside, wraps himself in
his King George Blanket,

Toohhoolhoolsote singing his heart into joyous anger,

Ollokot rigid on his cream-colored horse, staring forward like one
who is sick

as our young men, handing off their horses to the eagerest boys, surround the house,
and Sun Tied, the silent one whose sister, wife and baby the Bluecoats have killed
without reason, chambers a cartridge in his Sharps

—now Cut Arm will learn that we too may show the rifle!—
and they are shooting through the walls:

Pim!

    pim!........pim!

        Good Woman, Cloudburst and Sound Of Running Feet
        watching in excitement, holding their skittish horses,
        and Welweyas the half-woman, her face as heavy as a war-
        rior's, her lips as narrow but her eyes much wider, sits her
        pony quietly behind Cloudburst,
            Springtime sweating, holding her wounded arm,
        Toohhoolhoolsote's women happily singing their WYAKIN
        songs
            (their WYAKINS are NIGHT GHOSTS)
        while their careful husband watches back along the trail,
and from within, a shotgun begins to speak,
        our children covering their ears, for its snarling is nearly as loud as
        Wahlitits's buffalo gun:
        Heinmot Tooyalakekt leads them back (he is certainly no war
        chief).
Parting the shutters ever so slightly, a Boston shows his greenish eye, and we
shoot it:
        Tsálalal!
—the other Boston's shotgun barking like a terrified angry dog—
and from its voice we determine where he must be crouching behind the wall;
in this way we kill him also,
        remembering how Eya-makoot was pickaxed to death when her dog won
        a fight with a Boston's
            (now the murderer lives freely on our land);
then the young men discover two more Bostons riding foolishly toward us,
driving their hay wagon:
        Swan Necklace shoots one of them
            (gunsmoke fouling his grinning face)
        while the other flees into the willows,
        and Looking-Glass sits grimacing on his horse, while Heinmot
        Tooyalakekt turns away,
            the locusts singing *tekh-tekh-tekh!*
From the hayfield three more Bostons come running, then see the People and
begin to run away. Strong Eagle rides after them, and catches one, shooting him
in the liver so that he cannot die without screaming. The other two run into the
river, and in the quicksand their boots come off. This makes the young men happy.

9

Inside the house

(bloody handprints all over the walls),

hang rifles and pistols from nails just over the fireplace, on whose pallid ashes squats a sooty soup pot—

our hearts are now happy; we are taking whatever we please!—

one Boston lies powderburned and bleeding on the floor; the other has crawled in his blood to the bed

on the edge of which he used to sit and cross his knees so that the sunlight caught the greasy grime on his buckskin trousers while Arabella, clad in practical brownish-black, turned away from his stench, bending over her sewing and wishing she had never left Tennessee; to-morrow the neighbors will be condoling with her and saying: JEHOVAH *lift up His countenance upon thee & give thee peace,* and she will be thinking: Maybe I'll get peace now that I don't have to live there no more; it was never my notion to live there; he could of lived there without me and I would of just took the children, which will happen now in any event, so why not tell myself I never lived there and only he lived there

and died there, slowly enough for his fingernails to tear open the feather mattress:

Áhaha!

White Bird comes lightly in. His narrow-braided head turns from side to side; his deep, alert eyes are neither triumphant nor sad. Red Spy enters smiling. Shooting Thunder is peering under the bed, hoping to find some Boston cringing there. Wounded Head looks around, then leaves, touching nothing. Lean Elk searches vainly for ammunition for Shore Crossing's buffalo gun, while Over The Point and Strong Eagle take up the dead men's rifles.

Heinmot Tooyalakekt,

he who once fancied that he could make Cut Arm good by talking,

stands gazing down at the pallid and blackened face on the bed, then pulls a blanket over it. He says: Do not rob them. Cover them all with blankets,

and just as he has said, so it is done.

Then we strip the house of its curtains, blankets, bed-ticking, everything we can use for a bandage

(Good Woman comes quickly in to cut off a strip of quilt to help Springtime's arm

—when her husband first wished for a second wife, she said to him: How could I turn away from your desire? and indeed she has always loved Springtime as would an elder sister—

and Arrowhead gleans a dead man's handkerchief with which she can splint an orphan boy's shattered hand

as Towhee slits a pillowcase into something long and soft to tie around
   her daughter's bubbling, bleeding chest);
then we gather in all the dead men's horses, to enrich ourselves and impoverish
Cut Arm

—and some happy young men pile our horse-dung into a conical
   mound, to teach Cut Arm exactly how our hearts conceive of
   him—
while Looking-Glass and Heinmot Tooyalakekt stand apart
   and Toohhoolhoolsote insults his old women, who had hoped to
   join in the plundering,
as Lean Elk commences shouting: *Hurry, hurry!*
   —so that we fail to burn the place.

10

Heinmot Tooyalakekt says: We should not kill anyone for nothing,
but White Bird replies: A Boston must have no respect for himself. It makes no
matter how well we treat him; he will take advantage of us.

11

The hot day is cooling,
      and even the babies are silent; they are sleeping as they ride
      but two wounded old women cannot stop moaning
         (White Bird will sing over them again to-night)
and we ride on, loose-wrapped in striped blankets, hoping to smear our hearts
with enemy blood.

12

Just before sundown we find another ranch,
      our hatred rising steep as an antelope's horn,
         and Springtime's dog lays back his ears:
behind the barn is a gulch where some Bostons are placer mining, wounding OUR
MOTHER. At once they begin to flee, crying like children.
   White Thunder, who once learned some words of Boston talk from Tsépmin,
calls out: *Come back here! We good Indians, never hurt no white man!*
   so that one Boston removes his gun and slowly walks toward us with his dog,
   with his head down,
      while his brother watches,
         our horses still except for their swishing tails,
and the young men leap down laughing, handing the halters to the adoring
young boys.

Again Heinmot Tooyalakekt seeks to straighten them by talking
   —he is telling them three times!—
but they turn away, sometimes even smiling,
and neither White Bird nor the other chiefs will say anything, so fiery are their
hearts against all Bostons,
      even this trembling one here who grows as white as the pine tree mush-
      room called *lílps* as he slowly, sadly comes to us
         (he is not so tall):
            his dog is whimpering as it comes.
Swan Necklace shoots the dog: *Pim!*
   so that we can enjoy the Boston's face:
      Áhaha! Áhahahahahaha!
         (Good Woman and Cloudburst watching without pity, be-
         cause they remember Fair Land)
and when he falls to his knees (better plead than run), Red Spy raises his Springfield, with an exploding cartridge in the chamber:
   Let us do it!
   GODd——n you, Boston! *For what you mean killing our children?*
   Fellows, I swear to GOD I never—
      Pim! . . .
         flaming from the barrel, reddening the cottony smoke:
         Tsálalal!
            —his brains detonating into purple like the inside of an
            Oregon grape—
      Áhaha!
            —now we are beginning to get even with Cut Arm the Moldy;
but it is nearly dark,
   cooler and colder
as we pillage the ranch
      (Sound Of Running Feet now bending down to touch the dead Boston so
      that her heart may understand what her father and her uncle have already
      told her, that the Bostons were truly made in this other color, which does
      not rub off like paint:
         once we arrive in the Buffalo Country, where we shall be happy
         because no Bostons ever ride there, she will rest and then begin to
         remember this strange thing that she has now touched),
and because the chiefs wrap themselves in their blankets and turn away, we
forbear to sing the victory song;
then once more begin to ride
      southward toward the Lemhi Country
         (where Toohhoolhoolsote's father and Old Looking-
         Glass used to hunt buffalo, in the days before the Shin-
         bones came)

because Looking-Glass told us to ride to the Crows, and his
way is no good;
     if the Lemhis do not receive us well we can still go to
     the Crows.
We ride through the dark, and the wounded are groaning.
Lean Elk leaps down from his racehorse; we shall camp exactly here,
    lighting small fires, boiling soup,
    wrapping ourselves in robes and blankets,
      since Cut Arm has again devoured our lodgepoles.
White Bird is now singing over the two old women
and Peopeo Tholekt, whose WYAKIN is a WOODPECKER, elongates his index finger
to touch the curse-spot on Springtime's arm,
    because her nephew, his war-friend White Thunder, has asked this of him,
so that his Power begins to peck at the evil inside her, hammering it away as he
sings his WYAKIN song:
    This badness is going;
    this badness is going—
until the sad woman begins to feel better.
Now Fair Land's son is sleeping,
    and Springtime's child is suckling (perhaps we shall name her after my
    mother),
       and later in the deep night, knowing his women by touch and
       smell, Heinmot Tooyalakekt creeps to them, first Good
       Woman, then Springtime, comforting their tears
          as Ollokot, smiling in his sleep, Dreams of Dark
          Green Place back home on the north shore of the
          Enemy River, where he used to ride so many times
          with his father,
       and Sound Of Running Feet's dog licks her face.
At dawn we are digging more graves for our People;
    we are becoming bad; we shall soon be mean.

13

Looking-Glass takes no part; neither he nor Heinmot Tooyalakekt
    (whom the Bostons once baptized *Ephraim,* and now call *Joseph*);
from these killings those two stand aside like women:
    Heinmot Tooyalakekt, who was never more than camp-chief
      (he has never made himself brave)
     although after Cut Arm showed the rifle he presumed to tell us:
     Finish your talk,
       desiring us to become slaves and cattle, since he could not
       keep his own country from being sold,

and Looking-Glass, who also obeyed Cut Arm,

    penning himself up on a scrap of painted-off land, trusting the Bostons for nothing,

    trusting them again at Ground Squirrel Place, even after Wottolen told his dream:

it is he who killed us, I am telling you three times!

—while Heinmot Tooyalakekt is nothing; he cannot kill Bostons.

14

We are pleasing our hearts, punishing Cut Arm
while Looking-Glass
    (he who is unexcelled)
rides silently, treasuring his last dream, the Buffalo Country,
    where we were given our Owl Dance long ago;
and just as a buffalo shakes himself when he clambers out of the river, so Looking-Glass shakes off his grief; he will lead the People to the good far-off place where we shall all grow rich again,

    riding into the blooming of the yellow-green light

    and the fragrance of the golden grass on that bluff in early morning, with the Swift Water* streaming widely and darkly down below, showing few glints of white where the high rocks are, but many dark green wrinkles in its cool flesh as it curves around a wide crescent of pale gravel striped with tree-shadows;

    and Looking-Glass's rest has been as dark as the fallen cottonwood on that sand

        (its branches much paler, nearly as delicate as a mudsucker's whiskers);

now he is rising up from his rest, leaving until evening the one whose smile makes his penis as long as a deer's neck;

he is ready to hunt and wander forever

    through this morning striped with blue tree-shadow;

        already his friends have filled their pipes to him

        and offered their smoke to the SKY, to the EARTH and to the Homes of the FOUR WINDS;

        they have sung: *ACBADADEA, MAKER OF ALL THINGS ABOVE, hear my prayer!*

and looking out across the forested sandbars he sees goldfinches rising up from the cottonwood crowns and speaking each to his mate

    (smell of water and dust, mountains far away, the river hissing on and on, the near-full moon overhead, and now TRAVELLER THE

---

*Yellow Stone River.

SUN begins to warm the back of his neck as the golden grass dulls
down to brownish-yellow, the river to brownish-green and bluish-
brown, while to the west, the channel between the bluff and a cottonwood island shines sky-blue)
and once TRAVELLER begins to warm his shoulders, it reveals a hoard of
river-rocks in a stripe of shallows
    (they glow like green and yellow trade beads);
and he is wearing his blanket diagonally, in the style of his friends,
and they watch where the downstream edge of the wooded sandbar ta-
pers like the prow of a Boston ship
as three deer, reddish in the low sun, browse in single file across the
meadow on the far side, presently entering the wideness and cleanness of
that deep river
while he goes on watching with his Crow friends
    until on the very horizon it begins to show itself:
        that black smudge of buffalo, wider and more than the river
        itself, wealth beyond wealth.

15

Thus he dreams, but we have said that Looking-Glass's Medicine is no good
    (our hatred for him as visible as the flash of a Bluecoat's rifle);
his WYAKIN Power has altered into childishness.

16

We ride south,
    outdistancing Cut Arm again,
        Sound Of Running Feet on Helper, riding beside Wounded Head's
        wife, whose chest-wound still whistles when she breathes
            (her mother has become one who weeps at night),
        then Good Woman, Springtime and Cloudburst,
    and Over The Point,
        who always makes himself brave,
    mounted on a chestnut horse:
        he wears his lovely elkhide shirt and his necklace of grizzly
        bear teeth,
            pulling on a travois another dying child,
riding up through the pines to escape this valley,
our horses cropping at reddish-gold grass in the clearings
            (Red Spy, my brother, where have you been?
            On ahead),
    as a frightened deer's split rump dwindles,

this valley narrowing now, purple mountains to the east,
>a horse-carried child crying out at the way a branch suddenly darts past like a small dark animal;
>and Toohhoolhoolsote keeps mourning in his heart for his mountains,
>>grieving for the Chinook Salmon Water country;
>>>he is lacking it forever
as we enter the golden openness of meadows, resting, drinking at a round greenish-brown pool, then letting our horses drink,
>cleaning each other's wounds.
When some women pause to gather this year's first strawberries, Lean Elk shouts: *Hurry, hurry!*
—so that we must ride until we have ascended the slope of forest, whose sky is golden green between the lodgepole pines,
>and enter the highest bright pines and meadows,
>following a creek hidden in yellowing willows
>>where Looking-Glass, spying fresh scat, rides off the trail to hunt,
>>>Blackberry Person now picketing one of his packhorses,
>>and he creeps like a snake, calling upon his WYAKIN Power, waiting in the shadows at a meadow's edge until he sees
>>the large ears of a deer lifting slantwise as the animal peers back over his shoulder at Looking-Glass, his face three dots, the long neck not straining but raised, the white hindquarters like a stripe of dirt
>>—and Looking-Glass shoots; the deer leaps and is dead
as the People keep riding ahead, ascending that brown and cool creek which cuts through the sagebrush hills where here and there a stand of aspens has begun to turn yellow
>as TRAVELLER THE SUN declines
and so we are unrolling our blankets:
>Springtime's arm has grown as big as her thigh; she feels feverish and the baby is crying,
>>but Good Woman cuts soft grass for her to lie on and rocks the baby to sleep;
>>>and although Springtime's pain still annoys her, Peopeo Tholekt will return this night to help her with his Power,
>>>>(she is softening rawhide with one hand; she is making something secret)
>>and Good Woman is now thickening Cloudburst's soup with the last of her cous flour
as Looking-Glass brings in his butchered deer for the People,
who thank him with closed hearts;
>>>then it is full dark, so that Wottolen and his son Black Eagle go creeping off, hoping to kill a few of the turkeys which are roosting overhead

as Arrowhead wraps herself in her wolfskin cape
but Helping Another longs to die;
> the STARS are swimming, troubling her like the
> white spots on certain horses,
>> (her dead child must not be mentioned);
>>> Welweyas dreams of dancing the
>>> Rabbit Dance one more time,
> and after moonrise, Ollokot creeps under the
> blanket with Cloudburst:
>> for a long time they are silent;
>>> then she utters a sound like a mourn-
>>> ing dove.

17

Next morning the People reach the pass, coming into the Country of the Lemhis,
> who are almost the same as Lice-Eaters—
> Sacajawea's People:
>> it was she who brought the Bostons into our country
>> to spy out our riches
>>> and tell lies, eating our horses like beef, changing horses with
>>> Looking-Glass's grandfather
>>> while William Clark used Red Grizzly Bear's sister to make
>>> Tzi-kal-tza.
> Now we are decorating our faces
> (Springtime and Good Woman are hastily roaching their husband's hair),
> for their tipis stand below us in a great circle and their best men are riding toward us
>> so that Peopeo Tholekt halts his longnecked yellow horse, holding him-
>> self very tall, lean and still,
>>> with eagle feathers marching far down his back and a beadwork
>>> strap around his forehead;
>> he is wearing all his many necklaces, staring straight;
> and then Looking-Glass, pulling up the reins, throws back his gaze and stares out
> at these Lemhis from under his feathered hat.
> Chief Tendoy,
>> plump-cheeked and soft-faced,
>>> his metal trade-whistle the same color as the dark deerleather strap
>>> from which it hangs,
>> throws back his head, so that his white braids begin dancing on his chest
>>> (his wives are sighing with pity to see Springtime and Helping An-
>>> other),
> and he says: Looking-Glass, my brother, my heart is glad to see you;

but he is not glad, and when his little eyes begin to see that Lean Elk is head-chief, he continues thus:

Lean Elk, my dear brother, there are now bad issues with the Bostons; how will you settle them?

to which Looking-Glass replies: My brother, since my grandfather's time the Bostons have had confidence in me; it is only now, since they have decided to devour our lands, that there have been bad issues,

but it is as if Looking-Glass has not spoken.

Looking-Glass then says: Tendoy, how has it escaped your heart that my father and yours used to hunt buffalo exactly here?

Tendoy replies: There are no buffalo here anymore,

at which Toohhoolhoolsote,

glaring, his eyes half shut, the corners of his mouth angrily downturned, spits on the ground, then snarls as if to himself: Wherever the Bostons come, the buffalo go,

while Looking-Glass keeps silent,

and then Tendoy slowly says: When the Bostons were a long way off, my heart was not much troubled . . .

—and as the other People sit there in the horse-trampled grass
    (Toohhoolhoolsote's wives bewildered:
        Old Wolf Woman's white hair unloosed as she leans forward, smiling strangely, her hands shaking,
            Strong Eagle telling Red Spy, not softly: *We have always come here to pick camas!*,
        Place Of Arrival slowly turning over a rock),
Towhee tries to change her daughter's bandage, but Helping Another throws off her hand.

Lean Elk takes the pipe and says: If you wish us to, we shall go likewise,
        and indeed the Lemhis would not keep them,
            Toohhoolhoolsote clenching both fists, growling over his shoulder: This chief is a slave of the Bostons!
                —but even as Springtime, Sound Of Running Feet and Good Woman lassoo their family's horses, preparing to ride away,
                    and Arrowhead remounts her white stallion,
                Looking-Glass, whose heart still takes pride in his Boston friends, leaves Blackberry Person to hold his stallion while he visits a certain trader whom he knows will supply ammunition, should the price be high enough:
                    so he gets many cartridges in secret even from the People,

who ride on east into the mountains
>
> as Wounded Head tells Over the Point: I know this is not right,
> and Springtime asks her husband: Where shall we now live?
> to which he replies: I do not know where;
>
>> then, pitying the women and children, rides alongside White Bird
>> to learn his heart as to what might now be best;
>> but the old chief tells him: Brother, you remember very well that
>> after we made our peace treaty with the Bluecoats, I warned Looking-
>> Glass not to lead us south, but he would not desist, and you upheld
>> him. Now evil things have happened. What can we do? It is too late
>> to return to the Salish; Bostons and Bluecoats hunt us everywhere,
>>
>>> after which he knees his horse forward, so that Heinmot
>>> Tooyalakekt may understand his heart's angry sorrow;
>>
>> but White Thunder, seeing that Springtime has made herself sad,
>> says: My dear aunt, when we arrive in the Buffalo Country I shall
>> kill all the yearling cows you wish; again you will be rich in robes!
>> —at which she must smile, loving this young man's kindness
>
> as the People ride away,

farther and farther from home,

> Helping Another never groaning,
> Toohhoolhoolsote's old wives longing for fresh meat,
> passing muddy ovoids in the prairie grass where buffalo bulls have dug
> out wallows for themselves,
>
>> so that Over The Point and some other best men begin talking
>> about riding off the trail to go hunting

—until Red Spy, riding ahead, catches sight of the Big Dust,

> our children wailing,
>
>> Heinmot Tooyalakekt caressing Springtime's back, then
>> stroking one of Good Woman's braids,

the young men stripping off their leggings and deerskin shirts, calling eager
boys to hold their horses, then rushing forward along the ridgetops

> as Lean Elk rides round and round, seeking a hiding place for the women,
> wounded, old ones and children,
>
>> Burning Coals whispering to his anxious herd,

—but White Thunder comes galloping back: Nothing but a wagon train, I am telling you three times!

—the People now laughing *áhaha!*, our best men positioning themselves to receive these Bostons

> (Sound Of Running Feet feels afraid):
>> three wagons drawn by sixteen mules each and one trailer-wagon with
>> an eight-horse team;

they are coming straight here, to the creek's middle fork; it must be their cooking
time; we shall see if their horses please our hearts.

The young men ask Ollokot,
> he who now leads so many,

whether or not to kill them, but he replies: When it mattered, you never asked your chiefs what you should do. Now you may do as you please.

18

Thus certain young men (the others hiding) decorate their faces with friendliness; and these five Bostons smile at them; they are making themselves good.

The half-breed Bunched Lightning, who can speak Boston words, looks over these white men who have arrived at the place where they were meant to come, and he says: *Where going?*

Salmon, Idaho. D'you reds know where that is?

Sure,
> as a few more young men now come riding in,
> then a few more, peering into the wagons:
>> ever so many sacks, crates and canned goods for Salmon, Idaho,
>>> where we once used to have some villages, just for awhile, in the summers and winters before Cut Arm,
>>> when Toohhoolhoolsote's People roamed, fished, dug roots and Dreamed.

What tribe you fellers from?

Take a good look, Bostons!—
> the People gloating over the canned things:
>> Stripes Turned In now discovering two barrels of *getting-drunk liquid,*
>> and in the dark sit two scared Chinamen:
>>> bound for the mines.

You ain't Nez Perces, right?

No more talk here now, says Bunched Lightning. *Give food our children!*
> —and the kind Bostons obey, meaning no harm,
> unless they are sneaky and cowardly like the Bostons in the Bitter Root Valley who pretended that this war was over:
> such are the hearts of Bostons everywhere,
>> which is why our longhaired young warriors, as smoothfaced and lovely-eyed as girls, watch them with their hands clenched at their waists;
>> and Red Spy stares at them like a baby which refuses to be appeased by a certain woman's breast
>>> (the Bostons dreading his *hateful Indian eyes*)
>> and Toohhoolhoolsote begins rising up with the doggish spurious gentleness of a black bear,
>>> our other best men now readying themselves,
>>> so that Heinmot Tooyalakekt, whose sad heart again cries *qoh! qoh!*

qoh!, strides forward to warn them: If you do this, Cut Arm will surely choke us all in rope!

—but Looking-Glass, whose heart says the same, has no more Power

(he is glaring like an old chief guarding his pipe),

and Toohhoolhoolsote's heart is grimly indifferent: Cut Arm will choke us anyhow!

while White Bird hides his face behind his feather-fan:

for who is Heinmot Tooyalakekt now, he who sold his country for nothing and could not lead our young men? He is not even a failed war-chief like Looking-Glass, merely a camp-chief; he fled Ground Squirrel Place like a woman; what has he done of worth? So let him be silent now when we are not in camp,

which is why Good Woman calls Sound Of Running Feet to her; those two must walk, just for awhile,

taking Springtime by her good hand, leading her out into the golden prairie,

gathering prairie sage, which the Crows call *the wolf's perfume;*

dressing her arm with sweetgrass, to keep down the stench of the wound,

as Good Woman carries the cradleboard,

—our children meanwhile eating the Bostons' hardbread, our old ones creeping around the wagons, wondering what to steal:

candy, which we have always called *marrow-like,*

rice, which in our speech is *maggot-like,*

and even a sheet of glass, which we have named *ice-like*

(this last we give to the young boys for their entertainment: they shatter it with rocks, then try to cut things with the pieces, but mostly cut their fingers)

and Cloudburst puts a piece of *marrow-like* in the mouth of Fair Land's little boy: He is astonished.

Old Tzi-kal-tza, who lacks a wife to help him, cuts open a sack and crams uncooked *maggot-like* in his mouth,

Toohhoolhoolsote chuckling and coughing until his loop necklaces of bone beads convulse into fits of clattering,

the trembling *Americans* saying nothing.

Here are ten thousand rounds of ammunition!* We take them all, singing.

Once we lay hands on their horses, the Bostons begin to complain. Now we are instructing them; we are beginning to make them scared,

---

*Coincidentally, they were bound for Major Shearer's volunteers in Idaho.

levelling our rifles, driving them down into the coulee,
　　　the locusts singing *tekh-tekh!,*
although Geese Three Times Alighting On Water,
　　　remembering how when we commenced this war along the Big
　　　Salmon Water,
　　　　　after Swan Necklace came riding into camp on a white man's
　　　　　horse, and Heinmot Tooyalakekt grew so displeased,
he, Geese Three Times Alighting On Water, was pursuing a Boston
who tried to gallop away, with a little Boston boy riding behind,
clasping his arms around the man's waist,
and Geese Three Times Alighting On Water drew his bow
　　　　　(for Shore Crossing had not yet given him any dead Boston's
　　　　　rifle),
took aim between the father's shoulders, and loosed the arrow
　　　　　—a fine straight one which he had made from a serviceberry
　　　　　twig—
so that his arrow pierced the white child's arm;
and this child began to weep: *shlak, shlak!*
　　　　　at which Geese Three Times Alighting On Water, feeling
　　　　　painful in his heart, turned and rode away, allowing the boy
　　　　　and his father to live,
now turns away from our best men, who laugh at him, saying: Coward,
go stir ashes with your mother!
—thus he returns to the half-pillaged wagon, where Towhee slits a strip
of calico to make her daughter a new bandage
　　　　　because Arrowhead has already cut up a bolt of white cotton
　　　　　cloth;
we are admiring our new horses (this time Burning Coals gets one)
and Heinmot Tooyalakekt wraps himself sadly in his King George
blanket,
while the best men drive those Bostons like animals
　　　　　(just as Cut Arm seeks to drive us)
　　　　　—their misery as delightful to our taste as a buffalo's shoul-
　　　　　der-hump—
down and down,
　　　　　Bunched Lightning grinning like the miniature of his own
　　　　　WYAKIN,
down
until, just as the game requires, our first Boston turns, running
toward the creek,
　　　　　　where the spiny shiny leaves of Oregon grape have al-
　　　　　　ready begun to turn red, reflecting themselves in trem-
　　　　　　bling pink

and he runs, runs, runs:

    Red Spy, so accomplished at killing, shoots him from behind,
just once: *Pim!*

        at which he runs, runs, just like a lung-shot deer,

            blood blooming between his shoulderblades,

        nearly reaching the bank,

            our young men waiting here smiling,

        until he coughs red and tumbles down, his face in the
water,

            tsálalal!

and the second,

    who begins to remind White Thunder of Tsépmin,

        he who used to thank us for everything and laugh at
our stories

            (as when Red Spy told how a man can hear a BUT-
TERFLY or a MUSSELSHELL GIRL opening and
closing Herself—Tsépmin laughed until tears
came),

        yes, he who once hanged three of our People,

tries to draw, but Naked-Footed Bull breaks his gun across his
hand; as he gazes up weeping, Five Snows shoots him in the chest:

    Pim!

            —now once more we have wiped our buttocks on
Cut Arm's head—

while the third one, the saddest old Boston,

    like a broken-legged buffalo bull waiting for a bear to eat him,

him Five Snows shoots in the bladder:

    his belly explodes with blood and urine,

        áhaha!

        Is he completely dead?

        No, poor fellow! I'll help him:

            Pim!

        and from his mouth comes the sound made by a
woman who scrapes a dry hide, so that we laugh
again:

            Now we feel ourselves refreshed with
life! We shall suck out their marrow,

          as in the golden grass Springtime rocks her
screaming baby one-handed and Sound Of
Running Feet covers her ears,

while the fourth Boston frantically hits out with the butt end of his
mule whip until Rattle Blanket shoots him in the face:

    Qáw!

and the last one, tall and pale like Moss Beard, draws a hatchet
from his belt, whirling and swinging:

he wounds Bunched Lightning, then grazes Five Snows;

so Stripes Turned In shoots him in the heart:

Shláyayaya.

Thus we have killed them together,

satisfying the blood of Rainbow, Fair Land and the others

(whom we should not mention);

now we are gloating over their dead faces tattooed with powder and
burned by gun-flames:

*You Go*ᴅᴅ——*n Bostons!*

*Cut Arm, Go*ᴅᴅ——*n you! You should not have showed the rifle!*

we are singing the victory song;

and Red Spy,

he who once went night-hunting after women,

would now scalp them, but we dissuade him, and even leave their corpses
unrobbed, in order to please our chiefs,

who remain away,

Heinmot Tooyalakekt speaking apart with Lean Elk, who replies: Nor could you stop them on the Chinook Salmon
Water;

now our best men begin unloading the wagons, giving the People so
many fine canned things, some of which they have never before eaten

(*marrow-like* and Borden's dried milk):

the children are happy to fill their bellies

(Toohhoolhoolsote turning away from this food in disgust),

and the wounded are joyous that we have begun avenging ourselves as
we go,

hoping to find more *Americans* to kill,

our young men galloping their new horses round and round,

Heinmot Tooyalakekt trying again, warning them: This is not
the way to show bravery:

but indeed we lack a common heart on this matter,
and so his thoughts turn shallow, translucent, brown
and cool, like the Clearwater at Cañon's Mouth (Red
Owl's country): flowing away, gliding across the
whorled rocks, away and away—

and Good Woman is squeezing out the pus from Springtime's arm,
while White Bird sings over her, a little song of Power, as *Kate* begins softly drumming; when the baby begins to cry, Cloudburst
carries her away; then Sound Of Running Feet begins to sing

(Heinmot Tooyalakekt has paid White Bird two horses:

Springtime will never tell anyone that her heart preferred the Medicine of Feathers Around The Neck)
while Lean Elk counts cartridges for the great buffalo rifle that
Shore Crossing once carried:
only thirteen left
—but now the two Chinese (we forgot them) weep like children!—
so, pitying and despising them
(they are nothing; they cannot fight; at least they are not Bostons),
we compel them to dance like monkeys:
Áhaha!
—even Toohhoolhoolsote cannot help smiling—
after which White Thunder instructs them: Run away now, tiny little
yellow ones; go and see your grandmother!
—so they clasp their hands, bowing and bowing to us, then sprint into
the dying grass, never looking back;
we are laughing as they go; grim Toohhoolhoolsote is laughing.

19

Now we are drinking the Bostons' *getting-drunk liquid*
(White Thunder will not touch it,
Wounded Head scolds us
and Heinmot Tooyalakekt turns away,
remembering the way that Springtime used to
look at him, tilting her head so that her dark
braids caught fire in the sun
—her glance has now become as thorny as
the stem of a wild rose—
and the summers and winters when Sound Of
Running Feet used to laugh),
while we chuckle over that one Boston who just now died in
the same way that a woman scrapes a dry hide;
we are still wishing to kill Cut Arm and leave him exposed with a stick in his anus;
we are quarrelling over the Stick Game:
Coyote With Flints stabs Heyoom Pishkish
and two warriors shoot each other, each grazing the other's head
(no chief can do anything):
just as the hemorrhaging women at Ground Squirrel
Place reddened the river they died in, so now the faces
of our best men grow ensanguined from this happy
Medicine whose Power permits their hearts to be bad;

while Five Snows is singing and almost falling down
until Stripes Turned In, who fought so well at Ground Squirrel Place, cries out:
Hear me, young men! Your hearts are reckless; you are making yourselves foolish.
If the Bluecoats come now, they will kill us all!

Again and again Heinmot Tooyalakekt murmurs with the other chiefs, until
their hearts hear him at last, and they say: Let us pour out this *getting-drunk
liquid,*

which Stripes Turned In, White Thunder and Peopeo Tholekt begin to
do,

so that Five Snows draws a dead Bluecoat's Colt pistol
(a woman's toy; why has he kept it?)
—Stripes Turned In now crying out: Brother, I am telling you—
and Five Snows shoots Stripes Turned In, who falls down; his thigh has
exploded.

Now Five Snows's heart becomes ashamed, and so the chiefs finally begin to
make themselves heard:
We pour out the lovely brown drink
(although No Swan catches some in a dead Bluecoat's canteen),
take the dead Bostons' wealth, burn their wagons,
and ride again,
Lean Elk shouting: *Hurry, hurry!*
and Broken Tooth,
whom we once called White Feather,
she who has lost father and sister, sits silent in the saddle, chewing on a
piece of Boston hardbread.
Meanwhile the Lemhis, led by Tendoy, are already scouting for the Bluecoats,
following our trail.

20

Soon we shall have left behind the days when mint blooms.
as we ride on,

never again to Dream with Smohalla, watching his wide dark
pupils grow,
never to hear when WOWSHUXLUH comes down to tell us everything;
and Stripes Turned In grows feeble; he can no longer ride;
Five Snows has killed him;
so he says good-bye to the People, who must leave him to be scalped by
the Lice-Eaters
—but Springtime's arm has begun to heal.

21

The young men have all sobered themselves; once more they are healthy, laughing as they ride. Calling them, Heinmot Tooyalakekt says: I understand well what has now been done. You are spilling blood upon blood. Next you will be shooting women again. If you refuse to listen to me, I cannot help it. If our hearts cannot come together, I must be silent. Now surely Cut Arm will choke us all in rope! You saw how they killed our women and children at Ground Squirrel Place; do you suppose they will not be further angered now? You are devouring us, your own People! My heart is sad.

They fall silent

(Toohhoolhoolsote's warriors shoot hateful looks into his eyes);
and now we must creep away like snakes; in fear must we now go to seek our friends;
but now we are about to enter their country; they will take us in:
the Crows will come riding, riding, crowned with many widespread feathers,
with the fringe flowing from their long sleeves like waterfalls, raising their
streamered lances as they come.

THE GREEN LIGHT
AUGUST 14

*I*n the morning Wood can see the green light through the willows,
and the grass appears higher and more extensive than in the night, no
longer white except for its central veins,
and he looks back west into Big Hole and then across the hazy
snow-capped mountains which will soon be foregrounded with
cows and Progress.
Looks like more Bannocks coming to help us out, in care of a
couple of white men. I wonder how I could try a Bannock
squaw? I can't ever try a Nez Perce girl with that James Reuben sniffing around. And Wilkinson must never
Having gained leave from the general to draft another of his campaign sketches
(for he has a fast horse and can easily overtake the march), he approaches the river,
finding it easy and pleasant to walk out upon on a tongue paved with partly dry
gravel, setting up shop on the inevitable flat dry rock, with the river brown and
cold beside him, rippling around the reflection of a bushy alder in a great oval.

Completing his sketch ("Gen'l Howard's Army Breaking Camp"), he returns to the bank and seats himself on a cold rock, gazing at thistledown, sitting in sunshine just outside the shadow that encloses the river and its gentle banks. He will ride after the column in five minutes.

He picks up an oval white rock which has been pitted as if by insects.

Although he gazes steadily back at the mountains, he can see no one; he hears only the river's liquid heartbeats.

He exhales, and thistledown flutters away, catching in a willow.

HIS FATHER'S GRAVE
AUGUST 15

*S*o we keep riding away, but Heinmot Tooyalakekt remembers coming into Wallowa from Imnaha:

> first the blue-grey of the lake mountains, wide and sharp on the horizon, and the golden grass
>> pine tribes dispersing into solitaries, then vanishing
> as our horses breast that one rise of yellow grass, the threshold of the valley
> and we enter wide greatness all around
>> (the lake still hidden by forest),
> the valley widening into the entire world
> where our lodges stand pale and tall in the grass, and with their long black braids shining down, our women sit weaving baskets;
>> Springtime is dressing; she is putting on her robe; soon she will receive me by the lake;
>> then when Smohalla comes we shall Dream of WOWSHUXLUH,
>> and keep the Bostons out forever;
>>> Welweyas needs a new husband,
>>> and my daughter must soon be married;
> and my father's grave awaits my care.

BANNOCK CITY
AUGUST 15

1

*W*e'll try to intercept them from the east.

Yessir.

Wood, ride back with Captain Clark's courier, and explain to the captain that his proposed movement would result as a diversion in favor of the enemy.

Yessir.

Looky there. Those boys are too exhausted to play cards, cicadas roaring nearly as loud as the Transcontinental Express.

See that Blackie. Still mooning over his Fidelia—

No I ain't. I'm sick.

What do you mean, sick? Hey, Doc, give Blackie a swig of quinine from your black bottle.

Well, I hope they go down thisaway, southeast to Fremont's Peak! See, according to Colton's map, that's the loftiest in the whole mountain chain. Sure would be good sport to get into the shadow of that. Might be snowy and cool—

I hope we shoot 'em all to-morrow.

You feeling poorly, son?

Doc, I—

Shut up and drink this down. And you fellers make him drink all the water he can hold. You'll pull through, Blackie. It's not cholery or nothing.

Where's Captain Trimble? He's had words with Captain Clark.

Well?

They declined to follow your orders, general. I don't know why.

Thank you, Wood. That will be all. I need Wilkinson now. And here he is! Good morning.

General, we're all of us disgusted on account of those disloyal civilians—

Never mind. Do you see how the stage road runs on this map?

Yessir. A very practical march.

Once we get there.

General, if we stopped to-night at this Red Rock Stage Station—

Exactly! That's the strategic point. You have the makings of a staff officer.

Thank you, general, although I thought I was one, I mean, at least in a sense, being your—

Humor's not your strong suit, Wilkinson. Since the fine citizens of Bannock City are leaving us in the lurch, we'll ride out doublequick, and they can get back to abusing the Army. Speaking of grumblers, has Doctor Alexander been growling any more than usual?

Not sure, general. Some men have fallen out sick—

Examine the company commanders, especially Perry. Sound the move out in thirty minutes. No excuses.

Yessir, general!

Did you witness that, Fletch? He's like a bulldog. I'm truly fond of Wilkinson—

Excuse me, sir, but you look tired. Is it your arm?

Come to think of it, could you fetch the carbolic acid?

Of course, sir, and I'd be pleased to clean it for you.

Thank you . . . O, that feels better. You'd think it should have healed by now, Fletch. Fifteen years—

Sir, it never will. Shall I add this business of Bannock City to the field report?

I'm afraid so. Whenever we suffer in silence, the outcome is another slap in the Army's face. We're doing whatever we can humanly do.

Without a doubt, sir.

Has that Redington found his feet yet?

A hilarious young man, general! He's just crazy for excitement—

What does Chapman say?

O, he hates him, sir, since he's—

All right, then Redington must be trying to do right. He looks awfully young.

Yessir.

I'll pray for him.

Yessir.

To-day must be the fifteenth of August. Another month till Bessie's birthday. Six years old, she'll be,

> and the Board of Commissioners for Foreign Missions doubtless expects
> my attendance at this month's end, but what about Joseph? O, he's the
> question, right here at Red Rock.

Yessir.

Back so soon, Wilkinson?

They're ready to push ahead, sir, although Colonel Perry was in a black mood and said something about not being responsible—

What?

I pretended not to hear, since he was looking bleak. Anyhow, sir, you know he'll drive those men forward even if he has to pound them . . .

> Well, sir, the pack mules are suffering, I fear.

Trumpeter, blow "The General."
Yessir,
>as they form into columns of four, small clouds
>creeping toward them in the dusty sky
>>(dreamers who've never stopped running
>>from the coal mines,
>>hungry Irishmen
>>and German Communists from Cincinnati)
>—our country and flag forever!—
>the Gatling barrels too bright to look at,
>our general's blue suit fading but not yet much stained,
>Trimble prowling up and down the line of Company
>"H," wiping his forehead
>>(not the least little zephyr out here in this
>>Godd——n desert wilderness),
>Doc whispering to Blackie and pointing right, because
>westward of Bannock City all the way to the Rocky
>Mountains the map shows Big Hole Prairie and then
>GOLD, GOLD.

Perry can take up the rearguard.
Yessir. He's—
>"Boots and Saddles," boy—and blow your heart out!
>>Why the *fuck's* that shavetail still standing over there? Punish
>>him.

Right away, captain.
Pack wagons all buckled up, sir!
Then tell that lazy nigger over there—
Excuse me, sir, did you hear something?
>*They are the ones who killed our good children and our good*
>*young girls.*

I thought I heard Indian. That's just the wind, son.
Yessir.
Here comes that Wilkinson, sniffing around. Shut up and act busy;
d——n you, you'd better *be* busy!
>>"To Horse."

>Let's go, boys; let's get those d——d saddles on; *go, go, go*—
>>What a raggedy bunch. Driving them to Hell and
>>gone so the *Christian Soldier* can
>"Prepare to mount."
>"Mount."
>>*Advance*—
>>*Move out.*

And the long horsetrooper-shadows all bloom from one side of the column as

they inscribe themselves upon the blank prairie, the horses coughing dust, Blackie
wishing for just one more sip from Doc's cocaine bottle, and they march all day,
glaring at their officers like railroad strikers snatching up rocks to throw,

> the Japan wax melting out of the cannelures in their bullets,

> and even Captain Bendire the bird expert no longer aims his field-
> glass at every rustling bush

> > (This desert is as charming as can be!

> > Sure is, general . . .),

> the horses with their heads down, flies clinging to the dusty
> corners of their eyes,

> Perry's fingers sunburned nearly to the brownish-black of a
> Modoc's skin

> and Red O'Donnell scarlet and sweating there on the spring
> seat as he wearily whips his mules (at least the wagonsheet
> keeps some of the sun off);

> and a despatch rider pursues them all the way to their fresh-planted
> guidon:

2

Read this, Wood, and tell me how it squares with your notions.

> Did you hear about that despatch, what Mr. Joe's done now? That
> young fellow there just brought it. Blackie overheard it all. And
> then they cut the harness, so they must have been real close behind.
> And then they mutilated him, but good.

A tragedy, general.

Well, do you assert that Mr. Joe should be punished or not?

Anyone who murders should be punished, general.

> And two hundred horses stolen by the reds—

Ride out and get the latest from our scouts. Where's Jim?

Umatilla Jim, sir?

Right.

O, he must be out there—

That will be all. Well, well, Fletch. What did you make of that?

> as a result of which, Fletch, comprehending and pitying
> Wood's fickleness, remarks to Wilkinson: His thoughts
> change horses every fifteen miles, like the Cayuse stage!— to
> which Wilkinson replies: It's worse than that. He's been play-
> ing us, and especially the general, like a cynical whore who
> gets her hand in someone's pocket.— No, says Fletch, that's
> ungenerous.— Well, you believe that because he's playing
> *you*. Am I the only grown man here?

What is it now, Redington?

Well, general, the Bannocks are raring to attack Joseph. They can't understand why the Army's so far behind. I'd like to—

Young man, it's not for you to peddle advice, and I'm speaking kindly, on account of your lack of experience. O, me, but you do enliven this command! Now where is Joseph headed?

General, it's looking ever more certain that he seeks a juncture with the Crows. The Bannocks and our good Nez Perces both—

I agree, although he's fooled us before. Keep Buffalo Horn and his scalpers in hand until I order you otherwise. Has Captain Fisher said the same?

Yessir.

If they disobey me, they'll be punished.

Yessir.

Mason, I dislike the look of Trimble's line.

I'll take care of it right away, sir,

> their tongues cracking in their mouths while the general rides serenely
> along on Arrow, so that the thirstiest men long for him to die.

Now what's the holdup yonder? Wilkinson, straighten them out.

Sitting up late in camp there at Red Rock Stage Station, the evening sun brightening the clustered awnings of our wagon park, he experiences an inappropriate exhilaration flushing out of his skin, as if this were some fine hour he anticipated, even, for instance, his honeymoon with Lizzie. But there's Wood, whose heart appears to be as tight as the dried rawhide on a wooden Indian saddle. What does the boy want? A coyote wails. He has marked the maps and recapitulated his conclusions three times. It seems as if he could and ought to repeat this labor all night, until the hot darkness brightens up again into buffalo heat; but it hardly bears saying that the source of this happy energy is his body itself, which must in fact be overtired in order to play these tricks on him. Now he feels tired; the joy has drained out of everywhere but his spine—insulting life-jokes! Right now he'd like to ride and ride, until every man of them fell out of the saddle:

> Again that Indian Joseph has humiliated me. This time I thought to have
> him sure, but there's the fact, as stubborn as some thick-logged Confed-
> erate blockhouse anchored in the dirt.

Well, Sherman's interests here are still in pretty fair condition, I must say,
> like Captain Trimble's well-patched sack coat.

So Much Waste

1

*H*as Buffalo Horn gone yonder?

Yessir.

Wood, can you take dictation now?

I'll sure try, general.

All right. Now this is for General Sherman . . .

> and a single cirrus cloud as snow-white as the forehead and collar of President Hayes leads them until
>> I know Lizzie and Grace are praying for all of us.

Very favorable weather, ain't it, Doc?

Wish we could catch some breeze.

Or a piece of tail.

Or a better road . . .

What's wrong with this road, I'd like to know?

I'll tell you what's wrong. It hurts my feet.

It ain't ended yet. That's what's wrong with it, you d——d fucker.

You keep on calling me names, and one morning you might just wake up with your teeth beside you in the gravel.

Put that knife back or the sergeant's gonna—

Now you've got it, d——n you, keep it—left—left—left,

> a hundred ten paces to the minute,
>> back into Idaho Territory, maybe somewhere around here.

Sure is hot.

No it ain't.

This here's an endless day,

> each day past and gone another of the pale yellow flower-suns in the grass of the Buffalo Country, which now goes sandy again, reigning conterminously with the Sagebrush Empire.

No it ain't.

What time is it? We oughter stop pretty soon. Looks to be at least three- or four-o'-clock by the sun.

No it ain't. You shut up now.

How long we been on the trail, boys?

Wasn't it June twenty-third we rolled out of Lapwai

> and ain't you homesick for the sweet cool shade of locust trees way back there?

That's near about two months.

I said how long?

Fifty-odd days. Reckon it up for yourself.

Well, by September or October, maybe our sad old Christian General might take the initiative.

Pardon my doubts.

He got rolled up by Stonewall Jackson.

You said that a thousand times.

Anyway, it wasn't his fault.

Whose was it then? Besides, his best friends are niggers. He never takes a white man's word.

They say General Crook hates him worse than rattlesnake juice.

So do I. We could have ended this war without ever riding out of Lapwai. One crank of a Gatling, while all them d——d Injuns was lined up!

Fifty-two days.

Remember Grande Ronde? We got to meet all them villains then. And Captain Whipple wouldn't never—

He had his orders.

Which one do you believe's the worst?

Toohhoolhoolzote for the certain. He's got the evillest look,
> and a dead puppy, fawn-colored and surely belonging to the hostiles, lies
> on the trail with its head smashed in and flies on its muzzle—more proof
> of Mr. Joe's cruelty.

What are you talking about? From June twenty-third to the first is—

If you'd of asked me, I'd say he's ruled by them coupon-clippers and dove-traders from back East.

And the niggers.

After the Indians, we ought to put them down next, before they forget their place.

I said I count fifty-two days.

Well, it ain't but fifty-one.

He's *a man of moderate calibre.* I did hear an officer characterize him in that way.

Which officer?

None of your business.

We're toiling along without any credit. No glory for anybody.

Excepting our *Christian Soldier,* who's always whistling—

Well, I disagree.

You would.

I think we're making history.

What kind of history?

Well, *the field is the place,* right?

Do you suppose Joseph can be collecting other Indians?

I can't imagine those Indians know how to unite their forces. Because look at them and look at us. One time they owned all this country, and when we finish up they won't have nothing.

D——d right.

And what's our reward?

When we get to town, O, my word, there'd better be some young ladies who admire our brass buttons.

The men will cheer and the boys will shout,
The ladies they will all turn out,
And we'll all feel gay when—

What good would that do us? Mark my words: Behind every gal you'll find an uncle with a Bowie knife to quiz you on your intentions.

Like my Jennie always says, it's no use in longing.

And what was *she* longing for, might I ask?

Shut your filthy mouth,

and just then, caught in sagebrush, a cylindrical basket for berries; before some mule crushed it it might almost have resembled a hollow log—

What's that?

Squaw trash. Some Injun whore must be getting tired.

Is it good for anything?

You just pick that d——d thing up and you'll learn what it's like to be called *squaw man.* Besides, don't you know not to carry any extras but food? That's Marching Rule Number One.

Squaws don't have no hair down there. It's because they're primitive.

It's because all you diddle is ten-year-olds. I seen you that time in Lewiston—

Cut it out about squaws. I want a *woman.*

You'd think the young ladies would be longing for our society.

The men will cheer and the boys will shout,
The ladies they will all turn out—

You sing that nearly as sweet as a negro minstrel.

Are you claiming you enjoy the company of negroes?

They don't hurt nobody. They're just ignorant. They're not wily like Chinamen or hateful like Mr. Joe and his red devils.

Next thing he'll be telling us he's engaged to a nigger!

You ever tried a nigger gal? They call it the jelly roll.

They say General Custer did it with his cooking-wench, who was blacker than—

That's a lie about a great hero!

No it ain't.

Anyhow, they say that the way negro women are are made, they—

No thanks, brother. I'll stick with a nice pink piece of ass! Now, one time when I was in the Gem Saloon in Walla Walla, this blowsy tart strolled in, and she

The men will cheer and Howard will pout

When ladies' skirts turn inside out—

Fuck that God——d Howard! Can't even catch a no-account Indian encumbered with horses and squaws—

Look sharp, villains! He's a-riding up this way—

That's a fine white horse you're riding, soldier. You know, he resembles Jeff Davis's Arabian stallion, which we captured on the way to Cheraw, in Camden, actually.

Thanks, general.

How's his endurance?

Well, sir, he's getting tired . . .

Are you tired?

I, no, sir.

Keep up your best effort. What's your name?

Mulvaney, sir.

A Paddy, are you?

Yessir.

Got a little woman back home, do you?

Yessir.

How long have you been married?

Going on three years, general.

She must be proud of you.

Yessir.

Keep it up, Mulvaney. I'm expecting your best.

Yessir.

Captain, would you please return to the end of the line and ensure that no stragglers have fallen out?

Sure thing, general.

Lieutenant Fletcher, ride up here with me.

Yessir.

Fletch, do you think Colonel Perry is becoming erratic?

Not at all, sir. An admirable officer!

Of course that's what you have to say. I understand you were in the field with him last year.

Yessir. Last September when we scouted the country along the Saint Joseph River, I was lucky enough to be his topographical officer.

Good. Now, Fletch, strictly between you and me, at that time did Colonel Perry show any signs of vacillation or timidity?

None whatever, sir.

Thanks, Fletch. Return to your duties. Lieutenant Bomus, how many of Joseph's horses have we captured to-day?

None, sir. They've all been dead, probably due to these desert conditions—

The Indians do ride them hard, for a fact. Well, how many are currently branded and in service?

Not quite fifty, general. We had to shoot three more this morning.

Have you inventoried them onto Abstract "N"?

Not formally, general, since the situation—

No, you're right; there's no need for make-work. See if Lieutenant Otis can use any new service animals. And ask Jocelyn and Bendire; their companies are slow to-day.

Yessir.

When Captain Fisher comes in, I want a report on Joseph's whereabouts.

I'll tell him, general.

Lieutenant Parnell, is Captain Trimble still satisfied with you?

I hope so, general.

How's Company "H"?

Ready for blood, sir.

How would you rate our Nez Perces?

Well, general, if we keep harassing them, we'll demoralize them and then they'll beg for clemency.

And you're ready to keep harassing them?

Absolutely, sir.

Parnell, you've got "sand"! Carry on. Now, Wood, when's Buffalo Horn expected?

Any time now, sir.

He was having words with Jim, I understand.

You mean Umatilla Jim, sir?

Exactly. Perhaps our Jim's getting too far from home. Do you still trust him?

Not completely, sir.

All right. Well, see if you can find Buffalo Horn, or . . .

Yessir.

    Halt!

        for ten American minutes at streamside so that our troops can throw themselves down, straining drinking water through their dirty shirts, the horses sweating even as they drink; Umatilla Jim dips his filthy neckerchief in the water, then knots it back around his throat, opening his eyes a trifle rounder, instantly letting fall the dribbling corners of his mouth when he spies Colonel Perry,

            to whom he appears as presumptuously knowing as that tall scarred nigger doorman in the girlie place back at Fort Leavenworth:

            the nigger had a way of *seeing* you with an indifference to your continued existence which his steady half-smile (pinned on, no doubt, by the education of his slave years) pretended to deny, and although he generally sat near-motionless in that cane chair he could move pretty d——d fast to knock a man out as easy as emptying chamberpots, not that he ever scared

me; I do confess it pleasured my soul to see him crack that
one-legged corporal over the head when he pulled a Bowie
knife on Mollie for nothing more than being the whore she
was, because I was just as fond of her as the next man,

    which must have been why I remembered her when I
    first saw Theller's wife and she was wearing that green
    dress whose stuff must have come from someplace spe-
    cial back East,

and by GOD I wouldn't have tolerated her being murdered; all
the same, to stand by when a nigger does a white man violence is sickening—another reason why I can't respect the
general with all his pro-nigger talk; I'd like to see *him* take
orders from some stinking four-star Ethiopian!

    I disagree, Fletch. Gibbon was at Antietam, and
    he says that in absolute terms our casualties at Big
    Hole, however unfortunate, were *insignificant,*

while Jim, watching Perry whenever Perry is not watching him,
considers the following in his heart:

I have now been trying to become him,

    this one whose heart will always hate me although I
    have fought beside him in war

        —unlike Cut Arm, who pleases his heart by wish-
        ing to help me

        (Cut Arm is nothing)—

and two instants after Wilkinson has finished repainting his knapsack with tar they are moving out again in columns of four, with the
wagons behind them, the horses coughing and sneezing dust,

    deserters under arrest creeping along at the rear,

        soon to be returned to service after punishment detail,

and that bitter odor of yarrow,

    sickening Wood ever so slightly, since he has begun to associ-
    ate it with the dug-up children at Big Hole:

        Buffalo Horn's bunch scalped even those little ones—
        and they told me Joseph was the one who burned
        women!

            —as doubtless he did, LORD knows; and I won't
            forget Mrs. Manuel and those other Salmon River
            people,

            nor will I forget this; I am disgusted in my nos-
            trils—

            yet I do believe that the general can and will teach
            me that we were not wrong; for *he* is good, and
            even Fletch insists that it was for the best

(I wonder what Umatilla Jim truly thinks?),
aspens outstretching their arms over the whitish-green grass, and
then sagebrush and scree as the land rises away from the river:

Guy, ride ahead with me now, would you? Just up to that mound yonder and we can . . .

Is your arm paining you, father?

Well, I do notice it.

Shall I wash it for you?

Perhaps to-night. Now, how are you getting along?

Excellently. I'm enjoying the adventure and making a lot of friends. I wish we could send word to Mother that we're all right.

The ladies they will all turn out—

She's a soldier's wife. She and Mrs. Perry can shore up each other's spirits.

Why wouldn't Mrs. Theller remove to Portland?

Her folks are from California. I believe she wants to take her husband's remains there once this business is finished.

And we'll all feel gay when—

The enlisted men are getting tired, father.

Don't I know it! As soon as they go into action they'll be all right. First class men!— Son, we can keep chatting, but now we had better keep riding along.

What was the story you began to tell me this morning?

Which story?

About the cotton. And then Colonel Perry came to you and wanted—
a white-breasted, white-throated prairie dog standing erect, folding in its little arms diagonally across its breast.

O yes. Both armies were burning the cotton, you see. The Confederates seemed to think that we, being Yankees, wanted it for gain, and we believed that the Confederate government depended on this staple as the foundation for their revenue, so we burned it. One or the other of the parties was evidently making a mistake. That's how war is, Guy. So much waste.

All war?

I'm afraid so.

But how can this war be any less than essential? We have to punish those murderers and put the rest on a reservation.

That's right. We have our orders.

So where's the waste?

Every tipi that we burn on suspicion, every white man *they* kill simply because he's white . . .

But how in GOD's name could that be alleviated except by ending the war?

I would say through gestures of goodwill. Because— You there! *Unclose that wagon.*

General, there ain't nothing in here but—

Lieutenant Howard, get Mr. Calloway.

Right away, general.

Yes, General Howard, what can I do for you?

Mr. Calloway,

who wears a stovepipe hat as high as the pommel of a squaw saddle (what a dandy volunteer he makes! He's going to eat Joseph for breakfast, guaranteed!)

this man of yours declines to obey my direct order.

General, I'll bet he didn't mean no harm. It's mighty dry out here and—

Unclose that wagon.

Mikey, you heard the general. Open up your wagon.

Now open the bench box, doublequick.

See, general? Only ropes, leather and grub—

Now, what's in that barrel? Don't pretend it's molasses.

General, it's my own supply.

Whiskey, isn't it?

Well, actually it's rum . . . *general.*

Dump it out. Mr. Calloway, I'm going to count ten. If that man hasn't dumped out his rum by the time I reach ten, he'll be punished. *One.*

Do as the general says.

General, it's nothing but Blackfoot quality, hardly no more than—

Two,

the mules now lifting their ears and narrowing their strangely sweet dark eyes.

Right now, Mikey.

Three. All right. You're Michael O'Malley, aren't you?

That's who I am—*general.*

You're infamous in Bannock City. If you weren't a volunteer I'd have your pay. As it is, I'll confiscate your mules, traps and everything if you're in trouble again. Have you sold any liquor to my soldiers to-day?

No, sir.

If I find out you're lying, you'll be carried in irons. That's all. You can close up the wagon again. Mr. Calloway, make sure your men know about this. I mean business.

O, they'll hear about it pretty quick, general.

That Puritanic tyrant!

Watch it now. He's giving us the evil eye.

2

Look at them officers just sitting on their hams while we—

I'll bet it was Lieutenant Wilkinson who tattled on Mikey.

D——d Bible-kisser—

Like his master—

Where's Doc?

Doing business with Red O'Donnell.

And I'll bet you we have to bring in Crook
or Miles before Mr. Joe ever sees the gallows. Because Uh-Oh Howard—

Now, the Crows will pay a horse for seventy-five pretty earring-
shells. Jim helped me ask them—

Umatilla Jim?

That's right.

I think he's becoming my favorite Indian. Never complains or
fails to do his part.

He's teaching me sign language.

Show me how to say *woman*.

O, no, I shouldn't have castled . . .

What's done is done, Fletch.

Then I'll take your queen,

just like when your Colonel Miles tried to steal away the Indian
Territory from old Mackenzie and General Sherman stepped in—

Lieutenant, I'd be grateful if you said nothing against Colonel
Miles. He's not only our general; he's our hero.

No offense, lieutenant.

None taken.

So how is it out at Tongue River?

Pretty cold come winter. Other than that, not bad.

What about Sitting Bull?

O, he's dusted across the line, for now, anyway.

Fine. Checkmate.

A very pretty termination, Wood.

Thank you, general.

Was that a Scotch gambit?

Pretty near, sir. And what makes it hilarious is that Fletch taught me this
manoeuvre himself!

Just sitting on their hams, I said,

not unlike those grimy grim troopers, bearded like ancient men,
with stinking slouch hats pulled low over their sunburned foreheads and their eyes watching out of brim-shadow,

whereas Redington, who would sometimes rather be a cowboy
and who when he is alone likes to practice roping boulders
and saplings, is proud to have escaped from our command,
riding away across the grass until the train of mule wagons
reduces itself into a line of snake vertebrae with ragged flaps
of flesh, our cavalry, infantry and guns, not yet rotted off.

Some days he gets far enough away to assert to himself: For
all I know, the whole GoDd——d command has retreated,

in which case this happy war *could* go on forever!
Picketing his horse within reach, unrolling his blanket on the
ground, pillowing his head on his saddle, Redington, whose
tastes are simple, yearns for a sweet harlot with a turquoise
choker around her long white neck,

although even an Indian bitch would do;
the sun ripening Wood's sorrows, and the jewel-like glare as Guy
burnishes his Colt warming up the resentments of that proportion
of our soldiers who are in fact the merest runaway thieves and gold-
greedy vagabonds, maybe even almost Communists,

among them, naturally, Doc, who now broods again upon that
August afternoon at Farewell Bend when, wishing to slit Blurick's throat and get his barefoot whiskey, or even merely
break one spoke out of his wheel if he could but calculate how
to get away with it, which he could not, he bent down to splash
water over his sweaty hair and saw intermittently vanishing
and trembling the reflection of his grey-stubbled sunburned
face! Shocked by the extent to which this season's ride down
the Trail had aged him, he jerked his gaze away and across that
entire lukewarm, still and wide river which bore on its muddy
blue skin the fiery-orange reflections of the blackish-orange
ridges back there in Idaho, each sagebrush clump an upside-
down greenness upon the floating desertscape of sunshine or
shimmering copper foil, another wagon-train of gold-seekers
on the eastern horizon, a whole camp of them on the Idaho
shore—churned mud, mosquitoes and flies, shouting drivers
unceasing—and then our camp and a dozen more over here in
Oregon: mosquitoes by the river singing, mosquitoes in the
cottonwood shade, cattle bleeding at the nose, curses and
fights, campfires, turds everywhere, children crying, fevers
settling as soft as the cottonwood down in the grass. For all of
this, Blurick would be to blame, forever,

because what can I get now, what can I get, I'm old, and
if I could have had but one friend (for I don't count Wilbur), then it all could have come out right, but I'm going
to fix myself good in Wallowa and then don't see if I
won't prove myself more alive than any other man on
this GoDd——d stinking earth!
—none of them, I happily confess, incapable of being put to service
by the beautifully automatic machinery of our Government, which
will screw down Joseph's heart into goodness.

You'd better shut it, because our *Christian Soldier*'s on his way over here.

He's what?

Well, boys, still enjoying the soldier's life?

Yessir.

When we whip Joseph, I'll remember good service.

Yessir.

Who's that dickering with our Bannocks over there? Is that Jim?

Injun Jim? Yessir; he's been—

All right, boys. At ease.

What sign?

Another dead Indian pony in that draw down there, colonel, sir.

Looks like they ate some of it. Not so fresh; the vermin are at it.

Well, don't slack off.

Yessir.

Watch out for that cactus. If you fall into one and get enough spines in your face, you're a goner.

How do you know?

I heard about a man it happened to.

Yeah? I'll bet you a round silver dollar you don't know his name.

That one in the big slouch hat, Fletch, he's like all them cattle drovers we used to see all over Washington in the grand old war days. Kind of joys me to see that type again.

Yessir. You mean that Mr. Calloway?

Yep. How do you suss him out?

Well, captain, I'd say he's trouble. He doesn't respect our general.

Loyal to the core, ain't you?

Yes I am, Captain Jocelyn, *sir.*

All right. So you must be against Mr. Chapman, too.

Sir, I don't know about that.

Excuse me, Colonel Perry. General Howard would like to see your Sick-Book to-night.

What in hell for?

I think he's trying to estimate our present effective strength.

All right, Wood. I'll get it to him as soon as we encamp.

Thank you, colonel. I'll tell the general.

Sorry to bother you again, gentlemen, but when you get an instant, Fletch, would you send Jim to me?

Right away, general. Will you be in your tent?

That's right.

Good evening, Jim. Thanks for coming. How's everything?

Fine, general.

What's new with Chief Joseph?

His bunch are tired, general. I saw them to-day. Many wounded, and some sad children crying. But they still ride fast.

Joseph's a wonder, isn't he? The *Red Napoleon!*

Yessir.

How are your lot getting along with the Bannocks?

Not bad. We talk sign.

Give me an example.

Well,

> locking down his thumb against the second joint of his index finger, which assemblage points forward out of his closed fist,

this means *cartridge.* You see, general, the Bannocks want to trade for cartridges. They—

How many cartridges do you have, Jim?

O, just one or two every now and then that I beg off Lieutenant Fletcher, so I can defend myself.

How many do you have right now?

I got seven, general. I hope you're not distrusting me, because I did volunteer to chase Joseph.

I trust you, Jim. Now, what do our Bannocks want with cartridges?

Same as me.

But you've given them none?

That's right, general.

And you'll give them none? Promise me.

Sure, general. I promise.

All right, Jim. You can go.

> Sure is hot to-day.
>
> Well, maybe it'll be hotter to-morrow

CAMAS MEADOWS
AUGUST 19–20

1

*T*hey've gone up the north sweep of the meadow, general.

Their trail's hard to miss. Send for Buffalo Horn, if you please.

Yessir.

Wood, I'll need a clean copy of that letter to General Sherman.

Here it is, sir.

Thank you. We'll be camping on that knoll yonder.

The one like a castle, sir?

That's right. And I'll want the guards and pickets farther out to-night, despite the terrain. Norwood's cavalry ought to be on the west side. Calloway's volunteers can camp across the first stream if their precious town meeting permits them to do anything.

I'll pass on those orders, sir:

> *Plant the guidon!*

>> Yessir,

>>> our American flag now anchored on the ridge.

General, shall I post the infantry in reserve by the creek there?

That's fine, Mason.

Men are looking pretty tired, sir. I saw some puking on the trail—

I know. That's Indian service for you. Fletch, please take this note to Norwood. No, Guy, I'd better verify that first. Buffalo Horn, a fine evening to you, my friend. How are you holding up?

Very good, General Howard.

So you saw Joseph's Indians yesterday?

They were all here

> (his eyes shining like the rising and falling scalpels in a candle-lit field hospital).

Did they see you?

I don't think so.

Where are they now?

Well, general, maybe fifteen miles up that way

> as the cavalry and infantry creep wearily in, a hundred ten paces to the minute, waiting for the cool time when the yellow desert prairie will go green in the evening light:

>> *Fall in!*

> (Guy absentmindedly scratching his ankle through the wrinkled cavalry boot, his young face fixed wide-eyed and frowning upon this Indian):

>> *Roll call*

>>> (Mason and Sladen disagreeing about something; I won't interfere).

>> *Right face—*
>> *break ranks—*
>> *dismissed!*

and our muleteers breaking up the train, Red O'Donnell singing out some long ballad from the old country as they all hand down cargo bags,

uncinching the *aparejos*, peeling saddleblankets off their animals'
   shining, reeking backs,
   his sunburned soldiers falling out, glued to earth by their own sweaty
   dust.
Do you know this for sure?
I followed them. They mean to cross the pass.
Buffalo Horn, you're a very fine scout. Now go and get some rest.
I don't need any, general.
   And then with the light greening the golden sagebrush, the buttes stand-
   ing out, the sky finally bluer than blue-white
      O bury me not on the lone prair-ee
      Where them wild wild coyotes are howlin' over me
      In my narrow grave just six by three
   and to the north the pale blue mountains
   and the green willows and brown creeks where someday American cows
   will safely browse.
Gentlemen, what's your opinion of Buffalo Horn?
Seems to be a loyal Indian, sir.
Very young, isn't he?
And quite extravagantly decked out, sir,
   as the light suddenly decreases from glaring to dazzling, the sun now but
   a finger and a half above the mountains.
I suspect he's becoming quite attached to us.
Yes, sir.
Ah, good; there go Trimble's pickets
   across the low outcroppings as the rifle echoes and the bugle blows "Retreat," losing themselves in sagebrush, then ahead a sad stand of green
   forest, demeaned by the desert with the mountains so close now, green
   below and then bluish-grey and reddish-grey above in the twilight
   of small aspens so white and graceful, a dimple of sun on every leaf, and
   the leaves red-flecked in the northwest corner of the lava mound.
Orderly, you can pitch the tent now. Mind the poison oak.
      Ain't hardly no game hereabouts even as big as a mocking-
      bird.
Yes, sir.
Well, gentlemen, any card-games for you to-night?
Maybe one quick round of whist, sir. Guy, what do you say?
I'm nearly done in. Honestly, I'm not half the man my father is—
You flatter me, boy.
General, here's the ordnance tally you asked for.
Thanks, lieutenant.
Getting dark, sir.

Yes it is.

No sense asking Wood,

> who is still reading *The Old-Fashioned Girl* by Mrs. Alcott, sewing another patch on his uniform, then writing a poem
>
>> because the loneliness of rockscapes surpasses the loneliness of forests, yet it's less eerie, more serene; how shall I word it? What religion's in it? None in the first stanza; that's for certain! When we catch Joseph I hope to quiz him about the Indian faith. I'd best approach him when the general's not around,
>
> his notebook resting upon the taut-spread skirts of his greatcoat.
>
>> Blackie, there's trout in the creek!

It's all right, Fletch. If you can't get a partner I'll play.

Mighty white of you. Come on, Guy. Just one hand with me.

Agreed.

Then may the best man win! Orderly, could you please make clean copies of both slips? Thank you. Well, I think I'll stretch my legs and admire the view.

You're a man of iron, sir!

—Laughing, he strolls over the crest.

Good evening, soldier. Why isn't your horse saddled and bridled?

His back was getting galled, general, so I was fixing to rub him down—

With what?

Well, general, I was—

Soldier,

> you're as dirty as one of our vagabond shavetails who enlist only to get
>
>> through the winter and then run away to the gold fields, so

what's your name?

Josiah Smith, general.

With Company "L," I see.

Yessir.

Soldier, you know that when on duty with the supports, you're to keep your horse saddled and bridled. If Joseph attacked right now, you'd be no good to all of us who are counting on you. That's a serious offense. Where's Captain Whipple?

Up thataway, seeing to the pickets, general.

Get your horse in order right now.

Yessir. Please, general, sir, I'm already in trouble—

For what?

When my horse kicked me, general, I—

You allowed your horse to kick you? You shouldn't be in the cavalry. Whatever Captain Whipple may see fit to do to you, I'll tell you this: I'm going up that hill there. When I reach the top, I'm going to turn around. If your horse isn't in full trim, I'll have you arrested.

His arm-stump is already annoying him again. He strides out toward the pickets, gazing into the hill where Joseph's Indians must be, there where through some trick of dusk the topmost arid mountains are becoming more conspicuous in the sky. Biting insects swarm around the horses. In the scalelessness of that hot white sky they could be the silhouettes of high-flying birds.

I'm starting to have nightmares about his hateful eyes. Am I losing my "sand"? Must never let anyone know—

but the air chills, the lava pavement darkens; and that circle of darkness begins to widen on the sagebrush prairie all around:

If you were here, Lizzie,

your eyes burning within mine

and far away the grass and

a doe with her fawn and

What a delightful open view!

(devouring the lime-green, almost odorless aspen leaves: broad, lobular, pointed at the tip,

sagebrush bleeding white in the twilight).

I fear that if we don't get him soon, the men will start to say . . .

and now the lake goes *grey,* and the sagebrush greyer than greyish-white, so he turns sadly back toward his soldiers

(a hundred and fifty-odd effectives to-night, Lieutenant Bacon's detachment being absent):

my heart is good

and in that instant, the sun goes red, deforming into a pear, banded with blue by the cloud it glows through; and the air now almost freezes the backs of the soldiers' sweaty necks.

We'll do well to collect our strength to-night. Since Buffalo Horn's feeling so strong and proud, I'll send him out for more definite news of Joseph,

sky and mountains lost to each other, still peach-colored back where the soldiers came from,

the eastern enemy mountains now shades of blue.

OUR FATHER Who art

as white as aspens in the dusk

hallowed be

the white glint of a creek winding through the sagebrush at twilight, and the sweetly birdlike voices of prairie dogs,

then the red moon coming so rapidly over the purple ridge, mottled dark, rising almost perceptibly, so huge; and just as his gaze rises in expectation, it clears the ridge and comes into the sky

and now the world's a silhouette under the western sky, dust in the evening, the coyotes singing,

the sky nearly as dark as the blue-backed Webster's spelling book Gracie used to carry to school

(has she found a beau yet? Please, GOD, don't let her die an old maid)
and
then the moon turning orange with horizontal bands of darkness across
it as it rises into stripes of cloud.

You see that, Doc?

Sure do. Shinin' just like silver, like that song says—

Hey, Doc, can I—

When's taps?

We've been tenting to-night on the old camp ground,
Thinking of days gone by,
Of the loved ones at home that gave us the hand,
And the tear that said, "Good-bye!"

What did you see out there, father?

Nothing. And what have all of you been looking at through your field-glasses?

Mars. This is actually the closest it's been all century—

Fletch, was it you who told me that our new telescope at Washington has
found a Martian moon, and possibly two?

That's right, general—

And there's Venus, I believe. Lieutenant Wood, you're the most fanatical star-
gazer among us, aren't you?

It seems so, sir. I wonder if we'll ever find means to voyage there.

To Venus?

Yessir.

Still the dreamer!

Yessir.

Thinking of days gone by . . .

No, Fletch. Save your revenge for to-morrow.

So you beat him, did you?

Just barely, father. A tip of the scales—

Where's the orderly?

Scrubbing the frying pan, sir.

Never mind. Wood, you seem to be incubating some happy thought.

Tenting to-night—tenting to-night on the old camp ground,
tying the mules to the wagons, hobbling the bell-mares of each
pack train.

Well, general . . .

Something connected with your literary efforts?

Actually, sir, I was just deciding
to buy Nanny some fine gauze underwear like the sort I saw by
mistake that time in Madam Gillison's shop, and then I'll rip them
off her and wait for her to give me *the look* so that I know
to take off my pants to-night, as this is so safe a place.

Tenting to-night—

You're right. Joseph can do us no harm here. What do you say, Guy?

Tenting on the old camp ground—

I lent my pistol to a scout just now, so of course the Indians will come back!

Tenting to-night—

Ha, a pessimist! Well, gentlemen, chance it as you like. I think I'll leave off the pantaloons for once. Shall we turn in?

Tenting to-night—

Well, sir, if those volunteers would just be quiet—

Thinking of days gone by—

2

He awakes to night gunfire, and for much less than a second (which endures an hour) feels as betrayed and bewildered as on that July Fourth in Livermore when, exhausted by heat, nausea and the speeches of brother patriots, having already accompanied Lizzie and the children to the livestock show, the stench of prize goats and outhouses impelling him near about to fainting, heat glaring and dazzling on him like sun on cast iron, he excused himself for a quarter-hour because his stump had commenced throbbing in time with his heart, as why would it not?

Forward!

Forward,

to be free without servility,

the militiamen's white and red pompoms as gruesome
as wounded flesh,

James shrieking in his sister's arms (should get him fresh
cow's milk), Chauncey fast asleep on Lizzie's lap,

but where is all this?

A despatch station on the east shore of the Chick-
ahominy, right on their York River Railroad—

Yessir.

General, sir, you had better dismount and lead your
horses, for the dead and wounded are here.

Do I still have my arm?

Yessir.

And then if you go south, see, there's Bottom's Bridge
on the Seven-Mile Road—o, excuse me, general.

At ease. A hot night.

Yessir. General, sir, you're going to lose your arm.

All right. Miles, is that our picket line?

Another quarter-mile yet, general, but I fear you'll lose
your arm to-morrow.

General, your arm!

O, sir!

on this great occasion, even as our sons, brothers, husbands and fathers, rich men and poor, lay down their lives on the slaughter-field so that this America distilled out of Indians, women, corn-fields and armies may endure forever in despite of all those wicked Secceshes who would have burned our dear old Constitution to ashes, which is why our own native son, General Oliver Otis Howard, who as you see has already offered up a piece of his mortal body for a sacrifice upon the altar of Liberty, has come to tell all you folks to-day that

His soul goes marching on,
but why is my white glove red?
To arms! To arms! To arms, in Dixie!

An old woman in a Quaker cap stretched out her hands to him; he closed his eyes. Now came the parade, their rifle-barrels gleaming like thunderheads in the evening sky of Big Hole, Montana, but why couldn't there be a breeze? The maple leaves were drooping on the trees. Dust and sweat smelled fouler to him than ever before. This sepsis must be pretty well developed. Shall I see the doctor again? Lizzie doesn't understand why I won't take calomel. I'm sure my condition's less painful than any woman's lying-in. *In pain thou shalt bear children,* to recompense Eve's sin. These were the days and nights when she very lovingly kept up poulticing his wound, so that it seemed that the two of them would be intimately happy forever, the two elder children watching round-eyed, whispering: *Papa's sick. Where's Papa's arm?* Now Gracie was begging for an ear of Indian corn, which had come in early this year, doubtless on account of the heat. Lizzie didn't wish her to have it; he pitied the child, and thought the favor innocuous, but would not go against his wife. O, dear JESUS, please help me to endure the misery of my wound. Must practice writing with my left arm; to-night I'll despatch a letter to Miles, asking how his foot is coming along. Will they need to amputate? And is this all there is to life? Our FATHER, Who art in Heaven, O, my JESUS, I wish to be strong before these good people who know nothing about war. Well, our old soldiers marching here with their flintlock muskets, they know. A Winchester rifle is lighter than a Sharps, and practically any rifle is lighter than a flintlock musket, as I have occasion to know, and ten muskets are nothing compared to the weight of this missing arm of mine; dear sweet LORD, help me clear my mind, for the sake of my family and all these people here. The world swung clockwise and counterclockwise; is this what drunkards experience? Shall I take calomel after all? FATHER, give me strength. Guy, who being halfway through that interesting interval between six and seven should have outgrown such behavior, was pounding on his toy drum; his father smiled at him, scarcely able to endure the noise. A child vomited on the grass, at which flies arose from nowhere. He sat on a bench beneath the big elm tree while Lizzie refreshed the stump with carbolic acid; now Gracie was rocking James again and entertaining him most sweetly. What a dear child; I must never let on that she's my favorite—although once Guy grows up a little I may love him best. Rowland had despatched his re-grets; unfortunately some irregularity occurred at his church. Charley and his family must already have arrived, Guy being suddenly out of sight; well, the boy wouldn't go far. He was still shy of his father, not having seen him for a year. Ador-ing the child, the father kept his distance, as he would have with a new horse.

That's my Papa! He got his arm cut off in the war. Uncle Charley said he didn't even cry—

All right, Guy, that's enough. So you like that new drum of yours, do you?
Yes, Papa. Papa, who's your best friend?
Mama is.
And after her?
General Sherman. I pray you get to meet him someday. Lizzie darling, you look wilted in the heat,

in the family way again. If it's a boy we should name him Chauncey, or was Chauncey already born? Yes, he was, the day after I lost my arm. So where is he and why is this not right? If I am dreaming how can I prove it?

Let me take James for awhile—
But how can you, dearest? I mean—
I have to learn how to manage sometime.
You're very sweet. Don't worry; he's asleep now, don't you see?

A fat-cheeked, spoiled little boy being led on a pony didn't know how good he had it. Charley boy was recovering well; I'll feel ashamed if he returns to the line before me. I can nearly feel my phantom arm. Lizzie helped him pin to his breast that silver-plated medal badge with its all-seeing eye shining and glittering with rays: **THE UNION MUST AND SHALL BE PRESERVED.** Guy chased a seagull; honey-haired Gracie waved her American flag uncomprehendingly, after which he was introduced, most fulsomely I do admit, by a typical officer of the old school:

Where's Miles?

Dixie Dixie Dixie Dixie Dixie Dixie

Dixie

General—

Dixie Dixie

after which he commenced his own speech, calling upon the men of Maine to fill their quota of volunteers (several ladies already wearing black, I see):

Hurrah,

hurrah,

James sleeping open-mouthed in his mother's lap, Gracie staring up at her Papa, not having realized before that he was famous like JESUS

(sometimes she played with Guy's marbles, pretending that each one had a soul which could die:

Hurrah,
 hurrah!)
　　the sun more sickening than the lightning-glow within an
　enemy cannon's mouth,
　　and now let us bow our heads in prayer for our dear Republic:
　　hurrah!
after which he thankfully commenced toward Lizzie by descending a flight of
stairs, dizzy and on the verge of vomiting (Guy must have run off to Charley boy
again)—and slipped—and, beginning to fall, reached for the railing with the hand
which had been rotting among the surgeon's tidbits for a month now, and hence
did fall, O JESUS, striking the ground stump-first, the pain as loud as a shot (did a
picket fire the alarm?) and
　　　JESUS, dearest JESUS, I will not cry out—
　Thank GOD for the protection of that leather patch—
　　　　　　O JESUS
　　　the nightmare realized
　　　　　(mostly light carbines and one buffalo gun so far, but
　　　　　what if it's a diversion?)
　　the skirmishing still as indistinct as the dark scratches on his own dark
　belt—where did the moon go?
　Father, lie down or you'll be hit!
　　　　To arms!
　flickering lamplight, clatter of pistol belts,
　　　　To arms!
　and at once, that high "G" trumpeting out over and over, then the fast
　repeated triplets, then again the high "G" like an alarm:
　　　　　　For GOD's sake, men!
　　my cold bare feet
　　　　(the roar and reddish-violet flash of a Springfield)
　　and bullets humming through the wagons:
　　　Indians! Indians!
　　　　Sir, they've driven in our pickets—
　　my canvas overalls thankfully warm and dry as I pull them back up and
　　　Load with cartridges; load! Fire at will:
　　　　our guns flashing like stars!
　Well, Guy, I notice that *you're* not lying down. Shouldn't have lent that scout
your pistol, boy! Wood, have you forgotten how to put your pants on? All right,
let's go form the lines. No panic now. Come on, men! Don't disgrace your flag!
　　and that *Indian yell:*
　　　　Well, now. Ain't they as shrill as a heap of gut-shot mules!
　　　　Where are they, sarge? I can't *see* them red devils—
　　　They dodged in behind our reserves—
　　　　To horse!

Sir, the trumpeter's—
Over there,
cranking one Gatling with a will, and:
Look sharp now! You dropped your d——d percussion caps!
Sir, the line's given way—
(more blood-red rifle-flashes)
Please, father, lie close!
O, no, I must be up for this! Nothing can be better, if they'll only stay and give
us a battle—
So he's tricked me again! And now it seems as if I *knew* that he would, yet
sought this new disgrace—
(GOD will school me by means of my failures
but dear FATHER, if this must be our Last Stand, I
I)
Here they come—
*Fire! Fire! Fire, GOD*d——*n you!*
Over here, sir!
—(red and yellow explosions)—
Calloway's been killed.
Brooks took one—
Shot in the face with that buffalo gun!
No, he's—
Major Sandford, saddle up the cavalry.
General, sir, our volunteers are getting overwhelmed—
Why aren't I surprised? How many casualties?
Well, general—
Come on! They're getting us!
How shall I meet this threatening movement? If Joseph's plotted another
fiendish ambuscado,
Little Big Horn or White Bird Cañon—
Sir, the Indians have run our mules off.
The DEVIL you say!
Where's Buffalo Horn?
Sir, they
General, sir, they stole the mules!
Who did? The scouts?
Joseph and his—
Who's the officer of the day?
Captain Trimble, sir.
Is that the Indians coming across?
I think that's Calloway—
Are you sure?
. . . attacking our ammunition packs—

Hey you, Calloway!
Don't shoot! Don't shoot!
Now *that's* the Indian yell all right.
Fire at will.
So dark I—
Did you get him?
Don't seem to check 'em much—
Forward!
Forward!

On the flank of the command . . .

Horses won't behave.

Then tie their heads together.

Yessir.

Well, boys, we're peppering away right merrily. Maybe they'll bag Mr. Joe.
Yessir.

. . . Digging rifle-pits with their knives but the soil's mighty hard . . .
Wood, tell Captain Trimble to lay down his reserves in a line until daybreak.
Right away, sir.

I'd swear an oath it was Looking-Glass! And then he crawfished
into the scrub down there—

All right, Guy, take me to Norwood's wagons.
This way, father,
and within the night something touches him, something as velvety as the
skin of a poplar tree, and
I see our herd stampeding away, there by the first stream—
Yessir.
Where's Major Sandford?
Here, general.
All right. Take command of Norwood's, Carr's and Jackson's companies—

That ain't nothin'. Just a skin wound. Don't funk.

Yessir.
Recover the service animals. Go as soon as you're ready.
Yessir. Forward!
Forward!

as the moon takes on the yellowness of a bone breastplate.

Captain Wells, mount your artillery on that knoll yonder. Dig in your infantry,
who now fill the night with clatter and clamor, frantically piling up the
reddish lava-stones into semicircular or circular emplacements less than
knee high, and
Yessir.
Bendire, Wagner, saddle up your cavalry at once.
Yessir.
And now, gentlemen, we may as well take our breakfast,

spreading out our square of canvas here among the poison oak on that
sagebrush knoll, looking down north into a line of aspen and then a wash,
while we await Major Sandford's results. They say excitement's good for the diges-
tion. What do you think, Fletch?

Well, general, I don't rightly know—

(They look to me to do something instantaneously. As if anything
could possibly erase our negligence of last night!

I remember General Grant imperturbably smoking his cigar
at the battle's edge. We were all in suspense then, of course,
but nobody glared indignantly at him as they eternally do at
me, as cross as Homili's yellow Indian dogs, demanding to
know why the move out hasn't sounded! *Why am I different?*)

Did you hear that .44? a-comin' between
those rocks? Sure that was Ollicut.

Says who?

James Reuben swears it up and down. Got
me this brass for a souvenir.

Well, James Reuben's nothing to me.

General, sir, Major Sandford reports that Joseph has turned his left, and—

Gentlemen, we'll have to abandon our breakfast. Quickly now. Captain Wagner, Lieutenant Otis, await my signal. Wilkinson, ride ahead to reconnoiter
Sandford's line. Be careful.

Right away, sir,

sad to depart the commissary wagon's coffee-steam, I see.

Captain Wells, you take the right.

Yessir.

Move out!

Move out!

into the dying darkness and
my aching eyeballs

But if Joseph ran off our animals,
why can't I stop dreaming?

Sandford bears watching. Did he have something going with
Calloway? Must ask Fletch

because this setting moon shines like lovely sweat, the sweat on
Lizzie's throat when she was young and

Sorry, captain. I thought I saw something in that lava
bed.

O, it was only a scare.

We've repulsed 'em, boys! Give 'em another!
Hurrah!

and another volley, red and yellow in the
night,

enemy fire fading away,
and another *Indian yell*, closer than might
have been expected—
General, we'd better—
Watch out!
Where's Carr's company?
Sir, I—
Captain, sir, the hostiles must have run the mules
thisaway—
will I die this night and never see her again? It doesn't feel like
it. Well, what *do* I feel? I'm all in a
blue fog over the camas prairie at dawn, the men coughing, exhausted
and dirty, an unseemly number stopping to shit their guts out:
There they are, on the horizon there—
Ain't that Ollicut's horse?
One of Jackson's killed, and one of Carr's wounded,
but—
Major, how far away would you say they are?
Near about four miles, general—
a weary private discharging his gun by accident and therefore liable to
punishment;
and full morning, under whose tutelage the lava-founded sagebrush
swales go orange and grey, then by degrees green and grey:
and day, with a painful white horizon-line in the east, as if some salt lake
might be there—thus the battle's residuum presents itself, revealing
What's this? Why are they retreating? O, it's Major Sandford. Well, where's
Norwood?
General, that's what I'm trying to find out. They turned his left and—
What? You didn't leave him, did you?
There's Indians hiding right there in the aspens, sir, taking aim—
That's enough. Forward now!
into basalt like the cinders in the blacksmith's shop and then the sun as
they descend into a blue-grey bowl of dusty prairie, which turns purple-
blue, then olive, then green; the ground clear of any significant hostile
force:
O, GOD, o JESUS, o, no, no . . .
And because they've driven the mules into the mountains . . .
Lieutenant Benson's been hit, sir, and five enlisted—
All right. Mason, I'm told that Joseph's turned Sandford's left.
Unfortunately, that's so, general.
Yes, Wilkinson, what is it?
Sandford's right's also been turned, sir; there was a danger of his being trapped,
so he—

Then what?

Too difficult for Norwood to withdraw, so he dug in—

Well, I'm glad there's one man out there anyhow.

Excuse me, sir, but it's got to be thisaway,

> gashing their ankles on the lava, starting up a deer, sipping hot foul water
> from their canvas-skinned bottles,

because that's where Mr. Joe attacked:

> *No, no . . . JESUS, o, no; I can't stand it; o, my GOD, o, o—*

You there, rectify your formation.

Yessir.

There they are, sir, among those cottonwoods—

> *O JESUS, o, GOD, please, o, o, o, JESUS—*

So that must be Norwood's wounded up here.

That's right, general. Doctor Alexander's riding up now—

> *O JESUS, o, no! JESUS, JESUS, JESUS!*

How many?

Six wounded and one dead, sir.

> If I had Joseph in my hands right now I'd

General, Bendire's gone back thataway, because—

JESUS, JESUS! O—

Who was killed?

Brooks, sir. Captain Jackson's bugler—

O yes. His favorite.

And three or four others seem likely to pass on, sir, because—

You're shot in the lung, looks like.

General, Buffalo Horn advises us to chase the enemy.

Well, how far away are they?

He says maybe ten miles. Over by that Henry Lake—

> *O, my GOD—*

Return to camp. Joseph's bested us again.

3

Gentlemen, Joseph made a moderate demonstration against our lines. He startled us, which ought to be both a disgrace and a lesson. But the fact is that he failed to gain his very modest object. With the exception of a few mules and three horses, the service animals are back in our possession. Please pass on these thoughts to your individual commands. There will be an inspection in thirty minutes, followed by a funeral service. That will be all. Captain Trimble, I'd like you remain a moment with me.

Yessir.

Well, Trimble, this could have put us out of business.

Yessir.

The loss of those wagon-mules leaves us half crippled. We can't keep up with Joseph until we resupply.

General, I—

You were officer of the day.

Yessir.

Do you have anything to say?

No, sir.

In our service, Trimble, the responsible innocent suffer for the irresponsible guilty. You know this as an old soldier.

Yessir.

You're one of the most dependable officers in this command. That can't help you this morning. Substitutive penalties in military affairs are expedient, Trimble. By them men learn to govern their fellows.

Yessir. The responsibility's mine. I know I've let you down—

And all of us.

Yessir.

Volunteers don't understand this principle, of course. That's why a soldier such as yourself is worth ten of them.

General, I'm so sorry I can hardly—

Once at West Point when I was cadet officer of the day, the superintendent punished me because I was unable to end some disorder of the men beneath me. I found it unpleasant.

Yessir.

LORD, that was more than a quarter-century ago! Nearly thirty years—

Yessir.

Trimble, did I ever tell you that Robert E. Lee's son was in my class?

I've heard it said, sir.

You were at Gettysburg! And you allowed this to happen . . .

My fault, sir.

> So it is, Trimble, just as it was mine when I found myself unable to wish
> away the fact that for whatever reason my Eleventh Corps retreated at
> Gettysburg; I still don't know why. I will never tell you this.

Well, have you established yet how Joseph was able to get through?

Yessir. Strange to say, the mules didn't act restless beforehand. He—

I want a full report in an hour, explaining this incident and detailing the punishments meted out to those who were derelict.

Right away, sir.

Trimble, I'm going to reduce you from captain to second lieutenant, effective immediately. Do you have any comment?

No, sir.

> So I'm censured. Will I get cashiered? Perry must be gloating.

Good. I'll suspend your reduction for the time being. If you make amends for your mistake by means of superior work throughout the remainder of this campaign, I may revoke the penalty. That's all.

Thank you, general. I—

Go now,

> and restore yourself if you're able—you half-spent man with faded service cord still proudly on the arm of your blouse in spite of the regulation now three years old; for *that* I'll never censure you, poor Trimble: with the First since the Secession War
>> (well, the same goes for Perry,
>>> who, as I cannot forget, operates under quite a grey-bellied cloud nowadays, thanks to White Bird Cañon,
>>>> which is to say, thanks to Joseph's treachery and those *hateful Indian eyes*—
>>>>> why, they're DEVIL's eyes! how did I fail to realize that until now?— No, I must never think that, must not . . . !
>>> but Perry will pull through and resume his rise, perhaps to regimental commander if he cleans his record in future Indian service:
>>>> 1. Smohallie and all those River Renegades;
>>>> then
>>>> 2. sooner or later our lightfingered Bannocks
>>>>> Which way will Buffalo Horn jump then?
>>>> [or perhaps first 3. another lesson for the Apaches; Lizzie won't be happy about that];
>>>>> I'd soonest trust him against the Bannocks first, while he regains his confidence;
>>> OUR FATHER will help him, I'm sure; for he hasn't grown old in harness—whereas Trimble's in danger of becoming poor old Trimble);
>> well, we're all getting older. I'd be kinder to him if I could, but then he'd despise me.

And on your way out, please tell Lieutenant Wood to come here.

Yessir.

Well, Wood, an embarrassment and a half!

I'd say so, general,

> gazing at him with the same sad eyes of the shire horse which Father used to keep on the farm. Father would have

Are you ready to take dictation?

Yessir.

Who's Brooks's next of kin?

A mother, sir, in Pennsylvania.

After the service, the burial detail had better ride several horses over his grave in order to disguise it from Mr. Joe and his scalp-hunters.

        O, bury me not on the lone prair-ee—

I'll see that it's done, sir.

All right. *Dear Mrs. Brooks, my heartfelt condolences on the death of your son Bernard on August 20th, 1877, during a night attack by Nez Perce Indians. I can assure you that in an injury of this type there is very little suffering; death comes almost instantaneously. He was a favorite in Company "B" and will be greatly missed. You are in my prayers. If there is anything I can do for you, please command me. Yours sincerely.*

Yessir.

Such a sprightly, cheerful young man! Always forward in his duty—

Yessir.

Were you well acquainted with him?

Only slightly, sir.

Do you know if Doctor Alexander expects Trevor and Glass to pull through?

Sorry, sir, I—

Now, could you run over to Lieutenant Bomus? I'll want his ideas on how we're to manage with this unexpected deficit of service animals—

HENRY'S LAKE
AUGUST 22–28

1

*Y*ou'd better attend to your boots.

Yessir.

What's that grimace about, soldier?

Toothache, sir.

Report to Doctor Alexander to-night and get it pulled.

      Must ask Lizzie how Mrs. Perry is getting along—

          No, I don't want to.

          Why, Lizzie?

          You tired me out with all your guests, and now it's late. Besides, the children—

          But it's not late. It's only

              at which juncture he remembers the lesson of civilian life, especially as learned by military men: few things can be accomplished by persuasion, and fewer still by argument

> (her mouth working crossly even in her sleep, then beginning to suck like a child:
>
>> *She's getting old!* How can it happen so soon?
>>
>> Well, well; it's always going to be too soon).

Yessir.

Mr. Calloway, I assume that at least you can escort our wounded to the rear.

General, I resent that!

Shut your mouth, sir. You're a no-account insubordinate coward. That will be all. Wood, see if you can find four or five of this gentleman's volunteers who are brave enough to guide us on to Henry's Lake.

Right away, sir.

Major Mason, step aside with me.

Sure thing, general.

Mason, *entre nous,* did Perry make a good showing in the fight?

He was overcautious again, general. Had he only galloped his bunch up to Sandford—

So I feared.

I quizzed him about it, and he said he couldn't have lived with himself if he'd spent the lives of his command—

As at White Bird Cañon.

Yessir.

So he's through.

I wouldn't put it that way, general. And Sandford's said nothing—

You're very fond of Perry.

Yessir. You should have seen him driving the Modocs into the lake! And General Crook once told me—

All right, Mason. On another subject, what's your impression of Old George?

Of average intelligence for an Indian, I should say. He was moderately active last night. Chapman says his statements can be relied upon.

O, so you believe Chapman, do you?

I follow your lead, general.

Enough said. You'd better oversee the column. Guy, where's Lieutenant Fletcher?

Receiving Captain Trimble's report, father.

Good,

> the mountains where the Nez Perce have gone now wearing morning purple above the green ridge (so Joseph's bucks are indeed capable of night attacks, just like the Snakes),
>
>> Chapman already prancing like an idiot on his grey racing-horse,
>>
>> GOD help me to stop detesting that man (I grant he's useful),

as two shavetails cinch flour barrels to another mule
(Sound "The General"!
Yessir),
our other drivers fitting up the wagons,
Sandford's bunch cursing those yellow volunteers:
Why in hell did they come here? They must have been
the only men in town who could find saddle-horses and
rifles. Well, they sure enough left their balls at home!
Wood excited to now go deeper into the Indian country,
Wilkinson,
who frankly loves the general and thinks, as may be the
case, to understand him better than anybody else in the
Army, Guy Howard not excepted,
receiving Bomus's report;
our tame Indians breaking Joseph's ponies to work in harness
(Umatilla Jim can do it with no time lost, beating and choking
the animals for half an hour each morning while we're loading the wagon train)
and as for Perry and Pollock, one last cup each of the
Army's best: Rio green coffee,
then full sun as shocking as if Theller were to wrench off his moldy
blanket and leap daredevilishly up out of earth, and the bugle
sounds the move out:
left, left, LEFT,
with a shoulder-glance at Brooks's unmarked grave,
left, left, LEFT,
far in advance of our dusty wagons
—in one of which, happily out of our sight, poor
Glass lies jolting and screaming (shot through the
bladder by Mr. Joe)
and Trevor beside him, knowing that he too is a
goner, takes a herculean swig of calomel—
the men freshly irritated at Chief Joseph now that he
has rustled away their mules:
we're surely going to get him into the ground
(although Mason is not at all sure);
and ahead of these walking soldiers,
some of whom now commence to appear as motley as
Indians, with their patches of hide and gunnysack,
the S-curve of cavalry troops upon the prairie.
All through the forepart of this day we ride two abreast, gasping in dust
(and Perry, pulling his hat down low and wrapping his scarf
across his mouth in defense against the Big Dust, rests his

rifle across his lap, holding the stock in his right hand, the reins in his left, Diamond's ears upraised and tail spreading wide in the wind);

then, as the trail narows and steepens, we lead our horses one by one, infantry and artillery behind, scouts ahead, our cheeks muddy with dust-weeping, right up into those mountains

(aspens on our left, all white in the morning light,

and the creek as bright as sunlight on a warrior's hair-roach); and even through shut lids the sun presses in to burn our swollen eyeballs, on account of that march to Camas Meadows: at the next halt I'd better grease my eyes even though

The bold dragoon he has no care

—I'm unnerved for our advance guard, because Joseph might not have

(left, left, LEFT)

and the snapping of locusts in the sand might hide something worse

As he rides along with his uncombed hair

through lavender-blue blossoms of horsemint surviving past its time, the pine-forest closing in:

a boulder as grand as the desk of a senior clerk,

a silver river running through the olive grass:

Someday I'll stake my home right there, right where the ripples run (such a rich place it will be—my black cows around this mirror-white pool,

Wilkinson whispering to his spavined horse,

my tongue now drier than the clapper of a dusty bell; I *hate* this life, I hate it, and the general most of all, who tortures us to no purpose),

because I've never been to Wallowa and I want to get away from Doc, who won't never hardly let a fellow alone

(well, general, they haven't divided or doubled back at all!)

and from that Nigger-Loving Howard, who never takes a white man's word

to possess someday a drawing-room with a looking-glass on the wall,

picture windows for Fidelia,

and we'll breakfast on trout, and she'll always be happy

so that I can forget the way she looked at me at Farewell Bend when Blurick and I dug her mother's grave and then we lowered her down from the side of the wagon only to find tumbleweeds already rolling into the hole and I said the best I knew into the stench of dead fish, looking straight out where the white bank eroded vertically, a good twenty-five-foot drop I should reckon, with the great cottonwood roots exposed growing straight down through the air, and I knew what Fidelia was thinking, that before long her mother's grave would likewise wash away, and her sobs were like those hoarse bird-cries all around and the years ahead of us could have been round grey river-pebbles when she said it was I who had killed her mother by carrying the family out West;

and then, behind the slender white aspens, here come the arid enemy mountains, not far now beyond this green grass with its whispering white trees and fat black birds puffing out their chests

(when I look back now, the whole world has become a meadow)

and the grass moister, the aspens thicker, spruces coming, then a lodgepole pine forest upon the plateau and

Keep up your brightest lookout now, men!

because although it would never do to compare Joseph to the infinitely more impressive Stonewall Jackson, who used without any warning to burst in upon our intrenchments with thousands of screaming men, the fact of his guileful Indian treachery cannot be denied

(last night he blew away Will Clark's shoulder with an exploding bullet, and he got Sergeant Wilkins in the temple

so that I almost feel his hateful Indian eyes on me now, chilling the back of my head—is that a face between those pines?)

especially not now as we ride up out of the Shotgun Valley, through these gracious meadows of pines, aspens and yellow-orange grass, the disgrace of Camas Meadows safely out of sight, the morning sun golden on our right shoulders and all around the meadow grass in yellow splashes, then through a long winding meadow of trees,

*Now you've got it, d——n you, keep it—left—left—*LEFT!

Watch out!

No. Ad Chapman says it's all right.

Who are they then?

Just raggedy-ass Bannocks from Fort Hall.

General, they say that Captain Bainbridge of the Fourteenth is en route with more scouts—

Who sent him?

General Crook, sir.

Well, well. Bless his heart. Stay on the *qui vive.*

Yessir.

Should I buy Lizzie a sewing machine? She insists she doesn't need it and could never learn to use it, but her arthritis is getting pretty bad—for that

matter, LORD, does my arm hurt to-day! It's this
heat I suppose, and the sleeplessness,
and perhaps I should have waited to propose to Nanny,
but I was sure then, and I wanted her, and I know that
once I went West I would never if I could help it come
back, so unless I tied myself to her I might not see her
again, and o! to watch her hands plucking a flower!—
not that this sight, however lovely, comprises the best
grounds for marriage, but in fact I do love her not
merely for her perishable beauty but for her pride and
mirthful spirits, which I confess ladies do seem to lose
when they part with youth, but there is no *reason* on
earth why that ought to be so, if I cherish her as she
does her flowers, never forgetting the damage done to
women by rough men such as my drunkard father,
never mind that he claims I'll forgive and understand in
time; I know very well what he has done to Mother and
I won't forget it. And now Nanny glides on through the
pearl-grey limbo of an affianced belle, incontrovertibly
mine as I must remain hers on pain of disgrace and self-
punishment as a cruelly negligent Lothario; when I received that two-cent letter from her last summer and
was informed that she had resumed seeing her other
beau I was, if not wild with rage, resentfully annoyed
(more proof that I love her), and requited myself with
Sitka Khwan and those other interesting squaws, until
I had to admit that I have betrayed Nanny (and may
well continue to do so) not to pay her back for her own
lightness but because it pleases me to enjoy these adventures, so aren't we equal, she and I? I won't verify the
equation by confessing to her! (Although I love and revere the general, and her, too, in my fashion, still, how
delicious it would be to observe Mrs. Howard's thun-
derous disapproval should I inform her of my delirious
miscegenations!) Meanwhile Nanny entertains her
beau or beaux, and I await the post with some dread,
lest she break her engagement. Well, she deserves to
please herself no less than I. When she wrote me that
her people took her to the Centennial and bought her a
tropical banana dressed in metal foil (ten cents), I
wished that I could have escorted her myself, but did I
begrudge her her life's unfettered ongoing? May she
collect full measure of whatever pleases her; soon

enough, we'll both be in mortality's pit, and even if we're decently buried in some graveyard with marble over us if we died rich or cement if we were poor, what's the difference between that and lying swollen and fly-veiled in White Bird Cañon, whose hideousness I never can nor wish to forget? Now I begin not only to love the general more, but to feel closer to him, for this Nez Perce campaign remains so small a chore to him, however great in drudgery, that with each misery and atrocity I better perceive or at least begin to perceive how violently his spirit must have been forged in the flames of more colossal horrors whose screaming amplitudes doubtless reënforce his propensity to meditate on hell-fire—and, more to the point, render him partially incomprehensible (or perhaps invisible) to people who know only ordinary life and death: young children carried off one after another by yellow fever, wife hemorrhaging in childbed, or for that matter Mrs. Howard's father falling headfirst through an unsecured ship-hatch; these sad endings, *necessarily* sad if those who passed away were loved by anyone at all, have scant collateral or even token value in comparison to whatever the general must have seen and done at Chancellorsville.

Woolgathering?

Sure, Guy,

who will never be better or worse than innocent. I envy you. I know you do not envy me, because you mistake my isolation for sadness and because

Wood, don't you care about this campaign?

What does that mean?

You . . . I'm near about sick of you,

because I want to be the one whom Father can trust with anything, without him even telling me what it is, or even me telling him that I've done it. Redington,

who reminds Wood of a pallid coyote outstretching himself,

will ride up and say: Joseph's dead, general, and I'd like you to meet Mrs. Manuel tied to that Indian pony safe and sound, and all the bad Indians have surrendered to the last man—and do you know who carried all this out, sir? And then Fletch and Wood will say:

Lieutenant Howard, go complain to your father.

They're acting ugly, general.

Colonel Perry, do you mean to tell me that you can't control them?

Excuse me, sir, but I most certainly can,

    you contemptible old maunderer—stung by Joseph's sally, aren't you now?
        (if Crook were in charge, Mr. Joe would have been on his knees or
        in his grave long since. Crook has "sand" in him, whereas you're no
        d——d good at all, and your hangers-on—Wood, Wilkinson, Fletch
        and Sladen—remind me of those four hymn-humming negroes
        who operated the chewing tobacco machine at the Centennial Ex-
        hibition, LORD spare me and d——n *you* to hell for a crippled Chris-
        tian fool, no good, not worth a wooden dime, no fucking)

Good. Anything else?

No, sir.

They don't understand that we must be cautious as well as active,

    like Umatilla Jim, who even for an Indian is small of build, turtling down
    his head as he rides away on that little dun pony, fading into the scrub
    oak even before we'd finished blowing the Funeral March for that half-
    grown Brooks, who always ran shy of me. Once I saw him break off a
    piece of his biscuit for Jim—

        What is it about Jim and his sad greying braids that speaks to me?
        And he's nearly a Christian. With a little encouragement—
            but the men mistreat him on account of his race; they'll never
            like him, unfortunately.

You're right, sir.

Well, educating them is your department, Perry. That's all,

    wondering if poor Sergeant Garland will succumb to last night's wounds
    and watching for hostiles who are hiding our stolen mules and horses
    somewhere in the hills

        (which Captain Pollock hopes might be the metal-bearing
        kind; I'd sure like to strike it rich, for the children's sake),
        and there may be Sioux: the worst of the worst. Sitting Bull could
        be up in the next coulee. Well, he knows that,

            and the volunteers have finally realized it; that's why they
            failed us last night. Should have drummed them out right
            there if they hadn't already quit—

Yessir.

Captain Pollock, what are you grinning about?

O, general, I was just telling my bunch the squaws will have a jolly good time
cooking our mules.

Ha, ha! You're an entertaining addition to this campaign. Now where's Jim?

He's just coming up the line, sir. Should I fetch him?

Yes, please. There you are, Jim. You know, your horse has a lot of "dash" the
way you've decorated him!

Thanks, general.

Now tell me how Joseph played last night's trick.

Well, general, they came up from two sides. I could tell from the tracks. Maybe one bunch was led by Looking-Glass, because he and some Crows did the same thing one time to some Cheyennes and got their horses; he was always jawboning about it.

What about the other bunch?

Could have been anyone, general.

It must have been Joseph himself!

Yessir.

How many Indians in total?

Not many. Twenty, maybe.

You're an interesting Indian.

Thanks, general.

Jim, you often wear a sad face. Do you feel sad in the Army?

No, sir.

Why are you here with us? I'd like to understand you.

Well, my Daddy was on scout with Company "G" in '64. Grindstone Creek. They was hunting Snakes. There was Nez Perces helping us out, and then this one Lieutenant Noble—

Thank you, Jim. Return to your duties. Captain Jackson, how are your bunch?

Real sad about Brooks, general—

He was your favorite orderly, I hear.

Sure was. He died blowing his bugle. A glorious way to go out . . .

You're right about that, captain. Ever since White Bird Cañon, Joseph has consistently targeted our trumpeters. He's found our weak spot.

Yessir. Colonel Perry was thinking the same thing. Just now he reminded me that White Bird stayed awhile to watch our manoeuvres at Lapwai, so he could be the Indian behind this.

We'll see once we catch them. Wilkinson, ride along the column and report the stragglers to me.

Yessir.

Is something on your mind?

No, sir,

> because Wilkinson, who reads on Trimble's face a certain faded, cracked defiance, which might of course be mere weariness, cannot yet decide whether to leave the man alone, encourage him, or tilt the general against him.

All right then. Go ride the line and GOD bless you. By the way, Trimble, I saw one of your boys struggling to clear his weapon last night.

Yessir. Those brass cases sometimes—

Break during extraction. I know.

Yessir.

Your company is deficient. That will be all. Fletch, did that teamster just use foul language?

Afraid so, general.

Get his name and dock his pay.

For to-day only, sir?

Yes. For to-day. Now, where's Buffalo Horn?

He—

Is he away from the column?

No, sir.

Send an Indian to round him up.

Right away, sir.

And where's Lieutenant Howard?

In the vanguard, sir.

Did I send him there?

He—

Bring him back here, doublequick.

Yessir.

Camping that night on the north fork of the Snake, nearly suffocated by the evergreens all around

> (Umatilla Jim out on left flank, rubbing his weaselskin bracelet and whispering his secret song:
>
> he has begun Dreaming that White Bird's best men will kill him),

our troopers dare not take off their boots to sleep—all the more reason to hate Joseph, and here's another: "Reveille" at two a.m., rattle of pistol belts and bubbling of coffee, on the march before dawn, in hopes of cutting off their enemy before he passes Henry's Lake:

He has already vanished through the Tachee Pass, it seems.

> *Wakesh nun pakilauitin*
> JEHOVAN'M *yiyauki*—

That James Reuben never quits. A plucky, cheerful Christian man—

Yessir.

> Old Joe's exasperated us again!
> He sure knows how to skedaddle.
> Ain't that like an Indian?

Wilkinson, by all my faith in the Good Time coming, we *will* get Joseph.

I pray you're right, general. You and I can go on until it kills us, but some of these pampered shavetails—

Most will show their metal when they have to.

Yessir.

If not, the failure's ours. Now, where's Fletch? O, good morning. Any news from Captain Fisher?

Not yet, sir.

You look worse. Report to Doctor Alexander.

Yessir. I can hold out, sir.

Go to Doctor Alexander now.

Yessir.

Perry, how's your column?

Moving like a machine, general.

Glad to hear it,

> his love for them all rising like a crescent moon over the desert.

Yes, Trimble, what news?

General, in case they should attack us on the march—

I'm sorry, Trimble. You'll have to leave that to the officer of the day. All right, major, what is it?

> > Doc, you been right about everything.
> > Naturally.

2

Did you get a thrill the other night?

Yessir, Captain Pollock.

What an idiotic defense we had! We should have plugged Mr. Joe, and I told the general . . .

Yessir.

Well, that Brooks sure died a soldier! Tried to stand up after he was shot—

O, captain, he even caught his stirrup strap, hoping to get back in the saddle! Fletch and I were saying—

Wood, I need to make some money in this campaign. I know where to look for silver and gold, but so far there hasn't been much of that. Maybe there's other minerals to pick up. For all I know, there might be sapphires in these mountains. Now, who should I talk to?

Well, sir, Captain Whipple was prospecting in Wallowa—

For gold, Wood. Don't you know that?

Yessir. You want sapphires?

They might be a d——d sight easier to find, you see. And you're a young man who knows everything.

All right, captain. I'll ask around.

3

> > . . . Could do with some fruit. A nice peach or an apple or . . .
> > Don't get dreamy on me. Reds could be in that timber up there
> > > where hours ago Buffalo Horn studied the broken grass; now he is already patrolling Henry's Lake

(his one legal bullet ready in the pouch tied to his carbine, all the others hidden in his buckskin shirt).

After what Mr. Joe and all them River Renegades has done, we'll make it so them Indians won't show their faces off the reservation unless they've got a signed paper.

Well now. That'd sure be a start.

Doc?

What is it now?

Did you know that Brooks?

Nope.

Well, he was a real sweet young man. Never complained.

What's to complain about?

When Stonewall Jackson caved in his Eleventh Corps at Chancellorsville . . .

Doc, what's Buffalo Horn arguing about with our Nez Perces?

He's blamin' 'em for riding slow on purpose, to help their kin-folks out. See how his hand flies down like that? So the Nez Perces are getting mad, sending him to the DEVIL. See, that's good. We *like* that.

Why on earth . . . ?

Only two ways to fight savages, boy. Either we divvy up the savages and make 'em fight each other, or else we act like savages ourselves. Ain't many white men who have enough "sand" for that.

So you're saying that even our Bannocks and our Nez Perces—

Hush up now.

Doc, how'd you learn to speak Indian?

That's not your real question, is it, now? Because you're not wondering *how* but *why*.

Then tell me the why, Doc.

Sure I can talk Chinook and live as an Indian, but that's just a means to an end.

So what's the end?

Look at the color of your skin and think about it.

4

Sinking the guidon-pole so that our American flag flies up (and from a willow thicket straining out of mossy mud, many birds burst shudderingly, and fly over the lake, leaving nothing behind but the buzzings of flies), we water our mules and horses, curry them, then for newfound fear of Joseph we side-line them with strong chains; telling off work parties, we dig our sinks and fire-pits, pitch our

Sibley tents behind that broken-down wagon—headquarters over *there*—and await GOD's next move (General Howard has determined to refresh and recruit his command), the lucky men easing their carbines down; and just as ever so often in life when the cards glissade face down across the table, Lizzie's hand or Charley boy's drawing them out, so now at Henry's Lake, I.T.

> (romantic enough here, if it weren't for the leeches—
>> and Trimble shouting at Company "H"
>>> (never mind that even Doc's out of cocaine by now)—
>>> how I used to wish I could go fishing for pickerel on Androscoggin Lake! But there was so much work on the farm, especially after Father died—)

here where the Snake River commences, O, what a long way
> —and so long ago since Wilkinson and I steamed up the Snake to Lapwai: Mrs. Theller still unwidowed, Perry undisgraced, and I not yet betrayed and humiliated by Joseph—

and some few aspen leaves have already commenced to go yellow and purple.
>> Fine that man a month's pay. He delayed my column this morning.
>> Yessir.

Well, Fletch, did they find sign or not?

They did, sir, right where Company "F" is watering their horses.

O, I see. The southwestern shore—

Yessir. Mr. Joe certainly bivouacked here the night before last. Here's a Nez Perce arrow for Captain Fisher's collection—

Why didn't he find it himself? What's that man about? Never mind. I'll expect him in a quarter-hour. And go remind Captain Jocelyn that his Morning Report had better not be late to-morrow—

At the water's edge sits Redington on his bedroll, wearing shirt, hat and underdrawers, bathing his feet, weary-looking but grinning, with his horse blanket steaming behind him in the sun, sewing up the seam of his trousers with a bone needle from a dead squaw's sewing pouch,

> and Wilkinson,
>> who personally prefers the worsted trial stockings to the approved woolen type,
> is washing the aforesaid items, but with almost ludicrous rapidity, so that he can get back to the general before being called for,
>> as Chapman strides through the waist-high grass, gripping his rifle in both hands with the stock against his belly and the long barrel parallel to the ground, hoping to unearth something interesting

while Trimble draws up his report:
> Back in the years when the railroad agents contented themselves with pitching stores off the train wherever they liked, our men had to guard

every car, because there wasn't any storehouse, and that's how it feels, wondering where the general will attack me next;

and we had to scatter into loneliness, wondering when Mosby's raiders might ambush us from the dark, and now that's how I feel again, O my GOD, with the general against me,

> here in the algae'd gravel of Henry's Lake, the Continental Divide reddish-green, with patches of evergreens along its back,

>> the Nimrods among us making a creditable "barbeque" of eight-pound trout and giant swans,

> and a brown reflection in the lake, interrupted by ripples, and a mucky smell:

>> Get your horses on half lariat and picket them out.
>> Yessir,

and that coward Perry who got us all whipped by Mr. Joe wishing me out of the way before the Court of Inquiry, and Company "H" stinks, and now we'll never catch the reds. When we get back to Lapwai I'll resign,

and our tame Indians sucking the Government like horse-leeches, GOD——n them, as we send out sullen parties of detailed men to stand sleepless against another surprise from Chief Joseph,

> the undetached fellows filling their hats with huge black currants at the discretion of their officers, rinsing their overshirts and canteens in the lake, squinting bloodshot eyes, drinking fresh water as greedily as mosquitoes do blood.

> No, Fletch; you're incorrect. The general was only a first lieutenant in 1857.

> You sure have his career down cold.

> Well, the thing is

>> (for Wilkinson considers Fletch to be more nominally, which is to say less essentially, a Christian than the general and himself),

> you don't care about the general as much as I do.

> Wilkinson, that's a d——d lie! Now cut it out. We'll settle our differences at Lapwai if we have to. Do you want peace?

> All right, I'm sorry; let's shake on it.

>> Chapman, whose ranch is that?

>> Got to be Mr. Sawtell's, colonel. Looks like he's skedaddled on account of—

>> You ever been out here?

>> Not this far, colonel.

>> Then shut up.

Now let's tot up the results of almost exactly two months of steady application, eight hundred and twelve point eight miles out of Lewiston, and if we count from Kamiah, it's been twenty-six days without rest, for an average of one hundred and ninety-three miles a week

(useful to lay this out in my Supplementary Report, so that Crook and the others can't impress Sherman with their insinuations, which may by now have alloyed themselves to Agent Monteith's);

and Carr's company must now have ridden twelve hundred and fifty-six miles. Must commend them to Sherman.

Yes, Captain Miller, what is it now?

General, according to Surgeon Hall, at least fifteen men will have to be left behind if we ride out to-morrow.

Including our wounded?

I don't know, sir.

By the way, have you visited Trevor? A stalwart! Hardly even groans—

He's failing, sir.

We should all pray for him.

Yessir.

Captain, at the Battle of the Clearwater your charge was heroic. You helped drive Joseph out of Idaho.

Thank you, sir.

Must I alter my opinion of you?

No, sir.

How well do you know Surgeon Hall?

Well enough, sir.

Bring him and Doctor Alexander here at once.

Yessir.

Well, gentlemen?

General, unlike the officers, some of the men already suffer rheumatic pains. And I'm worried about foot-rot, given the deficiency of socks. Moreover, the food ration is—

All right. What about Trevor, Glass and the others?

Trevor's mortally injured, general. Glass has a bladder wound, which as you know—

Anything else?

Sir, without an issue of suitable clothing this command will rapidly become worthless.

Strong words, Doctor Alexander! Surgeon?

Nothing to add, sir.

Within half an hour I expect a complete list of supplies required. Thank you both. Mason, how many days to get resupplied from Virginia City?

At least five, sir.

Has anyone seen Lieutenant Howard?

Yessir, he was giving the engineers a hand—

Fetch him here.

Yessir.

The first tricks taken by each side are a book and don't count. Joseph won at White Bird Cañon, as did I (I think) at Clearwater. Each trick afterward is one point. Fort Fizzle doesn't count. Score one for me at Big Hole, and a very small one for Joseph the other night at Camas Meadows, and then right here two more of Joseph's meaningless murders which can't qualify as moves in the game:

Where were the bodies discovered?

Down thataway, sir.

I see,

stacking the cards of each trick taken so that all players can count them: Theller and Rains, to be sure, but how many of Mr. Joe's have we now totted up and laid aside in a row of neat little overlapping piles?

By GOD, we need a change. Uh-Oh Howard can't even keep Joseph from running off our mules.

All right, Wood. This will be to our men. General Order Number Six. *The General Commanding takes this opportunity of expressing to men and officers his thorough appreciation . . .*

Not his fault.

O yes it is. He don't have my fuckin' confidence *no more.*

The General is not ignorant that two companies are destitute of overcoats.

Yessir.

Men have given up their overcoats to the wounded, Wood. You've seen that.

Yessir. A fine bunch—

And, you know, we've driven Joseph out of the fertile valleys where he would have rested—

Yessir.

The seventh trick is called the odd, but I certainly hope there will be no seven tricks at this particular business! When one side ends two games, that ends the rubber; that probably applies here. Two more decent battles, and Joseph will be whipped.

How fine it will be to be telling Lizzie all about it! And then to sleep in her arms, O, Lizzie. She'll want to hear everything; she's naturally curious and preternaturally considerate, the best listener I ever knew, as I found by explaining the game to her before we married: I have five trumps, so I'd better lead them . . .

her poor father smiling at us behind his cards, so happy to see Lizzie engaged,

and now—what a sweetheart—she's more cunning at whist than I!

Lord, I'm tired!

> Two trumps, and weak cards in my plain suits, so I'd definitely better not lead trumps.
>
> A guarded king, and Lizzie out of sorts—

Yessir.

Well, Captain Fisher, how are your Bannocks holding up?

O, pretty darned well, general! The new lot are out for blood.

How's your bow and arrow collection coming along?

Got me some fine relics at Big Hole, sir. Frankly, I'm itching for something from Mr. Joe—

> > and picture windows for Fidelia to look out of every day, and our house will face eastward, now that there is no more new West to find, and so she and I will watch the sunrise as alone with these others I have done for so many days now in the course of chasing Mr. Joe—

Yes, that would be quite a *coup*, now, wouldn't it!

Ha, ha, sir, what a caution you are!

Now, Fisher, mind you don't impede the baggage train.

O, no, general. My Indians are carrying them all for me—

Good. Otherwise I'll have them burned. Now keep on.

Yessir.

Wood, what do you have for me?

Well, general, I've done this sketch entitled "Indian Chief," because the people back East—

O, that's Red Heart! A great likeness.

And this sketch of our bivouac just before we got to Weippe, and here are four drawings of our victory over Joseph at Clearwater—

Splendid! Pack them up, because they're going to the newspapers to-day. Then the civilians will see for themselves how arduously we labor at our Indian service. Unfortunately you'll have to be anonymous, because General Sherman—

That's all right, general. I'll bring them in five minutes.

Thanks.

Major Mason,

> whose innocent look does not convince me; what have you been hiding from me? O well,

> > scanning the grass:

> > > one private cropping another's hair:

> > > > Thanks, Doc. You're the best friend I ever had.
> > > >
> > > > Blackie, listen up. I'm a-tellin' you this because I've took a shine to you. You know what? You have the makings of a real Indian killer. But you got to get well. You been sick a long time. Don't worry. It ain't the cholery or

you'd be dead. To-night I'll get us some whiskey. That's your surefire cure.

Whiskey? How you gonna pay for it?

Remember that buckskin pouch I showed Blurick? Well, I got another one. Went prodding with my ramrod last month when we flushed them reds out of Clearwater. They hid gold dust in the ground—

Can I see?

Not here. If there's nobody down by the sinks I'll show you. And to-night you'll have you some whiskey, and I don't mean the barefoot kind. And once this campaign is done, I aim to take care of you. Listen, Blackie: Now them Nez Perces is run out of that good old green Wallowa Valley

and Redington is burning leeches off his ankle, that's fine; but where's Perry? I don't need him in earshot!—

another word, if you please.

Yessir.

Now, when you commanded Colonel Perry during the Modoc War . . .

Yes I did, general, although he was out in the field much of the time. A superb soldier, with much initiative.

So I've heard. How's he holding up nowadays?

Well, sir, he's pushing himself hard. Like all of us, he wants blood paid out for Lieutenant Theller.

Thank you, major. And what about yourself?

No complaints here, general!

You're a fine man. A credit to the service.

You're too kind, sir.

Doctor Alexander's uneasy about the men. What do you say about that?

They'll go wherever you lead them, sir.

All right, Mason. You might as well stay a moment. Lieutenant Howard, round up the officers.

Yessir,

the lake now a lucid blue-grey like the eyes of President Hayes.

Gentlemen, our scouts report that the hostiles are riding toward the Crow Agency. Joseph's final objective point must therefore be his hunting grounds in the Buffalo Country of the upper Missouri. We've been riding him pretty hard; he's got to recruit supplies and rest his women and children. Do any of you see it differently?

Well, no, sir—

Redington?

General, our Bannocks believe that Looking-Glass will make contact with the Crows, in which case Sitting Bull—

All right. Who's the Crow Agent? I'll expect him to keep our Crows on the sunny side of the Government. Fletch, prepare a draft letter on that subject. Wood, unroll the map. Gather round, please. As you can see, he must pass through the National Park, and then get to the Musselshell Valley either down *here* by the Stinking Water or else up *there* via Clark's Fork.

Yessir.

What is it, Sladen?

The National Park appears pretty trackless,

> (for even between Virginia City and this "Yellow Stone," Colton's map offers but beige emptiness squiggled here and there with barely-named creeks, while Yellow Stone itself might as well be Mars),

so if we can hire civilians from Virginia City to cut a wagon-road—

How does it compare to Lo Lo?

Not as bad as that, sir. But—

Spurgin, do your engineers have "sand"?

I sure hope so, sir.

Ride ahead to the National Park and despatch me a report on what you'll need. I'll sound out the good citizens of Virginia City. That's all for you, Spurgin. Our continued progress depends on you. Go now.

Yessir.

Where's Captain Fisher gone to? Still fooling with his artifact collection?

General, he's scouting around the lake, because Buffalo Horn—

Wilkinson, prepare a despatch to Captain Cushing. He's to lead his company, Norwood's and Field's to Fort Ellis right away, and operate in our advance while I pursue the direct trail. He's to recruit more scouts at the Crow Agency and send them out to harass Joseph's column.

Yessir.

I want him to draw on the Fort's commissary eight thousand rations of bacon or hardbread and four thousand rations of vinegar.

Yessir. When should they expect us?

As soon as supplies come in. I should suppose we'll be here a good three or four days. That will be all.

Yessir.

Fletch, I expect the blacksmiths to reshoe our service animals as needed. Make sure they receive all assistance. Lieutenant Bomus will help you there.

Yessir.

Lieutenant Howard, you and I will ride out for Virginia City in fifteen minutes. Pick the best team you can. Where's Captain Adams?

Here, general.

You're to come with us. Mason, you'll take command until our return.

Yessir.

Well, what is it?

General, that's a hundred and fifty miles round trip—

We'll be back the day after to-morrow if possible. I was advised it would take five days, but we aim to do better.

Well, general, that sure would be—

Recruit the men, but keep on the *qui vive*.

Of course, sir.

Gentlemen, that will be all. O, Doctor Alexander, I was just about to send for you. So that's your list.

Yessir.

All right. I'll see what I can do. Bomus, are your requisitions drawn up?

Here they are, sir.

I know how you feel, giving vouchers which don't even pledge the credit of the Government! A serious embarrassment.

Yessir. Our postwar Army—

Right you are. Good-bye, gentlemen.

Good-bye, general!

5

Thanks, father, for bringing me with you.

The pleasure's mine. How are you holding up?

O, I love this wild country! What about you?

A pleasant adventure, and we just may set a record. Poor Captain Adams is fast asleep. A wonder any man can doze jouncing over this boulder-field!

Father, how can you never get tired?

O, I get tired all right. That's all on that subject.

Looks like the Gallatin River ahead.

Correct.

Do you think Mr. Joe will get away?

His purpose is undeveloped so far as I can tell. He's squandered whatever advantage he had in delay and indecision. In my opinion, wild Indians are essentially opportunistic. If the Crows take him in, he'll join them; if not, he might ride for the British Possessions, or seek to winter at Yellow Stone. Now that we've driven him from home, he has no strategy, only tactics. That's why he's finished.

Thank GOD! By the way, father, I admire Wilkinson more and more.

Good. He's an upright, hard charging man . . .

6

How are you feeling, father?

Sadly disappointed.

About Camas Meadows?

O, about everything, Guy. Enough. It's in GOD's hands,
     the sun as crimson as a Crow brave's saddleblanket.

No, don't let him graze even in passing. When a horse tires is just when you can't
be slack. That's the ticket!

He's a real fine trotting horse.

So's the grey. We may have to work them to death.

Father?

What is it now?

What do you think about Mr. Chapman?

O, he reminds me of a Seccesh with his knapsack full of cornmeal "dodgers."
A simple harmless fellow who wants to be sly—

I worry that he plays you false.

How so?

I don't know, exactly. Just a feeling.

Never mind, Guy. Every soldier lies to his general. How are you holding up?

Fine, thanks,

> his face dusted as grey as the suits Mother used to make up for me out of
> milled wool from my stepfather's many sheep—but no complaint from
> him! Thank You, LORD, for his love and courage.

Happy to be with you, father—

Likewise. I'm so lucky to have such a son. Enough of that. What do you suppose that Mama's up to?

Riding all night and into the dawn, they descend into clouds as white as the
tops of new pioneer wagons, pass an island of aspens in a meadow, then roll into
Virginia City before noon. The citizens give them a hurrah. Three hours later they
set out again with a fresh team, carrying shoes and blankets, and drugs for Doctor
Alexander, with the mail following behind them, and fresh horses on order—all
at profiteers' prices. The following day they canter back down the Divide,

> Captain Adams taking the reins, Guy snoring heartily, the general swaying
> easily in his seat, with his mouth locked in a faint smile,

>> remembering the flowery breeze regaling him on the second-storey
>> porch of General Saxton's headquarters, the Fuller House in Beaufort, as
>> in lemonade we toasted our hopes of colored elementary schools
>> throughout our Reunited States, and inalienable negro homesteads in
>> Edisto, once upon a time, as Samuel Fullerton sat taking notes on the
>> President's behalf;

and into that wide bowl of sagebrush, which presently opens up into Henry's Lake
pale blue and wide, on the shore of which our city of grimy-pale Sibley tents has
been long since erected (every man hoping to be in at the death), sunshine sparkling prettily on Gatlings' bronze-jacketed breeches, and the suits flashing and
glittering like black and crimson beetle-swarms upon the painfully white fan-
arrays of playing-cards in the last quarter-hour before the bugle call to afternoon
fatigue.

7

Here at last come the two muleteers mounted on mules (of course) and leading a pack-mule full of mail. Many communications fall to him: three from Lizzie (the most intimate one is destined to be transferred to the breast pocket of his blouse), which he smilingly sets aside for some private instant, a dozen from his Department in San Francisco, one from Washington, another from Chicago, requesting the favor of his autograph; a packet of very worrisome confidential appreciations of those Communist-led strikes (which have tapered off, thank the LORD); an unfavorable press notice from New York, referring to Gibbon's attack on Joseph at Big Hole as a "massacre"—this good-intentioned journalist quite failed to see what poor Custer used to refer to as *the dark side of the Indian question*—an envelope from the *Chicago Advance* (Charley boy, no doubt); an anonymously mailed press notice from Washington accusing this campaign and more specifically its general of inaction and inefficiency in relation to Joseph (I've heard worse); one very urgent note from his lawyer about some new charge which might be preferred against him relative to the Freedmen's Bureau (this time his supposed peculations date all the way back to 1862, when Mr. Charles B. Wilder was Superintendent of Negroes); two direct from General Sherman, none whatsoever from Agent Monteith at Lapwai (which *proves* him to be intriguing against me) and a letter dated March first from the Northern Pacific Railroad Company, whose office is in New York: *I hear from Portland that you have delivered publicly a lecture on the Battle of Gettysburg, in which you complimentarily mentioned the dear boy and the brave officer, my son, who was killed in your first day's fight. I cannot express to you the sorrowful joy and the profound gratitude kindled in my heart . . .* Thank You, FA-THER, for permitting me who have never lost a son to console this sad old man; and thank You for taking from me so far only my arm. May You never take Guy from me, I beg you (this, only this)! *Dearest Father: We have all been praying for you, and Mother is becoming very blue.* O, that's very sweet from Grace! I do hope that she or Lizzie will inform me how Mrs. Perry is getting along. No word on this Captain Gray, I see. Is he serious about Grace? She's so tender-souled she needs an extremely sympathetic husband. When I consider how she still mourns for that colt she used to have (a well-broken animal named Topsy), I realize how she . . . O, suddenly I feel unwell—must never let anyone see. And has Wood received any missive from his intended? A lovely-haired belle, for a fact! Sometimes I worry that she is playing the field and will break his heart. *My Dear General: By the last mail I had received a letter from you informing me that you had received a letter confidential and private in character, stating that I am* constantly *under the influence of strong drink. I have resolved, on my bended knees before my GOD, that with the assistance of His sustaining grace I will refrain from drinking intoxicating liquors; hereafter, neither will I offer it to others. No one knows, but my GOD, the efforts I have been making . . .*

Yes, Guy, sit down. Roll up that map. Did you get any letters from Mother?

Dear Genl Howard, enclosed please find the signature card of my late
father, Mr. George Beauddry, who on your say-so placed all his savings in
the Freedman's Bank and lost it all in the crash, so I am hoping you can so
far redeem your promise as to return to his orphaned children their due,
sincerely yours, Mrs. Letitia Thompson, formerly Letitia Beauddry

the card made out to George Beauddry, with his master and mistress's names also written in (they being of course the original
Beauddrys), his height five foot five and one-fourth inches, his
complexion black, his plantation Edisto:

Yes, father; three or four at least—

—and a nickel's worth of side meat.
Where was that?

O, in Lewiston, of course. You know
that Sibley tent down by the river,
where them d——d officers sneak in,
and fancy they're real discreet? Well,
this one Blackfoot squaw, what she
did with me you wouldn't believe.
How many times?

Three or four at least. And if she's still
swishing around after we whip Mr.
Joe, guess what I'm a-gonna do to her?

Good.

And Glass has gone septic; he's about to expire—

So that is all the news of our bunch. Nobody cares anymore if Mr. Joe
dusts over the border and keeps his skin. How is Mother's cough? I
pray to GOD every night that our darling little Mary Elizabeth will
not be taken away from us like her brothers. Now you had better
address your letters, darling, to Fort Ellis, Montana . . .

Gazing into the still lake as if to count its leeches, Wilkinson holds his
envelope

(perhaps I am defective in some way, for Sallie's letter ought to be a treat
to me and she is plenty affectionate but I continue to find her passing
dull, perhaps on account of my own disappointment in being passed over
by the general);

Wood (not exactly one of us) perches on a boulder with his notebook on his lap, rubbing his head and then writing something
which resembles a squaw track cunningly doubled back on itself

—and a fish leaps:

extremely interesting the way the spiny knobs and scales of the Continental Divide manifest themselves as a reddish-brown fan on the lake! I
wonder if Professor Mahan could have explained it?

And pig iron's all the way down to $16.50 a ton. Could that
be true?

Don't know, sir.

If so, that's bad. The Silver Panic was just the beginning.
How're we supposed to live?

And on account of those *hateful Indian eyes,* and you
know what I'm talking about, well, that's why I believe
in phrenology

and just then Wilkinson receives a more substantial envelope! Wishing with all
his heart to save the general from distress, he has now unearthed (thanks to a
clipping service incarnated in his selfsame diligent Sallie) a number of unpleasant
new articles in the newspapers. While intimidating the storekeepers of the Bitter
Root Valley, Chief Joseph and his reds supposedly let loose impudent gibes about
"General Day-After-To-morrow," whom President Hayes would have sacked but
for our victory at Clearwater, and Governor Potts continues to deride to this day.
With each week the chase drags on, our poor general grows more risible. Wilkinson considers the slurs of the press to be nearly as disgusting as the dirty ribbons
on Sallie's corset, which he once discovered halfway by accident. And the root
cause is Perry's failure at White Bird Cañon! Concerned that in the forthcoming
Court of Inquiry this jackassical so-called colonel (whose brevet signifies no more
than one of Sallie's corset-strings) might drag our general down, and I mean *down,*
Wilkinson, his high forehead shining, has tabulated the reporters' insinuations,
then made certain investigations among the mule-packers, not to mention side-
trips to Perry's two most forthright enemies Ad Chapman and Captain Trimble:

General, I have certain information that Theller used to drink and run around
with loose women. Mrs. Theller doesn't know a thing.

Thanks, Wilkinson. I'll trust you to keep this in confidence. You'd best get
back to your duties.

Pappy's in a rage. His writing's all frazzled. There's been another
railroad strike, and they've called out the Army.

That's why our bunch ain't gettin' no help against the d——d reds.
Now they got the *socialists*

as Ad Chapman (who never receives letters) happily skins another eight-and-a-half-foot swan.

You know the way the Old Turnpike runs through Chancellorsville?

Sure. Lemme draw it in the dirt here. Now, this square's the Fairview Cemetery—

It weren't square, but—

Right. Then that's where we were that Sunday,

looking out across the slimy rocks of the lake bottom, across the leechy
blue which is pure looking yet mucky smelling. And Mr. Joe was over
there—

As for our *Christian Soldier,* well, unlike you others, I don't attach no blame
because we was all *told*—

And Empire Transportation has sold out to Standard Oil.

Then there's gonna be another French Revolution back East.

But them Secceshes must have been told *different.* Now, if we had Chancellorsville to fight all over again, and Sherman had *my* ear—

Blackie's mother died.

Put him on guard over that hill.

Yessir.

Them Indians is skulking over there, I'll bet,

like soldiers sitting around their campfires after mail call, and the ones who received no letters pacing sadly in the dark

(except for Chapman, who would only have expected trouble if he got a letter in the name of that Umatilla squaw he put away:

she can write her ABC near about as good as a mule),

all the tent-flaps open, men sharing home news with one another, sparks rising:

No, he gave it to me to hold. And since you know the mule-driver—

Now that there's getting pretty rare, like one of them old box-lock Sharpses, from before they started slanting the breech,

Perry,

whose bitter harshness of demeanor Wilkinson has always considered suspect,

wondering whether the general has just now been informed in some despatch that the Court of Inquiry has now been set in motion as it must be next year if not this year unless Mr. Joe does for me; I must study the general's face to discover whether he has yet begun to hide any fact; but no, I won't see anything because who can read so noble an idiot? Who will be my judges? They can trip up anyone they've got a mind to. I'll say the truth: that GODD——d Ad Chapman started it:

Is the mule-driver interested or not?

and here as so often Perry's thoughts take on the colors of dead men: black and yellow.

Captain Pollock, what news from Sara and the children?

O, Josie has been sick again, sir, but at least it's not the cholery—

Says it's worth whiskey, if the general don't—

Straighten up. Colonel Perry's staring at us—

—wanting to get my hands around Mr. Joe's throat, and, if he escapes, then some other dirty treacherous Indian will do (plenty of Indians all over the country).

Wrenching himself out of that maggoty pit, he entertains himself with a vision of Delia Theller,

with her brown hair falling smoothly around her wide fair oval face, then banged off at the neck, always with her silver hoop-earrings, her lace collar and that lovely single button under the throat, and me undoing it

—Delia, Delia, whom I have loved even more ever since she

realized she had become a widow and then covered her hair
in that black net cap—

and that Blackfoot squaw, as brave and determined as a quartermaster who must refuse some pushy officer, now gives me her
haughtiest once-over, so I practically want to hand her my last silver dollar: what a great show, and no wonder Theller's enchanted!
Talk about the best stock on hand!

—except for Delia:

D——n, I want a drink. And Delia with her legs spread. Soon as I get leave I'll
see if that squaw's still in Lewiston. When will that be? If Joseph doubles back
down into the Buffalo Country, it may be awhile before I can lay me down

with Delia underneath me
or even Theller's squaw in the tent, or
anyone but my GODD——d wife.

In the willow thicket growing out of the white gravel at the
lake's southwestern edge, a tiny creature moves, probably a
bird, although only a red would know for sure, and then he
hears a fly. From within the muck-scented greenness, a duck
dives down under the lake, then comes up pecking at something on its neck.

Now with Redington leading the general by the nose and me disgraced by
White Bird Cañon I'll never get to show what I can do. If I asked for permission
to scout ahead—

GOD HELP ME
AUGUST 24

1

*S*oldier, is that as fast as you can ride?
I been whuppin' her real good, sir, but she—
No excuses. You're falling behind.
Yessir.
And if I catch you mistreating that horse, you'll lose a month's pay.
Yessir.

I could sure use a squaw to make me some good elkskin
mockersins.
Well, you'd better get you some more burlap and be

your own d——d squaw.

I asked the sergeant if I could see Lieutenant Bomus and he—

Then go ask Doc and stop bothering the rest of us.

I could use some grease for my feet.

Go grease your asshole and see if we care.

Don't treat me mean. I always shared with you. My feet's gettin' all swoled up,

> Left—left—LEFT.

> Doc striding unweary with his elbows in, his hat at an angle.

If you won't do like the rest of us and wash your d——d feet whenever you can, you ain't got no sense.

Well, that softens up the skin.

Does not.

Anyhow, I seen 'em chaw that green leather in their teeth—

You never seen nothin'.

Where's Doc?

Somewhere.

Doc could trail that Joseph right across water.

Guy's right. They're looking sullen. Even Perry, GOD bless him, begins to complain of the old wound the Modocs gave him. Can I blame the man? If Lizzie were here to coax me, how could I prevent myself from lying down to rest? But this is mere weakness, nothing more; our desires need not bear on our actions for which we shall be judged. It may turn out that *I cannot whip Joseph.* LORD knows I'll keep trying! As yet every officer still holds the line, but Pollock and Jocelyn begin to bear watching; poor Trimble has failed, and even Miller is losing confidence—while good old Sladen could ride to the ends of the earth with his one leg! I can't deny that some enlisted men are getting cynical. I'd best nip all outward demonstrations in the bud—

> Jenkins, sing us a song.

> Nope.

> Why not?

> My mouth is all dried out—

> And Trevor's fixing to die to-night. He's gone delirious.

Anyhow, the croakers always find fault. They're lucky I pity them. If Sherman were here, he'd hang them up by their heels.

2

Did I mention Crazy Horse is dead?
O, was that in General Sheridan's letter, sir?
It slipped my mind to tell you. He resisted arrest—
At the Red Cloud Agency, sir? I thought he'd already surrendered.
Yes.
And how is General Sheridan otherwise, sir?
O, he's . . .

> O, they're building armories in all the important cities nowadays. That's what Blackie's uncle wrote.
> Well, in the letter I got—
> We're tired of your letter.
> But you see, after all them tramps and socialists has done, the Government can't let more strikes go on.
> Lazy bastards! What do they want to go on strike for? If my Daddy was still foreman he'd know how to get the work out of 'em.

>> When Mr. Joe put a spider in our dumpling back at White Bird Cañon—
>> That's right.
>> And then again at Cottonwood, and thumbed his nose at us at Kamiah—
>> For that matter, I say he got the best of us at Clearwater—
>> What in blazes are you talking about? That was a draw.
>> Well, even if it might have been a draw, it sure weren't no victory for us.
>> That trick he played us at Camas Meadows just goes to show—

>>> He's got no "sand" in him.
>>> Lounging like a Pasha in his big old Sibley tent . . .
>>> D——d right! Calls hisself a Christian when he's an idle one-armed bashi-bazouk!

> Sir, the flankers keep complaining they're hopping hot boulders for nothing when them Injun scouts already—
> Tell it to Colonel Perry if you're tired of living. I don't care to hear any more.
> Yessir.

>> . . . To keep all the Indians quiet . . .
>> And then we'll Christianize 'em, because

My stump aches. If Lizzie were here she could make it stop. She could even
>Shoot Mr. Joe! Ad Chapman says—
>That Chapman's a hard pill, all right.

I'm about ready to camp.

Who ain't?

Fixing to be a showery evening.

Looks that way.

What do you think, Jim? Say, what's your bracelet made of?

Weaselskin.

You make that yourself?

Sure.

Could you make me one?

No weasels around here.

Well, then, would you trade me yours?

For what?

What do you want for it?

No. You're the one trying to get it. You tell me.

O Godd——n you for a Godd——d sneaky savage! Always trying to get
the better of us—
>*Halt.*

3

Mason may know something about the Court of Inquiry
>(and it seems as if from what I overheard that rat Wilkinson squeaking
>to the general, there may even be a second one about my performance at
>Cottonwood,
>>in which case I am going to punch that so-called Major Shearer in
>>the teeth
>>>and have a word with Whipple, who looks as if he could
>>>use some cocaine
>>>>(I never thought he'd turn on me after I stood up
>>>>for him:
>>>>>It sure wasn't my fault about the Brave Sev-
>>>>>enteen! And what the fuck does he know?
>>>>>That jackass couldn't even arrest Looking-
>>>>>Glass! If I'm still post commander when
>>>>>this is over, I'll make his life worse than a
>>>>>nigger's)
>>>>and that skunk McConville deserves to get called out if I can
>>>>do it without getting in more shit with the Army),

so once he has brushed Diamond's coat and given him a grain or two of sugar he
looks up old Mason, who somehow is as trusty as a tin coffee pot,

the company street flying up behind them
> (lithe Chapman cocking glances all around)
>> as Red O'Donnell's bunch unhitches the mules from the high-covered wagons whose grimed canvas remains inexplicably paler than the dirt,

and after they have jawboned about nothing, neither one of them backstabbing the general, Perry begins to approach this topic as carefully as if he were creeping in on a line of Pi-Ute squaws gathering grass seed, when Mason catches sight of something:

> turning round, Perry spies that uncanny Umatilla Jim gliding out of the bushes

>> (excuse me, says Mason, but that man's sight is somehow obnoxious to me. Colonel, you should watch your back).

4

A tempting sortie for the queen's bishop, isn't it, Wilkinson?

Sure is, general.

You're fighting an uphill defense.

Sir, it's uphill both ways—

Life generally is.

Not for you, father! Anyhow, Wilkie's a hard man to conquer!

You're giving me a mighty good run, Guy. But it's time to finish this. So regarding that queen's bishop, watch me now!

Well, gentlemen, carry on. Who's general officer of the day?

Captain Miller, sir.

Again! Time surely rolls around.

Yessir.

It must be no joke for his troopers in the Fourth, pulling artillery all this way—

No, sir.

Would one of you go and find out if there's anything I can do for him? If their shoes are wearing out, I'll bend Lieutenant Bomus's ear . . .

I'll go, father.

Thanks. Where's Redington?

He came in, sir, looking very querulous, with two or three Bannocks staying on horse, nearly out of the firelight, and I heard him say to Captain Miller that the hostiles are miles and miles ahead. Then he rode out again.

Consistent little Redington! Was Buffalo Horn with him?

Beg pardon, sir, I didn't see.

Excuse me, Wilkinson. I believe Buffalo Horn's on detached duty to-day.

Please send him to me as soon as he rides in. I'll be in my tent.

Yessir.

5

Withdrawing himself behind the tentflap to study over Colton's map, and also because, declining to permit himself the raggedy buckskin livery of General Crook, he needs to reinforce the left seam of his trousers with a discreet strip of canvas tactfully obtained by Guy on his behalf,

> probably from Bomus, who is, after all, the emperor of such commodities
> > (Guy would gladly sew it up for me, but I'm squeamish to ask such
> > a favor of anyone, even my son),

and then to look after some expenditures

> > *(Dear General: Everything is paid up except the taxes for the current half*
> > *of the year. It is my duty to inform you that there has been a great decrease*
> > *in the value of property here . . .),*

he finds himself, as he so rarely does except in sleep, descending back into his Maine Woods with Charley boy and Rowland to cut firewood among the grand old oaks—real ones, not the Western imitations which can scarcely warm a kitchen half as long—and hemlocks and

> > *Glory, glory hallelujah—*
> > > how slowly and sadly they sing to-night! These iron bands of dolor
> > > behind my breastbone have nearly squeezed all the longing for
> > > glory out of me. I *will not* care. Should they poison my heart, I'll
> > > pass my heart by; I'll ride away to

archipelagoes of grey-green moss upon the ancient pines, silver raindrops on the jewel-weeds and on the ferns,

> > our Bannock scouts in their broadbrimmed white man hats
> > > (how soon will they try to steal the horses?)

and the trap rock in the mountains around Leeds, and

> > > > What's the password?
> > > > How the hell should I know?
> > > > Where are you from?
> > > > Helena.
> > > > Helena, Montana?
> > > > That's right.
> > > > Is this here Montana or Wyoming?
> > > > If you don't know that, how can you expect me to
> > > > guess your daily d——d password?
> > > > Well, it's *Liberty.*
> > > > *Liberty.*
> > > > All right; come on in. That's one blown-out horse
> > > > you're riding, boy.
> > > > Thanks.
> > > > What news?

I need a drink.

Not in *this* stinking Christian army. Now tell me the news.

Those *socialists* are striking again. The Army had to put 'em down.

Railroad strikes, is it? Godd——n Hunkies and Jews. Well, we'll fix 'em. (Hey, Blackie, water this man's horse.

—Yessir.)

Sure is fine to get some news around here.

Yeah.

Everything else well in the U.S.?

Lemonade Lucy's waxing fat in the White House.

Speaking of teetotalers. Well, so what?

And Brigham Young died.

Glory, glory hallelujah—

When was that?

O, sometime this summer. Heard it last month, guaranteed by a man from Missoula. Then our newspaper picked it up.

Well, soon's we whip Joseph we ought to march into Utah and get aholt of them *polygamist* gals. I'd bet they aim to please.

One thing I *will* say. I never met me a dishonest Mormon.

So are you with me on this, boy? We quit this cheapjack Army, ride for Salt Lake and conquer a few dozen of the fair sex?

Did you ever calculate how far Utah is?

Only about a million miles.

I will never forget the perfume of those woods: pine, sphagnum moss and
the smell of smoke, saddleblankets, stale piss and old sweat as
Trimble's boys fumigate their clothes for lice and

Glory, glory hallelujah—

most of all the rainy grey-green coolness of the New England forest. From what
Wood tells me, Alaska is all that. After we whip Joseph I'll take Lizzie and the
children to see that sector of my Department. Can Alaska truly have the same

Despatch for the general, sir. This boy's just ridden in
from Helena.

grey-greenness of rhododendrons, and so many brilliant orange and red toad-
stools shining like newt-slime?

Why, that's Headquarters!

Glory, glory hallelujah—

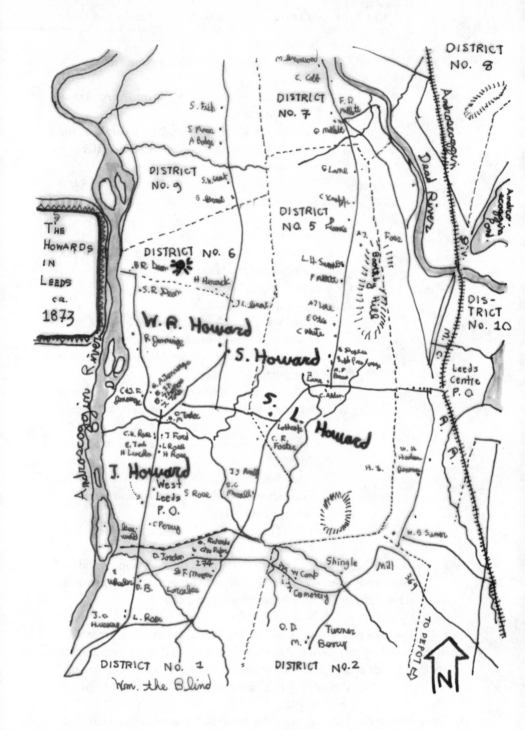

Yessir.

Since it had rained so heavily, Father thought it best to delay bringing in the corn. O, those cone-shaped stacks! How I used to dread that work! And Father let all three of us off to gather in huckleberries and blueberries for Mother. Charley boy kept teasing Rowland for the way he drove the spring wagon, and every time the bay gelding raised his ears I'd

> Fletch, you take him to the general and I'll find him something to eat—
>
> Thank you, sir. And it seems my horse lost his shoe back there in the lava beds.
>
> I'll have Doc take a look. See any hostiles out there?
>
> Made two good ones—

Blueberries by the pound, o, yes, and the fat smiles of jewel-green frogs,
> and Perry's voice as unmistakable as the stock of a Sharps carbine (he must be overseeing the pickets),
> and who's that out there?

and the way certain black old trees in Maine glow with whitish-green lichens (I don't hate the West, but, LORD, I'm tired!)—

General, sir, I've got a despatch rider just in from Headquarters.

Thanks, Fletch. Send him in.

Good evening, sir.

What's your name, son?

Kane, sir.

And you rode all the way in from Helena, did you?

Yessir.

GOD bless you! What do you have for me?

Here it is, general:

Headquarters—Army of the United States
Helena, Montana, August 29th, 1877

General O. O. Howard
Commanding Department of the Columbia in the Field, Head of Yellow Stone:

General:

I have just received from General Sheridan the despatch of which enclosed is a copy. You will perceive that he has three small forces east of the mountains to receive the Nez Percés when they issue from the mountains.

1st. General Sturgis with six companies on Clark's Fork.

2nd. Major Sloat, with five companies and a hundred scouts, on Stinking Water. and

3rd. General Merritt, with ten companies at Camp Brown.

Not much use for poor Gibbon, who of course is still nearly *hors de combat*—

Yours, as the pursuing force, requires great patience, but not much chance of a fight.

Glory, glory hallelujah—

There are many things in your Department about which I would like to consult you, and I will feel your absence much. Really I see not much reason for your commanding a Department after having driven the hostile Indians out of your Department, across Montana, and into General Sheridan's command.

So Sheridan is also my enemy
(sensing now, as if one had right-flank pickets posted all the way out to Washington, D.C., the influence of steady malice in the night, the horses snorting, the sentry on the verge of firing the alarm gun).
And I wonder if Sturgis has begun scheming to recover his career?

I find Lieutenant-Colonel C. C. Gilbert here who has served long in this Territory and is familiar with the Indians and the country in which they have taken refuge.

Is he one of Sheridan's tools? Or Crook's? If so, Perry might know him—
Glory, glory hallelujah—
Can this boy with the sun-faded hair perceive that I'm affected? *No.* Fair Oaks was worse than this. Can this truly be from Sherman or from one of his lackeys?
If GOD has no future use for me then so be it.

I don't want to order you back to Oregon, but I do say that

my heart is good; my heart is good;
The LORD is my shepherd. Ye that fear the LORD, praise Him, and

you can, with perfect propriety,

lie down in green pastures,

return to your command, leaving the troops to continue until the Nez Percés have been destroyed or captured, and I authorize you to transfer to him, Lieutenant Colonel Gilbert, your command in the field, and to overtake me en route, or in your Department.

Yours with great respect,
   Your friend,
      W. T. Sherman,
         General.

He remembers attending Sherman at the grand review of armies in Washington, riding slowly down Pennsylvania Avenue, the people offering flowers to their heroes, and Sherman turns to him, saying: Magnificent, Howard, simply magnificent! Our column's compact; our muskets glitter like a solid mass of steel . . . !— and then at Lafayette Square, Sherman doffs his hat to Mr. Seward, who of course remains in bandages after the assassination attempt; and then they take their posts upon the reviewing stand, Sherman at the President's side, and they stand for six and a half hours while their armies march by.

To Sherman's messenger he says: You must be tired, lieutenant.

I'm all right, general.

That's the spirit! Lieutenant Fletcher will take care of you now. Report to me straightaway after breakfast and I'll have a reply.

I sure will, sir.

         Why art THOU so far from helping me, and from the words of my
         roaring? My strength is dried up like a potsherd; and

By the way, how's General Sherman's health?

Excellent, sir. Same as ever.

That makes me glad. Fletch! O, there you are. Would you kindly take care of Lieutenant Kane until to-morrow?

Of course, general. Lieutenant, please come along with me.

Good night, lieutenant. O, and Fletch, based on the urgency which General Sherman has expressed, I'm appointing "Reveille" for three-thirty to-morrow morning.

Yessir. I'll let them know.

Good night, Fletch.

Good night, sir.

6

Once upon a time at West Point he was censured for maintaining a preexisting friendship with an enlisted man, from whom the regulations required him to separate himself; his friend Lothrop did become an officer in time; O yes, in time to die of typhoid during the Secession War. At West Point his fellow classmen first alleged, then firmly concluded against him, that he was an Abolitionist who associated with a "cut man" who was, furthermore, merely enlisted; moreover, that he had taken part in the Bible class, they said in order to ingratiate himself with the professor of ethics. Therefore his classmates refused to recognize him. He became suspicious and began to ignore the presence of others whom he suspected of "cutting" him, even if they were not doing so on purpose. Finally the Commandant of Cadets, Captain Alden, said to him *as a father to his son:* Howard, if I were in your place I would knock some man down.— This he did, and Captain Alden punished him as he had promised to do; afterward the oppression lightened.

But I cannot knock Sherman down; nor do I wish to. Whom then?

7

What precisely does he blame me for?

For Trimble's dereliction at Camas Meadows, of course—and Gibbon's half-cocked carelessness at Big Hole—never mind Perry's flying back in disorder from White Bird Cañon—and, most of all, for not catching Joseph, who—

I whipped him at the Clearwater—or nearly—

I rendered Red Heart safe, and drove Looking-Glass away from the settlers. I've been grinding Joseph down ever since. Who could have done more?

Once I sent Mason forward into that skirmish with Joseph at Weippe, that really ended the campaign within the limits of my Department. Rawn's failure at Fort Fizzle had nothing to do with me. Big Hole is certainly Gibbon's responsibility. Therefore—

GOD help me to run him down.

8

In Tampa during the Seminole removal campaign, he kept silent while Colonel Munroe whipped his colored boy. But he never forgot it. It was in that city that he announced he would never fight any duels.

Why, you would be proclaimed as a coward!

Major Mickinstry, that would not make me one. I am not a coward, and probably the time will come, if I live long enough, to show that I am not.

9

Some officers have proposed a game of whist, Whipple's lieutenants both gazing up at him with resentful anxiety, as if this Christian General would deprive or punish them should they attempt this pleasure. How can they not know him after all this? He smilingly wishes them a good match, then goes away, understanding that they will better enjoy themselves beyond his sight.

Lizzie would know what to tell me. Perhaps she's read aloud from Rowland's *Sermons of Consolation,* not that she admires my brother's writings, but she's aware how much I do love her voice

and Rowland

and her hair and

the mobility of her expressions, and especially the way she changes color:

as when he came courting a quarter-hour too early and Lizzie was still kneeling at her spinning wheel; she leaped up flushing, and that was when he truly fell in love with her. Twenty-three years ago now, her father not yet in the grave! And Rowland made me swear to always—

Now, the way they hang out tobacco to dry come autumn in Missouri, see, now what they do is—

offer me a turn with Mrs. Manuel. Since the reds have—

Cut it out. We're not in Missouri and we're trying not to think about that.

Not unless you've got some to share.

If you want some kinnikinnick to smoke, Doc's your man. He sold me some.

How was it?

It ain't cured.

If it ain't cured, then it ain't no d——d good.

Well, I'm from Missouri and I say—

I say go drink a gallon of castor oil. That'll keep you occupied—

Soldier, you didn't get that clean. Now do it over.

Yessir.

I didn't hear you.

Yessir!

All right. Boys, move away from the general's tent and let him be. On the double now.

All right, lieutenant.

Sherman has his glory and his glamour. I, humiliated, lack every alternative save only of being true to myself, for which I must thank You, FATHER.— But isn't Sherman likewise true to himself?

What was it Miles wrote me after I was acquitted? I wish I had that letter with me. *I think you must realize that "the LORD reigns."* That's more or less it.

10

Why, what's the matter, father?

Nothing.

The boys say that you're in trouble with General Sherman.

O, do they? I suppose they would—

I'll always believe in you, father.

Thanks, Guy. Let's sleep now.

It says here that there's Communist poison spreading through the railroads, and it comes from Europe.

Well, my brother-in-law's a railroad man, and he ain't never seen no *Communist.*

Maybe he has now.

You see, Gibbon's boys invented an elixir called *Rosebud punch.* It was champagne and—

That ain't quite it. It's champagne *cider.*

How d'you know?

And whiskey.

Exactly. That Lieutenant Kane was telling me all about it. He sure wanted a drink. And I had to tell him—

Careful. That's the general's tent up there, and he can—

Are they annoying you, father?

Sure could use a swig of that Rosebud punch!

Never mind. They suppose they're whispering . . .

Not in *this* army.

Where are you going, boys?

To the sinks, sir.

You know very well they're down thataway.

Yessir. Those down there are all filled up.

You read me well, Guy. General Sherman is impatient . . .

All right. You'd better hurry and finish your business before "Tat-too."

Yessir.

Sorry, father.

Will it disturb you if I light the lantern and study the map? I have a new idea to get at Joseph . . .

Of course not. Do you need help with anything?

You're not sleepy?

Not at all. I'd be grateful to do something helpful—

That despatch from Sherman was mortifying, I must say.

Father, what's been the most difficult moment of your career?

Without a doubt, Chancellorsville.

I see—

Not for the reason you think. Hooker's lieutenant-colonel ordered me to turn my artillery upon the men when they were running away—

My GOD! And did you?

No. Later Hooker accused me of being soft . . .

Didn't General Custer get court-martialed for shooting down deserters?

Yes. But let's not speak ill of him.

Father, may I ask one more question?

All right, Guy, go ahead.

Have you ever been afraid?

The one time was when McDowell made our troops a reserve force at Bull Run. We were all inexperienced, of course. It was our first battle. All morning and into the afternoon we had nothing to do but listen to the cannons. Of course we could hear shouts and screams.

What did you do?

I placed myself in His hands. What about you, Guy? Have you felt fear during this campaign? There's no shame in a feeling, only in being swayed by it.

No, sir. Well, I've sometimes felt anxious but not much. I've tried to profit by your example—

Thank you, Guy. Now I'd better look over the map.

11

Just as they finish breaking camp, dawn comes as grey as a cavalry blanket, burdening his weary men with a new misery of hours. Aspen leaves, hissing and almost chattering together in the low breeze, confuse and tire them like smoke.

Well, well, gentlemen, I haven't seen you since "Reveille." Any difficulties?

None at all, general.

Where's Lieutenant Kane?

Salving his horse, general.

Offer him one of Joseph's. By the way, the morning gun was late.

Yessir. I'll find out why—

And report it to me. I trust you all slept well?

Yessir—

What about you, Captain Trimble? Didn't you exert yourself yesterday? A sleepless man is a man who didn't push himself.

I'm all right, general.

Good. Because starting to-day, we'll need to push the men harder. The summer's wearing on, you know. Doctor Alexander, how are they?

They've recruited themselves somewhat, sir. Only four on the sick list—

Splendid! Remember this, all of you, and remind the men of it: In thirty-one days you have gained fifteen days on a body of the best mounted Indians in the world.

WHATEVER LIGHT THERE IS

1

*J*ust as our Crows ride faithfully to their Agency in season to receive annuities, so here comes Wood again (his beard growing longer over the months, his face becoming thicker and more ovoid) to gain wisdom and comfort of his general. (Euripides: *We show ourselves unhappy lovers of whatever light there is that shines on earth, because we are ignorant of another life, and the world below is not revealed to us.*)

General, I feel that I can ask you anything.

Of course you can, my boy.

Well, sir, what I've always admired the most about you is your sense of the right. You've stood up for the negroes at great cost to yourself, and protected the Apaches, and—

Yes, Wood, what is it?

Are we, I mean, sir, is putting Joseph on the reservation right?

You know that this policy did not originate with me. I could say *orders are orders,* and that would be enough for most soldiers.

Yessir.

Do you question orders, Wood?

Sir, I promise always to follow your orders without hesitation.

I should hope so. Now, what exactly do you expect me to say?

General, had the matter lain within your sole discretion, would you have undertaken to remove Joseph from his roaming-grounds?

Yes. I'm afraid that's not the answer you wished for. You'd like me better, perhaps, if I said: *The Government policy is cruel, and should be rescinded.*

Yessir.

We've all of us met with the bad goods that contractors foist upon the Army at inflated prices. Who knows how many of our soldiers have died as a direct or indirect result of such frauds? And of course, if we don't turn away our eyes, we see (yes, Mason, I'll be with you in five minutes) the far worse iniquities perpetrated by corrupt Agents upon helpless reservation Indians in their care: axe-handles sent without axes, brogans with paper soles, blankets made of shoddy and glue which fall apart when wet—I've heard some bad men laughingly call those *Injun-killing blankets,* Wood, and this winter GOD alone knows how many old people and children who depend on our Government will freeze to death in them—and, worse yet, the moldy bread, the barrels of putrid meat—and *we arrest them* if they dare to leave the reservation and hunt for themselves . . . !

Yessir.

Not a pleasant subject, I'm afraid.

No, sir.

But, Wood, consider: *The Indians are finished.* The Army has not the strength to patrol the treaty lines. Why, right now in the Indian Territory, hide men are conniving with the Agent to slaughter buffalo belonging to our Cheyennes—and we can't stop it, and couldn't even if there were two soldiers for every private American citizen. How much power could the President himself bring to bear? President Grant signed an executive order granting Joseph his range, and within two years they forced him to rescind it! Don't you see that if we left Joseph to his own devices in Wallowa, the settlers would come nonetheless, *as they have,* and within five years at the most, he'd be ruined?

I understand, sir.

As it was, we waited too long, so that he murdered eighteen people, not counting Mrs. Manuel.

Yessir. Of course he must hang—

I discussed our Indian problem with Commissioner Walker not too many years ago, and frankly, Wood, I—well, it was painful.

Yessir.

So, even though Joseph didn't want to go on the reservation, even though we may have felt sorry for him, it would have been best—buying him time, you see.

Yessir. But the *Injun-killing blankets* . . .

There are good Agents and bad Agents. The bad ones care only about profit. That's why President Grant decided to give the reservations to missionaries. And I think he was correct. Down at Lapwai, for instance, while Agent Monteith may sometimes act a trifle severe, he means well. Nobody's starving or freezing there. And the fact is, if he doesn't push them a bit, they won't change. We must make them realize that if they become farmers and homesteaders as our forebears had to, capable of owning individual property, and educated to preserve and defend it, then they'll have as decent a chance for prosperity as you or I.

Yessir.

Of course they do not *want* to realize it! When I find—as for instance in Arizona or Nevada, or for that matter in Oregon among the River Renegades, and Smohallie's band, yes, and Joseph's!—an Indian tribe very degraded indeed, as yet in the dimmest twilight of knowledge, full of maddening passions and unclean habits, I *never* see such a tribe growing better by its own motion. Never! They need patient and persistent eternal help, Wood.

Yessir.

All right. Now I want you to ride along our infantry and report on their discipline. Not much "sand" in them, I'm afraid.

No, sir. I'll go directly.

All right. Yes, Mason. O, I see. No, his report is unacceptable. Warn him not to fudge his returns again, or I'll punish him. And could you find out what's wrong with the artillery wagons? Thanks. Wilkinson, have your couriers returned from the Yellow Stone?

Not yet, sir.

You're looking stronger.

Thanks, general, I've thrown off this fever at last—

A cross to bear, wasn't it?

Yessir.

Your horse was jaded yesterday.

Yessir. He's not as strong as Arrow—

Now what was it? About Wood, I suppose.

Yessir. I fear he's turning Communist.

What *is* a Communist exactly? Don't they all speak French?

No, general. Communistic ideas are now widely entertained in America. I've read that the Communists might take over Philadelphia or New York—

And you seriously suppose that Wood is allying himself with strikers and tramps? Out here in the wilderness? That's nonsense, Wilkinson, and I won't hear any more of it. Now go make contact with the scouts and see where they propose to camp. Right away.

Yessir.

LORD have mercy! Yes, Fletch, what is it now?

Sir, Lieutenant Otis begged leave to tell you that the mountain howitzer is—

Naturally. He must have seen Mason coming. Well, his mules must be pretty blown, I suppose.

Yessir.

Tell him to switch animals with Calloway's remnant.

Yessir.

Fletch, how do you feel about Wood?

General, he's as solid as Gibraltar.

Good. And tell Lieutenant Howard to come here . . .

Just then Wilkinson appears, in order to silently and even shyly console his downcast general with a can of preserved oysters which he must have carried near a thousand miles.

THE LAND OF WONDERS
AUGUST 28–29

1

*J*oseph's foiled us again, sir!

True enough, captain, but he's running out of sap. Guy, to the list of Indian depredations please add: *Mr. Oldham, shot in face, and one of his companions.*

Right away, father. What dastards! Will Mr. Oldham recover?

That's in the LORD's hands. Their situation looks bad, I'm afraid. That's all. Sladen, ride yonder with me.

Yessir.

How do you think Spurgin's engineers are managing?

They work harder than beavers, sir! I'll sure allow they've got "sand"—

I wanted to show you this.

General, I've heard about it, of course.

From whom? Don't answer. Yes, of course. Nothing to be done.

General, may I shoot from the hip? You know I'm your friend—

Go ahead.

Sir, you can't blame Sherman. He's got the business men prowling round him, demanding that the Army do more for less—

I know all this.

Yessir. But one thing about you, well, you give others too much credit at the first, and then, when they abuse it, as human nature compels them to do, you feel betrayed. And that hurts you, sir, and I would pay my other leg, and both arms, too, if I could spare you that hurt, because after President Lincoln you're the best man I've ever known—

O, thank you—

President Lincoln I never met, of course—

Sladen—

General, please let me finish. You've done your level best in this campaign. If Mr. Joe's given us the slip so far, it's because you went out of your way to offer him a fair deal, and because every settler within a hundred miles of those reds keeps yelping for Army protection, which you give, while the reds ride farther ahead. The public doesn't understand what's not convenient.

That's so. Well, I guess we'll soon be seeing geysers and other marvels. Just like old times in Arizona.

Yessir. I wonder how old Cochise is getting on?

Keeping cool, I hope.

You said it, sir.

I was just reminiscing with Wilkinson—

Yessir.

Sladen, I feel about you exactly as I do about Colonel Miles. Did I ever tell you that he held my arm for me when they were cutting it off?

You sure did, sir, and I would enjoy to meet him. If we don't stop Mr. Joe in the National Park, I'll bet the colonel will need to come into the picture—

By the way, I'd value your opinion as to how well Guy's established himself.

From what I can tell, general, he's a hard charger; everyone gives him that.

What won't you say?

He's young and handicapped by being your son. He hasn't yet been lucky enough to distinguish himself. I saw him right after you got in from Virginia City—and no hint of weakness after that hard ride. I'm telling you straight, sir. No one says anything against him.

All right, Sladen. Thanks for your confidence. We'd best be riding back to the column or they'll be saying we're kidnapped by those *reds.*

A fine joke on our flankers that would be, sir.

Good afternoon, captain!

Afternoon, general. Afternoon, Captain Sladen!

How's everything with the Twenty-first?

Couldn't be better, general. The boys sure enjoy getting out of barracks.

Well, well! The former Blackfoot country! Who'd have thought we'd have come so far?

Who indeed, sir.

Captain Spurgin, you succeeded commendably in widening the Lo Lo road.

Thank you, general; that seems eternities ago—

It seems your company will be quite busy with road-building for some days yet.

Sure looks like it, sir.

The good people of Montana believe it's impossible to get wagons through here. You'll show them different.

Yessir.

Anything you need?

We'll do our best, sir—

Good man! Keep at it!

Good-bye, general! Good-bye, captain!

What a cheerful fellow!

Yessir.

Sladen, what do you suppose Joseph is thinking right now?

2

Coming into the beautiful country, the Land of Wonders ("Yellow Stone," they call it),

Major Mason's round face rising like a moon above the wagons as he rides the length of the column, dislikable though not exactly cruel,

> *Wakesh nun pakilauitin*
> *JEHOVAN'M yiyauki,*

they all take heart and pride, to think that this place pertains to our United States, and Wood tells himself: Anyway I'm leaving Big Hole behind, just like some dreamer in a prairie schooner who's fled his ugly life to come West:

> Ought to find us some upland plover, if the boys don't make too much racket. Could get the scouts to do it, I guess. Real good eating, and a d——d pretty bird,
>> grass as high as our stirrups

and even the general is heard to remark (to Trimble of all people): You know, we all felt like this when Sherman raised his magic wand and we commenced our March to the Sea—

3

Now, general, right here the Earl of Dunraven caught a trout on the fly, then cooked it in this very spring. It's called the Tea Pot.

What a marvel, Fletch! I suspect that Progress will find a profitable use for it.

Shall we give it a try, sir?

I'm afraid we'd best be pushing along. If we're lucky, perhaps Joseph will lead us to the Prismatic Hot Spring. Mr. Chapman, have you ever heard of geyser coffee?

4

The men are slow again to-day, father.

Well, after their discouragements and long marches it's no wonder we see some stragglers. Of course they must not be permitted to hold us up.

How would you rate Joseph as a general?

Inferior to Sitting Bull, for a fact! He hasn't yet wiped us out like Custer's men, now, has he?

He's led us a pretty good chase.

As an annoyance, he may be effective enough, but think, Guy, what can his object be? He can't whip the United States. He can't ever return home—

> *The men will cheer and the boys will shout,*
> *The ladies they will all turn out,*
>> *Left—left—left!*
> on Earth as it is in Heaven,
>> turn out and turn again;
>>> O, how blackly they all look at me: an index of their feelings.

Captain Pollock, how's Company "D"?

O, they're managing, sir.

And are you enjoying this country?

Well, general, we've seen quite a number of sulphurs.

Yes. Lieutenant Parnell, what news from Company "H"?

Sir, we're up for anything, because in '67 Colonel Perry went out for thirty days straight and rode twice as many miles as Crook, and we—

Ride ahead with me, lieutenant. You persist in believing that Colonel Perry's in trouble with me.

O, no, sir. He—

Parnell, I admire Colonel Perry. How could you think otherwise? Your company has nothing to fear. That's all.— What is it now, Fletch?

Sir, Captain Fisher's Indians found another of Joseph's victims.

Dead?

No, sir, he—

Bring him to me as soon as he's carried in. Even if he can't talk.

Yessir.

What's Captain Fisher's position?

On the south fork of the Madison, with the hostiles just ahead, he says.

Where's Redington?

On the trail, sir.

Good. Remind Wood he's tardy with Captain Jocelyn's returns.

Yessir. He—

That's all. Guy, what's your opinion of Mr. Chapman nowadays?

I sure admire him on a horse!

Yes,

> as we plant the guidon at last, the men turning out, currying horses and unrolling blankets with half-closed eyes,
>
>> Red O'Donnell unhitching his mules, thoughtfully painting white lead on their rawest sores,
>>
>>> Perry's bunch laughing and grumbling together as they stand in the stream, rinse their stockings and blouses together under the eye of their commander,
>>>
>>>> who as it turns out is still wearing his 1874 grey undershirt, now greyer than grey,
>>>>
>>>>> Umatilla Jim in the mountains four miles ahead, creeping alongside but never *on* the enemy trail and wondering if Strong Eagle or Red Spy might be hunting him,
>>>>>
>>>>>> or if Buffalo Horn would enjoy shooting him in the back
>>>>>>
>>>>>>> (the wind's voice reminds him of a song his wife sings when she is smoking deerskins to keep them soft);

Pollock detailing his unfortunates to dig sinks,
                none of them over-excited about the mud-pot ebul-
                litions of Wonder Land:
                        At least this'll bring us closer to the Union Pacific
                        Railroad.
                        And Colonel Perry looks at me as fierce as a Co-
                        manche, and he—
It gets dark much earlier now, father.

Yes. Would you mind trimming the lamp? And then fetch Wood here. Once you find him, send to Captain Fisher for news of the hostiles, and whatever he says, I want Wilkinson there. Afterward, take Ad Chapman aside and find out whether the Bannocks are intimidating our Nez Perce scouts. He knows the Nez Perces, and we'll need them at the end to convey surrender terms. Now listen to me, son. Chapman's a grasping bully. You'll need to learn to handle men like him. Be polite, but don't stand for his insolence.

I can manage him, father.

Go then, and GOD bless you.

Yessir; Lieutenant Howard sent for me—

It's eight-o'-clock p.m., I believe.

Yessir. I'll dateline accordingly.

You can read me like a book! All right, Wood, this despatch will be to San Francisco. *Indians still aim northward, bearing east to avoid my troops. Sent Cushing five days ago with three companies . . .*

Yessir.

This next will be to the commanding officer at Fort Ellis. *Please communicate with officer in command 7th Cavalry, probably Colonel Sturgis: News of Indians crossing Yellow Stone near Mud Springs, below Sulphur Hills . . .* Have you ever met Sturgis?

No, sir.

Entre nous, a most unfortunate person. Now look over the map with me. The Nez Perces must be somewhere about *here.* I don't suppose they'll ride to Wind River country unless we force them in that direction. What do you think?

I agree, sir.

Why do you agree?

Because this cañon here—

All right. Good. You do see the point.

Thanks, general. I suspect that much depends on the Crows—

Yes. Now telegraph General Crook . . .
                        What a busy Christian General!
General, sir, another Bannock seems to have deserted.

That's disappointing news, major! How do you know?

Well, we haven't seen hide nor hair of him since breakfast time yesterday, and he—

All right. Keep me informed. Back already, Guy? Then please prepare a clean copy of this message to Colonel Gibbon. Thank you. By the way, your horse wants rubbing down.

Right away, father.

Do you feel hungry? This crisp air does wonders for the appetite.

That it does. I was just thinking about the apples we used to—

Kill that thought. Wilkinson, have you seen Lieutenant Fletcher about?

Still with the quartermaster, sir.

Send him to me as soon as they finish that tally.

Yes, sir.

And here comes Jim. Bring him here. Halloo there, soldier! What's your latest impression of the scouting life?

Real good, general.

Have any of the boys mistreated you?

No, sir.

Good. Now what about Joseph?

The reason we can't find him is because he don't know where he is.

Ha, ha, ha! So you think he's lost, do you?

Yessir.

If you were me, where would you trap him?

The thing is, general, he don't know where he's going. Maybe he'll turn around, try and go back home, or maybe—

Fine. Jim, I'm going to ask you something.

Sure, general.

Have you ever met Smohallie?

No, sir.

Is he a bigger Medicine man than Toohhoolhoolzote?

General, they all go to Smohallie when they can.

Even Joseph?

Yessir.

No more, I hope! Now tell me this: What can Smohallie actually do?

Well, general, when big Dreamers sing, they can make people real strong mad, or strong brave, or whatever they want.

And you believe this?

General, I have always told the truth.

I hear some misguided Indians in your tribe have run away to be Dreamers.

We have our own Prophets, general. Wilatsi and Luls. They died and came back. Maybe they died again now.

What foolishness! Now I'm disappointed in you, Jim.

O, no, general, I don't believe in the Indian religion. If it had worked, Joseph wouldn't be on the run.

You can go.— O, good evening, Trimble. How are your bunch enjoying the Indian ponies?

Well, sir, even as little as they are ridden, they won't stand one-fourth as much as an American horse. No wonder Mr. Joe uses up so many of them!

So you believe he's using them up, do you?

Yessir.

Good. How are your men?

Excellent, sir, and itching to fight.

Just what I hoped to hear. Carry on.

Yessir.

Colonel Perry, your troops were straggling to-day.

Well, general—

I wish you to stir them up.

Yessir.

Are you digging in your heels against me?

Not at all, general.

Perry, this campaign has gone on long enough. As we used to say during the war with the Seminoles, *we haven't lost any Indians.*

We whipped them at Big Hole, sir!

We surely did. By the way, colonel, I'm told that Lieutenant Theller sometimes ran with fast companions.

O, is that right, general?

Well? Is it so? Could he have been *inebriated* at White Bird Cañon?

     at which Perry flares like a wolf at his kill, or a miner at his claim.

No? Then good night, colonel. Now, Wilkinson, would you unroll the map? If we place Sturgis here . . .

Yessir, although if Joseph then—

That would be impassable, even to Indians. Think on Joseph's women and children!

Yessir, but if the warriors—

Then Sturgis will need to guard three passes. How thin is he spread? You may be correct. Show this map to Captain Fisher, and you'd better also ask Chapman. Then report to me. O, hello again, Wood. What do you think of our new Crow scouts?

They'd like to meet you, general.

All right. Well, well—how brave they look on their horses! Infamous horse thieves, aren't they?

So I've been warned, sir.

And perhaps a trifle insubordinate to the United States? Colonel Gibbon praised them none too highly.

Well, sir, but from what I've read, they've been a peaceful tribe ever since '34. That was when they besieged Major Culbertson's trading post, and he showed them the light. It only took one cannon-shot to impress them. Right in the middle of all their tipis—

O yes; very good. Now, interpreter, what's that interesting-looking old buck saying?

Sir, he says: *The soldiers from Fort Ellis are our friends. Are you from Fort Ellis?*

Tell him we're from another Department altogether.

Sorry, sir; I don't think he understands what a Department is.

All right. What else does he wish to tell me?

I have something to say to you and the Great Father. We are not given enough beef.

Tell him I'll mention it to the Great Father next time I see him.

Perfect answer, sir! That'll flummox him—

I'm not joking. I'll certainly take it up next time I'm in Washington.

Yessir.

If we don't keep our promises, we're no better than they are.

Yessir.

What's he saying now?

Well, general, he informs us that he was thick with Half Yellow Face, who died with Custer.

That's good enough for me.

Yessir.

Ask him to describe his sensations after that battle.

He says, it was a black day, general; he was very sad that we got whipped by the bad Indians.

GOD bless him! Has he ever met Sitting Bull?

Never, sir, because Sitting Bull is the enemy! Very, very bad man, he says—

Ask him whether Sitting Bull might come south to make a junction with Joseph.

He says: Sitting Bull is very dangerous. Who knows what he might do?

That will be all. I hope he'll be satisfactory to Fisher and Redington. Now, Wood, who, having become bearded and bloodshot like a veteran of a real war, among all these fine sunburned troopers runs neck to neck with my son for the prize of handsomest—

Yessir?

We've heard nothing satisfactory from General Terry. I wonder if he's secured the Musselshell River yet?

It's a concern, sir. In fact, the map shows that all through Judith Basin—

Exactly. We'd better prepare another despatch to General Sheridan, to hold Terry's feet to the fire. A somewhat unenergetic officer, I'm afraid. Colonel Miles must still be occupied in mopping up the Sioux . . .

Yessir.

Miles, you know, was my adjutant at Fair Oaks. And he served on the Court of Inquiry which acquitted me of fraud and peculation in regard to the Freedmen's Bureau. A very loyal friend.

Yessir.

When I was found innocent, do you know what he wrote me? I'll always remember it. He wrote: *I think you must realize that "the LORD reigns."* What do you think of that?

That must have pleased you, sir.

Are you ready?

Yessir.

      Well, boys, we're bound to see some strange lands now.

        Let Bacchus's sons be not dismayed,

        but join with me, each jovial blade.

  How grand it all is!

Beautiful ain't no description,

    a dark green star of larkspur like a fanciful military medal

    and the white phallus of Liberty Cap, whose stuff seems to have been half shaped on a potter's wheel, the potter then called eternally away,

    then the Palette Spring, whose boiling water streams down its white and yellow-brown terraces, sickly trees struggling out of the stone which glistens like ice, making the clear water sparkling down its surface resemble sun-shimmers

      (Well, Mason, what do you think of this gusher?

      A fine place to wash clothes, general),

followed by Mammoth Hot Springs, where Mr. Joe murdered that music teacher and his friend right there at the hôtel in the tall sagebrush, chokecherries dead ripe around us as we march, the river as silver as a burnished rifle:

      enough buffalo and antelope for any man to live royally.

      When my enlistment's up, I'll get me a wife

          even as equivalent fantasies of Nanny alight on Wood like fireflies, whose night-dreams nonetheless have become dark as Joseph's hands,

          while Wilkinson joys to be every day riding into country he's never known before:

              What a treat it's been to cross the Rockies! And now this Yellow Stone! Quite pleasant to study the blank places in the map with the general as we determine which way to go. Pretty soon I'll know Yellow Stone; and once I know a place I never forget it. For instance, I have Lapwai in my head just like the multiplication table. When I go to sleep I like to glide over every cabin and tent; I peep in through Mrs. Theller's window, and watch the FitzGeralds' children taking their evening bath; even the wigwams of our good Nez Perces are *engraved in my mind* as they say; I would be happy, I think, controlling a post like that—and I would do a far, far better job than Perry,

              but it will be perfectly satisfactory to return to

Portland with the general, exchanging recollections with him on the beauties of the Yellow
Stone;
and the bugle sounds "Retreat" and the evening gun shoots,
Red O'Donnell still putting his lariat in order,
the sun as red as an angry buffalo's eyes,
our sentinels lying prone in invisible threes, and the evening
overwhelmed by the sucking sounds of cavalry horses grubbing up the grass.

5

In life as in whist, hearts can't go round twice without being trumped. Edisto
and the Freedmen's Bureau, wasn't that enough? And I'd already suffered Chancellorsville, compared to which the loss of my arm was insignificant. And now, so
it seems, I'm to be tested again. O LORD, give me fortitude and cheerfulness,
for Lizzie above all,
O my Lizzie,
and permit me to play high cards just a little while longer
looking up from the map whose half-told contours now appear so unlike
my prior detached pictures of Chief Joseph withdrawing over the aspen-
evergreen shoulder of Targhee Pass and down into unknown greyish-
yellow meadows on the way to Yellow Stone,
and withdrawing the tiny Bible from his breast,
or low ones after my highs have been exhausted.

6

Wood, what did you find out about minerals and sapphires?
Captain Pollock, I asked around but—
You don't care for me anymore. Now you're high up with the general—
No, sir, I swear it's not like that! I've asked around, but—
You never come around to sing nigger songs with the old bunch.
I'll stop by to-night if I can, sir,
GODD——n you.
Wood, I'm falling out of favor with General Howard.
Sir, I'm sure he values you as much as ever——
The thing is, he's nothing but a d——d professor—
Sir, I'll thank you not to swear at our general.
Excuse me, Wood. That's just my manner of speaking. Anyhow, if you could
put in a word, tell him that Company "D" could go ahead and get Joseph in a week.
You know we can ride like Indians! We'll finally wrap up this campaign—
Yessir.

7

Umatilla Jim has ridden out far past *Lédinton,*[*]
　　his heart wishing for good words from Colonel Píli,
　　but our enemies' trail now narrows, the forest closing gloomily in
　　　　—an ambush place!—
therefore, picketing his horse behind some trees, then tying his Medicine bundle
around his arm, he begins to whisper a song to his Takh:
　　the Spider, Who gives him the Power to kill others,
　　　　and creeps around the dark turn with his Springfield carbine point-
　　　　ing ahead,
　　　　　　finding no Pierced-Noses, but a meadow world whose hori-
　　　　　　zon is blackened by buffalo beyond counting.

8

Soon we'll see them gangs of buffalo! I always did want to—
Hey, Redington, how much are buffalo hides going for nowadays?
O, hardly worth the bother. Fifty cents for a summer skin, and maybe a dollar
sixty for a fine winter pelt. It's been a boom year, so the big buyers can jew us down
back East.
Then better we leave 'em alone until winter, I guess. After we whip Joseph—
You'll never get back here.
O yes I will.
When's your term up?
Two more years. That's nothing.
　　　　　　　　What a tempting pawn! But I won't take it.
And then what's your notion?
I'm a-going back to the Crows to buy a young squaw.
　　　　　　　　Very kind of you, Fletch, but I'll take your knight just
　　　　　　　　the same.
You fixing to be a *squaw man?* Why on earth?
I can get a nice one and good worker, sixteen years old, for forty dollars hard
money. The Crow scouts and I have been jawboning real good. That Horse
Rider, he's a white man and he's awful happy with his wife. I guess I'll civilize
my squaw or else she can Indianize me, I don't much care . . .
Well, that tears it!
　　　　　　　That reckless capture will cost you the game!
　　　　　　　Not if I can help it.
What about you?

---

[*]Redington.

O, I'm off to the gold fields. Eight more months . . .

Correct move, Wilkinson. That's absolutely the best defense against Cozio's Attack.

Excuse me, general, you surprised us! It's been a tricky game—

Is Staunton's chess chronicle still of value to you?

Sure is, sir. It's not a bit outdated.

Well, keep it as long as you like. Has anyone seen Colonel Perry?

He's down there with the howitzers, general.

O, so he is. Excuse me, gentlemen.

Good evening, sir. How does this weather compare to Maine?

It certainly compares, colonel. You're holding up well.

Thank you, general. I'd rather be here than chasing Modocs through lava holes.

Yes, that must have been quite an adventure. I wish I could describe how interesting it all was when I rode into Cochise's Stronghold . . .

Yessir.

Well, we should be getting in another crack at Mr. Joe pretty soon.

Sure looks like it, sir,

> O yes, and here comes that shitty d——d Chapman, riding high like the Admiral of Idaho's squawfucking Navy, telling the general what he craves to hear,

>> and Mason almost seems to see before him General Terry's narrow face, the beard and moustache stuck on for a joke, and that two-dimensionally cadaverous yet somehow not Lincolnesque frame:

>>> Had I been with him in the Dakota Column last year, I would have risen considerably faster. I am fond of General Howard, yes, but the way he is going about this campaign I won't ever get my star.

Perry, another despatch came in, and I'm afraid there will definitely be a Court of Inquiry about White Bird Cañon.

I see,

> as if you haven't already hounded me with this a hundred times. What exactly is your jackassical *aim*, you GODd——n Christian cripple?

Don't worry about it. These things are disagreeable, but of course the judges are always fair.

Of course, sir.

I speak from experience, Perry. As I'm sure you know, I faced something of the sort after Chancellorsville.

Yessir.

Perhaps you've heard it discussed behind my back.

Not at all, sir—

You know, on the evening before they broke through, General Hooker rode with me along my front line, and kept exclaiming: *How strong!* And at the very beginning I despatched Colonel Asmussen to ensure that all was right in the direction of the firing. And remember that we did detain Stonewall Jackson for over an hour; as a matter of fact, we stopped him forever. All the same, Perry, it has been customary to blame me and my corps ever since. Fourteen years now it's been and still they—

(Perry's mouth tightening)

Well, their imputations of—of neglect to obey orders, of *extraordinary self-confidence,* whatever that meant; of not strengthening my right flank by keeping proper reserves; of neglecting to send out pickets and skirmishers—far from true!

I'm sorry, sir.

I certainly did all which could have been done by a corps commander . . .

Yessir.

And so did you.

Thank you, general. I tried my best, and Theller—

I remember when my dear friend Captain Griffith of Philadelphia took his mortal wound. I went to his bedside, Perry, and I said to him: *Captain, your wound is a punishment to me and not to you.* And he . . . To you, Perry, I would say the same. What happened at White Bird Cañon was my failure, not yours.

Thank you, sir. That means a lot to me.

9

Fletch, do you know what I just heard from Major Mason? Apparently General Sherman just recently passed through here.

Yessir.

As a tourist!

Yessir, I did hear something of the sort. He was escorted by Company "L" from Tongue River—

O! Who told you?

Buffalo Horn, sir. He knows our every corps; it's almost unnerving. And it seems Mr. Joe has now kidnapped and outraged a party of tourists in the vicinity—

That's right. Redington's on their trail just now. What do you think, Fletch? Wouldn't it be splendid if we met General Sherman to-morrow with *good news:*

Joseph and his confederates safely in irons, Sherman striding rapidly toward me, smiling and puffing on his pipe

(he has just now decorated *thirty-one* of Miles's soldiers with the Medal of Honor for overthrowing the Sioux!—not us!)

as I turn out the guard to receive him, our drums beating *the long roll* just before I present my army to him with every compliment

just as he had ever craved to do, from the very first time they really crossed paths (although they had already been introduced at Chattanooga, during a conference of strategy presided over by General

Grant): a humid dawn when he surprised Sherman's bridgemen on the North Chickamauga, and Sherman himself was there, shouting cheerily: How are you, General Howard? That's right! You must have got up early . . . —at which he knew in his heart that here stood his true leader, no less resolute and indefatigable than he himself (GOD knows, not a soul on this earth could ever be more so!), but recklessly grim and mirthful all at once as he could never be; he knew how to spend himself to his utmost and had proven at Fair Oaks that he could laugh off his own most atrocious agonies; but to enjoy *hazarding* oneself like a gambler (it was well known that Sherman lacked Grant's faith in PROVIDENCE), to *feel,* and glory in the feeling, this pattern of being touched by some as yet unmatured consonance in the acolyte whose shrill voice, sadly brilliant eyes and myriad aloofnesses—from drinking together, from swearing, from expressions of rage and violence against the enemy, not to mention companionable nigger-baiting—left him too indrawn to *dare,* socially at least; how could he ever know spontaneity, except when he gave himself again and again in prayer to OUR SAVIOR, or in passion, succeeded by devotion, to Lizzie, or in lovingkindnesses and sweet sillinesses with his younger children? But here laughed General Sherman, whose greeting, so simple, recognized his ear-liness as a happy, natural characteristic of any zealous soldier-brother in this soon to be bloody morning of a relentless year—and in his affection for Sherman there might have been the protective-ness of the phlegmatic nature (which Howard in truth possessed, no matter that his enemies claimed to smell hysteria in him) to-ward the mercurial one—for everyone likewise said that Sherman was more perturbed by excitement than Grant. He yearned to shoulder still more misery, drudgery and peril for the sake of this open heart whose openness might someday be wounded—although if it actually had, would his ardor for Sherman have declined?

Yessir. It would be splendid indeed.

The men they will cheer and the boys they sure will shout,
    we officers in our fantailed dress coats trimmed with buff
The ladies, O, the ladies, how they'll all turn out!
    and Lizzie in her lilac Sunday dress, with Mrs. Perry on her arm
        (the brightness of this Yellow Stone country painful on my
        eyes):
And we'll all feel gay when—
By the way, Fletch, who's the officer of the day?
Captain Miller, sir.
O, that's right. Will you ask him how far he trusts our Bannock scouts?
Right away, sir. Sir, Buffalo Horn is sullen of late, he says.

Well, send him over. I'm sure I can coax him back into a good humor. Wilkinson, how would you rate Sandford's shavetails?

Not exactly neat from garret to cellar—

Exactly. Warn him there's to be a surprise inspection to-morrow, and everything had better shine like a silver dollar. I do hope he can pull them together. Hard marching is no excuse.

I agree, sir.

Then ride to the rear of the column and see how many men have fallen out.

Right away, general. And Sladen purposes that the three of us sing some hymns to-night.

Good. O, and Wilkinson?

Yessir?

Wilkinson, do you suppose that Fisher really knows the mind of his Indians?

10

Regarding Captain Fisher,
> toward whom Perry can't help but feel friendly because the man is bearded and wide-hatted just like General Crook
>> and almost exactly Perry's height: six feet,

it must be confessed that Wilkinson,
> to whom it is essential that this campaign be conducted in a spirit of integrity,

dislikes him because for the sake of his collection (although he claims inability to control his reds) he keeps digging up the graves of our enemies, who, evil though they surely are, ought to be left undisturbed until the Last Trump;
> truth to tell I do feel much disgusted at our ghoulish Bannocks; why the general won't punish them I'll never understand. But it's not my business; who cares about me anyway? Now he's practically put Wood in my place. I can't say I expected that. Well, he *is* my general just the same and I'll follow him without thinking about it. Please, GOD, give me patience with all these afflictions, and send me an opportunity to distinguish myself again even if I die for it; although in all honesty I was plenty brave enough at the Clearwater.

11

And then they move out, the cavalry riding single file on Spurgin's narrow road, the infantry marching at a hundred and ten paces a minute.

Mr. Chapman, the general desires you to see him.

Where is he, lieutenant?

At the rear. Some snaffle with the artillery wagons.

If only he could have travelled light! I feel the same as you.

What do you mean?

Looky here, Lieutenant Wood, we all know you're sick of this campaign.

That's not true.

It ain't, eh? All right.

By the way, Mr. Chapman, I'd like to ask you something.

Well? Am I in trouble with you now?

Why did you turn against the Indians?

Which ones? You mean Joseph's reds? They was fine to me. Treated me right, and all that. But they stood between me and my dreams, so that's why I done it.

12

General, Captain Robbins is bringing in another of Mr. Joe's victims.

O, and who is that?

I can't say, sir, but the captain's riding in just now. The fellow's still alive, it seems. Shot through the head.

Bring them both here.

Yessir.

Good afternoon, captain. Good afternoon, Mr.—

Cowan. The Nez Perces shot me in the head and then tried to brain me with a rock. My wife and her sister—

They're safe, thank GOD. You have my word. Now, Mr. Cowan, did you see Joseph himself?

That cruel red devil! Pretended to let me go—and Looking-Glass was there—

Wood, where's Doctor Alexander?

Standing by, general. I'll—

Wait a moment. Mr. Cowan, before you get medical attention, is there any information in your possession which will help us get Joseph?

Lots of 'em—on their horses, going fast, and the squaws yelling all the time—

Calm yourself. Did you see any other white captives? We're hoping that a Mrs. Manuel is still alive—

No, general, I—

All right, Wood, take him to Doctor Alexander. Stay with him awhile and see what else he can tell you.

Yessir. Please come with me, Mr. Cowan. It's not far.

My wife—!

Don't worry now. Who shot you? Was it Joseph?

My wife, she, her name is Mrs. Emma Cowan, and they've also kept her sister, in order to—

Wood can almost see those grim Indians levelling their weapons at Cowan while his wife and sister-in-law look on screaming

and Red O'Donnell, enthroned in the spring seat of his wagon, reaches back without looking, grubbing into his sack of dried apples.

What in myself should I repudiate?

The general is right, I see, and always was. My sentiments keep chilling me like cañon-shadows. Our arrest of Red Heart was certainly unethical—

but who are my friends,

and how can I stop wasting myself?

What should I do?

O, that stone cold murdering Joseph!

Don't I want to put all this behind me? That means getting through the campaign and—

Maybe Gibbon was also right. If the squaws were shooting back, what the hell was he supposed to do? And why won't Joseph surrender? I now hate him more than anyone.

THEY ARE THE ONES WHO DID WRONG THINGS

1

They are following us as perpetually as FROG stays glued to the MOON's eye, even now into late summer, when the male tree swallows have begun turning greener:

our women gathering serviceberries and chokecherries as they ride, no longer hoping to stop long enough to dry them into cakes,

whipping the mules our best men stole from Cut Arm

(these animals are strong, but cannot travel quickly, so let us beat and scare them until they die! That will punish Cut Arm the Moldy—

and if only he had not picketed his horses that night!

Peopeo Tholekt, whom the Bluecoats nearly killed, actually untied Tsépmin's grey racing-horse and stampeded him away, but in the morning he was not among the captured animals; who can say how that happened? Red Spy, scouting back upon the Bluecoats, is grieved to see our former brother once again riding that fine stallion:

Why can we never kill Tsépmin?),

our weary wounded children weeping
>(Mourning Dove has now begun to die; black blood blossoms on her deerskin dress);

and Over The Point is making us all homesick by singing,

although Looking-Glass grows easier in his heart, since we praise the way he led our night raid on Cut Arm

—whom we would tear apart with our hands!—

I am telling you three times, although he must not be head-chief anymore, Looking-Glass remains a good war-chief!

and now his Crow friends will take us into their country;

while White Thunder's heart continues proud that he injured those killers

and his great war-friend Wottolen, bruised below the ribs by an almost spent Bluecoat bullet, is laughing yet over how we scared them into the cottonwoods

>(they cannot make themselves brave);

>he jokes with Toohhoolhoolsote, who can steal a tethered horse from the hand of his sleeping enemy;

as for Ollokot, who led the young men of Wallowa so well on that night, he has begun to heal from the death of Fair Land, his matchless one,

>whose son he now carries all day on his roan horse

>and Cloudburst rides behind, driving the pack animals and worrying about

>how to do alone for her man and boy what Fair Land used to help her do,

>>White Bird turning aside to shoot mallards for his People

>>even as White Thunder kills a black bear cub so that his Uncle Yellow Wolf, his Aunt Springtime and the other wounded People can salve themselves with fat,

>>>all our People riding here and there as they please, delighted to have escaped from being penned up forever on painted land,

>>>longing to ride and hunt forever

as we drive our ponies into the Buffalo Country:

>a rich home where drying meat will dangle everywhere,

>>camas prairies and wild horses again at our hands, going this way farther than we know, and that way into the dead places which the Bostons have already made.

Even now,

>although Burning Coals has lost Long Ears and six more good stallions,

we remain horse-rich:

>black and ocher they accompany us, red and white, lovely palominos and strong Appaloosas, our jewels—

>>a thousand and more!

>and just as a silty stream flows into a clear green river, muddying it, our wealth pours onto the trail, sometimes half a dozen abreast, raising the Big Dust for Cut Arm, saying: *Hinimí!,*

our herders riding in and out of the horde, quirting the slowest: *kíw, kíw!*

Now we arrive at the place where White Thunder's grandfather Homas died while hunting buffalo. We ride up the river and cross it where the two big rocks stand, there on the south side of Tongue Water,*

> TRAVELLER's light greening the golden sagebrush, buttes standing out,
> the sky finally bluer than blue-white,

riding on as if we were thirsty and the river were receding,

but where we go is as obscure as the part of the forest where GRIZZLY BEAR WOMAN dwells all alone.

2

Meanwhile Looking-Glass, he whom the Crows call *Arrowhead,*
> who in his youth used to climb trees to kill eagles for their feathers,
now decorates himself,
>> his wives winding brass wire around the ends of his braids as he fastens
>> on his brass earrings, his daughters cleaning that tin looking-glass he
>> loves:
soon he will be smoking again with Blackfoot the *lucky man,* whom he aided against the Cutthroats
>> and Húsishúsis Kute pulls on his eagle-plumed headband of fine hard
>> rawhide;
>> Toohhoolhoolsote will likewise ride with them, for he is longing to eat
>> buffalo liver in order to improve his old eyes;
>> Strong Eagle,
>>> remembering a certain Crow woman who paints her face with
>>> white clay,
>> and his new war-friend Over The Point will also go
>>> (although Wottolen, Red Owl and Two Moons speak against it);
>> likewise Ollokot, because when his marriage dance with Fair Land was
>> held, Looking-Glass came to him, and gave many horses
and because he has said to Heinmot Tooyalakekt: Elder brother, stay here
and I shall go for you, in case they kill us;
>>> therefore, thanking and praising him, his brother chief,
>>>> who has travelled to the Buffalo Country only once
>>>>> (to Looking-Glass he is as ignorant as one who cannot
>>>>> recognize the coughing of a grackle),
>>> remains to help the weak,
>>>> whom Lean Elk leads deeper into the forest, shouting: *Hurry, hurry!*
>>>>> (Looking-Glass's heart is so happy to ride away from this man
>>>>> that he begins singing).

---

*"A big river which flows through Yellow Stone."

Riding their best fast horses northwest into the hot country of mourning doves,
and wondering how it will be,
they go easily, unworried about that pale old creeper Cut Arm:
Ollokot first, on the same cream-colored buffalo horse he rode at Sparse-
Snowed Place,
then Húsishúsis Kute,
and because Heinmot Tooyalakekt saved Looking-Glass's horses at
Ground Squirrel Place, and those good sister-wives Blackberry Person
and Asking Maiden have saved most of his ornaments, Looking-Glass,
wishing to rest his favorite stallion Home From Capture, rides a fresh
bay whose collar is of trade cloth dark blue, light blue and yellow, embroidered with white pony beads in diamonds and triangles outlined in
black,
while Toohhoolhoolsote's horse is ugly and old like him
and Strong Eagle's horse is as graceful as a woman,
and Over The Point rides a fine black stallion whose saddle is lightly
decorated;
so they ride on, their horses bending down to drink as they wade each cañon
stream,
until these emissaries presently see smoke and send word;
and just as a rider throws up his arms when he is shot in the breast, then
whirls off his horse, so the red SUN speeds out of the ground
as they enter the Crow Country,
watching for Lice-Eaters and Bostons to kill.
Looking-Glass the renowned one now paints his face red
and Over The Point and Húsishúsis Kute paint their faces in reds and ochers,
while Strong Eagle,
he whom we can always recognize from far away, from the lovely shoulder-
beadings on his elkhide shirt,
decorates himself in stripes of white and yellow,
but Toohhoolhoolsote makes himself more varicolored than anyone,
for he, farfaring Dreamer, has ridden west through the Umatilla country
to Painted Hills, treasury of pigments, where some mounds are scarlet,
and others violet-grey or else golden-green with rays of black descending
them; here are hills of ocher-brown which blends into pure red, and yellow
hills, and hills of broken white stone bearing leaf-images and shell-images;
this of all places is the place for a man who paints himself;
so now they have become ready;
and coming into Blackfoot's camp, leading three gift-horses, Looking-Glass smiles
to see a young girl riding alone on a pony behind her mother, both of them with
saddleblankets and blouses decked out in elkteeth
and the bleached buckskin fringe on her sleeves hanging and swaying
way down the horse's side

so that loveliness is shimmering in all our hearts:

> and one Crow has painted an X on his face, signifying that he has killed an enemy;

>> now here come the old men and the young boys and all our old friends:

>>> the Lost Lodges, Bad Honors, Bear's Paws, Ravens and Prairie Dogs

>>>> (even Horse Rider is here);

>> young women begin to smile at them,

>>> pretty ones who have painted their hair partings red and perfumed themselves with yarrow,

>>>> so that Looking-Glass, swallowing hard with lust, remembers the way that Crow women incite us to war by waving scalps;

Toohhoolhoolsote's leg-rattles are hissing; his fishbone necklace is chattering

> and a little Crow girl comes carrying her doll-baby on her back

>> while in the dying grass graze so many painted ponies (some with Mexican brands) that we can almost believe we have come back into the days when the Crows were rich in horses;

as from that sunbleached tipi painted with a golden-ocher SUN-device, circletted with outward-pointing white teeth, Blackfoot emerges.

Looking-Glass and his People give the Crows brass bracelets, and the Crows give them pretty parfleche bags of buffalo pemmican. Their hosts invite them to a buffalo feast, serving the meat in buffalos' shoulderbones,

> so we keep our hearts quiet as men should,

>> determined not to speak of the Bostons—or, as they are called here, the *Yellow Eyes*—

until it comes time to pass the pipe.

The Crow chief, whose hair is tied in a greying, feathered knot over his forehead, stares upon Looking-Glass almost in dread, the pair of great white shells upon his breastplate of necklaces trembling like a butterfly's wings, his cheeks drawn in, perhaps with illness, his lips silently parted to emit sad breath, his eyes wide yet dull

> and the vertical wrinkles between his eyebrows deepen

>> as beside him Curley Crow, who rode to Little Big Horn with Yellow Hair* last spring, and never disdains to take the Bluecoats' part, now squints into the sun, showing off his smooth bare chest and neck with the many white necklace-loops on them, his wavy brown hair braided almost like a white woman's; he is gazing at the ground

>>> (although even now Looking-Glass's eyes cannot help but seek a certain Crow woman whose forehead bears a circle tattoo);

---

*Custer.

and Yellow Hair's old scout, White Man Runs Him,

naked to the waist, crowned with eagle feathers,

frowns and flares his nostrils at Looking-Glass, who begins to speak in words
as sweet as the tight-clinging leaves of a sweetgrass bundle: My dear brothers, we are now here in this place so that we may know each other's hearts.

Taking the pipe, Blackfoot replies: Brothers, my heart is glad to see you. I wish
that we could stop this bad feeling between your nation and the Bostons, but it is
too late, because your young men have done evil things, and the Bluecoats will
hunt you down forever. Looking-Glass, ever since I have first seen you, my heart
has loved you, and I still have the same heart. Now I wish I could guide you
straight, or persuade Cut Arm to listen, but since I cannot, there is nothing for
you here. Now I am finished speaking; now I have opened my heart,

and the *lucky man*, with his many feathers radiating from his scalp,
draws in his blanket with his arm inside it, half-closing his eyes, lowering
his head, as if he could truly be sad

to which Looking-Glass replies: My brother, have my ears become addled, or have
you really spoken such words? Have you then forgotten your promises?

—speaking loud and long about this matter,

his words winding around: *pokát, pokát*—

until Blackfoot says: Why should you ride here to carry war to our fireside? Why
bring the Bluecoats upon us? You know that I do not lie; if we go against them they
will take away our country, I am telling you three times! But hear me, Looking-
Glass: Should Cut Arm require us to ride against you, we shall shoot in the air . . .

Blackfoot, I had not looked to find you such a cowardly old woman. You have
grown too fond of the Bostons' sugar. Blackfoot, you cower before them like a dog!

That may be so, Looking-Glass; but I remember how you refused to rise up
against them when we urged you; moreover, from what I have heard, you would not
help your own People when they struck the Bostons on the Chinook Salmon Water,

and Horse Rider, the "white Crow" who could never help us much, is not
much help to-day, either,

so Toohhoolhoolsote snarls: You too have sold your country,

and Ollokot widens his eyes, smiling at the Crows with extreme
hatred,

and White Man Runs Him finally takes the pipe only to say: My
heart falls to the ground,

so that once again Toohhoolhoolsote's heart finds occasion to say: *It is warped;*
and Strong Eagle, who should have left the talking to the chiefs, but like our other
young men has lately learned to speak yes and no, smokes the pipe, then slowly
tells the Crows: If you fight us, I shall make your women gash their foreheads with
arrowheads,*

after which the People take their gift-horses back again;

---

*In mourning.

their dreams have withered, just as the MUSSELSHELL SISTERS dry
up in the sun.

3

So we must ride to Sitting Bull. If we are straight in our hearts, perhaps he will
not kill us.

There remains nothing but to cross the Medicine Line to the far place, the cold
place, the Place Where Dead Trees Whistle,
but for all the ride back Looking-Glass is speechless, and even Toohhoolhoolsote,
      bowing his head, with his hands clasped across his chest and his white
      braids hanging still across his arms,
now says: I know not where to go.

4

Ollokot, my dear younger brother, please tell me exactly what has been done,
but before Ollokot can open his mouth, Toohhoolhoolsote explains: Once again
Looking-Glass has misled you. He promised that the Crows would save you. As
for me, I am a man, and so I expect nothing,
      and in much the same way that a woman knows that something bad has
      happened when her needle breaks while she is sewing, Cloudburst (al-
      though she has not been sewing to-day) understood already before she
      even saw Ollokot's face;
            now she is boiling soup for him, and for him she is cutting off a
            piece of Welweyas's gift to her,
               that dried huckleberry cake from the Salish country;
      while Looking Glass keeps silent; a headache is haunting him. Blackberry
      Person crushes up some sage leaves for him to sniff, and then he sits gri-
      macing on his horse.

5

Red Spy, who even until now believed in Looking-Glass, has been thirsting in
his heart to ride alongside the Crows, raiding and killing Shinbones, Big Bellies
and Walking Cutthroats,
            and tasting enemy women in much the same way as we crack bones
            and suck out their marrow,
      for before this war, when the People used to come together at Weippe and
      Split Rock, Looking-Glass many times told us how the great Crow chief
      Tattooed Forehead disguised himself as a Big Belly, spied two Big Belly
      maidens bathing naked in a river, and when they laughingly hid them-
      selves in the brush, caught one by the hair and quicker than you can

imagine cut off her head!—Red Spy, feeling hilarious over that joke, immediately thirsted to kill more enemies; and now that he has begun shooting Bostons, his heart has learned to laugh at the blood of others; he has made himself brave; why should he not kill Big Bellies?

Now we must ride north alone, hoping that these enemies will become our friends,

and so Red Spy grows enraged at Looking-Glass.

6

Now again we all ride together,

our young warriors still perfect with their tight braids and their roached hair shining with grease;

and Toohhoolhoolsote is listening to the creakings of trees as he goes (even after this he will Dream himself where he likes, no matter whether the Crows think to deny to us the Buffalo Country: like a green-grassed creek-groove down deep in the dry dirt always runs his Dream, cutting through the skulls of any who would tell him where he must go; because Toohhoolhoolsote, who knows the pale gold of the Buffalo Country in late afternoon and black buffalo in the golden grass, has what belongs to a man),

while Cut Arm must sit on the ground far behind, because we have got his mules!

Exactly here where pallid grey fans and pillars of rain connect the clouds across the pale whitish-grey air to the almost silhouetted pines along the soft green ridge, we find buffalo in a row, and kill three of them;

the women butcher the meat and pack it on ponies; to-night in camp we shall roast it. Asking Maiden and Blackberry Person are glad,

but as for their husband, once again he has grown silent:

treachery upon treachery undoes him!

Even now he can scarcely believe in Cut Arm's crookedness; the murders of our women and children at Ground Squirrel Place have grown almost unreal to his heart; and what the Crows have now done,

those very ones who have sung praising-songs for my war-deeds,

his heart cannot comprehend; closing his eyes, he feels himself galloping down, galloping down

through rimrocks and currant bushes, these junipers so still against the dark blue sky,

because we must all now pass through the sayings of Lean Elk's heart like mice running through dark narrow slits in sandstone,

Looking-Glass meanwhile waiting for some Power to fly down and re-store his luck.

7

Lean Elk shouts: *Hurry, hurry!*
—to which Toohhoolhoolsote replies: *I, a chief, will not be spoken to so.*

8

Our tired old ones become strong from eating so much meat, so Lean Elk makes us travel as quickly as the mules can go. Now we enter a valley where an-other herd of fat shaggy buffalo grazes like black stars on the sky of grass, munch-ing and slowly ambling, rolling on the ground as if they itch; white dust rises from them even in mist and drizzle.

Smiling, Toohhoolhoolsote stalks a buffalo cow who is ducking her head down against the heavy rain which has greyed every ridge down to outlines,

      riverbends of living white fog in the rain

         (even between the nearest trees there seems to be fog);
now he and the animal have both vanished as we ride on past bubbles, geysers and overlapping raindrop-rings in the puddles between sagebrush

      (Lean Elk is not certain which way to lead us):
here runs the wide, steel-grey river, rain-pimpled, wriggling over blue-grey rocks, and Looking-Glass is silent; then

        pim!
at which Toohhoolhoolsote's hungry old wives come grinning and galloping, ready with their knives.

9

We have begun to lose our way; even Lean Elk cannot explain why even the best men have come to this. He sends scouts in three directions to find a safely secret way to the Swift Water,

      which we must cross to get into the dry prairie

         (soon that place will be getting cold),

      through the coulees and into the marshes where the yellow columbine
      grows low and high,

      then around the snowy mountains to Place of the Cave of Red Paint
      and thus to Wolf's Paw*

        past Big Bellies and Walking Cutthroats

      to the Medicine Line

---

*What the Nez Perce called Bear's Paw.

—so far away!

Our wounded and our old ones will keep dying.

So our scouts ride out, northwest, north and northeast:

The other People follow, riding too far on weary horses, resting too little,

Dreaming horribly, awaking in fear to flee again

(as she begins to help Cloudburst pack Uncle Ollokot's horses, a stallion tries to kick Sound Of Running Feet, so she pricks him hard with her knife; he rolls his eyes and jerks; she clouts him on the muzzle as he skips and cringes; then the packbags go on him)

and Lean Elk yells: *Hurry, hurry!*

Strong Eagle spies a mule deer's outstretched ears in the golden grass:

Pim!

the doe falls dead; her chest explodes; to-night our widows will be praising him.

Over The Point and Swan Necklace ride back up to the pass:

Cut Arm is not yet in sight, nor any Lice-Eaters.

White Thunder's party,

watching down the winding pine-walls to the white river-pavement where the mourning doves are creeping,

finds an old Boston, evidently a miner. Gathering round their captive,

his face white as a new-peeled lodgepole,

they tell the half-breed Bunched Lightning what to say, and in the Boston language he shouts: *You Boston, answer quick! Can you find Elk Water?**

Since he can, they do not kill him. They take him to the People. We make him draw a map, to show us the marks of this country. Then we keep him, and make him drive our horses as if he were a woman

while the creek, reddish-brown and silver, alters rapidly but mutedly beneath the clouds, a great buckskin-colored bluff watching over, and beyond it taller cliffs with snow on them;

a few of us still have tipis; that night our women raise them on the sandbar

where Ollokot entices Cloudburst to open her butterfly

so that their hearts forget to grieve, just for awhile

and Toohhoolhoolsote Dreams of visiting Smohalla in a place which smells like home

(the Chinook Salmon Water)

but Smohalla will not ring the small bell:

covering his face with both hands, he keeps silent, as if I, his brother, were some crooked-hearted Boston.

---

*A minor river in Yellow Stone Park. Exactly which one is unclear.

10

On the next day, White Thunder and his war-friends,
    still longing to harm and punish the Horse People
    and to injure Cut Arm above all,
hear a noise like a musselshell cracking open in the fire:
    someone is shooting far away;
and so they find a camp of Bostons.

11

One man (he must be chief) offers his hand to White Thunder, who therefore no longer wishes to kill these people. First we take their flour, sugar and bacon. We search for *marrow-like* to bring our children, but they have none. Now we are admiring their horses:
    The chief Boston's stallion, tall and white, with a reddish undercoat and
    strong legs, looks too heavy for war, but strong and calm—good enough
    for Rainbow's widow
        (let her work him to death).
The Bostons stand there with their hands up. Bunched Lightning shouts in the Boston language: *We take you to the chiefs. You come now d——n quick!*
There are seven of them. Terrified of our warriors' smooth red-brown young faces and shining eyes, they rush to get ready. Then two women emerge from the tent,
    Emma and *Ida,*
        pretty ones,
        their hair dark brown like a buffalo's new coat.
            For what are they coming here? To spy for Bluecoats who kill
            us?
Once we begin to taste them with our eyes,
    grinning crookedly or staring with our mouths a trifle open,
        we young men to whom no Boston woman has ever said: *Taste me,*
        even though so many Bostons have raped our women
            (they have no hearts),
a certain Boston
    (he must be their husband or father)
grows angry and begins to shout. We shall certainly make him understand.
We take our captives to the People, and when other young warriors see them, they begin to tease these Bostons, just for fun, lassooing their horses, shouting: *Quick, fast, heap fast!* galloping round and round (*Ida* and *Emma* weeping almost silently), chasing them all when they dismount,
    saying: *What do you mean, killing our People?*

—so that they must run like children to Lean Elk and Looking-Glass, who cannot
tell us yes or no about this,

     not even about these Boston bitches

        (no matter what Heinmot Tooyalakekt may say);

        for just as male and female towhees wear the same blood-splash on their
flanks, so these Boston men and women are all bloody killers:

They are our enemies forever, and we shall treat them so,

     although Lean Elk,

        who dislikes to see the young men go wild,

     quietly leads two Bostons into the trees, murmuring: *You fellows run
away quick!*

        (in time they will find Cut Arm),

and the other People, all Boston-haters, go riding by,

   discussing how *Emma* and *Ida*'s female parts might be fashioned,

     joking about the noise of opening and closing which a MUSSELSHELL
WOMAN makes

        (One such lured COYOTE into Her clashing vagina, and squeezed
until She had killed Him):

      —can *Emma* do this? *Ida* appears not strong enough:

        Áhahahaha!—

the brownish-black oval of a distant bear crawling through the sagebrush
as our young men in their feathered top hats and their striped gorgets keep playing with their prey,

     sharing out weapons:

        a Henry rifle with two hundred rounds, a shotgun, two Ballard rifles,
three revolvers and two needle guns

and then:

Get'm off, mister. Me want ring.

No get'm off. My wife gave me this.

*My friend, me see'm ring. Get'm off, or I cut'm off! Áhaha! Good. You're a d——n
good little white man. Now me have ring, GODd——n you,*

     the Boston women staring at them so that they are reminded of how a
deer raises its ears before it leaps away:

        then the hearts of the Bostons become smaller and smaller,
and their women are weeping.

White Thunder says: My WYAKIN told me never to be cruel.

Yes, replies Red Spy, but they are the ones who did wrong things,

     the eye of his gun as black and round as a horse's opening anus,

and now Swan Necklace,

     he who first started this war

        (the other two with him lie dead and dug up at Ground Squirrel Place)
and whose sister lies buried or maybe dug up far back on the trail, in a
gravel place which the greyish-pink mourning doves will soon be leaving,

rides up,

with his long braids spilling neatly down to his blanket-robed lap, where his
pretty hands rest opened like knives, the long fingers clenched together, his
dark eyes shining with some unknown purpose,

quickly shooting the nearest Boston in his thigh,

only once and then just twice

(he is merely playing around)

so that this white man

(the one who shouted at us when we touched his women),

a tourist who came to see Wonderland, hunt swans and shoot bald eagles

(now he has become red-eyed like a towhee),

tumbles off his horse, his legbone shattered, and tries to crawl for the ravine,

his woman, awkward in her Boston bell-skirt, lowering herself from the saddle
as quickly as she may, wrenching herself away from us, running toward him,
shrieking: *O, George! O, George!*

Áhahahaha!

Let me pound now him to death,

and Swan Necklace (whose voice is beautiful) begins happily singing his
WYAKIN song

while Red Spy shoots another Boston in the side of the head: *pim!*

(and just as from the dark square cave of smoky heat in the square
white blacksmith's shop there comes an orange light more vicious
than the desert sun, so within his skull there suddenly enters pain's
illumination, brilliant beyond all his suppositions,

although his story is strange:

this one will hide, and live, and in great pain make his own secret
way to Cut Arm)

and his horse lowers his handsome white head, half-closing
his white eyelashes, and sneezes at the blood in the grass

while the enemy women keep screaming like female wood ducks
and the thigh-shot Boston's woman rushes to him, cradling his face in her arms,
crying: *Kill me, kill me first!*

(now she is convulsing bitterly)

until Strong Eagle pulls her away and shoots him in the forehead:

Áhaha!

and Shooting Thunder rides happily up the creek to whistle for elk.

12

We take the Boston women and the last Boston man to Heinmot Tooyalakekt,

he who saves the weak,

and when Swan Necklace ecstatically enlightens this chief's heart about the Bostons we have shot, he turns his back, wrapping himself in his King George blanket

(he is but a camp-chief; now it is for the young men to say yes or no);
and now Ollokot has killed another deer, which Welweyas has eagerly helped Cloudburst skin with her Wilson knife
as Peopeo Tholekt comes in from singing to his yellow horse;
we are eating roast meat,
although Looking-Glass's wives and daughters will not come
here; their hearts are ashamed that their man whom we once
admired has now overflowed with errors,
and the leftover venison Cloudburst, Good Woman, *Kate* and
Springtime now begin to pound with berries, hoping for time to
make pemmican, since we must keep riding forever, it seems:
we become horse-happy,
for Burning Coals now owns the short Boston woman's mare:
a fine white-footed roan, who bent her long neck so gracefully to graze while we began to torment those two sluts;
while White Thunder has got the other woman's horse:
a mare truly lovely to our hearts, for her coat is of a rare
reddish orange like some pigments that our best men
gather at Cave of the Red Paint;
I am telling you three times, we are all full of good meat, and would
be laughing at Cut Arm if we still laughed
but there was a way Fair Land used to pound meat that was
better than this way; Cloudburst should have learned it, so
now Good Woman is scolding her; in that moment those two
are hating each other, and as her baby yawns in the cradleboard, Springtime sits on a rock, pounding meat alone
as Heinmot Tooyalakekt watches the enemy people from across the fire; when the
man begins to plead with him, he turns away.
Red Spy,
who would sit beside these fine Boston girls and maybe pull back their heads by the hair
—were Heinmot Tooyalakekt only absent, I should take one of them with
me and use her on the trail
(as easy as slitting a dying deer's throat)—
keeps wondering how they might taste
(for Yellow Bull has shared his heart with me; it was his best men
who killed those Bostons in their homes by Chinook Salmon Water
and then raped their women; why shall I not do the same?)
Then the boy About Asleep cocks a pistol at the Bostons, shouting: *Good——n,*
Good——n no good! White man no good,
and the People laugh
(but not Heinmot Tooyalakekt).
Realizing at last that nothing is taller than a Nez Perce horseman
at twilight, with grey tipis rising like volcanoes behind him, the

last Boston stares into these warriors' eyes, desperate to learn
whether they mean to kill him; he cannot even tell if they can see
him; for a moment they appear to be dead; or it might merely be
that they are staring *through* him in that Dreamer way—and
nothing has changed in them; it is only he whose perceptions
cannot stay still; then all at once, with that same almost unwink-
ing gaze, they seem to look upon him as if he himself were dead.
He seeks to calm himself by remembering how Henry's Lake
shone brighter than Looking-Glass's mirror (he could see the
trout right through the water)

> and everyone danced the pigeon wing, drank root beer,
> then went swan-hunting.

Sitting on a fallen tree, a young brave with flowing black hair
watches him cruelly, with a rifle across his lap, imperial in his
fringed and beaded robes, with bearteeth at his throat and
two U.S. Army cartridge belts strapped on him. Half-smiling,
half-grimacing, he seems to see into the white man's skeleton

> (LORD JESUS, grant me a brave death! And if the last thing
> I'll see on earth is this grey spill of hair on the shoulders
> of an Indian's striped blanket, and that rifle swinging to-
> ward me, *I must look the villain in the face*—but I suppose
> what I'll actually see last is the heels of his moccasins
> when I'm lying in the grass and he walks off . . . although
> he might bend down and scalp me; don't they all do that?);

and Sound Of Running Feet is longing for her father to kill these Bostons! Wearily
he sits down between her and Good Woman,

> the young men watching among the trees, murmuring: *Let us be evil to them;*
even Ollokot (although he stands aside), craves vengeance for Fair Land,
who once beaded his rifle-scabbard red and black

>> and Arrowhead would wish to cut those long Boston dresses with
>> her skinning-knife to make new bandages for our wounded;
Looking-Glass lacks pity for them;
even Welweyas the half-woman, whose heart adores women everywhere,
would laugh to see the deaths of these two Boston bitches:

>> all the time their race keeps seeking to squeeze us into a
>> small place!

—and White Bird stares into the fire,

>> sitting with his wrinkled hands folded in his blanketed lap,
>> with lovely dark and white double bars of bone about his neck,
>> his hair roach akimbo and soot around his squinting eyes,
remembering how the creek back home in Sparse-Snowed Place
appears in this season:

>> wide and brown, with its white stones rising from the shallow

water, the humid sky white and purple-grey, and my father's
grave in the mound of dying grass where Tsépmin promises
to dig for gold after he has killed us,
as smoke obscures the rising moon, and the young men,
some of them joylessly playing at the Stick Game,
wait for what will happen,
and as Sound Of Running Feet crouches down, staring (her eyes strangely half-
closed) across the fire at the enemy women, Naked-Footed Bull says to Grizzly
Bear Youth,
who Dreamed so wisely that we should steal Cut Arm's animals:
Boston women are happy when the Bostons kill us! To-morrow let us kill them
on the trail . . .
—but who can account for what now occurs? She with the scarred arm and
sickly infant to whom the murders committed by the Bluecoats and Bostons
must surely stink worse than any deed of ours, she whose child, as she begins
to know, will never see the home in which it was conceived, whose husband,
who was meant to be her protector, cannot save her from Cut Arm's pursuing
terror, and whose elder sister-wife no longer understands her heart, why should
she for whom these near-worthless wailing days and nights are now an expected portion show in her heart any residuum of pity?
Yet Springtime now takes up her baby girl and seats herself by the Bostons.
Doing whatever he can to be liked,
terrified even of these squaws, whose gazes seem to him as faint as star-
light on Springfield rifles
(the warriors overgazing him almost gently, their eyes filled with
some meaning which it might save his life to understand),
the man lifts up the child and gives it to one of his women to hold. She makes a
disgusted face. He says: Pick up the baby, Emma. Don't you want to live?
She does; so will he. In his memoirs he writes: *I know I could have sat down on
that young one and smothered it, with a good deal of relish.*
She takes the child, who looks up at her wide-eyed, not crying; the Boston woman
wipes its snotty nose and all at once our women smile.

13

Almost weeping, the Boston man stretches out his hand to Heinmot Tooyalakekt, imploring: *Friend?*
Heinmot Tooyalakekt takes his hand, replying: *Citizens' friend.*

14

We keep these Bostons for some days. Some of Toohhoolhoolsote's young men
still wish to rape the women, then kill them like deer, but Heinmot Tooyalakekt

says: You have done many things against my advice. There will now be an end to this talk.

The next day, Lean Elk leads away the captives, gives them played out horses and sets them on the Bozeman Trail toward Fort Ellis.

15

As we ride, Heinmot Tooyalakekt comes to our chiefs and best men one by one, asking them to spare the Bostons—for who can say that this war will not keep going against us?—but some will not answer; and Toohhoolhoolsote replies: I am a chief. No one commands me.

16

Riding east through the stormcloud meadows, we shoot other Bostons and steal their horses, paying back Cut Arm wherever we can. (When they bleed, they go as pale as buffalo tallow.)

Heinmot Tooyalakekt keeps quiet. Since he cannot straighten the young men, they must straighten themselves as they see fit.

Over and over he hounds us: *Leave a clean trail,* but even his own dear nephew White Thunder is one of those who now often says: *Let us go and devour them,*

and farther up the trail Toohhoolhoolsote's best men, as cruel and furious as grizzly bears, corner a Boston who has come prospecting—

—let us help him so that he need not go on weeping!—

loot his corpse

(his open eyes already less blue than huckleberries),

then break, burn or bury his tools:

We do not sell or wound OUR MOTHER!

Here is the dead man's palomino grazing in pale yellow grass; let this animal begin to gladden our hearts!

—and that night Toohhoolhoolsote dreams of a grizzly bear, part tawny, who stretches out in the golden grass.

Far away, past a yellow stripe of sunlit meadow, we spy a herd of buffalo, and one bull alone; our best men ride there, we hear rifle-shots

(Welweyas and Springtime clap their hands)

and soon the women are butchering the meat

although Looking-Glass declines to hunt; keeping aloof like an old stallion banished from his harem by some snorting young challenger,

because now that the Crows have closed their hearts to us, he has begun to Dream of enemies ahead:

like some whirling snow-wind is the trailer bonnet of a

Painted Arrow* warrior, streaming straight out behind him as he gallops toward us on a fine brown horse, upraising a long lance decorated with streamers of red trade cloth; he wears a great white rectangle of bone beads across his chest and he is coming to kill us—

all the same, Lean Elk has uplifted our hearts; he has led us to a place where we have found our way:

we shall now ride upriver to the trail called Narrow Solid Rock Pass on the south shore of the Tongue Water; then we shall cross the Swift Water and pass quickly through the Country of the Crows, whose hearts no longer open to ours. But the Buffalo Country has no end; even before the Cave of Red Paint we shall be resting and wandering as we used to do,

just for awhile, before we ride to Sitting Bull.

And now all the berries are ripe, but we have lost our cedarbark baskets on the way,

and although the Medicine women are singing over her, blowing her sickness far from us, Mourning Dove cannot live anymore, so we bury her in her ragged blanket, and Tuk-le-kas rings the small bell.

AND THEN I CAN WRITE A PLEASING ARTICLE
AUGUST 29–SEPTEMBER 1

1

*G*eneral, Captain Fisher has news—

Bring him here. Well, captain, what is it?

Sir, our Bannocks have located Joseph right of Soda Butte; he's heading toward Clark's Fork—

Good. Sturgis will head him off. How's the mood of your Indians?

O, excellent, sir; they're looking forward to being in on the death.

We all are. I guess Joseph's back will be broken within another three or four days, once Sturgis gets in position.

Yessir.

What's the meaning of that look, Captain Fisher?

I was fixing to sneeze, general.

Return to your duties.

---

*Cheyenne.

Do they all laugh at me? Perhaps I should resign, but then what would I do? I should like to be a grandfather. How delightful it was when I used to sit Gracie behind me in the saddle and she sat smiling like such a good child! Anyhow, I need to help Guy get established. And when I whip Joseph, Sherman will smile on me again, GOD willing. Perhaps Miles and I can capture Sitting Bull. And then I can write a pleasing article about the Nez Perce campaign. Wood can polish it up. The *New York Herald* might take it. I should certainly like to pay off the balance of my legal expenses, then try once more to do something for the negroes.

2

Left,
    left,
        left they march,
shaded they ride and march,
recruiting their weary souls in this reposeful place, lusting to skylark
    although poor Captain Fisher, six feet tall and proud in his broad-brimmed hat and decorated deerskin jacket
        (a wonder his legging-buttons haven't snagged off)
    must now ride thirty miles ahead to see what he can see of Joseph
        (Redington setting off more eastward, jawboning in Chinook with one of our more likely Crows),
    singing the jingle from Thompson's Two-Bit House in Portland:
        Go to Thompson's Two-Bit House, no deception there!
        Hi, you muck-a-muck, and here's your bill of fare!
            That's hilarious, Doc.
            Well, now—
            I said, that's fuckin' hilarious, GODd——nit!
and even Perry's spirits lifting, strange to say,
    because the way this campaign is turning out—marching and marching to the end of everywhere, as if we've been rocking on our horses for a quarter of a million years—puts me in mind of the days when I was younger, riding and Indian-hunting way out in the wild country
        (Perry half-smiling to remember how in California when our rifles echoed over the lake and the Modocs screamed war-cries back at us, flocks of lake swallows used to fly up just far enough to dip their wings like oars into the blue-grey water, rowing themselves away from us in flittery panics, and then we'd all yell *Hurrah!* just to hear another echo)
        —the days before I was married, O yes!
        —and my days with General Crook, the freest genius I've ever known, his squarish yet ethereal face, his flowing moustaches and

bright sailor-eyes, his humor ready to harden against any challenge, and until then serene:

> d——n, but the man was no more stylish than a nosebag dangling from my saddle ring! . . .
>
> —well, I loved him for being so at peace with himself,
>> as I can never hope to be—
> but then why was Theller my best friend when he was so tormented? What don't I understand?
>
> O, if I could shake away all my sorry experiences, like Diamond rolling and rolling in the dust after the saddle comes off him . . .

while Umatilla Jim, having heard it sung that there is or can be a tiny light which we cannot see even as it shines, the light of SOMETHING

> (all we can do is ready ourselves),

sits down by the riverbank, watching the Lice-Eaters dishonor the dead

and he smokes kinnikinnick, waiting for the light of SOMETHING to come, Spurgin's engineers chopping ahead with their hand axes, so why shouldn't the rest of us recruit ourselves?

> (Whipple says this is worse than the road over the Blue-ridge—
> Well, of course it is. This ain't no road.)

—Blackie no longer caring whether we catch Mr. Joe, and accordingly up for travelling infinitely (which is by no means forever) through this yellow-grassed summer, accruing Government wages, learning new country, ensuring dreams for Fidelia,

Redington likewise loving the campaign life more every minute, riding in and out of camp with a *yip-yip-yip* password of his own invention

> (how heartily old General Prayer Book laughs at that!),

and it's still a treat to jawbone with Fisher, Jule and the other scouts.

> (The general's soft on Injuns, Fisher says. Well, they're nothing but animals, every last stinking one of them.)

As for Captain Pollock, who has served as a member of the San Francisco Vigilantes, he still yearns to ride ahead, even in advance of Redington's Indians, and take care of Joseph—

> *Halt,*

planting the guidon:

>> *About face.*
>>> *Dismissed!*

—Wood,

> dreaming of a certain dark plump Bannock squaw in a tightly beaded buckskin dress and a belt shining with nailheads
>> and then remembering that he needs to clean his pistol,

smiling meaninglessly while the general and Wilkinson sit on logs with Guy,

Ad Chapman and a few of the fellows, singing "The Battle Hymn of the Republic,"

> some enlisted men broiling deer meat on the cleaning rods of their rifles,
>
> a wide-eyed German with a handlebar moustache slowly moving his lips over an American New Testament,
>
> messmates sitting in the grass, playing cards on a stinking horse blanket:
>> Now, when you're setting out to paunch a buffalo, here's what you want to do—
>>
>> By my count, Mr. Joe's bumped off at least six citizens here in Wonderland alone.
>>
>> You can't even count how old you are,
>>> as, gripping Joseph's rebellious pony between his knees, Perry quirts him a few times, but cannot break him, so gives him over to Bomus to be shot.
>>
>> Doc, where'd you get that theodolite?
>>
>> Traded for it.
>>
>> You understand how to use it?
>>
>> You sad old horse's ass—

Where are you from, soldier?

From Hamburg, general.

What's your name?

Klughard, general.

And are you enjoying this campaign?

General, sir, that one don't speak good English. He's got in his head you asked him something else. Right now he's saying that his relatives have all booked passage on the "Hammonia" for this August; a slew of Klughards coming over from Germany, he says—

Thank you, sergeant. Carry on. Now, Guy, I'm afraid that Captain Jocelyn needs a nudge about his Morning Report.

I'll see to it, sir.

> Well, boys, thirteen years ago to-day, the Secceshes were evacuating Atlanta.
>
> Now I know for a fact that President Grant smoked half a hundred cigars a day. And when we were on the march—
>> No, Trimble, I'm with you. To get him quick, we should think Indian and play Indian. But all this GODd——d command ever does is follow staff orders and march, march, march.
>>
>> Pollock, my boy, you sure said it! But the trouble started before General Prayer Book, because when they deployed us at the Lava Beds, Canby even forbade us to—

But near about "Tattoo," while the rest of our command sits brightening up, recruiting itself back from out of fatigue and sorrow, Wilkinson, Mason and the general continue studying the map by the trembling light of the grease lamp.

3

Perry, how's your company?

Well, sir, they're holding up real fine.

I've had a talk with Trimble.

Yessir.

Reminded him that we were all in the Lava Beds together.

Major Mason, sir, I truly appreciate that.

Now how are you getting on with the general?

Not bad, sir, although between you and me I detest that little Indian lover he has buzzing about his tent—

You mean Lieutenant Wood?

Yessir. The boys are saying he puked at Big Hole.

Is that so?

I didn't see it, sir. But something's wrong with him. He's squeamish or something. Won't admit how things are

 —for instance, the way the Modocs used to prey on Shastas and Pi-Utes, selling their children to the Horse Indians at The Dalles, a boy for a pony, while a girl ripe for whoredom and concubinage might go for as much as five horses;

 and then once our settlers came in, the Modocs started raiding them instead,

 overreaching when they murdered Mr. Reed, carried off his two young girls, and before they had even become women began to rent them out, the elder one's performance earning her the accolade of a slit throat and a heave over the cliff-bank of Cottonwood Creek when two of her owners agreed to disagree about her earnings, the younger presently receiving a comparable reward from jealous squaws, although she was never found.

Perry, he's not the only one. I'll do what I can for you.

Thank you, major.

4

No word from Sturgis?

I'm afraid not, general.

Joseph could be giving us the slip again right now.

Yessir.

Fletch, what's your opinion of the situation?

Well, sir, I wonder if Captain Fisher's Bannocks are telling all they know.

Maybe they find one of our couriers dead, and they scalp him; you know their fondness for scalps—

I've warned them that that's prohibited.

Yessir. And then they might hesitate to tell us, for fear of being punished, and so—

You purpose to legitimate the murder and scalping of prisoners, for expediency's sake.

Of course not, general, but maybe Captain Fisher could tactfully interrogate his Indians . . .

I take your point. Kindly speak with him on this subject, and report straight to me. Sturgis's silence is becoming inconvenient.

Rest assured, general, I'll ride out straightaway.

Fletch, I'm aware that Fisher dislikes me.

Well, sir, I—

If he realizes how crucial it is to communicate with Sturgis, he might withhold information, simply to spite me. So don't let him realize it.

I understand, sir.

And, Fletch, I've just decided that you *must* give Fisher written orders to turn over all prisoners to the main column, *alive.* The murder of that poor old squaw continues to distress me. It's a blot upon the Army. So draft something and take it to him; I . . .

Yessir. General, is your arm paining you just now?

No, it's not that. Well, GOD bless you. That's all.

WHAT NEXT?
SEPTEMBER 2

1

*W*ilkinson, do you have a moment?

Sure thing, general.

I consider you extremely well informed on a number of subjects.

Thank you, sir.

Do you understand Communism?

Well, sir, in what sense?

Who are these rebels? What do they want?

O, an eight-hour working day, higher wages, you name it.

Bless us! What next?

General, if you don't mind my asking, has there been bad news from the States?

On the contrary. The railroad strikes have all been put down. There was an anti-Chinese riot in San Francisco, and the coal miners may walk out, but I think the Government has asserted itself.

In my opinion, general, we haven't seen the last of them. They're GODless, you know.

Well, well! I didn't realize . . . And they're in the Army?

Some of them, yessir.

Keep your eyes out. But don't accuse anyone without absolute proof.

I understand, sir.

GOD bless you, my boy! That's all.

2

General, the teamsters' extra horses have disappeared.

Fetch me Redington or Captain Fisher at once.

Yessir.

Well, hello there, general. Guess you heard—

Are any of your Bannocks missing?

About half of them, sir.

Arrest Buffalo Horn. He's to stay in custody until every animal has been returned. That's all.

General, sir, they've brought back the horses.

All right. Let Buffalo Horn go. It's in his nature; he can't help it . . .

3

So we follow Chief Joseph up the Yellow Stone to the Lamar, where the rugged road goes widely down to the jade-green, bouldery stream

> (could even Nanny be as lovely as these greenish-grey outcroppings along the Yellow Stone?),

> > Fletch riding ahead up Pelican Creek in search of Captain Fisher, remembering Wood's warning: *Don't let your Bannock get behind you!*

> > > (he finds Fisher,

> > > > who rides very well, as even Wilkinson will admit, but his ornamented Indian leggings are a bit unmanly,

> > > and they crawl over the ridge to spy on Joseph's rearguard;

> > > then they chase after their general by night, their horses breaking through a sulphur-crust on the way,

> > > > rejoining the command just in time to hear Wilkinson drive Ad Chapman out of the Headquarters tent)

—pine-and-sulphur wind on the trail high over the river:

 Black bear tracks again. And I think I smell honey.

 You don't say! Find us some honey, Doc,

  so that to-night Wood will dream that Nanny is crown-

  ing him with a circlet of dark bearclaws—

then east through the stormcloud meadows toward Icebox Cañon

 (far away, past a yellow stripe of sunlit meadow, another herd of buffalo),

past Pebble Creek up into the cañon whose cliffs seem in this rain more purple

than grey,

 Icebox Cañon's soft evergreens tottering out from river-cliffs

 and the slender reddish trunks of pines slowly flashing by . . .

  If you don't believe me, boys, look at the map. We're already in

  General Crook's Department.

  Well, if Sherman would simply telegraph him to take over—

  If Mr. Joe sneaks off by way of Wind River—

  James Reuben predicts he'll avoid Soda Butte Cañon.

  But Uh-Oh Howard will never—

Wearily, he remembers how the masses once stood up for him at the Christian

Commission rally in Philadelphia, awed by his empty sleeve.

BARGAIN WITH FLETCH
4–8 SEPTEMBER

1

*W*ell, Bomus, it used to be that sack coats were looked down upon by

most of us in the service. That changed during the Secession War . . .

So I remember, sir.

Now, Guy here has come to own a contrary opinion . . .

 —riding up the cañon, which the general has named after Captain Jocelyn,

 the black tail of Wood's horse swirling tightly in the wind as our flankers,

 drawn in perforce, warily, wearily eyeball these many reddish cliffs above

 belts of evergreen and wet meadow—

  Well, I for one agree with Mr. Vanderbilt. He said: *Building*

  railroads from nowhere to nowhere is not a legitimate under-

  taking.

  But a railroad turns nowhere into somewhere. Don't you

  want to see this country settled?

Right here's good for nothing but Indians and range cattle
(the milky greenish river flowing over its many-toothed
stones, the other bank, very steep, thick with lodgepole
pines which exude their fragrant morning gloom),
so—
So let's lose the Indians,
and stumps of old burned trees here in the neighborhood of Clark's Fork
(where the hostiles are, GOD alone knows, if not Fisher, Redington
and Buffalo Horn:
still ten miles away, more or less),
the sea-green river foaming slowly between gravel bars, O that lovely wide
river in the wide valley, and now the pale green going chocolate red, bluer
in the reflection-shadows of evergreens (and what's Mr. Joe planning for us
up in these mountains with their long narrow rock-grins?),
and Perry, who has lately developed wrinkles around the corners of his
mouth, cantering Diamond along Company "F"'s regulation-spaced column,
not looking over his shoulder even though he's weighed down by an
eerie feeling about those reds, as if they could be creeping up on our
rear—
for who could forget the time (ten years since) when Parnell
(whom Perry used to tease with *Dick's Irish Dialect Recitations,* back before Perry stopped enjoying anything)
got permission from General Crook to double back on some
mules the Pi-Utes had killed, and caught the Indians fair and
square, shooting five out of six? What if Mr. Joe's bunch are playing that game? Ollicut's probably the craftiest red of them all.
From what James Reuben says, it's either Ollicut or that Yellow
Wolf who did for Theller. (I wonder if Umatilla Jim would tell me
straight? He must know. They all do.) Now, under Crook we
would have crept up on them by night and gunned them all
down. It's a GOD——d marvel that Uh-Oh Howard won't let
Buffalo Horn off the leash, or even Pollock, or me; hell; there's
more than one of us who could have ended this business by now.
But the advantage of sack coats, you see, is for sleeping in, because—
well, well, it's turning out to be quite some chase.

2

Colonel Perry, did you get bad news from home?
No, sir.
You look discouraged. Is your wound troubling you?
Not at all, sir. And yours?

Touché! When the Modocs shot you, did you feel it right away?

Instantly, general. But I—

Of course you carried on. You're a fine and energetic officer. For me, I must admit, the unpleasant part was being carried to the rear. A jolting ride in that ambulance—

Yessir. I got to recruit myself at Camp Warner, so that wasn't bad—

With your wife there. You know, Perry, she's just about my beau ideal of an Army woman.

Thank you, sir,

     and I wish I could punch you in the teeth.

3

And then when General Hill pulled off Stonewall Jackson's gloves, one of 'em was full of blood.

Were you there?

> No, sir, Buffalo Horn reports them very near, with women and children lagging behind their column.

Sure.

> All right. Where's your pad, Wilkinson? You can make a clean copy in camp to-night. This is to Colonel Sturgis. *Colonel: It is imperative that you prevent Joseph's escape from the mountains.*

Which side were you on?

> *Of the three passes available to him . . .*

Which side do you think?

> Yessir, I've got that.

Then shut up. You don't know Stonewall from *nothing.*

> *Of the three passes . . .* I hear raised voices. We'd better see why those troopers are forgetting themselves.

Hey, you Johnny Reb, why the hell are you riding in the United States Army?

That's enough, boys; we're all Americans here. And no profanity; you know that.

Yessir.

I'll excuse you this time. If you'd slowed up our column you'd have been punished.

Yessir.

So you were at Chancellorsville?

Matter of fact, general, I was in your corps—

The Eleventh?

Yessir. And he was with *them.*

O, I see

> the flash flood of deer stampeding out from the wall of trees on that cloudless evening, then lightning blaring from the Secceshes' guns as my Germans turned tail.

Well, glad to have you both here.

Thanks, general. Say, I'll never forget how you turned us men around,
> silently draping our American flag over his armstump as they tried to retreat past him.

All right, soldiers; that war's over. Carry on,
> briefly re-haunted now, as if by a horsefly, by that night, when the woods caught fire from the shells and burned the wounded alive. *Long have they pass'd.*
>> I'm told that Stonewall would raise his hand to thank OUR SAVIOR for victory. No doubt he did so at Chancellorsville. Well, he's learned his mistake. Have I learned mine? Our FATHER, Which art in Heaven—

and smell of dewy sage, chirr of locusts as we hug the cliff-walls
> (no, sir, Buffalo Horn rode thataway),
> following this valley of evergreens
> deeper into Wyoming Territory,
>> a singular place where women are allowed to vote, and
>> where pines rise from crevices in the pale, slanting, lichened rock, the river hissing like wind, and feather-clouds over the mountains, the air cool enough to sting our noses (autumn's coming),

then sun-shots silently blasting our faces.

Wilkinson, what do you make of that mossback? Another veteran of the Eleventh!

A lifer, general. Like us.

Yes. He looks my age.

Or older, sir—

And the other one: also pretty hale . . .

He sure is, general.

I guess the weaklings have died out by now. Despatch continues: *My forces will soon be in position. Thank your officers and men for their vigilant coöperation.* Salutation, etcetera. Do you believe in luck?

No, general, only in PROVIDENCE.

Well said. But Sturgis is not a lucky man.

I never met him, sir. Does he have "sand"?

Well, he *is* from Custer's Seventh! He won't disgrace himself the way Rawn did at Fort Fizzle. And he's coming with thirty-six mule teams, so he can carry anything he wants. However . . . Yes, doctor, what is it now?

Thought you'd want to know, general. That fever case resolved itself. It's not typhus.

Thanks, and GOD bless you!— Wilkinson, *entre nous*, I'll pray that this courier makes it through.

Wood and I were just discussing that, sir. The boys are starting to call it a "suicide gallop" whenever we send any white man out of camp.

Not Redington!

Not him, of course, sir. But apparently our Bannocks have just found another dead man, or made one—

Enough. Your next despatch will be to Captain Cushing: *Indians are between me and Sturgis, and I hope we shall entrap them this time. By marching toward Clark's Fork you will be in position to reënforce either of our commands as needed,* salutation, etcetera, and the instant you've prepared a fair copy it must go off to Fort Ellis. Wood's penmanship is superior to yours, at least when writing in the saddle, so please take more trouble. Now where's Major Mason?

Up there, sir,

> where we've found sign:

>> not far west of Crandall Creek
>> where the sinking grasslands grow suddenly grooved by rock
>> planks between which the green river makes long white chevrons
>> while the clouds argue with the blue sky, and here Old George
>> kneels down to break apart two semi-dried horse droppings from
>> the enemy's herd; Ad Chapman calls him a good boy, a real good
>> Indian, and Redington canters in, joyously singing his customary
>> *yip yip yip;* he's followed Crandall Creek some distance along its
>> steepwalled rocky bed:

No, general, we can't box in Mr. Joe right here. See, on the map . . .

That's so. You're a quick study, young man.

Thanks. But, sir, if I explore Jocelyn Cañon up to this blank patch on the map, then I could tell you which way they'll be heading, and then—

Make contact with Sturgis if you can. Redington, I'm counting on you. As you know, the other couriers didn't get through.

I'm not afraid, general—

Doublequick now, and then back to me. GOD bless you.

Right away, general.

Thanks. A brash boy, wouldn't you say, Wilkinson?

Yessir. He's got rough orphan ways,

> for Wilkinson, who considers himself supremely entitled to point out the
> dangers of permitting Redington so long a leash, has lately begun to color
> his adjectives (subtly, to be sure) in the course of referring to this half-
> grown nuisance.

How old is he?

Couldn't tell you, sir. Looks to be about fourteen, but he—

Where's Wood?

With Major Mason, sir.

That fellow's a dazzler. Extremely talented.

That's so, general. You see good in everyone—

His poetry's impressive.

Yessir.

I'm aware that you dislike him. All the more credit to you for proposing him for promotion. Is he managing?

O yes; everything he does is well done—

You know, those sketches of his we've "leaked" to the newspapers have already increased public sympathy for this campaign.

I'm glad, sir.

You remember our last night at Lapwai, when you and I were gazing at Arcturus and chewing over our service in Arizona?

I sure do, general. Pasqual's camp—

We go back a long way now, you and I.

Yessir. It's been an honor—

I was much impressed with your brave initiative in the Battle of the Clearwater.

Thank you very much, sir.

I'm hoping Wood can distinguish himself in the next engagement. Would do him good.

Yessir.

Or do you think he wants courage?

It's not that he's lacking, general.

Tell me what's on your mind.

Sir, lately I've wondered whether he's tilting against the Army—

Look into your heart, Wilkinson. Most soldiers wouldn't understand me, but you and I can speak this way. I ask you to pray for better relations with your brother officer.

General, I promise to do better.

Thank you. Now bring that silly Mr. Chapman to me. I'll be up front with Mason. And then ride past that teamster O'Donnell or whatever his name is and look him over. I still suspect him of smuggling whiskey.

Yessir.

How's Bomus managing?

A stellar officer in my opinion, sir. He—

　　Blow a halt.

　　Halt!

　　　　　and Redington riding in from left flank on an unfamiliar Appaloosa pony, passing something into the fist of that colorful old soldier who calls himself *Doc.*

O, here we are already. Looks like a pretty enough headquarters:

　　　　　concave reddish pyramidal peaks green-stained with forest and purplestrewn with shadow, then the forest valley with its invisible river, and then the silver-yellow sagebrush on the plateau on which we will camp.

Yessir. Your horse looks tired—

　　Dismount.

　　　　Roll call,

　　　　　　　Wood already currying the general's horse,

right face, beautifully and nearly automatically,

Umatilla Jim, who walks almost silently in those moccasins of flint hide, following unnoticed in Perry's footsteps
so that our troopers nearly bust a gut laughing, then
whirling away just before the colonel turns around,

Sladen and Mason unwinding tack from their animals
and our jaunty Bannocks sitting on the edge of the dying grass, smoking kinnikinnick—how handsomely
they've beaded their shirts! Fisher claims that's called
the *Crow stitch;* I wonder if he could help me obtain a
souvenir for Lizzie before I'm

dismissed!

Well, Parnell, how's your company managing?

Real good, colonel. Captain Trimble sure keeps
our blood flowing—

Yeah.

You look snappy, sir. Everything smooth in Company "F"?

Smooth enough, given the circumstances. Parnell, you and I go back ten years and more. What's
your opinion of this campaign?

Colonel Perry, the way I see it, it won't end soon.

Correct. Well, we've pulled through worse incon-
veniences.

Yessir. Do you recollect that time we set out with
General Crook from Trout Creek and nine mules
disappeared right off?

Sure do. Pretty fine days. We managed without
this Christian sonofabitch,

and if we only rescued Mrs. Manuel our for-
tunes would be made.

That ain't likely, Blackie, considering how
Indians are. Didn't you ever hear about
when the Cayuses held onto white women
after the Whitman Massacre and *raped
them inside out?*

And Mrs. Benedict, see, what Ollicut did to
her, see, after he shot her husband and
tossed him in the crick—

Well, when the Indians smashed Mrs. Denoille's head between two rocks and then
burned her, we found bones and long flaxen
hair in the fire-pit but the bleeding hearts

back East still wept, *lo, the poor Indian;* and
even after we searched some captive Pi-Ute
squaws and discovered that they were wearing her silk stockings, chemise, dresses, you
name it, the holy Joes said there must be a
happier explanation, but at the end of spring
we caught an Indian who confessed, so we
shot him up good, and then Colonel Perry
said to General Crook, he said—

Dig that sink!

Right away, sir,

and as the rubber blankets unroll into company streets,
Captain Pollock, whose troopers, the best in this
GODd——d mulefucking Army, can arrange themselves
without constant direction, accordingly indulges his
favorite dream, never mind this shitty old whopper of a
headache he's got,

the general strolling out of camp, just for an instant, to stretch his legs and refresh
himself,

returning to his Bible with much the same expression on his face as when
one descends from a sun-blasted ridge into a crowd of silver-leaved whispering cottonwoods:

*"And they shall rebuild the ruined cities and inhabit them. I will
plant them upon their land, and they shall never again be plucked
up out of the land which I have given them," says the* LORD *your*
GOD.

Amen; it *must* be so! I'm going to whip Joseph. Now I'd best return and
look over the map . . .

the coffee wagon steaming, old Trimble shouting himself turkey-
red at his ever-loving bunch,

a wide-eyed German with a handlebar moustache
striding away from Red O'Donnell's wagon,

Parnell helping oversee the bivouac, a chore now so beautifully
automatic that the lieutenant's mind is left free to consider, re-
consider and ultimately tilt against Perry's criticism of the general, not only because the latter is a good man in a high place (too
kindhearted, in fact, to make himself as stern as old Sumner used
to be at Bull Run), not to mention that the general is *one of us*—
doesn't he know the shrillness of breaking shells?—but also because Perry has become, as Trimble has convinced him, *yellow:*

a coward at White Bird Cañon (that's why Joseph
whipped us)

and worse than that at Cottonwood: How could he bear

to stay within his defenses while the Brave Seventeen
were shot down?

O, I'll keep on being pleasant to him, and I'm even fond of
him, but I no longer respect him as a man!

General, if we close in on them from the north
side—

No.

How would you rate that Springfield, Blackie?

It sure don't compare to my Daddy's Winchester 1866.

—animal-lover Bomus meanwhile sadly detailing a teamster to
shoot another three of Joseph's ponies for which we have no use,

three sad shavetails from Company "F" now inventing themselves moccasins from the burlap in
which we wrap Army bacon,

as Captain Pollock, who sure hopes to become a business man, begins parting the buffaloberry bushes as if
to relieve himself, then clambers up a hill of rainbow-
colored clay to browse a vein of quartz—

Stable call!

(Perry smiling with pleasure at the clickings of the currycombs)

—and dropping three flecks of golden color in the miniature bottle of acqua-regia, he watches them fade away
(slipping on his spectacles for the best part), then pries
up the precipitate with a longhandled glass spoon,
draining the acid back, pouring water on what's left, at
which it too dissolves, leaving reddish crystals behind
in proof of *gold,* true gold!

If I got lucky I could make even a thousand dollars a day; then when I get it going I can bring in
Chinamen to nigger away at ten cents a day although Captain Whipple claims to hear that the
best ones now charge two dollars. D——n them, I
won't pay it!

So it may do to come back here after we whip Joseph,
because Pollock

(who now drops back the bottle in his breast-
pocket)

has a child or two to provide for:

Josie, Izatus, John, Lyle, Ella, Willie and Flora

—and on account of these dependents he
would have done better to consult Ad
Chapman, who knows near about as well as

Doc the way that pure gold sometimes shows itself in tiny cubical crystals . . .

Fetch the officers right after "Stable Call."

Yessir.

Is everyone present? Where's Captain Pollock? Well, well, just in time, captain. Wood, find out who wants coffee. Unroll the map again, Wilkinson, and would you kindly indicate Heart Mountain? As you see, gentlemen, if we connect our position with Sturgis's probable location by a right line, and then these two passes over here, one of which Joseph must take, we obtain an oblong figure. The distance from us to Sturgis will be less than a hundred miles through *here*. Yes, Mason, what is it?

Sorry, general. Does anyone know about this third pass down here? Colton hasn't marked it clearly—

I have reminded Sturgis to keep all three passes in his sights, but of course he can't scatter his forces irresponsibly. Mr. Chapman, what do our Nez Perce scouts know about Mason's pass?

Well, general, Old George he ain't never rid so far. Captain John he come out here once to hunt buffalo, but that place you put your finger on, he had no call to go through it. Looks mighty steep to me. Maybe I could get through it on *my* horse, and you ride pretty good on Arrow, but I don't know about the rest of you. You see, general—

Thanks, Chapman, that's all. Mason, are you satisfied?

Yessir, so long as Sturgis is on the *qui vive*. It's up to him, I guess.

All right. Now, gentlemen, I was disappointed at our meagre mileage to-day. The troops had their holiday at Yellow Stone. Starting to-morrow, we're going to drive them harder. Colonel Sturgis will do his best, I'm sure, but he can't keep the Nez Perces bottled up forever without reënforcements. Go ahead, Bomus.

General, if I have your permission to lean on the mule drivers, we can carry more of the unfit men in the wagons—

Have the muleteers been complaining?

Well, sir, they allege our ammunition is mighty heavy for the animals.

When did they start carrying ordnance?

From Yellow Stone until now, sir. Lieutenant Otis advised me that just managing his Gatlings in that forest—

You mean to say they're conveying our carbine rounds. A case is a hundred pounds, I believe.

Ninety pounds per thousand, general. And we haven't shot much off, since—

Don't remind me! Well, lay down the law to those muleteers, and report to me to-night. They'll have to make room for a few more weaklings. Sladen, how many soldiers fell out to-day?

Seventeen, general. Six punished. Some fevers, and then whenever their boot-nails work into the soles of their—

I didn't request a medical report. Perry, Trimble, Pollock, Jocelyn, how are the horses?

Not bad, general.

Captain Spurgin.

Yessir.

Without your engineers we would never have reached here. The Army thanks you.

I appreciate it, general, and I'll tell the—

Spurgin, I've decided to send the wagons home to Fort Ellis. You'll command the convoy. The genuinely unfit men will go with you. Bomus and Otis, it's for you to decide between yourselves how much ordnance we carry. From here on, everything the men don't carry must go by horse or mule. Report to me before "Tattoo."

Yessir.

You have some comment, Captain Pollock?

Yessir. On the subject of meagre mileage, I'd like to say that that old sonofagun Mr. Joe won't stay long enough in one place for the infantry to get a shot at him, so some of us ought to ride ahead and—

Thank you, captain. Now let's turn to that crucial subject. Captain Fisher, where's Joseph?

4

Wood, you seem down in the mouth this evening.

To tell you the truth, Fletch, I—

You what?

. . . A case of intermittent fever . . .

Do you consider it a nervous disorder?

No, sir.

I'll inform Doctor Alexander.

No need, sir.

Then do try to pull out of it.

O, well. How about a spot of chess?

Let me see. It can't be Nanny, because no one's brought the mails since Henry's Lake. And you're in no trouble, since the general's made you his pet. No, I can't guess. You'd better come out with it.

This campaign—

What are you talking about? Here, let's step away from these tents. The orderly . . . All right, Wood. Get it off your chest.

I can't.

You showed your metal at White Bird Cañon. I should say you looked sick all right, especially when we found Theller, but you stood it with the rest of us. At the Clearwater you didn't hang back for an instant.

Thanks, Fletch.

It's the Indians, isn't it? O, I'm right—I see it in your face. Quickly now. The general's going to call one of us momentarily, and then—

No, sir, Lieutenant Howard's with his father.

Promise not to tell a soul. You dragged it out of me.

What do you object to precisely? You agree that Mr. Joe and his gang are murderers?

Of course. But dead squaws and children give me an ugly feeling. And I don't see why we couldn't have left them alone in Wallowa.

But it's not just Wallowa they'd require, Wood. They're *wild.* They expect to roam wherever they please, living on buffalo and whatnot. That means nobody can farm there. It's got to be them or us.

I know you're right, Fletch.

And finally a lighter weight undershirt by next year, they say.

Yessir.

Why tear yourself up by the roots for the sake of a doomed race? It's already too late for them. What would you do—resign from the Army? And what good would that accomplish?

Fletch, you're a better Christian than I. Do you ever pray for the Indians?

This is ridiculous. But I'll make a bargain with you. You straighten up and stop agonizing over what you can't help, and I'll do as you ask. I know for a fact (and I'll thank you to keep it to yourself) that every night before he retires the general asks GOD to hold His hand over Joseph's head, and lead him to the light. And I do compassionate the Nez Perces in particular. Formerly they rendered many services to the United States. I suppose that Joseph, White Bird, and most of the other ringleaders will be hanged in the end. But the women and children—

foiled us again, sir!

No more of that talk.

All right, sir.

Yes, general, you sent for me.

Stay a moment, Wilkinson. Major Merrill, how's the Seventh enjoying this adventure?

Real good, sir. We're cavalry, after all! Like to roam near about as much as Injuns—

I'm told you know the country to the north of here.

Well, sir, not bad for a white man, if I do say—

Did you agree with Mr. Chapman's Indians about there being only three escape routes from these mountains?

General, that Mr. Joe's a genius. He could come out anywhere.

He may be, but we're going to get him. Now, major, I want to communicate with Colonel Miles.

General, do you really think Mr. Joe can evade us that far?

My thoughts are my business, major. But you'll note that I summoned you privately, and you'll govern your mouth accordingly.

Right. Well, general, the fastest way to communicate with Tongue River is by boat. If I may show you on the map—

Yes. Wilkinson, if it comes to that, I think Miles had better take the diagonal line of march through *here*.

Yessir.

What do you say to that, major?

I'd say it's plausible, general. But if Joseph gets into these buttes north of Cañon Creek, well, it's a labyrinth all the way to the Musselshell.

How long could he conceal himself in that country?

Well, sir, with autumn coming on, and the grass dying back, unless he gets lucky with a buffalo herd, which is plausible, for bison are still as thick as mosquitoes up there, but even so his horses will be getting weak . . . But the thing is, no army in the world could ring him round in these badlands I'm talking about.

Major, you have a low opinion of this Army. Perhaps we'll surprise you. At any rate, if Joseph crosses the Musselshell, where might he winter other than in the British Possessions?

I don't know, general. It gets pretty cold up there, and our Cheyennes would be hunting him. But, after all, Indians are Indians. He might have a few tricks left—

Thank you, major. Your assessment is appreciated. Where's Fletch? O, is that so? All right. Then instruct Lieutenant Otis to revise his report, and present it to me before "Tattoo." I expect his solemn oath that both Gatlings will be firing fifteen minutes after they're called for. Now, Wilkinson, if the enemy joins up with Sitting Bull's hostiles—

> The bold dragoon he has no care
> As he rides along with his uncombed hair,

at which melody Perry finds himself remembering that icy starry desert night in California when the two of them sat high in the rocks, awaiting the move out at moonrise:

Colonel, are you out of tobacco?

You know me well.— Thanks! How you are holding up?

Not bad, sir.

Quarrelling with Delia again?

Yessir. You know how it is between men: When you're friends, it's done; you can count on it—whereas between man and woman, whatever you say, she goes right on doubting you. Makes herself miserable for nothing until you finally—

A d——d shame, Theller. She's a peach, to look at, anyhow.

Yessir, but you don't know the half of it. Sometimes I wish—o, hell. At least she looks up to *you*. Well, when do you think this Modoc campaign will be over?

It would have wrapped itself up right away if Canby hadn't been so soft and trusting.

Sir, you can say that again. I did feel kind of low when he got himself shot. Not a bad sort, for a general.

Theller, if Crook were in charge, Captain Jack would already be feeding the buzzards.

You've told me so much about him, sir, I can almost—

He's the greatest Indian fighter the U.S.A. has ever produced. Any man wants to disagree, I'll punch him fair and square in the face.

Someday I hope to meet him, sir.

O, thanks, I will build myself another drag. Not quite straight tobacco, is it?

No, sir. Cut with kinnikinnick—

And I know where you got it, too. In that Sibley tent in Lewiston, right on the riverbank, the one where—

Yessir.

I recognize the savor.

Yessir.

Theller, you're my friend. I don't judge you, and I'll never tell a fucking soul.

Thanks for that, colonel. That little gal in there, she's nothing but a two-bit Blackfoot squaw, but she somehow gets me easy in my mind.

I understand. I've seen you riding back from there with a smile on your face.

O the bold dragoon he has no care . . .

D——d straight, Theller. Ha!

Sir, if you ever care to join me . . .

5

You're tired, aren't you?

A little, father.

I'm very proud of you.

Do you mean it?

Cross my heart. Now listen, Guy. This is for your ears only. Sherman has ordered General Crook out of Camp Brown, in hopes of completely investing Joseph. You know that Crook is my most poisonous enemy. He's never forgiven me for saving Cochise's Apaches from his murderers. Moreover, he hates negroes, so of course he hates me. He will do his utmost to obtain the credit for Joseph's capture. This is one of the reasons why I may ask help from Colonel Miles, who as you know is one of my best friends. Sturgis is his dependent, of course. You see, Guy, and I'm telling you this in hopes that it may be useful: In this world, and especially in the Army, it's not what you know, it's who you know. That's part of why I felt distressed when General Sherman turned against me. If you ever set out to become a general, son, and I hope that you will, you will make enemies. There is no way around it. Therefore, you need friends to guard you from your enemies. And if I do summon Miles in person, I hope that you will improve your opportunity and make a friend out of him, because he's young enough to help you after I'm gone, and he owes a great deal to me. Is all this clear?

Yes, father. Who's riding with Crook?

The Fifth and the Third, and some Sioux.

Camp Brown is pretty far away, isn't it? Maybe they won't arrive in time.

Well, GOD *disposes,* as we say. You know, when I was acquitted of malfeasance regarding the Freedmen's Bureau, Miles said to me: *I think you must realize that "the LORD reigns."* And He does, Guy—He does! There's no doubt about it.

6

Then comes "Reveille" and the morning gun, sunrise, roll call, breakfast
> (Fletch withdrawing needle, thread and beeswax from his tiny buck-skin bag),
"The General" bugled out most excellently, followed by the move out, everything beautiful and automatic,
> clouds and mist, then rain,
>> Sladen and the general riding side by side along the left flank of our column, rehashing that interesting sermon they heard in Portland on the topic: *Would a law prohibiting the sale and consumption of whiskey, rum and other such ardent spirits infringe upon our American tradition of freedom?*
>>> the Gatlings' nest of long slender barrels wavering behind galled mules,
>>>> drizzle dripping off hundreds of black-tarred rucksacks,
>>>> Captain Fisher unshakeably active on his roan horse, bawling out our Bannocks for some misdemeanor
>>>>> (general, I'd say that we'd better have our Bannocks called in and thoroughly quizzed on their loyalty, before some mischief happens)
—while Redington, luckiest man in the Army, gazes down through the tops of foreshortened pines on the dizzying cliffs, which fall blindingly sunnily at first and then narrow into shadow-walls through whose purpleness he can hear but not see the river, thinks: This sure is a thrill. Real good country, maybe the best, knowing that down there in the murk the river foams dully. Next time he gets down there, maybe to-night, he'll stop to catch some trout. Once he tires of this particular prospect, he continues up Joseph's trail, watching sharp shadows of pine-tops on the cliff-wall; now he can spy sunny white bights of foam in the river. O yes,

a hundred thrills an hour! thinks Redington, following the enemy upstream, but not far enough to get killed; anyhow, Buffalo Horn's Indians
are ahead. He turns back to see the river, brown, white and green, sizzling
down through the steep cañon, while,

> riding in patient misery at thirteen dollars per month, with cold
> water dripping out of the sleeves of their rain-darkened stable
> frocks, and the infantry marching out of sight behind them,
>
>> the general's faded overall suit rain-darkened almost back
>> into new blueness,

our cavalry kill Mr. Joe again and again in their hearts, mainly to stay
awake. The best they can expect to-night is hot weak coffee as they sit on
their rubber blankets in the camp-mud, while the drizzle tickles their
necks. When they get old they can blame their rheumatism on those cruel
and stinking reds. Mr. Joe's the worst! They'll cheer when he's hanged.

General, Mr. Joe's burned Baronett's bridge.

All right. Get the remnant of Spurgin's engineers together and have them re-
pair it.

Right away, sir.

What a beautiful ride.

Sure is, general.

I've always enjoyed the rain.

Yessir.

Wilkinson, do you remember that man from the Eleventh we met yesterday?

Of course, sir.

Could you find out his name?

I think I can, sir.

Had one of the old iron-barreled 1870s—

Yessir, a pound heavier than ours. But Colonel Perry swears by them.

You must be mistaken. He always carries the 1873.

Well, as post commander—

I suppose. In some things the Army could be more flexible.

> And Redington has linked up with Sturgis's scouts.
>
> That's not for sure.
>
> Well, I heard Captain Fisher say—
>
> He ain't told the general, so he ain't got nothing for the general.
>
> Umatilla Jim told me Redington has made contact.
>
> He did? Who's scouting for Sturgis, anyhow?
>
> Cheyennes from Tongue River.
>
> No, Canucks.
>
> Americans at heart. And I'll bet he's picked up some Crows.
>
> Could be.
>
> Well, let's hope Sturgis finishes it.

Wood, that envier of Redington, who must feel near about as free as the Indians he hunts, now wonders whether that young man, being out of the general's sight, is entertaining himself beneath some overhanging boulder, smoking pure kinnikinnick, watching the rain part on either side of him like a Nez Perce woman's braids when she bends over to kiss her lover. The column rides on, carrying and being in part carried by Blackie, who also longs for Redington's job, believing so faithfully in what he desires that for him the rain becomes sunlight,

> for I do mean most resolutely someday to ride down this long winding valley, through all the sagebrush flats at the river's edges, then down into green-gold sagebrush meadows, to find the perfect place to live and die with my Fidelia,

while everyone else enjoys counting on Sturgis.

Now Is the Time for Steelhead to Die
September 9

1

$\mathcal{E}$ver since her husband told her that the Crows turned us away, Good Woman has been Dreaming of her WYAKIN, the SHOVELER DUCK, she knows not why:

> blue wings, red belly, and round eyes whose irises are orange, like WOW-SHUXLUH, the metal-eyed Dreamers' bird:
>> Now is the time to dance here;
>> now is the time for steelhead to die,

and then as the People begin packing their horses to ride out of camp

> (her husband is scolding a young boy who let two ponies escape),

she hears White Bird speaking to Ollokot once again about the Old Grandmother's children, the Redcoats, who may perhaps protect us if we can only cross the Medicine Line

> at which her heart tells her that blue wings have to do with Bluecoats, and the red belly with Redcoats, so that her WYAKIN will help her both here and there so that once again she can make herself brave
>
> as they ride away, travelling together like flying geese
>
>> (Looking-Glass's wives have not yet lost their beargrass caps),

into the former Salish Country (long ago the Blackfeet and Cutthroats drove them west)

> and farther from Wallowa,
>> where her mother lies south of the lake beneath a rocky hill, desiring for her grave to be loved,

and from Ground Squirrel Place,
>   where we buried Fair Land and the others,
although the Lice-Eaters have surely dug them up.
She yearns to vomit
>   even as Springtime, who must have eaten something bad, grows likewise nau-
>   seous, so that the jolting of the mare beneath her (one of Ollokot's) disturbs
>   her belly, and even the smell of the baby's hair begins to seem vile; so she
>   comes to know that she will vomit unless she dismounts to rest, which no one
>   will do except the dying ones whom we must leave on the trail; a stench of pine
>   perfume roars oversweetly inside her; now she is throwing up as she rides
and Sound of Running Feet is ashamed.

2

White Thunder,
>   ever watching to see whether the Bluecoats might suddenly be down in
>   those white- and vermilion-walled cañons,
has been flying along ridgetops, but we are not all fashioned like him: our horses
are getting skinny from too much travelling. The women, children and old ones
grow heart-tired;
>   Ollokot shows a new streak of grey in his braid,
>   the babies crying, *shlak, shlak!*
and even Good Woman has become one of those who weep as they speak.
>   Springtime is still vomiting.

3

With sudden noiselessness White Thunder makes himself alarmed by something,
>   just as when his WYAKIN awakes him in the night, to save him from a
>   prowling grizzly,
but this time he discovers nothing but a mourning dove pecking for seeds
>   —soon now it must fly away—
while his mother Swan Woman begins Dreaming of deer meat;
Toohhoolhoolsote, as quiet as the SUN'S FATHER, rides on and on,
>   no longer wishing to sing the young men into anger,
>   and Sound Of Running Feet slaps Helper's nose to make him go;
Cut Arm will not stop following us.

4

So we make camp, arriving in grief, hunger, weakness and sickness,
>   Springtime's arm is getting better; now she can lay down bedding-grass
>   near as easily as she used to do;

and Good Woman makes thin soup while Heinmot Tooyalakekt repairs a lariat
for Rainbow's widow.

5

TRAVELLER THE SUN begins to touch the trees
   as Lean Elk shouts: *Hurry, you People!*
but old Kapoochas the Medicine man is febrile; wounded in his hip at Ground
Squirrel Place, he can ride no more,
  so we leave him under a buffalo robe, with two copper bracelets to comfort him
   (he is smiling after us like the smell of sunshine on fallen pine needles);
now we are riding and riding away.

JOSEPH'S GOOSE IS FINALLY COOKED
SEPTEMBER 9

1

*S*ure could use a pinch of Borden's evaporated milk in our coffee to-night.
And maybe some molasses—
 Shut up.
 And then some squaws for side meat—
 Quit it. General's coming,
   not to mention Wilkinson, who finds the most unpleasant aspect of
   Army life the low, base smuttiness of the enlisted men's minds—once
   upon a time he imagined that they could be educated out of it, but now
   he knows that *they're brutes,* riddled with the sin of Adam, polluted:
     dear LORD, it's not merely prostitutes who are, as the wise have
     warned us, *whited sepulchers!*
So that's my position on promotion, Fletch. Unfortunately the Government
sees fit to—
 Excuse me, general, but I thought you wanted to hear some good news.
 What do you mean by that, Captain Fisher?
 Well, sir, Redington just reported in, and he made contact with some Canuck
who's on scout for Colonel Sturgis—
 Go on.
 Seems the Canuck had no idea of Mr. Joe's whereabouts, but Redington put
him on the trail, so he went galloping back—

That *is* excellent news. Once Sturgis gets in position . . .

Yessir.

Where is he now?

Waiting for the hostiles, sir, and guarding all three passes as ordered.

Thank you, captain, and please assure young Redington that I won't forget his exertions. That's all. Wilkinson, go notify Major Mason, if you would. Well, Fletch, what do you make of this development?

General, I'd say Joseph's goose is finally cooked. Do you think he's aware that Sturgis is approaching from the other side?

Probably. But it won't do him any good to know what awaits him. What can he do but charge into our pincers, or else wander back into Yellow Stone, where at best he could delay capture for another week or two?

Who will capture him there, sir?

We will.

Yessir.

What's your opinion of Redington?

As you've said yourself, sir, a brash youngster. I like him. Insolent, amusing, capable, extremely daring so far as I can tell—

Well, after this campaign is concluded we ought to do something for him.

Yessir.

Perhaps even a recommendation to West Point . . .

General, sir, there's Mr. Joe's tracks, headin' right up the valley!

So I see, Captain Fisher. Right here at Crandall Creek, just as you've predicted. Now tell me something. Have James Reuben's bunch been exerting themselves?

Well, general, I know my Bannocks better than I do your Nez Perces, so I—

Tactful of you. How far ahead can we see yonder?

A good ten miles, sir.

Where's Mason? I sent Wilkinson for Mason. What is going on? Now, Fletch, unroll the map again. I purpose we follow this gorge up to Sunlight Creek right *here.* We won't prevent Joseph from ascending Heart Mountain, but we can harry his rear, and Sturgis will be waiting below whichever pass he chooses.

That's logical, general.

Where do you suppose he's heading?

Sir, he may swing south toward this Stinking Water River—

All right. Major Mason, are you as pleased as I am? Kindly look over the map with me . . . Wood, Fletch, Wilkinson, inform the officers. Captain Fisher, keep your scouts on the *qui vive.* This cañon would be perfect for an ambush, which we know is Joseph's specialty. That's all, captain; kindly return to your duties. Where's Chapman?

Right here, general.

Captain Fisher has implied that our Nez Perce scouts are holding back. Could any sympathy for their relatives in Joseph's band possibly hinder this campaign?

Well, general, speaking as someone who knows those Indians—

Go on, Chapman,

because in much the same way that alkali begins to shine out as one rides westward through Nebraska, so Ad Chapman's qualities increasingly bewitch our general's soul,

so that they all go over the map again together

(Wilkinson rolling his eyes,

Wood longing just then to marry a fine half-breed girl and spend his life deep inside her),

and then they rejoin the column, trailing the hostiles through this long wide valley in which the late summer grass is growing patchily on the high sunnier swales

although here the grass has been grazed down by Joseph's herds

and I see more dead horses in that marsh of jade-green reeds,

Glory, glory, hallelujah—

then many more brown marsh-pools,

Left,

left,

left!

clackings of pebbles under horse-hooves,

Arrow still yearning to chase after Chapman's grey,

cloud-piles here and there on the valley walls,

and my bladder is already full again and that arm-stump has commenced annoying me again (I won't take calomel unless it gets a lot worse):

O, how fine it would be to be sitting right now on Colonel Perry's front porch at Lapwai, listening to the cicadas while Mrs. Perry sets out her bowl of root beer, the FitzGerald children shyly playing, and gallant Perry helping Mrs. Theller with something, the moon rising fast, the soldiers already back in barracks, our good Indians softly singing

Wakesh nun pakilauitin

JEHOVAN'M yiyauki—

and presently it will come time to retire and read Lizzie's latest before reviewing the communications from Headquarters,

then re-approaching Montana Territory, passing through an aspen grove to where a knob-mountain perforates the sky

(and in the vanguard our Bannocks chanting; I must ask Fisher if all these Indians smoke the same mixture in their *kinnikinnick*

—and is *kinnikinnick* a word universally employed? It reminds me of the syllables I used to hear as a child from our Indians in Maine: Abenakis, Penobscots—

LORD have mercy, but my arm does ache! I'm getting old, evidently),

and coming down into the dry grass country, a butte-labyrinth in the aspens between the clouds, pellets of scrub, pancakes of buffalo dung, the country ahead ever wilder, the river almost invisible to our left behind the softly rolling swales not unlike Joseph's Imnaha country, the Army moves brightly on!

2

We'll plant our guidon *here* on the map, just before Sunlight Creek joins Clark's Fork. Do you follow me, Wilkinson?

Yessir. I see—

Then give the instructions. Lieutenant Howard could use some exercise. Send him forward to notify the scouts.

Right away, general. The boys'll be—

> Pim! Pim! . . . Pim!

What's that?

Sounds like shooting, general.

Wilkinson, ride ahead with me.

Sure thing, general,

> cantering so that in convenient time they arrive at the ordained halting-spot, so shady and so delightful by the sweetly rushing brown creek (a veritable oasis among the crags!),
>
> all quiet, so it must not be an emergency
>> (perhaps some careless trooper discharged his weapon in error:
>>> a punishable offense),
>
> fresh horse dung everywhere:

Joseph must have just vacated this camp, wouldn't you say?

Without a doubt, sir.

We merely need to keep bearing northeast on Joseph's trail . . .

Yessir.

O, *there* they are. Why do they stand around like that?

> as angry nest-guarding birds fly cheeping to the attack, accompanied by flies and mosquitoes
>
> although even more flies enshroud this dead Indian under the tree—

Captain Fisher, what's happened here?

Well, general, when I heard them three shots I wondered the same thing, so I rode up here quick as I could, and my Bannocks were just putting the finishing touches on this Nez Perce. Seems like Mr. Joe left him here to die, and when my Injuns rode in, he sat up like to draw a bead on 'em, so they—

Then where's his weapon?

Well, sir, my half-breed must've confiscated it. Them Cheyennes are crazy about toys like that. Hey, Jule, show the general that pistol of yours.

Captain Fisher, look me in the eye. Do you swear that your man's pistol was previously in the dead man's possession?

General, I absolutely swear by the sainted MOTHER OF GOD! See, he must've been holdin' up Mr. Joe's progress, with this hip wound of his, so they tucked him here—

Captain Fisher, this Indian has been scalped.

Well, gosh, general, now that you mention it, I do see that he's missin' hair—

Have you forgotten my prohibition of killing and scalping the wounded and infirm Indians we find in these camps?

Sure I've kept it in mind, general, but the thing is, when my Bannocks ride ahead of the column they sometimes forget the rules.— By the way, general,

> pointing up to the cañon-ridge where the cloud-puffs so quickly flow,

ain't that quite the Injun trail up there? I'd appreciate your opinion, because all the boys keep remarkin' on your eagle gaze.

That's your job, captain. I'm disgusted you'd even ask me. However, let me look through my field-glass,

>> while Fisher winks to Jule, who instantly kicks down the willow twig on which the Indian's scalp was drying, then throws a blanket over it, just before the general, having swept his glass across the river and up into the grinning green crags

>>> (this time even Wilkinson, who ordinarily must be counted the best observer in and of the general's circle, is fooled, and apes his master),

>> turns round, saying:

Nothing of the kind. Now, captain, henceforth you'd better keep a tighter rein on your Indians. I will enforce certain standards of humanity. Do you understand me, captain?

Yessir.

I see you've already stripped him. Doubtless for your *collection.*

No, sir, it was my Bannocks who—

Look into your heart, captain. Consider your conduct. From now on I'll be watching you.

Yessir.

This is the third time. Next time I'll have you punished. Wilkinson, go tell them to plant the guidon. Then send Buffalo Horn to me, and, Captain Fisher, I want you present,

>> and suddenly the cool air from the creek seems nearly as precious as the lovely clouds themselves which now whiten the gap of sky between river shrubs, so rich and cool—such a treat, a relief after the desert!

> as Wilkinson,

>> whose view of these Nez Perces is simply that they have to go,

> having finished gazing up toward the sky, inquires into the origin of a delightful cinnamon smell:

>> Is it this tree's crumbled whitish bark? No, in fact it derives from the resin of that tree's ovoid leaves

>>> (while our Bannocks, as innocent as house-cats, gaze up wide-eyed through leaves into the blue and white sky),

> mounts his horse, transmits the general's first order, which instantly registers upon our Army as follows:

> *Halt!*

>> *Dismount!*

then rides ahead to collect Buffalo Horn
>   (although Wilkinson, who has never trusted Buffalo Horn and lies
>   awake at night worrying that he might take advantage of our gen-
>   eral's kind heart, has little hope that any talking-to will improve the
>   Bannocks' natures),
and the river flows so loud
>   while Trimble's company forts up in the soft rye-grass under the
>   trees,
>   with Perry's bunch on their left and Jocelyn's on their right
and Ad Chapman rides up singing
as a fine breeze blows up the cañon.

WHEN THE THISTLES ARE BLOOMING PURPLE
SEPTEMBER 10

1

*T*hen coming down from the pass, across the shoulder of green and orange grasses in the reddish dirt, as the first riders begin to see far ahead where Heart Mountain glows in a notch of Buffalo Country, Springtime, who rarely speaks out, suddenly says to her elder sister-wife: Now that my baby is getting weak, it comes into my heart to kill her.

Good Woman,
>   she who once was rich in horses fitted out with many baskets,
is riding White Face, who keeps snorting and stumbling. She replies: My sister, you are tired; in camp to-night I shall look for rush skeletonweed to fatten your milk; that is all she needs,
>   while their husband, completing his heart, rides up to Looking-Glass to
>   say: White Bird and Lean Elk are right, I am telling you three times.
>   But if Sitting Bull will not smoke with us—
>   Then, my brother, we shall die. Where else can we ride now?
They ride through the light rain, the Buffalo Country glowing pale yellow ahead with blue shadows some of which might be water
>   (they are taking us far away),
into the arid loveliness of that other world, so vast that it must contain some country where the Bluecoats can never find us
—if not yet here, then somewhere;
if not before the Medicine Line

(only our best men know where that is, and nobody asks them)
then after
(there will someday be happy days of drying meat)—
but again Springtime speaks of killing her baby, because her breasts have gone dry;
      therefore Heinmot Tooyalakekt goes fishing with Ollokot, who then
      creeps away to chase a deer,
            while Good Woman watches for helping herbs as she rides
            and Heinmot Tooyalakekt kills two ducks for his family,
      Traveller the Sun low on the left like a Lakota warrior's quiver.

2

Riding side by side until night, hoping for buffalo,
      with the knife-ridged mountains just ahead resembling bear-gnawed
      deer vertebrae,
      and our horses greying in the rain,
            Good Woman, the excellent one, now becoming wrinkled,
                Cloudburst carrying Fair Land's son,
      we follow Lean Elk, our strict head-chief, longing to eat and rest
            (although Toohhoolhoolsote's heart does not care);
it is getting cold, and Springtime's baby no longer cries.

3

Up here in the green shadows we gaze down into the light,
      sorrowing as we ride
down the meadows into the windings among white-striped red-backed ridges
and the canted stripes of red sandstone,
      the foggy meadows beginning to bear the silver marks of sagebrush, es-
      pecially along the lips of the red-walled river gorges;
            when the chilly breeze springs up, the long deerskin fringes of his
            shirt begin pattering against Looking-Glass's shoulders,
and now between the spread thighs of rainy orange meadows shines the sky-jewel
over arid buckskin buttes
      and rain, low purple clouds over the dry orange hills, cool fat drops
            (this world goes on forever,
            this gently slanting world),
      rain singing down the carved gorges, pillared gorges, everything rounded and
      grooved
                as Strong Eagle rides up a side-coulee,
                  wishing to help our People, who are always hungry for meat;
              and Wottolen climbs a butte to look back, because he has Dreamed
              that Cut Arm will soon attack again

(and just as cowbirds pursue the buffalo herds, in order to eat the insects which afflict them, so Cut Arm's kindly Lice-Eaters keep after us, to relieve us of our horses and our weary lives);

while Looking-Glass keeps speaking against Lean Elk, *pókat, pókat,* although Toohhoolhoolsote,

whose heart informs him that just as no man can say exactly how and when old women become no good, so no one can tell us when Looking-Glass stopped being straight,

cannot make himself angry at this decayed chief:

we all must die, so why should Looking-Glass be considered worse than smallpox?

—but White Face keeps stumbling, and Sound Of Running Feet punches Helper's nose again and again

(for a moment we hear Looking-Glass's youngest daughter weeping)

and to the north, a purple murk of rain with a crack of blue sky just over the cañon ridge.

Now as we ride down into the sagebrush flats, with colored buttes ahead, Well Behaved Maiden,

who was lung-shot at Ground Squirrel Place,

slides off her horse;

although White Bird tried three times to suck the evil Power out of her, singing songs and inhaling her sickness through a leaf funnel, she kept failing, so that her brothers have now begun to say that White Bird is a wicked shaman

(all Arrowhead's poultices have failed;

Toohhoolhoolsote lost much of his helping-Power at Ground Squirrel Place;

perhaps Feathers Around The Neck could have healed her);

she can ride no more.

(Her WYAKIN is a BLUE GROUSE; that girl never could resist anything.)

Her mother and brothers are grieving over her; they wrap her in a buffalo robe and hide her away in a cave guarded by wild roses, leaving her to be raped, shot, scalped, stabbed and stripped by the Lice-Eaters;

White Bird does not look; *Kate* rides ahead quickly;

then down we ride,

so that when we spy some fleeing miners we enjoy to overtake them,

especially Swan Necklace, whom the Bostons have many times insulted in his heart,

and whose war-friends and sweet sister they have killed;

they are galloping away from their wagon—how easily we surround them!

soon we are shooting them in their hearts even as they begin to weep:
  Pim—pim—pim!
        Please, you Indians, have mercy! I swear to JESUS we never—
        Pim!
(although he turns away, wrapping himself in his blanket, not even Heinmot Tooyalakekt speaks against this:
        They are Bostons, so let us bleed them until they die):
              That poor one is still groaning. Let's help him!
              I shall kick him to death;
        I shall hit him hard;
              I shall crack him open
                        (dark stripe of blood from mouth to ear)
                    after which a few of us sing the victory song.
Thus have we comforted the blood of Well Behaved Maiden,
    who has not yet been killed,
        but whose name we should mention no more,
    and of Shore Crossing, Chief Eagle Robe's son,
        he who could climb nearly any mountain
        and led the Three Red Blankets:
            him we cannot stop thinking of.
Pillaging the wagon before we burn it, we find good things, giving our children
marrow-like to suck, and our shivering old ones handfuls of Borden's powdered
milk and dark salty hunks of smoked bacon,
            a canvas bandage for Helping Another,
        but what Sound Of Running Feet most wishes for is to see someone
        smash in these Bostons' skulls
            (she keeps quiet, for fear of her father);
        and Broken Tooth, that sweetly sunfaced girl, long-braided, her rich hair
        angling darkly across her temples so that her face is shaped almost like
        an arrowhead, folds her hands in her lap, with a striped blanket draped
        across her shoulders as she stares at the dead men, remembering her
        murdered father Grey Eagle,
        while Springtime leaps off Redhead and touches a Boston's pale hand;
            now she is touching his beard, surprising her hand with its mild
            roughness as of buffaloberry leaves:
                she is making herself brave.
Pouring out the Bostons' *getting-drunk liquid,* we take their rifles and cartridges
        (Swan Necklace sorrowing in his heart to not get more ammunition for
        his new needle gun,
        White Thunder crushing sagebrush between his leadstained fingers),
leaving them face down in the sand; then for a moment our young men play with
a buckskin bag crammed with glittering grey galena crystals.

4

Toohhoolhoolsote says: Heinmot Tooyalakekt, my brother, you are never satisfied with what our young men have done,
to which the sad chief replies: What were these Bostons to us, that we must kill them?

What were they? Open your ears! Have you forgotten the council at Butterfly Place, when Cut Arm stopped my mouth and showed the rifle?

5

Even now when we have ridden so far away from home, those rotten-hearted ones will not leave off troubling us. For White Thunder, Strong Eagle and Ollokot, scouting across the orange-grassed gravel and down the white-pillared purple cañon, smell new Bluecoats encamped, half hidden under rainclouds:
a faraway flick of lightning, the sky still blue behind it, then a bugle's call:
they too must be Cut Arm's slaves, hunting us.
They gallop back to warn the chiefs and other best men,
who pass the pipe while we rest the horses and the women brew willow tea
(even as from his Medicine pouch Peopeo Tholekt takes out that half-mummified woodpecker-head whose Power will draw worms from a baby; his war-friend White Thunder has told him about Springtime's child; he touches the relic to the small girl's forehead and sings a secret song into her ear; then she opens her eyes; at her mother's breast she begins to become strong);
and the council goes on talking: *pokát, pokát:*
If Rainbow and Five Wounds still lived, they would show us how to wipe them out!
—at which Looking-Glass, turning on him as suddenly as that Bluecoat's bullet which came spinning and hissing through Wounded Head's little son at Ground Squirrel Place,
says: Swan Necklace, you have no sense; it was you young men who made the Bostons our enemies forever.
We must kill more Boston women; that will grieve Cut Arm.
It is true what White Bird says: If we kill one Bluecoat, a thousand more will take his place. If they kill one of our best men, no one can replace him.
Looking-Glass, his words wide-spreading like box elder branches, advises us how to pass around these *Americans;* but he has no Power; he is nothing.
The young men and Ollokot decide what to do:
We must escape through the extremely steep place:

the hidden cañon, the chilly-shaded crack where low blue striated knobs
of pinkish grey rock barely occlude the sky
    (Bad Boy knows the way);
for us it is easy,
    the children quiet as we hold them,
    our blind grandmothers entirely silent;
    now we are riding down,
        quietly singing our WYAKIN songs,
    squeezing our knees with all our might to avoid flying over the horses' heads,
        old Tzi-kal-tza helped by his dear daughter Iltolkt,
        Welweyas leading both her horse and her murdered mother's,
            Towhee helping her daughter, whose wounded breast bubbles
            and bleeds, bubbles and bleeds,
        Red Owl descending as quietly as he departed his country forever
        after the Big Water fight,
        Looking-Glass's women leading all the family's horses except for
        Home From Capture, whom only the *lucky man* should be helping,
        and the warriors' long hair streaming in the wind:
any real human being could do it
    (two of Cut Arm's mules whirl down to death,
    one of Lean Elk's racehorses stumbles,
        Burning Coals gets his entire herd down
    and Helper breaks his leg, so we leave him for Cut Arm, and Aunt
    Cloudburst gives Sound Of Running Feet another horse, a fine yel-
    low one);
and then walking,
    White Thunder's old mother Swan Woman following the horse
    herd, whipping them untiringly,
and Heinmot Tooyalakekt guides the feeblest People down
    into the flats close by a yellow-clad butte, our horizon a rain-silvered
    ridge with many steep cañons gouged out of it,
        even Good Woman almost dizzy with weariness as she begins to
        unpack the horses
while Lean Elk sends warriors southeast, saying: Hear me, young men! The Bluecoats are like children; we can trick them. Tie branches behind your horses to
make the Big Dust. Ride your horses round and round. Then our enemy will believe
in their hearts that we are riding to the Stinking River. Young men, be careful! If
you fail to deceive them, many People will die. Return carefully; make no dust!
    And it is easy for them; they are all becoming best men;
    and it is easy for us; we are still flying up; even now
        in this time when the thistles are blooming purple although the juniper
        berries are still green,
we possess a few flint hides to sleep on.

VICTORY
SEPTEMBER 10

1

*L*ieutenant Howard, ride up there doublequick and ascertain the cause of their delay.

Yessir,

as the remainder of the column creeps miserably up the divide,

navigating between the carcasses of Joseph's abandoned horses

(Wood meaning to ask Umatilla Jim, the officers' favorite scout, about the parfleche bag painted with red and yellow hourglass-like designs he's found:

probably made by a Crow squaw)

—and here's another of our mules they stole at Camas Meadows and worked to death, GoDd——n them filthy reds!

Guess who's working *us* to death like niggers? Up and down, up and down—

What's the matter, Fletch? A little winded, are you?

I sure am, general, and my poor horse—

All right. On your feet now,

and up the orange-grassed slopes, the cañon now buckskin-colored below, the sky bruised with clouds

(flash of snow in the rock-slit between forest-peaks),

Trimble, sunburned and balding, his raggedy-ass sack coat practically falling off his shoulders, glaring across the column at the general,

not that he will ever consider my side of it. I've served in the First just as long as Perry, but that will never signify: Perry's his pet and will blacken my name to save his own. I'm aware how *that* goes,

Perry knowing all the men of his company as well as the white blazes on Diamond's back legs and watching them almost without looking, so expert a campaign commander has he become that he begins to hope never to return to Lapwai, but rather to ride endlessly up and forward through all these infinite new American lands

and into the chilly meadows:

close to the clouds now, smelling grass, their progress memorialized by a huge dandelion puffball,
clouds and peaks taking on each other's colors,
   the mules raising their ears, mincing and braying, the
   packers riding up and down the line, sometimes narrowly avoiding a tumble,
  Wilkinson staring forward, tautening his face
   (he reminds Umatilla Jim of one who has not eaten),
 and a chilled bumblebee creeping from bloom to bloom of the steep
 lupine slope,
 this universe of buckskin cañons awesome and eerie.

Chapman, I've never thanked you properly for this horse. That wouldn't have
looked right in the beginning, before I knew what kind of man you were. But this
Arrow of yours is a marvel to ride.

I'm glad to hear it, general, and you sure ride good for a one-armed man.

Now, how far have you explored this Stinking Water River?

Well, pretty much all the way, general.

Excellent. Your knowledge will be invaluable,
 and turns Arrow off the trail to receive his approaching son,
  peculiarly comforted, although no words are said, to see before him
  Wilkinson's high bright forehead and dark little eyes
  and wondering whether Fisher would truly dare to hinder this campaign. The man's insolent and perhaps treacherous, but surely not
  malicious! If only Guy were more capable of reading men, I could—

There you are finally.

Sorry, father. When I found Captain Fisher, he was perplexed, because Joseph's
trail bore toward the Stinking Water as we'd all expected, but after two miles the
tracks suddenly went every which way, so that even Buffalo Horn—

Well?

Captain Fisher has just doped it out, father, and it's a marvel to see how he—

All right, Fletch, I'll review that report in another instant. Lieutenant Howard,
which way has Joseph gone?

   That's just a squaw track,
   No, that's a buck track. Look here. Fisher showed me—

North again, sir, on what looks to be a steep trail—
  And around that ledge. He almost made a fool of us again. And you know
  what's fishy. Our tame Nez Perces kept pointing us toward the river, but
  Ad Chapman said—

Unroll the map. O, I see. Mason had better come here; yes, thank you, Fletch. So
they're bound for Clark's Fork Cañon, unless they can somehow double back again,
which looks impossible. Well, Sturgis will halt them until we reach the scene. Gentlemen, observe these contour lines. This may be a challenge for our pack-mules . . .

2

Here stand the muleteers, bearded and glum, wishing away Joseph's impossible tracks down that precipitous crack of a cañon:

> Red O'Donnell, longing to curse, spits instead, as if by accident, then
> wipes his bearded mouth on the shoulder seam of what five hundred
> years ago might have been a white canvas stable frock;

and Perry,

> gazing down into other cañons and mountains with their infinitely var-
> ied shadows
> (Diamond snorting again and again):

finally says: You're kidding me. Mr. Joe went down *here?* Well, well, I guess he did.

> Gonna call this the Devil's Doorway.
> Sure, soldier. You ready for hell?

Now, general, don't you be deceived! I'd advise you to—

Chapman, shut up. Where's Captain Pollock?

Right here, sir.

Captain, for some time now you've been itching to show us all what your
bunch can do. You'll take the lead, right with the scouts and A.D.C.s.

Thank you, sir.

LORD knows what you'll find down there. But remember, captain: Don't use up
your horses. Keep them fresh for the shock. If Joseph's braves are blocking the way,
hit them hard. But get away from the cañon as quickly as you can, so the rest of
us can aid you. You know all this.

Yessir.

> Sound the move out.

GOD bless you, captain.

> Not even twenty feet wide—
>> Sorry, colonel, but there's no way we can ride the animals.
>> Not even a red could—

Come on, bruisers!

>> This'll be Dead Mule Trail all over again.
>> I'd sure rather be climbing Heart Mountain.

Move out.

>> Father, please tell me how this will turn out.
>> With luck, we'll finish Joseph to-day or to-morrow,

that daredevil Ad Chapman riding ahead on his crazy grey racer and Redington
right after him, having slid his long rifle out of its Indian-beaded deerskin sling,
then Wood, eager to impress Wilkinson and the general in equal measure,
enjoying himself mostly because Chapman does, wishing Nanny could
glimpse him in some magic mirror,

> for I remember when my stretch of America extended not much farther

than from the library to the Riding-Hall, from where we made our horses leap over hurdles as we fired at mock heads, anticipating the melodies of the band at parade, and wondering when some local belle might allow one of us to squire her across the grass, when now I'm actually

leading his Indian pony, drawing his pistol, ready for anything, even to make his stand,

and tall Captain Fisher, proudly cramming extra .50 calibre cartridges into the star-patterned bag of a dead Nez Perce squaw which was unearthed by our Bannocks at Big Hole and then engrossed into his souvenir collection in exchange for a tin of of black powder, comes right behind on his roan horse,

along with Umatilla Jim and all that Indian crowd, right on the vanguard's heels

(Jim now quickly touches his weaselskin bracelet);

next comes Captain Pollock's bunch leading their animals, with pistols on full cock,

and then Diamond enjoying the wind, his back legs together, as Perry

(feeling irrelevantly qualmish just as always before close action)

begins to coax him down the steepest stretch,

because I aim to prove to the general that I've got more "sand" than all the rest of them, and I mean to pay back Mr. Joe for what he did to Theller, and to have a GODd——d good think about Delia,

these three considerations packed together as neatly and routinely now as saddle blanket, overcoat and rubber blanket

—and he touches the bridle so gently against the animal's neck:

You're sure the best horse ever! You trust me, don't you? Good boy, good boy! Even going down the Devil's Doorway, you never even flirt your head,

Trimble's company longing for a fight (every man a hero),

and the general's twin, jaunty one-legged Sladen, well in the saddle, clinging to the neck of his chocolate-colored horse

(that hero never even once swigged from a cocaine bottle),

then Fletch, so unique to us with his wide, slightly haunted eyes, and the thick dark moustaches interrupting his boyish face, leading Whitey down the cañon;

Sandford's boys and Jocelyn's bunch, with their dark blue blouses (preserved for inspection) strapped tight to their saddles, and their grey felt slouch hats rotting on their heads,

poor Lieutenant Otis shepherding his unwieldy pair of Gatlings

followed by Mason, who is still haunted by the siege of the Lava Beds,

as if Captain Jack, roundfaced and old, could possibly be grimacing at him right now, with his tooth necklace clattering and clawlike hands on his rifle!

(but this particular specter, unlike Perry's, cannot weaken him, for it comprises an enemy, not a friend; hence Mason pulls his horse forward with an air almost of disgust, as if to say: Nothing could be half as bad as the Modocs!);

while Wilkinson, knowing that Joseph is now trapped, feels so happy that he
could seriously burst out in a one-man chorus of "Stand Up for Jesus,"
the horses slipping, screeching and sometimes tumbling, our muleteers shouting, the whole command in wobbling, anxious disarray,

>> down,

>>>> and blue-eyed Captain Miller, our braveheart of the Clearwa-
ter, sucks in his cheeks, gripping his shiny Springfield, neither
sad nor angry but simply alert:

>>>>> Well, this sure is a real tingler—

> down,

>>> toward the light:

>>>> Clear our dead animals out of the way. Pack their loads
on your backs if you have to but don't hold up the line.
Mr. Joe's around the corner! *Doublequick now,*

and finally, at the cañon's mouth:

> Sturgis's campsite, and his tracks marching east,
> Joseph's tracks arrowing northward toward the horizon,
> and Clark's Fork River, lipped with willows which at this moment seem
> brighter than their cousins back along the Big Hole River, taking on the
> same muddy purple as the rainclouds.

THE OPTIMISTIC SCOUT
SEPTEMBER 10

*G*azing down northwest from the edge of a red earth mesa frosted with white
stones, on one of which he warms his buttocks, Redington sees neither smoke nor
flag, hears nothing of Sturgis's command—where in this world have they gotten to?
Lowering his field-glass, he stares across Clark's Fork River—Rotten Sun Dance
River, his Crows call it—and rain begins to fall on him. Well, the Seventh Cavalry's
sure going to be unpopular with our Christian Sourpuss—unless of course they are
fighting the Nez Perces somewhere. Tamping a pinch of kinnikinnick into his pipe,
the boy unbottles a Lucifer match, strikes fire, takes a draw, and wishes this life
could go on forever. Maybe it will. Once we whip Joseph we can go after the Bannocks and Crows. Besides, there's always Sitting Bull to be cleaned up. He watches
a fat drop strike an orange rock near his ankle. The wet place goes red. He kicks the
rock, which bounces down a runnel of greenish sandstone, down between greenish
and orange sandstone pillars, down into the little badlands.

Here the river curves like the grip of a prewar Volcanic pistol. The coyotes are singing.

Redington reaches into his pocket, breaks off another hunk from a crumbling greasecake of buffalo pemmican, and counts his lucky stars. Maybe to-morrow I'll get to shoot another deer, or an Indian, which is more exciting if not exactly a contribution to the larder (would I stand on principle, or would I be a cannibal if necessity called? That's easy!).

Again he plays his field-glass over the flat tops of all these little mesas, which are gently wind- or water-combed with east-west lines. No sign of Mr. Joe!

Enthusiastic, optimistic, he even yearns to plumb the wearisome winding crevices of the badlands.

I Would Give a Thousand Dollars
September 11

1

*F*olding up the collar of his overcoat against the wind, and gazing across flats and badlands toward the unseen cañon where Sturgis should have been, he interviews the wounded German under the bruised sky, while a contingent of Captain Fisher's Crow scouts sit on a log, whittling plug tobacco and additionally profiting by the time to be entertained by this half-broken white man who repeats: *Dead,* both of them! By *Joseph* murdered! They were good men; give meat to everybody. Now *dead.* *Murdered* by Joseph; *shot,* GODd——n him for a *bloody* red devil—

Sir, that sort of language is never called for. Rest assured: We are on Joseph's trail and he will soon be brought to justice with all his confederates. Now, after the Indians killed your partners, which way did they ride?

> Away, no doubt, from these Crows with their war bonnets on, some of
> them bearing lances or coup sticks frilled with feathers
>> (ought to ask Redington about their picturesque claptrap),
> their arms and faces so smoothly, darkly ochered as to resemble shad-
> owed stone, and

Right, fellows! the German grins, now perceiving the Crows, and, forming his right hand into a fist from which the index finger alone extends, he brings it first to his right cheek (which is still black with dried blood from his scalp wound), then passes it just under his nose in a refined approximation of cutting.

Why, the *nez-percés,* of course! An ingenious sign, isn't it, Wood? And all the Indians know it?

Yessir.

Remind me to inform Mrs. Howard. She'll be most interested.

> Impudently half-smiling, his Crows imitate the gesture, sticking out their index fingers as they whisk their knives across their tobacco boards (better not to take notice). Who's that self-important old buck who's tricked out his horse in the floral-patterned, crimson-beaded crupper fringed with brass jingles? And did that interesting Indian from Little Big Horn ride home to his reservation? I haven't seen him since Yellow Stone. What was it he said about the Custer fight? *A black day,* or some such. If I ask Wood again, he'll think me senile. A handsome piece of tack on that horse, actually! I wonder what Lizzie would say if I bought one for our dun mare? Now they are mixing kinnikinnick with plug-shavings, each brave preparing the afternoon's smoke in the way that suits him best. LORD, they couldn't care less if we never chased Joseph! Well, soon they too must meet a wholesome compulsion.

Yessir.

> Hey, fellows, did he get robbed?

Has Doctor Alexander examined this man?

> Naw. Mr. Joe, he don't use money.

> Well, Looking-Glass does. Remember them storekeepers who—

> But this Dutchman here—

> The reds sure broke his jug of acqua-regia. Look at that. What a shame; what a shame.

> He's fine.

> But did he find gold?

I don't believe so, general. I'll find him straightaway.

> All right. Then we won't take up a collection.

But where's Redington? And why haven't we heard any news of Colonel Sturgis?

> Anyhow, he's nothing but a foreigner.

They were *good* men, I swear! Never harm anyone. Even *niggers* they would feed. Now *dead.* Murdered—

All right, sir, good-bye and GOD bless you. We're on the march now; we'll teach them not to murder. Sound the move out.

Now *dead,* general! They plead to Joseph: *Please, save our lives.* Then Joseph turned away. The devils, they were laughing. In our faces they shot us. But we were *good* men. Very good—

Move out!

> —past cottonwoods, pines and a few spruces, the command of the column devolving once more upon Captain Miller, who if I were him would pay more attention to his advance guard, our infantry striding a hundred ten paces to the minute in sullen unbelief, our windburned cavalry riding

two by two, through rain on the yellow grass and afternoon light over the hill, over the hill where we all must go

(when I catch Joseph, perhaps I'll pass my finger across my nose like that, and study his reaction),

more or less north now, deeper into Montana where long lean snouts of crumbling rock snuffle in the yellow grass:

What's weighing Wood down? Wilkinson's accusation is absurd. But it's true that the boy cocoons himself. To young people, this or that issue can seem absolutely important, when maturity's light either exposes it as a trifling distraction, or else proves to be a manifestation of duty, love or GOD. I know all too well what devours him. Will he make anything of himself before the gilt wears off his buttons?

If only Guy could be kinder to him! I

can't help but admire that Bannock over there who rides the lovely white stallion with brown fringes of mane striping his neck: how I'd love to gallop that horse!

> Stand up for these, the wrong'd, the aggriev'd,
> In deepest pits of darkness found,
> Wakesh nun pakilauitin
> JEHOVAN'M yiyauki—

and considerably in advance of the turbid-watered dirt groove called Silvertip Creek (the tall mountains behind lost in fog), they halt, then resume their northeasterly march in good order,

Trimble's bunch in the vanguard to-day,

some men in corduroy, some in rags, one in calfskin trousers, and Fletch reminds Wilkinson: Joseph can keep this up for all eternity, excluding attrition. If we can just stampede him into doing something like the average Indian . . .

and Wood, who has felt a trifle deflated ever since Joseph gave us the slip in that steep narrow cañon, keeps considering something that his drunken father used to say: *Everything has to be met with courage, toil, misgiving and disappointment . . .*

Fisher scouting rightward with four Crows, Captain John and that Cheyenne half-breed,

Perry riding at the head of Company "F," his nightmares as thick as the reeds and flowers about White Bird Creek,

the general cantering Arrow up and down the line:

Sir, I caught this man with barefoot whiskey. I poured it out—

Where'd he get it?

He won't say, sir.

Whose is he?

Captain Jocelyn's—

All right, soldier. You've already lost a month's pay. Here's one opportunity, and only one, to remit a greater punishment. No? Wilkinson, write him up. A month at hard labor, remitted until our return to Lapwai,

Chapman posting diligently behind the general, hoping to win a prize

(knowing that General Howard needs him to keep this company organized against the enemy, he tells Wilkinson: Now let's see where them Indians might have dodged down to. That's exactly what we'd like to see, all right. Chapman, you're a caution),

Guy cantering happily up and down the column beside his father and on through the yellow-grassed flats, the low near horizon a series of buttes, the sky diagonally pillared with rain, until

Halt. Dismount. Fall in. Roll call.

Pickets out.

Right away, captain.

Pickets *right.* Pickets *left.*

Yessir.

You there! Where's your intrenching tool?

No, you d——d ape! You side-line the animals *every night!* Can't you remember Camas Meadows?

Bomus, how is our supply of hardbread?

O, tolerable, general.

Right face.

All right, boys. Encamp in battle lines. Campfires will be permitted to-night.

Yessir.

Now, that's not an ideal place to fetter your mules. You want Mr. Joe to sweep 'em up again?

Wood has practically disgraced himself, in my opinion.

Did you hear the joke about the darky who tried to marry Pocahontas?

No, sir. What about the bell-mare?

Well, he said to her, he said—

No, I'd rather be playing "base ball."

Graze her over there,

Perry mixing linseed oil and white lead as the painters do, then gently blotting the medicine onto Diamond's saddle gall, all the while murmuring to the horse and stroking his neck

as Trimble, whose animal is in better shape, turns his back to his accustomed enemy and sits on his saddle, tying up a tear in his boot with buckskin strings,

Fisher's Crows oiling their hair

and our army outspread upon a prairie like some stinking tent city or hell on wheels for the railroad.

Not to worry, general. Doctor Alexander assured me the wound was superficial. Evidently he was attached to his partners, and that's why he—

He must have been. Well, Wood, a sad case.

Yessir.

In your opinion, is German blood more excitable than ours?

I'm not sure, general. My father knew a German once—

All right. By the way, do you see that dust yonder? Near about due south, I'd say. Might be nothing more than a herd of buffalo.

General, you have eyes like an eagle. I'll have somebody check it out.

All right, sergeant.

Doc, could I kindly borrow your needle and thread?

Help yourself,

unrolling his cracked rubber blanket, glumly unhooking his tin cup, and to Blackie he appears, for the first time, lower-spirited than that prancing caution Mr. Chapman—in short, neither merry nor vicious but simply old.

Thank you. I got me an extra hunk of biscuit if you want it.

Keep it. We ain't done yet.

When do you suppose this campaign'll be wrapped up?

When Uh-Oh Howard gets dragged behind the woodshed.

Now what they did to Mrs. Manuel and Mrs. Osborne, see, first they stripped them buck naked, and then they twisted their titties south of sideways, and *then*, after they bashed the baby's head in, they . . .

. . . scalped that old squaw, then sold her night-shirt to Captain Fisher! He's mad for that trash!

Soldier, shine up your d——d rifle; it looks like you found it in some rotten old sink—

Yessir,

as Umatilla Jim, having curried his horse, removes a hunk of hardbread from his pocket, remembering how perfectly his wife mixes salmon flour with huckleberries in this season.

O, good evening, Fletch. Any more tantrums from Buffalo Horn?

He's on his best behavior, sir.

Where's Redington?

Just arrived, sir.

Bring him to me right away.

Yessir.

Good evening, Redington,
>whose neckerchief wraps palely across his shoulders, while his buttons march straight down to his grimy-gloved and folded hands, and his cartridges live neatly downpointed in a belt around his hips almost like a choker of elkteeth.

Evening, general.

I believe Captain Fisher's pleased with your behavior.

Thanks, general. I—

You know, I envy you. Adventuring out there in the Buffalo Country . . .

Yessir.

How is it really?

Glorious, sir.

Good man! Care to sup with our command?

Why not, general?
>There's ants in all my pilot biscuit!
>Well, fancy that.

Did you hear that, general? That man said there are ants in his biscuit. Now I'm real excited to try a chew. It's a thrill to have crawling condiments—

Ha, ha, ha, Redington! You're what we call *a card*. Now, where's Joseph?

Not too far ahead, general. This morning I caught a glimpse of his hindmost old squaw dragging along like Methuselah's grandmother. The Injuns were just about to cross the Yellow Stone.

Thirty miles, then.

Yessir.

All right. Go eat your insect-flavored biscuit. Maybe we can spare you some bacon and coffee with it.

Thanks, general.

That one's grown up into a real Western man! Wouldn't you say so, boys?

Yessir.
>And then they raped Mrs. Manuel. Now, what they did
>to her, see, was they cracked her legs *real wide* and they—

General, I see mounted men up there to the south.

You're as keen-eyed as an Apache, Fletch! Who could it be?

White men, general.

Sturgis.

2

Colonel Sturgis, I'm assuming command.

Yessir,
>his face piteous in the firelight, beyond which the night now goes as black as our corpses' faces at White Bird Cañon.

Well, what happened?

O, general, poor as I am I'd give a thousand dollars if I hadn't left that place! Joseph made a fool out of me—

I've often heard General Sherman remark on the necessity of appointing commanders who obey orders and execute them promptly and on time. Those were his exact words.

Yessir.

You had six companies. You could have deployed them to block all of Joseph's routes.

General, we waited a good week, and then we started worrying that he'd doubled back to the Stinking Water River, and my scouts never—

Well, colonel, it can't be helped now.

No, sir. And when Lieutenant Hare found both our flankers murdered, with Indian tracks coming in from the Stinking Water—

I believe we've met before. Weren't you general of volunteers at Antietam?

O yes. Yes I was, sir. The rebels showed a lot of fight. That's right. You'd just lost your arm, and—

Yes, I was on that scene, for a fact.

Thoughtful of you to remember me, sir! But after Bedford Forrest whipped me in Mississippi, I became forgettable,

> in his wide sloping hat, his long narrow beard, joined to his moustache, straggling more than two buttons' worth down his chest, his small eyes slightly closed as if by a headache.

> GOD almighty, Parnell, he's as blubbery as Captain Winters's wife! As you see, I didn't stay a general long.

My dear Sturgis . . .

General Sherman never forgives failure, they say.

Nonsense! Blame Congress for the postwar Army! Look at Miles and Gibbon— both reduced, simply for lack of positions. Poor Custer died a lieutenant-colonel—

Yessir.

Even my Colonel Perry is technically a captain, but one must respect the brevet, don't you think?

Yessir.

Enough of that, *general.* You look a trifle older than I. When were you graduated?

'Forty-six, general. And you?

'Fifty-four. You experienced the heyday of the old martinet system, from what I hear.

Well, sir, you know how it is—

I do; I do indeed. 'Forty-six! Then you must have been to Mexico?

That's right, general, but I scarcely saw action. The greasers captured me right away.

Well, well, and how was that?

Aside from their semi-savage habits, infinitely more relaxing than West Point, sir—

Sturgis, I have always advocated the paternal system over the martinet system. The general who cares for his men as the father cares for his children, doing everything he can for their comfort consistent with their strict performance of duty, will be the most successful. Do you agree?

Well, absolutely, sir.

You must have studied under Professor Mahan.

Yessir.

He's still there, I understand. I well remember that elegant red jacket of his with the gilt buttons. A very distinguished-looking man, wouldn't you say?

Yessir. And a genius.

For certain. By the way, my condolences on the death of your brave son—

Thank you, sir.

A death with honor.

Yessir.

Within our lifetime we'll have the West cleaned up.

I'm sure you're right, sir. Another ten years, perhaps—

I gather you knew General Custer well.

Yessir. The man who threw away my son's life!

Sturgis, that's no way to talk.

Of course, of course. Forgive me, general—

My dear Sturgis, the ways of PROVIDENCE . . .

Yessir.

I understand Custer was mutilated.

Scalped. That's a fact, general. But no worse. I'm told he lay there with a smile on his face,

> all Sturgis knew of that being what he had been told by friendly officers, for he lacked both funds and opportunity to visit his son's grave for many a year. It was not until long after the Nez Perce question had been satisfactorily adjudicated that he walked the ground of the Last Stand, on a rainy and sunny afternoon in late summer. Another downpour ceased. His trousers were sodden to the knee. Gazing out from the mound where Custer fell, down into the ravine in which among the dripping yellow grass grew yucca pods and already early rosehips like carnelian trade beads, he wondered whether his son had died down there or up here behind the breastworks of dead horses with Custer. He gazed out at the lovely clouds. Beyond the ravine, the long dark green line of the Bighorn River divided the world. Then he turned his back on that river, and stared the other way, across yellow and reddish swales to other clouds. It was the ravine, the bluish-grey ravine, which trapped his horror,
>> and rolls of cloud in the pale sky,
>>> and still a few bones and arrowheads in the grass.

Now tell me what happened with Joseph.

Well, sir,

staring emptily at me like the gunbarrel of a battery bereft of its horses, I was probably misled by some treacherous Crows . . .

3

How can I shore up this feeble officer? Dear LORD, afford me the patience and insight to, to, I'm so tired, please forgive me; help me, *Amen*.

4

Sturgis, I'll give you an opportunity to make up for your misfortune. From what our scouts report, Joseph's not far ahead. You'll take the advance.

Yessir.

Make sure you capture the herd. Getting ahold of their ponies will break Indians sooner than most anything.

Sir, I'll do my best—

I'm aware that you're nearly out of rations. Well, we veterans know what that's like!

Yessir.

My command will make a junction with Captain Cushing. That's imminent, Sturgis. It might even happen to-morrow. As soon as the beef comes in, we'll re-supply you.

Yessir.

Major Sandford will strengthen your force with his fifty cavalrymen. I'll also give you Lieutenant Otis's howitzer battery and twenty-five Indian scouts. Both howitzers are mounted on mules; they won't delay you.

Thank you, general; I'll—

Lieutenant Fletcher, you'll keep charge of those scouts and place yourself at Colonel Sturgis's disposal. For now, would you please get me Sandford, Fisher and Otis?

Right away, sir.

And Captain Bendire's to report here immediately.

Yessir.

> Fletch, between you and me, I'm not heartened by the energy that Colonel Sturgis has shown thus far. Do what you can to keep things efficient. If you need to coördinate with me, tact and discretion are essential. He's a proud, angry man.
>
> I understand, general.
>
> And while Captain Fisher is nominally in charge of those scouts, I expect you to manage them, and him.
>
> Yessir.
>
> He seeks to undermine this campaign—
>
> Yessir.

Colonel, I'll expect you on the road by five to-morrow morning.

5

It's quite an adventure we're on. I hope you're enjoying it.

Very much, father,

> his Crows, having tied willow-tops together into arches to make their impromptu tipis, now wrapping themselves in trade blankets, the tired horses scarcely nickering, the bugler blowing taps in the misty darkness

>> (as Old George, pitying Sturgis, says to Tsépmin: Bad fooling. Mighty bad,

>> to which that Boston replies: D——n bad.)

I'd thought that commanding the Army of the Tennessee under General Sherman would be the most fascinating event of my career. But I have to admit that Joseph has proved an interesting antagonist. You know, Guy, sometimes I lie awake and wonder what he might be thinking.

So do I.

Do you, son? Well, when we catch him, I'll arrange a chat, and if you like, you can be there.

Thanks, father. I'd like to know what goes through his mind when he murders people. I'll bet he enjoys it—

Perhaps. By the way, what's your impression of the Crows?

Much like all these other dirty Indians, I'd say.

They're actually less primitive in some of their views than Americans, even. At least so I've been given to understand. Do you know that they once permitted a negro to be their chief? Apparently the Crow squaws are not even averse to *marrying* negroes. That shows their—

Excuse me, father, but how would you feel if Grace married a negro?

Well, now, I suspect your sister has more expensive tastes! She'll pick a high-toned banker or something out of her various beaux. Probably not a minister, unfortunately.

If she likes any man right now, she keeps it secret—

What about this Captain Gray?

Well, I don't—

And I hope not a poor soldier . . .

Father, you're too much! Now tell me, please, *entre nous,* when will we catch Joseph?

The truth is that Sturgis has let us down. But you're never to allude to it outside this tent; do you promise?

Word of honor, father.

Now it may take a full month or more. The main thing is to keep our Nez Perces from escaping American territory. You're very protective of Grace, aren't you?

Yessir.

That's good. That's good . . . After I'm gone I know you'll take care of her—

Don't talk about that, father. You'll be here a long time.

We all have to be ready for GOD's call. Are you ready, Guy?

I hope so—

An honest answer! That's all any man can say. You're getting sleepy, aren't you?

I'm always grateful for these night chats with you, father.

As I get older, I find it more difficult to fall asleep. You're lucky to know nothing of that.

Yessir.

> *Waty maua athauin hanaka JESUS hiwayam,*
> *Ayawin kulukinyu, JESUS hiwayam.*

Well, well. Do you recognize that?

Of course, father. "Down Life's Dark Vale We Wander." I was four years old when you taught me that tune.

James Reuben is a good Christian man, don't you think?

He seems so, father, but didn't you say he's related to Joseph?

My heart bleeds for him. But he's never played us false. After we've whipped Joseph I plan to do something for his family.

Yessir.

Perhaps he'll even become a preacher.

Yessir.

You know, son, I often remind Wood to harden himself. He's too sensitive—you'll keep that to yourself, I know.

Of course. He's very disappointed that our bunch can't ride ahead with General Sturgis, and I'd say the same. Father, if you were leading them to-morrow—

But we all feel what we feel. The main thing is to avoid showing it. For instance, were you affected by that German this afternoon?

O, yes! I wanted to shoot Joseph then and there!

Well, of course there will need to be some hangings, Guy. Sherman himself has said so. But what did you feel for that German personally? I must tell you that I pitied him with all my heart. To be minding your own business, on your own property, and then meet with violence! Well, good night,

> imagining Lizzie knitting by the fire, and then

Good night, father.

To-morrow beyond Fromberg, following the milky river which glows in the rain, he will discuss with Mason the forthcoming junction with Cushing, and the base of his spine will ache as he sits expressionless in the saddle, impelling his troops toward the glitter of lightning.

NOT TRUE!
SEPTEMBER 12

1

*B*ut Wood, feeling sometimes so sensitive-ironic that he can barely speak to his brother officers when they stand down together in the evenings, cannot but hurt his general's feelings. In demeanor he's as smart as ever; he *loves* the general, who suspects all the more, now that Wilkinson has so asserted, that this young man is diverging from him. Not true, o, never! And whatever insult that Guy carves out of his own wooden heart to throw at me, I'm unmoved, and would surely remain so even if he weren't the general's son. What's my trouble? I don't dislike any of them, except for Guy and sometimes that prancing Redington when he puts on airs—although Captain Pollock's become an ass, and Perry's impersonally horrible in a way I manage not to think about. As for the scenery, if I could bottle it I'd make a million dollars! What could be a better adventure than this? And if I disagree with our Nez Perce policy, I know the general feels equally badly—or did, until Mr. Joe made a fool of him at Slate Creek, and doubly so at White Bird Cañon. Now how can he *not* be on fire? I love him, and my comrades, and these grand vistas we are passing through. (I wish I saw some way out but can only do my duty for now.) If the right and wrong can't always shine clear, well, isn't everything mixed up anyhow? Nanny, for instance, who could be perfect if she only chose to, but never stops saying

Checkmate, Trimble.

You're right,

and Captain Fisher sent word they've now crossed the Yellow Stone.

Would I rather be an Indian? Our Bannocks did such vile things to our enemies' remains at Big Hole—and can I forget our own pillaged corpses at White Bird Cañon? How foul of Joseph to steal Theller's watch!

Someday I'm going to write a poem about this, a *great* poem, and then they'll see that

Wood's dreaming again! Thinking of Nanny, are you?

He's the sort of fool who'd put a front wheel on a hind axle.

That's right, Wilkinson. Has anyone broken your chess winning streak?

Play a round with me and find out.

All right,

since you're offering me what little you can in the way of friendship—why won't you believe that I don't disdain you? We're all lonely out here, especially *him* in his tent (which he only started sleeping in around the time General Sherman humiliated him; I suppose he's hiding from us):

Still missing apples, Guy?

No, father, I've given that up.

Good man! I'll tell you a secret; after all these years I still sometimes get homesick for Additon cheese. You wouldn't have that
vice, not being raised in Leeds. Sometimes I wonder how the Ad-
ditons are getting through life.

Unless you'd rather be *dreaming*. Well, she's worth dreaming about!

Thanks. So's your Sallie. Pick a hand.

Then I'll chance your left fist. Black! Well, you'll need your little advantage,
Wood. Go ahead, dreamer!

There.

O, *that* was bold! I'd best let fly my knight, like *this!*

He's my friend, my genuine friend among all these lonely men, second
only to Fletch although I'd never look him up outside the Army, and the
vision of his descending on me in civilian life horrifies me near as much
as the way he talks about Sallie. How can I reassure him? I won't pray
with him, just as I decline to kiss up to Guy; that would make me false. If
the general were to ask me to pray, I would do it and believe in it on account of *him*, but Wilkinson, come to think of it, is not my friend.

If I could get away from all of them, and go scouting as Redington
does—

You know what, dreamer?

What?

I admire the way you love Nanny. You're not a lady-killer like so many of us—

Thanks.

No, he *is* my friend, and I'm evil.

2

And so Wood and Wilkinson go on playing chess, there being no news from
Sturgis or Cushing,

while Pollock sings the same old happy nigger songs with his bunch,
and, observing the match from the boulder on which he sits, wise Mason, not
without amusement, wonders whether Wood will quit the Army this year or next,
and on what path Wilkinson,

whose insinuations are as fluidly masterful as the shimmering reforma-
tions of a Sioux battle-line, which blows every which way like the dying
grass itself, then swirls back around our troops to probe for weakness,
will next guide our general,

while Perry ducks inside the wagon of the teamster Red O'Donnell
and Cushing appears no more lost than everybody else.

AND QUICKLY RIDING TO SOME FARTHER
PLACE
SEPTEMBER 12–13

1

*I*n the strong morning wind, the green and yellow grasses matted down by
dew,
> the locusts just beginning to sing *tekh-tekh-tekh!*,
they ride through the cottonwoods and chokecherries, tired, much poorer in
horses, and around their horses' necks fewer blue and scarlet belts of stripes and
triangles than before, but still laughing at the trick they have played on Cut Arm,
> who perhaps continues to hunt them along the Stinking Water,
> Strong Eagle
> > last of the Three Red Blankets,
> in advance, hoping to kill a swimming or shore-browsing moose,
> > White Thunder's war-party a full day ahead, spying out the country
> > for Bluecoats,
> and then Looking-Glass, who can recognize the algae-muddy odor of the
> Swift Water without opening his eyes;
> Grizzly Bear Youth, who Dreamed so wisely that we should steal Cut
> Arm's animals;
> and Toohhoolhoolsote in his many loop necklaces of bone beads, cheer-
> fully murmuring his WYAKIN song (although last night he was quarrel-
> ling with his wives),
> Heinmot Tooyalakekt helping the women to drive the animals,
> > Good Woman still riding White Face, leading one of Cut
> > Arm's mules,
> > Springtime on the horse she has finally named Redhead,
> > Sound Of Running Feet on Yellow One, her present from
> > Aunt Cloudburst
> > > (last night she most horribly Dreamed of that Bluecoat
> > > who rose up before her at Ground Squirrel Place),
> > the little dogs yelping, the horses saying *hinimí*, the babies sobbing
> > *shlak, shlak!*
until they reach the Swift Water
> where Young White Bird, seeing a certain half-sunk log where the water
> is reddish-brown, for some reason cannot help but remember the woman

at Ground Squirrel Place
　　(one of the Wallowa People)
who not long after his thumb was shot off took a bullet in her left breast,
fell into the river
　　(his mother took her in her arms and laid down her head on a soft
　　sandbar)
and quickly bled to death, the water reddening so richly around her,
Ollokot, Over The Point and the other young men now reading the Swift Water,
judging the dangerousness of its deep part, the *green water:*
　　indeed we shall surely cross it on our horses, even with the wounded
　　　　(news which gladdens Good Woman's heart:
　　　　　　she feels too tired to be plaiting serviceberry vines, making
　　　　　　rafts);
while some of White Bird's young men, distrusting even their own WYAKIN
powers, scout behind in angry dread of the willow-darkness where Cut
Arm's hired killers may wait:
　　they crept like wolves down through the dark willows:
　　　　we remember Ta Mah Utah Likt and her baby, Fair Land and
　　　　Shore Crossing,
　　　　　　who could lassoo two horses in one noose and be un-
　　　　　　moved by their bucking,
　　　　Grey Eagle, Five Wounds, Swan Necklace's dear sister Where
　　　　Ducks Are Around and Burning Coals's daughter, Kah-pots
　　　　and Rainbow and
　　our enemies crawling ever after us, sliding between hills like the blue
　　snake called *kuyímkuyim;* we hate them, we keep on fleeing, even
　　now into late summer when the buffalo gnats resemble black beads
　　　　(Lean Elk says that never again shall we watch the salmon
　　　　going up our rivers)
but White Bird's scouts, parting the smooth red chokecherry branches,
find no Lice-Eaters, much less any line of mounted white men with carbines; there is only blue sky
—maybe now we are almost free,
　　although Lean Elk tells us to keep spying behind, so that the Bluecoats
　　will never again deceive us
　　　　(we wish to kill them all)
and Ollokot's heart is uneasy, as if his WYAKIN might be warning him,
　　although when we crept up on our bellies at Camas Meadows to
　　steal Cut Arm's animals, and SOMETHING swayed over me in the
　　darkness like the scalp hanging from the bridle of a Minneconjou
　　warrior's horse, I reached up and felt nothing but a half-severed
　　branch with the leaves still alive;

while at Ground Squirrel Place my WYAKIN kept silent,
and Swan Necklace whips Cut Arm's mules.

2

It is summer's end, and the cormorants are flying away
(the breadroots growing here passed tenderness two moons ago; we
shall not gather them):
Smohalla's flag must have risen on the cottonwood pole for the Huckleberry Feast;
WOWSHUXLUH the wooden bird has awakened;
and now the flag goes down; again WOWSHUXLUH sleeps in His box, and
the Dreamers have dispersed
while we ride down to the wide grey river,
as the horses say: *Hinimí, hinimí,*
and the fishes splash: *Mokh!*
First our young men make for the gravel bar near the other shore, laughing
when the current draws the horses downstream of that,
and this *green water* is nothing for us; it cannot compare to our Chinook
Salmon Water or our Enemy River back home
or Looking-Glass's river, the Big Water, whose ripples are as
lovely as the beadwork stripes upon a young bride's dress
(had Shore Crossing not been killed,
he who liked to chase wild horses into the Chinook Salmon
Water, swim after the angriest stallion and ride him across
the river and back,
he would now be laughing at this Swift Water)
while our nervous women and hungry children snatch handfuls of chokecherries
from the trees, and Heinmot Tooyalakekt,
he who helps everyone,
counts children, mules and horses,
our dogs silently snarling,
some ponies pawing and anxiously side-biting,
while just before us, pale tan ovoids of stone glow up through the
grey-green water like eyes
and the widow Pellutsoo, whose baby is already tied to her body, makes
sure that his elder brother, almost two winters old, remains well-strapped
onto her last blanket-horse;
—and now the river goes frothy and murky with many struggling animals. The
young men flank them tightly, ready to save whomever the RIVER might seize.
Some women loudly sing their WYAKIN songs,
Springtime's baby staring down at the forest of horse-legs in the shining
water,

Ollokot riding with Fair Land's child in the crook of his arm,
Helping Another supported on her left by old Towhee her mother
and on her right by her husband Wounded Head, who swims a
string of horses behind him,
> Looking-Glass
>> (who has placed a bone in his hair)
> leading his wives and daughters safe through the *green water*,
>> his neck mirror sparkling with river-light as he rides
>> the bay, pulling Home From Capture,
> and Toohhoolhoolsote's old wives giggling like girls when
other horses splash them.
One of Cut Arm's mules drowns: no loss.
The wounded keep quiet.

By the time we have passed beyond the sandbar to the other shore, many suns
sparkle in the brightening shallows,
> and we are now another river from our country,
> while Lean Elk will never be going home to the Salish.
>> What is there but the Medicine Line? We must hurry, hurry
>>> even as Heinmot Tooyalakekt's women remember Wallowa, the
>>> place where something once was
>>>> and for no reason Sound Of Running Feet
>>>>> (she who is pleasing to look at)
>>>> slaps Yellow One on the nose.

3

While they await the wounded's crossing over, Springtime and Good Woman
go beating chokecherries out of the bush with their digging sticks,
> the baby wide-eyed on Springtime's back
>> and Sound Of Running Feet is holding the horses;
they have lost their berry-baskets, but it is easy enough to collect this food in a
dead Bluecoat's shirt:
> dark chokecherries whose juice, though sweet, dries out the mouth like
> fear.

Heinmot Tooyalakekt now says: My chiefs, here is my heart: shall we not ride
more slowly for those who are tired? Looking-Glass has said this already, and he
spoke straight,
but Lean Elk replies: My brothers, have you already forgotten who is head-chief,
and why? I have a heart even as you do; our weak and wounded deserve pity, but
we all understand the cause of their suffering. Young men, you set pity aside once
you began killing Bostons. Looking-Glass, you surely meant well; it was not you
who broke the treaty at Ground Squirrel Place. All the same, we must not rest
until we have crossed the Medicine Line. Now hurry, hurry!

Our smallest children have begun weeping. Springtime rubs new mud on her wound. Good Woman catches a trout and packs it deep under chokecherries; tonight perhaps she will smoke it over the fire;

and bending down to the river, Heinmot Tooyalakekt straightens without bringing up anything.

Then we are riding, riding,

into this far country north of the Swift River

exactly here where summer hailstones can kill even horses,

whipping the packhorses ahead:

Lean Elk in front

and then Peopeo Tholekt on his yellow racer

and Ollokot with his young men,

Strong Eagle and Over The Point, still brave in their decorated elkhide shirts,

Wounded Head with his wife and her mother,

About Asleep and his weary grieving father (we shall not say the names of those who haunt them),

Wottolen and Black Eagle,

Heinmot Tooyalakekt with the orphans, cripples and cachectic old women; then *Kate*

and Good Woman

(who is becoming angry at Springtime for not helping more,

while Springtime is sad because we arrive much too late to drink syrup from the box elders);

Cloudburst, who has now worn out the last pair of Fair Land's beaded moccasins,

Looking-Glass smiling to see the familiar plum-thickets and alder-brush of the Crow country

(as Toohhoolhoolsote, riding off the trail to shoot a buffalo bull in the ear, gets meat for his grateful women)

and White Bird,

his top hat wrapped round with a segment of striped blanket, bright shell-disks at his ears, white bead-loops round and round from his chin to his chest, feathers in his braids, the filthy ends of his blanket-coat beginning to fray,

and all of us,

passing among grassheads like the dull golden beads which sometimes separate bearclaws on Crow necklaces,

even as another mean wild Boston rises up out of his diggings, fires his revolver at us and misses

so that Strong Eagle shoots him in the mouth

and we take gun, gold, coffee, cocaine, blanket and boots

(he must have hidden his *getting-drunk liquid*),

kicking him down into the hole he made in OUR
MOTHER:
he lands on his teeth;
the babies sleeping in their cradleboards on their mothers' backs.
Sound Of Running Feet rides behind her father, who looks
not to right or left.
Welweyas feels thirsty. She wonders about her murdered
mother's dog, which ran away at Ground Squirrel Place.
Springtime feels as if she is waiting for something to happen.

4

And on this day,
one sun after he shot that tall Boston in the buckskin suit right off his
horse, then chased down another Boston on a fine grey horse until that
man leaped off and fired at him, grazing his head
(his war-friend Wild Oat Moss galloped up to make the killing
shot),
White Thunder,
chasing buffalo-silhouettes gathered down ahead on the grey-green plains,
first sees our friends the Crows riding together with Lice-Eaters
(Wild Oat Moss kills one of the new Bostons they bring);
so he gallops back to the People,
arriving just as they are driving in the horses for the night,
unpacking and unsaddling them, staking them down;
they are camping downstream of the fording-place,
settling in a circle,
and talking over where they must now go
(perhaps, if Lean Elk so decides, to the head of the Musselshell, a place which our Crow friends call *The Bad
Mountain*);
and Welweyas the half-woman is helping Cloudburst spread out some
river-sodden blankets on a chokecherry bush; then those two begin withering buffalo meat over the fire;
Red Spy is piercing new bearclaws to string them on a necklace of pale
golden beads;
Good Woman has just finished salving White Face's saddle-sores; now
she is stretching cloth
as Sound Of Running Feet goes apart to the river
because when we were tricking Cut Arm by going down the extremely steep place, where our animals kept falling, the girl, pulling
back the halter of a mule with all her strength, found herself bleeding for the first time:

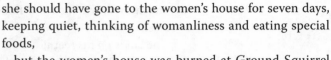

she should have gone to the women's house for seven days,
keeping quiet, thinking of womanliness and eating special
foods,
—but the women's house was burned at Ground Squirrel
Place—
and her mother, Good Woman, who used to know her, sees
nothing, asks nothing,
so Sound Of Running Feet,
    hoping that she will not bring bad luck to our fight,
will say nothing;
    her dark-dyed leggings do not show the bloodstains;
she feels herself to be unwell, but not even to Aunt Springtime will
she tell this secret;
and as Looking-Glass's four women unpack their horses, unroll their blankets and begin to prepare soup, he, their *lucky man*, sits silent, remembering
how it was when the Crows were our friends and at dawn he rode with them
out on the bar (actually less white than grey), where the brown-green water,
much darker than at sunset, swished rapidly through the channel, strong
enough to sweep a pony away, swelling and cresting almost like an ocean as
it rushed around the next bend, into the shadow of the Sacrifice Cliffs:
    he remembers that one moment after sunrise when parts of the
    cliffs turned the same pale pink as a peregrine falcon's eggs
    and midmorning when we were hunting buffalo on that plain of
    golden grass and cottonwoods on the east side of the Swift Water,
    the potter-tan cliffs black with caves and crowded with junipers
        (he is merely pretending to know something)
when Toohhoolhoolsote's dogs creep into camp stinking like skunk
and Wounded Head helps his wife down to the river to wash out her
chest-wound again
        (she is not herself, their little son being but recently dead);
leaping off his horse, White Thunder greets his mother
  (who smilingly begins to boil him a muskrat soup),
then draws Heinmot Tooyalakekt aside to say: It seems to my eyes that the Crows
are becoming Boston helpers! Shall we begin to kill them?
  My dear nephew, that would be a mistake. We are too weak to fight everyone.
Say nothing to the People, in order to keep their hearts at peace. Rest now;
    for indeed, Heinmot Tooyalakekt,
        listening to what will be spoken, knowing that some People are
        angry at him,
    hesitates to tell this news even to his own brother Ollokot,
      he who now bears so much trouble;
    for even as the long fingers of tree-shadows press down the flowery lake-
    meadows high above Wallowa, so this news darkens his heart:

When my father told me: *never sell the bones of your father and your mother*
and when my father tore the *thief treaty* into pieces,
he never imagined that in my time, stay or go, I would find all others our enemies!
—then he shoots four ducks for his women to make into soup.

Close Action
September 13

1

*T*his pursuit of Joseph may consume a very considerable time.
Yessir.
Another sullen drizzle, sir.
Looks like it. Stay dry if you can!
Yes, sir.

    Glory, glory, hallelujah—
    the sky as cool as the sweaty dark leather of a haversack strap.
        No, colonel, I'm afraid he's growing disaffected.
      I disagree. Just last night I heard him tell the boys—
    What he says to the boys is one thing. But what I've heard him say—
    Glory, glory, hallelujah—
Yes, Wilkinson, what precisely *did* you hear him say?
    Glory, glory, hallelujah—
O, hello, general.
      O, cut it out. I'm already saved.
Who's disaffected?
    My GOD, my GOD, is that *pity* in their eyes?
        Ain't you a Christian, Doc?
        Whatever I am ain't for you to know.
Well, sir—
Never mind, gentlemen. I know the code of loyalty. Has Mr. Redington reported in to-day?
Not yet, general.
That's fine. Keep me informed.
Yessir.
And this is my sketch of the mules climbing the trail from the Salmon.

It's very lively, Guy.

Are you cross?

Why should I be?

Because I wasn't there, and I know you fancy yourself a bit of an illustrator.

May the best man win!

That's the spirit, Wood! What's that magazine you're reading?

O, have you heard of Theodore Bland?

No.

He's not well known. This periodical is called *Council Fire.* He used to be employed in the Indian Department. Now he's turned against that. His series of articles is called "Abolish the Army," and—

Wood, you're too much!

Wood, why don't you go stand on a ridgetop with the sun on you? That'll give
Joseph an opportunity to abolish you.

"Abolish the Army," men! Did you hear that? Wood's getting peculiar.

Actually, I'm—

    To horse.

        Mount.

           Move out,

                led to-day by Perry, who is almost as perfect-visioned as
                an Indian scout.

Looky here. Another squaw pestle,

        but no Joseph,

and then the land swells up like the belly of an unburied corpse.

    Halt:

           up with the company street—

                Wood currying Arrow for the general

                and Chapman inspecting each of his grey racer's feet

                —but Trimble's horse keeps sneezing; the man looks
                worried

                (nowadays he always does)

                and heads for Red O'Donnell's wagon—

                while Perry has already finished with Diamond, whose
                eponymous white patch he strokes:

                    time now to go chivvy his men:

                        You villains move those bedrolls out of here
                        right now or I'll have you punished.

  (Pickets out!);

                as Trimble now begins doctoring his horse with bran
                soaked in lye

                    (all of us staying out of the general's way because
                    he's sure got a bee up his ass to-night)

and an hour later sees Perry leaning against a boulder, squinting or frowning, with his hat tilted back from his high forehead, and his trousers tucked into his cavalry boots, one hand on his hip, and the other, rope-burned, dangling free from an arm elbow-braced against that slanting rock behind him as the Crow scouts sit at his feet—strange that they enjoy the company of this red-blooded Indian hater!

Sir, a Bannock has just ridden in with this note.

Thank you, Wood. Well, well! Fletch informs us that Sturgis has finally engaged the hostiles! Get me Major Mason. Hello, Mason. Detail fifty active men to ride ahead with me. It'll be an all-night business, I'm afraid. You'll command the rearguard.

Now we're finally moving into close action, with GOD's help—

. . . Cañon Creek, right here on the map . . .

If he can halt them . . .

Maybe this will finish them off, general. The men are—

Forward.

Forward!

> *Gonna bring that steam drill out on the job,*
> *Gonna whap that steel on down, o, LORD.*
> *Gonna whap that steel on down.*

Now he's finally breathin' smoke and fire,

Perry's hope of whipping Joseph suddenly as glorious as a Comanche horsewoman.

Watch out. He's looking this way.

Keep tight at my heels.

All righty, Doc, I promise—

riding along the column's left side, almost smiling, his breast armored in sorrow (praise GOD, I can bear this),

Umatilla Jim in the vanguard,

wondering what the general would say to be informed that Jim has himself beaten sticks in two of Smohalla's Dreamer dances;

racing horses with Chapman, who knows that it can't be any worse to end up as some bloody corpse on the trail than to get a funeral and get interred in first-class concrete;

then Fletch, Wood and Guy cantering cheerfully away:

O, to return with Mr. Joe's head in an India rubber sack!

—the sky like a Crow woman's dark dress brightly constellated with elkteeth—

and they ride all night in their damp, reeking clothes (thirty-five miles), arriving at Cañon Creek just before eleven in the morning.

FINGERNAIL NOISES
SEPTEMBER 13

1

*W*here the stagecoach road parallels the Yellow Stone, the sharp brown and blue horizon across the river is close and clear, afternoon clouds scarcely yet beginning to bleach the sky above it; and now a little cotton-ball of dust manifests itself, presently elongating its comet tail across the flat orange grass country, half-way erasing the bluff's greyish-blue trees, and presently we can hear horses.

The stagecoach enlarges. It pulls up, and then,

> never forgetting that the Bluecoats have struck us again and again like rattlesnakes hidden deep in dead timber,

our warrior-horde gallop up, joyously shouting and shooting into the air,

> the actress Fanny Clark screaming inside,

horses rearing, the stagecoach almost tipping over, the doors exploding open, the driver and passengers bolting for the willows

> (when Fanny Clark's dog keeps barking—which attracts the warriors' bullets—a prudent Boston cuts its throat, in hopes of hiding from the *Red Napoleon*);

and now our best men, reeking, with their greasy hair loose, their hands filthy and their feathered heads thrust back in proud rage, begin to open the Bostons' various traps,

> hoping for *getting-drunk liquid,*
> sowing the dentist's false teeth in the road like optimistic husbandmen,
> broadcasting letters likewise;

following the Law of the EARTH, they wreck a mowing machine,
burn down the station, fire a fine haystack:

> Were the Bostons here and in our power, we would kill them all and leave them with their buttocks showing!
> But these miserable ones now crawling in the willows
> > (they cannot make themselves brave),
> we shall now leave them alone to terrify themselves,
> > although it might refresh our hearts to rape this woman,
> > > but we are not killers like Bostons; our hearts are good
> > > (I am telling you three times!) we never kill anyone who does not deserve it:
> > > > Even in the old days when we crept within the ti-pis of Snakes and Lice-Eaters to kill them, we

passed our hands across each sleeper's hair, because the women and children dress theirs differently from warriors, and we, COYOTE's People,
were too kind to harm them.
Some warriors mount the driver's box, squatting up on top, and away they go,
happily shouting all over the country
and a dozen brown quail start up out of the high grass
while other braves swerve east, following the gullied stagecoach road.

2

So we are riding out to rob the Bluecoats of horses, joy and life:
Earth Blanket,
grieving for Shore Crossing, who has but briefly been dead,
and wishing to pound Cut Arm's bones into powder;
John Mulkamkan, Iskiloom and Kalotas, Owhi and Old Yellow Wolf
(whose head wound from the Big Water fight has now healed);
and Rosebush gallops beside us, just for awhile
(we shall refresh ourselves with revenge),
riding east along the Swift Water,
the grasshoppers almost frenzied at the peak of this long summer;
and arriving first at Mr. Brockway's ranch:
we burn his corral and hay house
while his Bostons rush to dodge among the willows.

3

Joseph Cochran has made himself a homestead,
because to be an American is to believe in the notion of a better life:
someday he'll get a wife
and homemade shelves lined with calico:
someday we'll be sitting on the shaded, white-pillared
wraparound porch of our home, guarded by aspen
trees, the river flowing fast and steep just down the hill,
and no Indians to harm our children.
Clinton Dills and Milton Sumner are tenting at his place. If they keep wolfing
just right, someday they'll step into his shoes.
Now here come our warriors riding along the Swift Water to see what we
can kill,
our horses' manes waving like meadow-grass,
and by their tent these two Bostons are eating; they look up smiling, mistaking
the People for Crows, and we shoot them dead:
Pim! Pim!

and in the first rifle-echo, the cliff swallows by the Sacrifice Caves
all flee their nests, but only for a moment; their blood-hued throats
weary the People's eyes, and then they have flown home:
>   Please, I didn't never harm no red—
Pim!
> *Tsálalal!*
Áhahahaha!
>   grasshoppers already in the blood
>>   (for as the two dead men had just been remarking, this sure
>>   has been a boom summer for hoppers)
then prepare to burn the buildings.

4

Mr. Cochran has gone upstream with his loggers. Riding quickly but cautiously down when he hears the shots, with his rifle slung over his shoulder, he
finds these reds on his place,
>   his three dogs running along with him, then plunging into the pond,
>   their dark patches glistening more than do the white:
>>   Homer, the friendliest, fetches a stick to one of the Indians, who
>>   ignores it;
>>   the dog persists; the Indian kicks him, at which Cochran begins to
>>   take alarm,
swinging down from the saddle, wondering whether the Indians will shoot him
and when he should level the Winchester
>   (not now):
Well, boys, what are you doing around here?
We good Indians, mister, real good, just hunting here for awhile, replies the
half-breed (his courtesy as shallow as brown-green summer water flowing slowly
over white rocks), and they all grin at Cochran
>   (let us thoroughly kill him);
he keeps smelling gunsmoke. And Dills and Sumner are so quiet (the reds must
have scared them off)—
Instinctively he now does the one right thing, extending his hand. They hesi-
tate, then sourly shake it one by one.
What tribe are you?
Snake Indians, mister.
O, is that right? says Cochran, supposing that it might be true. You want some-
thing to eat?
We want your horse, explains the half-breed, smiling at him almost sweetly.
You no give us your horse *doublequick*, we kill you.
All right, he says slowly. You can have my horse. You want the saddle, too?

You give us horse, saddle, get down, go away *quick*, GODd——n you! Go run away quick now or we shoot you!

Nodding as if he likes them, he says: I give you this horse. Thank you for giving me my life.

They surround him and snatch away his rifle, plucking the Colt from his hip:

> expecting to die, he closes his eyes,
>> then slowly turns his back and begins walking, believing with all his soul
>> without ever knowing why that if he breaks and runs they will shoot him
>>> (they might shoot me anyway:
>>>> my GOD, could they be Chief Joseph's bunch?)
>> and should he look back, something equally bad will happen,

so he just keeps walking, and opens his eyes:

> *And though I walk through the Valley of the Shadow of Death, I shall fear*
> *no evil, but*
> *fear no evil*

his dogs barking loudly behind him, doubtless because the Indians have begun handling his horse

> (he prepares himself for the squealing and clubbing sounds that must
> soon come;
>> he has loved those dogs)

and now at last he can turn away from the road

> (at any moment the Indians may decide to hunt him),

coming into the sweet smell of water,

> the pods now well swollen on the milkweeds
>> (now they are killing his dogs),

and once he finds himself among the silver-green buffaloberry bushes

> (after the first freeze, put a sheet under the tree and shake the branches;
> the berries will have gone sweet),

he begins to run, craving only to hide,

>> the locusts singing *tekh-tekh-tekh!*

Hearing them gallop farther east, he lies low until gunshots come from Coulson Town, which proves that they must have left his property,

> so he doubles back,
>> his Russian olive trees coming along well, their narrow-bladed grey leaves
>> blending in with the buffaloberry bushes,

and finds his ammunition gone, his tools ransacked and half-pilfered along with clothes and food,

> while there behind their tent lie Sumner and Dills, and all three dogs,
>> a silent brown dragonfly hovering over the blood,
>>> at which point it crosses his mind that *the Indians might come back*
>>>> (or, still worse, the main detachment of Chief Joseph's killers might
>>>> now show up,

striding out through the brush behind this tall dead cottonwood whose bleached wood shines like evening:

they burn women alive, he's heard),

so that once again he takes it into his mind to hide

or maybe help the fellows at Coulson, if one man more or less, and him
without a gun, could somehow advantage the situation.

Shaded by sweet poplar trees, ducking into the yellow-green reeds

(the wild grapes now ready),

he flees northeast, running away through the immense dusty-grey cottonwoods
and the thistles and the sparkling milkweed pods, all the way to the Yellow Stone,
whose turquoise current is dark, sliming the edges of its white gravel-islands
brownish-green as it goes:

far away, between the bars, another fast deep narrow groove of river, then
another white pebble-plain

(Sumner's on his belly, but the pupils in Dills's dead eyes resemble
the black spots on baneberries);

and, far away, a blue-green ribbon, then white shore, cottonwood forest
and the Sacrifice Cliffs brown-green and grey-blue, nude cutaways of
dirt, the water-breeze blowing cool and murky in his face as he hides in
the grass, waiting for the Indians to ride away. From a yellow grasshead
which resembles many tawny cords glued together hangs a dead dragonfly in an absent spider's web. Something stings his shoulderblade. He
looks back west into the twitching stems of sage. The locusts are all one
note, almost like a Corliss engine. They pause, then stridulate again. A
redwing blackbird is singing. The Yellow Stone hisses and pulses, and the
locusts keep roaring between his ears. Now the cottonwoods are greenly
darkening,

not yet to silhouettes, sun still warming his back;

while farther down the riverbank the gravel bars continue brightening in
the lowering sun, the shining cottonwood foliage momentarily still, cicadas pulsing faster and faster; every bush on the cliffs across the river now
shadow-outlined

(ahead and to his right the rolling reddish rockhills of the Pictograph Caves);

and he crouches on the edge of that flat meadow of half-dried grasses, dreading
to turn back toward the dead,

alone beneath the darkening cottonwoods, the light on the river neither
hope nor help:

perhaps someone at Coulson is still alive and needing him, or else
the Indians are waiting.

Coldness rises in his heart, so that there remains nothing to do but think
clearly

(better clear than quick):

Shall I lie here all night and possibly get hunted down, or try to help the
Coulson people?

—grey-green darkness now oozing out of the trees, and the grinding of the river's stones more distinct.

Feeling too visible, he ducks back west of the river, into a clearing's bright
swelter (will they shoot me now?), then into the forest shade,

remembering his life's sunglow on the white limestone cliffs above the
shaded pine-tree river-cañon,

many leaves bleached already to the color of sunblasted canvas, a
few weeds going rusty, the tall poplars still leafed dark green, glossy
shining and glaring in the sinking sun,

and the river kept flowing, south to north, right to left, the
sandbars glittering, the locusts leaping in excitement.

5

Again Heinmot Tooyalakekt seeks to shame our bad men, but Toohhoolhoolsote

he whose young men are wildest of all,

remarks: My brother, you are doing nothing but making noise with your fingernails.

6

Here is an elk cow with her big reddish-brown ears high, lunging into green
scrub, chewing, then flashing her deep black immobile gaze, with her fawn beside
her; Heinmot Tooyalakekt shoots them both, so that we shall have meat.

Here is a lost buffalo calf. Swan Necklace takes pity on it, but kills a fine cow
which might have been its mother.

ANOTHER REUNION
SEPTEMBER 12–13

1

*G*et the fuck away from my horse, Jim.

Colonel Perry, sir, he's starting to go lame.

Then I reckon you stuck a pin in his hoof.

No, sir.

What do you want?

I can fix him, colonel. You want me to fix him?

And just how would you do that?

Get me some *anásh*, colonel. The top of a plant. Diamond, he's a good horse. I want to fix him.

He's a good horse, all right.

Yessir.

Well, you've got eyes, because he's getting lame for a fact, and I sure do hate to see it. These d——d long marches, Jim.

Yessir.

And you can fix him?

If I can find this one plant I know. When we're bivouacked I'll look around.

That's fine. Now get away from me.

2

I know that one.

My heart tells me he is one of Cut Arm's slaves. *Tsím,** is that so?

I shall not lie; I scout for Cut Arm.

You are hunting us now.

No. I seek *anásh* for a lame horse.

Hear me, Red Spy: *Tsím* kills our women for Cut Arm!

Then let us wipe our buttocks on his head.

He has also been Tsépmin's dog. When Tsépmin tired of his wife, *Tsím* carried her away and penned her up on painted land. *Tsím,* do I speak straight?

Shooting Thunder, I cannot contradict you.

And did you then fuck Tsépmin's wife? Did you take her for your *átawit?*[†] Listen: I can speak Boston. Hear me now: Godd——n you, *Tsím!*

Áhaha! Let us kill him.

Tsím, did she teach you how to dig roots like a woman?

No.

Tsím, to-day your weaselskin bracelet failed to enlarge your eyes!

You speak straight; I never saw you—

Tsím, you are now used up, like old dead grass—

Tsím, did Tsépmin fuck your wife? *Áhahahahaha!*

No.

How much did Tsépmin pay you to pen up his wife?

He paid me this:

the Rutherford B. Hayes Centennial medal,

---

*Jim.
[†]Shooting Thunder is entertaining himself by using the Umatilla word for "sweetheart."

whose tarnished relief offers the same comforting authority as those great round tokens that Lewis and Clark used to hand out to good Indians.

Perhaps if you give us that big coin we shall let you go. *Áhaha!*

GoDd——n you, you Tsím!

Please do not kill me. It would grieve your chief. I shall pay you this coin that Tsépmin gave me, and everything I have, because my wife

—and he now sees before him the way her wrinkled face began to shine with tears when he told her that he was riding to Butterfly Place to scout and fight for the Bostons:

much older-looking than he, a good hard worker, she goes to church for prudence's sake, with her hair tucked up in a shawl she once received from the missionary woman Kate McBeth; perhaps the Agent will help her if Cut Arm forgets to send money—

Your wife fucks Bostons for molasses. *GoDd——n her!*

She is the sister of Heinmot Tooyalakekt's cousin.

Then we shall certainly kill you. What do you mean, helping Cut Arm hunt down your own relations?

Shore Crossing knows me—

He is dead, and you helped kill him. Now you shall meet him:

Taq!

the .50 calibre exploding bullet making of Jim's skull something as red as a Crow woman's hair parting.

In Which We Learn That Our Grandfather Still Loves Us
September 13

1

*E*ven before all our raiders have returned from the Sacrifice Cliffs
(those steep bluffs, some squared off, some rounded, the hue of baked clay, where milkweed feathers sparkle in the pale sky),
White Thunder sees the blanket signal:
Bluecoats are coming!
and gallops down the dry river cañon to find Horse People dismounted into Walking Soldiers

(already he is nearly the last one, just as at the Big Water fight);
so he canters back up toward the narrows where the People are:

the Place Like Split Rock,

where a river flows in spring, inviting grebes and blackbirds and
avocets; now there is no river

and hastens back toward our other best men,

grasshoppers leaping up and crackling against the legs of his swift horse,

recognizing from far away Lean Elk waving the People quickly onward

(sunlight sparkling on his brass-buttoned trade vest),

and Heinmot Tooyalakekt,

White Thunder's good uncle and chief,

whose heart keeps screaming *qoh! qoh! qoh!* as if it has fallen
into the thoughtful grip of a cowbird's dark talons,

riding up and down the column, bending over the wounded, helping old
women whip their packhorses,

some of which remain laden even this late with rolled mats and tipi-
canvases, woven bags of dried berries, camas cakes, ammunition
(Cut Arm has not yet devoured all our treasures);

and he is handing young children up to their mothers

(some say that Springtime might be jealous)

as our young men strip for war

and Good Woman, making herself brave, remembers how her
mother used to say the words of the old story: *They are coming to fight, COLD WEATHER GIRL; they are coming . . .*

while Toohhoolhoolsote is now becoming angry against Cut Arm:
his WYAKIN will help him protect us;

and

while Loon, who keeps trying to make himself brave, gallops into a
coulee, pickets his horse, chambers a round in his Springfield,
creeps up from behind a boulder with his rifle pointing ahead, then
completes his heart, runs back to his horse and gallops after the
women,

once more Peopeo Tholekt blows his eagle-bone whistle five times to
make himself safe from bullets.

All alone, in a cave where the cañon narrows, No Leggings begins shooting at
the Bluecoats.

2

Although he worries about his dear mother Swan Woman and his tired Aunt
Springtime, White Thunder has no fear for himself. His WYAKIN, like Wottolen's,
has promised that bullets will not kill him;

moreover, even now he aspires to kill Tsépmin the Unkillable,

or Píli
or Cut Arm the Invisible, who never dares to show his face.
And now bullets come whirring like a flock of prairie chickens.

3

So again they have found us:
these Bluecoats, Bostons and their Government which seeks to see us
everywhere
(the *Americans* are our friends)
like SHE WHO WATCHES, high above the Distant River,* where we once
took salmon:
in the cliffs over Distant River Gorge goggles SHE WHO WATCHES,
tiny-white-pupilled within her many white concentric eyes, square-
mouthed, with small thick white eyebrows which are closed arches,
Her white gaze wide yet guarded upon the dark rock:
thus must be the stare of the wicked old Grandfather in Washington
(Rutherford B. Hayes),
who will never turn away his *American* eyes from us,
and the moldy stare of Cut Arm,
he who has shamed Toohhoolhoolsote and our young men,
and the sticky stare of Moss Beard
who would pen us up to stir ashes, then cut open OUR MOTHER's
breast!
They are the ones who deprive us of our country,
sending us their gifts of bullets:
Again they have wiped their buttocks on our heads.
Now we need not listen anymore to the old men making such a good talk about
their wars, for we have won a war that will not forsake us,
Red Spy shouting in anger, firing exploding bullets through his
Springfield
and our old ones fleeing wearily up the cañon.

4

Lean Elk,
he who takes good care without praise or thanks,
looks down the trail to see more Horse People dismounting to become Walking
Killers.
Quickly while they are still bunched up,
yet holding his breath

---

*Columbia River.

(wishing to cut them into pieces over and over),
he very carefully shoots with Shore Crossing's buffalo rifle, loving the roar of it:
> *timm!*

and just as their great wheeled gun begins to pound, another Bluecoat tumbles
tsálalal; his head flies away from his body.

5

Peopeo Tholekt, his rifle speeding out of its gorgeously beaded case, aims at a
Bluecoat officer and misses,
> while behind that squarish boulder which is larger than two hands'
> worth of horses, resting his .44 lever-action Winchester in the crack, with
> just the barrel peeking out and down, Heinmot Tooyalakekt sights on a
> Bluecoat who is ludicrously silhouetted against the golden grass, then
> shoots: *pim!*

his bullet diving down, down below the horizon, until it enters the Bluecoat's hat; he tumbles silently,
> > rain coming down, bringing with it the smell of sage, lichens begin-
> > ning to glow, the grass softening as it dampens,
> > > the wheeled gun pounding no more;

then Heinmot Tooyalakekt leaps onto Black Mane-Stripe's back, galloping ahead to see to his women
> > (Springtime and the baby have ridden far ahead, while Good
> > Woman is whipping Cut Arm's mules and Sound Of Running Feet
> > hands Fair Land's baby up to Cloudburst as she waits in the saddle)
> > > but Wounded Head's wife sways in the saddle, bleeding anew
> > > from her chest:

while the Bluecoats have now shot Silooyam in his ankle
—and now here comes a jaunty Bluecoat, surely an officer, who smokes a pipe and
carries a fishing rod as he rides:
smiling at him, Peopeo Tholekt takes aim again, holding his breath.

6

Looking-Glass says: This is how I would do it, only in this way,
> but no one replies,
> > not even Heinmot Tooyalakekt, who replies to all
> > > (to him Looking-Glass resembles a tree swallow pursuing an-
> > > other bird's fallen feather);

then creeping from boulder to boulder, Looking-Glass bravely shoots, but no one
is watching.

Young Grizzly Bear sings to his WYAKIN, the AIR BIRD; then like the AIR BIRD
he is flying up,

flying up
>to the ridgetop where he now aims down at Cut Arm's walking
>soldiers;

while Strong Eagle and Over The Point keep carefully firing the cartridges we
bought from the Bitter Root Bostons, spending the gold and money we took from
the Bluecoats we killed at Sparse-Snowed Place
and so we halt those Walking Soldiers
>who cannot even make themselves brave enough to catch our children and old
>ones,

>>the dying grass blowing in transient semblances of the beaverhair roach
>>Ollokot used to wear at Dreamer dances
>>(Cut Arm burned this treasure at Ground Squirrel Place),
>>seedheads stylized and golden,
>>the breeze blowing colder,

>>>Lean Elk laughing, Shore Crossing's buffalo rifle roaring out from
>>>the reddish-greenish rock knobs:
>>>>*timm!*
>>>Toohhoolhoolsote choosing for his victim a tired soldier like a
>>>bloody old buffalo bull with his tongue hanging out:
>>>>*pim!*
>>>and the man's mouth opens as he backflips off his horse:

Áhaha!
we are flying up; we are killing them
>until a bullet enters the hip of Animal In A Hole,
>>who is saved by Heinmot Tooyalakekt,
>>>he who is called *Joseph,*
>>and a cool breeze comes off the Swift Water, with mosquitoes in the
>>shade,

>>>>our women galloping up the red and yellow cañon:
>>>>>they have saved the horses,
>>>>>and they have nearly made our children safe.

7

Lean Elk fires the last cartridge from Shore Crossing's buffalo rifle:
>*timm!*
>—striking a wounded Bluecoat in the shoulder:
>>the man flies back *tsálalal*
>>>(his exploded chest already pink like deer meat broiled
>>>just right);
this good thing is now finished also,
>>purple rain falling through the yellow sky behind the western walls of the
>>cañon where the women and children have withdrawn the herd

(perhaps there will soon be snow),
our best men still sniping at the Bluecoats
—*pim!*... *pim!*—
(our hearts are now becoming happy),
then ducking their heads down
just as the enemy kills two of our horses
and Toohhoolhoolsote with all his WYAKIN Power
shoots a Bluecoat who is running;
and here is a young Boston on a ridge, spying for the
Bluecoats, his hair pale brownish grey like a prairie
dog's; yes, he is like a prairie dog, on all fours in the
mouth of its hole, its head up high to watch us,
but not even Looking-Glass can kill him, not even
with a needle gun;
therefore Lean Elk, crawling up into the rocks, digs a secret grave for this gun
which has spoken so loudly for us since the beginning, causing Cut Arm's killers
to throw up their arms in terror;
now this gun will speak no more,
and Lean Elk, crawling like a snake between boulders, descends into the
coulee where his horse waits
and gallops up the cañon,
his half-grey hair flying behind him,
around the bend to our People.

8

Choking the narrows with logs and boulders,
then riding after dark through sagebrush-lipped earth-grooves and salt-
grooves in the grass,
our children weeping in the wind,
we tell our People to camp for the night on the bank of Elk River,
always watching back in case the Bluecoats should foolishly come
(we wish to pound them all into powder which we could grind into
the dirt).
and Heinmot Tooyalakekt helps Tzi-kal-tza get down from his horse, and that
ancient man says: Now perhaps I am beginning to die from this long ride,
while Good Woman is already boiling soup as she weeps,
the MOON as white as a buffalo skull.

9

Well before dawn
(ridgetops pallid with frost),

Lean Elk begins shouting: *Hurry, hurry!*
so that our women can pack the horses in good time, and the old ones, wounded
and children can start ahead,

    for it is still far to the Medicine Line

        and Cut Arm is following us more closely

            (but where is he? We can never see him).

                Home From Capture, Looking-Glass's favorite stallion,
                has gone lame at last. The *lucky man* turns away when
                Asking Maiden slashes his hind legs so that Cut Arm
                cannot ride him.

Cloudburst is opening the saddlebag which Fair Land once made and carried,
    withdrawing for her husband that brave and old-fashioned collar of otter-
    skin decorated with beads and red cloth streamers,

    and Ollokot paints his face with the last of the red earth that Fair Land
    gathered for him in Wallowa,

while Heinmot Tooyalakekt is helping everyone

    (with her wounded arm Springtime has trouble mounting Redhead while
    holding the baby,

        whose hair has grown in; to him it feels as soft as the moss in the
        high forest behind Wallowa Lake;

    her father hands her up);

and his good daughter Sound Of Running Feet,

    she who has now become a woman after her mother's heart,

is helping old ones onto their horses

    even as elkteeth fall unstitched from her elkskin dress.

        Welweyas the half-woman,

            she who until now has been so strong,

        whispers to Cloudburst that she is cold and tired; her heart prefers
        to ride no more,

            as Lean Elk shouts: *Hurry, hurry!*

        but Cloudburst goes to Heinmot Tooyalakekt,

        who says to Welweyas: My dear niece, my dear younger sister,
        please keep on with your People who love you. The Lice-Eaters will
        scalp you and the Bostons will be glad.

        But hear me, my chief, I can go no further—

        Now let this talk be finished, Welweyas,

            and from his own body he unwraps his last King George
            blanket, placing it in her hand, so that she is shamed back
            into strength,

                and Good Woman quickly unpacks a black-striped grey
                blanket for her husband to wear, then leaps up on
                White Face, who has not yet gone lame,
                while he mounts Black Mane-Stripe.

Now as we all are quickly riding farther away from our home,
> up out of the arroyos, passing between hilltops where the softest
> hills split open in rock-grins and some ledges have rotted into pink
> honeycombs
>> (Helping Another begins to ride well again; her chest-wound
>> has finally scabbed over; her mother and husband take pride
>> in her strength),
> Looking-Glass gazes back over his shoulder, half hoping to see across
> country and river to the Sacrifice Cliffs
> —and cries out in anger!—
so that we who once admired him,
among them Wottolen, *he who remembers*
> (and will surely remember this),
also look back,
> spying not the Bluecoats,
>> who cannot leap onto their horses like men,
> but other mounted riders with many silvery necklace-loops slapping
> across their bare chests:
>> their silver beads proclaim them:
>>> now they too have begun killing us—
our fine friends the Crows.

MOST EXTRAORDINARY AND PRAISEWORTHY
EFFORTS
SEPTEMBER 14

1

*W*ood, draft a despatch to Sturgis explaining that we will ride down the Yellow Stone to Baker's Battle-Ground and the Musselshell while he is recruiting his command back to operational strength. As soon as he can, he should continue hunting Joseph along the direct trail.

> Do you remember those old twenty-pound Parrotts? I sure wish we
> had one of those here.

Yessir. Is he to meet us at the Musselshell?

Man proposes, GOD disposes. That's all, Wood.

> In confidence, father, do you feel dreadfully hurt that

Colonel Sturgis didn't halt the reds?

Not at all,

and across the silver-brown groove of Cañon Creek the Indian horses have already fled.

2

The object of whist is to take tricks, but the object of Indian warfare is to take horses, because without those, the savages can't get far away, especially when encumbered by their papooses and squaws. Accordingly, he'd reminded Sturgis to go for Joseph's pony herd, which would have been easy for any competent officer. Unfortunately, the poor colonel once more allowed his timidity to get away with him, still worrying about another Little Big Horn;

so again the newspapers must be calling me General Day-After-To-morrow. LORD help poor Lizzie! Well, she's had a dozen years of practice at being the wife of a "nigger lover." She'll keep her head high—

Wood, this next will be to Division Headquarters in San Francisco. *Our advance is having a running fight with Joseph over twenty miles. Indians' horses are now constantly dropping out, too lame and worn to go farther. More than four hundred of them have fallen into our hands. Sturgis has made most extraordinary and praiseworthy efforts* . . .

Yessir.

You think badly of him, don't you?

Not at all, general.

He marched eighty-five miles in two days to reach Joseph at Cañon Creek. Even General Sherman couldn't ask for more.

He sure couldn't, sir.

I'm impressed, as always, by Joseph's ease on horse. Just think what the United States could do if every trooper could ride like a Nez Perce!

On that subject, general, how's Arrow?

At Clark's Fork Cañon I was nearly ready to shoot him. But he seems to be picking up. He may well last out this campaign. Has Captain Fisher ridden in yet?

Yessir.

Go chat with him, please, and you two project our march to Pompey's Pillar. I'll expect your report in fifteen minutes. Wilkinson, how are you holding up?

Thank you, not bad, general—

Right now it seems as if SATAN is striving with all his helpers against the light, but I know the better side will conquer.

Yessir.

Send a rider to Colonel Buell, doublequick. I want to know when he can get our resupply to Baker's field. And this is to Colonel Miles. Make a good copy for me to sign at "Reveille" to-morrow. Has Ad Chapman come in?

No, sir; Fletch thinks he may be souvenir-hunting at Cañon Creek—

If he's not back by muster call, dock him a month's pay. Now where's our main command?

Not quite caught up, general. Apparently Cushing was lost, and, as you know, our bunch has some pretty jaded horses, so they—

I asked: Where are they?

Still a good seventeen miles from the Yellow Stone—

Have you received Sturgis's casualty return?

Just now, general. Three enlisted men killed, nine wounded.

Not bad. What about Joseph's losses?

General, Colonel Sturgis claims twenty-one Indians killed and four hundred ponies captured.

Perhaps Joseph carried all his dead off the field.

Yessir. And those captured horses—

Wilkinson, do try to trust in your fellow man!

Thanks for the advice, general.

Yes, Wood, what do you want?

Here's the projection, sir—

Thanks. Well, perhaps I'll turn in. Wake me at three a.m., would you?

Sure thing, general.

Wood, I'm sorry I snapped at you. Forgive me—

Don't think twice about it, general. Good night.

Good night, and GOD bless you!

> —so weary as to suddenly find himself nearly indifferent to everything (must never let on)

>> even as Wood, wishing to know our Crows better, and having for that very purpose stopped several evenings ago at Red O'Donnell's wagon to buy an ounce of Dandy Jim tobacco, now takes that offering to the scouts,

>>> from whom Captain Fisher, battle-worn but not in the slightest downcast, has just traded something in exchange for a parfleche bag (an item most commonly of squaw manufacture, so Ad Chapman has explained), and who have suddenly become morose about something,

>>>> so that without even knowing why, Wood himself commences to feel sad and dirty

>> —failing, however, to make his signs comprehensible to them until Old George says: All right, lieutenant, what you want to speak to these fellows, you speak it and I tell 'em straight!—so they all smoke the Dandy Jim in silence; then the Crows give Wood a bundle of pale greenish-grey plant-stuff, and that is how he first learns the way that a crumb of sweetgrass leaf can afflict the tongue's tip with peppermint numbness,

>>> (he feels too shy to show off his horn spoon from the Clearwater: what would they care anyhow?),

while Pollock's bunch are all laughing at the way our general's son, desperate to get in a lick at Mr. Joe, let fly with a howitzer that was still strapped onto a mule! The shell went one way (too short), and the mule flew back the other. Well, Lieutenant Howard may not be a hundred percent effective, perhaps, but no one can say that he lacks "sand"!

> and Trimble's horse, patiently doctored, has finally begun to sneeze out lye—a sign of recovery

—as the general wraps himself in his rubber blanket, his eyes unable to focus on the stars:

> *Now* what will General Sherman say?
>
> I can easily imagine the greedy delight of my rival Department heads. *General Day-After-To-morrow,* they call me.
>
>> Joseph still retains twenty-five hundred head of horses. He's getting away, and everyone knows it.
>>
>> While Terry tends to gaze over or through me, Sheridan narrows his dark eyes, firing silent suspicion at me from both barrels:
>>
>>> I loathe his ugly cheeks and double-wrinkled neck, the creases at the corners of his eyes—LORD forgive me; to-night I'll pray for him,

and preparing to pray for Mrs. Trimble with her children,

> and I trust that Lizzie's finally taken Chauncey to Doctor Pilkington, not that he's necessarily the best oculist
>
> ## (a fine stock of Artificial Eyes kept):
>
>> FATHER, thank you for giving me Lizzie

and for large-brooded Mrs. Pollock, and poor Mrs. Parnell at Walla-Walla

—but, O, that sad supper when nobody but I dared to talk to Sturgis,

>> who should have been some slim, elegant drawing-room colonel with gold braid on his shoulders and his elbow out as he leans on his sword,
>
> the officers drinking cool wind (having nothing more substantial to partake of) and looking back into the greenish-grey butte-horizon we'd come from
>
> as Sturgis kept gazing east, the buttes now strangely bleached by the evening sun so that they seemed snowed over,
>
> his weary infantry, far more beaten down than mine, greasing the insides of their cracked boots
>
>> while Wilkinson tended to the wounded most commendably, singing hymns with them;

by which time Captain Fisher was already returning down the sagey shoulder of the nearest butte: Colonel Sturgis, sir, they're solid gone!

But once Miles strikes diagonally across our front—

Can't you sleep, father?

Well, did you get enough excitement to-day?

Not hardly, since Joseph's got away again! If I whisper in your ear, may I ask you something?

Guy, that's not . . . All right.

Is Colonel Sturgis a "weak link"?

I'm afraid so.

Then what should a general do in such situations? Not that I ever expect to become one, but I—

O, it's a much larger question than that. It goes beyond the Army. When we finish building our United States so that they'll survive down the ages, we'll ensure every individual can be replaced by another, even the President.

Then—

Guy, I'll tell you something that General Sherman used to say. It much impressed me then, and still does now. He said: *Our Government should become a machine, self-regulating, independent of the man.*

Now Perhaps It Is Too Late
September 14–16

1

*T*he Bluecoats are coming up, four abreast:

they are driving us like animals; such is Cut Arm the Hateful, whom we sometimes call *People Herder,*

Cut Arm, whose many-Bluecoated will now begins to extend itself all the way across Our Mother

Whose grassy nipple studs the horizon, after which will come the *wrinkled land;*

but they ride and shoot like little boys; already they are getting tired; this fight is nothing,

except that now the Crows have also betrayed us,

which sickens our hearts,

Looking-Glass's wives screaming,

our children round-eyed like antelopes,

Sound Of Running Feet helping both her mothers to whip the horses and mules into a stampede

(just as buffaloberries cluster close to the stalk, forming a column of red within the long narrow, tapering green-grey leaves, so her desire to see the blood of these new killers partly conceals itself within the girl's quotidian actions, not that anyone is paying attention to her anyway)

while our exhausted young men,

whose fur-wrapped braids hang down stiff with dirt and grease, swinging against their chests, whose roached hair is dirty and whose deerskin shirts, stained with the blood of enemies and dead war-friends, have begun to fall apart upon their bodies,

now stare forward in uncomprehending sorrow

(again they believed the words of Looking-Glass):

Toohhoolhoolsote counts a hundred and fifty of our good friends,

many of them wearing hair longer than Lice-Eaters do

(they must hope to steal our horses),

their scouts *wolfing** ahead,

as he takes aim at the tasseled, beaded SUNdisk-ornament which hangs between the eyes of the nearest Crow's favorite horse:

Pim!

—but that warrior keeps coming—

and looking back, Looking-Glass spies the familiar white blaze between the ears of a certain Crow pony now bowing his long dark neck to drink from a dark stream,

the rider bright white with eagle feathers, hairpipes, shell-beads and dentalia:

White Man Runs Him, who until now was my brother

—even as White Bird, ever more of an enemy, trots up his buffalo horse to express his heart: Looking-Glass, again you have ruined us; you have led us down the Skeleton Trail! Until now I looked at the Crows as my own flesh, and I believed them when they said that they and our People were one. Once again I esteemed the words of Looking-Glass. Why should they shoot at their own flesh? But you, Looking-Glass, have misled us three times. When you first withdrew your People to stay out of the war, I considered you very wise, but after Cut Arm devoured your country, your heart has become crazy. In Left Hand's country you would not listen to my warning, when we could have gone safely to the King Georges. Then you commanded us not to watch behind us at Ground Squirrel Place, for fear of insulting the Bostons; so they killed our lovely girls, our old ones, our young boys and our best men. Even after that, you promised that the Crows would take us in, and we were as children to follow you—see how they now herd us like cattle! Looking-Glass, you have deceived us too often. Looking-Glass, I am finished with you. That is all I have to say,

*A Crow verb.

at which Looking-Glass, incensed, finished with *him,* gallops back to shoot at the
oncoming Crows while Lean Elk and Heinmot Tooyalakekt hurry the People onward,
  the Crows galloping closer, their brass necklaces jingling as they commence to
  shoot:
            Pim, pim, pim, pim, pim!
as if we were weak poor people without any family
—already they have killed Surrounded Goose and Fish Trap:
  old men who had no weapons.

2

Ollokot and his dear nephew White Thunder have stood shooting rifles side
by side, until, seeing the Crows preparing to attack our women and children,
     much as when our hunters force buffalo into a tightly wheeling circle,
     letting the old bulls go, shooting cows and mature calves
        —but these hunters would kill us all, even our old ones!
          (Fish Trap never harmed them; he was merely seeking a lost
          horse;
              while Surrounded Goose, they say, did not even stray
              from the People: his luck was simply finished)—
Ollokot, jumping onto his buffalo horse
  (it comes into my heart that I shall die now),
gallops to try and halt them, calling the young men to ride beside him, hoping to
see and taunt some former brother in order to make himself still braver with rage
     as they come on singing, with their long narrow parfleche bags cinched
     down low against their horses' flanks
        (now they have cut off two stallions from Burning Coals's herd),
     and we watch the enlarging of the beaded rectangles, yellow, blue, red,
     white and black, which decorate their stirrups:
        Pim, pim, pim, pim, pim!
Thus again White Thunder is alone, behind all the fleeing People, as enemies
close in;
so he jumps onto Grey One, riding away with slow contempt
     (loving the strangely small snakelike heads of certain enemy horses),
  because he has made himself brave and believes his WYAKIN's promise
as two Crows ride near, making themselves likewise brave
  as if they might even dare to count coup upon me with their elk-handled
  quirts! . . .
he fires his Winchester at the same moment that one of them also shoots,
  at which those bad Crows wheel back, riding away hard
    (hopefully he has injured one);
then a hundred more Crows and Lice-Eaters come riding,
    some of them in flannel shirts or cotton or buckskin,

shooting at him quick and sly from beneath their horses' necks:
        grazing his thigh
                (this is laughable),
        then creasing Grey One's mane
at which, remembering that his WYAKIN never promised horse protection, he
gallops forward.

3

Staking down his horse in a coulee, Strong Eagle,
        last of the Three Red Blankets,
                who fights in red no more,
crawls up a sandhill,
        startling a long-billed curlew,
to see
                (keeping his head down)
        the Crows
        and with them their new brothers the Lice-Eaters
                (whom we once drove like animals)
        and far behind them the first straggling Bluecoats just barely on the low
        grey-green tree-horizon of this world of orange grass:
                They have deprived us of everything. They have killed our country.
Scarcely raising himself, he aims the Springfield rifle that could not save some
nameless Bluecoat at Sparse-Snowed Place
        (now near three full moons ago, before any of us began to be killed):
                Pim!
But this enemy keeps approaching unhurt,
        the straps of his earth-colored saddlebag swinging as he barebacks, nod-
        ding as his horse sways, gripping lightly with his knees, splaying his feet
        out:
                how I long to kill him!
with others coming behind
                —his WYAKIN, whose reach was once as long as a grizzly's claws
                hovering small and silent above his head—
so he runs back down into the coulee, leaps onto Home Again
        (Shore Crossing's favorite horse)
and gallops forward,
        traversing the steep grass-hills in search of a better shot.

4

Now Grey One begins pawing strangely, so that when White Thunder rides in
among his rearmost war-friends to help guard the People, White Bull whips the

horse to make him quiet, until we realize that he is wounded, and Ollokot says:
Dear nephew, hasten to camp! If you end up on foot, the Crows will surely kill you!

    Leaving saddle and blanket with his uncle, in case Grey One should die, he
rides forward,

> while in this late afternoon OUR MOTHER THE EARTH shows the colors
> of Her skin:
>> from whitish-tan to walnut brown to orange and red
>>> (all the colors of leather on a saddle-blanket)

and into the chilling evening:

> sunset like the red stripe along the backbone of a newborn buffalo calf

and the dark.

    Lying down battle-stripped and hungry between two rockpiles, suffering pain
in his bones, he warms himself with rage,

> coyotes yowling all night
> and he finally sleeps, trusting in his WYAKIN,

until at dawn, spying the button-tail of an antelope behind a dead willow, he rises,
aching from his ankles all the way to his spine,

> his rifle burning cold,
> and since he who as a boy used to take joy in leaping among the high
> white boulders above Wallowa Lake remains WOLF-agile, he approaches
> quickly and quietly all confidence,

approaching downwind so that the cow takes no fear, watching him curiously
with her round eyes:

> *Pim!*

—hearing which, his cousin Charging Hawk comes for breakfast

> (he says that in the night the Crows stole a hundred ponies),

then leads him back into camp, where our women have already packed the horses:

> they are mourning Surrounded Goose and Fish Trap.
>> White Thunder begins to dislike his Aunt Springtime
>>> —her Power as poisonous as larkspur leaves—
>> because she makes his uncle sad,

and Lean Elk has already sent scouts forward while Heinmot Tooyalakekt sets out
with the wounded.

    But now our women begin screaming!

> We must lead them out of this killer prairie; we shall hide them in the
> mountains,
>> just for awhile.

Here come Lice-Eaters and Crows to kill our families,

> their brass necklaces jingling as they trot;
>> and pulling their knives from their beaded belt-cases to taunt and
>> terrify our women, they shout out what they mean to do.

    With no time to get a strong horse, White Thunder leaps back on Grey One,

> singing to his WYAKIN, Who is WOLF: *O You Who run round and round,*

and beside him, on some other warrior's high-blooded racing-horse, rides
Over The Point,
>Red Heart's son,
>>he who made himself so brave two moons ago at the Big Water
>>>(the cowards would not follow his counsel, and so Cut Arm
>>>devoured Red Owl's country)
>>and who rode with Ollokot and the other best men that night to
>>Camas Meadows,
>>>where our buffalo hunters once used to camp,
>>>>just for awhile,
>>>in the generations when we could ride where we wished,
>>and stole Cut Arm's mules:
>he has stripped off his elkhide shirt with the whorled circle of beads, but
>still wears his outward-pointing necklace of grizzly bear teeth;
this pair of war-friends will now join our best men:
>Swan Necklace, who can ride and shoot concealed on the side of his
>horse, and Strong Eagle, along with White Thunder's brave war-friend
>Wottolen, with his twelve-year-old son Black Eagle
>as Red Spy howls the *scalp halloo.*
So they charge the murderous Lice-Eaters,
who are as mosquitoes,
>and who dismount and hide
>>so that White Thunder can finally change Grey One for one of their
>>best horses,
>>>a handsome snakeheaded ocher buffalo pony,
>>then shoots and shoots, aiming at their bright blanket-coats;
as for Over The Point, he cannot halt his racing-horse, which careers straight to
the enemy,
>closer and closer:
>>when a Crow stands up to shoot him, Over The Point cannot turn
>>his eyes from the beaded star-patterns on the warrior's saddle
>>>(his WYAKIN, barred like the black mask of a ce-
>>>dar waxwing, has never promised him immunity
>>>from bullets):

>*Timm!*
>>—sage grouse rising up in panic—
>*Tsálalal!*
(how shall we no longer say his name?)
—then that riderless horse runs back toward the People, shouting: *Hinimí!*
>while Looking-Glass,
>>who has many times seen the Keeper of the Pipe untie the long-
>>fringed Medicine bag, which is beaded with red diamonds fishtailed

head and foot, each enclosing two yellow rectangles whose short
sides kiss at a white stripe,
keeps shooting wild.
(We never needed him or his WHIRLWIND-Power.)

5

Creeping through the dusk-misted gulleys, longing to escape this prairie,
Swan Necklace,
who once wished to make himself as brave as the Three Red Blankets,
and longs for the sound of Shore Crossing's buffalo rifle, which always
comforted us, that sound we shall hear no more,
doubles back into a coulee not far north of our last night's camp and sees from
behind one of his Crow enemies silhouetted on a dark ridgetop whose tall grass-
silhouettes resemble black knife-slits in the yellow sky, the horse's rump and the
warrior's shoulders all one, inset rather than bisected by the faint upturned cres-
cent gleam of the animal's back, and the warrior's many-feathered head, erect and
unmoving—a black fist in the middle of the lone sunset cloud.

6

Earth Blanket,
quick and careful killer,
riding up one of the sagebrush-speckled cone-hills to gaze back on our
pursuers,
and Heinmot Tooyalakekt, riding up to the backbone of this swale,
hoping to kill more of the head-blue* Bostons,
can see yesterday's battle-cañon as two low blue-grey jawbones in the land; the
leading Crow scouts are but two rises away;
behind them ride more Crows with their .50-calibre breechloaders,
spread out arrogantly or feebly across the plains
(now we shall call them *the Women Nation*,
at which Welweyas the half-woman smiles sadly):
They are all against us,
winding themselves around and around us.
and the old women are getting headaches from the wind.
(We are hastening them to the mountains, but even in the
mountains we cannot stay.)
Shivering, we flee to the grey horizon,
having thus renewed our sorrow
with sunshine on our knees,

---

*The color of their caps.

and swales rocky beneath the grass,
and flocks of darting little blackbirds
      (the bluebells already gone from the riverbanks);
          Springtime never takes off the beargrass cap that Good
          Woman made for her at Weippe
      and White Bird now puts on his wolfskin cap.
At last the Crows and Lice-Eaters,
   having captured more of our horses
      (three from Looking-Glass, one from Lean Elk, seven from Toohhool-
      hoolsote, twelve from Burning Coals, who will never cease to count
      the loss
         although they have not yet stolen Lucky One,
      six from Swan Woman),
begin to fall away.

<h1 style="text-align:center">7</h1>

Galloping forward into the cold night,
         our breath-steam rising,
       departing even the lonesome call of the long-billed curlew
we presently approach a village of our dear friends the Mountain Crows,
and then, unable to stop hating Cut Arm
    (although Heinmot Tooyalakekt insists that this is not straight:
      he is one who is always talking),
we kill and burn,
     like pounding meat on a flat rock,
stealing all their horses
    (they have stolen three hundred of ours)
      so that Springtime's heart is gladdened by the soft bleached deer-
      skin fringes of her new Crow saddle,
        although Redhead's hooves are becoming diseased;
packing their jerked buffalo meat onto Cut Arm's mules
        while Loon (who is as greedy as a shaman) now longs with all
        his heart to drink *getting-drunk liquid* and Red Spy cleans his
        hands in a dead man's hair
      and Toohhoolhoolsote has now finished singing the scalp song
        —Heinmot Tooyalakekt wrapping himself sadly in his grey
        blanket
        even as Looking-Glass, standing over the corpse of a Crow boy,
          this one whom I knew:
            in fun he used to shoot at his friends from beneath
            his horse's neck and miss them, such was his skill,
          this one whose dance-shirt sports yellow-waisted red

hourglasses in a sea of blue, and whose elkskin-sleeved
arms were just this day waving like stalks of grass,
gazes into the dead face and almost touches it, then turns
away grimacing,
and when the rawhide loop of his shoulder-slung old Winchester chafes his neck, he looks around for the beaded elkhide case which was lost at Ground Squirrel Place, then
remembers that it is gone—
then the People begin laughing *áhaha* and singing their WYAKIN songs,
happily inhaling the smell of blood:
We shall not kill your chief, because she is a woman. Hear us, you
Women Nation! We wipe our buttocks on your heads!
and ride rapidly on
(Lean Elk is disappointing us; he never lets the weak ones rest)
toward the ragged hunks of rock bursting out of the swales, and far ahead
the low blue mountains meagrely streaked with snow-diagonals
where forests will open to hide us, just for awhile,
and dark-stoned wavecrests curling out of the green and orange plain
as Peopeo Tholekt's favorite yellow horse first begins to limp;
then down into a rougher country of scattered dolmens, mesas and trees:
a single glittering aspen,
faint, darkly glittering shine of water at Big Coulee Creek
and on the horizon, the new river as wide as a woman's belt,
bearing muddy silver river bends, no more metallic than a carp's
belly, through cottonwoods and box elders:
the Musselshell.

8

Here we shall camp where the river-water is fluttering like butterflies:
bluish-green leaves of mountain death camas,
purple-specked red berries of false Solomon's seal,
gaillardia's small white flowers on their tall stems
(Looking-Glass, who has led a Crow war party to this
place, warns that we must now watch out, since we
soon shall be riding into the country of our old enemies
the Shinbones and Walking Cuttthroats;
at which Old Yellow Wolf says to White Thunder:
That one should not tell us who to watch out for!)
—and Peopeo Tholekt doctors his yellow horse with yarrow and WOOD-
PECKER Medicine
as Good Woman begins softening her husband's bed with good grass,

Welweyas, Cloudburst, *Kate* and Looking-Glass's women all
salving their horses' bleeding sores
(even now we are rich, with hundreds in our herd),
Looking-Glass's four women softening their last camas cakes
in clean river-water,
Towhee wrapping blankets around her dear daughter
Helping Another,
Springtime and Sound Of Running Feet seeking old roots to dig up.
Again some young men have painted themselves; they are drumming on their
untanned elkskin, singing their war-songs; Loon makes himself brave
(we have heard this too many times);
Strong Eagle shoots a blue and yellow kingbird for war-Medicine,
Toohhoolhoolsote, sucking on a handsome pipe, skins a muskrat from
the tail end
and Ollokot begins softly quarrelling with his remaining wife,
while the dead wife's child stares open-mouthed
as Sound Of Running Feet sweetly picks her tired father's lice, asking him: When
shall we ride home to Wallowa?

As Good as a Circus
September 16

1

Quite an interesting river, the Yellow Stone.
Sure is, general.
It's changed color from yesterday.
Refraction, sir.
Apparently Mr. Parker drowned here in the spring, carrying despatches to
Colonel Miles.
Yessir. Didn't know you were acquainted with him—
A brave, unfortunate fellow. I hear he leaves two children.
Yessir.
Could you bring Doctor Alexander to me?
Right this moment, sir.
O, good afternoon, doctor. How are you getting on?
No complaints, general,

alkali sugaring the sawbones' face. A fine soldier—must write him a commendation at the end:

Surgeon Charles T. Alexander has given complete satisfaction.

Or does he deserve better still? We'll see. An opportunity for bravery under Joseph's fusillades, or—

That's the spirit! Now, what about our troops?

Well, general, the cavalry are in better shape than the infantry, of course. Lately there's been more erysipelas of the ankles, due to all the marching. I've painted all the afflicted men with creosote and iodine, of which we still have plenty. Calomel's getting low, so I'm saving it for wounds.

You've mentioned boot nails penetrating their feet.

Yes, general. Even the officers say *as honest as a Leavenworth contractor.*

Thank you, doctor. You surely have patients to attend to. Someone bring Redington here.

Right away, sir.

Well, my boy, how was the battle?

Pretty lively, general. We made holes in a few Indians, and I had to dance around their bullets.

A battlefield's a ghastly place, Redington. I rode over the ground on the thirteenth, and Captain Bendire showed me where you charged. Dead horses, dead men—how can we not hate war?

Well, sir, that's a real brain-twister, all right.

It's a thrill to you, isn't it? Well, GOD bless you! Fletch says you were pretty brave up there on the ridge. Now, where have our Nez Perces gotten to?

General, they're still ahead with all their ponies, squaws and luggage. General Sturgis's command are disadvantaged without fresh horses, but once Captain Cushing—

I didn't request your opinions about General Sturgis.

Apologies, sir. Anyhow, Mr. Joe's almost reached the Musselshell.

What about the Crows?

General, they're better than a plague of locusts! You should see them cut horses out of Joseph's herd! As long as they can steal, they'll stay on his tail.

Good. You ride out now, and give Captain Fisher my compliments. Tell him he's got some fine scouts. O, and take this despatch to Lieutenant Fletcher. That's it. Guy, what do you think of the Yellow Stone?

O, father, it's as good as a circus!

Where's Lieutenant Wilkinson?

Here I am, sir.

What news from Cushing?

He's only three miles off now, sir.

What about Lieutenant Otis?

He's almost back from the battlefield, sir. Of course he can travel more quickly now—

That's so. After losing one of our two howitzers in this river!

That's right, general. I don't suppose we'll be commending him.

Possibly not, Wilkinson, although that's not your affair. Are Trimble's bunch finally ready?

No, sir.

Go find out why and report back to me immediately. *Immediately*, Wilkinson, who when he reëxamines the definition of culpability must admit, no matter how much his forgiving heart may thereby be pained, that Trimble's dereliction at Camas Meadows has met it; and so believes that not only the interest of the service, but also the general's, demands that the latter be reminded of this fact as needed, in order to protect O. O. Howard (Wilkinson and Fletch's dear old general and the finest Christian in the world), who bears so much on his shoulders, from being dragged down by yet another untrustworthy individual;

or, to recast the matter in more universal terms, Wilkinson, who dislikes no man and would get Trimble and Perry back on the square if he could, nonetheless cannot forbear from pointing out that Trimble has, and entirely though his own fault, rendered himself liable to punishment, while Perry for his part is an equally unworthy officer—although Wilkinson plans to intervene discreetly in Perry's Court of Inquiry if possible, in order to save the general (not Perry) any grief and embarrassment from which it may be possible for one human being to rescue another (and so far as he can make out, Perry has very little to fear, no matter how discreditable his behavior at White Bird Cañon, since it cannot be in the Army's interest to do anything but bury the whole affair).

Yessir. They're horsed up now, sir.

Your horse is failing.

Yessir; he's got a case of the trembles.

Would you like one of Joseph's ponies?

Thanks, general, but as long as I can keep good old Pacer going on lead and calomel—

Let's move out. As soon as we're underway, send Trimble to me.

Yessir. *Move out!*

Yessir. Bugler, sound the move out.

Command across the river, hurrah!

the horsemen fording the river with their rifles pointed diagonally upward on their backs, water up to the animals' tails, bandoliers pale in the rain, hats snugged down over bearded cheeks, a long crew rowing in a bullboat, and the ribbed canvas cylinders of wagontops floating across,

poor Mason so pallid and weary ever since Clark's Mountain,

Ad Chapman
>—a true Western man, I must admit, with
>plenty of "sand" in him—

swimming his horse gallantly back and forth,
seeking and not finding Lieutenant Otis's sunken
howitzer

>(the officer just mentioned acting—such is
>his embarrassment about the loss—
>ashamed of everything, even the scarlet ar-
>tillery insignia he bears);

our hostile Indians ever farther ahead, although
perhaps Sturgis will strike them another blow

>(O, I do hope Cushing hurries up!)

or the Crows will harry them sufficiently for
Miles to get in position
and I have gained fine instruction in not being
frantic, at Edisto not least, O, and Chancellorsville, never mind Fair Oaks, and my best and
hardest lessons of all being those times when I
must worry and show nothing when Lizzie was
brought to bed in our darkened room, patiently
risking her life to give me another child

>—sweet Lizzie, please don't die before I do!—

our mules swimming trustfully after the bell mare,
and on the near bank, Captain Jocelyn huddles with
Trimble while the general, who has lately forded this
river more times than he can remember, massages his
empty sleeve:
Hurrah, hurrah!
>Wade in, fellows.

Now Wood,
>whose dreams of Nanny are as handsome as the gleam of cartridges in
>Perry's gunbelt,

and Wilkinson, Mason, Sladen and the general have crossed; Perry and Trimble
impel their cavalry out of the water, employing curses so long as the general is out
of earshot, then expressing sincere feelings for some buffalo venison with buffaloberry jelly on it;
>a dozen enlisted men huddled together, entertaining one another with
>what appears to be some Irish or Bohemian tomfoolery:

>>Doc, this here Frederick wants to know how to buy a squaw.

>>For what?

>>What else?

>>I don't see no squaws around here.

I don't care from where. Maybe I'll find my opportunity. Blackie says you know the Indian language.

Here's what you do, says Doc,

    bringing down his outspread fingertips ever so gently from just above the crown of his head down around his ears and cheeks:

        combing imaginary hair

            (thus sign language, the *lingua franca* of our American aborigines);

as Pollock, whose bunch all swam across safe and fast and easy, and have been awarded a breather, strolls along the bank looking for minerals, even if for only ten minutes

    (What did the captain call you for?

    Well, to compliment for the way I organized that picket.

    Did he now!),

and Wood,

    remembering how not an hour since he took pity to see the general sitting on a rock outside his Sibley tent, all alone in that instant when Wilkinson had been despatched away and Sladen, summoned, had not yet arrived, so that there the general was, clasping his left knee, moving his lips, sweating beneath his slouch hat,

now feels jealous anger at the general's laying-of-hand on Wilkinson's shoulder!

    (I wonder how Fletch is getting along with that pathetic Sturgis? When's he coming back to us? He might be my best friend now. And what sign has Fisher found? The Seventh's horses are a d——d sight less jaded than ours. Will they finish Joseph before the Musselshell, or will we be in on the death? I'm grateful the general took me with him to sketch the battlefield. If the Crows and Bannocks haven't completely pillaged the dead, maybe I can finally get a souvenir. I'd like to own something of Joseph's. It's almost noble the way he keeps struggling on. Why is this crossing taking so long? No wonder the general's irritated. Poor old Pollock's looking blue over there; he must miss his family. I wish I could go chat with him, but it wouldn't look good to wander away)

as Cushing's detachment finally rides up with the beef (doublequick, thanks to Mason's exertions),

and here comes Chapman on his prancing charger, shaking water everywhere, happier than ever, and doubtless yearning (supposes Wood) to become as horse-rich as a Nez Perce

    while our general sits waiting, studying the map to see where Chief Joseph might be and on which diagonal Miles ought to strike

        (soon we'll be picking over that gruesome battlefield again:

            well, well, a decent effort poor Sturgis made; I hope they don't sack him), as, raging at the complaining, cowardly incapacity of our selfsame Sturgis, whom he considers in the light of some milquetoast hallooing *murder* at the moon (Christ, he's as rusty as Granddad's horse-pistol!), Perry (whose speculations merely pretend to be frozen, like a line of dark bison on a yellow ridgetop) now dopes out that Umatilla Jim hasn't been in camp for awhile:

Has he deserted? Never even cured Diamond! I'd sure love to hang that son-ofabitch,

while Fletch, having missed Redington, comes cantering up on a pretty Indian pony, courtesy of Joseph, exhausted but enjoying the morning well enough to wave his hat, perhaps ironically, to Chapman, who in return rides in tight circles round him,

and Captain Pollock, even when he puts on his seldom-used spectacles, has unearthed no trace of silver, gold or copper; and the general has not yet perceived Fletch,

who, as you might well imagine, arrives laden with topographic sketches, anecdotes (particularly about our played out horses), jokes, and of course Sturgis's entreaties and complaints,

Wilkinson humming "Nearer My GOD to Thee" as the general composes new memoranda, his disappointments as boulder-white as the naked corpses of Custer's command in the corn-yellow grass.

EVEN IF I MUST FORGO THE CREDIT
SEPTEMBER 17

1

*A*t dawn he returns startled to himself, believing himself home in Portland, as if Lizzie has awakened from her latest Indian nightmare, sobbing: O, how I hate them!— Rising with a sad smile, he meets the morning star, which the Crows call *Sees the Ground.*

We're punishing the enemy considerably.

But Joseph has no communications to interrupt, nor . . . O, good morning, general.

Good morning, Fletch. Good morning, Wood. What were you saying about Joseph? I relish debates of that sort,

> and the morning gun
> and the rapid sweet bugle-tones of "Reveille,"
> roll call

(sweet air on his windburned face),
>Perry towering over Company "F" to hear muster:
>>last night's war-dreams gibbering at him as si-
>>lently as the shadows between the withes of a cov-
>>ered wagon.

Good morning, Chapman.

Morning, general:
>I sure despise that holy fool. If he wasn't a one-armed old melancholic, I'd
>pound him flatter than Injun pemmican.

Thank you, Wood. Nothing on earth like steaming coffee!

That's so, general. Mr. Chapman, here's a mug for you.

Well, well, well. Mighty white of you, lieutenant.

You're welcome.
>Now looky here, general, the way I see this campaign—

Shut up, Chapman. Trimble, thanks for your Morning Report; it appears to be in
good order. Sladen, could you please fetch Major Mason here? Now where's Wilkinson?— No, Fletch, in fact I disagree with your argument. President Grant sincerely
wanted peace with the Indians. That's why he put those Quakers in charge. O, hello,
Mason. Have you any pearls of wisdom on improving to-day's rate of march?

Yessir. The artillery . . .
>Sound "The General,"
>>the bugle prattling away
>>>(but not the way that Brooks used to blow
>>>>—nor poor old Jonesey:
>>>>>*long have they pass'd*),
>>>>*Wakesh nun pakilauitin*
>>>>JEHOVAN'M *yiyauki,*
>>>>the wheels squeaking on the forge wagon,
>>>Guy still carrying with him always that nickel portrait medal
>>>of General Grant from before he was President:
>>>>I wonder when it will tarnish? I should have thought it
>>>>would on that miserably rainy march to Weippe. Maybe
>>>>it will last all my life. If I'm killed by the Indians, will
>>>>they take it? Would Father notice? Stinking old reds!

as Chapman's grey racing-horse prances hysterically up and down the line, under-
scoring these troops' no longer glittering evolutions:
>*Left,*
>>*left,*
>>>*left!*

on this hard-pressed march, chasing after Joseph, leaving behind camp after
camp of reeking sinks,

with braid-rows on their coatsleeves to memorialize years lost in the Army.
>Now, you should have seen the way Robert E. Lee's horse used

to carry him. *Traveller,* he was called. Best-mannered horse that ever lived.

O, shut up.

Well, now that we can move entire wagon trains by railroad, I'd sure like to know why General Sheridan can't just—

Quit it, jackass. Have you forgotten the labor strikes?

—and I see that Jocelyn and Mason have already cut canvas yokes to guard their shoulders from the strengthening night winds; shall I advise Guy to do likewise? No, he'd best learn for himself,

and a rounded brown ridge like an elk's shoulder, and on the horizon a grassy nipple

and then down over the horizon's greenish-silver sagebrush swales, sunshine warming our necks,

Trimble (half-confident that the general will rescind his punishment at campaign's end) high up on his gelding, with his chin wedged against his neck, glaring fondly down at Company "H" as they limp on through the sand at a hundred and ten paces per minute,

Mason,

who so far as Wilkinson is concerned appears to have gained a dangerous ascendancy over the general (didn't the Modoc campaign drag on disgracefully enough?),

wondering about the boys back at Fort Vancouver,

the general already needing to urinate, all the more so since Arrow keeps stumbling to-day,

Blackie dreaming of grazing fat cows and putting up winter vegetables for Fidelia,

Perry, who never stops riding back and forth along the line of Company "F," beginning to face the fact that Diamond is favoring his right back leg

(did Jim do something to him or not?)

and determining once and for all that the coaxings of our praying general are of the same species as the murdered Canby's strangely womanish face, or the hateful *Indian smiles* of Mr. Joe and his peace shammers,

and still hoping to show up that d——d Chapman with his Injun wives

(if Wilkinson sees that Diamond's gait is off, he might tell the general, and if he orders me to to put this horse down—

Red O'Donnell might have something to cure Diamond. I'm going to ask him right now),

Captain Fisher already anticipating showing off his latest Nez Perce souvenir once we pull into camp to-night: a fine pair of leggings decorated with quill-wrapped horsehair (never mind the bloodstains),

Pollock disappointed to hear from Jocelyn that Wood has criticized Mr. Joe's removal,

but Company "D" all in trim,

while the aforesaid critic, Wood, having lately perceived the way that in
each Alaskan springtime the floe ice melts from beneath, invisibly declining from a column of approximately uniform thickness to a mushroom
stem, so that where a man walked yesterday in safety, to-day he falls
through, has begun to suspect that when a woman falls out of love with
her sweetheart, or a soldier loses his general's favor, the mechanism of the
matter might be the same: Nanny tolerates me, apparently forever, then
without warning returns to Mr. Tracy Gould (if in fact she has done so;
how the hell do I know?); the general treats me as his pet, then from one
march to the next withdraws his fondness. Of course the spring thaw, my
established absence from Nanny, and my unwilling opposition to certain
aspects of this campaign, are all known phenomena, and their certain or
projected results may be predicted, although one prefers to think that the
ice will not give way just when someone strides onto it, that Nanny's fidelity will save us both, that certain other elements in the general's relation
to me (for instance his appreciation of my quickness, and his notorious
kindness) will preserve my standing, at least until we return from the
field—as indeed may turn out so. But this sick tension around my heart
and a certain barely perceptible dizziness (which may be nothing more
than dehydration) warn me that some ruinous change may soon over-
power me. I am selfish enough to desire the general's friendship even
while indulging my disloyalty to him and my brother officers. I do not
wish to give up anything! What poor creatures we all are, so greedy and
deluded . . . Must I butter up the general? The cunning way would be to
disparage Nez Perces in earshot of Wilkinson. No, I won't do it,
the land beginning to groove and mound again into badlands, softly at first,
grassed and rounded:
    Might be good barley land.
    What do you want that for? Can't feed a wife on that.
        O for the taste of cherries or even chokecherries in my cracked and
        stinking mouth—
then soft grassy flats, on the westward ridgetop, a dark and heavy dotted line:
buffalo grazing in a row,
small pools of dour brown water with jade-hued reeds
        (Fisher, Redington and the scouts already operating along the Mus-
        selshell River
        as our Crows gallop ahead to prey on Chief Joseph's stragglers),
and then ahead a few purple bluff-stripes on the horizon, on the far side of a
dark groove, which fails to be a creek; now even the horses are thirsty:
        Ask them Crows how far to water.
        Yessir, soon as I can catch 'em!
        O, indeed, they're all bloodlusted now. A pleasure to see them ha-
        rassing Mr. Joe, even if it's but nips in his rear—

and then breasting the low hills, the late grasshoppers striking up against the horses' legs as we hunt Indians through this country of prickly pear, white pebbles and golden grass,

badlands now in truth,

which brings to mind how that comical old Chief Homili, who wormed his way off the reservation whenever he could, always used to repeat in his wheedling, insinuating stupidity: *Bad lands, you say. I like best! Stones and sands and Indian tillicums always kind . . .*

—the Crows screaming and singing because they've shot down another old Nez Perce grandfather:
O, LORD help this brutal, sinful world!—
(must ask James Reuben if our Nez Perces also use the word *tillicums*)—
Praise the LORD, Homili lacks the daring to link up with Smohallie while we're away pursuing Joseph . . . !—

we meet the soft-furred white seedheads of thistles ready to disperse themselves.

Soldier, if you delay this column in any way you'll be punished to-night.
Yessir,
thistles blowing.

Now I lack any recourse but Miles, if I'm to prevent Joseph's junction with Sitting Bull in the British Possessions. Dear GOD, help me to capture Joseph even if I must forgo the credit. And, if it please You, preserve my dear son Guy from death or injury on this campaign. *Amen,*

dead thistleflowers like grey spidery skeletons.

THAT OFFICER WILL GET PROMOTED
SEPTEMBER 14–17

1

I hear that Colonel Miles is well established at Tongue River.
Yessir.
Men,
do your stares signify that even you in your patched once-blue uniforms

consider me worn out? Few of you can even keep up with this march, and yet you blame me for your failure to catch Joseph. Well, that's of no account to me, and

here are two copies of my despatch to him. Your bunch will ride overland, and the rest of you had better run the Yellow Stone. How soon can you set out?

In a quarter-hour, sir.

Good luck. GOD bless you.

Thanks, general. We'll do our best.

I know you will. Yes, Wood, what is it?

Arrow's shoe is back on, sir, and the blacksmith says—

On that subject, tell Colonel Perry to see to his horse. Incipient hoof disease, I suspect.

Yessir.

Frankly, he should have caught it before I did. I'm surprised.

Yessir.

Now, Captain Fisher, what news from that Redington?

He hasn't reported in since yesterday, general.

That's not like him. Kindly alert me the instant he rides in.

Yessir.

A shame if he should be killed. Such a lively young man!

Yessir.

Has anyone tracked down Umatilla Jim?

Afraid not, general.

A sad case. He'll have to be punished, I'm afraid. Wilkinson, take dictation now.

Ready, sir.

This is to General Sherman, usual salutation. *Had Cushing been at Clark's Fork with the force I had directed him to have, the escape of the enemy across the Yellow Stone would absolutely have been prevented. I was much annoyed that Colonel Gibbon saw fit to override my orders, so that Cushing received no assistance at Fort Ellis. All the same, we are doing all that can be done to harry Joseph to the finish.* Write out a fair copy for me. Wood, where's Doctor Alexander's report?

I'll go remind him, sir.

O, I've just learned that your sketch of Dead Mule Trail will be published in *Harper's Magazine.* Congratulations.

Thanks, general. That sure was a muddy uphill climb, coming away from our Salmon River Crossing . . .

Some while ago that was. July second.

Yessir.

By the way, you've not met Colonel Miles.

Haven't had the honor, sir.

Well, as I must have told you, he's my dear old friend, and a very fine soldier, too. You know what Sumner used to say about him right at the beginning of the

Civil War? Miles was a lieutenant then, and Sumner remarked to me: *That officer will get promoted, or get killed.*

Yessir.

He spurs himself; he's his own best horse

> and all my dead before the stone wall of Confederate sharpshooters, and Colonel Miles in a stretcher, holding his neck-wound shut with two fingers as he stops to give me some advice as to placing my troops, and

Yessir.

You know, he's a whiz at remembering names and ranks, even of men he's never met. I don't know how he does it, GOD bless him! (I used to be better than I am now.) On the eve of the Battle of Fair Oaks, he inquired as to how I supposed that General Huger would proceed against us, so I naturally asked whether he had known the general, and he replied something like: Wasn't he in your corps, sir?—as indeed he was, before he went Seccesh. And Miles *knew* this. Impressive, don't you think?

I should say so, sir.

A man of varied accomplishments. How like Miles to study up on General Huger!

Yessir.

He was in the hospital tent, holding my arm in position for the surgeon to amputate. Steadfast. Not that I remember clearly, of course—

Of course not, sir.

And he will surely turn over many a mossy stone to discover ways of getting at Joseph. A most energetic officer!

I hope I get to meet him, sir.

O, you will, you surely will,

> remembering when Miles, who was to him as Wood now is, met him at the edge of a swamp by Fair Oaks Station, to guide him to the lines; it was a Saturday night, the last night he ever possessed a right arm, and an uncanny feeling infected him like typhus when Miles, immediately after saluting, said to him: General, sir, you had better dismount and lead your horses, for the dead and wounded are here

>> in the darkness most populous with groaning obscenities and entreaties.

Any torpedoes in this section, corporal?

> and a lantern trembling far away.

Miles, is that our picket line?

Another quarter-mile yet, general.

> Shoot that horse.
>
> This one's gone.

O, sir!

and musket-rattle, round shot tearing brilliant wounds in the sky where

> The LORD is my
>
> Soldier, can you walk?

is my

       I shall not want

    my shepherd:

  D——n these mosquitoes on my face!

                  O!

as more bursts of round shot scuttle across the heavens like luminous corpse-
vermin, at which the wounded thousands recommence to groan as if in adoration

              O, sir!

    No, that's not the countersign!

    Union or death,

and the bluish-white faces

          O, sir!

    Where's your regiment?

          Longstreet must have taken the wrong road, so when
          we attack—

          O, sir!

    I said where's your regiment?

    They, they—

          No, that one's dead.

Miles, is that their railroad line?

Another half mile yet, general. Now, after that lone tree it may get dangerous.
Our boys should have challenged us right here. They might be done for . . .

    I said where's your regiment?

          He maketh me to lie down in

              rotting guts

          I shall not want. And deliver me from

          O, sir!

And around this oak grove, general. There may be a torpedo on the lefthand side.
All right.

        Do you feel all right?

          O, sir!

        all right, and deliver me from

          night,

              illuminated by helpful Miles, who possesses
              the face of a surgeon or perhaps a jurist:
              high, delicate forehead and twin-horned
              moustache.

    I feel fine now.

    Good. You're going home.

  Soldier, where's your regiment?

          Kind sir, come to me—

the creakings of the stretchers

          O, sir! Kind sir!

Just a moment, Miles. Let me see what can be done for that poor fellow.
He keeps calling to us—
General, we're in danger of being captured.
>   *Please, sir—*
Then we'll keep a lookout, won't we?
Please, sir—
Just as you like, general.
What regiment do you belong to?

>   *The Fifth Mississippi.*

>   Lantern across the Secessionist's face
>   and the fizzing whisper of gunpowder somewhere beyond the dark
>   trees
>   and
>   What do you want?
>   *O! O, kind sir, I'm cold—*
>   General, shall we continue on?
>   *O, sir, I'm cold—*
>   You have a good warm blanket over you
>   —as pale as Lizzie's forehead
>   *Cold! O, sir! O! O, I'm so cold—*
Once at West Point after he had taught his final mathematics classes of the
morning he was taking a walk with Lizzie when the nanny came running: O,
general, o, missus, your poor little lamb . . . and when they had rushed back they
found that Gracie had choked on one of her brother's marbles and lay apparently
dead; the corner of her mouth was clotted with blood and
>   You have a blanket on you, soldier.
*Yes, sir, I, yes, sir, some kind gentleman from Massachusetts gave, gave me his
blanket, but, sir, I'm cold—*
He tickled the marble out of the child's throat, at which she opened her bright
eyes and
>   and
>   and the enemy boy's blue and gasping face
>   . . . *Cold, sir!*
>   and Miles standing silent, holding their horses
and since there was nothing to do for him, they left him to die beneath his Union
blanket.

2

By God, Wood, you're looking fit! What can I do for you?

Captain Pollock, sir, the general wants your Morning Report.

Sure. Here it is. I've even signed it.

Thank you, sir. How's the company getting along?

We all miss you, my boy. But now you're too high and mighty for us—

Never, captain! And I miss you all as well. You've been good to me—

Now you're gone, it's no joke having to write these d——d reports. You know what? It's this fucking red tape that keeps us from getting Mr. Joe. That's what I say. Do you agree or not?

Well, sir, since when was the Army anything but lumbering?

Lumbering, eh? I like that! Now, Wood, come into my tent for a moment. Have a smoke. What's your view of this campaign?

I'd say Joseph's leading us a good chase—

Whose fault is that, by God?

Sir, I've heard it said that there's a theory of war which will forestall the imputation of blame to those who do not deserve it, because we've sure marched awfully hard—

I can d——d well guess who told you that theory. And you know what? He's the first professor I have had to follow and I hope he may be the last, God——n him! He spreads out his pickets and flankers all over the line of march, which delays operations, and every time we got close enough to launch an assault, he holds us back. Captain Jocelyn's of the same mind. You know what I think? To get right down to it, Wood, Howard's *yellow.*

Captain Pollock, I've got to be getting back to headquarters. I'm happy to see you again, sir; you'll always be my friend . . .

3

Here's my report, lieutenant, and please apologize to the general for me.

I'll tell him, doctor.

Was he much displeased?

I don't believe so. I told him you had some difficult cases.

Thank you! Lieutenant Wood, you're a brick!

Happy to help.

I must say, I'm beginning to admire Joseph's pluck. After all his battles and losses, to keep going like this, he almost deserves to escape into the British Possessions.

And what do the men say?

Mostly they're not as favorably disposed to the reds as you are.

As I am?

Come, lieutenant, everyone knows—

After all, doctor, no matter where our sympathies lie, the Government must carry its point. Excuse me now; I'll bring your report to the general.

4

General, you sent for me?

Happy returns, Captain Pollock.

Sir, that's mighty kind—

Your fifty-eighth, is it?

Yessir. Thanks for noticing.

You're very brave and cheerful, captain. Don't think I haven't noticed your energy. And I know very well you'd like to dash ahead with Company "D" and finish Joseph. I appreciate your zeal. That's all.

5

Barefoot like a Seminole woman, Blackie straggles head down, not so far behind as to be punished by Captain Trimble. (Doc will rescue him if possible.) His feet now swaddled in bloody burlap, he marches on and on, so that our Government will be able someday to bring Mr. Joe to justice. At Lapwai he used to be a file closer at a parade. Now he can scarcely keep in the ranks. General, shall we continue on? *Cold, sir!* My heart is good; my heart is good. I am telling you three times: My heart is good. My tongue is straight,

as Chapman and the general joyously plumb the inexhaustible subject of Kentucky blood-horses, after which Chapman canters to the vanguard wondering who is looking after his ranch (burned by Mr. Joe), how much trouble his Umatilla ex-wife has made, and whether his friend Major Shearer is running Mount Idaho yet

(Wilkinson, I like to think of you as a sartorial man.

Thank you, general.

You see, Grace wants me to consider going to Newberg's for custom shirts for the boys; she says it would be cheaper than making them ourselves, although I doubt it)—

while the general rides rearward past the mule wagons to inquire:

O, are you getting back trouble, Mason? I've heard that it commonly afflicts plump men like you. It's never troubled me, although I thought it might after I lost my arm, because compensation with the other arm must twist the spine slightly over time. Now, my brother has never put on weight, so that can hardly be the only factor. He rode a horse all through the Secession War, as you may remember; I'm extremely proud of Charley boy. Well, after the Government closed down the Freedmen's Bureau, he joined the

American Missionary Association, as I probably should have done instead of staying in the Army. And right about then his back began to trouble him. Charley boy would have sworn by Electric Oil, if he were a swearing man; it did wonders for his back! Now they don't seem to vend it anymore. Have you tried it?

No, sir.

Too soon dawn's yellow sky fades to blue

>(Wood, who is not very tired, half-smiling to remember how he used to throw pebbles at Nanny's window to stir her up for an early morning horseback ride);

that way of light has closed; while to the south brood a few fine young clouds. The sun, cooler and whiter than yesterday, expresses no interest in the cool air which tingles our noses; now the eastern gold has become white cloud; the bluffs' shadows remain, but on the flats another longish day has opened; soon the box elders will shed their leaves. Beautifully and almost automatically we move out; we march all day, Wilkinson still hoping that some benefit to our general will come out of this campaign. Patched once-blue uniforms define us. Would Lizzie and the children enjoy a reed parlor organ? I'd better wait until we relocate to the Vancouver Barracks. Our Bannocks scalp another old squaw; Buffalo Horn promises that she was already dead. Then up with the guidon; may our Sibley tents flower.

Guy, you're looking down in the mouth.

Sorry, father,

>the youth's expression suddenly recalling to him some quality pertaining to Lizzie's dark and cautious eyes. I hope he cannot see how greatly he moves my heart;

>>while four soldiers, steam rising up from their slouch hats, hunker over a dead horse, stretching its legs out, slicing back the hide, cutting through the spiderweblike shinings of the endodermis into the ribs and slicing out steaks.

Is something distressing you?

No, sir.

Remember, good nature is the best contribution anybody can make to society.

Yessir.

Sladen, how you holding up?

Very well indeed, general—

That's the spirit! And look how chipper our Mr. Chapman keeps himself! That man's a wonder, wouldn't you say?

Yessir,

>but where was that fucker when we were burying Theller at White Bird Cañon? I loathe all cowards without exception.

From the sagebrush not all the rosiness has bled. Buttes and bluffs remain in shadow, the grass glowing silver and gold. Coming up into the golden-green plains, we will be given quail and sunflowers.

What about you, Perry?

Well, general, we're coming into Cheyenne country. Never thought we'd ride so far—

What do you think of the Cheyennes?

I like them all right, because they're good to their horses.

Fine. Are you?

Just what do you mean, sir?

Diamond's faltering. He may fail you in a charge. I know you're fond of him, but if you can't fix him up, we'll have to shoot him. Now, Wood, is Captain Whipple field officer of the day again?

He sure is, general,

> and I hope that my conduct has been irreproachable to you and the whole Army, never mind how the Indians must see it; I do take pride in the patriotic evil I have done, because I entered into this work with trust and no understanding, and to abandon it would have disgraced me without benefitting Joseph, so I have done bravely if evilly and deserved your love, general, no matter whether you comprehend it.

All right,

> and are you likewise conning me sidelong, pitying or condemning me for a worn out relic? I suppose I do appear old
>> like frost-bearded Solomon Lothrop clutching his curvehandled cane, staring down into my eyes—had I been late for church?— while his equally ancient wife, Sarah, his cousin's daughter, whose dark dress went nearly up to her wrinkled neck, frowned into the sky, her hair decently concealed by a black bonnet:
>> they married, I believe, twenty years before I was born, and when Father explained that he had been the first postmaster in Leeds, I could hardly imagine any world before him; he must have been about the age I am now.

By the way, was Josiah Smith punished for dereliction of duty?

At Camas Meadows, sir?

That's right.

Yessir; he was flogged.

I don't recall that Trimble ever sent me word of it. And could you bring me all the consolidated Morning Reports?

All of them, general, or only Captain Whipple's?

Yes, all the books since we first went on the march against Joseph.

As quick as I can, sir.

Thank you, Wood. That'll keep you busy enough, I'm afraid. Now, Guy,
> whom I love too much,

could you come here a moment, please?

Yes, father, what am I to do?

I have a tricky commission for you. Go hunt up Captain Sladen. The service animals have been looking pretty seedy lately, and understandably so, after all this wild country we've been dragging through. But that doesn't excuse the responsible parties, especially now when we're running out of time to stop Joseph. We'd better study all forage and equipage requisitions, and if need be have a word with Bomus. But you understand that the responsible company commanders will resent it if you demand the reports in the wrong spirit.

Then what should I say, father?

Use your initiative, and then inform me how you handled the business. Go now. And where's Wilkinson when I need him? Fletch, have you seen the man?

He'll return momentarily, sir. He's—

Fine. Tell him to prepare an abstract of our casualty returns since White Bird Cañon. We'll want that in order when we turn in our final report.

Our final report, sir?

That's right. General Sherman will expect one as soon as we've whipped Joseph. Please see to it.

I understand, sir.

Fine country yonder.

Yessir.

I'd like to bring Lizzie and the children out here, so that they could enjoy themselves and put up some buffaloberry jelly . . .

6

Once upon a time, the general asked his son to define *discipline*, then answered himself as follows:

Nothing but *the spirit of self-sacrifice for the good of the community.*

In this frame of mind they creep on.

BESSIE'S BIRTHDAY
SEPTEMBER 19

1

*D*id you sleep well, father?

Form up!

Not bad. You were tossing in your blanket—

Sorry if I disturbed you, father.

You didn't.

I suppose Bessie's not awake yet.

She loves a birthday, that's for sure! And when it's her own—six years old already, O my LORD!— Guy, how well do you know her?

Well enough to call her an angel, father. She's the sweetest little sister anyone could have.

And a worry to her mother, because, as you may have noticed, she—

> *Roll call!*

right here beneath the morning star, which the Crows call *Sees the Ground.*

2

You know, Mason, I think the Crows connived in Joseph's escape.

From Yellow Stone, sir?

Yes. Didn't that prospector say that there were Crows with the Nez Perces who attacked him?

He surely did, sir.

That tribe's going to bear watching from now on, I'm afraid.

They don't seem formidable to me, sir. We'll take care of 'em when the time comes.

Right you are. What a world!

> —actually, a forbearing world, in which Wilkinson,
>> who wishes to re-inform his general that the manner in which Wood has lately been performing his duties leaves something to be desired, at least in spirit,
>> and who to Wood frequently appears as silly as some half-frozen soldier embracing a stovepipe,
>
> decides to bite his lip, at least for now, since his present concern is the smooth execution of the campaign, which promises finally, should a few more i's get dotted, to become somewhat beautiful and automatic,
>> O for rich milk, fresh butter, rich butter, buttermilk,
>> rich fresh milk butter, anything but this d——d pilot bread! And if Nanny were here, with a pink ribbon in her hair . . .
>>> *The bold dragoon he has no care*
>>>> except that Red O'Donnell has exhausted his stock of Dandy Jim tobacco for sale:
>>>> *Stable call!*
>>> —and Theller's blackened face haunting me and the general half-tightening his screws of insinuation and that nosy Wilkinson, whose deportment reminds me of a prairie dog standing full length behind its hole, and nancy-boy Wood and all the rest of them, but above all the general, who's got my balls in his hand; maybe Trimble's worse, especially after his disgrace at Camas

Meadows, for every time he reports to the general I can't help but wonder if that cocksucker's putting another spider in my dumpling so that when that Court of Inquiry convenes—

Lieutenant Bomus, I want fifty pairs of socks.

All right, captain; I'll need a requisition.

But as soothing as it would be to gaze on Nanny right now (I could look on her just once and then lay me down), Theller's squaw would signify equally well. After all these months I'm near about ready to meet the wandering eye of a heathen Chinee or a jaunty negress!

Now, Mason, how are they holding up?

Still strong to march, sir, and out for Joseph's blood

(Perry's dark deepset gaze like unto a Snake Indian's:

I'll grant that his horse has not yet delayed the column)

and pickets out,

Chapman gazing up at the summit of his dreams,

which are about real estate since it's too late to be a hide man no matter what Doc says

(he's just an old scoundrel; someday I just might teach him right from wrong);

and the breeze carries down chlorine stench of Captain Pollock's acqua-regia: he must already have gone gold prospecting again,

the coyotes singing as they did that night below our vantage-point, when they were feasting on Theller's command; I suppose they've dug them up again by now.

Very good. No more deserters?

Nowhere to desert to, sir!

Except to Joseph.

Ha, ha! You're a witty one, sir—

All right, Mason, I'll let you go now. Yes, Wilkinson, what is it?

General, last night I prepared this card, since—

Good LORD, you remember everything! Bessie's sixth birthday, yes; I recommended Lizzie to send to Saint Louis for one of those children's white coney capes, reduced to forty and fifty cents.

Yessir, I believe Mrs. FitzGerald was also interested, although by now she must have—

Really, Wilkinson, I'm touched by your attention to my family. I frequently feel closer to you than to many of the other officers.

Thank you, sir. Was it D. Crawford & Co.?

Of course, because Mrs. Sherman as I happen to know was very satisfied with the black lynx muff her husband ordered. All right. And here's a note to Bessie, not that she can read it, but her mother will be pleased. Send it to Fort Benton with the despatches, and GOD bless you!

Right away, general.

May I ask you something in confidence?

Yessir.

Are you acquainted with a Captain James Gray?

The steamboat man, sir? When Captain Wolf is otherwise—

Exactly. I have reason to think him interested in Grace.

I'll check him out when we get back, general. So far as I know there's nothing against him.

River men tend to drink.

Not necessarily, sir.

It's getting on time for Grace to make her own way in life. Who knows how long—

General, I'm betting on seeing you in the twentieth century.

Ha, ha! An old cripple like me! Well, GOD disposes.

Amen.

I do worry about Grace.

An adorable belle, sir, and worthy of a fine marriage.

She lacks her mother's talent for weaving, unfortunately. Tries to prove that storebought cloth is better. I fear she may be a disappointing wife in that regard . . .

O no, general. The ladies of my family have pretty much given up weaving.

Have they really? And what about your Sallie?

Well, yes, Sallie still weaves occasionally—

I thought as much! A fine girl. Anyhow, we can't stand against Progress,

> and the way we think about Joseph
> and dusk and mist like the smoke of a Parrott gun
> —but to-night will prove as velvet as Custer's trousers.

RIVER SEASON
SEPTEMBER 21–22

1

*D*awn bleeds orange upon the dark river, which only our best buffalo hunters have ever seen before; dark tree-hands grope at the yellow sky. The chin of the MOON is as round as Toohhoolhoolsote's. Now our women have caught and packed all the horses. They loose the lame ones, having sliced into one leg of each—another gift for Cut Arm the Moldy—

> as two fishes splash: *mokh!*

in this river called *O-pumohat Kyai-is-i-sak-ta*[*]

> (Looking-Glass, Lean Elk and White Bird know what
> that name means)

and Peopeo Tholekt gives his yellow stallion more strong Medicine
as Good Woman catches a trout with a forked stick, guts it, throws
it in her lodgefire's ashes: a treat for her husband,

> who finishes cropping Baldface's tail, then helps the wounded
> mount their horses

> (coyotes singing on our back trail)

while White Thunder, Wottolen, Swan Necklace and those other young men,
rubbing their swollen legs with infusions of the season's last tarragon, dip
Bluecoat canteens into the river, choose horses and ride away:

> now they are creeping behind like snakes to watch for Lice-Eaters, Crows
> (our newest enemies),

> Bostons, Bluecoats and crooked Butterfly Place enemies
> as one locust sings: *tekh!*

even as Toohhoolhoolsote's braves ride ahead to spy out Painted Arrows, Big
Bellies, Shinbones, Cutthroats and Walking Cutthroats
and Lean Elk rides up and down, shouting: *Hurry, hurry!* Do you wish to be killed
by Crows and then dragged behind a horse?

—and so our remaining People,

> families overseen by chiefs and warriors whose hearts are now as wide
> apart as the tips of an anxious deer's ears,

must again set forth,

> away from the MUSSELSHELL SISTERS and

northwest toward the Medicine Line

> (sorrowing as they go),

> Looking-Glass's heart singing:

> > *I am galloping down, galloping down*
> > > *(my dreams have floated down from the air);*
> > *They have thrown me down,*

and so we ride,

> Burning Coals on Lucky One (he still keeps most of his herd),
> John Dog low on a stolen Boston horse, resting his bleeding fore-
> head on the animal's neck as he rides,
> and all our women in their beargrass caps,

accompanying a creek whose name most have never before heard

> (Toohhoolhoolsote's People already many bends ahead)

as snowy mountains raise up their heads on the horizon
and the horses lower theirs, snortingly snapping up mouthfuls of dying grass,
our dogs running off to hunt for rodents, or else mincing along on sore paws.

---

[*]The Musselshell River.

Good Woman canters alongside her husband, passing him that fish nicely
roasted and leaf-wrapped; he smilingly whispers: Thank you, *síikstiwaa,*
> which she sees more than hears;
then turns her horse's head back to help Springtime and Sound Of Running
Feet drive Cut Arm's mules, in company with Cloudburst, who is looking ill,
> and the People keep riding
> > northwest, west, north and northwest with the creek-swerves,
> > > here where his father once rode with White Bird and Looking-
> > > Glass's father
> into the country called *O-to-kur-tuk-tai*
> > (a name understood by our oldest buffalo hunters, not by us;
> > > my father would certainly have known it:
> > > > twenty summers ago, he told me, one could kill
> > > > many hundred buffalo here),
> watching on all sides for new enemies and old
> > (Red Spy running secretly along the hilltops, longing for
> > other Bostons to shoot with exploding bullets),
> > > the mountains growing more slowly than sickness,
> > > > with the Medicine Line still farther beyond than death
> as Heinmot Tooyalakekt now rides alongside Ollokot,
> > this quickly smiling one who keeps quiet, in his own way
> > surely remembering their father
> > > (whose name we rarely mention, for fear of causing sad-
> > > ness and bad luck)
> > and his dear wife Fair Land,
> > > she who fed every guest,
> > and that spring in Wallowa when they stood him next to her
> > so that they were married
> > and danced the wedding dance,
> the elder brother growing likewise sadder within his heart (perhaps
> Ollokot can tell),
> for now is River Season, when steelhead salmon ascend our rivers
> back home
> > in Wallowa
> > > (last spring, when Fair Land bent down over Wallowa
> > > River to breathe in its breath and listen to its voice, it
> > > was she who met the first red salmon coming)
> and in this creek we see no salmon;
> nor do we hear the *kek-kek-kek* of the black-necked stilts; they have
> already flown away for winter;
> while the avocets have also gone; they gouge the mud with their
> long black beaks no more;

my brother is half-widowed, my wives weary and my daughters always cold.

2

Ollokot, my brother, show me your heart. I know not what to do.

Elder brother, you know very well that when our father lay dying, he told us to look to you. Lead us. You are my chief.

3

He rides up to White Bird, who smiles at him and says: In that draw there we killed a fine buffalo cow; she was almost snow-white,

and he sees that this tale is about his father.

White Bird, my dear brother, hear me! *The People must not divide their hearts.* Now with so many of our best men killed, we are growing weak. If we go in different ways, the Bostons will devour us one after another until we are finished.

Then you are content that Lean Elk is head-chief?

Lean Elk or you, either way I am satisfied. Now it is Looking-Glass who in his addled heart once more makes trouble. Speak to your young men! It is the young men who say yes or no. Advise them to follow whoever is head-chief . . .

Your words are good; I shall tell them even though they never listen.

4

Toohhoolhoolsote,

he who Dreams by himself,

flying up past the lodgepole pines and beyond red scree and silver scree to the crags, snow and eagle-caves,

now rides along the ridgetop, smoking kinnikinnick which he has made from the irregularly ovoid leaves of chipmunk apples. This is strange, for usually it is only Bostons who smoke as they ride.

Heinmot Tooyalakekt canters alongside him. The young men fall back.

Grinning with all his teeth, the bear-hearted chief repeats: The Bostons have taken my country but they will never pen me up.

Hear me, my dear brother. They will pen you up if they divide us. Are your young men satisfied to follow one head-chief?

Brother, you speak entirely without sense. Who is there to follow but Lean Elk or White Bird? They both say the same: We must ride to the Old Woman's Country. You have no experience, and Looking-Glass is broken in his heart. As for me, I refuse to lead these quarrellers.

If Cut Arm sends more killers—

Heinmot Tooyalakekt, you fear the Bostons too much! Every man must die. When he attacks again, we shall fight again. But he is helpless until his slaves bring him more mules and horses.

That may be so, but will your best men remain one-hearted until we are safe?

Am I then Cut Arm, to tell People what they must do?

5

Heinmot Tooyalakekt rides wearily back to Lean Elk, telling him what indeed he knows: The People have begun quarrelling, *pokát, pokát,*

to which news Lean Elk, whose exhausted eyes resemble those bright-hued poisonous mushrooms which always turn grey, replies: They can carry away my chieftainship whenever they like,

as the horses say: *Hinimí,*

and Heinmot Tooyalakekt replies: My dear brother, it was never in my heart to remove you, but to ask what we should now do.

What is there for me to do but what I am doing? And what can you do but keep thanking us all for nothing?

Lean Elk, hear me! Looking-Glass gives us no rest; you know his jealous heart; and now that we blame him for the loss of our best men, he hates himself. Day and night I keep warning the young men to follow you . . .

Warn them as you wish. When they tire of me, then they may have another chief,

at which Lean Elk knees his horse forward, the sun sparkling rather than glaring on the brass buttons of his trade vest.

6

In Looking-Glass's band the women ride more sadly than others,

because Cut Arm robbed them first, at Kamnaka,

even before our losses at Big Water and Ground Squirrel Place,

and ever since Looking-Glass has caused the People harm and grief, his wives and daughters live unspeakably ashamed,

but that brave woman named Arrowhead, who always rides with a wolfskin over her shoulders

(she who stopped to bandage Peopeo Tholekt's leg-wound after the Bluecoats attacked Kamnaka)

now says: My People, be cheerful! Soon we shall be free forever beyond the Medicine Line!

All the same. Looking-Glass, whom the Crows called friend, *Arrowhead* and *Lucky Man,* and once was nearly adopted into the Tobacco Society, continues silent,

dreading that this last place where we must now ride,

the Country of Redcoats and Cutthroats,

may be fatal,

like mistaking death camas for wild onion, which certain foolish or
desperate women have done in autumn, when only the bulbs remain
        (not even Old Wolf Woman could tell food from poison then);
so as he rides he pleases his heart by remembering a certain Crow woman
softening quills in her mouth,
      her hair parting painted crimson, her small hands quick and lovely;
then he Dreams his way back to Kamnaka, the riverine home which Cut
Arm once painted off for him
      (my heart once thought to sit in peace within this morsel of my
      country, but Boston dogs dragged me down),
and as his women watch him
      (how can this sad one smile as he rides?),
he remembers one summer day before he had more than one wife, when
he and his Crow friends came riding homeward after killing many Cutthroats, and left their horses down at the creek with the young boys and
clambered up the sandstone cliff to have a smoke in Two Eyes Place; from
below, these caves resembled two eyesockets in the rock, one of them
shallow, and the other, which they entered, opened into nostrils continuing back into the rock in smaller channels like guts; and here in the tan
coolness of the cave they sat gazing out at the river cañon and junipers
and pallid rimrock, a few small clouds coming over the beautiful land
where if he must give up his home he would have wished to dwell forever;
and as I, William the Blind, sit beside the river at Pompey's Pillar, I wonder how to know who Looking-Glass was; through my binoculars, the
stripe of a sandbar on the far side of the Yellow Stone becomes an ag-
glomeration of tan rocks sufficiently distinct to enumerate if I so wished,
and I can count the leaves of the chokecherries behind them, and nearly
distinguish the fruit; this might be the difference between my eyes and
Looking-Glass's, and my knowledge and his
as he now rides toward the Medicine Line,
  longing to kill a fat buffalo cow for the People,
  hoping for Crows and Bostons to kill
      (all his life he has proved himself,
         which becomes difficult once one fails),
      hating Cut Arm, Bluecoats and the Crows, but hating Lean Elk still more,
      since of all that Looking-Glass has lost
        (our future now as unbranched as the antlers of a half-grown deer),
      it is only what Lean Elk took from him that he may win back:
        this he loathes him for;
      and should he not regain it, he might well become some maggot-produc-
      ing thing like Cut Arm's heart.
Now he must give himself to the Cutthroats. They are cruel but do not lie. As
Sitting Bull has famously said, *the white men are all liars.*

Heinmot Tooyalakekt,
> the feebly crooked-hearted, who favors White Bird and Lean Elk,
>> pretending all the while that just as falling snow sometimes conceals the trail of a bleeding deer, so that the hunter cannot find it, so all that has fallen upon us now obscures our way:
>>> a chief must never so believe!
>> (Ollokot should be the Wallowa chief),

rides up alongside him to say: Looking-Glass, my brother, how is it with you?

You ask, so I shall tell you. The People are all fools. My women and daughters are sick; how much farther can they ride? Ollokot's son is weak; your baby daughter wastes away. The wounded ones are tortured as they ride. We must rest!

Thank you, my brother; I shall not contradict you . . .

Good, for in what I now say there is no error. Listen: I alone have crossed the Medicine Line! Even Toohhoolhoolsote has never gone there. If White Bird claims to have hunted there, he lies. He is jealous of me; he has no sense. Hear me, Heinmot Tooyalakekt: In the Old Woman's Country it is very cold. If the Cutthroats' hearts are poisoned against us, how far can we ride before we freeze to death? I am telling you three times: Before we go on, we must kill meat, doctor our horses and prepare the People. If not, all but the best men must die! What do you say now?

Looking-Glass, I am but one chief; I know not what to do.

7

So all day they ride on, and Heinmot Tooyalakekt keeps quiet because he has done all he can and will not further trouble the warriors and other chiefs
> (as his father used to say, *it is all talk, and nothing coming*),

they are riding, hungering, fearing and sorrowing as they go,
> lowering their buffalo horns on strings into the creek whenever they feel thirsty
>> (their hands and necks are cold),
>>> and when Redhead stumbles, nearly throwing Springtime, it is only Good Woman who comes to her,
>>>> receiving a smile like a death-grin,
> while Looking-Glass's wives keep singing softly into the horses' ears the song their husband taught them, the song that a Crow girl sings to her horse:
>> *Horse will help.*
>> *Horse has a WYAKIN.*

at which their horses walk a trifle more quickly;
> somewhere behind, a wounded woman is groaning

and Springtime wavers in the saddle.

8

Spying backward, cantering through coulees, picketing his horse and creeping up the twisting grassy grooves in the sagebrush until he has reached a broken outcropping from which he can peer down invisibly,

    or climbing up a steep ridge of rusty scree,

        watching across those wide shallow cañon lands

            (cool wind, and pale brown small prairie chickens in the rocks),

White Thunder can see far southward the dust of oncoming Lice-Eaters (after stealing our horses, the Crows have all ridden away) and a few dark dots of Bluecoats

        (from far away he can smell those *Americans* who stink as if they never clean themselves):

Cut Arm is farther behind than before! Poor fellow, he is no good for anything; he should go home to eat soup with his wife (may she cut off his head!)

        and, blowing on his numb hands, White Thunder circles down into the salt- or sand-caked flats of sagebrush and dying grass, where the land splits open, rockily grinning for many a crooked cañon, in case there might be other Bluecoats or Lice-Eaters advancing murderously,

            but there is only cool wind.

9

Thus the mountains enlarge, until dusk hides them as we ride on

        (Lean Elk shouting: *Hurry, you People! Do you want the* Americans *to get you?*)

while finally, when the old ones can go no more, we loose our horses, picket Cut Arm's mules and make camp

        (an easy thing without tipis and lodgepoles, our dried meat and pounded roots nearly gone),

            as Peopeo Tholekt sings softly over his yellow horse, who is now strong again

            and White Bird, who is fishing-skilled, goes down to the creek,

the women gathering rosehips to make the children stronger, then patching their ropes of horsehair

        (now that the sunflowers have completed themselves, they gather the seeds and pound them)

even as the young men wonder what is best:

        what if we are going round and round for nothing?

—the old men smoking kinnikinnick, with nothing to say

                as in a place apart, Toohhoolhoolsote makes a circlet of willow branches sleeved in crimson King George cloth and decorated with eagle feathers; perhaps it will help us;

and our dead sing the soft song of Tuk-le-kas's small bell
as Sound Of Running Feet, with three white necklace-loops about her short
throat, clasps her hands and stares into the fire
and White Bird has a toothache
while Springtime, having suckled her child and salved her husband's bleeding
packhorses, braids Good Woman's hair.

10

My dear husband, my heart wishes for Feathers Around The Neck to sing over
our daughter.
Star Doctor has cured many young children.
I am telling you three times!
Síikstiwaa, as you wish, so shall it be done,
and Heinmot Tooyalakekt pays the shaman two horses:
now he is carefully singing
as Good Woman, Sound Of Running Feet, Cloudburst and
Welweyas begin singing and tapping long sticks together,
he sucks away the baby's sickness through a rolled-up leaf and in-
censes her with herbs;
when she opens her eyes, her mother, believing that she already appears stronger,
smiles and silently weeps.

11

The young men are arguing with Ollokot. They know more than their chiefs.
Heinmot Tooyalakekt says: Now let this talk be finished,
and they stare, falling silent.
That night he goes in to Good Woman. She is making him stiff; she is pressing
him erect.

12

Now it is dawn. We cannot get warm (some children are weeping). Lean Elk is
already calling. With numb fingers the women pack the mules and horses. We ride
ever nearer to the Medicine Line, and a light hail strikes us with the clicking as of
a buffalo's dewclaws.
All day we ride,
finding buffalo droppings, but not fresh,
White Bird and Heinmot Tooyalakekt beating grouse out of the
sage, so that the women and children will have something to eat;
the old ones begin to speak against Lean Elk.

13

Looking-Glass has shot a browsing elk, and the People are glad,
    while Ollokot skins five minks
and the young men hope to kill more buffalo
    as Canada geese keep crying out of sight,
        because it is the season to ride home, away from the Buffalo Coun-
        try, riding, riding to the home we have no more;
our old women cannot stop shivering; they are digging up sagelily bulbs to eat
    as Heinmot Tooyalakekt sits on a stump, his face smooth, his cut's half-closed,
    with the slender pigtails which his wives have made for him falling straight
    and neat down his chest, while Springtime sews up a hole in his blanket;
        then some of the young men begin striking a tree with sticks, all in
        time, and singing as they strike:
            We are flying up!
    so that Toohhoolhoolsote, smiling, sings: *Death is in the light;*
then Good Woman spreads over Springtime's heart a yearling buffalo blanket, to
keep the baby warm.

It Certainly Is a Lovely Stream

September 20

1

*A*nd to the west, steep pale bluffs look down on the blue Musselshell. His army awaits the bugle, each man preparing coffee in his cup.

Well, general, it certainly is a lovely stream. And millions of buffaloberries to refresh us. They must be the best puckerers on earth—

Always the humorist, Redington. Now, where's our Mr. Joe?

At least as far away as Camp Lewis, sir. One of my Injuns is due back from Fort Sherman any hour now—

Fort Sherman's been decommissioned.

General, that's so. Major Reed bought the buildings, I've heard. He and his partner run a pretty exciting trading post out there. Lots of firewater—

Your Indian had better not ride in drunk, or he'll be punished. What's his name?

Do you suppose Mr. Joe likes firewater, general? Some of them Nez Perce bucks sure do. If Reed and Bowles let the taps flow freely, that might slow the enemy down a trifle.

I see your meaning. By the way, that's a fine buckskin you're riding.

One of the best buffalo-running horses in the world, general. My Crows cut it out of Joseph's herd.

They're extremely handsome Indians, by the way. Do you think they ride as skillfully as our Nez Perces?

O, about the same, general.

Redington, I asked for the name of your scout.

It's Bear Heart, general.

That will be all, thank you. My regards to Captain Fisher. Now, Wood, could you take a spot of dictation, please?

Yessir.

Dear Mrs. Glass, my condolences on the death of your brave son Samuel, who passed away on August 24th, 1877, from wounds sustained during a night attack by Nez Perce Indians at Camas Meadows, Idaho Territory, on August 20th, 1877. You may be sure that he received the best medical care available, so that when the end came he was not in great discomfort. I understand that Company "L" have taken up a collection in his honor. If there is anything I can do for you, please feel free to command me. Your family is in my prayers. Yours sincerely.

Got it, sir.

When shall we date it?

Shall I make it August thirtieth? Then she'll—

All right. Now we'd better look in on Sturgis. He doesn't seem capable of great exertions.

I think he's at the field hospital, sir.

Heartening his wounded, no doubt. Commendable. Well, then, let's visit him.

Right away, sir.

Well, Sturgis, how are you bearing up?

General, my men are all in, and my horses have hoof disease—

I'm sorry to hear it, colonel,

> pitying him in truth,

>> because on the fourth of February 1865, when I marched my army along the Augusta & Charleston Railroad, with the two-tongued Edisto River ahead, Sherman having commanded me to take Orangeburg, and we had to struggle through deep water, with our cartridge boxes tied around our necks, not one man fell out of the column; no one whatsoever complained of being all in,

>>> or have I forgotten?

>> I wonder why Lizzie wants to put up green curtains all of a sudden? We've never used that color before. And why on earth did that occur to me? O, I see, it's this wall of foliage trembling

>>> and this brisk breeze, almost chilly, the willows and

grasses thrashing even as the crowns of the pines up on
the bluffs remain nearly still.
Poor Sturgis—*all in:*
unfit for command,
but we have got to keep on fighting it out!
Yessir,
a wounded man closing his eyes.
After all, we've brought you five hundred pounds of beef! What else do you need?
You see, general—
Colonel, why are your bunch so run down? My troops have been marching
since June, and they're much ruddier . . .
Well, general, first our supply steamer sank, so we had to send all the way to
Bighorn Post—
Unlucky man! Tell me, didn't General Custer come through here in '73?
I believe so, sir, en route to Fort Abraham Lincoln.
I spied his old traces at Pompey's Pillar.
Yessir—
A very fine body of water, this. Such an enthusiastic sportsman—he must have
improved his time here. His brother was also a great huntsman, I remember. Well,
we'd better be up and after Joseph, or General Sherman will be after *us!*
Yessir,
as behind him a private lies on his side, his knee bandaged with a length
of red trade cloth (where did he get *that?*), while four other privates play
euchre, and a bandaged corporal sits mending a stirrup with deer sinew,
nodding and jerking,
like poor old Trimble whom I once supposed to be as solid as the
limestone blockhouse at Fort Hays.
He can't be very satisfied with us just now, Sturgis.
No, sir. General, I—
Despatch an explanation to Tongue River.
Yessir. I have one here—
All right. Now, on the map Tongue River looks to be less than three hundred
river miles from Fort Buford . . .
Yessir. Two hundred seventy-two miles by the Yellow Stone, and a hundred
seventy-five by wagon trail. You're considering resupply?
Yes. Joseph is now free to make a junction with Sitting Bull. They could wipe
out the entire garrison at Tongue River, as you must be aware. What will Colonel
Miles think of you now?
He'll be passing disappointed, sir.
Sturgis, look me in the eye. *Why* can't you pull your troops together?
If I'd ever demeaned myself like him, Rowland would have said: *O, Otis,
please do try again!* And Charley boy would—
General, I'll keep doing my best

there amidst the wilting whitish seedheads and the failing flowerheads with the glossy white spider-legs, there on the edge of that sunny thicket beside the Musselshell.

They'd better burnish their weapons. I'll inspect them before the move out.

Yessir,

> and Mr. Joe's dusted out for the British Possessions, I'll bet. My wounded can't even get a swig of cocaine. And this d——d Howard will drive us all the way to the line. He despises me, but I don't care. He's the nigger-loving asshole who got whipped at Chancellorsville,

>> and since I've been whipped more than he ever has, I've won the right to be honest about everything, and by GOD I don't have it in me to be as unctuous as Wood, Fletcher or Wilkinson, who dive for crumbs of divine grace brushed off the plate of their Christian General!

I want them shinier than a silver dollar, Sturgis.

Yessir.

That's all. Fletch, please take this note to Colonel Perry. Find out if Redington's Indian has ridden in. Send the officer of the day to me. And then see to your horse; he wants combing.

Yessir.

Doctor, have you examined that private over there?

Yes I have, general. I've done what I could for him.

All right.

Would it insult your profession if I asked you to do a bit of horse doctoring? Colonel Perry's much attached to his charger. *Diamond,* I believe he's called.

General, I tried. Only a month in pasture will heal that horse.

I see. That's all, doctor.

Where sunlight strikes the river, it goes a crystalline green. The general seats himself in a warm spot on the grassy bank, and before he knows it begins to lose himself in the tumulus-shaped reflections of the cottonwoods on the southern bank, which resemble images less than shrouds. They are brownish-red on the green water, which ripples over them. *No.* I won't get into a funk like Sturgis, GOD bless him! But my back hurts

> and Joseph

>> and General Sherman,

>>> Fletch brewing more coffee over the campfire,

>>>> Blackie in the willows, scrubbing out his underdrawers with a bar of soap,

>>>> Trimble cutting a scrap of white canvas into a patch

>>>> as Sergeant McCarthy sees to it with shouts, roars and kicks that the troopers of Com-

pany "D" are grooming their horses' coats
nearly to sunshine,
Mason and Sladen inspecting the bayonets, wagons, forges, in advance of their general:
Shit, here he comes! Yeah, yeah, I know. It
has to shine like a GoDd——ned silver dollar.
No, that ain't him. That's just his son,
the blacksmith fixing every broken shovelhead in the
tool wagon (must commend him),
Trimble now sewing that new patch onto
his sack coat,
our tame Nez Perces hanging back now that the Bannocks and Crows have ridden out, huddling behind the
general
(to tell you the truth, Blackie, the way they crowd
around, they remind me of the prairie dog vendors of Columbus, Nebraska),
and Joseph and Joseph and
sweet Lizzie:

My dear Wife:

*We are stopping just now on the bank of the Muscle Shell River, about 120 miles
east of Helena. The men seem tired, and express considerable disappointment that
once again Joseph has slipped through our hands. Really poor Sturgis has not fared
as well as he might, and it becomes ever clearer why Gen. Sherman has not seen fit
to promote him. But that of course must remain* entre nous. *I think you would
agree with me that the country hereabouts would be a most excellent place for a
pic-nic. A number of the men have started fishing just now, & in this lovely virgin
country I should be surprised if they didn't catch something to lay on top of their
hardbread. Do you remember how Guy used to carry Chauncey on his shoulders
all through the South Field to scare away the birds? There are quite a number of
winged creatures hereabouts; this morning we got screeched at by eagles on high
until we could scarcely think; all the same it was very amusing. Wood asks me to
remember him to you and everyone. To tell the truth, he seems discouraged—not
on his own account, of course, but the necessary loss of life on both sides has told
on his sensibilities. I don't know what will become of him. Meanwhile Guy proves
every day a finer and finer soldier who I am sure will never fail to make us proud.
He and I live comfortably together in our tent*

and in the tree- and rock-shadows, where the river goes opaque green,
and sometimes the wind-tortured grass bows down to touch it. How
tired I am!
General, do you need anything?
Doc's still got a few buttons in his bag. He might
sell you one.

No thank you, Wood. I'm writing Mrs. Howard just now.

Yessir. Please give my respects to her

who is very kind to me, whom I love, and who, however acquiescent to the fate which she had married, resists it by treating it as unreal, accordingly becoming unreal or at least inaccessible to others,

whatever happened between her and the general when they were alone being unimaginable

(for if I, William the Blind, may be permitted to insert something here, I would remark that Wood in his state of youth, which is to say his condition of desperate hope that the world is not as it is,

the idea of glory which eased that hot and anxious long ago evening at Norton's ranch (Theller yet unburied), now resembling one of Captain Fisher's souvenirs: a greasy Indian belt, probably from the shortness of it a squaw's, studded with brass and tin, bloodstained along the edge,

cannot bear to believe that there is neither more nor less between the Howards than he sees)

so that sometimes she seems to diminish into her children when it is only the general and me at dinner, the others timid nearly to silence, except of course for Guy, who would hate me if he took me seriously enough to know me but whom if the general and society were more honest the Howards would supplant with *me* as their best son

and if Nanny ever becomes like Mrs. Howard I will shoot Nanny or myself.

It now seems as if the campaign will soon be wound up one way or another. I have high hopes that we, or if need be, our old friend Colonel Miles, will prevent Joseph from crossing into the British Possessions, and then it will be over quickly. Miles, so I hear, has forted himself up in style at Tongue River, on the old Cheyenne hunting ground. I hope his wife is not too lonely there. At any rate, from Tongue River he might readily intercept Joseph, altho' I hesitated to call on him before now. General Sherman has expressed a bit of impatience, but I pray day and night to OUR FATHER *for a result which will be satisfactory to all of us,*

but that teamster standing waist-deep in the river, washing the putrid saddleblanket of his galled horse, how does he expect to dry it? He'd better have a spare, or his poor animal

unless, of course, it got killed at Cañon Creek, Mr. Joe being extremely

How is Mrs. Perry holding up? Please let her know that her husband excites every man's admiration by his energy & perseverance. And have you heard from Mrs. Theller since she removed to San Francisco?

I expect your green curtains will add cheer and elegance to the windows, espe-cially the big one in the parlor.

If you can do so without embarrassing Grace, see what you can find out about Captain Gray. Which church does he go to, and how regularly? Are his parents alive? Wilkinson has heard nothing against him.

Please pray for us and know that I remember you and everyone at home each night without fail,

for the Musselshell might be a lovely spot to stay forever, but it's not ex-actly home; therefore,

To horse,

drawing up the company line:

Prepare to mount.

Mount.

Advance,

riding and marching now beyond beginning and end,

Redington (wide-eyed, young, excited and handsome, with his slouch hat pulled low, his neckerchief loose, and cartridges march-ing all around his waist), hiding despatches in his flannel shirt, then waving good-bye as he rides out: *yip-yip-yip!*

now he has dwindled into dust;

Sladen's chocolate-colored horse limping and stumbling, then recovering on the broad trail,

Ad Chapman teasing our Bannocks, chasing them up the trail, pretend-ing to be merry, with his face tilted back, his hair thinning and his eyes narrowing, his moustache lengthening but not yet greying, ready to avenge any insult,

and a cottontail rabbit fleeing across the trail, nearly doglike;

Perry wild and watchful as his general rides past

(he's getting as grimy, grim and unkempt now as Crook always is in the saddle, but that can't improve him out of being a GoDd——d crippled-armed Christian milksop who's set his face against me,

or has he? How can I tell? He continues as mild with me as a tipple of Blackfoot rum, pretends to be my GoDd——d father,

As he rides along with his uncombed hair.

but it must be an act; at the Court of Inquiry

—inevitable as the screech of our wagon wheels—

he'll cover his GoDd——d Christian ass!

And will he make me shoot Diamond?),

west along the Musselshell, where pale yellow rock-pillars burst out above the steep grey scree,

the orderlies riding at regulation distance to the rear of their officers

(I pray we won't be called upon to corduroy this stream for the wagons);

and there's that villainous old soldier again (actually, he's only two years older than I). I wonder how many times his captain has hung him up by his thumbs? From Fort Laramie, he said, and

> *The bold dragoon he has no care*
> *As he rides along with his uncombed hair.*

Pete, I believe his name was,

> up in a tree, a dead Crow wrapped in buffalo robes,
> and sunlight on the river like the sweat shining on Lizzie's throat when she

No. It wasn't *Pete;* it was *Doc.* Why do I so dislike the look of him? After all, he's apparently indefatigable,

> although I imagine him to be one of those men who must have lived in a hole in the hillside, like a coyote, who can miss a deer at fifty paces, and whose attempts to emulate Indian pemmican end up crumbly and scorched,
> or is he as good a woodsman as Captain Fisher? He habitually appears angry, which in my experience is a sign of failure—

well, what if he's perfect in his way? Come to think of it, he reminds me of Ad Chapman, without whom the Indians might have surrendered at White Bird Cañon, turning in their ringleaders, coming peacefully on to the reservation:

> my heart is good, I am telling you three times—

although Mr. Chapman is an energetic sort of man who knows this country and our Indians and has made good his error.

> Arrow's teasing for a run! What about that gelding of yours?
> He's rarin' for a chase, general.
> Good man! Now where's Fletch?

And the Musselshell sinks deep and rocky-lipped into the dry ground, then continues, upstream or downstream, I'll never tell you, west through the steeper swales,

> then up onto the high plains of buffalo grass,
> Perry riding hard ahead of Company "F," not sparing Diamond; and the five brass eagle buttons still shine on his chest, as if he's just departed the energetic laundresses of Lapwai;
> Wood gazing sidelong at the faraway sunken blue eye-holes in the domino of Perry's face, then cantering past in search of Mason
> (who inquires: How would you rate the view, lieutenant?
> Rather somber, sir.
> O, nonsense! You've been reading too much of your poetry!);
> then, collecting Mason's report, Wood rides forward to deliver it,
> wondering whether sorrow's weight must inevitably increase as we age:

Look how sad the general is! And my mother . . . ! No, I won't allow myself to be sad with Nanny!

    —and then allows himself to grow homesick for all the steamboats running on the Columbia and the young ladies gathering at The Dalles to flirt,

—Perry swinging back to terrorize his stragglers (one of whom is as goiterous as a Snake Indian):

then comes the narrow dark-shining groove of Careless Creek, crossing the Musselshell at a near perpendicular,

  where the hunters turn to chase their prey into a weary wilderness of cañons.

2

Well, Doc, them Indians are getting to timber now,

    the sunset as white, yellow, blue, red and pure as the beadwork which frames certain Sioux saddleblankets,

        sounding "Retreat," lowering the flag.

Looks like it.

We gonna catch 'em? Doc, what do you say?

I say shut up,

        the river hissing like a dead horse getting kicked in his bloated belly;

           Buffalo Horn riding back into camp, his long braids flying behind him,

         autumn coming, almost here: the days still too hot, the nights verging on too cold:

           I'd give a good ten dollars for a buffalo overcoat like our Colonel Perry's got.

           Jackass, you never had ten dollars in your life.

                Unfortunately, general, I'd have to say our boys are no longer worth much.

                Don't worry. When I reorganized the Eleventh Corps after they gave way at Chancellorsville . . .

           And Sturgis's bunch say this whole valley was black with buffalo last time they rode here.

           No wonder the grass is eaten up.

        My Mama asks after you in her latest.

        O, thank you, Guy. A finehearted Christian lady! And how is she getting on?

        Pretty blue. But Grace keeps her entertained. I've got to say, my sister's got backbone.

        She sure does.

By the way, Wilkinson, have you heard from your Sallie?

O yes.

How long ago?

When the general brought the mail to Henry's Lake—

Then you're updated!

Sure—

And how is she?

As usual.

It's pretty damaging circumstances on him, I'd say.

When are you two tying the knot?

It all depends on Captain Trimble's testimony—

We haven't set a date. I don't want to interfere with my Indian service. Excuse me now, Guy,

whose relation to his father embarrasses more than offends Wilkinson, on account of its public awkwardness (specifically, its continuous and, at least so far as Wilkinson is concerned, strident denial of nepotism—a denial which can never be proved and which indeed can only sustain itself by making itself forgotten).

Bomus warns me that the commissary wagon's running low—

I'm sick of this.

Better than sitting in a rooming-house, paying out your last cent and no work on the horizon! When the Silver Panic started, I told myself I'd better run to the Army.

No, you're mistaken. It was "I" Company that carried away them officers' remains from Little Big Horn, because my brother-in-law—

Well, *I* say they buried all them officers right there except for Custer himself. That's what *I* been told. They was afraid of Sitting Bull by then; they'd had a fine fright—

Bet you a pair of boots you're wrong.

Lieutenant Bomus, I was sort of hopin' you'd oblige me with a new pair of boots. You see, the toes on these ones is mostly rotted off.

Sorry, Chapman. You'll have to make do like the rest of us.

But I got me a voucher right here.

That's no good. For the last three years, all vouchers from the Indian service must be dated. That rule comes straight from Washington, and I can't change it.

Well, that's not right. I'm a volunteer, and I'm the only white man around who can speak Nez Perce, so GODd——nit, lieutenant, you ought to show some consideration.

You heard me. Go over my head if you dare.

Why, I never knowed you was such an infamous tightwad!

I'll meet you anytime you require satisfaction, sir. Now get out of my face or you'll see what I can do.

    D——d skunk!

        Doc, that Ad Chapman wants a pair of boots.

        What's he got, kid? What's he got for me?

        I'll find out.

Pair of boots for seven dollars goes for—seven dollars. I don't bet that much,

    the moon rushing up high over the cañons and a north wind blowing.

        Now, the old grey flannel undershirt, Union cloth, we used to call it.

        Yessir.

            Watch out! There goes that sour Lieutenant Wilkinson, tattletaling to his master:

General, right after "Stable Call" I spied those two mule-drivers selling barefoot whiskey to the infantry.

That pair yonder?

O yes, general. Them. I've been—

Are you sure?

Positive, sir. And they're some of ours, from Lewiston. When Bomus put them under contract—

        See, I told you. That cocksucker Wilkinson does bear watching.

Count off six men and search both wagons. If you find liquor, arrest the sellers and lay them in irons. They'll forfeit all their pay, and then I'll see what else they deserve.

Yessir. It may inconvenience our march to-morrow—

But this is too much, especially after so many warnings and examples. Their professions cannot screen them from the punishment they deserve.

Yessir. Shall I inform Major Mason?

Of course. Perry, what is it now?

General, I know one of those muleteers pretty well. His name is Red O'Donnell. If you let me at him, and nobody present, I believe I can find out his confederates.

Why must there be nobody present?

Well, sir, because he knows me—

And why should you be known to a man like that? All right. You can have him out of jail for a half-hour, on your personal responsibility.

Yessir.

How's your company?

Blood-crazy, general, and well dug in for the night. No complaints—

Report to me before "Tattoo."

Yessir.

Perry, look me in the eye. I overlook what I need to, but I don't forgive lying disobedience. You say you know Mr. O'Donnell. Did you have any part in this?

No, sir,

> Diamond raising his ears as a teamster's halter swishes not far away.

Enough. What now, Captain Fisher?

General, my Indians confirm the Nez Perces have speeded up. If our Bannocks don't attack—

No. Where's Joseph to-night?

His forward bucks must be in sight of the Missouri.

Well, that doesn't signify, so long as we can seize his women and children. How long's his column?

Still a good five or seven miles, general, and the dead horses—

We've thinned down his herds.

Looks like we have, sir.

So don't be alarmist. Now, have you finally gained control over your Indians?

The point is, general, they keep teasing me to let them scalp some other reds.

If you don't keep Buffalo Horn reined in I'll have you punished. Do you understand me?

Sure do, general.

On your way out, find Old George and send him to me. Any news of Umatilla Jim?

Yeah, our Crows found him two miles south of Cañon Creek. Shot in the back.

Joseph, or your Bannocks?

Can't say, sir. Anyway, he was a deserter, right?

Was he scalped?

Afraid so, general.

That's all. Fletch, come here for a moment.

Yessir.

When I sent you to that livery stable in Lewiston last spring—

Yessir, for kerosene.

What was the sutler's name?

Red O'Donnell, sir, and with him another sullen fellow who declined to give his name. He kept out of the light, but I'd stake ten dollars that the other teamster whom Wilkinson apprehended—

But you found no proof that they were supplying Lapwai.

No, sir.

You're sure of this.

Yessir.

Among the drunkards did you see anybody you knew?

> Throw some dirt on that sink, private. It's a disgrace.
> Yessir.

Yes, sir.

Was it Colonel Perry?

No, sir. Lieutenant Theller was there, not far gone, and off duty, so I considered it not my business. Forgive me for not peaching on a brother officer. Now that he's dead . . .

Wilkinson would have informed me, Fletch.

Yessir.

And then I would have sent Theller to Lapwai instead of Bomus. You do recall that I sent Bomus for the mule teams?

Yessir.

Was Lieutenant Theller a habitual drunkard?

Sir, I never saw him so on duty.

Nor I. But you saw him so on more than that one occasion?

Yessir, once in Lewiston, in a certain tent—

Enough. Forgive me, Fletch, but please do look into your heart: Do you feel any responsibility for the disaster at White Bird Cañon?

> Why, them clouds is greyer than Sapolio soap! We got
> winter creeping up on us—

> > He told me our Bannocks are pooping out.
> > Sure you'll find some mighty fine whorehouses in
> > Cheyenne, maybe even with white gals.
> > I'd rather have good bread and butter.

General, in my opinion Lieutenant Theller was a brave and effective officer. They say he was never in his life thrown from a horse—

Perry informed me that the last sight of him he ever had was of a disoriented man who had lost control of himself.

I wasn't aware of that, sir.

You think my temperance is a mania, don't you?

No, sir. You have never said a word against General Sherman, who drinks heartily, so I hear—

Fletch, on your honor, is Perry a good officer?

He drives himself hard, sir. I've never seen him drink. The men are afraid of him. I suspect his home life is unhappy—

Well, poor Mrs. Perry is rather . . . Continue, Fletch.

Sir, he means to redeem himself for White Bird Cañon and Cottonwood. I'm sure he'd be crushed not to be in on the death.

There might be no death but a natural one, if Joseph escapes across the line! You understand that there must be no more errors in this campaign.

3

They're pretty tired, father.

I know. And Sturgis was good for nothing, I'm afraid. *Entre nous,* a disappointment, that officer!

He sure made it hard on us.

Is that a complaint, Guy?

No, sir.

All right. Then I'll overlook it.

4

Bide a minute, blacksmith. The prisoner's coming out with me, general's orders.

Yessir.

All right, you, get walking,

> with his hat aslant and his bandolier clanking, and the captive sweating, our detail of sink-diggers turning to look:

>> But Gibbon was at Second Manassas, and he swears that the Secceshes—

>> . . . sent out Fisher's Indians to make another scout—

>> Where's he taking Red?

>>> —a fascinating question also entertained by Trimble, who happens to be out his long wool socks,

>>> while Pollock, who should be sewing a bit of gunnysack down the seam of his trousers, is already hosting his bunch to sing the same old nigger songs in that Sibley tent,

>>>> which induces in the general a melancholy mem-

ory for which he momentarily lacks a caption:

a circle of negresses in calico dresses and
bonnets, sitting around their lunch-basket
in the dust *of the cotton field:*

o, of course, Edisto . . .

as Wood, hunched over that journal of his, looks
up at me in a way so reminiscent of the time I
caught Lizzie trying to remove her freckles with
buttermilk

—Chapman's sharply triangular face and bare forehead suddenly flashing (that feller sure don't miss nothing!)

Captain Fisher cleaning the upturned ends of his moustache as Redington keeps grinning away, his eyes shining,
and on the perimeter, our alert pickets half expecting Nez Perces, painted and feathered, to
come bursting out of the timber like a forest fire

—while James Reuben, Old George and Captain John,
the latter of whom somewhat reminds Wood of Uncle Phil,
our negro gardener back home

(as a boy I used to pull the miniature plow he made me),

sit smoking kinnikinnick, watching everything,

the wheel-spokes of the Gatlings silhouetted in the evening

and Wilkinson leans against the wagon, crossing his arms,

unable and certainly unwilling to deny Perry's weakness, complic-
ity, incompetence, cronyism, and, above all, untruthfulness

(Wilkinson, who is proud to have never uttered a lie ever
since he reached the age of discretion, now considers Ad
Chapman a necessary evil and therefore declines to influence
the general against him, simply because Chapman is Perry's
enemy, and Perry is *an unfit man*)

when the poor general, whose goodness Perry continues to abuse,
will not spare himself; has everyone forgotten that not much more
than a week ago he rode all night through freezing winds at the
head of fifty men to be in at the death should Sturgis succeed in
cornering Joseph

(which is to say hateful Mr. Joe, imbrued with blood)?

—as of course Sturgis *didn't*, and if I were a GODD——n
ing sort I would say (LORD forgive me), GODD——n
him!—

and while the rest of us got to wait for Cushing to crawl into Clark's
Valley, that one-armed old man forded the Yellow Stone as soon as
the sun came up and rode straight for Cañon Creek, as I know since
I of course was with him; I was at his, so to speak, right hand!

No, general, that can't be an Indian scalp. Know how you can tell?

No.

By the nits. If there's no vermin crawling in it, then it's not Injun. So our Bannocks are behaving themselves.

Well, then what is it?

Well, general, that I can't tell you.

Captain Fisher, I won't be made a fool of. You're going to be watched from now on. Now get out.

As Perry leads the prisoner away, a prairie falcon rushes overhead, his wings striped white and brown,

Wakesh nun pakilauitin
JEHOVAN'M yiyauki,

pickets on perimeter and the wheel-spokes of the Gatlings silhouetted in the twilight.

Praise your lucky star he was late with your irons. No, shut up and keep walking, doublequick. Here's a likely coulee,

and so they descend into a little cañon, where beneath three box elders some grand milkweeds, their sticky pods nearly ready to burst, strain up at the moon,

more or less as if Parnell and I were reliving our summer evenings on the trail ten years ago in Nevada Territory:

the Snake War, and glorious old General Crook

and Pi-Ute squaws fanning the chaff out of grass-seed that they used to mush up for their food; we put them all on the reservation.

Now they can't hear us. O'Donnell, what can I do for you?

I don't know, colonel.

Who pinched you?

Who else but Wilkinson? You know how he's always like some pushy little officer trying to draw a revolver for himself at Uncle Sam's expense—

Shut up. John Thomas wasn't carrying?

No, sir, he unloaded when he caught that look on Lieutenant Wilkinson's face—

O, how I know that look! Who's with you in this?

Colonel Perry, I—

I'm trying to do you a kindness. Now listen. The only way to get your ass out of this is to give up a name to the general. Ruin one to save the others. Do you want me to stash some barrels for you?

There ain't but one now.

Holding out on me, aren't you? Well,

grinning tall and terrifying,

I'd do the same in your shoes. Is Chapman with you?

O no.

Good, for he's a horse's ass. Keep him out. My advice is have John Thomas unload it somewhere, in case the general gets a bug up his ass and searches that wagon again. Now what name shall I turn in? Or do you want to take it all on your shoulders? Speak up, man; we have to go back.

Then, sir, let's pin it on that Mikey O'Malley of Calloway's, since that bunch is long gone—

Good. I'll get you out soon as I can. Here:

a heel of wormy hardbread.

Kindly done, colonel. They didn't feed me nothin.

Now let's doublequick to your irons. And be more careful around Wilkinson.

Thanks, colonel, and soon's we get back to Lewiston we'll have an entertainment like old times. Sure was a shame about the lieutenant—

Yes,

for those old days had been not half bad. When he and Theller used to ride down for cockfights at the livery stable in Lewiston, drinking barefoot whiskey and singing songs, they never hitched their horses out front, because who the fuck could guarantee that it wouldn't get back to Pruneface Mason or that d——d *Christian Soldier*? The only quality that this aforesaid jackass shared with Crook was teetotaling, which Perry and Theller refrained from holding against Crook since *he* otherwise had so much "sand," but which certainly made one more deficiency for which to hate Uh-Oh Howard, the Yellow-Hearted Nigger of Chancellorsville—not that they wasted breath on that fool when they sat at their ease with Red O'Donnell and that other mick sutler who went by John Thomas, a name unlikely to be legitimately possessed by any man who rolled his r's so; well, those were pleasant tipples, all right, the more so after a canter up the Lewiston Hill's tilted ocean of green and golden grass-waves, O, and spying round the whole world through their field-glasses, as happy as Presidents, or Senators at least—and then down that great hill, riding through the wind, the Clearwater and the Snake both twinkling below, every now and then the basalt showing through on the riverbanks, and the tents of the city as tiny ahead as painted squares on a Crow parfleche bag, and then that livery stable where last year's chromolitho explained: **OUR BOYS IN BLUE, WE GO FOR HAYES**—and it was true that both Perry and Theller had voted for him, not that he'd proved good for much. Red O'Donnell was a good man who scarcely watered down the whiskey, while that John Thomas kept his mouth shut and had a way with sick horses. And yes, Chapman was sometimes there. He was a mean one, a backstabbing opportunist, but at least no coward. Lots of men came there; even Tattle-Tale Trimble called once on Red O'Donnell and John Thomas, whose eyesockets were as sooty as the filth-blackened wheel-rims of their wagons, and who both paid attention when Perry revealed a certain thing which he had learned in Crook's army about Comanche women (secondhand, of course). There was a crib behind the harness room where a fellow could bring a woman if he hankered for more privacy than the joy tent offered, but Theller's squaw never came there where the madam's authority and protection could not reach, nor even to the dry goods tent to buy hairpins or candy, so brutally dangerous being the men of the town, and indeed this proved convenient to Theller and Perry since they could shop there for their wives without embarrassment; one afternoon they encountered Mrs. FitzGerald browsing for calico, and after that they made sure to fulfill their wives' errands first, and only then drop by the livery stable to liquor themselves up, enjoying themselves until it almost seemed that Lewiston had become once more the capital of Idaho; and if they could further avoid Lapwai without demerit they afterward sometimes slipped away, knowing that Red or else John Thomas would mind their horses, to the joy tent, which in fact had been new to Perry, who did not particularly hunger that way, until the first time he accompanied Theller, after which that Blackfoot squaw each time haunted him more, but mainly because she was Theller's (her other claim on his attention consisting in the question of which sad chain of stories had dragged her here from her old home up by the Medicine Line; had she been enslaved, married, traded or otherwise engaged?); in and of herself, although in face and form, to be sure, she appeared pert and smart enough, she meant nothing to Perry, since Delia Theller was the one he pined for. It consoled his fantasies that Theller was near about done with her anyway. But Delia, he knew full well, had long since distrusted him, however intermittently, smelling the whiskey on her husband's breath on those nights when the two soldier-comrades rode back late to Lapwai, and now outright condemned him for White Bird Cañon, so that when he now thought of her he grew as defeated as if she had actually caught him and Theller coming out of the joy tent. But Delia, twenty-three years old and no place to go

> (when Theller proposed she never looked back, since even being a military wife couldn't be as awful as niggering all day in a Massachusetts cotton mill where one gal can't even talk to another. She still had nightmares about the McKay stitching machine)

has told me that she was so grateful to get out of there, into the wild country

> (I'd pay a three-cent nickel for an empty bottle of her White Magnolia perfume
>
> or ten dollars hard money to be around her Cape Jassamine scent one more time)

and she must have been, as I was; I'll never forget the way red whiskey

seemed nearly black in that bar-tent where Theller and I used to go drinking, and the way that Blackfoot squaw glowed both red and black, not to
mention both together.

When she gets him reburied, I'll give him a closed oak wreath on a white
metal token. That won't hardly set me back.

GODD——n her; what did she lead me on for?

5

Wood, I have heard of an organization called the American Indian Aid Association, for the Protection and Civilization of the American Indian. You might
wish to turn your energies there. I believe they sometimes petition Congress for
a redress of wrongs committed against the red men . . .

Thanks, Fletch. Anyhow, I've turned over a new leaf. No more pointless mop-
ing from me.

Good man!

Has the general said anything?

So you'd ask me to peach on his confidence!

No, I'm sorry; forget it.

Look. You know who your friends are.

6

Perry, I hope you didn't hurt him.

No need, general.

Well?

Sir, he swore up and down he didn't carry any contraband until that Mikey
O'Malley from Calloway's bunch was with us just before Camas Meadows, and
when you caught him with the hooch, he knew it was no good to him, so he unloaded it on O'Donnell without asking any money for it, just so he'd be out of his
scrape. Of course O'Donnell said he'd turn over some share of the profit once he
got back to Lewiston, but that's—

Perry, was Lieutenant Theller a drunkard?

No, sir.

Did you and Theller ever ride together to O'Donnell's establishment to drink
hard spirits?

No, sir.

Wilkinson, bring Lieutenant Fletcher here. Yes, lieutenant. Please sit down.
Colonel Perry, I'd like you to repeat what you just told me.

Sir, Lieutenant Theller and I never drank together at Mr. O'Donnell's place.

On your honor?

Yessir.

Any comments, Lieutenant Fletcher?

No, sir.

Thank you, gentlemen. Wilkinson, see to this: Sean "Red" O'Donnell is to be dismissed from our service without pay. He'll remain in confinement until Lewiston. His mules and equipment will be kept by the Government. Tell Lieutenant Bomus to sign a chit for them. Find a soldier who can manage his wagon. After this campaign, Mr. O'Donnell may apply for relief from the Government, but he'd better not come to me. As for you, Colonel Perry, of course I accept your word as an officer. The case is closed.

What about the other prisoner, sir?

O, I'd forgotten. Yes; give him the same punishment. What's his name?

Frank Haley, sir.

Yes. Write him up. Now, Fletch, since Lieutenant Otis has lost half his artillery, he must not have enough to do. To-morrow at sunrise you and he are to ride back to Cushing's camp on a pair of Joseph's horses, get a wagon and team, and bring us all the beef you can, doublequick.

Yessir. Shall we shoot our horses on arrival?

Unless Cushing can use them. Now tell me what you think of this (Wood, unroll the map): If Miles marches rapidly from Tongue River to Carroll . . .

7

Good night, father.

Good night, son, and GOD bless you,

> smiling to remember those fine spring nights at Lapwai before Chief Joseph broke his parole, and o how we used to enjoy those occasions on Colonel Perry's porch, with Mrs. Perry bringing coffee and pie; usually Mrs. FitzGerald had also cooked up some treat, and Mrs. Theller (who, truth to tell, did not appear to be greatly loved by Mrs. Perry) never failed to make herself useful, scrubbing china and cutlery, dipping water out of the great barrel, kind Perry invariably prepared to aid her by carrying the heavy coffeepot, should her husband happen to be engaged in joke-telling with his comrades—interesting to see how "magnetic" she was! The officers could scarcely prevent themselves from watching her. After Theller was killed, Mrs. FitzGerald had remarked in the hearing of Wilkinson, who dutifully tattled to his general: Poor woman, hasn't her life already been sad enough?—and neither he nor Wilkinson could puzzle out what she could have meant,

> and then "Taps,"

> after which he glissades into a long bad dream in which he stands once more in the Senate, facing the fourth, fifth and sixth charges against him, relating to the fact that he was a stockholder of the company which furnished patent-brick to the Howard University—and then suddenly, inex-

plicably, his accusers all turn into negroes! He's the only white man there, and the negroes are accusing him:

> a weary old ex-slave, seated, lays left hand across right wrist, opens his knees, leans forward and stares, ever so slightly shaking his head. A young negress, probably his daughter, stands behind him, holding a baby against her heart, her wariness not yet converted to rage. Beside her stands a hulking negro, resting his arm on the old man's shoulder. They squint, or gaze in poleaxed wonder; I must be back in Edisto,

from which he's rescued by "Reveille" and the morning gun

> (Wood waking up happy, as he promised Fletch, longing ever more for each dawn, essaying not to care for the cause itself—
>
> his thoughts as tangled as the trees of Yellow Stone).

Roll call,

> and another cloudbank as dark as the case hardening on a Winchester 1866.

Well, Fisher, what news?

Joseph's pulling farther ahead, sir, and Buffalo Horn's in a rage—

I do expect you to manage your Indians. Is Redington giving satisfaction?

Yessir.

Have I ever told you that he's a brash young man?

First time I've heard it, sir.

Well, well. The nights are getting longer. Still not sunrise . . .

Any new Indian curios in your collection?

No, sir.

Now show me Joseph's position. Thanks, Fletch; unroll it there; that corner needs another bullet or it won't stay down in this breeze. Now.

General, the reds are strung out down along *here.*

So. From there to Colonel Miles . . .

Yessir, but that's as the crow flies, and Joseph—

And this is verified—

By Old George and Buffalo Horn both, general, and if *they* agree—

Thanks, captain; return to your duties. Fletch, I want this army *on the march* forty-five minutes. Go make that known.

Right away, sir,

> and so they move out,
>> left,
>>> left,
>>>> *left,*

over weary dry bluffs and sometimes down into cañons,

> their eyes dazzled by alkali
>> —buffalo left and right: fresh meat every night for every man!

—Blackie and Doc organizing their future in Wallowa (peaches, horses and gold; blood-red salmon and undying grass), as this moon sinks like a single silver tear,

the general riding straight and easy in his faded blue overall suit,

wishing to urinate, his arm-stump on fire and his hips grinding in the saddle,

a few more troopers certifiably unable to march on their bloody feet

(they can ride in the wagons),

another man febrile

and Trimble and Perry both slipping up, with even Wood now perhaps on the verge of descending a bad road:

(all this is what General Crook calls good and necessary, *working off the soft material,*

through sickness, death or desertion,

rain working through the worn spots in our infantry's long-ago-tarred rucksacks:

O, me! There must be kinder ways!),

while Careless Creek bisects the hot flat desert down on which gaze blue buttes not unlike those of Camas Meadows:

Well, Sladen, does this landscape remind you of anything?

The Arizona Territory, general—

Exactly! O, those prairie hens roasted over a sagebrush fire!

Yessir,

crawling and riding across the world's back, wishing for more bacon and salt and a rocking chair for Fidelia to nurse our baby when it comes and butter and sugar or even just a cup of nigger-heel molasses:

I sure could use a can of oysters.

I remember a real good oyster salon in Portland. It's called the Hard Case. One time I hitched my horse and went on in to drink a beer, so I saw this gal, real pretty little squaw, and in them days I was fleet with that Chinook jabber. Well, first thing I says to her, I told her—

Cut it out. We don't care where you stuck your prick once upon a time, or more likely didn't stick it.

Anyway, Doc was right there with another squaw, and when I drops my pants he looks over and says to me, he says: *Load with cartridges; load!*

—the blue mountain-horizon approaching, the country as callused as an old squaw's hand,

buffalo like black clouds lumbering in their own dust and flat red shards of desert pavement ringing beneath the horses' hooves.

Wilkinson, how are you holding up?

Couldn't be better, sir. From the instant I was born my parents car-

ried me from one revival meeting to another, so this is a comparative *pic-nic.*

Your father was an extremely captivating preacher, I understand.

Yessir, he was. Must have known a thousand hymns.

Well, he's in Heaven now, for a fact.

Yessir.

Entre nous, what's your prediction about Joseph?

We'll whip him for sure, general. I've been praying over it.

Your birthday's the fourteenth of next month, I think.

Good of you to remember, sir.

I suppose we'll be back in Portland by then, whatever happens.
You'll be forty-one?

Forty-two, general.

Well, well. Mrs. Howard and I must have you over for dinner,
and now as we continue north the land goes orange and olive, as interminable
as the necklace-loops of our Crow scouts

    (the northern mountains closer but still low upon the yellow grass of the
    buffalo plains)

because this continent goes forever and we will make our lovely and glorious United States of America reach forever

        (and we're going to get our Solid South no matter what
        card you nigger-loving Republicans plunk down),

O glory glory:

forever,

        Wood's thoughts as clear against his desires as the chocolate-
        brown of Sladen's horse against the silver sagebrush:

            I wish I could be as proud of anything as Chapman is of
            his grey;

        sad Trimble mentally flying all the way to home and across
        Lapwai's parade ground to the pallid arc of tipis along the
        creek:

            when I get back I'll see how it goes, and if they're deter-
            mined to blackball me I know where I can get a real fine
            Indian pony for thirty dollars and then

        —but he cannot even wrench his fantasies out of sight of the
        narrow-roofed whitewashed two-storey house where the
        FitzGeralds and the Perrys live

            (I remember that time on the porch when Mrs. Perry
            and Mrs. FitzGerald kept looking through that little
            book of Centennial pictures from last year, and then
            Mrs. Theller said something real nice to me; she said:
            Captain, you're such a *loyal* man . . .),

        and Wilkinson, regarding whose opinion of Theller's charac-

ter no less forceful a word than *outraged* will now do, counting that deceased officer lucky to be buried with grief and
honor, praying that through his death Theller might have
atoned for his filthy sins—and determined to verify Perry's
word of honor by interrogating Red O'Donnell himself

> (by the way, Wilkinson can barely cover up his utter
> scorn for Sturgis, who once again has dragged down the
> long-suffering general into discredit, *adeptly* and *mali-*
> *ciously*),

Pollock dreaming of gold nuggets on quartz ledges,
and I'll follow them all the way across the Medicine Line. What do I care if it goes
till winter? This is the rarest fun I ever had. The general likes me now! He won't
forget me. I'm a-gonna be famous. I might even be in the newspaper. D——d if I
won't snare a few of Mr. Joe's horses, and sample his harem (that Springtime's a
fetching young bitch), and all the while I'll let him know my opinion of him and
his stinking Dreaming reds. Not even Toohhoolhoolzote will talk back to me now.
If he don't get hanged for breaking his parole, it's the Indian Territory for sure!
And Mr. Joe's gonna dance from a rope, and all them bucks that did for Mrs.
Manuel and the others. Then I'll get my piece of Wallowa, if I don't find something
better. How much gold dust do those Nez Perces carry? Lew Wilmot always swore
that White Bird's bunch was sitting right on the mother lode; that's why they took
so sour when the miners came in. I'll bet me there's a vein of pure gold in White
Bird Cañon somewhere, maybe higher up the crick from my place. I know how to
put a bug in White Bird's ear until he tells me where it is! If that don't pan out, at
least I'll put in for a higher daily rate at Lapwai. I'm gonna be somebody now. Ain't
nobody gonna talk down to me no more, not even that bitch I kicked back to the
reservation. Hope her and her five brats all die from the cholery. Wonder where
they sell them blankets infected with smallpox? I'll get her that for our anniversary. And Lieutenant Bomus is on my list; I'll do him dirt. And Lieutenant Wood,
and that snotty Lieutenant Wilkinson who'd pray me into hell just because I've
forted up with a few squaws, and all them weaseling interpreters back at Lapwai
who've tried to crowd me out. I'll be doing the talking from here on. And maybe
someday I'll get silver spurs cheap from some greaser, I mean real solid silver, with
rowels like pointed stars, and once I stop having to sneak up on Indians I'll hook
on the grandest silver jinglebobs so all the fine squaws will know it's me coming,
me, Ad Chapman.

A Mighty Interesting Woman
I Have to Say
September 23

1

$\mathcal{A}$nd now the mountains shine greenish-orange in triangles at or near their peaks, their lower facets shadow-purple,

> our general as stiff and stern as Sherman himself, who could almost be the prow of a ship,

and to the west, a low blue horizon like frozen ocean is so beautiful that Perry feels tears

> and that first time I caught him in that tent in Lewiston he looked as shocked as some fool who's just got bit by a wild stallion, but then when I saw that squaw, a mighty interesting woman I have to say, nearly as haunting in her looks and ways as Delia, I understood the why of it, so I said, Theller, any man can get attacked by a stallion's teeth,
>> and, sir, that's why Colonel Miles is—
>> Why not Fort Buford? We've got five companies there.
>> That's so, general, but projecting Joseph's line of march—
>> I know, Wilkinson, I know!

and he said, I know, and I wish I could give her to you; I believe you and she could be near about as happy as when you and I go galloping down that Lewiston Hill, and if you were any other man I'd kill him, but since it's you
> O God
>> since it's you

and sunset stormclouds like Rees painting their faces black and red for a Scalp Dance:

> *Halt!*
>> as we plant our guidon,
>> tightly drawing in the wagons, whose off-white tops shine out from the sagebrush like stripes of morning sunlight on an Indian's forehead:
>>> *Fall out!*

and rain and lightning just for two dozen breaths,

then calm dusk,

> the general sitting outside the doorway of his Sibley tent, with a map on the folding table and Wilkinson across from him, both of them bowing over it,

Chapman oiling his forty-pound saddle

as Perry curiously and cautiously commences probing with a stick
in the tar bucket under what used to be Red O'Donnell's wagon

—no hidden jug there—

the other muleteers sitting sullenly in their spring seats,
turning away;

Redington (off duty until four a.m.) lighting a tiny grease lamp,
studying a newspaper borrowed from Lieutenant Wood;

Bomus receipting for eight more captured Indian ponies whose
backs are badly galled:

They sure do treat their animals rough!

—and just as in the rolling grasslands there can be cañons and gorge-
mazes almost invisible until you get right up to them, so comes twilight
and three white-necked antelope raise their heads on the plain.

2

A single thunderhead, very low above the grass, and a brown butte like a giant-
ess's comb, and sometimes the cool yellow light on the orange and olive-hued
hills, whose lower reaches remain muted (actually, the light is less than yellow, a
gentle, pallid glow which cannot dazzle the eyes), and Careless Creek's twisted
trees and shrubs, very green against the faded autumn sky, and white stripes of
autumn light on the reddish grass, and flocks of little brown partridges flying up
from under the horses' hooves just like grasshoppers,

but the grasshoppers are gone now as this summer ends in the smell of
grass and dust in the wind, the grassheads waving endlessly

(the yellow and purple prairie flowers have already died; the strawberries are all gone)—

these comprise the Stations of the Cross for our U.S. Army

of blistered, malnourished, doubting men,

whose march is beautiful and just about automatic:

Send more scouts to our left. There may be some hostile
countermove . . .

Yes, sir,

and Doc keeps hoping to glimpse ore as yellow as blanketflowers

(likewise Captain Pollock,

whose acquaintance Wood first gained from that ride so long ago
now across the Harney Desert to Fort Vancouver, before Joseph had
lost his country),

Perry riding high up on Diamond

(praise God he's still keeping up!),

staring at the Judith Mountains, weary, his face sunburned and his eyes stinging from dust but still unable to stop loving whatever the horizon may bring,

and Chapman, who never could wangle new boots out of Lieutenant Bomus, has now cut strips of fur and stretched them inside the moccasins his cast-away wife once made for him:

> he rides along singing,
>> while Captain Fisher heads for the horizon on his tired roan horse,

our general continuing hatefully active

> (excepting him, Doc, Chapman and Wilkinson, nobody hopes for action anymore),
>> our infantry stumbling like Bowery sailors who've drunk a pint too much of foul beer,

Redington singing out to Captain Fisher: This has got to be the best grass country on earth!

—Wood and Wilkinson solving all the problems of our great Republic:

> Wood, that's simply immoral. Next you'll be supporting trade unionists,

Captain Pollock chewing the fat with his officers every night in his Sibley tent, before they sing their happy nigger songs:

> No, Sturgis didn't see it for himself. Evidently he heard that Nowlan had found his son's shirt in the Indian village and there was a bullet hole in it.
> And Sitting Bull was the murderer?
> Could have been any of them. And maybe next week Joseph will swell his evil hosts.
> That won't happen.
> Why not?

I believe in Colonel Miles. He's a better general than Uh-Oh Howard, while Trimble (now almost tramplike in his patched-over-patches sack coat) blinks his sad eyes at dandelion galaxies or skeleton-seeds.

> Father, do you think they'll get away?
> Sooner or later, we're going to whip Joseph.
> What if he gets across the line?
> He won't.
> But he's—
> You know, Guy, about ten years ago, when General Sheridan led a winter campaign against some Indian renegades, he discovered that their ponies weren't good for much at that season. In the summer, when the grass grows thick on the plains, the Indians can outride us. We have to carry feed for our mules at least, and often for our horses. In the winter, we're still carrying feed, but the Indian ponies have hardly anything to graze on. Custer made use of this fact to achieve his famous victory at Washita.

But if he does cross—

Then our diplomats will have to lean on the British, and we'll ride home,

and then O to glide with Lizzie and all the children across the lawn's walkways at Saratoga Springs, approaching the domed portico where the source emerges

as we ride toward Judith Gap where a great lady with a purple diamond-head spreads her lavender skirts:

the mountain,

the nights growing as long and dark as cavalry rifles, silently exploding with stars.

RELATIVE TO ABSTRACT "N"
SEPTEMBER 27

1

*L*ieutenant Bomus, how are the animals?

They're managing, sir. Of course they're not what they were.

What about the new batch of Indian ponies?

Sir, I'd say that at least one-quarter are lame, but if they're not abused they'll come around. The rest are spirited enough creatures: very handsome Appaloosas in all colors. We caught them so fast, Joseph had no time to cut their tendons. An excellent addition to our transportation—

Have you entered them all onto Abstract "N"? That's captured property, as you certainly recall.

Right, sir. Well, not quite yet, I'm afraid. Ever since the condition of our infantry's shoes has become a priority—

Never turn in untimely paperwork, Bomus. The Army won't forgive that.

Excuse me, general. I'll attend to it within the hour.

This once, a delay might be just as well. Detail your squad and get it over with. We can't use them and we don't want Joseph to get them back.

Yessir. The ones we've kept have—

I know how it is, Bomus. You love horses, don't you?

Very much, sir.

I feel the same. But even the teamsters won't accept more service animals. O, but is there one that might suit Colonel Perry? He's pretty tall, you know.

There sure is, general. They're a beautiful lot!

He's to choose his pick. Then take his worn out animal and shoot it. Did I ever tell you about the Arabians I bred at West Point?

No, sir.

O, there was one bay who used to . . .

> a well-broken mare for Grace
>> (Bomus's breath-fog hanging in the air, and my sweaty collar threatening to become a ring of ice)
> and eight hundred captured Cheyenne ponies screaming when General Custer's men began to destroy them after the Battle of Washita,
>> some of them worth considerably more than twenty-five dollars each, Sturgis assured me,
> and the day I kept feeding apples to Charley boy's grey charger at Chancellorsville and he
> and the Sunday I whipped Guy for being cruel to his pony
>> (Lizzie peeping out the window in horror, as if I were murdering the boy:
>>> of all my memories this is one of the awfulest)
>>> *Wakesh nun pakilauitin*
>>> JEHOVAN'M *yiyauki—*

And then you can tot up what's left, and enter the balance of enemy animals acquired onto Abstract "N."

I'll see to it right away, sir.

Now, what's the state of our equipage?

Well, sir, that too is getting, I won't say perilous, but with winter coming on—

What's your greatest deficit?

As I mentioned, sir, the men's shoes. If we had an official inspection just now, many of them would be condemned.

It was the same in the Secession War. You served with General Hooker?

Very kind of you to remember, sir.

Well, I suppose that in a very few years the factory system of the United States will have whipped this problem once and for all. Meanwhile we're stuck in the present, aren't we?

Yessir. I spoke with Doctor Alexander, and he informed me that some of the men's feet—

Bomus, I'm aware that your duties are trying just now. Please be assured that no one blames you for the deterioration of our supplies and matériel. Now let's not start fearmongering.

Right, sir.

I consider you one of my best and most motivated officers.

Thank you, sir.

What I'm going to ask of you now is confidential. I want you, Bomus,
> smiling sweetly at the young man, while building this sentence as carefully as a Nez Perce decorates his horse's mane,

to project the effective decline of our transportation, subsistence, ordnance and equipage from now through the end of December, broken into biweekly intervals.

Yessir.

Don't give me that face! *Entre nous,* this campaign must end within a month, one way or another, unless Joseph doubles back on his tracks. But he could, you know. Have you read what the newspapers are calling him?

The Red Napoleon, sir.

That's right. But even Napoleon lost the war against General Winter, and he wasn't encumbered with squaws and children!

Yessir.

Prepare the worst reasonable case, but you'll need to justify it to me. No alarmism, do you hear?

Yessir. Am I to factor in encounters with hostiles, sir?

There'd better be, or I'll be mighty disappointed in this command!

Yessir.

Assume one battle on the order of Clearwater every two weeks. As Joseph's women and children continue to tire, we'll be striking them more readily, poor creatures . . .

Yessir.

Then calculate for each interval how many men we'll be compelled to muster out, in order to keep the remainder effective. I'm releasing Sandford's bunch to-morrow.

General, as the temperature falls we'll need to increase the rations.

Isn't that the concern of the Subsistence Department?

Yessir; please forgive me—

You care for our men like a father, Bomus. That's commendable,

> although you cannot yet envision the men on whose account we act, the longbearded American paladins back East who accept no excuses; soon they will found new dynasties out in this country, and they will never, ever say to us:

Thank you, sir.

I suspect that you and Doctor Alexander have been chatting most frequently.

How did you know, sir?

Well, well! Lay out your co-diagnosis.

They're on the cusp, general. Soon the meat will be freezing hard at night. The flour and coffee are nearly gone. Even those vegetable bricks they used to curse at Lapwai would—

But they do their duty, don't they? Speak to me straight, Bomus.

Well, some seem to be getting a little bit demoralized, sir.

Bomus, in this army we're Americans. That means we have no excuse, absolutely none, not to whip Joseph. Don't you agree?

Yessir.

I know how their hearts burn to give Joseph the finish, but they must be patient.

Yessir.

So the time may come for shorter rations. If so, I'll direct the officers to explain the necessity. In the meantime, we'll send out more hunting parties. Still plenty of buffalo in this country . . .

Yessir.

Short rations are not starvation rations. Consult with Doctor Alexander on this question if you like, but not in front of the men.

Yessir.

During the Secession War we sometimes lived quite contentedly on cornmeal.

Yessir.

Do you have another question?

Sir, in this calculation shall I suppose that we'll capture other unmaimed service animals from Joseph? He seems to be hemmorhaging horses nowadays . . .

His forces are in decline. So are ours. I'd like your report in two hours. That will be all. Fletch, I need you for a moment.

Yes, general, I'm ready.

By the way, how you are holding up?

Itching for a fight, sir.

That's the spirit! Now, right here in Trimble's report—where was it?

       as Joseph's horses begin to scream, the Springfields discharging
       almost thoughtfully.

2

General, we've struck a large trail of Indians up thataway.

Fine. Wood, how rapidly can we communicate with Colonel Miles at present?

General, in my best judgment—

Excuse me, father. This just came in from Colonel Miles.

Thanks. Where's the courier?

There are two of them, father, and they'll be here directly. They're pretty done in.

All right. Just a moment. Yes, it seems that Miles is making steady progress. A promising despatch entirely. Sladen, assemble all company commanders and higher.

Right away, general.

Which scouts are present?

Fisher and Redington have just arrived with Buffalo Horn, sir. I don't know how many of the other Bannocks are here. The Nez Perce scouts are absent, except for Captain George—

Fine. Summon Captain Fisher, but it's probably just as well to leave him responsible for informing the Indians as needed.

Yessir.

Father, Colonel Miles's couriers are outside now.

Get them a meal and a place to rest, and inform them we'll call on them as soon as they're needed—within half an hour, I should say.

Yessir.

Guy, could you come here a moment?

Yessir.

I thought you might be interested in this despatch from Colonel Miles. You see, he's a trueheart. *Do not let* <u>*anything*</u> *influence you to turn over the command to some one else, for you will soon drive them into submission, or out of the country. I know you are very tired and deserving of rest, but I am convinced you should see it out.*

What a loyal friend!

Yes he is. Could you take dictation, please?

To Colonel Miles, father?

You understand me. *Dear Miles, there is no one here to relieve me from command, and I am strong and well* . . . What is it now, Wood?

General,

> whose face is now sunk in whiskers up to his ears,
>
>> whose sad blue overall suit has now faded almost greyish-white
>
> and who as it may prove is no enigma after all, nothing but *himself,* in which case I have neither more nor less to learn from him than from the breath of sweetgrass in a squaw's mouth . . .

How can he be himself and not *vicious?* When GOD knows he's the best man I've ever known—the best! So how can my attempts at lovingkindness not cross swords with his, he being fundamentally good and even ashamed of his goodness, since he cannot but believe in

> the Army,
>
>> our Government,
>
>>> the United States
>
>>>> (as do I),

all three of which consider kindness as cowardice or worse whenever it gets in the way of success! O, I know how much Mrs. Howard has suffered for his sake, her mouth ever more bitter and angry a warning every time I see her, because she must once have believed in him without understanding and now she's getting tired—wife of a nigger lover!—which must be why Guy has grown up into such a squalid tinheart and Grace into the good daughter who exceeds all expectations of filial submission, so that I could never desire her, unlike Nanny who prefers to reign over everyone although she too must fade,

> and when I disappoint her, how will *she* stand up to it? (No question but Grace would be an easier wife!
>
>> —at least so long as I stay loyal to the Army);

and whom should I expect to suffer on my account when I am quite aware, thank you, of being immoral in my soul, which thank GOD the general cannot see? I who consort with squaws and seduce farmers' daughters make my unblinking peace with being his younger self whose tilt toward lonely righteousness he would open approve if he ever stopped being shaded from knowledge, because I formerly delighted in pleasing him at least as greatly (so I flatter myself) as Guy still does, while my understanding surpasses Guy's; hence my submission must be a finer thing:

> For instance, I comprehend as neither one of them ever will that our cause is, to put it fairly, *evil*, which is why my hands are more bloodstained than anyone's, even Gibbon's or Joseph's: We do not expect of the untutored heathen what we do of him who *knows*
>> of Sitka Khwan what I do of Nanny,
>
> never mind the heroine of *The Old-Fashioned Girl* by Mrs. Alcott
>> (and Mrs. Howard's thin, cruel mouth then, and her skirt grandly rounded like a Sibley tent, and her mother-love for me);
>
> and of Joseph what I at least pretend to of Rutherford B. Hayes;
>
> but I do now restlessly, methodically and desperately divert myself from that knowledge.
>
> LORD, may I return home to my ignorance, or, far better, be taught by You through the general that we are in the right

and I know that he is one of the best, yes, the best of all, infinitely better than I, braver and more decent. How could I ever tell him if I quit the Army? Why can I not be sustained of the LORD? Our Father Which Art in Heaven, hallowed be Thy name. Our Father Which Art in

> America,
>> even Fletch harbors gratitude for Your miraculous works. Why can't I feel relief?

Well, I'll stay in the Army until he dies, O GOD,

and never question him,

not until my day comes and I must show myself to be a murderer like the rest of them or else fall out of his esteem, unbefitting myself to receive his legacy

> (I'm nothing but a mimic).

Thank you, Wood. Now, gentlemen, as you might have noticed, autumn is coming on, and once winter settles in, our mobility will be compromised. We need to whip Joseph soon, or he'll escape into the British Possessions, where Sitting Bull's murderers and renegades will doubtless welcome him. We lack the authority to pursue fugitives beyond the borders of the United States. If we fail now, Joseph and Sitting Bull will be emboldened, and their coalition of hostile Indians will constitute a significant annoyance to our Government, and a threat to our citizens, perhaps for the rest of this century.

I know that all of you in my command have done your best effort throughout this campaign. I could not have asked more of you. Your men are footsore and your service animals approach exhaustion. The fact is, gentlemen, that Joseph has practiced remarkably sagacious generalship! Although he suffered a reverse at Big Hole, he eluded us then, and continues to do so now. Captain Fisher here has accomplished fine service in keeping track of the hostiles and harassing their rear.

He travels far more fluently than can we poor Army men with our wagons and ordnance. Captain, if I'm not putting you on the spot, would it be fair to characterize your feeling about our progress as one of exasperation?

Well, general, you said it.

All right. I have good news for you, captain, and for all you officers. As of to-day, we'll travel easier. We can't catch Joseph at the pace he is keeping, and we're no longer going to try. Instead, we'll make shorter marches so that the horses and mules can recover and the men can recruit their strength. Joseph has come to despise us. Our task will be to increase his contempt and complacency. Captain Fisher, up till now I've told you to practice reconnaissance in force. From to-day, I want your scouts to break contact the instant that they sight the enemy. Joseph's conclusion, I hope, will be that we're giving up the fight. It was when we lagged behind at Lo Lo that he gave his people a rest, allowing Colonel Gibbon to surprise him. If we repeat the exercise, Colonel Miles can catch him unawares on our side of the line. Unroll the map, Wilkinson. Joseph's up *here,* and you see our position. Questions, gentlemen?

You remember all them monte games we used to run at Gillem's Camp? A hundred dollars a card! Them days are a-comin' back now while we rest our feet. And Uh-Oh Howard won't even—

Good. Tell your subordinates what you think best. It's your responsibility to ensure that our plan not reach Joseph's ears by any channel. Doubtless you comprehend my meaning. Fisher, that goes especially for you. Gentlemen, that's all.

3

How soon can Miles be in position?

I don't know, sir.

I won't accept that answer. Consult with Chapman, Old George, Fisher, Redington, anyone who might have some notion of the country up yonder. I'll expect you in half an hour. Go now.

4

Once upon a time (he had already parted from his arm, although he still possessed but two pale stars on each dark band of his epaulettes), he happened to be riding along the rear of his deployed line in company with General Sherman, when the musket-rattle from the enemy began to swell; next came a cannonade; grapeshot severed branches overhead, and he remarked: General, there will be a battle soon.— I don't think so, his friend curtly replied, to which he answered: See, general, Logan has halted his advance!—but Sherman merely fixed his low-browed gaze on the enemy position (his greying beard and moustache lichening the stiffness of his face, his hair matted back), then tucked his hand into his breastcoat, pulled out another cigar, lit it and stuffed it into his mouth

(*John Brown's body lies a-molderin' in the grave,*

John Brown's body lies a-molderin' in the grave
       —a tune which in those days always somehow reminded Howard of the
       tapering-petaled pale orange trumpets of the Canada lily);
therefore, turning away from Sherman, he said: Captain, it's time to cover our front
with whatever logs and rails we can find, doublequick. That old field there offers plenty
of fencing.— I'll give the orders, general.— Thank you, captain. And bring three batteries forward.— Yes, sir.— Fine, Howard, said Sherman. I hardly think there'll be any
battle. But in case of need, Morgan's division will cover your right flank. Good afternoon to you.— And he went riding back to the center of our lines, not long before the
Battle of Ezra Church began:
       Hurrah! Hurrah!

Having just been promoted to command of the Army of the Tennessee in substitute for the dead McPherson, and therefore inclining to prove himself rather than
(as would be the case later, for instance in the Nez Perce War) resist challenge, he
felt more sad than insulted by Sherman's disbelief. He listened to the rebel yells of
the massed enemy, who were led by his own West Point classmate, Lieutenant General Stephen D. Lee. Closing his eyes, he called up Lee's face, which helped him to
consider how the man approached war. Lee was reckless by nature and sometimes
neglected his flanks.— So many men are the same! In fact, the more recklessness is
called for in life, not to say demanded, the more dangerous it becomes. Even General
Sherman loses a dice-throw sometimes.— As for General O. O. Howard, he drove
off the Secceshes, killing them by the hundreds and capturing five of their battle
flags. When it was all over he walked the line to congratulate his men, who showed
him considerable affection. His greatest pleasure of all, I suspect, consisted in writing an understated report of victory to General Sherman.

A decade and a half later, he has confirmed the value of this lesson, and learned
an adjacent one: Caution may well win the race, to be sure—but haste gets the
credit.— Well, LORD, let it be so,
    let them despise me for a sluggard, and despise my judgment, if only Miles can
    halt Joseph,
        the last battle already rising up out of time's earth.

THE FIRES

SEPTEMBER 28–30

*W*ell, Fisher, why the long face?
General, we've lost Joseph's trail.
Whatever do you mean, captain? Here we are in Judith Basin. The British frontier's

straight yonder. You know that's where the hostiles are heading. They've got nowhere else to go; they've got to ride to Sitting Bull, unless he cares to come to them. Frankly, I'm disappointed. Your Bannocks are out for blood, and that Cheyenne half-breed of yours will certainly take more scalps if I don't stop him. Redington would do anything for a thrill. So the morale of your scouts must be high. Therefore . . .

Yessir.

So?

General, when the wind changes you'll smell it. The prairie's afire. The tracks have burned away.

That's Lieutenant Doane's work, I'd expect. General Sheridan sent him to drive all the game away in honor of Joseph's arrival.

I see, sir.

Although it could be prairie lightning.

Yessir.

Wood, get me Major Mason.

Yessir.

Hello, Mason. How are you getting on?

Just about ready for a new horse, general.

We all are, except for the incredible Mr. Chapman. Even Arrow's faltering a bit. A fine charger, I must say. Well, Mason, Fisher here has missed the trail, on account of some fires ahead. What do you purpose?

General, I—

Well?

Sir, some of us have heard that General Sherman gave you secret instructions back at Henry's Lake. Could they possibly bear on this situation?

Major, my instructions are to pursue Joseph as far as possible, right up to the line if need be, and either defeat him or drive him out of the United States.

Then, sir, all we can do is our best.

My philosophy also. Captain Fisher, you're a master scout. When Joseph tried to outwit us back at Clark's Mountain—and did outwit Sturgis—you recovered his traces. I recognize how much you've done for this campaign.

Sir, I don't know what to say.

Just because we're not personal friends is no reason for me not to appreciate your efforts. Now, Fisher, we all depend on you. We no longer have a trail to follow. So be it. Lead us forward without a trail.

VII

Detached Pictures

September–October 1877

. . . at this late life I cannot strengthen my early stories with witnesses to show that I am telling only truth . . .

TWO MOONS, 1909

You can only get suggestive glimpses of the past; for the fullest memory only yields detached pictures, leaving the blanks between them for the imagination or other memories to fill.

BRIGADIER GENERAL OLIVER OTIS HOWARD, U.S.A., 1881

A CALL AGAINST THE WIND
JUNE 1–SEPTEMBER 30

1

*B*uffalo Horn repeats to Cut Arm: *I am telling the truth!*—but Cut Arm, who once hoped that our Bannocks were becoming attached to him, no longer pretends to significant faith in Buffalo Horn's sayings. Moreover, the discovery that Theller was a drunkard and a debauchee, and that Perry may for all his honor-sworn denials (which would have been believable—and preferable—without Wilkinson's uncalled for investigations) have taken part in the late lieutenant's unseemly doings calls into question the integrity not only of Perry but also of several subordinates; not to mention ever so many other persons, places and matters; for just as after promotion an officer's knowledge of the force he must employ grows almost instantaneously more complete, and his awareness of the enemy's force enlarges, while the risks he will soon adventure assert themselves no more as theories, but practical questions, so as the general rides ever closer to winter and the Medicine Line (lovingly, proudly amused at Wilkinson, who last year managed to "snag" one of the few knit undershirts remaining from the Secession War, right before the Army closed them out!),

> another nauseous breakfast gagged down in darkness, then "Boots and Saddles," the move out, two-note walking-music, foreheads aching in the wind, boot-nails pricking half-rotten feet at a hundred ten paces per minute under the eye of our hatefully tireless general, men's heads dangling down as if they were exhausted horses, our horses going lame,

>> even Doc now hunching forward as if his rucksack weighs him down, reaching out with both hands to exchange something with a muleteer

>> (pretty soon I'd better release Whipple's, Trimble's and Jocelyn's companies back to Lapwai),

> Redington for his part loving so much to be alone that if this d——d Indian war rolled on a century, that would be fine with him

>> (never mind the queasy terror of riding down into night cañons all alone, seeking what he dreads, this ultimately unavoidable horror has not yet embittered or otherwise coarsened him):

> he's got no pity for Mr. Joe, because Progress must shunt the Indian aside in order to develop; moreover, Progress is the direct result of his own prairie thrills,

the Judith Mountains so lavender-grey across the prairie, whose lavenders,
oranges, blues and yellows are even more grey,
our column long and loose like a Snake Indian's hair,
and his yearning for Lizzie completes itself, his son's faith in him grows grimmer,
if grander, while his own sorrow, I will not say despair or disillusionment, widens.

2

To a military mind, the Columbia gorge—wide, flat and soft between steep
rocks thickly grown with evergreens—leads almost irresistibly to considerations
of blockades, walls, forts, ambushes. Human passage through this section can be
controlled in a manner entirely impossible in the plains of the Buffalo Country.
While, being itself human, that mind may not be utterly insusceptible to the
black dolmen hard by Bridal Veil, especially if it imagines a ramble there someday
with Lizzie and the children to gather blackberries, it cannot but take prudential
note of that steep, dark forest wall where Starvation Creek comes down into the
river. In such a place, hostile Indians could accomplish murderous outrages
against our shipping. All the more reason to remove the Indians. And now near
The Dalles the golden grass begins to shag the lowest hill-pubises between river
and forest. Not until Hood River will patches of basalt and golden grass more
seriously assert themselves against the evergreens and aspens, but the military
mind already observes and records the impending change, which has certain consequences for pack mules (more fodder), Indian camps (easier to set them afire),
infantrymen (greater danger of rattlesnakes), and dozens of other gaming pieces,
after which we enter the dying grass:
Wallah-Wallah, Lewiston, Lapwai, White Bird Cañon,
> when they all looked at me, as if I were to blame for Perry's dereliction!
> Well, that scarcely touched me. I remember when the Assistant Adjutant
> General seized my safe in order to seek evidence that my service for the
> Freedmen's Bureau constituted embezzlement from the Government, at
> which Lizzie blushed—even she felt ashamed of me!—and then Sherman,
> bless him, praised me for being true to my post when I could have
> > *left—*
> > > *left—*
> > > > LEFT,
the Salmon River like bright metal on a new rifle, and Joseph's Indians flaunting
their red blankets with obscene pride and scorn,
> > —and reburying Perry's dead at White Bird Cañon; *long have they*
> > *pass'd—*
Norton's: the death of Rains with all his bunch, then the lonely fight of the Brave
Seventeen (poor Perry twice more disgraced),
the Clearwater

(where Perry fails again),
Kamiah, Weippe, Lo Lo, the Bitter Roots at a hundred ten paces to the minute,
Wilkinson only now beginning to worry about Wood

> *(Stand up for these, the wrong'd, the aggriev'd,*
> *In deepest pits of darkness found)*

Rawn's disgrace at Fort Fizzle, and the general and his picked bunch rushing ahead to reënforce Colonel Gibbon:

> Wood astonished even now to remember how we descended the Lo Lo Trail standing in our stirrups, hoping not to be dashed over our horses' heads
>
> > (a wonder that our general can manage so well—
> >
> > > and Sladen with one leg—
> > >
> > > > and how many times have we wondered all this before?):
> > > >
> > > > > Well, general, it sounds like a serious affair at Big Hole.
> > > > > Joseph's finish, no doubt.
> > > > > Yessir,

and then Big Hole,
Bannock City, Camas Meadows, Henry's Lake

> (memories of Lizzie shining like the well worn walnut grips of an old Colt Navy revolver,
> the cantles of our saddles cracking and wilting),

the pale turquoise cone-mountains of Yellow Stone, Clark's Mountain, Sturgis's failure at Clark's Fork River, the Yellow Stone River

> (all now transformed into detached pictures:
>
> > Now, Mitch Boyer, sir, there was a character! Died with Custer— real courageous for a Crow. Plump-cheeked and always smiling, and he wore two stuffed bluejays on his cap. Must have made a nice souvenir for our Sioux),

Cañon Creek

> (we certainly were in close pursuit, but d——d Sturgis . . .),

the Musselshell,
and now

> *The hope of final victory*
> *Within my bosom burning,*
> *Is mingling with sweet thoughts of thee*
> *And of my fond returning,*
>
> > so for Delia's sake, I swear to rescue Theller's bones from the flames of that yellow grass, and freight them to San Francisco, although if she can accomplish it by herself—
> >
> > > and forever d——n the general for putting down Diamond!

—dark buffalo lying down to browse on a swale,
> Guy posting up and down the column, helping Mason hunt down
> stragglers,
>> Trimble, Pollock and Jocelyn combining in low voices,
the general's longing for Lizzie even more lovely than the reddish-
orange paintbrush flowers in this virgin prairie
> and the yellow flowers of heartleaved arnica
> and the bluish-lavender flowers of horsemint surviving here
> and there in mild coulees
>> where Captain Fisher keeps finding old obsidian arrow-
>> heads for his collection
>>> (the sun as red as cuprous gold),
> our column marching on, its upraised rifles wavering with
> seeming purposefulness, like the legs of an overturned mil-
> lipede; they have learned to lift their feet as little as possible,
> and only certain officers sing anymore:
>> O, you s'pose *you're* in pain. Where were you back in '68?
>> What the hell do you mean, Doc?
>> Delaware Creek, Republican River, mid-September,
>> when we was besieged by Indians and our breastworks
>> was dead horses, and our food was horsemeat, which
>> was rotting to heaven, so we salted it with gunpowder,
>> which didn't improve the flavor none, and so there we
>> lay a-waitin' for relief from Fort Wallace, day after
>> GODD——d day. Until you can top that, *shut up,*
Perry's determination to run down Joseph and his Indians so complete as to resemble indifference or grief
> while the Plains nights keep chilling down
>> (even our hearty general must finally throw a sack coat
>> over his faded blue union suit)
and Wood canters ahead to take Captain Pollock's report,
Wilkinson, who like Chapman never gets tired, growing nearly cordial to
Wood again because the general has finally awakened himself to that
young man's failings, which goes again to show that Wilkinson's discreet
and moderate course of insinuations has finally told, thereby saving the
general from another bad association
> (in Wilkinson's summation, Mason should be watched, Wood side-
> lined, Sladen rewarded and retired, Trimble disgraced and de-
> moted, and Perry perhaps cashiered, but the only Christian thing
> to do is to labor, however thanklessly, to cover up their defects,
> except of course to the general)
and we gather in still more of Joseph's ponies:
> Now there's a real fighting horse.

O, I can handle him, lieutenant. See, when you're aiming to control
a vicious half-broke buckskin, and you've got him partway choked,
you don't let up until *he* does.

Well, if you can't break him in camp to-night, shoot him,

> the locusts silent,

>> Mason riding wearily alongside (I fear there is not much to be
>> done for his back pain),

>> Guy's hopes eternally off the ground, like a horse's hocks,
>> while Pollock,

>>> who, truth to tell, wishes to someday become as adept
>>> as Wilkinson at the Terpsichorean art,

>>> tries to get Company "D" to belt out just one more nigger song
>>> (Ad Chapman says: Come on now, captain, teach *me*
>>> the words!)

but Fletch, knowing that it will be difficult ever to put behind him
a certain conversation, and therefore trust the general as a friend,
finds himself feeling less rather than more sympathetic to Wood,
whose character we have all begun questioning; for by the principle
of magical contagion, a wise officer who foresees the possibility of
losing the affection of his superior (without which he can scarcely
be) guards himself against others with that taint: as soon as the
general used words each as heavy as a loaded Navy pistol to accuse
me for White Bird Cañon, or at least to invite me to blame myself
for not peaching on Perry, well, I lost a degree of interest in riding
and drudging for him: What do *I* care if we never catch Joseph?

> —and this same thought may well have occurred to our limp-
> ing infantry (whose faces have long since been blacker and
> greasier than the muleteers' chaps):

Captain Pollock, sir, this man he done his best, but the nails in his
shoes—

All right, soldier, rejoin the line. You there. Let's see your feet.
That's right. Good old Fort Leavenworth contractors—worse than
Mr. Joe and all his reds! What's your name?

Well, sir, they call me Blackie—

I'll let you ride in one of the wagons to-day. To-night go see Doctor
Alexander, and then come tell me what he says.

Thank you, sir.

Get a move on and find a wagon; don't hold up my GoDd——n column,

while Guy rides here and there in hopes of coördinating with Captain
Fisher

> (How are those two managing together?

> O, general, I should say middling well),

and Wood, his testicles swollen and aching because it's been so long

(in homage to this new country we're coming into, he has begun
dreaming of Cheyenne squaws—virgins, of course, wrapt in con-
cho belts of German silver:

O for a winsome one, wide-eyed, hanging her head, braided
and beaded, practically armored in her trade cloth dress with
its hairpipe and dentalia accoutrements! And then she),

defends feminine honor:

Matter of fact I seen her in Lewiston, buying two yards of calico.
Going to make herself a bright new dress, most likely, or maybe sell
it to some other gal that don't get out much, maybe too busy in that
tent with her legs spread—
O quit it.
What, are you sayin' you sweet on some lice-eating squaw? How
about it, Wood? Is that what you're sayin'? Maybe we don't want
you in our future.
She used to be Theller's gal.
Well, that's different!

Now there's a full-barrelled Indian pony! Thank you, Mr. Joe!
Don't shoot that one; I want him.
You can have him. The reds lamed him up,

—Wilkinson rubbing his sunburned nose

(although he would never admit it, even he has begun to long for a
double handful from that big glass butter jar back at Lapwai)

and Perry, walrus-bearded and formidable in his old style twelve-buttoned
overcoat, glowering as he rides this Appaloosa formerly belonging to Joseph and now supposedly compensating him for Diamond, who currently
feeds the buzzards, raises his field-glass

as we approach the Judiths:

rising swales growing green and a few sawtoothed ponds
flashing in the coulees,
and then cottonwoods and aspens, dark coolness of pines

(well, he can pray day and night until the bugler blows
"Payday," but he can't whip Mr. Joe!),

wrapping our blankets inside our overcoats as we
march a hundred ten paces to the minute,

the Judiths now fading into grey, with blue-green patches at crest
and hollow

(the usual disappointment attendant on nearing mountains);

and Fisher and Redington still trail-bewildered, together with all their Indians:

Now you've got it, d——n you, keep it

(Colonel Perry, did I hear profanity just now?
No, sir!)—

left—

    left,

until even Chapman wouldn't mind if right now
he could be riding his grey racer up Mount Idaho's wide main street, which is demarcated by
fences and steep-roofed houses, and instead of
continuing upward toward the cemetery knoll
where our innocent victims of Indian barbarity
await the resurrection, it might be pretty d——d
sweet to hitch the old grey to a post right here and
take a sip or two of barefoot whiskey with Major
Shearer, toasting the Brave Seventeen or even the
Lost Cause, why in shit's name should I care, then
running down Colonel Perry's cowardice at
White Bird Cañon and maybe reconnoitering
whichever Celestial beauties might presently be
in evidence in the back crib of the laundry, although if the Temperance killjoys get their way
we won't have a single pleasure
left,

up the wide windy swales, a few pools of
dark water, the Judiths falling away to the
left, and behind, some lost buffalo in a hollow—

LEFT.

3

Guy, I'd like to ask you something.

What is it, father?

Have you ever been ashamed of me?

Whatever do you mean?

I remember one evening long ago—o, in Washington it must have been—
coming home to your mother, who I'm afraid was wringing her hands, while Gracie was in tears because her schoolmates had called me a *nigger lover.* And you—

Please, father, how could I ever be anything but proud and grateful to be your
son?

Of course that's how I would have answered my father, whatever my feelings.

May I ask a question?

All right.

Well, what *were* your feelings about him? You never say much about Grandfather.

I must have told you any number of times about the Sunday he called me away
from the upper grain field to come and dress for church.

No, sir, you never told me.

I never did? You see, he almost never prayed, so in those days I saw no reason to, either. But that one Sunday he must have been touched by GOD. He wanted me with him, Guy—but I preferred to stay home, so I pretended not to hear him. We worked so hard on the farm; and for once I felt like running away, or . . . It was quite a blustery morning; I could barely hear his voice. But I did hear it. He called and called—

After all, you were only a child—

He sent Uncle Rowland to find me, but I was cunning, and poor Rowland was only seven. I crawled inside the haystack, where I fell asleep. When I woke up, all was quiet. Only the cold Maine wind, Guy; I do remember that. Much worse than this . . .

And Grandfather gave you a whipping?

No. They rode home early in the afternoon. I could hear the horses far away on the road. And then I heard him coughing, coughing! And your grandmother was weeping. While they were at church his lungs had hemorrhaged, and, I'm certain that the cause was overstrain from his calling and calling my name against the wind. He was never well again. Thirty-seven years now it's been. April thirtieth, 1840; that's when he passed on. I can't ask his forgiveness, so I ask yours—

Please don't, father!

I did the best I could. Well, son, we'll both be wise old soldiers by the end.

4

Well, Mason, it's time to prepare our quarterly return of deceased soldiers.

Here it is, general, as up to the minute as it can be, given that anything can happen up to the thirty-first.

A sad duty, isn't it?

Yessir. Mr. Joe's quite the widowmaker.

He's a very impressive Indian, wouldn't you say?

I'd like to get my hands on him, sir.

5

Chapman, what will you do after this campaign winds down?

Make money, general.

Recently my family and I heard an interesting sermon on the topic *Worship Not the GOLDEN CALF*. Have you reflected on your soul as well as your pocketbook?

Sure, general.

What was your conclusion?

General, that's a real poser.

6

Perry, will your men hold a little longer?

Sure, general,

> because *you're* the one who can go home, retire and play with your pet niggers. Sherman wants you out; you've got the golden fucking ticket. We're the ones who have to be here.

Wilkinson, is anything wrong?

No, sir.

How are you managing, Wood?

Just fine, sir. And of course you're looking as strong as ever.

Thank you.

Well, sir, the hostiles are still showing a lot of fight.

True enough.

General, how do you think they can keep it up? What's Joseph's secret?

You see, Wood, a tribe of Indians usually takes its character from the head-chief. If he loves them as a father should, then they follow and do as he says, and

> *The men will cheer and the boys will shout—*

7

Rain stinging their cheekbones like sand, they march on to save America:

> What's the matter, soldier?
>
> Well, captain, I'm a mite freezy.
>
> I don't want to hear that. Pull yourself together.
>
> Yessir.
>
> Let's see your feet.
>
> Yessir.
>
> JESUS! GODd——d weakling. I'm disgusted. Fall out, and go see Doctor Alexander.
>
> Thank you, Captain Perry.
>
> O, go to hell,
>
> > remembering that April night in '68 in the Malheur country when we made fifteen stream crossings and then stood perfectly still in the snow until near about midnight in order to attack the Pi-Utes by moonlight:
> >
> > We made "good" Indians out of twelve bucks and twenty papooses and squaws, then destroyed five thousand pounds of dried salmon in their campfire without any d——d weaklings getting a mite freezy
> >
> > > and I was young and had not yet gazed into Delia's face.

8

His breath is frosting the rubber blanket,

> the platinum brilliance of the moon and all its light first a joy, and then, because he cannot escape his numb shivering, inimical, as if not the cold but this fiendish light were to blame for his sleeplessness—how it dazzles his tired eyeballs! If only Nanny were on top of me, or, better yet
>
> > —but why better?—
>
> some hot and vigorous squaw who—
>
> > (or home with Nanny under a goosedown comforter, a fire on the hearth and
> >
> > > —but even in my visions she and I can't be alone anymore, given the way that Guy watches me all the time now, while even Fletch misdoubts me in his earnest sad stupidity! *D——n them!* What is it that I am called upon to do or refrain from doing? I cannot stop a single thing, and anyhow Joseph is evil, because Mrs. Osborne and Mrs. Manuel
> > >
> > > > [if Nanny were in his clutches I'd]
> >
> >)
>
> Why they don't make pockets for our overcoats, I'll never understand.
>
> That's because you don't understand nothing.
>
> The new issue have got a breast pocket. That's what I heard. I—
>
> Watch out. Here comes the Christian Fool,
>
> > happily plain and simple in his 1858 sack coat—
>
> What's that black bottle over there?
>
> Well, general—
>
> You're under arrest.

9

What's on your mind, soldier?

General, do you think we'll be spending Christmas at home?

We can certainly hope for that. The end doesn't seem very far off. In the meantime all we need to do is to carry out our duty patiently.

Yessir.

> Why's he staring up over our heads like that?
>
> Cut it out. Generals hear whispers better than anybody.

10

All right, Mason. Shall we release First Cavalry?

I'm afraid we'd better, sir. They're in bad shape, and our supplies—

I only required a yes or a no.

Sorry, general—

No, Mason, old friend, *I* am. Forgive me . . .

Of course, sir.

It's becoming a long campaign.

You said it, sir!

Then draw up the orders. They'll be relieved to get out of this mud—

Yessir. I'll tell Sandford's bunch—

Excuse me, general—

What do you need, Wood?

General, a rider is here. He says the Indians have attacked the depôt at Cow Island—

Lean Elk and the *Lucky Man*
September 21–27

1

*S*craping out the pale inner bark of pine trees to eat as if it were now winter's end, and chewing on the last dried buffalo meat
>(our present from those women-cowards the River Crows),
the People ride north in their tattering deerskins,
>Lean Elk's admonitions losing flavor like old camas bread
>>(he too has become one who is no longer eager to speak),
>>>the sky behind us black as baked camas bulbs (some People say that the Bluecoats have set this prairie fire, in order to drive the game away from us)
>>>>and the next butte silhouetted along with its pines: black jaw of tree-teeth;
>so that Looking-Glass,
>>who on the very summer before she was enslaved and sold to the *Americans,* as he went riding with his Crow friends to steal horses, saw from ambush and tried to kill Theller's squaw, because she was

BRITISH POSSESSIONS
UNITED STATES

Milk River
Bear's Paw
Fort Benton
Cow Island Depôt
Carroll
Missouri River
Fort Buford
Missouri River
Musselshell River
Cañon Creek
Yellow Stone River
Tongue River Cantonment
<COLONEL MILES>
Clark's Fork
Stinking Water
Little Big Horn
Tongue River
Powder River
Little Missouri River
Yellow Stone River

CUT ARM'S
LAST CHANCE
(September - October
1877)

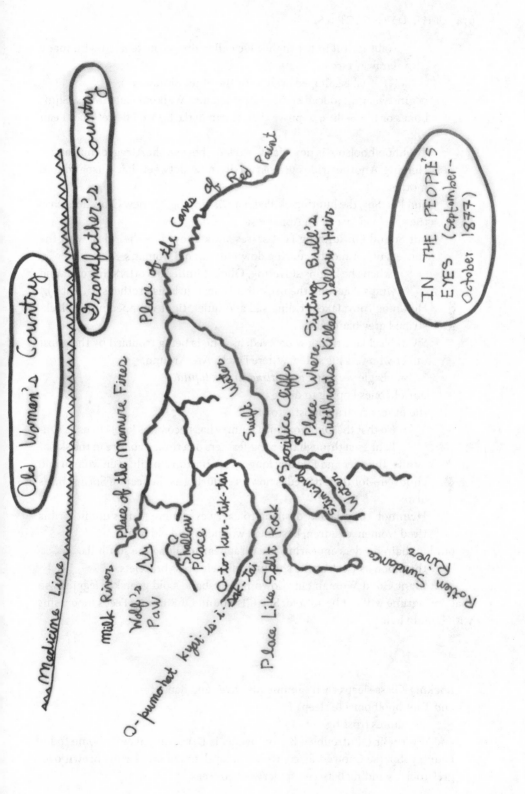

Old Woman's Country

Grandfather's Country

IN THE PEOPLE'S EYES (September – October 1877)

Medicine Line

Milk River

Place of the Manure Fires

Place of the Caves of Red Paint

Wolf's Paw

Shallow Place

Sweet Water

Sacrifice Cliffs

Place Where Sitting Bull's Cutthroats Killed Yellow Hairs

O-pumohet kyji-is-i-O-to-kun-tuk-tai Dak-Tai

Place Like Split Rock

Stinking Water

Rotten Sundance River

so beautiful in her night-blue calico dress constellated with many
faraway circles

(she galloped away with the other Shinbones),

begins wishing to lead some People against Walking Cutthroats, Shinbones or Big Bellies, to prove that he can make himself better than Lean
Elk;

Toohhoolhoolsote is now riding a deep-chested, shortlegged mustang,

Helping Another rides almost easily now between her husband and
mother

and Red Spy, the hunting-skilled man, is singing; his new Crow horse has
the speckled face of an Appaloosa;

but Sound Of Running Feet stares sunken-eyed as she rides, with the
corners of her mouth curving down like an old woman's

(when she begins shivering, Ollokot unties his otterskin collar and
wraps it around the neck of this dear girl, his brother's daughter),

Heinmot Tooyalakekt riding sad and quiet, tight-wrapped in his black-
striped grey blanket,

Swan Necklace riding wide-eyed, as if he is being troubled by the ghost
of her who was his sister, Where Ducks Are Around,

Strong Eagle yearning for *getting-drunk liquid*,

our old ones hoping to die,

the others desiring mostly to arrive

(so that the Old Woman's Country has become as lovely to us as sunlight seen through the wing-feathers of a turkey vulture in the sky),

White Thunder and Red Spy longing for Bostons to kill, even women and
children—for their hatred is now as enduring as the scar on Springtime's
arm;

Heinmot Tooyalakekt desiring to carry ever more things uphill for his
tired women, children, best men, wounded and old ones,

our longhaired riders appearing and disappearing along the soft hills,

the moon as weak as the shinings of their brass bracelets.

That night Good Woman cuts down her husband's old goatskin leggings so
that Springtime will not be so cold. She fills Sound Of Running Feet's moccasins
with buffalo hair.

2

Looking-Glass sleeps easily among his wives and daughters
and Toohhoolhoolsote sleeps,

his snores frosting out,

and White Bird, untroubled by toothache, is Dreaming his way home to his
country: Sparse-Snowed Place, whose steep-banked creek runs brown over
grey rocks, winding between spiderwebbed trees,

down the narrow gorge of trees between steep grassy walls exactly here
where we first prepared to kill Cut Arm's slaves,
then deep down into the hazy blue morning cañon of the Chinook
Salmon Water;
> to awake is to fly up into the high dry grass and bare rock above the
> treetops,
> up to the yellow-grass ridgetop with piney hollows (sky above and
> below);
> then finally it is all evergreens, mostly tall cones of spruce and pine
> crowded together with brownish-grey darkness between their
> branches
>> where spruce branches fan down like spiderwebs;
while to sleep is to catch our blood-red salmon;
and Strong Eagle now finds himself Dreaming of a halfnaked Painted Arrow
enemy on a pony,
> whose long loose hair, and the striped feather in it, has been pulled horizon-
> tal by the wind; his nipples are hard with cold, his eyes and mouth unmov-
> ing as he lifts his "Yellow Boy" Winchester and aims at Strong Eagle,
>> whose WYAKIN will not come;
and White Thunder is sleeping; so too his mother Swan Woman and his war-
friend Wottolen, beside the boy Black Eagle,
as Heinmot Tooyalakekt dozes anxiously beneath the blanket with Good Woman
> while Springtime lies apart, holding the baby, terrified to close her eyes.

3

In the dark of the moon, Swan Necklace catches a Crow boy among our horses,
and takes him to the chiefs, saying: Shall I kill him?
No, this child is but a little girl. Cut off her hair and send her home to the
Women Nation on a bad horse—
> *Áhaha!*
>> Girl, show us how you piss like a woman!
>> Let us ride her like a horse!
Crow bitch, hear me! Shall I put a baby in your belly? Go home and give birth
to human beings!
> *Áhaha!*

4

Before dawn,
> while *Kate* gathers yarrow for her husband to chew, since his toothache
> has come back,
>> and Ollokot and Cloudburst inhale each other,

Heinmot Tooyalakekt
      (he whom the Bostons call *Joseph*),
    waking up when Good Woman yawns and scratches her breasts,
tracks a buffalo by its breath-frost
      (discovering a small herd not far away:
          the dark animals on the snowy plain black and white like the bead-
          work on Fair Land's old cradleboard),
until like some walking cloud, this fine bull, darkly bearded, with his upturned
horn-crescents shining against the fur nearly as brightly as his huge eye-whites,
comes pawing toward him;
now as Heinmot Tooyalakekt raises the Winchester, the animal is lowering his
head and snorting;
he aims:
      Pim!
mud-clots stinging his face as the fleeing bull kicks them up;
now he is dead;
      then the young men kill two tender cows
          (any human being could do it; it is as easy as teasing Bluecoats un-
          til they shoot wild)
so that our women ride quickly to cut up the meat
      (Welweyas first and proud with her Wilson skinning knife),
and by sunrise
      (horses sneezing and shivering)
the People are smiling at the sizzling fat;
   Heinmot Tooyalakekt gives meat,
      seared grey outside and blood-red inside
   to each orphan and to all the old blind ones;
they eat until they feel warm, and strength and hope rise back up into their hearts;
then they feel sleepy,
   but Lean Elk is shouting: *Hurry, hurry!*
      even though Cut Arm's spies, slaves and murderers must surely be falling
      away;
         hence Looking-Glass,
            he who now well earns his name of *Wind-Wrapped*,
         begins murmuring to Peopeo Tholekt,
            whom he twice persuded to ride to Cut Arm's Bluecoats on
            that morning when they stole our country from us:
            Kamnaka, our Kamnaka—
My dear nephew, Lean Elk is not one of us
      (I am telling you three times),
     for he has closed his ears to the weeping of our children; and our
     oldest uncles waver on their horses,
        our grandmothers growing as fragile as pine moss;

soon we must cross yet another coldly boiling river before the Medicine Line; and on the other side of that river, trees withdraw themselves, so that new Enemy People will surely see us:
> the Painted Arrows
> and the Cutthroats (Sitting Bull's People)
>> —although it is to them that we must come hoping to
>> smoke the pipe—
> not to forget the Walking Cutthroats who have always killed
> us,

so that then we shall be riding and riding without rest. Speak to the
chiefs, my dear nephew! You all know that my heart is to do right
always. I am telling you, unless we soon rest now, our horses will be
no good, and our children will fall from the saddles.

But Peopeo Tholekt, holding tight the long ancient pipe which Looking-Glass
once gave him, replies mildly but with a closed heart to his chief,
> who has deceived us so many times,

and the other young men, who have become the ones to say yes and no, still prefer
Lean Elk; and will keep on in that way unless Looking-Glass stops being silent;
hence he now becomes one who cannot stop talking;
> so we laugh at him.

5

Leaving their fires, catching and packing their sore animals
> (another of Lean Elk's racehorses, a fine spotted stallion, must now be
> tendon-cut for Cut Arm),
>> having heard what has been said,
> this light snow already almost melted,

the People ride on north,
> toward *Ah-ki-ne-kun-scoo,* which means *Snow Hole*
>> (explains Looking-Glass the much-knowing one)

and through wet places where the baneberries grow up around their horses' necks:
> (baneberries like insect eyes, many-seeded, black-speckled, sometimes
> red, sometimes white),

riding through morning,
> Welweyas the half-woman travelling adoringly near her chief, so proud
> to wear the King George blanket he gave her
>> (he rides silently between his wives),
> Wounded Head seeking to turn away his thoughts from his dead boy,
> moisture sparkling on Toohhoolhoolsote's bone bead necklaces,
>> a horned lark flying restlessly,
> the meadow rue already bloomed and gone, the virgin's bower long bereft
> of its white flowers,

riding into afternoon,
>> the sun warming them almost like summer
>> but no more do the locusts sing *tekh-tekh-tekh!*
and now they are approaching Reese Fort.

6

Lean Elk says: Wait,
> although our best men long to burn and murder.
Who has met these Bostons?
—They are my friends, replies Looking-Glass; I am telling you three times!
> —and the other chiefs
>> (it is they who ought to decide these things)
> believe that this might even have been so,
but now all things are changed.

Peopeo Tholekt says: Hear me, Looking-Glass! You are my chief; it is on your account that I rode twice to the Bostons at Kamnaka; because you hid yourself like a woman, they shot me in my leg exactly here. Looking-Glass, I am telling you: A Boston's promise runs away like a river. It flies away like a strong wind.

Now Looking-Glass begins to make himself angry,
but Heinmot Tooyalakekt steps in between them to say: My dear brothers, we must not quarrel anymore
as Strong Eagle and some other best men conceal themselves in a coulee, quieting their horses
> (soon now we shall kill more Bostons),
>> all the People coming slowly on behind:
>>> the Wallowa People looking south toward the lavender dip between this world and its purple horizon
>>>> and the last prairie coneflowers and the wilting pink blossoms of gayfeather
>>> while White Bird's People look north, where a dark mountain hunches low over the grassland
>>>> (*Kate*'s piebald horse swishes his black tail, his white head low in the grass)
>>>>> and Good Woman has gathered peppermint and is boiling it so that White Thunder's old mother Swan Woman can steam away her headache;
>>>>>> beside them some child grimaces, his hand laid open by a bowstring through his carelessness;
>>>>> while Wounded Head's wife dismounts her horse without help
>>>>> and Looking-Glass's women are digging tough late yampah roots;

but the men who must now talk are riding toward a green line of cottonwoods by
the white-pebbled stream
> (Cottonwood Creek),
and for seven heartbeats they stand watching the log-and-mortar cabin of the
trading post
> and its Z-planked door,
>> which opens.

7

Unlatching the door, Bowles sees a rectangle of yellow light and silver-green trees,
> that sweet little creek with plenty of brown-green water in it even now
> when the cottonwood leaves are going yellow
>> and gulls begin to crowd the lakes
> and he sees swallows flittering suddenly up behind his cords of seasoning
> cottonwood logs:
>> Indian summer,
>>> with Indians in it . . .
my GOD, *here they come:* murderers, Nez Perces,
> men in grey-green stinking shirts of deerskin.
What can he do but invite them in? He wishes Reed were here.

8

Now the reds are squatting on his greasy dirt floor, beneath the three pillars
and the several ceiling beams. He is terrified of them, especially of Chief Joseph,
who burns women and children alive, more so yet of Toohhoolhoolzote, who lowers his head like an angry bull, but most of all of White Bird—the one who shot
George Cowan in the head at Yellow Stone. Which is which? Unfortunately, the
only one he knows for sure is Looking-Glass.
> If Reed were here . . . !
>> —but Reed, since business has scared itself away
>>> (Yellow Stone River buffalo at lump weight, four cents a pound),
>> has gone clambering up the wet mountain outcroppings to the north, search-
>> ing for nuggets in the pale rock but finding only bluish-black crystals, dream-
>> ing, hoping, his white horse peering out at him from under a dripping pine
>>> while Bowles lay hoping for a return visit from that Cheyenne
>>> squaw who was willing to do anything, I mean anything, to get
>>> another golden eagle button
—and now here are these killer reds with Looking-Glass,
> and behind them a deerskin robe, beaded and shelled, hangs limply off
> the wall
>> (Bowles got it from an Assiniboine for a pint of barefoot whiskey)

and Looking-Glass, who until now has demeaned himself like one who conceals the stick most excellently when he gambles (LORD, save me from his hateful Indian eyes!), now says: My brother, we mean you no harm. Have you flour, coffee, bacon or ammunition to sell?

—directing the half-breed Bunched Lightning to carry this into Boston speech
(words with the hollow irregularities of deer toe leg rattles),
so the latter says: *Give whiskey, hurry up quick!*

and just as at sunrise on a dusty morning a line of white will sometimes appear where the pallid blue mountains join the earth, running all along them, making a brighter horizon, so his WYAKIN's smile-gash now grins across the edge of the earth
—but Heinmot Tooyalakekt, who understands this word, grows angry, and says,
(his tone as sharp as the tip of a reed arrow)[*]
If one more time you fail to speak straight, I shall treat you as an enemy,
so this time Bunched Lightning does his best,
at which Bowles inquires: Are you sure you don't want whiskey? I've got a real good batch.

No whiskey, says Heinmot Tooyalakekt.

If you're Nez Perces I'm not supposed to sell you ammunition.

How much? says the half-breed. *We pay good real quick.*

So he sells them ammunition, only a pound or two, so that they won't kill him; then he sells them a sack of moldy flour;

and they vanish back into the thick brush along the creek.

9

Our buffalo hunters know what should now be done in these grey and white rainy days at summer's end
(yellow-clad swales going green again, the mountains almost hidden in cloud)
as Red Spy scouts backward for Cut Arm, looking down at the low green buttes whose tops touch the bluish-white stormclouds,
gathering the last leaves of kinnikinnick to make tobacco, hunting for sego lily bulbs to eat, craving to eat marrow or birds' eggs or anything
(better still, he'll drink Cut Arm's blood),
while Strong Eagle and Shooting Thunder scout ahead for Walking Cutthroats
as Heinmot Tooyalakekt, hearing the speech of pheasants, creeps into the brush and kills three for our hungry orphans,
other warriors frenetically scaling evergreened precipices to spy out Cut Arm's killers,

---

[*]Used to kill small game.

White Thunder sniffing the air for the scent of Bostons
and Wottolen creeping with his dear son Black Eagle, vainly
hunting someone to shoot.
Now here is a black shaggy bison head down on the green grass;
there is the herd,
but Lean Elk keeps shouting: *Hurry, hurry!*
so that Ollokot and his young men yearn to break away:
this head-chief of ours resembles Cut Arm, who unceasingly
tells us what we must do!
—and now ahead the horizon is all butte tops, the greatest ones touching
cumuli, the others each bearing a glowing white stripe of air between
their grey-green backbones and the swirly clouds
as we turn our horses east through the wet green grass
(prairie coneflowers like pallid suns),
and along the creek and up the meadow between pine forest hills, huckleberry swamps shine like metal.
Toohhoolhoolsote leads his riders along the steep mountain wall of pines and
aspens
(the latter paler at a distance than the former),
and up the wet foggy cañon, our trail steepening:
he listens to a flock of piñon jays in the mossy pines, speaking quietly to
one another,
and he spies out the dark-tipped wings of the otherwise white snow goose,
the black beak and white breast of the long-billed curlew,
but no brothers or enemies
even exactly here where one dawn twenty snows ago he and his warriors found and fell upon the darkstriped tipi of a Shinbone family
(they allowed the woman to run away with the children)
—nothing but the blue-shadowed triangular tips of the dark pines trun-
cated by cloud,
as our scouts seek ahead and behind,
Shooting Thunder straining down into blue fog, unable to find Cut Arm,
White Thunder hoping to steal some Boston horses for his mother,
and on the edge of the scree, yarrow, and then purple-blue harebells dangling
down their tender lobes.

10

Up the sloping orange prairie they ride,
up the low hills toward the clouds
(low wavering mountain-islands on the yellow horizon),
the mountains opening into purple-topped green and orange ridges
shadowed by many cañons,

wide greenish dimples in the land ahead,
> Springtime, weary-dizzy, looking around as she rides, won-
> dering which roots she might dig exactly here

as they come down into a grassy coulee

into the shaggy green shoulders and backbones of the country:
> purple blossom-strings of gayfeather,
>
> fat pale grasshoppers
>> (too late for the blue-black whortleberries)

and they begin to feel safe in the green coulee whose sides are occasionally striped with white gravel.

Lean Elk cries: *Hurry, hurry!*

but Looking-Glass has killed a deer, so that the hearts of the hungry return toward him.

11

Now as we near our last great river, the Place of the Cave of Red Paint,[*] the long summer returns once more from its dying; and when Lean Elk halts us to rest our failing horses by a huge lone cottonwood growing out of rabbitbrush, grease-wood and snow-white alkali, we almost seem to be back near Sparse-Snowed Place, with nothing lost, and our hopes still possessing all the lucent green-greys and olive-browns of this prairie after a rain

> as we drink out of dead Bluecoats' canteens
>
> (the water here is no good)

and Looking-Glass says: We shall arrive at Shallow Place[†] by evening,
> our young men restless, caring little for any chief, even Lean Elk; longing
> to rob and kill
>> even exactly here by this twisting pond rimmed with alkali where
>> Heinmot Tooyalakekt now shoots seven ducks for our orphans and
>> old ones
>>> as Springtime digs weakly for roots,
>>>> with the baby apathetic in the cradleboard behind her,
>>> and Cloudburst feeds crumbs of cous bread to Fair Land's son.
>>> Our hearts are longing for buffalo robes from the year-
>>> ling calves which the best men have promised us, but
>>> although we see more buffalo every day, Lean Elk, the
>>> morose one, forbids us from stopping to flense their
>>> hides;
>>>> he is strict; his ways become nearly as cold as Cut
>>>> Arm's; he is straight without mercy.

---

[*]The Missouri River.
[†]Cow Island.

Now again we are riding over the gold-and-silver prairie:

> knobby outcroppings to the south, horizon to the north where the country drops off,
>
>> and a lesser horizon straight ahead;

indeed we are riding east down toward the sky,

> spreading out like a line of dark trees in a coulee
>
>> horse-poor, ammunition poor
>>
>>> —hungry, swallowing the spittle that springs up in the backs of our throats—
>
> coming into the late afternoon light:
>
>> that gentle yellow-green glowing which has begun in the southern country,
>>
>> while to the north, small sharp buttes remain white-banded and brown, not yet touched by this new light;
>
> and now the land flattens out, so open that we cannot hide
>
>> (but our best scouts, turning their sunburned faces from side to side, have spied no enemies exactly here in this prairie between Crows and Painted Arrows)

as we ride and ride toward the Place of the Cave of Red Paint,

> Heinmot Tooyalakekt still on Black Mane-Stripe, the good one who understands whispers,
>
> Welweyas the half-woman happy on her strong horse
>
>> (but Ollokot's cream-colored stallion, his lovely favorite, has finally begun limping),
>
> Lean Elk ahead of all,
>
>> his grimace gashed downward like a trout's mouth,
>
> as Good Woman and Cloudburst whip their tired packhorses
>
> and Toohhoolhoolsote's old wives beat one of Cut Arm's mules
>
>> (even up to now they have saved two lodge-skins and a heavy basket of woven bark, which Cut Arm's creatures must help them carry),

passing ribbons of alkali in the tall grass

>> (to the west in the lowering sun, a wide splash of alkali shines like a lake)

and OUR MOTHER's lovely low blue jawbone to the northeast, and silver-green buttes bursting out of the grass.

We are riding over red ridges, while to the south the country is softening and flushing pink

>> (horizon all around),
>
> world-edges sharpening,

and then pines begin to rise out of the rock ahead.

So we cross another ridge, coming into a fire-gold plain to see at last the north rim of the great cañon blue in the haze far ahead and below,

which then conceals itself again

>> (hot light in our faces,

humidity in the dust-streaked sky, dust in our eyes
and cicadas singing, seedheads dancing on the grass)
until we cross over a long low pine-topped butte,
Sound Of Running Feet looking back west where the pine-buttes are going grey
and White Bird looking east where all is dusty-green:
warm pine smell, perfume of juniper, and between the pines we
find again the banded cliffs of the cañon,
locusts snapping in the sagebrush,
the sky not yet black with Canada geese flying south:
and hobbling our horses, we walk out the last tongue of meadow,
with the river before us, the Place of the Cave of Red Paint:
so far down from the locust-snapping grass we stand
on, beyond the tops of lodgepole pines to where the
golden-grey EARTH opens up in many deep folds from
one of which rises a river-voice like an echo, presently
mixing with the sound of evening wind in the trees;
so many horizons below us, then the Little Rockies and their cañons
and at the extreme left of where our ridge
drops down, the two easternmost pale blue
pads of the Wolf's Paw Mountains (all removed in the blue-grey atmosphere):
we shall ride there, then cross the
Medicine Line;
and so we stand here in the canted grey dirt at this world-edge
at the end of the former Salish Country
(the Cutthroats drove them out; how will they act toward us when
we meet them in the Old Woman's Country?);
but Heinmot Tooyalakekt keeps looking back across the grey-green grass into the
westering SUN.

12

Toohhoolhoolsote, squatting on the red-gravelled ledge of a great beehive of
white clay as the crickets begin to sing, looks back west across the yellow world:
mourning doves flying darkly up against the sunset,
white alkali beginning to turn milk-blue,
another lonely cottonwood, becoming paler and yellower
(hardened mucus in his nose as sharp as flint),
and his women have gathered a few sunflower seeds which they now grind between rocks in order to season what soup can be made from moldy camas flour.
Long before now we should have drummed and danced, but

Cut Arm's killers will never stop chasing us. It has come time and high time to Dream of WOWSHUXLUH sitting high on His single round leg; of WOWSHUXLUH, Who is Smohalla's Medicine.

We are settling in a circle; we are making camp,

Sound Of Running Feet and Welweyas cutting grass for bedding,

Cloudburst murmuring a sad song as she pricks the horses' blisters,

Good Woman mending her husband's moccasins,

Springtime desperately trying to suckle her child.

White Bird paints his cheeks yellow with powdered buffalo gallstones; he has lost his red paint; perhaps to-morrow he will get more exactly here by the river, if no Bostons molest us.

Helping Another boils soup for her husband and her mother; her chest-wound scarcely smarts.

Now we are all lying down,

longing as always to beat Cut Arm with a stick until he is entirely dead,

and at night there are red rays in the sky.

13

Heinmot Tooyalakekt, he who has never wished to come between disagreeing chiefs, was long ago warned by his father that such quarrels advantage the Bostons, who pit nation against nation, devouring the loser, then gnawing at the winner;

so it has proved among our People:

thief treaty!

and yet we have also been bitten no matter how we chose:

we lost Wallowa at once and for nothing, when Cut Arm showed the rifle, giving us thirty days to pen ourselves up,

while Looking-Glass lost his home for obeying Cut Arm;

we abandoned Red Owl's country only because our best men quarrelled at the Big Water fight

—it was our own fault that Cut Arm burned our lodges and treasures!—

and our treaty with the Bluecoats at Narrow Place advantaged only them:—we trusted them as if we were children!—

so that they could kill our People at dawn;

then the Salish refused to help us

(we must not blame them; they hoped to stay free for awhile, just for awhile);

likewise the Lemhis,

and the Crows,

whom the Bostons have bought for sugar, tobacco, and lying

promises of protection:
Sitting Bull spoke straight last summer when he called us to become of
one heart, and unite against the Bostons. Now it may be too late, but
perhaps in the Old Woman's Country we can all live quietly together;
 if not, why then, Sitting Bull and his Cutthroats will quickly kill us,
 or else we shall die along the way. Then all will finally be
 straight.
 Looking-Glass and I should each give Sitting Bull two
 horses and a fine bracelet of elkteeth. Has White Bird
 decided what to offer?
If Looking-Glass and Lean Elk cannot be of one heart, then again the Bostons
will take advantage.
But must we live like Bluecoat slaves, all marching and fighting in the same
way? Then we would not be free.
He hears White Thunder riding in with four horses well stolen from the Bostons
 (how many men has my nephew now killed?)
and Black Mane-Stripe greets him: *Hinimí.*
Burning Coals snores loudly
 as an owl speaks from down in the cañon
while a very few wives and husbands laugh quietly together within their blankets,
giving each other joy,
 but to-night once again Springtime will roll away from her husband
 while Good Woman, not expecting to be touched, has already begun Dreaming of some unknown Boston's face:
 high black collar, thin, ungiving lips
 —and Sound Of Running Feet begins to Dream just a little of her
 WYAKIN
 (perhaps It will bear the many painted colors of a wood duck),
 but Springtime and the baby are sleeping
 and Good Woman is too tired even to oil her hair.

14

 Lean Elk shouts: *Hurry, hurry!*
so we must ride down toward the Place of the Cave of Red Paint,
 the morning cloudy, windy and cold
 and the sky as greenish-white as the eggs of the yellowheaded
 blackbird
 (Looking-Glass pitying our old women's chilly aching bones),
 OUR MOTHER now brown, naked, grimy and curved, like one of many
bearclaws on its deerleather necklace-thong
 as we decorate our faces most bravely

and Heinmot Tooyalakekt leaps onto Black Mane-Stripe, slides his
feet into the rawhided willow stirrups which Good Woman made
for him long ago when we still lived in our own country, levels his
Winchester carbine
and we ride across Her flesh to the river.

15

As we wait for all our People to arrive,
    the grass as yellow as the tongues of Painted Arrows' moccasins
    and TRAVELLER beginning to descend in the sky,
we gaze over Shallow Place to the cottonwooded island, then to the north shore,
    seeing canvas houses there
        and a mountain of food
            (our hungry children begin remembering the hardbread,
            marrow-like and *maggot-like* we took from those Bostons we
            killed after Tendoy turned us away:
                perhaps there will also be meat)
    —and we hear men speaking the Boston language: Bluecoats again!
        —Toohhoolhoolsote folds his hands over his belly like a black
        bear standing.
So our careful chiefs send twenty men across the water,
        among them Red Spy, Strong Eagle, Shooting Thunder,
        and Red Moccasin Tops's father Yellow Bull, who attacked
        Píli's right flank at Sparse-Snowed Place,
        Old Yellow Wolf
        and his famed nephew White Thunder,
            who, determined to watch, warns himself: I must keep
            my heart clean,
            seeing my WYAKIN always:
they strip off their leggings and deerskin shirts, pointing chambered
Winchesters, Springfields and Sharpses ahead
        —gifts from our good friends the *Americans*—
        and sing their WYAKIN songs,
            ready for the Bostons to shoot them,
leading their best horses through the brown water,
    which is thick with dead and dying grasshoppers,
            our other warriors waiting here, their hearts crying
            qoh! qoh! qoh!
—but the Bostons forbear.
    (They are the ones who have made all this trouble.)
    And so now we all swim our horses and mules through this easy water,
        flanking the Bostons upstream and downstream,

with our dogs panting and paddling among our children and women,

      Blackberry Person and Asking Maiden keeping their daughters
      close, gazing back anxiously at their dear husband Looking-Glass,

      Ollokot riding Short Tail, rope-pulling the tired cream-colored
      horse behind,

      Springtime on Redhead, riding safely between Good Woman and
      Sound Of Running Feet,

      Helping Another wondering if her husband can save her if she slips
      from her horse

      while Toohhoolhoolsote's wives keep beating Cut Arm's nasty
      mule, swimming their horses forward, singing their WYAKIN songs
      with hatchets upraised;

thus we are helping our wounded, children and old ones to arrive exactly here,
around the island over the other channel to the north shore,

      where we now hear those Bluecoats whispering and digging holes like
      prairie-dogs:

      they can never make themselves brave!

Heinmot Tooyalakekt leads the women and children behind the creek trees
and up the trail, safely far from our enemies; he will protect us with his .44 Winchester carbine

      (Springtime is trembling)

as Lean Elk sends scouts forward and back to watch, waiting until all the People have passed

and Looking-Glass and the half-breed Bunched Lightning,

      two who love to talk to enemies

          (Lean Elk knows not how to speak; he is nothing but a horse-
          breeder),

tie on their Medicines

      —Bunched Lightning's a pierced thunderstone which he attaches to his
      braid,

          while Looking-Glass conceals around his neck the beaded flower-
          sun closure of a parfleche Medicine bundle decorated with blue
          columns and circles and fringed down the sides with soft deerskin

              (it was not ready when Cut Arm's killers attacked Kamnaka,
              nor when they struck Ground Squirrel Place, but he found
              time to affix it at Big Water and Place Like Split Rock)—

and approach the Bluecoats' canvas houses

      (so I have always said: these Bostons, these *Americans*, whoever they are, they
      have never done anything but hurt me),

and Looking-Glass waves his hat at them while his companion begins to speak in
Boston words:

Soldiers, we Indian People want eat. You give us, we give money.

No.

Soldiers, listen! We good Indians, never harm white men, just riding through here for awhile. You give us eat, give bullets, then we pay you gold.
No!
Soldiers, last time we ask you like friend, like brother! You give, we take, pay money. You no give, we take. Now give eat, hurry up quick!
and one Bluecoat, tall, pale, and beaknosed, gives hardtack and bacon, but only a little

        (not as if we were friends or brothers),
so that Red Spy begins to strip himself for battle
and White Bird pulls on his wolfskin cap
and we then begin shooting very happily:

      pim! pim! pim! kíw!

           because all Bluecoats are killers who will not end their big
           fight against us,
               shooting our women and children,
               roasting them like meat
        (already Yellow Bull has killed one foolish Boston; may our best
        men now shoot others!
           —never mind that Looking-Glass the renowned would have
           it that we began firing too soon, like careless children dis-
           turbing the eels their elders meant to catch);
and by nightfall
      —*Hasten; evening shadows be!*—
the Bluecoats are staying almost quiet, hiding behind their dirt wall (we hear them digging); hence we take whatever we wish:

        more hardbread, coffee, sacks of beans and flour, sugar, more bacon,
        marrow-like and *maggot-like,* bullets and matches,
        even pots and kettles for our women who lost theirs at Kamnaka, Big
        Water and Ground Squirrel Place
           (and Wottolen's son Black Eagle snatches a pair of soldier shoes too
           large for his feet, which for fun he puts on nonetheless;
        while Springtime, Welweyas and Cloudburst, exultantly daring,
        creep down from camp and through the willows:
        laughing warriors give them a cartridge belt for Heinmot Tooyalakekt,
           he who stays to help the children and women,
         a bottle of matches, *maggot-like,* molasses for Fair Land's child
           —as Red Spy shoots another Boston:
               from his mouth we hear the hissing that comes
               from musselshells when we bring them up out of
               the river—
             and Good Woman and Sound of Running Feet, coming
             down to watch, are laughing *áhaha,* because they who
             helped bury our People at Ground Squirrel Place have

seen how the Bluecoats shot Sun Tied's woman, and her
midwife, then crushed the skull of the baby just born,
and Welweyas gladdens her heart with a bolt of calico, which she
winds around herself beneath the fine King George blanket that
Heinmot Tooyalakekt gave her):
now we are making Cut Arm recompense us
(even Toohhoolhoolsote's women finally get enough!)
—we are flying up!
But the best thing we may not have:
Heinmot Tooyalakekt has now come frowning; he
makes us chop up the barrels with axes,
at which Five Snows and our other bad boys throw
themselves down into the frozen mud and lap up the
getting-drunk liquid like dogs
and we laugh at them.
Having taken most of what we wished, we burn the rest,
molasses jugs blossoming with flame,
children laughing,
the Bluecoats learning their lesson
(they should never have showed the rifle),
jars of matches exploding with sparks,
bullet trails painting the black sky
—perhaps it is like this when COYOTE throws up His eyes into the
air one after the other—
flames shouting all night and only a few Bluecoats shooting feebly,
so that again we sing the victory song,
feeling bright and brave.

16

Now Good Woman and Sound Of Running Feet are sleeping under a blanket,
full-dressed, with even their moccasins on, in case these Bluecoats should begin
to kill us. Good Woman's hatchet lies by her side.

Springtime is shivering, with the baby in her arms. Her husband whispers:
Síikstiwaa. She smiles a little.

He is stroking his baby's hair. About him the Three Red Blankets used to jeer:
He is always fondling his wives.

17

At dawn,
beating the ice out of our blankets
and fearing that the Bluecoats might now creep forth from their

holes to get even,

the women pack our horses quickly,

cutting out twenty dull-eyed lame ones to give Cut Arm,

Lean Elk sharply calling the warriors away from their bonfire

(Bluecoats whispering miserably in their holes);

then as our dogs run before and behind and under the horses' bellies in hopes of
meat, the horses say: *Hinimí*

and we depart the northern bank of this Place of the Cave of Red Paint, riding up,

eager to get out of the Bostons' jaws,

White Thunder, Wottolen and Black Eagle watching behind, just for

awhile, to make sure that our enemies will not come up from the river,

Toohhoolhoolsote's wives taking turns clouting their mule's

head with some Boston's frying pan,

Burning Coals chasing his herd

as otter-faced Heinmot Tooyalakekt, appearing almost young again, canters
up the trail on Black Mane-Stripe,

who knows that he must quickly ford each creek, not stopping to drink,

and the morning light gleams cleanly on the sad chief's forehead

and diagonally down his chest runs a wide bandolier (a precious gift from

Springtime and Good Woman) patterned with leaf-sprouting diamond

forms vaguely resembling the decorations of playing cards;

he rides yet more gracefully than Ollokot.

So we have left Shallow Place,

with still more best men scouting behind, ready to shoot the Bluecoats if they rise
up treacherously from their holes, but those enemies tremble like children

(we are mocking them as we ride)

—and now we ascend the great river's bluff

(and White Bird, who has Dreamed evilly, will not stop at the Cave of Red Paint);
riding up,

but Ollokot's cream-colored horse, limping behind on a long rope, struggles

feebly up the trail, his back legs slipping

(Cut Arm's mule is biting him),

so that at the top Ollokot jumps off Short Tail, leaving him with Cloudburst,
walks aside and whistles to the cream-colored horse, who comes limping with
sad eagerness:

Ollokot strokes his mane, whispers, hugs his neck, then quickly slits his

throat, so that Cut Arm can never mistreat him;

he steps back, watches him sink to his knees, panicked and bleed-

ing, tossing his head,

then turns away when the life begins to go out of his eyes;

now he is striding back to the trail; he is leaping up on Short Tail's back

while the dogs run to lap up the blood, nipping at the twitching legs
as we ride wearily on.

18

Looking-Glass cries out: My People, now be watchful, for exactly here I have met Walking Cutthroats!

    —indeed it once happened that when Blackfoot the *lucky man* was still a man, not some slave who had sold himself to Cut Arm for coffee and tobacco, he and Looking-Glass killed an enemy chief not far from this ridge, sharing out his horses and quarrelling over his horned headdress.

        (White Bird's toothache worsens; now it is a headache, and he pulls his wolfskin cap down tighter,

            gathering no red river-dirt with which to paint himself;

        but Springtime is happy again:

            she has given the Bluecoats' cartridge belt to her nephew White Thunder, who praises her;

            and to-night perhaps she will make a fire with one of her new matches;

        while Looking-Glass, his admonition unanswered, rides wearily, squinting as he wonders how many horses he should give Sitting Bull.)

Riding as if we have become heavy,

        chilly between our shoulderblades,

    cantering, striding, limping and trotting toward the Medicine Line,

        TRAVELLER THE SUN as cool and pale now as the little creamy yellow-white flower clusters of the grass-leaved death camas

        and hail thicker than August grasshoppers,

we make our best pace so that Lean Elk will not yell,

        our skulls heavy with sleeplessness,

            the world suddenly dark brown with buffalo all the way to the horizon (Lean Elk will not let us stop to kill any of them),

        the young men scouting ahead for Walking Cutthroats

        and for Shinbones

        (proud enemies who have ochered their faces red and yellow),

    our dear women searching for rosehips on the desiccated stalks, hoping to strengthen the children,

    our old ones silent or groaning,

        our ponies weakening on willow bark and late grass

—but now again we steal some horses from careless Bostons, laughing to leave those Crooked Hearts alone here

    (it is as if we never tired)

—then Strong Eagle rides quickly toward us:

Another wagon train!

    —Toohhoolhoolsote gnashes his teeth—

so we must strip for battle,
galloping
    (anxious about Painted Arrows),
      so that we kill the three Bostons who dare to meet us
         (they all mean to cheat us into misery)
      while five others flee into the willows like children:
         Áhaha, we shall make Cut Arm cry!
—then we attack the wagons and kill two more Bluecoats before we burn everything. When will they leave us in peace?

19

Red Spy waves the blanket: *Bluecoats are riding after us!*— We shoot at them,
and one flies off his horse; then they run away. Cut Arm is now getting feeble; soon
we shall never again be afraid.
    Riding through the rainy windy coulees of OUR MOTHER,
        some trees of Whom are still beaded light green, like the edge of many a
        Cheyenne knife-sheath,
we creep toward the Old Woman's Country. The horses are tired, and Toohhoolhoolsote cannot stop coughing.

20

Silhouettes of boulder-nippled swales pretend to be buffalo
and buffalo become silhouettes
as the eastern sides of buttes darken in early evening;
        we are camping early, eating Boston bacon and sugar but longing for buf-
        falo,
            and Looking-Glass says: Lean Elk was never any chief! He is killing
            our old ones!
                so the old ones say: Looking-Glass speaks straight,
                    and our best men begin thinking.

21

In the sleety night, Good Woman screams beneath her blanket,
        tortured by a nightmare of hearing the fat bubbling out of our women
        and children whom the Bluecoats shot and roasted at Ground Squirrel
        Place
            (it is only the river saying *mululululu*).

22

Yellowish-red like a young buffalo calf creeps TRAVELLER THE SUN up over the trees, and the People flee on, hating Lean Elk, who warns: Listen to me, Looking-Glass and all you chiefs! I am telling you three times. Unless we hurry and hurry, we shall all be killed.

But our Boston food makes us heavy and happy, all of us
    except for Toohhoolhoolsote's wives, who never eat much:
        they long to make a tea from the sagebrush which grows far away
        in our country, along the Chinook Salmon Water;
            then their husband's coughing would stop;
    and except for our old ones and children
    and Springtime, who cannot keep her baby warm.

23

We wind toward Wolf's Paw,
        our copper bracelets still gleaming,
    wrapping our blankets tighter as we ride
        (the ice-breeze says: *tsss!*
        —soon the buffaloberries will be ready):
            and down in that draw, exactly there, another Boston is rid-
            ing alone on a fine horse.
            All white men are spies, so let us kill him
                —*pim!*—
    and take his treasures:
            Red Spy pulling off his boots
                (no need for pounding: he is quite dead, poor fel-
                low!),
            Young Eagle Necklace shouldering his old Sharps,
            Tomyahnin buckling on his cartridge belt,
                Ollokot finding .44 rimfire ammunition for his
                dear sad chief and brother,
            White Bird's *Kate* happily wrapping greenbacks into
            her braid-ends:
            while Black Eagle, Wottolen's brave son, takes his
            brown and white pinto pony
                 (whose shoulder has been heart-branded)
            and we share his sack of *marrow-like* among the chil-
            dren,
                 but when we wish to strip off his clothes, Hein-
                mot Tooyalakekt forbids it.

Now that the Crows and Lice-Eaters have fallen away, and the Bluecoats remain far back by the river called *O-pumohat Kyai-is-i-sak-ta*, it begins to seem to the People

(excepting Wottolen,

whose nightmares of Cut Arm have again become as terrifying as the Painted Arrows who roam ahead in their tall war-bonnets,

and White Bird,

whose heart has come to hate Looking-Glass)

that Lean Elk has hurried too many of us to death;

our horses are tired, their hooves diseased

(Burning Coals worries about his herd; even Lucky One gets quickly winded now);

and as for Looking-Glass's follies, just as we wash colored earths in a vessel of water so that the gravel settles out, then pour the cloudy water into another vessel which the fine pigments will settle in, so now if we but sift and refine his words we may gain the best of him,

for his follies are truly ours: he has never told us what we desired not to hear,

and in just the same way that earth pigments settle in swirls when we wash them

(and since Heinmot Tooyalakekt's heart cannot tell him how he should speak in this matter, he murmurs aside with Ollokot, who replies: Elder brother, if you say yes, then I shall follow your words.

White Bird, are you determined to keep quiet?

What others hide in their hearts is not for me to spy out),

so our longing to rest awhile, just for awhile, sinks grain by grain within us, falling silent upon itself, building up into something sure and bright:

Looking-Glass, who even now remains a *lucky man*,

and who when he comes before Sitting Bull will be wearing his best hairpiece decorated with Crow beads as large as tears

(while Lean Elk dresses like a poor man),

shall again be chief

—to which Lean Elk repeats in council: I have done my best for everyone. Now indeed you may again be head-chief, but my heart tells me that we shall all be captured and killed.

ROSETTE PORTRAITS
OCTOBER 1–3

1

*M*ason, Sturgis, you'll remain here in charge of the command. I'll take Miller's artillery on the "Benton." Captain Miller, you're to lead the infantry along that old Indian trail, doublequick. Head them toward the Milk River until I send other orders. Lieutenant Fletcher will be your aide-de-camp. Captain, I'm counting on you! Should Joseph succeed in making his junction with Sitting Bull, your reënforcements may tip the scales.

Yessir. We can head out in an hour.

GOD bless you. Chapman, how's that magnificent horse of yours?

Real good, thanks, general. How's yours?

You'll ride out with us in half an hour. I don't need to tell you, *I hope*, how great a moral responsibility you bear as interpreter. The Government depends on you to express our words to the Nez Perces, and theirs to us, with exemplary fidelity. Do you understand?

Upon my honor, general—

Whatever do you wish to say now?

Just that you can count on me, because I been out here in Indian country for twenty-two years, and I'm a brother in good standing of the Order of the Eastern Star—

Go now. Well, Perry, Mrs. Howard informs me in all her letters that your wife is bearing up exactly as expected.

Yessir,

>as watchful as a Crow scout.

Have you received news directly from her?

Not since Henry's Lake, sir, but I'll bet she's managing.

Mrs. Howard gets a bit *blue* at times, as she puts it. She's quite exercised at Joseph for leading us so far from home!

My wife probably feels much the same, sir,

>the whore.

>>Someday before I get too old or get killed I'm going to resign this chickenshit Army and leave that harridan; then I'll make us a love-seat out of tamarack wood and Delia will quilt the cushions for it and plait a back out of red cedar. And in the evenings we sit there, except that *I'd* get blue doing nothing at home.

Now, what should I know about Old George and Captain John?

Knowing them as I do, sir, I would not trust them in any way.

Then whom should I trust? Not Chapman.

Take me, general! If I can be in on the death—

For Theller's sake.

Yessir.

I'm sorry, colonel. Your company needs you here. They can't keep up. How are they?

They sure appreciate the slowdown, sir.

Good. Your new horse has a lot of "dash." Wilkinson thinks him somewhat rawboned, but I disagree. You chose well.

Thank you, sir.

All right, Perry; that will be all.

Yessir,

> staring at him, his collar faded to the hue of the Big Dust, his forehead
> smudged with soot and shadow, his beard, still neat, going grey
> as they both listen to someone's water bottle cracking from internal ice-
> pressure.

2

Lieutenant Wood, Lieutenant Howard, you'll come with me. Wilkinson, re-mind Chapman and the scouts that they're to embark in thirty minutes.

Yessir.

Walk with me for a moment.— Don't be downhearted, my boy! Most officers I'm leaving behind because they don't have enough "sand" in them for the final push. (I won't name names.) You're staying here because I trust you more than anyone to keep an eye on everything.

Thanks, general—

Wood needs his chance, don't you see? You've already distinguished yourself. I'll never forget your courage at Clearwater!— Pull yourself together, Wilkinson, and the LORD be with you.

Yessir.

Good-bye now,

> turning away from him but still seeing through closed eyes Wilkinson's
> despair as bright as the calcium lights of New York City.

3

Old George and Captain John are ready first. Leave it to the d——d reds.

Throwing on their triple-buckled blankets, leaving behind the shining pyra-mids of our Sibley tents and the almost empty commissary wagon, each of them

> (excepting Old George, Captain John and Ad Chapman)

meditates as follows: O, a cold chase this will surely be!

4

As the "Benton" draws away,
        her smoke blowing behind us over the swales,
                the boys slamming logs into both boilers
            and our horses neighing belowdecks,
the sun goes as red as the nosebleed of a lung-shot buffalo, but in that strange
evening light, the dying grass, frosted and matted down, seems as pallid white as
new lace at the milliner's:
        forty miles yet to Cow Island
as the general and the captain keep jawboning with that grubby courier from
Colonel Miles,
        the low-compression engine loudly farting and pig-snorting,
                so that the rest of us feel safe from being overheard as we backstab
                the men we've left behind
                        (gazing like lords across the paddlewheel while the crew does
                        all the work):
        Well, he was all instinct and impulse. The way he instantly took against
        Wood—
        But don't you remember how much he loved Lieutenant Theller?
—and as the general strolls to the pilot house, Wood looks back once more at our
bunch
        (just in case I'm killed)
to find Colonel Perry standing among them as tall as the flagpole on Lapwai's
parade ground
and Wilkinson, already shrinking and darkening, leads the abandoned ones in
three cheers.

5

This has not been as short a campaign as I expected, but now comes the finish,
one way or another, and I do hope to regain General Sherman's confidence.
        Miles's command will surely be a match for Joseph in his present dete-
        riorated state, unless Sitting Bull . . .
                I cannot get over the effects of that despatch at Henry's Lake. But I must
                believe that once we close this war, even if merely by running Joseph
                across the line, General Sherman and I will restore our friendship:
                        cinders rushing from our towering two funnels, painting the
                        dusk with orange stars.
                                Poor Wilkinson! What can I do for him? He'd be per-
                                fect overseeing a boarding-school for Indian children.
                                I'll write the Department.

I must pray again to-night for Mrs. Manuel; could Joseph be saving her as his bargaining-chip? Custer once told me that when he stormed that Indian village on the Washita, some hideous old squaw was holding a white woman captive, and upon his entrance she stabbed her prisoner in the heart . . .

Now if we can but prevent Joseph from fording the Milk River, which must now be mortally cold for his women and children— that should delay him!—

unless it has already frozen solid—

. . . well, that also is in GOD's hands.

How dark this river is!

O, this certainly *feels* like the finish, the death of something, and we have all been condemned to wait for death—first of all—our own; and then (far worse) to sit at the deathbeds of those we love:

Poor father was so afraid of suffocation at the end!

It may have been a mistake to tell Guy about it. *No.* He's a soldier,

his purpose still as white as a cadet's linen collar.

He needs to show "sand." He'll be no good unless he can face every horror.

I'll never forget that time I came into that dim and pestilential sick-chamber and Mother and Rowland were sitting him up so that he could breathe; he kept gasping and staring at us as if we could help him . . .

. . . wheezing and coughing, choking on his own blood, with no relief, that same panic I have seen so many times in my dying young men . . .

O dear GOD, and the way his throat kept rattling at the finish! It sounded like some fiendish Dreamer shaking a gourd!

(I must not hate Toohhoolhoolzote; it is not for me to hate.)

I did my best to hide how fearful I found it, but since I was his own flesh he must have known.

He needed to die! How could we have ever wished to let him go? But we did; only death could relieve his agonies and ours

to which then must succeed the first import of loss, then the second, and third, when pain eats deeper into our heart-roots—

But this finish here and now will not be sorrowful, not even if the Indians wipe us out,

although for Lizzie of course . . .

It will be the *true* finish, just as when at a prayer meeting our burning eyes and choking sadnesses surrender to ethereal joy.

6

Wood keeps dreaming
>—as if any dream could be as proud as the white horse on the roof
>of Sherlock & Bacon's livery stable in Portland, or as hopeful as
>Theller's Blackfoot squaw when some greasy miner promises her
>two bits for opening her legs!—

of some kind of glory,
>not least because the instant he saw the Missouri Breaks his breast
>ached for joy, and it seemed to him that his heart would never stop
>laughing:
>>Why shouldn't I make my stand here? Live out my life and . . .
>>Because isn't that what every American feels, the yearning for
>>a beautiful home? If I could be here every morning forever,
>>and shoot birds for Nanny to roast
>>>(two gunshots far away,
>>>>white frost on our black-tarred backpacks),
>>while she
>>>—but might I prove incapable of happiness? I really
>>>ought to make myself pray
>>—since if nothing else it looks as if I'll be in on the finish:
>>What if it's me who captures Joseph?
>>If it's a duel between him and me, could I shoot him, feeling
>>as I do?
>>Well, wouldn't it be best for the Indians if I do whatever it
>>takes to end their sufferings?
>>Or how would it be if I led them safe into the British Posses-
>>sions, and married Joseph's daughter? Then I'd be the White
>>Chief. They'd teach me how to live like an Indian, and I'd . . .
>>Ad Chapman says she's twelve years old, and they marry
>>around thirteen. Nanny would

shoot herself, but we got the pistol out of her clutches. Seems she'd gone hysterical
after some Blackfeet murdered her husband, so we
>>>>never should have left Nigger Lover
>>>>Howard in charge of this campaign.
>>>>Quit it or he'll—

No, Guy, it should be all right. Miles has a Hotchkiss and a Parrott gun.

WILKINSON WAITS
OCTOBER 3–4

1

*W*ilkinson, abandoning himself to prayers for his general's better success
(if he could get any wish whatsoever in the world, it would be for
his dear general's triumph and gratification)
and fearing now even more than does the general that our reds will manage to slip across the Medicine Line, thereby discrediting this campaign
—worse yet, embarrassing Mrs. Howard, an outstanding woman
whom he frankly would choose for his own mother any day,
not to mention Grace, who for all her stupidity is at least not
arrogant
(and he will freely admit her to be far more beautiful
than his own Sallie, despite the latter's brown eyes),
kneels down behind the general's forsaken Sibley tent and asks the LORD OF
HOSTS to help us defeat Chief Joseph, for the sake not only of every man here but
our entire United States, and then Christian decency,
since even before Joseph put himself in the wrong by murdering and raping those white people on the Salmon River there was the fact of his
Dreamer idolatry, for which Wilkinson is sufficiently bighearted to blame
not Joseph but Joseph's dead apostate father, yet which all the same remains a canker which must be gotten rid of.
Soon as we whip Joseph and I get leave, it's me for Lewiston! I want
a Dutch apple pie from Skookum's bakery. Until this moment I
never noticed how hungry I am. After that Dutch apple pie I might
eat a huckleberry one without help.
Wilkinson,
not to split hairs,
asserts to GOD that although Joseph may well differ from, say, Toohhoolhoolzote in
both intentions and character, he has certainly long since declared himself for the
evil side; as for any so-called military genius, Wilkinson after scientifically considering the facts believes this *Red Napoleon* to be at best (if one may borrow from
Edgar Poe) a Red Imp of the Perverse, for which reason his continual survival in the
field frustrates and, he stints not to confess it, outright angers Wilkinson, who
would like to see Joseph pay: drop the trap, hiss out rope, stretch his neck!—followed
by Toohhoolhoolzote, the latter being irremediably SATANIC. To be sure, even Joseph may someday come to the LORD, in which case a course of lifelong humble

penitence in the Indian Territory (and a mandate to keep his bucks quiet) might suffice for punishment, Wilkinson being of a forgiving and forbearing disposition; but the first thing is to defeat this woman-burner, and in this regard Wilkinson cannot help but worry about the general's associates:

> Chapman's intentions have never gone beyond the simple lusts and greeds which one must expect of any man in his fallen state;
>
> Guy is no use, and our tame Nez Perces unreliable;
>
> moreover, without ever meeting him, Wilkinson has always hated and distrusted Colonel Miles, of whom the general speaks with such guileless generosity.

Finally, Wilkinson,

> > who on more than one occasion has confided to Fletch that he for one finds it baffling why the general shows so much favor to Wood,
>
> would really like to know just where Wood stands nowadays, which is to say (putting the matter more pointedly) the location of his allegiance to our Indian service.

Now he prays. He could not, even if he wished, ever daydream the way that Wood does; he can never escape his own presence in the world, except when he sleeps; but suddenly he cannot shut out a memory of Grace Howard yattering on about Vassar College, as if she thinks us all so primitive.

BACK IN TIME
OCTOBER 1–2

1

*A*nd arriving the next morning at the Cow Island ford
(the reds have wrecked and pillaged everything,
> just as our doughty Bannocks entertained themselves at Big Hole
> by kicking about a child's calcined skull),
we interview the sad troopers of Company "B"
(two of them now wounded)
who sought and failed to withstand Joseph
(another blot, however unavoidable, on Custer's shining Seventh Infantry!):

> You see, general, they killed Stoce, Barker and Bradley; then they shot Parker in the back. Except for Stoce, those fellers was just mule drivers. They never did no harm!
>
> All right,

and we inventory the enemy's dead animals
(among which lies a mule branded 𝕌 𝕊 ; doubtless Red O'Donnell would recognize
this one)
as Wood recopies despatches like mad for his general to correct, redraft, approve
and sign before the "Benton" departs:

> Miles need not split his command, for thanks to Mr. Joe's work here, we
> can track his approximate position on the map, to-day and to-morrow,
> > using mathematics
> > > (my true calling, as Lizzie loves to remind me:
> > > > another reason I went into Ordnance),

and perhaps even halt him before he crosses the line.

> Next, we verify our detachment
> > —the Brave Seventeen again!—
> > > > But, father, you've always said that we should at-
> > > > tack Indians with superiority of numbers.
> > > > GOD disposes, Guy,
> > > thawing the bits in warm water so as not to hurt the horses' tongues,
> > > steam rising from our saddleblankets,

and after one more map-lookover with Mile's rider:

> > > You see here, general, Mr. Joe's likely gonna slip *here* between the
> > > Bear's Paw Mountains and the Little Rockies.
> > > And where's Colonel Miles?
> > > Sir, he was someways down over *here* when I rode out,

we set our best selves forward:

> *Load with cartridges; load!*
> And picture windows for Fidelia!
> > —seventeen cheery Troopers of CHRIST
> > > > (I know what they call me.
> > > > Well, if they ever say anything in my hearing, fa-
> > > > ther, I'll sure knock them down!),
> > > crossing to the north shore,
> > > > frost greying down our black-tarred rucksacks
> > > > and our horses churning up the shallow water like buttermilk
> > > > > (no slush ice yet: another week, perhaps),
> > > and coming up onto the *wrinkled land;*

sixteen lost men following Colonel Miles's hollow-eyed courier, commencing to
burn distances, hunting Miles and Joseph through the Missouri Badlands.

2

> Very cold, general,
> > the stars dull yellow like the tacks hammered into the stock of a deco-
> > rated Indian carbine.

Well, it'll moderate, or not. Anyhow, the season's not far advanced.

Yessir.

They'll fight desperately enough this time, I should suppose. This is the last battle,

> and a cold ride indeed, the general blowing his nose (he is enveloped in the newspaper correspondent's bearskin coat), Guy well buttoned up, Wood frankly shivering
>
> —for some reason his knees are the coldest—

trying to distract himself by remembering Sitka Khwan, and Theller's squaw

>> (yearning to buy her some pretty stone of a turquoise color like the Musselshell River, and see what kind of smile she makes),

and that dear sweet nigger woman whose name he never learned, and that rancher's daughter Mary who called it dancing the quadrille, and Nanny of course

>> (to what degree would she forgive me?),

> and, reader, I may as well inform you that Wood, so practiced at such observations, has on several of his supper-visits to the general's home at Tenth and Morrison noted Grace's lovely ankles peeping out from her many snowy petticoats:
>
>> What would *she* be like? *A maiden wrapp'd in dreams?* I don't think so, but a girl can have a wooden head and still be silk down lower!
>>
>>> —even as Guy glares at me, Bessie leaps into my lap and old Mrs. Battle-Axe Howard sits embroidering another horsehair cushion

while Ad Chapman, who'd never until recently hoped to get this far in life, rides happily ahead on his grey charging-horse, with a plug of kinnikinnick in his cheek, and our two good Nez Perces at his right, the entire party riding doublequick, the painful, pallid moonlight disturbing their eyes in late afternoon, and sleet stinging their faces like a cloud kicked up by fleeing buffalo:

> O, what a fine horse my Arrow is! I'll have to give him back to Chapman when this campaign ends—

Guy, how are you holding up?

Very well, thanks, father, and you?

Fine,

> his testicles aching and his bladder already nearly in spasms although how can there be any fluid already in it?

Somehow this journey makes me imagine your grandfather's ride.

Yessir. When he—

Sorry, son. I realize I've told you a dozen times,

> looking pointlessly back toward Cow Island (already unseen)
> and then our wavering line of fog-hidden Sibley tents at Carrol,

then Lapwai,

their eyelashes freezing shut in this snowy, icy wind.

But think, Guy, a child of six on horse all the way from Bridgewater, Massachusetts,

the family removing to Leeds:

Captain Seth Howard and his wife Desire, who was John Bailey's daughter, with their seven children, off to finish taking up what I grew up hearing called *the old Captain Seth Howard farm*

(since Father was six it must have been 1801, back when there was still a richness of bluejoint grass around Androscoggin Lake, and Chief Pocasset's village remained unburned);

and now that I gaze over at you, Guy, riding your Appaloosa like a Westerner, as weary as the rest of us, and like the rest of us endeavoring not to show it, I somehow begin to see in you neither myself nor Father but the frowning, deepset eyes, protuberant lips and high, waxy forehead of Father's brother, Stillman Howard, Captain Seth's eldest son,

who frightened me.

I wish you could have known him.

Grandfather? Yes, father, I wish that also,

and then they ride in silence awhile, both thinking unknown to each other: May I die before I finish my days on *the old Captain Seth Howard farm!*

but Guy is merely chilly, excited and happy

(I do wonder if cocaine would warm me up?),

whereas his father rides into a landscape of various dreads and griefs not unlike the long parallel shadows oozing across the floorboards from the treadles of Lizzie's loom;

perhaps right now she is winding another warp.

A penny for your thoughts, Chapman!

Well, general, I was thinkin' on beefsteak and eggs for breakfast, with wheatcakes afterward. More of the same for lunch. Soon's we've whipped Mr. Joe—

Yes. Is our pair of Indians bearing up all right?

Them? O, don't worry, general. They don't never complain.

Wood, whom do you feel sorry for now? Joseph's Indians?

Colonel Perry, sir.

I see.

His eyes, general—

Entre nous, he missed the opportunity to distinguish himself.

So they ride on,

following pilfered packages of coffee and finecut tobacco dropped from Joseph's animals,

and then by a small lake lies one of our couriers, some poor negro from Fort Hall, shot through the heart by the *Red Napoleon,* with ravens on

his head, and his despatches and cigars torn up as if by children (why
have they left his needle gun in the dead grass beside him?)
and phlegm invades the general's throat; well, I'm getting old, or at least so Sherman opines; how pleased I'll be to see again a *truer* friend,
smiling to envision shaking Miles's hand,
and tinged by melancholy joy to find that he still knows by heart (as undoubtedly does Miles) the way that the Pamunkey River wriggles thinly
northwest upstream from the York (wasn't it somewhere around here
that Captain Argall kidnapped Pocahontas?):
four bends to Indian Town, and then one more to White House
where the Richmond and York River Railroad shoots southwest and
then nearly due west to the enemy capital
when Miles and I were still volunteers in French-grey overcoats
and I was young and had two arms
(these detached pictures comparable to the results of
the game he used to play with Sladen as they followed
slender, bearded Jeffords on the cañoned trail into
Cochise's Stronghold, preferring not to dwell on whether
the Apaches would murder them on the way, which was
why they simply compared fancies while pointing out to
one another the variously perceived shapes of the Peloncillo Mountains: sombrero or sugarloaf),
Fair Oaks Station lying on the railroad: South to the parallel-curving
Williamsburg or Seven-Mile Road, with Seven Pines there just about
due south of Fair Oaks Station
—although Miles reminded me that we'd have to watch out
for that White Oak Swamp—
my beard freezing in this icy wind, the night darker than the inside of a gun-
barrel,
as I remember canoeing with General Saxton in John Seabrook's
grand fishpond at Edisto,
in the days when we both believed we had the Government's
ear
(was my inability to do for the negroes what Lincoln
promised I could do the greatest disappointment I ever
experienced?
—or was it when the Government overturned my bargain with the Apaches—
or Joseph's dishonesty to me
—I sincerely wished him good!—
or that last communication from General Sherman?);
while Old George and Captain John are likewise riding back in time,

back to when the People could roam wherever they pleased without being
molested by the Bostons,

    digging camas at Weippe,

        Dreaming with the Salish and Smohalla,

           hunting with the Crows,

while Wood rides on,

    remembering the general at "Reveille" drinking coffee by a tallow can-
dle's light

        and the white tents at dusk when we were bivouacked by Henry's
Lake,

           and Wilkinson in that single-breasted shortcoat of his, with
the five brass eagle buttons flittering in front and one miniature eagle button on each sleeve as he stood loudly reading
from the Book of Common Prayer (whose entirety I'm sure he
could recite) when we buried Bugler Brooks at Camas Meadows (then taps, and all of us quickstepping away),

               thus back and back to when I used to carry a pair of
two-bushel sacks of wheat or rye for Father, who of
course would have been drunk, so Uncle Phil, my favorite darky all through childhood, helped me load up so I
could set out riding all the way to Owings Mill to get
them ground

                   (it was always like this, riding on and on and
dreaming,

                      but what did I dream about before I dreamed
about women? Maybe if I could dope that out,
I'd finally know myself;

                        also, there was something about my
father, and a secret inside that yellow
brick building where he used to be
Surgeon General of the Navy):

one sack tied to the cantle and the other to the front of the saddle

    and o, when I think about how rapidly that negro John John-
son could cradle wheat, and how kind he was to me when I
was a child . . . !

        (But I adored Uncle Phil the most sincerely. He was a
real man; he taught me how to carry weight.)

        And the reason I love the general more than my own
father is that he has actually tried to do something for
the negroes,

and so Wood rides on, rides on,

    seeing before him whenever he closes his tired eyes the pallid Z of bygone
Perry's gunbelt, shoulder sling and wind-pulled scarf

and ever-lost Wilkinson's buttons,
        looking on this campaign as it might actually be, no longer seeking to
        falsify life but to steadily sorrow and even to do evil steadily as much as
        I must, just until I get to the end of this;
                although afterward I may well need to become a stranger to this
                whole bunch:
                        Since I have now chased, killed and suffered nearly all the way
                        to the Medicine Line, can I not live as I wish? Do I not know
                        how or do I simply not dare?
—and Guy rides beside him, back to the days before Father favored Wood,
        Chapman easy and eternal in his Denver saddle,
and Miles's courier rides sadly
and the general rides on
        back to that time when Lizzie, pregnant with Chauncey, was sewing the
        gores on a skirt and Gracie was mopping the kitchen (she must have been
        about seven); then Guy came in to inform me that his sister had saved up
        ten cents to donate to the American Missionary Association, and I felt
        proud beyond words, and therefore—had no words for Gracie, who
        flushed as she went on mopping and scrubbing, equally proud and em-
        barrassed that I now knew her secret
        and the time before that when Lizzie was still a fine young fair-complected
        lady with a clean white collar riding her dark dress like a yoke, o, and those
        dark globular little earrings she had from her Mama . . . !
        and her short hair
                —too shy even to smile at me—
                (I wonder whatever happened to that bracelet she used to wear with
                the rosette portraits of Lincoln, Sheridan and Stoneman
                        —and where's Stoneman anyhow?)
                        LORD, it's cold! After this is finished, I long to stretch
                        out on my back in our featherbed while Lizzie reads
                        to me,
                                just for awhile,
                        or withdraws into the kitchen to boil soup while I
                        think of nothing.
        Enough of this.
—Wood,
        who continues to be a disappointment, unfortunately
                (he needs a victory to pull him together),
how are you holding up?
    Pretty good, sir, and you?
    Fine. Now, Wood, you know that you have my entire confidence.
    Yessir,
        that chain from Nanny formerly showing from within his open-necked

blouse which to-night he's had to cover in extra canvas

      (obtained from Lieutenant Bomus).

Do you understand the battle plan?

I believe I do, sir,

    or does this general of mine in fact know and keep me as I would a squaw
    or prostitute, to scare away the loneliness which bares its yellow teeth in
    that icy leafless serviceberry thicket right over there? And should he re-
    quire of me to shoot down squaws and children in cold blood—

Very good, my boy, because if I should fall to-morrow,

    and all our march come to ashes

        (Joseph and his SATANIC cohorts laughing at us from behind the
        Medicine Line)

    and Guy tumble unhorsed with an arrow in his throat

        although he will bravely receive whatever GOD sends him

    but Lizzie, O my Lizzie,

you'll need to represent me on the field and issue the orders I would have given . . .

        Charley boy will look after her; he's always called her *sister*—

        and I so want Grace to have a brilliant wedding.

GOD forbid that should happen, general!

Until Miles takes command.

Yessir.

GOD bless you.

And you also, general:

    Of course I'll do it, even that, anything to end this, because even if Joseph
    escapes to the British Possessions—

        No sign thataway, sir.

        Well, keep a bright lookout, because in this fog, you understand . . .

        Yessir.

        You're doing a good job, soldier.

        Thank you kindly, sir,

            the other men faintly coughing,

                shivering in their wool coats, blankets, canvas overalls
                and grimy stable frocks

                    (Old George longing for *getting-drunk liq-
                    uid* as he will do all his life):

                    Remember, that buffalo overcoat of yours is quar-
                    termaster property.

                    Yessir,

            as we rush after our hostile Indians on this night so cold that
            the stars almost cast shadows upon the flat bitter darkness

                which in the Civil War we called *that dark and bloody
                ground.*

3

Soldier, how far have we come?

From the Missouri? I'd say seventy miles, general.

Not bad,

     his arm-stump burning miserably with cold

        (I should have thought it would be dead by now; well, it must be the
cut edge of the living part that feels).

Sir, but from here on it's guesswork. They could be anywhere.

Well, keep on! Everything's in His power,

      wondering whether Joseph has pulled off another massacre

        (if it's White Bird Cañon all over again, at least that's not my
responsibility),

      and should Miles have fallen on the field, with our reënforcements
still far away

        —that horrible old Toohhoolhoolzote no doubt would enjoy
offering me up in sacrifice to his MOTHER EARTH!—

then

        the LORD is my Shepherd, and I shall not

           (O, but his *hateful Indian eyes!*)

        think about it,

           bringing to mind that pleasant occasion when he
once went sleigh-riding with Lizzie and her folks,
in the Christmas season before they married; it
was good cold Maine weather, so he and Lizzie's
Papa dragged a feather mattress inside

—then realizes that he is not certain whether or not Miles's courier said
yessir.

4

From far away come three rifle-shots. Miles's rider replies in the same way. Then they continue up the dark trail.

At last they hear two galloping horses. From whom could they derive but Miles?

His hopes grow warm as the Chinook wind which comes to our relief in the middle of a Montana winter. The jury's still out, but so is the infantry.

So Near the Medicine Line
September 29–30

1

*R*iding up into the snow-light, swaying on their stumbling horses, their feet swelling, the dogs limping,

> Springtime's shell-earrings shining, her long black braids streaming horizontally behind her and her collar of teeth and shells whisper-clicking as she canters quick and steady on her husband's dark Appaloosa
>> (for Red One grew lame yesterday; Good Woman slit his back leg-tendons for Cut Arm)

> passing old rings of tipi stones,
>> with Wolf's Paw snowy behind them,

they arrive at Place of the Manure Fires,

> the old ones shivering and the babies weeping, *shlak, shlak!*

—and gratefully make camp, the women unpacking the horses,

> who lower their long dark necks,
>> grazing on the low plateau to the west
>>> as the young girls seek out herbs to heal saddle-sores,
>>>> the wind singing *tsss!*

Certain best men, sent ahead by Looking-Glass to watch out for Shinbones, Crows, Big Bellies and other enemies, have already shot four buffalo cows. Whose heart cannot now love our new head-chief?

The women establish our lodges. Now they are cutting grass to make us all sweet soft beds,

> gathering buffalo dung for fires,
> and broiling steaks
>> (in the morning they will flense and smoke the hides),
>> —but Welweyas the half-woman, having neither husband nor mother to care for, goes away early, wishing to follow the white glint of water in the dark mud beneath willows until she can hang her King George blanket from a branch and commence admiring her reflected shape, parting her lips, pretending at breasts
>>> (shall I someday become what I wish?),
>> widening her eyes at herself as she stands longhaired, necklaced and tight-wrapped in that bolt of calico she received from the generous Bostons at Shallow Place

while Ollokot, unmoving, gazes down from the horse herd
into this wide-turning shallow cañon, watching Cloudburst
make their lodge, his ears going numb,
aching for Fair Land, fearing for his little son,
asking his heart what shall now be done about Cut Arm
(his heart will not answer);
presently he turns to watch back over our trail:
over the brow of the snowy hill he sees buffalo
as Toohhoolhoolsote's wives wander bent-backed, seeking
sticks and rocks with which to raise up their home against
the wind, cursing Cut Arm the Moldy, who has devoured
their lodgepoles;
Springtime's mouth begins watering for meat, and the baby is feebly crying;
they have both sickened from too much fleeing,
the child's arms and legs skinny white like a camas root,
the mother's face whitening like an old woman's eyes
(her husband says: *Síikstiwaa,* make your heart happy, for
Looking-Glass has now brought us into a good country!);
and her roan pony keeps trembling and sneezing,
Black Mane-Stripe is almost lame
and even Good Woman, worrying about White Face's hooves
(and still unsuspecting that Sound Of Running Feet is no longer a
child),
prefers to rest,
just for awhile
exactly here in this maze of wind-sheltered coulees so near the Medicine Line;
perhaps to-night we shall cut a few green branches, to keep the rain off our faces;
we shall help Toohhoolhoolsote's wives.

2

Once more White Bird urges our best men to rush on to the Old Woman's
Country,
to which Ollokot is willing
(his brother will watch over Cloudburst and the boy),
while Wottolen likewise says: There is no reason for us to stay here. I
smell death around here
—but Lone Bird,
he who sensed evil before Ground Squirrel Place,
remains easy in his heart:
this country is good, with many buffalo,
and his last horse will soon be lame, and his grandmother longs to rest;

while Toohhoolhoolsote and Heinmot Tooyalakekt wish the
horse herd to become well;

moreover, for the past seven nights, Grizzly Bear Youth's
WYAKIN, the AIR BIRD, has not flown down into his dreams
to warn him of anything, so that he who once followed the
People to Ground Squirrel Place against his own argument in
council takes no alarm just now,

and Sound Of Running Feet, restless, crumbles buffalo
chips upon her newborn fire, on which she sets the
kettle, then snaps off a hard dry stalk of buffaloberry for
nothing

while Lean Elk says: If you wish to die here, so be it; I shall do no
more for you;

but Looking-Glass,

he whom we sometimes call *Black Swan,*

has brought back our old life,

when we could rest or not, as we pleased:

so let us then rest,

our women longing once again to clothe lodgepoles with
skins,

and our best men desiring to hunt that double line of dark,
reeking buffalo browsing in the tawny grass

(plenty of game in this country);

knowing that we shall be safe, because his WYAKIN with the grebe's glowing
red eyes has promised him; squinting down, he says: Hear me, all my People!
The old ones are tired. Our children can go no more. They shall now rest; we
can cross the Medicine Line to-morrow,

at which Toohhoolhoolsote narrows his eyes, hunching down his head,
staring silently at everyone, then says: Yes, it is good

(he is one to know a place and Dream about it; to his ears all of us
have long since taken on the barking voices of geese in autumn);

and White Bird's woman *Kate* yearns nearly as much as Looking-Glass's pampered wives to rest, heal her horses, eat hot fat meat and salve her cracked lips
with buffalo tallow;

Springtime, tired of dreading, begins hoping to put on her best dress for
the Cutthroats, the one with double rows of dentalia shells across her
breasts,

across which her husband was once so welcome to run his hand;
in this country her milk will surely come back, so the baby may finally
begin to grow fat;

Burning Coals whispers happily among his herd, salving blisters,
trimming manes, stroking Lucky One;

even Heinmot Tooyalakekt,

who kept speaking against so many of the things we have done,
now says: We have made our freedom! Here not even Cut Arm can pen us up
on painted land. If we stay safe in this place and talk straight to the Bostons,
someday they will give us back our home.

3

And so those few who have them raise up their tipis in the dying grass,
while the rest do what they can with sticks and soldier cloth:
Toohhoolhoolsote's People by themselves between two creek-forks
in the northwest
(fifteen lodges),
then White Bird's People from Sparse-Snowed Place
(eleven lodges by the three trees,
White Bird's home beside Nah-How's),
Looking-Glass's People
(nine houses)
and then over the creek from them and across the low wide rise of
dying grass
to the village's southern edge:
Húsishúsis Kute's Palouses with the Wallowa People
(fourteen lodges up here in the higher flat:
Heinmot Tooyalakekt will sleep just here with his
daughters and wives);
as our busy old women now gather more buffalo dung, cutting and breaking willow branches from the creek,
then once again patching their worn-out horsehair ropes,
Cloudburst already boiling soup at Ollokot's lodge,
seeking not to think Fair Land's name,
some horses darkly huddled in the creek, drinking, churning mud with
their hooves, pawing at ice-crust along the bank, while the herd nickers
down at them,
most families unrolling buffalo robes and scraps of half-frozen Bluecoat canvas,
wrapping up their children in horse blankets, the wind blowing through
rips in the cloth,
the few trees decorated with red and yellow, like Lakota warlances
as Blackberry Person comes slowly from Looking-Glass's lodge to ask for
cous flour from Springtime,
who has none to give but presents her with a quarter-loaf of camas
bread
(once we enter the Old Woman's Country, everyone will find
food);

while Heinmot Tooyalakekt cleans his carbine
and the Medicine men and Medicine women all share
a smoke to drive crazy-making GHOSTS away.
Now an icy wind begins to blow, and from any distance the pale conical lodges
resemble trembling sails on that sea of withering, freezing grass:

Hasten; evening shadows be!

—yes, another cold evening of coyotes singing
(our scouts must stay out on the prairie to-night to keep them
off our kills):

we are looking toward the yellow sky,
and behind us spread the snowy pads of the Wolf's Paw,
where our enemies the Crows were created.

(Strong Eagle, who will lead our scouts
north and east against Crows, Big Bellies
and Walking Cutthroats, shyly watches
Looking-Glass's daughters as he awaits his
brave war-friends. Perhaps he will marry
that pair of girls. But as he stands in the
wind, turning over this desire, sudden grief
for the two slain Red Blankets,
who should not be mentioned,
bites him like a bad dog, and he looks away
from those lovely ones, tracking cloud-shadows on the cottonwoods down in the coulee,
hoping to kill a sleeping Crow this night,
—although any Boston will do—
then he remembers Split Rock, Wallowa
and Sparse-Snowed Place,
and wonders how it might be for us in the
Old Woman's Country.)

Now snow has begun to fall, so that this cold far country grows as
white as a fine new buckskin not yet smoked.

4

Toohhoolhoolsote, his eyes half closed in weariness, stares at the unseen end:
the Medicine Line.

5

Good Woman is telling some orphan children how COTTONTAIL BOY swept
THUNDER from the sky
(all the while she is longing for some blue grouse soup)

and Sound Of Running Feet feels jealous, then goes to clean
her little sister
as our old men, too cold and weary to gamble at the Stick Game, sit
smoking kinnikinnick,
hoping that we shall kill buffalo all the way to Sitting Bull's
country:
Buffalo meat is the best. Only buffalo meat
will do.
Looking Glass's wives perfume themselves with dried yarrow leaves, as the
Crow women often do:
their hearts are longing to please their husband and help him clear his
mind;
and Sound Of Running Feet is shivering: *í-tsitsitsititsits.*
Springtime throws her a rope to mend.
Red Spy, White Thunder and Strong Eagle
ride away.
Already comes night,
fat stars scattered like the ducks on Wallowa Lake,
and Heinmot Tooyalakekt counts them, lying in Good Woman's lap while she
picks lice from his hair.

6

Before dawn, he goes to Springtime
whose love once tasted as sweet as the humpmeat of a buffalo calf,
to tell her: *Síikstiwaa,* once we are safe past the Medicine Line, our daughter will begin
to grow, and I shall make her a toy digging-stick and you will paint it, my *síikstiwaa . . .*

7

TRAVELLER THE SUN begins to pale the horizon:
dark dawn, grey sky;
and frost thickens all over Toohhoolhoolsote's bone-bead necklaces; silently he
pulls them on
while Looking-Glass is parting his hair.

8

Toohhoolhoolsote comes out from under the sheet of mildewed canvas which
now comprises his lodge. Raising his hands, be begins to sing: *You, OLD MAN
SUN, Who ride forever across my country and all the countries of others . . .*

9

Springtime begins boiling buffalo bones
    (the baby still sleeping on the cradleboard)
as her husband, wrapping his blanket tighter, gazes down at the three trees by
White Bird's camp,
then turns toward the rolling hills to the south, finding nothing but dead grass
iced down and dying grass bending in the wind.

10

Sound Of Running Feet keeps shivering: *i-tsitsitsititsits.*
From one of his last packbags Looking-Glass takes a pretty King George blanket. He gives it to her, saying: Be warm now, my child,
    at which she weeps.

11

Her father says: Come now, my lovely one; let us go catch horses,
so she leaves her lovely blanket at home with Springtime, just for awhile, to save
its newness until we break camp;
they climb the hill
    where the buffaloberries are ripe but not yet frozen sweet,
    and her dog follows happily.

12

Good Woman and Cloudburst have already set out at the sky's first greying,
    catching White Face and Short Tail, leaping on them bareback, then
    trotting to the plateau just east where Red Spy has killed another fat buf-
    falo cow:
here in the bloodstained frost they will butcher the meat with Welweyas
the half-woman
    (vain one, she cannot forbear to bring her King George blanket
    with her, although she has at least spread it out to air a few steps
    away from the slaughtering-ground)
and with tiny old Towhee, who rarely gets tired,
and her daughter, Wounded Head's wife:
    Helping Another, that sad one who saw her little boy slowly die on
    the trail
        (now her chest-wound is healed over; she no longer breathes
        with whistling sounds);

their life-steam rises up;
>they have already erected stick frames on which to flense the hides
>while on the low horizon, Broken Tooth, Swan Woman, Blackberry Person
>and Wolf Old Woman, silhouetted against the yellowing sky, are bending
>over the buffalo bull that Strong Eagle has shot, whisking out their knives,
>drawing out half-frozen guts.

Picketing their horses away from Helping Another's pinto pony, who bites, the two sisters* take off their blankets; now they are ready to bloody their hands,

>>although Good Woman is slow and weary, for last night after her
>>husband fell asleep there came to her a nightmare of SOMEONE
>>Who outlined His eyes in white clay;

>Welweyas is already whirling her Wilson skinning knife between the
>flesh and pearly underside of the half-frozen hide, which she pulls away
>as she goes

>>(putting forth her man's strength),

>while Helping Another squats barefoot upon the carcass, holding it still
>on its back, gripping its forelegs as her mother cuts loose the anus and
>ties it off

>>(she has promised some liver to Toohhoolhoolsote)

>>>and the ravens are coming, crying: *Qoh, qoh, qoh!*

Cloudburst has left Fair Land's child with Springtime,

>>to whom she will bring the blood-rich heart to make her strong;
>they must quickly finish:

>>no time to cut the narrow red strips of meat to be smoked from
>>wooden frames,
>>for Looking-Glass might set us on the trail.

13

As for Sound Of Running Feet and her father, they walk west,

>along the windy ridge
>then toward the flat place which is so black with our wealth of horses.

Delighting in this woman-child of his, with her perfect hair-parting and lovely round face, Heinmot Tooyalakekt takes her hand

>>(she cannot stop smiling over the blanket that Looking-Glass has given
>>her)

as TRAVELLER THE SUN begins to warm them
and the horses say: *Hinimí.*

>>But now her dog begins to snarl, laying back his ears.

---

*That is, sisters-in-law.

14

Then White Thunder's old war-friend Wottolen,
    he who Dreamed of danger at Ground Squirrel Place,
now strides through the camp crying: *I have Dreamed! Enemies are coming*
    exactly here where the matted golden grass resembles a horse's sweaty
    mane
        as clouds lower over the red willows;
but Looking-Glass, as serenely rigid as a baby in a cradleboard, replies: I have told
you all three times: May your hearts now be at peace!
        and when his good wives Blackberry Person and Asking Maiden
        leap up anxiously, and the two daughters with them, he rises as if
        to strike them—he has now begun making himself angry!—so that
        they all decide to go help butcher buffalo with those other women
    —while certain warriors whose women have not finished packing sit un-
    easily playing the Bone Game
                (Yellow Bull and Shooting Thunder talking about
                scouting ahead and maybe buffalo hunting or
                horse-stealing:
                    now that it grows cold, everything is easy:
                    one can see a buffalo cow by her steam)
      as Young White Bird and the other boys play something like the
      "base ball" they have seen at Butterfly Place, batting lumps of mud
      with sticks

            and *Kate,* having packed up the lodge, scrapes the hair
            off a deerskin, meaning to make clothes for Young
            White Bird
            (now she has begun singing)
            and even Toohhoolhoolsote, whose heart well knows
            the sadness of returning to hot meadows of dying grass
            after flying up in Dreams, feels no narrowing of the
            world
                —but suddenly the baby begins to cry, so that
                later Springtime will be wondering whether it is
                certainly true what the People say, that the young-
                est child can often see what is hidden from the
                others,
      and Black Eagle, unafraid of his father Wottolen's nightmare,
      amuses himself by strutting around the camp in his loose
      soldier shoes;
even now when Red Spy and White Thunder come galloping up from the south,
shouting: *Stampeding buffalo! Bluecoats coming!*

and Lean Elk sits slowly down, with his face in his hands,
        Húsishúsis Kute pulling tight his striped blanket,
Looking-Glass shouts: Complete this talk! You saw buffalo but no Bluecoats. Bluecoats cannot come here. Hear me, you People! I am head-chief—

15

Whether his blindness has grown since Ground Squirrel Place
        (perhaps senility now begins to grow up like a mushroom through his
        overripe heart, so that all that remains left to him is childish opposition
        to Lean Elk)
cannot be known; but the way to understanding his fatality may be simply this:
When one is a *lucky man* whose luck has bled away
        (Cut Arm devoured him; now he is nearly as poor as the meat of a salmon
        that has spawned and died),
habit may well be all that is left, and one goes on acting as if the luck will return,
since without it one is certainly lost,
        when he is lost regardless:
                luck, like life itself, is no certain thing, but a loveliness which may
                alight upon my shoulder but more often seems to be some un-
                known brilliant quantity in motion.

16

Still our women, trusting Looking-Glass, carefully continue to pack the lovely
bloody steaks of buffalo meat onto their horses and Cut Arm's mules,
                a pony cropping at dying grass,
                and our forgotten old men smoking the pipe and uttering nonsense
                like magpies, *pokát, pokát,*
until Strong Eagle comes galloping, waving his blanket to show us: *Bluecoats are
here!*
    Some women begin screaming
        (remembering Ground Squirrel Place),
            the chiefs shouting: *Young men, pack your horses and ride!*
                and the few women who are ready lift up their children onto
                the packed horses and begin to gallop north
                    as Wottolen runs for the horse herd
                    and White Thunder begins to feel something almost
                    gleeful in his heart like a MONSTER swimming under-
                    water: Now all this will be finished
    —and White Bird remarks slowly: My heart is sad that we kept no scouts
around our camp. Too late now!

while to his best men he murmurs: Looking-Glass is worse than nothing; he is a dead and wormy dog,

at which we do not even laugh, for it is so;

once again they have surprised us as if we were a herd of hoofed and hunted creatures running round and round:

therefore Looking-Glass has made himself to be not even nothing

(turning away, he pulls on his beaded gauntlets);

our best men,

who yet again believed him like children,

run into the southern coulees to prepare hidden welcomes for Cut Arm,

Ollokot among them, wishing that he could have painted his face one more time with the red earth that Fair Land used to prepare for him:

we are making the war-cry:

now we shall be quickly dead:

they are causing us to die

—while Strong Eagle, leaping off his horse, strips off his leggings and deerskin shirt; even if Ollokot will not do so, this man,

last of the Three Red Blankets,

pauses to paint himself black and red, then says: Now in only a brief time those Bluecoats will be here. I am going to collect their bones,

to which Toohhoolhoolsote replies: I am certainly ready,

as our dogs commence howling and snarling.

Now the first enemy,

newest of Cut Arm's slaves,

begins to shows himself:

first his war bonnet,

then his grinning head, his painted face and shouting mouth puffing clouds of frost-breath as he screams his war-song,

then his naked shoulders

and the tip of his Springfield rifle already swinging toward us

as he comes galloping over the bluff on a spotted horse well decorated for war:

a Painted Arrow!—

with the hats of Bluecoats beginning to rise up behind him like mushrooms.

IT CANNOT SEEM RIGHT
SEPTEMBER 30–OCTOBER 4

1

*A*bout Asleep's father shouts: My son, get your horse and ride away quick!
You are yet too young; you cannot fight—
> and Wottolen's brave son Black Eagle begins running for the horses:
>> *Save the horses! Save the horses!*
> (frowning in fury, he throws off his soldier shoes),
>> Young White Bird fleeing from the bullets of the Bluecoats
>> and Painted Arrows, swimming across the icy creek
>>> (his thumb-stump almost crazing him with chill-pain),
>> running, running,
>>> barefoot and naked but for his deerskin shirt,
>> until finally a kindhearted woman sweeps him up onto her horse
> even as Black Eagle, still unhorsed, runs up toward the frantic herd,
>> hears buffalo thunder from the south
>>> (it is not buffalo but the Bluecoats, the Horse People, charging
>>> down),
> tears his blanket into strips
and knotting them into a rope, he catches Peopeo Tholekt's fine yellow
horse, leaps up, and rides after the stampeding horses down into the coulee
>> where he sees many People already mounted,
>>> shouting, milling, trying to catch our other horses,
>>>> because if Cut Arm gets them we are finally finished
>>>>> (Looking-Glass's daughters longing for Rainbow and
>>>>> the Three Red Blankets to live again and save us),
>> as Painted Arrows swoop in from the west:
but Peopeo Tholekt's mother demands this horse, which Black Eagle
must give her;
then she returns to him his blanket rope so that he can lassoo his own horse
and another woman gives him a leather strap with which he bridles the
animal
> as Heinmot Tooyalakekt,
>> he who was called *Joseph,*
>>> and has been catching horses with his daughter,
>>>> whose round face and low forehead make her
>>>> seem younger than her big strong hands,

throws her a rope, calling: Sound Of Running Feet, my brave one, my lovely one, hear me now: Catch a horse and ride away!

—to which she, wise and good young woman, wastes no time replying
(he will never see her again)
but looks for Yellow One,
Aunt Cloudburst's gift,
and not finding him, lassoos one of Burning Coals's quick stallions
(if he lives, the mean old man will be angry)
even as her father, seeing Black Mane-Stripe, runs to rope
him for himself,
bullets singing like flies;
then, leaping up lightly onto her animal's back, Sound Of Running Feet looks back once to see her father gazing directly at her, his eyes glittering almost as if in tears, which her heart will now remember together with that rectangular charm at his throat, and the V-necked fringe of his jacket
(on each of his sleeves a diagonal thick white stripe of quills, which gives way to dark stripes of quills)
as the rest of these People trapped there with horses begin to gallop away
from enemy guns shooting *pim, pim, pim* and *kiw, kiw, kiw!*
—uncaught horses stampeding with dilated nostrils and
Wounded Head's stallion running loose in terror
as Sound Of Running Feet, now looking back for the
second time, finds her father out of sight
(his heart is near exploding with sorrow);
and she is shivering as she goes
(wishing to be riding so brightly in that King
George blanket given her by Looking-Glass),
and a Painted Arrow begins to chase her but is lured
away by Cloudburst's horse
(it is well that Sound Of Running Feet wears no
pretty blanket);
while About Asleep keeps chasing the horse he has roped, pulling until the stallion finally braces his legs, snakes back his head and snaps his teeth at the boy
who struggles to leap onto his back as the Painted Arrows now ride up screaming:
About Asleep is too short to leap up like a man, but finally
pulls himself on like some clumsy Boston
even as a Painted Arrow begins to level a Winchester
at him:
this enemy's mouth has opened as wide as it will
go in a scream of triumphant murder,

so that About Asleep's heartbeats begin to slow down; as his death approaches, each instant elongates, rendering him ever wealthier in life; there is now time to see everything:

his killer's moccasins are so richly beaded as to be nearly ice-white, with lovely zigzag fissures showing the dark hide beneath

as he swings the Winchester around;

and About Asleep gallops away through the bullets

—*kíw-kíw-kíw-kíw!*—

to sweep up his younger brother, wheeling down into the soft low cañons in order to head north

and silently calling on his WYAKIN:

I am encircling; I am enclosing; I am circling as I go

—but as they flee, a bullet shoots off one of his younger brother's braids just below the ear:

two Bluecoats are chasing them but this horse can gallop well;

... circling as I go ...

the enemies fall behind;

but just ahead a Painted Arrow on a cream-colored horse is shooting at a woman

(his favorite sport):

Pim!

—she is galloping, galloping—

pim!

now she is flying down

to break her skull on OUR MOTHER'S frozen breast

so that the Painted Arrow, singing, vaults off his pony,

whisks out his knife,

bends over her and

then About Asleep and his brother have escaped beyond the rolling ridge

—but by now the People cannot catch more horses!

The Bluecoats and Painted Eagles are chasing them; they are driving them

as in bitter desperation we remember our name for Cut Arm:

People Herder:

now he has herded our lovely horses,

the ones who have helped and saved us,
our friends, our wealth,
almost half of them,
so that our children and women and old ones can no longer flee;
hence the young men, wide-eyed and braided, gallop off to die.

2

Brave Cloudburst, who remembers how she once brought her husband a fresh
horse when the Bluecoats were shooting at him at Cottonwood Place
(Fair Land, the one he loved better, still lived),
once more does exactly this,
minding Ollokot's good counsel not to turn her horse broadside to enemies
spewing cotton-smoke at her from their carbines
(she longs to kill them all);
so she brings Ollokot's stallion back down into camp,
but Heinmot Tooyalakekt has not come back, and Springtime crouches weeping,
with the two children in their cradleboards beside her.

3

Wounded Head leaps onto a staked horse, cuts the rope and gallops toward
camp to get his rifle,
coming upon that Painted Arrow who on a cream-colored horse chases
another of our women, who tries to whip her horse away
(she is pleading as she rides):
Wounded Head still lacks his gun to help,
and so the Painted Arrow shoots her:
Tsálalal!
and now he is counting coup on her corpse; surely he will scalp her; he is
singing his war-song;
and Wounded Head gallops past, raging in his heart,
while Two Moons keeps galloping round and round the
camp, holding back Bluecoats and Painted Arrows as best he
can.

4

As for the Bluecoats charging four abreast from the south, our warriors, hiding
prone in flanking coulees, begin to receive them,
dropping down, creeping back over the wide ridge of frozen grass
toward the clouds,

looking up over the gentle wide shoulder of the coulee, to the east,
where the plain almost flattens, and cloud-shadows stripe the rolling swales of white grass:
here they come, the Riding Soldiers, the Horse People!
—now our best men are raising themselves up just a little but staying low
in the dying grass,
taking aim,
preparing to shoot from left and right as they gallop near,
the bugle screaming:
Cut Arm is galloping down! Where did he come from?
Where is his blue suit?
Kill the trumpeter!
No, it cannot be Cut Arm. Those are other Bluecoats.
Then why do they kill us?
—and as these enemies halt where OUR MOTHER suddenly steepens,
their horses rearing back, slipping in the icy grass,
with the Wallowa People's lodges in sight below,
our best men leap up in a line to shoot point-blank.

5

Praying to THE ONE ABOVE
and singing his WYAKIN song,
Heinmot Tooyalakekt, leaping on Black Mane-Stripe,
gallops straight toward the Painted Arrows,
who are parading around, pretending to be brave,
seeking to catch stray horses and bridle them with brittle dead grass:
so he is met by a scout in a white shirt on a white war pony,
his long loose white shirt cinched around his waist by a full
cartridge belt which shines like the autumn sun: he is singing
a Painted Arrow song and raising his rifle and
then rides through them all
(they are screaming in disappointment),
next passing the Bluecoats
as they shoot holes in his clothes and wound his dear horse;
indeed he has returned, down into the Place of the Manure Fires,
hastening along the dark creek,
passing the lodges on the east bank,
galloping up onto the tongue of flat land southeast of White Bird's
People,
who are running and shouting all together so that for an instant their bewilderment infects him,

then across the small dip, the creek wriggling at his left,
he comes home
>	where Ollokot is not
>	and Good Woman cannot be seen
but Springtime, his lovely *síikstiwaa,* stands waiting
>	(she has finally made herself brave),
holding out his rifle: My husband, here is your gun. Fight!

6

Rushing south toward the guns' voices in the smooth hills, despairing for
the People and himself
>	as Bluecoats fall dead off their horses
>	and their dead horses come tumbling down,
>>		*tsálalal!*
>	so that our enemies now dismount again to fight
>>		just as at Sparse-Snowed Place
>>		and Place Like Split Rock
>>>			(we have shot their bugler; we are killing their of-
>>>			ficers),
he leaps off Black Mane-Stripe to meet Ollokot,
>	he who leads the young men,
but Ollokot is already dead, with a bullet in his skull.

7

Cloudburst and Good Woman are not here to know; Springtime has not yet
been told; but our young men's hearts are raging and grieving,
>	Lean Elk running toward this fight
>>		(longing for Shore Crossing's buffalo gun),
>>>			and Two Moons showing the young boys where to begin dig-
>>>			ging rifle-pits before he too comes running, with his Spring-
>>>			field upraised and a round chambered in it:
>>>>				on that high bluff the Bluecoats now try to fire their big
>>>>				gun, but since they cannot depress its barrel, the shell
>>>>				flies laughably over our heads.
Seeing his younger brother thus dead in the stiff grey grass, Heinmot Tooyalakekt tells the warriors: We must complete our hearts without him. Since we have
left our home forever, we can do no better than die for our women and children.

8

Even our oldest chiefs are now shouting, riding, fighting,
    the Bluecoats firing ever more pressingly,
the first of them now galloping into our camp:
    we kill three of them
        (Heinmot Tooyalakekt shooting well)
but they kill six of us before we drive them out
                (Red Owl is now dead: first he lost his country, then his life);
             so we are stripping rifles and cartridges from the Horse People's
             corpses
                        (Lean Elk is digging a rifle-pit on the brow of the hill
                        and White Thunder keeps aiming at each Bluecoat until
                        his bullets are gone):
             for a raven's wingbeat our hearts are clear
    unwrapping our Medicine bundles, we put them on for the last
    time,
        and for the last time Red Spy sings out the *scalp halloo*
as White Bird says: We must send word to Sitting Bull.
                  Hear me; I saw a woman escape; perhaps she is now
                  already among the Cutthroats—
                    Where is my husband? Tell me, where is my niece?
My People, we must dig in and wait.

9

    As an officer in a light shortcoat
        (his white charger already dead)
kneels down to reload his pistol, White Thunder shoots him in the neck:
    Áhahhahahahahahahahaha!
        (with this Winchester it is easy)
        —Bluecoats falling *tsálalal,* horse-holders taking their places,
            loosed horses whinnying back to the Bluecoat chief's house
                 and Red Spy shooting away the last of his .50 cal-
                 ibre exploding bullets
            as another Painted Arrow,
                 his face painted yellow, with an oval black outline
                 under his parted, unbound hair and around his
                 cheeks and chin, a scarlet feather shooting up
                 from his head, his cartridge belt cinching a striped
                 blanket round his waist, powder horn at his shoul-
                 der, his mouth a screaming oval of hate-songs,

riding up close,
> tries to strike Looking-Glass with an elkhorn quirt, but
> Peopeo Tholekt shoots him in the face:
>> *Pim!*

and now at last some Bluecoats find sense to throw themselves down on their bellies, shooting down into the coulees at our best men,
> so that Five Snows,
>> he who loves *getting-drunk liquid,* and killed Stripes Turned In
>> when he was drunk,
> now swallows a fat lead bullet, and his death with it,
>> his throat exploding as he tumbles backward,

proving that the rest of us must put Ollokot out of mind while we save ourselves.

10

Toohhoolhoolsote, silently snarling, has crowned himself with that carefully dressed wolf's head which he once lovingly belled and beaded:
> indeed my death will be as delicious as black bear meat!

He is preparing to shout; exactly now he is singing the scalp song
> —then sings his WYAKIN song.

Closing one eye to take aim with his Sharps
> *—pim!—*

he sees the long trailer of red trade cloth streaming straight behind the Painted Arrow he has just killed, and on its upper edge, a row of eagle feathers standing straight up, dark-tipped like something charred,
> the warrior's angry ageing face exploding as the bullet enters his screaming mouth
>> the horse galloping right through camp before the rider falls.

11

Although he has now made himself still more despisable, Looking-Glass is brave; no one can say otherwise; he retains a few cartridges still in that fringed, red-bordered, blue-hourglassed beaded pouch which his Crow friends once gave him. Grimacing, he unties the mirror from his scalp-lock.

Among the oncoming riders he now recognizes his old enemy Two Moons, who helped kill Yellow Hair's soldiers at Little Big Horn and who now, boulder-wide and grim, comes at a gallop, the corners of his mouth angling sharply down and his eyes narrowed.

Looking-Glass shouts his name. Two Moons rushes toward him, levelling his Winchester.

They both fire, and miss.

12

Bear-hearted, wolf-headed Toohhoolhoolsote,
>scorning these others who behave as if they are bleeding from their hearts
>>(they have forgotten that we must all die)
>and longing to kill Cut Arm, who caused him to be ashamed at Butterfly
>Place
>>>—I shall shoot three fingers down from the star on his hat—
has led seven warriors exactly here:
>>Tohtohaliken, Tomyahnin, Timlihpoosman, Lakoyee, Young Eagle
>>Necklace, Old Eagle Necklace and Grizzly Bear Lying On His Back;
>they are all lying down at Red Rock Place,
>>>straight across the side-coulee from White Bird's lodge,
>>>where the three trees stand;
>>fighting as eagerly as young men look for women
>>>(we say to the lovely ones: *Shall we inhale each other?*).
Lakoyee shouts: *Tsépmin!* but his eyes are mistaken;
>>exactly here in the iced dead grass below this small pink-rocked
>>cliff they lie shooting at Bluecoats and Painted Arrows,
>>>>whose violence is so vast that Lakoyee remembers the
>>>>story we tell our children about when the MONSTER
>>>>swallowed so many People:
>>already Young Eagle Necklace is wounded in his leg
>>>(Timlihpoosman shoots at an officer but the shot goes
>>>wide);
>>then a bullet opens Lakoyee's forehead:
>>>>his life is pouring out into the dying grass—
but Toohhoolhoolsote
>(who is so strong that eight men cannot hold him when he is drunk)
smiles to remember the mountains of his home country between the Enemy River
and the Chinook Salmon Water
>>(the land where he was young
>>and married his women:
>>>once he had little sons and daughters running eagerly into his
>>>presence; now they are dead);
>and chambering another cartridge in his Sharps, he swings up the barrel
as lightly as a heron raises its head,
>>unceasingly singing his WYAKIN song:
>>>*So I am becoming crowned with bearclaws—*
>and shoots a Painted Arrow off his horse,
>>>but Old Eagle Necklace has missed a Painted Arrow
>>>who is wearing an *American* flag

as yellow lights wink from distant rifle-barrels
and Tohtohaliken and Timlihpoosman lie dying in the grass
(their WYAKINS have left them)
as Grizzly Bear Lying On His Back, aiming his Winchester,
declining to be no more than a mule with his head low
in the grass,
takes a bullet to the hand;
now the Bluecoats are pouring bullets exactly down
here at Red Rock Place
where Toohhoolhoolsote,
getting drunk on his own necklace-rattling
chuckles as he now breaks out his last package of .44 calibre explosive bullets from
Cottonwood Place,
levels his Sharps, pulling the trigger even as the
barrel still swivels:
Pim! . . . taq!
—the bullet detonating just before it reaches the
Bluecoat's face, riddling his brain with lead hailstones;
and Old Eagle Necklace leaps back dead as Grizzly Bear Lying
On His Back gets shot in the throat
—*tsálalal!*—
so that now only Tomyahnin and Toohhoolhoolsote are left.

Toohhoolhoolsote has not yet been wounded even now when they shoot Tomyahnin in the shoulder.

Gnashing his teeth, he stamps his foot so that his leg-rattles hiss and whisper:
I am turning round and round, enclosing OUR MOTHER in my arms—

Chambering the next exploding bullet, he says to his heart: I who have seen
the stone corpse of SUN MAN, in the place called Red Mineral Paint, where Smohalla once lived,
just for awhile,
must now die;
then he shoots and misses
(laughing at himself: *I am ageing; I am rotting like wood*):
the sizzling bullet now detonates in air.
So he chambers another round,
and as he lifts up his head to kill another Bluecoat,
yearning with all his heart for all our dead warriors to be here at
this fight,
indeed death enters his face.

13

Cleaning his rifle, frowning down at the fouled barrel, White Thunder says: The Painted Arrows are the Crows' enemies. What do they mean, hunting us together?

Naked-Footed Bull replies: Ask Cut Arm.

14

Once TRAVELLER THE SUN has gone halfway down the sky, Bluecoats begin to charge from the east and southwest, so we shoot their officer and they retreat in terror,

    but word comes to us that Lean Elk,

        who led us best,

    has just been killed in error by our best men;

    and Húsishúsis Kute,

        he who spoke so bravely to Cut Arm at the Butterfly Place council,

      now thinking to see Painted Arrows,

        whom White Thunder on his skittish horse has tried and failed to drive away from our women,

    has mistakenly killed Kowwaspo, Koyekown and even Lone Bird,

      that wise young man who Dreamed that the Bluecoats would soon kill us

      (Looking-Glass would not listen);

but here is the worst: they have captured nearly all our horses!

        —Cut Arm, you moldy coward, why hide again? Cut Arm, come down here so that we may kill you!—

so that we instantly become nothing,

    our freedom now and forever the merest memory-image, like the white-outlined, black-and-yellow-striped hourglass of beadwork on the elkhide rifle case which once belonged to Looking-Glass

    (and now travels in Captain Fisher's collection).

15

Still we have some brave men left:

    Strong Eagle,

    Peopeo Tholekt,

    Wounded Head,

    Two Moons

      (no longer caring whether he keeps his life)

and his half-brother White Cloud, who has fought in every battle;
Black Eagle,
White Thunder and Wottolen,
Red Spy and Shooting Thunder;
> Heinmot Tooyalakekt calls to the young boys to fetch them water;
we shall fight on, throwing back our feathered heads, pointing our rifles out and
up at the Bluecoats, watching always to both sides;
> while some boys and women have already set out toward Sitting Bull,
> who killed Yellow Hair last summer:
>> he is a truly *lucky man,* having Power
>>> (he must be luckier than any of us);
>> it would be easy for him to ride here with his Cutthroats and finally kill
Cut Arm—

16

So we are fighting on,
> the smoky sky flushed with twilight, pearl-clouds and ice-clouds pending,
>> warriors sniping at the enemy from any coulee until darkness
>> comes
>>> (never again the monstrous roar and flash of Shore Crossing's
>>> buffalo gun, but still unsilenced the five far and feeble notes
>>> of Peopeo Tholekt's bird-bone whistle).
Again White Thunder cries out: First the Lice-Eaters, then the Salish, the
Crows and now the Painted Arrows! Why are they all helping the Bostons to kill
us? It cannot seem right,
but his uncle, Old Yellow Wolf, reproves him: You promised me that if you went
to war you would never whine like a woman.

17

Six hundred People remain alive,
> the women, children and old ones now digging in along the creek near
> where Toohhoolhoolsote's People have placed their lodges,
>> frantically scratching into the frozen earth with skinning knives,
>> digging sticks, camas hooks and those trowel bayonets we stole
>> from Ground Squirrel Place,
>>> Welweyas the half-woman throwing great hunks of
>>> mud over her shoulder with a man's strength,
>> families grabbling out lodges for themselves like prairie dogs,
>>> laying down saddles over the doorways and burying
>>> those in dirt,
>>>> reënforcing the entrances with dead horses,

patching ropes with numb fingers, in case
we should recapture our herd,
as our best men dig rifle-pits in the hillsides.
The children are crying;
White Thunder, who has eaten nothing, digs furiously
with a Bluecoat's intrenching tool;
White Bird's ears are aching; he cannot get his wolfskin
cap; the Bluecoats' guns can see his lodge.
Wailing for our new dead, the women fetch water and serve
what dried food they can,
longing to make secret fires, so that the cold would
bleed out of children's knees and fingers, but they must
not give any light to the enemy's well-seeing guns.
Cloudburst has painted Ollokot's ruined face red, and Toohhoolhoolsote's
wives paint his dead face red, black and yellow; our kind women paint Lean Elk's
face also, since he had no wives;
they cover our dead where they can, hiding them from the
Bluecoats, Painted Arrows and Lice-Eaters.
All night we are digging connecting tunnels
as our best men creep up among the wounded Bluecoats to take their
guns, cartridges and money
(Heinmot Tooyalakekt made us promise not to harm them; indeed
we are even bringing water to the thirsty ones)
but Wounded Head, barefoot and battle-stripped, must hide
in the snow all night, among the scaring-stones on the eastern rise where other People before us once drove buffalo
(now there is ice on his braids, and the coyotes are singing);
he will try to enter our camp at dawn.
We are sorrowing as we dig,
dreading the dawn:
Heinmot Tooyalakekt, feeling unsteady, is remembering Ollokot
and then Fair Land,
the kindly one, who was always eager to give others the best
to eat,
in her dress of red King George cloth decorated with many white
shells,
—while Springtime, who still has one deer-gut bag filled with
dried fat
(Good Woman saved it from Ground Squirrel Place),
is giving orphans small handfuls of the dried buffalo meat which
we took away from our fine friends the Crows, and to *Kate* she gives
all the bacon she got from the Bluecoats at Shallow Place

—but Strong Eagle, last of the Three Red Blankets, withdraws himself into the darkness, sits down, closes his eyes, calls upon his
WYAKIN and presently Dreams of two reddish stallions with rich
black tails; each horse is lovely enough to bestow a necklace on;
now he is galloping, riding up; he will grow rich.

18

Wounded Head,
      worrying over his wife Helping Another and Towhee her mother
        (they did not return from butchering buffalo),
prepares to seek them,
at which Heinmot Tooyalakekt then says: My dear nephew, from my heart I ask
this: Learn what you can about Good Woman and Sound Of Running Feet.
    Indeed I shall look for them,
replies the warrior,
      who now crawls into the eastern dark.
        Cloudburst and Springtime are weeping,
        but Toohhoolhoolsote's women sit silent.
    It has become dawn,
      the snow falling already a hand's width deep,
and
          just before Wounded Head creeps back in to the People like a snake,
            having found nobody he sought,
            leading his horse through a deep and winding coulee so that
            the enemies will not see
              as we all wait on Sitting Bull's coming
                (he who has been our enemy forever is now the
                only one for whose friendship we can even yearn,
                  although Looking-Glass tells his heart: as
                  cruelly proud as Sitting Bull may sit, with
                  that great eagle feather rising from his fore-
                  head, when he rides here I shall make my-
                  self prouder),
for the first time their big gun begins to speak,
      shooting down:
it says *timm!*
      —a great gout of frosted stony mud rising up,
        hailing gravel,
          thudding down smoking and stinking,
        (women screaming, holding buffalo robes over their heads in hopes
        of not being killed):
and in much the same way that when the fat brown grasshoppers of the

Buffalo Country fly up from the summer dirt, their wings flash out so
vibrantly that they momentarily resemble butterflies, so these howitzer
shells send up lovely brightness when they explode,
    but even as the People's gazes first begin seeking to comprehend this
flowering color, it has become but dust and smoke, the concussion now
killing, deafening, dismembering—and then dirt, mud, ice, snow and
rocks come back down:
        this gun seeks to bury People alive!
          but only one pit does it find,
            closing OUR MOTHER,
              suffocating a mother and child
                (the *Americans* are our friends).
So we live through another day of ice beneath snow while old Swan Woman
mourns her horses,
        gunsmoke twisting down into our cañon, and
    the golden grass bent down by wind, frozen where it has kissed the snow
        (now after the freeze is the time for our women to beat the bright
        red buffaloberries off the branches, catching them on their spread-
        out sleeping-robes;
        then our women would break through the creek-ice to wash the
        berries clean, and our mouths would be contented:
           for once the frost arrives, these berries get sweet;
              there are more of them here than back home
                in Wallowa);
and looking across the stiff red willows and up the gentle white ridge-ocean to
where the Bluecoats are, our best men long as ever to kill Cut Arm or this other
chief
        while our children, peering out of caves and holes at the creek's rosy steel,
        crave water
              as White Thunder, preparing to be killed, remembers Wal-
              lowa Lake
              and Looking-Glass's heart hopes northward to the grey wall
              of the Medicine Line;
           and just as Ollokot once used to caress Fair Land and Cloudburst,
           running his fingers down their unbraided hair, so this death-wind
           now strokes our cheekbones, noses, necks and coughing throats; so
           it makes love to the shrunken breasts of our shivering old women
           in their ragged blankets and deerskins, chilling their hearts, slip-
           ping long ice-fingers around their coughing lungs
        as our old men sit miserably in the clammy icy pits we have dug, too worn
        out and hungry to play the Bone Game
           (smoking kinnikinnick warms them, just for awhile)
and Heinmot Tooyalakekt, longing to lie down, just for awhile

(or else to be killed, and meet his father and his dear brother),
helps the young men tunnel from hole to hole.

19

Now a white flag rises on the southern hillcrest, and the Bluecoats' voice shouts down in Chinook: Hear me, *Chief Joseph!* I speak for Bear Coat, who is chief here. Bear Coat says: Come here and give me your rifles. Then this fight will be over, and I shall carry you back to your country. I have no wish to kill your women and children! *Joseph,* what do you say?

Our best men are laughing.— Heinmot Tooyalakekt, he thinks you are head-chief!

He has no sense!

Let us thrust a stick up his anus!

Joseph, Bear Coat awaits you. His heart longs to meet you. Come up here quickly, before he makes himself angry—

May he eat mice!

My People, now I shall speak. If I must play the head-chief's part, then let me ride up to meet this Bear Coat. Maybe he speaks straight. If he kills me, Looking-Glass and White Bird can defend the People.

Uncle, you must not go or they will trick you forever—

Joseph, are you coming or shall I kill you? Bear Coat says: You must answer me quickly.

White Bird now says: We cannot go on in any way. We have no friends; now we are starving. Heinmot Tooyalakekt, you always spoke against this war. But Looking-Glass kept quiet in his country, and Cut Arm devoured him! We made a treaty with the Bostons, and yet they killed us at Ground Squirrel Place. Why should you trust Bear Coat? He must be an *American* like the others. And yet we cannot stay here, nor can we ride away anymore. My dear brother, do as you choose.

Joseph!

Looking-Glass, what do you say?

I say there is no good in a Boston's heart, and Sitting Bull will surely come to help us.

Then for now I shall not go,

and so we begin to fight again,

our best men laughing: *Joseph!*

20

Shooting Thunder has been longing for exploding bullets; with them he can kill the Bluecoats' horses even when the range is bad;

but now that does not matter; the Bluecoats have become like us at last,

lying low, shooting carefully, seeking not to show themselves.

21

At sunset of that second evening we hear a wagon train coming to bring food
and tents for the Bluecoats
        (although still no friend has come for us)
and were we still wealthy in horses, we could ride out to destroy that train
            as we nearly did at Big Water,
or steal the Bluecoats' mules
            as we did at Camas Meadows,
                although it is true that they had no Painted Arrows to help them
                there;
instead we live on, with our best men well dug in, shooting at the Bluecoats,
            whose gun says *timm!* but cannot see to kill
                (this day no more of us have died);
now we are creeping to the creek at night to get water, quietly filling our canteens
and buffalo horns
            which the young boys carry to the warriors;
            our women cook secretly together in one wide pit,
                the bravest bringing hot meat to the men
                    (the last Crow beef, Boston food from Shallow Place, steaks
                    from our dead horses),
                and Looking-Glass's wives and daughters hang their heads as
                they help
                        (their hearts are ashamed of him by whom we now suf-
                        fer this)
while Heinmot Tooyalakekt,
            who if he could would carry everything uphill for all his People,
crawls from hole to hole,
                through snow as bright as his eldest daughter's hair-parting
                    (perhaps she is not yet dead),
            helping wherever he can,
after which again we wait for nothing,
Kate sitting in a hole alone, Toohhoolhoolsote's widows digging quietly in another hole
            (soon they must desist from saying his name),
and White Thunder's mother Swan Woman, fierce and prematurely ancient,
        wrapped tight in faded blankets both plaid and striped, with their fringes
        mangy, and thorn-made holes in them around her calves
            (her white hair is parted neatly beneath her bonnet);
squinting, grips her stick, ready to bash in a Bluecoat's face,
while Springtime, the lovely one, sits underground next to Looking-Glass's daughters:
they are all rocking babies in the deep pits,
        falling asleep sitting up,

living into another dawn
> of sharp black shards of open water around the willows,
> numb fingers, running noses, hungry bellies
>> (but Good Woman, most provident of all wives—has she now
>> been killed?—kept even until now a last bag of hard white
>> cous roots, which thus belongs to Springtime),
>>> a dead pony in a coulee,
>>> the Bluecoats' big gun thundering *timm!* just as at Big
>>> Water . . .
>>>> —and now a new gun shouts: *titálin!*
>>>>> (we must wait until our ears no longer ring)—
> and the faint hissing of the water beneath the snow.

22

So this is war:
> sleet stinging our best men's cheeks,
> wet snow sticking,
>> snow half-melting against Strong Eagle's ankles and then freezing,
>> ice thickening on the backs of his knees
>>> (closing his eyes, he sees the dawn sky shining through sil-
>>> houetted willow-branches at Ground Squirrel Place,
>>>> in that time when Rainbow and all Three Red Blankets
>>>> remained alive to save us),
> long parallels of wind-beaten grass frozen down against the snow,
> Looking-Glass's daughters, the pampered ones, trying not to weep with
> hunger, remembering how we used to bake eels on sticks
>> when we still had our home
while in that cave of icy mud; Springtime,
> who loves roasted shoulder-meat,
sits dull-eyed, rocking her baby between *Kate,* who still holds Fair Land's son, and
Swan Necklace's wife, who is mending a horsehair rope,
>> until Heinmot Tooyalakekt creeps in like a snake to bring more of that
>> dried buffalo meat which we took from our dear hosts the Crows
>>> (when Springtime asks for news, he wraps himself tight in his grey
>>> blanket),
> then crawls out again to visit his young men in the southwest-facing rifle-
> pits; they are all longing to shoot
> —but the Bluecoats remain careful, rarely showing themselves above our
> coulees;
so that we wait for nothing, grieving for our dead, dreaming of lost horses, hoping
for the Cutthroats to save us:
> Why should we not have one friend?

23

As Traveller the Sun begins to go under the horizon, Heinmot Tooyalakekt speaks to the warriors

> (who are no longer stripped for war, since they cannot ride or run, but only crouch by night and day):

Young men, now you have had what you desired. You named me *coward;* you called your own chiefs crooked-talkers! So you beat the elkhide and made your war. I warned you that in the end we must obey the Bostons and be quiet—living or dead! Young men, you would not listen! When we all met at Split Rock, we numbered seven hundred. Now a hundred and more have been killed. Young men, what do you say now? Young men, have your hearts yet been satisfied?

> —while they stare wide-eyed and rigid into his face, their braids unravelling as they pull their blankets tighter over their ragged deerskin shirts, their pallid necklace-loops hidden against their skin to avoid drawing fire
>
> > (in their silent hearts they are saying:
> >
> > > Although you talk as if *we* have done this, only once since this big fight began
> > >
> > > > —not here
> > > >
> > > > > nor at Place Like Split Rock, Ground Squirrel Place, nor even Big Water,
> > > > >
> > > > > > since Cut Arm's killers always came on so quickly—
> > > > >
> > > > > only at Camas Meadows, where Looking-Glass and Ollokot led us to win
> > > > >
> > > > > > —hear us, Heinmot Tooyalakekt, you would not ride with us then, but stayed behind, stirring ashes with the old women!—
> > > >
> > > > yes, only once since we rode away from home could we beat the green hide and sing war-songs to make ourselves brave!);
> >
> > then quickly their eyes swim back toward the southern bluff, in case some enemy might have raised his head,

when White Thunder replies: And so, my uncle, after all we have accomplished and suffered, you would have us now lay down our anger at Cut Arm's feet?

Thus once more the sad chief finds himself silenced,

> wrapping himself tighter in his grey blanket, turning away from our best men who wish to fight on,
>
> > his mind no longer on the Bluecoats
> >
> > > (he is fearing for Springtime, expecting her baby to die; he cannot cease grieving for Ollokot, nor give up wondering

whether Good Woman lies raped and scalped and Sound Of
Running Feet has frozen to death);
so he tries to clean his Winchester, but his fingers lose their
cunning as sunset bleeds away between the snowy hill-
breasts

—*hasten; evening shadows be!*—

and just before dark, bullets begin pelting them all like sleet

—so that White Bird, who has scarcely fought until now

(excepting only our victory at Sparse-Snowed Place)

takes aim at some gliding thing

—merely a black spot in his sun-dazzled old vision—

lowers his rifle, then crawls through a tunnel to an ice-rimmed nest where his
shivering warriors crouch and watch, not far from Toohhoolhoolsote's blanket-
wrapped corpse,

and in a rifle-pit to the northwest, Looking-Glass sits beside Wottolen and those
other best men, still lusting to kill Cut Arm the Moldy

(or at least Tsépmin, wherever *he* is):

but just as even the blackest crows can appear purple in the sunshine of the Buffalo Country, so this fight too begins to brighten in
the light of Looking-Glass's unfailing hopes.

I See You've Studied Geography
October 4

1

*G*ood morning, Miles!

Well, good morning, general. We have the Indians corralled down yonder—

No, Wood. I'll summon you when needed. Now, colonel

—blue-eyed, broad-shouldered, all the more so thanks to that bear coat,
and according to most of the newcomers appearing—especially in comparison to their own sad Christian General—even taller and cooler than
a steamer shining on the half-forgotten Columbia—

what were you saying about our Mr. Joe?

I believe we have them blocked up, general.

When did you engage them?

I moved up my command at nine a.m. on September thirtieth. First I sent in
my Cheyennes . . .

Miles, shall we tour the field? By the way, this is Lieutenant Wood, my aide-de-camp, and Ad Chapman, our interpreter. Those two Indians are treaty Nez Perces from Lapwai. My son here you've met when he was small—

Delighted. Well, general, Joseph's dug himself in. We have ourselves an actual frontline.

You don't say! A resourceful Indian!

I have him sewed up. We'll keep on grinding out Gatling shots until he sees reason. Now follow me, general,

> the frozen mist crystallizing on our moustaches and the horses' hair, on Wood's eyelashes, on the bearskin coat the general borrowed from that correspondent (it's not as impressive as Miles's),
>> our dead laid neatly out
>>> (two officers and nineteen men so far)
> while the Plains wind screeches down our necks.

A comfortable and pleasant camp.

Sure is, general. Have you met my adjutant? Lieutenant Baird, one of the most energetic officers in our Indian service—

A pleasure, lieutenant.

Likewise, general.

Well, Miles, it's been a long time.

So it has, general,

> unbuttoning his coat for the sake of fresh air.

That red blanket-shirt becomes you.

Well, general, and you certainly look fit for your age.

Thanks. How's Mrs. Miles?

No complaints. And Mrs. Howard?

The same. What about that delightful Cecilia of yours? She must have just turned nine, if I'm not mistaken.

> *Watch out!*

That's so, general; thanks for remembering. She rides near about as well as an Indian now. I started her off with a captured Kiowa pony.

An excellent policy. You've put on weight, I see.

My sedentary life, general—

> Well, that was a close one!

What a joker you are!

> Yessir.

Yessir,

> in a voice exemplifying the crunching of Army boots in soft snow, which is ankle-deep, mostly, except on shaded slopes, where men sometimes sink up to their knees.

Now we're close enough, general. They killed another of ours last night, not ten yards from here.

Lieutenant Howard, venture ten yards with me.

Gladly, father. Here's your field-glass.

Well then, general!

Miles, you rascal, I *knew* you couldn't keep away from gunpowder! Now I see. Past that line of willows, is it? Joseph's been digging indeed! Who would have thought it?

You see, Chapman, Mr. Joe's all forted up now.

Pretty good, for an Injun. I was his neighbor once.

When Uncle Billy* hears about this, he'll take off his hat to Mr. Joe—

I dunno about that. Ain't never met him.

Fire!

Your Parrott guns are doing good execution among the Indians.

That's so, general. If they don't learn their lesson we'll soon rub them out.

If we could have deployed such artillery at the Clearwater, I shouldn't have troubled you here. We had a howitzer and two Gatlings. In confidence, Miles, our Lieutenant Otis was a disappointment . . .

See, general, that's where we charged. Right down there. As soon as my Cheyennes softened 'em up, the Seventh went in like bloodhounds. We could have rushed 'em, but the cañon walls were too steep, so the reds had the advantage. You've heard that Captain Hale was killed—

Owen Hale?

Yes, general, right in the forefront. And you know he was in the Seventh all the way back to '66.

Get down! Shoot me that Indian! Behind that red rock—

A fine soldier. I knew him by reputation. And who's that man there?

General, I don't know every last private. You there! You look familiar. What's your name?

Doc, general. I was with you both at Chancellorsville—

Miles, enough of this. Now, where's Joseph's horse herd?

We've captured most of it. Near about seven hundred head.

O, I'd thought those ponies belonged to your Cheyennes. Good work, Miles! So you made a clean sweep?

Their remaining animals are in those coulees down there. Not many. Now, general, for Mrs. Howard's sake, let's withdraw a few paces. Mustn't tempt GOD.

All right. Yes, thank you, Guy. No, Wood, put that away. Miles, I do wonder if Sitting Bull will show up?

Don't think I haven't considered it, general. They'd probably try to get around us over there and up thataway, the way they did with Custer. But I got me some fine Cheyennes with plenty of "sand" in them. No rabble of Sioux can surprise me.

That's the spirit! But in a pitched battle, by night, with some mischief by Joseph—

---

*General Sherman.

General, I believe we can whip them every time.

You've parleyed with Sitting Bull last winter, I believe.

Yessir. After he refused to come in and obey the Government, his bucks tried to burn us out.

Well, I suppose he must be a very interesting old fellow. What was your impression?

A wild, reckless warrior, general; make no mistake. And a cool, cruel scowl on his ugly Injun face—

What does he want?

O, the same as all the others, general—to live as an Indian.

Naturally.

To tell you the truth, general, the whole time he sat near me I was bracing myself to get what the Modocs gave poor Canby.

That's in the LORD's hands, Miles. Canby didn't suffer. Anyhow, we whipped the Modocs—

Amen! And next year, general, I'm going to whip the Sioux. You'll see.

Commendable, Miles. You're a firebrand. Well, well; what's my Lieutenant Howard about?

He rode to the west side of Joseph's diggings with Baird. On the other side, where it's still pretty safe, there's an interesting overlook—

All right. Young men . . . !

See, I told you my Cheyennes had "sand"! Look how they ride! What do you think of 'em, general?

Very fit and vigorous, for a fact. Most interestingly painted up—

General, they're the finest species of wild men in the world.

   I wonder how many of 'em were killing our boys last year at Little Big Horn.

   Button that mouth, soldier.

Well, our Nez Perces may keep them occupied.

I'll whip the Nez Perces to-day or to-morrow, guaranteed, unless Sitting Bull—

Yes, you probably will,

   their youth now haunting them like the perfume of Grant's Havana cigars.

2

Wood, having observed through his field-glass the pastel stubble of grass and willows down there in those gently wandering white coulees, presently extends himself to Lieutenant Baird,

   a true Indian fighter, who will do anything to win,

  and they chat about buffalo

   —still half a million within a hundred fifty miles of Tongue River, where we often shoot them for meat

(in fact Lieutenant Baird appears enviably warm, not to mention "dashing," in his lovely purple-brown cloud of a buffalo-
hide jacket with its four leather tabs to connect the eight
brass-buttons in double columns down the chest:
    Wood wishes he had one)—
and Indians, commands and adventures,
    happily laying blame for our failure at Big Hole
    —Gibbon tried to do too much without enough men—
    and at Cañon Creek:
        —all Sturgis can shoot is tobacco juice!
        He lost six hundred men at Antietam,
        and no trueblue officer can forget that time when he
        rushed to Centerville and Pope told him: *Too late,
        Sammy, too late!* LORD's sakes, Wood, and then after
        Chief Joseph fooled him at the Stinking Water—
until Wood must break away, on account of Baird's contempt for Wood's
general, the kindest man in the world
    (Baird for his part assuring his new friend that General Miles, who
    soon again *must* be a general in rank as well as in name, is the best
    American soldier now active,
        since General Sherman has become an ancient despatch-
        shuffler);
then we fall back on waiting for Chief Joseph to break,
    or the general's reënforcements to arrive from Carroll
    or Sitting Bull to come mix things up;
and Wood traverses his field-glass across our front:
    snow on a dead Indian's face,
    white snow on a dead brown horse;
        groans from Doctor Tilton's open-air hospital
        (four officers and forty-six men wounded at present);
and that night occasional bullets come glowing up from the cañon like the gas-
light chandeliers of Wanamaker's department store.

3

A bit of a sharp wind, general.

The women and children must be suffering greatly. With GOD's help, they can't
hold out much longer.

Yes, sir. They're almost in British America, sir.

I see you've studied geography, soldier.

Yessir.

Haven't you?

Yessir.

Fire!

—shelling over the snowy coulees and past the river-willows into the Nez Perce dug-outs:

A ten-pound Parrott gun will shoot three hundred yards straight, four hundred and fifty at one degree of elevation, six thousand and two hundred yards at thirty-five degrees.

Bull's eye.

I'll bet we got us some more "good" Indians.

Sure wish I had a bear coat like Colonel Miles.

More'n one way to keep warm. You know how that Chapman does it? He's a *squaw man.*

Where's his squaw, then?

He left her for another one.

And where's she, then?

O, he traded her for another one.

Wood, have you prepared the clean copy for General Sherman?

Here it is, sir.

Did the ink freeze down here?

Yes it did, general. I'm sorry.

Wood, you're a well-prepared officer.

I appreciate the compliment, sir.

I'd like to ask you something in confidence.

Of course, general.

Have I been remiss in any aspect of this campaign?

Absolutely not, sir. We've had some stinking luck, that's all.

Thank you for saying so. You know I'm your friend—

As I am yours, general, and will always be.

It won't be much longer. They simply can't hold out anymore.

That's how it seems to me, sir.

You compassionate them greatly, don't you, my boy?

Yessir; it's pitiful to watch them get ground down. They've showed such pluck.

That they have. Believe me, Wood, I feel as you do. Do you know the Twenty-second Psalm?

Of course, general—

Verse twenty-seven: *All the ends of the world shall remember and turn unto the* LORD; *and all the kindreds of the nations shall worship before Thee.*

Yessir.

And remember Mrs. Manuel; she's in my prayers every night. Do you suppose she's still alive?

That would be a pretty long chance, sir.

All right. Ready for dictation?

Yessir.

This will save Colonel Miles the trouble, and since I'm in command, hopefully will mean more to the family. Corporal Haddo's next of kin is a wife, I believe?

Correct, sir.

Best to keep up with these sad obligations, before they . . . *Dear Mrs. Haddo, my sincere condolences on the death of your husband John, who fell bravely on the field of battle in the Bear's Paw Mountains, September 30th, 1877. Please be assured of my prayers, and let me know if I can do anything for you. Yours sincerely.*

Yessir.

And Miles, you see . . . The other three were also from the Fifth?

Private Irving was with the Seventh, sir. Company "G."

All right. And here comes Lieutenant Howard! Back from your tour of the front, I see.

Yessir.

Well, what's your assessment?

Colonel Miles has it all sewed up. O, father, I wish we could have seen him in action against Crazy Horse! Lieutenant Pope tells me he's never witnessed such courage—

Yes, Guy, truly; he's got a lot of iron in him—

And he held your arm when they cut it off?

That's so. A true friend. Ready, Wood?

Yessir.

As for this Geogehgan, I don't see a next of kin.

I'll look into it, general.

Fine. And Peshall leaves a father.

Yessir.

Dear Mr. Peshall, my condolences on—

I suppose this weather will hold on.

Yessir.

Fire,

shooting down into the reds.

O, nothing can live within that gun's range.

But we can't see their hidey-holes—

Fine work down there, Miles!

Yep, they're just about whipped—

General, just now I was approached by Chapman—

Really, Wood, is this important? My apologies, Miles. Well, out with it then!

Sir, he reminds me that both Captain John and Old George have daughters in Joseph's band, possibly still alive, and if we were to let them wander down there and warn the Indians that your army's only a day's march away . . .

Do you think I'm in my second childhood? Why do you suppose we carried them all the way here?

Sorry, sir—

Where's Chapman?

I'm right here, general! Why, you near about overlooked me! Now, the thing is, knowing Mr. Joe the way I do—

Shut up. Miles, I understand you've parleyed with Joseph?

Correct, general. On the morning of the first, I hung out the white flag and directed one of my Cheyennes to call him in Chinook. He showed up pretty quick. Well, we jawboned awhile, and he even gave up a couple of guns, so I thought he was in the bag. But he had some fight left in him. His excuse was that he didn't mind surrendering, but he had to convince the other reds. When he refused to come to terms, I called him back and rolled him up in two blankets! Kept him on ice all night.

Miles, I advise you not to mention that in your report. The press back East . . .

Anyhow, general, that should have ended this campaign, but unfortunately Lieutenant Jerome was visiting Joseph's works during the truce, to learn where I could best drop my shells, and he overstayed, so the reds took him hostage, and I had to exchange him for Joseph!

You don't say! You know, I had to leave Captain Sladen as a hostage with Cochise when I rode for Fort Bowie to establish a truce. The Apaches liked him very well. Cochise's son became his *bueno amigo*, as they say down there. A handsome young lad—

General, the point is that Lieutenant Jerome obstructed my victory. But what's another day or two given the way this campaign has dragged on? Joseph is whipped, and he knows it. I'm going to finish him to-morrow.

With GOD's help!

Amen, general!

4

Doc?

Doc?

Doc?

What is it now?

What's supposed to happen next?

What do you think's supposed to happen? We're gonna whup them Injuns.

Doc, do you ever read the Bible?

Sure I do. I learned me the entire Bible near about by heart. And there's a verse you ought to keep in your heart as an Indian fighter: Isaiah 46:13, and it runs like this: *I bring near my righteousness; it shall not be far off, and my salvation shall not tarry; and I will place salvation in Zion for Israel my glory.* Now stop sniveling and start showing me your metal, do you hear?

Yeah . . . Doc, I'm cold.

Have a swig of this.

That's real good. Can I have another?

Nope.

What is it?

Just Blackfoot rum. All right now; one more swaller and then quit your whining.

Thanks, Doc. I'm feeling warmer now.

Watch out for that one-armed Puritanic tyrant. One dark night that killjoy's liable to get his CHRISTly old throat cut.

Ain't you afeared of nothing?

Nope.

Ain't you cold?

Nope. What about you, boy? Did that rum fix you up?

Yes, thanks.

Now you have fun and git you some Injuns.

This ain't fun.

More fun than ripping up railroad tracks in Atlanta. Can you sing?

Sure.

Then sing us a song, boy.

Mine eyes have seen the glory of the coming of the LORD . . .

5

General, he's an extremely able Indian.

That's as may be, but he's been completely invested, Miles. Once our reënforcements arrive, the field is ours.

He might be the ablest Indian I've ever met. A real *Red Napoleon.*

And how does he appear these days?

Well, general, I'd say he wore a pretty sad look on his face—

6

And now the clouds have come down, covering the colored twilight,
     the world going dark, swathes of pale red grass
          (whose snow can no longer be seen)
closing in on the pearly sky:
   Fire!
—shooting down into the Big Dust:

I am flying up.

I am leaping up.

I am worshipping,

and at this very moment Lizzie may be playing whist with the children if they're not too tired,

the moon as roundfaced as a Kiowa warrior over and under whose arrowhead-shapen cheekbones shine ovoid seas of light; light beams out of his wide, cratered forehead, and darkness from his eyes, O, those *hateful Indian eyes.*

Our Dread of This Day
October 4–5

1

Since Bear Coat has proved himself to be as cruel and crooked-hearted as Cut Arm

(after raising the white flag, he penned up Heinmot Tooyalakekt, who is our chief!

—We remember when Cut Arm showed the rifle at Butterfly Place and his tall killer laid hands on our Toohhoolhoolsote:

Now indeed we certainly begin to understand the hearts of these Bostons!),

the young men insist that their way is certainly best:

still it is they who say yes or no,

and they refuse to offer our People to these Bluecoats

who will lie, rob us and choke us in rope.

Because we hope for something good, and the Bluecoats are so bad, some of us still wait on Sitting Bull,

who Looking-Glass promises will soon come riding exactly here

(remembering the singing of tin tinklers on the shirts of Cutthroat warriors, our *lucky man* sits listening, expecting soon to hear again that sound of metal snowflakes dancing in a blizzard of horse-wind),

although our old ones and children will presently be freezing to death

(Springtime's baby whimpers *shlak, shlak*).

We can no longer become new.

Indeed these young men whom Ollokot once led

(those to whom less has happened)
continue to expect the Walking Cutthroats
(and the young boys who bring water and watch our few hidden horses will not
look ahead to see themselves penned up forever, never to become men);
as for Heinmot Tooyalakekt,
just as the hair peels off an old hide, so his last hopes fall away.

2

My dear younger brother,
he who was chief with me, and led the young men,
lies out in the snow day after day. We can make him no grave. And Good Woman
is gone. The best men can no longer clear their minds. Cloudburst will not eat.
Springtime's heart longs to die,
the same cares chattering in all our hearts, *pokát, pokát.*
Sound Of Running Feet has passed to unknown enemy lands,
pokát, pokát,
Pulling his blanket over his head, he Dreams himself back into the southern
reaches of our home:
morning in the mountains, the lodgepole pines on the far side of the
creek now golden-green in this place where my father and I rode horses,
a wall as of sunlight, the sky pale, chilly here where we've camped in the
soft golden grass, our horse-hordes calling: *Hinimí,*
mountain cliffs above us shining brighter and brighter:
TRAVELLER THE SUN has almost reached us.

3

On the night when Bear Coat confined him, Heinmot Tooyalakekt told the
Painted Arrows, speaking Chinook: It is good to talk straight on both sides. It is
not us we speak for, but the children who follow us.
Then a certain Painted Arrow opened his mouth. Was he now speaking
crooked or straight? Heinmot Tooyalakekt could not understand.
Tightlipped, narrowfaced Bear Coat replied in the Boston language; then that
same Painted Arrow,
tilting his tanned old face, the quillworked stars on the shoulders of his
fringed shirt as faded as his hair
(Looking-Glass might know his name)
and his eyes squinted so nearly shut that there was nothing but shining
darkness between the lids,
explained in Chinook: *Joseph,* you must stop fighting, or we shall kill all your
People. Cut Arm is angry, and will soon be coming exactly here.
On the next day, when his People came to exchange him for the Bluecoat

officer, Wottolen laid down a black-striped white blanket; after which both Heinmot Tooyalakekt and this Bluecoat stepped on the blanket together to shake
hands; then the Bluecoat went back to Bear Coat and Heinmot Tooyalakekt returned to camp,

      where the young men shouted: *Now we shall never surrender!*

4

Evening comes again,
    the big gun no longer shouting,
as we wait and watch in our rifle-pits,
            cold even through our spines,
      our words as abundant as grasshoppers in late summer,
    while Looking-Glass is wondering how Sitting Bull will be when he ar-
rives and we offer him our council pipe to bite on
and again, although he strives not to,
     pokát, pokát,
Strong Eagle, last of the Three Red Blankets, begins remembering his two best
war-friends, who commenced this war:
    they too have been killed:
        he is gone; he cannot help us: Shore Crossing, who could shoot
        golden eagles from the sky;
        and gone, Red Moccasin Tops, who fought so well always;
then as he watches through the curtain of sleet at the whitening ridges of night,
the reddish-grey grass fading into the fog, Strong Eagle,
    although it is better not to remember those who are dead,
now also sees in his heart two more for whom he grieves:
    Rainbow, who tricked Cut Arm so hilariously into crossing the Chinook
    Salmon Water twice
      (Rainbow has left us; his WYAKIN could not protect him before
      sunrise),
    and Over The Point, who was so brave at Big Water
      —had our cowards obeyed his counsel, Cut Arm could never have
      devoured our lodges!—
        now he has been killed by our good friends the Crows.
        Now we are nearly finished. Now I shall speak.
    Strong Eagle therefore says: Hear me, my best men and chiefs! What do we
mean, sitting around here? Let us creep and kill Bluecoats to-night. If they kill us,
then we are free. If we kill them, we are free also. Now I have told you my heart.
    Still the chiefs keep quiet:
      White Bird,
        whose heart perhaps never believed in peace,
      and Looking-Glass,

who ever since his blindness again betrayed us has ceased playing head-chief

(we have no war-chief anymore),

and Heinmot Tooyalakekt, the quiet one,

toward whom we feel ashamed, for he warned us not to kill.

He has given to Toohhoolhoolsote's shivering old widows the King George blanket that Looking-Glass presented to his daughter.

(His thoughts are as wide-spaced as the tracks of a running horse.)

At last he replies (since the other chiefs keep silent): Strong Eagle, my dear nephew, we must not now go up there. I say this without bad feelings. You are one of our best and brave men. For you it has been easy to make your life into a weapon. But if we should all be killed, what would the Bluecoats do to our women and children? Your heart knows exactly how they would heal the wounded!

Heinmot Tooyalakekt, I should not contradict your words. But must we now give up everything?

My nephew, just this I will ask you: What remains for us to give up? They have already cheated us out of our country.

5

White Bird has been listening. He now says: Strong Eagle has spoken straight: *For what do we lie around here?* But what Heinmot Tooyalakekt says is also right. Therefore, let us all creep away like snakes to-night. Those who wish can stay here and surrender. The rest can leave this place with us. Cut Arm will soon bring death here. If he fails to shoot us, he will choke us all in rope. Is it not better that the Walking Cutthroats and Big Bellies should kill us on the way, or that Sitting Bull should put us all to death in the Old Woman's Country?

You must listen to your heart, White Bird. Ask your young men—

6

Strong Eagle speaks again, saying: I am a warrior, not a woman, and I say let us fight to-day.

—but Loon, who like so many cowards remains alive (never again will he seek to make himself brave) cries out: Without our horses, what can we do against Bear Coat?

Loon, you are nothing, and this very night I shall go away from all of you, for Bear Coat can never pen me up on painted land!

So TRAVELLER hides within OUR MOTHER, and we watch cold stars

as Strong Eagle goes out,

and with him, White Hawk, Hide Scraper, Calf Of The Leg and Wamush-kaiya,

braves ones who will not be Cut Arm's slaves,
    creeping through the ring of Bluecoats,
and White Bird says: Now again my heart thinks on leaving,
    while the People crouch in their holes until dawn.

7

Again Bear Coat's slaves wave the white flag and call down in Chinook;
    the People warn: Heinmot Tooyalakekt, our dear chief, you must not go;
    again he will trick you!
        and Springtime says: Husband, if they kill you, your baby and I
        shall soon starve,
but he says: We cannot run away. White Bird spoke the truth: Cut Arm will soon
be coming;
    and so a second time he rides out on a borrowed horse, holding up a white cloth.

8

Again Bear Coat says (the same Painted Arrow speaking for him): Hear me,
Joseph! If you fail to lay your rifle at my feet, all your women and children will soon
be killed. Cut Arm's heart is angry, but we can make him forget this war. Let us
all have peace.

Bear Coat, I have been listening to you; what you say is good. But sometimes
you *Americans* use words in a way that we People cannot understand. We People
are ignorant; we know only how to speak straight from our hearts. Therefore I am
now asking you: What *peace* shall we have?

Joseph, listen! I shall feed your women and children; none of you will get
hanged. In the spring I shall give back most of your horses, and then you will all
be carried to Butterfly Place to be penned up on painted land with your friends.

What you have said pleases my heart, but have you kept count of our horses,
so that all will be straight?

This will certainly be done, but first we have promised the Painted Arrows that
they may choose from the animals now captured . . .

Bear Coat, that is well. My father always told the Bostons that we own too
many horses and cows to live in one small country; you have now relieved us of
this difficulty.

Heinmot Tooyalakekt, Bear Coat is asking: Do you make fun with him? Bear
Coat is proud; do not make his heart angry.

Tell Bear Coat that I have opened my ears. Now let me go back to tell the young
men. Lately it is they who say yes or no.

9

Night comes
>> as White Bird sits in a hole, Dreaming of a snow-white sandbar dark with buffalo,
>> and Heinmot Tooyalakekt seeks to count stars in GHOST'S TRAIL,* just for awhile
>>> while White Thunder wonders if his mother still lives
>>> and Springtime holds the baby
>>>> (who never cries anymore).

Heinmot Tooyalakekt goes away to listen to his heart
> —not far (he must watch for Painted Arrows and Cut Arm's other crooked slaves)—

and between two boulders he sits, gazing up at GHOST'S TRAIL,
listening to the wind.
>> His heart cries *qoh! qoh! qoh!*

10

Father, forgive me that I now name your name in my heart:
> you whose name was *Elder Warrior*
> and whose name was *Hair Knotted in the Back of the Head,*

father, hear me! You will not be dead, even after we have died without a home, and
our children live penned up and hungry, never knowing you:
> Still they will be saying words from your mouth,
>> even when the red salmon have gone;

their hearts will sorrow with yours whenever the Bostons dig up OUR MOTHER'S
bones
and our best men will follow your trail forever, I am telling you three times:
> helping our People until all is ended,
>> giving up all else,
>>> as I have.

My father,
> you who were my chief,

you know how I waited on your last words, opening my ears.
> I never sold our country, I am telling you three times!
>> They took it; we could not fight.

My father, I have followed you by not following you;
> for the People I have abandoned your grave forever
> and left our country to the Bostons.

---

*The Milky Way.

11

So comes dawn
when Springtime says: My husband, I would now speak.

What is your heart?

You yourself have said that White Bird spoke truly. Cut Arm is coming here! Let us rapidly leave this place. The other chiefs have failed us; you cannot save the People.

Síikstiwaa, we cannot alter how it ends.

You who once promised yourself to me, take pity; do not stop your ears! Will you take no care for your family? Good Woman and Sound Of Running Feet, are they still alive or have the Walking Cutthroats devoured them? Let us now go to them. My dear husband, listen to my heart! We are all dying. Save your women! Save your baby, I am telling you three times,

> holding up the baby,
>> whose face is almost blue.

Síikstiwaa, have you forgotten that morning in Wallowa when I spoke to you from the root of my heart? I asked you: *Shall our People be killed?*

They betrayed you! After you spoke for them at Butterfly Place, they killed those Bostons. At Big Water you would have met Cut Arm, and they called you *enemy—*

That is so. But as I have always said, the Bostons were the cause of all our trouble.

My heart cannot yet understand you—

I shall not leave them.

> Withdrawing her arms inside her blanket, she hugs her heart, gazing down;
>> no longer will she speak.

12

Not long before noon, the traitors Tsoka-y,
> now called *Kaptin Tsán*
>> (he was at Weippe when we ambushed Mason's scouts—if only we could have killed them all!)
and limping Meopokit,
> known to Cut Arm and Moss Beard as *Ol Tsolts:*
—both crooked Butterfly Place enemies, yet weary and bloody as we are—
come carefully riding down, flying the white flag,
> desiring to see whether their daughters still live
> and whether we shall surrender forever to Cut Arm,

who promises that no one will be rope-choked.

    Shall we punish them?

    White Bird has said—

    But whenever any Bostons sought to buy our country, the old chiefs always—

            Pokát, pokát.

Heinmot Tooyalakekt receives them in front of the frozen hole where he lives with Springtime, her baby, Cloudburst and Fair Land's child. He has decorated his face red and yellow.

White Bird will not come at first; Looking-Glass says: *Prevent these spies from prying about here!*— But some do wish to meet these slaves of Cut Arm, wondering what their lying mouths might say.

As is his way, Heinmot Tooyalakekt thanks them for nothing, saying: Yes, indeed I am grateful for what I have heard.

Allutakanin, one of our bravest young men, has yet survived his brother Over The Point. He says: Meopokit, how is it with my father Red Heart? How are my mother and sister? How are my two brothers? They surrendered to Cut Arm in Kamiah, and I have heard nothing about them.

Meopokit closes his mouth

    (his sixteen-year-old daughter likes her husband, so she refuses to come here)

        as White Bird, lately arrived, watches him from behind a fan of feathers,

            Looking-Glass's younger wife Asking Maiden hoping that we shall become rich again,

      and *Kate* raises her beautiful small head, wondering how he has permitted himself to become a slave of these Bostons who have made a filthy thing of our land;

      and Welweyas wipes her nose and listens, wondering whether Moss Beard

          (whose moustaches and whiskers flow in such a way as to make his mouth seem eternally open)

      will compel her to dress like a Boston man

      —but White Thunder's old mother Swan Woman crouches in a corner, longing to brain Meopokit with her horse-whipping stick,

until Allutakanin raises his voice: Tsoka-y, hear me now. Your brother fears to answer. You must know very well how it is with my family. I am asking: What has Cut Arm done with them?

Allutakanin, my dear nephew . . .

Our best men therefore say: Let us kill them.

To them speaks Heinmot Tooyalakekt: Your actions have come to nothing. You will not harm these two who speak with Cut Arm's voice. May your hearts now be silent.

13

Looking-Glass creeps to White Bird's cave and says: Heinmot Tooyalakekt has completed his heart; to-morrow he will give his rifle to Bear Coat.

—Even now he does not know these *Americans!* Looking-Glass, what will you do?

We shall go away to-night. I know that we shall never again lay eyes upon our home.

14

The chiefs are smoking kinnikinnick with our best men in the rifle-pits.

Looking-Glass says: Heinmot Tooyalakekt, hear me! I speak for myself and for White Bird. We are older than you; we have met two-faced and two-tongued men. Should you surrender, you will sorrow in your heart; and in your sorrow you will wish to be dead.

No doubt, but Bear Coat has made a good talk. Our People are naked and freezing, our women suffering with cold, our children weeping. For myself it makes no difference; I shall surrender for these others.

I myself shall never surrender to a crooked Bluecoat, I am telling you three times!

Just then he sees a silhouetted rider coming from the northeast.

Rising up from his pit, he looks across the wide shallow cañon, stretching out his hand as he cries: *Look, my People! Sitting Bull is here!*

      and even though he is not wearing his shining mirror, a bullet now finds
       his forehead:
         Taq!
           (they have made him explode)
and he tumbles downhill, *tsalalál!*
         (Already his wives and daughters are screaming.)
   Looking-Glass, who always expected the best
      and who knew each river by its smell,
his blood is now spreading.
   . . . Even yet we others keep hoping that the rider
      (who now returns to Bear Coat's camp)
might be Sitting Bull,
       the grass standing even as the snowy wind strengthens
         and sleet keeps pelting the Bluecoats along the ridgetops.

15

   After this the young men begin more darkly to sorrow in their hearts at last;
it begins to be clear that this last battle they cannot escape,
        unless they leave the weak ones to be devoured by Cut Arm;
indeed White Bird now repeats Looking-Glass's words: I shall never surrender to
a deceitful white chief,
to which Heinmot Tooyalakekt likewise repeats: Am I then to leave the People all
alone? Our horses are lost; the children cannot walk; I shall not cause the old men
to wrap their blankets over their heads and walk away from me.
   —Yes, my dear nephew, whatever you do is all right; as for my young men,
        the ones who began this war,
Cut Arm promised to choke them in rope, and only that promise does he ever
mean to keep . . .
   No, White Bird, he cannot harm them, for they are mostly dead! And now that
Strong Eagle has fled his reach . . .
   My nephew, now listen: The Bluecoats always punish the innocent with the
guilty. Why shall I make myself like some deer for them to kill? But if Cut Arm
speaks straight, then come False Flowering Time we shall all ride back home.

16

   We are waiting for TRAVELLER to hide beneath the world,
        so that White Bird may lead away whoever will not give himself to Cut
        Arm,
        and the two new widows may safely wrap up their husband's corpse,
                remembering when he was young, and his dark and naked chest
                was smooth, his bone-earrings shining brighter than the sunlight
                under his eyes, and the Crows called him *Arrowhead,*
        while the two daughters wail softly, just for awhile
                (they long to be quickly riding away with White Bird before the
                Painted Arrows come to scalp their dead father)
and Heinmot Tooyalakekt now gives Wottolen many of his best old pipes, whistles
and necklaces to be taken safe into the Old Woman's Country
                (perhaps they may smooth the way with Sitting Bull, and in any event the
                Bostons will not succeed in devouring them)
and the small red wool blanket which Captain Lewis gave the People seventy-two
snows ago, when the *Americans* were our friends;
from around his neck, he gives a wampum bead to White Bird, then another to
Peopeo Tholekt;
then White Bird

(whose toothache no longer troubles him)
says: Now you will be head-chief after all.

17

Cloudburst will go with White Bird,
        since she does not wish to become a slave to those who killed Ollokot and
        Fair Land;
and because the way across the Medicine Line may be difficult, she gives Fair
Land's son to Springtime, perhaps forever; Heinmot Tooyalakekt will adopt him.

18

So we have completed ourselves,
            our dread of this day as tall as a Shinbone's coup-stick deco-
            rated with scalps and miniature horses;
        we are burying money and rifles, so that Cut Arm will not get them,
    the twilight going orange
            (soon some of us shall be creeping across the hard snow, hoping
            that the Painted Arrows remain too delighted with our horses to
            chase us),
the sad People watching Heinmot Tooyalakekt leap onto his borrowed horse
            (the young boys will look after Black Mane-Stripe in case their chief
            should return)
and Peopeo Tholekt hands up to him surrender's white cloth:
        Springtime turning her back
            —she is as white as a young horse's teeth—
        whispering to the baby,
        then withdrawing into her icy hole to weep with Cloudburst
            (who has helped him decorate his face, since Springtime re-
            fused to do it);
he shoulders his Winchester
    (perhaps Cut Arm's heart will joy in it)
            as Geese Three Times Alighting On Water,
                the only one of us Wallowa People to follow Shore Crossing
                when he began this war,
            now looks up at the one he disobeyed,
            and his heart is as sad as this grey-blanket-wrapped chief's who
            now goes away;
            most People say that Heinmot Tooyalakekt's heart is bravely
            straight
                but Many Wounds does not forgive him for what he is now
                doing; fifty years later he still will not forgive him.

Now he is riding up toward the yellow-trimmed sky of mussel shell, where a hand's
worth of Bluecoats pace silhouetted, among them the unmistakable Cut Arm
> (I shall be remembering White Bird as he goes; my heart will
> be speaking to him as he rides away),
> > the wind worse on the ridge, but much of the dead grass still erect
> > > (he knows how it will be; he remembers the V-shaped forma-
> > > tion of Bluecoats he had to enter, and Bear Coat waiting at the
> > > point,
> > > > then the little ravine where Bear Coat hides his com-
> > > > mand at night).
Keeping in his heart what Toohhoolhoolsote always used to tell our young men:
> When I was born, I grew to be a boy; I learned to use the arrow and bow.
> I hunted the birds and the rabbit. When I killed them, I saw that their
> lives went out with their blood. This taught me for what purpose I am
> here. I came into this world to die,
he rides upward, slowly waving the white flag
> as a few young men sadly follow him,
> his heart crying *qoh, qoh, qoh.*
> > Now indeed the Bostons will wipe their buttocks on our heads.

19

We wait. Heinmot Tooyalakekt does not return; all gunshots have ceased:
> White Bird has crept away with his People;
here come Bluecoats and Painted Arrows; they are already digging up our hidden
things.

How to Earn a Star
October 5

1

A mighty keen wind, Miles,
> the foggy dawn cold and green like a hunk of fluorite, our infantrymen
> coughing and shivering even before we fire the morning gun;
> > Miles delays to answer.
> > > Well, well. Looks like Mr. Joe's strengthened his lines.
> > > He's mighty active, even in this cold—

It must be wearing their women and children down. Did I say that already?

That's right, general. I believe it's fixing to snow again.

I pray we can finish this quickly. My word, this landscape is as charming as can be, don't you think?

Well, sure, it's as white as the top of a new covered wagon,

> the sun bloody-gold like an autumn pumpkin

>> as we slam another one-point-six-five-inch shell into the breech of the Hotchkiss;

> and faraway down there in their diggings past Snake Creek the squaws have recommenced weeping and moaning in their customary savage fashion:

>> we must have made some more good Indians.

I want you to know something.

What is it, general?

I have not come to rob you of any credit, Miles. I know you are after a star, and I shall stand back and let you receive the surrender, which I'm sure will take place to-day or to-morrow.

> What's the counter-sign?
> *Freedom.*

I appreciate that, general, because I deserved my star a long time ago. All right, boys, start shelling those reds!

Right away, colonel.

O, hello, Guy. The coffee's ready, I hope.

Yessir,

> wiping his nose.

Father, what do you think of Joseph after all this time? I mean, what sort of man is he, to—

O, he's brave and cunning, all right. But he can't keep this up.

You said it, general! My Cheyennes will

> *Fire!*

>> and the first shell-screech and

> *Infantry, fire at will,*

>> respecting the laws of greatness which both prove and proclaim us the best.

>> Now, Sammy, you see that Indian right down there? He's got his head stuck out like a partridge. Just watch me,

>>> thumbing the extractor firmly backward, then flipping up the trapdoor so that the bulletless shell tumbles down among the rocks and pebbles, thumbing in the next round and then:

>> *Pim.*

> Doc, you sure can shoot!

—and there lies Looking-Glass, his face nothing but crimson

meat, his legs drawn in like a grasshopper's at rest—another good Indian!

2

General, I worry that you may have made a mistake.

About what?

About not assuming command.

Wood, have you forgotten that Miles was my aide-de-camp in the Secession War? I got him his first command. I trust him as I would trust you.

Sir, you know best.

3

Evening recruits the sky into a lovely warm pink

> (ice under the smoothest snow,
>
> the sleet strengthening),

as Miles once more trains his field-glass down into the snowy coulee,

> waiting, as men will do while their wives are behind the door giving birth, listening to the silence, the midwife's murmuring and the anguished screams, waiting for the infant's cry;

>> so it is that our Parrott guns, operated by these kindly medical men, ease open the secret womb of this place, so that America can come out,

Wood's face numb because he must stand toward the leaping sleet,

> the breeze meanwhile insufficient to stir the willows down in Joseph's valley

>> (No, Guy. You see, up until now, the Indians had no ranks to open up with our guns),

> and the burn of the cold, cold copper bracelet on Wood's left wrist makes it no use to think of Nanny:

Get up here, Chapman.

Don't talk that way to me, you sissy punk—

Shut up and hurry. General wants you,

> so Chapman, his hair now shoulder-length, hands easy at his sides, strides forward with that same sway of hips and shoulders as if he were riding that grey racer of his. From Miles's Cheyennes he has already obtained a plug of liquorice tobacco, and his left cheek bulges out as he walks. His trousers are as fabulously cracked as anyone else's, but he has managed to patch them.

>> Old George and Captain John come riding slowly back:
>> *Load with cartridges; load!*
>> Joseph wants to parley.

4

And his Bible says: *Take heed to thyself, lest thou make a covenant with the inhabitants of the land whither thou goest, lest it be a snare for thee: But ye shall destroy their altars, break their images, and cut down their groves,*

as Chief Joseph, wearing buckskin moccasins, a blue wool shirt, a grey blanket with a black stripe, and a bullet-measled grey shawl

(his braids frozen against his face),

rides slowly up the snow-hill, with his .44 Winchester carbine over his shoulder,

attended and perhaps consoled by three or four walking braves,

fixes the rifle in the crook of his arm, rides forward away from these best men,

leaps off his shivering spavined horse, letting the bridle fall,

the well-trained horse remaining still;

now is walking up past the Hotchkiss and our blanket-wrapped dead;

hesitantly he extends his hand.

And now he wants a surrender.

I can get him with a good shot.

General says no.

Which general?

Both of 'em.

How do you know?

Easing his hand into his shortcoat pocket, where a cocked pistol waits to fix Joseph should that savage seek treachery against the man whom he, Guy Howard, loves most, the young lieutenant stands a few steps behind Colonel Miles and his father,

who now, as Joseph pulls his blanket tight and slowly, sadly offering his Winchester, gestures to Miles to receive it:

General Miles, sir, he may be dangerous. Remember how Lame Deer tried to kill you even when he was waving the white rag—

Poor Shrenger, he sure took that bullet! Don't worry. We won't let Mr. Joe try any such tricks!

—then Joseph hesitates, holding his rifle a little longer, with the barrel pointing downward and toward himself

(Guy now crouched and ready)

and begins murmuring alien syllables:

No, Doc, he don't speak English.

Sure he does. He was even baptized once. *Ephraim,* they called him. He's just faking,

Wood writing Chapman's words with numb fingers on his little pad, a courtesy which no one has asked him to perform:

Tell Cut Arm I know his heart . . .

Joseph staring straight ahead, his eyes and mouth three slits, his throat guarded by a collar of bearteeth,

his face far thinner than at Lapwai, the creases at the corners of his eyes longer, his braids beginning to turn white

(for some reason I remember the way that Ollicut used to set his mouth)

and his gaze shining away somewhere:

I must say he comes off worse in any comparison, even of dignity itself, to Cochise, who listened to me, kept his word, and saved his tribe,

remembering the Apache chief's long, high-cheekboned face, with vermilion paint on his cheeks, his hair likewise beginning to grey,

and the Indians offering me their gratitude for having placed them safely on the reservation:

O, so much better than this!

What he told me before I have in my heart.

That's truly Mr. Joe?

Well, disease and starvation makes wild Indians grow rapidly old in appearance.

What's he jabbering, boys?

I am tired of fighting; our chiefs are all killed; Looking-Glass is dead; the old men are all killed . . .

Can you hear what he's saying?

For a red, he's almost a gentleman. You remember the way Robert E. Lee slammed his hands together after *he* surrendered?

Hey you, Chapman, what's he saying?

From where the sun now stands . . .

O, go home to your squaw wife, you greasy fool.

I'm pickin' me a fresh one just now and ain't nothin' you can do about it. Now shut up; I'm interpreting Mr. Joe.

You would.

Cut it out, boys; I want to hear this.

I will fight no more forever.

I *like* that.

Well, I say that villain's layin' it on too thick.

Anyhow, we were in on the finish!

Amen.

Wood, prepare a tent for Chief Joseph.

Yessir.

Praise GOD. Praise GOD. But why on earth was this campaign necessary? I must have been too trusting, I suppose. Lizzie's so much more canny about people than I. She would have seen through him at Lapwai,
> this man who condemns the LORD of Glory:
>> O yes, I meant to pass my finger across my nose and see if he knows the *Nez Perce* sign.

That was a pretty good little speech, wouldn't you say, general?

Yes. No, Chapman; he's to give his rifle not to me but to Colonel Miles.

I wonder how many Americans that Winchester has laid low! Well, it's my souvenir now. I'll have Mary hang it over the stove. Come to think of it, Chief Joseph may be one of the ablest Indians on the continent! General, are you tired?

Not at all, Miles.

Chapman, is Mr. Joe done surrendering?

Sure is, colonel.

Tell him his horses will be returned to him next spring at Lapwai.

Colonel, he asks about his women and children.

Tell him I'll do everything I can for them.

Yessir.

Mr. Chapman.

How can I help you, general?

Have any of White Bird's bunch come in yet?

No, sir.

Ask Joseph where they are.

He says White Bird is a chief and speaks for himself—

Remind him that the surrender is to be complete and unconditional.

Sure, general; I'll make him understand—

After they've all come in, I want to examine Joseph and all the sub-chiefs about Mrs. Manuel.
> If he threw himself entirely on my kindness, would I be more inclined to aid him? *No,* because he tricked and humiliated me, and because I can see how pride glints even now in his *hateful Indian eyes.* The will to do us evil persists within him! I'll warn Sherman that
>> little Maggie Manuel was shivering on that hot afternoon in Brown's Hotel at Mount Idaho when she told me how Joseph shot her mother and her brother right in front of her; could any child lie about so grave a matter? She said the Indians made her stand there barefoot while her mother's blood ran between her toes. I can read sincerity in a child's eyes! Hence
> he's a fine candidate for the Indian Territory.

Well, Guy, you get along with Colonel Perry, I gather.

O yes, father. He's a friend to me. A shame he couldn't be here with us—

He ought to be satisfied that Theller's murder can now be avenged.

Yessir.

And how do you feel?

Exultant, father!

Good. Would you like to see them settled in the same place as Perry's Modocs?

Hanging's the ticket for them, father! At least for Joseph and his—

No doubt. And the women and children removed to Quapaw, perhaps, or Baxter Springs . . .

O, father, I suppose that's fine enough for Indians. But when the colonel told Joseph he could return to Lapwai, as if he deserved anything like that—

That's if they all come in. And the murderers must be indicted, of course. Wood, take charge of Chief Joseph as a prisoner of war. See that he is made comfortable and in no way molested.

Yessir. Mr. Chapman, could you please tell Joseph that I will conduct him to a tent and wait on him there in case he needs me?

Sure thing, lieutenant. I'll make him understand. Yeah, he says he's at your orders.

5

White Bird has not come in.

No, sir. Chief Joseph says—

Miles, whatever Joseph may presently deny, the fact is that he surrendered unconditionally.

And Mrs. Manuel—

I'll bet you a silver dollar the squaws did for her. They're monsters of jealousy. A white woman in their vicinity would—

Whenever Pi-Ute squaws lied to us, we'd just lead 'em to the nearest tree and noose their necks until they talked sense. Now in this case . . .

I'll take care of that. Lieutenant Baird, round up our Cheyennes and put the word out. White Bird's renegades are loose!

Can we ride with 'em, sir? We're itching for more excitement.

I need you here until Joseph's bunch are all secured. The Cheyennes know what to do. They'll hunt them down in detail.

6

Rather a forlorn procession of Indians.

Not Mr. Joe! He's as handsome as a cigar store Indian!

What do you say, Doc?

He ain't nothin' compared to one of them old-time Injuns who ride in with scalps a-streamin' at the sides of their painted beaded war-shirts, and their hair a-blowin' in the breeze—

I sure would enjoy to have one of his necklaces. Or maybe his mockersins.

Look at them lame skinny ponies we caught! How could they make it so far?

They weren't lame and skinny before; that's how.

Those reds sure showed a lot of "sand."

They were as good sports as any white man.

Well, I'd say they was agreeable.

And Doc reckons maybe a hundred skedaddled.

O, don't you worry about that. Our Cheyennes'll get them.

Well, Miles, your wife will be relieved, no doubt.

That's right, general. She's been beside herself.

Here comes a longhaired, hollow-cheeked man with a beadwork belt cinched high above his hips and a striped blanket folded across his hand; he totters, and the general inexplicably remembers the way that General Sherman laughed at the Seccesh prisoners who trod the road so gingerly when he set them to digging up their own torpedo-mines. Why should this come into my mind? LORD JESUS, please forgive me, and help me to feel compassion for

this stately squaw in calico, folding her arms across her high waist, with her children kneeling in the frozen grass beside her,

(the babies sobbing, *shlak, shlak!*)

Chapman eyeing them like some nasty-looking lounger.

Well, Doc, here's one of your own sort! Quite a hardy Indian, I must say—

Where's White Bird?

He must have got his.

Nope. He skedaddled last night.

You don't say! What's the general's reaction?

Which one?

Miles, of course.

O, he let fly a few words; our *Christian Soldier* weren't none too happy then—

Ha, ha, ha! D——d old fool—

Watch out; here they—

and Wood, seeing among the shivering, broken-down squaws a young woman, no matter her rags and dirt, of such fierce and angry beauty that when her eyes lock contemptuously onto his, he nearly staggers, electrified by what seems at that moment to be neither more nor less than the most irresistible lust of his life: for her unseen female parts, for her powerful thighs clamped painfully tight around his hips, her lower lip clenched between his teeth—but now she has passed on; and her impression lingers upon him as if he had been literally incensed by her unwashed body; and he wishes to seek her among the prisoners and marry her.

Now she is making desperate gestures; she must need to relieve herself. Two laughing soldiers lead her toward the sinks, and they go out of sight:

She'd be an amusing little companion.

O, they're just miserable, deformed creatures.

Hey, you, *kloochman!**

No, she don't understand.

> That's why if we can't honor our treaties at the beginning, it's best to exterminate the reds straight off.
>
> I for one feel sorry for 'em.

Well, missy, let's see what's under that buckskin dress. You came here to shit anyhow. You want to eat? Here's a hunk of stewpot meat. Pull up the dress. Pull up the dress. Don't you get it, you redskinned bitch?

> You're picking up some education now, Georgie boy.
>
> O, she's quite the hellcat,

as Wood remembers her eyelashes like fern shadows,

and Nanny, of course,

> but why should it harm Nanny if I allowed myself to be inspired by this or that Muse along the way, that Nez Perce girl for instance, or even Theller's squaw?
>
> Were I on better terms with Perry I should request her name.

Dear LORD, I thank You for permitting me to live to this day, holding Your hand over my head to shade me from harm. And thank You for sparing our general, who means so well by the Indians;

> General Crook would have gunned them all down, so I hear.
>
> Well, *we* can't. What Congress has done to the Army, it's not a square system.

Here comes a weary old lady in a blanket-coat pinned across the breast, and her wrinkled head shrouded in a bleached rag; her gaze seems nearly blind, and her thin lips smile flatly with heartbreak or apathy

> (Lizzie would be nauseated by the shrivelled faces of these old Indian squaws)

and then Looking-Glass's daughters,

> their ragged filthy trappings all the sadder in the bright snow,

and a blind man,

followed by a bleeding old man who upraises a copper medal depicting Lincoln and Johnson in the protective shadow of an eagle in whose beak a scroll reads **FREEDOM TO ALL MEN**.

> Where on earth did he get that?— From some horse-trader, I suppose.
>
> And here comes old Hushush Cute.
>
> What a sly look he wears!
>
> That's why the general wouldn't sign his pass back at Lapwai—

the Bluecoats standing with their white-gloved hands crossed upon their

---

*Chinook jargon for "woman."

breasts, steam and smoke from campfires, smell of food, Ad Chapman happily counting captured horses:

> one thousand five hundred and thirty-one:
>> three hundred to our Injun scouts,
>> the rest back to Tongue River, and then we'll see!

while Lieutenants Wood and Baird jointly inventory our new chattels:

> eighty-seven bucks,
>> (several of them fixing to die),
> a hundred eighty-four squaws
> and a hundred and forty-seven papooses,
>> this one nearly as weak-looking as Captain Winters's little daughter Kate.

Father, you must be feeling satisfied.

O yes, Guy; I suppose I am:

> They almost remind him of his own silently patient wounded soldiers during our Secession War—never complaining, wasted, dull-eyed. But there comes to him a better comparison: in the way they accept bread from the hands of their captors they are, at last, as simple and grateful as negroes.

7

Walking the field with Miles and several other officers, he smiles admiringly at Joseph's fortifications, which show evidence of skill, however merely instinctive. The first souvenir hunters are already excavating here and there. Lieutenant Baird begs to show them the dead Looking-Glass, brushing snow off the exploded face for the convenience of his general, who like any decent Christian would prefer to sorrow over his violent end, but, remembering the way that Looking-Glass laid down his gentleness last spring at Lapwai, and commenced answering him insolently, he cannot but believe that this renegade's killing serves the interest of peace. Likewise, what American could grieve over that murderer Ollicut, the wicked counselor Toohhoolhoolzote, and all Joseph's other various bloodthirsty subalterns who fell here, and at Big Hole and Clearwater and other skirmishing-grounds along the way?— Besides, it has already grown apparent that Joseph, as usual, did not keep his word: a good one-third or more of the Indians have decamped, no doubt to make common cause with Sitting Bull. We'll have to stop them.

Guy follows eagerly at his heels. Wood strides at his left side. On the right strides Miles with tolerant good humor, his customary blue ribbons streaming from the crown of his hat.

> Litter carriers into all these d——d trenches down there.
> Yessir, General Miles.
>> I dug up this here squaw necklace—
>> Then I beat you out! See, this pouch is full of gold dust! Must have carried it all the way from Oro Fino—

Or took it off one of ours at White Bird Cañon, more likely.

Well, Miles, your boys seem very much up to snuff.

Thanks, general.

In the snow he spies something which reminds him almost irresistibly of Charles's pocket Gospels, one of the most familiar objects of his life: half the size of a man's hand, bound and clasped in dark leather softened by use and saltened with sweat. Rowland's copy is less worn, his own a trifle more so. Here's another. He picks it up: an Indian child's right foot.

This too must be laid at Joseph's door, he says bitterly. If they'd only listened to the Government and gone upon the reservation . . .

Yessir.

What do you think about all this, Miles? A sad sight—

You said it, general! But we've both seen worse. For instance, Fair Oaks . . .

Interesting that you should mention the war. Of course one can't help comparing the past to the present, and then trying to locate the precise rung we've reached on the ladder of Progress. Do you realize, gentlemen, that notwithstanding our great improvements in arms, the aggregate casualties at Gettysburg were no greater than at Waterloo?

I Shouldn't Be Surprised If General Sherman Changed His Mind
October 5

1

Well, Wood, we did it after all! We whipped that Joseph—

Yessir.

You know, I often hear the expression *American* or *That is an expression of our American life.* It covers so much; energy in preparation; fearlessness in undertakings; bravery in action; endurance under every hardship.

It certainly does, general.

And I'm not ashamed to say that this war against the Nez Perces was a very American campaign.

Yessir.

I shouldn't be surprised if General Sherman changed his mind now and sent his congratulations.

Let's hope so, sir.

Or President Hayes himself! What do you think of him?

Well, general, an extremely handsome man . . .

He's certainly all of that!

What's your opinion of him, sir?

They say he's generous. I expect that he rewards valor.

Yessir. Do you think they'll hang Joseph?

Depends on what's proved against him. As for me, Wood, well, to be honest I don't know what to think. Anyhow, you look tired.

O, not at all, general. But I wonder if Mrs. Manuel's alive.

Perhaps White Bird is dragging her with him into the British Possessions as we speak. Poor lady! And that would be the best case. Wood, I can tell you're all in. Take a rest, my friend; you've earned it. Or, if you feel the inclination, some sketches of Joseph and the battlefield and so forth might prove extremely interesting.

Well, then, general, until to-morrow.

Right. Yes, Guy, what is it?

Father, your arm—

That's what it does, when . . . When we reach Tongue River there ought to be carbolic acid. Anyhow, how are you holding up?

Excellently, thanks. Father, I'm very proud of you.

Step over here with me.

Yessir.

Guy

> (peering down into the rolling cañon:
>> no sound but sleet and the screaming of an unseen horse
>> —someone should have shot that poor creature),

there's something I want to tell you.

Yes, father.

I'll only say this once, no matter how many campaigns you share with me, or serve in after my retirement, which may not be far off . . .

Father, I'm listening.

I've never shown you favoritism and never will.

Of course, father; that's best for us and everyone.

But in my nightly prayers I always give thanks that you've been spared. I'm grateful to have been given you for my son. Now shall we take another ramble together through Joseph's intrenchments?

2

That night, the trumpeter blowing "Cease Fire" to inveigle any remaining wild Indians in the vicinity, he shares a tent with Miles, to whom he confides all the best parts of the adventure.— Guy and I have calculated, he remarks to his friend, that this campaign was *one thousand three hundred and twenty-one miles in seventy-five days!*

More than seventeen miles a day, general—

Correct!

A very respectable average, considering the nature of the country. Glad I was able to step in. Now it's over, I can tell you about a little scare I had. You see, the day before you showed up here, one of my scouts cried out: *Indians!* Of course I thought it was going to be another Little Big Horn. I said to Baird: Well, our hour's come. Do you know what it was? Not Sitting Bull, but a buffalo herd!

Oh, me! The little comedies of our Indian service . . .

By the way, general, I'm dissatisfied with General Sherman.

And why is that?

I want a command in accordance with my rank. My wife has approached him any number of times—

I should think the assistance you've rendered here should be just the ticket. And of course I'll say a word in General Sherman's ear. But White Bird—

O, I can hunt him down on foot. My Cheyennes have already destroyed a few of his followers.

That's fine. Now, Miles, what do you propose to do with the Indians we have? I trust you still reject the old Army doctrine of destroying the whole race.

You'll soon see my mind on that, general. I won't hesitate to protect the innocent.

You certainly demonstrated Christian spirit with those Cheyennes.

Well, general, they took Grey Beard away from me. I made a stink, but nobody would sustain me. Now he's confined in Florida with the rest of them. I should have gone to the press—

You meant well, I know. Have you kept up with Grey Beard?

No, sir.

I'm afraid he was shot during an attempted escape.

They were probably starving him. This Indian policy's idiocy, general, as I know I've said to you. Getting back to these Nez Perces, the women and children are one thing. But they must be taught not to murder.

Of course.

You see, general, they'd be better off in the Indian Territory, at least until all their outrages have been forgotten. But they expect to return to Lapwai.

It will be difficult for them at first, to be sure. But I pray it will be for the best.

They rely on me for justice, general.

Well, Miles, that will be up to the Government, after all.

Excuse me, general. I'm being called on to give orders about my prisoners.

What's the trump suit?
Clubs.

Whose prisoners, Miles?

HAPPILY EVER AFTER
OCTOBER 6

*H*aving buried our dead, and permitted them to cover theirs, we are now
loading forty wounded Indian bucks into brush-filled wagons
>   (Miles's sawbones Doctor Tilton extracts bullets from the worst cases,
>   and offers medicinal vinegar around),

after which we hitch up our oxen, heading back for Tongue River
>   (allowing the able-bodied prisoners to ride the horses that no longer be-
>   long to them);

so that everyone who matters is happy:
>   Ad Chapman has claimed the pick of Joseph's horses, not that he will get
>   most of them;
>   Doc wears around his neck a broad bison horn spoon, shining and pale,
>   which he took off a Nez Perce (it don't matter how),
>   Wood gets to pump the prisoners for folk tales,
>   while Captain Fisher (just arrived with Captain Miller's reënforcements)
>   has arranged to take receipt of an entire wagonload of interesting squaw
>   trash for his souvenir collection,
>   Redington, who has burned through seventeen horses on this campaign,
>   winds up with the .44 Remington pistol said to be Ollicut's,
>   and bright-eyed Fletch (another member of Miller's bunch) completes a
>   topographical sketch to embellish the general's final report
>>   (in the end every battlefield on the campaign will be delineated by
>>   him, Wood's portraits and such being a trifle too artistic)
>   while Guy unearths a Nez Perce skull
>>   (won't his sister have a good scream!),
>   Miles anticipates his well-earned star,

and the general, who desires that his Indians be well treated, is told:
No worry, sir. We'll feed 'em good, till they're as fat as jailhouse flies.

VIII

I RAISED MY EYES

1877–78

I raised my eyes above the criticisms and well-meant advice of my companions in arms; I looked to the GOOD SHEPHERD.

BRIGADIER GENERAL OLIVER OTIS HOWARD, U.S.A., 1907

WISHING FOR A HACKNEY
OCTOBER 1877

1

*M*iles, so it transpires, pretended he would share the credit, but then sent the following despatch to General Terry: We have had our usual success. After a severe engagement, the hostile camp of Nez Perces, under Chief Joseph, surrendered at two-o'-clock to-day. Since heretofore *our usual successes* have been accomplished without General Howard, what might one infer about the indispensability of that gentleman?

We now remove to the "A" tents and mud-chinked log barracks of Tongue River Cantonment, Miles's Stronghold, where in a dark doorway sits Joseph, looking very small, wide-eyed, compliant and alert. Now his heart has grown straight at last. Once Fort Keogh is completed, our usual success will grow all the more amazingly American, but here at Tongue River, arrangements aren't half bad: We store our prisoners (one or two have died since we last tallied them, and a dozen more, freshly captured by the Seventh, are now en route from Milk River) next to the ordnance, and the hospital is flanked on the left by our Academy of Music (built up proudly out of mudded cottonwood logs), on the right by the band's quarters. From this latter edifice now file the keepers of our musical ordnance. Which tune will they strike up first? I wonder. Marching past our rectilinear arrays of infantrymen who shine like silver dollars, our dismounted cavalrymen at attention in a double row, with their hands at their sides in once-white gloves, their knee-high boots cracked but smartly shining, and Old Glory flying over hardpacked dirt!—not to mention our victorious Crows in their most crimson war-shirts and their brass necklaces and eagle-feather bonnets, beadwork ringing their horses' heads—tame Sioux and Cheyennes gawking alongside, and our Bannock and Nez Perce scouts well painted for this occasion, *Amen* (even Buffalo Horn's nearly joyous)—they ascend a planked platform, take formation, cock their weapons and let fly this salvo:

The men will cheer and the boys will shout,
The ladies they will all turn out,
And we'll all feel gay when
Johnny comes marching home!
  Hurrah,
  hurrah,
  hurrah!

A heartfelt production, boys! That's for certain,
> like the suppositions of Wood (who will never forget
> from Big Hole the open mouth and closed eyes of the
> dead squaw whom in his waking nightmare's eternal
> present tense our Bannocks have disinterred and will
> now be scalping forever, worrying at her as do dogs any
> dead meat which requires more than one bite, the head
> flopping and twitching as they pull at it to cut off her
> earrings; now they are unrolling her bloody muddy buf-
> falo robe, laughingly stabbing her arms and legs, cut-
> ting away that beaded deerskin dress from her extruded
> guts, in order to dishonor her more obscenely):
>> What deserves my best attention is the determi-
>> nation, however hypothetical, of *how I once
>> wanted this to be* (my dreams as poor a fit as any
>> soldier's boots),
>>> *Wakesh nun pakilauitin*
>>> JEHOVAN'M *yiyauki—*
> and when I get back to Nanny I wonder if I'll even
> feel anything after all this—and, by GOD, if this
> time she still refuses to let my tongue inside her
> mouth . . . !
>> O, they always say they just wish to be left
>> alone.
>> Well, they're a dying race.
>> Help them along is what I say!—
and Chapman's realization that even after all his valor
(the Army has awarded him two of Mr. Joe's Cayuse
ponies), he may not necessarily come out as horse-rich
as the Walla-Wallas used to be, let alone the Nez Perces,
> but I'll stick with Mr. Joe and worm something
> out of him, just see if I don't! Get me his war-
> shirts and other trash, and sell to a souvenir
> dealer, just you wait. And tell him what to sign
> and not to sign, and someday get inside that
> daughter of his, or else some other fresh young
> squaw. And I want to visit Philadelphia, just once,
> and see Wanamaker's department store,
and Perry's fair-minded appreciations of the situation:
> I thought I knew something about Trimble, but
> just because we're in Indian service together don't
> mean a thing, evidently. After all I did to advance

him! That sly traitor must've had it in for me from the first. Now it's adding up.

> And there's Joseph. Holds himself high, I see. No remorse. About all I can do not to draw a bead on him and let drive. Maybe that's why the general kept me away from the finish. Well, fuck 'em both.

The thing is, I need to do Trimble discredit before they convene my Court of Inquiry. Can't go to the general anymore. I'll see Major Mason. He's been on my side ever since the Lava Beds. Then I'll lay me down and sleep, or—

Lapwai won't be the same, of course, with him dead and her in San Francisco by now

> (to hell with that squaw of his)

and Fletch's near-innocence

> > (you straighten up and stop agonizing over what you can't help):

Yessir,

> as Miles, waiting for his jolly wife, breathes down at the black rubber buttons of his new double-breasted buffalo overcoat, and watches the vapor freeze them silver.

> > And Mr. Joe won't confess about Mrs. Manuel.

Why the sour face, Wilkinson?

Nothing at all,

> but here's what I have against Wood. He has been a dead beat on the Army. And the general allowed him to be in on the death. Just for that, I don't feel the same about the general anymore. He's

> > > much inferior to the bugle corps at Fort Lincoln, I should say . . .

> > Now right over that away, that's where Red Cloud killed Fetterman.

> > Remember, boys, that's how to get ahead in life and have a fort named after you. Just let them reds massacre you—

> > I seen Red Cloud one time and he's a real—

> > Never should have taken *his* surrender.

> > Paid off by Uh-Oh Howard—

> > A load of cowards in the Government.

Maybe even Communists. That's how they let Howard in.

I'm going to recommend that you be cited for meritorious conduct.

Father, I don't deserve it!

You showed a lot of pluck, Guy, and I mean to boost your career while I can.

Mr. Chapman, the Government will pay you for your service in good time. You can put in your claim for eighty-one and a half cents per day, but don't hold your breath. Now sign here.

Sure now, I spoiled it there. Went too far down, I guess. Sorry I write such a powerful poor hand . . .

Now *there's* a red with interestin' charms:

a pretty young Cheyenne woman, earringed and braceleted in good cold German silver, holding a bunch of sweetgrass, smiling with excitement, with her chin up high

(near about as saucy as some yaller nigger wench),

and her ribbon-hemmed calico dress decorated with many dewclaws of deer and cinched tight over her hips with a brass-tacked leather belt.

And Mrs. Miles looks enchanting! Why, she—

—played Theller for a good two or three years; oughter be taken out and shot for a crazy-making Indian.

Fine tall grass hereabouts. A man might get five tons to the acre.

We'll do the best we can.

Them prisoners sure stink,

pointing to a Nez Perce mother whose iridescent shell-disk earrings reach down to her chin, which is underlined by beads black and white; her doubled braids march down her blouse of beads and squares; her baby daughter splays the fingers of her right hand upon the mother's wrist which first guards her on her lap, then crosses the other wrist; staring into our eyes, the mother begins to close her hands into fists.

What do you expect? They're Injuns.

Barnum would make a fortune if he got them in his circus,

> which might be so, for even Perry softens to see a young Nez Perce boy weak and shivering yet expertly riding a painted horse.

Barnum's broke.

No he ain't.

They have dressed him in fringed, embroidered Crow clothing since his own is too raggedy for the satisfaction of the photographer, Mr. John H. Fouch. His hair-peak glares white, and on his dark braids twin white adornments touch his cheeks. He sits with his wrists tightly crossing on his blanketed lap. His head is tilted. Ad Chapman interprets malignantly; in reply he smiles. He puts our boys in mind of a wild horse's second or third meeting with the snubbing post. At Bear's Paw, Miles promised him that he could return to his good old home, because the Americans are his friends. Instead, that fat, drooping-eyebrow'd bully General Sheridan will ship him off to Leavenworth. And so the *Bozeman Times* declaims: *Too much praise cannot be placed to the credit of Gen. Miles and his officers who crushed out the power of the Nez Perces to do evil.*

> *We will welcome to our numbers the loyal, true and brave,*
> *Shouting the battle-cry of freedom,*
> *And though they may be poor, not a man shall be a slave,*
> *Shouting the battle-cry of freedom.*

(Well, well; soon the snow will be blowing in here again, and we'll be busy with our picks and shovels.)

> *Hurrah,*
> *hurrah,*
> *hurrah!*

> The telegram should not have been altered so as to leave out the fact of my being there at Bear's Paw.
> I agree, sir.

> > His eyes half closed, a headbanded Cheyenne scout uplifts his face at jolly Mrs. Miles,

> > > and, O, my Lizzie, if I could but lay my head down in your lap and weep—
> > > O, dear GOD.

> You know, Wood, Miles was my devoted friend. I just don't understand it—
> General, he's played you false, I'm afraid.
> Did I tell you that he held my arm while it was being amputated? He—

Hurrah for General Miles!

> *Hurrah,*
> *hurrah,*
> *hurrah!*
> *Long have they pass'd, hurrah, hurah, hurrah!*

The cannon roars out, scaring twelve hundred captured horses and shaking the alkali cliffs, and the smile of Tzi-kal-tza is the smile of a knife slicing meat off the bones of a thing.

2

Do sit down, Miles. It's said that you gave Joseph your word that he wasn't subject to removal. Is that the case?

It might have been his impression, sir.

I've interrogated poor Howard, who naturally is death on the idea of permitting Joseph to remain in his former hunting ground. He's out for blood!

Naturally, sir.

Did I ever tell you about the time that Custer and I were putting pressure on the Kiowas? At first, of course, they wouldn't hear of coming in to the reservation at Fort Cobb. Well, we had Lone Wolf and Santana in custody by then. They kept demanding to speak with me. I knew they had to be taken down a peg, so I refused. Finally I said to poor Custer, I said: You tell those two chiefs that we shall wait until sundown to-morrow for the tribe to ride in. If by that time the village isn't present, Lone Wolf and Santana will be hung, and the troops despatched in pursuit of the Kiowas.

Yessir. That came out pretty well, sir.

Correct. One sometimes needs to follow a hard line. And the fact is, Miles, that those Kiowas were playing us false, *and the same goes for that d——d Joseph.* For two cents I'd take him out back and shoot him.

Yessir.

Well, well. Public opinion wouldn't permit it, I suppose. The world isn't always as we'd like it to be, is it, Miles?

That's for sure, general. For instance, I've repeatedly asked General Sherman about my—

How's he behaving?

Joseph? Smiling a blue streak, sir.

Now, we're going to put the squeeze on him. He might as well be informed that until the rest of his confederates come in, he can rot. And whatever promise you might have made him at Bear's Paw doesn't signify.

In fact, general, I always considered it the merest stratagem of war.

Right you are, Miles. And if you flattered his pride to make him surrender, you did a good thing. Those squaws and papooses of his were pretty broken down. They should be grateful.

Yessir.

And thank GOD he didn't make it into the British Possessions! The press would have *savaged* us, so to speak . . .

Ha, ha, ha!

Now, Miles,

       sweetly and deliberately smoking his cigar,

How dangerous is this White Bird? You tell me he's definitely managed to cross the line.

That's so, general. Those d——d Cheyennes disobeyed my direct order and—

Scalped a few of Joseph's squaws, no doubt.

Yessir.

Got to give them that.

General, the point here is that I caught the big fish.

Yes, yes, *the Red Napoleon.*

Yessir. White Bird is a vicious, cunning Indian and no mistake. I have no doubt that Sitting Bull can make use of him to disturb the country thereabouts. But compared to Joseph he's—

Why did you let the sonofabitch get away, Miles?

I—

Don't blame your stinking Cheyennes, at least not to *me.* You know d——d well an officer takes responsibility for his command.

See here, General Sheridan, sir, I demand to go on record—

I've been fighting Cheyennes since '68. I know how to keep them in line if you don't. And if you want to quarrel with me, Miles . . . Would you like a quarrel?

No, sir.

Good. Keep your brightest lookout for stray Nez Perces up that way, especially the bucks, of course. And remind Joseph that since he's now enjoying the unmerited protection of the Government, he'd better induce White Bird to come in before we run out of patience.

I'll do that, sir.

And light a fire under those Cheyennes of yours.

O, I certainly shall, general.

Why give me that look? Have you forgotten that I was best man at your wedding?

No, sir.

A most delightful event! Has it already been, what, eleven years?

Yessir, and my wife expected to see me in a far higher position by now.

Of course. Good LORD, that's what any decent wife would—

General Sheridan, sir, not a single one of the mistakes in this campaign was mine. I have authority for what I say.

No one's against you, Miles! If anything, you're liable to win your star at long last. With your connections—

I should hope so, general. You wouldn't believe how many times I've asked General Sherman for my own Department. And if anybody impugns me for winning the Nez Perce War at the eleventh hour, I'll stand on my rights. I've been patient for far too long, sir. I'll go to the press if I have to.

Easy there, Miles. In your opinion, who did commit those mistakes?

I believe you understand me, sir.

I do. Just between us, how would you characterize old Howard? A couple of words will do.

He's my superior in rank, sir, and has always advanced my—

To hell with that.

In a couple of words? *An embarrassment,* sir.

A sad case. He was never good for much. Thank you for your honesty, Miles.

3

Next come the slanders and insults in the newspapers back East, one after the other, like Indians galloping in tightening circles around a wagon train

(my conscience acquits me)

and when Miles in his public pronouncements (as offensively retrogressive as lead shot twined into a Tlingit rattletop basket) declines to thank any but his own troops for the victory:

What about Theller, for the love of GOD? He could at least have gratified the widow, and recognized his sacrifice

(Hooker and Crook must have gotten to him; now even Sheridan's against me:

my future's as long and narrow as a Winchester)—

I'd think he'd show an ounce of consideration for me, who

comes mar-ching home!

and Fletch, and Perry, Wood

(who is already yearning to put his hair up like a Dreamer)

and Bomus, Trimble (forgiven now), Mason, Miller, Whipple, Sladen, Guy and

(Captain Jackson's bugler, what was his name? I hope the hostiles failed to disinter him for his scalp)

and a reception concert in honor of Brigadier General O. O. Howard at the New Market Theatre in Portland this Monday evening, November 12, 1877, featuring

Mrs. C. Richlings Bernard from the Grand English Opera; she will perform the grand sesella from "Lucia di Lammermoor" while Lizzie and the children sit in the front row, and a solo and chorus will acquit themselves of "The Star-Spangled Banner," after which someone will sing "Let Me Like a Soldier Fall"

—decency as forgotten an invention as the coffee-mill Sharps—

and all the brave men who
        even Sturgis
     nor will I descend to political maneuvering
and

           Stand up for these, the wrong'd, the aggriev'd,
           In deepest pits of darkness found . . .
        (How much longer do you suppose that old man can sit a
horse?
        Poor one-armed fellow!)
he takes up his pen and begs to differ, for the sake of his own army
        (I was never put on Earth to be a business man)
and for Lizzie, who weepingly disparages him for never standing up for
himself and his children
        Father?
        Not now, Guy.
(Will she never see what I do stand up for? No, never,
        praying for us, baking our bread in her wrought-iron pan;
that's not for me to ask of her, much less of anyone else, including
so-called Christians such as General Sherman who
        does he *pity* me now?
unlike me never hesitates to be pitiless, I'm called upon only to
defend Him to the best of my capability, no matter when I cannot
answer all they ask:
        Toohhoolhoolzote demanding to know, perhaps even in good
        faith if I may profane that phrase in relation to such a thick-
        headed old villain, why I should presume to remove him from
        his so-called MOTHER
        and Lieutenant Hazzard in his stifling office during the Sem-
        inole campaign
           [exactly twenty years ago now it's been since I *felt* GOD's
           grace]:
        Well, then, Howard, how do you account for these discrepan-
        cies in the Bible?
           grinning at me, lighting his pipe, slapping a mosquito
           on his cheek—
        I cannot tell right now, Hazzard. But perhaps I'll be able to
        explain them at some future time,
        and Hazzard flummoxed, myself proudly, courteously un-
        moved),
but Miles coolly declines to express any consideration for our effort. Who would
have thought it? Just as in whist the partner of the player winning the first trick
gathers the tricks for that deal, so my good friend Miles now sweeps in the honors
which, strictly speaking . . .

How was Wood able to size him up so accurately? Frankly, I have sometimes been too credulous,

> trusting for instance in the word of Joseph,

and believing as I do that one must endure with men of bad habits, even profane men, I may have forborne too much.

LORD forgive me, I never desired but to be of service! Hence I hoped to be a good man in a high place—

Wood, would you please come in for a moment?

Yessir.

With your talents, I think you could do a fair job presenting a true account of the surrender to the press.

I'll get right on it, general.

> *Colonel Miles, I am astonished at your accusation—*
> *General Howard, you virtually gave up the pursuit—*

His brother in CHRIST Reverend Cooke sends him, no doubt out of kindness, an issue of a newspaper from Helena, Montana. Governor Potts has addressed the Legislative Assembly as follows: *The Indian situation in the Territory has been very unsatisfactory. The raids of the Nez Perces and Bannack Indians were very destructive of life and property. Nothing so much retards the settlement and growth of a country as continual trouble and depredations from Indians. The most intelligent estimate made by the United States authorities, places the number of hostile Indians, with Sitting Bull's camp near the northern line of the Territory, at between fourteen and fifteen hundred lodges. The people, capable of bearing arms, should be organized, drilled and disciplined. The present situation of this Territory appears to warrant the consolidation of the two Military districts into a Department, and the public sentiment of the people points with entire unanimity to Brevet Major General Nelson A. Miles, Colonel of the 5th Infantry,*

> with entire unanimity, O yes. I see.

I'll need to retire now. No. I won't bow, not ever. But perhaps in five years, I'll leave the Army. Then what? I'll show Lizzie all the love whose existence she has learned to doubt; and the instant the debts of the Freedmen's Bureau are finally liquidated, I'll farm. No, I'll breed horses once again. Shall I buy Arrow from Chapman? No, it wouldn't look right. Besides, this campaign has begun to wear him out. Joseph's Appaloosas are fine, but I'd like a trick horse, perhaps a hackney show horse with a cheerful mincing prance. GOD forgive him. *I* forgive him. Do I? Dear LORD, I humbly request of You the Christian forbearance and fortitude required to truly and fully forgive Colonel Nelson Miles, who used to be my friend.

Well, boys, our Christian General sure took a tumble into the ditch this time. Serves him right,

> GOD forgive him. GOD forgive him. GOD forgive him.

If he'd just hauled Mr. Joe behind the woodpile and whipped him, right at the start, all them people round about Mount Idaho would still be kicking—

And our boys at White Bird Cañon—

And Cottonwood—

And—

The biscuit's full of worms again, boys.

O shut up.

They *raped* that Helen Walsh. Just about ripped her open is what *I* heard. And Howard stood aside and—

He could have saved Mrs. Manuel if he'd—

I'll bet you White Bird's using her this very instant, over there across the line.

No, they strangled her before Lo Lo. Mr. Joe confessed—

He did?

And Uh-Oh Howard—

Just like at Chancellorsville. Should have been cashiered.

Dragging us across Hell and gone—

Even at Camas Meadows he couldn't keep one eye open. That Mr. Joe he come right in and—

And Howard won't never take a white man's word for nothing.

He's nothin' but a GODD——d old ass-fucker.

Yeah, how'd *you* know?

JUST DESERTS
NOVEMBER 1877

1

*G*ood morning, general, says his best friend.

Good morning, general.

So you concur with General Sheridan.

I do, sir.

Now what about this half-assed promise that Colonel Miles supposedly made to Joseph? You were present.

Yes, general. He did make it in my hearing. But the terms of the surrender were violated by the Indians' conniving at White Bird's escape—

General Howard, I know you for a true gentleman. Joseph may have made a fool out of you, but that don't matter for *shit.*

General—

As far as I'm concerned, he ought to be hanged, and all his redskinned devils exterminated right down to the last GODD——d squaw. We'd better make an example of them.

General, I hope there will be fair trials.

Howard, you were always soft.

But I do agree, general, that we can't send the Nez Perces back to Lapwai. It wouldn't be fair to the good Indians who have obeyed the Government.

Right. So I'm going to override Miles. The Secretary of the Interior will follow my recommendations. Miles will be mortified, of course. He's gone to me over Sheridan's head—

O, *did* he?

I suppose you'll feel a certain satisfaction, general. *Vengeance is mine, saith the* LORD.

Not on my account, sir!

Or do you now entirely believe that GOD is love? Mrs. Sherman used to opine that.

I certainly do not, general.

By the way, general, it's time to consider your health. You're worn out—hardly any good to the Army—

General, I hope to prove the contrary.

All right, Howard. That will be all. You can keep your Department. As for those d——d Nez Perces, we'll bury them deep in the Indian Territory.

So long, Mr. Joe!

IX

THE AMERICANS ARE
YOUR FRIENDS

1877–1904

The Americans are your friends, and want you to go back to your old home, and if you don't, you will go to some other good Reservation.

Lieutenant George W. Baird, to White Bird, 1878

The reservation system is a system under which the Indian people can never make much progress. It is a system plainly for the benefit of white men—settlers and Indian employees.

Brigadier General Oliver Otis Howard, U.S.A., 1907

It would be a hardship which our white frontiersmen could not bear to shut them up together upon a ranch, however fertile, and keep them there by military force in order to convert them from shepherds and herders into successful farmers. They would in time doubtless come to it by some such pressure, especially if attended by a reasonable degree of starvation. Such inhumanity is plain when whites and not Indians are concerned.

Brigadier General Oliver Otis Howard, U.S.A., 1907

I think if I should dwell a year or two with any savage tribe I should live as they live; I should dress as they dress . . . and I should probably eat out of the common pot, and be, to all intents and purposes, an Indian.

Brigadier General Oliver Otis Howard, U.S.A., 1907

I have endeavored to show how my grandfather's stories of the wild Indians with whom he had to do, affected my childhood; how these tales became almost like a nightmare to me and continued to haunt me even when I was a cadet at West Point.

Brigadier General Oliver Otis Howard, U.S.A., 1907

In dealing with Indians we must neither fear nor hate them. After instructions are given by the proper authorities, see to it that the Indians are made to understand the orders. Afterwards, see to it that they are carried into execution without hesitation or delay.

Brigadier General Oliver Otis Howard, U.S.A., 1907

THE MEDICINE LINE
OCTOBER–NOVEMBER 1877

1

*I*n the fog, with TRAVELLER THE SUN orange-brown like an old grizzly bear tooth, they ride and walk toward the Medicine Line as they can. Then TRAVELLER goes away. They flee together or alone, days and horizons apart. Some are barefoot, many lack blankets and a few go nearly naked. They are all hungry. Huge wet snowflakes cling to their shoulders. Then the snow begins to freeze
>as they sing their WYAKIN songs,
>>walking frozen-toed or stick-whipping their shivering horses,
>>>wondering whom they will see again,
>>Black Eagle struggling to make himself brave for his lost father Wottolen
>>>(after three suns, some Crees will give him clothes and moccasins),
>>About Asleep comforting the little brother behind him on his horse
>>>(tonight those lucky boys will stop farther down the creek and kill two buffalo),
>>Sound Of Running Feet knowing only where north is, and afraid that her mothers and her father are all dead
>>>(her hands and feet have become nothing but frozen bones);
>>about her baby sister her heart feels nothing: that silent little blue-faced creature has been dying for a long time;
>>Sound Of Running Feet is wishing for her mothers,
>>>especially Good Woman,
>>and weeping for her father
>>while fearing to fall asleep on Burning Coals's horse in case she should see again behind her eyelids that Painted Arrow raising his Springfield carbine to kill her
>>>(now she is menstruating for the third time: her mothers or Aunt Cloudburst would tell her what to do with this blood)
>>and watching for enemies, MONSTERS and killers,
>>>hoping that one of our best men will have killed Cut Arm;
>she is one of all these fleeing People who keep longing for fire and meat

(but they must make no flame where Cut Arm and Bear Coat
might see);
at night they can see no stars.
Dawn comes strangely clear: to the north, beyond
glowing yellow stripes of low prairie, blue hills
shine beyond the Medicine Line
(maybe even there the white people's hearts
will be bad);
then the snowy wind comes back.
Welweyas the half-woman counts herself warmest of all in her King George blanket
that gift from her loving chief,
he who will now forever be called *Joseph,*
and her heart keeps so happy with Good Woman, Helping Another, Towhee
and the other buffalo-butchering wives, grandmothers, sisters and nieces who
galloped away on that morning when the Painted Arrows attacked,
the Bluecoats then chasing us like wolves, peeling off horses from our
herd as our men screened us
(White Thunder was bravest)
so that we could ride farther and farther away from our People,
watching out for the tipis of Shinbones,
shivering, hungry and sleepless
(we have only misery to eat and even TRAVELLER THE SUN
has become like the huge dark hole in a deer's heart when our
men shoot it from close ambush);
indeed Welweyas's heart is happy:
Now we are all women here; why should my WYAKIN not complete
me at last?
I am going, I am going
—and across the Medicine Line I shall find a strong husband—
but Good Woman weeps for Sound Of Running Feet,
who is now creeping not far east of her;
while Cloudburst, travelling behind them with White Bird's
band, cannot turn her mind from Ollokot,
who has gone across the river with Fair Land:
they are all sorrowing as they go,
scattering, hiding, hurrying, hungering,
fearing enemies ahead.

2

Hearing that Sitting Bull has come, and seeking his own dear wife, Wounded
Head escapes, stripped for a war, and when a Bluecoat rises up to challenge him,
he clubs him dead and takes his horse and clothes,

travelling toward the Medicine Line,
>meets another Bluecoat,
>>shoots him, takes his horse and clothes likewise;
>>and next morning, still expecting Sitting Bull, sees a black-capped
>>chickadee hopping weakly from tree to tree, hungry for seeds;

then, fording creeks and rivers, he arrives at a Plains Cree camp, where to be kind those People trade clothes with him, so that Bear Coat will not kill him on sight;
>so he rides on, seeking his dear wife Helping Another, and her mother Towhee
>>—happily finding them, thanks to his unfailing WYAKIN.

3

Those who first galloped away, and those who escaped each night until the last day
>when Heinmot Tooyalakekt gave up his rifle
>>(Hahtalekin has now been killed, they say),

indeed they hunt for each other,
>shaking a few frozen buffaloberries into their blankets
>>(in this time when we should be rich in venison and other winter food)

>while nightmares, Bluecoats and coyotes conceal the songs of wolves and the soft noises of moccasins in hard snow:
>>Grandmother, I can walk no more.
>>Make yourself brave. If we leave you here, Cut Arm will eat you!
>>Grandfather, please carry me.
>>Then climb onto my shoulders. My dear granddaughter, how you are strangling me! You should behave more gently. Yes, hold on exactly like that.
>>Thank you, grandfather.
>>Never mind, dear child.
>>>Looking back, they cannot see Wolf's Paw in the fog.
>>Grandfather, when shall we go home?
>>Be silent; you are getting heavy.
>>Now I am rested—
>>Good. Get down. Now you are acting brave,

and some get WYAKIN-luck, but too many remain bewildered and alone as they seek the Old Woman's Country,
>the land widening out, smooth and cruel: the wind will get them wherever they go;
>>and milk-grey cloud devours the blue-grey wall of sky.

A few wander northwest to the snow-stripes of Box Elder Creek; while certain wretched ones, forgetting the warnings of the dead Looking-Glass,
> who never listened to ours,
flee straight north to reach the Medicine Line sooner,
>> their hearts carrying them up across the Milk River, toward the gunmetal sky and wide swale that will become a plain across which we must creep to Sitting Bull;
and on a steel-grey morning of freezing wind
>>> —small hard snowflakes beating against their faces, constellations of snowflakes upon the dark grey ice-puddles—
>> as they approach Fort Belknap
>> (a bad Bluecoat place),
certain shivering People—two women and three men—hear horses calling: *Hinimí!*

Growing homesick, they seek these voices,
>> glimpsing patched tipis whose crooked stick-fingered crowns glitter with icicles, and then exactly here stands a stained tipi from which smoke comes
>> (a woman sits outside beating her dog);
>> as the warriors of this place come riding up on half-starved ponies, so that the People begin to recognize them for Big Bellies and Walking Cut-throats,
>> who feast them on buffalo meat,
>>> old men in smoke-tanned deerskin shirts half-smiling at them across the fire:
>>> now they are showing their hearts, offering us the pipe
>>>> as we tell our long war story
>>>>> but our two women keep quiet, feeling shy; it best becomes them to gaze away from these others with the eagle feathers in their hair,
>>>>>> who until now have been our enemies,
>>>>> although exactly here sits a lovely Big Belly girl who has quilled her buffalo robe white, yellow, brown and black, crossed with red wool yarn; our two women smile at her, and she touches her heart, so that all five of the People now feel easier toward their hosts,
>>>> who give them more and more to eat,
>>> then guide them to a sandbar on Milk River
>>>> (we have almost crossed the Medicine Line)
>>>> where the People's hearts begin to say *qoh! qoh! qoh!*
>>>> as a Big Belly warrior named Long Horse
>>>>> (until now he has kept silent)

raises up his 1873 Winchester
> (the younger woman is the only one of us who begins
> weeping for her life)

and in his gaze there is merely carefulness:
> *pim—pim—pim—pim—pim!*

as he ensures that the Big Bellies will keep Bear Coat's friendship.

4

But Sound Of Running Feet, with her long black braids wrapped tight and falling down to her waist, stares ahead, crying out. Her heart is as happy as if someone had given her a deerskin bag filled with meat!

For on this morning of dark winds and clouds
> —it could have been no worse on the bygone day when COYOTE killed
> TRAVELLER THE SUN—

she has found her mother, who indeed still lives—likewise broadshouldered Welweyas, who loves her, and Helping Another, Wounded Head's wife; No Swan, who knows how to run, and these other women and children whom she knew from the days when we all had horses. No longer will the lonely girl be suffocated by ghosts.

5

Although the Bluecoat sentries who spied White Bird's last People creeping away must have pitied them, since they forbore to shoot, now all has changed. Bear Coat and Cut Arm, we have heard, rage against those who refuse to be penned up on painted land with Heinmot Tooyalakekt. So the Bluecoats, Painted Arrows, Walking Cutthroats and Big Bellies are all hunting us
> along with our dear friends the Crows,
>> and the Shinbones who have always been our enemies.
>>> (No one will ever know which tribe killed Speaking Water; as
>>> for Fatal Throat Wound, the Painted Arrows, Shinbones or
>>> *Women Nation* could have done for him.)

It rains and snows. At night we cannot see the stars. We go on,
> wind singing through dead branches: *tiyé-pu—!*
>> (and in a coulee some ancient Painted Arrow woman is pounding
>> a skunk to death for her dinner:
>>> we creep beyond her like snakes;
>>>> she does not hear us);
>> and in the snow ahead we sometimes seem to see Walking Cutthroats in white wolfskin caps, their eyes outlined in white clay,
>>> but this is only snow
> and we creep on toward the Medicine Line.

6

Far ahead lies a thick blue line, too even to be a mountain.

Then this blue line grows grey and a notch begins to show.

7

Red Spy, letting his striped blanket hang down the side of his spotted horse, swings up the barrel of his Springfield carbine and pulls the trigger all in an instant:

the shot goes wide, but the Shinbone warrior gallops away,

after which Red Spy, lithe victor of battles,

he who hunted down Bostons for fun in our hot summer past at Cottonwood Place,

rode against Cut Arm at Toohhoolhoolsote's side at Cliff Place

and killed the traitor *Aplaham Pluks* from a bush

—*áhaha!*—

wraps himself back up in his blanket and canters on, wishing again for exploding bullets

(soon he will be wishing for any bullets at all)

and the ice-wind strokes his chest.

8

Far away, a yellow horizon-line causes Welweyas to ask: Is that the Medicine Line?— Not yet, my dear younger sister; indeed you must grow more patient.

9

We are journeying vainly:

Sound Of Running Feet,

my precious child,

she who prefers not to trouble my heart by speaking,

cannot ride anymore; now she is walking bravely.

I remember when her dress was once well decorated with quilled horsehair.

Good Woman warms the aching cold in the bones of her daughter's fingers, as Welweyas clumsily, adoringly offers her the King George blanket she wears.

10

The night before Heinmot Tooyalakekt gave his rifle to Bear Coat, the Big Bellies had already killed five more of our warriors on the south fork of Box Elder
Creek
     (and caught our women and children to be their slaves).
          It has always been so. Someday perhaps we shall revenge ourselves;
          then all will be straight.

11

Heinmot Tooyalakekt has said: My dear nephew, creep around these Bluecoats
and find Good Woman, and your dear mother Swan Woman, and my lovely
daughter Sound Of Running Feet. Ask Cloudburst if her heart has changed; she
should come live with her child. Bring them here so we may all dwell together at
Butterfly Place,
    and so White Thunder creeps out, but never comes back,
        for he thinks it a pity to pen up his relatives on painted land
           —but let my uncle go stir ashes for Cut Arm if he likes! Surely he
           should follow his own heart.
Calling upon his WYAKIN, he presently finds the tracks of his mother's horse.
And the world widens around him, all the way to the newest end of everything,
so far from our home
          (even here the Bostons will soon be coming to suck away every-
          thing good with their leech-mouths).
Now his heart begins to wonder what present ought to be offered to Cutthroats. For what does he possess but a necklace of dentalium shells, that pistol
which he has carried so far, and his two cartridge belts?
    Through the night comes the smell of a white bear. He cannot stop to hunt it.
    As he rides north on a bad horse, ready with his old Winchester, wondering
whether his mother still lives, he keeps watching out for Walking Cutthroats,
        so many of whom have been killed by Rainbow, the bravest of our best
        men
           (who now lies half out of his grave at Ground Squirrel Place; the
           Lice-Eaters have dug him up and scalped him, but the Bluecoats
           buried him again, then some Bostons dug him up once more in
           hopes of souvenirs),
and longing to kill a Big Belly for a warm black hat and beaded gauntlets,
        sorrowing and grieving,
           remembering our vast herds
            (thief treaty!),
creeping through the snow with his pistol out,

feeling as eerie in his heart as when he shot the SPIRIT DEER that went on
grazing, untouched,
and grateful indeed for Wottolen's advice back at Sparse-Snowed Place, for without such words he would have given this toy to a woman, and the rifle is too heavy
to point ahead always,
especially now that his belly grows hungry.
As he pursues Swan Woman toward the Medicine Line,
hoping that Wottolen has looked after her again,
and wishing for a saddle, with one of his mother's long cous breads dangling from it,
dreaming about the Enemy River on a summer evening
and Wallowa,
shivering,
he warms himself with the memory of the day last summer at Cottonwood Place
when we crushed that Bluecoat's head with our clubs, *taq!*
—his heartbeats now as highpitched as war cries.

12

White Bird knows the way as well as did Looking-Glass:
he has been even here with his father and Old Heinmot Wellammoutkin,*
hunting buffalo;
exactly here has he killed Cutthroats and Walking Cutthroats
(but he is wishing for his wolfskin cap);
from ambush on the Milk River he has seen a Shinbone vermilioning his
wife's face.
From Place of the Manure Fires he has saved a hundred and three men, sixty
women and eight children,
some of them wounded and bleeding,
some walking, most riding on horses hidden from Bear Coat:
Looking-Glass's widows and daughters
and Broken Tooth (she whom we once called White
Feather),
Toohhoolhoolsote's grim old widows,
Ollokot's widow Cloudburst
and ancient Tzi-kal-tza, together with his loving daughter,
following Snake Creek to the Milk River,
walking and riding for ten suns, wolf-wandering
toward tilting grey westward-blowing strings of snow on the
horizon
and an ovoid silver ice-pond;

---

*Old Joseph.

even now he has kept his fish-headed whistle whose voice can summon eagles and coyotes. Perhaps it will be a helper.

Behind him, White Thunder's mother Swan Woman never stops; she keeps her horse-whipping stick ready to crack a bear across the face or break a Big Belly's nose

> and Grizzly Bear Youth, whose forehead will always grin with that scar from a Boston
>> (who clubbed him with the butt of a needle gun at Ground Squirrel Place)
> strides on and on,
> but Hunts No More, many-necklaced, taller than White Bird, gazes forward with his lips slack and his eyes dulled,
>> our children grabbling down in the crackly clumps of sage-brush to get out of the wind, hugging the dead grass beneath,
>>> snow breaking under them, cutting their thighs—

a simple journey for the People: any human being could do it,
even delicate little *Kate* will survive to fold her hands across her blanketed lap in the Great White Mother's country and stare bitterly across the Medicine Line;
> only seven warriors with us will be killed by the Walking Cutthroats and Big Bellies.

On the third sun they even begin to get food: pronghorn antelopes.

White Bird then says: My People, will you sit down here in the snow and wait for Big Bellies to kill you? Soon the Bluecoats will be here! Will you wait for them to pen you up? If that is what you wish, you should have surrendered with Heinmot Tooyalakekt.

> He should have been our head-chief
>> (I Dreamed he was packing away his necklace of shells).

Now they come to the Milk River, and finding a camp of half-breeds, White Bird comes forward to speak in signs: My friends, who will take us to Sitting Bull for money?

What money?

I shall pay you a gold button from a Bluecoat's jacket, or five paper dollars unwrapped from my own woman's braids.

Gold! says a half-breed.

Just before the Medicine Line, at the bank of a frozen creek, White Bird kneels, smooths away the snow, then scrapes out a hunk of white clay with his knife;
> and softening the white clay against his body, he goes on,
>> wrapping his striped blanket back around his waist,
>>> secretly touching his fish-headed whistle,
>> wishing and calling upon his WYAKIN,
>>> hardening his roach of hair with this good white clay,
>>> so that the Cutthroats will know him for a man who respects himself;

while *Kate*, having made a new pair of beaded moccasins for herself, now hopes to give them to one of Sitting Bull's women.

So they are crossing the Medicine Line,

among them brave Arrowhead, she who always rides with a wolfskin over her shoulders

and who once lived at Kamnaka for awhile,

just for awhile,

until Cut Arm sent killers to arrest her chief, Looking-Glass

(now they have shot him):

even until now this massive woman has saved her white horse, whose bridle and other tack she has embroidered with red triangles and black diamonds, the saddle-blanket fringed all the way to the ground,

and hanging from her belt is a large white root-digging bag (now empty) figured with many triangular-bodied deer;

what becomes of her on the other side I cannot tell you,

for all these People's stories are now ending,

like Shooting Thunder's:

He has ridden ahead into the snow,

but we never see him on the other side of the Medicine Line.

13

Red Spy comes into a village, craving to warm himself

—indeed they are Walking Cutthroats in white wolfskin caps, with their eyes outlined in white clay—

and they say: If you are our friend, lay down your rifle!

—so he does; then they shoot him

(Bear Coat will be pleased; he will give them tobacco).

14

And now Strong Eagle,

last of the Three Red Blankets,

fleeing with White Hawk, Hide Scraper, Calf Of The Leg and Wamushkaiya,

breaking through the snow into water or ice, falling, struggling up wet and silent to creep on,

until by midmorning the wide-spread fingers of the leafless trees return to distinctness as the snow stops whirling,

runs northward,

and so those five warriors, murmuring their WYAKIN songs, approach the Medicine Line,

arriving in the Land of Brightness.
Entering a village; they make the sign for food:
it is our good friends the Walking Cutthroats who receive them,
>   white-eyed and white-hatted,
>   these wealthy, many-wived men
>>   —laughing woman-chasers who vermilion their faces whenever
>>   they wish to marry again
>>>   (Strong Eagle is smiling because these men have decorated
>>>   themselves to resemble the Shinbones' wives)
>   and who hang abalones in their ears, roaching their hair, braiding
>   false hair behind them to their feet;
>>   they are pleased with us because we are now at war with the
>>   ones they name *the Raven Enemy*,*
and these jolly-hearted ones, having taken the People's rifles, invite them to a
feast,
>   entertaining them with woman-fights:
>>   for they hold it great sport to watch their wives marking each other
>>   with clubs or knives;
and just as a hawk bends forward on his branch, scanning uneasily from side to
side, hunching his wings, then opening them and shaking off featherdown, Strong
Eagle watches his hosts,
>   who now teach the People how to say *wittko wiyon*, a slut,
after which (keeping their guests' weapons) they kindly put them on the way to
the Big Bellies
>   —down into the pale treetops in the creek-gulleys
>>   as they sing their WYAKIN songs, hoping to become invisible this
>>   one last time,
>>>   the grey clouds turning black and the night becoming a black
>>>   cloud—
ride after them,
shoot and scalp them
>   (now all will be straight),
their pilfered bloody corpses resting finally against a swale of frozen grass which
helps stop the wind.

15

The Walking Cutthroats have been hunting us for thirteen days;
>   the Big Bellies have been killing us or chasing us out,
>>   their women seated outside the tipis, wrapped in blankets, gazing hate-
>>   fully at us, saying nothing,

---

*Crows.

and the Painted Arrows keep after us;
Bear Coat has sent three Bluecoat detachments to pursue us, both Horse People and Walking Soldiers
    (they have caught forty-five of us among the Red River half-breeds)
—but Swan Necklace has now escaped with five other men, two boys and two
women
    (Half Moon arrived first, with some other old men,
    and then, on his longnecked yellow horse, Peopeo Tholekt,
        who now and through all the years lost in the Indian Territory will
        hide in a deerskin pouch tied within his leggings a greenstone pipe
        from Ollokot, a wampum bead from Looking-Glass, a redstone
        pipe that White Bird gave him at the war dance long ago at Split
        Rock, when we all still had our country, and the short bead from
        around the throat of Heinmot Tooyalakekt;
    and with Peopeo rides his war-friend Welehwoot, who can speak Crow
words with the Cutthroats);
and White Bird's People will soon likewise arrive:
        our home can now be in the Old Woman's Country, where we can
        surely ride and wander as before.
Black Eagle has fled safely; so too his father Wottolen,
along with Good Woman's sorrowful ones;
and crossing the Medicine Line, we all come presently into the valley of snow,
pines, aspens and spruce, with the tall log fort of the Queen's Children grey in the
flickering snow.

THE AMERICANS ARE YOUR FRIENDS
1877–81

1

*S*itting Bull, roundheaded and many-wrinkled, with his waist-long braids
spilling down his crumpled shirt and two pale feathers rising high from his scalp,
stares into White Bird's heart, frowning neutrally, sucking in his translucent
cheeks. Yes, they have been enemies, but on this day he has pity; he will not kill
them. His People incense their sad guests with sweetgrass. They sing, waving their
long, horse-headed dancing sticks so that bells jingle and eagle feathers sway. But
some of the Nimiipu women will not stop weeping. Their home is gone forever,
their nation devoured by the Bostons! The babies sob *shlak, shlak!*

Meanwhile the Lakota remain wealthy: fringed, feathered and beaded, owning many horses. They still dream of buffalo thunder. They share with the People their own lodges, outside of which thin dogs lie sleeping. Presenting them with King George blankets, they feast their guests on fat buffalo meat, well roasted—although they have not much themselves. To the women who need it they give the blue tea of the rush skeletonweed that Lakota and Painted Arrow mothers drink to bring out their milk.

White Bird is the People's only remaining chief, so his heart must now offer thanks to these good friends, these *Cutthroats*.

Sitting Bull remarks: I don't want to have anything to do with people who make one carry water on the shoulders and haul manure.

Smiling, White Bird replies that indeed the hearts of white men are bad. Even the women of that breed are evil-hearted, so it seems. They should all be killed.

They have made your People as poor as snakes!

White Bird agrees that Sitting Bull has said exactly what is true.

Sitting Bull stares across the fire at him with morose mistrust.

(It may be advantageous that Looking-Glass is not here—he who killed so many of Sitting Bull's best men.)

2

Red Cloud and his son *Jack* are present, the father grimly staring White Bird down, the younger man, from whose loose hair rise eagle feathers like the spread lodgepoles atop a tipi, peering through him with the same distant skepticism which he would bestow on any Boston; while farthest away from the fire sits an old warrior wrapped in a blanket painted with the image of a reddish hand: this means he has been wounded.

Peopeo Tholekt draws near, standing before Sitting Bull, whose eagle-feather war bonnet nearly reaches the tipi's dirt floor. Sitting Bull extends to him the longhandled peace pipe. Peopeo Tholekt bows down to take it, wondering whether these People, too, will someday wipe their buttocks on our heads.

But they do not. Sitting Bull shakes everyone's hand, down to the last little girl.

3

I, William the Blind, have read that Sitting Bull failed to save the People at Wolf's Paw because the first news he gained of the battle, from Half Moon and those other old men, was in hand-signs; and he mistook Snake Creek for the Place of the Cave of Red Paint, which his Cutthroat riders could never have reached in time. It is written in these yellowing books whose word-ashes I have dug and stirred like an old woman in order to write *The Dying Grass* that Sitting Bull came with warriors to meet White Bird's People as they came into his new country, and that Sitting Bull was then the first to leap off his horse and lament the doom of his old enemies, the People, the Nimiipu, the ones who once were rich in rivers, mountains, camas and horses.

I have also read that the Redcoat chief came to the Lakota and said: Sitting Bull, hear me! You know that I do not lie. I shall now speak words which the Grandmother herself has placed within my mouth: If you lead your young men south across the Medicine Line to make trouble for the Bluecoats, I shall certainly drive your People back into the Grandfather's Country without pity, even your children and old women. Sitting Bull, now I have spoken,

> after which the Lakota concluded in their hearts that it was better to save their own People than to help these Pierced-Noses who could not be helped.

In any event, it is told that Sitting Bull said to White Bird: My dear brother, what a pity that we could not understand the speech of your old men! Had I known, I could have saved you. From here to Wolf's Paw is no farther for me than from my head to my pillow!

Reader, only you can judge whether his heart was straight or crooked when he said this. In any event, it was most handsomely said.

4

White Thunder first fears that Sitting Bull will murder them all. Clapping hands and crying out, his hosts ask him to smoke with them, but he refuses, because his WYAKIN will not allow it. Once he explains, they forgive him. His mother Swan Woman is cold and starving. Sitting Bull's women give her pemmican in a quilted bag figured with a crimson horse.

Growing suddenly warm, Sitting Bull repeats: Had I known that you were in the Wolf's Paw Mountains, I certainly would have helped you! What a pity, what a pity!

Smiling very rapidly, White Bird replies that it is a pity indeed. He has lost his eagle-feather fan; he cannot hide his face behind it.

But now that you are here, I shall not permit the *Americans* to take even a child from you without a fight.

Sitting Bull, you are a great man, I am telling you three times . . .

A great man? O, I used to be a kind of chief, but the *Americans* made me go away from my father's hunting ground.

White Bird gives him seven starving horses. Sitting Bull presents him with seven buffalo robes.

5

Sitting Bull says: Why did you refuse to join us last year? We could have killed many *Americans*.

The Crows were against it.

Yes, they have always been our enemies. Now they are yours.

White Bird agrees that this is so.

I have heard that you sold your country to the *Americans.*

Some crookedhearts from Butterfly Place sold what they had no right to sell. My People never sold OUR MOTHER—

As for me, brother, I did not give the *Americans* my country, but they followed me from place to place, and I had to come here.

So I have heard. You are the greatest warrior of all. We were laughing and singing when you killed Yellow Hair—

Sitting Bull says: Did you speak with Bear Coat?

White Bird murmurs that he found it best not to do so.

When Bear Coat marched through my country, he told me that the Grandfather had commanded his coming.

Perhaps that is so.

Now tell us about this battle, says Sitting Bull. We are opening our ears.

6

Wottolen presents to Sitting Bull many of the beautiful old Nimíipu things which Heinmot Tooyalakekt gave him. Then the Lakota give gifts to their guests. Across the fire, a warrior watches White Bird. The eagle feather standing in this Cutthroat's hair has been triangularly notched to show that he slew and scalped some enemy—perhaps one of our best men.

Shyly, Sound Of Running Feet offers her Bluecoat pistol to Sitting Bull, who gives it to one of his women.

Black Eagle says to his family: Sitting Bull is very good with us.

And so they live together until the dirty snow melts away,
>   but there is not enough to eat:
>   not many buffalo are coming
>   (they must be somewhere else).

White Bird remembers how Looking-Glass always used to say: *Buffalo meat is the best. Only buffalo meat will do.*

7

The yellow grass grows green again. Snow clings to shady slopes. Again White Bird praises Sitting Bull for killing Yellow Hair, while the Lakota grow joyous in their hearts to hear again how we slaughtered Bluecoats at Sparse-Snowed Place, in the days when none of us had yet been killed in this war.

Wondering how well the Wallowa People are now living penned up at Butterfly Place, he asks Sitting Bull what he has heard, but no news comes.

He passes the time among old men tattooed upon their naked chests, their faces all muscle and bone, like mummies; they frown into space whenever Sitting Bull speaks,

remembering the long, sweeping drop in their yellow and golden land
where they killed Yellow Hair's soldiers, and never can go again:
                green stripes of shadow and the blue and purple butte-horizon;
and then *Kate* sits quietly, chopping wood and boiling bone soup. An old woman
spits into the ashes,
                and White Bird, following the fashion of the Hunkpapa in order to please
                them, paints white stripes across his upper arm to express his escape
                from captivity
                        (perhaps someday he will even smoke the Medicine pipe with our
                        ancient enemies the Shinbones
                                and should he desire a second wife, there is a certain full-
                                lipped Lakota girl whom he sometimes watches across the
                                fire; he would like to slide his hand around one of her braids),
                                        while Hunts No More sits with his wrists in his lap
                and Welweyas the half-woman acquires tinklers and jinglebobs to
                wear; her heart knows how to make men happy; moreover, she can
                carry as much wood as two men.
Every now and then we still Dream;
                we are flying up,
                going round and round,
                        smoking sweetgrass mixed with tobacco so that the good
                        Powers will come;
and at night White Bird's People tell stories about the Three Red Blankets
                (some of us still hope that Strong Eagle and those four war-friends will
                come down to us exactly here).
Wottolen,
                who has given the Lakota his only shirt as a present,
now Dreams to more perfectly remember this war for us with all its tales
                (across the fire, his son Black Eagle sits listening, knowing that his gen-
                eration will never be able to ride all across the Buffalo Country, nor make
                war, catch horses or gamble at Weippe and Split Rock Place,
                        racing horses and attracting women, hunting, riding far whenever
                        we like:
                                sometimes Wottolen smiles to tell of something lovely that is
                                gone)
and Good Woman sits hungry and quiet beside Sound Of Running Feet,
                who never asks about her father;
they help and work whenever they can,
                Cloudburst fetching wood and water in deepest silence,
                        grieving for Fair Land, her dear sister-wife
                        and for Fair Land's son
                                (now he must be walking and running very well, unless he
                                has died),

worrying about Sound Of Running Feet, who seldom looks at anyone,
remembering Ollokot,
who should not be named, and
who once picked for her the flower called *wind's tears.*
Asking Maiden and Blackberry Person whisper into their daughters' ears; these four keep busy and quiet, for fear that the Lakota will remember the hateful deeds of the dead Looking-Glass;
and *Kate* begins to sew quilled rawhide stripes to make a fine breastplate for her husband, who will then appear more like a Lakota chief.

8

Sometimes we like to fool the Redcoats, just for awhile
(there is no evil in our hearts),
and ride back across the Medicine Line to seek buffalo. Even Sitting Bull now admits that we know how to hunt. Whenever we find a herd, we drive it into the Old Woman's Country, to enrich ourselves and punish the Big Bellies and Walking Cutthroats:
now those enemies are likewise getting hungry:
Áhaha!

9

Sound Of Running Feet remembers when we still lived in our home, and she rode Little One, leading Spotted Head, who might have become her favorite horse.
When she made her first dress in error, so that it was no good, her mother helped her put it right.
Now she can decorate herself; she can make any dress or shirt
and is well able to weave a basket.
Her mother tells her to grease up her black braids, and when she does, the Cutthroat braves begin to look her over, so that when they are outside fetching water from the half-frozen creek the young woman murmurs: My mother, has it come into your heart to give me to the Cutthroats?
It is too soon for such talk.
My mother, does my father still live?
Be silent, for I shall now close my ears.

10

Snow creeps away by night, oozing and crawling away, clinging only to cañons, creek-banks and trees. Cows bow their heads in the shining new fields south of the Medicine Line, which our People and Sitting Bull's sometimes cross to kill them. Now we are hunting together almost like one People—but there is never enough food in the Grandmother's Country.

Peopeo Tholekt,

    wearing the coat he has made out of a blanket which our sad chief
    gave him at Wolf's Paw,
 rides out to hunt buffalo, but returns ashamed, unable to find any.

In mid-spring when the willows bud and the bunchgrass grows up in the Buffalo Country, some of us break our promise again, riding back across the Medicine Line to see what can be found in the lands which used to be ours. Perhaps there will be buffalo. We certainly should not kill Bluecoats, for that might anger our good friends the Redcoats, but there may be a lone Crow or Walking Cutthroat to murder

    once we have first silently looked down into the turnings and along
    the length of that softgrassed coulee where Our Mother will
    drink in our blood and eat away our bones:
      exactly here was Heinmot Tooyalakekt's lodge; from here he
      rose with his daughter to catch horses
        (he whose heart was not bravest in war but unfailingly
        straight through all sorrows),
      as a hawk darts over the coulee—
 while far away, dream-white, the Wolf's Paw Mountains squat on the
horizon,
    where Bear Coat came down to kill us;
 and if we keep riding south,
    back into the country called *O-to-kur-tuk-tai*,
      where the Crows stole our horses,
our hearts may begin to become joyous again, as if we were riding back into time.

 Before they know it, our best men have already returned to the Swift Water,
    exactly here where we once had fun teasing the Bostons just a little,
      burning their stagecoach, shooting them dead and shouting orders,
      the locusts singing *tekh-tekh-tekh!*
      (this year there will not be many locusts)
and find a place which our good friends the *Americans* now call *Terry's Landing.*

 White Eyes is one of these warriors; he wishes to uplift his heart again. Finding two Bostons in this place—tall, quiet men who keep their Winchesters close—he kills one and wounds the other: *Áhaha!*— Now we are fleeing home to Sitting Bull,

 laughing as we ride,
    our hearts already expecting to see the Cutthroats' nine-pole-clawed tipis rising at last on the far side of the foggy plain,
but White Eyes falls behind;
 our fine friends the Crows catch him and put him to death.

11

Sitting Bull stays good to us: We dwell in the shadowed stare of his oval face:
> two deep vertical grooves above the bridge of his nose;
>> we have learned the shallower lines on his moon-bright forehead,
>> the dark wrinkles from his nostrils down to the corners of his
>> mouth, and his many-stranded, pefectly combed black braids, his
>> multitudes of necklaces, the fringes on his hide shirt.

He helps us, but sometimes we are all hungry.

Even until now Cloudburst still kept the dead Bluecoat's breastplate that Ollokot gave her at Sparse-Snowed Place; now she gives it to Sitting Bull's youngest
wife, who now opens her heart, presenting her with a hunk of dried buffalo meat,
> and this she takes to her dear niece Sound Of Running Feet, who has
> grown ever more sad and pale,
> and who thanks her in a whisper, turning the gift round and round in her
> callused hands.

12

Now in the season called *Towering Plants*,
>> when the bindweed first comes out at Butterfly Place
>> and we used to ride to the higher place so that our women could dig
>> cous,
> when the redwinged blackbirds throng back to the rivers and swamps,
> males calling females to come and follow them,

White Bird, wishing to wrap his braids in otterskin after Sitting Bull's fashion,
rides to the creek to kill whichever animal he desires;
> later there will be a dog feast,
> and the whispering of the tin tinklers on the Lakota's clothes;
>> and at last we must smoke the pipe with our old enemies the Shinbones,
>> for they are Sitting Bull's friends.

He finds no otters, but kills seven muskrats,
> and after dawn, when Sound Of Running Feet comes down there to fetch
> water, she sees the old chief skinning them,
>> so that her heart remembers that story we tell our children:
>>> MUSKRAT's tail is naked because it got caught by the shutting
>>> of the dying MONSTER's anus after the rest of us had all
>>> rushed out
>> —so her father told her when she was small,
> and White Bird, looking up, now says: Sound Of Running Feet, my lovely
> niece, your father still lives, I am telling you three times!

Feeling shy, she smiles, flushes, then runs away to fill her pot and kettle.

13

Slumped, pallid and glaring, General Sheridan, richly buttoned, locks his elbow on the table, presses his pale spread fingers against his ear, sinks his head between his epaulettes, with his hand on his hip, never ceasing to remember Sitting Bull with the balefulest hatred and White Bird with rage,

but now he has orders;

hence General Terry,

whom the Sioux call *Star,*

and Colonel Miles get theirs,

so that Lieutenant George W. Baird,

who remembers his wife's red-rimmed eyes and moaning nightmares when he rode out with Miles's column in hopes of avenging Custer

(for the third time—such is the lot of an Army wife—she had to give birth when I was far away: for myself I don't care if that d——d Sitting Bull gets me, but as for *her . . .*)

and whose ear still appears a trifle nasty from the wound Chief Joseph's bunch gave him at Bear's Paw,

receives Miles's order and sets out for the British Possessions,

carrying with him Húsishúsis Kute,

whom Cut Arm still imagines to be chief of the Palouses,

Yellow Bull,

the father of our slain hero Red Moccasin Tops (he is White Bird's nephew),[*]

and Estoweaz,

called *Thunder-Eyes*

—all on loan from the Indian Territory:

Maybe they'll make White Bird see daylight.

14

It is the time when serviceberries have just begun to turn purple back home in the Chinook Salmon Water country. By now our women would have finished digging camas at Split Rock; soon we would be riding away to meet the Salish at Weippe. Up on this side of the Medicine Line, it seems, rather, as if summer has just opened.

Of course Sitting Bull declines to come, hunkering himself away in his lodge,

---

[*]His relative by marriage.

just as a buffalo will wallow in summer mud to armor himself against sun
and flies,

    while Wottolen sits half lost amidst the snakelike and ladderlike tattoos
of the old men, unnerved by the loosehaired young warriors who sit almost smiling with murder-dreams

        (he is telling himself the deeds of Rainbow at Big Water
and counting up the murders of our People by the Bostons before
this war:

           now his heart begins too late to understand
              —although many other best men dispute this, prefer-
              ring White Bird, who planned our victory at Sparse-
              Snowed Place and led us across the Medicine Line—
           that our greatest chief was Heinmot Tooyalakekt,
           he who never had hope,
              desiring only to help our women, children and old ones:
                when Toohhoolhoolsote spoke against him at the
                Split Rock council, because he had sold OUR
                MOTHER, he replied: *I shall go against my promise
                to him who was my father and chief. I shall now
                live and die on painted land, never to go out*).

  as *Kate* sits weeping with Good Woman, fearing that Bluecoats will now
carry off her husband,

      and perhaps her heart whispers what is straight,
           for indeed this Lieutenant Baird, rereading his instructions
           for one last private instant in the Redcoats' sleeping room
              (Sitting Bull has supplied the buffalo robes on their
              beds, so they have sometimes allowed him a slice of the
              dark tobacco cake beside the two-handled chopper)
           is now meditating on that dawn raid last May when Lame
           Deer, surprised and defeated, had already shaken hands with
           Colonel Miles,
              so that Baird could begin coaxing Iron Star to lay down
              his rifle,
                when one of our d——d Cheyennes saw fit to
                snatch at it,
                  at which point Lame Deer, thinking the
                  worst, shot at Miles,
                    so that history must take its course:
                  fourteen Minneconjous killed
           (General Terry later said: It is the best thing that has been
           done since hostilities commenced).
           Now what I'd like to do is get the drop on White Bird, if these
           Britishers will stand for it. Why should they care anyhow? It's

not as if he's one of their Indians! I'll bet General Terry would commend me—

But I can't do it here. If my Nez Perces can talk him into surrender, maybe something can happen on the way back to Tongue River.

But Miles might say it ain't right. He's awfully soft on Joseph's whole bunch.

All the same, wouldn't it be for the best?

No,

        spitting into the square spittoon filled with sand.

I'm not going to get in hot water just to bump off some lousy Indian. What do I care?

15

Next to the half-breed interpreter I see smooth-faced many-necklaced White Bird sitting watchful, with pale beads on the ends of his dark braids and his hands clasped into almost-fists upon his blanketed lap. Behind him, a mosquito squats on the whitewashed wall of logs.

Across the table I find Commissioner Macleod next to his American guest, that selfsame Lieutenant Baird, who again remembers his wife's red-rimmed eyes and moaning nightmares when he rode out with Miles's column in hopes of avenging Custer,

        and from General Howard's report he recollects how at that fateful council at Lapwai last spring, this same White Bird persisted in hiding his face behind an eagle's wing;

    and Baird scans the long dark cracks between ceiling-planks.

By the door stands James Morrow Walsh, the Mounted Police superintendent: very handsome, open-faced, almost delicate of skin, with a pretty moustache and wavy hair, looking innocent and kind for a policeman,

    as indeed he is: even Sitting Bull likes him,

        hoping that the Lakota may dream away their lives here in the White Mother's country just as quietly as the grass grows on the roof of the North-West Mounted Police station at Wood Mountain, killing buffalo and perhaps stealing horses or shooting Crows.

A bull train of flour, bacon and coffee comes on toward the fort. Soon traders will ride in from the town. Heavily, the sentry's relief ascends the plank-steps of the Southeast Bastion.

Lieutenant Baird now explains to White Bird: The Americans are your friends, and want you to go back to your old home, and if you don't, you will go to some other good reservation.

White Bird listens, jibberjabbers something in Injun, and then the interpreter says: If the Indians and the Government have made treaties already, it is not my place to interfere.

I don't understand what you mean by *interfere,* replies Lieutenant Baird.

I want Joseph to come back to our own country. I see how the hearts of both Governments are toward the Indians. I am so happy. My heart is open . . .

He doesn't *look* happy, remarks Lieutenant Baird to the interpreter; at which Commissioner Macleod rubs his projecting bearded chin.— Tell White Bird the following: The Great Father sent me up here to give you the opportunity to go to Joseph. If you want to go, you ought to make up your minds at once.

We are all glad to hear it. I am glad the other chiefs surrendered. When they surrendered

       (this sure is one logical Injun!),

it showed that they did not want to fight anymore.

Mr. McDonald, this is not to the point. Please make him understand that if he comes over the line with us to Joseph, there is a very good prospect that they will all go back to their old home, but if he stays here, Joseph's prospects may not be so good. This is because the Great Father may say: *White Bird and his people are living with my enemies, the Sioux.*

I don't care for the Sioux; I just camp there to pass the time, just for a little while. My heart is very good; there is not a bit of bad in it.

At this reply, which could not contain any more equivocation even if White Bird still possessed a fan to hide behind, good Lieutenant Baird, who is tall, pale, bearded and exhausted, like a Union soldier from our late Secession War, or perhaps like President Hayes when he was younger, peers at him, then rubs his swollen ear, while White Bird ponders the fancy ropes arcing down from the lieutenant's epaulettes almost like overlapping Indian necklaces.

After making marks in a book whose pages are creamy-white like the crown of miniature death camas flowers, Lieutenant Baird tries again, saying: I know you are brave men, and I like to hear brave men talk, because I know they will tell me the truth.

Wishing to aid his American colleague, Commissioner Macleod assures the Indians: You have a splendid chance.

I understand, says White Bird very delicately, that Chief Joseph and his people do not want to go south of Leavenworth, where the country is bad for them. If Joseph comes back to our part of the country, to a good reservation, we shall join him.

Now Lieutenant Baird seems to be out of sorts. Gazing away from his hosts, as if the gilt chevrons on their scarlet coats make him feel shy, then stretching himself like some MONSTER preparing to hunt upstream, he says: Tell him that those who slip back one at a time will be treated as hostile Indians.

Yellow Bull, still permitted to wear his Dreamer's peak, watches everyone with a wary desperation in his hard face, his long hair shining loosely down his shoulders. A mosquito crawls upon his Hudson Bay blanket-coat of many stripes. The other two prisoners, Húsishúsis Kute and Estoweaz, seem not very interested. In confidence they have informed White Bird of how it truly fares with the People in the place where they are kept. Soon Lieutenant Baird will hale them back there.

White Bird says: I shall not go.

16

Nearly weeping, she cries out: Husband, you have returned! My heart is glad. How were his words?

Like a blanket not good enough to be a present.

Did he make himself angry?

Síikstiwaa, he is nothing; he resembles some nasty creature eating mice,
>   and soon our best men ride secretly back across the Medicine Line with Sitting Bull's best men to hunt buffalo,
>>   with a little reddish-grey coyote trotting along for blood,
>   although White Bird, always cautious, declines to go.

17

In the fort he has seen a sack of biscuits, and canned corn, peaches, salmon and pears from Fort Benton; this he remembers when he tastes *Kate*'s thin bone soup and watches the old men sitting hungry and silent across the fire.

His People still Dream along with Sitting Bull's, flashing skinny thighs as they dance around the fire:
>   their heads upraised, their gazes mild, bead-circlets in their ears:
>   we are all flying up, circling round,
>>   remaining hungry.

18

Once the People understand in their hearts that the Old Woman will never feed them, nor allow them to take a reservation here, they begin to slip away
>   —some of them, most of them, but never White Bird and *Kate*—
>   back across the Medicine Line,
>>   disturbing the brown mirror of the Milk River and then
>>   creeping like snakes through the great new enemy country, the Boston, *American* country
>>>   where wild roses are in full flower,
>>   and at Wolf's Paw they stop to rebury their dead
>>>   (Painted Arrows, dogs and souvenir hunters have played with them);
>>   then, camping along the creek, butchering buffalo, watching out for Big Bellies and our former friends the *Women Nation*,

        dandelion down blowing and caught in spiderwebs,
they point out to one another where White Bird and *Kate* once had
their lodge:

        exactly here on the creek's wide eastern lip, fifty paces from
        the coulee's white-grass wall

            (through the thick green line of Snake Creek the locusts
            snapping);

                and from there where the wide round grass-hill
                meets the clouds the Bluecoats first came gallop-
                ing
                and our hearts began once again to hate Looking-
                Glass, who has now left us,

but the rifle-pits still show in the pale yellow grass on the gentle
ridge to the east of the creek;

so then down where the ridge fans out into pale-grassed fingers
outspread by Snake Creek they stand atop Red Place, where
Toohhoolhoolsote and his warriors died:

        dead yarrow, gayfeather flowers both purple and white

—and vaulting off their horses, they descend the pink rock, which
is lichened orange, black and white, and the bees, flies and grasshoppers are singing:

            —a few steps now to where they were killed, and then
            the orange meadow flattens out to the pale grey-green
            lips of Snake Creek, whose flow cannot here be seen.

        Welweyas the half-woman wraps herself tighter in her grubby
        King George blanket.

Now the People's story is tapering like a bullet or Nez Perce moccasin

    as they follow the Place of the Cave of Red Paint, riding west, then south
as the river curves,

although some of them go farther south and then west to Ground Squirrel Place,

        where the hair has been ripped off our women's skulls and
        our children's teeth lie scattered like the lovely white cluster
        of miniature flowers which form a spoonlike crown on spring
        beargrass,

then back over the Lo Lo Trail

    to our homes,

            avoiding Lewiston, which used to be Riverfork
            and Ripple Place;
            while at Sweat Lodge Place the Bostons are grow-
            ing potatoes;
            at Crossing Place they have found and burned our
            secret treasures;

at Old Woman Place they are gashing OUR
MOTHER beside the bridge they have built;
everywhere they hunt us without pity,
until our women grow tired, our men despair, and in
small groups the People surrender at Butterfly Place,
expecting to be scolded by smoothfaced
Tsams Lúpin, then maybe whipped and
fined by Moss Beard until we must cut our
hair and go to church,
but their days become far worse than that—for
Heinmot Tooyalakekt, their last chief, is not there!
Bear Coat broke his promise.
(White Bird never told them what he
had learned from Yellow Bull and the
others. He feared to hurt their hearts.)
And the Bluecoats take them far away, to the Hot Place where Heinmot Tooyalakekt has been penned up.

19

Meanwhile the Lakota begin to starve; for the Old Woman will not help them,
either.

INDIAN TERRITORY
1878–85

1

*T*hey have penned us up in a hot place, in a country like a worn out winnowing basket that cannot even be given away. As Heinmot Tooyalakekt keeps
telling the Grandfather (whose wife pours them another lemonade), this is a country like a poor man, a country which has nothing. We are ringing the small bell
and tying our blanketed dead to tree branches exactly here where Salt River meets
Deer Creek,
for Bear Coat has said: *Joseph,* I spoke straight to you at Wolf's Paw! You
must not blame me that the Government has stopped my promise. If I
now give up my star and go away, it will make no difference; still they will
send you to the Hot Place,

to which he replied: My heart cannot understand how a Government
sends you out to fight us, then breaks its word.

2

Among our many *American* friends, Tsépmin the Unkillable
    (who still wears that dark old deerskin coat thickened with grease)
has become first,
    so that Heinmot Tooyalakekt must smile and shake his hand,
        even his,
    thanking him for nothing,
for he will now be our voice: Whatever we wish to tell the Bostons, Tsépmin will
say it for us
    (he who once whipped our boys for picking fruit from land which was
    ours);
and should we make his heart angry, he will say what is bad, to make the Bostons
hate us more
    (he will always be lying when we cannot understand);
hence Heinmot Tooyalakekt must give him gifts:
    first a snow-white buffalo robe,
    then the pipe which once belonged to his grandfather.

3

The Bostons rush to stare at him whom they call *Joseph.* For our People's sake,
he keeps smiling, thanking them, too, for nothing,
    fighting not to remember Ollokot,
    smiling, smiling on the rear platform of the train, wearing the ribbon-
trimmed black hat some Boston has given him; he is trying to shake
hands with them all,
    his eyes hysterically wide and his hair roached straight up by
    Springtime, who does not yet understand anything
        (perhaps she is longing for the richly bloody taste of deer
        meat):
    my heart is good, I am telling you three times
—and slender double necklaces sway against his throat when the train
hoots eastward:
    Bismarck, North Dakota,
        (three babies born, thirteen children dead)
      where the *Americans* invite him to a banquet appropriately
      commemorated by a paper negative (later to be signed by Ma-
      jor Moorhouse) captioned "Chief Joseph":
        his stiffly curving peak of hair very white against the

blue-greyness of the doorway, his eyes seemingly off
center, his mouth tight, a blanket striped round his
waist, his twin braids darkening below his throat, a
rectangular beaded gorget just above his fringed breast
—and then that night, to surprise us for his own fun, Tsépmin announces where we shall now be going
(thus it has been done:
Áhaha!),
after which (since horses are not permitted on this train) the
Americans part Heinmot Tooyalakekt from Black Mane-
Stripe, paying thirty-five dollars cash money as he turns away
(now it has become Buffalo Calf Season);
then Jamestown, Dakota Territory,
as we think on Cut Arm, who is and must remain exactly as he was made,
and Springtime is vomiting down the toilet hole;
Brainerd, Minnesota, and the Northern Pacific Junction,
where his sore heart falls back and back,
going southeast along the Chinook Salmon Water,
that flat wide river squirming southeast and southwest
down to the Enemy River,
to the place where my father still rides fast horses:
soon we shall set out for Eel Place, where Ollokot will
take Fair Land for his wife;
then we shall ride to Split Rock Place to gamble
while our women dig camas,
and Saint Paul, Minnesota, the Bostons swinging around their
wagon teams on Main Street to help their children better enjoy the
Red Napoleon's arrival.

4

Springtime rarely speaks:
our baby daughter becomes as white as that mushroom which we used
to gather beneath pine trees
because in the places where they pen us up, we can get neither yarrow nor snowberries to heal her;
but on the train, when she returns from squatting over the toilet hole
(terrified of the speeding tracks beneath)
she says: My dear husband, now my heart begins to realize how you have always
preferred Sound Of Running Feet
(perhaps even now the coyotes are chewing her bones)
as the Bluecoats carry us farther from our home

(it has come the season to wean our colts):
Austin, Minnesota
> —three more dead:
> They should have gone onto the reservation when they had the chance.
> Now they're at the disposition of our Government, and lucky not to be
> hanged!
> I say the Government does too much for 'em—
Mason City, Iowa
> —cigars for Chief Joseph, with our best American wishes!
>> My husband, will you keep doing nothing all the time?
>>> —and behind the depôt, a mound of frozen buffalo bones as
>>> white as the ring on our sad chief's dark and wrinkled hand—
Des Moines, then Council Bluffs,
> where Springtime
>> (with Tsépmin's help)
> trades away her narrow white leggings with the calves beaded blue and
> yellow; in exchange the bespectacled Boston (who makes her strip them
> off before his and Tsépmin's eyes, so that he will not be cheated) gives her
> a tall brown bottle of medicine guaranteed to save the baby;
and finally Fort Leavenworth
> (a camp by the river cesspool):
> we are settling in a circle to get tuberculosis and malaria
>> —no herbs to help; twenty-one deaths:
>>> warriors' wounds going septic, children's fevers shooting up
>>> like Progress—
and Mr. Joe in a longtailed war bonnet, his face withered, posing for nickels, wearing a plaid blanket-skirt like a Scottish Highlander, his ankles skinny in their
white-bordered leggings, he leans upon a rifle as if it were his staff, his head
sunken down—ain't he the living image of a *Red Napoleon?*
> —while Springtime has certainly become one who strings secret matters
> together within her heart.
>> Now it is Cous Cake Season at home
>>> (Springtime is raising up her arms),
>> while in Smohalla's country
>>> (if Smohalla has not yet been killed)
>> the seven Dreamer women will be gathering the first roots, wearing
>> eagle feathers on their hats as
Springtime hugs her heart, gazing at the dirt; Heinmot Tooyalakekt
turns away and her throat keeps working beneath the loose-knotted Boston handkerchief
>> as Feathers Around The Neck leads drummers and singers:
>>> we are burning sweetgrass Medicine until the next SUN
>>>> as Springtime sings with all her strength

and her husband's desperate heart says *qoh! qoh! qoh!*;
calling upon all Power to save this baby girl, our lovely one,
who now begins to leave us for the last time
as TRAVELLER begins to rise:
now she is going away:
we who have become poor can hardly expect to wrap her in a King George blanket.
Springtime cannot stop groaning for her child,
who has no name:
we must never say it:
and gruesome Bostons keep watching.

Heinmot Tooyalakekt says: Tsépmin, my dear brother, you know that it is not straight to disturb our hearts here.

Joseph, you now must do as you are told. Only if you pay me money shall I make them go away.

His braids are so nicely wrapped with rings of string of deerskin that the *American* ladies sigh: How I'd love to touch his hair!

—but Chief Joseph, dark and wild, stares away, flashing his dark *Indian eyes.*

5

Tsépmin's tent has become a museum of souvenirs. Tsépmin is all-seeing; he knows how to devour our last treasures. For a nickel, any Boston can see White Bird's wolfskin cap, and the pipe which once belonged to Heinmot Tooyalakekt's grandfather,

Toohhoolhoolsote's bone whistle to call the ANIMAL PEOPLE
and the false-embroidered triangles of red, green, blue and pink on a Nez
Perce bag of Indian hemp and cornhusk (never mind that bloodstain),
dead men's beaded quivers
and a Nez Perce dress yoke of deerskin, beaded with converging columns
of black and white beads, then horizontal stripes of larger brass beads
below
(Fair Land's work; every woman knows it)
—and if you want to see more curiosities, right over there by the sinks stands Chief Joseph, who nearly whipped the U.S. Army! I'd sure like to shake his hand
(the other surviving chief, Húsishúsis Kute, who was actually never a
chief, can barely make a nickel)—
while our young boys, so adept at leaping onto fast horses, will now shoot a Boston's nickel out of a forked stick if he permits them to keep it
(near as good as a nigger show)
and old Tzi-kal-tza sometimes gets a piece of hardbread by showing himself off to the Bostons, saying: *Me Clark!*

—Star Doctor and Wolf Head grimly glowering at the way he has lowered
himself, but his daughter plenty grateful to crunch up his bread.

Although Tsépmin's tent may be the best place to spend a nickel, our women,
who do not understand why nickels should not also come to them, make beaded
things to sell,

Injun things, squaw trash

(I might get twenty dollars for this back East),

and sometimes the Bostons want other things:

they are tearing our young women's dresses: *khattát!*

after which come shameful diseases. Now how may
they be married?

6

We are wrapping her in a stinking rag of blanket

(Springtime as helpless as a horse in quicksand; Looking-Glass's
wives must hold her back)

and the Bluecoats command: Down by the sinks,

and Star Doctor

with that wide-eyed yet wary Indian gaze which to some Caucasians
speaks of ecstasies, to others of secrets, and to the rest of reptilian evil

rings the small bell, just as Tuk-le-kas used to do,

so that the Bostons pay Tsépmin a nickel to watch the fun,

admiring the fringework and trade beads on Springtime's grubby
deerskin dress,

lifting up their children so they can observe how a squaw weeps

(pay attention, Annie, because there won't be none left by the
time you have children of your own!),

until White Cloud, the brave one who fought in every
battle of this war, whispers: My chief, shall we not now
kill them? Then they will kill us, and our troubles will
finish,

but Heinmot Tooyalakekt says: Enough of such talk!
You could have died like a warrior. Now we must live.

My dear little daughter, you too I shall see
no more.

7

In the time when the camas will have just begun to extrude its six sky-blue
petals at Split Rock Place

where the brown pond-frogs must now be singing and our women would
be dipping baking-grass in the lake

(Good Woman used to bring a basket of alder leaves with which to
        sweeten the roots as they steamed beneath the ground),
Looking-Glass's hollow-eyed widows approach the sad chief, saying: Uncle, please
hear us; we cannot keep the Bostons away from our daughters. What shall we do?

Unless you can marry them well, you must find yourselves a new husband to
protect them—

Uncle, you are now our only chief! Will you not help us?

My sorrowing ones, if you can find no one else, I shall certainly marry you.

Springtime's heart may be thrown down—

Enough. Wait awhile; then we shall see.

8

Wondering about our People in the Old Woman's Country,
        and hungering for our home,
we pass the time,
        just for awhile and awhile
                (we are no longer COYOTE's children);
as Springtime, seeking to make herself brave, sits plaiting a basket which she
hopes to sell to the Bostons, but because she now dislikes everything, fever begins
to weigh down her eyelids, so that she finds herself Dreaming as she sits:

a breeze overpasses the rapid green creek, stirring currant-heavy leaves, the
ripe dark berries glittering;

now wind has begun waving across the cloud of sagebrush on the far bank:
        my heart longs to be carried exactly to this unknown place forever.

And indeed the *Americans* are our friends!—for in the season when we have
always ridden to Weippe to meet the Salish and Crows, digging camas, gambling,
courting, racing and Dreaming
        (red salmon already darkening the streams of Wallowa),
they send us farther away—all the way to the Hot Place.

9

On the twenty-first of July, 1878, we pack off some four hundred and forty
prisoners to the Indian Territory. (I note five children buried at Baxter Springs,
then uprooted and devoured by pigs.)— Chief Joseph's squaw appears too ill to
walk; the heat does not agree with her. Well, she should have thought about the
consequences of murdering people!

Our chief says: If I am to speak—

at which Tsépmin explains: You must now place your words out of sight:

Áhaha! Now indeed he is beginning to understand!

Our orders require us to unload them at the Quapaw Reservation in the north-

east, on land previously assigned to the Modoc prisoners of war; let the reds work
it out between them:

    sixty-three tipis in the Modocs' oak grove,

          settling in a circle this last time,

Springtime wringing her hands, Dreaming that the Bostons have dug up our
baby to get souvenirs

        (since after a steamer is wrecked one naturally returns to the sand-
        bar to see what property might have washed up)

    and right away Tsépmin finds a Modoc wife.

By year's end, seventy-nine have died from sickness, wounds and sadness.

10

    Heinmot Tooyalakekt is wearing a shoulder-sash decorated with leaves and
diamonds, and that subdued double-stranded necklace to which he has taken
since his capture, evidently wishing not to look too wild,

    and although it is hot, Springtime keeps shivering: *Í-tsitsitsititsits:*

    she has malaria; her heart desires to die

        (and mine also, *síikstiwaa*):

            Tsépmin has not entirely emptied his black bottle of
            quinine, but only his favorite Indians get to sip from it,
                living on, spending their days, living SUN after
                SUN for nothing.

Tsépmin, my brother, I know not whether your Medicine will help her—

Joseph, you must pay me:

    one greenback for a real good swaller,

and Springtime keeps night-raving for her child; she has become one who cannot
stop speaking at night:

    Síikstiwaa, you're not eating

        (they lose their way when they speak to each other,

           although it grieves her heart to hurt him when speaks what is
           exactly true;

             she will soon separate herself from him),

thus he begins longing still more for Good Woman, whose love is as soft as a sage
leaf after rain.

11

Tsépmin,

    he who helped make the big fight against us,

now says: Listen, you People! I have always helped you. If you now pay me cash
money, I shall speak good words to the Bostons so that you may go home,

even to Wallowa.

But hear me! They must have money; their hearts insist upon it!

—Believing him, our women unwrap the last greenbacks from their braids;
even Heinmot Tooyalakekt gives twenty dollars in gold
(in Wallowa it is now time for serviceberries, huckleberries, wild
gooseberries),

after which Tsépmin says: The Bostons made their hearts angry! You paid too
little. Now you must stay here forever.

12

Nearly every day the Bostons come
(certain ladies will pay Tsépmin to see the way the sunlight sometimes
glistens in downpointing triangles beneath Chief Joseph's eyes),
while Springtime keeps frantically digging into sleep like that
woman at Ground Squirrel Place who tried to burrow into the riverbank so that the Bluecoats would not shoot her;
she is seeking to get lost;
when Bostons peer into her lodge, she refuses to open her eyes.

Forbearing with her, Heinmot Tooyalakekt goes out to remind the others: My
People, we must shake hands with them and all the time thank them for nothing,
so that perhaps they may someday keep their promises.

So there we dwell, just for awhile, trading *squaw trash* for *getting-drunk liquid*,
gambling with the Modocs and Potawatomies, racing sick horses with the Sene-
cas, just dying and passing the time.

13

Now deepvoiced *Tsams Lúpin*
(one of those who sold our country
so that Butterfly Place might be left untouched just for awhile)
arrives from that nest of evil—
indeed, it is he, the *Christian* one,
who never looks so well as when Moss Beard stands tall behind
him, with a hand on his shoulder, opening his ears to the Grandfather's newest orders, so that he may steal our last things from us,
he, the hateful one who scouted for Cut Arm
and who called us cowards at the Chinook Salmon Water
(our hearts are joyful that we wounded him on the trail).

He says: You warriors who were too proud to open your ears, many of you now
lie rotting on the trail!

He says: Tsépmin, you are finished! People, I who know the Book of Light shall
now be your voice to the Bostons,

at which our best men chuckle secretly: *Come and see the way he is!*
while Springtime whispers: *Let me hear.*

Let her hear, then; let her choke on it.

He buttons his suit and combs his hair and shines up his plump cheeks, preparing to insult us: He will be teaching *Christian* school.

He makes himself nasty, loudly calling on JESUS, Whom he loves like a wife,
and bowing just as an elk lowers his head as he drinks from the river. Indeed he
hopes to cut us in two. His heart thirsts for us to sing:

> *Wakesh nun pakilauitin*
> JEHOVAN'M *yiyauki—*

>> High Mountain Maiden whispers: We shall soon be
>> afraid.

> Our sad chief says nothing
> (desiring to shelter us from new trouble)

while *Tsams Lúpin*'s speaking is pointed exactly like *this,* to hook us as does
that magic MAN Who raises His hair with clay and doubles up His knees,

> walking up out of the water:

>> soon we shall be going up out of the water side by side
>> to give ourselves forever to JESUS,

>>> Whose blood we must now drink.

Heinmot Tooyalakekt has withdrawn himself, like some animal who tastes his
own blood,

> wishing to Dream with Smohalla one more time, just for awhile, so that
> WOWSHUXLUH will tell us everything:

>> he sits very still, crossing his blanketed wrists, his hair braided on
>> the left and let down loose on the right, the nine-looped necklace
>> of white beads reaching all the way down his chest to his inward-
>> turned elbows, a dappled eagle feather rising diagonally from the
>> back of his head, his forelock not roached as high as Ollokot's used
>> to be,

>>> in another photograph later to be attributed to Major Moor-
>>> house;

or else he stands still among the oak trees,
or cares for our sick orphans, hoping to die from malaria.

Our best men now approach him, saying: Hear us! Our hearts dislike for
Tsams Lúpin to make us new.

What then is your wish?

You who are our only chief, please inform the Bostons that we prefer Tsépmin.

14

Despite his adoption of what I should call a semi-Indian manner of dress, Mr.
Arthur "Ad" Chapman,

whose new squaw wife, Addie B., stands faithfully behind him, with her arms at her sides and her neat-combed hair organized into twin water-falls falling to her belt

(sometime he might even give her a red silk handkerchief),

has become friends with Agent Jones,

an energetic Quaker appointed with all good intentions by President Grant, in order to improve the Indians,

deeply cutting into their hearts

with help from the Quaker missionaries Asa and Emeline Tuttle

(and watching how that pair behave together, we re-member the way that Looking-Glass and Blackberry Person used to admire each other's faces):

together they shall cast down the Dreamers forever, thereby civilizing this errant tribe

(and indeed, just as strips of buffalo meat begin to draw in and darken when we dry them in summer, the fat hardening and growing translucent, so our People-scraps shrink into ever harder loneliness:

so let's keep dragging them to the Cross

—which resembles a woman's dig-ging-stick),

a mighty kind endeavor, which, like General Howard's, can be facilitated by Chapman,

because Chief Joseph prefers him to James Reuben

and because he keeps good and bad Indians straight:

Well, what is it now, Chapman?

This time John Fur Cap and Charley Moses are the ringleaders,

because they once came onto my horse ranch without my say-so and acted d——d saucy, telling me I'd thieved away their land, *ha!* Ad Chapman don't never forget. Now I'll learn 'em something.

Are you sure about this?

As sure as the Good Time comin'

—a line he's borrowed from General Howard.

And *Tsóns** now bans the Sun Dance: He means to stop us all from Dreaming, breaking us by stretching us ever thinner

(he has decided: we shall be stirring ashes forever).

He makes our sad chief sign the ration sheet without permitting even Tsépmin to tell him what it says. Who knows what we are pretending to receive?

Star Doctor, who for more than a year has kept in his Medicine bundle a men-strual rag which he stole from White Bird's wife *Kate*

---

*Jones.

(White Bird is a shaman, so *Kate*'s blood must have Power),
sings a curse, then, when night has made the sand as pallid beneath his feet as the
dried leaves of a sweetgrass bundle, pays Tsépmin's Modoc wife to hide this thing
in *Tsóns*'s bed,

    but *Tsóns* will not die.

15

At first Emeline Tuttle

    (she who has been raised to believe in the Power of LOVE)
cannot help but feel almost lovestruck by the glamorous *Red Napoleon*. I fear she
was corrupted by the whinings of the Eastern press.

    Ad Chapman sets her straight: Ma'am, I been out there in *wild* Indian country
for twenty-two years an' more, and I got so's I could see right through Mr. Joe. He's
double-dyed wickeder than Sitting Bull by a long shot! *Now take it from me:*

        —pantomiming how his good neighbor George Dempster sank down to
        the ground once he saw what the reds had done to his place
        and how James Silverwood lost everything
            (thank the LORD we saved Mount Idaho),
        hinting (rolling his tongue in his mouth) about what happened to Mrs.
        Chamberlain
            (you'll sleep better not knowing)
        and how they ambushed the Brave Seventeen—
        and *then,* now he's prepared her, giving it to her straight as to *exactly*
        what Mr. Joe did to Hattie Chamberlain
            (three years old, ma'am—how could *she* have wronged an Injun?)
        and when the lady still stubbornly wonders, he retails the *fate worse than*
        death of Mrs. Manuel:
Then he burned her alive! *I was there* when they raked away the embers; I seen her
bones, I swear by the Holy Bible—

    After that, he's got Mrs. Tuttle where he wants her—and no more interference
with his plans for Mr. Joe,

        and soon Tsépmin has somehow obtained the pattern-pricked, salmon-
        hued deerskin shirt of the dead Looking-Glass; he goes busily around
        trying to sell it to the Bostons
            (it is well; my heart is content; the widows must have given it
            to him).

16

Bunched Lightning, our half-breed one who during this war whose heart grew
so proud to tell our captive Bostons what they must do
        (*áhaha!*),

enters the hot and stinking tent just when the Government inspector is announcing: And you Indians must not be afraid to inform us of all your desires and grievances,
>   which *Tsams Lúpin,* turning upon us the spurious gentleness of a
>   horse's gaze, now interprets to say: *Joseph,* if you do not follow your
>   Agent exactly, the Government will punish you!
—at which Bunched Lightning
>   (he who has always made himself brave)
rises up to tell the People what the inspector has truly said.

*Tsams Lúpin'*s face grows red like deer blood; his eyes become rounder than a
screech-owl's!— He shouts: *Where is a policeman? Put that man out!*

So Bunched Lightning goes out, and just to help him, the Indian policeman
shoots him in the side: *taq!* He lives on for a week, buys *getting-drunk liquid,* and
sits in a rocking chair, rocking and drinking, drinking and rocking
>   (I am now going where we are catching red salmon),
until his holstered pistol goes off, removing the top of his head:
>   *Áhaha!*

17

Heinmot Tooyalakekt has taught himself what Bostons do when one of them
cheats another. He says: Hear me, Tsépmin, you who are our friend and our
brother! Take us to the notary's office, and say my words straight, so that we may
send a letter to the Grandfather in Washington.

But *Tsams Lúpin*
>   (even he once gazed down upon the woven platters of First Foods, while
>   Smohalla's men and women and children awaited the ringing of the
>   handbell so that they might begin their chant and give thanks:
>>   now his heart hungers to make us droop our heads and murmur:
>>   *What is your law?*)
has opened his ears. He flies between Tsépmin and the sad chief
>   like a rapid narrow creek cutting through sagebrushed sand, changing a plain
>   into a cañon
to say: *Joseph,* you proud bad Dreamer, you must go out, while Tsépmin and I
write to the Grandfather. *Joseph,* you have told many lies; your words are no good
forever!

Tsams, you have now told us your heart. For this I am grateful. But have you
forgotten that you married my sister? Your angry speaking hurts your own
family—

Joseph, you who should never have been chief, until you accept the Book of
Light we shall never be related anymore! You must surely go underground to be
pounded and broken; then you will be burned. You have named this *the Hot Place.*

Now do you begin to understand what is in store for you? *Joseph,* the Grandfather hates you and so does JESUS. So stay away.

Heinmot Tooyalakekt replies: *Tsams,* my father made the tracks for me to go in and I intend to walk in them.

Tsams then makes himself angry, but Tsépmin carries our sad chief to the notary just the same, with old Yellow Bull for a witness: he is a knowing-hearted man who has seen how our People live in the Old Woman's Country. There they speak their letter to the Grandfather, and Tsépmin picks his teeth as it gets written down on lovely paper. They pay the notary five dollars and Tsépmin five dollars. As they sit waiting to be carried home to their painted land, playing the Stick Game, Yellow Bull stands up, pointing through a hotel window, so that they see Tsépmin and *Tsams Lúpin* in the lobby, correcting their letter to the Grandfather. They go in. Not rising, Tsépmin says: *Joseph,* this is precisely what you deserve.

> We are rolling down. Soon they will be eating us raw like
> liver.

18

Heinmot Tooyalakekt says: Tsépmin, my brother, now let me write a letter to Cut Arm and remind him of his promise.

Joseph, my nephew, it was not Cut Arm who promised you anything, but Bear Coat.

I must not contradict you. But Cut Arm is Bear's Coat's chief.

He pays Tsépmin with a beaded camas bag that Fair Land once made for Good Woman, and Tsépmin therefore writes Cut Arm, promising to keep all words straight. After a long time Cut Arm's reply comes and is read aloud by Tsépmin: *Joseph, my heart is glad that you are now becoming Christian. Keep quiet on your painted land forever.*

19

Heinmot Tooyalakekt is sick and raving again; perhaps he is dying
> (I seem to see a campfire like a mountain, and Good Woman is
> blowing on the flames),
because here in the Hot Place are no snowberries from which we could
make fever-tea;
> his heart is longing for the Land of Brightness named in the Death
> Song that Dreamers sing
>> for him it will be easy: no need to make himself brave.
>>> He is speaking to both daughters, the dead and the ab-
>>> sent, but no sound comes from his mouth.
Springtime, who has been sitting beside him with her legs folded sideways

(she is listening to his skeleton),

now goes to Tsépmin, whispering: Have pity! Save my husband; he has surely learned his lesson—

Springtime, my *síikstiwaa* bitch,

and he spits tobacco juice,

you have spoken well, so that I shall surely come.

He gives the sick chief

(whom he actually considers pretty near done for,

but he always did pay me pretty good)

two big swallows from that tall black quinine bottle, and six drops of cocaine, so that Heinmot Tooyalakekt may once more open his eyes

—at which Springtime resumes weeping,

longing to flee into the women's house,

but there is no place like that anymore.

Her husband says: Tsépmin, my brother, you have saved my life—

What'll you give me?

Springtime tries to slip into his hand a huge brass Federal eagle button torn from an old Army blouse. (A Boston at Bismarck presented it to her.) Tsépmin explains: That is not gold. You must pay me some other thing.

She shows him the baby's cradleboard.

You made this?

My husband.

Good. I can sell it. *Joseph,* what would you now say?

Tsépmin, hear me! You have helped me; now help all our People! You know very well that *Tsóns* is stealing our food and Medicine. He gives us rotten beef. Now he is telling the Bostons to make us pay double and triple for everything; I have seen white men come riding here to pay him a share of what they rob from us.

Joseph, you brought this on yourself by not going quietly onto painted land.

Did Looking-Glass then bring it on himself? You cannot deny that he stayed quiet at Kamnaka until Cut Arm attacked him—

Joseph, you must contradict me no more, for although Looking-Glass refused to join you at first, White Bird sent killers coming and going through that place. They are the ones who ambushed me at Weippe—

Tsépmin, my brother, this is a lie, I am telling you three times! When we had our country we always helped you. Now what do you wish from us? Is it truly in your heart to let us all perish?

Then Tsépmin, who until now has been as successful as the horse who can bite and kick all the others,

and who has considered taking payment from Springtime, just for thrills—*shooting his arrows inside her* as these savages would say,

and who bears a mind polished to answer even unanswerable questions,

such as: *Why is it that the mineralizing agent in apatite is fluorine rather*

than chlorine? and: *How did our Nez Perces become bad Indians? Can blood be overcome?,*
looks up from patching his calfskin trousers, strangely moved by the pleadings of this superannuated red, who has finally learned humility,
so that in season he writes a letter all the way to the Grandfather, in words that are truly straight, alerting him that in a single week *Tsóns* often steals more than five thousand pounds of beef from these poor reds
(it ain't their fault they're plumb ignorant)
and perhaps someday the Grandfather may even answer.

Learning of this matter, *Tsóns* makes his heart angry. He expels Tsépmin, but this action gets overturned by his superiors in the Government, so that life now grows perfect exactly here in the Hot Place.

20

Now indeed as we feared when Cut Arm showed the rifle at Butterfly Place, there is nothing to do but stir ashes like old women;
four from Red Grizzly Bear's family have already died
(working off the soft material),
and six children from Yellow Bull's
(Tsépmin is sorry, for he and that chief once shared the same house like brothers),
while our young girls who still live are forgetting how we pile wet rye grass over hot stones in order to steam camas bulbs and which child can now say why the heart of HUMMINGBIRD is sometimes a white feather up in a tree and what MOSQUITO saw when he spied through CRICKET's smokehole
(*Tsóns* dislikes it when we tell our old stories, and *Tsams Lúpin* threatens us with eternal burning);
they are bending us into a circle, biting us to death,
as Springtime ever more resembles the one who walks up and down within her tipi, singing and weeping, giving away everything, in order to become a Medicine woman—what will *she* become?
(All night she hears *qiqaw, qiqaw:*
the noise of skeletons moving.)

21

Getting even with all of us, the *Americans* now bring more People who surrendered at Butterfly Place:
bygone hunters, defeated warriors, who wish only for *getting-drunk liquid* in order to forget themselves here in the Hot Place

where our children sit quarrelling and dying, never to acquire
good names
> (nothing for them to do but civilize themselves as pa-
> tiently as Mexicans shaking gold-dirt in their wooden
> bowls):

indeed they are beginning to forget the way our home ridges
fold and bend
and the high lonely ripples of the grassy snowy lakes in the
Wallowa Mountains;

as our good friends the *Americans* bring in the rest of us from winter to winter.

Swan Necklace has returned from Sitting Bull's country; they caught him in
Montana; now they have penned him up here

(we keep quiet to save him from getting choked with rope:
> the Bostons will never learn how he began this war:
> he will die lucky, penned up on painted land, bored and weak from
> being lonesome).

Next come Hoof Necklace and Little Man Chief, Ip-na-mat-we-kin, Ko-san-yu
and Eye Necklace
> (all of these indicated by Moss Beard as *especially dangerous
> Indians*)

White Thunder and old Swan Woman;

then Two Moons and his wife Hat On The Side Of The Head
> (to the Bostons they will in coming decades almost resemble two
> frail, wrinkled, nut-brown women, one with thin dark braids and
> the other in a bonnet, both half draped in blankets, the braided one
> in a checked shirt and leggings which widen at the cuff almost like
> a dress, the other in an ankle-length skirt as they stand before their
> wide pale tipi on a plain of dying grass),

and Allutakanin, Red Heart's son
> (still he mourns his brave brother Over The Point, whose name
> must not be said),

Cloudburst, who once was Ollokot's wife just for awhile
> (she keeps Dreaming of SOMETHING as darkly rich as the inside of
> a meat-hung tipi)

Welweyas the half-woman
> —this one keeps especially quiet, so that *Tsóns* will not compel her
> into man's clothes—

and Peopeo Tholekt,
> who once traded Heinmot Tooyalakekt a fine horse for an otterskin
> and whose eyes will in time take on a shine of nearly hysterical
> incredulity and watchful rage as he sits on display with other pris-
> oners for the *Sunday Oregonian,*
> > remembering his yellow horse,

wondering how well the Bostons have destroyed his
home,
his braids joined together in a fringed rawhide ornament upon his
chest, his striped blanket long since traded for a coarse grey one,
his shirt of the white man's type, his hair still roached and his face
still bright if not young and serene, while behind him, Chief Joseph,
that grimacing dark nonentity in white man's clothes, stands wearily beside Mr. James McLaughlin,
sun-drowsy like some weak old Boston.

22

But Animal In A Hole,
he who first fought for Cut Arm, then
(once we informed him that the Bluecoats had killed his father at
Cottonwood Place)
came over to us during the battle at Big Water,
yes, he who then fought so bravely for the People all through this war,
winning wounds and trouble,
escapes the Hot Place with two men and two women,
for they cannot cease Dreaming of the red salmon we used to catch:
they walk all the way home.
In the evening, when they leave the Chinook Salmon Water behind,
exactly here in the place where Toohhoolhoolsote's People used to winter
(they seek the old caches of camas cakes, cous and weapons, but
Bostons have devoured them all),
the yellow grass-hills are pulsing with cool dark bushes,
and then again a cool grey-green veil of evening tree-hills stands out above the
yellow rolling of OUR MOTHER,
and after them, the open depths of the sunset cañon lands
with the bluffs and rises and breasts of the EARTH split and twisted by grinning precipices
as the fugitives creep on into the light green and dark green forest and the rich fat
green grass
and a wine-brown deer with a white rump stands atop a steep slope of tall grass;
then down through the ponderosa forest they see again the yellow country they
left behind,
their home,
intermittently speckled blue with trees down the wall of pines and to the
Enemy River,
as the wind blows uphill
where petroglyphs ripen on the rough dark chimney-rock above
the white rock that bulges with shell-shapes

and they can almost hear again the hollow hoof-clatter of our horizon-wide horse-herds

    exactly here at the dark water of all and no colors beneath its reddish-brown and silver-blue, eddying hissingly between rapids and bends, with the grey-green hills of the country now called *Oregon* towering in the twilight beyond

—and then our valley: *Wallowa!*

and our lake

and the place where our sad chief's father is buried.

    Now they are flying up,

        and out of this story forever.

23

But into this story the Bluecoats now deliver Good Woman herself—yes, exactly here in the Hot Place, where she is meant to be.

My strong one, tell me quickly: Is Sound Of Running Feet alive?

Husband, they have kept her at Butterfly Place to punish your heart. Moss Beard promised me three times: *Joseph* will never see her again!— They have penned her up in the Agency school until she makes her heart *Christian.*

Síikstiwaa, I must thank you for explaining everything.

Springtime, my lovely younger sister, my heart has been longing for you! How well have you and our husband been living?

Elder sister, all the time my heart says *pokát, pokát!,* therefore I say nothing . . . Are you tired? I remember how far you have come . . .

I begin to see that you are ill. I am not at all tired; let me now boil bone soup for you.

Do not help me, for my heart is no good. I am telling you three times: Our little one has *gone away*—

Springtime, how this news wounds my heart! Indeed I saw that she was not here—

After Bear Coat broke his promise, it was worse than the fighting. Our husband would not open his ears, and so she has now left us. I keep Dreaming that pigs are eating her—

My dear sister, you need not speak recklessly—

He said *pokát, pokát!* Now she is dead. *She is dead!*

. . . *Tsams Lúpin* makes himself pleased at her divorce, for a man must not keep more than one wife. He gives Springtime a new Christian name: *Magdellenia.* She will make Cut Arm glad.

And *Tsams Lúpin* becomes the Government interpreter; he will be our new best friend.

24

The Government desires us to sell them Wallowa. They will pay us with land exactly here in the Hot Place where we are all sorrowing and dying. *Tsóns* is happily wagging his head.

Heinmot Tooyalakekt explains: I promised my father never to sell OUR MOTHER.

But, *Joseph*, here is your best chance! The Grandfather has pity on you; he would forgive all your murders and even give you everything that you see exactly here—

I have my own opinion about this country.

The People stand around listening (they were not invited to sit). They say: Let us send again the Grandfather in Washington. He will straighten everything.

So our sad chief speaks from his heart to the Grandfather, and Tsépmin writes down his words. Since we have nothing more to pay him, Tsépmin takes pity: People, I am satisfied thus to help you; you have become as my own children.

The Grandfather replies in a letter, which Tsépmin reads out: *Come then, my dear grandson Joseph, and surely all will be made straight.*

Heinmot Tooyalakekt asks Yellow Bull to come. He asks Tsépmin to come. *Tsams Lúpin* says: No, *Joseph,* surely I have become the one to speak for you
　　　—how he makes his heart angry!—
　　　　　all the same, our sad old chief has spoken: it will be Tsépmin
　　　　　and Yellow Bull who accompany him.
　　　　　　　Tsépmin's heart is pretty d——d thrilled; he never
　　　　　　　thought he'd see this,
　　　　　　　and Yellow Bull, whose son was Red Moccasin Tops
　　　　　　　　(now a Lice-Eater plays with his scalp)
　　　　　　　merely says: If they kill me, my heart hopes they will
　　　　　　　not stay long alive.
　　So they are riding away on the train, all the way to *Washington*
　　　　(our chief is trying to fold up his arms and enlarge his heart to tolerate
　　　　the lies and thieveries of these Bostons who keep killing us all here in the
　　　　Hot Place)
and with these brothers he enters the great white house of President Rutherford B. Hayes,
　　　　who has long since made up his mind what to calculate on,
and he shakes hands with the Grandfather,
　　　　then learns the way that Lemonade Lucy parts her hair to make of her
　　　　forehead a wide white triangle;
　　　　he wonders at the ruffled collar around Lemonade Lucy's neck; he shakes
　　　　hands with brown-eyed Lucy,

then says: Grandfather, hear me three times! I never sold my father's bones to anyone. I did not sell OUR MOTHER,

> which words Tsépmin speaks for him in the Boston language,

after which all goes on as before.

25

In the spring, somewhere around False Flowering Time, he goes before the Government in Seneca, Missouri. He says: My heart feels that there should be one law for everyone red and white.

26

They invite him to be their guest at the Cowley County Fair. After all, he's an interesting Indian; he's the *Red Napoleon!*

Tsépmin explains for him: *He wants you to know now that he knows how to make friends.*

27

Wishing to be kind, the Government moves the People to the Ponca Agency in Kansas,

> where there will soon be a suicide or two

>> (plenty of Indians all over the country);

surely the Grandfather's heart is good.

Helping with all his heart, Heinmot Tooyalakekt leads the People as they load and unload their wagons on the way,

> wearing his broadbrimmed Boston hat slightly canted, his face soft and round, his necklace of teeth shining white, his hair black under the shadow of his hat and white in the sunlight, his vest faded over his plaid shirt:

>> by now he has become as brawny as a silver miner in Nevada,

and here I now see *Magdellenia* in church with *Tsams Lúpin:*

>> one night she finds herself Dreaming within a wall of red, of a white horse and two turquoise-centered, white-fleshed, blue-walled rectangles, all beaded, so she must now be scolded; she must apologize to JESUS,

>>> Who has promised that her baby girl is decorating herself in heaven.

> She grows as pallid as the SUN over Wolf's Paw

>> —but Good Woman continues Dreaming about Wallowa, Fair Land, and camas—and Ocher One, who was her favorite horse

>>> (once Looking-Glass placed a necklace on him),

while Loon, who once thought to make himself brave, has likewise accepted
Jesus;
as Chief Joseph (whom some once called *Heinmot Tooyalakekt*) sits in a horse and
buggy outside Sherburne's trading post, cursed by drunkards
   who once were our best men,
waiting for money or promises to emerge from that black square doorway:
       I have made myself too brave to be miserable;
       perhaps my WYAKIN will help me, or else I shall easily die;
   and Asking Maiden and Blackberry Person,
      Looking-Glass's widows,
   sit at the roadside with their daughters, trying to sell beadwork,
         longing to get their husband's shirt back,
            dreaming about Kamnaka and Eel Place,
            remembering how Home From Capture, their husband's favorite
            horse, used to run snorting, gnawing up moonlight and dusty sun-
            light;
while Grizzly Bear Youth, whose AIR BIRD sent him that wise Dream of raiding
Cut Arm at Camas Meadows, has learned to drive a mule wagon. Whenever Bostons insult him, the scar on his forehead
   (his souvenir from Ground Squirrel Place)
glows blood-red.

28

Here dirty squaws sit on the ground, trying to sell us their elktooth-beaded
blouses for almost nothing; next time we come, this time bringing our fascinated
children (Papa, how wicked are these Indians?), they are hawking bags and baskets
they have made, in the geometric patterns so characteristic of savage races.

They have finally learned what money is, and will not part with their handi-
works when some grinning American tries to fool them with a pewter campaign
medal for Rutherford B. Hayes: **HONEST MONEY HONEST GOVERNMENT**.

29

Star Doctor, who has patiently pretended to be just another grey-braided Indian gazing up silently, sadly and roundfaced at the white people, now ties on his
Medicine bundle; and as softly as a horse pulling up his picket pin at midnight he
too creeps away,
     away,
        away,
all the way back to Idaho
     (avoiding Chinese miners' pack trains around Riverfork, and all Bostons
     and our crooked enemies from Butterfly Place);

then Oregon,

> hiding forever on the Umatilla reservation
>
> (the last Palouse to dwell there, I have heard),

where he can once more be a Dreamer shaman, with many skins hanging from his belt and porcupine quills on his hat. By the time he dies, he will have twenty-five wives.

30

Here we are, dwelling at the Oakland Subagency on the Cherokee Strip, near the Painted Arrows who attacked us at Wolf's Paw. The Grandfather removed them here. Even though they went to war for Bear Coat,

> shooting our horses so that they screamed and their guts fell out,
>
> killing our women as they fled,

the Bostons have penned them all up,

> > and why these things must be done to them or to the People, who never sold their fathers' bones, I cannot exactly tell you (although Doc and Tsépmin might know); once upon a time the People had a tale that tells why GRIZZLY BEAR WOMAN stabbed children with Her needle, but now that cause has also been forgotten,
>
> and Two Moons, who fought against us in that last battle, now squints straight ahead, with his long hair loose around his shoulders and the corners of his mouth folding sharply down;
>
> > he has lost most of his ornaments and he wears a faded Indian Department blanket.

Heinmot Tooyalakekt makes peace with these enemies (so his father would have acted). Although *Tsóns*'s heart grows angry, our sad chief leads a few old warriors here, and together they dance the Sun Dance,

> Painted Arrow women looking joyously on
>
> > (a few still wear their beadworked trade cloth dresses),
> >
> > his thoughts of Springtime beginning to vanish into thickets like hunted deer
> >
> > > although his heartsoreness has now grown even up into his throat,

the fasting, painted men now stripping off their Boston shirts, upraising mirrors and charms, hanging from the calico'd center pole beneath TRAVELLER THE SUN so that the women will cry out in pride and encouragement

> (we are blowing eagle-bone whistles;

thus they hang and hang until the hooks and thongs tear loose from their breasts or their backs; then they fall free, *tsálalal!*

> > —while inside his tipi, where the Agent cannot see, Two Moons shows us his lovely buffalo-skin shirt braided with horsehair and human scalps.

31

Then he who is called *Joseph* begins to Dream of a sun or many-spoked wheel fashioned out of eagle feathers.

32

And now it is exactly like this:

Awakening pressed against Good Woman, he gently squeezes her buttock, and she opens her eyes, saying: Springtime spoke straight! You should not have given us to Bear Coat! Why did you do it? Now we must be slaves forever.

He rolls away.

33

For four drought years we break sod and cut tinder; now our men are becoming teamsters,

> trimming each animal's eartips so that it can be distinguished in the dark
> > (this amuses the Bostons):
> > > Chief Joseph manages pretty d——d good with a one-shafted double harness; if he keeps being a good boy we'll teach him how to hook up a single horse on a two-shaft,

our cleverest women meanwhile selling leather gloves in Arkansas City

> > (some Boston women's hearts grow jealous, because they cannot make gloves half as well)

while GHOST-smothered *Magdellenia* gets skinny and ancient as she creeps to church,

> > where Húsishúsis Kute will now likewise save his heart
> > > —*hallelujah!*—
> > for the Book of Light has brought him from the darkness
> > > and he cuts off his hair (but only for awhile)

as White Thunder smokes the pipe with failing brothers, waiting to die,

> > Dreaming of a lovely longnecked horse
> —and at night our chief is still sometimes pillowing his head upon Good Woman,

> > who continues Dreaming of the many-fingered leaf-hands of cous plants:

> > > back home it is now the season to dig up their short fat roots).

34

Our women begin to wear dresses like *Americans;*
> although Welweyas keeps to her striped blanket-dress. Still the Bostons
> do not know what hangs between her legs. Kind Tsépmin keeps the se-
> cret, pitying her,

and sometimes even our chief has begun to wear a suit when he must go before
the Government
> (always remembering the bitterness with which Toohhoolhoolsote in-
> quired of Cut Arm: *do you have ears?*);

all the time we are becoming more like Bostons,
for *Tsams Lúpin*
> (whom Peopeo Tholekt calls *the Judas Indian*)

never stops shouting at our best men to cut off their long hair like Christians
> (a few more now bow their heads and say as Cut Arm should have: *I have*
> *ears to hear you*);

he cries out: Proud ones, you must now accept the Book of Light! Consider what
I have said,
> and indeed some of us can believe in the transubstantiation of JESUS's
> blood into wine
>> (even Good Woman begins to listen),
> because when ELK boiled His wife's sleeve, it became good fatty meat for
> COYOTE to gobble down; moreover, ELK once turned His excrements into
> delicious camas for COYOTE to take home to His wife,
>> while Looking-Glass's younger daughter, who once wore her hair
>> long and loose around her oval face, in her maiden days when her
>> father was going to live forever, so that her dark eyes could be in-
>> terested and even friendly without any promise, and the striped
>> blanket wrapped loose around her up to the throat, has now
>> changed most magically into just another GODd——d stinking red
>>> (Tsépmin keeps sneaking around, trying to go inside her but-
>>> terfly; Addie B. can skedaddle for all I care),
>> while the elder one seems to have died.

In season *Tsams Lúpin* will persuade our most docile mothers and fathers to
send their children to Carlisle School: *I believe in killing the Indian and saving the*
man:
>> boys in fawnlike suits, girls in ruffled darkish skirts and white
>> aprons, everyone's hair trimmed and combed.

And so Heinmot Tooyalakekt, who sought to straighten the young men over
time, finds that most of them will not listen. They sit silent on the floor. *Tsams*
Lúpin's heart becomes joyful: He has more Power than ever before to refashion
these *blanket Indians.*

35

He lives quietly with Good Woman, who makes gloves and raises chickens and pumpkins, nursing him whenever his malaria returns.

(She is tying his hair in the back without braiding it.)

It pleases his heart when she mentions Sound Of Running Feet.

Sometimes he passes *Magdellenia,* with whom he once exchanged hearts

just for awhile.

Again he is Dreaming of his brother's young round face,

his hair roached just so by Fair Land, and white necklace-beads shimmering in the leaf-light

(gentle manly calmness in his gaze—more like our father's than mine),

so that Good Woman, who always knows his heart, goes unbidden to Cloudburst,

who used to sing when she was pounding cous with Fair Land,

to discover how she is living:

She too begins to make herself Christian,

sitting with her hands folded across her grubby skirt, fearfully gazing into the Agent's face—a fast-ageing bitch he thinks her; the world will be better with her underground—her narrow eyes now watching him with an expression which he has never been able to read—then let's raise a toast to *hateful Indian eyes!*—the corners of her mouth drooping down, and yet something about her oval face echoes the prettiness which she was once said to have—how many horses did that villain Ollicut pay for her?— Well, well, this one may be used up nowadays; but at least Ollicut got a lifetime value for his investment.

Good Woman is blowing on the fire. Again they speak of Sound Of Running Feet, hoping and believing that she has not yet died.

Good Woman asks: Does your heart love her the most?

He replies: *Síikstiwaa,* I have Dreamed that you too will divorce me,

but Good Woman closes her mouth.

So he turns away,

remembering her in the eagle-plumed woven hat which Toohhoolhoolsote's wife Wolf Old Woman had once made for her; at that time there had been no grey threads in Good Woman's long braids, and he had not yet taken Springtime; Good Woman stood holding the platter of camas for their First Foods feast, and the shell earrings were good to see against her black hair; he rang the handbell as Ollokot began to beat the drum.

In a photograph from the period, captioned and signed by Major Moorhouse, we see him in a faded vest and a checked shirt, his braids still thin and neat,

his desire for all that has died as well worn as the grooves which buffalo
engrave from gorge to riverbank;
he continues to wear a double-looped necklace of white beads, but his face is more
barren than before.

A Boston looks him up and down, then remarks to Tsépmin (Heinmot Tooyalakekt does not understand): I guess everybody's got to get his piece of country
to live in.

36

Heinmot Tooyalakekt sits on his horse, listening to the tiny bells ringing on
the grave-sticks.

He says to the Bostons: Take me back to my old home, where I can see the tall
mountains and count the stones at the bottom of the mountain streams.

Then Toohhoolhoolsote's widows both die from malaria.

37

Again and again he sends his words to the Grandfather; once Bear Coat comes
to visit him (Cut Arm never)—and in the Hot Place they stay,
        never again to dance the Broken Circle Dance:
        two hundred and sixty-eight Nez Perces, Palouses and Cayuses still alive
            (their hearts are putrid).
Why the Government permits them to return at all (aside, of course, from its
usual fidelity, compassion and charity) can be deduced from the remarks of Representative Thomas G. Skinner of North Carolina, who while busily warming his
Capitoline seat in 1886 nonetheless kindly finds time to choose the American
Indian's future: *Shall he remain a pauper savage, blocking the pathway of civilization? Or shall he be converted into a civilized taxpayer?*

Besides, Chief Joseph has grown antique and harmless now; like your
late father's Colt Navy 1851, whose long narrow barrel is prettily damascened
with rust.

In the engraving in *Frank Leslie's Illustrated Newspaper,* June 20, 1885, these
dark women in their shawls and calicos and dark men in cheap clothes, all carrying bundles as they mill around the Santa Fe passenger train, have come to take
on still more of the appearance of freed slaves, an effect reënforced by the line of
white men watching
        (troopers and an onlooker in striped trousers who keeps his hands on
        his hips:
            Now I can tell the folks I've seen Mr. Joe! He's about as calm as a
            king in a deck of playing cards,
                thirsting for the foam on mountain creeks in Wallowa

and the dry white granite boulders in the high creeks in
Salmon Spawning Season,
he chuckling of grasshoppers as they leap there
—smell of sunshine on rock, sunshine on pines),
our Nez Perces now well and truly beaten, sitting with clasped hands, their sullen
eyes variously bright with suspicion and rage or dull with weariness,
and even Chief Joseph,
he who once imagined that he could make Cut Arm good by
talking,
has locked his mouth.
Now we are going away; we shall be afraid no more
(faded squaws in raggedy blanket-dresses
and Peopeo Tholekt, who once wore a whirl of nested beargrass circles
on his shirt—
gold, with red ocher patterns superimposed:
on the left, a segment of arc bristling with rays or spokes;
on the right, two inward-pointing triangular teeth—
and then Tsépmin, who has wearied of his Modoc wife);
rolling through Pendleton on a Tuesday, two hundred and sixty-four of us now,
guarded by Special Agent Faulkner, twenty privates, two captains and a second
lieutenant,
and toward Colville, whose prisonlike torpidity is unlikely to be soon impaired
by the Northern Pacific Railroad
(there we shall be broken apart once more),
but first (and here the good ones who have chosen Progress will stay) they will
convey us all the way to Kamiah
(we are being moved in single file;
we shall yet join hands before we part),
exactly here where Chief Broken-Arm used to live with his People, just for
awhile,
and some old Indian, his thin white hair roached only a finger or two
high, then falling loose to his neck, no farther, stares frowningly, his lips
clenched, his narrowed eyes expressing an anger alloyed with grief's vacancy, this old man who no longer has braids wrapped in lovely otterskin
and whose necklace-loops are nearly plain; he looks out of the train as if
in bitter surprise already giving way to resignation.
Now the Bluecoats say that we must choose: Go to Butterfly Place in order to
believe in JESUS and dress in enemy style—or go to Nespelem with wicked old
Chief Joseph!
—and just as beargrass stays green all year, so it is with Wallowa in his
heart
(they are pitiless; they will keep leaving us out).

38

Wottolen and Black Eagle will go to Nespelem with their chief,
> along with Red Grizzly Bear, Feathers Around The Neck and so many
> damned souls,

along with lonely old Yellow Bull, who cannot stop telling everyone: *On Cut Arm's account I have lost all my children;*
> likewise Peopeo Tholekt, who was a boy with Heinmot Tooyalakekt at
> Butterfly Place,
>> where Reverend Spalding used to whip the People and teach the
>> Book of Light;

with them goes About Asleep, who held our best men's horses during the war
> (then he was twelve; now he is twenty;
> in his Dreams he is painting his face yellow)
>> after *Joseph's* death he will become chief after him.

Tsams Lúpin assures them all: You will surely be taken to the Low Place.[*]
Our hearts long to boil soup-broth from his bones.

39

But Welweyas the half-woman becomes Christian; she will die at Kamiah,
> because her heart has grown afraid.
>> Her WYAKIN (stripe-winged like a nighthawk) now flies away
>> forever:
>>> *Kuna, nakai,*
>>> *Tem-naktsha init nakaikahi.*
>>>> O, that's one called "The Home Over There." A
>>>> mighty good tune. I used to sing that one with
>>>> Lieutenant Wilkinson,

and Húsishúsis Kute will take land at Lapwai, just for awhile
> (he will die at Nespelem),

and Looking-Glass's youngest daughter becomes a good girl forever
> (I sure know what to do with her),

but White Thunder's heart does not take joy in something so large and so
long and so high as JESUS, so he departs for Nespelem with his Uncle
Heinmot Tooyalakekt,
> the one who has foreseen our ending
> —and now marries Looking-Glass's sad widows
>> (who have kept telling each other: *We are going to make a*
>> *husband for ourselves; we have made him our husband:*

---

[*]Hell.

we gave buckskins and horses for baskets and beaded
bags on the day when Fair Land and Ollokot were married, but on this occasion we find nothing to give),
and those three adopt Fair Land's son, who will be called Ollokot,
and who will die of malaria at age sixteen;
while Cloudburst for her part becomes *Mrs. Susie Convill:*
Will you *look* at that squaw! Jaws like an old bullet mold!

40

Some Bostons are waiting at the landing, meaning to take Heinmot Tooyalakekt and hang him
so that he will be a decent citizen at last,
but our Government prolongs his life,
and then Good Woman leaves him
(his Dream has come true):
she yearns to live near Sound Of Running Feet,
who has now married and become *Sarah Moses,*
forgetting COYOTE and BUTTERFLY; she will Dream no more of the
WORM PEOPLE or the WOMEN AT THE HEADWATERS;
she never met her WYAKIN;
soon she will die of malaria.
So it has come time to uproot Good Woman from himself. The Bluecoats are
waiting. He tells her: Now I shall hear what your heart has to say,
but she turns away in tears.
As for *Magdellenia,*
who also used to be his wife, just for awhile
(she resembles a wounded deer that defecates as it flees),
she says: It used to be difficult. Now I am understanding how to die.
So they have completed their hearts;
and he goes away with those few People who will not make themselves new. When
they reach Nespelem, their welcome will be as sour as an old wet blanket.
We have all learned our lesson.

CONGRESS SOLVES OUR INDIAN PROBLEM
1877

> Our attitude toward the Indians in General Grant's peace policy and
> in giving them lands in severalty; our intervention in Cuba and our
> subsequent neighborly action toward the people of that island; our na-
> tional efforts to lift up the people of Porto Rico, and our sending in-
> structors in large numbers to set in motion the work of education in
> the Philippine Islands: these and other benevolences suggested by this
> reference make the people of to-day feel that at last we have a Nation
> that cares for its children.
>
> BRIGADIER GENERAL OLIVER OTIS HOWARD, U.S.A., 1907

MR. MAGINNIS: My friend from Missouri says the Indian war is over;
Joseph captured and Sitting Bull gone. Why, sir, when Congress adjourned last
spring who ever dreamed you would have a war with Chief Joseph?

MR. TOWNSEND: Had we five thousand men in proper condition in the neighborhood of Idaho in the spring of 1877, the massacres by which fifty men lost their
lives in Idaho would never have occurred this year, and the war would not have
broken out, and my noble friend and neighbor, Captain Owen Hale, who perished
so gloriously in the attack on Chief Joseph, would now be alive.

MR. BRIDGES: I ask the gentleman from Mississippi whether, if the Indians had
been treated fairly and honestly at the trading-posts on the frontier and in the
intercourse of our people with them, there would have been any necessity for a
standing Army exceeding fifteen thousand men.

MR. SINGLETON: That is true, sir, so far as my knowledge extends. I believe that
these Indian difficulties do arise from the fact of the Indians being maltreated by
persons sent out by our Government. The gentleman talks about massacres which
have taken place. Yes, sir, General Custer and his men were sacrificed, and why?
You had troops in the South for unlawful purposes which if sent to him would
have enabled him to protect himself, and he would to-day be a living man. It was
because you scattered your military force all over the South to coerce men at the
ballot-box and intimidate our people and keep them under the bayonet rule, from
which, thank God, we have emerged, that Custer and his men were massacred.

MR. ATKINS: That's not to the point. What are the real and true uses of our
regular Army in times of peace? Simply to furnish a small force to take care of our
ordnance and forts upon our ocean front, and to protect the border settlements

upon our Indian frontiers, and to repel the cattle-thieves along the Lower Rio Grande. Transfer the control of the nomadic and hostile tribes of Indians from the Interior to the War Department, and very soon their raids would cease and their savage nature would be tamed.

MR. PHILLIPS: But I wish to ask the Chairman of the Committee on Appropriations* if being reduced by these bloody combats, by the fatigues of these long marches, and by the terrible incidents of the war of this year and by numerous desertions of an unpaid soldiery whose families might be starving, you will make use of this chapter of accidents to cut the Army down to the standard to which it has been reduced by Chief Joseph and Sitting Bull, and make a change in the law from twenty-five thousand to twenty thousand men in this bill?

MR. ATKINS: The idea of a large standing Army, Mr. Chairman, is un-American. It is borrowed from monarchical countries of the Old World. "It is not an American idea," and it is an insult to the American soldier to make a policeman of him.

MR. THROCKMORTON: It may be a pleasant thing for gentlemen who have constituents that are not in danger, over whose heads the tomahawk of the savage has not flashed, that they shall prate about economy and about a standing army.

MR. TOWNSEND: There is but one other thing to do, sir, with these savages. We might possibly withdraw the Army and conciliate them. *[Laughter.]*

GENERAL HOWARD EXPLAINS
1878

*F*ather, tell me something. Did we fail Joseph and his Indians in any way? Because to hear Wood tell it—

Fail them? No.

But you admired him in a sense—

I still admire his wild courage, and I can't help but wonder at his native ability. He reminds me of a Scots Highlander who leads his clan into battle when the madness comes on him.

But—

You know, Guy, his tendency to evil was doubtless inherited.

From whom?

From his mother. He had that Cayuse blood, remember? The blood of those

*Mr. Atkins.

who murdered the missionaries. One must never forget that. The rule is as fixed as the stars, that the sins of the fathers shall be visited upon the children unto the third and fourth generations of the men who hate GOD.

PHOTO BY BOWMAN
1890

*I*n this portrait, which will soon be credited to Major Moorhouse, we see him with three of his eight children, the braided young boy standing next to him with many pallid necklace-loops across his chest being Young Ollokot, whom as you know he has adopted in his brother's memory, while at his left, utterly still, sits Looking-Glass's elder widow Blackberry Person, now his wife (she will live to be a hundred), with her knees pressed together beneath the dark plaid skirt, her shell-earrings shining like moons against her thin braids, and her face now much drawn in beneath her cheekbones—and on the other side of Young Ollokot, the broader-faced lady in pale attire, whom Bowman imagined to be Cloudburst, for the boy rests his hand on her knee, is actually Looking-Glass's other widow Asking Maiden, since we are (unreliably) informed that he married the full pair; in any event, she is identified as a wife of Chief Joseph's. Why do we not know their names? Well, his friends wished to help him by presenting him to Progress as so saintly (in fact, nearly as much so as Harriet Beecher Stowe's Uncle Tom) as to be practically a Christian monogamist; while his enemies could not care less. Reader, as this edifying little history draws toward its close, won't you pray along with me for poor Chief Joseph, who had we only known more or less about him could have been one of us?

LATE AUGUST 1900

*T*oo late now for the strawberries back home in Wallowa; their many-pointed trios of leaves must have already begun to redden, first in birthmark-like patches or along the edges; suddenly entire leaves go crimson; meanwhile the People must keep crawling like snakes, because the *Americans* are your friends

but the lake in Wallowa
and the snowberry bushes
well known to us who now live in Nespelem
like snakes
your friends:
Wakesh nun pakilauitin
JEHOVAN'M yiyauki—
and the sparkle on our lake
which opens out like its own world of dark turquoise
now cools my eyelids even here
on the grass, within the oversight of the Agency buildings, where a
wide circle of pallid tipi-triangles is crowned by the silhouetted
outspread fingers of lodgepoles, and a cañoned ridge decorates the
horizon
exactly here in Nespelem, where just now the river is as pallid as the light on Joseph's face,
brighter than the grass,
and your friends the *Americans*
and summer gardens of bees, tomatoes and sunflowers
through which, beginning to forget the word which signifies guessing wrong in the Stick Game (our children are forgetting it),
we pass like snakes:
our hearts are good,
our hearts are good,
and the *Americans* are our friends.

In that side view copyrighted by Moorhouse in 1901, the backdrop is a blanket with the trellis beyond not cropped out, and he stands with his left hand partially clenched by his hip, while in his right he raises a tomahawk so that the handle is nearly vertical and the double-bladed head is level with the top of his forehead. A long white blur dangles from just below the haft. It may be a rabbit pelt. He wears a feather in his hair, a gorget of shells, bones or beads at his throat. Many white necklace-ellipses decorate his chest. From belly to ankles he has wrapped himself, or been wrapped, in a blanket patterned with rectangles and crosses—probably a Pendleton. The dark grip of a revolver shows itself from a holster affixed to a narrow belt whose awl-holes seem approximately as alert as a serpent's eyes. His pale forehead slopes whitely back to his peak of hair, and his thin lips press together as he smiles or grimaces.

NESPELEM
1885–1904

1

*H*e stands looking south, past houses and into the clouds, because that
way,
> over the river-bluffs where the grass goes down and down
>> in the willow-darkness where once the Bluecoats crouched, prepar-
>> ing a dawn without pity,
> down into the river's bowl of sagebrush, grass and rain,
> beyond the three black boulders like stubby fingers
> (and more behind them)
> then down into Elmer:
>> grass, haybales, horses and even fruit trees
>>> (I turn around; I am worshipping; I am turning round as I
>>> sing)
> and around the river's curve where the Grand Coulee Dam will rise:
that way lies Wallowa.

2

> Wallowa, Wallowa
>> where he once passed some years
now boasts many a cabin of tamarack lumber
>>> exactly here in the place we once called White
>>> Soil
and antlers bleaching on nails within the dark shacks,
>>> a new water trough at the courthouse square,
>> and for benefit of tourists Charley Turner runs a steam yacht on
>> Wallowa Lake (he'll also rent you the schooner "Never Sink")
and a schoolhouse with a piano exactly here where Springtime and Fair Land
used to lassoo the horses
>> (the teacher at her podium with the blackboard behind her, her right
>> hand accomplishing mesmeric passes across a baby American flag),
> and
>> Captain Pollock, honorably discharged, is trying it out here, to see
>> if this is the sort of place where a fellow wouldn't mind getting old
>> in the bosom of his family,

living a life like tea that is too weak,
with the addition of a slickhaired dog that sure can catch a
deer or an Indian
(bites his heels)
—but there's no gold to speak of and never was,
nor sapphires in Montana (that was quite
the pisser);
in fact, all I ever see around here are
churches and
a chestnut-braided pioneer lady with a rainbow Pendleton blanket over her
shoulder and a child in her arms:
scent of tub-washed wool.
I see a happy old rancher, getting on sixty-two or -three; a popular sage who
sure can shoot; if you ever find yourself up Wallowa way, just ask for Doc and
he'll tell you how everything used to be before the land was ours. He's a joker;
I hear he's the one who talked that dentist into digging up Old Joseph's skeleton. If you want to see it, pay the man a nickel.

3

Joseph
    (he who was once called *Heinmot Tooyalakekt*)
rides to Lapwai, his face as pleasant and quasi-meek as ever, holding his hat across
his belly, with his braids neat and tight and his faded neckerchief knotted loose;
when he sadly narrows his eyes into a smile, his face seems to widen. He stands
very still in the grass, leaning a trifle forward, no doubt out of courtesy to the Allotting Agent, who clasps her white hands across her middle, gazing levelly at his
chest. The interpreter, James Stuart, kneels in the golden grass, with his hat on
his knee.
    My heart is good; I do not lie, says Joseph. My heart is good; my heart is good.
    The Allotting Agent, who resembles Queen Victoria and whose companion
Jane Gay refers to her as Her Majesty, believes very much in her work. The two
ladies smile at him, their dresses hissing like a silver-green shimmering of cottonwoods. Every Indian man will get a hundred and sixty acres just like any
American homesteader. His wife can expect a comparable amount, and his minor
children less. (Springtime's baby, for instance, received her niggling allotment of
dirt when she died at Leavenworth.) Then all the surplus lands of the reservations
throughout our United States can be sold off, and we'll all be equal at last. For her,
most Indians wait by the church in their white hats. It is not too late for even such
a one as Joseph to be benefited.
    But Jane Gay writes: *He cannot be persuaded to take his land upon the Reserva-
tion. He will have none but the Wallowa valley,*

Wallowa, Wallowa,

WALLOWA COUNTY, OREGON

The Best Country in the Northwest for the Home-Seeker and the Capitalist

---

from which he was driven; he will remain landless and homeless if he cannot have his own again. It was good to see an unsubjugated Indian. One could not help respecting the man who still stood firmly for his rights, after having fought and suffered and been defeated in the struggle for their maintenance.

4

In Wallowa there is a photograph of A. C. Smith and Chief Joseph, dated 1900 or 1904, the two men standing grim and straight for the long exposure, Joseph a trifle plump now, on his face an expression of endurance, his mouth downturned, and a middling peak of dark hair; always the same mouth, like the multiply downcurved dead branches of pines. The Indians are getting shy now hereabouts; we scarcely ever see them. But we sure do remember them. On the wall behind the cookstove, Mr. Smith keeps his old Sharps breechloader hung up for a souvenir. He served with Captain Cullen's volunteers back in '77. He enjoys to talk over the old times, even with Joseph, against whom he's got no hard feelings. It sure is a grand valley, Mr. Joe, and I'd be right pleased to ride you through it, and show off our improvements. (Maybe you shouldn't come back again.) From what I hear, you people also lucked into good soil up where you live. What are you growing up there? If you keep at it, someday you might own a house as big as mine.

5

He visits President and Mrs. Roosevelt. Again he speaks of Wallowa.

6

In 1904, invited to Pennsylvania for the commencement ceremony of the Carlisle Indian Industrial School, he encounters Cut Arm. He says: Friends, I meet here my friend, General Howard. I used to be so anxious to meet him; I wanted to kill him in war! To-day I am glad to meet him. Now all is straight . . .

7

In Nespelem, where our good Indians decorate their horses with parade blankets on the Fourth of July, order reigns beautifully. There may be some who still Dream the dance and watch over the flesh of OUR MOTHER, but they'd better be awfully discreet or they'll get fined!— Our good friends the Americans will garrison Fort Colville for so long as needed. It remains prudent to watch the Medicine Line, and the Blackfeet—while the War Department certainly expects us to oversee the old Nez Perce warriors until they die off. Joseph continues stubborn, for a fact. (You will presently read how Lieutenant Wood sent him his son, so that he might learn how to live as an Indian.) Joseph won't even live in the house that the Government built him. But the century's turn finds most other Nez Perces settled down and already exhibiting signs of improvement. Some worship decently on Sundays at the Agency church, although that is more common at Kamiah, where Jane Gay decides that *it was interesting to see the dark faces lighted up with a glow of some kind of inspiration; it was pleasant to think that the Indian was able to relax his habitual scowl of bewilderment in the contemplation of one simple idea.*— Reader, shall I inform you what that simple idea consists of?— They have begun to understand that private property signifies the right to fence off a spring.

Some years ago, I grant, we had to watch them more closely than now, when Joseph's warriors began to turn themselves in. Why do you think they didn't flee to Canada and work their mischief over there among White Bird's renegades? Well, as might have been expected, White Bird came to a bad end: murdered by Nez Perce Sam in 1892. I suspect that was a healthy lesson for Joseph and the others. Anyhow, to Nespelem they all went in time, since, in the Olympian words of Francis Haines (1955) *there was no other place for them to go. Once they had submitted to the agent, every effort was made to break them of their old ways and of the bad habits . . . from their wild life . . . Monteith was able to handle these problem cases with little difficulty and no violence. He realized that the best method was to strip them of their glamour, so he forced them to wear ordinary coats instead of blankets and to cut their long hair. This simple change in costume robbed them in one stroke of most of their romantic appeal.*

8

The next step was to teach them better table manners. Hence Circular no. 153 1/2, direct from the Office of Indian Affairs in Washington: *I desire to ask your special attention to the beef issue. You are directed to give to this matter your most careful consideration, with a view to devising some general plan of slaughtering animals on reservations that shall remove all unnecessary cruelty, filthiness, and waste. The "beef issue," instead of being an object lesson of savagery, as it now too often is, should be a means of educating the Indians in the ways of civilization.*

9

Of course not every fault lay with the Indians. Sometimes even our good friends the Americans will bear a little watching. Thus Circular no. 140:

Information having reached this Office that certain persons are availing themselves of their positions as Indian traders to influence, by gifts or otherwise, leading men of Indian tribes to lease to them large tracts of reservation land for grazing purposes, all such practices are here by strictly prohibited. And they all lived happily ever after.

10

He stands looking south,
    remembering when Sound Of Running Feet lived every day in his lodge,
    and Springtime and Good Woman were peeling camas with their knives;
        Good Woman used to soften food in her mouth when Sound Of
        Running Feet's teeth were first growing in;
    and once Springtime was pregnant; once she was as tender as cotton-
wood bark
        (in the nighttime she is now counting thirty strands of beads,
        ninety strands of beads, but she does not have any)
    and Ollokot, Cloudburst and Fair Land still lived
        in Wallowa,
            where Tuekalas my father lies within the hill by the river
                (pay the man a nickel; some things it's a kindness to
                hide from Mr. Joe).

11

Patiently he cares for Lieutenant Wood's son Erskine, who would learn a trifle of how to live as an Indian. Neither this boy nor his father can be blamed for anything.

One day Erskine hunts beyond his strength; he has made himself tired. On the next morning Heinmot Tooyalakekt says: My dear nephew, please stay at camp to-day.

12

Asking Maiden has become feverish. Blackberry Person is caring for her,
    just as Good Woman used to help Springtime;
        he smokes kinnikinnick by himself, remembering the night
        when Good Woman first painted his face red, so that he be-
        came married to her.
Now Blackberry Person
    (although she will not open her mouth)
has made herself sad, so his heart believes,

wondering whether she sorrows to dwell exactly here in this lodge which is so much less beautiful than Looking-Glass's tipi, whose hides were colored with alder-bark and pine smoke, then decorated and painted, or whether she esteems him less brave than Looking-Glass:

Síikstiwaa, tell me your heart,

to which she replies: My husband, I was remembering Eel Place, where Looking-Glass used to bring us . . .

My dear wife, indeed I remember when Looking-Glass's father used to winter exactly there, just for awhile . . .

Sometimes old warriors still curse Looking-Glass in his hearing. (His wives withdraw themselves to weep.)— He always says,

pulling the blanket sharply in across his breast:

To me his guilt is absent. I am missing him.

13

Looking-Glass's daughter rides with her little boy to Kamiah. Agent Monteith has graciously given her a pass, revocable for bad behavior. Her child is dying; she wishes to have his photograph.

She gets the photograph, rides home, and her son soon dies.

14

White Thunder asks: Why should I be badly treated by the whites? They robbed us of all our country, our homes. We got nothing but bullets.

You're making trouble, Yellow Wolf.

No.

Yellow Wolf, if you don't get off the reservation right now I'll put you in jail.

And so White Thunder rides away with his sad wife Ayatootonmi and his children; wrapping their blankets around their shoulders, they pick hops in Yakima for day wages all summer, and every summer for the next twenty-five years.

15

The young girls learn to button up their dresses neatly at Indian school. As General Howard informs us: *The friendly Nez Perces now for the most part are dressed as white men; the hair . . . is cut short. This gives them much the appearance of the Mexican ranchers who live along our southern border.* Welweyas the half-woman had made herself old; she lives quietly at Kamiah, wearing a man's clothes so that the Agent will not whip her. At Lapwai the missionary Kate McBeth teaches the ladies how to make beaded cornhusk wall pockets. She can scarcely rest, nor can her sister, for Lapwai remains in her estimation *the moral cesspool of*

the tribe. But by 1895 we find ourselves able to pull our soldiers out of Nespelem.
After that the Indians were fined by the agent, the amount ranging from five dollars
for fighting to thirty dollars for unlawful cohabitation.

16

Resting on a rock, with the steep bank at his back, he sees white-bellied swallows swirling low over the still, clear brown river, and he smells the sagebrush more than the water even there at the river's edge,

        letting his hair hang loose,

            his skin coarsening like that of an old fir tree,

the river-cliff darkening, the air suddenly cooling,

      just as in the river-gorge the last light yellows a single stretch of cliff
      around the bend.

Now he will touch the sky with his hands.

Nespelem at dusk is blue clouds, yellow clouds,

      and my heart is bad,

riverline and old yellow grass gums in the jaws of the long-grassed skull of rock.
Here comes a weeping willow tree in Elmer (in time there will be a Mormon church).

    Through the clouds a gash of sun strikes the dark river.

        My heart is

cloud-light and far away golden grass like dawn.

NOT EVEN A HORN SPOON
1885–2012

That simplifies my position very much.

      TALLEYRAND, upon being told that his wife had died (1835)

*A*nd so our country progresses nearer to a perfect pacification upon such principles and by such measures as will secure the complete protection of all its citizens in the free enjoyment of all their constitutional rights,

    hear, hear!

another Indian problem solved, the land rising back up out of indigenous possession into our United States as we shake off old war-dreams, the water deep down

in the yellow and pink depths of the earth, Chief Joseph rotting safe away from us
in Nespelem, with all the badness leached from his heart:

    I pledge allegiance to the flag

              from the Clearwater to the Snake, from the Snake to the Columbia;

              from the Yellow Stone to the Missouri to Bear's Paw.

The Americans are your friends, and want you to go back

      to go back

      to go back

      to go back to your old home

          and if you don't

              —why then, to some other good reservation,

the drunk-making smell of a cold creek at dusk blending with the smell of green
irrigated fields

    of the United States of America,

      where they keep digging up our graves just as we once opened camas pits,

                    Wakesh nun pakilauitin

                    JEHOVAN'M yiyauki—

a green river-garden drinking from a single tall pipe

    (there is not a bit of bad in it),

and coming down the cañon to the town of Joseph, Oregon, at night between the
immense walls of sheepgrass-grown rock hardening into darkness where the river
trees clump into a winding forest, I'll bring you to horses, box houses, manure
smells and fresh-cut fields less dense but more solid than sky. The trees which
could not shade me by day now begin to stand upon the cañonsides as flagpoles
of the night

    with liberty and justice for all

    and not even a horn spoon left,

    but do help yourself to that box of faded campaign medals from the archives,
or, if you'd rather, to a cracked old journal containing the transcription in
some clerk's elegant hand of Governor Curry's letters during the Yakima War
of 1855–56, a citation of valor from the Nez Perce War; a certificate which
proclaims: *This is a good Indian;* a war bonnet whose dark-tipped almost-
white eagle feathers, their quills still whiter, grow out of now grey leather (it
once belonged to Yellow Bull, so they say); and the orange, wrinkled, sweetish-
smelling, dried-out newspaper clippings in General Howard's scrapbooks,

        a memento from the American Board of Commissioners for Foreign
Missions. *This certifies that* Gracie Howard *has contributed* Two *dimes for
the new* **MISSIONARY PACKET, MORNING STAR,** June 1866

and three newspaper clippings from World War I,

        beads from Lewis and Clark: red, blue and green,

      old bones wrapped in a smoke-tanned buckskin,

        White Bird's wolfskin cap,

            the foxed barrel of Doc's old Sharps,

the dense double ribs of Peopeo Tholekt's bone
necklace, and

INDIAN RIFLES. From lot surrendered by Sitting Bull Indians after the Custer Massacre to U.S. Army officers
and by order of the U.S. Government sold at auction in
1885 as Indian relics. Price, $20.00 each,

the bright-colored triangles and squares on a Nez
Perce root-carrying bag,

holographic notes by Lieutenant Wood, evidently for some poem: *Here
on Joseph's Peak I learned to worship the sun with my red brethren,*
and Wood's private diary from the Bannock War of 1878, in a thin but
heavy-boarded leatherbound book, worn at the edges, whose spine reads
RECORDS and whose page-edges are burned orange by acid; decay is circling in, and the ink on the first and last pages has begun to fade
and Wood's copy of Kent's *American Law*, whose leather covers are riddled and stained, and whose flyleaf is inscribed four years before the Nez
Perce War
and two Nez Perce scalps dug up out of graves by our Bannock scouts (my
heart is good), their black tresses dried into brittle wire; and in the neighboring box another scrapbook trussed with stained string, the tooled suede on the
heavy coverboards sloughing off in globs as if of muddy red moss, and that sad
sweet smell of old books

*Sir, I have the honor to submit the following report of the march,
battle and its results:*
leather flakes at the bottom of the folder, like dirt,
and subsidary results of
summer dusk glowing on the yellow brick of the post office in Walla
Walla
and it is raining in Joseph
(my heart is very good)
and in the cool darkness
the flags are still out on Main Street.

HERE ENDS THE FIFTH DREAM.

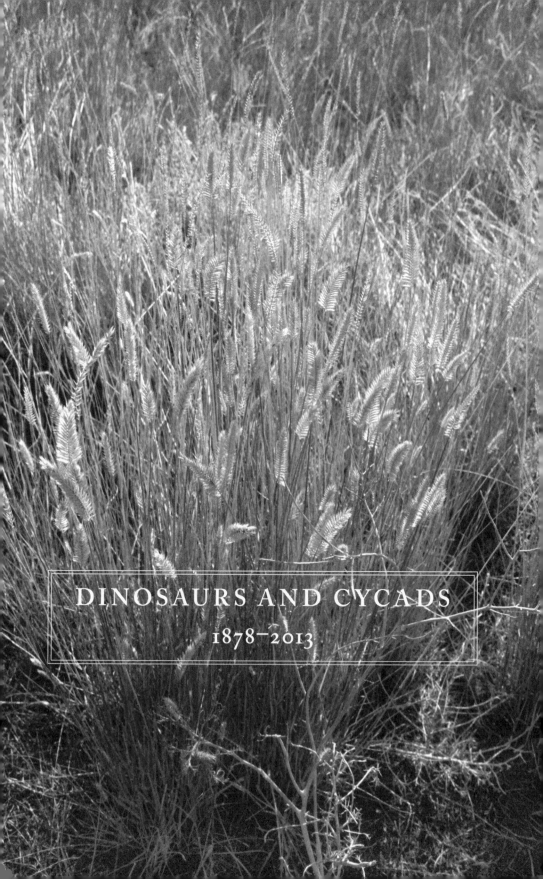

DINOSAURS AND CYCADS
1878–2013

FURTHER HISTORY OF
THE UNITED STATES OF AMERICA
(1878)

> So onward still we press, and nothing stays
> Our steps, now guided by the waning light,
> Until cold shadows from the level solar rays
> Are falling fast from off the western height.
>
> Colonel John Gibbon, "A Vision of the 'Big Hole'" (*ca.* 1882)

By 1878, I see, the United States had re-entered a period of prosperity . . .

FURTHER HISTORY OF THELLER'S SQUAW
(1878–2013)

> In the last analysis the real test of greatness is how an individual bears defeat.
>
> Helen Addison Howard, *Saga of Chief Joseph* (1941)

*T*he last Perry ever saw of her was before he got back to Lapwai and went out on leave to Lewiston en route to collecting his wife—in short, she had disappeared from his ken even before Theller was killed—but one rainy day around the date of his own wedding anniversary, Wood, now entering into that time when the brittle bridge of life begins to crack underfoot, glimpsed her on the dirt streets of Portland; she was tippling with a couple of Clatsop whores at the river's edge, and although she looked far gone he wished to approach her anyhow, such being her never to be explained allurements over him, but on that occasion he happened to be hurrying at the general's heels, en route to Vancouver Barracks, so it wasn't as if he could have said or done anything. If I told you that none of the characters in this book ever again laid eyes on her, I would be reducing the truth to something convenient. They did see her, but with Chief Joseph rendered harmless they had *reentered a period of prosperity*, which in Wood's case entailed Nanny's petticoats, richer than cumuli, and the translucent pinkness of Nanny's face as she commenced to gaze away from him. Not without fortitude, Theller's squaw lived out her own prosperity, without tears and for all I can ever know without expectations. As parallel as the two stripes on each of Wood's sleeves were the two women in his soul: Nanny and the other unknown person who should he ever know her would inevitably become unable to save him from that mixture of despair and extreme boredom with his sensations which he had first experienced when pursuing Joseph, especially on that horrible stretch along the Lo Lo Trail; there had then come a time when he would have nearly rather given up and died than continued to march—not that he felt that way now, of course, being so happily married. Which men inhabited the soul of Theller's squaw remains unwritten—not Theller, I suspect; what could he have meant to her? No man ever painted vermilion on her face, the way a Blackfoot husband would have done. Wilkinson saw her and—never mind that he had so frequently advised Wood not to distress himself on these Indians' account, since all they needed to do was request the help of church and Government in getting out of their ancient Satanic pit—prayed for her and with her, then gave her a silver dollar, which she spent on strong drink. I myself caught sight of her once in 2013, when I was visiting Tom Robinson and he showed me that rusty-lidded biscuit tin which encoffined the cracked and edge-frilled glass plate negatives he'd scored the previous weekend at a flea market—ten dollars cash for the lot—and as we sat on his front porch holding each one up to the sunlight by turns, I came across a nude of her, glaring at me, sullen, ancient and hunch-shouldered, with a Pendleton blanket for a backdrop, her breasts too shriveled to droop, her privates shaved, her right arm badly scarred (unless those were scratches on the emulsion), and in her hair a wilted eagle feather, doubtless planted there by the photographer. The caption read *The Old Squaw, copyright Major Moorhouse.*

FURTHER HISTORY OF COLONEL PERRY
(1878–1908)

> One hardly can command men and go into battle often and still keep an altogether sunshiny face.
>
> BRIGADIER GENERAL O. O. HOWARD, describing Colonel Perry (1881)

*H*e was acquitted at the Court of Inquiry, after which he regained the outward respect of most troopers in our Indian service—for written Government approbation is nearly as stress-proof as the thread that Pi-Ute squaws fashion from the bark of a certain bush. Dissatisfied all the same, Perry consulted the general, then demanded the second Inquiry himself. Of course he would rather have been in the field chasing reds, but he could no more live out his career while officers made a hobby of insulting him than we could have allowed Nez Perces to roam around like dangerous tramps. So three days before the sessions opened, he steamed down the river with Captain Gray, who appeared ever more likely to marry the general's daughter, and arrived in good time at the Government docks of Fort Vancouver. Perry hated it there; he felt closed in. His few friends told him: Colonel, if you keep up that sour face we're going to start calling you *Old Skull and Crossbones.*— Fortunately, the general and Mrs. Howard invited him home for supper—along with Mrs. Perry, of course, with whom he was endeavoring his utmost to get along. In short, the Perrys sat there like lumps. Grace served everyone all round, while her mother dipped out root beer. Captain Gray was absent; he had to pilot the "Lurline" on her midnight run. I forget whether Chauncey and Bessie were there, but Guy was well in evidence, as his father had ensured, for the young lieutenant adored Perry— who, wondering how soon he could get out of this, might nonetheless have proved unable to animate his own tall, awkward and sunburned effigy, were it not for the fact that Mrs. Howard had long since grown expert at drawing men out. Before he knew it, he was telling everybody how it had been when, just recuperated from his wound, he led Company "F" unhorsed at two a.m., the night illuminated by the frozen explosions of stars as they marched toward the peninsula a mile west of Captain Jack's Stronghold, accompanied by Lieutenant Cresson's Troop "K," arriving in position before sunup when Captain Miller's command began to march, as Theller sat horsed and quietly smoking his pipe.— Heavens, colonel! cried Mrs. Howard. Those horrid old Modocs sure gave you a frightening campaign!— I, William the Blind, wish I were as clever as Wilkinson, to analyze for you exactly why who next said what to whom while Grace and Bessie cleared away the plates, but perhaps it doesn't matter, since Perry's aftermath bears little on my biography of that evil genius, the *Red Napoleon.* Suffice it to say that after a month and more (the duration of the first Court of Inquiry), the judges agreed to believe that he had been

outnumbered by Chief Joseph's villains; moreover, the reductions in men and matériel of our feeble skeleton Army rendered his defeat as excusable as Custer's. The
insinuations of that sonofabitch Trimble he successfully overcame with expressionless patience, even *smiling* at his accuser (during the sessions he kept daydreaming,
sometimes of Delia Theller, who had already removed to San Francisco for good, but
far more often of his happy marches with General Crook). What mattered was who
stood *for him*—and just as he used to be able to tell Diamond's mood by the inclination of his ears, so Perry could read his general by the bleakness or sentimentality of
his eyes; and the instant he first entered the court-martial chamber, he knew that
old Prayer Book would take care of his own. It helped that Ad Chapman, taking no
part in any of the trouble he caused, had long since tucked up his yellow tail and
gone into the insurance business. I won't say that Chapman took the fall for White
Bird Cañon, but he did provide excellent if unrecorded help for our judges, who
naturally preferred not to blame the Army for anything. What most gratified Perry
as he sat there enduring the testimony of all those bastards was that even that foul
old Seccesh of a so-called "Major" Shearer, who had denounced him about Cottonwood, now came out saying that Colonel Perry had set up a pretty fine skirmish line
over there and had sure done plenty to rally the men! No doubt Shearer was hoping
to get elected to something. So far as Perry was concerned, he resembled one of the
drummers one sees drinking in the livery stable at Lewiston; I'd d——d well rather
vote for Umatilla Jim!— For his own part (and this again came at our other-cheek-
turning general's urging), Perry refrained from running down the conduct of his
accusers, including even lying stinking Trimble, who had (O my goodness! cried
Grace) actually *skedaddled* once Mr. Joe turned our line. This forbearance went over
well. Cross-examinations came and went; Perry sat in court, wishing himself far
away across the Musselshell, approaching the snowy mountains on Diamond, and
his eyes glowing with windburn.— Colonel, said the general, I'm praying for you
every night.— Thank you, sir.— Mason arrived to put in a good word, as well he
should; likewise some former volunteers. After the verdict, the two protagonists
walked out together, and the general, saying nothing, laid his only hand on Perry's
shoulder, which brought the younger man nearly to weeping, a state which as a rule
only came over him when he happened to be in someone's parlor peering into Lincoln's sweet, sad, chromolithed eyes. So that wrapped up White Bird Cañon.

Next year came that other Court of Inquiry, the one he had demanded regarding his refusal to aid the Brave Seventeen at Norton's; and again the general came
to his rescue—for the record, Perry's troops had saved those volunteers *immediately!*— so that McConville, Shearer and various other sacks of shit whom some
call *citizens* were consigned to fester indefinitely in commerce or civilian politics.
By then Perry was a major in Sixth Cavalry, with a beard as long as an Indian's
scalplock. Unfortunately, he'd merely earned another brevet! One might have expected him to become a time-server, simply dreaming, as he had done during both
Courts of Inquiry, of riding away forever in company with General Crook, who sure
knew how to wear a slouch hat, with that hard merriment in his eyes and his filthy
greatcoat buttoned up tight, his fur collar blending in with his beard as he hunched
down, seeking new Indians to chase. But it turned out nothing like that. Without

regard for grief or rage, believing he could make this right if he only bore up, Perry had come out standing; and even if his re-ascending self-esteem might be challenged by the occasional nightmare (for instance, momentarily shaded by a stolid horse, one of Theller's bunch, stripped down to his drawers and lying on his face, blackish-yellow and swollen, with his left hand over his heart, rolled over and then *reached up* as if to pull Perry down on top of him), all our dreamer had to do was remind himself that many other men, the general for starters, had suffered worse.

The long march in pursuit of Joseph had left a peculiarly shallow imprint on his mind. In later life he thought more often about the Modoc War.

Whenever he saw Red O'Donnell or John Thomas on the streets of Lewiston, they pretended not to know each other, at least until Wilkinson had shipped out to run that shitty little boarding school for reds. Then it appeared safe once more to duck into the livery stable, where Perry still found it pleasant to sip barefoot whiskey and hear Red tell about that time he won a Chinese girl in a poker game and had a hell of a time losing her. But after the third time Red told that story, Perry realized that he didn't care. He could finally drink at home in Mrs. Perry's sight; the old girl wouldn't tell on him.

Once upon a time he had collected more thoughts in his skull than those pertaining indirectly or not to Lieutenant Theller and his wife. Now those good days were coming back. He kept getting promoted. He might as well have been. Just as a Sioux celebrates his murders and horse-stealings with hanks of hair sewn to his buffalo-hide shirt, so Perry kept exteriorizing his own accomplishments, which kept the missus blissfully busy with needle and thread. In a mere seventeen years he had replicated his brevet rank; he was colonel of the Ninth! Did he mind that they were colored troops? Perhaps he had learned a few things about negroes from General Howard.

Redington wrote him a letter once, *just for laffs.* The dolt wanted to jawbone about our old times in Montana, when we slept under the stars and puckered up on Oregon grapes. Redington had failed to improve himself. Perry remembered his boyish jinks and his *yi-yi-yip!* of a password; these had never impressed him. So he didn't answer or even show the envelope to his wife, even though she collected stamps. Montana times, hell. Bannocks, Crows, Cheyennes: *thieves!* Perry preferred to remember the dark and silent Warm Springs Indian scouts, faithful in appearance to his idea of Arabs, who'd helped us chase Captain Jack.

Sometimes he did still enjoy to think about the time when he and Theller were riding their horses up the Lewiston Hill, up toward Wawai where the Palouses used to be, and after so many years the sorrow merely spiced the sweet pleasure of remembering. He dreamed of fat flies buzzing over everything. By now he had lost touch with the general, and, truth to tell, looked nearly as decayed as the old Mandan graveyard by Fort Berthold. Guy being out of the picture, nobody cared about him except for Mrs. Perry. Whenever she asked him when he would catch up with Howard, Miles and the other important generals, he would say: Well, darling, *the dung is still fresh on their trail.*

So it came time to enter the retired list, and they put him down as brigadier general. Then he died.

FURTHER HISTORY OF JOHN W. REDINGTON
(1878–1915)

Old soldiers never die.

American proverb

*T*he little scout, who called himself a colonel, received his pay in yellow vouchers redeemable at thirty cents on the dollar. All the same, he signed up again for the Bannock campaign, because he couldn't ever get enough excitement! A year later he went off with some Umatillas to the Sheepeater War. Right about then he became Assistant Adjutant General of Oregon. Could he have even been twenty-one yet? You will be happy to hear that he married the beautiful Nellie Meacham, whose father's machinations had helped bring about the Modoc War. They had four daughters and lived in Tacoma, so all should have been peachy, but in 1915 Redington wrote his friend Mr. Hines: *Times have been so tough psychologically for a long while, that a man has to cut his own hair or become a freak.*

FURTHER HISTORY OF MRS. MANUEL
(1878–2013)

The horrible story is told that Mrs. Manuel was outraged by twenty Indians and then burned at the stake.

The Morning Oregonian, July 6, 1877

Well, where's the blood then, Drake? You're used to blood; you'd like to know.

THOMAS WOLFE, "The Hollow Men" (bef. 1938)

*N*o one ever found her, although Wilkinson, believing it to be far from unjustified to investigate more deeply the baseness of Joseph's morals, hated to hear that we had stopped searching. Maggie Manuel went on swearing all her life that she had seen Chief Joseph stab her mother to death, although it might have been Ollokot who did the deed, never mind that our volunteers turned over the ashes of the burned cabin without discovering any bones—but maybe they did find her earrings and a piece of her skull (Ad Chapman, who did the digging, first said he had only turned up bits of animal bone, then revised his report to please our best Indian haters)—while Peopeo Tholekt confided to a certain Boston many years later that the lady in question had died on the Lo Lo Trail, for which Joseph felt *very very sorry;* as a matter of fact, sometime in the middle of the twentieth century a souvenir hunter around Big Hole uncovered a female skeleton which had not yet shed every last hank of yellow hair—while long before that, one of Gibbon's former volunteers, who surely had fun in his investigations, reported: *Recently I dug up the leather robe of a woman, which had been richly trimmed with many beads, and right where the head of the skeleton should have been, I found the braid of hair, fine in texture, probably golden at one time.*— Wood, who as we know was always easily gulled by Chief Joseph, finally persuaded the general to suppose that Red Wolf might have stabbed her before her cabin door, for when that villain threw her onto his horse, meaning to carry her off toward Rocky Cañon, she had leaped off and attacked him—or anything else might have happened. Of course the general never fixed on what to *absolutely* believe. In the absence of a corpse, SATANic Joseph escaped the noose—just one more instance of the over-leniency of our generous American system.

FURTHER HISTORY OF BROKEN TOOTH
(1877–78)

ADMETUS: Ah, what then shall I do separated from you?
ALCESTIS: Time will heal you. One who is dead is nothing.

EURIPIDES, "Alcestis" (438 B.C.)

*U*nable to keep up with her fleeing People, she found sanctuary with the Walking Cutthroats, who strangely refrained from killing her. (She was pretty; perhaps she became some warrior's woman.) Presently she removed to the Pend d'Oreilles, where she met and married a Boston—a goodhearted fellow, if maybe a bit wild. What it was about her that touched his heart he never could say. To him she was as happy-making as the first sight of evergreens in the Grande Ronde mountains. In other words, he was a no-account *squaw man.* When he lay ancient, grizzled and dying, and the names of the women he'd had after her grew fainter than the pencilled hoofprints on Peopeo Tholekt's drawings, he confessed to himself that he had loved her best. Perhaps her sufferings during Chief Joseph's War had increased his tenderness to her.

Their story was short: They decided to travel to Kamiah and settle down with her folks, who had done the right thing and turned Christian. So they started west.

But the nearer to Idaho they drew, the more hatred they met. O, our friends the *Americans* sure remembered the Nez Perces, all right! They did not care to lay eyes on any more of those reds—who anyhow were better off in the Indian Territory. And Broken Tooth had been with Joseph—and escaped. Who could guarantee she hadn't been one of those cruel squaws who mutilated our troopers at White Bird Cañon? Check out her *hateful Indian eyes:* She might have even helped burn Mrs. Manuel—

Well, they kept right on westward, and her faithful Boston even helped her locate the grave of her father Grey Eagle, whom Gibbon's boys had done for at Big Hole—Ground Squirrel Place, she called it. Bannocks and souvenir hunters had dug up the old boy a few times, more for a joke than for anything else, and then the foxes played around; Broken Tooth and her Boston hid him once more within OUR MOTHER.

Where they should now dwell bewildered their hearts. Fortunately, this difficulty was soon removed, for her Boston got involved in a harmless little raid, as a result of which the Shinbones killed her.

FURTHER HISTORY OF THE BANNOCKS
(1878)

The Shoshone or Snake Indians are fairly honest, peaceful and intelligent, but the Bannocks showing more of slyness, cunning and restlessness, and the Sheep-eaters naturally less active and demonstrative than either of the others.

HIRAM T. FRENCH, M.S., *History of Idaho* (1914)

*B*uffalo Horn turned against us, sure enough, and on the twenty-eighth of May, 1878, the Bannocks fell upon some Americans who, declining to keep their promises to them, grazed livestock on Camas Prairie. Even General Crook felt obliged to write: *This root is the main source of their food supply. I do not wonder, and you will not either that when these Indians see their wives and children starving, and their last sources of supply cut off, they go to war. And then we are sent out to kill them. It is an outrage.* Well, but didn't they attack a Mormon mission back in '58? Besides, they comprised a sub-nation of the Shoshones, whom Lieutenant Humfreville assures us were *some of the lowest and most degraded people in the world.* By the eighth of June we happily succeeded in wounding Buffalo Horn, who died not many days after. It was General Howard's last real Indian war. He and Miles worked together, suppressing their differences so that their Indian service remained beautiful and automatic. The reds fought on until October, but of course we whipped them, and for their punishment confiscated Camas Prairie, which we had needed anyhow. Thus we made those Indians over. In December a Congressional report explained: *The discontent among the Bannocks . . . appears to have been caused by an insufficiency of food on the reservation.*

FURTHER HISTORY OF THE UMATILLAS
(1878–2013)

> Now, therefore, it is hereby ordered that so much of the existing Umatilla Reservation in the State of Oregon as lies within the following described metes and bounds is hereby declared to be, and is established as the diminished reservation . . .
>
> WM. F. VILAS, Secretary, Department of the Interior, 1888

*A*n Army hospital should only last ten years; after that its walls grow poisoned with disease. Perhaps that is how to manage a reservation. At any rate, Americans like to alter them, generally by shrinking them down.

The first step, as usual, was to gather them in. Certain bands of Umatillas were still Dreaming and wandering unconscionably;

> I wish I could have seen the way that the eagle-feather headdresses of Umatilla warriors caught the light even when they and their horses were silhouetted by the sun, and the way their tipis glowed like white triangles beneath their silhouetted topknots of sticks;

we took care of that. A few fled to the Flathead reservation, which in due time we also cut up.

During the Nez Perce War our boys in blue made sure to guard the Umatilla reservation so that no one could leave; some of the inmates starved.

There was a Umatilla War in 1878, but that was really only a side-adventure of the Bannock War—and just as the crude unity of a cannon has given way to the slender multiplicity of a Gatling's barrels, so Progress sometimes likes to engage in several small wars. Pouring in lead, we gave several Umatillas what Wilkinson's favorite preacher, Dwight Moody, calls *instant salvation.*

It is not my place to tell you much about these Indians. Apparently they used to subsist on chinook salmon and steelhead, trout, eel, squawfish and crayfish. Should you wish to learn more, I refer you to Major Moorhouse, who took some photographs of them. In the museum I have seen his lovely portrait of a Umatilla woman smoke-tanning a buckskin. (The caption: "Anonymous squaw, said to be wife of Umatilla Jim.") About the war he wrote: *The steamboats were patrolling the upper river looking for Indians. They had bales of wool piled around their decks for protection.*

Whenever they saw a canoe load of Indians they would fire at it and sink the boat and kill the Indians, if possible.

In 1885, Progress further improved the dusty pastel hills of the Umatilla country, for as the newspaper explained: *The Protestant Indians on the Umatilla reservation have a new preacher to look after their spiritual welfare. He comes from the Indian Territory, where he had been teaching and preaching to Joseph's Indians.*

I have seen Moorhouse photographs of Indian girls learning to sew, Indian boys scowling shyly in their school band uniforms. Pretty soon the Umatillas were calling themselves *Shikèmnúvit,* which means horseless.

There is a casino there now. But some Dreamers remain, holding a Root Feast in the fall, somewhat as Smohalla might have done.

FURTHER HISTORY OF THE FLATHEADS
(1891–1997)

The Indian can be made self-sustaining . . . Of course, you have got to use a little force.

GENERAL GEORGE CROOK, *Autobiography* (*ca.* 1885)

*W*e finally got around to clearing them out of Stevensville. Chief Charlot might have denied sanctuary to Chief Joseph, as was only right, but all the same he remained in our way. So we packed him and his Indians off to the Jocko reservation, where Americanization was already succeeding:

Agent Ronan (Looking-Glass's old friend) banned all Dreamer ceremonies. The children were placed in schools which punished them for speaking Salish. And in due time they were all civilized: *By 1997, the number of completely fluent Salish speakers had probably declined to 1–3 percent of tribal membership.*

FURTHER HISTORY OF THE CROWS
(1868–2012)

> Ready to co-coperate with the whites—kindly disposed toward the new
> road—beginning to appreciate the fate of the red man who shall oppose
> the progress of civilization . . . they regard with something like hope the
> strong arm of that progress and stand ready to perpetuate their own life
> by a just conformity to its reasonable demands.
>
> MRS. MARGARET I. CARRINGTON, *Absaraka (Ab-Sa-ra-ka),*
> *Home of the Crows* (1868)

I love the white man, the *lucky man* named Blackfoot (another former friend
of Looking-Glass's) told Colonel Gibbon in 1876. We want our reservation to be
large, we want to go on eating buffalo, and so we hold fast to the whites.*— The
whites therefore held fast to them, doing unto them as they did unto all Indians,
and so the history of the Crows went on as level as the parade ground at Old Fort
Laramie. *They are now settled to the number of some 1800 on a reservation . . . to the
south of the Yellowstone river,* which most Americans considered just as well since
these Indians *have ever been known as marauders and horse-stealers, and, though
they have generally been cunning enough to avoid open war with the whites, they
have robbed them wherever opportunity served.*

I was once there on Crow Native Days, admiring the horseback-riding girls, who
wore all colors of trade cloth, polka-dotted with elkteeth. There came a truck
heaped with antlers, blankets and buckskin garments; children on ponies were
scattering candy, waving turkey-feather fans; here came another line of lovely wide-
faced dark girls in red dresses decorated with shells. An old woman in a red blouse
covered with elkteeth slowly waved her turkey fan. On top of a pickup truck's cab
rode a young boy in Plains Indian headdress, waving a bluehandled buckskin-
fringed quirt.

I cannot call them friendly; no one told me: *I love the white man.* But the Crow
do say that there are colors which must not touch.

---

*The Earl of Dunraven explained to us: *Blackfoot may fairly be regarded as a representative man. Superior
to the mass of Red Indians, he is a good specimen of the ruling class among them.*

FURTHER HISTORY OF THE SIOUX
(1877–1901)

The destiny of the white race in America is to eat up the red men, and in this rising tide of population that rolls toward the setting sun there is no one who is backward in taking his bite—no one except the government that temporizes and buys peace, to avoid doing the duty that the individual is doing from choice or from necessity.

PHILIPPE RÉGIS DENIS DE KEREDERN DE TROBRIAND (1867)

*T*he Bluecoats bayonetted Crazy Horse in September; he had surrendered four months before. Nor was this the only augury of Progress. At the end of the following year, our dark horse, President Rutherford B. Hayes, in his State of the Union address informed us that Sitting Bull's followers *are apparently in progress of disintegration.* Once more across the Medicine Line they rode, doomed to the hunger and sickness of the reservation. Many were already showing signs of civilization: Red Horse, for instance, put on his trade shirt, although I admit that he preserved a pair of eagle feathers in his hair. In 1881 even Sitting Bull came back, with his residuum of a hundred and eighty-seven people. *Long have they pass'd.* His Dreamer Power, some said, might bring back the buffalo. Hence the Ghost Dance, whose suppression, as it turned out, required us to make a few more good Indians at Wounded Knee.

To General Howard's old friend General Miles must be given full credit for energetically initiating Sitting Bull's arrest. It not infrequently occurs during a surrender conference with Indians, or when it comes time to transfer our prisoners into the next stage of confinement, that some misunderstanding, occasioned perhaps by a scout's or trooper's brusquely leveled weapon, instills needless alarm into the vanquished, so that they strike out at us, in which case our anxious or enthusiastic soldiers shoot them. While we deplore such incidents with all our hearts, their result—the removal of dangerous and recalcitrant chiefs—can only be a benefit to Americans and Indians alike, there being, after all, no way forward but the way of Civilization. Such was the outcome in this case, although I admit that when Sitting Bull perished, thirteen other men on both sides likewise received their death-wounds. Reader, don't be sorry for him! In a book for children, General Howard laid out Sitting Bull's epitaph: *He had practised cruelty to animals and men from his childhood, and as long as he lived; he was full of passion, and often very angry.*

Perhaps the reduction of the Sioux was a trifle sad, since, as even an old cavalryman admits, *they had a language of their own.* (Who would have thought it?) *It was rich in words, soft and pleasing to the ear, and could be more readily acquired than any other tongue of the aborigines . . . In characteristics and customs they were the furthest advanced for Indians of all savage people in North America.* But it wasn't as if we killed them all! In 1901 I saw Rain In The Face selling autographs at Coney Island. And even now, if you are inclined that way, please feel free to observe how our typical Sioux decorate their horses' hooves with beadwork red, blue and yellow for the Fourth of July.

FURTHER HISTORY OF SMOHALLA
(1878–95)

HOW TO BREED AN OUTBREAK
If we cannot have an Indian policy vigorous enough to take all such vagrants to the reservations and keep them there, then let the government quit dealing with the Indians entirely and allow the settlers to have it out with them . . . Nothing could be so absurd as to allow them to wander at will in bands all over the country . . .

The *Wallowa Chieftain* (Joseph, Oregon) (1877)

*T*he old hunchback Dreamer prophet who had defied General Howard, he whom Toohhoolhoolsote and Chief Joseph had admired and whose religion exercised considerable influence on the Ghost Dance, outlived Wounded Knee by nearly five years. By then he was blind, and only one of his ten wives remained to him: Hair Cut Like Bangs, who could understand the language of weeping babies. When he expired, this faithful woman and her sister painted his face, then wrapped him in tule mats.

Cut Arm was relieved; he said as much to Lizzie. Joseph, imprisoned at Nespelem, never heard about it. The Indian Agent for the Sioux considered that a significant obstruction to Progress had exploded itself, for Smohallie above all others had been the evil genius of roaming tribes such as the Nez Perces, who might long ago have come to reason without bloodshed, had it not been for his pernicious doctrine.

We have now dammed up Smohalla's birthplace; it is underwater, and much of the land downstream of it is contaminated with plutonium.

FURTHER HISTORY OF THE APACHES
(1874–1914)

A minority of white men, when united in a common purpose, never fails to drive from power a semi-barbarous majority.

The *Augusta Constitutionalist* (1877)

*C*ochise died peacefully in 1874. He'd sure been a good Indian; he'd killed no more Americans. Maybe he raided Mexicans from time to time, but nobody's perfect. Needless to say, General Crook never cared for him: Cochise was General Howard's success story. (About Howard he wrote in his memoirs: *I was very much amused at the General's opinion of himself.*) Well, well, and now Cochise was gone! Two years later, very near about when Custer's boys were eating lead and arrowheads at Little Big Horn, our Government decided to concentrate the Apaches in a smaller reservation, and pack Cochise's band off to San Carlos. I suppose they'd expected to stay on the painted land of their own choosing, but through some accident nothing had ever been written down, Cochise and Howard being men whose word was as good as gold, and anyhow two Americans had been Indian-murdered lately, and besides, now that we had gotten the tribe under an Agent's thumb, how did it profit us to be obsequious? Crook again: *As soon as the Indians became settled on different reservations, gave up the warpath, and became harmless, the Indian agents . . . now came out brave as sheep . . . and commenced their game of plundering.* And so the Agents corrected their scales in favor of the superior race. Thus at Beale's Spring one Hualapai family designated to receive ninety-five pounds of beef got fifteen. The Apaches enjoyed equally enlightened treatment. But what could Crook do about that?

As for General Howard, he told Sladen: *Every promise you and I made those Apaches, through Jeffords, was afterwards broken by agents of our Government.* I suppose you could look at it that way. At least our *Christian Soldier* had kept all *his* promises. He had nothing to blame himself for.

So the Chiricahuas returned to the warpath. Geronimo led the jailbreak. In spite of Crook's most exhausting efforts, they kept us busy until Geronimo's final surrender in 1886 (for which we must thank General Miles, who concluded: *The Chiricahua Apaches are the lowest, most brutal, and cruel of all the Indian savages on this continent*). To punish them for the trouble to which they'd put us, we shipped them off to Florida and suchlike places. Some died, but wasn't that just as well? We despatched their children to the Carlisle school in Pennsylvania, in hopes of civilizing them, but it can be difficult to beat savagery out. Nobody can say we didn't try our best.

In 1914, we permitted the survivors to return to New Mexico.

FURTHER HISTORY OF THE HOWARD FAMILY
(1878–1909)

And as I started for my home so far away I felt very happy . . .

GENERAL O. O. HOWARD, 1907

*I*mproving the draft of his autobiography, which will soon be issued in two volumes, he lingers, struggles unavailingly to forbear, then finally inserts: *By some singular clerical error Sherman in his memoirs puts Gordon Granger in for me in that Knoxville march.* In the kitchen, Lizzie is boiling a calf's head to make mock turtle soup—her most luxurious dish. Poor thing, she always seems so old and tired now; when I wake up in the small hours and find her sleeping like a helter-skelter bag of bones, her knees and elbows pointing every which way, I long to rescue her from her infirmities; of course, that's not what OUR LORD planned for us. How can I save her? For myself I ask nothing; my life has been full; praise GOD; praise GOD!

Before bedtime he must correct the manuscript at the very least as far as December of 1864, when Sherman despatched him to cross the Ogeechee and storm Fort McAllister, a nasty redoubt guarded by marshes and by hidden torpedoes which could send an entire ambulance flying up into pieces: mules, wheels, wounded and all. *The reason I am thus particular in reciting the preliminaries is because in General Sherman's memoirs he conveys the impression that he himself did what I as wing commander began, continued, and accomplished—of course in complete agreement with Sherman and in keeping with his instructions*

as we forgive those who sin against us, even in the emerald doors of the Senate chamber. Forgive us this day our daily

Dinner, Otis!

All right, dearest.

The men will cheer and the boys will shout,
The ladies they will all turn out—

but as for her, she's

in complete agreement with Sherman

or should I say *in utter fulfillment of Sherman's instructions?*
Who can say I didn't see to everything?

I should have kept Toohhoolhoolzote under arrest.
Those SATANIC Dreamers always—

I wish I'd never come back! Better killed by Joseph's Indians than

My GOD, forgive me! What am I thinking?

Dearest, what's wrong? Did something in the newspaper upset you?

Pass the salt, please, Lizzie.

We ought to plant more flowers on Guy's grave.

All right.

It's nearly the anniversary.

So it is.

Only three more days until the twenty-second:

> *Born December 16, 1855 at Augusta, Maine.*
>
> *Killed in action, October 22, 1899,*
>
>> defending our interests in the Philippines; Thou leadest me to lie
>> down in green pastures
>>
>> for America, my America,
>>
>> an ideal life, O my GOD,
>>
>> my son.

That's correct, Lizzie. Three more days. Shall it be a rosebush?

O yes, dearest, a red one, because he gave his blood—

Lizzie—

Then what's troubling you? I know you take his loss so much to heart—

Not anymore. I'm certain that Guy's

> as sad as a sagebrush knoll at dawn and

in Heaven.

Well, Otis, what is it? Is it that horrid old Joseph again?

No, it's

> an item from the *Congressional Record* regarding a letter, blandly
> damaging, from the Secretary of the Interior: rent due and overdue
> to the Trustees of Howard University for buildings once employed
> as the Freedmen's Hospital, because if you allow a one-armed Chris-
> tian to pour our GOD-given dollars down a nigger rat-hole, then you
> deserve to get not only *shot* but also referred to the Committee of
> Appropriations, which is to say

the state that our Government's fallen to.

You're fretting over the negro question again, aren't you?

If only Lincoln had lived!

LORD knows you've done your dead level best to help those poor creatures!

Would you like to read Gracie's letter now? She's

> in arrears to the Trustees of Howard University and

very, very happy with that Captain Gray, thank goodness,

> and once upon a time there had been a fine fire in the furnace and little
> Gracie teething in the night.

Yes.

Are we in money trouble again?

I honestly don't know, Lizzie.

So that's why you've taken on all those speaking engagements.

Well, that's right.

I thought your Medal of Honor would—

Never mind.

Sometimes you look so tired when you come home . . .

The soup is excellent, dear.

I know you like it. That's why I . . . Are you still working out the warfare of the future?

No, dearest. I finished that one. But thank you for remembering—

You promised to read it to me.

Well, there's a line I rather like. Where did I put it? Yes: *The wars of the future, so far as our country is concerned, will, I think, in the main, be contests like that which the Salvation Army are trying to wage.*

I think that's lovely and much to the point.

Thanks, Lizzie.

I do hope they remunerate you well for it.

With GOD's help—

And then perhaps we could all go to eat ice-cream and drink buttermilk at one of those "Wild West" exhibitions.

You'd like that, would you, darling?

With all the children—

Why not?

But are we in financial trouble again? I'd really prefer it if you told me.

You can leave those matters to me, dearest.

I know. And it's not as if we can turn to General Sherman anymore—

That's quite enough about Sherman. Excuse me now—

> right behind my eyes is where it hurts
>> in America
> and it pursues me

>>> just as the reflections of white thunderheads follow at our shoulders as we ride down to the Big Hole River, I am telling you three times,
>>> and then we ride and ride, all the way to Bear's Paw,

and we ride year after year to save and perfect America, day and night, till death do us part. By day I first set out against Joseph and by night I ferried Stone's brigade across the river to cover the building of my pontoon bridge to Columbia, which the Mayor duly surrendered on the following morning, and then we waited on General Sherman, who led his horse across the bridge first, followed straight after by me, of course; next by envious, emulous Logan, and after him the entirety of the Fifteenth Corps, while puffs of cotton blew like snowflakes up out of the burning bales, and that was when the tallest man in the crowd handed General Sherman a fair copy of the new ballad about his March to the Sea:

> *Still onward we pressed, till our banners*
> *Swept out from Atlanta's grim walls,*
> *And the blood of the patriot dampened*
> *The soil where the traitor-flag falls*

on earth as it is in Heaven as it is in America, America, O America.

Whether he ever learns of Sherman's letter to President-elect Garfield, calling him *easily used and influenced,* and concluding: *As a business man I have not the faith in him our President has,* I, William the Blind, cannot tell, but come 1891 we do find him loyally heading Sherman's funeral procession. His eyes shine with tears.

Until his final fit of apoplexy he revises and explains. Over his head in a frame roosts a yellowing letter from an inspector of the Indian Office, dated the year after he whipped Chief Joseph:

> Few men do as much toward the cause of Christian enlighten-ment, in the sum of the allotted years of life. If you were to come through this country now—the Indians from far and near would come to see you—and greet you as their best friend.

FURTHER HISTORY OF GENERAL MILES
(1878–1925)

I . . . have fought and defeated larger and better armed bodies of hostile Indians than any other officer since the history of Indian warfare com-menced, and at the same time have gained a more extended knowledge of our frontier country than any living man.

COL. NELSON A. MILES TO GENERAL SHERMAN, 1877

1

*I*nterestingly, Grant wrote to Sherman: *I read one of your interesting letters to the Sec. of War with great interest.* These interesting words were datelined hôtel Bristol. Paris. Nov. 17th/77. Grant continued: *Miles has done good work since, which, with what he had done before, must rank him high with our young officers.*

As part of his *good work,* Miles shot off another letter to General Sherman, proposing himself again for promotion to brigadier general. After all, his uncle-in-law was getting old, his glare now a wintry, half-stricken stare out of crow's-feet and snowy bristles. He was almost GOD. Miles knew that in comparison he himself appeared both sleek and anxious; he was always lifting up his head to be proud, but somehow that only made him resemble a horse caught in the midst of drinking. General Sherman did not love him; hence Miles declined to call him Uncle Billy, even though his marriage gave him more cause to do so than our grinning enlisted men. Who ran Sherman anyway? Was it the President, the Congressmen out West or those shadowy loafers in Washington, D.C., who sit under summer awnings watching parades and horsemen pass by like Time itself? There was, to be sure, a Government, with undoubtedly beautiful and automatic policies—which, however, swayed with the tides of democracy. For instance, what were we supposed to do with our Indians? Sherman knew, and acted undeviatingly. But he was not President; he was constrained, since the Army was. Preferments and perks remained difficult to gather, no matter that Miles was the greatest Indian fighter on earth! If anyone could help him it was his darling little Mary, who practically alone, it seemed, touched her uncle's heart. Why shouldn't Miles finally attain to the rank which he deserved, especially now that he had saved Uh-Oh Howard's bacon and fixed Crook's Apache blunders? And wasn't he literally versed in every chord to play? He'd known enough to be there with a band playing "Garryowen" when Custer rode in with the Seventh. Buffalo Bill, who would help him to bring about the death of Sitting Bull, considered him *a man, every inch of him, and the best general I ever served under.* Returning the favor, Miles gave him a fine chestnut horse which he rode on Nebraska's first-ever "Cody Day."

2

White Bird's survival embarrassed the Government. Being, as General Sheridan termed him, *a good, pushing officer,* Miles proposed, through expeditious interpretation of the doctrine of hot pursuit, to raid the Sioux and Nez Perces across the Medicine Line, just as we do when we punish escaped Indians in Mexico. General Sherman countermanded him: Mexico was not the British Dominions, and Miles d——d well ought to realize that, d——n him!— To Miles it seemed but the matter of a few more years before both of these countries had been joined unto our United States. Why did Sherman always put the brakes on?

Miles had quite a head for politics. He planned to improve everything. For instance, he proposed that we honor our surrender agreement with the Nez Perces, because *Joseph is by far the ablest Indian on the continent.* Why did everyone smile when he said that? General Sherman preferred to keep Joseph in the Hot Place. But ignorant missionaries kept whipping up the Eastern press until Sherman was more or less spent, so he lost out, and the Government sent Joseph to Colville to die.

Miles had gone out of his way to visit Mr. Joe in the Indian Territory in 1881. It was a little sad to see how little the Nez Perces had made of themselves. A touch ungratefully, the *Red Napoleon* sought to hold him to his surrender promise. Miles prayed on it; he kept doing whatever he could.* He went over Sherman's head to President Hayes, requesting the tribe's return to the Idaho Territory—never mind that this act was bad for his career; Mary at least saw it his way—and even visited the notorious troublemaker Helen Hunt Jackson, whose speciality was making us feel sorry for our Indians.

Truth to tell, Miles probably did more for the reds than General Howard ever accomplished—which is peculiar, given the former's more worldly nature. I can only say with Wilkinson: *Judge not, lest ye be judged.*— He aided the Pi-Utes, Pimas and Mohaves in reëstablishing themselves on a reservation more to their liking,

---

*About the Nez Perces he writes in his Autobiography: *I frequently and persistently for seven long years urged that they be sent home to their own country, but not until 1884, when I was in command of the Department of the Columbia, did I succeed . . .* In that work he hardly mentions General Howard. If you read it you will learn that Miles was wounded at the Battle of Fair Oaks; his old commanding officer, whose arm he held as it was being amputated, has been expunged.

and even supported reservation Cheyennes against ranchers and our own Government. When Major Forsyth of the Seventh Cavalry ignored his command not to approach the Minneconjous too closely, thus precipitating the Wounded Knee massacre, Miles reacted in fury and sorrow, convening a tribunal on his own initiative and seeking to prosecute Forsyth. Needless to say, the authorities agreed with General Sherman, now retired, who remarked: *If Forsyth was relieved because some squaw was killed, that was a mistake, for squaws have been killed in every Indian war.* And so in due course Forsyth became a general.

No one worried much about Indians by then. The new enemy was socialism.

3

The *Wallowa Chieftain,* whose editors had cogitated on both evils, explained the danger as follows: *Poverty breeds socialism. But what breeds poverty? Indolence, stupidity, intemperance, want of prudence and foresight, lack of intelligent energy.* In 1894 we will find Miles repeatedly demanding permission, which he cannot obtain, to fire upon the socialists and other foreign elements who are masterminding the Pullman strike in Chicago. If only Nelson Miles were in charge of everything! Then America would hum as straightforwardly as an Aetna Centennial sewing machine!

Interestingly, he wrote to General Sherman: *In my opinion what is needed is for some friend in Washington to interest himself fortunately in my interest.*

4

Bit by bit, even as Tongue River enlarged itself into Miles City, he won his heart's desire. His renown grew as thick and glossy-furred as do buffalo hides at the end of the year. In 1878 we find him in charge of the Military Equipment Board, which recommended the reissue of canvas overcoats after the fashion of Howard's enemy General Crook. Accordingly, the blue "Miles pattern" was approved by General Sherman and adopted in 1880. That year he made full general, presently taking over the Department of the Columbia formerly commanded by Old Prayer Book. Presiding over the court-martial of the black West Point cadet Johnson Whittaker, who was discovered tied and beaten in his room, and therefore must have faked it, Miles pronounced, as he was expected to do, the sentence of guilt for the presumptuous nigger, but he waived the year of hard labor. As you can see, there was something a trifle softhearted about Miles, perhaps because he was a Baptist. Was it this particular defect which annoyed his father-in-law? If so, that would have been unfair; Mary went so far as to be a Suffragette, and the old fellow never insulted *her.* All Miles could do was keep on plugging. Pushing diligently, like all of us Americans who seek our happiness ever ahead, he despatched explorers to Alaska, explaining to General Sherman why he could not entirely support the annexation of Canada: *I think it too soon to occupy the Boundary line now, when we are ready for that the North Pole may be the boundary.* In short, he had matured; he had learned moderation; so why should old men hold him back now? In time he managed to feud with Gibbon, Crook, Terry, Sheridan, and, of course Uh-Oh Howard—who beat him out in the contest to command the Department of the Atlantic! *That* particularly annoyed him, because, as you well know, he'd rescued Cut Arm a second time in '78, halting the fleeing Bannocks exactly as he had the Nez Perces.

In these great times when history was as busy as is a buffalo robe black with vermin, Miles performed his part. Very cheerful, bluff and candid in appearance, with his moustache trimmed just so and his eyes smiling, he knew far better than Old Prayer Book how to give us all *the look.* Near the end of 1894, while he was breaking railroad strikes, Miles looked sharp: General Howard's retirement allowed him to take over command of the Department of the East. A year later he assumed supreme command of the United States Army!

In 1900 he became lieutenant general. That was when he met Chief Joseph in New York, at Buffalo Bill's Wild West Show. Mr. Joe's bunch made a fine impression on the public, and Buffalo Bill remarked: *I thought my Sioux Indians were very fine, and so they are, but alongside the Pacific coast Indians they look rather cheap.*

5

He dragged his feet in the Spanish-American War, calling the Army unready, but eventually conquered Porto Rico.

Demanding to investigate war crimes committed by our Government in the Philippines, he won the hatred of President Roosevelt. In 1902 his report on torture by Americans was quashed.

In 1917, long retired, he volunteered his services against the Kaiser, but the War Department had business to attend to. On the street he was mistaken for some broken down barber.

He proudly hung onto the rifle and shawl which Joseph had on him at Bear's Paw. Poor Mary had long since gone to her MAKER.

In 1925, eighty-five years old, he took his grandchildren to the circus. All rose to salute the flag. His heart stopped, and he crashed down dead.

FURTHER HISTORY OF LIEUTENANT WILKINSON
(1878–98)

> I know that the chaplain in the regiment is the man whom all the men look up to for the cause of our common MASTER.
>
> GENERAL O. O. HOWARD, 1864

*A*s you can guess, he fought for his beloved general once more, in the Bannock War. His loyalty was solid-colored like the coat of a quarter horse. Wood was also present, but Wilkinson had finally, utterly and irrevocably lost interest in that officer. I once saw a photograph, caption by Major Moorhouse, of the general with his hand in his pocket, gazing fondly down at Wilkinson, who had just then asserted that in any event there can be little to fear in dying for the right cause, even while looking the oncoming bullet or arrow in the eye, so to speak—and bullets, at least, do have eyes; arrows are more contemptible in every way. Shall I now confess that the subject of this chapter sometimes smiled at Wood with much the same contempt? Wilkinson, who believed himself capable of apologizing to anyone, even the lowest heathen negro (in the sole event, of course, that apology was warranted), had recently decided on a new course: *Never do any act which requires an apology*—an extremely Christian policy, which, had he troubled to drag it into the sunglare of truth, might have required him to assess the general more poorly. But the general would soon be disassociated from Wilkinson's biography.

Not long after Buffalo Horn had been rendered harmless, Wilkinson, who always came immediately to himself in the morning, spent the interval between "Reveille" and muster call in categorizing the characters in this book:

Mrs. Howard, whose cooking, if Wilkinson might be permitted to say so, surpassed any other woman's, not least that of Wilkinson's mother, who, poor soul, had performed to her utmost, but never really measured up,
the general himself, whose so-called scruples constituted an annoying miscalculation of an issue which, objectively considered, must be supremely unimportant to civilized man;
Grace, who, if Wilkinson were to be exact, did not appear to have inherited her father's intelligence,
one-legged Sladen, so likeable and admirable for his cheerful, stoical continuance in Army life, and scornful of any earthly reward,
Chapman, whose presence Wilkinson had frequently experienced with repulsion, contempt, embarrassment, suspicion and a hint of rivalry,

not that Wilkinson held anything against earning an extra dollar or whatever per day, as Chapman purposed to do as an interpreter
(and he certainly knows his Indians);

nor would Wilkinson himself be averse to promotion, although he understood that to make that happen some higher-ranking officer must retire or die; such is the way of the world, O LORD;

meanwhile the amount accruing to his monthly credit, while modest, did indeed accrue, without deductions, which was a pleasant thought; perhaps he would buy Sallie something,

although Sallie, in spite of her adorable brown eyes, was not precisely the girl who, at least in Wilkinson's estimation, promised to make a perfect wife;

Wood, who in Wilkinson's opinion had by now revealed a nearly unforgivable trend in his thinking
and Theller's squaw, whom he grudgingly confessed to be irresistible.

Although he promised himself that if and when he married Sallie he would purchase one of those extra-accurate new Smith and Wesson revolvers made for the Russian trade, the nickel-plated sort whose barrel, cylinder and appointments shine silver and gold like a brass instrument in a high-class orchestra, he never acquired that firearm. Come to think of it, he never acquired Sallie, either.*

There seems to have been an earlier period when Wilkinson hoped and expected more; after all, once upon a time even COYOTE found opportunity to dress himself in the SUN's clothes.

But I would be doing him an injustice were I to leave you with the impression that his career disappointed him. While those schemers like Perry and Miles were getting ahead, and his dear old doddering general forgot him

> (although, to be sure, when that happened he did experience a sensation not unlike that of any good quartermaster's when we open up a package of provisions for our troops and find it filled with stones, courtesy of contractors at Fort Leavenworth),

Wilkinson kept taking satisfaction in the rapid sweet bugle-tones of "Reveille," the relatively longish melody of "Tattoo," the urgent brevity of "Boots and Saddles," whose notes rise, peak, then descend to an unresolved plateau at high "C," the way the last note of "Assembly" is repeated four times and the happy grandeur of "The General." So what if he would never be a general himself? Blessed, o, blessed are the meek!

In 1880 Old Prayer Book despatched him to Forest Grove, Washington, to establish what is now called the Chemawa Indian School. Most of the first pupils were Puyallup Indians. The boys learned wagonmaking, blacksmithing and suchlike useful trades; the girls were taught domestic arts. Of course they were forbidden to speak their own languages or engage in any pagan cults—for Wilkinson was not the only American disinclined to tolerate such expressions! Their parents were threatened with arrest if they refused to surrender them. Wilkinson's procedure was as bold as Major Moorhouse's signature upon an Indian negative, and in its way successful: In five years, forty-three children died there, the majority of them girls, and mostly from tuberculosis.

Longing above all to find something in his fellow men to forgive, he soldiered on, as reliable as Army standard wool, praying that maybe even in his own lifetime this entire country would be settled and prosperous from the Atlantic to the Pacific, after which we could do our best for the red men.

In 1898 certain difficulties ensued with the Pillager Band of Chippewas at Leech Lake, Minnesota. Wilkinson led the assault. Although the Battle of Sugar Point went against the Indians, Wilkinson received his death-wound. He was sixty-three years old. The highest rank he had ever attained was brevet major.

He is remembered for founding the Portland, Oregon, branch of the Young Men's Christian Association. He labored sincerely and successfully to find positions for unemployed men.

---

*Redington, who never liked him, put it about that among his effects was found a tintype of Grace from the 1880s, looking very lovely in oval spectacles, short hair and a hat of black feathers. Perhaps Guy gave it to him.

FURTHER HISTORY OF COLONEL GIBBON
(1878–96)

In the fight with General Gibbon we lost fifty women and children and thirty fighting men . . . The Nez Perces never make war on women and children . . . We would feel ashamed to do so cowardly an act.

CHIEF JOSEPH, 1879

*I*n time the hero of Big Hole commanded the Departments of the Dakota, the Platte and the Columbia. Promoted to brigadier general in 1885, retired 1891, died 1896—how well does that sum him up? Nowadays his military lustre (so fickle is posterity) has gone as greenish-grey as those August afternoons at Big Hole between hailstones and rainbows; that sure was a fine adventure Mr. Joe led us on.

Sometime after 1890, he wrote up a minuscule anecdote entitled "Enemies Become Friends." It seems that in 1889 he had met Chief Joseph on the shore of Lake Chelan. By then the *Red Napoleon* had become a trifle fat, and in the portrait some photographer, probably Major Moorhouse, made of him as he sat beside Gibbon,

> which he had to do because just as in the land of the dead a living soul feels himself alone on a dark prairie, and must pretend to eat serviceberries or raise a doorflap out of faith and obedience to the SHADOW PEOPLE's command, so Mr. Joe must now obey the Bostons,

we see him in a military blouse whose top button only is closed, his belly bulging out underneath. Gibbon remarks that in that suit of Army bluecloth with metal buttons, not to mention the broadbrimmed felt hat, Mr. Joe appeared as good as you or I. *He would take his food with the white man's knife, fork spoon napkin and cup with as much nicety as the most civilized gentleman. He was not much of a talker, for he could not speak English, but he could look the gentleman and act it. Little children flocked about him and were petted and loved by him.*

FURTHER HISTORY OF LIEUTENANT WOOD
(1878–1918)

> Stories of machines increasingly penetrating into the human being usu-
> ally prove to be reductionist complements to the paradigm of alienation.
>
> GERALD RAUNIG, 2010

*T*he year after our Nez Perces had been brought to reason, he helped General
Howard whip the Bannocks, married his silken Nanny (fascinated to more intimately investigate the conditions under which her spirit of coquetterie became
diablerie) and carried her West on the railroad. (Sure thing she was fooling around
with that Tracy Gould when I graduated.) Perhaps our continent had begun wearing thin now, showing blood beneath her skin, like the polka-dots of crimson trade
cloth shining through the leather-holes on an Apache saddlebag; but then again,
perhaps not yet; there were still buffalo in those days. It thrilled Nanny to glimpse
three or four hundred of those brutes (who had evidently gotten separated from the
main herd) as they sat looking out the window of their private car. Her husband
smiled patiently, hoping she would like it out West.

To please her, he now removed his copper bracelet forever; she'd thought it
rather gauche. Now she was sleeping. It would sure be swell to introduce her to the
general and all that bunch! He could hardly wait to get back outdoors.

More prairie rolled by. To pass the time, he reread Custer's interesting passage
on the Kiowa girl whom the martyred author had considered to be our most beautiful squaw ever: *Her graceful and well-rounded form, her clearly-cut features, her
dark expressive eyes fringed with long silken lashes, cheeks rich with the color of
youth, teeth of pearly whiteness occasionally peeping from between her full, rosy lips,
added, withal, to a most bewitching manner . . .*

Sitka Khwan had looked nothing like that. Still, she had given him plenty of
thrills. She'd actually been exquisite in her way.

General Howard signed the guarantee on their first home. Needless to say, at the
housewarming party no alcohol was served.— Thank GOD West Point taught me
dancing!— Mrs. Howard embraced the new couple; Guy led everybody in three
cheers. Wilkinson, each of whose insinuations was as understated as the bend between the receiver and stock of a Winchester 1866, gave the Woods a silverplated
visiting card receiver from Eugene Jaccard. (He found a great deal to whisper into the
general's ear.) Loyal old Fletch commissioned their studio portrait, which I believe was
later credited to Major Moorhouse. (As it happened, Perry and Trimble could not leave
their obligations at Lapwai.) Nanny and Grace passed a lovely quarter-hour by the
punchbowl, discoursing on Wood's bravery and poesy; Nanny, much interested in
Grace's opinions, privately resolved to keep her husband far from that seductive bitch's

claws. Meanwhile Wood got the general away from Wilkinson, and for his reward got buttonholed by Guy, who demanded a straight judgment, as between colleagues, of his artist's rendering of the Nez Perces on the knolls at Norton's, massacring the wagon party: the horse already down but raising his head as if playfully, while a female figure (was she supposed to be Mrs. Manuel or Mrs. Chamberlain?) waved her sleeve vaguely, and a dead man lay on his back, very dead-looking indeed, as some other fellow meanwhile crawled on hands and knees across the prairie, with the barrel of the rifle in his mouth. The Nez Perces were all cigar store Indians.— There was only one opinion appropriate to Guy's expectations, and Wood provided it.

Now the punchbowl had run dry. Captain Pollock longed to go home. Although he too had commenced to suspect that Wood was naturally doomed, just like any soldier who gets separated from his command, why piss on the parade? So he banged on the table, initiating three more cheers for Mr. and Mrs. Wood.

Pollock intuited correctly: Gazing away from the general's high square forehead, Wood was already planning to quit the Army. (But, Wood, we can't make the Government liable for the deeds of a few bad white men!— Yessir, that's so.) His soulful eyes were now underlined by a beard as thick as a musk ox's. He kept trying to improve his cooking, for the sake of his brother officers; he learned new jokes to tell them; but they now thoroughly distrusted him; even Pollock felt out of place, suspecting with ever increasing bitterness that Wood, for whom he had done so much, looked down on him for singing nigger songs.

Nanny *loved* Portland—but at Vancouver Barracks, her husband overheard certain comments about his loyalty. He knew what the general would have advised: Punch those who insult you, then accept your punishment. But this counsel made sense only for a lifelong Army man.

When Grace finally married Captain Gray, the pilot of the "Lurline," Wood gave the couple one of his watercolors, while Nanny, playing extra sweet, presented them with a set of silver napkin rings. It was a pretty bright affair, I must say: The bride wore satin-trimmed ivory white silk, and her veil was festooned with orange blossoms. And the groom turned out to be equally impressive: Wood was speedily informed that he had once roomed with the famous composer Whitney Coombs. And, speaking of music, the entire Twenty-first Infantry marching band now burst into Mendelssohn's wedding march! The general got tears in his eyes. There were flags and evergreens and flowers. Mason, Sladen, Whipple and Wilkinson made splendid offerings. When Wood, who in sign of the general's continued favor had been the groom's principal attendant, now strolled over to inspect the painted ebony panel from Chauncey, Wilkinson slowly turned his back, while Fletch supplied him with that famous *knowing look*, as if to say: Do you remember that bargain we made at Clark's Fork? Well, you didn't keep it! Wood did not reply: You hate me because I see through you.

In 1879 he accepted Chief Moses's surrender on the general's behalf. He sure found it pleasant to see again the sun shining through the frame of a tipi! As Whipple twitted him: Even you must admit that Indian service isn't all bad!— As he had leisure (tasting Nanny's tender little lips), he memorized Kent's *American Law*, in case he should glimpse a chance to improve himself. When that chance did come, he went to West Point as the general's adjutant, explaining to his wife: You see, darling, he has borne with me for my sake and loves me still. He made sure that even I got a brevet for the Clearwater, when all I did was fetch water one night. So I must stick with him.— Of course, said Nanny. She was happy enough to see her folks again; her father was failing. And how could she turn down a trip or two to Wanamaker's department store?— So it happened that in more or less the same locale that Mrs. Howard had given birth to Grace, Nanny brought little Nan into the world. Meanwhile her husband studied law at Columbia.

Nanny was wearing a very pretty dress like noon sun on the syrupy green coils of the Musselshell River. He would have liked to paint her standing beside Custer's Kiowa squaw. Nanny was willing, o yes; she would have posed for him, smiling among her cut flowers.

It took him seven years before he found enough "sand" to resign, but he did. The truth is that having imbibed the Communistic poisons of Indian "rights" and the eight-hour working day, he was falling morally ill. A few of his brother officers held a farewell party, which the general and Mrs. Howard graciously attended (Pollock, Wilkinson and even Fletch sent their excuses); then Wood became an active member of the state bar, his hopes as voiceless as dead Indians.

Influential men had begun calling to restrict voting privileges, in order to save the United States from Communism. Wood came out against even this prudent measure.

Loving the pale hands of his dark-skirted girl who sat by her sewing machine, he knew that they would live happily ever after; and indeed they had five children, who, taking after their mother, grew as sleek as horses in summer. In due time he left her for a poetess. That was how Nanny learned the lesson that when we are young we may dress to allure others, and when we are old we dress only to trick ourselves, while the vendors of satin and rouge laugh behind their hands. As for her former spouse, he lived on and on, as cheerful as Uh-Oh Howard greeting possibly hostile Apaches with a *how, amigo.*

FURTHER HISTORY OF LIEUTENANT WOOD
(1893–1944)

In my youth, as an Army officer I chased and killed Indians driven to revolt by the oppressions of the vague thing called "the Government." Looking deeper, I saw that "Government" was in fact a corrupt gang which defrauded the Indian and drove him to open revolt . . . I found I must obey the orders of men whose intellects I could not respect, who were themselves only puppets and were idolaters of "the Government" and its emblem "the flag," regardless of acts done in violation of all the traditions of the flag.

C. E. S. WOOD, *ca.* 1927

*I*n 1893 he had sent his fourteen-year-old son to live with Chief Joseph at Nespelem, learning how to break wild horses and hunt deer. Nanny came out against it at first, but the boy pleaded with her, and her husband persuaded her that the *Red Napoleon* was not only kindhearted but also (this being his single point of agreement with General Miles) one of the greatest Indians of all time. And by then Nanny was exerting herself ever more anxiously to retain her husband's affection. So Erskine got his opportunity. From his diary, I gather that he was already accomplished at trapping and bird-hunting, like so many Western boys of that period. He loved the reservation's landscapes, and frequently explored them by himself. Sometimes he photographed the Indians. He would have liked to make a portrait of Joseph's two old squaws (who had made his moccasins), but they hid their faces from the camera. One brave offered to take him hunting all the time if the boy gave him his knife, which he did—a provident bargain. General Custer and even General Howard had sometimes yearned to live like Indians, as Erskine's father had told him; there was in fact a certain melancholy on the old man's face when the son set out from Portland. They shook hands, and his father said: I wish I could go with you!— What Erskine actually learned at his Indian school I cannot say for certain; maybe words can't explain it. In a glass plate negative from this period, signed by Major Moorhouse, we see that babyfaced young man posing hand on hip, with a cartridge belt buckled around his belly and a rifle in his hand; his shirt is fringed like an Indian's, and he's got holes in his trousers. I should call him proud and happy. In his diary he wrote, as do many ungrown persons, in flat and solitary style, detailing the number of prairie chickens he killed, sometimes the weather, and very occasionally some quarrel he undertook with an Indian. Every now and then he mentioned Chief Joseph, whom he would gratefully remember for the rest of his life: *He stands so tall and straight but rarely looks straight at anybody. He wears a striped blanket draped over his arm . . .*

Truth to tell, the general and Mrs. Howard were disappointed in Erskine's father. Of course they wished Joseph well, and considered that the Government had behaved handsomely in allowing him to come back to the West at all when there were so many indictments on his head. But his promise to become Christian at last (relayed through the reliable Ad Chapman) did not appear to be kept. The Howards demanded to know whether it was true that Joseph lived in sin with both of Looking-Glass's widows. The Agent replied that it was. And what if young Wood came back full of Dreamer notions? From what they heard via Wilkinson, Joseph continued to gamble and race horses. A fourteen-year-old should not be exposed to such influences. Praise JESUS, his mother, whom they agreed was just about the beau ideal of an American woman, was a right-living sort; she would set Erskine straight; and together these three wise people made certain that his second stay with Joseph was his last.

It has already been hinted that the father disappointed them in other ways. (When Mrs. Howard expressed a willingness to oversee the social education of his wife, he replied: I beg you not to submit me to Nanny's criticism.) In much the same way that the rocks and forests which flank the Clearwater River soften the redness of its reflected sunsets, so the various boulders already encountered on Wood's descent through life dimmed down his bright American colorations—for mysticism had attainted him; he had practically begun believing that if he were a poet or an Indian he might almost know what the river said.

He said to himself: Nanny's perfume cannot compare to the scent of sagebrush after the rain.

He still adored America, whom I love as I would a tired old woman or a baby girl who cannot yet speak; someone who ahead of or behind her is connected to beauty and greatness, like that Lady Liberty in the statue which the French lately sent.

In due course we find him representing the anarchist Emma Goldman, and even Margaret Sanger, who espoused some obscene doctrine called *contraception.* General Howard would have admired his decision to resign from the Oregon State Bar because it denied entrance to a negro, but by then the old soldier was in the grave.

Another unsavory cosmopolitan, Dr. Sigmund Freud, once wrote that true life begins with the death of the father, and indeed it was now that Wood's outspokenness began to flower into gentle denunciations of his deceased commander. His own drunken violent father had once said: Erskine, my son, someday perhaps you will understand better and be more tolerant.— Since his father was likewise dead, he tried to apply his understanding and tolerance to the general, whom he had loved far more. In 1942 he wrote the general's son Harry: *Your father was very liberal and kind-hearted.*— But by the end of his life, old and blind, speaking into wax recording cylinders, he was referring to *my ignorant superior officer, General Howard.*

Meanwhile, he revised and improved Joseph's surrender speech. The story goes that an Army functionary in Washington wished to borrow his transcription, which then got lost; Wood then wrote it down from memory:

> From where the sun now stands, ~~I shall fight no more~~ ...
> ~~I shall never fight again~~ ...
> Joseph will fight no more forever! Now that's it!

In his poems he dreamed his way into heaven and across the painted desert and even as far away as Wallowa: translucent blue horizons under white clouds, as one sits on a granite boulder, listening to drowsy flies.

He still had his war trophy, that horn spoon from the Clearwater. He despatched it to Tiffany's to be set in silver.

Sometimes when he was alone he whispered: *I am going to fly. I am flying; I am flying up* ... But this he could not do.

I have mentioned his other woman, whom he met in 1910. In a photo made too late to be signed by Major Moorhouse, who could travel only backward in time, this elegant, slender brunette in a a flowing striped robe and floppy hat leans fondly over her white-bearded soulmate, who slightly resembles Karl Marx. Her name was Sara Bard Field Ehrgott, and when they first met she was a Baptist minister's wife. Unlike Nanny, she tolerated the slightly bitter tartness of Oregon grape, with its dirty, stinging aftertaste. That told Wood what he wished to know.

In 1918 Nanny refused him a divorce. Eventually she gave in.

His was one of those cases when enlightenment, instead of being something we achieve, is a felony committed upon us. But he, like his old general, finally turned away from what he could not help, and tried to be happy with Sara. In 1941 he wrote to Molly O'Shea: *I have come to think of this Universe as cradled in the arms of the* GREAT MOTHER.

FURTHER HISTORY OF WHITE BIRD
(1877–92)

The Nez Percés . . . believed that things would be different in Canada, and so, to some extent, they were. But the distinctions were more apparent than real. The techniques of dispossession were different, but the end result was the same: the Indians were left without enough land to maintain a livelihood.

The Cambridge History of the Native Peoples of the Americas, 1996

Sometimes *Kate,* whose braids were always long and neat, whose blouse was as clean as the Chinook Salmon Water itself and whose plaid blanket-skirt looked almost new, spoke to him of riding so far west as to find the smooth naked stalks of death camas, crowned by yellow-white flower-clusters; then they could eat it and be free, but in the end he had no need for that; a certain man's child, dying in fever, named White Bird; and when the man's next child, also dying, whispered *White Bird!,* the father lay in wait with a gun. I have seen a photograph of this murderer, who soon perished in prison, leaving only a silver gelatin image of the slouch hat and long shoulder-locks of Nez Percee Sam in a white man's vest.

FURTHER HISTORY OF WHITE THUNDER
(1877–1935)

We are of the Anglo-Saxon race, and when an Anglo-Saxon wants a thing, *he just takes it!*

THE CHAIRMAN OF THE ENDS OF THE EARTH CLUB (1905)

1

I have told you that he ended up picking hops: here is his story.

In the spring following the war, he sometimes kept company with those who raided back across the Medicine Line,

> the grey creek-ice sobbing out fresh water, zigzag snow-stripes still enduring across the deeper, harder frozen streams

>> as Good Woman sat outside Sitting Bull's house, picking nits from Sound Of Running Feet's hair, longing for roots, Dreaming of purple-blue towers of camas flowers rising from home's meadows;

so they found new grass and willows blooming back red and yellow in the frozen creeks,

and clouds as golden-white as fine-flensed rawhide which has been scraped into translucent thinness.

Joyfully riding down the slanting golden-grassed arms of the melting coulees, they hunted buffalo between the parallel shallow snow-striped cañons:

> instead of buffalo they found Bostons' cows and horses, and stole whichever animals pleased their hearts.

Then they rode home to be hungry.

2

That summer, craving meat, he took leave of Sitting Bull's shrinking multitudes in the Old Woman's grasslands,

> his Lakota brothers gazing after him:

>> eagle feathers in their hair, the quillwork still bright upon their deerskin shirts, their eyes shining with sadness,

then recrossed the Medicine Line with a remnant of home-hungry People:

> Swan Woman, Sound Of Running Feet and Aunt Good Woman,
> some old men and warriors.
> Peopeo Tholekt,

>> to whom White Bird now gave away his fishheaded Medicine whistle, to call birds, coyotes, eagles

>>> (I shall see you no more),

> and Black Eagle (now twelve years old) with his weary father Wottolen:

all these children of OUR MOTHER now set out for Butterfly Place, discovering right away that the war was not over after all

> —their story no different than for others,

>> death shining like a bear's eyes in darkness,

>>> even here in the place called Antelope, where my grandfather Homas lies buried.

Protecting the others, White Thunder and the warriors rode homeward along the sides of the orange-grassed hills, safely below their crests, to watch for Cut Arm's killers

—Bostons on horseback, Lemhis, Crows, Walking Cutthroats, Big Bellies, Salish, Bluecoats, ranchers and miners

(they are shooting up after us, following us!)—

and skulking from cañon to cañon,

confusing their pursuers with magic fogs,

waiting below the red sand-grin of many a grey-green cañon for deer or wild horses

(for White Thunder, who has handled fire at the Winter Spirit Dance, is very clever at finding animals),

extorting food from whichever enemies they caught alone

(White Thunder leaping down off his horse into the knee-high grass, upraising his old 1866 Winchester repeater:

he is strong with WOLF Power, and his face and shoulders have been ferociously painted),

and so they carried off horses and meat, creeping up on the squarish hindquarters of silhouetted cows, clubbing and sometimes killing Bostons who meant them harm (my heart is good; I am telling you three times).— This world of rivers and fading buffalo was America now. GOD bless you, Cut Arm; GOD bless you!

3

White Thunder could have become a mountain fugitive, eking out some outlaw years, one of a very few lonely riders in the mountains, or he could have married into some tribe still overlooked by the Americans—but which tribe would that be?—or bend his knee at Butterfly Place, where Moss Beard might consider accepting his Christian submission: neither WYAKINS nor Dreams—or he could surrender in some other place to the Government, one nation indivisible under GOD, the President and Cut Arm, to maybe get hanged, with liberty and justice for all. So he rode toward Wallowa,

the place where my chief's mother and father were once buried,

back in the time when we had enough of everything, even dirt to rot in:

the place for which my great-grandfather Eye Necklace died

(the Pokatellas cut off his arms and legs before they slew him),

avoiding the new ranches at Asotin,

where Old Looking-Glass's People used to live, just for awhile,

as long ago as when SKUNK seduced EAGLE's women FROG and EAGLE GIRL,

wondering how *Tsams Lúpin*'s heart would be

and riding through the dying grass

toward Wallowa,

where my mother Swan Woman gave me birth,

Wallowa, which is my home no more.

Remembering where we once cached bags of camas—at the confluence of these rivers, in this meadow, in that cave—they too found opened pits, burned places, black cows switching their tails in the golden grass.

So they rode east of Butterfly Place
      exactly here where my father Horse Blanket sometimes used to live,
hiding up on Faraway Mountain
      where my parents sent me to meet my WYAKIN,
then down to Cottonwood Place:
        here remains the skeleton of White Cloud's horse, and the skeleton of that
        Boston's horse which fell in the same battle:
          my ears can almost hear Red Spy giggling as he creeps up on Blue-
          coats to kill.

4

Wherever they rode, the Bostons tried to kill them,
      so they surrendered in twos and threes,
        telling the women to go first and make themselves new;
        the Bostons would not hang them—
finally, White Thunder himself,
        forgetting Tsépmin, Bear Coat and Cut Arm,
          whose heart is as cold as a northeast wind,
      longing indeed merely to kill Moss Beard with his war club, which con-
tains THUNDER's Power
        (my heart is heavy because the Bostons have been bad),
painted his face red and black,
then rode into slavery.
        Tsams Lúpin taunted him, then rode away.

5

If it ain't Yellow Wolf! Returned from the warpath, I take it? Quick—get me an
Indian. Speak to him in Chinook. Ask him which of us he means to scalp next.
    Mr. Montís,* he can't speak Chinook.
    Then speak Nez Perce.
    Yellow Wolf says: *I have come to surrender. Hang me or not.*
    I smell defiance. Ask if he's hiding any weapons or other dangerous bucks.
    He says: *I have given up everything. I have always told the truth. I am telling the
truth now.*
    Look at me. Yellow Wolf, I know you. You're a real good boy,
      and Moss Beard shakes hands with the prisoner,
        who had intended not to let himself be touched. Now he too must
        learn his lesson:
          Áhaha!
    Yellow Wolf, you must tell me everything you know. You were fighting General
Howard. Just now some soldiers killed six of you.
    No.

---

*Monteith.

Yellow Wolf, you're a pretty good boy.
Montís, you will get fat when you hang me.
That fall they sent him to the Indian Territory with the others.

6

Upon their return, White Thunder kept quiet. For the rest of his working life, as I have told you, he picked hops in the Yakima Valley: a dollar per hundred pounds. In time he met a warmhearted Boston who wrote down his war story over a period of years. After he died, this Boston erected a monument on his grave, which lies beside Chief Joseph's.

FURTHER HISTORY OF PEOPEO THOLEKT
(1904–35)

Then bad DEVIL white people come and Indians treat them good

PEOPEO THOLEKT, 1935

*H*e lived until the same year as White Thunder. Almost to the end, he kept a lock of Mrs. Manuel's lovely blonde hair for Medicine. After Chief Joseph died, he began to Dream backward much in Wottolen's fashion. Holding tight the short wampum bead which Heinmot Tooyalekekt once wore around his neck, he decided to make pictures of the war.

Because I, William the Blind, was once lucky enough to please the librarians of Pullman, Washington, they brought those vast drawings out from the cage for me and unrolled them. I have seen how his pines and People march horizontally, then continue up curves, roaming every perspective at once, while parallel to the earth stand Bluecoats with upraised rifles, smoke twisting out of the barrels.— At Bear's Paw he made himself tallest of all, sitting in profile on his giant yellow horse, whose white ears are raised straight up. He wears a shirt of blue, and his headdress of many feathers crowns his head, then marches at horizontal parallels down his back, along the side of the horse and below his feet, like an immense cartridge belt. He bears painted pencil-dots on his cheek below his single eye. A white gorget whose parallel pencil-lines might be bearteeth armors his long neck, and short diagonal parallels outline the back of his leg. Now he is aiming a rifle at the dismounted Painted Arrow whose black robe has opened itself on purpose to show us a grey shirt and blue and vermilion leggings, and a long narrow pelt of yellow dangles from one shoulder. All is straight; these two enemies are shooting bullets at each other without fear, and the bullets hang pencilled in air!

At Big Hole we find his likeness in the second row of tipis, once more incarnated superhumanly large, as a one-eyed profiled Indian head with many necklaces and very broad shoulders, still believing in Looking-Glass's lie-treaty with the Bostons, awaiting surprise from within the curtain of vermilion and the open doorway of yellow. And in the third row, inside a wide blue tipi with blue-enclosed white stripes crowning it, we see the immense one-feathered head of Chief Joseph, who wears a throat-disk mounted to one of his necklaces.— Meanwhile, at the top of this great sheet, upon a cloud of greyish-blue earth with pen-strokes for grass, a reddish-or-ange antlered stag faces a doe, wide-eyed, her muzzle white while his is pencil-greyed; and to their left and right, in graphite sometimes colored green, march pinnate-leaved, spriglike lodgepole pines, all in a row; then, just beneath the deer couple, there descends an irregular column of those evergreens, so that upon the tan blankness of the page there floats a letter "T" of forest, and sheltering beneath its righthand arm stand three rows, again irregular and sometimes broken into segments, of Bluecoats, some one-eyed in profile, the rest in fullface. With their huge round eyesockets and vertical-slit nostrils they resemble triangular-headed skulls. They hold red rifles, which point up or down. The killer on the far right bears a greyish triangle, perhaps an epaulette, on his left shoulder; I suppose he is Colonel Gibbon. One hatless soldier with a splash of red on his blank chest stands spreading his arms to die beside a buffalo twice his size which has already upended itself, its legs straight out parallel to the ground as if in rigor mortis, a yellow puddle behind it and its tail curving down into the tan paper.

Most carefully realized of all are the seven mules and horses that we captured, their manes a blend of reds, oranges and yellows, outlined in grey pencil-hairs— and one of these animals, saddled and stirruped, advances up a crosshatched hill-line, from Conchalic River to the Yellow Stone, toward a cavalryman who stretches out his hands encouragingly. Above that pair and below the bottom line of Blue-coats winds a thinly pencilled scattering of horseshoe-hoofprints.

Gibbon's yellow-barrelled howitzer sports a gearlike wheel at top and at bottom; here the perspective has twisted so that we are gazing *down* on this weapon, which unti now has been pulled by its four mules in traces, with a diminutive Bluecoat in a little box—but an immense warrior with five pencil-stranded necklaces, long hair and red leggings—surely this is Peopeo Tholekt himself—has effortlessly seized the gun by the barrel, which only comes up to his waist; the Bluecoat is not even a quarter his size!— And so it appears to end rather happily.

FURTHER HISTORY OF THE NORTHERN CHEYENNES
(1884)

...the history of man shows that the progressive increase and force out the weaker or lower races...

J. LEE HUMFREVILLE, 1899

*R*ewarded for chasing the Nez Perce at Bear's Paw, they were sent to the Indian Territory—and for his collection, which he hopes someday to turn into a paying proposition (ten cents each to see my Indian relics), Captain Fisher obtained on extremely good terms a Cheyenne buffalo-skin shirt braided with horsehair and human scalps.— In '84, since they had been pretty good reds, they got a reservation near the tract set aside for the Crows, and this place (with General Miles's help) they exchanged for a crumb of their old country from the middle of Tongue River to the Northern Pacific Railroad Company grant; O, they were sitting pretty, all right,

and now as it became day in America the Bostons were cheering as at a Scalp Dance.

FURTHER HISTORY OF THE MODOCS
(1878–2013)

When we are elated with noble joy at the sight of slaves... when the soul retires in the cool communion of the night and surveys its experience and has much exstasy over the word and deed that put back a helpless innocent person into the gripe of the gripers or into any cruel inferiority... then only shall the instinct of liberty be discharged from that part of the earth.

WALT WHITMAN, 1855

*W*hen Captain Jack told Judge Roseborough: *I know that I and all my people are doomed,* he was not far wrong, but note this:

Oregon Historical Society.
Order # 016550. Date *ca.* 1873, location Oklahoma, "3 Modoc Indians in Their New Home," stereo by McCarty of Baxter Springs, Kansas:

> three women and two men, all grey-faced and glum against a grey wall.

So those reds actually had it pretty good,

> many of the Modoc boys still remembering how they used to watch the lake grass so that when it swayed they would know where to shoot their arrows at chub-fishes.

That was why General Howard opined about the Nez Perces: *Let them settle down and keep quiet in Indian Territory, as the Modocs have done, and they will thrive as they do.*

After 1900 those who wished returned West to affiliate with the Klamaths. The rest stayed at Quawpaw, memorialized as follows:

> **Modoc Oil, fifty cents a bottle, relieves pain instantly**
> (not to mention **Nez Perce Cattarh Snuff, fifty cents a bottle**).

As for the Modoc country we had seen fit to fight them for, strange to say, it never amounted to much. A few ranchers took it over; they drained six-sevenths of the lake; great American things were supposed to happen; and yet when I, William the Blind, motored through that section in 2013, I found dying towns, fields for sale or fallow—several nice green parcels left, to be sure (doubtless the possessions of our wide awake business men), but mostly it all felt empty,* as if lava kept tainting the grasslands like poisoned shadow—why, if the Modocs had been left out there, they'd be no bother to anyone! As General Howard would say, GOD works in wondrous ways.

---

*Here stood the cross where General Canby was murdered. (Just down the way, the most complete array of Modoc petroglyphs had just been vandalized.) Late afternoon light struck a bluff of yellow-greenish grass. Evening came on at Captain Jack's Stronghold and birds were rising off what remained of Tule Lake, the wind now rushing like a river from that cañon over the low lava-studded rise of dying grass. Golden grass danced on the forehead of Captain Jack's cave, within which rock-shadows grew and grew. (Hunting in there for souvenirs, Mason, so I have read, considered the silence, then said to Perry, who merely grimaced: *This is what it must be like to be dead.*) Behind me, something pretended to be gurgling water; it was wind coming through the grass. On the high ground behind lay the ring of lava stones where the warriors and shamans danced a magic dance, promising their People that the Bluecoats could never break through; and far away on that horizon studded with blue buttes rose the white jewel of Mount Shasta, wide and snowy, her crown hidden in the clouds. Turning back toward the lake and its decrepit towns, I smelled wild rose and sage in the freshening evening breeze.

FURTHER HISTORY OF THE NEZ PERCES
(1882–2013)

Leaving the rest to the sentimentalists, we present freedom as sufficient
in its scientific aspects, cold as ice, reasoning, deductive, clear and pas-
sionless as crystal.

WALT WHITMAN, 1892

I have already told you about the Allotting Agent, whose advances Chief Joseph
refused, since she could not give him land in Wallowa. No matter; she continued her
work, Americanizing Nez Perces wherever she could, from the Clearwater to the
Snake, from the Snake to the Columbia (forget those benighted rebels out there in
Nespelem). After all, it had been decided in Congress: For the betterment of all parties,
the Americans would now further grid, checkerboard and subdivide the reservations,
as if they were cutting meat into smaller and smaller strips: Once they grew entirely
civilized, the Indians would require reservations no more. Just as a long expedition
over buttes and sagebrush gradually tires even Army mules into some semblance of
obedience, so this Government-anointed whipping-march toward civilization tamed
down most Indians in time, from Sioux horse-inveiglers to the heroes and heroines of
each Dream. In Kamiah they told her: We do not want our land to be cut up into little
pieces. We have not told you to do it.— Again, no matter. They came around. Down
at Lapwai they were still more resistant. She knew how to handle them. The Commissioner of Indian Affairs announced that nobody who refused allotments would be
permitted to go hunting off the reservation. Anyhow, she meant well; she truly wanted
every Indian to get a nice agricultural parcel. (Yellow Bull insisted on keeping the Red
Rock Spring even though it was on bad land, because he had drunk of that water when
he was young. She did as he asked.)— Now came the moment which justified all her
labor: surplus lands were opened for sale to the Americans who ringed them round.
Seventy-three percent of the Nez Perce reservation got sold off.

Reader, don't you think those d——d reds got their just deserts? Let me quote
that card Redington:

> Much credit has been given to Joseph's Nez Percés for humanity shown dur-
> ing the war. Well, there certainly were some people whom they did not kill
> during their bloody foray, and some they killed but did not mutilate.

Outside the reservation it was the same or better. A pioneer woman writes:
*Later on my husband and I learned of homestead land on the Nezperce prairie in
Idaho, so in 1897, we took our three children and migrated there by covered wagon.
It was at Nezperce that three more children blessed our home.*

Now the People were being changed; now they must cut their hair and make themselves different. The Government was charging them to hunt and fish on the lands they had ceded. The allotments shrank through inheritance; the lessees did not always pay.

In 1910 the Nez Percés (with the accent) were reported as *of a high intellectual type (seen in children); suffering much from disease and white contact. Amount uncertain.*

In 1994, not even thirty Nez Perce could speak their language with any fluency.

They have now become good. We sometimes turn up trade beads, glass vials, a child's beaded bracelet and other squaw trash when our real estate men find cause to bulldoze their graves, and here and there a few early skeletons pale against the golden-brown grass.

FURTHER HISTORY OF MOUNT IDAHO
(1878–1914)

... the world is growing old. We are so advanced in the Arts and Sciences, that we live in retrospect and doat on past achievements.

WILLIAM HAZLITT, "The Spirit of the Age" (1825)

*S*o too fades Mount Idaho, and when I wandered there, hoping to find some earthly trace of Ad Chapman's glory, I ascended the pale green fields toward Mount Idaho, gave myself over to blue-green ridges of forest, passed horses grazing, spied other blue mountains down below the ridge of pines; and there, turning toward the setting sun, the sky white, my forehead hot, the horizon of blue hills washed down to white, I found the old graveyard, whose inscriptions thirteen decades had commenced to rub out:

JOHN CHAMBERLIN
BORN 8 . . . 1847
HE AND HIS DAUGHTER
HATTIE
AGED 3 YRS
WERE KILLED BY THE
NEZ PERCE INDIANS
JUNE 14, 1877

(a weeping willow carved on that marble headstone)
and

JAMES BAKER

Killed by Indians

June 15, 1877

AGED

24 Years

Gone but not Forgotten

and the smell of resin, the songs of birds and flies, the grass of the cemetery sloping down toward other green fields, then far away arid grassclad mountains which as dusk draws on pretend to be blue, and

LEWIS DAY

BORN

JULY 10, 1821

DIED

JUNE 29, 1877

A VICTIM OF INDIAN BARBARITY

all white marble, their headstones as white as one of those sandbars on the Snake down by Farewell Bend.

FURTHER HISTORY OF WALLOWA
(1890)

> To be camped at the southern end of Silver Lake, more commonly called Lake Wallowa, and there to behold a July sunrise, is a privilege not soon to be forgotten. The golden rays of Sol first illume the snow capped summit of Mount Joseph . . .
>
> WILBUR BROCK, "On Wallowa Lake" (1890)

A. C. Smith will loan school moneys at eight percent per annum, accepting patented lands as security, and the man who knows what's what will buy his sulky plow from D. McCully. Now what about you, ladies? Don't think history has forgotten you! Here at Wallowa you can obtain Chichester's English pennyroyal pills for feminine relief. Make sure you get the variety with the blue ribbon. The pink-wrapped pasteboard boxes are dangerous counterfeits. And **To Married Women Only:** *You can get Medical Literature by mail sealed, that will teach you how to obtain happiness, pleasure and prosperity, by sending your address and two 2-cent stamps to Dr. E. M. CLEMENTS, Enterprise, Wallowa County, Oregon.*

We now have five thousand residents in Wallowa County, and it's only going to get more perfect from here on out, because the old undesirables have nearly finished fading away. *Congress adjourned last week and the Indians are leaving Wallowa. There is no particular connection between these two facts, except that both occasion a feeling of slight relief...*

So settle in, get initiated tonight at Joseph Lodge, No. 81, of the A.F. and A.M., and, above all:

$ MAKE MONEY! $

Nearly all our wealthy men can trace their

SUCCESS

to dealing in **REAL ESTATE**. Try it.

Buy when Land is Cheap,

And Sell in Prosperous Times.

This advice cost you nothing. For further particulars

enquire of

THE CHIEFTAIN REAL ESTATE AGENCY,

Joseph, Oregon.

Further History of Montana
(1896–2012)

The law of necessity, in Military Service as elsewhere, is a sufficient excuse for any act or measure, provided the necessity can be made apparent to others.

> August V. Kautz, *Customs of Service for Officers of the Army* (1865)

1

*B*y 1896 and probably even before, the Anaconda Express arrived daily at Butte at 9:45 a.m. and 4:15 p.m., so that was progress, the flags soon drooping atop the skeletal black headframes of Butte, and tall narrow wooden houses standing greyish-white or quasi-verdigrised or silvered, their brick companions blotched with dirt. South of that city, the so-called *landless Indians* (Crees, Métis, and GOD knows who else) sojourned for a decade or two in their canvas tipis, until we finally ran them all off. To the west, Big Hole's now mostly uncontested tall green ranchgrass bowed in the wind-gusts, the mountains steely-blue, with clouds above them and the first few home-fires below them, Indian skeletons still lying half out of their graves, hacked, scalped and yellow-white like a wood duck's eggs. By the way, the town of Wisdom was coming along, O yes, Amen. And in spite of starving Indian cows stealing our forage (sometimes not even fences stop them), history became the tale of the stockmen *versus* the grangers.

Near about Jocko, Montana, circa 1900, I see a family of Flathead Indians in their trade calicos and homespuns, posing in front of their tipi with three dogs, patient and still, the mother with her hands hidden behind her narrow waist, copyright Major Moorhouse.

Good old Redington was still alive in 1924, living the fast life in Los Angeles. But he still kept up with Montana; O indeed; he had a soft spot for that locality. On his typewriter he pecked out a letter to Mr. Hilger: *I am glad to note how the white people have developed Judith Basin, and realize how it would stand around there a million years with its hands in its pockets b4 the red man would develop it.*[*] American-ness is going up like walls of Montana corn.

In the 1930s, the Pictograph Cave was excavated and presented to posterity. Whether its images faded or hid under new mineral deposits is beyond my ken; but I assure you that when I, William the Blind, visited the place in 2010, all that remained of the figures were a few red fringemarks and some dashed black lines here and there.

To the military historian John Keegan, who begins and ends one of his books with *I love America,* Progress had worked out beautifully and automatically. *Montana, the "unceded Indian territory" of the 1870s, is a state of the Union. I cannot say that I feel things should be otherwise . . . the pretensions of the Plains Indians to exclusive rights over the continent cannot, it seems to me, stand. Their claim, the claim of less than a million people . . . is the claim not of oppressed primitives but of the selfish rich.*

Thank goodness the Plains Indians have lost their grip on the dirty orange crystals of calcite from Gallatin County, Montana! Now we are fencing in rough pasture, breaking in horses for the Dakota market, with yellow and green hill-fields glowing under purple rain; we are exactly here by white cloud-masses and blue mountains, in our grey shacks roofed with blonde grass; and the grass is tautly horizontal like Custer's long blond hair when he galloped after buffalo bulls at dawn.

2

Following the Nez Perces down through the Bitterroot Valley (whose name, as you notice, has now folded two words into one), you will see the elevated irrigation lines with their high sloppy water-squirts, black cows over the grass; and this grass, this yellow grass in the soft blue light of morning, must be similar to what once upon a time met those Indians, in whose honor the car conveys me back toward 93 on Looking Glass Road; I see Five Wounds Way and Two Moons Road; now we've got *them* out of the way. Not far north of Hamilton, a red arrow-sign on a truck points to FUN. Reader, shall we cross the trestle bridge over the Bitterroot River? O yes. Just south of Hamilton, an American flag pulses in front of Quality Supply, with the tines of the Bitterroots breaking greyish-white out of their forests. Now here comes the Never Sweat Ranch as we approach the smoke of many forest fires,

---

[*]In 1930 we find him putting the Secretary of the Interior straight: *But your ideas of assimilating the Indians do not seem to take. Most white people do not care to mix with them, as the Pocahontases and Longfellow Hiawathas are rather rare, and the assimilation would include too many coyote-dogs and odors from the wigwam. The nobility of the nobile* [sic]. *red man is The Bunk to most western people, especially those who have seen the mutilated remains of the victims of Indian atrocities.*

with train tracks following us, a Stars-and-Stripes-adorned tipi before the blurred forest, the smell of smoke, black dead trees, some fallen on the golden grass, the hills ahead grey-green with smoke; then around a bend, everything greyer and blacker, a fisherman on a river-rock, the grey fringe of upsloping tree-horizon on the ridge near the fire, a tent city of firefighters at the **INCIDENT BASE**, eyes stinging from the smoke.

FURTHER HISTORY OF WASHINGTON
(1881–2011)

I have frequently seen in the Territory instances of white men living alone for most of the time, in a big hole dug in the side of a river bank or foothill. At times a white man will take a squaw into partnership; then she teaches him to live like an Indian and not like a Cayote [*sic*] in the ground! It is a matter of regret that many of these men will after the lapse of a year or two abandon these women entirely and go to some other part of the country, leaving the woman who has been to him a hard working wife, to the tender mercies of a cold world.

ALFRED DOWNING, U.S. Army (1881)

*N*ot long after Chief Joseph died, Walla Walla got a shiny red fire engine with a huge nickel-plated jug of water. And just as young buffalo bulls drive away their elders who made them, so we sent off our precursors, the Indians.

I see Klickitat Peter, Yakima, old and frowning, feathers drooping down from his ears, claws on his head and around his throat, wearing a white man's vest,
> and then sky through the tunnel of a covered wagon
> and Nez Perce hop-pickers slouching on horseback in castoff Boston hats
>> and Yakimas stooping between the rows of white man's strawberries
>> on the Columbia for piecework wages
>>> and then tractors and Mexican field workers.

But in the Palouse country, White Thunder, Chief Joseph and Peopeo Tholekt live on archivally in the McWhorter Collection up in Pullman, ringed round by wheatfields, ryefields and churches; the country is orange, yellow, emerald, turquoise, beige, all zones maintaining distinct lines between them, and each one combed neatly by the plow.

Joseph dwells quietly underground at Nespelem, and at Colville the farmhouses are infested with wood-rats.

FURTHER HISTORY OF IDAHO
(1878–1914)

When the LORD your GOD brings you into the land which you are entering to take possession of it, and clears away many nations before you . . .
and when the LORD your GOD gives them over to you, and you defeat
them, then you must utterly destroy them; you shall make no covenant
with them, and show no mercy to them.

DEUTERONOMY 7:1

*T**he native tribes of Idaho are now chiefly of historic interest.*

FURTHER HISTORY OF OREGON
(1878–1992)

I dismounted . . . and found he was soon to be a good Injun. [As I was]
taking out my knife, he signed to me not to scalp him until he was dead,
but I had no time to spare; for there was much to do—it seemed to be a
busy time of year.

SOL REESE (recollection *ca.* 1907)

*J*ust as lodgepole pines (so I am reliably informed by Indians) cannot open
their cones until a fire comes, so we residents of American states and territories can
scarcely hope to unfurl our schoolhouses, parades & c until the cleansing blaze of
an Indian war has passed through. Rich in such purifying events, Oregon grows up
into greatness. From Kansas City departs another cavalcade of covered wagons as
white as the dawn mist which rises from bends and pools of the Big Hole River, the
leader being one *Travis* or *Captain Travis*, whose six scouts sure can shoot; they're
bound for Oregon; and behind them comes another, whose missionaries dream of
the turquoise loveliness of morning mountains, and another, ready to claim their
Wallowa acres. Before you know it, they'll be at Farewell Bend.

Here come more Americans, smoothing away the People and their old hillside
graves,

and Meadow Place, where the Wallowa People and their brother bands used to dig camas, is now yellow with civilized fields and grass.

In Canada, runs my encyclopaedia, *no prohibition of marriage between whites and Indians exists, but such unions are forbidden by law in the states of Arizona, Oregon, North Carolina and South Carolina.* This wise policy has borne its expected fruits. That alien, Indian quality has largely departed from our state. Oregon's stablest crop is young American schoolgirls as pink as nodding onion flowers. Three cheers for cottonwoods, scrub oaks, fishermen and salmon! In 1930, so improved is Oregon that the *Medford Mail Tribune* is reduced to reporting on supernatural eeriness:

MOONLIGHT VIEWS OF CRATER LAKE CREATURE AT NIGHT,
the sky-blue mirror of Crater Lake fuzzed with fog.

By 1992 a handbook for leisure travels sees fit to explain: *With their 10,000-foot peaks and rugged terrain, Oregon's Wallowa Mountains and Eagle Cap Wilderness have earned the nickname, "the Switzerland of America." The Nez Perce Indians once called these lands home; now they are beloved by vacationers, artists, and outdoors enthusiasts.*

FURTHER HISTORY OF THE INDIAN TERRITORY
(1889–1907)

The Indian is capable of recognizing no controlling influence but that of stern arbitrary power.

GEORGE ARMSTRONG CUSTER, *My Life on the Plains* (1872)

*O*ne August day in 1890 I was reading in the *Wallowa Chieftain* that Missouri was the only state left where you could still get land at a dollar and a quarter an acre. That was when I knew that it was just about over.

The Indian Territory, that convenient dumping-ground for the human refuse popularly known as *reds*, still offered possibilities for Americanization; and indeed I have read that another reason our kindhearted Congress allowed Mr. Joe's bunch to return West was to make room for white people. By sweet tricks we pried land away from the Creeks and Seminoles. The opening of the Cherokee Strip in 1889 had been a fine spectacle: the starting-gun was fired, and twenty thousand members of the superior race literally sprinted to file their claims. In 1890 we pulled the territories of the Five Civilized Tribes into our Oklahoma Territory. At that time the population was still one-third *Indians and negroes*. The Creeks, Osages, Kaws, Poncas and Otoes remained to be gobbled up; and in 1907, when the proportion of

Indians and negroes had been safely reduced to thirteen percent, the State of Oklahoma entered the Union.

At the end of *War and Peace*, Tolstoy presents his two great antagonists, Napoleon and Alexander, as objects rather than subjects of their time. *And far from having to explain as* chance *those petty events, which made those men what they were, it will be clear to us that all those petty details were inevitable.*

The same must be said of the protagonists of the Nez Perce War. The prudent and trusting submission of Looking-Glass, the violent resistance of the Three Red Blankets, the flight of White Bird and the restraint of Chief Joseph all produced the same result. So did General Howard's kindheartedness and General Sherman's pitiless fury.

From the East to the West it had now been done, and the admission of Oklahoma was our crowning ritual; together we had accomplished the long miracle of Indian subjection—all of us:

> Crook in his tilted slouch hat, with his wrinkled coat pulled right up around his whiskers,
>> living light and striking hard, leaving his rides, raids and massacres to be followed up by columns, forts, towns and everything else that can be carried within the narrow white arches of Army wagons
>
> and Custer, who once said: *If I were an Indian, I often think that I would greatly prefer to cast my lot among those of my people adhered to the free open plains rather than submit to the confined limits of a reservation . . .*
> then Gibbon, Miles and even poor Sturgis,
>> their Indian scouts like well-trained setters ranging and beating the ground,
> not to mention our boys in blue,
>> dropping down on their knees to aim their Spencer carbines
>> then their Sharpses, and Springfields
>>> (for the Philippines they shouldered great Krags, whose roar approached that of Shore Crossing's buffalo gun)

so that buffalo could be magicked into mules, sulkies, vanners, expressers, bussers, drafts, thoroughbreds and even French coach horses

> while we transformed Indians into souvenirs:

M. E. TAYLOR,
DEALER IN
Hides. Pelts. Furs. Tallow.
Ginseng and Indian Relics,
Furs a speciality in season.

Some of our American dreams were white with black blotches like Holstein cows; but we also established on our new landscapes the brownish-orange white-islanded coats of Guernsey dairy cows,

> and then cities,
>> always craving more and more,

so that just as we slice away strips and stripes from a rawhide,
so we trimmed down the reservations,
> correcting treaties until each ranging Indian nation was
> as long gone as a melodeon
>> (moonlight on our sleeping America, Indian
>> ghosts silently leaving her forever)
—preparing the way, uplifting the trumpets
—here comes the general!—
so that now, in Panama, Hawaii, Grenada or Iraq, our grand old American dream
may again unroll itself in a still more perfect array, exactly as a column of march
straightens itself out upon leaving its old bivouac.

FURTHER HISTORY OF AMERICA'S INDIANS
(1902)

Indian warfare is horrid; but Indian massacres, outrages and brutality,
and Indian rule, which is war, is a thousand times worse.

O. O. HOWARD, Brigadier General, U.S. Army (1881)

*Notwithstanding all that has been said about the progress the Government
is making in civilizing the Indians,* explains a veteran employee at the Indian Office,
*the full blooded Indian of to-day is right where he was one hundred years ago . . . Our
experience has been that the Indian never rises above the intellectual and mental
status of a child of fourteen years.*

FURTHER HISTORY OF PRESIDENT RUTHERFORD B. HAYES
(1878–CA. 1885)

It is true that a dollar a day is not enough to support a man and five children, if the man insists on smoking and drinking beer . . . Man cannot live by bread, it is true, but the man who cannot live on bread and water is not fit to live.

HENRY WARD BEECHER, sermon (1877)

Spade-bearded and gracious (Lemonade Lucy peering curiously in), he twice met Chief Joseph and listened kindly to his complaints, but of course little could be done for the poor fellow. Foggy-minded sentimentalists such as Lieutenant Wood have sometimes presumed to criticize our reservation system, under which, I do admit, certain unscrupulous Agents have enriched themselves at our Indians' expense.— All right, a few redskins might have starved to death. However, as President Hayes was starting to realize, the Indians were no worse off than any number of other little people. Now that America had become so beautiful and automatic, our negroes, coal miners and railroad men, the German proletariat, the pallid young women in the textile mills, the Chinamen, were all under the sway of reservations. If only we could establish a reservation for buffalo!— Or for citizens!— After he left office, Hayes wrote in his diary: *This is a government of the people, by the people, and for the people no longer. It is a government of corporations, by corporations, and for corporations.* But Lemonade Lucy was calling him; she required assistance with one of her earrings; so he contented himself with adding: *How is this?*, then closed the book.

FURTHER HISTORY OF THE UNITED STATES OF AMERICA
(1911)

... whenever I travelled, particularly on horseback, I used to continue, in imagination, peopling the hills, ridges, groves, forests, and ravines with soldiers, and laying off everything, for purposes of offence and defence, into military positions for cavalry, artillery, and infantry.

BRIGADIER GENERAL OLIVER OTIS HOWARD, U.S.A., 1881

And pre-eminent usage, reports the Encyclopaedia Britannica, has now made its citizens "Americans," in distinction from the other inhabitants of North and South America.

FURTHER HISTORY OF CAMAS
(1877–2010)

Labor is the straight trail that leads to pleasant places full of wheat and corn and potatoes instead of Kowse, Kamas and bitter root; where the cow, the sheep and hen take the place of the buffalo, the deer and the curlew; and melons and fruit that of weeds and thorns.

GOVERNOR CALEB LYON, to Chief Lawyer of the Nez Perce (1864)

*E*ven after their lands were allotted, the Nez Perce still travelled to dig camas every June and July, but there was less and less of it
 (as the People would say, it is becoming smooth),
 the Bostons plowing and grazing on all the camas meadows,
and so through scarcity our Indians were all the better guided to reason.

FURTHER HISTORY OF THE BUFFALO
(1878–84)

> As nearly as I can estimate, there were in 1865 about nine and one-half million of buffaloes on the plains between the Missouri River and the Rocky Mountains; all are now gone, killed for their meat, their skins, and their bones. This seems like desecration, cruelty, and murder, yet they have been replaced by twice as many cattle. At that date there were about 165,000 Pawnees, Sioux, Cheyennes, and Arapahoes, who depended on these buffaloes for their yearly food. They, too, have gone, but they have been replaced by twice or thrice as many white men and women, who have made the earth to blossom as the rose, and who can be counted, taxed, and governed by the laws of nature and civilization. This change has been salutary and will go on to the end.
>
> GENERAL WILLIAM T. SHERMAN, to Buffalo Bill (*ca.* 1887; in a letter proudly hung on the wall of Bill's "Welcome Wigwam" in Nebraska)

*I*t was in the country around Judith Basin that the Crow woman first perceived what was happening: Not even the flowers masked the stink of decaying flesh: *Our hearts were like stones,* she said. *And yet no one believed, even then, that the white man could kill* all *the buffalo.*

Likewise, no one now believes that once upon a time a Comanche could hamstring a buffalo at full gallop.

Long have they pass'd, faces and trenches and fields, into a white banner with red and blue lettering hung over the street between Shooters Sports Bar and the revolving sign which glares: REMEMBER OUR TROOPS NEAR AND FAR, shining all through the night before the Lewiston Roundup; and come morning there'll be a beautiful blonde flagwaver, who might even smile at you on your way out of town; you'll be coming down from the gas station past Nez Perce Drive, not far from Nez Perce Grade; my heart is good, O yes; *long have they pass'd* into Idaho's yellow rangeland.

Long have they pass'd, those centuries when old women made rope out of Indian hemp. *Long have they pass'd,* the buffalo.

On his deathbed, Buffalo Bill boasted of having done for more than forty thousand buffalo all by his lonesome. His favorite gun was a .48 calibre breech-loading Springfield named Lucretia Borgia.

The buffalo-skin overcoat was almost the universal winter costume of street car drivers, teamsters, and cabbies, who had to brave the sub-zero weather without the protection now afforded to motormen and chauffeurs . . . The relative cheapness of these coats put them within the means of the great multitude doing outside work and was the cause of the buffaloes' passing.

Once upon a time, the Crows paid eight buffalo robes for a knee-length red coat trimmed with silver and gold. I wonder why they can't afford those red coats nowadays?

When Columbus arrived, there might have been as many as a hundred and twenty-five million buffalo within the confines of what is now the United States. It took awhile to chip away at those. Pennsylvania's last herd avoided extermination until 1799. Reader, wouldn't you have supposed that we could have finished the job before? Well, we didn't. Come to think of it, I remember a pioneer mother in long skirts, a shawl around her head, pushing a wheelbarrow full of buffalo chips, her grimy little blonde daughter at her side. She might have had a use for the buffalo. But buffalo herds are the commissaries of our wild Indians. If you want to corral those savages onto some nice little reservation, it's best to starve them.

At first, Custer's widow admits, *the bleaching bones of thousands of buffaloes were rather a melancholy sight to me, but I soon became as much accustomed to the ghastly sockets of an upturned skull as to the field-mouse which ran in and out either orifice with food for her nest of little ones . . . All evidences of death are sad to a woman.*

The bones were gathered up by enterprising white men and sold for fertilizer. As for the manure, there were Montana homesteaders still burning it in their stoves as late as 1900.

Kill an old bull for a shield, a fine young cow for a tipi wall or a bed robe. *Long have they pass'd.*

If you've ever wondered why we couldn't have improved the breed until they were almost as good as beef, I have two definitive answers. First of all, Buffalo Bill's disciples assure us *that it is death for the domestic cow—due to the hump on the calf—to breed with the buffalo bull.* Secondly, Mr. Buffalo Jones, who tried the experiment on a ranch out by Dodge City, did manage it without fatal results, but *the cattalo turned out a singularly unsightly beast, without the majesty of the buffalo, the swift balance of the longhorn, nor the smooth compactness of beef stock. But Jones planned to improve the strain.* Let's leave those two Buffaloes to quibble, while history blazes on, rendering our domains ever more American.

The Union Pacific Railroad had begun to push west from Omaha upon the termination of our Secession War. In four years it accomplished its collateral result: the Plains buffalo had been subdivided into northern and southern herds, the former more numerous. Two lines of track through Kansas easily disposed of the southern herd. O yes; American sunshine drove away those dark shaggy clouds. Now for the northern residuum:

In our centennial year, when Custer fell and the People passed their last summer in Wallowa, the Northern Pacific Railroad reached Bismarck. Here came the first long train, as pretty as an Apache squaw riding on a fast horse, with her night-dark braids whirling behind her! Before Thanksgiving, Bismarck held a noteworthy fête, showing off Chief Joseph, Yellow Bull and other Nez Perce captives at the Sheridan House Hotel. They were very up to date there; they even had a chromo portrait of President Hayes on the wall. A mirthful American lady kissed Joseph on the lips! (Springtime, fumbling in a bluish-grey cornhusk bag decorated with diagonal stripes of dull reddish-brown, found no more yarrow for the baby's fever.) Then off went those savages to the Indian Territory; *long have they pass'd.* On other trains came our buffalo hunters. The price of buffalo hides had fallen, so they had to kill more buffalo to make up the difference. Then there was the unfinished business with Sitting Bull (not to mention that renegade White Bird).

SITTING BULL: As long as there are buffaloes, that is the way we will live.
REPORTER: But the time will come when there will be no more buffaloes.
SITTING BULL: Those are the words of an American.

Accordingly, we stationed our half-breeds, tame Indians and hide men just this side of the Medicine Line. Whenever the buffalo tried to cross, our proxies shot them and scared them back. *It was there, some said, shut in by this line of prairie fire and guns, that the greatest slaughter of the northern herd took place.* Had the Canadians pulled this trick on us, continues the lady just quoted, how we would have trumpeted our national fury! But I, William the Blind, wonder whether the Canadians thought that it was just as well? After all, sooner or later, their Indians must likewise be confined in reserves. Why not send a little hunger their way? And so in 1879, the Prime Minister up there in the British Possessions expressed something between resignation and equanimity when he concluded: *The best authorities agree in representing five years as the maximum period for which the food wants of the Indians of the Plains may be to any reasonable degree supplied from the buffalo.* One year later, the Northern Pacific arrived at Terry and Sully Springs, Montana, elevating the summer butchery of herds from a possibility to a convenience. In 1881, Sitting Bull's Sioux in Canada were reduced to eating their dead ponies. Accordingly, most of them went back across the Medicine Line to surrender to their kind friends the Americans. That was the year the Kiowas postponed their Sun Dance from June until August, because only then could they find a single buffalo. In 1882, no buffalo came to the Kiowas, who accordingly cancelled their Sun Dance. Meanwhile, two hundred thousand buffalo hides departed from stations between Mandan and Miles City. The following year, forty thousand hides went out. That was when Standard Railroad Time settled throughout our United States. One year later, the hide men sent one carload, *the last shipment ever made.* And in that year I see Sitting Bull gazing wearily down at the tomahawk in his lap, a feather in his hair, his eyes sunken deep in, his face round and wrinkled, photograph copyrighted 1884 by Palmquist & Johnson.

From a newspaper, 2011:

OREGON CITY, Ore.— As long as American Indians have lived in the Pacific Northwest, they have looked to a jawless, eel-like fish for food.

Tribes once harvested the lamprey from rivers throughout the Columbia Basin, which stretches from the Oregon coast up into Canada. But with dozens of hydroelectric dams in the way, the fish has followed the path of the buffalo . . .

One of the fundamental facts of life is the dominance of man over the lower animals, and the further dominance of civilized man over his primitive brother dwelling in savagery . . . If we really believe that the civilization of the white man is superior to the savagery of the red, we must of necessity believe that this conquest was a desirable thing . . . Nor can we blink at the fact that this good could be realized only through the destruction of the life—whether human or animal—which flourished in the wilderness . . . The wild buffalo was no less antipathetic to the white man's culture than were the dinosaurs and the cycads of the Jurassic Age . . .

> MILO MILTON QUAIFE, Secretary of the Burton Historical Collection (1938)

Our whole conduct towards them [Indians] has been marked by a greed that knew no bounds, a rapacity that has never been staid, and a cruelty more ferocious than savages ever inflicted upon their enemies . . . If it be the purpose of the Government to continue this monstrous policy until the extinction of the race is accomplished, then it is wiser, cheaper and more humane to select and put into operation the agencies that will attain this end as quickly as possible . . . Let us finish the work, commenced so many years ago, by a sharp and decisive stroke. Send the Army out over the plains and into the fastnesses of the mountains, to strike down and destroy the Indians of every age and sex until not one of that unfortunate people shall be left to tell the melancholy story of their wrongs . . .

CONGRESSMAN J. SMITH YOUNG, 1878

After our rebellion,* when so many young men were at liberty to return to their homes, they found they were not satisfied with the farm, the store, or the work-shop of the villages, but wanted larger fields . . . It is probable that the Indians would have had control of these [Western] lands for a century but for the war. We must conclude, therefore, that wars are not always evils unmixed with some good.

ULYSSES S. GRANT, 1886

. . . and from the soul's birth until it soars into Heavenly Spheres it has to seek for, and be clad in, an armor fitted for warfare, until it meets and overcomes the foes to its innocency, to its progress, and to its ultimate attainment.

BRIGADIER GENERAL OLIVER OTIS HOWARD, U.S.A., *ca.* 1895

---

*The Civil War.

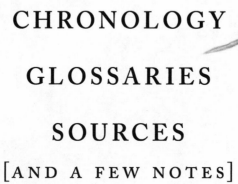

CHRONOLOGY

GLOSSARIES

SOURCES

[AND A FEW NOTES]

A CHRONOLOGY OF THE
SEVEN AGES OF WINELAND

✫✫✫✫

V. THE AGE OF DYING GRASS

✫✫✫✫

ca. **8,000 B.C.** **End of the last Ice Age. Possible date of arrival of the Nimiipu (Nez Perce) in their pre-Contact homeland.**

1492   Estimates of buffalo population in what is now the United States vary between 50 million and 125 million.

ca. 1770   Miner's dip compass introduced in Sweden.

1786   **Tuekalas (Old Chief Joseph) born.**

1805–6   **Lewis and Clark become the first known Euro-Americans to meet the Nimiipu, by whom they are kindly treated. Their homeland extends "more than 13.5 million acres."** See entry for the Walla Walla Treaty of 1855.

1806   John Coulter, formerly with Lewis and Clark, makes what might be the first Euro-American contact with the Crows.

1815–20   **Smohalla (Smohallie or Smowhala) born in Wallula, Washington Territory, sometime in this period.**

1818   Establishment of Fort Nez Perce, "Gibraltar of the Columbia."

ca. 1822   About five thousand Crows (half the population) massacred by Sioux and Cheyennes in one day.

1822   **Rutherford B. Hayes born. He will be President during the Nez Perce War.**

1824   Creation of the Indian Department (which belongs to the War Department).

1827   **John Gibbon (who will lead the Big Hole attack) born in Philadelphia.**

1828   **George Crook born near Taylorsville, Ohio.**

1830   **Oliver Otis Howard born in Leeds, Maine.**

1831   Four Nimiipu travel to Saint Louis, requesting Christian instruction.

1833   Howard's father brings the Negro boy Edward Johnson to help with farmwork.

1834   Congress creates the Indian Territory, which will become (approximately) the state of Oklahoma.

1834   Fort Laramie built by William Sublette. Bought by Army in 1849.

1834   Hudson's Bay Company constructs Fort Boise (abandoned in 1855 due to Indian troubles). Meanwhile, in Montana, the American Fur Company establishes a trading post in Blackfoot country. The Crows, enemies of the Blackfeet, attack the post but are beaten off. "Thus ended the first, last, and only warlike attempt ever made by the Crows . . . upon the whites."

1836   Marcus and Narcissa Whitman establish their Cayuse mission at Waiilatpu. Henry and Eliza Spalding establish their Nez Perce mission at Lapwai.

1838   Old Chief Joseph becomes a Christian and sets up his lodge by Lapwai.

ca. **1840**   **Chief Joseph (Heinmot Tooyalakekt) born, and christened Ephraim.**

1839   Nelson A. Miles (the future captor of Joseph) born in Massachusetts. (Some sources give 1840.)

1842   **Nez Perce tribal government invented by Spalding and a Dr. Elijah White (Indian subagent for Oregon) who (kind souls) draft laws for the Nimiipu.**

The first head-chief they impose is a convert named Ellis. Not surprisingly, he is unpopular, and according to some sources presently departs for the Buffalo Country.

1843	Foundation of first Oregon militia.
1843	A measles epidemic impels the Cayuse to murder their missionaries (this is the "Whitman Massacre").
1844	Foundation of Oregon Rangers.
1847–50	Cayuse Indian War in Oregon, initiated by the Whitman Massacre.
1848	Upon the death or departure of Ellis, Richard becomes Nimiipu head-chief.
1848	Gold discovered at Sutter's Mill, California, precipitating an immigration "rush."
1849	Richard resigns, to be succeeded by Lawyer (Hahlalhotoost).
1849	Oregon Territory created.
1849	Control of Indian matters transferred from Department of War to Department of the Interior. The new organization is now called the Bureau of Indian Affairs. Looking back on this event in 1878, one bleeding heart Congressman will consider soldiers to have been better to the Indians than "their present guardians of the Interior Department, whose amazing villainies would astound the sturdiest felon."
1850	Ostensible ringleaders of the Whitman Massacre hanged.
1850	Lee (Thomas Leander) Moorhouse born. Many Nez Perce photos will be stamped with his name.
1850	Howard graduates from Bowdoin College and enters West Point. Robert E. Lee's son is in his class.
1852	**Charles Erskine Scott Wood born.**
1852	Moses Milner founds Mount Idaho, the town which will play so significant a part at the beginning of the Nez Perce War.
1853	Creation of Washington Territory (split off from Oregon Territory).
ca. 1854	"Finding the buffalo diminishing in their own country," the Sioux begin to encroach westward on Crow country.
1854	Bannock and Shoshoni attack emigrant train along the Snake River.
1854	Howard graduates from West Point, fourth in his class. Commissioned a brevet second lieutenant.
1855	Howard marries Elizabeth (Lizzie) Waite on Valentine's Day. Guy Howard born at Augusta, Maine (December. 16). Howard will write about this son: "His was an ideal life from his babyhood to his death in the service in the Philippines."
1855	**Walla Walla Treaty sets aside a joint use area for the Cayuse, Walla Walla and Umatilla. Nimiipu sign a treaty whose provisions (following Spalding and White's edicts of 1842) require them to relinquish some traditional territory for the transcontinental railroad. They retain 12,000 out of almost 30,000 square miles (7 million acres). The English-speaking convert Lawyer becomes head-chief.**
1855	Head-chiefs also established for Cayuses, Flatheads, Kootenais, Pend d'Oreilles, Walla Wallas and Yakimas.
1855	Washington Territory invalidates marriages between whites and Indians.
1855–56	Rogue River Indian War in Oregon. About its causes General Crook remarks: "It was of no unfrequent occurrence for an Indian to be shot down in cold blood, or a squaw to be raped by some brute. Such a thing as a white man being punished for outraging an Indian was unheard of. It was the fable of the wolf and lamb every time." (In this description Crook conceptualizes a whole series of Rogue Wars spanning 1850–58.)
1856	**As Chief of Ordnance in the field, Howard takes part in the military removal of the Seminoles from Florida.**
1856	Nez Perce aid the U.S. Army in the Yakima War.
1857	**While in Florida, Howard comes forward in a Methodist revival meeting and finds salvation.** Around this time his second child Grace is born. When the Seminole campaign concludes, he teaches mathematics at West Point (1857–61).

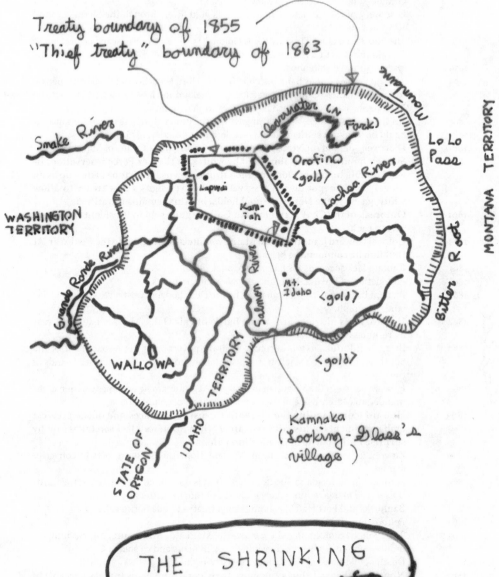

Treaty boundaries of 1855
"Thief treaty" boundary of 1863

Snake River

Clearwater (N. Fork)

Mountain

WASHINGTON
TERRITORY

Lapwai

•Orofino
<gold>

Lochsa River

Lo Lo
Pass

MONTANA TERRITORY

Kam-
iah

Bitter Root

Grande Ronde River

Salmon River

•Mt.
Idaho <gold>

<gold>

WALLOWA

IDAHO TERRITORY

STATE OF OREGON

Kamnaka
(Looking-Glass's
village)

THE SHRINKING
RESERVATION
(1855, 1863)

1857	Grande Ronde reservation created in Oregon.
1858	Discovery of the Comstock Lode spreads gold fever through the Sierras around Virginia City.
1858	The Nez Perce chief Timothy helps Colonel Steptoe's troops escape encirclement by Yakimas, Coeur d'Alenes and Spokanes.
1859	Oregon granted statehood.
1859	The soon to be famous Bannock chief Buffalo Horn leads five hundred of his people to Fort Brigadier in hopes of getting a homeland in the Utah Territory, but the Eastern Shoshoni chief Washakie refuses to share land.
1860	"In the year 1860 there was nothing within the limits of what is now Montana that could be termed a settlement . . ."—Lt. James H. Bradley, 1876.
1860	**Discovery of gold on Nimiipu lands, near eponymous Orofino, Idaho.**
1861	**Sixteen hundred gold claims filed by whites on the Nez Perce reservation. Illegal establishment of Florence and Orofino towns. Lewiston springs up as an illegal supply depot on the reservation. Lawyer signs a new treaty to allow white access to the Nez Perce gold fields, but this remains unratified.**
1861	**Outbreak of the Civil War. First ten Gatling guns sold to President Lincoln at $1,300 each.**
1861	**Colonel Howard leads the Third Maine volunteer regiment into the Civil War. At Bull Run he commands a brigade.**
1861	Captain Jack succeeds his father as Modoc chief.
1861	Foundation of Dakota, Montana and Nevada territories.
1862	Birth of La Barge City, Montana (the future Deer Lodge); construction of the Overland Telegraph.
1862	**Howard loses his right arm at the Battle of Fair Oaks** (May 31). Later that year he resumes active duty.
1862	Brig. Gen. Rufus Saxton becomes military governor of the Department of the South, and begins to establish free black labor and education in the Sea Islands of the Carolinas.
1862–63	Howard serves in the Virginian campaign. At Antietam he becomes division commander; in March '63 he becomes major general of volunteers.
1863	**Howard (commanding the Eleventh Corps) experiences one of the greatest embarrassments of his military career when Stonewall Jackson takes him by surprise in the Battle of Chancellorsville.**
1863	Lincoln issues the Emancipation Proclamation. The Union resorts to conscript armies.
1863	Foundation of the Idaho Territory. Lewiston is the capital for one year (afterwards Boise). The first governor receives charge of Indian matters.
1863	Bannocks and Fort Hall Shoshonis sign a treaty at Soda Springs, I.T.
1863	Foundation of the Arizona Territory.
1863	Thirty-eight Sioux hanged *en masse* in Mankato, Minnesota, after a hunger-induced uprising in which they killed 644 civilians and 93 soldiers.
1863	Death of Old Looking-Glass at age seventy-eight.
1863	**Nimiipu at Lapwai sign away more than 13 million acres (ninety percent) of their land [see entry for 1805–6] in what White Thunder will later call a "thief treaty." (Bill Gulick: "So one-third of the tribe signed away seven-eighths of the reservation as its boundaries had been laid out in 1855.") (Emily Greenwald: "Government agents devised the 1863 treaty to protect the lands of 'friendly' Christianized bands but to dispossess the non-Christian bands . . .") As a result, the tribe splits into treaty and non-treaty factions, the former headed by Lawyer, the second—who never signed—including Old Joseph at Wallowa and White Bird in the Salmon Valley. Taking heed of the latter group, President Lincoln declines to ratify the treaty.**
1864	William Pitt Fessenden, Secretary of the Treasury, establishes "Freedmen's Home Colonies" for former slaves in Confederate-free parts of the South.

1864	Howard commands the Fourth Corps and helps conquer Atlanta. During this campaign he is wounded again. Upon the death of General McPherson he is chosen by Sherman to lead the Army of the Tennessee.
1864	**Massacre of Cheyenne civilians at Sand Creek, Colorado, by Col. J. M. Chivington with the Third Regiment of Colorado Cavalry.** See source-note to p. 631: "Without a shadow of excuse . . ." on p. 1313.
1864	Nevada admitted as thirty-sixth state. Montana Territory formed from parts of Idaho and Dakota. Most of Wyoming is likewise split off.
1864–68	**Snake Indian War plays out across the Great Basin. Among the troopers fighting the Snakes is David Perry, who will lose the Battle of White Bird Canyon in 1877.**
1865	**"Until 1865 government policy meant what it said: an America for whites east of the Mississippi and west of the Rockies, and a red America in the 'desert' in between."—John Keegan.**
1865	Sioux and Cheyennes raid the Powder River in Wyoming to avenge the previous year's Sand Creek Massacre.
1865	**Chief Joseph's elder wife Good Woman (conjectural name) gives birth to a daughter, Sound Of Running Feet.**
1865	**Howard teaches Sunday school to freed Negroes while stationed at the Sea Islands. Sherman issues his Sea-Island Circular turning over the islands, abandoned rice fields and certain other lands near Charleston to black settlement.**
1865	Helena, Montana (founded a mere year before), now contains 8,000 inhabitants.
1865	**Lee surrenders. The Civil War is over. General Howard becomes a brigadier general.**
1865–1920	**Lincoln establishes the Bureau of Refugees, Freedmen and Abandoned Lands (March 3, 1865). After the President's assassination, Howard disregards Sherman's advice and becomes the bureau's first head (commissioner), beginning in June 1865. By December 1868 the institution has been effectively undermined and paralyzed by President Johnson's administration. It limps along until its abolition in 1872. The associated Freedman's Savings and Trust Co. (incorporated by Congress 3 March 1865) fails in 1874; a final accounting of its assets will not be completed until 1920. Howard is charged with malfeasance and spends many years and much money to clear his name.**
1866	Captain Fetterman's 81 troops massacred by Cheyennes and Sioux.
1866	Gatling guns officially adopted by U.S. Army.
1867	**Placer mines in Nez Perce ceded territory are mostly exhausted.**
1867	Custer and Hancock ride against the Cheyennes, but succeed only in burning one empty village.
1867	Buffalo population within limits of present U.S. estimated at 50 million. See entry for 1492.
1867	Kansas Pacific constructs a railroad line to Abilene, Kansas, allowing Texas cattlemen to sell beef to parts east.
1867	Foundation of the Dominion of Canada.
1867	The U.S. Peace Commission concludes that the best policy is to place all Indians on reservations. Meanwhile, Sherman writes Grant: "This conflict . . . will exist as long as the Indians exist, for their ways are different from our ways, and either they or we must be masters on the Plains."
1867	**President Johnson ratifies the Lapwai Treaty of 1863.**
1868	Young Joseph visits the Buffalo Country with his father. Meanwhile, Nelson Miles, Joseph's future antagonist at Bear's Paw, weds Sherman's niece Mary.
1868	**Nimiipu land treaty of 1863 signed in Idaho and ratified. Lawyer goes to Washington to amend it but evidently ignores the concerns of Joseph, White Bird and the other "non-treaties."**
1868	In Chicago, the Peace Commission (controlled by General Sherman et al.) advises Congress to stop treating with Indians as "sovereign dependent nations" and make them subject to U.S. law.

1869	Union Pacific and Central Pacific railroads meet at Promontory Point, Utah, completing the transcontinental route and thereby dividing the bison into northern and southern herds.
1869	Sherman placed in command of the U.S. Army.
1869	**President Grant puts Bannocks on Fort Hall reservation. His well-intentioned "peace policy" takes authority over reservations away from the Army and gives it to missionaries, with the hope that promises to the Indians will thereby be better kept. John B. Monteith, Presbyterian, becomes Indian agent for the Nimiipu. Henry Spalding goes back to Lapwai to be the school superintendent.**
1869–73	**Howard co-founds Howard University and becomes its first president.**
1870	"The 1870 census, for the first time in American history, counted American farmers as a minority work force . . ."
1871	One out of four horses in the U.S. dies of pestilence.
1871	**Congress ceases making treaties with Indian tribes.**
1871	Spalding baptizes Lawyer.
1871	President Grant signs order to remove Flatheads and other Indians from the Bitterroot Valley of Montana (the site of "Fort Fizzle" in the approaching Nez Perce War) because it "has proved, in the judgment of the President, not to be better adapted to the wants of the Flatheads than the general reservation . . ."
1871	**White settlers arrive in Wallowa.**
1871(?)	**Death of Old Chief Joseph Tuekalas.** This might have been in 1870.
1871–79	Southern bison herds exterminated.
1872	**Howard persuades the Chiricahua Apache chief Cochise to come onto a reservation. This result, perhaps the greatest success of Howard's Indian career, comes quickly undone following the death of Cochise two years later. When the U.S. decides to relocate the Chiricahuas to a reservation not of their choosing, war breaks out. Howard later writes his former aide-de-camp: "Every promise you and I made those Apaches . . . was afterwards broken by agents of our Government."**
1872	Malheur reservation created in Oregon.
1872	**Whites begin to settle illegally in Wallowa. Joseph orders them out. Agent John Monteith and T. B. Ondeneal, Indian superintendent of Oregon, are appointed to arbitrate the land question between non-treaty Nimiipu and settlers.**
1872–73	**Modoc Indian War in California. Among others mentioned in this book, Capt. David Perry, Capt. Joel Trimble, and Lt. Edward Theller, who together will lose the Battle of White Bird Canyon during the Nez Perce War, take part in the Modoc campaign. (Maj. E. C. Mason, another Nez Perce campaigner, is Perry's superior during the Modoc War.) "The conditions existing in the Lava Beds that made [Captain] Jack," the Modoc chief, "fight were identical with those in the Wallowa Valley . . ."**
1872–74	American and Canadian survey parties mark the "Medicine Line," the boundary between their nations, moving westward from Minnesota to the Pacific.
1873	**President Grant issues an executive order creating a "Wallowa Reserve for Roaming Nez Perce."**
1873	Idaho Territory established.
1873	After a falling-out with Monteith, Spalding removes to Kamiah, exchanging his title of school superintendent for a missionary's proselytizing crown.
1873	Jay Cooke of the Northern Pacific Railroad goes bankrupt, precipitating the Panic of '73; one result of this is that Congress reduces Army appropriations. In 1866 the Army mustered about 54,000 men. After 1873 the Army consists of only 25,000 men.
1873	"Beginning with the depression of 1873, agricultural prices began a quarter-century-long slide . . ."
1874	Howard is finally acquitted of misappropriation of Freedmen's Bureau funds, then appointed to command the Department of the Columbia.

1874	Spalding dies, to be succeeded by the sisters Sue and Kate McBeth.
1874	Grangeville (Idaho) supplants Mount Idaho. These two settlements will furnish volunteers and victims at the beginning of the Nez Perce War.
1874	Death of the Apache chief Cochise. Geronimo replaces him. War with the U.S. Army resumes.
1874	Wood graduates from West Point.
1874	Rich gold strike in the Black Hills of South Dakota.
1874	**Nez Perces and Flatheads reject Sitting Bull's proposal for a pan-Indian uprising against the whites. Looking-Glass aids the Crows in a great battle against the Sioux.**
1874–75	"The Red River campaigns . . . with their endless pursuits, demand for vigilance on the part of the Indians, and numbing cold . . . rendered most of the southern plains peoples destitute," including the Kiowas, many Cheyennes, and Kotsoteka and Kwahadi Comanches. Col. Nelson Miles takes a prominent part in these operations.
1874–81	**Howard commands the Department of the Columbia.**
1875	**Grant revokes his 1873 order of recognition of the Wallowa Reserve.**
1875	Civil Rights Act requires hotels, vehicles, etc., to be made as available to Negroes as to whites; furthermore, whites cannot prevent Negroes from being seated on juries.
1876	"By 1876 the Grant administration had all but collapsed in a shambles of corruption and ineptitude."
1876	**Custer and his troops, together with some Crow scouts, massacred at Little Big Horn (total killed about 260) by Sioux under the leadership of Sitting Bull. The Army's retaliatory operations fail to prevent Sitting Bull's escape into Canada.**
1876	John and William H. Blurick, whom I have conflated and distorted for my fictional character of Wittfield Blurick, ride the Oregon Trail, in company with a scout named Doc, who promises to shoot the first Indian he sees. "There was plenty of Indians all over the Country."
1876	Colorado becomes the thirty-eighth state.
1876	Fort Macleod established in present day Alberta, Canada, as Mounted Police headquarters, mostly to interdict American smuggling. Fort Walsh, built soon thereafter, 160 miles to the east, will become the HQ post in 1878. Sitting Bull's Sioux settle in this latter jurisdiction.
1876	Death of Lawyer.
1877	Miles receives the surrender of many Cheyennes at Tongue River, and causes or facilitates the surrender of Crazy Horse's band as well as many Sans Arcs and Minneconjous.
1877	**Lapwai councils with non-treaty Nez Perce. On May 3, General Howard "shows the rifle" and confines Toohhoolhoolzote in the guardhouse for opposing Nez Perce removal. Aubrey L. Haines: "The council was a mockery."**
1877	**Nez Perce War:**

White Bird Canyon, June 17.
Skirmish on the Salmon River, June 28.
Attack on Looking-Glass's camp, July 1.
Skirmish on the Cottonwood, July 3.
Skirmish at Norton's ranch, July 4.
Misery Hill, July 9.
Clearwater, July 11–12.
Skirmish at the Clearwater ford, Kamiah, July 13.
Skirmish at Weippe, July 17.
Fort Fizzle, July 28.
Big Hole, August 9–10. (Nimiipu casualties, according to Joseph: 18 men and 51 women and children killed. Other estimates are higher.)
Camas Meadows, August 20.
Canyon Creek, September 13.

> Cow Island, September 23–24.
> (Sitting Bull's people parley with Miles and then cross over to Canada.)
> **Bear's Paw, September 30–October 5.** At Bear's Paw, Montana, some 418 tribespeople surrender with Joseph. About 233 escape to Canada with White Bird, joining Sitting Bull.

"In brief, bands of Nez Perce stockmen were disposed of to make room for white ranchers."

—MERRILL D. BEAL, 1963

1877	Thanks to the military's poor showing against Sitting Bull and Joseph (not to mention labor unrest on the railroads), Congress re-expands the army.
1877	Official U.S. poverty line is $506 per year.
1877	Edison invents the phonograph.
1877–1937	"Government repression in 1877 set the standard for the next sixty years . . . When not using the U.S. Army to maintain complete control of the workplace, American corporations could call on the militia, police, the Pinkerton Agency, or simply hire thugs as needed, free from any government regulation or inquiry."
1878–80	**Most of the Nimiipu refugees in Canada return to the U.S.**
1878	**Nimiipu prisoners removed to the Indian Territory.**
1878	**A U.S. commission visits White Bird in Canada, seeking his surrender. He refuses.**
1878	Umatilla Indian War in Oregon.
1878	Escape attempt by Northern Cheyenne. Some killed, some returned to the Indian Territory.
1878	**Howard takes part in the Bannock Indian War in Oregon (his last active campaign). Like the Nez Perce War, this lasts from May until October. Buffalo Horn fights against the Army and is killed.**
1878	**"By 1878, all the Native peoples of the American Plains had been forced onto reservations."**
1878	Bodies of Lt. Rains and others slain by the Nimiipu at Cottonwood reburied at Fort Lapwai.
1879	Grace Howard marries Capt. James T. Gray.
1879	President Hayes vetoes the Chinese Exclusion Act.
1879	Robert Williams becomes the first Nimiipu to be ordained.
1879	The U.S. goes to war with seven Ute tribes.
1880	**President Hayes reports to Congress: "We are now at peace with all the Indian tribes in our borders."**
1880–83	Northern bison herds essentially exterminated.
1880	Howard appointed to command the Department of West Point.
1881	Sitting Bull surrenders to the U.S. (July 18). He is taken to Fort Randall and imprisoned for two years.
1881	Garfield becomes President; assassinated that same year; Arthur succeeds him. Chinese exclusion passes.
1881	Umatilla tribal police force established.
1881	Lewistown, Montana, begins municipal life as Reedsfort, named after Maj. A. S. Reed whose trading post the non-treaty Nez Perces visited in 1877, en route to Bear's Paw.
1881	**Howard publishes *Nez Perce Joseph*.**
1881–82	Howard is Superintendent of West Point.
1882	**Some non-treaty Nimiipu widows and orphans permitted to return to Lapwai.**
1882	The Umatilla sell 640 acres to the municipality of Pendleton.
1882–86	Howard commands the Department of the Platte.
1883	**"Wild bison were almost eliminated by 1883 . . ."**
1883	The Supreme Court rescinds the Civil Rights Act of 1875.

1883	The Indian Bureau promulgates its "List of Indian Offenses," which, among other things, subjects practicing shamans to prosecution.
1884	Northern Cheyenne assigned a reservation in their traditional homeland near Tongue River.
1884	Fort Lapwai decommissioned.
1884	Guy Howard, aged twenty-nine, marries Miss Jeannie Woolworth.
1885	**Joseph and some other non-treaty Nimiipu sent to Colville reservation in eastern Washington.**
1885	Congress passes an Umatilla allotment bill.
1885	Arrival of the Statue of Liberty.
1886	Howard promoted to major general and appointed to Military Division of the Pacific in San Francisco.
1886	**Geronimo surrenders to General Miles, and with him the Chiricahua Apaches formerly led by Cochise. They are shipped off to Florida and other places, their children acculturated at Carlisle School.**
1886	Congress decides that reservation lands may now be allotted (see **Dawes Act, 1887**) with Indian consent.
1886–87	Blizzards kill off many range cattle in the West; the era of the open range approaches its close.
1886–88	Howard commands the Department of the Pacific.
1887	**President Cleveland signs the General Allotment Act (better known as the Dawes Plan or Dawes Act), which seeks to replace reservations with forced integration of Indians into mainstream white culture and society. "Surplus" reservation lands can be sold to non-Indians, and communal lands will be subdivided into individual allotments. Indians receiving allotments automatically become U.S. citizens. By 1934, Indian lands have shrunk from 138 million to 55 acres.**
1888	Umatilla reservation reduced in size for sale.
1888–94	Howard commands the Military Division of the Atlantic (Department of the East) at Governors Island, New York.
1889	North and South Dakota, Washington, Idaho and Montana all become states, raising the total to forty-one.
1890	Wyoming becomes a state.
1890	Army decommissions Fort Laramie.
1890	General Crook dies in Omaha.
1890	Sitting Bull killed while "resisting arrest."
1890	**The Ghost Dance religion (based in part on Smohalla's Dreamer teachings) reaches its zenith, emboldening Native Americans to resist white authority and terrifying various Indian agents. Through the negligence or worse of Colonel Forsyth of the Seventh Cavalry, the Wounded Knee Massacre, "the last major armed encounter between Indians and whites in North America," kills at least 150 Sioux.**
1891	Howard heads Sherman's funeral procession.
1892	**White Bird murdered by Nez Perce (or Percee) Sam.**
1893	Howard receives a Congressional Medal of Honor for bravery in the Battle of Fair Oaks.
1893	Death of Rutherford B. Hayes.
1894	Howard retires.
1894	"The last . . . performance of the sun dance among the Indians took place at Havre, Mont., June 19, 1894, despite the Government's efforts to prevent it." (In fact the Sun Dance continues as I finish this book, in 2015.)
1895	Unallotted Nimiipu reservation lands made available for white settlement.
1895	Howard founds Lincoln Memorial University in Tennessee, in hopes of serving whites in the Appalachians.
1895	**Death of Smohalla.**
1899	Howard's son Guy, now a colonel, killed in the Philippines, leaving his wife and two children. (Some sources say 1900.)

1904	**Chief Joseph dies in Nespelem, Washington.**
1905	Lee Moorhouse publishes his *Souvenir Album of Noted Indian Photographs,* containing among other images portraits of Joseph.
1907	The Indian and Oklahoma territories become the State of Oklahoma.
1907	**Howard publishes *My Life and Experiences Among Our Hostile Indians* and the two-volume *Autobiography of O. O. Howard.***
1909	**Howard dies in Burlington, Vermont.**
1914	**Chiricahua Apaches finally permitted to return to New Mexico. (See entry for 1886.)**
1916	Wallowa Lake dammed.
1925	General Nelson Miles dies of a heart attack which strikes him during the Pledge of Allegiance.
1926	Lee Moorhouse dies in Pendleton.
1927	Nez Perce Tribal Council inaugurated on the reservation at Lapwai.
1929	**Joseph's elder widow Wa-win-te-pi-ksat (formerly one of Looking-Glass's wives) dies at Nespelem at nearly a hundred years of age.**
1934	Repeal of Dawes Act (replaced by the Indian Reorganization Act, which prohibits the sale of so-called "surplus" lands).
1934	John Collier, Bureau of Indian Affairs Commissioner: "No interference with Indian religious life or ceremonial expression will henceforth be tolerated."
1935	**Death of White Thunder (Yellow Wolf) at Colville.**
1935	**Death of Peopeo Tholekt.**
1941	Two Nez Perce lawsuits against the U.S. dismissed.
1944	**Death of C. E. S. Wood, Howard's former aide-de-camp.**
1944	Death of Lucullus Virgil McWhorter, who wrote *Yellow Wolf* and *Hear Me, My Chiefs.*
1949	Umatilla tribe establishes a constitution.
1954	All western Oregon tribes terminated.
1956	Grande Ronde reservation closed.
1960	Three million dollars owed to Nimiipu from the "thief treaty" of 1863 finally paid.
1976	K. Ross Toole writes: "If one were to pick one theme which more than any other has remained a constant in the white attitude toward the Indian it would be 'removal,' removal from where they *are,* meaning land which for one reason or other we want, to some land which, for one reason or another, we do not want."
1995	John Keegan writes: "Only the Americans have succeeded in creating a society of complete cultural uniformity."

GLOSSARIES

I have tried to define every term which may not be readily comprehensible. (1) Because this is a novel, not a treatise in linguistics, the words are entered as they appear in the text, not necessarily in their nobly correct and inertial forms. In the text, however, their form is never the result of my own caprice, but of someone else's. (2) Sources for terms are not in any way exhaustive; they merely indicate where I have seen them in my reading. Thus, for instance, it is entirely possible that a term described as of Nimiputumít (Nez Perce) origin might have been Umatilla as well. (3) The same word is often spelled a variety of ways in this book (e.g., "Espawyas," "Powyes," "Sepowyes" and "Spowyevas"). Every spelling in this book, as always, is taken from a primary source. Rather then be a totalitarian, I have preferred to let the variants stand in all their charm. Cross-references from one glossary to another are noted as, for example, [G 2] (that is, "See Glossary 2").

1. GLOSSARY OF PERSONAL NAMES
Including Yellow Wolf's true name.

2. GLOSSARY OF ORDERS, ISMS, NATIONS, PROFESSIONS, HIERARCHIES, DIVISIONS, RACES, SHAMANS, TRIBES AND MONSTERS
From generals to chiefs, not to mention the Freedmen's Bureau. Brevet ranks are explained.

3. GLOSSARY OF PLACES
Updated from Horn's Guide.

4. GLOSSARY OF TEXTS
Less to the point than in previous Dreams, but retained for sentimental reasons.

5. GLOSSARY OF CALENDARS, CURRENCIES, FORMS, LEGALISMS AND MEASURES
Useful for surveyors and military men in our American wilderness. Monetarists will wish to know about shinplasters, and missionaries may care for a definition of Indian policy. Some Nez Perce seasons are also listed.

6. GENERAL GLOSSARY
The sound of a crying baby, or of icicles striking each other.

1. GLOSSARY OF PERSONAL NAMES

> Names occurring only once in the text are not glossed.

About Asleep—*(Anglicized Nimiputumít.)* [Eelahweemah.] A fourteen-year-old boy who carried water up to the warriors at Clearwater. His mother was killed at Big Hole. He lived out the war and went to Nespelem, succeeding **Joseph** as chief.

Agate Woman—See **Welweyas**.

Joe Albert—See **Animal In A Hole**.

Allutakanin—*(Nimiputumít.)* [Meaning unknown.] One of **Red Heart**'s four sons; unlike the two younger brothers, he fought alongside the non-treaties, survived the Indian Territory and died at Lapwai. See also **Over The Point**.

Animal In A Hole—*(Anglicized Nimiputumít.)* [Also: "Animal Entering A Hole".] One of the treaty Nez Perces. His Christian name was Joe Albert, which the Nez Perces might have pronounced *Tso Alpít*. A U.S. Army scout. He was captured at White Bird Canyon and released under condition that he would not fight against the non-treaties anymore. Breaking his promise, he accompanied the Army to the Clearwater. When the non-treaties informed him that soldiers had just killed his father at **Cottonwood** [G 3], he switched sides. Injured at Clearwater, and again at Canyon Creek, he survived the war and actually escaped from the Indian Territory, walking all the way back to Idaho along with a few companions.

Arrowhead—*(Anglicized Nimiputumít.)* [Etemiere.] A woman of the **Looking-Glass** band who bound up **Peopeo Tholekt**'s leg wound after the attack on **Kamnaka** [G 2]. [Coincidentally, one Crow name for Looking-Glass himself meant "Arrowhead".] Aside from this one episode, she does not appear in the sources familiar to me, so her escape from Bear's Paw is invented.

Asking Maiden—See **Looking-Glass**.

Blackberry Person—See **Looking-Glass**.

Wittfield Blurick—A mostly invented character of mine, based on a Blurick of another sort (actually, there are two other names involved: John and William), whose 1876 ms. in the Oregon Historical Society mentions a scout named **Doc** who promised to shoot the first Indian he saw. I couldn't bear to part with the original Blurick's last name. (Only the few directly quoted phrases in the "Indian Service" chapter are genuine.) Blurick has ridden into this book only because he comprises the nail-flick of accident, whose childish fun launches a halfpenny nail through the bull's eye glass of Doc's mental parlor, will never know his own purposelessness, because when Eliza Bell Blurick at last escapes her pain by virtue of getting crushed by it, crushed like the chest of Old Johnson when the tree fell on him and like the heads of barren hens when we grind them under our boot-heels, he, unable to stop believing in everything, stakes his faith in a better place for her beyond the sky and for him a high green country of pears beyond rivers and deserts, not recognizing himself as the merest dreamer dreaming and dreamed, for as he steers his prairie schooner west in Captain Travis's caravan, Hood River begins to open herself up for him, flower by flower and pear by unborn pear, with the snowy white mountain decorating his fancies forever: he's becoming *free* from his ghosts and failures back East, free even from Eliza Bell whose adorable whimperings when she was young and he could pleasure her usually turned into what she in embarrassment would later apologize for as screams, when actually they resembled the soft pallid weeping of a rabbit when the life is about to be choked out of it; once she was worn out, old and dying, she made the same noise, whose other meaning came to roost in his mind as horribly as vultures landing on a Plains Indian scaffold burial, and the Secession War tainted everything else, so where was he to go but forward, working at living out something better for himself since so much of his life had been eaten up already? The sooner he got to Hood River, the sooner he'd enter the perfect times. And if he were easy to ridicule as a dully careful reckoner of small advantages, the only ones he expected as opposed to aspiring to (for even Hood River might turn out to be a single dead pear tree), well, didn't he have his reasons? Weren't his advantages as worthy as mine? He was, if anything, more likely to succeed, since Eliza Bell's ghost was surely riding in the next wagon behind, never mind an orphan girl and a few ripe pears might help him with the sorrows he could not drive away.

Lieutenant Bomus—The post quartermaster at Lapwai. **Theller** was sent to White Bird Canyon in his stead. From Howard's account, Bomus was a brave and effective man, and I brought him along for the pursuit of **Joseph**, conflating him with several of his real-life equivalents, such as Lieutenant Ebstein, "who came speedily out of difficulties," and after whom the camp at Henry's Lake was named.

Lieutenant Boyle—Perceived as a "boy" by Nez Perce chiefs, this fellow was one of **Howard**'s mouthpieces.

Lieutenant James Bradley—One of **Gibbon**'s most liked and trusted officers. He was in the anti-Sioux operation of 1876 and saw the dead at Little Big Horn, his ms. about that campaign being published posthumously. He scouted out the Nez Perce camp at Big Hole. During the assault on the following morning, he was killed almost immediately.

Broken Tooth—*(Anglicized Nimiputumít.)* Formerly White Feather [In-Who-Lise], this beautiful eighteen-year-old got her new name at Big Hole thanks to a soldier's rifle-butt. Her father and sister were both killed. She escaped from Bear's Paw and later married Andrew Garcia, one of **Howard**'s men, who wrote *Tough Trip Through Paradise* about their idyll together, which was soon terminated (along with her life) by Blackfeet.

Bugler [Bernard] Brooks—Killed by Nez Perce at Camas Meadows.

Buck Antlers—*(Anglicized Nimiputumít.)* [Allahkoliken.] A warrior who defected to the Army on the first day of the Clearwater battle.

Buffalo Horn—*(Anglicized Bannock?)* A renowned **Bannock** warrior from Fort Hall who became one of **Howard**'s scouts, following the Nez Perce from Kamiah across the Lo Lo Trail and beyond. The following year he became one of Howard's principal adversaries in the Bannock War, in which he was fatally wounded. I have no reason to believe that he could actually have spoken English with Howard as he does in this novel.

Bunched Lightning—*(Anglicized Nimiputumít.)* [Heinmot Tosinlikt.] A half-breed who interpreted when the Nez Perces kidnapped a prospector in Yellowstone National Park. I have given him a more extended role than he probably had, making him interpret in other captivity situations, and conflated him with the half-breed Henry Tabadour aka Henry Rivers, who was probably but not certainly the same man. Loyal but vicious-tempered, he took an active part in the war, and died as described, in the Indian Territory in a drunken accident with his gun.

Burning Coals—*(Anglicized Nimiputumít.)* [Also called Blacktail Eagle.] An old man whose stingy refusal to lend his horses to the warriors on the day before the Big Hole battle might have saved the Nez Perce from being taken by surprise. His unnamed daughter was fatally wounded at Big Hole.

Brigadier General E. R. S. Canby—Like Howard, he removed the Seminoles and fought in the Civil War (the capture of Mobile laid to his credit). He was a well-meaning but inflexible (or powerless) negotiator in the Modoc War: The Modocs must go on the reservation no matter what. The Modocs murdered him during a truce parley on 11 April 1873. General Howard presently took over his command: the Department of the Columbia.

Ad Chapman—"A low-principled scoundrel, wedded after the tribal ritual to a Umatilla woman. Speaking the Nez Perce language fluently, he became General Howard's interpreter . . ."—L. V. McWhorter. But **Howard** wrote: "Ad Chapman is at once one of the most intelligent and bravest men in the command. He is generally acknowledged to be the best horseman in northern Idaho."

He and **Wood** are jointly responsible for the final form of **Chief Joseph**'s poetic surrender speech. Of course I can never know how he and **Perry** actually got on, but a newspaper article from 1877 remarks: "It is told us that among the people of the garrison, Perry is reported to have attributed his defeat at White Bird to the conduct of Chapman and his volunteers." The Nez Perce would have pronounced his name "Tsépmin."

Charging Hawk—*(Anglicized Nimiputumít.)* [Hekkik Takkawkaäkon.] **White Thunder**'s cousin. Mentioned in connection with the Canyon Creek fight.

Charley boy—See **Charles Howard**.

Charlot—*(Flathead.)* A Flathead [Salish] chief (*ca.* 1830–1910.) [Also: Charlo, Charlos, etc. His name meant "Small Grizzly Bear's Claw."] In 1877 he still refused to go on the reservation (although the future President Garfield helped forge his mark on a treaty to that effect), and the greater part of the Flathead nation stayed with him in his camp outside Stevensville, where he gave the non-treaty Nez Perces a cool welcome. He was forced onto the reservation in 1891.

Cloudburst—*(Anglicized Nimiputumít.)* [Wetatonmi.] **Ollokot**'s younger wife. She survived him, and the war, but some sources say that she had a child which did not live out that long conflict. In this novel she has no child of her own. Her maiden name was Tahmokalona. She fled Bear's Paw with **White Bird**'s band and presently returned to the U.S. At some point she remarried and became Mrs. Susie Convill, giving birth to at least one child.

Cochise—*(Apache.)* Chief of the Chiricahua band, in southeastern Arizona Territory. Wrongfully arrested by the U.S. Army in 1861, Cochise became a dangerous enemy of the settlers until General **Howard** persuaded him to come onto a reservation more or less of Cochise's choosing. After the chief's death, the U.S., breaking Howard's promise, decided to concentrate all the Apaches on one reservation. This precipitated another war.

Jay Cooke—A famously ruthless railroad financier. When his toy, the Northern Pacific Railroad, went suddenly bankrupt, this went far to cause the "Silver Panic" of 1873. Many reviled him; a few zealous "business men" thought the world of him.

General George Crook—An effective and enthusiastic Indian fighter, who subdued Paiutes, Apaches and others. The Crows called him "Three Stars." **Sherman** thought very highly of him. **Rutherford B. Hayes** was with him at the Civil War battle of Cloyd's Mountain; he considered him the best of generals. Crook was once **Perry**'s commanding officer. In 1877 he commanded the Department of the Platte. Since he was so close to President Hayes, **Howard** had reason to fear that Crook might replace him if he continued to be "General Day-After-Tomorrow" in his pursuit of the Nez Perces. The two men were antagonists for much of their careers. Howard thought him bloodthirsty, especially against the Apaches, while he thought Howard an interfering Christian namby-pamby. What was Crook actually? In his autobiography he wrote: "The trouble with the army was that the Indians would confide in us as friends, and we had to witness this unjust treatment of them without the power to help them. Then when they were pushed beyond endurance and would go on the war path we had to fight when our sympathies were with the Indians."

Lieutenant Colonel George Armstrong Custer—Our dead-victorious equivalent of the Serbian Prince Lazar (killed by the Turks in 1389). To the Sioux who killed him he was "Yellow Hair." The Crows called him "Son of the Morning Star." "He never acquired . . . the reputation either of **George Crook** or of **Nelson Miles,** the leading practitioners of plains warfare . . . In a different, truly colonial or imperial society, Custer might have gone on from the Civil War to greater things . . ."—John Keegan.

Richard Dietrich—See **Naked-Footed Bull**.

Doc—For his genesis, see **Blurick**. I have entirely invented him, based on that manuscript's charming one-liner. His presence in every battle, where no one could actually have been, proves him the counterpart of Argall in Dream 3, and his creatures (Blackie, Johnny and Georgie) are pretty d——d interchangeable.

Eagle That Shakes Himself—*(Anglicized Crow.)* A Crow chief who urged **Looking-Glass** to join a pan-Indian alliance with the Crows and Sioux against the Americans. The Sioux killed him.

Elder Deer—*(Anglicized Nimiputumít.)* [Wehmastahtus.] A friend of **White Thunder**'s whom the latter mentions in connection with the Clearwater fight.

Fair Land—*(Anglicized Nimiputumít.)* [Aih-its Pal-o-ja-mi.] Alternate meaning: "Of Fair Land." The elder of **Ollokot**'s two wives, who was mortally wounded at Big Hole, leaving behind a baby boy whom **Joseph** probably adopted.. The other wife was **Cloudburst**.

Feathers Around The Neck—*(Anglicized Nimiputumít.)* [Wap-tas-wa-hiekt, which possibly means "gives healing." Later called Frank Thompson.] A shaman involved in the unsuccessful curing ceremony for **Springtime**'s baby girl in May 1878. The infant died before 21 July.

Captain Stanton G. Fisher—This tall, very competent woodsman and an effective organizer of Indian scouts joined **Howard** just after Camas Meadows, bringing with him some Bannocks from **Crook**'s Department. He did not scruple to distract his softhearted commanding officer's attention when the Bannocks were killing and scalping the Nez Perces they found on the trail. A zealous relic collector.

Fire Body—*(Anglicized Nimiputumít.)* [Otstotpoo.] A brave warrior and excellent shot who killed Trumpeter **Jones** at White Bird Canyon and fought at the Clearwater battle.

Five Snows—*(Anglicized Nimiputumít.)* [Pahka Alyanakt.] After murdering some teamsters in the mountains south of Big Hole, the Nez Perces got drunk on the whiskey found in the wagons. Five Snows then injured **Stripes Turned In**, who was trying to dump out the whiskey. The latter died of his wounds. Five Snows was killed at Bear's Paw. His earlier activities at Clearwater are invented.

Five Wounds—*(Anglicized Nimiputumít.)* He and **Rainbow** were perhaps the most prominent young warriors and buffalo hunters. A war leader at Clearwater, where he was wounded in the hand. Killed in a suicide charge at Big Hole.

First Lieutenant Robert H. Fletcher—**Howard**'s aide-de-camp. This active member of the Twenty-first Infantry is credited by his general as first spying the Nez Perce village on the Clearwater, although other accounts dispute this. He drafted simple and not unbeautiful sketches of each battlefield for Howard's final report. His character in this book, his friendship for **Wood** and his nickname of "Fletch" have been invented.

First Lieutenant A. G. Forse—He supported **Colonel Winters** of "E" Company at the Clearwater battle, remaining on the skirmish line day and night until the final charge.

Geese Three Times Alighting On Water—*(Anglicized Nimiputumít.)* [Lahpeealoot.] The only one of **Joseph**'s warriors to participate in the Salmon River raids. He also fought the **Brave Seventeen** [G 2] at **Cottonwood** [G 3]. His later career is obscure, but I presume he lived out the war and possibly went to Lapwai since he was later called Philip Williams.

Colonel John Gibbon—This Civil War veteran commanded the military District of Montana. His **brevet** rank [G 2] was general. He was involved in the anti-Sioux operation of 1876, but obviously was not at Little Big Horn. He led the attack on the Nez Perce at Big Hole, where he was badly wounded. The Crows called him "The Limping One."

Good Woman—*(Anglicized Nimiputumít.)* [Aye-at-wai-at-naime, or perhaps Heyume-yoyikt, in which case her name would mean "Bear Crossing."] Conjectural name of **Joseph**'s elder wife, the mother of **Sound Of Running Feet**. [For Joseph's marriages, see the third source-note to "And the World Keeps Getting Wider and Wider."] She escaped from Bear's Paw to **Sitting Bull**'s camp and returned to Lapwai the next summer with **Peopeo Tholekt** and others. Sent to the Indian Territory, she finally separated from Joseph when he went to Nespelem, evidently preferring to stay at Lapwai with her daughter.

Tracy Gould—A prenuptial love interest of **Wood**'s first wife Nanny.

Grizzly Bear Youth—*(Anglicized Nimiputumít.)* [Transliteration not given.] Possibly the same as "Ugly Grizzly Bear Boy," who might or might not be identical with "Black Hair." Having scouted for **Miles** in northern Montana, this brave then returned to the Bitterroot Valley, where he met the fleeing Nez Perces. His counsel to go straight north to **Sitting Bull** was ignored, but he accompanied the tribe anyway, fighting at Big Hole, where he was wounded, at which juncture "Red Owl's son" (possibly **Over The Point**) saved his life. He later dreamed about raiding **Howard** at Camas Meadows, and this dream was acted on under the half-resurrected leadership of **Looking-Glass**.

Hair Cut Upward—*(Anglicized Nimiputumít.)* [Witslahtahpalakin.] A warrior who fought alongside the **Three Red Blankets** at Clearwater.

Hair Cut Short—*(Anglicized Nimiputumít.)* [Alikkees, whose Christian name was Alec Hayes.] A well-reputed warrior who defected to the Army at Clearwater.

President Rutherford B. Hayes—The *New York Sun*, 1876: "He is a candidate whose weakness and unimportance are his principal recommendations to the Republican party." Mark Twain called his accession "one of the Republican party's most cold-blooded swindles of the American people . . . I was an ardent Hayes man, but that was natural, for I was pretty young at the time." While Hayes very likely did steal the election of 1876, he was no worse than his Democratic opponent Tilden, and perhaps a trifle better. He did veto Chinese exclusion, and once remarked in an address to Congress: "Many, if not most of our Indian wars have had their origin in broken promises and acts of injustice upon our part . . ." All the same, he approved the removal of the non-treaty Nez Perces. In my opinion, his worst act as President was to "compromise" by withdrawing Federal troops from the South, thereby permitting racist legislatures to undo most of Emancipation. But before that, when he was Governor of Ohio, Hayes helped pass the Fifteenth Amendment, which gave black men the right to vote; so he was not all bad. "In his honesty and high sense of duty Rutherford Birchard Hayes belonged more to the period of his Connecticut and Vermont forebears than to the generation over which he now presided. But in other respects he suited his own times . . ."—Robert V. Bruce.

Heinmot Tooyalakekt—See **Chief Joseph**.

Helping Another—*(Anglicized Nimiputumít.)* [Penahwenonmi.] The wife of **Wounded Head**. She and her young son were both injured at Big Hole, the child fatally.

Horse Rider—*(Anglicized Crow.)* Thomas Leforge, a Caucasian "squaw man" who came to consider himself a Crow. In his memoirs he claims to be an acquaintance of **Looking-Glass's**, so I have imagined that Looking-Glass actually did turn to him among others.

Charles Howard—Called "Charley boy." **Oliver Otis Howard's** brother, and one of his aides-de-camp during the Civil War. Brevetted brigadier general of volunteers. Helped Otis establish Freedmen's Bureau schools. Later became western secretary of the American Missionary Association, after which edited the *Chicago Advance*.

Lieutenant Guy Howard—Son of **Oliver Otis Howard**, and his aide-de-camp from Kamiah to the end of the Nez Perce campaign. In Howard's autobiography I seem to read (as one might expect) a great proud grief behind the soldierly reticence with which he describes Guy's death in the Philippine campaign (1899 or 1900). From this and other indications (see Chronology entry for 1855), I have imagined their relationship as especially close. Some of Guy's campaign sketches were published by the army. They are mediocre whereas **Wood's** are sensitive. In the Grace Howard scrapbook at the Oregon Historical Society, there is a sketch of Guy's which depicts **Toohhoolhoolzote** threatening his father at the fateful council at Lapwai, when of course matters took the opposite turn. Guy (who was not present at the council) portrays Toohhoolhoolzote as a generic Indian. I have envisioned Guy as more tone deaf to the Indians' grievances than his father. Since both he and Wood were aides-de-camp, and Wood must have had more intellectual and artistic talent—and, moreover, Wood turned against the military, while Guy stayed in it until he was killed—it seems not implausible that those two young men, both competing for the general's attention, disliked each other.

Brigadier General Oliver Otis Howard—Called "Otis" by his wife and brothers, and by the Nez Perce "Cut Arm" ["A-timkí-wnin," literally "arm cut"] and "A-tim," which means "armless." (Occasionally they also called him "Sleeveless" or "People Herder," the latter being my hopefully improved version of what has been translated as "the Indian Herder.") Accounts of the Nez Perce War tend to depict him as (*a*) a bigoted blusterer who (as he most certainly did) derailed the Lapwai conference by arresting **Toohhoolhoolzote**, and (*b*) a semi-relevant buffoon who never could have caught **Joseph** on his own. Here is one military historian's assessment of his latter aspect: "Howard was a world-class military incompetent, often inclined to lie or shift blame for his failures . . . He had no head for a war of maneuver. He consistently failed to understand either the terrain or the enemy and drove his long-suffering troops as if they were a pack of mules." That such dispraise was by no means universally expressed we can see in the following *New York Times* dispatch relating to the disgrace of his Eleventh Corps at Chancellorsville: "General How-ARD, with all his daring and resolution and vigor, could not stem the tide of the retreating and cowardly poltroons." In 1963 one historian wrote: "Howard's conduct of the Nez Perce war was probably the best one possible." As to the former side of Howard, a sympathetic biographer remarks: "His basic thesis that it was possible to maintain peace with the Indians was fundamentally sound" (this I consider absurd), "but even he knew that because of distrust and misunderstanding on both sides and because of the selfishness of some white men, there would continue to be trouble as long as the Indians could carry on a separate, semi-dependent existence. Hence he became an advocate of as rapid assimilation as possible . . ." I myself find much to admire and compassionate in this man, who paid a significant price for his kindness to oppressed people. Many of the blunders laid at his door in the Nez Perce campaign were made by trigger-happy, undisciplined **volunteers** [G 2], subordinates such as **Perry**, and panicked civilians who demanded his protection, which he gave, after which they blamed him for not chasing the enemy more effectively. This cannot excuse his part in the unjust war against the Nez Perces, and his vindictiveness toward Joseph after the surrender; nor does the fact that had he recused himself from it, the outcome would have been no better. For discussion of how I constructed his character, see the note "Howard's personality" in the source-citations to the chapter "Their Hearts Have Changed." For consideration of his views on African Americans, see the note on the chapter "Washington, D.C." in the source-citations to the "Edisto" section.

Rowland Bailey Howard—**Otis Howard**'s brother; a minor character.

Húsus Kute—*(Palouse.)* [Also: Húsishúsis Kute. Howard called him "Hushush Cute."] His name means "Bald Head"; he so named himself when a cannonball took off some of his hair in the Cayuse War. He spoke for the **Palouse** [G 2] [see also **Nez Perce**, G 2] at the fateful Lapwai council, although the real chief was Hahtalekin. At Bear's Paw he managed to kill three warriors by mistake, including Lone Bird. He survived the war and was sent to the Indian Territory with Joseph.

In-Who-Lise—See **Broken Tooth**.

Captain Jack—*(Anglicized appellation, obviously.)* The Modoc chief Kintpuash, who fought impressively against the U.S. Army in 1872 in vain defense of his people's homeland, the lava beds around Lost River, California. Having been the victim of American intimidation and dishonesty, he was persuaded to murder **General Canby** under flag of truce. Among his opponents in the cavalry were **Perry**, **Theller** and **Mason**. He was eventually worn down, captured, sentenced and hanged.

Joakis—See **Captain John**.

Captain Stephen Jocelyn—He led Company "B," Twenty-first Infantry, beginning when **Howard** took the field after the Battle of White Bird Canyon. Although some officers were certainly hostile to this general, I have no evidence that Jocelyn was in fact one of them; in this novel I have made him so. He fought bravely at the Clearwater.

Captain John—*(Anglicized appellation.)* [Joakis or Tsoka-y, meaning "Relaxed."] A Christian Nez Perce. He and Old George [Meopokit] served as **Howard**'s scouts from Kamiah all the way to

Bear's Paw; they may have set out with Howard even earlier. These were the only two Indian scouts to go so far. Since each one "had a daughter with the hostiles," they were considered good truce intermediaries at the last battle. How their own people perceived them is debatable. The Nez Perces might have pronounced "Captain John" as *Kaptin Tsán,* and "Old George" as *Ol Tsolts.*

Bugler Jones—[Jonesey.] A drunk who struck up an unlikely friendship with **Toohhoolhoolzote** when the latter was confined by **Howard** at Lapwai. Killed at White Bird Canyon by **Fire Body**.

Chief Joseph—*(Anglicized appellation, obviously.)* [Heinmot Tooyalakekt, "Thunder Travelling to Loftier Heights."] The missionary Kate McBeth translated his name "The Sound Of Thunder Coming Up From Water," which McWhorter rejects "since no syllable of it appears to denote water." However, Aoki's dictionary has "Hinmató-wyalahtq[']it" (absolutive case), meaning "As One Travels Out Of The Water." A contemporary newspaper gave his name as "In-mut-too-yah-lat-lat."] His boyhood baptismal name was Ephraim. "He has been called the 'Indian Napo-leon.' . . . Chief Joseph was by nature destined to be the leader of his people in their futile struggle against the encroachments of the whites." In fact he seems to have been less the general and more the advocate, diplomat and caregiver. For information on Joseph's wives and children, see the third source-note to "And the World Keeps Getting Wider and Wider."

Old Joseph—*(Anglicized.)* **Joseph**'s father, whose real name was Wellammoutkin—a reference to braided hair tied in a bun at the forehead in testimony of great knowledge. His final name might have been Tuekalas or Tewetekas. [Aoki gives his name as Tiwí-teqis, or Senior Warrior.] For a time he lived near the whites. The missionary Marcus Whitman wrote of him that "Joseph one of the two oldest Members distinguished himself for his discretion & Christian zeal." He even permitted Young Joseph to be baptized. After the infamous *thief treaty* of 1863, Old Joseph rejected Christian teachings (some say he tore up both his Bible and his copy of the treaty of 1855), and withdrew to the area by Wallowa. He caused boundary posts to be erected all around the Wallowa territory; these of course were disregarded by the Americans. He was lucky enough to die before the Nez Perce War.

Kate—*(American name.)* **White Bird**'s wife. If he had only one (which I don't know for sure), then she must have been the woman called Hiyom Tiyatecht. She escaped with him to Canada.

Kapoochas—*(Nimiputumít.)* [Kapochas.] A sick or wounded old shaman left behind by the Nez Perces at what is now accordingly called Dead Indian Campground, Montana, because one of **Captain Fisher**'s Bannock or Cheyenne scouts shot him. He might or might not have been the shaman Kah-pots who was wounded at Big Hole, then quickly finished off by the Bannocks.

Kaptin Tsán—See **Captain John**.

Kulkulsuitim—*(Nimiputumít.)* A peace emissary, possibly duplicitous, from the non-treaty Nez Perces at Kamiah after the Clearwater battle. His parley made poor **Howard** believe in **Joseph**'s imminent surrender.

James Lawyer—*(Anglicized Nimiputumít.)* [Hallalhotsoot or Hahlalhotoost.] This chief signed the treaties of 1855 and 1863. Therefore, according to Alvin Josephy, he "presided over the destruc-tion of the cultural pride, dignity, and heritage of large numbers of Nez Perces, and . . . robbed them of their self-respect as humans." But his fellow "treaty Nez Perces" tended to opine that he had done the best that he could.

Lean Elk—*(Anglicized Nimiputumít.)* [Wahwookya Wasanaw (or Wasaäw).] Also known as "Poker Joe" [Hototo] or "Little Tobacco," this half-breed Nez Perce (he was partly French) lived near Corvallis (to the south of Missoula). Following the **Fort Fizzle** affair [G 3], he joined his countrymen in their war against the United States, becoming head-chief after **Looking-Glass**'s disgrace at Big Hole. As the Nez Perce approached Bear's Paw, he was deposed in favor of his rival. Had the Nez Perce followed his advice over Looking-Glass's, they might well have reached safety in Canada—not that that would have saved them. He "owned fast race horses and was clever in other sports and games." Killed at Bear's Paw.

Left Hand—*(Anglicized Flathead?)* A Salish chief on whose land the fleeing Nez Perces held a council the night after they broke out of Fort Fizzle. His unenthusiastic hospitality encouraged them on their way.

Lemonade Lucy—The teetotaling First Lady. One contemporary account called Lucy **Hayes** as "jolly as a plain country girl."

Lightning-Struck—*(Anglicized Nimiputumít.)* [Tomyunmene.] A brave warrior who fought at the Clearwater. He seldom appears in the records.

Lone Bird—*(Anglicized Nimiputumít.)* While in the Bitterroot Valley this young man uttered one of several unheeded warnings that the Americans might not respect the "treaty" of Fort Fizzle. He was accidentally killed at Bear's Paw by **Húsus Kute**.

Loon—*(Anglicized Nimiputumít.)* A man's name taken from Aoki's dictionary. Since the primary source documents decline to specify which young men were "cowards" at Clearwater, I have invented two such characters. (The other is **No Swan**.)

Looking-Glass—*(Anglicized Nimiputumít.)* Called "Arrowhead" by the Crows and "Allalimya Takanin" or "Flint Necklace" by his own. [This was also his father's name, and his grandfather's, although the latter was called We-ark-koomt by Lewis and Clark.] To the Flatheads he was Big Hawk. He was also known as "Black Swan" and "Wind-Wrapped." His eponymous mirror is variously described as being worn around his neck or fastened to his hair, so I have had him mix it up. McWhorter calls his leadership "unduly praised"; it "proved the utter undoing of the patriots, assuring for all time the silent, undying hatred of the war party for the very memory of this leader's name." This may be. But he if anyone was a true victim of the war, having first obediently trundled off to his reservation, which **Howard** treacherously violated, then trusted to the apparent friendship of the Montanans who repaid his forbearance toward them in the Bitterroot Valley with the Big Hole massacre. He led the mule-stealing raid at Camas Meadows with considerable success. Of course the Indians' surprise at **Miles**'s attack at Bear's Paw must be blamed mostly on Looking-Glass. The names of his wives, Blackberry Person and Asking Maiden, are both invented (taken from women's names in Aoki's dictionary). Their real names were transcribed as Wa-win-te-pi-ksat [or Wa-win-te-pe-tal-e-ka-sat] and I-a-tu-ton-my [or I-a-to-we-non-my]. These cannot be found in Aoki's dictionary, so I have tried to at least give the reader two vivid and accurate female names. Given his success against them in war, Looking-Glass would not have been a favorite with the Sioux, and it is easy to see why he kept arguing against taking refuge with Sitting Bull. His death at Bear's Paw might therefore have facilitated Sioux compassion for the Nez Perce refugees.

Mrs. Jeanette Manuel—[Also: "Jenett."] One of the victims of the Nez Perce raids which opened the war. Her corpse was never found. According to **Peopeo Tholekt**, she was carried eastward with the Indians on their flight and died (or was killed) on the Lo Lo Trail. Her daughter Maggie swore an oath that she was murdered before her eyes at their home, but no skeleton was found in the ashes of the cabin. **Ad Chapman** claimed that **Joseph** stabbed her in the breast. Mc-Whorter writes: "This imputation of a crime of which he was wholly innocent, darkened Chief Joseph's entire life."

Many Coyotes—*(Anglicized Nimiputumít.)* [Ityiyi Pawettes.] A companion of **Peopeo Tholekt** at Clearwater, who spotted the Army and rode down to camp to give the alarm.

Major Edwin C. Mason—Twenty-first Cavalry. Led two companies in the Modoc War. **Howard**'s chief of staff in the Nez Perce War. In *Nez Perce Joseph*, Howard calls him "Colonel Mason," which was his actual rank at retirement; major was his **brevet** rank [see G 6]; in 1877 he was a captain. He was commended for bravery against the Modoc War (although in that campaign he evinced timidity bordering on disobedience of orders) and commended again in the Clearwater battle. His letters home are one source for this novel.

Sergeant Michael McCarthy—The sole escapee from White Bird Canyon. I had expected to expand upon his story here; it would make a fine novella.

Colonel McConville—A leader of civilian volunteers, and later a firm enemy of **Perry**'s as a result of the Cottonwood affair.

Mean Man—*(Anglicized Nimiputumít.)* [Howwalits.] A brave warrior at Clearwater.

Meopokit—See **Captain John**.

Major Merrill—Seventh Cavalry. A cipher.

Captain Marcus P. Miller—Fourth Artillery. He graduated West Point in 1858, serving in the Civil War, and also in the Modoc campaign, which means that he must have been well known to **Perry**. Brave and calm. Accompanied **Howard** on much of the Nez Perce Trail; distinguished himself at Clearwater.

General Nelson A. Miles—Technically he was a colonel during the Nez Perce War, but he was a leader, hence in contemporary speech a general, which he indeed became. **Howard**'s aide-de-camp at Fair Oaks, and, so far as the latter knew, his friend. He had risen to **Brevet** Major General of Volunteers [G 2] at the end of the Civil War, and then was assigned to be CSA President Jefferson Davis's over-jailer. Afterward he became a colonel in the regular army and married **Sherman**'s niece. Veteran of the Red River War (1874–75) and Great Sioux War (1876–77). In September 1877 he was placed in command of the new District of Yellowstone. The Indians often called him "Bear Coat." A very brave and effective officer, who plausibly if unfeelingly considered himself the main victor of the Nez Perce War. Served in the Bannock War (1878) and Chiricahua Apache War (1886). The Wounded Knee Massacre at Pine Ridge happened on his watch ("Sioux operations," 1890–91); he tried and failed to get the responsible officer punished. He was commanding general of the U.S. Army in 1895. "Nelson Miles was a poorly educated, extraordinarily vain man who exasperated each and every one of his superiors." To his credit, he tried to intervene on behalf of the Nez Perces during their exile in the Indian Territory; and their eventual repatriation had something to do with him. In comparison, Howard's postwar callousness toward **Joseph** is shocking.

John B. Monteith—The Indian Agent at Lapwai from 1877. A bullying proselytizer. The Indian sobriquet "Moss Beard" I have invented for him, after the style of "Cut Arm." I'm sure the Nez Perces had a pretty good name for him. After he died, his brother Charles succeeded to the post. The Nez Perce might have pronounced his last name *Montís*.

Major Lee Moorhouse—An Indian Agent turned trader. He worked on the Umatilla reservation and died in 1926. Some people claim he had a habit of attributing others' photographs to himself, a fitting trait for the robberies chronicled in this novel. How much Moorhouse actually stole is beyond my ken. In the Source-Notes I have faithfully indicated which images are genuinely captioned as his, and which I have stuck his name on, with an ever mounting pride in absurdity. A portrait shows him nicely buttoned up, with the light shining tall and narrow on his dark top hat, his pale narrow-chinned face and his well-trimmed dark moustache.

Naked-Footed Bull—*(Anglicized Nimiputumít.)* A warrior whose sister and three younger brothers (since I do not know their names I have invented them) were all killed at Big Hole. Embittered, Naked-Footed Bull later murdered or helped to murder the music teacher Richard Dietrich in Yellowstone National Park.

No Heart—*(Anglicized Nimiputumít.)* [Teminisiki.] **White Thunder**'s cousin, who warmed a young woman in a rifle-pit during the night of the Clearwater battle, and meanwhile fought bravely. White Thunder implies that the interlude with the woman may have violated a **WYAKIN** (G 2) taboo. No Heart was killed at Big Hole.

No Swan—*(Anglicized Nimiputumít.)* See **Loon**.

Sean "Red" O'Donnell—This whiskey-smuggling mule driver is both fictional and plausible.

Ol Tsolts—Old George. See **Captain John**.

Old George—See **Captain John**.

Old Joseph—*(Nimiputumít.)* Look under Old **Joseph**.

Ollokot—*(Cayuse.)* ["The Frog."] [**Howard** writes his name as "Ollicut." Another variant: "Alo-kut."] Before this he was called Tewetakis, whose meaning remains unknown. Meanwhile, Aoki writes his name "Álokat. Young mountain ram . . . McDermott's etymology, frog, for this name may be on the basis of a Sahaptin word." Evidently one of the main war-chiefs, and certainly more effective and prestigious on the battlefield than his brother **Joseph**. An appealing, energetic, handsome man in his prime. The names of his two wives are not invented. He was killed at Bear's Paw.

Lieutenant Otis—Fourth Artillery. A disappointment to **Howard** at Clearwater, he probably did the best he could with heavy guns on horrible terrain.

Larry Ott—See **Shore Crossing**.

Place Of Arrival—*(Anglicized Nimiputumít.)* **Toohhoolhoolzote**'s younger wife (invented by WTV; name taken from Aoki's dictionary).

Over The Point—*(Anglicized Nimiputumít.)* [Teeweeyownah.] Also: "Over The Hill Point." Son of **Red Heart**. One of the older war leaders of **White Bird**'s band (so perhaps he was in his thir-ties? His parents were still alive). At the Clearwater battle he called for a continuation and an escalation of the battle, but was refused by "cowards." He took part in the Camas Meadows raid, and was the only warrior killed (as it happened, by Crows) in the aftermath of Cañon Creek.

First Lieutenant William R. Parnell—This British Lancer, a survivor of the Charge of the Six Hundred at Balaclava, fought in the American Civil War, then enlisted with the First Cavalry and fought the Paiutes with Crook. He was second-in-command to **Trimble** at White Bird Canyon and beyond.

Peopeo Tholekt—*(Nimiputumít.)* [Chief George, Peo-peo-tah-likt, Piyopyo Talikt.] His name means "Bird Alighting," or "Landing Crane." [In Aoki's dictionary the "general word" for bird is "payó-payo," while "piyó-piyo" refers to a now extinct "crane-like bird," this latter being the relevant part of Peopeo Tholekt's name, as well as **White Bird**'s. Since "White Bird" is a well-established English equivalent for the latter chief, I thought it best not to change his name to White Crane. For consistency I followed the same policy with Peopeo Tholekt.] A prominent warrior in the **Looking-Glass** band. He is said to have parleyed on Looking-Glass's behalf with **Captain Whipple** before the latter's volunteers fired into the camp. He fought in all the war's battles, endured exile in the Indian Territory and survived into the 1930s. His beautiful drawings of the Nez Perce War and several transcripts of his recollections are now in the Holland Library in Pullman, Washington.

Colonel David Perry—In fact he was, like **Trimble**, a captain, but had won the **brevet** [see G 2] for Indian fighting under General **Crook**. This imposingly tall Civil War veteran (he was more than six feet) generalled both First Cavalry units, his own Company "F" and Trimble's Company "H," during the Battle of White Bird Canyon. Defeated there, and then overcome by indecision at Cottonwood when the **Brave Seventeen** [G 2] were attacked, and finally dilatory during the final assaut at Clearwater, he must have disappointed **Howard**. (**Wood** claims that at Clearwater, Perry's cavalry remained so demoralized from White Bird Canyon that "they returned after a few puffs from **Joseph**'s rear-guard. I forget Perry's excuse, but he was reprimanded on the spot by Howard . . .") He had served with **Crook** and (with **Theller**) in the Modoc War, where he was seriously wounded. There is no reason to suppose that he possessed the haunted, ruthless soul I have attributed to him, and no reason not to. His marital difficulties are invented, but in real life Mrs. Perry was notorious for her anxious disposition. Because Howard subdivided his command, Perry, like so many other characters in this novel, actually departed center stage once Joseph's pursuers set out on the **Lo Lo Trail** [G 3]. [In this Dream I made, after much hesitation, a decision to deviate from the historical truth in Perry's case, and in the case of several other Army men.

Without my so doing, Howard's troops would have been even more monotonously "beautiful and almost automatic" than they really were.] The shock and horror of the defeat at **White Bird Canyon** [G 3] must have been extreme for the surviving Bluecoats, just as the trauma of Big Hole must have followed the Nez Perces to the end. I wanted to enter into the mind of Perry, or someone I imagined to be like him, and portray that stress. The further anxiety he must have been feeling about the impending court of inquiry, and Howard's own uneasiness about the bad showing that had been made throughout the campaign—alloyed, no doubt, with the latter's paternalistic kindness—deserved to be dramatically worked out. The basic facts about Perry in his "Further History" chapter are accurate. The Nez Perce could have pronounced his name *Píli.*

Píli—See **Perry**.

Captain Robert Pollock—**Wood**'s commanding officer before he got promoted to aide-de-camp. He enlisted in 1844, fought in Mexico and was commended by Zachary Taylor. He became full colonel during the Secession War, a rank he of course lost in the postwar army. Promoted to captain in 1869. This brave, profane Indian fighter, who fathered many children and liked to prospect for gold, was at first, as he wrote in one of his many informative letters to his wife, a "favorite" of **Howard**'s (evidently he watched his language), but presently, when he could not conceal his disgust at the length and manner of the campaign, the general came to dislike him. During the Nez Perce War he was in charge of Company "D" of the Twenty-first Infantry. Retired in 1883.

Qapqapó-nmay—*(Nimiputumít.)* ["Strong Leader of Women."] **Chief Joseph**'s mother; **Old Joseph**'s wife. She died before 1877.

Rainbow—*(Anglicized Nimiputumít.)* [Wahchumyus.] A renowned buffalo hunter who returned to the Nimiipu after the Battle of White Bird Canyon. He is credited with the successful strategy of making **Howard** cross the Salmon twice. A war leader at Cottonwood and also at the Clearwater, he sought to keep the young warriors dug in against the U.S. Army at the latter place, but was unsuccessful. His **WYAKIN** [G 2] promised him immunity in battle, but only after sunrise. He was killed before dawn at Big Hole. The cameo appearances of his widow are my interpolation; as a renowned warrior and buffalo hunter he was probably married, but this is only a guess.

Second Lieutenant Sevier Rains—He overlapped with **Wood** at West Point, graduating two years later (1876). It was he who found **Theller**'s body. Killed by the Nez Perce in one of the three Cottonwood attacks which occurred before the Clearwater battle. Like **McCarthy**, he is someone who deserved to become a more major character.

Captain Darius Bullock Randall—A leader of the Mount Idaho volunteers. It seems that he had settled illegally on Nez Perce land. He led the "Brave Seventeen" out to escort a dispatch rider to Norton's ranch, and was soon killed, along with another volunteer, in the last of the Cottonwood attacks. **Perry** delayed in sending relief to the Brave Seventeen, for which he was accused of cowardice, but acquitted by a military tribunal.

Rattle Blanket—*(Anglicized Nimiputumít.)* A warrior who challenged **James Reuben** together with **Howard**'s other scouts as they prepared to avenge the defeat at White Bird Canyon and cross the Salmon River. He figures only rarely in the accounts.

Captain Charles Rawn—The commander of "A" Company, Seventh Infantry, and the Seventh's seniormost captain. He arrived in Missoula not long after the outbreak of the Nez Perce War and began to build a fort there. When the Nez Perce arrived in Montana, he set out with troops and volunteers to halt them, but they intimidated him into letting them pass unmolested. The affair became known as "Fort Fizzle." The Nez Perce for their part misinterpreted his action as a sort of peace treaty. Rawn was with **Gibbon** at the Battle of Big Hole.

Red Feather Of The Wing—*(Anglicized Nimiputumít.)* A boy who helped the warriors in battle by holding their horses and changing tired animals for fresh. I know little else about him.

Red Heart—*(Anglicized Nimiputumít.)* [Tememah Ilppilp.] A subchief of the **Looking-Glass**

band, he might have been in the Buffalo Country at the outset of the war, or then again he could have been present at **Whipple**'s attack. His two elder sons **Over The Point** and **Allutakanin** became radicalized and fought; the younger two [Tememah Ilppilp, named after the father, and Nenetsukusten], along with his wife and daughter, surrendered to **Howard** shortly after the Clearwater battle, and were cruelly imprisoned. The band was kept at Fort Vancouver until April 1878, and finally brought back to Lapwai by Federal order.

Red Moccasin Tops—*(Anglicized Nimiputumít.)* [Sarpsis Ilppilp.] One of the three who began the Nez Perce War by murdering white settlers. See **Shore Crossing**. A member of the **Three Red Blankets** [G 2]. Killed at Big Hole.

Red Owl—*(Anglicized Nimiputumít.)* [Koolkool Sneehee.] This half-brother of a certain **War Singer**, who was half Flathead, has been described as a "sub-chief" of **Looking-Glass**'s band. Red Owl was on his reservation after **Howard** attacked Looking-Glass, who came to him for food and shelter. After the other non-treaties converged here, the Battle of the Clearwater began. In the Bitterroot Valley, Red Owl spoke in favor of going north, but was outvoted by Looking-Glass and others. Wounded or killed at Bear's Paw.

Red Spy—*(Anglicized Nimiputumít.)* [Seeyakoon Ilppilp.] A very cunning and active warrior. After the Nez Perces had led **Howard** over the Salmon River and back, Red Spy killed the young scout Charles Blewett, thereby luring out **Rains**'s detachment. He may have been part of the ambush of **Mason**'s scouts at Weippe. At Big Hole he and **Red Moccasin Tops** unsuccessfully petitioned **Burning Coals** to lend them horses in order to scout back on the trail. Had they been successful, the slaughter at the hands of **Gibbon** might have been averted. Some of Red Spy's later doings in this book, while plausible, are invented, but he was indeed killed by enemy Native Americans en route to the Medicine Line.

John W. Redington—A very young (around fifteen), very brave and brash thrill-seeker who departed Salem, Oregon, for Mexico but lost track of his companions en route, so he went to Salt Lake, where he heard of the Nez Perce War, then rushed back to Idaho, serving under Captain **Fisher** as one of **Howard**'s scouts. He joined the campaign not long after Big Hole, and continued nearly to the end, serving under Howard in the Bannock War of the following year. His letters and the memoir he wrote, "Scouting in Montana," are vivid, amusing and quite racist; he showed little sympathy for the Nez Perces. His middle name was "Watermelon."

James Reuben—A Christian "treaty Nez Perce" who scouted for the cavalry during the war. "Widely disliked." His original name was Tip-ia-la-na-te-skin ("Eagle Which Speaks All"). His wife Elawitnonmi was **Old Joseph**'s daughter. At the ambush at Weippe, a rearguard of the re-treating Nez Perce wounded him in the arm, after which he was sent back to Lapwai. Following the surrender he went to the Indian Territory to replace **Chapman** as interpreter, and to teach and proselytize the exiled non-treaties. The Nez Perce might have pronounced his name *Tsams Lúpin.*

Roaring Eagle—*(Anglicized Nimiputumít.)* [Tipyahlahmah Elassanin.] One of the warriors who nearly captured the Army's pack train at Clearwater.

Tom Robinson—He taught me a lot about cameras and printing, and I acknowledge him in several books. Here he appears as a semi-fictional character, on account of his lore concerning Indian negatives at the Oregon Historical Society.

Major George M. Shearer—A leader of volunteers at Mount Idaho during the Nez Perce War. Probable ally of **Ad Chapman**. The events at Cottonwood made him **Perry**'s enemy. His rank derived from the Confederate Army. **Howard**'s communications to him in *The Dying Grass* are indebted to true originals (see the Source-Notes). His memory of meeting a neighbor's runaway slave in a Civil War battle is my invention. Near the beginning of the war he brutally crushed in a wounded Indian's head.

General Phil Sheridan—As **Howard** would say, an energetic officer. In March 1856, when only a lieutenant, he disembarked his subordinate killers from the steamer *Fashion* and marched on the Indians at Middle Cascades, conquered at Bradford's Island, and hanged Old Chenoweth, Tecomoec, Captain Joe, Tsy, Sim Lasselas, Four-Fingered Johnny, Jim, Tumalth and Old Skein. He fought bravely in the Civil War and kept rising. He had supreme command in 1868–69 in the campaign against the Kiowas, Arapahoes, Cheyennes, Comanches and Apaches. In 1877 he commanded the Division of the Missouri [G 2, **military divisional organization**]. I am impressed by his wrinkled, shadowed cheeks and bitter eyes. He had an angry meager look, a high forehead and low thick brows; he could have been a policeman in some small French town.

General William T. Sherman—In 1877 he was the commanding general of the U.S. Army. A ruthless, racist, angry strategic genius (and a surprisingly gifted writer), he was **Howard**'s mentor and idol. To Sherman the Indian wars were an inglorious sideshow. He sometimes advocated, although did not put into practice, extermination for such determined enemy tribes as the Sioux. But he said much the same about Secessionists. He frequently spoke of "dispossessing" Southerners, and once wrote: "The whole people of Iowa & Wisconsin should be transported at once to West Kentucky, Tennessee & Mississippi, and a few hundred thousand settlers should be pushed into South Tennessee." He gloried in the notion of a businessman's America, and if he lived today might be running some multinational corporation.

Shooting Thunder—*(Anglicized Nimiputumít.)* [Yettahtapnat Alwum.] The warrior who killed **Richard Dietrich**. The primary sources give him very little mention, so most of his doings in this novel (and his disappearance) are invented.

Shore Crossing—*(Anglicized Nimiputumít.)* [Wahlitits.] Also: "Crossing," or "Springtime River Ice Strong Enough To Be Crossed," or "Crossing In Spring Along The Ice." McWhorter calls him "an athlete with the trim faultless form of an Apollo." The son of Chief Tipyahlanah Siskan ["Eagle Robe"], who gave land to a settler named Larry Ott. When Ott took more land without asking for it, Tipyahlanah Siskan attempted to stop him from plowing it, at which point he killed the chief with his six-shooter. Shore Crossing was accordingly incited (by and with at least two others: **Red Moccasin Tops** and **Swan Necklace**) into killing whites in 1877, precipitating the Nez Perce War. He then became one of the **Three Red Blankets** [G 2]. He fought well at White Bird Canyon and Clearwater, and died at Big Hole.

Dan Sickles—Another one-legged war hero (who truly did donate the amputated part to a museum). He helped pull the strings so that **Hayes** became President. It would be slander to say that he managed to put his mistress's boyfriend out of the way.

Sitka Khwan—*(Anglicized "Esquimau," as Wood might have put it. [Exact language unknown].)* Conjectural name of **Wood**'s Alaskan Inuk paramour.

Sitting Bull—*(Anglicized Sioux.)* Once his proposal for a pan-Indian uprising against the whites was rejected by the Nez Perces, this former enemy nonetheless took them in after Bear's Paw. His career touches theirs only briefly in this book, which cannot do justice to him. In 1878 a *Chicago Times* correspondent described him as bow-legged and limping, with a hooked nose and wide jaws.

Captain Joseph Alton Sladen—**Howard**'s adjutant during the Nez Perce War, who was also with him at Chancellorsville. He had served him closely and bravely during the capture of **Cochise**. Between then and 1877 he lost a leg after a riding accident. He served Howard in the Bannock War and kept him company until 1885—twenty-two years in all. His Nez Perce adventures in this book are almost entirely fictional, but I wanted to keep him with Howard for as long as possible. He adored his commander, and said of him: "His enthusiastic confidence in the ultimate outcome of his mission, and his ultimate faith in God's personal providence, made him brush away every obstacle as though it was a cob-web in his path."

Smohalla—*(Wanampum.)* [Also, as **Howard** writes it: "Smohallie."] An influential practitioner of the **Dreamer** religion [see G 2], which had much to do with the Ghost Dance (horrifically suppressed at Wounded Knee), this man resisted General Howard's machinations to put him on a reservation. "He is not a chief . . . but a *yantcha*, a leader and spiritual adviser." Howard first met him at **Wallula** [G 3], and described him thus: "He was the strangest-looking human being I had ever seen. His body was short and shapeless, with high shoulders and hunched back; scarcely any neck; bandy legs, rather long for his body; but a wonderful head, finely formed and large. His eyes, wide open, were clear, and so expressive that they gave him great power over all the Indians that flocked to his village." Since the Dreamers resisted removal from their nomadic lives, the whites called the roaming bands affiliated with him and certain other shamans the "River Renegades." Many non-treaty Nez Perces respected him and followed his teachings. He died blind and almost isolated but not defeated.

Sound Of Running Feet—*(Anglicized Nimiputumít.)* [Whepwhepomni, Hophop Omni or Kap-kap Pomni.] The only child of **Chief Joseph** who survived infancy. She would have been eleven or twelve in 1877. Her mother was **Good Woman**. After Bear's Paw she escaped to Canada (where one account calls her Jean-Louise), and eventually returned to Lapwai with her mother. Her father was never allowed to see her again. In 1879 she married a Nez Perce on the reservation named George Moses (he surely must have been Christian) and took the Christian name Sarah.

Captain W. F. Spurgin—Twenty-first Infantry. He commanded a company of engineers who proved especially helpful when pursuing the Nez Perce through the tracklessness of Yellowstone National Park.

Springtime—*(Anglicized Nimiputumít.)* [Conjectural meaning of "Toma Alwawinmi" or "Tom-ma-al-wa-win-mai."] "This definition is questioned by a Nez Perce interpreter of considerable ability." Younger wife of **Chief Joseph**. Wounded at Big Hole. Unlike **Good Woman**, she surrendered with Joseph at Bear's Paw. After her baby girl died in the Indian Territory, she divorced Joseph, and **James Reuben** renamed her "Magdellenia."

Stripes Turned In—*(Anglicized Nimiputumít.)* [Ketalkpoosmin.] A brave warrior who helped capture the howitzer at Big Hole. Killed a few days later by **Five Snows** in a drunken fight subsequent to the murder of some white packers. His earlier activities at Clearwater are invented.

Strong Eagle—*(Anglicized Nimiputumít.)* [Tipyahlahnah Kapskaps.] **White Bird**'s stepson. The last of the **Three Red Blankets** [G 2] to die. Wounded in the hip when he rescued **Red Moccasin Tops**'s body. Killed by the Assiniboines after Bear's Paw.

Colonel Samuel Sturgis—Seventh Cavalry. An unlucky mediocrity, who was slightly older than **Howard**. He was unsuccessful in both the Civil and Mexican wars. In 1869 he became **Custer**'s commanding officer in the Seventh. His son died at Little Big Horn. **Miles** dispatched him to help capture the Nez Perces as they emerged from Yellowstone; the Indians tricked him and escaped. He fought in the Battle of Canyon Creek without success; after that his command was effectively worthless. Staying in service for a brief while after the Nez Perce War, he rose to lieutenant colonel. "Colonel Sturgis displayed energy and determination" during the Nez Perce War. "Perhaps he erred in being overly eager to intercept the Indians."

Sun Tied—*(Anglicized Nimiputumít.)* [Weyatanatoo Lapat.] His wife, her midwife (his sister) and the newborn child were all killed by soldiers at Big Hole. In one account, Sun Tied fought back along with **White Thunder** and others. In another, he spent the day burying his family. His later brief appearances in the novel are inventions.

Swan Necklace—*(Anglicized Nimiputumít.)* [Um-til-lilp-cown. Also: Weyat-mas Wa-hakt.] One of the first three Salmon River raiders, but not one of the **Three Red Blankets** [G 2]. Accounts of the first raid vary. He might have been an instigator as I portray him, or he could have been the merest young horse-holder. His mother was **Shore Crossing**'s sister. He does not figure largely in the oral histories collected by McWhorter, so much of what he does in this novel is invented. He escaped from Bear's Paw to Canada, but was captured upon his return and sent to the Indian Territory.

Swan Woman—*(Anglicized Nimiputumít.)* [Yiyik Wasunwah.] **White Thunder**'s mother. She survived Bear's Paw.

Tendoy—*(Lemhi.)* "One of the great Lemhi chiefs of the mid-nineteenth century."—Robert and Yolanda Murphy. He was half Bannock and half Shoshoni. He refused the Nez Perces shelter as they fled Big Hole, and his people later scouted after them for the Army.

Mrs. Delia Theller—All I know about her is that she was **Edward**'s wife, and that she was overcome with disbelief and rage at his death. She removed to her parents after White Bird Canyon (and eventually got a job at the San Francisco Mint). I have imagined her as very attractive. Her marital unhappiness and Perry's interest in her are invented. Having assigned her childhood to a McKay stitching machine in 1862, I made her twenty-three in 1877.

First Lieutenant Edward R. Theller—**Perry**'s second-in-command at White Bird Canyon, and the highest-ranking soldier to die there. He had also served under Perry in the Modoc War. I have imagined, without knowing for a fact, that they were close friends.

Three Feathers—*(Anglicized Nimiputumít.)* A sub-chief of the **Looking-Glass** band, who was present at **Whipple**'s attack. Whether or not he fought at Clearwater is unknown to me. At Weippe he decided to surrender with "his small following" and rode to Kamiah, where he was promptly imprisoned.

Thunder Travelling To Loftier Heights—*(Anglicized Nimiputumít.)* [Heinmot Tooyalakekt.] Conjectural name of Young **Chief Joseph**.

Samuel Tilden—**Hayes**'s Democratic opponent. "The contemplation of Mr. Tilden's career will always repay the student of great disappointments . . . He had sharp, clerkly qualities, which would have been useful in a cheese-paring administration."

Tiwí-teqis—*(Nimiputumít.)* ["Senior Warrior."] A name for **Old Joseph**.

Toohhoolhoolzote—*(Nimiputumít.)* ["'Sound,' such as is produced by striking any vibrant metal or timber with a hard substance . . . probably a Flathead name." Aoki transliterates the name "Tukulkulcú-t" and writes that it means "antelope." Other renderings: Toohulhulsote, Toohhoohoolsote, T-whool-we-tzoot.] The leader of a non-treaty band in the Salmon River Mountains. Many non-Indian sources portray him as favoring war; McWhorter claims that he did not. General **Howard**'s arrest of him for speaking his mind at the Lapwai council undoubtedly contributed to the anger of the young men who began the war. This immensely strong and active old man was a war-chief at Clearwater. He died fighting at Bear's Paw. Howard thought him to be a shaman, but this might not have been true. His marital status is unknown to me, so I gave him two wives, Wolf Old Woman and Place Of Arrival.

Towhee—*(Anglicized Nimiputumít.)* Mother of **Helping Another**. Although in real life this woman did more or less as she does in *The Dying Grass*, her name is one I have lifted from Aoki's dictionary.

Captain Joel G. Trimble—Another veteran cavalryman. His company ("H," First Cavalry), with **Perry**'s, took part in the fiasco at White Bird Canyon. Trimble's second-in-command there was First Lieutenant William **Parnell**. Like Perry, Trimble had fought in the Civil War, and in the Modoc War; he was the one who took **Captain Jack**'s surrender. At Perry's court of inquiry, Trimble testified against him. His supposed default at Camas Meadows is entirely my invention; who was officer of the day on that occasion I never learned.

Tsams Lúpin—See **James Reuben**.

Tsépmin—See **Ad Chapman**.

Tso Alpít—See **Animal In A Hole**.

Two Moons—*(Anglicized Nimiputumít.)* [Lepeet Hessemdooks. His name might in fact have meant "Sun And Moon," or "Two Celestial Orbs."] A warrior in **Chief Joseph**'s band who first informed him of the Salmon River raids, fought at Big Hole and other battlefields, survived the war, and verified some of **White Thunder**'s narration to the historian L. V. McWhorter. He is not to be confused with a Cheyenne warrior of the same name, who makes a glancing appearance during the Bear's Paw battle, and briefly reappears in the Indian Territory.

Tuk-le-kas—*(Nimiputumít.)* A shaman mentioned in J. Diane Pearson's ***The Nez Perces in the Indian Territory*** [see G 4] as ringing the small bell for a funeral ceremony. After Big Hole he must have had plenty of work.

Tzi-kal-tza—*(Nimiputumít.)* Also called Halahtookit, which means "Daytime Smoke." A by-blow of William Clark's by Chief Red Grizzly Bear's sister, he was seventy-two in 1877. He survived the war and was deported to the Indian Territory, where he died.

Umatilla Jim—A U.S. Army scout, entirely invented. Some of his memories (a wife mixing salmon flour with huckleberries; a mother singing while digging roots) derive in part from a certain linguist's pattern sentences in the Umatilla Sahaptin dialect. The Nez Perce could have pronounced his American name something like *Tsím.*

War Singer—*(Anglicized Nimiputumít.)* One of L. V. McWhorter's informants.

Wahlitits—See **Shore Crossing**.

Wellammoutkin—*(Nimiputumít.)* One of the names of **Old Joseph**.

Well Behaved Maiden—*(Anglicized Nimiputumít.)* An invented character, standing in for other real people whose names we have lost. Wounded at Big Hole, she faded away and was left behind on the trail near Heart Mountain. I took her name from Aoki's dictionary.

Welweyas—*(Nimiputumít.)* "Coulee." A "half-man-half-woman" mentioned briefly in one of the oral histories. Most of her doings in *The Dying Grass* are my invention, as is her mother Agate Woman. [Although I use female pronouns for Welweyas, McWhorter notes that "the gender" of the word "is neutral, neither masculine nor feminine."] Apparently she always wore female dress. Deward E. Walker, Jr.: "Transvestites were sometimes seen but not typically taken as second wives." She was with the party who were away from camp, bringing in a beef-feast for the people at Tolo Lake, when **Swan Necklace** and his fellow raiders began killing whites on the Salmon River. There was two such transvestites when the war broke out; neither was captured; one died at Kamiah and the other "was killed in Lewiston during the gold rush," which is odd since the gold rush in Lewiston happened a decade before the war. I have imagined that Welweyas was the one who died at Kamiah, after having made it to Canada and back. This would imply (given the habits of Indian Agents) that she became nominally Christian and stopped cross-dressing.

Wetwhowees—*(Nimiputumít.)* Sister to **Wounded Head**. Her husband Red Sun is invented. Through physical strength she saved herself from a soldier's bayonet at Big Hole. Later she was called Lucy Ellenwood.

Where Ducks Are Around—*(Anglicized Nimiputumít.)* An invented character; one of the women who died at Big Hole. I have imagined her to be **Swan Necklace**'s sister.

Captain Stephen G. Whipple—This commander of the First Cavalry (Company "L") was charged with keeping an eye on the **Joseph** band during their final winter of freedom (1876–77) in the Grande Ronde Valley. After the war started, **Howard** dispatched him on the imprudent and unjust raid on **Looking-Glass**'s village. His communications show him to have been intelligent, perceptive and educated.

White Bird—*(Anglicized Nimiputumít.)* [Peop[p]eo Hihhih.] Another translation is "White Goose," but see the entry for **Peopeo Tholekt**. A prominent chief among the Salmon River band. White Bird Canyon, or **Sparse-Snowed Place**, was in his territory. He was an experienced buffalo hunter. In 1877 he was quite old, so it is said that he fought in no battle except Bear's Paw—although I must believe that he took some part in the White Bird Canyon fight. Most of the Salmon River raiders originated in his band or **Toohhoolhoolzote**'s, only one being from Joseph's. He was the sole Nez Perce chief to escape to Canada, where he was eventually murdered. According to a private in **Miles**'s army, he had two wives; however, a photograph of White Bird in Canada shows but one, the woman called **Kate**. Since Private Zimmer probably never saw White Bird, I have discounted his assertion and made White Bird a one-wife man.

White Cloud—*(Anglicized Nimiputumít.)* [Sewattis Hihhih.] A brave and diligent warrior who took part in every battle. Wounded at Cottonwood. He survived to return to Colville with **Joseph**.

White Thunder—*(Nimiputumít.)* His maternal grandfather was the brother of Old **Chief Joseph**'s mother. A prominent fighter in the Nez Perce War. This book relies in part upon his autobiography [see G 4]. "The whites call me Yellow Wolf, but I take that as a nickname. My true name is . . . Heinmot Hihhih, which means White Thunder." On the next page he relates his spirit-vision of a yellow wolf, from which he derived his more commonly known name. He survived war and exile, dying many years after Joseph, beside whom he is buried. His monument reads: *Yellow Wolf (1855–1931). Patriot Warrior of Nez Perce "Lost Cause" 1877. Marker Placed by White Friends.*

Wild Oat Moss—*(Anglicized Nimiputumít.)* [Otskai.] (Conjectural meaning of this difficult word.) A companion of **White Thunder**, whose life he saved by killing a citizen with whom he was gun-duelling not long before the Canyon Creek battle. Since his name might have been Flathead, I imagine him as having Flathead relatives.

First Lieutenant Melville Wilkinson—Third Infantry. This devout Methodist artilleryman distinguished himself at Clearwater. According to **General Crook**, **General Howard** had "an aide-de-camp named Wilkinson, whose stock in trade was religion." Wilkinson is stated to have been a captain at that time (1872), evidently by virtue of a **brevet** [G 2]. At Fort McDowell, Howard informed the commanding officer that he had been requested to deliver a speech to the soldiers. The CO, who disliked him, inquired who had asked for this speech, and he had to admit that the responsible party was Wilkinson. Everything that I have Wilkinson doing and saying between Clearwater and Bear's Paw is a fiction, because Howard actually sent him to Spokane to keep the Indians quiet. There is no evidence that he was the scheming fault-finder I have made him; in fact he was more likely a bluff innocent, given his habit (not mentioned in *The Dying Grass*) of waking up his comrades early in the morning by bellowing out hymns. His subsequent career is as I give it in the "Further Histories."

Colonel William H. Winters—This commander (Company "E") was actually a captain (see **Brevet Ranks**, G 2). He led an assault at the Clearwater battle.

Wolf Old Woman—**Toohhoolhoolzote**'s elder wife (invented by WTV; name selected from Aoki's dictionary).

Second Lieutenant Charles Erskine Scott Wood—Lived 1852–1944. An aide-de-camp to **General Howard** during the Nez Perce campaign and the Bannock War of 1878. The basic facts of his life and participation in the pursuit of **Joseph** are accurately presented here; his thoughts and words, of course, are mostly invented. He and **Ad Chapman** between them must have had a lot to do with Joseph's famous surrender speech as we know it. An admirer of **General Miles** assures us: "Wood was known to be a heavy drinker and a spinner of wild yarns." I see him rather differently. For discussion of how I constructed his character, see the note "Wood's personality" in the source citations to "Alaska Sounds Fine and Cool."

Wottolen—*(Nimiputumít.)* ["Hair Combed Over Eyes."] A close comrade of **White Thunder**'s. Evidently a member of **White Bird**'s band, although he was often with **Looking-Glass**. The father of the warrior Black Eagle. His **WYAKIN** [G 2] promised him safety from bullets. One of the war leaders at Clearwater. A prophetic dreamer (whose dreams warned of disaster at Big Hole and Bear's Paw), and after the war the tribal historian. (He lived to approximately a hundred and one.) His whereabouts at the beginning of the Nez Perce War are not entirely clear to me, so I have him keep White Thunder company at the Battle of White Bird Canyon, and then ride insouciantly home to **Kamnaka** [G 3] so that he can witness the cavalry raid on Looking-Glass—and verify **Howard**'s suspicions that Looking-Glass was not neutral. This may well be what happened.

Wounded Head—*(Anglicized Nimiputumít.)* [Husis Owyeen.] [Also: Shot On Head.] His name at the beginning of the war was Wettusolalumtikt [Last Time On Earth]. A brave warrior. His wife (wounded at Big Hole) was **Helping Another**. His sister (who turned aside a soldier's bayonet at the same battle) was **Wetwhowees**.

Wounded Mouth—*(Anglicized Nimiputumít.)* [Mimpow Owyeen.] The father of **Animal In A Hole**, who was scouting for the Army, he was the first Nez Perce to die in the war (at Cottonwood, mortally wounded by the **Brave Seventeen** [G 2]).

Yellow Hair—See **Custer**.

Yellow Bull—*(Anglicized Nimiputumít.)* [Chuslum Moxmox.] The father of **Red Moccasin Tops**. This warrior had fought against the Sioux with **Looking-Glass** and the Crows at the great battle of 1874. He was probably a leader in the second Salmon River raid, when the Nez Perces committed atrocities. McWhorter's sources mention him in regard to White Bird Canyon and Bear's Paw. After the surrender he accompanied Lieutenant **Baird**'s peace mission to Chief **White Bird**, then was returned to the Indian Territory. He accompanied **Joseph** to Nespelem, but eventually relocated to Lapwai.

Yellow Wolf—*(Anglicized Nimiputumít.)* See **White Thunder**.

Young White Bird—*(Anglicized Nimiputumít.)* **White Bird**'s nephew, aged about nine years. Wounded at Big Hole, his mother and sister being killed. He escaped from Bear's Paw with his little brother.

2. GLOSSARY OF ORDERS, ISMS, NATIONS, PROFESSIONS, HIERARCHIES, DIVISIONS, RACES, SHAMANS, TRIBES AND MONSTERS

Acbadadea—*(Crow.)* "The One Divine Being."

A.D.C.—Aide-de-camp.

Ahkunkenekoo—*(Nimiputumít.)* McWhorter translates this variously as "Deity" and "Land Above; Happy Hereafter."

Air Bird—*(Anglicized Nimiputumít.)* "A great bird, that . . . rests only the clouds." The **Wyakin** of **Grizzly Bear Youth**.

Americans—The Indians' best friends.

Army—See **Military divisional organization**.

Assiniboin(e)s—*(?)* Called "Walkarounds" or "Walking Cutthroats" by their enemies the Nez Perces, some of whom died at their hands in 1877–78, these people have named themselves Nak'óta. They "speak one of the four dialects of Sioux." During the Nez Perce War several of their bands were roaming northern Montana near the international border.

Bannocks—*(Euro-American corruption.)* [Also: Bannacks. From "Banakwut," which is what they called themselves.] Employed in the Nez Perce War as Army scouts. "A part of the Shoshonee nation . . . but they spoke a dialect of their own. Their principal hunting grounds were west of the Bitter Root Mountains and south of the Coeur d'Alene River. They acquired the name of Root Diggers from the fact that a large portion of their food consisted of roots . . ."—Humfreville, 1899. Apparently only some bands were actually called Diggers. Some Shoshoni called them "Punnush." [*Cf.* Lewis and Clark's word for the Nez Perce: the Chopunnish.]— According to Christopher Tower, their dialect of Numic is very close to Northern Shoshoni. "The Bannock are actually related to the Northern Paiute."— "The Bannock were Northern Paiute speakers who had migrated from Oregon . . ."—Robert F. Murphy and Yolanda Murphy. In the early 1700s they got horses and moved to south central Idaho by the Snake River in order to be near to buffalo. By 1840 Bannock and Shoshoni were said to be a single tribe.—"The Bannocks were Northern Paiutes who had intermarried with the Shoshoni and allied with them during times of war. They . . . were a horse culture, but caught fish lower down the Snake River at Shoshoni Falls and dug roots in Idaho's Camas Prairie."—Michno, 2007. In 1873 there were a hundred Bannocks and Shoshoni at Fort Hall, nine hundred in other places. The women were renowned for beautiful basketry. The Nez Perce word for "Bannock" meant "enemy." Another derogatory word for them was "Lice-Eaters." The Crows called them "Worthless Lodges."

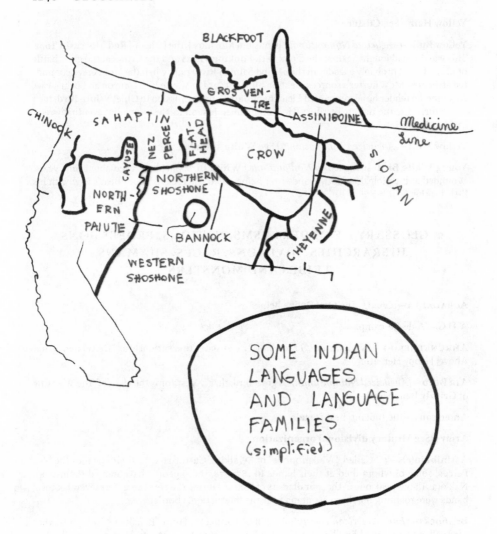

Big Bellies—*(Anglicized Nimiputumít.)* See **Gros Ventres**.

Blackfeet—*(Euro-American.)* This nation is divided into the following tribes: Bloods [Kainaio-was], Blackfoot [Siksikas], North Piegans [Pikunis] and South Piegans [Blackfeet]. They were enemies with the Crows, and sometimes raided the Nez Perces, Flatheads and Kootenays for horses. The Nez Perces referred to them by a word meaning (approximately) "Legs" or "Shin-bones." According to Alexander Henry, *ca.* 1810, they were "the most independent and happy people of all the tribes E of the Rocky mountains. War, women, horses and buffalo are their de-lights, and all these they have at command."

Bluecoats—*(Anglicized Nimiputumít.)* American soldiers, especially cavalry.

Bostons—*(Anglicized Nimiputumít and Chinook jargon.)* White Americans; settlers. The Crow name for them was "Yellow Eyes."

Brave Seventeen—Fifteen volunteers under **Captain Randall**, along with the dispatch rider they were escorting to **Colonel Perry** at Cottonwood. They ran into Nez Perce warriors and two of their number, including Randall, were killed. Perry hesitated to relieve them, for which he was accused of cowardice.

BREVET RANKS

A brevet rank was, in effect, honorary. It marked meritorious service. Many Civil War volunteers were brevetted, but so were regular Army soldiers; for instance, several of Gibbon's officers who fought at Big Hole received this honor—which effected no increase in pay or command power. As such, it was a perfectly expedient reward for members of the under-manned, underfunded post-1865 Army. Here are the brevet and actual ranks of the following characters as of 1877 (Custer of course died in 1876).

	Brevet	Actual
Custer	General	Lieutenant Colonel
Gibbon	General	Colonel
Mason	Major [& Brigadier Gen.]	Captain
Miles	Major General [& Brigadier Gen.]	Colonel
Miller	Colonel	Captain
Parnell	Colonel	Lieutenant
Perry	Colonel	Captain
Sturgis	Brigadier General	Colonel
Trimble	Major	Captain
Wilkinson	Captain	Lieutenant
Winters	Colonel	Captain
Whipple	Colonel	Captain

For this book I decided to have Howard address Perry as colonel, which indeed he often did. Since Perry was in actual rank senior to Parnell, Trimble and Whipple, I thought it best to have Perry and Howard commanding them according to their actual ranks, rather than, for instance, to have Perry call Trimble a major. For much the same reason I let Captain Miller stay a captain. Fletcher, Wilkinson, Wood and Guy Howard were all lieutenants and aides-de-camp, therefore equal colleagues, so I made no reference to Wilkinson's brevet rank. I transformed Mason from a brevet major (and major is what Howard politely called him in *Nez Perce Joseph*) into an actual major, so that I could make use of the regulation about majors inventorying the property of dead soldiers, which grows relevant at White Bird Canyon (there is no reason to believe that Mason actually performed this gruesome task). On the other hand, I thought it best for Howard to refer to Custer, Gibbon, Miles and Sturgis as generals, not only out of politeness but also because, according to 1877 usage, any commander of a detached unit was its "general." Hence in this book, Gibbon's men call him general. When after Sturgis's several failures I have Howard begin to call him colonel, this is a mark of the latter's disappointment and irritation. In real life he might have been too gentlemanly to do this. Meanwhile, there was no impediment to letting Winters be called "colonel."

Cayuse—Weyíletpu is "the Nez Perce term by which the modern Cayuse refer to themselves." Closely related to the Nez Perce, although their language was different. By 1837 younger Cayuse had lost their language, and spoke Lower Nez Perce instead. After some Cayuses murdered the Whitmans in 1843, the tribe was often stigmatized (by **Howard** among others) as "the worst of the whole," "crafty, cunning, and troublesome."—Humfreville, 1899. By 1877 the lower-cased "cayuse" had become a descriptor for Indian ponies of less than high quality. In 2013 a rancher in northeastern Oregon (not far from Wallowa, in fact) told me that this usage was still active. See also **Umatilla**.

Cheyennes—Called "Painted Arrows" or "Arrow Marks" by the Nez Perce, these people served as scouts for **Miles** on the Bear's Paw fight. At least one of **Captain Fisher**'s scouts during the pursuit through Yellowstone and after may have also been Cheyenne. Needless to say, this tribe won no great benefit for helping the Anglo-American conquerors, and once the scouts had "cleaned up" the northern plains, it came time to apply the adage about the Moor who has done his duty, and they were shipped to the Indian Territory with the rest of their people. To his credit, Miles eventually succeeded in getting them a reservation on their own homeland. [Following the lead of the Nez Perce informants in McWhorter's two oral histories, I have not differentiated Northern from Southern Cheyennes in this book.]

Clatsop—[Also: Klatsop.] They lived near the mouth of the Columbia and were mentioned (not glowingly) by Lewis and Clark. In 1877 some could be found in Portland.

Columbia River Renegades—See **River Renegades**.

Cous Eaters—See **Nez Perces**.

Coyote—This trickster protagonist of ever so many Plains Indians myths figures in a great number of Nez Perce legends. Very often he spoils life for himself and others as a result of his own greed and ignorance, but sometimes his trickery has benefited others [see **Monster**]. The Nez Perces sometimes called themselves Coyote's children.

Crows—The Absaraka or Up-sah-ro-ku. A common spelling at the moment is "Apsaalooke." The **Assiniboines** called them "the Raven Enemy." **Lieutenant Bradley** (1876) believed that at contact their homeland extended from the North Platte to the mouth of the Yellowstone and north into the Judith River country, and that prior to this they (and the **Gros Ventres**) may have derived from the Paducas who dwelled on the headwaters of the Kansas River, and these in turn from a tribe of "white Indians" dislodged from Georgia by the Cherokees. In Bradley's time there were already two subtribes: the Mountain and River Crows. "The Crows became mercenaries of the United States—according to native informants—in order to save that tribe from extinction." After they helped the U.S. Army against their friends the Nez Perces, the latter called them the Women Nation.

Cutthroats—*(Anglicized Nimiputumít.)* See **Sioux**.

Department—See **Military divisional organization**.

Diggers—See **Snakes**.

District—See **Military divisional organization**.

Division—See **Military divisional organization**.

Downstream People—"The Nez Perce have been divided into Upper and Lower divisions, primarily on dialect grounds. The Upper Nez Perce were oriented more toward a Plains lifeway." The Downstream People, who used salmon more, and went to trade at Celilo Falls, included dwellers at Lapwai, Spalding, Lewiston, Asotin, and along the Snake and the Clearwater; the Upstream People, who often went to the **Buffalo Country** [G 3], hailed from Orofino, Ahshaka, Kamiah, Kooskia and Stites. **Chief Joseph** is said to have identified with the Downstream People, who were also called "Tied Back Hair."

Dreamers—The pan-Indian Ghost Dance religion, which was so horrifically suppressed in the Wounded Knee Massacre of 1890, grew out of the Dreamer doctrine that **Mother Earth**

should not be gashed by cultivation, mining, irrigation, etcetera, and that if the Native Americans respected Her enough, wandering the land, hunting, gathering and giving thanks, all their dead would presently be restored to life, and the white people driven out. **Smohalla** was an important prophet and practitioner of this faith, which is now sometimes called the Seven Drum religion.

Enemy—*(Anglicized Nimiputumít.)* When capitalized, this word refers to the people called Bannocks, Shoshonis and Snakes. The Nez Perce word is *tiwélqe.*

Flatheads—*(Anglicized Chinook jargon?)* These relatives of the Nez Perce, some of whom once wintered in their territory on the west side of the Lo Lo Trail, lived near Missoula. In 1877 the people who followed Sub-chief Arlee had but recently been removed to their reservation. The ones who followed Chief Charlot stayed free until 1891. The Shoshoni called them Tatasiba, "the shaved-head People." They called themselves (and the Nez Perces followed suit) the Salish. The Flatheads and Pend d'Oreilles were "two groups of Salishan-speaking people with dialects mutually understood . . . They had separate but somewhat overlapping geographic locations." When the fleeing Nez Perce left Yellowstone National Park, they came into the former Flathead zone, and stayed there until they reached the Missouri.

Freedmen's Bureau—*(Post–Civil War American.)* Benjamin G. Humphreys, first postwar governor of Mississippi, 1865: "To the guardian care of the Freedmen's Bureau have been trusted the emancipated slaves . . . Look around you and see the result . . . From producers they are converted into consumers, and, as winter approaches, their only salvation from starvation and want is Federal rations, plunder, and pillage."— General Grant, 1865: "Everywhere general **Howard**, the able head of the bureau, made friends by the just and fair instructions and advice he gave; but the complaint in South Carolina was that when he left, things went on as before."— W. E. B. DuBois, 1901: "Foredoomed to failure. The very name of the Bureau stood for a thing in the South which for two centuries . . . better men had refused even to argue—that life amid free Negroes was simply unthinkable . . ." Perhaps if Lincoln (who had called for the establishment of the Bureau, and recommended Howard for its chief) had lived, the Bureau could have accomplished something. As things turned out, its legacy was false hopes for the freedmen and shame, impoverishment and litigation for Howard.

The Grandmother—*(Anglicized Sioux and various Indian.)* The Queen of England, and therefore of the British Dominions, which in 1877 included what we now call Canada.

The Grandfather—*(Anglicized Sioux and various Indian.)* The President of the United States.

Gros Ventres—Once they lived between the North and South Saskatchewan rivers, but by the mid-nineteenth century they had been driven into northern Montana. Apparently their language, a member of the Algonquian family, was similar to Arapaho, although when they and the Arapaho parted ways no one knows. Allied and confederated with the Blackfeet. Called by the Nez Perces "Big Bellies" or "Atsinas," these people wandered and hunted north of the Missouri much as the non-treaty Nez Perces still aspired to do in their own homeland. The Gros Ventres and Nez Perces were sometimes enemies. Gros Ventres "believed that menstruation occurred subsequent to sexual relations . . . ," and who am I to say that it doesn't?

Horse People—*(Anglicized Sioux and various Indian.)* Cavalry.

Hunkpapa—*(Sioux.)* Sitting Bull's nation.

Indian Agent—"The chief duty of an agent is to induce his Indians to labor in civilized pursuits."—U.S. Government circular, 1878.

Jayhawkers—*(Civil War American.)* Militant anti-slavery advocates who sometimes murdered pro-slavers in their beds. After the war this term was sometimes used to refer to the opposite sort of vigilantes: Ku Klux Klan–like types.

King Georges—See the same in G 6.

Klamaths—*(Anglicized Upper Chinook.)* [*Shlamashl,* "They of the River."] Neighbors, occasional allies, and eventual enemies of the **Modocs**. There were thirty-four Klamath Marsh villages, and fourteen more of the Klamath Falls subgroup. Between them lived the Agency Lake, the Lower

William River and the Pelican Bay peoples. To the east, the Upper Klamath people lived along the upper Sycan and Sprague rivers. The few Modocs who finally returned from exile in the Indian Territory were confederated into the Klamath nation.

Lemhis—"Linguistically the same as the Bannack Shoshsoni." "Salmon Eater and Sheep Eater Indians affiliated with the Bannocks." [See **Bannocks**.] Considerably before 1855, when Fort Lemhi was built, the Lemhis assisted a Mormon missionary expedition. Hence their name. **Looking-Glass** evidently considered them his friends. However, former buffalo-hunting allies of the Nez Perces though the Lemhis were, they turned them away on their flight, for fear of punishment by the U.S. Army.

Lice-Eaters—*(Anglicized Nimiputumít.)* See **Bannocks**.

Military divisional organization—In 1877 **General Sherman** had supreme command. Beneath him, the states and territories were divided and subdivided, each part having its own head. The largest zone was a division. Irwin McDowell (HQ San Francisco) commanded the Division of the Pacific, which encompassed the area from the Pacific to the Bitterroot Mountains. Just east was the Division of the Missouri, commanded by **Phil Sheridan** (HQ Chicago). Each division consisted of departments. **Howard**'s was the Department of the Columbia (Alaska, Washington and Oregon). The much larger Department of the Dakota, commanded by Alfred Terry, covered the northern Great Plains. Departments were organized into districts. Within the Department of Dakota, **John Gibbon** controlled the District of Montana, while (as of September 1877) **Nelson Miles** had the District of Yellowstone, in which **Samuel Sturgis**, commander of the Seventh Cavalry, was a cog. See p. 70 for map.

Musselshell Sisters—*(Anglicized Nimiputumít.)* Certain dangerous Powers who sometimes killed males (including the half-pathetic trickster **Coyote**) by sexual means.

Modocs—*(Anglicized Klamath-Modoc; older sources say Anglicized French.)* [Mo:wat'a:k-khni, the Southern People.] There were three distinct groups: around the Lower Klamath Lake and Tule Lake, along the upper Lost River to Goose Lake, and along the lower Lost River. They signed the obligatory cession and reservation treaty in 1864. Mistreated both by the **Klamaths** and **Snakes** on whose land they were placed, and also by the agency system, they returned home. For some reason the whites did not like this. The Modoc War of 1872–73 was gruelling and vicious, one memorable incident being the Modoc murder of the Army peace commissioners under flag of truce. After their inevitable defeat, the Modocs were shipped off to the Indian Territory. Modoc was one of two "closely related dialects" of the Klamath-Modoc language. "As of 2006 there were no fluent native speakers of either dialect."

Monster—*(Anglicized Nimiputumít.)* He swallowed up nearly all the ancestors of animals and people. **Coyote** managed to be gulped down and then killed Him from within. As the Monster was dying, everyone fled through His anus. (The Muskrat has a hairless tail because the anus closed just as He was coming out.) The heart of the Monster, an important site in Nez Perce folklore, is a great rock near **Kamiah** [G 3].

Nami Piap—*(Wanapum.)* A Creator of the **Dreamers**.

Negroes—*(Anglicized French, Spanish, etc.)* "Army people like the negroes, and find a quality of devotion in them that is most grateful . . ."—Custer's widow. In *The Dying Grass* I have lower-cased this word as she did, to indicate their miserable status in nineteenth-century Amercian society.

Nez Perces—*(Anglicized French.)* [Also: Nez Percés. This purer French spelling is still found in some contemporary dictionaries, but I have not heard the accent pronounced on the reservation.] The Nimiipu [or Neemeepoo]. More strictly, the Nimí, "Pu" meaning tribe or people. (According to **Wood**, who cites **James Reuben**, "the name of the Nez Perces is *Te-kaw-ten*—We the people.") Their occasional enemies the **Bannocks** called them "the Cous Eaters." The Crow may have called them the *pókholokátu*, meaning untranslated; they also signified them by "Paddles," and *apupé* or "Pierced Noses," while the Lakota employed a comparable name. In the eternal words of Indian Agent Cain (1860), "the Nez Perces are characterized by mental power, energy of will, bravery and docility, and are larger and more muscular than most of the other tribes . . . Many of their young men annually hunt the buffalo on the headwaters of the Missouri." The "treaty" or Christian Nez Perces were headed (at least as the whites saw it) by **Lawyer** (Hallalhotoost). The "non-treaties," who never signed the agreement of 1863, were:

1. Joseph or Wallowa band [Wallowa Valley, Grande Ronde and environs]. According to McWhorter, they were the *Kammooenem*, or "People of the Hemp Place of Snake River." About 55–60 fighting men.
2. White Bird or Lahmatta (Lahmtahma) = "Sparse-Snowed Place" band [White Bird Canyon]. No more than 50 fighting men.
3. Looking-Glass band [Clearwater River, Asotin and around]. No more than 40 fighting men.
4. Toohhoolhoolzote band [in hills between Salmon and Snake rivers]. About 30 fighting men.
5. Palus [**Palouse**] band [Lower Snake River. Chiefs: Húsus Kute (who might have been a subchief, or simply an orator) and Hahtalekin]. Probably 16 fighting men.

The total number of non-treaty Nez Perces was 600–700. For details on this number, their war casualties, the number who surrendered and the number who escaped from Bear's Paw, see the source-note to "It Cannot Seem Right," below, p. 1329: "Numbers of non-treaty Nez Perces in Joseph's (invented) speech." See also **Downstream People**.

Nimiipu—See **Nez Perces**.

Our Mother—*(Various Native American, Anglicized.)* The earth.

Painted Arrows—See **Cheyennes**.

Paiutes—Also [in 19th cent.] "Pi-Utes." See **Snakes**.

Palouse—In the entry under **Nez Perces**, this band appears as a subtribe, and **General Howard** seemed to see it as such. According to Cheryl Wilfong, they shared a language with the Nez Perce and intermarried with them, especially with the **Looking-Glass** band; but the two were in fact "closely related tribes." Their homeland lay west of what is now Clarkston, Washington. According to McWhorter, their "ancestral home," which was close to Pullman, was called Wawai.

Pend d'Oreilles—See **Flatheads**.

Piegans—See **Blackfeet**.

Pit River Indians—A northern Californian tribe now known as the Achumawi.

Raven Enemy—See **Crows**.

Red Mineral Paint—*(Wanapum.)* Name for a **Dreamer**.

River Renegades—**General Howard**'s term (and possibly that of other whites) for the roaming tribes along the Snake and then Columbia who resisted removal to the reservation. Their most famous chiefs were Moses and **Smohalla**. Most were **Dreamers**.

Salish—See **Flatheads**.

She Who Watches—*(Anglicized Chinook?)* Tsagigla'lal, a petroglyph over the Columbia River Gorge. On Lake Pend d'Oreille "are the wonderful painted rocks . . . upon which, at the height of several hundred feet, are the figures of men and animals, which the Indians say are the work of a race that preceded them."—Caroline Leighton, 1866.

Shikèmnúvit—See G 6.

Shinbones—See **Blackfeet**.

Shoshoni—*(Euro-American.)* [Also: Shoshone.] The language is a "continuum" of "mutual intelligible dialects" stretching "from southern Nevada to western Wyoming with no significant break."

Sioux—*(Euro-American.)* The Nez Perce word for them meant "Cutthroats." Their confederation consisted of a number of tribes; this long book must give them short shrift. In the summer of 1878, the figure-eight-shaped Sioux camp in Canada was laid out along tribal lines as follows: Hunkpapas (**Sitting Bull**'s people, Oglallas and Sans Arcs in the upper loop, Yanktons [or Yanktonais], Santees and Miniconjous (along with the Nez Perce refugees) in the lower.

Snakes—*(Euro-American.)* Name used by settlers to refer to the Paiutes of Oregon's Great Basin—and sometimes also to Shoshoni, **Bannock** and Southern Paiute of Idaho, Nevada and California. Being enemies with the **Blackfeet** and friends with the **Flatheads**, they were (sometimes, excepting their Bannock groups) friends with the Nez Perces. They "occupied the territory in and around the Snake River Valley, and . . . eastward to the foot of the Bitter Root Mountains, and as far south as the Ute country." According to another source, "the northern Great Basin and Snake River Indians were generally lumped together by the whites . . . as 'Snakes.' In the southern Basin, they were the 'Diggers.'" The homeland of the Snakes contained enough grass to support a horse culture. The Diggers' country did not. Snake bands had extremely divergent languages. The camas prairie referred to in "Further History of the Bannocks" was near what is now Fairfield, Idaho. Snake braves were said to be able to run down a deer.

Sun Man—*(Wanapum.)* One of the Dreamer Powers, possibly associated with creation.

Three Red Blankets—*(Anglicized Nimiputumít.)* **Shore Crossing**, **Swan Necklace** and **Red Moccasin Tops** were the three warriors who commenced the Salmon River raids which opened the Nez Perce War. However, Swan Necklace, the only one of these to survive the war, was the least prominent of the trio, and almost at the outset he was replaced in it by **Strong Eagle**. These three renowned warriors liked to wear red blankets when they fought, to draw the attention of the Army and thereby show their bravery. The loss of Shore Crossing and Red Moccasin Tops at Big Hole was a serious psychological blow to the non-treaty Nez Perce.

Takh—*(Umatilla.)* The **Umatilla** version of a **Wyakin**.

Tiwata-át—*(Nimiputumít.)* Shamaness.

Tiwét—*(Nimiputumít.)* Shaman.

Umatilla—"The Cayuse, Umatilla, and Walla Walla are people who long associated and in 1855 agreed by treaty to dwell together on the Umatilla Reservation." Before and after the Nez Perce War, **Howard** persuaded and intimidated some wandering Dreamer bands of Umatillas to go back onto the reservation.

Volunteers—"General McDowell transmits a telegram from Aide-de-Camp Lt. Keeler, in which he says volunteers of the character and status of those operating with General Howard would be worse than useless."

Walking Cutthroats—See **Assiniboines**.

Walking soldiers—*(Anglicized Sioux and various Indian.)* Sioux name for U.S. infantry.

Wanapums—*(Wanapum.)* River People. A tribe in what is now eastern Washington State. Their language is in the same family as Nez Perce. Little information is available to me on this group and their language, the best source being Click Relander's book. The great Dreamer **Smohalla** was one of their number. Only a handful of members now remain.

Wowshuxluh—*(Wanapum.)* The sacred wooden bird (Bullock's oriole) of the Dreamers, which only **Smohalla** could touch.

Wyakin—*(Nimiputumít.)* Relating to the specific power of fearsomeness or invulnerability in war, or success at hunting or other difficult things, achieved through the fasting and sleeplessness of a vision quest. In effect, the WYAKIN was a guardian spirit. Each man or woman lucky enough to meet one was assigned a personal taboo (for instance, **White Thunder** was not permitted to smoke). A WYAKIN could be anything from shore ice to a wolf (as was White Thunder's) to a beetle or a night ghost.

3. GLOSSARY OF PLACES

> Including stars and planets, although the Nez Perce would have thought of them as Powers, and hence fitting entries for G 2. Nez Perce–style place names invented by WTV are mostly not given here, since they occur only once; they may be found in the appropriate Source-Notes.

Ah-ki-ne-kun-scoo—*(Language not stated.)* Local name for the country around what is now Lewistown, Montana, which in 1877 was a trading post ("Reese Fort") and a very occasional military detachment.

Aipadass—*(Nimiputumít.)* A cous flat not far from **Split Rock**; at Craig's Ferry, also known as Luke's Place.

Asotain—See **Eel Place**.

Bear Claw Place—*(Anglicized Nimiputumít.)* [Wé-pukeletpetpe.] Spot east of the **Clearwater River**, between Kooskia and **Kamiah**.

Bear Sneaking Up—*(Anglicized Nimiputumít.)* A star in the Big Dipper.

Bear's Paw—*(Anglicized various Indian.)* Low mountains near the Montana-Canada border, near Snake Creek, where the Nez Perce fought their last battle. The Nez Perce called these mountains "Wolf's Paw."

Big Hole—*(American English.)* [Ross's Hole.] Called by the Nimiipu "Ground Squirrel Place" [Izhkumzizlalkik or Iskumtselalik Pah], this valley campsite in southern Montana, not far east of the Continental Divide, was the setting of **Gibbon**'s bloody dawn attack. The translation may be approximate, since one source notes: "Named after a small animal resembling a ground squirrel." Another source translates it: "Place of the Buffalo Calf."

Big Water—See **Clearwater River**.

Bitter Root Valley—[Nowadays, "Bitterroot."] Between the Rockies and the Continental Divide, this part of Montana was sparsely populated by whites in 1877. The Nez Perces emerged here from the **Lo Lo Trail** en route to **Big Hole**. For the meaning of the name, see **spatlam** [G 6]. The valley's western perimeter is the Bitter Root Range, through which the Nez Perces descended on the Lo Lo Trail.

Blue-ridge—*(American English.)* The Blue Mountains around **Wallowa**.

British Possessions—*(American English.)* Used here, as it was in my originals, to refer to Canada, although of course the British would have also applied it to India, Australia and other territories of the Empire. Sometimes called (by Indians) the Old Woman's Country, the Grandmother's Country or the White Mother's Country, all in reference to Queen Victoria.

Buffalo Country—*(Various Indian, Anglicized.)* At one time the buffalo (or, technically speaking, bison) could be found over most of the continental U.S. In 1859 an Army officer noted that "upon all the [emigration] routes north of latitude 36° the animal is still found between the 99th and 102d meridians of longitude." He also remarked that "a few more years will probably witness the extinction of the species," and he was very nearly right. In 1877, when buffalo bones remained prominently visible in Omaha, Nebraska, the Buffalo Country still included the plains of eastern Montana where the Crow, Sioux and Northern Cheyenne traditionally ranged. Although buffalo were still then to be found in Wyoming, the Dakotas and parts of southern Canada, it seems to have been Montana that the Nez Perce referred to by "Buffalo Country." A sojourn there meant much to the self-respect of a young Nez Perce man. **White Thunder** remarks: "Buffalo hunters were the best warriors, bravest fighters."

Butterfly Place—*(Anglicized Nimiputumít.)* "**Lapwai**" [q.v.] means "butterfly" (which in turn can also mean "vulva," as noted in G 6.) In this novel the Nez Perce characters call "Butterfly Place" what the whites call "Lapwai."

Camas Meadows—*(Various Indian, Anglicized.)* Site of a Nez Perce raid upon **Howard** whereby he lost most of his pack-mules. The place is near modern Spencer, Idaho. The Indians were fleeing the **Big Hole** battlefield, en route to Yellowstone. The name seems to have no Nez Perce equivalent.

Canada—*(Various Indian, Anglicized.)* See **British Possessions**. The origin of this name is discussed in the Third Dream, *Fathers and Crows*.

Cañon's Mouth—*(Anglicized Nimiputumít.)* [Pettahyewahwei or Peeta Auuwa.] The site of the Nez Perce village when the **Clearwater** battle began. Where the Clearwater's south fork meets the Cottonwood. Home (and reservation) of **Red Owl**.

Canyon Creek—See **Place Like Split Rock**.

Chinook Salmon Water—*(Anglicized Nimiputumít.)* The **Salmon River** (q.v.).

Chipmunk Mountain—See **Meadow Camp**.

Clark's Fork River—As you might have guessed, Lewis and Clark named it. The Crows called it "Rotten Sundance River" or "Rotten Sundance Tipi."

Clearwater River—*(American English.)* Site of an important battle in the Nez Perce War; Lewiston, Idaho, is also on this river, which the Nez Perce followed upward on their flight toward **Lo Lo**. Aoki's dictionary reports that the river itself is called *himekhí-cku-s* (Big Water); the middle fork is *himeqisníme* (the Great River) and the south fork is *tukúpe* (no meaning given; "named after a spring near Stites, Idaho"). Lewis and Clark heard the Nimiputumít name for the Clearwater as "Koos-koos-kee." Hence the town named Kooskia.

Columbia River—*(American English.)* More important to the **Downstream People** of the Nez Perce than to the bands who took part in the Nez Perce War. Aoki gives two words for it in his dictionary. One, which would be more germane to this story, is left untranslated; the other, used by the Downstream People, contains the prefix *eteyé* [see **Craig's Mountain**], meaning "distant," "deceased" or "unbelievable," so I have compromised with "Distant River."

Cottonwood Place—*(Anglicized Nimiputumít.)* [Qápqapí-n qáp.] Cottonwood, Idaho. In the vicinity of the Cottonwood battle. Cottonwood and Norton's ranch were the same.

Cow Island—*(Anglicized Nimiputumít.)* The highest consistently navigable point on the Missouri River; hence the site of an isolated depot (Fort Benton is about 120 miles upriver). My name for this spot, "Shallow Place," is a pseudo-Nimiputumít invention, since I don't know what the Nez Perce really called it. It was indeed a traditional fording point. Here the Nez Perce crossed on their way to **Bear's Paw**, and engaged in a fight for supplies with the personnel of the little depot on the north shore. The island itself (some sources say there were two islands) played no part in the fight.

Craig's Mountain—This place, which figures in the early part of the Nez Perce War (it was often in view, and **Howard**'s troops had to ascend it after their useless Salmon River crossing), was where many Nimiipu teenagers went on vision quests to meet their **WYAKINS** [G 2]. Here I have translated the Nimiputumít word *eteyé* [see **Columbia River**] as "faraway," since that seems to combine "distant" with hint of the eerie "deceased." Hence "Faraway Mountain."

Crossing Place—*(Anglicized Nimiputumít.)* Pittsburg Landing on the **Snake River**. It was here that **Toohhoolhoolzote**'s People wintered for several years before the Nez Perce War, and here that after the Battle of **White Bird Canyon** the volunteers found and destroyed a huge cache of food and supplies.

Dark Green Place—*(Anglicized Nimiputumít.)* Site of a Nez Perce village on the northern bank of the **Snake**, closely downstream from Truax, Washington.

Distant River—See **Columbia River**.

Edisto—One of the Carolina Sea Islands. Here the plantations of the masters were first turned over to their former slaves, and colored schools began to thrive—a trend which **Howard** believed he could continue and even facilitate as head of the Freedmen's Bureau. Unfortunately, his work was undone by the Johnson administration, and Edisto was returned to the planters.

Eel Place—*(Anglicized Nimiputumít.)* [Asotain.] Also: "Eel River." Site of present day Asotin, Washington.

Eewahtam—*(Nimiputumít.)* Another name for **Split Rock** (Tepahlewam).

Elk Water—*(Anglicized Nimiputumít.)* A minor river which flows through Yellowstone Park. Exactly which one is unclear.

Enemy River—*(Anglicized Nimiputumít.)* The **Snake River**.

Faraway Mountain—See **Craig's Mountain**.

Farewell Bend—*(American.)* Just south of the present day town of Huntington, Oregon, this fording-place on the **Snake River** marked the spot where some emigrants turned off toward California and others continued on into Oregon.

Fish Trap Place—*(Anglicized Nimiputumít.)* [Nahush.] The spot by Kamiah where the non-treaty Nez Perces crossed the **Clearwater** after the battle of July 11–12.

Fort Buford—*(American English.)* "At the confluence of the **Yellowstone** and the **Missouri** (five [Army] companies)." Description written in 1867.

Fort Fizzle—*(American.)* Derogatory name given to the place where the Seventh Infantry and some volunteers failed to stop the non-treaty Nez Perces from streaming past them off the **Lo Lo Trail** and into the **Bitter Root Valley**.

Fort Lapwai, Idaho—*(Anglicized Nimiputumít.)* Lat. 46° 24′, long. 116° 48′. Established 6 August 1862 on Lapwai Creek at its confluence with the **Clearwater**, and twelve miles from **Lewiston**. "Sit'd within Nez Perce Indian Res'n . . . Daily stage from Lewiston, and semi-weekly steamboat route over Snake River, dist. 12 miles . . . Area of [military] reserve 640 acres and of Hay [*sic*] reserve 586 acres. Abandoned 1 Oct. 85(?). Turned over to Ind. Dept. for Ind. [illegible] purposes Nov. 17. 85."—Adjutant General's Office inventory. See also **Butterfly Place**.

Ghost's Trail—*(Anglicized Nimiputumít.)* The Milky Way.

Gillem's Camp—Army field headquarters during the Modoc War. On southwest side of Tule Lake.

Gorge Place—*(Nimiputumít.)* Hell's Canyon, Oregon.

Grandmother's Country—*(Various Indian, Anglicized.)* See **British Possessions**.

Grande Ronde River—*(Cheyenne.)* Used by the **Joseph** [Wallowa] band as a wintering place. The Nimiputumít word is *welíwe*, for which no meaning is given.

Greasy River—*(Cheyenne.)* The **Missouri River**.

Great River—See **Clearwater River**.

Ground Squirrel Place—See **Big Hole**.

Heart of the MONSTER—*(Anglicized Nimiputumít.)* See **MONSTER** [G 2].

Heart Mountain—*(?)* [Also: Hart or Hart's Mountain.] A prominence in southeastern Montana, east of Yellowstone, this place was a landmark marking (in 1877) the near beginning of the **Buffalo Country**. It was very near here that the non-treaty Nez Perces came down a narrow canyon and got past **Sturgis**.

Imnaha—*(Nimiputumít.)* The canyon and river to the east of the **Wallowa** Valley, descending into the **Snake River**. The meaning of the name does not seem to be known.

Indian Territory—*(American.)* In **General Howard**'s words, "a country west of Arkansas and north of Texas," where Seminoles, Cherokees, Chickasaws and Chocktaws had been confined. One book on the Dawes Act defines it simply as "present-day Oklahoma," but the geometry was not quite the same. The Modocs, Cheyennes, Nez Perces and others were deported there. The Nez Perces learned to call it the Hot Place.

I.T.—Idaho Territory.

Izhkumzizlalkik—*(Nimiputumít.)* See **Big Hole**.

Kamiah—*(Nimiputumít.)* [Also: "Kamlahpee." Possible meaning: Many Camas Roots.] Now a town on the north fork of the **Clearwater**. In 1877 some missionaries, ranchers and treaty Nez Perces resided there. After withdrawing from the Clearwater battle, the non-treaties crossed at that spot, pursued by **General Howard**. Ironically, seven decades before then the Nez Perces had helped Lewis and Clark cross the river near this very place

Kamnaka—*(Nimiputumít.)* Name of **Looking-Glass**'s village (destroyed by **Captain Whipple** at the beginning of the war). Meaning unknown.

King George's Country—*(Various Indian, Anglicized.)* See **British Possessions**.

Lalac—*(Wanapum.)* **Smohalla**'s vision quest mountain.

Lewiston, Idaho—*(American, of course.)* Established illegally on the Nez Perce reservation in 1861; on the site called **Simí-nekem** ["Riverfork"]. Another Nez Perce location now swallowed up by the town was called Ripple Place. Named after Meriwether Lewis; Clarkston across the river in Washington honors William Clark.

Lewistown, Montana—See **Ah-ki-ne-kun-scoo**.

Lochsa River—*(Transliterated Flathead?)* This river flows out of the middle fork of the **Clearwater**. Aoki suspects that *láqsa* may be a Flathead word referring to pine trees; hence I have called it Pine Tree River.

Lo Lo Trail—*(Nimiputumít.)* [Also, and nowadays exclusively: Lolo.] Said to be named after a French-Canadian prospector named Lora or Lulu who was killed there by a grizzly in 1852—but apparently *lolo* means "to carry" in Chinook jargon. Lewis and Clark followed this route coming and going. It was the Nez Perce's northerly way to the **Buffalo Country**. The non-treaties took it when they fled the Army subsequent to the **Clearwater** battle. It "runs along the ridge or divide between the North Fork of the **Clearwater** . . . and the **Lochsa** . . . , primarily in Idaho County."— Gary E. Moulton. From Lewiston to Missoula along this route is about two hundred miles. Once they reached Lo Lo Pass, the Nez Perces were out of the Idaho Territory (and the core of their traditional homeland) and—so they thought—into the United States, with whose citizens they imagined they were not at war. (In fact, Montana remained a territory until 1889.) Following Lo Lo Creek down into the **Bitter Root Valley**, they won a nonviolent victory over the Army at **Fort Fizzle**.

The Low Place—*(Anglicized Nimiputumít.)* Hell. LOW PERSONS are DEMONS and DEVILS.

Meadow Camp—*(Anglicized Nimiputumít.)* [Woutokinwes Tahtakkin.] A well-grassed marshy resting point on the **Lo Lo Trail**, near the ranger station on Rocky Ridge, a place which the Nez Perce called Chipmunk Mountain [Motsqosmots].

Meadow Place—*(Anglicized Nimiputumít.)* The Joseph Plains between the **Snake** and **Salmon** rivers. A camas-digging place not far from **Split Rock**.

Medicine Line—*(Various Indian.)* "Completed by August 1874, the demarcated boundary" between the U.S. and Canada "thereafter became a visibly recognizable entity . . . at the approximate midpoint of the line" between Minnesota and the Pacific. A hundred-mile length of mostly treeless plain touching both present Blaine County, Montana, and the Cypress District of Saskatchewan, was regarded as a "Medicine Line" by Native peoples crossing in either direction. The line came to possess 'magical political power' among the tribes . . ."—Jerome A. Greene.

Missouri River—Called by the Nez Perce "the Place of the Cave of Red Paint" [Seloselo Wejanwais] and by the Cheyennes "the Greasy River," this important military and civilian route was plied by steamboats up to **Cow Island**, and, when water level permitted, all the way to Fort Benton. Between this river and the **Medicine Line** was a No Man's Land of Cheyennes, Assiniboines, Gros Ventres, Sioux and buffalo hunters.

Modoc Lava Beds—*(Various Indian.)* The area south of Tule Lake, California (which then, before draining, also stretched into Oregon). Site of the Modoc War, whose purpose, wrote the *Portland Oregonian*, was "to drive a couple of hundred miserable aborigines from a desolate natural shelter in the wilderness, that a few thriving cattlemen might ranch their wild steers in a scope of isolated country, the dimensions of some several reasonable sized counties."

Monster-Udder Place—*(Anglicized Nimiputumít.)* Site of a former Nez Perce village, near **Kamiah**, on the eastern bank of the **Clearwater**. See **Heart of the Monster**.

Mount Idaho—Once a contender to be Idaho's seat of government, in 1877 this place was a nest of Indian-hating volunteers.

Mount Misery—Name for the place near **Kamiah** where the Nez Perce besieged some volunteers, shortly before the Battle of the **Clearwater**. The Nez Perce name for the place was Possossona, or Water Passing, so called from a spring nearby.

Musselshell River—Where the heart went out of Sturgis, and the non-treaty Nez Perces began to feel almost safe from soldiers.

Narrow Solid Rock Pass—Exact location not known to me. A trail on the south side of the **Tongue Water**, followed by the Nez Perces as they fled the cavalry in Yellowstone National Park.

Nespelem—By Colville, Washington, near the Grand Coulee Dam. Final reservation for the non-treaty Nez Perces who refused to become Christians after their exile in the Indian Territory. Chief **Joseph** and **White Thunder** (Yellow Wolf) are buried here.

Night-Fishing Place—*(Anglicized Nimiputumít.)* Smith Creek, ten miles up the **Clearwater**'s middle fork near what is now Kooskia. This would have been in **Looking-Glass**'s traditional "country," and might have been in (or else very near to) his reservation.

Norton's ranch—See **Cottonwood**.

O-pumohat Kyai-is-i-sak-ta—*(Language not stated.)* Local name for the **Musselshell River**.

O-to-kur-tuk-tai—*(Language not stated.)* Local name for the Judith River and Mountains.

Old Woman's Country—*(Various Indian, Anglicized.)* See **British Possessions**.

Old Woman Place—*(Anglicized Nimiputumít.)* Site near or at the present day bridge from **Kamiah** across the river. Apparently it was not a village.

Oro Fino—*(From Spanish.)* Now spelled Orofino, this settlement, not far from **Weippe**, was realizing between ten and fifteen dollars a day for its most skilled gold miners in the spring of 1861. By 1877 the gold was pretty much played out. The Nez Perce Chief Twisted Hair used to live here.

Our Mother—*(Various Dreamer, Anglicized.)* The earth.

Pine Tree River—See **Lochsa River**.

Place Like Split Rock—*(Anglicized Nimiputumít.)* [Tepahlewam Wakuspah.] Canyon Creek, Montana, where the eponymous battle was fought. So named (as you might guess) on account of its similarity to **Split Rock**.

Place of the Cave of Red Paint—See **Missouri River**.

Place of the Manure Fires—*(Anglicized Nimiputumít.)* [Tsanim Alikos Pah.] The place on Snake Creek to the east of the **Bear's Paw** Mountains where the Nez Perce camped on 29 September 1877. Here they were surprised by **Miles** and **Howard**, and fought their last battle.

P'na—*(Various Dreamer.)* A sacred place near Priest Rapids, Washington; important to **Smohalla**.

Portland, Oregon—*(?)* Lat. 45° 30', long. 122° 27' 30". "Hdqrs. Department of the Columbia. AG.O. 1877 and 1874. See Ords. 10. 11th Mil. Dept. May 28, 1850 . . ."—Adjutant General's Office inventory.

Rawhide Place—*(Anglicized Nimiputumít.)* The indigenous site that became **Mount Idaho**.

The Redfaced Talking Star—*(Anglicized Nimiputumít.)* Jupiter.

Ripple Place—See **Lewiston, Idaho**.

Riverfork—See **Lewiston, Idaho.**

Rocky Cañon—See **Split Rock**.

Rotten Sun Dance River—See **Clark's Fork River**.

Sacrifice Cliffs—Just across the Yellowstone from Billings, Montana, this spot supposedly marks the site of a suicide by Crow braves whose families had died of smallpox. They rode their horses over the edge.

Salmon River—*(Anglicized Nimiputumít.)* A powerful natural barrier—to the Army, not to the Nez Perces, who after the Battle of **White Bird Canyon** crossed it, then crossed back again, leaving **Howard**'s troops frustrated and humiliated. It lay in **Toohhoolhoolzote**'s and **White Bird**'s Idaho homelands. The Nez Perce called it "Chinook Salmon Water." For the sake of euphony I have altered the name of Toohhoolhoolzote's country (which was evidently "Tamá-nma," or "Place Where the Chinook Salmon Water meets the Enemy River") to "Chinook Salmon Water Mountains," further simplified to to "Chinook Salmon Mountains."

Sapachesap Cave—*(Nimiputumít.)* [Also: Apaschesap.] A rock shelter on Cottonwood Creek, Idaho, near **White Bird Canyon**, where the Nez Perce once burned some Snake warriors alive.

The Sayak Stars—*(Half-Anglicized Nimiputumít.)* The Little Dipper.

Shale-Rock Mountain—*(Anglicized Nimiputumít.)* Exact location unknown.

Shallow Place—See **Cow Island**.

Simí-nekem—*(Nimiputumít.)* [Also: Shimenekem.] The confluence of two rivers, or the land between them. One place with this name (which I translate "Riverfork") is now **Lewiston**, which lies where the **Clearwater** meets the **Snake**.

Snake Creek—See **Place of the Manure Fires**.

Snake River—In Nimiputumít, the Enemy River—presumably so called after the **Snakes** or **Bannocks** [G 2]. According to Aoki, however, it has another name derived from the same "big" or "grand" as the **Clearwater**. [Gulick gives the Nimiputumít name as "Ki-moo-e-nim."] Also referred to as something approximating "Twining River" (name for the Snake "as far up as the forks of **Salmon River**"). Compassionating the reader, I have used only "Enemy River" in this text.

Soaring Up Like Birds—*(Anglicized Wanapum.)* [Wahluke.] A slope above the White Bluffs on the north side of the **Columbia**. Apparently this was a sacred **Dreamer** site.

Sparse-Snowed Place—See **White Bird Canyon**.

Split Rock—*(Anglicized Nimiputumít.)* [Tepahlewam.] Meaning conjectural (Aoki, who writes it "Tipakhlíwamiwatam" [thus simplified by WTV], defines it as "head of rocky bluffs," while McWhorter believes it to signify "split rocks" or "deep cuts"). The camas ground between Rocky Canyon and **Tolo Lake**, Idaho. Here the Nez Perces, Flatheads and other Indian groups used to meet in June to dig camas, gamble, flirt, make political decisions, etcetera. The non-treaty Nez Perces all came together here in 1877 to consider **Howard**'s ultimatum. Ultimately they decided to bow to superior force, and go on the reservation. But a few young warriors scotched this by killing settlers. Hence the Nez Perce War.

Stinking Water River—The Shoshone River, Wyoming. So called by **Howard**.

Sunflower Place—*(Anglicized Nimiputumít.)* Site of Boise, Idaho, which lay near the extremity of the traditional Nez Perce roaming grounds.

Sweat Lodge Place—*(Anglicized Nimiputumít.)* Where the **Grande Ronde** meets the **Snake**.

The THREE SISTERS—*(Anglicized Nimiputumít.)* Three stars in the handle of the Big Dipper. This interpretation of the Three Sisters is conjectural.

Timí-map—*(Nimiputumít.)* The place at at Bruce's Eddy, near **Orofino**, "now under an artificial lake." Aoki, p. 743. Meaning not exactly ascertainable.

Tipsusleimah—*(Nimiputumít.)* "Name of an edible root." Site on John Day Creek where **Shore Crossing** and **Swan Necklace** opened the Nez Perce War by murdering white settlers.

Tolo Lake—*(Nimiputumít.)* I am informed that at this time the lake had no native name; "Tolo" is an English corruption of "Tulekats Chikchamit," the name of the Nez Perce woman who warned the miners of Florence that her nation had risen up against theirs. Hence when I have the whites refer to Tolo Lake in "Should Be a Pleasurable Fight," my use is probably anachronistic; the war had just broken out, so it is unlikely that the lake would yet have received this name.

Tongue River Cantonment, Montana—*(Anglicized Chinook?)* The semipermanent base of **Colonel Miles** during the Nez Perce War; **Colonel Gibbon** likewise set out from here en route to the operation at **Big Hole**. Established 28 August 1876, the year of Little Big Horn. After surrendering to **Miles**, **Joseph** and the other captured non-treaty Nez Perces were temporarily brought here. "Situated at the mouth of Tongue River in the Yellowstone, about 272 miles Southwest of Fort Buford, Dakota, by the Yellowstone and 175 miles by wagon trail. Temporary reservation, 20 miles square, made by Interior Dept., Jan. 20 1877 at request of War Dept—for desc. see Post G.O. No. 2 of 1877 Reservation of suitable size to be surveyed and decld—letter Jan. 26, 1877 to Gen. Sheridan. Troops transferred to Fort Keogh (near by) Nov., 1877."—Adjutant General's Office inventory.

Tongue Water—*(Anglicized Nimiputumít.)* [Pahniah Koos.] A big river which flows through Yellowstone. See **Yellow Stone River**.

United States of America—A lovely idea, even if its continued expansion required the displacement of Native Americans. **Miles** thought it should extend to the North Pole. When the Nez Perce War erupted, our nation wasn't quite so large as that; the flag still bore only thirty-eight stars. It is strange for a twenty-first-century American to reflect on how much of what we now consider part of the U.S. was then an ever altering conglomeration of territories. Emigrants on the Oregon Trail would regularly write about leaving the United States. Oregon had been a state since 1859, but Washington, Idaho, Montana and Wyoming were still territories. (In Wyoming Territory, and there alone, American women could vote in 1877.) In Montana, Oregon and Idaho, as this book shows, many Native American groups and nations still held on. Perhaps it was this cultural variation which led **Looking-Glass** and other non-treaty Nez Perces to (falsely and disastrously) believe that upon entering Montana they were now in the U.S., and therefore beyond the jurisdiction of **General Howard**'s Idaho-based troops.

Walla Walla—[also: Wallah-Wallah, Walla-Walla.] Let's say it was Walla Walla.

Wallowa—*(Nimiputumít.)* "Winding Water." Then again, it might be named after Nez Perce fish-traps. The homeland of the **Joseph** band, containing the eponymous valley in the northeast corner of Oregon. Wallowa County, which covers much of the same area, is 3,145 miles square. Governor Grover, 1873: "This State has already much of its best soil withheld from being occupied by an industrial population in favor of Indians. The region of country in Eastern Oregon now settled and to which the Wallowa Valley is key, is greater in area than the state of Massachusetts. If this section . . . which is now occupied by enterprising white families, should be removed to make roaming ground from nomadic savages, a very serious check will have been given to the growth of our frontier settlements . . ."

Wallula—*(Wanapum.)* ["Coming Down the River," or "Where Waters Meet."] Six hours by railroad from Walla Walla, Wallula was "the head of navigation" in 1877. **Smohalla** was born here, and **General Howard** came here en route to the fateful **Lapwai** conference. This important **Dreamer** site is now underwater thanks to damming.

Weippe—*(Nimiputumít?)* Possible corruption of a word meaning "Unstrung Beads," or of a name of unknown significance assigned to this place by a Grizzly Bear Person. [McDonald calls it "Wyap-p."] An ancient camas ground for the Nez Perces, Flatheads and Umatillas. After the **Clearwater** battle, the non-treaties retreated here from **Kamiah** and then conferred, most of them eventually choosing to take the **Lo Lo Trail**. There was still camas there when I visited.

Welíwe—See **Grande Ronde**.

Weir Place—*(Anglicized Nimiputumít.)* On the **Clearwater**, near Stites, Idaho. Needless to say, the Nez Perce used to trap fish here. Some non-treaties fled here after the **Salmon River** raids, then joined their brethren at **White Bird Canyon**.

White Bird Canyon—*(American English.)* [Lahmotta or Lamáta, meaning "Sparse-Snowed Place" (although McWhorter believed the name meant "Wearisome Place" on account of the labor required to ascend it). People from Lamáta were called "Lamtápo."] The American English name, of course, reflects the fact that it lay in Chief **White Bird**'s homeland. The site of the first battle of the Nez Perce War.

White Mother's Country—*(Various Indian, Anglicized.)* See **British Possessions**.

White Soil—*(Anglicized Nimiiputit.)* [Tom-mah-talk-ke-sin-mah.] The site of the town of Enterprise in the **Wallowa** Valley. Formerly a salt lick that attracted game.

Willows—*(Anglicized Nimiiputit.)* [Takseen.] The place about 12 miles south of **Big Hole** where the Nez Perce first camped after the battle. **Fair Land** died here.

Wolf's Paw—See **Bear's Paw**.

Yellow Stone River—[Nimiiputit: Koos Kap-wel-wen or "Swift Water".] Nowadays: "Yellowstone." A big river which flows through Yellowstone National Park, then northeast to the **Sacrifice Cliffs**, then up to the **Musselshell**. The Crows called it "Elk River."

4. GLOSSARY OF TEXTS

> A very few contradictory primary and secondary sources, to prove the muddiness of the waters.

Nez Perce 1877: The Last Fight, Robert Forczyk—After killing four settlers, "warriors from the White Bird group . . . went on a two-day spree of murdering, raping and burning along the Salmon River, which resulted in the deaths of at least 14 more Americans, including two infants. Four women were brutally raped. These Nez Perce raids were among the worst massacres of American settlers in the post-Civil War West . . ." As for Ad **Chapman**'s firing on the Nez Perce who bore a truce flag at White Bird Canyon, "Perry's troops had no reason to believe that the Nez Perce were anything but hostile after the deaths of those civilians" on the Salmon, "so firing on the supposed parley group was not as unjustified as has been claimed." I do not agree.

Nez Perce Joseph: An Account of His Ancestors, His Lands, His Confederates, His Enemies, His Murders, His War, His Pursuit and Capture, O. O. Howard—An historian of the Big Hole battle calls this book "a self-serving account with a romantic tinge." But it shows **Howard**'s well-meaning side, and gives much otherwise unavailable information about command decisions, life at Lapwai, etcetera.

Hear Me, My Chiefs!, L. V. McWhorter—"It is only fair to the Indians to call attention to the fact that the outrages against women and children did not occur until after the raiders became beastly drunk on whisky found by the barrel at Benedict's store-saloon."

Chief Joseph & the Flight of the Nez Perce: The Untold Story of an American Tragedy, Kent Nerburn. A fairly good read, but not especially scholarly or reliable. For instance, Nerburn claims that the stagecoach which the Nez Perce hijacked was unoccupied, whereas other sources all describe the passengers running to hide in the willows, the killing of the actress's dog, and so on.

The Nez Perces in the Indian Territory: Nimiipuu Survival, J. Diane Pearson—A very detailed account of what happened to **Joseph**'s band after their surrender, containing much information unavailable elsewhere. It is, however, as partisan in its way as Forczyk's book. For instance, here is how Pearson recounts the beginning of the war: "In order to avoid war, the bands would try to make the best of conditions [on the reservation.] But the next day, Mrs. FitzGerald [the army surgeon's wife at Lapwai] complained to her mother that the Nimiipuu had not gone to the reservation. Events spiraled out of control after several young Nimiipuu men killed a white man to avenge the murder of one of their relatives, and on June 17, 1877, troopers attacked a Nimiipuu group who were protected by a flag of truce." This is all she can bring herself to say about the rapes and murders committed by the Nez Perce before June 17.

Yellow Wolf: His Own Story, L. V. McWhorter—A sincere attempt by a local white rancher and autodidact, who seems to have been trusted by the non-treaty Nez Perce and was adopted into the tribe, to relate the autobiography of this warrior whom the author befriended and admired. For this book **White Thunder** (the preferred name of the man more commonly known as Yellow Wolf) was interviewed by McWhorter over the span of a quarter-century. Aubrey L. Haines calls it "at some points, contradictory, and at others, not in agreement with known facts; and yet, it is a useful, even indispensable work." Along with *Hear Me, My Chiefs!,* the same author's half-posthumous work, this may be the most imporant book on the Nez Perce War.

Howard's Campaign Against the Nez Perce Indians, 1877, Thomas A. Sutherland, volunteer aide-de-camp on Gen. **Howard**'s Staff—This slight, partisan work of "embedded journalism" makes no attempt to analyze the causes of the war, or to consider **Joseph**'s motives. It presents Howard in an almost glowing light. A few details of the campaign are mentioned in no other source. Sutherland implies that he accompanied Howard all the way to Bear's Paw, but he says little about the surrender or Joseph himself.

5. GLOSSARY OF CALENDARS, CURRENCIES, FORMS, LEGALISMS AND MEASURES

Nez Perce seasonal terms are here.

Abstract "D"—*(U.S. Army.)* An inventory of requisitioned property.

Abstract "N"—*(U.S. Army.)* An inventory of captured enemy property.

Assembly parade—*(U.S. Army.)* Sometimes dress parade. Often a quarter-hour before sunset.

Buffalo Calf Season—*(Anglicized Nimiputumít.)* Around December.

Cous Cake Season—*(Anglicized Nimiputumít.)* May and June.

Dawes Act—*(American.)* Also known as the Allotment Act (enacted 1887; see Chronology for that year). Divided up reservations into a checkerboard of private holdings (some of which were sold to non-Indians) for the purpose of further "civilizing" the Indians by assigning them American-style small homesteads. Of course the result was another American land grab.

Department—*(U.S. Army.)* A military district. Like the Territories, Departments altered rapidly in name, shape and extent during the 1870s and 1880s, based on patterns of settlement and Indian wars. See G 2, **military divisional organization**.

Eel Season—*(Anglicized Nimiputumít.)* Around July.

False Flowering Time—*(Anglicized Nimiputumít.)* Around March.

Greenback—*(American.)* A paper dollar. Sometimes accepted only at discounted rates. See **shinplaster**.

Indian policy—*(American.)* "Like the man who beat his wife, the government believes it has the right to maltreat the red man to the top of its bent, but that no one else shall be allowed to do so."

Morning Report—*(U.S. Army.)* Pretty much how it sounds.

"Retreat"—*(U.S. Army.)* Lowering of flag at sunset, generally accompanied by the second roll call of the day.

Reveille—*(U.S. Army.)* Wakeup call, generally accompanied by a "morning gun." The time varied from post to post. It might be set for 6:00 a.m., or for sunrise.

River Season—*(Anglicized Nimiputumít.)* Approximately equivalent to September, when steelheads ascend the rivers in the Nez Perce country.

Salmon Spawning Season—*(Anglicized Nimiputumít.)* Approximately the same as August. The word literally means something like "Head of Creek Season," since the salmon swim upstream to spawn. I have altered it to something more easily comprehensible to salmon-less people.

Sapalwit—*(Nimiputumítized English.)* Sunday; the Sabbath.

Shinplaster—*(American.)* Paper change for a **greenback**. The lowest denomination was five cents. Out west at this period, shinplasters were often honored only at a discount value.

"Taps"—*(U.S. Army.)* Call of lights out. At a military post, taps was often blown at 9:30 p.m. Enlisted men had to be silent afterward; officers did not.

"Tattoo"—*(U.S. Army.)* Call to quarters, followed by the final roll call of the day. Often at 9:00 p.m.

Towering Plants—*(Anglicized Nimiputumít.)* An extreme simplification of Aoki's three defini-tions of *tustimasá-tal* (p. 803), which is related to "very high up." The word could refer to the time when plants rise up, or the time when the sun is high, or when the Nez Perce rode to higher places to dig roots. Perhaps equivalent to April.

6. GENERAL GLOSSARY

And just as dealers in Indian relics may also sell Confederate money, calla lily seeds, and pills to solve or bring on female trouble, so I, William the Blind, will alongside my vending of the Nez Perce War offer for purchase various Americanisms and a few half-breed sayings.

Áhaha—*(Nimiputumít.)* Noise made when laughing.

Anásh—*(Umatilla.)* The top portion of a plant.

Átawit—*(Umatilla.)* Sweetheart.

Aparejo—*(Mexican Spanish.)* A cargo saddle for mules. As one soldier explained: "It's like two leather cushions hinged together at the top . . . First, a couple of saddle blankets are put on, then the aparejo is sat astride the animal's back . . . Now the boxes or sacks are laid on as near the top as possible & fastened together with a rope." Then comes a girth, and the *aparejo* is cinched.

Acqua-regia—*(American English version of Latin.)* One part nitric acid to three parts hydro-chloric acid. Used to dissolve gold, which will not dissolve in either of these acids alone.

Barefoot whiskey—*(Tennessee slang, according to Walt Whitman.)* The undiluted kind.

Blackfoot rum—*(Canadian and American.)* A watered-down variety concocted by traders, which cheaply served the purpose of intoxicating the Blackfeet.

Bitterroot—See **spatlam**.

Bone Game—See **Stick Game**.

Book of Light—*(Anglicized Nimiputumít.)* The Bible.

Buffalo—*(American Western colloquial.)* Bison, really, but I would be even more pedantic than usual to speak of the Bison Country, bison soldiers, etc. In unfixed usages I have not hesitated to interchange "buffalo" and "bison" from time to time.

Butterfly—*(Anglicized Nimiputumít.)* Vulva. "Lapwai" means "butterfly." So does "káyayayaya."

Calomel—*(Various English and American.)* A medicine containing, among other ingredients, opium and mercury. Used by the U.S. Army well past 1877; my 1911 *Britannica* still recom-mends it.

Camas—*(Nimiputumít and other languages.)* There were several different varieties of this edible tuber, which was a staple in the diets of many Indians from British Columbia down to California. The most useful kind, common camas, is *Camassia quamash*. (Lewis and Clark often spelled the name "quamash.") Camas was used in a tea by **Blackfoot** [G 2] women to induce labor. The flow-ers of this plant were usually blue or purple. "It looks like a little hyacinth-bulb, and when roasted is as nice as a chestnut. We have seen it in blossom, when its pale-blue flowers covered the fields so closely that, at a little distance, we took it for a lake." (Several varieties of the appropriately named death camas sport white flowers.) White settlers sometimes used pigs to destroy the camas meadows to deny Native Americans this food supply; more often, however, the whites were simply indifferent, and since the meadows were fine for grazing stock and such uses, that was that.

Cantenisses—Flapped saddle-pockets, often loaded up with cartridges.

Chá-á—The call of a bluejay, per Meriwether Lewis, whose orthography is "cha-ah, cha-ah!" I have made it look more like Nimiputumít.

Cous—*(Nimiputumít.)* [Lewis and Clark often spelled it "cows," so we can pronounce it accordingly. Other spellings: "khouse," "couse."] Also known as biscuitroot or breadroot, this tuberous plant was almost as useful to Nez Perce as camas. Lewis informs us that "the cows is a knobbed root of an irregularly rounded form not unlike the Gensang . . . This root they collect, rub of[f] a thin black rhind which covers it and pounding it expose it in cakes to the sun . . . The noise of their women pounding roots reminds me of a nail factory." Root oil could be applied to sores, and the plant was sometimes smoked. The Crows called it "bear root"; the Latin name is *Lomatium cous*. Several related species were also employed.

Crease—*(American English.)* To shoot a wild horse in a certain portion of the neck near the withers, in order to stun and capture it.

Dodger—*(Confederate slang.)* Cornmeal bread or biscuit.

Eye necklace—*(Anglicized Nimiputumít, invented.)* Field-glasses. Aoki's dictionary gives no term for this (or for "binoculars"), so I have made this up.

File closer—*(U.S. Army.)* An officer or NCO at rear or flank to supervise men in ranks.

Flint hide—*(American English.)* The skin of a buffalo, cow, or other leather-producing animal, prepared simply by scraping it, soaking it in a stream, and then drying it in the sun. Used where hardness and stiffness were paramount, as in moccasin soles, tipi covers and the pegged-out drumheads which are beaten on by the stick musicians at a Sun Dance.

Gangue mineral—*(Various English and American.)* "Associated with the ore minerals there are usually certain common ones, chiefly of non-metallic character, which carry no values worth extracting," including quartz, fluorite, feldspar, & c.

Getting-drunk liquid—*(Anglicized Nimiputumít.)* Whiskey.

German silver—*(American.)* First manufactured in 1863, this trade item "really contains no silver, but is an alloy of nickel, zinc, and copper."

Government—*(Various English and American.)* To **Howard**, a living American entity, so I always capitalize.

Guidon—*(U.S. Army.)* A swallowtailed American flag on a pole, taken with a regiment into the field and planted each night at camp.

Hairpipe—*(U.S. Army.)* Long cylindrical bead made of clamshell or bone.

Hik'íseyce—*(Nimiputumít.)* "It [the land] is wrinkled." I have used this in reference to the country around White Bird Canyon.

Hinimí—*(Nimiputumít.)* Sound of a horse's neigh.

Í-tsitsitsititsits—*(Nimiputumít.)* "Particle that describes shivering from cold."

Kaa náko haamankhnáawyanikh kaakíne hilkilíinenikh?—*(Nimiputumít.)* Why are they acting brave and milling around here?

Khattát!—*(Nimiputumít.)* Noise of something being ripped.

King George—*(Anglicized Nimiputumít.)* A product of the place we now call Canada. [Aoki's dictionary, from which I got this, does not say when it entered the language, so I have felt free to imagine its use in 1877.] And (so I imagine it, anyhow) by extension from "Boston," a Caucasian inhabitant of what is now Canada.

Kinnikinnick—*(Chinook jargon?)* A leaf which was sometimes smoked by itself, or sometimes mixed with tobacco, to make the latter more mild. The identity of the leaf seemed to vary widely. In the Lewis and Clark Botanical Garden of the arboretum in Boise there is an herb labeled as such. But to the Crows, kinnikinnick was often or usually red willow bark.

Kíw—*(Nimiputumít.)* A hammering sound.

Kloochman—*(Chinook jargon.)* Woman [a pioneer woman's transliteration]. "Young woman" is "Ten-as-clooch-man."

Kuseyn—*(Nimiputumít.)* The Buffalo Country. [See entry on **buffalo**, above, this glossary.] Aoki notes: "It sometimes refers to today's Montana, and sometimes to the country east of the Rocky Mountains [*sic*] divide." The buffalo hunters were called Kuseynutitoqan.

Kuyímkuyim—*(Nimiputumít.)* Blue racer snake.

Lílps—*(Nimiputumít.)* A certain edible white mushroom which grows beneath pine trees.

Marrow-like—*(Anglicized Nimiputumít.)* Hard candy. See note to "Red Salmon Season" on the "like" Nimiputumít words for American commodities, p. 1316.

Mokh—*(Nimiputumít.)* Sound of a fish splashing.

Mululululu—*(Nimiputumít.)* The noise of a bubbling river.

Paq—*(Nimiputumít.)* A marten's cry.

Parfleche—*(Nimiputumít.)* Translucent pieces of rawhide, often painted with earth pigments and hide glue in geometric shapes, and assembled into pouches, saddlebags and the like. The Crows are masterful at this art.

Pátskh—*(Umatilla.)* To fuck.

Pokát—*(Nimiputumít.)* "Sound of MAGPIE pecking COYOTE's eye-fat."

Pim!—*(Nimiputumít.)* The noise of a small drum. I have used this sound to represent a small caliber gunshot.

Qiqaw!—*(Nimiputumít.)* The noise made by skeletons moving.

Qáw!—*(Nimiputumít.)* A pounding noise.

Qoh!—*(Nimiputumít.)* The cry of a raven (McWhorter's orthography).

Recruit—*(American English.)* To restore to health, as in "recruit his command."

Red—*(American English.)* In 1877 this meant an Indian, not a Communist.

Reservation—*(American English euphemism.)* "The Reservation system a good one for everyone but the Indians and the people."—Lieutenant C. E. S. Wood.— It is especially saddening to consider that even the meager "reservation" onto which a given band of Indians were removed did not necessarily remain theirs in perpetuity. Note for instance President Buchanan's executive order of 1857 concerning the Grande Ronde reservation: "Set apart as a reservation for Indian purposes *until otherwise ordered.*"

Rocky Mountain fever—*(U.S. Army; general American English.)* A mild fever accompanied by painful swelling of the feet; believed to be altitude dependent.

Shikèmnúvit—*(Umatilla.)* Horseless.

Shlal—*(Pseudo-Nimiputumít.)* The sound of a fetus moving inside its mother. Invented by WTV.

Shlap—*(Nimiputumít.)* The sound of a raven's wingbeat.

Shláyayaya—*(Nimiputumít.)* The sound of icicles striking each other.

Shlokh-shlokh—*(Nimiputumít.)* Noise of footsteps in dry grass.

Sibley tent *(U.S. Army.)* "A patented tent copied from the Plains Indian's teepee . . . conical . . . , some eighteen feet in diameter, and had an iron stove in the centre . . ." This Civil War invention could sleep up to twenty soldiers if they lay spoon-fashion on their sides. It saw moderate use in that conflict, and very occasional use in the Plains Indian Wars.

Side-lining—*(U.S. Army; general American English.)* "The fastening of the hind and forefoot on the same side of the animal together; side-lines had a chain between the feet to prevent the Indians from cutting them and releasing the animals."—J. Lee Humfreville, 1899.

Síikstiwaa—*(Nimiputumít.)* Darling.

Silk buffalo robe—"A three year old calfless cow pelt and one of the most value."

Sink—Latrine.

Spatlam—*(Chinook jargon?)* "In May they get the *spatlam*, or bitter-root. This is a delicate white root, that dissolves in boiling, and forms a white jelly. The Bitter Root River and Mountains get their name from this plant."—Caroline Leighton, Washington Territory, 1866.

Stick Game—*(Various Indian, Anglicized.)* A form of gambling which involved concealing two sticks (one black and one white) in any of four hands. A bettor had to guess where each stick was. The Bone Game was similar.

Taq!—*(Nimiputumít.)* The noise of a thing getting crushed.

Taqaqaq—*(Nimiputumít.)* Sound of a crackling fire.

Tekh!—*(Nimiputumít.)* Noise made by a locust.

Timm!—*(Nimiputumít.)* Sound of thunder.

Titálin!—*(Nimiputumít.)* Extremely loud noise, as of an artillery shell.

Tiyé-pu—*(Nimiputumít.)* Sound of wind whistling through dead wood.

Tóq—*(Nimiputumít.)* Actually, not an onomatopoetic sound as so often, but a C-class verb. To crackle.

Tsálalal—*(Nimiputumít.)* The way a thing tumbles downward (Aoki gives the example of a shot eagle).

Túmm—*(Nimiputumít.)* Sound of many katydids.

Wakesh nun pakilauitin / Jehovan'm yiyauki—*(Nimiputumít.)* The refrain of the first hymn in the Nez Perce gospel book of 1897. In her introductory note the author informs us that "Rev. Robert Williams loved this Hymn and he sang it with his dying breath." Williams was first pastor of the First Church, Kamiah, and called by Miss S. L. McBeth "the St. Paul of the Nez Perces."

Wa-láhsasa—*(Nimiputumít.)* "I am flying up. I am jumping up. I am worshipping (as a Dreamer)." This definition of Aoki's I have slightly "retranslated."

Wapato—*(Chinook jargon.)* Duck potato or arrowweed.

Wá-wa—*(Nimiputumít.)* A mosquito. I have (plausibly, I hope) imagined this to also represent the mosquito's sound.

Wind's tears—*(Anglicized Nimiputumít.)* A flower, species not given.

Wittco Weeon—*(Assiniboine.)* [In the text I have altered the mid-nineteenth-century spelling to the more currently plausible *wittko wíyon*.] "Fool woman," a slut.

Woodhawk—*(American English.)* Woodcutter-entrepreneurs who sold their haul to passing steamboats.

NOTE ON NIMIPUTUMÍT ORTHOGRAPHY:

I have relied on the *Nez Perce Dictionary* of Haruo Aoki (Berkeley: University of California Press, University of California Publications in Linguistics, vol. 122, 1994), which employs an orthography similar to the International Phonetic Alphabet. Since this system might prove bewildering and even intimidating to nonlinguists (what does that slash through the "l" mean, and why should "c" be pronounced "ts" and what about those strange dots?), I decided to simplify these transliterations into approximations more practical for Anglophone usage.

Aoki's "x" accordingly appears as "kh." In fact, Nimiputumít employs two "kh" sounds, but since most native English speakers (including me) will not be able to hear the difference, I could see no reason to transcribe it. You may approximate this "kh" with the "ch" in "Bach."

Lateral fricatives (those barred "l"'s you were just reading about) have been represented by "shl." Glottalization was not represented at all. The glottalized affricate, which Aoki writes with the Greek letter gamma, appears in this book as "tl."

Aoki's apostrophes (as in "wiye-k'uyx") have been eliminated.

Nimiputumít vowels may be long or short. I represent a long vowel by repeating it; for instance, "ii" should be said for twice as long as "i." I have left in Aoki's accents. If you see a double "i" with an accent over the first, this does not mean that one "i" is accented and the other is not, but simply that the extra long vowel should be stressed. And on the subject of "i," in Nimiputumít this vowel is pronounced as we would pronounce an "e" in "eel." (The linguist Dr. Teresa McFarland, who kindly advised and oversaw all these simplifications, expressed such utter repulsion when I proposed to substitute "ee" for "i" that I yielded to her.) The letter "a" should be pronounced like the "a" in "father," not like the "a" in "wagon."

As the reader can see, many Nimiputumít words would be considered sentences in English. My dilemma here was whether to be scrupulously accurate, and use Aoki's translations verbatim, or "retranslate" a bit, in order not to be a copycat. In the end I decided to do whichever suited me at the moment.

Although Nimiputumít words can be challengingly polysyllabic for Anglophones, after much consideration I elected (except when replacing Aoki's dot separators) not to break up syllables with hyphens, fearing that the result might be a sort of baby talk. If you wish to read my simplified transliterations aloud, the best way might be to speak slowly. Although considerable acoustic meaning has been lost in my versions, you might at least hear Nimiputumít as it would sound to you in the absence of specialized training.

I have relied considerably on the dictionary as a basis for Nimiputumít dialogue, but there I have begun with Aoki's English renderings (for instance, of the noble word which means "the scraping of the inner bark of trees caused whoever [ate it] to have diarrhea") and modified them freely, trying to respect thought constructions and verb forms without merely parroting them. Thus when in certain Aokian verb forms a woman decorates herself with beads, to me the significant and beautiful core of this is the decoration, and so I sometimes have somebody simply decorate herself, or decorate herself with something other than beads. And I have further extended the conception as in this sentence about Chief Joseph: "And let me now decorate my heart with a memory of Wallowa."

Dr. McFarland, having studied Nimiputumít sounds as given in Aoki's dictionary, has transliterated for me the following American English proper names as the Nez Perces might have pronounced them (these are all listed in G 1): Joe Albert, Abraham Brooks, Jim, Captain John, John Levi, Old George, Robinson Minthon, Monteith, Perry and James Reuben. However, "Tsépmin" for Chapman comes from Aoki's dictionary.

P.S. "Mosquito's words do not follow the vowel harmony rules."—Aoki, p. 293 (entry for *k'uy*).[*]

NOTE ON UMATILLA ORTHOGRAPHY:

For most of the words in the native language of my fictional character Umatilla Jim, I have relied on the *Handbook of North American Indians*, vol. 12 (Theodore Stern, "Cayuse, Umatilla, and Walla Walla"), and on Virginia Beavert and Sharon Hargus, *Ichishkíin Sinwit: Yakama / Yakima Sahaptin Dictionary* (Toppenish, Washington: Heritage University, in assoc. w/ University of Washington Press, 2009). The following information comes from pp. xviii–xix (Bruce Rigsby, "The Origin and History of the Name 'Sahaptin'"): Sahaptin is a language in the Sahaptian language family. Sahaptin is related to Nimiputumít. Its dialects include Umatilla, Walla Walla, Yakima and Warm Springs. From 1811 until fairly recently, Nimiputumít was called by Euro-Americans "Sahaptin" and Sahaptin was called by them "Walla Walla."

I have re-transliterated as for Nimiputumít above. Thus my *pátskh* actually appeared in the dictionary as *pátsx*.

NOTE ON ENGLISH ORTHOGRAPHY:

In 1877, standard American English was obviously closer to the English of my own period than was the case for most other volumes in *Seven Dreams* thus far published. One can read memoirs of the Nez Perce War without noticing many orthographic archaisms other than a somewhat more generous capitalization of such nouns of hierarchical position as "Chief," "Government" or "Lieutenant." (Since Howard lower-cased them, so did I.) As in every period, some diarists and letter-writers spelled English as they heard it. For instance, here is how a soldier at Little Big Horn described what happened to Custer: "Their the Bravest General of Modder times met his death."

---

[*]And did I tell you that the language has the same word for an empty rifle-shell, a coffin and a turtle shell?

Some late-nineteenth-century words of American English read just oddly enough to early-twenty-first-century American eyes as to be considered possible errors: "Cashmire" (for Kashmir or cashmere), "intrenchments," "lustre," "coöperate," "reënslave," "to-morrow." A few are definite errors—for instance, the carbine frequently referred to in the possessive as a "Sharp's" was named after Christian Sharps. I have left most of these forms as they were (but corrected "Sharps"). General Howard frequently lower-cased the word "negro" and others upper-cased it. Howard did not, as many did, upper-case "Abolition," but because the word in isolation has lost much anti-slavery signification, I thought it best to represent his understanding of the term by employing upper case.

Howard's usage varied between "dispatch" and "despatch," so I have chosen the more exotic one. The year 1877 appeared to be one of orthographic transition for Howard and others for what I will call the "de-compoundization" of words. Thus "Looking-glass," so written in Howard's *Supplementary Report*, became "Looking-Glass" in his later book on the campaign. Place-names were in flux from, for instance, "Rocky cañon" and "Jackson's bridge" to "Rocky Canyon" and Jackson's Bridge." I have compromised on "Looking-Glass," "Rocky Cañon," "Jackson's Bridge," etc. In *Argall* and *Fathers and Crows* I took pleasure in spelling words any which way, as my sources did; but the narrowing trend of American English in 1877, combined with the challenge already faced by the reader in remembering that, say, Joseph is Heinmot Tooyalakekt, which purportedly means Thunder Travelling To Loftier Heights but might mean something slightly different, induced me to simplify a trifle.

The English of Lewis and Clark, being older than General Howard's, was spelled and punctuated delightfully every which way, and frontier orthography partook somewhat of this character right up into the twentieth century. I have sought to respect these varying forms during their rare occurrence in *The Dying Grass*.

SOURCES

[AND A FEW NOTES]

I think explanations and defenses are bad things.

RUTHERFORD B. HAYES, to his campaign manager, *ca.* 1876

Whether or not you agree with that President, I myself prefer to reveal what use (defensible or not) I have made of my sources. My aim in *Seven Dreams* has been to create a "Symbolic History"—that is to say, an account of origins and metamorphoses which is often untrue based on the literal facts as we know them, but whose untruths further a deeper sense of truth. Here one walks the proverbial tight-rope, on one side of which lies slavish literalism; on the other, self-indulgence. For an example of my difficulties, see the entry for Colonel Perry in Glossary 1. Given these dangers, it seemed wise to have this source list, so as to provide those who desire with easy means of corroborating or refuting my imagined versions of things, to monitor my originality,[*] and to give leads to primary sources and other useful texts for interested non-specialists such as myself. I have tried to do this as fully as seemed practical. In the twentieth century, Lieutenant Wood's son once composed "A Pleasunte and Wittie Worke . . . ," which was "Written by Erskine Wood After He Hadde Read Master Raphe Robynson's Translation of More's Utopia and Who When It Liked Hym Hath Boldlye Taken Some Phrases from That Booke." Like my other Dreams, *The Dying Grass* steals with comparable boldness; at least it foot-notes when it does.

This is one of those novels which attempt to present the mutual alterations of human beings over time. In its "real" form, the Nez Perce War was not conducive to such a project. As always in these Seven Dreams, the Indians appear fitfully and incompletely. No source is consistent as to the name and number of Chief Joseph's wives; about the other Nez Perce chiefs we usually know even less. Who travelled with whom, what (if anything) was said around the campfire, most of this remains beyond our ken. As for their pursuers, the fact is that Howard split his command after the Clearwater battle, the result being that a number of the men whom we know most about, thanks to recollections of the White Bird and Clearwater affairs, left the story forever. During the war, the Nez Perces encountered several different military groups: Perry's at White Bird Canyon, Howard's on the Salmon, then Lieu-tenant Rains's detachment (not to mention some volunteers before and after), Howard's at Clearwater, Mason's at Weippe, Rawn's at Fort Fizzle, Gibbon's at Big Hole, Howard's again at Camas Meadows, Sturgis's at Canyon Creek and finally Miles's at Bear's Paw.

Accordingly, I altered history. Of course all my Seven Dreams do, but this one more than any of the preceding volumes rejiggers events. Each deviation from historical truth is noted in an appropriate source-note. However, let me summarize my alterations here.

Because Perry's disaster at White Bird Canyon must have been so important to Howard, and be-cause his subsequent failure to immediately reinforce the Brave Seventeen at Cottonwood, and his strange dilatoriness at Clearwater, are thought-provoking, I wanted to give his character time to work itself out, so I kept him with Howard all the way to Carroll, when in fact he was out of the picture after Kamiah. Likewise, Howard's brave and pious aide-de-camp Wilkinson, who had been with him to the Yumas and who shared his outlook, was in reality dispatched to Spokane to deter other Indians from joining the Nez Perce combatants, but I could not bear to let him go, and the more I elaborated him, the more I enjoyed him. There is no evidence to indicate that he was the Iago I have made him, just as Perry's great friendship with Theller is a fiction, although not necessarily a lie, since, as noted, those two served together on previous Indian campaigns. Likewise, Mason and Sladen never followed the Nez Perce Trail as I have them do.

---

[*]See, for instance, the "Experience of Two Moons" source-note, p. 1312, to the chapter on the Big Hole massacre.

Wood's development from a would-be Indian killer into an antimilitaristic poet follows the facts, but just when he tilted against the Nez Perce War is unclear. He was loyal to Howard (who had been very kind to him) while the latter lived. My supposition that the attack on Big Hole shook him is just that, but it is not implausible. His dialogues about the matter with Howard, Fletch and Wilkinson are all invented, but it is good to remind ourselves that under some circumstances nineteenth-century (white) Americans enjoyed more freedom to be eccentric, nonconformist, oppositional, etcetera, than we do. It is instructive to read the memoir of almost any Indian-fighting general of that period, and compare it with the corporate blandness of some military functionary's autobiography from the beginning of this millennium; the latter's judgments are no more nuanced than Wilkinson's.

I invented Toohhoolhoolsote's wives, and made my best conjecture about the name of Joseph's elder wife. All the private family politics among the Nez Perces had to be made up. The incident when Springtime was nearly left behind at Clearwater, and Joseph's later separation from her and from Good woman, are attested. I guessed what I could.

Looking-Glass has been reviled for his arrogant blindness, which twice brought the Army upon the Nez Perces when they were unprepared. I tried to see things from his point of view—which is not to excuse him. His embassy to the Crows [see "They Are the Ones Who Did Wrong Things"] may well be "one of the romantic myths"; yet to me it makes such strong psychological sense, given what I think I have gathered about his character, that I decided to let it happen.

Very often the names of Indians who murdered civilians are not known. I chose to attach their roles to this or that real character (such as Red Spy) who seemed capable of committing such acts.

As in other Dreams, I have generally privileged the weather and light conditions I met with at historical sites over the ones described in primary sources. Since this series has much to do with the effects of specific landscapes on our consciousness (hence the series subtitle), when I visit, say, the Camas Meadows battleground, I can best bring the place to life by describing what I see and feel. The Nez Perce attack took place on a moonless night; I happened to encounter a spectacular moon, and recorded matters thus. Global warming prevented me from ever experiencing the early August night frosts which afflicted Gibbon's soldiers on their approach to Big Hole; and when I arrived at Bear's Paw on an early autumn day the place was quite hot. Since the Bear's Paw episode is associated with cold, I had to make another trip there in late winter to describe the place as I wished to do. But when the weather divergences from 1877 were not so extreme as to alter the fundamentals of a given scene, I have generally let them stand.

My hope is that all these imaginings bring a kind of life to the raw sources, and help a reader feel not that this was not precisely how it was, but simply that the situation was all too real, as were the various motives.

THE DYING GRASS

Epigraph: "For the most part, a civilized white man . . ."—Francis Parkman, *The Oregon Trail* and *The Conspiracy of Pontiac* (New York: Library of America, 1991; orig. text 1849 [1st ed.]), p. 242.

The maps I have drawn for this book are based in part upon nineteenth-century originals, in part upon contemporary commercial maps and driving atlases of the relevant states, and to some extent upon James Truslow Adams, editor-in-chief, and R. V. Coleman, managing editor, *Atlas of American History* (New York: Charles Scribner's Sons, 1943). I highly recommend this clear and elegant volume of line drawings, for its beauty as much as its information value.

Grass-Texts: A Speech and a Report (1877–78)

Grass-Text I: An Inaugural Speech (1877)

Extracts from the President-elect's speech—[U.S. Congress], *Congressional Record, Containing the Proceedings and Debates of the Forty-Fifth Congress, First Session, also Special Session of the Senate*, vol. VI, Part VI (Washington, D.C.: Government Printing Office, 1877), p. 3.

Whitman's lines—Walt Whitman, *Complete Poetry and Collected Prose* (New York: Library of America, 1982; orig. texts 1855–92), p. 593 ("Old War-Dreams, 1865–66, rev. 1881).

Description of President Hayes—After Lally Weymouth, *America in 1876: The Way We Were*, designed by Milton Glaser (New York: Vintage, 1976), p. 107. Various descriptions of Washington, D.C., are drawn from illustrations, etc. in this book. I have taken a few Hayes word-constructions from Charles Richard Williams, ed., *Diary and Letters of Rutherford Birchard Hayes, Nineteenth Presi-*

dent of the United States, vol. III: 1865–1881 (Columbus: Ohio State Archaeological and Historical Society, 1924).

"The dark horse from Ohio . . ."—Weymouth, p. 120 (*Louisville Courier-Journal,* June 17, 1876).

Summary of events culminating in Hayes's inauguration—After the same source, pp. 122–43.

Footnote: Congressional reduction in army size from 54,000 in 1866 to 25,000 in 1876—John M. Carroll and Colin F. Baxter, eds., *The American Military Tradition from Colonial Times to the Present* (Wilmington, Delaware: Scholarly Resources Inc., 1993), p. 99. See also Arthur A. Ekirch, Jr., *The Civilian and the Military* (New York: Oxford University Press, 1956), p. 114.

"I can myself almost remember negro slaves in New York . . ."—Whitman, p. 1173 ("Some Diary Notes at Random").

My understanding of the lay of the land at Chancellorsville, Yorktown, Fair Oaks and Gettysburg, here and throughout the book, is partially indebted to (a) Capt. Calvin D. Cowles, 23d U.S. Infantry, comp., *Atlas to Accompany the Official Records of the Union and Confederate Armies. Published Under the Direction of the Hons. Redfield Proctor, Stephen B. Elkins, and Daniel S. Lamont, Secretaries of War,* by Maj. George B. Davis, U.S. Army, Mr. Leslie J. Perry, Civilian Expert, Mr. Joseph W. Kirkley, Civilian Expert, Board of Publication (Washington, D.C.: Government Printing Office, 1891–1895), especially Plates XVII, XVIII, XX and XLI; (b) Department of Military Art and Engineering, United States Military Academy, comp., *The West Point Atlas of the Civil War,* chief ed. Col. Vincent J. Esposito (New York: Frederick A. Praeger, 1962 abr.? repr. of 1959 ed.), Map 43; and (c) William C. Davis and Bell L. Wiley, under direction of the National Historic Society, *Civil War: A Complete Photographic History* (New York: Tess Press, 2000 repr. of orig. 1981–84 6-vol. ed.), pp. 408–15.

Fleeing deer at Chancellorsville—Bevin Alexander, *Lost Victories: The Military Genius of Stonewall Jackson* (New York: Hippocrene Books, Inc., 2004 repr. of 1992 ed.).

"When you're forbidden to call a man *tyrant* . . ."—Common pro-slave appellations for Lincoln at this period were "mountebank," "old ape," "consummate tyrant." See the *Autobiography of Oliver Otis Howard, Major General United States Army* (Freeport, New York: Books for Libraries Press, Black Heritage Library Collection, 1971; orig. pub. 1907), vol. 2, p. 169.

Crow mutilations of Dakota corpses—Parkman, p. 117.

Grass-Text II: A Report (1878)

"The 'Report of Civil and Military Commission' . . ."—*Supplementary Report (Non-Treaty Nez-Perce Campaign) of Brigadier-General O. O. Howard, Brevet Major-General U.S. Army, commanding Department of the Columbia. January 26, 1878.* (Portland, Oregon: Assistant Adjutant-General's Office, Department of the Columbia, 1878), p. 3.

I. Indian Service

Epigraph: "The Indian service now devolving upon our army is necessarily arduous and unpopular . . ."— Oliver Otis Howard, Brig. Gen. U.S.A., *Nez Perce Joseph: An Account of His Ancestors, His Lands, His Confederates, His Enemies, His Murders, His War, His Pursuit and Capture* (Charleston, South Carolina: BiblioLife, n.d.; *ca.* 2009; facsimile repr. of: Boston: Lee & Shepard Publishers, 1881), p. ix.

Many of my descriptions of U.S. Army routines, drills, ranks, tactics, etc., are derived from August V. Kautz, Capt. 6th U. S. Cavalry, Brig. and Brevet Maj. Gen. of Volunteers, *The 1865 Customs of Service for Officers of the Army: A Handbook of the Duties of Each Grade, Lieutenant to Lieut.-General* (Mechanicsburg, Pennsylvania: Stackpole Books, 2002; org. ed. [w/ slightly different title] 1866). A helpful introduction (which I have drawn on much less) is Jeremy Agnew, *Life of a Soldier on the Western Frontier* (Missoula, Montana: Mountain Press Publishing Co., 2008). You will find a few specific tidbits from these two books sourced in the following notes.

Descriptions of buffalo are based in part on my own observation, in Yellowstone and other places, and in part on information in Parkman and in Mari Sandoz, *The Buffalo Hunters* (Lincoln: University of Nebraska Press/Bison Books [very appropriately], 1978 repr. of 1954 ed.).

The diction used is as much as possible contemporary to the Nez Perce War, and drawn from too many different sources to list, from Walt Whitman's essays to soldiers' diaries and letters. Very occasionally I have hazarded borrowings from such later sources as the Montana poet Badger Clark's *Sun and Saddle Leather, Including Grass Grown Trails and New Poems,* 9th ed. (Boston: Richard G. Badger/Gorham Press, 1922; orig. copyright 1915). Since he seemed to be helping himself to the phraseology of old cowboys, and since veterans of the Nez Perce War were certainly still alive in 1915, I saw no reason to deny myself the pleasure of "let's go a-courtin' in the mountains."

And the Water and the Grass

Descriptions of water—After a visit to Lake Easton State Park, Washington, in August 2009.
Description of the dying grass—First seen going farther east in that state, where the forest country ends.

Plenty of Indians All Over the Country

Descriptions of the Grande Ronde Valley, here and throughout—After visits in 2006, 2009, 2011.

Re: Nez Perce: "Don't ask me how they got their name."—But see Gary Moulton, ed., *The Definitive Journals of Lewis and Clark* (Lincoln: University of Nebraska Press, 1983–2001, 13 vols. incl. index), vol. 7: "From the Pacific to the Rockies," p. 223 (Clark, Wednesday May 7th 1806), in which Chief Cut Nose is mentioned. The captains also describe an occasional fashion of affixing a "wampum shell" to a nose-piercing. [Note: Cited "Lewis and Clark."]

"An immense tract of six thousand square miles . . ."—Dennis Baird, Diane Mallickan and W. R. Swagerty, eds., *The Nez Perce Nation Divided: Firsthand Accounts of Events Leading to the 1863 Treaty* (Moscow: University of Idaho Press, Voices from Nez Perce Country ser., no. 1, 2002), p. 36 (letter from Indian Superintendent Edward Geary, March 1st 1860). I have added a comma out of kindness.

George Catlin's map of 1833—Derek Hayes, *Historical Atlas of the American West, with Original Maps* (Berkeley: University of California Press, 2009), p. 146. Below the river of the Nez Perces live the Shoshonies [*sic*]. A second band of Shoshonies seems to dwell in the Rockies, east of the Snakes. South and southwest of the Shoshonies are two bands of Shosokies.

The long snake of Nez Perce riders—Description after Robert H. Ruby and John A. Brown, *Indians of the Pacific Northwest* (Norman: University of Oklahoma Press, The Civilization of the American Indian ser., vol. 158, 1981), p. 136 (sketch: "Nez Percés arriving for the Walla Walla Council in May, 1855").

Charles Preuss's map of 1846—Derek Hayes, p. 92.

Descriptions of Farewell Bend, here and throughout—After a visit in August 2011.

Sherman to Grant, 1868: "The chief use of the Peace Commission . . ."—Quoted in Robert M. Utley, *The Indian Frontier 1846–1890*, rev. ed. (Albuquerque: University of New Mexico Press, 2003; orig. ed. 1984), p. 117.

Joseph's boundaries—Information from Scott M. Thompson, ed., *I Will Tell of My War Story: A Pictorial Account of the Nez Perce War* (Seattle: University of Washington Press, in assoc. w/ the Idaho State Historical Society, 2000; orig. cashbook ill. *ca.* 1879–82), p. 18.

"Certainly no right to the soil can be obtained before confirmation by the Senate."—Reports on the Aftermath of the 1863 Nez Perce Treaty by Chief Lawyer, Governor Caleb Lyon, General Benjamin Alvord and Indian Agent James O'Neill, transcribed from the original ms. in the National Archives. Editing and intro. by Dennis Baird. Published by the University of Idaho Library. Transcription and introduction copyright 1999, University of Idaho Library. Northwest Historical Manuscript Ser. Original source: NARA, RG 393 (Continental Army Commands), Dept. of the Columbia Letters Received (1860–1870) and Fort Lapwai Letters Received, and RG 75 (Indian Affairs), Letters Received by the Office of Indian Affairs from the Idaho Superintendency, 1863–1880. Microfilmed as Project M-234, Roll 337 (1863–1867). Page 5 (Benjamin Alvord to Governor Wallace, 1863).

Description of orchards in the Hood River country—After a visit there in August 2009.

"And at that time we had 105 men able to handle a rifle . . ."—Oregon Historical Society, Mss. 1508. Blurick, John. Blurick, William H. Recollections 1876. Page 21. I have turned him into Blurick, Wittfield, and made up almost everything about him. Some details of his journey derive from the 1876 crossing made by Amanda Wimpy Nelson, ms. repr., in *My Sister and I* (Fairfield, Washington: Ye Galleon Press, 1973), and a few matters relating to wagons generally, which I have also applied to Army muleteers, from Washington State University Libraries, Pullman. Holland Library Archives. Cage 3080. Wimpy, Mary Ann Sida Anderson, 1844–1948.

The softness of the voice of the Crow squaw Kills-Good—Information from Frank B. Linderman, *Pretty-shield: Medicine Woman of the Crows* (Lincoln: University of Nebraska Press/Bison Books, 2003; orig. ed. 1932), p. 13. [Since there is as much of Linderman as of Pretty-Shield in it, this book, in contradistinction to my usual practice for such edited volumes of testimony, will be cited as "Linderman."]

The Flathead belief that our shadows are our souls—Information from H. J. Lee Humfreville, *Twenty Years Among Our Hostile Indians: Describing the Characteristics, Customs, Habits, Religion, Marriage, Dances, and Battles of the Wild Indians in Their Natural State . . .*, intro. by Edwin Sweeney (Mechanicsburg, Pennsylvania: Stackpole Books, 2002; orig. text 1903 rev. of 1899 1st ed.), p. 233.

Naked-Footed Bull [whose name I have written in this book as "Naked-Footed," in nineteenth-century fashion] to White Thunder: "My young brothers were not warriors . . ."—simplified and otherwise altered from Cheryl Wilfong, *Following the Nez Perce Trail: A Guide to the Nee-Me-Poo National Historic Trail with Eyewitness Accounts*, 2nd ed., rev. & exp. (Corvallis: Oregon State University Press, 2006), pp. 317–18 (words of Yellow Wolf [White Thunder]). I have folded in another account of this murder told in L. V. McWhorter, *Hear Me, My Chiefs!: Nez Perce Legend & History* [inside book, this subtitle reads *History & Legend*], ed. Ruth Bordin (Caldwell, Idaho: Caxton Press, 2001; orig. ed. 1952), p. 439. The names of Naked-Footed Bull's siblings are invented.

Details on White Thunder's parents—L[ucullus].V[irgil]. McWhorter, *Yellow Wolf: His Own Story*, rev. enlarged ed. (Caldwell, Idaho: Caxton Press, 2000; orig. ed. 1940), p. 25. The book's account of Dietrich's murder occurs on pp. 177–78. My version makes some use of it.

"Concealed by the thick timber of the mountains . . ."—John Gibbon, *From Where the Sun Stands: A Manuscript of the Nez Perce War* (Texas: Friends of the Sterling C. Evans Library, Keepsake Number 17, 1998), p. 39. Bancroft call numbers are genuine, but for clarity I have altered "his camp" to "Joseph's camp."

"By noon we top the main divide of all . . ."—*A Vision of the "Big Hole," by John Gibbon, Colonel, 7th Infantry.* Facsimile. Privately printed? Signed [to?] A. Snelling, August 9th 1882. Poem refers to "five years past," so wr. *ca.* 1882. Montana Historical Society call numbers in my text are genuine. This verse comes from p. 4.

Shooting Thunder's Winchester—McWhorter, *Yellow Wolf*, p. 11. [Catalogue copy in 1875 for Winchester rifles: "The pioneer, the hunter and trapper, believe in the Winchester, and its possession is a passion with every Indian."—Harold F. Williamson, *Winchester: The Gun That Won the West* (Washington, D.C.: A Sportsman's Press Book pub. by the Combat Forces Press, 1952 "by association with the U.S. Army"), p. 71.]

Comanche lassooing and torture-killing of U.S. soldiers, 1867—Humfreville, p. 178.

Behavior of thirsty horses—[Walter Mason Camp.] Kenneth Hammer, *Custer in '76: Walter Camp's Notes on the Custer Fight* (Salt Lake City: Brigham Young University Press, 1976; orig. interviews early 20th cent.), p. 58.

General Canby: "Listen to me, you Indians . . ."—Jeff C. Riddle, *The Indian History of the Modoc War* (San Jose, California: Urion Press, 1998 repr. of 1914 ed.), p. 65.

"The bold dragoon he has no care . . ."—Elizabeth B. Custer, *Following the Guidon* (New York: Harper & Brothers, Franklin Square, 1890), p. 50.

Doings of McLaughlin & Co.—*Idaho [Semi-Weekly] World*, vol. 2, Friday, March 9, 1877, and Friday, April 20, 1877.

Charles Nordhoff [of the *New York Herald*] to Hayes: "The darkies you'll have any how; the white Whigs are what you want to capture."—Quoted in Michael A. Bellesiles, *1877: America's Year of Living Violently* (New York: New Press, 2010), p. 29.

Notice of sheriff's sale—Altered and abridged from *Saint Louis Dispatch*, number 221, Tuesday evening, January 4, 1876, p. 3.

"CHEAP LANDS"—Ibid., Wednesday evening, January 5, 1876, p. 1.

Comparative costs of Chicago laborer's cottage and Nebraska dugout (1872)—Thomas J. Schlereth, *Victorian America: Transformations in Everyday Life, 1876–1915* (New York: HarperPerennial/ The Everyday Life in America ser., 1992 repr. of 1991 ed.), pp. 90–91. The exact price of the dugout was $2.78.

Blurick's food—After Louis M. Bloch Jr., comp. and ed., *Overland to California in 1859: A Guide for Wagon Train Travelers* (Cleveland: Bloch and Company, 1984), p. 19. A few bits of emigration-craft in the Blurick section, horse- and wagon-craft in the military sections, and hunting-craft here and there, derive from Randolph B. Marcy, Captain, U.S. Army, *The Prairie Traveler: A Hand-Book for Overland Expeditions, Published by Authority of the War Department* (Bedford, Massachusetts: Applewood Books, 1993 repr. of orig. 1859 ed.).

Nez Perce horse-trading with emigrants, to the Indians' frequent advantage—Archer Butler Hulbert and Dorothy Printup Hulbert, eds., *Overland to the Pacific*, vol. 8: *Marcus Whitman, Crusader,*

Part Three, 1843 to 1847 (Denver?: The Stewart Commission of Colorado College and the Denver Public Library, 1941), p. 14.

The horse die-off of 1871—Information from Schlereth, p. 21.

Caulking wagon boxes—Judith E. Greenberg and Helen Carey McKeever, *In Their Own Words: A Pioneer Woman's Memoir, Based on the Journal of Arabella Clemens Fulton* (1864), p. 50.

"Our fan-shaped advance guard of scouts"—"To the Sioux and Apaches, the military are greatly indebted for the present manner of throwing out the advance guard in the shape of an open fan."—Humfreville, p. 173.

Description of Moorhouse photographs—In this chapter, most of them come from a visit to the Oregon Historical Society in the company of Tom Robinson, Portland, 2003. [By the way, some cataloguing data from this institution seems to have changed before my visits of 2009 and 2012.] I have made up one or two images here. Generally my Moorhouse citations are not inventions. Many of my descriptions of Nez Perce and Umatilla Indians in this book derive from *Peoples of the Plateau: The Indian Photographs of Lee Moorhouse, 1898–1915*, ed. & comp. Steven L. Grafe (Norman: University of Oklahoma Press/Western Legacies ser.; pub. in cooperation w/ the National Cowboy and Western Heritage Museum, 2005). In keeping with my usual practice, I will cite this book "Moorhouse" rather than "Grafe," given that Moorhouse did most of the work (he took most of the pictures, or at least is credited for them). Some Moorhouse photos referred to in *The Dying Grass* are from Tom's personal collection. A number of formal portraits of postwar Nez Perce appear, surprisingly well reproduced given the text stock, in J. Diane Pearson, *The Nez Perces in the Indian Territory: Nimiipu Survival* (Norman: University of Oklahoma Press, 2008), various inserts.

Price of buffalo bullhide in Texas, 1876—Sandoz, p. 348.

Senate impeachment ticket—Oregon Historical Society. Manuscript Collection. Mss [*sic*] 6049. Gray, Grace Howard Scrapbook. Box 1 [of 2; second is merely a photocopy of Box 1]. [Henceforth cited simply: Grace Howard Gray Scrapbook.] Folder 1/5.

Various details on Nebraska, especially Omaha, in 1877, which is close enough to 1876 for me—Richard Reinhardt, *Out West on the Overland Train: Across-the-Continent Excursion with Leslie's Magazine in 1877 and the Overland Trip in 1967* (Secaucus, NJ: Castle Books, American West Publishing Company, 1967). The detail on easy-to-come-by buffalo bones comes from p. 57.

"The men will cheer and the boys will shout . . ."—Encyclopaedia Britannica, Inc., *The Annals of America*, vol. 9: 1858–1865: The Crisis of the Union (Chicago, 1868), p. 461 (no. 109, Patrick Gilmore, "When Johnny Comes Marching Home," 1863).

The horse painted on the blockhouse wall of Fort Laramie (in 1846)—Parkman, p. 97 (*The Oregon Trail*).

Doc's lamented horse, Star, and all the other horses in this book are dreamed up by me, with the exception of Lee's horse, Traveller, who gets two mentions, and Chapman's grey racing horse, whose name I never learned. Horse names of the cavalry and settlers are invented based on exemplars in the primary sources (such as Custer's horse, Dandy, who was lucky enough not to go to Little Big Horn and so was cared for by the fallen "general's" father). Having Howard call his black stallion Arrow pleased my sense of irony. Some of the Nez Perce horse names are taken from Aoki's dictionary, and the rest invented by me in imitation.

Some of my horse tropes are indebted to information in George P. Horse Capture and Emil Her Many Horses, eds., *A Song for the Horse Nation: Horses in Native American Cultures* (Washington, D.C.: National Museum of the American Indian, Smithsonian Institution, in assoc. w/ Fulcrum Publishing, 2006); Sir Walter Gilbey, Bart, *Concise History of the Shire Horse*, "2nd ed. re-issued" (Hill Brow, Liss, Hampshire, U.K.: Spur Publications Company, 1976 rev. repr. of orig. 1889 ed.); Don Worcester, *The Spanish Mustang: From the Plains of Andalusia to the Prairies of Texas* (El Paso: Texas Western Press, University of Texas at El Paso, 1986), pp. 57, 59–63; Harold B. Barclay, Dept. of Anthropology, University of Alberta, Edmonton, *The Role of the Horse in Man's Culture* (London: J. A. Allen, 1980), pp. 2, 4, 156–57, 161, 169, 170, 172–75, 178–79, 181; Elizabeth Atwood Lawrence, *Hoofbeats and Society: Studies of Human-Horse Interactions* (Bloomington: Indiana University Press, 1985), pp. 4, 6–10, 15–18, 21, 50; and Margaret E. Derry, *Horses in Society: A Story of Animal Breeding and Marketing, 1800–1920* (Toronto: University of Toronto Press, 2006), pp. 83, 85, 90, 122.

Probable silver and gold to be found in the Wallowa Mountains' quartz deposits—*Wallowa Chieftain* (Joseph, Oregon), vol. VII., no. 15 (August 14, 1890), p. 1, Wilbur Brock, "On Wallowa Lake."

Information (here and throughout) on precious metals, alloys and ores which a late-nineteenth-century gold-seeker might know—Ernest A. Smith, Assoc. R.S.M., *The Sampling and Assay of the Precious Metals: Comprising Gold, Silver, Platinum, and the Platinum Group Metals in Ores, Bul-*

lions, and Products (London: Charles Griffin & Company, Ltd., 1913), pp. 67–69. I have also profited from Heinrich Ries, Ph.D., and Thomas L. Watson, Ph.D., *Engineering Geology*, 1st ed. (New York: John Wiley & Sons, Inc., 1913), pp. 590, 592, 596, 600–601, 607.

J. M. Miller's lucky afternoon—Melvin D. Wikoff, *Chinese in the Idaho County Gold Fields: 1864–1933*, Master of Science thesis, Texas A & I University, May 1972, p. 8.

Names of Mrs. Johnson's children; "the Confederate Bushwackers who shot my brother in the back . . ."—After the following: Washington State University Libraries, Pullman. Holland Library Archives. Cage 3018. Lederer, Alice Mooney.

The suicide of J. C. Hearan—Mentioned in the *Saint Louis Dispatch,* number 221, Monday evening, January 17, 1876.

Procedure for drawing quicksilver out of gold amalgam with a potato—The Editorial Staff of the *Engineering and Mining Journal, Handbook of Milling Details*, 1st ed. (New York: McGraw-Hill Book Co., Inc., 1914), p. 398 (Guatemalan process).

Details on price of flour at Big Sandy and Fall River (in 1853, when the cost of riding the Oregon Trail was $368.04), Nez Perce cow trade with Sioux, length of Oregon Trail—Margaret Booth, ed., *Historical Reprint: Overland from Indiana to Oregon: The Dinwiddie Journal* (sources of Northwest History no. 2, State University of Montana, Missoula, repr. from *The Frontier,* vol. VIII, no. 2, March 1928).

Further Blurick citations—Loc. cit. & ff., through p. 31.

Prints from Compartment Four

Descriptions of photos, and Tom's remarks—From notes taken in Oregon Historical Society, September 2002.

Duration of buffalo stampede (2 hours)—*Autobiography and Reminiscences of Sarah J. Cummings* (pvt. pr. in Freewater, Oregon?, 1914), p. 24.

Photo of Bannocks "sitting with their children in the golden grass"—Description after Ruby and Brown, p. 28 (photo: "Family of Bannock Indians in front of a grass lodge"). The copyright was not by Wesley Andrews.

Photo of Bannocks mustered in, supposedly by Moorhouse—My invention.

Killing of the "helpless old squaw" at Squaw Lake—Wilfong, p. 304 (words of John W. Redington).

"DEMOCRATIC PARTY DIED OF TILDENOPATHY . . ."—Edmund B. Sullivan, *American Political Badges and Medalets, 1789–1892* (Lawrence, Massachusetts: Quarterman Publications, Inc., 1981 rev. ed.), p. 437, which reproduces a brass medal against Tilden.

Inscription on William Foster's grave—Copied on site by WTV, 2006. He was killed in the Battle of the Cottonwood.

Actions of Ben Wright and Chetcoe Jennie—Keith A. Murray, *The Modocs and Their War* (Norman: University of Oklahoma Press, The Civilization of the American Indian ser., 1959), 5th pr., p. 31.

Texas Red's remarks on Nez Perces, Walla Wallas and Dr. Whitman at Powder River—Information from *Autobiography and Reminiscences of Sarah J. Cummings*, pp. 35–37.

Loam at Oro Fino, lode below Clearwater Forks—Baird, Mallickan and Swagerty, p. 80 (report by Dr. A. J. Thibodo, April 13th 1861).

Thousand-dollar claims on Rhodes Creek—Ibid., p. 93 (*Pioneer and Democrat* [Olympia], May 31, 1861).

Description of Pendleton, and the advertisement for Chief Joseph in a Pendleton blanket—After a visit in August 2009.

Cutting down poles from Indian scaffold burials—This mean trick was very common among white emigrants in their wagon trains, according to Humfreville, p. 129.

Information on the movements and antipathies of Indian-fighting generals, summer 1876—Robert Wooster, *Nelson Miles and the Twilight of the Frontier Army* (Lincoln: University of Nebraska Press, 1993), pp. 70, 79–82, 97.

Sheridan's dainty enjoyment of his cigars—Jasper Ridley, *Maximilian and Juárez* (New York: Ticknor & Fields, 1992), p. 251.

Crook's abstemious habits in drink—Captain John G. Bourke, *With General Crook in the Indian Wars* (Palo Alto: Lewis Osborne, 1968; first published in March 1891 issue of *The Century Magazine*), p. 38.

Where You Want to Be

Description of the country between the edge of the forest and Nespelem inclusive—After a drive from Seattle to Nespelem and back, August 2009.

Euphrata's two former names—Click Relander (Now Tow Look), *Drummers and Dreamers: The Story of Smowhala the Prophet and His Nephew Puck Hyah Toot, The Last Prophet of the Nearly Extinct River People, the Last Wanapums* (Seattle: Northwest Interpretive Association/Caxton Printers, 1986), p. 314.

"A worn and weathered pipe," & c (Burials 52, 93, 20), "the beads of an unstrung necklace . . ."—Michael J. Rodeffer and Stephanie Holschlag Rodeffer, with Roderick Sprague, *Nez Perce Grave Removal Project: A Preliminary Report* (Moscow: Department of Sociology/Anthropology, University of Idaho, 1972), p. 68.

Wallowa

Description of Colville Indians catching salmon—After an illustration in Ruby and Brown, p. 32 ("Colville Indians trapping salmon . . .").

Description of the Wallowa Valley—After a visit in September 2006.

Descriptions of plants beginning here and continuing throughout—After Lewis J. Clark, *Wildflowers of the Pacific Northwest from Alaska to Northern California*, ed. John G. Trelawny (Sidney, B.C., Canada: Gray's Publishing Ltd., 1976). This book contains information on flowering seasons, Native American use of various plants (including camas), etc. For further information on camas, see *The American Herb Association Quarterly Newsletter*, vol. XVIII, no. 4 (spring 2003), p. 3 (Gale Cool, "The Herb Report: Camas: *Camassia quamash*"). [See also the source-note on baking camas, below, in "And Black Birds on the Lake."] For various other uses of plants I am indebted to Jeff Hart, *Montana Native Plants and Early Peoples* (Helena: Montana Historical Society Press, 1996 repr. of 1976 ed.) [pp. 48–50 are useful on cous], and the very helpful pamphlet "The Hidden Basin Wildflower Trail," designed and illustrated by Raven O'Keefe, Lewis & Clark National Forest, Judith Ranger District.

"The Department Commander purposes . . ."—Howard, *Supplementary Report*, January 26, 1878, p. 4.

Howard's telegram of March 1, 1877—Ibid., pp. 4–5.

Summary Report Blank—On display at the Wallowa County Museum, 2006.

When Red Cloud walked right out of the council—Events of 1866 at Fort Laramie, as described in Utley, pp. 100, 104–5.

Loving Indian couples combing each other's hair—*Forty Years a Fur Trader on the Upper Missouri: The Personal Narrative of CHARLES LARPENTEUR 1833–1872*, ed., with many critical notes, by Elliott Coues, in 2 vols. (New York: Francis P. Harper, 1898), vol. 2, p. 396. [Henceforth: Larpenteur.]

"The LORD your GOD is bringing you into a good land . . ."—Deuteronomy 8.7 (abridged).

The horse-boarding rates of Jerry Despain—*East Oregonian* (Pendleton), June 30, 1877, p. 1.

Description of Horn's map from Fort Walla Walla to the coast—After Hayes, p. 97 (Map to Illustrate Horn's Overland Guide to California and Oregon, Published by J. H. Colton, No. 86, Cedar Street, New York, 1852).

"I've seen him stock a bower and an ace."—Here and throughout, many of my cardsharping phrases and procedures (especially in regard to whist and euchre) derive from "A retired professional," *How Gamblers Win; or, The Secrets of Advantage Playing Exposed . . . As Practised by Professional Gamblers upon the Uninitiated . . .* (New York: Dick & Fitzgerald, 1868). Many references to whist are derived from R. F. Foster, *Encyclopedia of Indoor Games* [partially conjectural, since much of title page has fallen off], 8th ed. (New York: Frederick A. Stokes Co., 1897), pp. 1–48.

As tiny as a Snake squaw—Snake women were described as petite in Lewis and Clark, vol. 3, p. 488 (Lewis, Fort Mandan Miscellany).

Extracts

"Those people treated us well . . ."—Lewis and Clark, vol. 5: "Through the Rockies to the Cascades," p. 219 (Clark, Course Dist. Friday 20th Septr 1805).

"I think we can justly affirm . . ."—Ibid., vol. 7, pp. 196–97 (Lewis, Thursday May 1st 1806).

"The Nez Perces . . . make many promises . . ."—Narcissa Prentiss Whitman, *My Journal 1836* (Fairfield, Washington: Ye Galleon Press, 2002, repr. from 1836 ms.), p. 57 (Oct. 18th). All entries in these Source-Notes referring simply to "Whitman" have to do with Walt, not Narcissa (or her husband Marcus; see next entry).

Hulbert and Hulbert, p. 142 (Marcus Whitman to Rev. David Greene, Secretary of the A.B.C.F.M., dated at Waiilatpu July 22d. 1844).

"In one day the Americans became as numerous as the grass."—Ruby and Brown, p. 138.

"When the Indians hesitated . . ."—Loc. cit.

"The Nez Percés received a reservation . . ."—Ibid., p. 139.

"I have just received your note of 25th inst. . . ."—Baird, Mallickan, and Swagerty, p. 51 (dated Nov. 26th, 1860—10 oclc [sic] a.m.).

"There is gold in the Bitter Root Mts . . ."—Ibid., p. 52 (dated Nov. 27th 1860).

"Before the end of this century . . . the Africans among us in a subordinate position . . ."—The Annals of America, vol. 9, p. 195 (no. 37, Georgia Debate on Secession, [1]: Robert Toombs, 1860).

"A single empire embracing the entire world . . ."—The Annals of America, vol. 9, p. 233 (no. 42, James Russell Lowell, "E Pluribus Unum," 1861).

"The Nez Perces are the most intelligent . . ."—Bill Gulick, Chief Joseph Country: Land of the Nez Perces (Caldwell, Idaho: Caxton Printers, Ltd., 1981), p. 148 (Dr. G. A. Noble, ca. 1861).

"The truth is, the close of the war with our resources unimpaired . . ."—The Annals of America, vol. 9, p. 622 (no. 154, John Sherman to William T. Sherman, November 10, 1865).

Letter in the Lewiston Radiator—Reports on the Aftermath of the 1863 Nez Perce Treaty . . . , p. 13.

"I do not apprehend a Genl Indian War . . ."—Michael Fenman, Citizen Sherman: A Life of William Tecumseh Sherman (New York: Random House, 1995), p. 261 (Sherman to Grant, August 1866).

"This valley [Wallowa] should be surveyed as soon as practicable"—Grace Bartlett, The Wallowa Country 1867–1877 (Fairfield, Washington: Ye Galleon Press, 1984), p. 14.

"All who cling to their old hunting grounds . . ."—Fenman, p. 263 (Sherman to John, Sept 23, 1868).

"I told him [Joseph] that it was useless . . ."—Ibid., p. 25 (Superintendent of Indian Affairs, Idaho, 1872. Microfilm).

"The American cannot keep his arms folded . . ."—Encyclopaedia Britannica, Inc., The Annals of America, vol. 10: 1866–1883: Reconstruction and Industrialization (Chicago, 1968), p. 281 (no. 60, Count von Hübner, Promenade autour du Monde, 1871 [Paris, 1873]).

"Congress have the exclusive right of pre-emption . . ."—Commentaries on American Law, by James Kent, vol. I, 11th ed., ed. George F. Comstock (Boston: Little, Brown & Co., 1867), p. 270. This was Lieutenant Wood's copy, whose flyleaf he inscribed in 1873.

"Custer, of course, was delighted . . ."—A Corps of Competent Writers and Artists [actually, most of this book is lifted unattributed from Custer's My Life on the Plains], Wild Life on the Plains, and Horrors of Indian Warfare . . . Superbly Illustrated (Saint Louis: Continental Publishing Co., 1891, copyright by W. L. Holloway; repr. by Robert M. Fogelson and Richard E. Rubenstein, advisory eds., Mass Violence in America ser.; New York: Arno Press and the New York Times, 1969), pp. 346–47.

"The great barrier to the settlement of the Wallowa . . ."—Bartlett, p. 34 (letter published in The Mountain Sentinel, La Grande, March 8, 1873).

Grant's orders establishing and revoking the reservation in the Wallowa Valley—Executive Orders Relating to Indian Reservations from May 14, 1855 to July 1, 1912 (vol. 1 of 2) (Washington, D.C.: U.S. Government Printing Office, 1912), p. 156 (WALLOWA INDIAN RESERVATION, Executive Mansion, June 16, 1873, and June 10, 1875). Three or four descriptors of the reservation (e.g., "Range No. 46 east") are taken from this document and inserted into Doc's mentions of Wallowa here and there in "Indian Service."

"Read White Men . . ."—Bartlett, p. 38.

"Should Government decide against locating the Indian reservation there . . ."—Ibid., p. 48.

"I think it a great mistake to take from Joseph . . ."—George Venn, Soldier to Advocate: C. E. S. Wood's 1877 Legacy (La Grande, Oregon: Wordcraft of Oregon, LLC, 2006), p. 15 (citing Howard, in Maj. Henry Clay Wood).

Orders and instructions of Howard to Whipple—Somewhat after Howard, Supplementary Report, pp. 5–6, 9–10.

Their Hearts Have Changed

Description of the Columbia River Gorge—After visits in November 2002, August 2009.

General Howard's journey up the Columbia—After Howard, Nez Perce Joseph, pp. 37–40.

"The day will come, sir, when this property will be very valuable."—Almost verbatim (but in another context) from Lieutenant James H. Bradley, The March of the Montana Column: A Prelude to the Custer Disaster, ed. Edgar I. Stewart (Norman: University of Oklahoma Press, 1961; orig. pub. 1896; journal wr. 1876, expanded 1877), p. 30.

That ancient Indian graveyard—Caroline C. Leighton, West Coast Journeys 1865–1879: The Travelogue of a Remarkable Woman, intro. and notes by David M. Buerge (Seattle: Sasquatch Books, 1995; orig. ed. 1883), p. 33: "We were shown a high, isolated rock, rising far above the water, on which was a scaffolding where, for many generations, the Indians had deposited their dead" in some unspecified place on the Columbia between Portland and Umatilla City, 1866.

"You can see the fins of speckled trout forty foot down."—Information (or allegation) from the *Wallowa Chieftain* (Joseph, Oregon), vol. VII., no. 15 (August 14, 1890), p. 1, Wilbur Brock, "On Wallowa Lake."

Howard's personality—"He was always busy at his office, and would be signing his name while some-one was talking to him, and he never had a meal at home without hurrying."—Oregon Historical Society, MSS 2094. Grace Howard Gray. [This is not the Grace Howard Gray Scrapbook cited elsewhere.] General Oliver Otis Howard, 1936, Interviews. James T. Gray (Grace Howard), inter-viewed by Dorothy O. Johansen. Page 2. To try to imagine Howard's personality, speech and man-nerisms I have relied greatly on his writings. Howard's religious views are very openly and sincerely stated in most of his non-military publications. Intelligent as he was, he lacked both grace and subtlety in his expression, and the sympathetic reader, finding frequent evidence of the sensitive, subtle raptures which must have impelled him, wishes that he had said more about them. To assist my envisioning of this aspect of the man, I have made occasional use of the ideas (and a phrase or two) in Mary Kupiec Cayton and Peter W. Williams, eds., *Encyclopedia of American Cultural & Intellectual History*, vol. 1 (New York: Scribner's, 2001), pp. 379–88 (Mark Y. Hanley, "Evangelical Thought"). A few phrases of his militant Christian righteousness in *The Dying Grass* are inspired by the *Radical Abolitionist*, vols. 1–4 (1855–1858) (New York: Negro Universities Press, 1969). I imagine that like many older people, Howard might have continued to think and speak in tropes that had gone slightly out of date, especially since this language informed the great causes of his life, the Civil War and the Freedmen's Bureau. The brief entry in the *Encyclopedia of the Civil War: A Political, Social and Military History*, vol. 2, ed. David S. Heidler and Jeanne T. Heifler (Santa Barbara, California: ACL-CLIO, Inc., 2000), may help any reader who wishes a summary of his career. Howard was close to his two brothers, each of whom served with him in the Civil War. (Both Charles and Rowland named a child "Otis," but that was their mother's maiden name.) Some family information in *The Dying Grass* (birthdays of Howard's children and those of his two broth-ers, along with marriages, deaths, and some career data, derives from J. C. Stinchfield, et al., *History of the Town of Leeds, Androscoggin County, Maine, From Its Settlement June 10, 1780* (No place of publication given: Press of Lewiston Journal Company, n.d.; intro. dated 1901), pp. 182–90, with some cross-verification and supplemental information from a handwritten list in the George J. Mitchell Department of Special Collections and Archives, Bowdoin College Library. O. O. Howard papers [henceforth: Bowdoin, OOH papers], call number M91, Box 43. Most of my allusions to the people, topography and institutions of Leeds are indebted to Stinchfield (who includes a number of photographs of prominent men, Androscoggin Lake, etc.).

Descriptions of Portland, Walla Walla and Missoula here and throughout—After John W. Reps, *Pan-oramas of Promise: Pacific Northwest Cities and Towns on Nineteenth-Century Lithographs* (Pull-man: Washington State University Press, 1984). I have occasionally based descriptions on lithographs up to twenty years older than 1877, but then only for solid edifices which probably survived into the time of the Nez Perce War. Descriptions of Helena, Philadelphia and Washington, D.C. (including Howard University and the Houses of Congress), are occasionally indebted to plates in Gloria Gilda Deák, *Picturing America: Prints, Maps and Drawings Bearing on the New World Discoveries and on the Development of the Territory That Is Now the United States*, 2 vols. (Princeton: Princeton University Press, 1988).

Young ladies and Indians at The Dalles—The presence of both is mentioned in Wood's diary (Venn, p. 29; June 21).

The letter signed by some unknown person reading: "This is a good Indian"—Somewhat after William F. Zimmer, *Frontier Soldier: An Enlisted Man's Journal of the Sioux and Nez Perce Campaigns, 1877* (Helena: Montana Historical Society Press, 1998), p. 19 (March 12th).

One horse for a squaw-axe—After Lewis and Clark, vol. 8 (Ordway and Floyd), p. 318 (Ordway, 1 June 1806), in reference to Nez Perces. The bit about blue beads is my interpolation.

Description of places on Howard's map rolled out at The Dalles—These appear in Colton's map of Oregon, Washington and Idaho, 1877.

"The Roseburg citizens aim to put in an oil mill."—Information from the *East Oregonian* (Pendleton), June 16, 1877, unnumbered p.

The Standard Oil strike in Cleveland (April 1877)—Information from Robert V. Bruce, *1877: Year of Violence* (Chicago: Ivan R. Dee, 1989 repr. of 1959 ed.), p. 204.

Fox's Ethiopian Comicalities—Advertised in the back of "A retired professional," as were the following volumes mentioned in this novel: Martine's [name not italicized in this instance] *Sensible Letter*

Writer, Black Wit and Darky Conversations and *Dick's Irish Dialect Recitations.* So these books would have been nine years old. It is easy to imagine them kicking dismally around for that long.

Descriptions of Crook's appearance and mannerisms, here and throughout—After Bourke, *With General Crook,* esp. pp. 13, 24, 38.

Cicero—Slightly "retranslated" from Marcus Tullius Cicero, *Letters to Atticus* (works in 28 vols., vols. XXII–XXIV), trans. E. O. Winstedt (Cambridge, Massachusetts: Harvard University Press, Loeb Classical Library, 1980–87 reprs. of 1912–18 eds.; orig. letters B.C. 65–44); vol. II (vol. XXIII in the Loeb complete works), pp. 42 (Latin) and 43 (English): VII.7. (Cicero to Atticus, Formiae, Dec. 18–21, 50 B.C.). I cannot say whether Howard actually knew Latin, and Cicero might have been a trifle highbrow for the reading circle at his Officers' Club; Dumas truly was more their speed.

"Sir, I don't know who you are"—Much after the author's account of what he said to a drunken ruffian in Major-General O. O. Howard, *My Life and Experiences Among Our Hostile Indians: A Record of Personal Observations, Adventures, and Campaigns Among the Indians of the Great West . . .* (Hartford, Connecticut: A. D. Worthington & Co., 1907), p. 417.

Description of Cape Horn and the railroad tracks—After Maria Morris Hambourg et al., *The Waking Dream: Photography's First Century: Selections from the Gilman Paper Company Collection* (New York: Metropolitan Museum of Art, dist. by Harry N. Abrams, Inc., 1993), p. 167 (Plate 122: Carleton E. Watkins, "Cape Horn near Celilo," 1867).

Remarks on the Boxer cartridge—Closely after Major T. J. Treadwell, Ordnance Department, Commanding Frankford Arsenal, *Ordnance Memoranda No. 14: Metallic Cartridges (Regulation and Experimental), as Manufactured and Tested at the Frankford Arsenal, Philadelphia, PA.* (Washington, D.C.: Government Printing Office, 1873), p 12 (with additions).

Description of the blind Umatilla man—After a photo in Thomas W. Kavanagh, comp., *North American Indian Portraits: Photographs from the Wanamaker Expeditions (from the Wanamaker Collection at the William Hammond Mathers Museum, Indiana University)* (Old Saybrook, Connecticut: Konecky & Konecky, 1998; orig. photographs 1908, 1909, 1913), p. 42 ("Tin-tin Meet-sa [Cayuse Umatilla], W1636"). [Note: In this book the "W" sometimes does and sometimes does not run on into the four-digit code. In case there is some significance to this, I have kept the variation.]

Interview with Smohalla's representative—Much expanded from Howard, *Nez Perce Joseph,* p. 40.

Events at Walla-Walla—Condensed and altered from Howard, *Nez Perce Joseph,* pp. 42–67, but some conversation between General Howard and Toohhoolhoolzote after McWhorter, *Yellow Wolf,* p. 39. When the Nez Perce say "Aa, aa" to the words of White Bird, I have borrowed that detail from Helen Addison Howard, *Saga of Chief Joseph* (Lincoln: University of Nebraska Press/Bison Books, 1965 rev. repr. of 1941 ed.), p. 122 (response to the words of Toohhoolhoolzote). Howard did apparently see the new Gatlings here; however, the Army had first adopted them in 1866.

Howard's remarks to Ollicut about Skimiah—Somewhat after Howard, *Supplementary Report,* p. 12.

Antecedents of Andrew Pambrun—Ruby and Brown, p. 138.

Howard to Wilkinson on blankets and feathers—Slightly after Howard, *Supplementary Report,* p. 12.

Establishment date, extent and situation of Fort Lapwai—See citation to Glossary 3 (Places), entry for Lapwai. Miscellaneous details and Lapwai and its inhabitants (such as the fact that Mrs. Perry wore a dotted black veil) have been raided from Emily FitzGerald, *An Army Doctor's Wife on the Frontier: Letters from Alaska and the Far West, 1874–1878,* ed. Abe Laufe, preliminary editing by Russell J. Ferguson (Pittsburgh: University of Pittsburgh Press, 1962).

Major Mason's appearance during the Modoc War—After Woodhead, p. 259 (group photo by E. Muybridge).

Descriptions of Monteith here and throughout—After a photograph in Venn, p. 38 (Plate 2.10); and a photograph in Pearson, p. 215.

Spalding's thirty-pound melons at Lapwai—Baird, Mallickan and Swagerty, p. 37 (letter from Indian Superintendent Edward Geary, March 1st 1860).

Monteith: "I sent out James Reuben to Wallowa . . ."—Somewhat after Howard, *Supplementary Report,* p. 17.

Monteith: "General, I am as fond of these Nez Perces as I would be of my own children."—Fairly closely after E. Jane Gay, *With the Nez Perces: Alice Fletcher in the Field, 1889–92,* eds. Frederick E. Hoxie and Joan T. Mark (Lincoln: University of Nebraska Press, 1981; orig. text privately bound as *Choup-nit-ki* in 1909), p. 17 (quoting a Scotchman in Lewiston on the subject of the Nez Perces).

"You well know that we cannot that we can take the offensive at all . . ." + "I am glad indeed that you did not fix any time . . ."—Somewhat after Howard, *Supplementary Report, January 26, 1878,* p. 5.

"with great parade and tragic manner"—Howard, *Supplementary Report,* p. 13.

Dialogue between Howard and Monteith: Father Cataldo—Somewhat after the same source, p. 15.

Monteith and Howard on the number of Indian churchgoers at Lapwai, Reverend Spalding's activities, greater assimilation-resistance at Lapwai than at Kamiah, and the agency attitude to the subchief Jacob—Information from Emily Greenwald, *Reconfiguring the Reservation: The Nez Perces, Jicarilla Apaches, and the Dawes Act* (Albuquerque: University of New Mexico Press, 2002), pp. 52, 54.

Spalding's belief that the Catholics bore responsibility for the failure of his Lapwai mission—*Reports on the Aftermath of the 1863 Nez Perce Treaty . . .* , p. 1.

"LORD JESUSNIM . . ." + "*Kaih kaih . . .*"—J[uliet]. L. Axtell (?), *Gospel Hymns in the Nez Perce Language* (Lake Forest, Illinois: no publisher given, August, 1897). Pages unnumbered. Hymn 4: "Whiter Than Snow."

Notion of Nez Perce as "Welsh Indians" who may suffer from a speech impediment—After Lewis and Clark, vol. 8 (Ordway and Floyd), p. 219 (Ordway, 5 September 1805).

Mrs. Symington at euchre—Howard, *Autobiography*, vol. 1, p. 71.

Whipple's tale of Indians playing cards with "the boys," and their readiness to gamble away ponies and wives—Somewhat after Zimmer, p. 21 (March 14th). Zimmer was writing about gambling on the Crow Agency. However, Nez Perce were similar in this enthusiasm. And I assume that what American soldiers did with the Crows they might well have done with the Nez Perce.

"We Army officers can't expect to be our own masters . . ."—Loosely after William S. McFeely, *Yankee Stepfather: General O. O. Howard and the Freedmen* (New Haven: Yale University Press, 1968), p. 34 (Howard to his mother, 20 December 1852).

When the Walla-Wallas and Cayuses rode circles round the treaty ground (in 1855)—Information from Ruby and Brown, p. 137.

Merchandise of Mrs. Sanford in Pendleton—*East Oregonian* (Pendleton), June 30, 1877, p. 1.

Tale of Howard's pure white Arabian named Mallach—After his *Autobiography*, vol. 1, p. 70.

"All our father's uncles are our grandfathers . . ."—Verbatim from Gay, p. 53 (September 1st, 1889).

Sherman's near murder at Fort Sill (1871)—Information from Utley, p. 143.

Toohhoolhoolzote defies Howard—His words are usually given: "I am a man . . ." But I rather like this alternate version: "I have a prick, and I will not go on the reservation."—Martin Stadius, *Dreamers: On the Trail of the Nez Perce* (Caldwell, Idaho: Caxton Press, 1999), p. 93.

"They want to know if you'll race with them."—Actually, White Bird challenged Lieutenant Wilkinson to a race (Helen Addison Howard, p. 128).

And the World Keeps Getting Wider and Wider

A few descriptions of Nez Perce material culture here and throughout are derived from information in Caroline James, *Nez Perce Women in Transition 1877–1990* (Moscow: University of Idaho Press, 1996).

Certain forms of speech which I put in the mouths of my Nez Perce characters are indebted to Aoki's dictionary (see "Note on Nimiputumít Orthography," above, p. 1640), and also to Haruo Aoki and Deward E. Walker, Jr., *Nez Perce Oral Narratives* (Berkeley: University of California Press, University of California Publications in Linguistics, vol. 104, 1989). Thus when it is said (p. 549) of one villainess, a GRIZZLY BEAR WOMAN, that "she must be the one who killed our good young girls," I have applied this accusation to Gibbon's soldiers at Big Hole: "They are the ones who killed our good young boys and our good young girls." Few written accounts of the war are in Nez Perce voices, and these tend to appear in pidgin English. So I have tried to filter them through "traditional" phrases and imitations thereof.

Nez Perce customs for expectant mothers—Deward Walker, ed. *Handbook of North American Indians*, vol. 12: Plateau (Washington, D.C.: Smithsonian Institution, 1998), pp. 421–22 (Deward E. Walker, Jr., "Nez Perce").

Joseph's wives and children—A surprisingly obscure subject. The most complete mention I have discovered is in Helen Addison Howard, p. 83: "Joseph, like his father, married four times in his life. His various wives were Wa-win-te-pi-ksat (or Wa-win-te-pe-tal-e-ka-sat), I-a-tu-ton-my (or I-a-to-we-non-my), Aye-at-wai-at-naime (Good Woman)"—whose name both Venn (p. 79) and Mc-Whorter (*Yellow Wolf,* p. 239 fn.) give as Heyume-yoyikt—"and one other whose name has been lost to history." The first two ladies listed were the widows of Looking-Glass, whom Joseph supposedly married out of loyalty to that chief's memory. (Beal, however, writes: "Having lost his first wife, Joseph married two widows of fallen Nez Perce warriors" [p. 298].) Aye-at-wai-at-naime might in fact have been Iatowinnai, meaning "Woman Walking." Lieutenant Wood's son Erskine, who sojourned twice with Joseph at Nespelem, mentions (if I can read his handwriting) a Mawantip[s] or Wawantif who was "Joseph's elder wife" (entry for Thursday 5th), and an "Iyat too we awetnomy" who was "Joseph's younger wife" (Sunday 8th). [OHS MSS 2445. Wood, Erskine 1879–1983. Diary of a Fourteen-Year-Old Boy, Days with Chief Joseph 1893.] Meanwhile, Helen Addison Howard goes on to say that Joseph had five girls and four boys; only two girls did not die in babyhood. Only one of these two lived to marry; she became known as Sarah Moses and was born in 1865 (ibid., p. 82). Howard believes her to have been Joseph's first child; the mother, who must have been one of the last two women of the four listed by H. A. Howard, was "a daughter of Chief Whisk-tasket of the treaty Nez Perces at Lapwai." Since McWhorter tentatively identifies the younger of Joseph's pre-war wives as "Springtime," or "Toma Alwawinmi" (see Glossary 1), in this novel I have called the elder wife (who must have been the mother of Sarah Moses, or, as I call the girl in this book, Sound Of Running Feet) Good Woman, and the younger wife Springtime. Sound Of Running Feet was permitted or required to stay at Lapwai after the war. (McWhorter [op. cit., p. 288 fn.] believes this measure was intended to punish Joseph.) After the Nez Perce exiles were allowed to leave the In-dian Territory, Good Woman evidently chose to live at Lapwai with her daughter when Joseph went to Nespelem (Venn, p. 79). Venn notes (loc. cit.) that in the 1885 census Joseph declared two wives, one aged thirty-five and the other thirty-two. Since Good Woman and Springtime were both out of the picture, one or both must have been Looking-Glass's widows. Dr. Edmond S. Meany visited Joseph in 1901 and reported that he then had two wives: Wa-win-te-pi-ksat, aged forty-six, and I-a-tu-ton-my, aged thirty-nine (Helen Addison Howard, p. 363). These ages and Venn's do not square up. If Venn's figures were correct, then in 1877 these women would have been about twenty-seven and twenty-four. Venn asserts (loc. cit.) that Joseph married an unnamed "young woman" at Fort Leavenworth in 1878. If so, then he would have had five wives that we know of. Helen Addison Howard quotes Meany (fn., p. 83): One child "died since living at Nespilem [sic], two died in Indian Territory and the rest died in Idaho." In addition, according to Bartlett (p. 80), settlers believed Joseph to have buried a little son near Wallowa Lake. In this book I have supposed the following marriages for Joseph:

1. Good Woman, before 1865 (since that was Sound Of Running Feet's birth year).
2. Springtime, between 1865 (since she was a second wife) and 1877.
3. Wa-win-te-pi-ksat (who died in 1929, "aged nearly one hundred years"—H. A. Howard, p. 367).
4. I-a-tu-ton-my; both of these after Looking-Glass's death in the last battle.

In the end I decided not to imagine the following marriage:

5. Cloudburst [Tamalwinonmi], Ollokot's surviving wife. It seems plausible that Joseph would have married her after Ollokot's death at Bear's Paw, since we know he adopted Ollokot's son by Fair Land, Ollokot's elder wife who was fatally wounded at Big Hole. Why not let Cloud-burst be the nameless young spouse at Fort Leavenworth? But by the end of the People's exile in the Indian Territory she had become, or was about to become, Mrs. Susie Convill.

We know that Springtime divorced Joseph and Good Woman separated from him, preferring to live at Lapwai, presumably in order to be with Sound Of Running Feet, but I have not been able to learn why these two marriages actually ended.
In addition to Joseph's two wives at Nespelem, one supposedly single woman was also living with the family for a time. These three could have been the last three wives on the list above, although the third woman could have been one of Looking-Glass's two daughters.
I could not find the names of Looking-Glass's wives in Aoki's dictionary. To make it easier for the non–Nez Perce–conversant reader to keep track of them in this novel, I substituted two other women's translated names from Aoki's dictionary: Blackberry Person for Wa-win-te-pi-ksat and Asking Maiden for I-a-tu-ton-my.
"These Bostons who came here were the cause of all our trouble."—After Bartlett, who quotes Joseph as saying: "I told Monteith he was my friend and I did not wish to talk to him so, but these Bostons here in Wallowa were the cause of all our trouble" (p. 25).
Caching of cous; cattle rustling of Nez Perce herd by whites—McWhorter, *Hear Me*, p. 176.
Now "the sage hens have already finished dancing in the Buffalo Country"—April, according to Linder-man, p. 39.

Make of Joseph's rifle—Detailed in Jerome A. Greene, Jerome M. Greene, *Nez Perce Summer 1877: The U.S. Army and the Nee-Me-Poo Crisis* (Helena: Montana Historical Society Press, 2000), p. 486, fn. 116.

Faraway Mountain—See Glossary 3.

Toohhoolhoolsote asks the identity of Washington—After Linwood Laughy, comp., *In Pursuit of the Nez Perces, As Reported by Gen. O. O. Howard, Duncan McDonald, Chief Joseph* (Kooskia, Idaho: Mountain Meadow Press, 4th pr., 2002), p. 230 (Duncan McDonald). [Henceforth cited: Howard et al.]

Fraudulent branding of Nez Perce cattle by the settlers—Ibid., p. 284 (Joseph).

Fashioning of grass bridles by the boys—Information from Kent Nerburn, *Chief Joseph & the Flight of the Nez Perce: The Untold Story of an American Tragedy* (New York: HarperOne, 2005), p. 63.

Toohhoolhoolzote "came here to excite our young men."—After Howard et al., p. 288 (Joseph). In the original it is unclear whether Toohhoolhoolzote speaks for war in Wallowa or at Split Rock.

Young children lashed to the horses—Leighton, p. 38 (1866): "Strapped to one of the horses, with a roll of blankets, was a Nez Perces [*sic*] baby. This infant, although apparently not over a year and a half old, sat erect, grasping the reins, with as spirited and fearless a look as an old warrior's."

Frequent appearance of brass (and copper) bracelets among Nez Perce—Information from Ronald P. Koch, *Dress Clothing of the Plains Indians* (Norman: University of Oklahoma Press, The Civilization of the American Indian ser., no. 140, 1977), p. 69.

Colors of Nez Perce women's clothes—After Pearson, pp. 29–30.

Description of the descent of Hell's Canyon to the Snake River (at Dug Bar, Oregon, with Washington State on the other side)—From a journey by car and on foot in September 2006.

The Modoc boys shooting frogs with bows and arrows—Information from Malcolm Margolin, ed., *The Way We Lived: California Indian Stories, Songs & Reminiscences* (Berkeley: Heyday Books & California Historical Society, 1993 rev. of 1981 ed.), p. 14 ("When I Was a Child," Peter Sconchin, Modoc).

The People as COYOTE's children—Deward E. Walker, Jr., in collaboration with Daniel N. Matthews, *Blood of the Monster: The Nez Perce Coyote Cycle* (No place of publication given: High Plains Publishing Co., 1994), p. 55.

And Black Birds on the Lake

Descriptions of Tolo Lake—After a visit there in August 2006.

The Stick Game and the Bone Game are described in Lewis and Clark, vol. 7, pp. 137–38.

Shore Crossing's aquatic exploits, running speed, etc.—McWhorter, *Hear Me*, p. 188. My description of his doings and motivations is partially indebted to the remainder of this chapter; but here, contradicting other accounts, McWhorter makes Swan Necklace a young follower rather than an instigator. There is much variance in people's memories regarding the first Salmon River raid. For instance, Two Moons claims that there were three men and they were drunk (op. cit., p. 201); McWhorter himself (pp. 191–93) says that there were two men who were sober. So I have tried to steer my own wavering middle course.

Description of the petroglyphs along the Snake River—After a trip to Buffalo Eddy, Washington, in September 2006. These were 4,500–300 years old. There were also petroglyphs at Pitttsburg Landing and Geneva Bar. These sites were all in Hell's Canyon.

Re: Toohhoolhoolzote's outfit: Common use of bone-bead loop necklaces among Nez Perce—Information from Koch, p. 66.

White Bird's outfit—He was old, and possibly set in his ways. The fashion I describe dates back to Lewis and Clark, vol. 5, pp. 258–59. I suspect that this would have been rare in 1877, but since the Nez Perce were both highly individualistic in their attire and also ancestor-loving, why not?

Information on Red Heart's family—From McWhorter, *Hear Me*, p. 333.

Description of Looking-Glass—After a photograph reproduced in Wilfong, p. 176 (W. H. Jackson, 1871).

Looking-Glass's "two daughters, both husband-ready."—Carson (p. 138) quotes a volunteer at Fort Fizzle who hears Looking-Glass say: "I have two good looking daughters up at the camp. Come and see them."

Ollokot's collar—After information on Lewis and Clark, vol. 7, p. 224 (Clark, Wednesday May 7th 1806): "The article of dress on which they appear to bestow most pains and orniments [*sic*] is a kind of collar or brestpate [*sic*]; this is most Commonly a Strip of otter Skins of about six inches Wide . . ." This may be an anachronism, since Ollokot does not appear to be wearing this in the portraits I have seen. But perhaps it was an old style item still sometimes employed on formal occasions. If so, the scene in which I imagine Ollokot giving his collar to Sound Of Running Feet to keep her warm may be more plausible.

The blue and green paints used on Looking-Glass's tipi—That these colors (which must have been mineral pigments) were available is surprising, but Lewis and Clark reported their widespread use among the Nez Perce even in 1805 (vol. 5, p. 259).

Description of baking camas—After information from Leighton, p. 38 ("between the Snake and Spokane," 1866); Lewis and Clark, vol. 8, *Over the Rockies to St. Louis,* pp. 14–16 (Lewis, Wednesday June 11th 1806).

List of women beginning with Cloudburst [Wet-a-ton-mi] and Niktseewhy—Taken from Jerome A. Greene, *Beyond Bear's Paw: The Nez Perce Indians in Canada* (Norman: University of Oklahoma Press, 2010), pp. 178–82 (Appendix C: Nez Perce never captured after Bear's Paw battle).

Digging baneberry roots—Hart, p. 10. This author mentions the practice in connection with the Cheyenne. I have supposed that so useful a piece of knowledge would also have been in the Nez Perce repertoire, since the plant was in their traditional homeland.

Description of Nez Perce horse racing and gambling—After Edwin Bingham and Tim Barnes, *Wood Works: The Life and Writing of Charles Erskine Scott Wood* (Corvallis: Oregon State University Press, 1997), pp. 65–68 ("An Indian Horse-Race"); and occasional passages in Humfreville, who did not personally know Nez Perce life very well but who saw many Plains Indian horse races during his Indian service. The Nez Perce are known to have been expert at leaping sideways on their horses.

Discussions of the chiefs there, and subsequent doings—After McWhorter, *Yellow Wolf,* pp. 41ff., Jerome M. Greene, *Nez Perce Summer,* pp. 30–31. The estimate of 120 warriors comes from McWhorter. Greene (p. 28) puts the figure at "say 95."

When COYOTE cunningly entreated the MONSTER—Information from Walker and Matthews, p. 10.

Roster of warriors—Once again I have taken some names from Appendixes A–C of Greene, *Beyond Bear's Paw,* where various Nez Perce escapees from Bear's Paw and their fates are listed.

"And soon they will wipe their buttocks on our heads!"—"A formulaic expression of abuse and mistreatment," says Aoki, p. 946 (slightly altered by WTV).

"We need a wide country, so that we can always find meat."—Sentiment expressed in Linderman, p. 10. [Henceforth, in defiance of my usual practice (since there is as much of him as her in it), Linderman.] I suppose the Nez Perce thought much the same about this as the Crows.

"They want to put us in a small place."—Somewhat after McWhorter, *Yellow Wolf,* p. 35.

Prevalence of buffalo-hunting journeys: Ruby and Brown, p. 188: "After 1860 the Nez Percés went less to buffalo, depending more on the Salish to do their hunting for them." For meat and hides they traded watertight bags.

Description of Smohalla—After Relander, photo insert 2, following p. 96.

Description of WOWSHUXLUH—Based on photo insert 10, loc. cit.

Grandfather Looking-Glass's helpfulness to Lewis and Clark—Information from Lewis and Clark, vol. 7, pp. 202 (Lewis, Saturday May 3rd 1806), 206 (Lewis, Sunday May 4th 1806), 215 (Lewis, Tuesday May 6th 1806).

Looking-Glass's words at the council of 1874—After Helen Addison Howard, p. 100.

Looking-Glass: "For every white man you kill . . ."—Gulick, p. 147.

"Talking slowly is good."—Verbatim from Gulick, p. 107 (speech of Old Joseph, 1855).

Joseph's speech: "My People, you ask me to show my heart . . ."—First two sentences somewhat after Howard et al., p. 279 (Joseph). The rest is invented.

The feast in honor of Springtime's baby—In another version, Joseph's party were going to kill eleven head of beef and share them out as the bequest of Looking-Glass's father. See McWhorter, *Hear Me,* p. 197 (testimony of Camille Williams).

Hanging of Red Moccasin Tops's grandfather—Howard et al., p. 218 (Duncan McDonald).

"When Lawyer sold our country, my father was not there . . ."—Abbreviated and slightly altered from Pearson, p. 18.

Joseph's memories of riding toward Asotin and Anatone with his father—After a trip from Grande Ronde to Lewiston, August 2011.

Toohhoolhoolsote: "I must not anger HIM WHO LIVES ABOVE . . ."—Somewhat after his speech at a previous winter's council, given in McWhorter, *Hear Me,* p. 163.

Promise of General Palmer to Looking-Glass's father [in 1855]—McWhorter, *Hear Me,* p. 92.

Colonel George Wright to Cayuses, Nez Perces and Tenino chief Stockwhitley (October 1856): "The bloody shirt shall now be washed . . ."—Ruby and Brown, p. 157.

Wottolen: "Why submit to this wrong? . . ."—Quoted in McWhorter, op. cit., pp. 167–68.

Description of Looking-Glass, White Bird and Ollokot breaking a horse—After procedure given in:

Oregon Historical Society MSS 2445. Wood, Erskine, 1879–1983. Diary of a Fourteen-Year-Old Boy, Days with Chief Joseph, 1893. This was Erskine's second stay with Joseph. Here he was describing the actions of Joseph and two other men, so I have imagined that Looking-Glass had two companions in his own effort.

When Coyote invited his EXCREMENT CHILDREN to poke out each other's eyes—Recounted in Walker and Matthews, p. 51.

Description of the ornaments of Blackfoot's buffalo pony—After an illustration in George P. Horse Capture and Emil Her Many Horses, eds., *A Song for the Horse Nation: Horses in Native American Cultures* (Washington, D.C.: National Museum of the American Indian, Smithsonian Institution, in assoc. w/ Fulcrum Publishing, 2006), p. 26.

The murder of Utsinmalihkin—A rumor only, reported in McWhorter, *Hear Me*, p. 113.

Catalogue of Nez Perce murdered by whites—Ibid., pp. 118–31.

The murder of Black Eagle and his wife—Ibid., p. 23.

"We came from no country, unlike the whites. We were always here."—Closely after McWhorter, *Yellow Wolf*, p. 18 (words of White Thunder).

List of Joseph's companions en route to Buzzard Mountain—McWhorter, *Hear Me*, pp. 195–96 (testimony of Wetatonmi).

The inveigling of Shore Crossing into murder—This is only one version of events. In other versions, Swan Necklace is not an instigator but a follower.

Description of Swan Necklace—After a photograph in McWhorter, *Yellow Wolf*, p. 45 (undated).

Killing of the old white man (Richard Devine)—According to McWhorter (*Hear Me*, p. 192), he was not in bed. The sources differ.

Descriptions of the next two murders—After the same, pp. 193ff.

"They kill those two dogs."—On this point the testimony in *Hear Me* is slightly confused, claiming that one of the two men got away but that the Nez Perces killed two men. The one who found against the Indians in the blacksnake whipping case and who supported Larry Ott's murder of Chief Eagle Robe, saying: "He should not be prosecuted for killing a dog," was Henry Elfers.

"Blood darker than Salish cherries." In Montana farmers' markets one often sees Flathead cherries for sale. These delicious fruits are deep crimson and so is their juice.

The Time Has Passed

Description of Toohhoolhoolzote turning away and wrapping himself in a buffalo robe—After W. Raymond Wood, Joseph C. Porter and David C. Hunt, *Karl Bodmer's Studio Art: The Newberry Library Bodmer Collection* (Chicago: University of Illinois Press, 2002), p. 146 (plate 22: Figure in a Bison Robe).

Shore Crossing's new Sharps buffalo rifle—Detailed in Greene, *Nez Perce Summer*, p. 450 (fn. 90).

"If they conclude to become slaves of Cut Arm . . ."—Somewhat after the words of Kamiakin to Owhi, 1856, quoted in Ruby and Brown, p. 156.

"Peopeo Tholekt said we could never win."—Information from McWhorter, p. 167 (testimony of Peopeo Tholekt).

Description of Shore Crossing as a "smoothly moonfaced young warrior . . ."—After Scott M. Thompson, p. vi (photo of Henry Eneas, National Park Service, Nez Perce National Historic Park, NEPE-HI-1171).

Red Heart's wife—"The Bostons never did anything to hurt me . . ."—Somewhat after Oregon Historical Society MSS 800. Wood, Charles Erskine Scott. Private journal transcription photocopy. 1878. Box 1, t 2.03.03. Henceforth cited: Wood diary, 1878 or 1879 (1879 pp. follow p. 28 of the original). This then is Wood diary, 1879, p. 32 (Chief Moses parley).

Looking-Glass: "You have acted like children in murdering these Bostons . . ."—Somewhat after Howard et al., p. 230 (Duncan McDonald); abbreviated, expanded and embellished.

"Lewiston, where we once had a cemetery"—Somewhat after Lewis and Clark, vol. 7, p. 219 (Clark, Tuesday May 6th 1806, re: "the Mouth of the Kooskooske" = Clearwater).

Some Kind of Peace

Two Moons comes to tell Joseph the news of the raids—Based on the account in *Yellow Wolf*. Two Moons himself tells the story differently, in McWhorter, *Hear Me*, p. 202.

White Bird's Dreamer song—Invented by WTV, roughly after the import of the monitory "Dream Song" in McWhorter, *Hear Me*, p. 84.

Beating an untanned elkskin while singing war-songs—The untanned skin, called *quilílu,* could be either elk or buffalo (Aoki, p. 585).

"White Bird rides his horse round and round . . ."—After Howard, *Report—In the Field,* p. 1.

Participation in the raids of Geese Three Times Alighting On Water—McWhorter, *Hear Me,* p. 199.

"If we stay in this place until the Bluecoats come, we shall make some kind of peace with them."— White Thunder quotes Joseph: "Let us stay here until the soldiers come. We will make some kind of peace with them" (McWhorter, *Hear Me,* p. 196).

Kate's crossed shoulder-sashes of trade beads—After Lewis and Clark, vol. 7, p. 253 (Tuesday May 13th 1806).

Wounded Head's trade of a horse for a gun—Somewhat after McWhorter, *Hear Me,* pp. 204–5.

Moss Beard—My own invented Nez Perce nickname for Agent Monteith.

"His blood is on fire."—After Howard et al., p. 290 (Chief Joseph).

Two Moons's flight to Weir Place—McWhorter, *Hear Me,* p. 203.

Advice of Old Yellow Wolf: "If you ride to war and get shot, no weeping!"—Somewhat after McWhorter, *Yellow Wolf,* p. 89.

Description of Kalkalshuatash—Somewhat after a portrait of the same, in Gulick, p. 158 (dated 1868, so of course he would actually have looked older in 1877).

Just for Awhile

Ollokot: "If Cut Arm troubles me, I shall fight him at once!"—Almost verbatim from Howard et al., p. 234 (McDonald).

The tale of the MUSSELSHELL SISTERS—After Allen P. Slickapoo, Sr., Nez Perce Tribe, director; Leroy L. Seth, Nez Perce Tribe, illustrator; and Deward E. Walker, Jr., University of Colorado, technical adviser, *Nu Mee Poon Tit Wah Tit (Nez Perce Legends),* 2nd ed. (n.p.: Nez Perce Tribe of Idaho, 1972), p. 85. [Henceforth cited: Slickapoo, Seth and Walker.]

Description of the route from Split Rock to Driving-In Cave—After a trip from White Bird Canyon to Cottonwood, September 2006.

The burning of the Snake warriors in Driving-In Cave—McWhorter, *Hear Me,* p. 15.

Relating to Red Grizzly Bear and Koolkooltom—Ibid., pp. 18–19, 21.

Joseph's smoking of the war pipe, and his oration on that occasion—Somewhat after Peopeo Tholekt/ Sam Lott, pp. 4–5. The latter was not actually present at any such scene, having withdrawn to the Clearwater with Looking-Glass's contingent.

Joseph: "Now we will have to fight . . ."—A little after Howard et al., p. 227 (Joseph).

The murder of Chief Pah Wyan and his wives—McWhorter, *Hear Me,* p. 22.

White Bird: " . . . you must do the best that you can . . ."—Substantially after Howard et al., p. 235 (Duncan McDonald).

Well, Colonel, This Means Business

Dialogue between Howard and his officers until the entrance of Mr. West—After Howard, *Nez Perce Joseph,* pp. 96, 94, 91, some verbatim.

Corruption-related difficulties contingent on Lieutenant Bomus as quartermaster, alluded to here and there throughout *The Dying Grass*—A few specific issues, situations and references to matériel derive from Charles Leib, late captain and assistant quartermaster, *U.S. Army, Nine Months in the Quartermaster's Department, or, The Chances for Making a Million* (Cincinnati: Moore, Wilstach, Keys & Co., Printers, 1862).

Howard's telegram—Slightly abbreviated from the same work, p. 98.

"Some of" Perry's Company "F" "helped Crook clean up the Pi-Utes ten years ago."—Information from Gregory Michno, *The Deadliest Indian War in the West: The Snake Conflict, 1864–1868* (Caldwell, Idaho: Caxton Press, 2007), p. 233.

"The canny ones rub soap or tallow inside their shoes."—Information from Agnew, p. 122.

Price of cocaine at Lapwai—Erwin N. Thompson, *Historic Resource Study: Fort Lapwai, Nez Perce National Historic Park, Idaho* (Denver: Denver Service Center Historic Preservation Team, National Park Service, United States Department of the Interior, July 1973), p. 95. According to the *Britannica,* 11th ed. 1910), vol. VI (Châtelet to Constantine), p. 615 (entry on Cocaine), the stuff is "much used in ophthalmic practice."

"You women have the harder part . . ."—Slightly after Howard, op. cit., p. 99.

"We both know that ninety-odd men may not suffice . . ."—and the good-byes of Perry and Howard—

After pp. 98–99. I have added the "-odd" to reconcile the troop count with Greene's (see below, "a hundred and three effectives").

Sherman on "Quaker policy"—William Tecumseh Sherman, *Memoirs of General W. T. Sherman* (New York: Library of America, 1990 repr. of 1886 ed.), p. 926.

"We did forget, I think, that even in the veins of Joseph . . ."—Almost verbatim from Howard, *Nez Perce Joseph*, p. 75.

The difference between local time and railroad time—"In 1876 time was not yet a commodity that was measured, adjusted, and distributed through the country." Noon was taken by observation. "Sacramento, California, for example, was . . . 3 minutes and 56 seconds later than San Francisco." In 1883 Standard Railroad Time was effected throughout the U.S. "without benefit of federal law or public demand."—Schlereth, pp. 29–30.

"A hundred and three effectives."—Number from Greene, *Nez Perce Summer*, p. 34.

Armaments of Howard and his antagonists—A few details here and throughout derive from Robert Forczyk, *Nez Perce 1877: The Last Fight*, ill. Peter Dennis (Oxford, U.K.: Osprey Publishing Ltd., 2011). Many others (the Beecher's Bibles, box-lock Sharps, Sharps buffalo guns, trapdoor Springfields, Remingtons, etc.) derive from illustrations and catalogue copy in Francis Bannerman Sons, Inc., *Bannerman Catalogue of Military Goods 1927*, repr. (Northfield, Illinois: DBI Books, 1980); and in Norm Flayderman, *Flayderman's Guide to Antique American Firearms . . . and Their Values*, 8th ed. (Iola, Wisconsin: F + W Publications/Gun Digest Books, 2001; orig. ed. 1977). For the trapdoor Springfield in particular, and for information on its performance in the field, I am indebted to Kenneth M. Hammer, *The Springfield Carbine on the Western Frontier*, rev. [4th] ed. (Bozeman, Montana: Little Buffalo Press, 2002). I have cited this book specifically once or twice below.

"*Wakesh nun pakilauitin . . .*"—Axtell, Hymn No. 1 (no title).

The village called Ridge Crossing—"Yénene-spe" is a "village site located at the northern edge of Lapwai," and "yéwnepe" is "the place one goes over a ridge" (Aoki, p. 946).

Should Be a Pleasurable Fight

The march from Fort Lapwai to White Bird Canyon—After Greene, *Nez Perce Summer*, pp. 34–35.

"He ought to do missionary work, not hinder us."—Somewhat after *Hawks and Doves in the Nez Perce War of 1877: Personal Recollections of Eugene Tallmadge Wilson*, review and interpretation by Eugene Edward Wilson (Helena, Montana: Montana Historical Society, in assoc. with the Eugene E. Wilson Collection, U. S. Naval Academy Library), p. 6.

Description of the country along the way—After a visit in August 2009. Description of Grangeville based in part on information in Wilfong, p. 129.

The doomed trumpeter's nickname: "Johnnie Jonesey"—McWhorter, *Yellow Wolf*, p. 56.

Accident with the mountain howitzer at Wallula—Oregon Historical Society MSS 1039. Robert W. Pollock, M.D., "Grandfather, Chief Joseph and Psychodynamics," p. 36 [Henceforth cited: Pollock.]

Twenty-nine settlers killed by Nez Perce in Salmon River raids—This was the figure given in the *East Oregonian* (Pendleton), June 23, 1877, p. 1. It is almost certainly exaggerated. For other figures, see Glossary 4.

"John Henry"—According to *The Annals of America*, vol. 10, p. 300 (no. 64), this folk ballad originated in an incident "during the construction of the Big Bend Tunnel, in West Virginia, sometime around 1873." So it would have been current in 1877. Rather than slavishly reproduce the version printed there, I have made up my own, since it is a folk ballad, after all.

Tale of Sioux stealing a hog in Saint Joseph—After *Autobiography and Reminiscences of Sarah J. Cummings*, p. 12.

Description of the settler (Ad Chapman)—In part after Relander, photo insert 15, after p. 96 ("Occupying the Indian Land").

"This place must have a shorter growing season than Lewiston."—Defendant's Exhibit No. 2, Indian Claims Commission, Docket No. 175-B, *Appraisal of Nez Perce Tribal Lands in Northern Idaho Before the Indian Claims Commission, Docket No. 1775-B, Valued as of August 15, 1894*, prepared for the United States Department of Justice by Homer Hoyt, M.A.I. (Washington, D.C.: October 12, 1959), p. 11: Grangeville, elevation 3,409 feet, had in 1959 a growing season of 134 days, and Lewiston at 743 feet had a growing season of 204 days. (This source is henceforth cited: Hoyt.)

Looking-Glass as "leader of the malcontents"—Howard, *Supplementary Report*, p. 10.

"Lynn Bowers she took off her skirt to run faster . . ."—Much after John D. McDermott, *Forlorn Hope: The Battle of White Bird Canyon and the Beginning of the Nez Perce War* (Boise: Idaho State Historical Society, 1978), p. 25 (words of Hill Norton).

"Mrs. Benedict asked me where I was going . . ."—Closely after Montana Historical Society. SC 183.
E. R. Bosler, Reminiscence. N.d. Transcript of partial ms., p. 1.

Shooting and rape of Mrs. Chamberlain [or Chamberlin]—Mentioned in McDermott, p. 32.

The rapes of Mrs. Walsh and Mrs. Osborne—Ibid., p. 22.

"O[h], colonel, you can easily whip the scoundrels."—Verbatim from Howard, *Nez Perce Joseph*, p. 108.

The lay of the land on the Bluecoats' map: Rocky Canyon, Tolo Lake, etc.—*Reports on the Aftermath of the 1863 Nez Perce Treaty . . .*, p. 40 (E. Giddings, "Map of the Washington Territory East of the Cascade Mts.," 1862; "Detail of Gold Rush Region").

Parnell's knowledge of "what it's like to charge Pi-Utes in the Infernal Caverns"—Information from Michno, p. 257.

The name "Tolo Lake"—Probably anachronistic as I use it. See Glossary 3.

Accomplishment of Toohhoolhoolzote's arrest by Howard and Perry—McWhorter, *Hear Me*, p. 168.

Flashbacks to the Modoc War, here and throughout—Information from Daniel Woodhead III, comp. and ed., *Modoc Vengeance: The 1873 Modoc War in Northern America and Southern Oregon, as Reported in the Newspapers of the Day* (Fresno, California: Linden Publishing, Inc., 2012); and Murray.

Information on Ad Chapman's wife: Umatilla—After information in McWhorter, *Yellow Wolf*, p. 47.

The ordeal of Mrs. Benedict—Information from McDermott, pp. 17–18, 23–24, 79–80.

"It would make your heart ache to see the little children hereabouts . . ."—Abridged and altered from McDermott, p. 13 (letter from Slate Creek).

Remarks on Nez Perce atrocities committed upon Jack Manuel's wife and Mason—Allegations from Wilson, p. 3.

"Stand up for these, the wrong'd . . ."—*Radical Abolitionist*, vols. 1–4 (1855–1858) (New York: Negro Universities Press, 1969); vol. III, number 7 (New York, February, 1858), p. 87 ("Stand Up for Jesus," composer: Dudley A. Tyng). Three stanzas of this hymn are used in *The Dying Grass*.

Description of White Bird Creek and Canyon—After a visit in September 2006, and another in August 2011.

"A succession of steeps, with pointed or rounded tops"—Verbatim from Howard, *Nez Perce Joseph*, p. 109.

Phases of the Battle of White Bird Canyon—After Greene, *Nez Perce Summer*, pp. 34–43.

Description of Ollokot—After a photograph in McWhorter, *Yellow Wolf*, p. 46 (dated 1876). His red-painted eyes and forehead are taken from Pearson, p. 29 (description of the Lapwai council by Emily FitzGerald, 1877).

"Can't go on to Salmon River, Trimble.— No, that's annihilation."—Verbatim from Howard, *Nez Perce Joseph*, p. 116.

"That snarling old bear who's wearing a wolf's head"—After information from Koch (p. 96) about Nez Perce war dress: "the entire skin of a wolf's head . . ." As will become clear later on in the text, I imagine this "old bear" to be Toohhoolhoolzote.

Penetration of seasoned white pine by a Sharps .55 carbine: 7.27 inches—Philip Katcher, *The Civil War Source Book* (New York: Facts on File, 1982), pp. 304–5.

News

Theller's bad companions (and his love of fast horses, mentioned in "Well, Colonel, This Means Business," p. 151)—McDermott, p. 59.

Sherman's facility in offering brilliant plans—After Howard, *Autobiography*, vol. 1, pp. 475–76.

Howard remembers Antietam—Ibid., pp. 302, 305.

"LORD, bow down Thine ear . . ."—II Kings 19.16.

White Bird disguises his face—Loosely after Major-General O. O. Howard, U. S. Army, *Famous Indian Chiefs I Have Known*, ill. George Varian (New York: Century Co., 1908), p. 192.

Howard's lesson from Bull Run: Extra discipline—Howard, *Autobiography*, vol. 1, pp. 269–70.

Ollicut's reluctance to promise anything at the council—Howard, *Supplementary Report*, p. 12.

The Indians "pursued Perry's men all the way to J. M. Crook's lane"—Verbatim from the *East Oregonian* (Pendleton), June 23, 1877, p. 1.

"Threw out their horse herd to cover their movements" + "deployed his skirmishes"—After Humfreville, p. 287 (referring secondhand, and very inaccurately, to the White Bird Canyon battle).

Howard's talk with Father Cataldo—Somewhat after Howard, *Supplementary Report*, p. 13. This conversation actually took place before the Nez Perce War, but I can imagine Howard extending the olive branch to the Nez Perce, or the appearance of one, even at this juncture.

Four murder victims at John Day Creek—Howard, *Report—In the Field*, p. 1.

"Extra good peaches this year in Hood River"—Information from the *East Oregonian*, June 16, 1877, unnumbered p.

Whereabouts of Sergeant McCarthy—As I imagine this scene, Howard would be trying to assess the magnitude of the White Bird Canyon disaster on this day, the 18th. He would have heard something about it on the previous day. Presumably he learned of Theller's death on or before late morning of the 18th. Sergeant McCarthy did not reach his comrades until the 19th.

"Blessed be GOD . . ."—II Corinthians 1.3 (slightly abridged).

Cretonne "with the frill fully pleated on"—After Elizabeth B. Custer, *Following the Guidon*, p. 252 (she was speaking of lounges).

II. Edisto

Epigraph: "GOD has limited the power of man . . ."—John A. Carpenter, *Sword and Olive Branch: Oliver Otis Howard* (Pittsburgh: University of Pittsburgh Press, 1964), p. 83. [Henceforth cited (to avoid confusion with Frank D.): John A. Carpenter.]

Epigraph: "My good mother . . ."—Howard, *Autobiography*, vol. 1, p. 20.

Some of the events relating to the Freedmen's Bureau are related out of order for narrative reasons.

A Good Man in a High Place

Description of Howard's doings at Cheraw—Somewhat derived from Sherman, p. 773.

Physical description of Howard: "bearded, slender," etc.—After the illustrated plate in his *Autobiography*, vol. 1, facing 112 (Howard as Colonel, Third Maine Regiment, 1861).

Incident with General [Thomas John] Wood at camp near Cassaville—Howard, *Autobiography*, vol. 1, 537–38.

Sherman to Howard, Savannah, January 16th, 1865—Bowdoin, OOH papers, call number M91.14, v. 3 [manuscript volume folio]: Diary of Major T. W. Osborn, U.S.V., "Operations of the Army of the Tennessee, in the Carolina Campaign, 1865," p. 2 (abridged by WTV).

Sherman, Howard and the Mayor of Columbia—Ibid., vol. 2, pp. 122–27.

"If any of your foragers are murdered . . ."—Ibid, vol. 2, p. 130.

"Each corps overlined its march with black smoke."—Information from Fenman, p. 225.

Description of the feather patterns on the Nez Perce root storage bag—After Mary Dodds Schlick, *Columbia River Basketry: Gift of the Ancestors, Gift of the Earth* (Seattle: University of Washington Press, a Samuel and Althea Stroum Book, 2002 corr. repr. of 1994 ed.), p. 160. A few other descriptions of Nez Perce and Umatilla baskets derive from plates in this book.

Incident at Mr. Lynde's church and aftermath—Howard, *Autobiography*, vol. 1, pp. 82–83.

Description of Howard after Gettysburg—From plate in same vol., opposite p. 448 ("Major General Howard . . . after the battle of Gettysburg").

Scene at the field hospital—Somewhat after pp. 473, 547 (Cassaville).

Incident with Col. [John] Munroe and the colored boy—Ibid., pp. 78–79. From the author's account, it seems that he said and did nothing. I have invented the dialogue between him and Munroe.

Incident of the fugitive slave at Bull Run—*Autobiography*, vol. 2, pp. 165–66.

"Their army is the strangest . . ."—John Rhodehamel, ed., *The American Revolution: Writings from the War of Independence* (New York: Library of America, 2001), p. 205 (Ambrose Serle, Monday, 2d. September [1776]).

"Should there be any amongst the negroes . . ."—Ibid., p. 85 ("To the Virginia Gazette, November 24, 1775"), slightly abridged.

"Sir, pass these acts . . ."—Howard, op. cit., p. 174 (considerably abbreviated).

Howard court-martials a young officer for speaking offensively against Abolition and the President—Ibid., p. 181.

Emancipation and Elisha's call—Ibid., p. 180.

Henry Ward Beecher's praise of Howard (actually in reference to his work for the Freedmen's Bureau)—Slightly abbreviated from McFeely, p. 87 (address to the Cooper Union, New York City, 8 May 1866, quoted in *American Missionary*).

Howard's speech to the Methodists—After *Autobiography*, vol. 2, pp. 318–19.

"I like niggers well enough as niggers . . ."—Verbatim from Femman, p. 160 (but said in the fall of 1864, and not to Howard).

"Four million . . . from Maryland to Mexico"—Much after Howard, vol. 2, p. 164.

"The Southern man lets go of slavery inch by inch . . ."—Ibid., pp. 310–11 (extracts from address delivered at Springfield, Mass., February 19, 1866; abridged and slightly altered by WTV; the interjections are fictions).

Edisto as "that former Tory Stronghold"—During the Revolutionary War a Tory assured us that from Charlestown all the way "to what is called the Ridge betwixt Saluda and Edisto Rivers on the road to Ninety Six," the people remain loyal to their King. Rhodehamel, pp. 762–63 (Robert Gray, "Observations on the War in Carolina," re: May 1780—February 1782).

Description of freedmen establishments in the Sea Islands—Derived in part from *The Atlantic Presents: Special Commemorative Issue: The Civil War,* December 2011, "designed by Plutomedia," pp. 80–81 (Charlotte Forten, "Life on the Sea Islands," May–June 1864). Other descriptions of Beaufort and Edisto are indebted to the plates in Davis and Wiley, pp. 170–81 ("Mr. Cooley of Beaufort and Mr. Moore of Concord: A Portfolio").

"From the course pursued by the Inspectors"—John A. Carpenter, p. 119 (August 1866: Howard to President Johnson).

"Mr. Johnson is giving up the law pretty fast . . ."—Ibid., p. 109 (Howard to Lizzie, 9 September 1865).

"Yet the President is cordial to me . . ."—Loc. cit. (Howard to Lizzie, 13 September 1865).

"General Butler has got a bill through Congress . . ."—Information from Bannerman, p. 257.

Brig. Gen. Henry J. Hunt: "As to the '*Christian Soldier*' . . ."—Harry W. Pfanz, *Gettysburg—Culp's Hill and Cemetery Hill* (Chapel Hill: University of North Carolina Press [Civil War America ser., Gary W. Gallagher, ed.], 1993), p. 10.

Meeting with Douglass and others (also there: Stella Martin, Henry H. Garnett, John M. Langston)—After Howard, *Autobiography,* vol. 2, p. 317 (somewhat altered; dialogue invented).

"Did they beat the negro when they pulled him out of jail? . . ."—Somewhat after *Testimony Taken by the Joint Select Committee to Inquire into the Condition of Affairs in the Late Insurrectionary States: Alabama,* volume III (Washington, D.C.: Government Printing Office, 1872), p. 1573.

Hiring of Joseph S. Fullerton and "men of integrity . . ." (Howard's words)—After John A. Carpenter, pp. 95, 97 (the latter altered and abridged).

Won and Fortified

Burning of Sioux property after vanquishing their village—Mentioned in Zimmer, p. 51 (May 8th 1877), p. 90 (August 1st).

When the night riders murdered Joe Bell—Information from Bellisles, p. 22. The actual last name was Johnson, which I changed to avoid confusion with President Johnson.

"You exert a dangerous effect upon our negroes."—Phrase somewhat after *Testimony Taken by the Joint Select Committee,* p. 1494.

"The negroes must be employed . . ."—First and third sentences somewhat after John A. Carpenter, p. 93 (an authentic letter from Howard to Lizzie, but actually written earlier—soon after the Atlanta campaign). I have altered and expanded it.

Richmond's ordinance of June 1865—McFeely, p. 95 (J. S. Fullerton to Orlando Brown, 15 June 1865).

Howard's proposal to the President on conditional pardon for slaveholders—John A. Carpenter, pp. 108–9.

His supposed instructions to Bureau agents (actually, nothing but a policy set out in one of his letters)—Ibid., p. 108.

Howard's pledges to Howard University, the YMCA and the church; Ketchum's encomium—Ibid., p. 237.

The firing of Rufus Saxton—I find myself on Saxton's side. He wrote Howard: "It seems to me as not wise or prudent to do injustice to those who have always been loyal and true, in order to be lenient to those who have done their best to destroy the Nation's life."

Description of Howard's office in Beaufort—After a photograph of the Freedmen's Bureau in Beaufort, South Carolina (165-C-394), p. 2, of Reginald Washington, comp., *Black Family Research Records of Post–Civil War Federal Agencies at the National Archives: Reference Information Paper 108* (Washington, D.C.: National Archives and Records Administration, 2010 rev.).

"You are right in wanting homesteads . . ."—John A. Carpenter, p. 110. Dialogue inserted by WTV, including Howard's "return home . . ." Of the entire exchange, only Howard's first two sentences are genuine.

Information on SB 60—McFeely, pp. 229, 236.

The riots in Memphis and New Orleans (May and July 1866)—Ibid., p. 273.

Use of Bureau agents as strikebreakers—Ibid., pp. 312–13.

Information on the Freedman's Savings Bank—John A. Carpenter, p. 323.

Howard's summons to the Senate—Bowdoin, OOH Papers, M91 Box 43, folder: Courts-Martial and Military Investigations Material (subpoenas, etc.), 1876–77.

The Bowdoin entrance examination—Howard, *Autobiography*, vol. 1, p. 29.

The charges against Howard, here and below; information on Fernando Wood and Hiram Barber—Bowdoin, OOH Papers, E185.2, P4, 1871. "Charges Against General Howard. SPEECH of HON. LEGRAND W. PERCE, of Mississippi, in the House of Representatives, March 2, 1871" (Washington: F & J. Rives & Geo. A. Bailey, reporters and printers of the debates in Congress, 1871). The charges are sometimes verbatim and sometimes not. The characterizations of Fernando Wood ("the gentleman from New York")—"a leader in the most corrupt political organization known to American history . . ." are verbatim but condensed.

"A nigro wench is as good as a white lady."—Somewhat after T. J. Stiles, comp. & ed., *In Their Own Words: Robber Barons and Radicals* (New York: Perigee, 1997), p. 47 ("Persecution," by Albert T. Morgan; alleged of Morgan himself, not Howard).

"God knows my heart and my life. It is better to go to prison than to deceive Him."—Almost verbatim from Howard's letter to Rowland (February 19, 1874), quoted in John A. Carpenter, p. 229.

Howard's rescue by Grant and Sherman—Ibid., pp. 229–31.

The presence of Colonel Miles on the panel, and his letter to Howard—Wooster, pp. 61–62.

The War Department's three civil suits against Howard—Ibid., pp. 243–45. In the same place is noted that Howard's legal expenses were seven thousand dollars; Congress never reimbursed him. In 1879 the civil suits were settled in his favor or withdrawn.

The Secretary of the Navy's opinion of Howard—*Diary of Gideon Welles, Secretary of the Navy Under Lincoln and Johnson, with an introduction by John T. Morse, Jr.* (3 vols.), vol. iii: January 1, 1867–June 6, 1869 (New York: Houghton Mifflin Co., 1911).

General Crook: "I was at loss to make out whether it was his vanity or his cheek . . ."—*General George Crook: His Autobiography*, ed. & annotated by Martin F. Schmitt (Norman: University of Oklahoma Press, 1960 rev. repr. of 1946 ed.; ms. wr. 1885–90), p. 170.

"After years of thinking and observation I am inclined to think that the restoration of their lands to the planters . . ."—Howard, *Autobiography*, vol. 2, p. 244.

General Crook's Assessment

"He told me he thought the CREATOR had placed him on earth . . ."—John A. Carpenter, p. 212.

Washington, D.C.

Dialogue between Howard and Walker—Walker's arguments, and many of his phrases, are based on *The Annals of America*, vol. 10, pp. 292–98 (no. 62, Francis A. Walker, *Report of the Commissioner of Indian Affairs*, Washington, 1873), much altered, expanded and abridged. In the original, Walker of course says nothing relating to black Americans. There is no reason to think that he ever met Howard. But one of the questions which most haunted me during the writing of this book is why Howard was so humane to the former slaves, whom he struggled at great personal cost to aid, no matter that the aid proved mostly ineffective in the end, while he treated Joseph so harshly. In part it must be that so many Afro-Americans were nominally Christian, while Indians were often to Howard's mind pagans. Their nature-worshipping justifications for refusing to leave their homeland enraged him. Then, too, he must have felt duped and betrayed by Joseph when Shore Crossing and the other young men went on the warpath. The Nez Perce War was a significant embarrassment to Howard in several ways. But the general seems to me to have been such an upright, kind and even noble man that when it came to Indian removal he must have victimized himself with some sort of mental trickery, much as when in reference to Edisto he was able to persuade himself as follows: "After years of thinking and observation I am inclined to think that the restoration of their lands to the planters proved for all their future better for the negroes." Hence the imagined dialogue with Walker, whose report is so chillingly prescient and self-satisfied all at once. Walker had no illusions about the policy he was implementing. He knew, and said straight out, that his Department was pauperizing hundreds of thousands of Indians. But it would all be for the best. If this was the Department's mindset in 1871, then it might well have been Howard's in 1877. He certainly deferred to Indian Agents with saddening alacrity. By the way, the physical description of Walker is based on the photoportrait on p. 295 (by B. Kimball).

III. The Burial of Lieutenant Theller

Epigraph: "Many officers fail with large commands . . ."—Howard, *Autobiography*, vol. 2, p. 57.

We Have Now Seen His Deeds

"There is always a theory of war . . ."—Nearly verbatim from Howard *Autobiography*, vol. 1, p. 375.

"The most crushing defeat ever inflicted upon us by the Indians."—Point made by Major General John K. Herr, U.S.A. (Retired), Last Chief of Cavalry, and Edward S. Wallace, *The Story of the U.S. Cavalry 1775–1942* (Boston: Little, Brown & Company, 1953), p. 182.

Military and civilian casualties (killed by Nez Perce)—From *Report of Brigadier-General O. O. Howard, Brevet Major-General U.S. Army, commanding Department of the Columbia,—In the Field. August 27, 1877.* (Portland, Oregon: Assistant Adjutant-General's Office, Department of the Columbia, 1878), p. 2.

Mrs. Theller's previous marriage to Mr. Butler—Information from Fanny Dunbar Corbusier, *Recollections of Her Army Life, 1869–1908*, ed. Patricia Y. Stallard (Norman: University of Oklahoma Press, 2003), p. 27.

Perry on Trimble: "He did seem in a hurry to get away," and Perry's refusal to prefer charges against that officer—Much after McDermott, p. 200 (Perry's testimony at court of inquiry).

Failure of some Springfield breechblocks to close at Little Big Horn—Hammer, pp. 7–8.

"Unfortunately, the assault was not successful . . ."—Howard, *Report—In the Field*, loc. cit.

"To fight savages successfully . . ."—Almost verbatim from Bourke, *With General Crook*, p. 36.

Sherman's bypassing of Sheridan in Nez Perce campaigns—Newton F. Tolman, *The Search for General Miles* (New York: G. P. Putnam's Sons, 1968), p. 80.

So This Was Joseph's Plan

"To start the war through a series of outrages, in the usual style . . ."—To end of sentence, nearly verbatim from Howard, *Nez Perce Joseph*, p. 122. Two or three of Howard's remarks on strategy in this conference are after Howard, *Supplementary Report, January 26, 1878*, p. 8 (somewhat altered; actually from March 1877, three months before the commencement of the Nez Perce War).

"A large, thick-necked, obstinate old savage of the worst type."—Howard, *Supplementary Report*, p. 18. Who knows if any such conversation as I have imagined occurred when Howard was briefing his officers before setting out on the pursuit of Joseph? If it did, I can well envision him as being "correctly" humane in general, but betraying his temper on the subject of Toohhoolhoolzote, whom he clearly hated.

Details of companies assembled at Lapwai by the 22nd of June, and strategy in the paragraph beginning "Gentlemen, I'm taking the field in person"—After Howard, *Report—In the Field*, p. 3.

"When Crook is doping out what to do"—Information from Bourke, p. 24.

"From them being half-breeds and *squaw men* . . ."—Altered and abridged from Aubrey L. Haines, *The Battle of the Big Hole: The Story of the Landmark Battle of the 1877 Nez Perce War* (Helena, Montana: Twodot, an imprint of the Globe Pequot Press, 2007 facsimile repr. of 1991 ed.), p. 11 (James Mills, Secretary to the Governor of Montana).

"Father Cataldo says his Injuns are all quiet up on Hangman Creek."—Altered from the *East Oregonian* (Pendleton), June 23, p. 1.

"This is the first such language I've heard since arriving here . . ."—After Pfanz, p. 10 (description of Howard).

Grace's Birthday

The rich bunchgrass around Imnaha—Specifically mentioned in Howard, *Among Our Hostile Indians*, p. 235.

Description of Umatilla Jim's mind-flight from Wallowa to the cave where Joseph was born—After a trip in September 2006, from Zumwalt Road, Wallowa Valley, Oregon, to Joseph Cave, Washington. When I went there, I saw sprinklers in the yellow grass on the far side of the Grande Ronde.

The visiting card receiver from Eugene Jaccard—Advertisement in the *Saint Louis Dispatch*, number 221, Tuesday evening, January 4, 1876.

Descriptions of Grace Howard's dress and hairstyle before and after puberty—Based on general information in Schlereth, p. 279.

Information on current military clothing, here and throughout—After Lee A. Rutledge, *Collector's Guide to Military Uniforms: Campaign Clothing: Field Uniforms of the Indian War Army 1872–1886* (Tustin, California: North Cape Publications, 1997). As this authority freely grants (p. 3), "the subject of U. S. Army field uniforms—even in the narrow confines of 1872 to 1886—is amazingly complex and confusing."

"A total force of two hundred and twenty-seven effectives."—Howard, *Report—In the Field*, p. 3.

Wood's dancing skills—Venn, p. 7.

Description of Elizabeth B. Custer—After a photograph in Weymouth, p. 56.

"Naturally, a civilized white man is lowered . . ." Almost verbatim from Howard, *Among Our Hostile Indians*, p. 525.

Howard and Wilkinson's visit to Pasqual—Howard, *Famous Indian Chiefs*, pp. 42, 40, 53.

Alaska Sounds Fine and Cool

This chapter distorts two facts: Howard did not join the march out of Lapwai on 22 June, but on the next day, so all the dialogue here is erroneous; and he probably saw very little of Lieutenant Wood at this stage (although he was certainly very fond of him).

"Joseph called it a good country."—Somewhat after Howard, *Famous Indian Chiefs*, p. 194.

Wood's description of metals in Alaska—Loosely after Venn, p. 12 (letter from Wood to Howard, Sitka, May 16, 1877).

"Go in and kill 'em all, boys . . ."—Ibid., p. 28 (diary entry for June 20: Astoria to Portland).

Descriptions of Gatling guns here and throughout—After John Ellis, *The Social History of the Machine Gun* (Baltimore: Johns Hopkins University Press, 1986 pbk. repr. of 1975 ed.), illustrations on pp. 21, 27.

Contents of the tool wagon—Information from Manigault, p. 164. Although this inventory was a good decade older than the Nez Perce War, I have supposed that the shrinkage of the postwar Army would have kept such collections at (or perhaps even below) their Civil War levels.

General plan of Lapwai—After Wood's sketch in Venn, p. 31 ("Fort Lapwai, Idaho Territory").

"When the Oregonians murdered our Modoc prisoners"—Event described in Woodhead, p. 186.

"Let's allow our train to elongate a trifle."—Idea from Howard, *Nez Perce Joseph*, p. 131.

Captain Miller and his duties—Mentioned in the same book, p. 133.

The general's "one blue overall suit which will fade"—Joseph Wall: "Howard wore a faded blue overall suit, and only his military hat with the star on the front proclaimed his rank."—Merrill D. Beal, *"I Will Fight No More Forever": Chief Joseph and the Nez Perce War* (Seattle: University of Washington Press, 1971 repr. of 1963 ed.), p. 255.

"Left Portland 5 A.M. . . ."—Wood wrote this not in 1877 but the following year during his far more extensive diary of the Bannock campaign; i.e., Wood diary, 1878, p.1. I have altered and abbreviated this passage.

Sladen's accident (12 October 1875)—*Making Peace with Cochise: The 1872 Journal of Captain Joseph Alton Sladen*, ed. Edwin R. Sweeney (Norman: University of Oklahoma Press, 1997), p. 109. [Henceforth: Sladen.]

The murder of Chief Tipyahlanah by Larry Ott—After McWhorter, *Yellow Wolf*, p. 44.

Situation at Norton's ranch—After Venn, p. 32 (entry for June 26).

Wood's state of mind from Lapwai until White Bird Canyon—Based on the same source, pp. 31–32. (The diary entries are brief.)

Wood's personality—The diary reprinted by Venn is very sketchy. Wood later complained that after the Nez Perce War, General Howard simply took all the notes he had made and used them himself. So Wood's actual state of mind and development during the campaign must be worked out by implication. We know that at the beginning Wood was credulous as to nonexistent Nez Perce atrocities (the reality at Slate Creek was bad enough) and that he was very fond of and respectful toward Howard. His diary from the Bannock War of 1878 is much fuller and helps bring his turns of thinking and speech to life. By then he seems to have already been somewhat estranged from Howard, who is hardly mentioned in its very personal passages. We also know that even in 1878 he was sorry for Joseph and the other exiles, and that he later sent his son Erskine to be mentored by Joseph. We know that he resigned the military and became a rather radical lawyer, then a poet. So I have taken the liberty of imagining the Nez Perce War as commencing his radicalization, which at that stage he had to hide a bit even from himself, in order to stay in the good graces of Howard and the other officers. I have learned a great deal from the C. E. S. Wood papers at the Oregon Historical Society.

The Old-Fashioned Girl by Mrs. Alcott—Mentioned in Zimmer, p. 157 ([December] 17th).

Wood's copper bracelet—Pollock, p. 63 (letter of July 22); he states that the bracelet's purpose was to ward away sickness. The bracelet's Alaskan origin is my surmise.

Half as many growing days at Norton's as in Lewiston—According to Hoyt (p. 11), the elevation of Cottonwood is 3,411 feet, and the growing season 123 days. See earlier Hoyt source-note for Lewiston in "Should Be a Pleasurable Fight."

Chapman's prior ownership of Manuel's ranch—McDermott, p. 15.

Wood's spoon-proof of his connection to Elizabeth Erskine—Information from Oregon State Historical Society, Mss. 800, C. E. S. Wood papers, box 1, folder 18, excerpts from 1912–1916? autobiography.

The Nez Perce will "operate on the settlements in the Wallowa."—After the *East Oregonian* (Pendleton), June 30, 1877, p. 1.

"A horse needs a full dozen quarts [of oats]."—Information from Zimmer, p. 59 ([May] 31st).

Size of a scalp: comparable to a silver dollar—Howard, *Famous Indian Chiefs*, p. 300. However, McWhorter's procedure in *Hear Me* (p. 38) would imply a greater area: Cut over eyebrows and straight around above the ears, then give it a good pull. Perhaps the extra skin is trimmed off later. The old scalps I have seen in museums do not show vast hanks of skin.

Battle Without Music

The shelling of the military band at Fredericksburg—Mentioned in Howard, *Autobiography*, vol. 1, p. 314. How many band members were killed is not stated.

Lowe's weeping about Custer's Gatlings—Camp, p. 53 (Interview with Winfield S. Edgerly).

"Everything had better shine like a silver dollar."—Closely after Zimmer, p. 149 ([November] 11th).

Parnell: *"That's Indian character for you . . ."*—Loosely after Michno, p. 330 (Parnell's words).

"Au namotihu SAVIOURNA . . ."—Axtell, chorus of hymn no. 2, "Yield Not to Temptation."

Shearer's thoughts—Some phrases taken from Idaho Historical Society, MS 42, George M. Shearer, Folder 7 (undated letters). Here are some other good ones: "If you were frightened by my letter of the twenty-seventh, well, what do you suppose was the effect produced by your reply to it?" and "But heavens! How can I bear up beneath the load of it all?"

"I do hope Johnny and Ella . . ."—Pollock, p. 31.

"Two boys killed a cougar in Lane County"—Information from the *East Oregonian* (Pendleton), June 16, 1877, unnumbered p.

Ads for Drake's Plantation Bitters—Information from Schlereth, p. 161.

A Happy Recollection of the "East Woods"

Professor Mahan's definition of common sense—After Howard, *Autobiography*, vol. 1, p. 385.

Distance from Johnson's ranch to White Bird Canyon—Howard, *Report—In the Field*, p. 3.

Doctor Alexander's treatment for rattlesnake bite—Information from Elizabeth Custer, p. 301 (ammonia on the bite, and whiskey to guzzle in order to slow the circulation).

"Leading the column with the regulation twenty-eight-inch step, a hundred ten paces to the minute"—Closely after Bradley, p. 12.

"Where are my brisk and hearty troopers?"—The last four words are verbatim from Howard, *Nez Perce Joseph*, p. 137. The sentiment is also his; he says that Perry's survivors are diminished both in numbers and in morale.

Mr. Croaesdale's creditable improvised field-works—All of these words lifted from *Nez Perce Joseph*, p. 138.

The theft of Croaesdale's explosive bullets—Information from Greene, *Nez Perce Summer*, pp. 315, 490 n. 146. Both .44- and .50-caliber cartridges were obtained.

"There's been a dozen strange Indians hanging around Celilo . . ."—Somewhat after the *East Oregonian* (Pendleton), June 23, 1877, p. 1.

Captain John's career experience—Information from Gulick, p. 242.

Old George's characteristics: "He has an Indian look, but at least his hair's short . . ." + "They say he's real good-natured."—Loc. cit. (quoting Howard, *Nez Perce Joseph*, which I have altered a bit here).

Shearer "already caught one of them hostile reds and bashed his head in"—Information from McDermott, p. 33; the Indian (part of a Nez Perce pillaging party) was a lame old man named Jyeloo, whom Shearer had already shot.

Howard's memory: Sleeping among corpses in the "East Woods" of Antietam—After Howard, *Autobiography*, vol. 1, p. 307.

Duty of a major to inventory the property of deceased soldiers—Kautz, p. 265.

Burial

Description of the battlefield—After Venn, p. 33 (entry for June 27). "Ravishing and burning women!" is verbatim. Of course the Nez Perce did not actually burn anybody.

Pollock: "All that has got to be done is to catch the leaders and hang them."—Wilfong, p. 59 (July 22).

Five bodies past the stage road—After recollections of a volunteer named Swarts, quoted in Greene, *Nez Perce Summer*, p. 388 (fn. 39).

The corpse in a thorn tree with its testicles in its mouth—Loc. cit.

"Unidentified. Two bullet holes in skull . . ."—Somewhat after the format of Dr. Lippincott's report on the Elliott massacre, in George Armstrong Custer, *My Life on the Plains, or, Personal Experiences with Indians*, with intro. by Edgar I. Stewart (Norman: University of Oklahoma Press, 1962; orig. book pub. 1874; orig. serial pub. 1872), pp. 288–89. [Henceforth cited (to avoid confusion with Elizabeth): George Armstrong Custer.] I have altered descriptions to fit my understanding of the situation at White Bird Canyon. For instance, all of Dr. Lippincott's corpses had names. I suppose that due to the hot weather many of Dr. Alexander's remained "unidentified."

"I've long since learned not to show my head twice when an Indian's watching."—Montana Historical Society. SC 520. John B. Catlin reminiscence. Typescript: "The Battle of the Big Hole, by Col. J. B. Catlin." [Henceforth "Col. J. B. Catlin."] Page 6.

"And alsoe Tobacao the wead that a soldier likes eaven better than he does Whiskey."—Verbatim from *I Buried Custer: The Private Diary of Thomas W. Coleman, 7th U. S. Cavalry*, ed. Bruce R. Liddic (College Station, Texas: Young West Series Creative Publishing Company, 1979), p. 13.

Dialogue about supposed mutilation of corpses by Nez Perce women—After Eugene Tallmadge Wilson, pp. 5–6.

Location of Theller's body—Information from Greene, loc. cit.

Perry's ride with Theller along the Clearwater from Lewiston to Lapwai—After a journey that way in August 2011.

Visualization of the deaths of Theller and his squad—Somewhat after the illustration in Forczyk, pp. 38–39 ("Lieutenant Theller's Last Stand, June 17, 1877").

"Human ghouls"—Coleman, p. 132 (Gibbon remembers the "human ghouls" who rifled the Sioux dead in their abandoned village just after the Battle of the Little Big Horn).

Howard's command to Wood about Captain Hunter's volunteers—Norman B. Adkison, *Indian Braves and Battles, with More Nez Perce Lore* (Grangeville: Idaho County Free Press, 1967), p. 15.

"Send out your cavalry to scout, and then corral the train."—Procedure after Bradley, p. 31.

"We're fewer than a single regiment of the Secession War"—Information from Bowdoin, OOH papers, M91.8: Indians: Articles & Addresses, "An Indian Battle (Nez Perce)," p. 7.

Bivouac procedure—Information from George Armstrong Custer, p. 99. This book was published five years before the Nez Perce War, so the procedure might or might not have been archaic.

James Reuben: "I told Cut Arm that if he wished to move our relations . . ."—Much altered from Howard et al., p. 230 (Duncan McDonald); but this was indeed Reuben speaking in the original—of course not to Umatilla Jim, who is an invented character.

The Negro songs in Captain Pollock's tent—"But everybody seems very cheerful. While I write, all the young officers are singing nigger songs in my tent" (Pollock, p. 44; letter to Mrs. Pollock evidently written at this time and place).

"Please ask General Sherman to send one (1) regiment . . ."—This was actually datelined June 30, or three days later. Abridged and slightly altered from Howard, *Report—In the Field*, p. 31.

"They were as the grass of the field . . ."—II Kings 19.26.

Howard's dispatching of Wilkinson and Mason to Norton's—This detail is invented. I needed them both at their general's side for much of the action around here, but Wood's diary states (Venn, p. 34) that those two "came up" to the Salmon on 30 July, so this seemed a good compromise.

Chapman's detail: Wettiwetti Houlis led the truce party—Information from McWhorter, *Yellow Wolf*, p. 54.

"On the twenty-sixth we successfully accomplished a reconnaissance . . ."—Somewhat after Howard, *Report—In the Field*, p. 3. Captain Paige sometimes loses the "i" from his last name in various sources, including this one; I have kept it throughout.

Wood's encounter with Theller in summer 1876—Wood was nowhere near Lapwai when he set off for Alaska, so this meeting could not have happened.

The Blackfoot prostitute's muslin dress—After an illustration in Horse Capture and Her Many Horses, p. 50 (the text says "possibly" Blackfoot but it may not be, so I have eliminated the battle pictures in the original).

Salmon Crossing

The hanging of Heyoom Tookaitat—Recounted in McWhorter, *Hear Me*, p. 117.

Captain Paige's news—After Howard, *Report—In the Field*, p. 3.

"Hear, O Israel . . ."—Deuteronomy 9.1.

"The reds have removed their plunder . . ."—This sentence slightly altered from the *East Oregonian* (Pendleton), June 30, 1877, p. 1.

Hunter's discovery and burial of Nez Perce victims—Adkison, p. 16.

"Now with the blowing of the trumpet . . ."—A line from a Nez Perce hymn written by Rev. Spalding; verbatim from Aoki.

Howard on different appearances of Nez Perce and white horsemen—Howard, *Nez Perce Joseph*, p. 21.

"Do they hope to turn my flank at Rocky Cañon?"—See the same book.

Chapman's willful mistranslation of Nez Perce challenges—No evidence that this happened here, but the claim has often been made (for instance, by Pearson, who considers him quite the villain) that at the end of the war, once he got power over Joseph and the other exiles, he altered their words to suit him.

Official pay of Indian Office interpreters as of 31 May 1877 (eighty-one and a half cents per day)—National Archives Microfilm Publications. Microfilm Publication M1121: Records of the Bureau of Indian Affairs, Record Group 75: 1854–1955 (17 reels). [Henceforth: National Archives microfilm M1121.] Roll 5: Miscellaneous Circulars, 1854–1885. Circular [unnumbered]. Department of the Interior, Office of Indian Affairs, Washington, May 31, 1877.

Dispatch of Miller, Perry and Paige (or Page) to Lapwai—Howard, *Report—In the Field*, p. 4.

"Indians flaunting their blankets from the bare hillsides"—Thomas A. Sutherland, volunteer aide-de-camp on Gen. Howard's Staff, *Howard's Campaign against the Nez Perce Indians, 1877* (Portland, Oregon: A. G. Walling, Steam Book & Book Jobber, & Bookbinder, 1878), p. 3.

"These Indians . . . scatter to the four winds at the approach of troops . . ."—Somewhat after Michno, p. 232 (Parnell's words).

"A foaming torrent rushing through desolation"—Wood diary, 1878, p. 1.

Location of the ford—Greene, *Nez Perce Summer*, p. 45.

Sunday ice-creams in Baltimore—Information from Bellesiles, p. 14.

Wood's night mission—Wood diary, 1878, p. 21.

Mr. Wilmot's haul from Nez Perce caches at Deer Creek—Abbreviated from Wilfong, pp. 112–13.

Cleaning Out Wallowa

Descriptions of Wallowa and Imnaha after various visits in 2006–10.

The mission of the volunteers in this chapter is invented, but draws on the experience of Captain John W. Cullen, who commanded a small detachment of Oregon volunteers at this time in an effort to discover the whereabouts of the non-treaty Nez Perces. "If I were an Indian I'd fight for this valley to the last ditch," and the allusion to Captain William Booth's cowardice, are both closely after Cullen's remarks (*Hear Me*, pp. 278–79). Cullen and his five men did not and could not have "cleaned out Wallowa." They did not coordinate with Shearer as far as I know.

The placer mines in the Nez Perce country: "All played out, ten years ago and more."—C. Marc Miller, Seattle, February, 1954, *Appraisal of Nez Perce Ceded Tract, Oregon, Washington & Idaho 1867, Cases 175 and 180 Before the Indian Claims Commission, Prepared for the Lands Division, United States Department of Justice*, p. 33. Doc was a liar. See also p. 27: "By 1867 production [of gold] in the Nez Perce region had declined to a low point."

Sign of a Nez Perce graveyard: horse bones on a hill—Information from Lewis and Clark, vol. 7, p. 219 (Clark, Tuesday May 6th 1806).

IV. I Am Flying Up

Epigraph: "It was those Christian Nez Perces . . ."—McWhorter, *Yellow Wolf*, p. 35.
Epigraph: "It was always hard to love a Government . . ."—Howard, *Autobiography*, vol. 1, p. 203.

Here at This Dance

Non-treaty Nez Perce's actions between the Battle of White Bird Canyon and the encounter with the cavalry at the Salmon—Somewhat after information in McWhorter, *Yellow Wolf*, pp. 62–64.

Nine hundred elkteeth—Koch (p. 47) says that Crow women could wear three to eleven hundred elkteeth.

The actions of Yellow Bull, "who helped rape those two loosehaired Boston bitches"—He was evidently one of the leaders of the second Salmon River raid, in which white women were gang-raped.

The accomplishment of Going Alone—McDermott, p. 33.

Rainbow, "he who can never be killed after sunrise"—Information from McWhorter, *Yellow Wolf*, p. 387.

The Dreamer (Washat song)—After Relander, p. 84; much "retranslated" by WTV.

"As if she has bewitched him with beaver-musk and camomile"—*Palakh* is "love perfume" from powdered camomile and beaver-musk, rubbed on body. Simplified from Aoki, p. 563.

Non-treaty Nez Perce *vs.* cavalry and treaty Nez Perce from the Salmon until the killing of the Rains party—After McWhorter, *Yellow Wolf*, pp. 67–71.

"The threats and taunts of the Lapwai People"—Joseph writes that "through all the years since the white man came to Wallowa, we have been threatened and taunted by them and the treaty Nez Perces. They have given us no rest."—Howard et al., p. 285 (Joseph).

Where the Enemy River Goes

"Loathsome old man . . ."—Somewhat after part of a song given in Aoki, p. 646.

When BUTTERFLY opened and closed Herself—Walker and Matthews, p. 23.

Description of the place where Fair Land picked cous—Based on a visit to Couse Meadows, Washington, not far south of Rattlesnake Summit (which in turn is south of Asotin), August 2009.

Flashback: Descriptions of the Nez Perce atrocities committed on the Salmon River settlers—After McWhorter, *Yellow Wolf*, pp. 196–ff.

"I am flying up. I am jumping up. I am worshipping" [as a Dreamer]—Aoki's translation (p. 299) of the word *wa-láhsasc*.

V. The Rest of My Days

Epigraphs: "Emma was kneeling . . ."—Wilfong, pp. 297–98 (Ida Carpenter).
" . . . My desire for life returned . . ."—Ibid., p. 302 (George Cowan).

We Gave Looking-Glass an Opportunity

"I'm glad to hear that Looking-Glass remains at home . . ."—Verbatim from Greene, *Nez Perce Summer*, p. 51 (quoting Howard to James Lawyer).

The report of Umatilla Jim—Based on information from "our friendly Indians," in Howard, *Nez Perce Joseph*, p. 148.

"Captain Whipple, go with your cavalry . . ."—Abbreviated from Howard, *Nez Perce Joseph*, p. 149.

The Chinese laundry at Mount Idaho—There were two in 1880 (Wikoff, p. 60), so maybe there was at least one in 1877.

The troops singing of "Turn Back Pharaoh's Army"—Information from Fairfax Downey, *Indian-Fighting Army* (New York: Scribner's, 1941), p. 237.

Description of Looking-Glass's camp on the Clearwater—After a visit to the site in August 2009.

The Gatlings—According to Greene (*Nez Perce Summer*, p. 51), for some reason Whipple actually left them at Mount Idaho.

"This place called Kamnaka"—Information from Greene, *Nez Perce Summer*, p. 52.

Description of Umatilla Jim's cape—After a cape on display in the Tamastlikit Museum on the Umatilla reservation in Oregon, August 2009.

The Hayes medal reading "CENTENNIAL AMERICA"—Sullivan, p. 425.

Description of Peopeo Tholekt—After Greene, *Beyond Bear's Paw*, p. 122 (National Park Service photo, Nez Perce National Historic Park).

"Looking-Glass is my chief!" and remainder of italicized speech—Slightly altered from Greene, *Nez Perce Summer*, p. 54.

Account of the attack—After Greene, *Nez Perce Summer*, pp. 52–57.

"He has stolen twelve hundred horses!"—Information from Howard et al., p. 239 (Duncan McDonald).

The bayonet-pierced kettles—Detail from *Hear Me*, p. 270.

Whipple's report—Somewhat after Howard, *Nez Perce Joseph*, p. 149, abbreviated and colloquialized. Whipple and Howard were not actually face to face at this moment.

"Perhaps I expected too much of your tired horses . . ."—Almost verbatim from Greene, *Nez Perce Summer*, p. 58.

Nez Perce casualties—Greene, *Nez Perce Summer*, p. 372 (Appendix B). The number of victims is not consistently reported. The women's names have not been recorded; I have called them Far Mountain and Big Old Woman (a female name from Aoki's dictionary). Rifle is a man's name taken from the same source.

Information on Grandfather Looking-Glass (Bighorn)—Lewis and Clark, vol. 7, p. 202 (Lewis, Saturday May 3rd 1806).

Old Looking-Glass at the treaty ground in 1855—Ruby and Brown, p. 138.

Looking-Glass: "My People, I will never make peace with the Bostons . . ."—Somewhat after his words quoted in Wilfong, pp. 126–27.

Killing of the Crow warrior by Red Owl's grandfather—McWhorter, *Hear Me*, p. 557.

The Black Arabian

Dispositions of troops in talk with Whipple—After Howard, *Report—In the Field*, p. 4.

"Leave no stone unturned" and "I expect of the cavalry tremendous vigor . . ."—Verbatim from Greene, p. 58 (Howard to Whipple).

Whipple's thoughts about Sully and Crook—This is the point of view in Forczyk, p. 41. It is not at all clear to me that Howard was so worried about getting replaced at this point.

"I hear from Mr. Cornoyer . . ."—Information from the *East Oregonian* (Pendleton), June 10, 1877, p. 1.

Chapman's gift of a horse to Howard—My invention.

Taking the Shortest Line

Wilkinson's assertion: Randall helped himself to fifty acres of the reservation—Information from McWhorter, *Hear Me*, p. 288.

Howard's dispatch to Perry—My invention, based in part on the general's reasoning in *Nez Perce Joseph*, p. 154.

"Mr. Reuben's ration check"—Whether he actually had one I cannot say, but like a canny bureaucrat I now refer you to National Archives microfilm M1121, Roll 5, Miscellaneous Circulars, 1854–1885: Department of the Interior, Office of Indian Affairs, Washington,——, 187——, handwritten, evidently sent out in 1876. "It is the purpose of this office, on January 1, 1877, or as soon thereafter as the instructions herein can be carried into operation, to commence a new system in issuing subsistence supplied to the Indians . . . Having thus obtained a list, showing the head and number of each family, every such head should be provided with a Ration Check . . . It should be clearly and forcibly impressed upon the Indians that no supplies whatever will be issued without the presentation and 'punching' of such check . . . and that its loss, or any attempt to use it, or to overreach you in obtaining increased rations, will only result to the detriment of the Indian thus careless or dishonest."

"Your orders are to cross the Salmon at or near Horse Shoe Bend . . ."—After Wilson, p. 6 (orthography slightly modernized).

Description of Doc and his accoutrements—After a drawing of an infantryman in Bourke, p. 51.

Larry Ott's hair—McWhorter, *Yellow Wolf*, p. 45.

Description of Deer Creek, Cottonwood, Camp Howard, Grangeville and vicinity—After a visit in September 2006.

"Hogback" and "table-lands" are both borrowed from Howard, *Nez Perce Joseph*, pp. 149, 154.

"What a mule has done is known . . ."—Verbatim from Sladen, p. 37.

"Right now the folks will be haying back home."—Information from Schlereth, pp. 38–39, farm routine for July in Iowa (from diary of John Savage).

"Our shortest line may be to turn back via White Bird Cañon."—Closely after Howard, in McWhorter, *Hear Me*, p. 281.

Fourth of July

In case you have not heard of it, this is the day when civilians and other children take joy in parades and ice-cream, while soldiers remember the Revolutionary War, which was truly the First Civil War: Whigs tarring and feathering their Tory neighbors and sometimes murdering them, Hessians stealing people's hay and cows and every once in awhile likewise murdering them, Americans burning Iroquois cornfields and occasionally skinning the Indians' corpses for boot-leather, both sides executing deserters, hanging spies; soldiers marching, marching, sometimes dying of dysentery or heatstroke, both sides charging each other with fixed bayonets, and on and on, frozen misery at Valley Forge, trenches and bombardments at Yorktown.

Fourth of July treats in Portland: Arctic soda, shooting match, etc.—*Morning Oregonian*, vol. XVII.—no. 130, Portland, Oregon: Friday, July 6, 1877 (pp. unnumbered).

Tale of Howard and Bullard (Howard's words verbatim)—Sladen, p. 48.

"And this month Congress has stopped paying the Army."—Information from Bruce, p. 88.

"Now that was one determined and successful campaign! . . ."—Very loosely after Michno, p. 339 (Parnell's words).

"Those who are really the servants of the LORD should work together."—Paul A. Cimbala and Randall M. Miller, eds., *Union Soldiers and the Northern Home Front: Wartime Experiences, Postwar Adjustments* (New York: Fordham University Press, 2002), p. 272 (address by Howard to U.S. Christian Commission, 1864).

Pollock's assessment of Wood—Wood's duties with Pollock are described in Venn, p. 7.

Pollock in El Dorado County—Pollock, p. 32.

Events relating to Damon Lodge and John McGuiness—Information from the *East Oregonian* (Pendleton), June 23, 1877, p. 1.

Description of the petroglyphs in the Modoc Lava Beds—After a visit to Petroglyph Point (near Tulelake) in June 2013.

Trimble and Theller at Fort McDermitt—Their proximity there is mentioned in Corbusier, p. 20.

The fate of Hattie Chamberlain and her relations—Information from McDermott, p. 32.

Description of the skull of Little Bear's squaw—After a photo in Weymouth, p. 113.

Details of the Fourth of July in Maine—Information from Bowdoin, OOH papers, M91.8: Articles and addresses. Folder 10: "Warfare of the future." Vol. 6, no. 10. Subject, "Warfare of the future." Typescript (probably wr. 1895), p. 12. [Henceforth cited: OOH papers, "Warfare of the future."]

The color of Independence Day turnout in Charleston—Information from Bellisiles, p. 12.

"When I was a cadet, our muskets were still loaded in ten motions."—Information from OOH papers, "Warfare of the future," p. 15.

Howard's remarks about his grandfather's father—Somewhat after OOH papers, "Warfare of the future," pp. 3, 5.

He Could Have Made Money Anywhere

Perry's recollections of fighting Paiutes—Information from Bourke, pp. 26–30.

Responsibility of Dutch Holmes and Osterhout for firing without orders at Looking-Glass's camp—Somewhat after McWhorter, *Hear Me*, p. 273, fn. 13. It is unclear which of them actually fired first.

Perry's dispatch to Lapwai—Abbreviated from McWhorter, *Hear Me*, p. 287.

Whipple to Perry: "Colonel, I sent out two citizens to reconnoiter the country . . ."—Abbreviated and altered from Whipple's communication to Howard, quoted in Kevin Carson, *The Long Journey of the Nez Perce: A Battle History from Cottonwood to Bear Paw* (Yardley, Pennsylvania: Westholme, 2011), p. 82.

Description of the Nez Perce's journey until Red Spy kills Blewett—After a trip from White Bird Canyon to Cottonwood, September 2006.

"When COYOTE and FOX got hungry . . ."—After Walker and Matthews, p. 97. The tale does not actually specify whether COYOTE raped the sister of His own husband or of FOX's.

Killing of Blewett and theft of his field-glass—McWhorter, *Yellow Wolf*, p. 70; and Greene, who tells the story slightly differently (*Nez Perce Summer*, p. 60).

Description of Rainbow—Somewhat after Brian W. Dippie, Therese Thau Heyman, Christopher Mulvey and Joan Carpenter Troccoli, eds., *George Catlin and His Indian Gallery* (Washington, D.C.: Smithsonian American Art Museum/W. W. Norton & Co., 2002), p. 111 ("Hee-Oh'ks-Te-Kin, Rabbit's Skin Leggins," Nez Perce, 1832).

"The flat place where . . . the women may dig cous"—It was called Aipadass and located at Craig's Ferry, where Whipple had sent the two scouts.

The destruction of the Rains party (the eleven Bostons and Foster)—Ibid., pp. 282–86; Carson, pp. 82–86.

"Perry and Whipple determine that they must be in communication with sympathizers at Lapwai"—Perry, at least, claimed to believe this: Anon. repr. comp. [originally brought together by Cyrus Townsend Brady as a portion of *Northwestern Fights and Fighter*, 1907], *The Soldiers' Side of the Nez Perce War: Eyewitness Accounts of "The Most Extraordinary of Indian Wars"* (Wallowa, Oregon: Bear Creek Press, rev. ed. 2003), p. 38 (Brigadier-General David Perry, "The Affair at Cottonwood"). [This volume henceforth cited: *The Soldiers' Side.*]

The battle with the Brave Seventeen—Somewhat after McWhorter, *Hear Me*, pp. 288–92; Carson, pp. 89–95.

Description of the Corliss Steam Engine—After an engraving in Weymouth, p. 21.

"The reds are hoping to draw us out."—Perry's opinion, stated in *The Soldiers' Side*, p. 39 (again, in "The Affair at Cottonwood").

Nez Perce curing ceremonies, here and throughout—Somewhat after Pearson, p. 122, *Handbook of North American Indians*, vol. 12, various parts of Nez Perce entry.

Avoidance of the dead man's name, etc.—*Handbook of North American Indians*, vol. 12, p. 424 (Nez Perce entry): "Typically the surviving spouse and relatives attempted to minimize memories of the deceased." His name was unmentioned, his house destroyed.

The one who found Jyeloo's body—McWhorter, *Yellow Wolf*, p. 49.

"Through his field-glass Perry discovers the blond head of Lew Wilmot."—In real life this could not have happened; the battle was two miles away.

Dialogue between Perry and Whipple: "Colonel, what's the excitement . . . too late."—Somewhat after McWhorter, *Hear Me*, pp. 292–93 (abbreviated and embellished).

The face paint of Perry's "lively Pi-Ute squaw"—Information from Lalla Scott, *Karnee: A Paiute Narrative*, annotated by Charles R. Craig (Reno: University of Nevada Press, 1966), p. 19.

Misery Hill

Description of Camp Misery (Misery Hill)—After a visit in August 2009.

When He Hears the Whisper

Cleaning (hide) clothes with white clay—*Memoirs of the American Anthropological Association*, vol. II: 1907–1915 (Lancaster, Pennsylvania: "Published for the American Anthropological Association," n.d.), pp. 165–274 (Herbert Joseph Spinden, "The Nez Percé Indians," November 1908), p. 216. [Henceforth cited: Spinden.]

When the world turned yellow for Peopeo Tholekt—Information from McWhorter, *Hear Me*, p. 269.

Toohhoolhoolzote's plans for decorating his new horses—After Spinden, pp. 229–30.

The "oldest women" who "still wear white beads and brass as their grandmothers did"—The grandmothers' generation is described in Lewis and Clark, vol. 5, p. 227 (Clark, Thursday [NB: Saturday] 21st Septr. 1805).

White Thunder's doings: Seeing the dead soldier, watching the races, hearing the first shell—Simplified from McWhorter, *Yellow Wolf*, pp. 85–86. Cloudburst's doings, and Peopeo Tholekt's, may be found in *Hear Me*, pp. 294–310, which covers the first day of the battle. The actions of many characters in the battle are of course embellished and invented by WTV.

Looking-Glass: "I have always said, Bluecoat, you are my elder brother . . ."—Somewhat after Wood diary, 1878, pp. 29–30 (remarks of Chief Moses).

Peopeo Tholekt: "If the Bluecoats had found Looking-Glass . . ."—Much after McWhorter, *Hear Me*, p. 271.

I Don't Expect This to Drag On

Description of the Clearwater country—After a visit in August 2009. In this vicinity, in the town of Stites, I have seen the following sign, whose import deserves to be immortalized: SMOKY COW BEHIND.

Elk City—Built in the gold rush of 1861. Succeeded by Independence Flat, which became Clearwater.

"Degenerated into a Chinese camp"—By the late 1860s Elk City was mostly being worked by Chinese. Wikoff, p. 30. I imagine this is how a typical 1877 Anglo-American would have put the matter.

Building of the blockhouse in Elk City—*Morning Oregonian*, vol. XVII.—no. 130, Portland, Oregon: Friday, July 6, 1877 (pp. unnumbered).

Magruder's ranch; Squaw Hill—Gertrude Maxwell, *My Yesterdays in Elk City* (Grangeville: Idaho County Free Press, 1986), pp. 2, 1.

Description of Wall Creek—After a visit in August 2009.

"And Colonel Perry swears he rushed his front line . . . right away" to save the Brave Seventeen—Closely after Perry's own claim in *The Soldiers' Side*, p. 39 ("The Affair at Cottonwood").

"Kamiah people say the bad Indians are dancing the war dance"—Information from Helen Addison Howard, p. 152.

"Crook knew every packer by name"—Information from Bourke, *With General Crook*, p. 45.

"Those poor women in the hands of fiends."—After Pollock, p. 87.

Howard's memories of December 1864—Somewhat after Sherman, pp. 675–76.

Sitting Bull's skeleton-pictures—Mentioned in Howard, *Famous Indian Chiefs*, 302.

Dialogue between Wilmot, Perry and Howard—Much is invented, and some sentences are nearly verbatim from Wilmot's account in Wilfong, pp. 144–45.

Howard's entry into the Ordnance Department—After his *Autobiography*, vol. 1, p. 60.

Trimble's scouts' sighting of Nez Perce herders—Information from Helen Addison Howard, p. 153.

The "red" attack on the Oregon Stage Road, 1864—Humfreville, p. 421.

Events of the beginning of the Clearwater battle as reflected in WTV's dialogue—Sometimes more and sometimes less after Howard, *Report—In the Field*, p. 7, with additions and interpolations; and Howard, *Nez Perce Joseph*, pp. 157–61. Some descriptions of the battle are based on Wood's drawings in Venn, pp. 41–44. The Nez Perces claimed to have fielded fewer than a hundred warriors at this engagement, while the soldiers imagined that they were fighting three hundred.

"Back in their old home ground"—After Wilfong, p. 134 (Lt. Harry L. Bailey: the Army was surprised "to find them in their very comfortable old home ground by the gurgling stream . . .")

"Mine eyes have seen the glory," etc.—*The Annals of America*, vol. 9, p. 306 (no. 64, Julia Ward Howe, "The Battle Hymn of the Republic," 1862).

"That Injun's got the cannon!"—Based on an assertion in McWhorter, *Yellow Wolf*, p. 93.

The doings of Lieutenant Forse—Bowdoin, OOH papers, M91 Box 43. Indians—Campaigns, Battle of the Clearwater, transcript of Capt. A. G. Forse.

"Shot him through the brain"—From Wilfong, p. 137 (Wood: "One man, raising his head too high, was shot through the brain . . .").

Howard's anecdote about Adairsville—Somewhat after Howard, *Autobiography*, vol. 1, pp. 521–22.

Captain Jocelyn's observation of a gap in the lines—After Helen Addison Howard, p. 204.

Captain Miller's charge—Howard, *Nez Perce Joseph*, pp. 161–64. His pipe-smoking is mentioned in Helen Addison Howard, p. 204.

"Savages ain't supposed to intrench themselves."—Helen Addison Howard, p. 203 (an exaggeration, I suspect): "Such tactics as rock entrenchments, and the besieging of superior numbers of troops, were never known before in Indian warfare."

High shooting of Springfields (at close range)—Alleged by J. W. Reilly, Captain of Ordnance, 1876 (re: Little Big Horn), in Hammer, p. 9.

Wood's company's experience: "Worm-crawling through the dying grass . . ."—After Bingham and Barnes, p. 76, "crawling around in the parched grass without water."

Nez Perce doings on the first day of the Clearwater battle—After McWhorter, *Yellow Wolf*, pp. 86–93. For "Cliff Place," see note on Dizzy Head, this chapter, below.

White Bird: "You wished for this war and you began it . . ."—Much after Howard et al., p. 230 (Duncan McDonald); actually said to the whole band just before White Bird Canyon.

"Let us kill these Bostons who have stolen our country . . ."—Somewhat after Howard et al., p. 235 (Duncan McDonald).

"Come and fight in a man's way . . ."—The original reads: "Come and fight like a man you big white SOB; don't play like a little boy; me no scared, you General Day-After-To-morrow."—Holland Library, Washington State University, Pullman; ms. 1218 (CM Brewster/Peopeo Tholekt), p. 3.

The promise of Wottolen's WYAKIN—McWhorter, *Hear Me*, p. 316.

Description of the water-carrying boys—After a photograph in Gulick, p. 155 ("Two Nez Perce braves").

Red Feather Of The Wing and his revolver—His possession of it and the fact that he sometimes swapped out tired horses for fresh are mentioned in Pearson, p. 49. The rest is my invention.

Events of the night—After Helen Addison Howard, pp. 205–6.

Ammunition and pancakes for the soldiers—Information from Bingham and Barnes, p. 76.

Wood's worries about Mrs. Manuel: The lot of a (female) Indian captive—Information and sentiment after General George Armstrong Custer, p. 374 (description of the fate of two white women captured by Cheyennes); with a few interpolations from the tales in Hugh A. Dempsey, *The Vengeful Wife and Other Blackfoot Stories* (Norman: University of Oklahoma Press, 2003).

"Squandered lives of men that meet lonely and awful deaths"—Wood diary entry for July 20, 1878.

Wood's journey to the spring—Howard says only (*Nez Perce Joseph*, p. 162) that several officers made this perilous trip.

Howard's hateful notoriety as "the Indian herder"—Information from Howard et al., p. 244 (McDonald).

Joseph's memory of the Dream Dance at Walla Walla—After an illustration in Relander, following p. 288, plate 10 ("Call to Washat Worship"). My own daughter, who is now fifteen (about the age of Sound Of Running Feet), always used to open her eyes and peek at me whenever we found ourselves in a situation of closed-eyed group prayer.

Nez Perce doings on the battle's second day—After information in McWhorter, *Yellow Wolf,* pp. 95–101; *Hear Me,* pp. 311–25; Wilfong, pp. 139–40 (memories of Wottolen).

The location of Mean Man's wound is not specified in the sources.

"The man who howls in the Wolf Dance"—Information from Aoki and Walker, p. 7.

"Why fight when the Bluecoats have not attacked our lodges?"—Sentiment after Wilfong, p. 139 (recollections of Roaring Eagle).

Description of the family in Ollokot's tipi—After a photograph in Gulick, p. 63 ("Indian woman with children in front of hide teepee").

The tale of About Asleep is taken (and slightly altered for narrative purposes) from his own testimony in McWhorter, *Hear Me,* pp. 317–18.

Dr. Alexander's report of the casualties at Clearwater—Thirteen men were killed and twenty-seven wounded (Greene, *Nez Perce Summer,* pp. 362–63), so I made the figures less, since the battle was still in progress.

The routing of the Nez Perce at Clearwater—Howard, *Nez Perce Joseph,* pp. 165–67.

The beetling cliff that Blackie stares at is Dizzy Head. "The battle took place above and on the next point north of Dizzy Head."—Wilfong, p. 132. For this topographic feature I have invented the Nez Perce–like name "Cliff Place."

"General, we've captured nearly thirty of Joseph's horses."—Trimble disputed this, saying there were only "about half a dozen crippled horses" on the scene (Wilfong, p. 141).

Parnell's opinion of Perry at Clearwater—Helen Addison Howard, p. 211.

We Rode Away Exactly When We Wished

"Cut Arm has burned eighty lodges"—Information from Howard et al., p. 291 (Joseph).

Description of Ollokot—Somewhat after the photo in McWhorter, *Hear Me,* p. 172 (taken June 1877).

"Toohhoolhoolzote lost twenty of his own horses at the Clearwater."—Information from Pearson, p. 49.

High Rock Place—Invented by WTV.

"Water is Medicine for everything."—Verbatim from McWhorter, *Yellow Wolf,* p. 29 (except that I have capitalized the "m" in "Medicine").

Looking-Glass: "All their promises to me about my reservation have been no good . . ."—Abridged, altered and embellished from Wood diary, 1879, p. 45 (Chief Moses).

COYOTE marries His daughter—Walker and Matthews, p. 135.

Looking-Glass's former ability to pay a high bride-price in horses—Price range from Harold B. Barclay, Dept. of Anthropology, University of Alberta, Edmonton, *The Role of the Horse in Man's Culture* (London: J. A. Allen, 1980), p. 171 (re: Crows).

Toohhoolhoolzote: "You were a fool to enslave yourself to some hardtack . . ."—First sentence much after the words of Sitting Bull, to reservation Indians quoted in Utley, p. 175.

Kamiah, "where our People once helped Lewis and Clark from one bank to the other"—Lewis and Clark, vol. 7, p. 252 (Lewis, Tuesday May 13th 1806).

Description of Old Joseph—After Gulick, p. 108 (sketch by Gustavus Solon, "Taowi-Tak-Hes, Joseph the Elder").

Kamiah

The boatloads of relic-hunters from the Clearwater battlefield—Information from Pearson, p. 46.

"Colonel Perry insists that the attack on the Brave Seventeen was diversionary"—Perry's own assessment, in *The Soldiers' Side*, p. 39 ("The Affair at Cottonwood").

"Trimble says there was nothing extraordinary about Joseph's defense . . ." + "the advantage of the river"—Ibid., p. 54 (Major J. G. Trimble, "The Battle of the Clearwater").

The deaths of Workman and Marquardt—Information from Greene, *Nez Perce Summer*, p. 361 (Appendix A: U.S. Army Casualties, IV). Unless otherwise stated, all condolence letters in this novel are invented.

Howard's instructions to Colonel Miller, and his dispatch to Headquarters—After Greene, *Nez Perce Summer*, p. 100.

Colonel Miles's intervention on behalf of Grey Beard—Wooster, p. 72. In fact, as was usually the case in such matters, all effort on the Indian's behalf was unsuccessful. I have imagined that Howard conveniently forgot this, or tactfully kept mum about it.

Perry's memory of serving under Crook in 1866—After Crook, p. 144.

"Even [Crook] admits there is another side to the Indian character."—See Crook, p. 69.

"In savage warfare the personal qualities of the voluntary soldier . . ."—Somewhat after the *Encyclopaedia Britannica*, 11th ed. (1910), vol. II (Andros to Austria), p. 605 (entry on Army).

Howard and the Seminole woman Mattie—After his *Autobiography*, vol. 1, pp. 84–85.

Sherman's dispatch of the Second Infantry—Howard, *Report—In the Field*, p. 32.

"Only two crops out of five seasons" in Kamiah—Information from Gay, p. 34 (July 18th, 1889).

Wood's browsings in the newspaper—*Morning Oregonian*, vol. XVII.—no. 132, Monday, July 9, 1877.

It Now Becomes My Duty to Change the Direction of My Operations

Number of men under Major Shearer's command—Idaho Historical Society (Boise). AR0012 MS0042, George M. Shearer. Folder 2: "Roll calls, supply & lists of Idaho militia."

Howard to Shearer—Idaho Historical Society (Boise). AR0012 MS0042, George M. Shearer. Folder 3: "Nez Perce War: Indian and Horse Policy 1874–1877." Dispatch datelined "Headquarters, Department of the Columbia, Camp M. P. Miller, Kamiah I.T." Much abridged but otherwise nearly verbatim.

Howard's instructions to Mason—Information somewhat after Howard, *Nez Perce Joseph*, pp. 169–70.

Howard's suspicions concerning James Reuben—In fact he "had been somewhat under suspicion by the volunteers and settlers of Camas Prairie, but he had the confidence of General Howard and carried a better gun than was furnished us, all of which did not tend to decrease the haughtiness with which we looked upon the civilians." McWhorter, *Hear Me*, p. 326 (Lieutenant Wilson).

Time from Kamiah to the Buffalo [in this case, Flathead] Country: six days—Information from Baird, Mallickan and Swagerty, p. 99 (Portland *Weekly Oregonian*, June 22, 1861).

"See Associated Press despatches . . ."—Almost verbatim from McWhorter, *Hear Me*, p. 324.

"We've defeated Joseph's treacherous allies . . ."—Howard, *Report—In the Field*, p. 12.

The Berries Will Now Be Turning Red

When GOPHERS used to bake camas—After Walker and Matthews, p. 15.

Ripening season of wild onion and wild carrots at Weippe: mid August—*Handbook of North American Indians*, vol. 12, p. 421 (Deward E. Walker, Jr., "Nez Perce").

Proposed destinations of the various chiefs—Information from Greene, *Beyond Bear's Paw*, pp. 8–9.

Route through the Bannock lands, past the hot springs and so to the Buffalo Country—Information from a COYOTE myth in Walker and Matthews, p. 69.

Descriptions of Blackfoot the Crow chief, Horse Rider [Thomas H. Leforge], and other Crow individuals, events and customs, here and throughout—After Thomas H. Leforge (as told by Thomas B. Marquis), intro. by Joseph Medicine Crow and Herman J. Viola, *Memoirs of a White Crow Indian* (Lincoln: University of Nebraska Press/A Bison Book, 1974; orig. pub. 1928). [Cited: Leforge.] Blackfoot's status and duties are mentioned beginning p. 128.

"The warriors whose hair touches the ground"—Information from Humfreville, p. 226.

Burning of settlers' ranches and slaughter of their cattle—Wilfong, p. 164.

Description of the Lakota warrior with the masked horse—After an illustration in Horse Capture and Her Many Horses, p. 13.

Heinmot Tooyalakekt: "My chiefs, do we fight to keep our lives? . . ."—Somewhat altered and embellished from Wilfong, pp. 164–65.

Looking-Glass: "Hear me, my chiefs! The Crows are my own brothers . . ." + Hahtalekin's response—Somewhat after McWhorter, *Hear Me*, p. 334.

The tale of Eagle That Shakes Himself—Much abridged and somewhat altered from Howard et al., pp. 225–26 (Duncan McDonald).

Five Wounds and Rainbow both agree with Looking-Glass—Information from McWhorter, *Hear Me*, p. 277.

Description of Joseph's mental journey up to Couse Meadows, Washington, and then south to Wallowa—After a journey along that route, August 2009.

"A horseload of roots"—Stolen from Lewis and Clark, vol. 5, p. 226.

Joseph: "Brother, if I am killed, remember this . . ."—Much altered from Howard et al., p. 282 (Joseph).

"I wonder if this ground has anything to say?"—Verbatim from Gulick, p. 106 (speech of the Cayuse leader Young Chief, 1855).

Family Reunion

The names of the five ambushers do not all appear in the sources. Some are my guesswork.

Dialogue between Red Spy and Sheared Wolf—Slightly after Gulick, p. 226, in which the killer was Watz-am-yas, and referred to "the happy hunting grounds," a name which McWhorter implies is highly inaccurate.

American Secrets

The events concerning Red Heart actually took place on the 16th and 17th, not the 20th and 21st. I altered the time frame in order to make the Nez Perce council at Weippe segue directly into the ambush.

Description of Red Heart—After Venn, p. 45, Plate 2.17 (sketch by Wood, "Indian Chief," who "may be Red Heart").

The circular which Howard reads to Chapman—National Archives microfilm M1121, Roll 5: Miscellaneous Circulars, 1854–1885. Circular to Indian Agents and Others. Treasury Department, Department No. 1, Second Comptroller's Office. February 26, 1875, clauses 16 and 19.

"We adjourned for want of witnesses."—Verbatim from *Adjutant Journal*, July 17, 1877; quoted in Venn, p. 46, fn. 70.

Tally of Red Heart's band—Wilfong, p. 153 (*Lewiston Teller*, July 17). Captain Keeler's report to Headquarters gives a slightly different number.

"And now the can-makers have gone on strike in Baltimore."—Information from Bruce, p. 100 (the strike took place in the second week of July).

Wood's soliloquy on hard female hands—Considerably indebted to two sentences in Wood diary 1878, p. 4.

Information on Dr. Jacques—After his advertisement in the *Saint Louis Dispatch*, number 221, Tuesday evening, January 4, 1876, p. 4.

Howard's telegram: "Majority of hostile Indians have fled by Lo Lo Trail . . ."—*Morning Oregonian*, vol. XVII.—no. 142, Friday, July 20, 1877, p. 1.

Transport to Fort Vancouver: Weeping of the women; removal of bead ornaments for daughter and for wife—After FitzGerald, p. 288 (August 5). Of course these things actually took place when the prisoners were taken out of Lapwai.

"Called out the Maryland National Guard."—Information from Bruce, p. 102.

Pairing of the men; sixty miles to march—McWhorter, *Hear Me*, p. 333.

Wood's diary: "Musings on the unhappy people . . ."—Much abbreviated from Venn, p. 46 (entry for July 17 [East Bank, Clearwater River at Kamiah]).

Description of the terrain over which the departing prisoners are conducted—After a visit to Kamiah River Park, August 2009.

Pollock's melancholic major—After Pollock, p. 26.

Description of Wally Scanlon—After Pollock, p. 20.

Pertaining to Mrs. Theller's Bonnet

Information on Maggie and on Chapman's five half-Umatilla children—After Pearson, p. 262.

They Called Me *Dreamer*

Wood's promotion (July 22)—Mentioned in Venn, p. 50.

Wood's remarks on Afro-Americans—Altered and abridged from Oregon Historical Society, Mss. 800: C. E. S. Wood. Box 2, folder 20, selection from biographical sketch by Wood for Max Hayek's German trans. of *The Poet in the Desert* (1927?), p. 22. [Henceforth cited: OHS Wood papers, Hayek.] A few other unsourced small details of Wood's life and memories, such as the toy made by Phil, the Negro gardener, derive from information herein.

Wood's father's drinking; Wood's record at West Point (drawing and demerits)—Venn, p. 5.

His encounter with Sitka Khwan—Mentioned on p. 13. The woman's name is not known, but I have described her after a sketch by Albert Brennan which "may have been commissioned to illustrate Wood's visit with the old Hoonah chief" (p. 15).

The tasks of Jack Carlton and of Wilkinson—Sutherland, p. 14.

Howard to Shearer—Idaho Historical Society (Boise). AR0012 MS0042, George M. Shearer. Folder 3: "Nez Perce War: Indian and Horse Policy 1874–1877." Dispatch of July 25, much abridged but nearly verbatim. Original reads "Crasdaile," but to make it consistent with the name in Howard's *Nez Perce Joseph* I have altered it to "Croaesdale."

Shearer's letter to Mason—I have examined a typescript copy of this at the Idaho Historical Society, dated "Mt. Idaho July 26, 1877," so I assume that a mounted courier brought it to Kamiah before the departure of Howard's command on the thirtieth. Howard's conversation with Mason is invented, as is his response to Shearer.

Extra salt rations to use on dead mules—The "Indian-fighting Army" had resorted to this before. See James A. Huston, *The Sinews of War: Army Logistics 1775–1953* (Washington, D.C.: Office of the Chief of Military History, United States Army, Army Historical Series, 1966), p. 266.

Guy's arrival is mentioned in Venn, p. 36.

"It's Harry's eighth birthday."—Guy's youngest brother's birthday was 25 July.

Accidents Do Happen, Sir

Conversation between Howard and Umatilla Jim: Description of camas meadow at Weippe—Lewis and Clark, vol. 8, pp. 7–17 (beginning with Lewis, 10 June 1806).

"No man could equal Sherman at that study . . ."—After Howard, *Autobiography*, vol. 1, pp. 57, 475–76.

Description of Mrs. Howard's Indian basket—After several illustrations in Schlick.

How Howard lost his arm—After Howard, *Autobiography*, vol. 1, pp. 246–50.

Words to "Dixie"—Taken from *The Annals of America*, vol. 9, p. 146 (no. 26, "Dixie," "improved" version by Albert Pike, sometime betw. 1859 and Appomattox).

"John Brown's Body"—Ibid.; p. 145 (no. 25, "John Brown's Body," slightly altered by WTV).

Information on the two kinds of bullets which wounded Howard's arm, and on the lack of standardization in military calibers (which, following Howard, I spell "calibres" in the text)—Bowdoin, OOH papers, "Warfare of the future," page 16.

Colton's older map—Colton's map of Oregon, Washington, Idaho and British Columbia, no. 68, 1860. Original at Oregon Historical Society.

"The Indians are reported reënforced by Smohallie's River Renegades . . ."—Considerably altered from McWhorter, *Hear Me*, p. 345 (Senate Document 257, 56th Cong. 1st Sess.). Howard actually wrote this on the night before I have him do so.

Career of James Reuben's father—Venn, p. 38, quoting Joseph, *Nez Perce Indians*.

"Dear General: Please see if you cannot give D. J. Richardson . . ."—Closely after one of the letters in Bowdoin, OOH papers, M91.7, vol. 8 [folio]: Copybook of letters sent, 1873.

"Every man is, in judgment of law . . ."—Kent, p. 63.

The arrest of Black Otter's small band—Invented based on the passing mention of Three Feathers's arrest in McWhorter, *Hear Me*, p. 334. The date of the arrest is not given. It is more likely that Three Feathers was arrested along with Red Heart, as described in *Nez Perce Summer*, p. 100. But even though he too was a chief, Three Feathers is not mentioned in many other sources (such as Beal, pp. 79–80). Furthermore, Red Heart might in fact have been coming back from the Buffalo Country as he claimed, while Three Feathers seems to have been at Kamnaka with Looking-Glass. In a typically poor novelist's compromise (and to portray the progressive hardening of Howard's attitude), I decided on two arrests, one of Red Heart and a subchief named Three Feathers, and another of Black Otter.

Endorsement of Francis Mills—Verbatim from a letter in the OOH papers copybook cited for Richardson immediately above.

"The LORD hath opened His armoury . . ."—Jeremiah 50.25–26.

"Left—left—left my wife . . ."—Elizabeth B. Custer, *Following the Guidon*, p. vii.

Wages of a fireman on the Baltimore & Ohio, 1873–77—Bellesiles, p. 147.

Description of Sladen—After Sladen, p. 28 (photograph of him in 1872).

The yellow stripe on a captain's grey trouser-leg—So it was in the Mexican War.

The way an Apache strikes a match on the sole of his bare foot—Information from Bourke, p. 34.

Description of the country from Kamiah to Weippe—After a trip from Kamiah to Weippe, August 2009; with some information from Howard, *Nez Perce Joseph*, pp. 175–76.

"When the Pacific railroads shall be completed . . ."—Almost verbatim from Howard, *Nez Perce Joseph*, p. 136.

And Perry Contemplates the Mountains

Jack Carlton and his road-wideners were actually still en route from Lapwai, not cutting ahead as I have them doing here. See Howard, *Nez Perce Joseph*, p. 174.

"Father, just say what you want me to do . . ."—Slightly reworded from Howard, *Autobiography*, vol. 2, p. 476.

"The best timbered region left in the U.S." (said of Lo Lo Trail)—Lynn and Dennis Baird, *In Nez Perce Country: Accounts of the Bitterroots and the Clearwater after Lewis and Clark* (Moscow: University of Idaho Library, Northwest Historical Manuscripts ser., 2003), p. 155 (Edward P. North, 1870). [This book will henceforth be cited: Baird and Baird.]

Whenever a Child Slips

Description of the Idaho side of the Lo Lo Trail—After a visit in August 2009. I was not able to take the rough old Lolo Motor Way, which more closely follows the trail than the modern highway along the Lochsa, whose beauties I occasionally mention here and in the next chapter, always hoping that the Nez Perces or the Army might have seen them. Some walks in the forest hereabout helped me to appreciate a little of the mountains' darkly, verdantly rugged character.

Old Man Place—Invented by WTV.

"This trail which he once rode with his father . . ."—Information somewhat after Pollock, p. 6.

Description of Tzi-kal-tza—After a photograph reproduced in Wilfong, p. 165 (Montana Historical Society), n.d.; see also Lewis and Clark, vol. 5, p. 241, fn. 5.

Looking-Glass's memory of his father and the miners—Gulick, p. 147.

The difficulties experienced by Animal Entering A Hole—McWhorter, *Hear Me*, p. 310.

Description of Wallowa in Joseph's memories—After a visit to the Wallowa Valley, August 2009.

Secret Rock Place—Invented by WTV.

Description of Wellammoutkin and of the significance of his name—Information from Baird, Mallickan and Swagerty, p. xix.

"There is where I live, and there is where I wish to leave my body."—Ibid., p. 24.

Fair Land gathers beargrass—Spinden (p. 191) reports that this plant was often collected on the Lo Lo Trail.

Description of Lo Lo Hot Springs—After a visit in August 2007; and Lewis and Clark, vol. 8, p. 62 (Lewis, Sunday June 29th 1806).

Narrow Place—Invented by WTV to signify the end of the Lo Lo Trail just west of Fort Fizzle.

Fairly Reliable Is Not Good Enough

Guy's pen-and-ink drawing—Oregon Historical Society, Grace Howard Gray Scrapbook, folder 1/5.

New York slang for codfish balls, ham and beans—Information from Whitman, p. 1168.

Specific chess strategies, games and turns of phrase here and throughout—Many, such as the match between young Prince Ouroussoff and Jaenisch, and the words "Black would have marched on his pawns to certain victory," were stolen fair and square from Howard Staunton, Esq., *The Chess Player's Chronicle for 1852, Containing Upwards of Three Hundred and Fifty Games and Problems by the Most Eminent Players* (London: C. Skeet, 21, King William Street, Charing Cross, 1852). To be sure, this might have been a trifle musty in 1877, as I have tried to indicate here and there. In short, it would have been about right for General Howard.

The death of Captain Dessaur—Howard, *Autobiography*, vol. 1, p. 377.

The entertainments of the Apaches in Washington, D.C.—Somewhat after Howard, *Among Our Hostile Indians*, p. 176.

Description of Wanamaker's—After Schlereth, p. 152, figure 4.6.

Parnell's memory of "that October ten years since" (i.e., in 1867) "when Perry and Harris were sent away to Camp Harney . . ."—Information from Michno, pp. 252–53.

Dialogue between Howard and Mason on Wood's performance as A.D.C.—Much after Montana Historical Society, mss. no. 80, p. 199 (Mason's letter home).

"No man living can get as much out of a horse . . ."—Slightly altered from Howard, *Nez Perce Joseph*, pp. 179–80 (quoting Chapman).

Pollock's hope that after Missoula "we will take up the line of march back to Vancouver"—Closely after Pollock, p. 73, letter dated July 28, left bank of the Clearwater.

Dwight Moody's hymn—Dee Brown, *The Year of the Century: 1876* (New York: Charles Scribner's Sons, 1966), pp. 26–27.

Jack to Canby: "I am a true Modoc . . ."—Riddle, p. 64.

Modoc taunt: Jack is a fish-hearted squaw—Ibid., p. 72.

"Why, Jack, you have no law . . ."—Ibid., p. 67.

Description of the Lo Lo (now spelled Lolo) Trail—After a trip from Missoula to Lolo Pass (i.e., Montana side of the trail) in August 2007, and Kamiah to Lolo Pass (Idaho portion) in August 2009.

The "narrow winding [ridge]crest," and the difficulty in finding forage for horses—Howard, *Report—In the Field*, p. 15.

The wire grass on which the horses subsisted—Sutherland, p. 19.

Description of Chief Victorio—After a photo in Sladen, p. 32.

"My GOD, Wood, you'll never get through . . ."—Abridged and altered from OHS Wood documents, Hayek, p. 22.

"His weaselskin bracelet gives him the Power to see everything."—According to the Peopeo Tholekt/ Sam Lott ms. it provides this, and also quickness.

"The original Martin design, without the reëntrant fold . . ."—Verbatim from Treadwell, p. 11.

"As fine a cartridge as the Berdan . . ."—Ibid., p. 10.

Use of Abstract "D"—Information from Kautz, p. 183.

"I have not always done right. In many things I ought to have been more careful."—After John A. Carpenter, p. 229 (letter to Rowland B. Howard, February 19, 1874).

Description of Lizzie mixing dough—After a photo in Randall, p. 87 ("Self-portrait of Evelyn Cameron").

Umatilla Jim's pouch—After a photo in Gulick, p. 166 (portrait of Molly Minthorne, a Umatilla beader, then over a hundred years old and blind).

"Our couriers" who brought news of Rawn's failure on the morning of 4 August were actually James L. Carley, who bore a dispatch from Rawn at 1:30 p.m. So much for the accuracy of *Seven Dreams*.

Peace Treaty

Description of the area around Fort Fizzle—After a visit there in August 2007.

Approach by the Nez Perce under flag of truce—Accounts differ. Some sources claim that it was Rawn who took the initiative. Readers who prefer long books may be disappointed to be informed that I have much simplified and abbreviated this encounter.

Description of Looking-Glass's mirror within the "great star"—After a "Looking-Glass family object" displayed at the museum in Lapwai.

Looking-Glass: "We are riding to the Buffalo Country . . ."—Somewhat after Duncan McDonald's version of his words, in Aubrey L. Haines, p. 18.

Joseph's words—After Howard et al., p. 291 (Joseph). According to Howard et al., p. 249 (McDonald), only Looking-Glass and White Bird were actually present at this first council.

White Bird's words—Much abbreviated from Howard et al., p. 249 (McDonald).

Rawn's and Rainbow's words—Somewhat after Wilfong, p. 181.

Subsequent dialogue between Joseph and Looking-Glass in camp—Much abbreviated from Howard et al., pp. 250–51 (McDonald).

Description of Lawyer: After an illustration in Utley, p. 18 (sketch by Gustave Sohon, 1855).

Description of Looking-Glass's horse collar—Somewhat after one of the photos in the *Handbook of North American Indians*, vol. 12, p. 428 ("Nez Perce").

"I have two good-looking daughters at camp . . ."—Slightly altered from original. See note on Looking-Glass's daughters, above, "And Black Birds on the Lake."

Looking-Glass to the prisoners: "Go home, my friends . . ."—Loc. cit., abbreviated.

Aubrey L. Haines, p. 27, claims that both Joseph and Looking-Glass imagined that the soldiers' acquiescence to their passage by Fort Fizzle constituted a peace treaty.

Tale of the girl Wet-ka-weis—Holland Library, Washington State University, Pullman; ms. 1218 (CM Brewster/Peopeo Tholekt), p. 10.

Looking-Glass's Dream

Description of Looking-Glass being wrapped in buffalo robes—After Wood, Porter and Hunt, p. 130 (plate 6: Funeral Scaffold of a Sioux Chief).

Looking-Glass's Flathead name: "Big Hawk"—Howard et al., p. 223 (McDonald).

Situation and description of the Flathead reservation—After information from Ruth B. Moynihan, Susan Armitage and Christiane Fischer Dichamp, *So Much to Be Done: Women Settlers on the Mining and Ranching Frontier*, 2nd ed. (Lincoln: University of Nebraska Press, 1998 rev. of 1990 ed.), pp. 212–26 (Mary Ronan, "No door or window was ever locked").

Description of Left Hand—After an illustration in Ruby and Brown, p. 85 (Peter Adams, a Flathead Indian).

"They make snowberry poultices"—This was a Flathead form of Medicine; the Nez Perces used snowberries differently.

Division in the council: Buffalo Country *vs.* Canada—McWhorter, *Hear Me*, pp. 357–58.

Description of Lean Elk—A composite. According to Pearson (p. 43), he was a "neutral," who lived in the Bitterroot Valley. Aubrey L. Haines (p. 14) finds him more ambiguous.

Red Owl: "They are so far off that perhaps my heart will never reach them."—Much after Wood diary, 1879, p. 30 (Chief Moses).

Joseph: "Much has been said . . ."—A little after Howard et al., p. 280 (Joseph).

White Bird: "If we go to the Crows, we all must go."—Information from Greene, *Beyond Bear's Paw*, pp. 9–10.

Shoshoni name for Flatheads—Lewis and Clark, vol. 8, p. 55, fn. 11.

Description of the river where Joseph watches Good Woman catch a fish—After a visit to Chief Looking Glass Recreation Area, not far south of Missoula, in August 2007.

Description of the routes of Looking-Glass, Gibbon and Howard through the Bitterroot Valley—After a visit there in August 2007. The approximate campsites of all three parties may be seen in a helpful map at the beginning of a pamphlet entitled "The Flight of the Nez Perce . . . through the Bitterroot Valley—1877," n.d., no author given, but credited to the United States Department of Agriculture, the [U.S.] Forest Service and the Bitterroot National Forest. [Cited: USDA pamphlet RI-75-79.]

The Salish "never pound meat together with berries"—*Handbook of North American Indians*, vol. 12, p. 299 (Carling I. Malouf, "Flathead and Pend d'Oreille").

"If we are good to them then they should give us good presents."—Somewhat after a line in the Peopeo Tholekt/ Sam Lott ms.

"Even now I would give my own life . . ."—Somewhat after Howard et al., p. 290 (Joseph).

Situation around Stevensville—According to Aubrey L. Haines (p. 7), eleven Nez Perce families under the chieftainship of Eagle Of The Light (White Bird's predecessor) coexisted with about three hundred and fifty Flatheads whose chief was Charlot or Charlos; they all rejected the Jocko reservation.

Charlot to Looking-Glass: "Why shall I shake hands with men whose hands are stained with blood? . . ."—Closely after Howard et al., p. 256 (McDonald).

The Salish berry-pounder—After a photo in *Handbook of North American Indians*, vol. 12, p. 303.

Photo of Chief Charlot—After a photo, ibid., p. 307 (dated 4 July 1907 but said to show the military coat and sash given Charlot's predecessor by Governor Stevens in 1855).

Lone Bird: "We should keep riding, riding fast! . . ."—Much abridged and somewhat altered from McWhorter, *Hear Me*, p. 364.

"Grizzly Bear Youth, whose WYAKIN is the AIR BIRD . . ."—Information from Howard et al., p. 266 (McDonald).

Looking-Glass's ultimatum to the merchants—Somewhat after Aubrey L. Haines, p. 40.

The young women "unwrapping five dollar bills from around their braids"—Information about this Nez Perce mode of money-carrying from Fred G. Bond, *Flatboating on the Yellowstone 1877*, from a manuscript in the New York Public Library (New York, 1925 no call number; digital version), p. 7. [Cited: Bond ms.]

"The Bostons mark up the prices" of goods sold to the Nez Perce in Stevensville—See USDA pamphlet RI-75-79, p. 9 (Washington McCormick to Governor Potts, 1877).

Description of Espowyes—After plates in Moorhouse, pp. 174–75.

The pin reading "OUR CENTENNIAL PRESIDENT"—Sullivan, p. 428.

White Thunder's two cartridge belts—Information from McWhorter, *Yellow Wolf*, p. 86.

The Missoulian: "HELP! HELP! . . ."—Moynihan, Armitage and Dichamp, p. 220.

Episode of the whiskey—Aubrey L. Haines, pp. 40–41.

Theft and vandalism of Lockwood's house, and the forced gift to him of seven horses—Somewhat conflated with other minor events.

Gibbon at Missoula

Descriptions of the appearances and habits of Montana birds from here on (since the novel has just entered Montana)—A few are from life, some are derived from the anecdotes in primary sources, and many come from the beautiful photographs (and occasionally from written information) in Stan Tekiela, *Birds of Montana Field Guide* (Cambridge, Minnesota: Adventure Publications, Inc., 2004).

Description of Missoula—Based in part on information in Aubrey L. Haines, pp. 7–8. I have relied considerably on this book for my envisioning of the Big Hole operation.

Description of competing Flathead braves—After an image in Ruby and Brown, p. 15 (Flathead Indians playing the Ring Game).

Some details of the military and civilian situation in Missoula upon Bradley and Gibbon's arrival— Montana State Historical Society Archives: SC 1616. James H. Bradley family papers, folder 1 of 4. [Henceforth: MSHSA, Bradley papers.]

"They outnumbered us three to one."—Verbatim from Aubrey L. Haines, p. 34 (letter to the editor from W. B. Harlan, local rancher, 4 August 1877).

Letter of Gibbon to Governor Potts—Abridged from the same, p. 35.

Date of Flathead removal from Bitterroot Valley: 1871—*Executive Orders Relating to Indian Reservations*, p. 89 (MONTANA, BITTER ROOT VALLEY RESERVATION, Executive Mansion, *November 14, 1871*).

"The Pend d'Oreilles have promised to behave themselves"—Information from Moynihan, Armitage and Dichamp, p. 221 (Mary Ronan).

Rawn assesses the peacefulness of the Flathead chiefs—Information from Aubrey L. Haines, pp. 12–13.

Nez Perce column: "Five miles long passing through Stevensville."—Information from Nerburn, p. 137 (actually, the column was passing in front of Stevensville, and was only sometimes five miles long).

"Indian Outbreak in Idaho . . ."—Abridged from *The New North-West* (Deer Lodge, Montana), vol. 8, no. 51, June 22, 1877, p. 2 ("Wednesday's Telegram").

Miles appointed official guardian for the German sisters—Wooster, p. 70.

Conference between Terry, Gibbon and Custer; the six scouts—After Bradley, p. 143. This author simply writes that "it is understood that if Custer arrives first, he is at liberty to attack at once if he deems prudent." I imagine that after Little Big Horn, Gibbon and Terry might have been happy to blame Custer for rashness.

Recipe for Rosebud punch—Information from Bradley, p. 128.

"Exhilarating compound" + "Here's how!"—Ibid., p. 133.

"Mr. Joe murdered a hundred and ninety-one whites in an ambush"—Newspaper allegation quoted in Aubrey L. Haines, p. 12.

"Nearly a civil war" in Pittsburgh—Bruce, p. 135 (*Pittsburgh Leader*, July 20: "This may be the beginning of a great civil war in this country, between labor and capital").

"I'm going to get me a warrior's fancy jacket . . ."—A little after USDA pamphlet RI-75-79, p. 11 (Amos Chaffin).

Henry Buck's observation—Information from Aubrey L. Haines, p. 42.

Wooden Nutmegs (and other nicknames for the inhabitants of various states)—Information from Whitman, p. 1168.

The fears of the Hunter family at Yellowstone—Somewhat after Bradley, p. 30.

Soon We Shall Be Riding Through the Golden Grass

Path of Nez Perce and their pursuers out of Bitterroot Valley and into Big Hole—After a walk on the Nee-Me-Poo Trail, Montana, in August 2007, and a drive from Sula over Gibbon's Pass and then down to Big Hole in August 2010.

Specific placements of tipis—Somewhat after: Washington State University Libraries, Pullman. Holland Library Archives. Piyopyo Talikt. "Battle of the Big Hole, Nez Perce Camp." Drawing. Cage 55, no. 135B (135.1 is the newer number for this item).

Facing direction of a Crow tipi—Leforge, p. 144. I have no evidence that Looking-Glass actually did this, but it seemed a nice expression of his Crow-philia.

Treading on half-dried meat to squeeze the blood out—Linderman, p. 78 (Crow procedure; I am hoping that the Nez Perce procedure was similar).

"Rubbing the deerhide with watered brains, then smoking it into yellowness"—According to Spinden (p. 215), a hide was soaked in brain-water overnight; however, White Thunder told McWhorter that Nez Perces could prepare an entire carcass in a single night; therefore I have compromised above. Yellow-smoking is a mentioned Nez Perce procedure in Aoki's dictionary.

Toohhoolhoolzote to Howard: "Are you trying to scare me? . . ."—Somewhat after Howard et al., p. 232 (McDonald).

Dialogue between White Bird and Looking-Glass—Much abridged and altered from Howard et al., pp. 258–59 (McDonald). This conversation actually took place on the trail a little before Big Hole.

The Rabbit Dance—Deward E. Walker, Jr., ed. [this vol.], *Handbook of North American Indians*, vol. 12: Plateau (Washington, D.C.: Smithsonian Institution, 1998), p. 429 (Deward E. Walker, Jr., entry on Nez Perce).

Lieutenant Bradley Scouts Ahead

The Gatlings in Pittsburgh—Information from Bruce, p. 142.

Description of Custer before his tent—After a photo opposite p. 87 in Bradley ("General Custer in Montana Territory in the 1870's").

Route of the cavalry—Major General John Gibbon, *Adventures on the Western Frontier*, ed. Alan and Maureen Gaff (Bloomington: Indiana University Press, 1994), p. 188. Evidently there was fine grass for the horses in the meadow slope of mallow, the meadow slope of grass, then resin-crystal-studded pines ahead, closing gently in upon the grass, wildfire smoke stinging the eyes (when I came there a hundred and thirty years later, I, William the Blind, found the narrow golden grass and black trees bejeweled by the gleam of a metal shed in the silver smoky air).

The murder of McDonald—*Army Life in Dakota: Selections from the Journal of Philippe Régis Denis de Keredern de Trobriand*, trans. George Francis Will, Vice-President, North Dakota State Historical Society, ed. Milo Milton Quafe, Sec'ty of the Burton Historical Collection (Chicago: Lakeside Press, J. Donnelly and Sons Co., Christmas, 1941; orig. journal wr. 1867–69), p. 291.

Dialogue between Gibbon and Blodgett—Very loosely after Aubrey L. Haines, pp. 47–48 (Will Cave).

Dispatching of 22nd Infantry to Chicago (July 24) and 23rd to Saint Louis (July 24th?)—Information from Bruce, pp. 245, 259.

Bradley reassures Gibbon that he'll come back—Events in his anecdote loosely after Bradley, p. 90. Bradley's scout actually involved more men and took him farther ahead than for narrative reasons I have made it seem here. See Aubrey L. Haines, pp. 47–49.

Bradley and his interpreter desecrate a Sioux grave—Bradley, p. 112.

Dialogue between Gibbon and Humble—Very loosely after Aubrey L. Haines, p. 47 (report of Gibbon to Assistant Adjutant General, Department of Dakota).

"I'd rather have nobody than an unwilling soldier."—Bradley, p. 43 (Gibbon to Crows).

"May the military operations that are now in progress . . ."—Verbatim from Bradley, p. 113.

Bradley's letter to his wife—Closely after the ending of the one he had actually written to her earlier, en route to Missoula, dated August 1, with a slightly altered insertion from one written in Missoula, dated the third. Transcribed from originals in MSHSA, Bradley papers, SC 1616.

Gibbon: "Men who want to sleep in their tipis every night . . ."—Verbatim from Bradley, *The March of the Montana Column*, p. 44.

Description of Gibbon in dress uniform—After a photo in Nathaniel Philbrick, *The Last Stand: Custer, Sitting Bull, and the Battle of Little Bighorn* (New York: Viking, 2010), insert following p. 70.

Passivity of Gibbon, Custer and Terry in spring 1876—Information from the same source, pp. 76–77.

What Icicles Say

The howitzer's crew—Information from Aubrey L. Haines, pp. 75–76.

Description of Big Hole—After a visit in August 2007.

A few details about Big Hole—After Lewis and Clark, vol. 9 (Ordway and Floyd), p. 331 (Ordway, 6 July 1806).

"Now stick together and fight like heroes"—Somewhat after Zimmer, p. 45 (May 7th); it was actually "fight like brave men."

Letters to Mrs. Bradley—Much abbreviated and slightly altered from, in order: M. J.(?) Reed (Camp Baker M.T.; August 14th, 1877), G.(?) E.(?) Fisk of the *Daily Herald*, Fisk Brothers, Publishers (Helena, Montana, August 14, 1877), and from Bradley's mother in Ohio (August 15th, 1877, and October 29th, 1877), transcribed by WTV from originals at MSHSA, Bradley papers.

Description of a Northern Cheyenne horse mask—After an illustration in Horse Capture and Her Many Horses, p. 19.

"All they that go down to the dust . . ."—Psalms, 22.29.

The experience of Pahit Palikt—Pearson, pp. 38–39.

Speeches of White Bird and Looking-Glass—After Howard et al. (McDonald), p. 260; altered and abridged.

The deaths of Shore Crossing and Rainbow—McWhorter, Hear Me, pp. 386–89. The man who shot Shore Crossing, and was killed by his widow, was probably Captain William Logan, Company Seven, Seventh Infantry; hence the physical description in the text. "Has she been shot to die?" derives from Yellow Wolf, p. 135, testimony of Eloosykasit, in which Shore Crossing allegedly says: "My wife is shot to die! I will not leave her . . . I am staying here until killed!"

Experience of Wounded Head—After McWhorter, Hear Me, pp. 371–72. His Medicine bundle is depicted on the last unnumbered p. before p. 373.

A Bluecoat gives money to two little boys—Information from the same, p. 381.

Grizzly Bear Youth is saved by Over The Point—Howard et al., p. 262 (McDonald).

Experience of Two Moons: After McWhorter, Hear Me, pp. 384–89.

Dialogue between Kah-pots and the unnamed woman (whom I have called Well Behaved Maiden)—After Pearson, p. 39 (slightly altered).

"Now Five Wounds has parted from us; now we shall see him no more."—It was a temptation for me to plagiarize the far more beautiful original: "His mind no longer on the battle, his Wyakin power had left him" (ibid., p. 388).

Experience of Young White Bird—Hear Me, pp. 375–79.

Experience of White Thunder—From Yellow Wolf, of course. But (like every other Boston) I have altered many details. For instance, White Thunder states that he began the battle with only his war club (p. 115). But I needed to have him keep his pistol up until the Medicine Line. His simile of Shore Crossing's wife lying dead across his corpse as if to protect him is his own (p. 133). The restoration of his Winchester to him is a fiction.

No Heart's transgression at the Clearwater—Information from McWhorter, Yellow Wolf, p. 93.

The soldier's transfer of a baby from a dead woman to a living one—Ibid., p. 37.

Sound Of Running Feet's duel with the soldier—Invented by WTV. If it had happened, the girl might not have told it.

Fire Body's inspiration to White Thunder at the Clearwater—Information from McWhorter, Yellow Wolf, p. 91.

"Heinmot Tooyalakekt and No Heart have saved our horses"—Claimed in the same, p. 385, fn. 44.

"You who began this trouble . . ."—Somewhat altered and abridged from the same, p. 390.

Death of Ta Mah Utah Likt—Pearson, pp. 38–39.

"perhaps a hundred have been killed."—Casualty estimates vary. This one, on the high side, is from Peopeo Tholekt (Hear Me, p. 393). McWhorter himself sets the casualty list at sixty to ninety (ibid., p. 403).

Ollokot's advice to Cloudburst at Cottonwood—Information from McWhorter, Hear Me, p. 288.

Tale of Grey Eagle and other wounded—Information from Pearson, pp. 38ff.

The flour-looting women of Pitsburgh—Information from Bruce, p. 172.

Fouling of Springfields; prying out spent shells with hunting knives—Common to Custer's troops a year before, so most likely still problematic at Big Hole. See Williamson, pp. 51–52.

Howard Morton's wound—Described in George Armstrong Custer, p. 142.

Description of Dr. Nelson G. Blalock (fl. 1873–1914)—After a pharmacy exhibit seen at Fort Walla Walla, August 2009.

The killing of Kah-pots—Somewhat after Pearson, p. 38.

At Least Idaho and Oregon Are Safe

Gibbon's wound—The same bullet that broke his horse's forelock entered and exited his leg without breaking the bone. See Gibbon, Adventures, p. 212–13.

"Well, we might have been whipped . . ."—Somewhat after Col. J. B. Catlin, p. 7.

Atrocities committed by the Nez Perce upon the Chamberlain family—Bowdoin, OOH papers, M91.8 v. 3. Letterpress Copy-book: Articles and Addresses: Nez Perce, pp. 175–76 [part of a long extract in quotation marks, so these are not Howard's own words].

"G" Company of the Seventh Infantry's losses: Fourteen out of twenty-five at Big Hole—Information from Zimmer, p. 153 ([November] 26th).

Description of Professor Thomas C. Upham—Howard, *Autobiography*, vol. 1, p. 33.

"Without a shadow of excuse the Colorado cavalry fired straight at them and into the Indian village" + "the indiscretion of Colonel Chivington"—Howard, *Among Our Hostile Indians*, p. 488. For details on this atrocity (28 November 1864), see *The Annals of America*, vol. 9, pp. 550–53 (no. 134, E. A. Wynkoop, testimony to 39th Congress, 2nd Session, Senate Document No. 156). Page 552: "Women and children were killed and scalped, children shot at their mother's breast, and all the bodies mutilated in a most horrible manner . . . the dead bodies of the females profaned in such a manner that the recital is sickening." Page 553, Wynkoop concludes: "All this country is ruined; there can be no such thing as peace in the future but by the total annihilation of all these Indians on the Plains."

Gibbon's justifications for shooting Nez Perce women and children at Big Hole: Cf. Col. J. B. Catlin, p. 7: "You may ask why we did kill the women and children. We answer that when we came up on the second charge, we found that the women were using the Winchesters with as much skill, and as bravely as did the Bucks [*sic*]. As to the children, [comma thus in original] (though many were killed), we did not think that a citizen or soldier, killed a child on purpose. They were there with their fathers and mothers, and their fathers and mothers were violating the laws of our land; and we as soldiers, were ordered to fire, and we did."

Looking-Glass Is Silent

John Dog wounded in forehead at Big Hole—Greene, *Beyond Bear's Paw*, Appendix C, pp. 178–82 [Nez Perce never captured].

Joseph: "Now, my beloved sister, you are going away for the last time . . ."—Somewhat after Gulick, p. 94 (Timothy re: Mrs. Spalding, 1848).

The death of Fair Land—Briefly told in McWhorter, *Yellow Wolf*, pp. 159–62.

Ollokot's arrival—In fact, say his warriors (*Hear Me*, p. 394), "It took us two days before catching up with the rest of the tribe, near the Lemhi reservation."

Description of Joseph regarding Looking-Glass—After a photograph in Gulick, p. 267 (Charles M. Bell, *ca.* 1897, "Chief Joseph with his nephew Ahlakat . . .").

Description of the lake near where Fair Land used to gather earth pigment (this detail is my invention)—After a visit in August 2013 to Hoffer Lake, in the Wallowa-Whitman National Forest, actually considerably west-southwest of Wallowa.

Revivifying the dead by stepping over them—Belief mentioned in Aoki, p. 645.

Use (among Nez Perce, by men only) of willow sticks as strength-giving emetics—Hart, p. 116.

"The sister of Swan Necklace"—We do not know who the second dying woman was. Inventing a kinship to someone we know seems better than simply imagining her as "a woman." Her death is mentioned in McWhorter, *Yellow Wolf*, p. 164. "Where Ducks Are Around" is a female name from Aoki's dictionary.

Joseph: "We could have killed their women and children . . ."—Somewhat after Pearson, p. 39.

Nez Perce burial procedures here and throughout—After description in Pearson, p. 58 (burial of a Nez Perce prisoner en route to Tongue River). The name of the Medicine man in this recounting is George Washington. His Nez Perce identity is unknown, but on p. 66 Pearson lists some possibilities, one of whom is Tuk-le-kas.

Death of Grey Eagle—McWhorter, *Hear Me*, p. 405.

The death of Running Eagle—Dempsey, p. 58. She was of the Blood tribe, but since the Blackfeet and the Nez Perce were enemies, I have assumed that the latter would not have been especially interested in which kind of Blackfoot she was. Apparently she became a warrior after the Crows killed her husband. Such was her success that she was the only Blackfoot woman to receive a man's name (her birthname was Empty Valley).

VI. Very Beautiful and Almost Automatic

Epigraph: "The machinery for production of metallic ammunition . . ."—Treadwell, p. 7.

Epigraph: "As I looked upon the battalion for the first time . . ."—Howard, *Autobiography*, vol. 1, pp. 46–47 (describing his arrival at West Point as a cadet).

Skinner Meadows

Description of Skinner Meadows—After a visit in August 2007.

"SERENE AMIDST ALARMS"—Sullivan, p. 341.

The firing of Mr. McFinn's house at Cottonwood—Adkison, p. 20.

Perry's vision of Theller's death—Somewhat after the illustration in Forczyk, pp. 38–39.

Information about Hardee's son—After Howard, *Autobiography*, vol. 2, pp. 151–52.

Immediately following dialogue between Howard and Mason—Somewhat after Montana Historical Society, mss. no. 80, p. 199 (Mason's letter home).

The best place to aim at buffalo, and the color of its blood when shot—Closely after John R. Cook [ed. by Milo Milton Quaife, Secretary of the Burton Historical Collection], *The Border and the Buffalo: An Untold Story of the Southwest Plains* (Chicago: The Lakeside Press, R. R. Donnelly and Sons. Co./ The Lakeside Classics, Christmas 1938); previous copyright 1934 (orig. pub. 1907), p. 126.

"Our meat it was of buffalo hump . . ."—After *The Annals of America*, vol. 10, pp. 372–73 (no. 83, "Work Songs"), half a verse out of the seven in "Buffalo Skinners," slightly altered by WTV.

"Tacoma, Washington Territory. Drinking whiskey has never been a fault of mine . . ." Abbreviated from a letter to OOH (March 26, 1877?), in Bowdoin, OOH papers, M91. Box 13. M91.4: Correspondence, western command period, May 1, 1875–Dec. 20, 1877, folder March 20–31, 1877.

Dandy Jim tobacco at a dollar a pound at Lapwai—Erwin N. Thompson, p. 97 (1878 price).

Description of Ad Chapman—After a photo in Pearson, p. 110.

Trimble's men think to "readily discern the different phases of" Nez Perces' "emotional expressions"— *The Soldiers' Side*, p. 55 (Major J. G. Trimble, "The Battle of the Clearwater").

Lice-collecting habits of Indian women—Actually retailed to ladies not by Wilkinson, but by another soldier mentioned in Wood diary, 1878, p. 2.

"Tha never hav no dissease . . ."—*The Annals of America*, vol. 9, p. 171 (no. 32, Henry Wheeler Shaw ["Josh Billings"], "An Esa on the Muel," 1874).

Description of Perry's ride down the Lewiston Hill with Theller—After a visit to that country in August 2011.

John Taylor and Bolatoe Ross—Names (and residences) from Ronald Vern Jackson, A.I.S. Senior Archivist, ed., *Montana 1870 Territorial Census Index* (Salt Lake City, Utah: Accelerated Indexing Systems Inc., 1979).

"Now, if you find a dead soldier in the Sioux country . . ."—Information or misinformation (accounts differ) somewhat after remarks of Sergeant Kanipe, in Coleman, p. 131.

"And the widows of Ashur are loud in their wail . . ."—David Perkins, ed., *English Romantic Writers* (New York: Harcourt, Brace & World, Inc., 1967), p. 792 (George Gordon, Lord Byron, "The Destruction of Sennacherib," 1815). As is my practice throughout these Seven Dreams, I have impartially block-lettered the names of both deities mentioned.

The tale of Howard's Negro boy who was murdered—Loosely after McFeely, pp. 41–42 (as told by Howard's brother Charles; Howard later denies that the boy was in his service).

"We will welcome to our numbers the loyal, true and brave . . ."—*The Annals of America*, vol. 9, p. 304 (no. 60, "Patriotic Songs of North and South," George Frederick Root, "The Battle-Cry of Freedom").

Excerpts from Turgenev review—Marjorie Longley, Louis Silverstein, Samuel A. Tower, *America's Taste 1851–1959: The Cultural Events of a Century Reported by Contemporary Observers in the Pages of the* New York Times (New York: Simon and Schuster, 1960), p. 99 (review of *Virgin Soil*, July 2, 1877).

The seven white lead mills of Pittsburgh—Information from Bruce, p. 120.

Red Salmon Season

Description of Sound Of Running Feet's surroundings when she relieves herself—After a walk in Jackson, Montana, in August 2009, just before dawn.

White Bird's fishheaded Medicine whistle—Mentioned in Holland Library, Washington State University, Pullman; ms. 1218 (CM Brewster/Peopeo Tholekt), p. 1. Its later transfer to Peopeo Tholekt in "Further History of White Thunder" follows the tale in this source.

Lean Elk's schedule—According to McWhorter (*Hear Me*, p. 406), he would move the caravan out "early in the morning," rest the horses from about 10:00 a.m. to 2:00 p.m., and then set out until around 10:00 at night.

The breakfast: camas porridge & c—Described in Frank D. Carpenter, *Adventures in Geyser Land*, repr. from *The Wonders of Geyser Land, Edition of 1878*, ed. Heister Dean Guie and Lucullus Virgil Mc-

Whorter (Caldwell, Idaho: Caxton Printers, Ltd., 1935), pp. 138–40. The source of the hardbread is my imputation; it could have been purchased in Stevensville.

"Cloudburst trims Ollokot's hair in mourning for Fair Land"—After information in Deward E. Walker, Jr., ed. [this vol.], *Handbook of North American Indians*, vol. 12: Plateau (Washington, D.C.: Smithsonian Institution, 1998), p. 424 (Deward E. Walker, Jr., "Nez Perce").

"Wounded Head keeps whispering to him the winter's tales . . ."—"After [children] had reached a sufficient age to understand, stories, myths, and didactic accounts of arts and technology were told them on winter evenings by the men."—Spinden, p. 247.

Death of Wounded Head's son—McWhorter says (*Hear Me*, p. 374) that he lived four days after Big Hole.

"on the Lo Lo Trail the birds will be eating the scarlet berries of the mountain ash."—Information from Lewis and Clark, vol. 5, p. 223, fn. 2.

Death of Only Half Grizzly Bear—Invented by WTV. This man's name was taken from Aoki's dictionary. Theft of eighty-seven horses [from the Pierce Ranch]—Information from Wilfong, p. 246.

Description of the country between Big Hole and Horse Prairie—After a visit in August 2009. The creek where I have imagined Looking-Glass as killing the deer is Bloody Dick Creek. The pass before Horse Prairie is Lemhi Pass.

Killing of four Bostons [at the ranch of Montague and Winters]—McWhorter, *Hear Me*, pp. 407–8; Wilfong, p. 247.

Swan Necklace's hatred of women—The exact composition of the Salmon River rapists is unknown. Since Swan Necklace was one of the three who began the war by murdering whites, perhaps he raped them, too.

Murder of Eya-makoot by a settler—Howard et al., p. 227 (McDonald).

Description of the interior of the ranch house—After Judith E. Greenberg and Helen Carey McKeever, *A Pioneer Woman's Memoir: Based on the Journal of Arabella Clemens Fulton* (New York: Franklin Watts, In Their Own Words ser., 1995; abr. of orig text. [wr. bef. 1934]), p. 124, photo of "the interior of a typical home in the Idaho Territory." I am hoping that Montana was not too different.

Piling up of horse dung to show disdain for Howard—*The Soldiers' Side*, p. 95 (H. J. Davis, "The Battle of Camas Meadows").

"A Boston must have no respect for himself . . ."—Somewhat after McDonald, Howard et al., p. 262 (McDonald). Although other commentators sometimes quote this remark as being White Bird's, the text is unclear as to whether he said it or whether it is Duncan McDonald's interpolation. It was supposed to have been uttered right after Big Hole.

Killing of the man and dog—McWhorter, *Hear Me*, p. 408; Wilfong, pp. 248–49.

Crow invocations to the SKY, ACBADADEA, etc.— After *Yellowtail, Crow Medicine Man and Sun Dance Chief: An Autobiography* as told to Michael Oren Fitzgerald (Norman: University of Oklahoma Press, 1991), p. 3. [Cited: Yellowtail.]

Peopeo Tholekt's WOODPECKER Power—This Power is described in *Handbook of North American Indians*, vol. 12, p. 427 (Deward E. Walker, Jr., "Nez Perce"). Since Peopeo Tholekt informs us in his Pullman ms. that he kept a mummified woodpecker's head with him for the sake of its Power, why not make his WYAKIN a woodpecker?

Description of the Buffalo Country as Looking-Glass envisions it—After a visit to Big Timber, Montana, in August 2012. This place was described because it it is not on the Nez Perce Trail. I wished to suggest how much more of the country than that one route must have been known to at least some of the men, such as Looking-Glass, who had adventured so often and so widely in Montana.

"The Buffalo Country, from where we gained the Owl Dance long ago"—Somewhat after Aoki, p. 505 (he says it simply comes from "the Plains").

Lemhi as an early-nineteenth-century buffalo-hunting site for the Nez Perce—Information from Gulick, pp. 18–19.

Miscellaneous descriptions of Crow regalia, etc., from here until after Cow Island—Some of these are after illustrations in Molloy Tribal Art et al., *Apsaalooke: Art and Tradition* (New York: Molloy Tribal Art, 2006).

"Where have you been?"—"On ahead."—Almost verbatim from McWhorter, *Yellow Wolf*, p. 197.

Reception of the fugitives by the Lemhis—After McWhorter, *Hear Me*, pp. 408–9.

Description of Tendoy—After a group photograph from 1880; reproduced in Warren L. d'Azevedo, ed. [of this vol.], *Handbook of North American Indians*, vol. 11: Great Basin (Washington, D.C.: Smithsonian Institution, 1986), p. 290 (Robert F. Murphy and Yolanda Murphy, "Northern Shoshone and Bannock").

"Wherever the Bostons come, the buffalo go."—Actually said in slightly different words by another Indian in a different place; recounted by Trobriand, p. 187.

Looking-Glass's secret purchase of cartridges—McWhorter says only (loc. cit.) that this could have happened; the idea that Looking-Glass worked the deal is plausible, given his experience in this country and his success at Fort Fizzle; all the same, it is my invention.

Ollokot: "When it mattered, you never asked your chiefs . . ."—Somewhat after Howard et al., p. 239 (McDonald, re: Salmon River).

The murder of the citizens in the wagon is not originally described in much detail, but the number of victims and the drunken outcome are as I have them.

The "like" Nimiputumít words for American commodities—Aoki, p. 850.

The ten thousand rounds for Shearer's volunteers—Adkison, p. 13.

Geese Three Times Alighting On Water's shooting of the white boy on the Salmon River—McWhorter, *Hear Me*, pp. 213–14.

Murder of the five mule packers—After McWhorter, *Hear Me*, pp. 409–10; Wilfong, pp. 251–52. The original sources do not state the names of the killers.

Relating to Butterfly and Musselshell Girls—Aoki and Walker, p. 594.

Chapman as "he who once hanged three of our People"—Aoki (p. 451) gives two of their names.

The days when mint blooms—July and August.

Description of "the Crows . . . riding, riding"—After Wood, Porter and Hunt, p. 154 (plate 30: Crow Indian Men and Horses).

The Green Light

"Gen'l Howard's Army Breaking Camp"—Invented by WTV.

His Father's Grave

Description of Joseph's imagined homecoming—After a visit to Imnaha and Wallowa in August 2009.

Bannock City

Immediate tactical purpose of march when leaving Bannock City, and the refusal of Captain Clark to follow Howard's instructions, and the route to Red Rock Stage Station (or, as Howard wrote it, "Red rock stage station")—Howard, *Report—In the Field*, pp. 19–20.

"German Communists from Cincinnati"—Information from Bruce, pp. 231ff.

The map depicting GOLD, GOLD—Colton's map of Oregon, Washington, Idaho and British Columbia, no. 68, 1860.

"two hundred horses stolen" by the Nez Perces—Information from McWhorter, *Hear Me*, p. 411.

So Much Waste

"Behind every gal you'll find an uncle with a Bowie knife . . ."—Loosely after *The Annals of America*, vol. 10, p. 282 (no. 60, Count von Hübner, *Promenade autour du Monde, 1871* [Paris, 1873], descr. of American Western towns).

Anecdote about Jefferson Davis's stallion—After Howard, *Autobiography*, p. 122.

Fletch's assignment as Perry's topographical officer in 1876—Donna M. Hanson, comp., *Frontier Diary: The Army in Northern Idaho, 1853–1876* (Moscow: University of Idaho Library, 2005), p. 163.

Parnell: "Well, general, if we keep harassing them . . ."—Somewhat after Michno, p. 339 (Parnell's words).

"Both armies were burning the cotton . . ."—Almost verbatim from Howard, op. cit., p. 129.

A horse for seventy-five earring-shells—Information after Carrington, p. 218.

Indian sign for cartridge—W. P. Clark [Captain, Second Cavalry], *The Indian Sign Language, with Brief Explanatory Notes of the Gestures Taught Deaf-Mutes in Our Institutions for Their Instruction, and a Description of Some of the Peculiar Laws, Customs, Myths, Superstitions, Ways of Living, Code of Peace and War Signals of Our Aborigines* (Lincoln, Nebraska: Bison Books, 1982 repr. of 1885 ed.), p. 97.

Camas Meadows

Howard's orders, and his dialogue with Buffalo Horn (which might never have taken place)—Loosely after *Nez Perce Joseph*, pp. 176, 219–25.

"Ain't hardly no game hereabouts even as big as a mockingbird."—Somewhat after Elizabeth Custer, p. 166. At least there were lots of trout.

Description of Camas Meadows—After a visit in August 2007. I spent the night in Dubois, Idaho. The closed library's window still said **FREE CHILDREN'S BOOKS**, and half Main Street was for sale but nobody was buying. In the empty park an informational sign explained that more than ninety percent of the sagebrush in the American West had been obliterated. The opal shop, direct from the miners to us, had gone to heaven. One pay phone remained, in the convenience store by the freeway. And on that hot afternoon where the sprinklers played over arid lawns, a train track with half a dozen empty Union Pacific boxcars crowned an embankment, and far off on the other side, leftwards of a church, an American flag stood firm.

"the blue-backed Webster's spelling book Gracie used to carry to school"—A pioneer emigrant (Oregon Historical Society [Portland] MSS 233, "Virginia Watson Applegate, Recollections 1840–1852," p. 6) mentions her "blue-backed Webster's spelling book." She was born in 1840, and Grace Howard in 1857.

The moon—Actually, Howard specifically remarks that the night was moonless (loc. cit.), but when I was at Camas Meadows there was a spectacular moon, and so by God I am going to put it in.

"We've been tenting to-night . . ."—*The Annals of America*, vol. 9, p. 502 (no. 122, Walter Kittredge, "Tenting on the Old Camp Ground," 1862).

Information on Mars's proximity to Earth, and the discovery of at least one moon—After Whitman, p. 804.

Dialogue between General Howard and Lieutenants Wood and Howard re: sleeping pantaloon-less—Fairly closely after *Nez Perce Joseph*, p. 225, with a few interpolations.

"THE UNION MUST AND SHALL BE PRESERVED"—Plate in Sullivan, p. 263.

Howard's fall in Livermore—After his *Autobiography*, vol. 1, p. 254.

"Father, lie down or you'll be hit!"—After Howard, *Autobiography*, vol. 2, p. 476.

"Lie close . . ." + Howard's rejoinder—Howard, *Nez Perce Joseph*, p. 225.

Dialogue and events until return to camp—Somewhat after the same, pp. 225–29.

Colloquy with Trimble—Entirely invented. Howard does not state who was responsible. The real life Trimble would probably not have been caught like this.

"The responsible innocent suffer for the irresponsible guilty . . ."—Somewhat after the *Autobiography*, vol. 1, p. 136.

The death of Brooks—Information from Greene, *Nez Perce Summer*, p. 366 (Appendix A: U.S. Army Casualties, IV).

Henry's Lake

Calloway's withdrawal with the wounded—Mentioned in Howard, *Report—In the Field*, p. 23.

Injuries of Glass, Trevor et al.—*The Soldiers' Side*, p. 97 (H. J. Davis, "The Battle of Camas Meadows").

The country from Camas Meadows to Henry's Lake inclusive—After a journey through this area in August 2007.

Arrival of the Bannocks from Fort Hall—Howard, *Report—In the Field*, loc. cit.

The four blacks at the Centennial Exhibition—Information from Bellesiles, p. 10.

"The squaws will have a jolly good time cooking our mules."—Much after Pollock, p. 77. However, this exchange could not have occurred since Pollock's company was actually forty-one miles in the rear when the Camas Meadows raid occurred (ibid., p. 76, datelined Henry's Lake, August 25).

Jim's story: Grindstone Creek—Information from Michno, p. 42.

Bugler Brooks tries to get back in the saddle—*The Soldiers' Side*, p. 99 (Colonel J. W. Redington, "Story of Bugler Brooks").

Doc's theory: "Only two ways to fight savages, boy . . ."—Paraphrased from Bourke, p. 36. ("To fight savages successfully, one of two things must be done—either the savages must be divided into hostile bands and made to fight each other, or the civilized soldier must be trained down as closely as possible to the level of the savage.")

Location of the Nez Perce camp at Henry's Lake: Southwestern shore—McWhorter, *Hear Me*, p. 434.

The huge black currants along the lake—Frank D. Carpenter, p. 37.

Meat available at Henry's Lake—Information from the same, p. 41.

Location of Mr. Sawtell's ranch—Ibid., p. 35.

Distance from Lewiston to Henry's Lake—Howard, *Report—In the Field*, p. 68. Distance, average mileage and days in march since Kamiah are from the same source, p. 24; likewise the distance covered by Carr's company (which had travelled the farthest).

Medical assessments of the army at Henry's Lake—Howard, *Report—In the Field*, p. 36.

Wounds received at Camas Meadows—Information from Helen Addison Howard, p. 268. There were eight casualties in all.

Five days to get resupplied from Virginia City—Sutherland, p. 31.

General Order Number Six—Howard, *Report—In the Field*, p. 38 (actually, dated August 28, Camp Cañon, Wyoming Territory, so it would have been issued just after the Army departed Henry's Lake).

Captain Fisher's souvenirs—Somewhat after information from Pearson, p. 46.

Wood's sketches—Ten of them were published on 3 August "in the New York Press," says Venn (p. 45), in which case they must have been sent off from Kamiah or thereabouts (before Lolo and after Clearwater). For narrative reasons I thought it better to have Howard more anxiously looking after his "media image" nearer to his unpleasant communication from General Sherman.

Howard's explication of Joseph's intended direction—Howard, *Report—In the Field*, p. 34.

Howard's orders to Cushing, Field and Norwood—Ibid., p. 23.

"giving vouchers which don't even pledge the credit of the Government"—After Howard, *Report—In the Field*, p. 24.

Howard's trip to Virginia City with Guy and Captain Adams—Mentioned in *Nez Perce Joseph*, chapter XXXIV.

Description of muleteers bringing the mail—After Elizabeth B. Custer, p. 53.

"the dark side of the Indian question"—George Armstrong Custer, p. 270.

"I hear from Portland that you have delivered publicly a lecture . . ."—Bowdoin, OOH papers. M91. Box 13. M91.4: Correspondence, western command period, May 1, 1875–Dec. 20, 1877. Folder: March 1–20, 1875. The letter truly was dated March 1, but I have pretended it was written in 1877. (There seem to be very few letters dated from the Nez Perce War period.)

Letter about strong drink—Abbreviated and slightly altered from the same folder. Letter from Harry M. Smith, dated March 8th, 1875.

Information on George Beauddry—He is fictitious, but the format of his signature card derives from a facsimile in Washington, p. 5.

Fall of pig iron to $16.50 a ton—Bellesiles, p. 7.

The wingspan of Ad Chapman's swan—Based on the measurements of Cowan's trophy bird in Frank D. Carpenter, p. 40.

"And Empire Transportation has sold out to Standard Oil."—Information from Bruce, pp. 300–301.

God Help Me

The dialogue at the beginning of this chapter implies that Howard's army was on the march between Henry's Lake and the receipt of Sherman's message. In fact the message came while they were still recuperating at Henry's Lake. I chose to alter reality in this way in order to give the men's fatigue more prominence.

Death of Crazy Horse—Information from Utley, p. 180.

"Everything is paid up except the taxes . . ."—Bowdoin, OOH papers. M91, Box 13 [M91.4: Correspondence, western command period, May 1, 1875–Dec. 20, 1877]. Folder: June 11–30, 1877. Letter from John H. Cook, dated June 16.

Sherman's letter to Howard—Ibid. Folder: August 1–31. Letter abridged by WTV. I have capitalized the first letter of "department" in order to conform to other usage in this book.

Howard's recollections of himself and Sherman at the grand review—After Sherman, p. 805.

"Why art THOU so far from helping me . . ."—Psalms, 22.1, 22.15 (abridged and concatenated).

Howard's travails at West Point—After his *Autobiography*, vol. 1, pp. 51–53.

Howard's belief that Mason's skirmish with Joseph at Weippe "really ended the campaign within the limits of my Department"—Howard, *Report—In the Field*, p. 11.

Events in Tampa—Howard, *Autobiography*, vol. 1, p. 80.

"there's Communist poison spreading through the railroads . . ."—After Bruce, p. 225. (The *National Republican*, July 21: "Communistic ideas are very widely entertained in American by the workmen employed in mines and factories and by the railroads. This poison was introduced . . . by European laborers.")

Chancellorsville: The order from Hooker's lieutenant colonel—Burke Davis, *They Called Him Stonewall: A life of Lt. General T. J. Jackson* (New York: Rinehart & Co., Inc., 1954), p. 423.

The one time Howard felt fear before battle—Information from *Autobiography*, vol. 1, p. 154.

"In thirty-one days you have gained fifteen days . . ."—Much after Howard, *Report—In the Field*, p. 39.

Whatever Light There Is

"We show ourselves unhappy lovers . . ."—Euripides, vol. II, *Hippolytus*, p. 141.

List of substandard reservation goods, and mention of arrest for hunting off-reservation—U.S. Congress, *Congressional Record, Containing the Proceedings and Debates of the Forty-Fifth Congress, Second Session*, vol. VII, Part III (Washington: Government Printing Office, 1878), p. 2796 (Transfer of Indian Bureau to War Department).

"When I find—as for instance in Arizona or Nevada . . ."—I consider the rest of this paragraph so important to understanding Howard's motivations that it seems worthwhile to quote its original: "When he [the Bible man] finds, as in Arizona, Nevada or Alaska, an Indian tribe very degraded indeed, as some are, as yet in the dimmest twilight of knowledge, full of maddening passions and unclean habits, he never sees, if he looks with carefulness, such a tribe growing better by its own motion."—Bowdoin, OOH papers, M91.8: Articles and addresses. Folder 6: "Christianity Among Indian Tribes," p. 3. The remaining sentence in my paragraph is lifted verbatim from the same typescript, p. 6.

"Communistic ideas are now widely entertained in America."—*Washington National Republican*, 1877, quoted in Bellesiles, p. 144.

"Communists might take over Philadelphia or New York."—After Bellesiles, p. 145.

The Land of Wonders

"Mr. Oldham, shot in face . . ." + the two dispatches to San Francisco and Fort Ellis, August 29—After Howard, *Report—In the Field*, p. 37 (abbreviated).

"The former Blackfoot country"—According to Humfreville (p. 211), the Yellowstone River once marked the boundary of the Blackfoot hunting grounds.

The Earl of Dunraven's cookery—Information from Frank D. Carpenter, p. 49.

The Prismatic Hot Spring [now Mammoth Hot Spring]—Ibid., p. 56.

"a number of sulphurs"—Pollock used this last word in a letter to his wife (op. cit., p. 91).

Parnell: "in '67 Colonel Perry went out for thirty days straight . . ."—Information from Michno, p. 306.

Fisher's position on the Madison—Montana Historical Society. SC 692. S. G. Fisher Diary. "Journal of S. G. Fisher, Chief of Scouts to Gen. O. O. Howard during his campaign against the Nez Perces . . . ," p. 23.

"even as little as they are ridden, they won't stand one-fourth as much as an American horse."—Much after Zimmer, p. 108 ([August] 27th).

The Crow uprising of 1834—Information from Bradley, pp. 81–82.

"The soldiers from Fort Ellis are our friends" + complaint about beef—Verbatim from Bradley, p. 42 (said to Gibbon the previous year). "Are you from Fort Ellis?" is my addition.

Death of Half Yellow Face—Information from the same source, p. 154.

"Let Bacchus's sons be not dismayed . . ."—From "Garyowen," the signature tune of Custer's Seventh Cavalry. The band played this during the dawn raid which commenced the Battle of the Washita. It also sounded during Colonel Chivington's massacre of the Cheyennes at Sand Creek, Colorado. Lyrics from Elizabeth Custer, p. xix.

Mason's judgment of the hot spring (useful for washing clothes)—Abbreviated from Montana Historical Society, mss. no. 80, pp. 199–200 (Mason's letter home).

Prices of buffalo hides, 1877–78—Sandoz, p. 317. Of course at this point in time Redington would have been anticipating a little. The season was still in progress; the extent of the boom, and the price slide, might not have been known for another couple of months.

"I'm a-going back to the Crows to buy a young squaw," & c—After Zimmer, p. 66 ([June] 24th): "White is going back to the Crows & buy a young squaw. He says that he can get a nice one & a good worker, 16 years old, by giving the old folks about $40 worth of presents . . . He can speak the Crow language quite well for the time he has been there, so he says, & by getting the squaw will soon get it thorough." Indeed, he married a girl named Yoho-na-ho, and stayed with her until she died in 1921.

Description of General Terry—After a photo in Philbrick, insert following p. 70.

Howard's excuses to Perry about Chancellorsville (until then the greatest blemish on his record)—Howard, *Autobiography*, vol. 1, pp. 365, 372, 374–75.

Incident involving Captain Griffith of Philadelphia—Ibid., p. 443.

Sherman's escort to Yellowstone: "L" Company—Zimmer, p. 81 ([July] 18th).

Sherman's decoration of 31 of Miles's soldiers—Zimmer, loc. cit.

Description of turning out the guard to receive Sherman—Procedure from Kautz, pp. 33–34.

Howard's meeting with Sherman at Chickamauga, the conference at Chattanooga, and comparisons between Sherman and Grant—*Autobiography*, vol. 1, 481–82, 473–76.

They Are the Ones Who Did Wrong Things

Peopeo Tholekt's temporary capture of Chapman's horse—McWhorter, *Hear Me*, pp. 420–21.

Mourning Dove—An invented character. This female name was taken from Aoki's dictionary.

Description of the line of horses—Information from Frank D. Carpenter, p. 97.

Description of Yellowstone National Park—After a trip there in August 2010.

The embassy to the Crows—Helen Addison Howard (p. 298), whose book occasionally contains details (possibly erroneous) not to be found in McWhorter, writes that Looking-Glass "reportedly rode ahead to hold a conference with the Crows." McWhorter (*Hear Me*, pp. 459–60) calls this "one of the romantic myths that has [sic] developed around the Nez Perce war," arguing that "it is unlikely the Nez Perces clung to any conception of the Crow country as a refuge after the battle of the Big Hole . . . Instead the Nez Perces apparently met a few Crow warriors while en route from Yellowstone to Canyon Creek. These proved friendly . . ." I have chosen to imagine otherwise, because why else would the Nez Perce have taken the long way to Canada? Looking-Glass must have been desperate to redeem himself; the possibility of refuge with Tendoy probably seemed remote; perhaps Lean Elk did lead the People in this very roundabout way simply in order to avoid capture, but I see no reason that some delegation would not have "reached out" (as modern corporate types would put it) to the Crows. See also Greene, *Beyond Bear's Paw*, p. 11.

Description of Looking-Glass's ornaments—Somewhat after Helen Addison Howard, p. 276 (Frank Carpenter).

Húsus Kute's headband—After a description in Koch (p. 102) of the "stand up" headbonnet employed by Nez Perce and others.

Benefits to eyes of eating buffalo liver—Information from Leforge, p. 156.

Ollokot to Joseph: "Elder brother, stay here and I shall go for you . . ."—A bit after McWhorter, *Yellow Wolf*, p. 36. When Howard summoned the Nez Perces to Walla Walla, Ollokot persuaded his brother not to go, saying: "You stay here. I will go see what is wanted."

Description of Painted Hills—After a visit to Painted Hills National Monument, Oregon, in August 2013.

Meaning of the Crow's X-painted face—Koch, pp. 29–30.

The Lost Lodges and other Crow clan names from 1877—Raymond J. DeMallie, ed. [of this vol.], *Handbook of Nothern American Indians*, vol. 13, part 2 of 2: Plains (Washington, D.C.: Smithsonian Institution, 2001), p. 702 (Fred W. Voget, entry on Crow).

The way that Crow women incite men to war by waving scalps—Information from Leforge, p. 258.

Mexican brands on many Crow horses—Montana Historical Society. SC 683. John W. Redington papers. SCOUTING IN MONTANA. By Colonel J. W. Redington, U. S. Scout and Courier in Nez Perce and Bannack Indian Wars, and Assistant Adjutant General of Oregon, 1879–83 [henceforth: Redington, "Scouting in Montana"], p. 6.

Serving meat in a buffalo's shoulderbone—Linderman, p. 14.

Crow name for white men: "Yellow Eyes."—Ibid., p. 22.

Description of Curley's bare chest and neck—After photos in Philbrick (insert following p. 294).

Description of White Man Runs Him—After a photo in Kavanagh, p. 27 ("White Man Runs Him [Crow]").

Crow chief to Looking-Glass: "Brothers, my heart is glad to see you . . ."—Wood diary 1878, p. 28 (somewhat after speech of Chief Moses to the Army and the Indian Agent, as recorded by Wood).

Description of the *lucky man*: Wood, Porter and Hunt, p. 155 (plate 31: Pachtüwa-Chtä, an Arikara Man).

"My heart falls to the ground."—Verbatim from Linderman, p. 20.

When a woman's needle breaks—Walker and Matthews, p. 158.

The tale of Tattooed Forehead—Bradley, pp. 120–21.

The capture of the prospector (Shively) and the group with the two women (these people became known as the Cowan party)—McWhorter, *Hear Me*, pp. 434–36; Helen Addison Howard, pp. 273–85.

The way Smohalla covered his face before speaking with a white man (or at least with General Howard)—After Howard, *Famous Indian Chiefs*, p. 334.

Intimate peculiarities of a MUSSELSHELL WOMAN—Aoki and Walker, p. 526.

Inventory of the Cowan party's weapons—Information from Frank D. Carpenter, p. 96.

Dialogue about the ring—Somewhat altered from the same, p. 107.

"My WYAKIN told me never to be cruel."—McWhorter, *Yellow Wolf*, p. 29.

The shooting of the two white men—Somewhat after Frank D. Carpenter, p. 116.

"now it is for the young men to say yes or no"—Much after a line in Joseph's purported surrender speech.

"GoDD——n, GoDD——n no good! White man no good."—Verbatim from the same, p. 121. The unidentified speaker was "a fifteen-year-old boy." About Asleep was around fourteen.

The Boston's memory of Henry's Lake—Information from Frank D. Carpenter, pp. 35–37.

Dialogue between the Boston (Carpenter) and Joseph—Verbatim (abbreviated) from Frank D. Carpenter, p. 134.

Grizzly Bear Youth's dream of mule-stealing—Howard et al., p. 266 (McDonald).

"I know I could have sat down on that young one . . ."—Frank D. Carpenter, p. 136 (verbatim).

Joseph: "Leave a clean trail."—Heinmot Tooyalakekt in Helen Addison Howard, p. 213: "I wanted to leave a clean trail, and if there were dead soldiers in that trail I could not be held to blame."

Toohhoolhoolzote's murder of the prospector—Invented. However, Toohhoolhoolzote's band might have been the most aggressive, and the number of "Bostons" killed in the park by the Nez Perces is undetermined; some bodies might never have been found.

And Then I Can Write a Pleasing Article

Captain Fisher's news: Location of Joseph—Information from Howard, *Report—In the Field*, p. 42 (September 4).

Description of Captain Fisher—Information from *The Youth's Companion*, New England ed., October 15, 1891, pp. 546–48 (General Oliver O. Howard. U.S.A., "A Phenomenal Scout"), describing Fisher.

The jingle from Thompson's Two-Bit House—Wood diary, 1879, pp. 37–38.

The tiny light which we cannot see—This trope based on a Walla Walla prophetess's "worship song," in *Handbook of North American Indians*, vol. 17, p. 666 (Rigsby and Rude, "Sketch of Sahaptin").

Chief Tattooed Forehead's funny little prank on the Assiniboine maidens—Information from Bradley, *March of the Montana Column*, pp. 120–21.

Klughards on the "Hammonia"—Ira A. Glazier and P. William Filby, *Germans to America: Lists of Passengers Arriving at U.S. Ports*, vol. 33: October 1876–September 1878 (Wilmington, Delaware: Scholarly Resources, Inc., 1984), p. 165.

"To get him quick, we should think Indian . . ."—Much after Pollock, p. 46, dated at Craig's Ferry, Salmon River, when Pollock was still in high favor with Howard, and had not yet turned against him. Here he was writing his wife (without expletives) in response to her letter of 25 June which arrived on 1 July.

Modoc predation on Shastas and Paiutes, and their attack on the Reed party—Murray, pp. 12, 25, 28.

Howard's order to Fisher, via Fletcher: No more killing and scalping of prisoners—Quoted in Wilfong, p. 104.

What Next?

Fletch's mission to Fisher—Redington, "Scouting in Montana," pp. 4–5.

Bargain with Fletch

Description of the country from Cooke City to Laurel—After a journey along that route in August 2010.

Cornelius Vanderbilt: "Building railroads from nowhere to nowhere . . ."—Quoted in Bellesiles, p. 6.

Stonewall Jackson's blood-filled glove—Burke Davis, *They Called Him Stonewall: A Life of Lt. General T. J. Jackson* (New York: Rinehart & Co., Inc., 1954), p. 427.

Howard's recollections of Chancellorsville—Ibid., pp. 418–20, 423.

Sturgis's thirty-six mule teams—Greene, *Nez Perce Summer*, pp. 205–6.

"Indians are between me and Sturgis . . ."—Ibid., p. 200, slightly altered and abridged. The previous dispatch to Sturgis is invented.

The Crow stitch employed by Bannocks for beading—Information from Koch, p. 54.

The fate of Mrs. Denoille (1867)—Michno, pp. 280–81, 288, 325–26.

"And they shall rebuild the ruined cities . . ."—Amos 9.14–15, slightly altered and abridged.

Moccasins from bacon-burlap—Redington, "Scouting in Montana," p. 18.

Wages of Chinese gold miners: ten cents to two dollars a day—Wikoff, p. 39.

Catalogue of Pollock's children—Pollock, p. 94.

Howard would have sent Spurgin and the wagons away the day before (for narrative reasons) I pretended that he did.

Crook's movements against the Nez Perce—Ibid., pp. 203–5.

Redington's view—After a visit to Sunlight Picnic Area, Crandall Creek, Wyoming, in August 2010.

Now Is the Time for Steelhead to Die

White Thunder's WYAKIN's grizzly-rescue—McWhorter, *Yellow Wolf,* p. 184.

The abandonment of Kapoochas—McWhorter, *Hear Me,* p. 405.

Joseph's Goose Is Finally Cooked

Redington's contact with Sturgis's French-Canadian scout—Actually, Redington was not alone, and it was not he who rode back to report the good news to Howard. But the incident is told by him, in Wilfong, p. 328.

Description of the spot where the Nez Perce was murdered—After a visit to Dead Indian Canyon, Wyoming, in August 2010.

The murder of the Nez Perce, and the concealment of his scalping from Howard—Described by Fisher, in Wilfong, p. 330. I have altered some details. For instance, it was Fletcher, not Wilkinson, who accompanied Howard, and (so Fisher claims) the Nez Perce was actually shot by a trooper named Sumner.

When the Thistles Are Blooming Purple

"her elder sister-wife"—Not the best description of the relationship, but Aoki's word, "co-wife," sounds too clinical.

Description of Broken Tooth—After Gulick, p. 230 ("A survivor of the Big Hole Battle . . . ," probably In-Who-Lise).

Peopeo's woodpecker-head—Mentioned in his ms., p. 5 (?).

"If we kill one Bluecoat, a thousand more will take his place . . ."—Actually, White Thunder, quoted in Carson, p. 152.

The narrow canyon route through which the Nez Perce outwitted Sturgis does not appear to be exactly known despite Wilfong's assertions; see Greene, p. 111. Landscape descriptions in this section and the next are after a journey toward Belfry, passing through the Bearstooth Mountains and then down into Wyoming toward Heart Mountain, August 2010.

Bad Boy's [Ilatakut's] help—Greene, *Nez Perce Summer,* p. 113.

Lean Elk's instructions to the warriors—Invented by WTV. However, Carson writes (p. 198) that dragging sticks behind the horses to make a dust cloud was Lean Elk's idea.

Victory

The dead horses and mules en route—Information from Howard, *Nez Perce Joseph,* p. 254.

Fletcher's fatigue—Loc. cit.

"Gonna call this the Devil's Doorway."—Information from Carson, p. 272, fn. 15.

"Don't use up your horses. Keep them fresh for the shock."—Information from the *Britannica,* 11th ed. (1910), vol. V (Calhoun to Chatelaine), p. 568 (entry on Cavalry).

"when my stretch of America extended not much farther than from the library to the Riding-Hall . . ."—Some of this flashback is indebted to: Oregon State Historical Society, Mss. 800, C. E. S. Wood papers, box 1, folder 18, excerpts from 1912–1916? autobiography.

The Optimistic Scout

Description of Clark's Fork River—After a visit there in August 2010.

Crow name for Clark's Fork River: Rotten Sun Dance River—Leforge, p. 143.

I Would Give a Thousand Dollars

The German's situation—Greene, *Nez Perce Summer,* p. 212; Howard, *Nez Perce Joseph,* p. 251.

Indian sign for Nez Perce—W. P. Clark, p. 269.

Description of the crimson-beaded crupper on the Crow's horse—After an illustration in Horse Capture and Her Many Horses, p. 26.

Description of Crow procedure: chopping plug tobacco and mixing with kinnikinnick—After Leforge, p. 162. For definition of kinnikinnick, see Glossary 6.

"Everything has to be met with courage . . ."—Somewhat after OHS Wood papers, Hayek.

"As keen-eyed as an Apache"—Apache eyesight is extolled in Sladen, p. 74.

Description of the country in which Howard and Sturgis met—From a visit to Belfry, Montana, in August 2010. Wilfong (p. 337) informs us that Howard "camped on the Clarks Fork a few miles south of Belfry on the evening of September 11 . . ."

"poor as I am I'd give a thousand dollars if I hadn't left that place!"—Almost verbatim from Greene, loc. cit.

"commanders who obey orders and execute them promptly and on time."—Closely after Sherman, p. 559 (in fact, he said this regarding his appointment of Howard to lead the Army of the Tennessee).

Description of Sturgis "in his wide sloping hat . . ."—After Coleman, p. 127 (photoportrait of Sturgis).

Captain Winters's weeping wife—Information from Pollock, pp. 26–27.

Howard's paragraph of remarks on the paternal system *vs.* the martinet system—Somewhat after his *Autobiography*, vol. 1, p. 94.

Description of Professor Mahan's jacket—After a painting reproduced in Ron Field, *Forts of the American Frontier 1820–91: Central and Northern Plains*, ill. Adam Hook (Oxford, U.K.: Osprey Publishing Ltd., 2005; Fortress ser., no. 28), p. 14.

The smile on the dead Custer's face—After Coleman, p. 21. Bradley says much the same (p. 173), but does not express himself clearly as to whether Custer was scalped. That story gets told both ways. It seems that most of the corpses were stripped and many were scalped.

Sturgis's memory of Little Big Horn—After a visit there in August 2010.

"misled by some treacherous Crows."—Howard, *Nez Perce Joseph*, p. 255 (Howard's words, not Sturgis's).

Howard's instructions to Sturgis and Fletcher re: pursuing Joseph—Somewhat after Howard, *Report—In the Field*, p. 44, expanded and embellished by WTV.

"*Waty maua athauin hanaka JESUS hiwayam . . .*"—Axtell, Hymn No. 10 ("Down Life's Dark Vale We Wander").

Guy and Wood's disappointment about staying behind—Howard, op. cit., p. 256.

And Quickly Riding to Some Farther Place

Description of the Yellowstone crossing—After a visit to Riverside Park, Laurel, Montana, in August 2010.

Description of buffalo gnats in late summer—After Humfreville, p. 436.

Description of the Huckleberry Feast—After Relander, p. 72.

Description of WOWSHUXLUH—Loc. cit.

"north of the Swift River . . . where summer hailstones can kill even horses"—Information from Leforge, p. 282. One such hailstorm occurred in the summer of 1877.

Incident of White Thunder and Wild Oat Moss against the whites—McWhorter, *Yellow Wolf*, pp. 182–84.

Crow name for the head of the Musselshell—Linderman, p. 54.

Traditional isolation of a Nez Perce girl at menarche—*Handbook of North American Indians*, vol. 12, p. 423 (Nez Perce entry).

Close Action

The project of Theodore Bland—Information from Ekirch, p. 117.

Trimble's lye-soaked bran treatment (the horse will sniffle it out of his nose if the only thing wrong with him is a cold)—Coleman, p. 158.

Fletcher's dispatch: Sturgis engages Joseph at Canyon Creek—After Howard, *Report—In the Field*, pp. 46–47.

Fingernail Noises

Description of the landscapes of the stagecoach robbery and of Brockway's, Cochran's and Coulson's ranches—From a visit in August 2010 and August 2012 to Josephine Lake and neighboring sites around Billings, Montana, where these incidents occurred. Ditto for the Sacrifice Caves.

Murder policy: Sleeping Snake women—Information from McWhorter, *Hear Me*, p. 27.

Occurrences surrounding the same—Greene, *Nez Perce Summer,* pp. 214–15. The identities of the raiders (based on McWhorter's notes) are given in the same, p. 444 n. 46.

"a boom summer for hoppers"—Information from Bond ms., p. 8.

In Which We Learn That Our Grandfather Still Loves Us

"They are coming to fight, COLD WEATHER GIRL . . ."—Aoki and Walker, p. 63.

Description of SHE WHO WATCHES—After a photograph in Leighton, p. 45, whose discussion informs my brief discussion of this entity in Glossary 2.

Description of the Canyon Creek battlefield—After a visit there in August 2010—which is to say: Up out of Laurel over the swale, past the veterans' graveyard, and suddenly into mesa country which but for its angularity resembles the far off Umatilla lands where Smohalla and his River Renegades first incited Joseph to commence his murders, rainclouds on the left, white cumuli and blue sky on the right, left, right, left, right, Sturgis hurrying us on to make good our previous indiscretion; and crossing the horizon of orange-and-silver mesas, we bear toward the rainclouds, along the Buffalo Trail, then down into a wide and shallow yellow valley which someday we shall plow and shave, toward the greenish-grey buttes ahead—but the valley is wider than it looked, although buttes are easy—or are they? As we ride closer, the tiny shrubs which crown them grow into pine trees. Between two buttes, left and right, a cañon's mouth opens. And now the Nez Perce begin to shoot at us, from hidden rocks up under the clouds.

Basic events of Canyon Creek battle—Somewhat after McWhorter, *Yellow Wolf,* pp. 185–94; Greene, *Nez Perce Summer,* pp. 228–30.

The trooper with pipe and fishing rod (Benteen)—Greene, *Nez Perce Summer,* p. 227.

The fate of Shore Crossing's buffalo rifle—Ibid., p. 450 (fn. 90).

Identification of silver-faced beads with Crows—Koch, p. 63.

Most Extraordinary and Praiseworthy Efforts

"Our advance is having a running fight with Joseph over twenty miles . . ."—Abbreviated from Howard, *Report—In the Field,* p. 47.

"it seems as if SATAN is striving . . ."—Somewhat after Howard, *Autobiography,* vol. 2, p. 470.

Guy's experiment with the mule-mounted howitzer—Ibid., p. 15.

The Nez Perce herd at Cañon Creek: twenty-five hundred head of horses—Redington, "Scouting in Montana," p. 7.

Description of General Sheridan—After a photo in Philbrick (insert following p. 70).

"But once Miles strikes diagonally across our front . . ."—Much after Howard, *Nez Perce Joseph,* p. 258.

"Our government [uncapitalized in original] should become a machine . . ."—*The Annals of America,* vol. 9, p. 433 (no. 101, William Tecumseh Sherman, letter to his brother, August 3, 1863).

Now Perhaps It Is Too Late

Events between Canyon Creek and the Musselshell—McWhorter, *Hear Me,* pp. 465–68; *Yellow Wolf,* pp. 187–94. Neither one of these sources mentions the Nez Perce attack on the Mountain Crow village. Nerburn does (p. 202), although his book, like mine, is not always literally accurate. For instance, he presents Looking-Glass's visit to the Crows as a certain fact (p. 188).

The Crow term *wolfing:* Leforge, p. 230.

The SUNdisk-ornament—After an illustration in Horse Capture and Her Many Horses, p. 35 (Crow).

White Bird to Looking-Glass: "Until now I looked at the Crows as my own flesh . . ."—Rhetoric a little after Wood diary, 1878, p. 30 (remarks of Chief Moses, who was not talking about Crows; much altered and embellished).

Keeper of the Pipe—A Crow conception.

"To be killed by Crows and then dragged behind a horse"—Procedure from Leforge, p. 182.

Description of the silhouetted Crow seen by Swan Necklace—After illustration in Kavanagh, p. 33 ("A Vanishing Race [Gray Bull] [Crow]").

"Crows with their .50-calibre breechloaders"—Information from Vaughn, p. 22.

Crows as "the Women Nation"—Howard et al., p. 224 (McDonald).

White Bird's wolfskin cap—Mentioned as in Chapman's possession in 1878, in Pearson, p. 88.

Attack on the Mountain Crows—Greene, *Nez Perce Summer,* p. 135 (information from Redington). It is surprising that McWhorter never mentions this incident.

As Good as a Circus

Some events in this chapter are based on Howard, *Nez Perce Joseph*, pp. 256–62. Howard first crossed the Yellowstone (ahead of most of his command) at dawn on the 14th. He then remained camped in the area until his troops had caught up on the 16th.

Parker's drowning—Information from Zimmer, p. 31 (April 2nd).

"Surgeon Charles T. Alexander has given complete satisfaction."—Abbreviated from Howard, *Report— In the Field*, Appendix: "Officers and Enlisted Men Specially Commended . . . ," p. 6.

Treatment of erysipelas—Crook, p. 8 (describing his own condition).

Description of the soldiers crossing the Yellowstone—Somewhat after a Guy Howard drawing, "Crossing the Yellowstone river," in the Grace Howard Gray Scrapbook, folder labeled "14" and "1/12."

The Indian sign for woman—A combination of "female" plus "height." W. P. Clark, pp. 171, 407. Sometimes the copulation sign was also used to convey the female gender.

Boulder-whiteness of Custer massacre corpses—Humfreville, p. 369 (observation of Captain Weir).

Even If I Must Forgo the Credit

Crow name for the morning star—Linderman, p. 127.

Captain Fisher's latest Nez Perce souvenir—Invented by WTV after information in Koch, p. 141.

"Bad lands, you say . . ."—After Howard, *Famous Indian Chiefs*, pp. 338–39.

That Officer Will Get Promoted

Howard's instructions to his men: Two parties to seek Miles—Howard, *Among Our Hostile Indians*, p. 297.

"Had Cushing been at Clark's Fork . . ."—The first sentence is almost verbatim, slightly abbreviated, from Howard's report to the Secretary of War, in Helen Addison Howard, p. 307. The rest is invented in light of this source's explication.

Publication of Wood's sketch of Dead Mule Trail—Information from Venn, p. 307. It was a cover illustration, revised by others, which appeared on 29 September. I have no idea when Wood and Howard actually learned about it.

"That officer will get promoted . . ."—After Howard, *Autobiography*, vol. 1, p. 187.

Description of Miles in a stretcher holding his neck-wound closed—Howard, *Autobiography*, vol. 1, p. 342.

Incident of the dying Confederate soldier—Ibid., pp. 240–41.

"He's the first professor I have had to follow . . ."—This and half the next sentence (with obscenities added by WTV) much after Pollock, p. 94 (letter dated at Camp on the Yellowstone below Clark's Fork, Montana, September 16).

Howard's happy returns to Pollock—His fifty-eighth birthday fell on September 17.

Description of the four soldiers and the dead horse—After Paul L. Hedren, *With Crook in the Black Hills: Stanley J. Morrow's 1876 Photographic Legacy* (Boulder, Colorado: Pruett Publishing Co., 1985), p. 18 (figure 9: Soldiers Cutting Up Abandoned Horse).

"good nature is the best contribution . . ."—Somewhat after *The Journals of Josiah Gorgas 1857–1878*, ed. Sarah Woolfolk Wiggins (Tuscaloosa: University of Alabama Press, 1995), p. 5 (Jany 12th, [1857]).

Howard's definition of discipline—Verbatim from the *Britannica*, 11th ed. (1910), vol. V (Calhoun to Chatelaine), entry on Cavalry; p. 524.

Bessie's Birthday

Howard's belief that the Crows helped the Nez Perce to escape Sturgis at Yellowstone—Information, or hearsay, from Theodore W. Goldin, *A Bit of the Nez Perce Campaign*, ed. E. A. Brininstool and John M. Carroll (Bryan, Texas: privately printed, 1978; orig. wr. 1927), p. 12. Goldin served with Sturgis at Canyon Creek. It is natural that he would have sought to lighten the discredit which stained his commander after the Nez Perces hoodwinked him.

Information on women's and children's fur goods—*Saint Louis Dispatch*, number 221, Tuesday evening, January 4, 1876, front page, advertisement from D. Crawford & Co.

Decline of weaving and spinning in 1870s—See Schlereth, p. 89 (case study of Savage family).

River Season

"O-pumohat Kyai-is-i-sak-ta," according to the Central Montana Museum, Lewistown, is the local name for the Musselshell River. The museum's obviously Anglicized transliteration functions here to accentuate the difference between this language and Nimiputumít.

Old Joseph's buffalo-hunting in Judith Basin—Information somewhat after Pollock, p. 6.

"O-to-kur-tuk-tai," again according to the Central Montana Museum, Lewistown, is the local name for the Judith River and Mountains.

"twenty years ago . . . one could kill many hundred buffalo here" in the Judith River country—Information from Gulick, p. 115 (re: 1855).

The phrase "River Season" and its time and meaning are all simplified (and slightly embellished into something like a seasonal name) from Aoki, p. 537.

The tale of Arrowhead—McWhorter, *Hear Me*, p. 269.

"Two Eyes Place"—My invention. I did see a pair of caves like this, overlooking the Yellowstone not far from Custer, Montana, in August 2012.

Description of Pompey's Pillar—After a visit there in August 2010.

Sitting Bull: "the white men are all liars."—Stanley Vestal, *Sitting Bull, Champion of the Sioux: A Biography* (Norman: University of Oklahoma Press, The Civilization of the American Indian ser., n. 46, 1957 rev. ed.; orig. pr. 1956), p. 192.

Old Joseph: "it is all talk, and nothing coming."—Almost verbatim from Baird, Mallickan and Swagerty, p. 24.

The Crow girls' horse song—Somewhat after Elizabeth Atwood Lawrence, *Hoofbeats and Society: Studies of Human-Horse Interactions* (Bloomington: Indiana University Press, 1985), p. 48.

It Certainly Is a Lovely Stream

Description of the landscape between Canyon Creek and the Musselshell—After a trip in August 2010.

"it certainly is a lovely stream . . ."—Much abbreviated and somewhat altered from Wilfong, p. 354 (Redington).

The death of Glass—Information from Greene, *Nez Perce Summer*, p. 366 (Appendix A: U.S. Army Casualties, IV).

Events of 4 February 1865—After Howard, *Autobiography*, vol. 2, p. 109.

The sinking of Sturgis's supply steamer—Greene, *Nez Perce Summer*, p. 207.

Custer's doings on the Musselshell, 1873—Information from George Armstrong Custer, p. xxv (intro. by Edgar I. Stewart).

Distance of Tongue River from Fort Buford, by steamboat and stage—See citation to Glossary 3 (Places), entry for Tongue River.

Regulation distance of orderlies from officers—After Elizabeth Custer, p. 145.

The goiterousness of Snake Indians—Alleged in Humfreville, p. 207.

Description of "the beadwork which frames certain Sioux saddleblankets"—After an illustration in Horse Capture and Her Many Horses, p. 24.

Role of "I" Company in carrying away some officers' bodies from Little Big Horn—Zimmer, p. 67 ([June] 26th).

The rule about dated Indian service vouchers—National Archives microfilm M1121. Roll 5: Miscellaneous Circulars, 1854–1885. Circular [unnumbered]. Department of the Interior, Office of Indian Affairs, Washington, D.C., August 15, 1874. Effective as of September 1, 1874.

Description of Paiute women winnowing grass-seed—Information from Scott, p. 3.

"OUR BOYS IN BLUE, WE GO FOR HAYES"—Sullivan, p. 435 (lithograph).

Prevalence of buffalo—"From the Musselshell on north it was almost impossible to look anywhere without seeing bunches of buffalo."—Redington, "Scouting in Montana," p. 17.

The McKay stitching machine—According to Schlereth (p. 56), this device was being used in 1862 in Lynn, Massachusetts. Let's say that Delia Theller was eight years old then. So she would have been born in about 1854, making her twenty-three in 1877.

Perfumes for three cents (1876 prices)—Schlereth, p. 84.

"working off the soft material"—Crook, p. 76.

Wilkinson's birthday—He was born on 14 November 1835.

A Mighty Interesting Woman I Have to Say

Sturgis's son's shirt after Little Big Horn—Information after Camp, p. 87 (Charles DeRudio, February 2, 1910).

Anecdote about Sheridan and the Indian ponies—Information from Carroll and Baxter, p. 108.

Relative to Abstract "N"

The use of Abstract "N"—Information from Kautz, p. 183.

Miles to Howard: "Do not let anything influence you . . ."—Quoted in Wooster, p. 101.

"Dear Miles, there is no one here . . ."—Much after Howard's reply to Miles, loc. cit.

The high-value monte games at Gillem's Camp—Woodhead, p. 115 (April 5, 1873).

Howard and Sherman just before the Battle of Ezra Church—After Howard, *Autobiography*, vol. 2, pp. 19–26.

VII. Detached Pictures

Epigraph: " . . . at this late life I cannot strengthen my early stories . . ."—McWhorter, *Hear Me*, p. 32.

Epigraph: "You can only get suggestive glimpses . . ."—Howard, *Nez Perce Joseph*, p. 121.

A Call Against the Wind

The growth of an officer's post-promotion knowledge—Closely after description of Burnside's promotion, in Howard, *Autobiography*, vol. 1, p. 324.

The situation at Delaware Creek, Republican River, September 1868—Information from George Armstrong Custer, pp. 139–40.

Description of Howard's father's call to him, sickness and death—Events, and a few phrases, from Howard, *Autobiography*, vol. 1, p. 14.

"a tribe of Indians usually takes its character from the head-chief . . ."—Somewhat after Howard, *Famous Indian Chiefs*, p. 314.

Perry's memory of "that April night in '68 in the Malheur country"—Information from Michno, p. 308.

Orders regarding First Cavalry—Information from Howard, *Report—In the Field*, p. 54.

Lean Elk and the *Lucky Man*

Capture of the Crow horse-thief—Information from Nerburn, p. 202.

Description of the landscape between the Musselshell and Reese Fort [the Ur-Lewiston], of Reese Fort itself, and of the mountains north of Lewiston—After a trip in August 2010.

Peopeo Tholekt: "A Boston's promise runs away like a river. It flies away like a strong wind."—Closely after Peopeo Tholekt/Sam Lott, p. 8.

"Yellowstone River buffalo at lump weight, four cents a pound"—Almost verbatim from Bond ms., p. 4.

Description of the landscape from the Judith Basin to Cow Island—After a trip from Roy to Winifred, Montana, then from Winifred toward Cow Island on the Missouri, August 2012 (most of the Wilfong route, 1–2 miles past the West Bottom sign).

Description of the darkstriped Blackfoot tipi—After Kavanagh, p. 143 ("Blackfoot Camp at Two Medicine Lake, Glacier National Park, W 3540").

Shallow Place—My invented name for the ford at Cow Island.

"the sky not yet black with Canada geese flying south"—Information from Bond ms., p. 9. He did see the sky blacken this way about a month later, when he flatboated some Nez Perce prisoners of war down this river.

Buffalo gallstones for yellow paint—Information from Koch, p. 26.

White Thunder's four new horses—McWhorter, *Yellow Wolf*, p. 197.

Joseph's stirrups made by Good Woman—Pearson, p. 285.

Looking-Glass's Medicine bundle—My description is based (I hope fittingly) on a Crow example, in Molloy Tribal Art et al.

The river "thick with dead and dying grasshoppers"—Bond ms., p. 8. This actually happened on the Missouri several weeks later that year.

Events at Cow Island (really, Cow Creek on the north shore)—McWhorter, *Yellow Wolf*, pp. 197–202; Greene, *Nez Perce Summer*, pp. 236–38. The non-treaties crossed the river at about 2:00 in the afternoon, and

while "two of the Nez Perces" (whom I have imagined to be Bunched Lightning and Looking-Glass) parleyed with the garrison, "the procession moved two miles away and went into camp."
Deaths of Sun Tied's wife, midwife and baby—Aubrey L. Haines, p. 56.
Episode of the whiskey at Cow Island—Helen Addison Howard, p. 309.
Events between Cow Island and Bear's Paw inclusive; the change in leadership—Somewhat after Mc-Whorter, *Hear Me*, pp. 469; however, this source states that Looking-Glass took over on 24 September, the very first day out of Cow Island. For narrative purposes I have made this occur slightly later.
The enemy chief's horned headdress—After Kavanagh, p. 158 ("Hawk Feather [Assiniboine], W3621").
The sagebrush from the Salmon River—Hart, p. 93, says that this unidentified species was used to make a tea against tuberculosis.
Murder of the lone Boston (between Birch and Eagle creeks)—Greene, *Nez Perce Summer*, p. 241. The branded brown and white pinto was actually seen by a white observer a day or two earlier, and the brand was different (ibid., p. 242).
"I have done my best . . ."—Much altered from McWhorter, *Hear Me*, pp. 473–74.
Information on Nez Perce hairpieces—Koch, p. 94.

Rosette Portraits

Howard's instructions to Miller—Information from Howard, *Report—In the Field*, p. 55.
Details about the layout of the "Benton"—Information from Trobriand, p. 20 (Tuesday, August 6, 1867), who describes "a plan that is uniform with all the vessels that navigate the Mississipi and the Missouri."
Death of Howard's father—This episode follows the *Autobiography*, with embellishments. Poor Howard really seems to have gone through life imagining that he brought on or substantially contributed to his father's final illness.

Wilkinson Waits

The pies from Skookum's bakery—Wikoff, p. 54.

Back in Time

Names of men killed by Nez Perces at Cow Island—Adkison, p. 13.
Joseph's projected course "between the Bear's Paw Mountains and the Little Rockies"—Information from McWhorter, *Hear Me*, p. 476.
"churning up the shallow water like buttermilk."—Simile from Bond ms., p. 5.
The ride from Cow Island to Miles—Howard, *Report—In the Field*, pp. 55–56. In fact Miles and some horsemen met Howard's party on the trail the night of their arrival.
The litter left behind by the Nez Perce pillagers, and the dead Negro courier—Redington, "Scouting in Montana," pp. 11–12.
The game with Sladen in Peloncillo Mountains—Information from Sladen, p. 50.
Funeral procedures for Brooks—Based on a service for one of Crook's soldiers in 1876, in Vaughn, p. 16. However, Wilkinson did not read Brooks's burial service; it was actually Mason. See *The Soldiers' Side*, p. 99 (Colonel J. W. Redington, "Story of Bugler Brooks").
Wood's childhood memories: Uncle Phil & c—Based on OHS Wood documents; autobiographical transcriptions.
The bracelet of rosette portraits of Lincoln, Sheridan and Stoneman—Sullivan, p. 303.

So Near the Medicine Line

Description of the camp at Snake Creek (Place of the Manure Fires)—After visits there in August 2012 and March 2013.
"old rings of tipi stones" and (in next chapter) "the scaring-stones on the eastern rise where other People . . . once drove buffalo"—Montana Historical Society Archives. 978.615 An239L 2005. Andy Anderson, Box 1229, Chinook, MT 59523, "Nez Perce Trail Cow Island Landing to Bear Battlefield . . ." Local Battlefield History 1902–1996. Field and Research Notes. Unnumbered typescript reads: "East of the Battlefield [*sic*] on Henry Gordon's land, we discovered a buffalo drive lane which was possibly used in the time before the Indians had horses to lead the bison to a cliff or to an ambush kill." Anderson also mentions the "ancient tipi rings of stone."
"Certain best men, sent ahead . . ."—Information from McWhorter, *Hear Me*, p. 478.

Events from here to the surrender—Based in part on the same source, pp. 478–507; Greene, *Nez Perce Summer*, pp. 260–318.

Joseph: "We have made our freedom!"—Heinmot Tooyalakekt in Helen Addison Howard, p. 213: "I sat down in a fat and beautiful country. I had won my freedom and the freedom of my people . . . We were in a land where we would not be forced to live in a place we did not want. I believed that if I could remain safe at a distance and talk straight . . . I could get back the Wallowa Valley and return in peace . . ."

The few tipis—McWhorter claims (ibid., p. 478) that "only an occasional canvas shelter" was available, but the painted scene at the Bear's Paw battlefield shows tipis, and White Thunder alludes to green lodgepoles.

Layout of the village—Greene, *Nez Perce Summer*, pp. 261–62.

Bear's Paw as the creation site of the Crows—*Handbook of Nothern American Indians*, vol. 13, p. 695 (Fred W. Voget, entry on Crow).

Experience of Helping Another, Good Woman and Cloudburst—Somewhat after Helping Another's testimony in McWhorter, *Hear Me*, pp. 508–9.

I have never butchered a buffalo, but I have had some practice when it comes to cows, pigs and chickens—knowledge employed in the description of the women preparing buffalo at Bear's Paw.

"the youngest child can often see what is hidden from the others"—Information from Walker and Matthews, p. 202.

White Bird: "My heart is sad that we kept no scouts . . ."—Abridged and much reworded from Howard et al., p. 269 (McDonald).

White Bird on Looking-Glass: "Looking-Glass is worse than nothing . . ."—Invented, but not entirely implausible since those two were probably at loggerheads and the latter had just brought disaster upon them one more time.

The first enemy: A Cheyenne on a spotted horse—So seen by Young White Bird, in McWhorter, *Hear Me*, p. 479.

It Cannot Seem Right

Description of the Bear's Paw battlefield—After visits in August 2012 and February 2013—the latter perhaps approximating conditions in October 1877, thanks to my era's warmer temperatures.

Joseph's farewell to his daughter, and his return to the camp—After Howard et al., pp. 293–94 (Joseph).

Description of Joseph "gazing directly" at his daughter for the last time—After Montana Historical Society Photo Archive negative 955–971.

Cloudburst brings a horse to Ollokot at Cottonwood—McWhorter, *Hear Me*, p. 288.

Two Moons's circuits of the camp—Wilfong, p. 383 (testimony of Two Moon [she spells it without the "s"]).

Death of Red Owl—He was wounded or killed at Bear's Paw. Howard et al., p. 224 (McDonald).

Description of the yellow-and-black-painted Cheyenne scout—After Hook, p. 19 (Wooden Leg).

Toohhoolhoolzote's hat: After information from Koch (p. 96) about Nez Perce war dress: "the entire skin of a wolf's head . . ."

Description of the Cheyenne warrior named Two Moons—After a photo in Kavanagh, p. 57 ("Two Moons [Northern Cheyenne]").

Red Rock Place—My invented name for the bluff of red rock where Toohhoolhoolzote and the five warriors were killed.

Description of Swan Woman—After a photo in Gulick, p. 239 ("Yellow Wolf's mother").

"White Thunder . . . remembers Wallowa Lake"—Information from McWhorter, *Yellow Wolf*, p. 212.

Numbers of non-treaty Nez Perces in Joseph's (invented) speech: McWhorter estimates "about six hundred" at the beginning of the war, while Howard estimates seven hundred (*Hear Me*, p. 185, fn. 27). Probably Howard was more correct, since 418 surrendered, and perhaps 233 (about 70 at the beginning, around 100 during the siege, and 50 with White Bird) fled the Bear's Paw battlefield (ibid., pp. 313, 499), which is around 600 in total; and Greene calculates that between 96 and 145 of them died during the war (*Nez Perce Summer*, p. 350). Hence I have taken an initial seven hundred to be a reasonable figure. (Greene in *Beyond Bear's Paw* [p. 48] proposes 700 people including 250 warriors.) It seems plausible that Joseph would have discussed the casualty rate with his young men, and employed round numbers.

White Bird "has scarcely fought until now . . ."—Information from McWhorter, *Hear Me*, p. 185. Many Wounds claims he did not fight at all, but since White Bird Canyon was in his own home territory, and his young men began the war, I suspect that he must have at least done a bit of generalling.

I See You've Studied Geography

Howard's contingent actually arrived on the night of October 4, but since he plays so conspicuous a part in this novel, I thought to please his shade by having him arrive on the morning of that day, so that he could observe operations and jawbone about them in his inimitable (although I have imitated it) fashion.

Description of Miles and his outfit—After Greene, *Nez Perce Summer,* pp. 263–64 (testimony by "two civilian guides").

Miles to Howard: "We have the Indians corralled down yonder . . ."—After Wooster, p. 105.

Age and birthday of Miles's daughter Cecilia (born September 1869)—Wooster, p. 59. As for her learning to ride on a captured Kiowa pony, we learn from p. 69 that the animal Miles first intended for her died. I imagine he would have gotten her another.

Dialogue between Howard and Miles: Sitting Bull—Based on words by Miles to others, and other general information, all in Wooster, pp. 88, 84–85.

Cheyennes as "the finest species of wild men in the world"—Closely after Humfreville, p. 240.

Number of buffalo near Tongue River (1881 figures, so in 1877 there might have been even more)—Sandoz, p. 345. In 1882 the buffalo were still being shot there for meat (loc. cit.).

Description of Baird's buffalo-skin coat—After a fine one I saw on display at Fort Walsh, Saskatchewan, in 2012.

Sturgis's losses at Antietam—Crook, p. 98.

"Too late, Sammy, too late!"—Ibid., p. 94.

Range figures on the Parrott gun—Philip Katcher, *The Civil War Source Book* (New York: Facts on File, 1982), pp. 304–5.

Deaths of Haddo, Geogehgan, Peshall, Irving—Information from Greene, *Nez Perce Summer,* p. 368 (Appendix A: U.S. Army Casualties, IV).

Guy's admiration for Miles—I have imagined this, but it is plausible. Wooster (p. 89) remarks on Miles's nearly suicidal bravery against Crazy Horse.

Captain John and Old George's daughters in Joseph's band—Information from Oregon Historical Society, Mss. 800, C. E. S. Wood, Box 1, folder 12, "Excerpts from 1925 autobiography re: Nez Perce Campaign . . . ," p. 4.

Miles's detention of Joseph—See Greene, *Nez Perce Joseph,* pp. 297–300. I took a middle course in my relation of the event. Nez Perce sources (e.g., McWhorter, *Yellow Wolf,* p. 217) claim that Joseph was hobbled and kept with the mules. Joseph himself discreetly avoided details of the incident, perhaps because he hoped for Miles's help in returning from the Indian Territory. Wood (who hated Miles) says: "The account that General Miles hobbled Joseph and had him coraled with the mules until after the surrender is absolute rot . . ." OHS Wood papers, folder 12, letter to Harry Howard, February 20, 1942.

Our Dread of This Day

Joseph's memory of the South Wallowas—After a visit there in August 2013.

Joseph to Miles: "It is good to talk straight . . ."—Much after Gulick, p. 107 (speech of Old Joseph, 1855), abridged.

Description of Miles's Cheyenne interpreter—After the frontispiece in Kavanagh (W 3602: White Hawk, Northern Cheyenne).

Details of the exchange of Joseph for Lieutenant Jerome—Holland Library, Washington State University, Pullman; ms. 1218 (CM Brewster/Peopeo Tholekt), pp. 3–4.

"I am a warrior, not a woman, and I say let us fight to-day."—Actually said by Kamiakin in 1856. Ruby and Brown, p. 156.

Description of the two treaty Nez Perces: "weary and bloody as we are"—In Moynihan, Armitage and Dichamp, pp. 223–24 (Mary Ronan), Old George (there called Captain George) is portrayed (six months later) as "a grim, bruised, battered-looking man with a soiled and bloody-looking bandana around his forehead."

Dialogue between Looking-Glass and White Bird: "Heinmot Tooyalakekt has completed his heart . . ."—Much reworded from Howard et al., p. 271 (McDonald).

Looking-Glass to Joseph: "Hear me! . . . We are older than you . . ." + Joseph's response and Looking-Glass's answer—Somewhat after McWhorter, *Hear Me,* p. 495 (altered and embellished).

White Bird: "I shall never surrender to a deceitful white chief . . ."—Almost verbatim from the same.

My version of the surrender negotiations is much telescoped.

Joseph gives Wottolen "his nice old Indian things" (as the original puts it) before the surrender—Brewster/Peopeo Tholekt, p. 18.

Joseph gives Wottolen the small red wool blanket from Captain Lewis—Washington State University Libraries, Pullman. Holland Library Archives. Cage 4681. Lot, Sam (Chief Peo-peo-Tah-Likt or [*sic*] Chief Many Wounds. Historical Sketches of the Nez Perces, 1935), p. 12.

Description of the Blackfoot coup-stick—After an illustration in Horse Capture and Her Many Horses, p. 39.

Many Wounds refuses to forgive Joseph for surrendering—Pearson, p. 136.

Toohhoolhoolzote: "When I was born, I grew to be a boy . . ."—Abbreviated from his speech of the winter council, in McWhorter, *Hear Me*, p. 163.

How to Earn a Star

Dialogue between Howard and Miles, Howard and Wood—Closely after Greene, *Nez Perce Summer*, p. 482, fn. 87 (testimony of Wood).

"Take heed to thyself . . ."—Exodus 34.12–13.

Joseph's dress at the surrender—Pearson, p. 52, with the addition of the black-striped grey blanket, which Wood remembered.

Joseph's approach—Somewhat after OHS Wood files, excerpts from 1925 autobiography, re: Nez Perce Campaign . . . , p. 4.

Incident with Lame Deer—Zimmer, p. 49 (May 7th). Shrenger was Miles's orderly.

Description of Cochise—After a photo in Sladen, p. 63.

Joseph's surrender speech—A somewhat syncretic excerpt, taken from the famous "official" version, translated by Chapman (which Wood almost certainly embellished and in parts may have invented; his field-notes do not survive, and what we have he wrote down many years later, saying: "much reflection has brought to my mind what I believe to be a clear memory of the speech" [OHS Wood files, excerpts from 1925 autobiography, re: Nez Perce Campaign . . . , p. 3]); and the version in McWhorter, *Hear Me*, p. 498. Wood (op. cit., p. 4) notes that some of the surrender negotiations were kept secret from him and the other soldiers. Wood stood waiting with his memorandum pad, but the general did not call him over, so that all the rest of his life he would wonder whether the general, or perhaps Miles, who so handily manipulated him, preferred for there to be no written record of any proposals or promises to Joseph. I hope this was not so. Anyhow, if you like, see the official surrender speech of Chief Joseph—"translated from the Nez Percé by Arthur Chapman, in Herbert J. Spinden's 'The Nez Percé Indians,' Memoirs of the American Anthropological Association, Vol. II, Part 3, 1903, p. 243." This citation and the speech itself both appear in John Bierhorst, ed., *In the Trail of the Wind: American Indian Poems and Ritual Orations* (New York: Farrar, Straus & Giroux: A Sunburst Book/Michael di Capua Books, 1971), pp. 194 and 153, respectively.

"Disease and starvation make wild Indians grow rapidly old in appearance."—Somewhat after Sladen, p. 31. Of course he was speaking of Apaches. But ain't all them reds the same?

No one agrees regarding whom Joseph offered his rifle to, or who accepted it.

Maggie Manuel's allegation: Joseph murdered her mother and brother—Elliott West, *The Last Indian War: The Nez Perce Story* (New York: Oxford University Press, 2009), p. 127. The girl might have fabricated this, since her mother's bones were never found in the burned house.

"Wood, take charge of Chief Joseph . . ."—Verbatim from Wood, op. cit., p. 6.

"Rather a forlorn procession of Indians . . ." + following 3 lines—Somewhat after Howard, *Among Our Hostile Indians*, p. 299.

Howard's recollection of Sherman's laughter at rebel prisoners—From Sherman, p. 670.

"nauseated by the shrivelled faces of these old Indian squaws"—Libbie Custer said she was.

The copper medal depicting Lincoln and Johnson—Sullivan, p. 271. Like the Nez Perce child's foot in the text below, this object never to my knowledge actually appeared at Bear's Paw.

Ad Chapman's tally of captured horses, and the count-off to Indian scouts—Information from Pearson, p. 49.

Looking-Glass answers insolently at Lapwai—Somewhat after Howard, *Famous Indian Chiefs*, p. 192.

Aggregate casualties at Gettysburg *vs.* Waterloo—Somewhat after OOH papers, "Warfare of the future," p. 17.

I Shouldn't Be Surprised If General Sherman Changed His Mind

"I often hear the expression *American* . . ."—Nearly verbatim from Howard, *Autobiography*, vol. 1, p. 61.

Distance and length of Howard's Nez Perce campaign—*Among Our Hostile Indians*, p. 300. (Here too Howard mentions that Miles shared his tent.) In his *Report—In the Field*, p. 68, Howard calculates that "from the beginning of the pursuit" on the Lo Lo Trail until embarkation on Missouri River going home, which is to say from July 27 to Oct. 10, his army made 1,321 miles in 75 days, averaging 17.61 miles per day.

Miles's belief that a buffalo herd was a Sioux war party (he later called it the worst scare of his life)—Tolman, p. 83.

"I want a command in accordance with my rank."—Wooster, p. 60 (Miles to Sherman, 1870).

"I can hunt him down on foot"—After Wooster, p. 86 (re: Sioux).

"the old Army doctrine of destroying the whole race"—After Wooster, p. 74 (Miles to Howard, 1874; re: Indians in general).

Happily Ever After

"loading forty wounded bucks into brush-filled wagons."—Information from Pearson, p. 56.

Redington's using up of seventeen horses—Montana Historical Society. SC 683. John W. Redington papers. Letter of October 12, 1924, to Mr. Hilger, p. 2.

VIII. I Raised My Eyes

Epigraph: "I raised my eyes above the criticisms . . ."—Howard, *Autobiography*, vol. 1, p. 378.

Wishing for a Hackney

My bringing together of the various military protagonists at Tongue River to celebrate their victory over Joseph is the merest fictional hocus-pocus. Shame on me! As you may remember, Perry's column never even got as far as Missoula. Howard's bunch set out for home on October 13; Miles and his prisoners did not reach Tongue River until the twenty-third. I hope you may find some artistic merit (or even human "truth") in what I have imagined.

Dispatch from Miles to General Terry, 5 October 1877—Greene, *Nez Perce Summer*, p. 312.

Inventory of prisoners—Information from Greene, *Beyond Bear's Paw*, pp. 57, 60.

Description of Tongue River Cantonment—Information from Zimmer, p. 38 (April 25th), diagram on p. 40.

"tame Sioux and Cheyennes"—"By July 1877, there were at least forty-eight lodges of American Indians living at Cantonment . . . including the Northern Cheyennes and Sioux . . ."—Pearson, p. 29.

Guy's citation for valor—This must have been pure nepotism. Greene calls it "perhaps the oddest recognition of all" in *Nez Perce Summer*, p. 316.

"Sure now, I spoiled it there . . ."—Closely after Wood diary 1878, p. 18 (July 3).

Deer dewclaws on a Cheyenne woman's dress—Information from Koch, p. 45.

Estimate of grass acreage near Tongue River—After Zimmer, p. 110 ([August] 28th): "This grass is so tall you might get five tons to the acre."

Description of Joseph at Tongue River—After a photograph in Greene, *Beyond Bear's Paw*, p. 110.

Description of General Sheridan—Ibid., p. 114 (U.S. National Archives photo).

"Too much praise cannot placed to the credit of Gen. Miles . . ."—Zimmer, p. 162 (article dated 8 November 1877).

"The telegram should not have altered . . ." & c—Altered and embellished from Wooster, p. 107.

Tongue River's alkali cliffs—Wooster, p. 80.

Sheridan's instructions to Custer on ultimatum to captive Kiowa chiefs—Abridged and altered from George Armstrong Custer, pp. 104–5.

Sheridan as Miles's best man—Information from Wooster, p. 50.

The reception concert for Howard at the New Market Theatre—Details from the invitation, in the Grace Howard Gray Scrapbook, folder 1/5.

Dialogue between Howard and Hazzard—Closely after Howard, *Autobiography*, vol. 1, p. 83.

Howard to Wood: "With your talents, I think you could do a fair job presenting a true account of the surrender to the press."—Much embellished from information in Wooster, p. 108.

"Colonel Miles, I am astonished at your accusation" + "General Howard, you virtually gave up the pursuit"—Both closely after letters quoted in Wooster, p. 109.

Governor Potts to the Legislative Assembly of Montana: "The Indian situation in the Territory . . ."—Much abbreviated from the *Council Journal of the Eleventh Session of the Legislative Assembly of the Territory of Montana* (13 January–21 February 1879). N.d. Transcription printed by Color World of Montana, Inc. Copy in Montana Historical Society Archives. Page 2 (Benj. F. Potts, Executive Department, Helena, January 13, 1879 [Message of the Governor of Montana]).

Just Deserts

Conversation between Howard and Sherman—As far as I know, they never met on this subject. But the two men's points of view are derived from the information in Pearson, pp. 69–70. "The terms of the surrender were violated by the Indians' conniving at White Bird's escape" is verbatim (abridged) from Howard to McDowell, May 1878 (loc. cit.). In August 1877, Sherman did not actually propose, as he had for the Modocs, exterminating all the Nez Perces, but he did call for "trials and executions, and what are left should be treated like the Modocs" (Beal, p. 336). In this hypothetical private conversation his language might well have been more intemperate.

Howard did meet Sheridan, with whom he quarrelled on the subject of Miles's victory claims and his own unauthorized counterclaims in the press. Later he wrote Sheridan that he was "sorry if I have compromised you in any way." Sheridan wrote Sherman: "I do not feel much compromised. It seems to me that General Howard compromised himself" (Beal, p. 233).

IX. The Americans Are Your Friends

Epigraph: "The Americans are your friends . . ."—Greene, Nez Perce Summer, p. 345.
Five succeeding Howard epigraphs—Howard, Among Our Hostile Indians, pp. 456, 454, 11, 8, 251 (re-punctuated).

The Medicine Line

Description of the country between Bear's Paw, Montana, and Fort Walsh, Saskatchewan—After a visit in August 2012. In this season it is rain and loneliness, fences on either side of the highway, prairie all the way to the clouds.

Some of the incidents described in this chapter are based on information in Greene, Beyond Bear's Paw, pp. 54–56, 58, 60–63, some on McWhorter, Hear Me, pp. 508–24, with embellishments, alterations and inventions. As one might imagine, no one tells the story quite the same way, and the secondary sources are even more variable. Beal, for instance, asserts that only fourteen men "and a comparable number of women" escaped with White Bird (p. 230).

Description of the Assiniboine village: patched tipis, etc.—After Wood, Porter and Hunt, p. 132 (plate 8: Assiniboine Camp).

When COYOTE killed TRAVELLER THE SUN—Walker and Matthews, p. 17.

Description of Assiniboines' white accoutrements and face paint—After information from Koch, pp. 34, 96.

Accoutrements of the Gros Ventre men—Information from Josephine Paterek, Encyclopedia of American Indian Costume (New York: W. W. Norton & Co., 1996 repr. of 1994 ed.), p. 99 (entry on Blackfeet). Description of the Gros Ventre girl's robe is after information in Handbook of North American Indians, vol. 11, p. 682 (entry on Gros Ventres).

A Blackfoot man's vermilioning of his wife's face—Information from Larpenteur, vol. 2, p. 396.

White Bird hires the half-breed—Howard et al., p. 272 (McDonald). The dialogue and payment are invented.

Description of the woman Arrowhead—After Schlick, 2nd p. of color insert following p. 96.

More description of the Assiniboines—Information from Larpenteur, vol. 2, pp. 397, 401, 405.

The way a man can become invisible when he sings his WYAKIN song—See Linderman, p. 55, for the Crow equvialent.

Peopeo's gifts from others—Information (slightly altered and embellished) from Washington State University Libraries, Pullman. Holland Library Archives. Cage 3073. Peopeo Tholekt, 1857–1935; p. 3.

The Americans Are Your Friends

Description of Sitting Bull—After a photograph in Greene, Beyond Bear's Paw, p. 111 (from Little Bighorn Battlefield National Monument). My telling of postwar cross-border raids and other events at Fort Walsh is indebted to this book's information.

Description of [Hunkpapa Lakota] dancing stick—After an illustration in Horse Capture and Her Many Horses, p. 68.

Sitting Bull: "I don't want to have anything to do with people . . ." + "as poor as snakes"—Larpenteur, vol. 2, p. 429.

Description of Jack Red Cloud—After Kavanagh, p. 53 ("Jack Red Cloud [Oglala Lakota]").

Symbolism of the red hand on the blanket and the triangularly notched eagle feather—Information from Koch, pp. 14, 12–13.

Description of Sitting Bull offering the peace pipe to Peopeo Tholekt—After a photograph of a tipi painting of this event by the latter, in McWhorter, *Hear Me*, p. 444.

"Sitting Bull shakes everyone's hand . . ."—Information from Gulick, p. 273.

Sitting Bull's miscommunication with Half Moon—McWhorter, *Hear Me*, p. 513.

The quilted bag figured with a crimson horse—After an illustration in Horse Capture and Her Many Horses, p. 47.

"Had I known that you were in the Wolf's Paw Mountains . . ." to White Bird's presentation of seven horses to Sitting Bull—Sitting Bull's words slightly altered and somewhat abridged from those cited in Greene, *Beyond Bear's Paw*, p. 203, fn. 46. White Bird's replies are my interpolations.

Sitting Bull: "O, I used to be a kind of chief . . ."—From an interview at Fort Walsh; reported by A Corps of Competent Writers and Artists, p. 396.

"I did not give the Americans my country . . ."—Reworded from Vestal, p. 217 (Sitting Bull was actually speaking directly to the American peace commission in October 1878, some months after the commission which came to treat with White Bird).

"When Bear Coat marched through my country, he told me that the Grandfather had commanded his coming."—After Vestal, p. 200.

Description of the tattooed old men with Sitting Bull—After Wood, Porter and Hunt, p. 126 (plate 2: Psihdja-Sápa and Tukán-Hátón, Yankton Men, righthand figure).

Description of *Kate*'s "fine breastplate"—After Koch, p. 39.

Effects on Assiniboines and Gros Ventres of transborder buffalo hunting by the Sioux and Nez Perces—McWhorter, *Hear Me*, p. 516.

"when the willows bud and the bunchgrass grows up"—Information from Zimmer, p. 25 (it was March 25th, and they were hunting Sioux in eastern Montana).

Towering Plants—For my rendering of this ambiguous season-word, see Glossary 5.

Origin of the Muskrat's hairless tail—Walker and Matthews, p. 11.

Description of General Terry—After a photograph in Greene, *Beyond Bear's Paw*, p. 115 (U. S. National Archives).

Mrs. Baird's nightmares—Embellished from Wooster, p. 79 (who says she was "distraught").

Names of the Nez Perces with Baird's delegation—Beal, p. 338 n. 5.

The time when serviceberries begin to turn purple—July. Baird's mission met with the Nez Perce on 1 July 1878.

The death of Lame Deer and Iron Star—Wooster, pp. 92–93.

The "half-breed interpreter" was Duncan McDonald, whose testimony in Howard et al. I have quoted from and embellished here and in this novel.

Description of Superintendant Walsh—After a photograph in Greene, *Beyond Bear's Paw*, p. 120 (Glenbow Archives NA-1771-1).

Dialogue between Baird and White Bird—Much abbreviated from Greene, *Beyond Bear's Paw*, pp. 135–50, with a few substitutions from Greene, *Nez Perce Summer*, p. 345, and some embellishments and alterations by WTV. "Reservation" begins with a capital in the original.

Description of Lieutenant Baird—After a photo in Greene, *Beyond Bear's Paw*, p. 123 (Greene's collection).

Description of Yellow Bull—After a photo in Greene, *Beyond Bear's Paw*, p. 124 (National Park Service, Nez Perce Historical Park).

"the Old Woman will never feed them, nor allow them to take a reservation."—Information from Vestal, p. 219.

Indian Territory

This chapter is so indebted to Pearson's book, which deals specifically with the Nez Perce exile, that I have not cited every little incident. Her relation of events is the main framework I have built on. Of course the dialogues are greatly embellished, abridged or (more often) invented; likewise this or that small event, such as Chapman's pay-per-view procedure at the funeral of Springtime's baby (which could easily have happened, but probably didn't). The more graphic horrors at Leavenworth (the abuse of the women, the grubbing up by pigs of the dead) are all true.

"My heart cannot understand . . ."—Howard et al., p. 297 (Chief Joseph), somewhat altered.

The paper negative of Chief Joseph, supposedly at Bismarck—Montana Historical Society Photo Archive, no. 955–961. The image was not actually signed by Moorhouse, and it could have been taken anytime after the surrender.

Ad Chapman as the bearer of bad news—Pearson, p. 69.

The journey from Bismarck to Quapaw—After Pearson, pp. 71–101, 117.

Events in Leavenworth—Information from Pearson, pp. 84, 88. She mentions the rape and venereal disease.

Description of Joseph in a longtailed war bonnet—After Montana Historical Society Photo Archive, negative 955–969.

"the seven Dreamer women will be gathering the first roots . . ."—Information from Relander (p. 75), who notes on the following page that seven is a sacred number for the Wanapums.

"Chief Joseph's squaw appears too ill to walk."—She and Chapman were both "prostrated." McWhorter, *Hear Me*, p. 532.

Number of lodges at Quapaw—Pearson, p. 125.

Seventy-nine dead at Quapaw—Ibid., p. 121 (I have deducted the five children who died at or before Baxter Springs).

Chapman's Modoc wife—McWhorter, *Yellow Wolf*, p. 289. Her name is unknown to me; "Addie B." is my invention.

Description of James Reuben—After a photo in Pearson, p. 214.

"You warriors who were too proud to open your ears . . ."—Reuben actually said something very similar to this to White Thunder when the latter surrendered at Lapwai (*Yellow Wolf*, p. 279). I have abbreviated his words and recast them in this novel's Nez Perce style of English.

Description of Joseph sitting—Gulick, p. 297 (Chief Joseph, 1901, supposedly by Lee Moorhouse).

Agent Jones's antecedents and frauds—Pearson, pp. 127–29.

Chapman fingers John Fur Cap and Charley Moses—Information from the same, p. 42. The cause of his accusations is actually unknown. Emeline Tuttle's fascination with Joseph is my invention, as is Chapman's possession of Looking-Glass's shirt. The anecdote of Chapman, James Reuben and the notary is told by Pearson.

The curse of a shamaness's menstrual rag—*Handbook of North American Indians*, vol. 12, p. 427 (Deward E. Walker, Jr., "Nez Perce").

"my father made the tracks for me to go in and I intend to walk in them."—Bartlett, p. 47 (actually said by Joseph to Monteith in 1874).

Chapman lets Joseph drink from his quinine bottle—According to Pearson (p. 122), he performed this kindness for "favored prisoners."

Chapman rats out Agent Jones—Ibid., p. 130.

Deaths in Red Grizzly Bear's and Yellow Bull's families—Ibid., p. 121.

Re: the heart of HUMMINGBIRD and what MOSQUITO saw (if you are wondering, He saw CRICKET copulating with Her husband COYOTE)—Walker and Matthews, pp. 23, 47.

The patience of Mexican gold-dirt-shakers [in the Arizona Territory]—Information after Fanny Dunbar Corbusier, *Recollections of Her Army Life, 1869–1908*, ed. Patricia Y. Stallard (Norman: University of Oklahoma Press, 2003), p. 28.

Fate of Swan Necklace—McWhorter, *Yellow Wolf*, p. 44.

List of warriors selected by Monteith as especially dangerous—Information from Pearson, pp. 43–44.

Description of Two Moons and his wife in old age—Gulick, p. 239 ("Two Moons and his wife, Lets-Koho-kates-Wenien: 'Hat on the Side of the Head'").

Description of Peopeo Tholekt et al.—From a group portrait photograph in Pearson, p. 221 (*Sunday Oregonian*, June 24, 1900).

Escape of Animal In A Hole—Ibid., p. 187 fn. 6.

The journey from the Salmon to the Snake—After a visit to Pittsburg Landing, Idaho, in September 2006. This was indeed the Toohhoolhoolzote band's wintering place in immediately previous years.

Springtime leaves Joseph—Pearson, p. 201. The reason has not been recorded.

"our chief is trying to fold up his arms and enlarge his heart"—Wood diary, 1879, p. 47–48 (Chief Moses): "Now if I say I do right these Yakima City men are looking toward me to bite me; they will shoot me down like a dog; I think you might look after such things and take care of my People . . . I am trying hard to get up a big heart, but the whites bother a good deal, but I am trying to fold up my arms and let the past go by."

Description of Lucy Hayes—After a photograph in Emily Apt Geer, *First Lady: The Life of Lucy Webb Hayes* (Fremont, Ohio: Kent State University Press/Rutherford B. Hayes Presidential Center, 1984).

"after which all goes on as before"—Joseph and Yellow Bull signed a document giving up their home-land in exchange for land in the Indian Territory, plus $25,000 in U.S. bonds. It was never ratified.

Description of Joseph in his broadbrimmed hat—Montana Historical Society Photo Archive, negative 955–963.

Grizzly Bear Youth's life in the Indian Territory—All invented.

The Hayes medal: "HONEST MONEY HONEST GOVERNMENT"—Sullivan, p. 427.

History of Star Doctor—Relander, pp. 104–6.

Description of the Cheynne brave Two Moons—After Kavanagh, p. 56 ("Two Moons [Northern Chey-enne], W1780").

Description of the Sun Dance—Somewhat after Pearson, pp. 238–50, although she mentions only suspension from the back; I am told by participants that nowadays suspension through the breast is common, so I put that in, not certainly knowing, however, whether it occurred in the 1880s.

Peopeo Tholekt's definition of Reuben: "a [I have made it *the*] Judas Indian"—Nerburn, p. 75.

When ELK boiled His wife's sleeve . . .—Information from Walker and Matthews, p. 83.

Description of Looking-Glass's younger daughter—After Kavanagh (with the exception of the striped blanket), p. 138 ("He-Yume-Wah-Pah-Lilpt, Jennie Lawray [Nez Perce], W3491").

"I believe in killing the Indian and saving the man."—Quoted in Pearson, p. 233.

"Take me back to my old home . . ."—Moynihan, Armitage and Dichamp, p. 222 (Mary Ronan).

"Toohhoolhoolsote's widows both die from malaria."—Invented, like everything else about them, in-cluding their existence.

Number of Nez Perces, Palouses and Cayuses left alive in 1885—Pearson, p. 209.

"Shall he remain a pauper savage . . ."—Much abbreviated from Greenwald, p. 30.

Description from *Frank Leslie's Illustrated Newspaper*—After an illustration in Pearson, p. 250.

Numbers of Indians and composition of their escort at Pendleton—*Pendleton Tribune*, 29 May 1885, p. 3., col. 1.

Chief Broken-Arm—Information from Gulick, p. 20.

"Kuna, nakai . . ."—Axtell, No. 6.

"Cloudburst becomes Mrs. Susie Convill"—Information from McWhorter, *Yellow Wolf,* caption to photo insert by p. 136.

Joseph's hanging party at Lapwai—Beal, p. 295.

According to Pearson (p. 296), Joseph and his (unnamed) wives arrived at Nespelem with two daugh-ters (presumably Looking-Glass's), ages fifteen and two, which does not quite jibe with Looking-Glass's invitation to the Bostons at Fort Fizzle to come meet his two eligible daughters.

Congress Solves Our Indian Problem

Epigraph—Howard, *Autobiography,* vol. 2, p. 203.

All dialogue—[U.S. Congress], *Congressional Record, Containing the Proceedings and Debates of the Forty-Fifth Congress, First Session, also Special Session of the Senate,* vol. VI, Part VI (Washington, D.C.: Government Printing Office, 1877), pp. 287, 292, 297, 294, 324. I have abridged many remarks, and rearranged the order to please my notions of logical and dramatic effect. (Original order: At-kins, Phillips, Atkins, Throckmorton, Bridges, Singleton, Maginnis, and Townsend—whose ora-tion I have broken in two; originally everything of his quoted here appeared in one [longer] speech.) At one point I have begun Mr. Atkins's remarks with "That's not to the point." Otherwise, all is verbatim.

General Howard Explains

Howard's opinion of Joseph's courage and inherited sin—Fairly closely after *Nez Perce Joseph,* p. 15.

Photo by Bowman

Description of Joseph's family—Gulick, p. 301 ("Photo by Bowman," "Chief Joseph with two of his wives . . . about 1890 at Nespelem").

Late August 1900

Descriptions of Nespelem—From a visit to Nespelem, Elmer and Grand Coulee, Washington, August 2009.

Description of the "wide circle of pallid tipi-triangles"—After Gulick, p. 300 (D. Edwin Latham, "Chief Joseph's home, Nespelm, Washington, 1902").

Description of the "side view copyrighted by Moorhouse"—After a negative labeled "'Chief Joseph' nezperce Tribe Copyright 1901 by Lee Moorhouse." Collection of Tom Robinson.

Nespelem

Tourist amenities on Wallowa Lake—*Wallowa Chieftain* (Joseph, Oregon), vol. VII., no. 15 (August 14, 1890), p. 1, Wilbur Brock, "On Wallowa Lake." (In the original, "Charley" is "Charles.")

Pollock's retirement in the Wallowa Valley is my invention.

Description of Joseph with the Allotting Agent—After a photo in Gay, facing p. 91.

"He cannot be persuaded to take his land upon the Reservation . . ."—Ibid., p. 90 (June 24th, 1890).

"WALLOWA COUNTY, OREGON. The Best Country in the Northwest for the Home-Seeker and the Capitalist."—*Wallowa Chieftain,* Thursday, Oct. 23, 1890, p. 1 (advertisement).

A. C. Smith's service in the Nez Perce War—McWhorter, *Hear Me,* p. 278.

"Friends, I meet here my friend, General Howard . . ."—Helen Addison Howard, p. 365. I have added an ironical "now all is straight . . ."—At this event, Howard said: "I would have done anything to avoid the war, even to giving my life. But the time had come when we had to fight. There come times when a fight is a mighty good thing and when it's over let's lay down our feelings and look up to God and see if we cannot get a better basis on which to live and work together."—*The Red Man and Helper,* printed every Friday by apprentices at the Indian Industrial School, Carlisle, Pennsylvania, vol. XIX, no 33, Friday, March 18, 1904.

"It was interesting to see the dark faces lighted up . . ."—Gay, p. 14 (June 8th, 1889; abridged by WTV).

"there was no other place for them to go . . ."—Francis Haines, *The Nez Percés: Tribesmen of the Columbia Plateau* (Norman: University of Oklahoma Press, The Civilization of the American Indian ser., 1955), p. 300.

Admonition on "the beef issue"—National Archives microfilm M1121. Roll 1: Circular No. 153 1/2, Department of the Interior, Office of Indian Affairs. Washington, November 1, 1889. Abridged by WTV.

"Information having reached this Office . . ."—National Archives microfilm M1121. Roll 1: Circular no. 140, Department of the Interior, Office of Indian Affairs. Washington, October 18, 1884.

Looking-Glass's daughter goes to Kamiah—Gay, p. 41 (July 26th, 1889).

"Why should I be badly treated by the whites? . . ."—Almost verbatim from McWhorter, *Yellow Wolf,* p. 29.

White Thunder's quarter-century of picking hops in Yakima—McWhorter, *Yellow Wolf,* pp. 13–14.

"The friendly Nez Perces now for the most part are dressed as white men . . ."—Howard, *Nez Perce Joseph,* p. 20. These words were published in 1881.

"the moral cesspool of the tribe."—Greenwald, p. 58 (McBeth said this in 1885).

"After that the Indians were fined by the agent . . ."—Francis Haines, pp. 301–2.

Not Even a Horn Spoon

Description of the war bonnet which might have been Yellow Bull's—This object was on display at the museum at Big Hole Battlefield in 2007.

Certificate from the American Board of Commissioners—Grace Howard Gray Scrapbook. Box 1, folder 1/5.

Colors of beads given by Lewis and Clark—Washington State University Libraries, Pullman. Holland Library Archives. Cage 4681. Lot, Sam (Chief Peo-peo-Tah-Likt or [sic] Chief Many Wounds. Historical Sketches of the Nez Perces, 1935), p. 8: "And Lewis give lots red beads to woman and blue beads like sky yellow bead color like flower and green beads color grass and other kinds."

"INDIAN RIFLES . . ."—Bannerman, p. 41.

"Sir, I have the honor to submit the following report . . ."—Bowdoin, OOH papers, M 91.7, v. 1, folio: "G. orders & special orders, Apr. 2 1863–July 12 1864" (although it actually begins in 1861 with Bull Run and seems to go only up to April 1864). Page 3 (Battle of Bull Run, July 21st, 1861).

Dinosaurs and Cycads

Further History of the United States of America

Epigraph: "So onward still we press . . ."—Gibbon, *A Vision of the "Big Hole,"* p. 2.

"By 1878 . . ."—*The New Encyclopaedia Britannica in 30 Volumes,* 15th ed., Macropaedia, vol. 18 (Tonalite to Vesuvius) (Chicago: Encyclopaedia Britannica, Inc., 1976), p. 975 (entry on "United States, History of the").

Further History of Theller's Squaw

Epigraph: "In the last analysis the real test of greatness . . ."—Helen Addison Howard, p. 333.

Further History of Colonel Perry

Epigraph: "One hardly can command men . . ."—Laughy, p. 64 (*Nez Perce Joseph* . . .).

Description of Paiute thread—Information from Scott, p. 65.

"Old Skull and Crossbones" as a nickname for a gloomy man—Elizabeth B. Custer, *Boots and Saddles, or, Life in Dakota with General Custer* (Lincoln: University of Nebraska Press/Bison Books, 2010; orig. ed. 1885), p. 223.

Perry advances Company "F" against the Modocs—Murray, pp. 205–7 (April 15th).

Shearer's favorable testimony—McDermott, p. 190 (from the cross-examination on December 27, 1878).

Description of Crook in his slouch hat—After Hedren, p. 6 (Figure 2: General George Crook).

"that time he won a Chinese girl in a poker game"—For a true instance of this, see Wikoff, p. 60.

Further History of John W. Redington

"Times have been so tough . . ."—OHS MSS. 2333, Redington, John W. Letters to and from Redington . . . letter dated at San Diego, Cal., April 5, 1915, to Mr. Hines.

Further History of Mrs. Manuel

Epigraph: "The horrible story . . ."—*Morning Oregonian,* vol. XVII.—no. 130, Portland, Oregon: Friday, July 6, 1877 (pp. unnumbered).

Epigraph: "Well, where's the blood then, Drake?"—Francis E. Skipp, ed., *The Complete Short Stories of Thomas Wolfe* (New York: Charles Scribner's Sons, 1987), p. 488.

Various theories about Mrs. Manuel's fate—Some come from McWhorter, *Hear Me,* pp. 214–16, and McDermott, pp. 157–60. Peopeo Tholekt's version, which appears in that Pullman ms. 1218, p. 1, asserts that after she died or was killed on the trail, Joseph himself took her scalp—which Peopeo then showed the interviewer.

"Recently I dug up the leather robe of a woman . . ."—Adkison, p. 6 (T. C. Sherril, one of Gibbon's volunteers).

Further History of Broken Tooth

Epigraph—Euripides, vol. I, trans. and ed. David Kovacs (Cambridge, Massachusetts: Harvard University Press, Loeb Classical Library no. 483, 2005 corr. repr. of 1995 ed.), p. 191.

This little chapter summarizes Andrew Garcia's *Tough Trip Through Paradise.* It was he who married Broken Tooth.

Further History of the Bannocks

Epigraph: "The Shoshone or Snake Indians . . ."—Hiram T. French, M.S., *History of Idaho: A Narrative Account of Its Historical Progress, Its People and Its Principal Interests,* vol. 1 (Chicago and New York: Lewis Publishing Co., 1914), p. 44.

"This root [camas] is the main source of their food supply . . ."—Crook, p. 222.

Bannock attack on a Mormon mission in 1858—Information from Ruby and Brown, p. 161.

"some of the lowest and most degraded people in the world."—Humfreville, p. 315.

"The discontent among the Bannocks . . ."—D. S. Benson, *Presidents at War: A Survey of United States Warfare History in Presidential Sequence 1775–1980* (Chicago [printed by BookMasters, Inc., Mansfield, Ohio], 1996), p. 402.

Further History of the Umatillas

Epigraph: "Now, therefore, . . ."—*Executive Orders Relating to Indian Reservations*, p. 154 (UMATILLA RESERVATION, Department of the Interior, Office of the Secretary, December 4, 1888).

"An Army hospital should only last ten years . . ."—Information from Huston, p. 255.

The gathering in of the Umatillas, and several other historical bits: "Finally, during the Nez Perce War of 1877 and the Bannock and Northern Paiute War of 1878, the absentee tribesmen were swept back upon the reservation . . ."—*Handbook of North American Indians*, vol. 12, pp. 410, 414–16 (Theodore Stern, "Cayuse, Umatilla, and Walla Walla").

"Instant salvation"—Dee Brown, p. 40.

"The steamboats were patrolling the upper river looking for Indians . . ."—Moorhouse, p. 5.

"The Protestant Indians . . ."—*Pendleton Tribune*, 29 May 1885, p. 3., col. 1.

Further History of the Flatheads

Epigraph: "The Indian can be made self-sustaining . . ."—Crook, p. 229.

The removal of Charlot's band—Information from USDA pamphlet RI-75-79, p. 17.

"By 1997, the number of completely fluent Salish speakers . . ."—*Handbook of North American Indians*, vol. 12, p. 311.

Further History of the Crows

Epigraph: "Ready to co-operate with the whites . . ."—Mrs. Margaret I. Carrington, *Absaraka (Ab-Sa-ra-ka), Home of the Crows* (Chicago: Lakeside Press, R. R. Donnelly & Sons Co., Christmas, 1950; orig. ed. 1868), p. 8.

"I love the white man . . . We want our reservation to be large . . ."—Bradley, p. 42 (Blackfoot, to Gibbon, 1876). The Earl of Dunraven's compliment to Blackfoot comes from the same source.

"They are now settled . . ."—*Encyclopaedia Britannica*, 11th ed. (1910), vol. VII (Constantine Pavlovich to Demidov), p. 514 (entry on Crow Indians).

Further History of the Sioux

Epigraph: "The destiny of the white race . . ."—Trobriand, p. 13. Citation continues: "For example, in Montana, in the very heart of the Indian country, wherever the presence of gold attracts and holds the miners, the Indian must flee or disappear. If he attempts to defend his land, he is exterminated! The miner, interrupted in his work and in his dreams of fortune, is in a terrible temper. He must have complete security, sheltered from hostile raids. Therefore he spares no one, and when he meets the red-skin, their women and children as well as warriors are left to fatten the land or the wolves."

President Hayes: Sitting Bull's followers "are apparently in progress of disintegration."—Benson, p. 405 (address of December 1880).

Apparel of Red Horse—Richard Hook, *Warriors at the Little Bighorn 1876* (Oxford, U.K.: Osprey Publishing, Men-at-Arms ser. no. 408, 2004), p. 8.

Sitting Bull's return, and the number of people with him—Wooster, p. 127.

Sitting Bull's magical link with the buffalo—Sandoz, p. 354.

The role of Miles in Sitting Bull's capture—Wooster, p. 184.

"He had practised cruelty to animals and men . . ."—Howard, *Famous Indian Chiefs*, p. 311.

"they had a language of their own . . ."—Humfreville, p. 315.

Rain In The Face at Coney Island—Hook, p. 15.

Sioux hoof-beadwork—After an illustration in Horse Capture and Her Many Horses, p. 28.

Further History of Smohalla

Epigraph: "HOW TO BREED AN OUTBREAK"—*Wallowa Chieftain*, vol. XVII, no. 134 (July 11, 1877). The extract continues: "Nothing could be so absurd as to allow them to wander at will in bands all over the country, coming in contact with all classes of whites, finding opportunities to get drunk, trading horses, buying arms and ammunition, and exposing themselves and their women to forms of vice, which they embrace with all the eagerness of low natures."

Smohalla's end—Information from Relander, p. 238.

Further History of the Apaches

Epigraph: "A minority of white men . . ."—Quoted in Bellesiles, p. 30.

"I was very much amused at the General's opinion of himself."—Crook, p. 169.

Howard *vs.* Crook—Eventually, I am pleased to report, they formed an alliance—against General Miles, whom by then they hated more than each other. General Howard sent his son Guy to Fort Marion, and he wrote as damning a report as could have been hoped. The impoverishment, sicknesses and deaths of the Apache captives were to some extent Miles's fault, for hadn't he captured Geronimo and didn't he advise against returning them to Arizona? See Wooster, pp. 172–74.

"As soon as the Indians became settled . . ."—Crook, p. 184 (abridged). The case of the Hualapai family was told on the following page. Crook further explained: "Every year we kill so many, and a process of extermination goes on which will finally wipe them out. They'll fight again, and their numbers will be again lessened. You can't prevent them from fighting, and the only thing you can do with them is wipe them out."—A Corps of Competent Writers and Artists, p. 490.

Howard to Sladen: "Every promise you and I made those Apaches . . ."—Sladen, p. 108.

Miles: "The Chiricahua Apaches . . ."—Wooster, p. 174.

Further History of the Howard Family

Epigraph: "And as I started for my home so far away . . ."—Howard, *Famous Indian Chiefs*, p. 136.

"By some singular clerical error . . ."—Howard, *Autobiography*, vol. 1, p. 492.

"The reason I am thus particular . . ."—Ibid., vol. 2, p. 87.

Dates relating to Guy Howard's military service and death—Howard, *Among Our Hostile Indians*, p. 309.

Overdue rent to the Trustees of Howard University—Somewhat after [U.S. Congress], *Congressional Record, Containing the Proceedings and Debates of the Forty-Fifth Congress, Second Session*, vol. VII, Part III (Washington: Government Printing Office, 1878), p. 2017 (March 26, 1878).

". . . contests like that which the Salvation Army are trying to wage."—Verbatim from OOH papers, "Warfare of the future," p. 25 (but "war," not "contests," in original).

Description of events at Columbia, and excerpt from the "March to the Sea"—After Howard, *Autobiography*, vol. 1, pp. 759–60. Logan was followed by Woods, whose name I have omitted here to avoid confusion with C. E. S. Wood.

Sherman's characterization of Howard—John A. Carpenter, p. 272 (Sherman to President-elect Garfield, Dec. 30, 1880).

"Few men do as much toward the cause of Christian enlightenment . . ."—Abridged from the same, p. 219 (E. C. Watkins to Howard, April 18, 1878).

Further History of General Miles

Epigraph: "I . . . have fought and defeated . . ."—Wooster, p. 90.

Letter of Grant concerning Miles—*The Papers of Ulysses S. Grant*, vol. 28: November 1, 1876–September 30, 1878, ed. John Y. Simon (Carbondale: Southern Illinois University Press, 2005), p. 313.

Playing "Garryowen" when Custer rode in—Information from Wooster, p. 59.

Buffalo Bill Cody on Miles: "a man, every inch of him . . ."—Helen Cody Wetmore and Zane Grey, *Last of the Great Scouts (Buffalo Bill)* (New York: Grosset & Dunlap, 1918; orig. copyright 1899), p. 287.

Miles's gift of the horse to Buffalo Bill—Ibid., p. 308.

Sheridan on Miles: "a good, pushing officer"—Wooster, p. 127.

Miles to Sherman: promotion, hot pursuit—Greene, *Beyond Bear's Paw*, p. 79.

"Joseph is by far the ablest Indian on the continent."—Wooster, p. 109 (Miles to Sherman, October 28, 1877).

Miles's efforts for Joseph in 1881—Information from Pearson, pp. 160–62.

"I frequently and persistently for seven long years urged . . ."—*Personal Recollections and Observations of General Nelson A. Miles* (Chicago: The Werner Company, 1897), p. 217. One adoring chronicle of our Indian-fighting Army asserts that Miles "never rested until in 1884 he had succeeded in arranging the return of the tribe to their home lands. There Joseph lived to old age, the patriarch of his people, counselling them against fire-water and other vices and keeping his promise to *fight no more forever*."—Fairfax Downey, *Indian-Fighting Army* (New York: Charles Scribner's Sons, 1941), p. 252.

Miles's aid to Paiutes, Pimas, Mojaves and Cheyennes, and his stance against Forsyth after Wounded Knee—Ibid., pp. 132, 166, 140, 184–91.

"Poverty breeds socialism . . ."—*Wallowa Chieftain* (Joseph, Oregon), Thursday, Oct. 9, 1890, unnumbered p.

"In my opinion what is needed is for some friend in Washington . . ."—Wooster, p. 116.

Mile's appointment to the Equipment Board, and its recommendation—Rutledge, p. 36.

Court-martial of Johnson Whittaker—Wooster, pp. 151–52.

Miles's expectation that the U.S. would soon annex Canada—Not just Miles's sentiment. Seward, for instance, had said much the same thing in 1846. See Jasper Ridley, *Maximilian and Juárez* (New York: Ticknor & Fields, 1992), p. 113.

Miles to Sherman: "I think it too soon to occupy the Boundary line . . ."—Ibid., pp. 136–37.

Description of Miles giving us "the look"—After Zimmer, p. 30 (photo of Miles in 1878).

Buffalo Bill: "I thought my Sioux Indians were very fine . . ."—*Pendleton Tribune*, 17 May 1900, p. 4.

Later events of Miles's career—Wooster, pp. 216–17, 200–1, 204, 228–29, 238, 241, 245, 264.

Miles's souvenirs of Joseph—Pearson, p. 46.

Further History of Lieutenant Wilkinson

Epigraph: "I know that the chaplain in the regiment . . ."—Paul A. Cimbala and Randall M. Miller, eds., *Union Soldiers and the Northern Home Front: Wartime Experiences, Postwar Adjustments* (New York: Fordham University Press, 2002), p. 272 (address by Howard to U. S. Christian Commission, 1864).

A stony surprise in a provisions package—George Armstrong Custer, p. 64.

Further History of Colonel Gibbon

Epigraph: "In the fight with General Gibbon . . ."—Howard et al., p. 292 (Joseph).

Gibbon's various Departments—Beal, p. 256.

"Enemies Become Friends"—Gibbon, *Adventures*, p. 219.

How it is in the land of the dead—Walker and Matthews, p. 123.

"He would take his food with the white man's knife . . ."—Gibbon, *From Where the Sun Stands*, p. 38.

Further History of Lieutenant Wood (1878–1918)

Epigraph: "Stories of machines . . ."—Gerald Raunig, *A Thousand Machines: A Concise Philosophy of the Machine as Social Movement*, trans. Aileen Derieg (Los Angeles: Semiotext(e), 2010), p. 32.

Description of the Apache saddlebag—After an illustration in Horse Capture and Her Many Horses, p. 25.

Description of the Kiowa girl—George Armstrong Custer, p. 338.

All the details on the housewarming party for the Woods are invented. There might not even have been one, although Howard did sign the guarantee on their home, and it seems likely that some sort of party would have been held to celebrate Wood's marriage. As for Grace's wedding (to Mr. James T. Gray, on Wednesday, September 17, 1879, at eight-o'-clock, Vancouver Barracks, W.T.), the guest list and gifts are accurate, thanks to: Oregon Historical Society. Manuscript Collection. Mss [sic] 6049. Gray, Grace Howard Scrapbook. Box 1 [of 2; second is merely a photocopy of Box 1], folders 1/5, 1/8 (for Guy's drawing of the Norton's massacre).

The Communistic poison of the eight-hour working day—After Bruce, p. 227 (*The Nation*, 1872).

"Influential men had begun calling to restrict voting privileges . . ."—Information from the same, p. 317.

Howard's greeting to Apaches: "how, amigo"—Sladen, p. 60.

Further History of Lieutenant Wood (1893–1944)

Epigraph: "In my youth . . ."—OHS Wood papers, Hayek, unnumbered early p.

Description of Erskine—Gulick, p. 299 ("Erskine Wood at the age of 14"). The photo was not signed by Moorhouse.

Erskine's diary: "He stands so tall and straight . . ."—My invention, based on photoportraits of Joseph.

Some details of Wood's life are from Bingham and Barnes, pp. 5, 9–18, 24.

"Your father was very liberal and kind-hearted."—OHS Wood documents, folder 12, to Harry Howard, February 20, 1942.

"my ignorant superior officer, General Howard."—OHS Wood documents; autobiographical transcriptions, carton 59. Excerpts from 1925 autobiogaphy re: Nez Perce Campaign . . . , p. 6, to *Century Magazine:* "I think it also negatives General Howard's argument that any promise, express or implied, was cancelled by Joseph's consent to White Bird's escape, Joseph having no control over

White Bird's actions and no right to speak for him. I must say my difference of opinion with my chief never blinds me to the fact that he was sympathetic with the Indians from first to last . . . and was always sincere in his opinions and persuaded himself that he was right."

"cradled in the arms of the GREAT MOTHER"—Wood documents, folder 12, Sept. 16, 1941, to Molly O'Shea. Small caps are my addition.

Further History of White Bird

Epigraph: "The Nez Percés . . . believed that things would be different in Canada . . ."—Bruce Trigger and Wilcomb E. Washburn, eds., *The Cambridge History of the Native Peoples of the Americas*, vol. 1, North America; Part 2 (Cambridge: Cambridge University Press, 1996), p. 156.

Death camas blooms in meadows late May or early June in southern central British Columbia.

Description of Nez Percee Sam—After a photo in Greene, *Beyond Bear's Paw*, p. 127 (Glenbow Archives NB-9-13).

Further History of White Thunder

Epigraph: "We are of the Anglo-Saxon race . . ."—Twain, pp. 345–46.

According to Adkison (p. 8), en route to Wallowa White Thunder's party killed two ranchers, A. L. Cottle and John H. Wareham, and three miners, Jack Hayes, Amos Elliott and William Joy.

White Thunder's antecedents in Wallowa—McWhorter, *Yellow Wolf*, pp. 25, 26.

When SKUNK seduced EAGLE's women—Slickapoo, Seth and Walker, p. 28.

Dwelling place of Horse Blanket—Ibid., p. 24.

The skeletons of the two horses at Cottonwood—McWhorter, *Hear Me*, p. 290.

"I have always told the truth. I am telling the truth now."—Verbatim from McWhorter, *Yellow Wolf*, p. 35.

Dialogues with James Reuben and Agent Monteith—Much after the same, pp. 279–82.

Wages for hop picking in Yakima Valley (1890)—Ruby and Brown, p. 181.

Further History of Peopeo Tholekt

Epigraph: "Then bad DEVIL white people come . . ."—Peopeo Tholekt/Sam Lott, p. 6.

Peopeo keeps Mrs. Manuel's hair—Ibid., p. 1.

Description of the Pullman drawings—Washington State University Libraries, Pullman. Holland Library Archives. Cage 55; 135.1 Piyopyo Talikt. "Battle of the Big Hole, Nez Perce Camp." Drawing. Cage 55. 562 [Drawings] (Top) Combat between Peo-peo Tholekt and a Cheyenne at Bear's Paw Battle (Bottom) Capture of Cannon at Battle of Big Hole. Drawing by Peo-peo Tholekt. (One original, one copy), with explanatory notes.

Further History of the Northern Cheyennes

Epigraph: ". . . the history of man has shown . . ."—Humfreville, p. 379.

Situations of the two Northern Cheyenne reservations—*Executive Orders Relating to Indian Reservations*, pp. 101–2 (NORTHERN CHEYENNE RESERVATION, two entries).

Further History of the Modocs

Epigraph: Whitman, p. 18 (preface to 1855 ed. of *Leaves of Grass*).

Captain Jack's words to Judge Roseborough—Riddle, p. 60.

Where to shoot their arrows at chub-fishes—Information from Margolin, p. 14 ("When I Was a Child," Peter Sconchin, Modoc).

"Let them settle down and keep quiet . . ."—Beal, p. 274.

Return to Klamath reservation after 1900—*Handbook of North American Indians*, vol. 12, p. 461 (article on Modocs and Klamaths). The next page says that by the end of the twentieth century, "in religion, Christianity was dominant, while shamanism was rejected as a thing of the devil."

Ads for Modoc Oil and Nez Perce Catarrh Snuff—*Daring Donald McKay, or, The Last War-Trail of the Modocs: The Romance of the Life of Donald McKay, Government Scout, and Chief of the Warm Springs Indians*, repr. ed. by Keith and Donna Clark (Portland: Oregon Historical Society, 1971; orig. ed. 1884), p. xv (advertisement, late 1870s?).

Further History of the Nez Perces

Epigraph: "Leaving the rest to the sentimentalists . . ."—Whitman, p. 948 (*Collect*, "Democratic Vistas").

"We do not want our land to be cut up into little pieces . . ."—Gay, p. 63.

Situation of allotments in Kamiah and Lapwai—Ibid., pp. 63–65.

Episode of Yellow Bull's land—Ibid., p. 78.

Percentage of reservation sold off—Ibid., p. 81.

"Much credit has been given to Joseph's Nez Percés . . ."—Oregeon Historical Society. Bound commonplace book of articles and clippings: "Indian Book." pp. 361–62. J. W. Redington, "When We Fought Chief Joseph," pub. 1905 possibly in *Sunset* or *American Catholic Quarterly Review.*

"Later on my husband and I learned of homestead land on the Nezperce [*sic*] prairie . . ."—Washington State University Libraries, Pullman. Holland Library Archives. Cage 3080. Ms. of Wimpy, Mary Ann Sida Anderson, 1844–1948, p. 11.

Information from 1910—*Encyclopaedia Britannica*, 11th ed. (1910), vol. XIV (Husband to Italic), p. 463 (entry on Indians, North American).

Literacy in 1994—Walker and Matthews, p. 2.

Further History of Mount Idaho

Epigraph: ". . . the world is growing old . . ."—Perkins, p. 689 (William Hazlitt, "The Spirit of the Age").

Description of the graveyard and its surroundings—After a visit to Mount Idaho in August 2009.

Further History of Wallowa

Epigraph: "To be camped at the southern end of Silver Lake . . ."—*Wallowa Chieftain* (Joseph, Oregon), vol. VII., no. 15 (August 14, 1890), p. 1, Wilbur Brock, "On Wallowa Lake."

Miscellaneous factoids and advertisements—From the same issue, unnumbered pp. 2–3; and from Thursday, August 14, 1890; Thursday, Oct. 9, 1890.

Further History of Montana

Epigraph: "The law of necessity . . ."—Kautz, p. 348.

Timetable for the Anaconda Express—*The Butte Miner*, Wednesday morning, January 1, 1896, p. 1.

The stockmen *vs.* the grangers—Randall, p. 115.

Moorhouse photo of Flatheads—Ruby and Brown, p. 189.

"I am glad to note how the white people have developed Judith Basin . . ."—Montana Historical Society. SC 683. John W. Redington papers. Letter of October 12, 1924, to Mr. Hilger, p. 2.

Footnote: "But your ideas of assimilating the Indians . . ."—Ibid. Letter to Hon. Ray Lyman Wilbur, Sec. of the Interior, Sept. 20, 1930.

"Montana, the 'unceded Indian territory' . . ."—Keegan, p. 313.

Description of the Bitterroot Valley—From a visit to Lolo, Montana, and environs, August 2007.

Further History of Washington

Epigraph: "I have frequently seen in the Territory . . ."—Alfred Downing, topographical assistant, U.S. Army, *The Regulation of the Upper Columbia and How I Saw It* (Vancouver, Washington: J. J. Beeson, 1881), p. 32.

Rat infestations of Colville farmhouses—Ibid., p. 8.

Further History of Idaho

"The native tribes of Idaho are now chiefly of historic interest."—French, p. 42.

Further History of Oregon

Epigraph: "I dismounted . . . and found he was soon to be a good Injun . . ."—Cook, pp. 424–25 (recollections of Sol Rees).

"In Canada . . . no prohibition of marriage . . ."—*Encyclopaedia Britannica*, 11th ed. (1910), vol. XIV (Husband to Italic), p. 467 (entry on Indians, North American).

"MOONLIGHT VIEWS OF CRATER LAKE CREATURE . . ."—*Medford Mail Tribune*, August 18, 1930, nap. (prob. cover story).

"With their 10,000-foot peaks and rugged terrain . . ."—Julie Fanselow, *Traveler's Guide to the Oregon Trail* (Helena, MT: Falcon Press, 1992), p. 165.

Further History of the Indian Territory

"The Indian is capable of recognizing no controlling influence . . ."—George Armstrong Custer, p. 148.

Price of Missouri homestead lands in 1890—*Wallowa Chieftain* (Joseph, Oregon), vol. VII, no. 15 (August 14, 1890), unnumbered p.

Details of the Indian Territory's conversion into Oklahoma—*Encyclopaedia Britannica*, 11th ed., (1910) vol. XX (Ode to Payment of Members), pp. 61, 59 (entry on Oklahoma). There is less information on the Indian Territory than one would expect. For a visually arresting presentation of this land's earlier history, see John D. Spencer, *The American Civil War in the Indian Territory*, ill. Adam Hook (Oxford, U.K.: Osprey Publishing, Elite ser. no. 140, 2006).

"And far from having to explain as *chance* . . ."—Count Leo Tolstoy, *War and Peace,* trans. Constance Garnett (New York: Modern Library, n.d.), p. 1055.

"If I were an Indian . . ."—George Armstrong Custer, p. 22.

"like well-trained setters"—Custer's simile (ibid., p. 46, almost verbatim).

Sulkies, etcetera—All these were common breeds of horses in turn-of-the-century America.

Advertisement of M. E. Taylor—Washington State University Libraries, Pullman. Holland Library Archives. Cage 55. Box 20. Folder 160. Notebook c. 1893–1898. [Contains names & addresses of dealers & collectors of Indian relics.] 4?/24/1893: "Below is two views of Pipe offered me the other day for $2 is made from dark slate and is a work of considerable skill for a pale face . . ."

Further History of America's Indians

Epigraph: "Indian warfare is horrid . . ."—Howard, *Nez Perce Joseph*, p. 211.

"Notwithstanding all that has been said . . ."—Humfreville, pp. 126–27, quoting *Washington Post*, July 1902. "Government" is lowercased in the original.

Further History of President Rutherford B. Hayes

Epigraph: "It is true that a dollar a day . . ."—Bruce, pp. 312–13.

"This is a government of the people . . ."—Ibid., p. 320.

Further History of the United States of America

Epigraph: ". . . whenever I travelled . . ."—Howard, *Nez Perce Joseph*, p. 142.

"And pre-eminent usage"—*Encyclopaedia Britannica*, 11th ed. (1910), vol. XXVII (Tonalite to Vesuvius), p. 612 (entry on United States, The).

Further History of Camas

Epigraph: "Labor is the straight trail . . ."—*Reports on the Aftermath of the 1863 Nez Perce Treaty . . .* , p. 12.

"the Nez Perce still travelled to dig camas every June and July."—Information from Greenwald, p. 77 (dateline 1888).

Further History of the Buffalo

Epigraph: "As nearly as I can estimate . . ."—Helen Cody Wetmore and Zane Grey, *Last of the Great Scouts (Buffalo Bill)* (New York: Grosset & Dunlap, 1918; orig. copyright 1899), pp. 275–76. According to Sandoz (p. 34), "some put the total buffaloes in 1867 at fifty million, probably much too high, although it was said that General Crook, long in the Indian country, favored this number."

"Our hearts were like stones . . ."—Linderman, p. 144.

Hamstringing ability of a Comanche horseman—Humfreville, p. 185.

Buffalo Bill's achievement: More than 40,000 buffalo killed—Wetmore and Grey, p. 325. Of this number, he claimed to have killed 4,862 buffalo in a single eighteen-month period "for the Union Pacific builders." This book also informs us (p. 316) that from 1868 to 1881, Kansas paid $2,500,000 for buffalo bones to be used in carbon works.

"The buffalo-skin overcoat . . ."—Cook, *The Border and the Buffalo*, pp. v–vi (publishers' note).

Eight buffalo robes for a knee-length red coat—Information from Bradley, p. 116.

Estimate of buffalo population in what is now the U.S., *ca.* 1492—Sandoz, p. x (the lower bound of the estimate being 50,000,000).

Buffalo misfortunes, 1799–1884, including "the last shipment ever made"—Cook, pp. xx–xxiii.

Description of the pioneer mother gathering buffalo chips—After a photograph in Greenberg and McKeever, p. 35.

"At first . . . the bleaching bones . . ."—Elizabeth B. Custer, *Following the Guidon,* p. 186.

Use of buffalo manure by Montana homesteaders, 1900—Daniel M. Vichorek, *Montana's Homestead Era* (Helena: Montana's Geographic Ser., vol. 15, pub. by *Montana Magazine,* 1987), pp. 27–28.

"it is death for the domestic cow . . ."—Wetmore and Grey, p. 327.

"the cattalo turned out a singularly unsightly beast . . ."—Sandoz, p. 316.

"as pretty as an Apache squaw riding on a fast horse"—Information from Sladen, p. 101.

The fête in Bismarck—Pearson, p. 69.

Dialogue between Sitting Bull and reporter—A Corps of Competent Writers and Artists, p. 397.

"It was there, some said, shut in by this line of prairie fire and guns . . ."—Sandoz, p. 340.

"The best authorities agree in representing five years . . ."—Greene, *Beyond Bear's Paw,* p. 81 (Prime Minister John A. MacDonald).

Situation of Sitting Bull's Sioux in 1881: Eating dead ponies—Ibid., p. 91.

Postponement of the Kiowa Sun Dance in 1881–82—Pearson, pp. 241–42. According to Humfreville (p. 442), thirty wild buffalo remained in the U.S. in 1902.

Photograph of Sitting Bull in 1884—Weymouth, p. 55.

Article about lampreys—*Moscow-Pullman Daily News* [Idaho and Washington]. Wednesday, August 3, 2011, p. 2A (Jeff Barnard, Associated Press, "NW tribes drive effort to save primitive fish").

Epitaph: "One of the fundamental facts of life . . ."—Cook, pp. xxiii–xxiv. This charming passage is, again, part of the "publishers' note." I am assuming that it was composed by the editor, Milo Milton Quaife.

Textual Apparatus

First epigraph to textual apparatus: Congressman Young—*Congressional Record, Containing the Proceedings and Debates of the Forty-Fifth Congress, Second Session,* vol. VII, Part III (Washington, D.C.: Government Printing Office, 1878), p. 2794 (April 24; Mr. Young re: Transfer of Indian Bureau to War Department).

Second epigraph: Grant—Ulysses S. Grant, *Personal Memoirs & Selected Letters* (New York: Library of America, 1990 repr. of 1885–86 ed. and 1967–85 ed., respectively), p. 778.

Third epigraph: Howard—Bowdoin, OOH papers, "Warfare of the future," p. 1.

Chronology

Several entries derive from information in Jeff Zucker, Kay Hummel and Bob Høgfoss, *Oregon Indians: Culture, History & Current Affairs: An Atlas & Introduction* ([Portland?]: Press of the Oregon Historical Society, 1983).

Entry for 8,000 BC—Possible date of arrival of the Nimiipu—Pearson, p. 9.

Entry for 1805–6: "More than 13.5 million acres"—Pearson, p. 9.

Entry for *ca.* 1822: Massacre of Crows by Sioux—Bradley, pp. 78–79.

Entry for 1834: Attack by Crows upon whites—Bradley, p. 82.

Entry for 1849: "amazing villainies"—Same speech as in first epigraph to textual apparatus.

Entry for *ca.* 1854: Diminishing buffalo—Bradley, p. 83.

Entry on Guy Howard (1855)—Howard, *Autobiography,* vol. 1, p. 69.

Entry for 1855–56: "It was of no unfrequent occurrence . . ."—Crook, p. 15.

Entry for 1860: Bradley's remarks—Op. cit., p. 24.

Entry for 1861: Sixteen hundred gold claims—Pearson, p. 15.

Entries for 1861, 1866: Gatling guns—Ellis, p. 25.

Entry for 1863: A "thief treaty"—McWhorter, *Yellow Wolf,* p. 35. Gulick: p. 157. Greenwald: p. 51.

Entry for 1865: "Until 1865 . . ."—John Keegan, *Fields of Battle: The Wars for North America* (New York: Vintage, 1997 repr. of 1995 ed.), p. 282.

Entry for 1865: Helena—Bradley, p. 26.

Entry for 1867: Sherman to Grant—Femman, p. 263.

Entry for 1870: Schlereth, p. 35.

Entry for 1871: Flathead removal—*Executive Orders Relating to Indian Reservations*, p. 89.

Entry for 1872–73: "The conditions existing in the Lava Beds . . ."—Keith A. Murray, *The Modocs and Their War* (Norman: University of Oklahoma Press/The Civilization of the American Indian ser., 1969 repr. of orig. 1959 ed.), p. 313.

Entry for 1873: "Beginning with the depression of 1873 . . ."—Schlereth, p. 35.

Entry for 1874: Rejections of pan-Indian uprising—Ruby and Brown, p. 188.

Entry for 1874–75: "The Red River campaigns . . ."—Wooster, p. 69.

Entry for 1876: "By 1876 the Grant administration had all but collapsed . . ."—Utley, p. 152.

Entry for 1877: Lapwai councils—Aubrey L. Haines, p. 2.

Entry for 1877: Nimiipu casualties, according to Joseph: Pearson, p. 35.

Entry for 1877: Summation of war—Beal, p. 247.

Entry for 1877: Official poverty line—Schlereth, p. 34.

Entry for 1877–1937: Bellesiles, p. 254.

Entry for 1878: "By 1878, all the Native peoples . . ."—Trigger and Washburn, p. 22.

Entry for 1880: Hayes's report—D. S. Benson, *Presidents at War: A Survey of United States Warfare History in Presidential Sequence 1775–1980* (Chicago [printed by BookMasters, Inc., Mansfield, Ohio], 1996), report to Congress, December 1880.

Entry for 1883: Wild bison—*Handbook of North American Indians*, vol. 12, p. 307.

Entry for 1887: Shrinkage of Indian lands by 1934 due to the Dawes Act—Utley, p. 258.

Entry for 1890: Wounded Knee Massacre—Utley, p. 248.

Entry for 1894: Supposed last performance of Sun Dance—Humfreville, p. 333.

Entry for 1934: John Collier—Relander, p. 61.

Entry for 1960: Pearson, p. 17.

Entry for 1976: K. Ross Toole, *The Rape of the Great Plains: Northwest America, Cattle and Coal* (Boston: An Atlantic Monthly Press Book. Little, Brown & Co., 1976), p. 40.

Entry for 1995: Keegan, p. 5.

Glossaries

1. Personal Names

Lieutenant Bomus—Howard et al., p. 184 (Howard on Ebstein).

Lieutenant Boyle—Ibid., p. 36.

Bunched Lightning—McWhorter, *Yellow Wolf*, pp. 303–6.

Burning Coals—Ibid., p. 109.

Ad Chapman—McWhorter, *Hear Me*, p. 215; Howard, *Report—In the Field*, Appendix: "Officers and Enlisted Men Specially Commended . . . ," p. 45. The newspaper article on Perry's estimation of him—*Morning Oregonian* (Portland), vol. XVII.— no. 142, Friday, July 20, 1877. Nez Perce pronunciation of his name—Aoki, p. 842.

Crook—Crook, p. 16; Linderman, pp. 128–29, 138.

Custer—Keegan, p. 298; Linderman, pp. 128–29, 138.

Feathers Around The Neck—Pearson, p. 83.

Gibbon—Linderman, pp. 128–29, 138.

Good Woman—McWhorter, *Yellow Wolf*, final glossary [for He-yoom Yo-yik].

Grizzly Bear Youth—Howard et al., pp. 262, 266 (McDonald); McWhorter, *Hear Me*, p. 357 (Ugly Grizzly Bear Boy) and p. 417 (where the Camas Meadows dreamer is identified as Black Hair).

Hayes—Encomium in the *New York Sun*—Quoted in the *East Oregonian* (Pendleton), June 24, 1876. Twain's characterization—*The Autobiography of Mark Twain*, ed. Charles Neider (New York: Harper and Brothers, 1959, p. 303. "Many, if not most of our Indian wars . . ."—Benson, p. 402 (address of December 1877). Bruce's description—Op. cit., p. 85.

General Howard—Aoki, p. 979; Forczyk, p. 15; *New York Times:* Writers and reporters of the *New York Times, The Most Fearful Ordeal: Original Coverage of the Civil War* (New York: St. Martin's Press, 2004); Beal, p. 255; John A. Carpenter, pp. 267–68. For "the Indian Herder," see Howard et al., p. 242 (McDonald).

Captain John [and Old George]—McWhorter, p. 493. For the meaning of "Tsoka-y," see Aoki, p. 49.

Chief Joseph—Helen Addison Howard, p. 9; McWhorter, *Hear Me*, p. 178, fn. 15; Aoki, p. 155. For "In-mut-too-yah-lat-lat," see Howard et al., Part III.

Kate—See White Bird.

Lawyer—*Reports on the Aftermath of the 1863 Nez Perce Treaty . . .* , p. 1.

Lean Elk—Beal, p. 252.

Lemonade Lucy—Dee Brown, p. 211.

Looking-Glass—McWhorter, *Hear Me*, p. 183; and [for Grandfather Looking-Glass] Lewis and Clark, vol. 7, p. 207 (Clark, Sunday May 4th 1806). For "Big Hawk," see Howard et al., p. 223 (McDonald). His other names of "Black Swan" and "Wind-Wrapped" are given by Aoki, pp. 861 and 987.

Mrs. Manuel—McWhorter, *Hear Me*, p. 215.

Miles—Wooster, pp. 272–73.

Moorhouse—Description after a photo in Relander, insert 16, after p. 96 ("Pilgrimage to the Nation's Capital").

Old Joseph—Baird, Mallickan and Swagerty, p. xix; Aoki, p. 769. Whitman's praise of him—Hulbert and Hulbert, p. 112 (Marcus Whitman to Rev. David Greene, Secretary of the A.B.C.F.M., dated at Waiilatpu, Oregon Territory. July 22d. 1845).

Ollokot—McWhorter, *Yellow Wolf*, p. 36; Aoki, p. 967.

Peopeo Tholekt—Aoki, pp. 520, 552 (for "bird" and "crane-like bird").

Perry: Wood's claim about his timidity at Clearwater—*The Spectator* [Portland, Oregon], vol. XLVI, no. 5, Saturday, September 14, 1929, p. 23 (Charles Erskine Scott Wood, "Indian Epic is Re-told").

Qapqapó-nmay—Baird, Mallickan and Swagerty, p. xix.

Reuben: "Widely disliked."—Pearson, p. 228.

Sheridan—Ruby and Brown, p. 155.

Sherman—Michael Femman, *Citizen Sherman: A Life of William Tecumseh Sherman* (New York: Random House, 1995), p. 167 (April 11, 1864, writing to his brother John).

Shore Crossing—McWhorter, *Hear Me*, p. 186.

Sitting Bull—See citation for Sioux.

Sladen—Sladen, p. 111.

Smohalla—Relander, p. 67; Howard, *Famous Indian Chiefs*, pp. 332–33.

Sound Of Running Feet—McWhorter, *Yellow Wolf*, pp. 239, 288.

Springtime—McWhorter, *Yellow Wolf*, pp. 97, 320.

Sturgis—Beal, p. 257.

Tendoy—Warren L. d'Azevedo, ed. [this vol.], *Handbook of North American Indians*, vol. 11: Great Basin (Washington, D.C.: Smithsonian Institution, 1986), p. 290 (Robert F. Murphy and Yolanda Murphy, "Northern Shoshone and Bannock").

Three Feathers—McWhorter, *Hear Me*, p. 334.

Tilden—*Morning Oregonian* (Portland), vol. XVII.—no. 133, Tuesday, July 10, 1877.

Thunder Travelling to Loftier Heights—McWhorter, *Yellow Wolf*, p. 36.

Toohhoolhoolzote—Ibid., pp. 36, 320; Aoki, p. 792.

Tzi-kal-tza—McWhorter, *Hear Me*, p. 498 (for "Daytime Smoke").

The pattern sentences relating to Umatilla Jim—Ives Goddard, ed., *Handbook of North American Indians*, vol. 17: Languages (Washington, D.C.: Smithsonian Institution, 1996), p. 678 (Bruce Rigsby and Noel Rude, "Sketch of Sahaptin, a Sahaptian Language"). "This sketch is based primarily upon the Umatilla Sahaptin dialect" (ibid., p. 666).

Welweyas—McWhorter, *Hear Me*, p. 197; *Handbook of North American Indians*, vol. 12, p. 423 (Walker).

White Bird—McWhorter, *Yellow Wolf*, p. 36; *Hear Me*, p. 181; Greene, *Nez Perce Summer*, p. 489 n. 126 (Private Zimmer on the two wives, including Hiyom Tiyatehct).

White Thunder—Ibid., pp. 26–27.

Wilkinson—Crook, p. 169.

Wood—Tolman, p. 91.

Wounded Head—McWhorter, *Hear Me*, p. 204.

Yellow Bull—McWhorter, *Hear Me*, pp. 208, 254.

2. *Orders, Isms, Etc.*

ACBADADEA—Yellowtail, p. 211.

AHKUNKENEKOO—McWhorter, *Yellow Wolf*, p. 19.

AIR BIRD—Howard et al., p. 266 (McDonald).

Assiniboines—Kavanagh, p. 154.

Bannocks—Humfreville, p. 211; Sharon Malinowski and Anna Sheets, eds., *The Gale Encyclopedia of Native American Tribes*, vol. II: Great Basin, Southwest, Middle America (New York: Gale Research, Inc., 1998), pp. 7–9 (entry on Bannock by Christopher Tower); Warren L. d'Azevedo, ed. [this vol.], *Handbook of North American Indians*, vol. 11: Great Basin (Washington, D.C.: Smithsonian Institution, 1986), pp. 284–87 (Robert F. Murphy and Yolanda Murphy, "Northern Shoshone and Bannock"); and Michno, p. 7; Leforge, p. 155 ("Worthless Lodges").

Blackfeet—After Dempsey, p. ix; Nez Perce term (*Hayáyo*) from Aoki, p. 104; Alexander Henry's assessment from Utley, p. 22.

Bostons (as Chinook jargon)—Washington State University Libraries, Pullman. Holland Library Archives. Cage 3080. Wimpy, Mary Ann Sida Anderson, 1844–1948.

Cayuse—*Handbook of North American Indians*, vol. 12, pp. 395 and [for Weyíletpu] 417 (Theodore Stern, "Cayuse, Umatilla, and Walla Walla"); Humfreville, p. 290.

Cheyennes—McWhorter, *Hear Me*, p. 483 (for "Arrow Marks").

Crows—After Bradley, pp. 74–77, 83–84. An earlier source not too dissimilarly informs us that the Crow country lies through the Rocky Mountains, along the heads of the Powder, Wind and Big Horn rivers, along the south side of Yellowstone, as far as Laramie's Fork on the River Platte and sometimes on the west and north sides of that river as far as the head of the Musselshell and as far down as the mouth of the Yellowstone.—Edwin Thompson Denig, *Five Indian Tribes of the Upper Missouri: Sioux, Arickaras, Assiniboines, Crees, Crow*, ed. John C. Ewers (Norman: University of Oklahoma Press, The Civilization of the American Indian ser., vol. 59, 1961, wr. bef. 1858). "The Crows became mercenaries . . ."—Ruby and Brown, p. 185. "The Women Nation"—Howard et al., p. 224 (McDonald). For "Raven Enemy," *Handbook of Nothern American Indians*, vol. 13, part 2 of 2, p. 714 (Fred W. Voget, entry on Crow).

Downstream People—*Handbook of North American Indians*, vol. 12, p. 420 (Deward E. Walker, Jr., "Nez Perce"); Emily Greenwald, pp. 43–44; Baird, Mallickan and Swagerty, p. xix.

Enemy—Aoki, p. 768.

Flatheads—*Handbook of North American Indians*, vol. 12, p. 297 (Carling I. Malouf, "Flathead and Pend d'Oreille"). Shoshoni name for Flatheads: Lewis and Clark, vol. 8, p. 55, fn. 11.

Freedmen's Bureau—Humphreys: *The Annals of America*, vol. 9, p. 627 (no. 156, Benjamin G. Humphreys, address to the legislature of November 20, 1865); Grant: Ibid., p. 637 (no. 158, Ulysses S. Grant, report to the President, December 18, 1865); DuBois: *The Atlantic Presents The Civil War*, p. 124 (W. E. B. DuBois, "The Freedmen's Bureau," 1901).

Gros Ventres—Raymond J. DeMallie, ed. [this part-vol.], *Handbook of Northern American Indians*, vol. 13, part 2 of 2: Plains (Washington, D.C.: Smithsonian Institution, 2001), pp. 677–82 (Loretta Fowler and Regina Flannery, "Gros Ventre"); Paterek, p. 96, Greene, *Nez Perce Summer*, p. 259 (for "Atsinas").

Indian Agent—National Archives microfilm M1121, Roll 5: Miscellaneous Circulars, 1854–1885. Department of the Interior, Office of Indian Affairs, Accounts, Circular No. 10, Washington, March 1, 1878. The civilized pursuits included plowing, fencing, railsplitting, haycutting, harvesting, and gathering crops, some for the benefit of settlers.

Klamaths—Victor Golla, *Californian Indian Languages* (Berkeley: University of California Press, 2011), pp. 133–36.

Lemhis—McWhorter, *Yellow Wolf*, p. 206 fn.; Virginia Cole Trenholm and Maurine Carley, *The Shoshonis: Sentinels of the Rockies* (Norman: University of Oklahoma Press, The Civilization of the American Indian ser., no. 74, 1964), p. 151.

Modocs—Golla, pp. 133–36.

Nami Piap—Relander, p. 306.

Negroes—Elizabeth Custer, pp. 227–28.

Nez Perces (as defined by Indian Agent Cain)—Baird, Mallickan and Swagerty, p. 37. The meaning of "pu" in "Nimiipu" appears in Aoki, p. 489. Bannock definition (the Cous Eaters)—*Handbook of Northern American Indians*, vol. 12, p. 438 (Deward E. Walker, Jr., entry on Nez Perce). For Crow and Lakota words, same vol., p. 419 (Theodore Stern, "Cayuse, Umatilla, and Walla Walla"), and pp. 437–38 (Deward Walker, Jr.); for "Paddles" see Spinden, p. 172, fn. 1. Wood's derivation of "Te-taw-ken" appears in Venn, p. 39. "Kammooenem" comes from McWhorter, *Hear Me*, p. 177, fn. 14. I have slightly emended the definition in the interest of what strikes me, at least, as common sense.

Palouse—Wilfong, p. 34; McWhorter, *Yellow Wolf*, p. 36.

She Who Watches—Leighton, pp. 44–45.

Shoshoni—Language information is from Golla, p. 175.

Sioux—Information on layout of camp is from Greene, *Beyond Bear's Paw*, pp. 86–87.

Snakes—After Zucker, Jummel and Høgfoss, pp. 11–12; Humfreville, pp. 207–8; Michno, p. 9; *Hand-*

book of North American Indians, vol. 11, pp. 284–87 (Robert F. Murphy and Yolanda Murphy, "Northern Shoshone and Bannock").

Tiwata-át; tiwét—Aoki, p. 768.

Umatilla—*Handbook of Northern American Indians,* vol. 12, p. 395.

Volunteers—*Morning Oregonian,* vol. XVII.—no. 145, Monday, July 23, 1877, unnumbered p. [since this copy damaged].

Wanapums—Relander, p. 306.

WOWSHUXLUH—Relander, p. 72.

WYAKIN—McWhorter, *Yellow Wolf,* pp. 295–300.

3. Places

Ah-ki-ne-kun-scoo—Central Montana Museum, Lewistown.

Asotin—McWhorter, *Yellow Wolf,* p. 37.

BEAR SNEAKING UP—Aoki, p. 696.

Buffalo Country—Marcy, p. 234; McWhorter, *Yellow Wolf,* p. 62.

Clark's Fork—Linderman, pp. 129–30.

Clearwater—Gulick, p. 23 (for "Koos-koos-kee").

Crossing Place—Aoki, p. 872.

Dark Green Place—Aoki, p. 504.

Eewhatam—McWhorter, *Hear Me,* p. 176.

Fish Trap Place—McWhorter, *Yellow Wolf,* p. 65.

Fort Buford—Trobriand, p. 17.

Fort Lapwai, Portland, Tongue River—National Archives. National Archives and Records Service. General Services Administration. Washington: 1966. National Archives Microfilm Microcopy 661 (8 rolls). Historical Information in Relation to Military Forts and Other Installations *ca.* 1700–1900, "part of the records of the Adjutant General's Office, 1870's–1917, Record Group 94." Lapwai: Roll 4 (Volumes I–L). Portland: Roll 6 (O–P). Tongue River: Roll 7 (S–T).

GHOST's TRAIL—Aoki, p. 67.

Gorge Place—Aoki, p. 623.

Grande Ronde—Aoki, p. 852.

Greasy River—Thomas B. Marquis, comp., *Cheyenne and Sioux: The Reminiscences of Four Indians and a White Soldier,* ed. Ronald B. Limbaugh (Stockton, California: Pacific Center for Western Historical Studies, University of the Pacific, Monograph Number Three, 1973), p. 13 ("Iron Teeth, A Cheyenne Old Woman").

Indian Territory—Howard, *Among Our Hostile Indians,* p. 99; Greenwald, p. 17.

Izhkumzizlalkik—McWhorter, *Hear Me,* p. 368.

Kamiah—McWhorter, *Yellow Wolf,* p. 102 fn.

Lalac—Relander, p. 306.

Lochsa River—Aoki, p. 311.

Lo Lo Trail—McWhorter, *Hear Me,* p. 343, fn. 1. Lewis and Clark, vol. 8, p. 55 (note by Moulton[?]). Chinook meaning of "Lo Lo"—Gulick, p. 4.

The Low Place; LOW PERSONS—Somewhat after Aoki, p. 990.

Meadow Camp—McWhorter, *Hear Me,* p. 344.

Meadow Place—Aoki, p. 730. If you go there now, you will see a barn with a hole in its wall, a cattail pond surrounded by cows, an empty house and many fields.

Medicine Line—Greene, *Beyond Bear's Paw,* p. 15.

Missouri River—McWhorter, *Yellow Wolf,* p. 198.

Modoc Lava Beds—Murray, p. 110.

MONSTER-Udder Place—Aoki, p. 569.

Mount Misery: Possossona—McWhorter, *Hear Me,* p. 295.

Narrow Solid Rock Pass—McWhorter, *Yellow Wolf,* p. 26.

Night-Fishing Place—Aoki, p. 718.

O-pumohat Kyai-is-i-sak-ta and O-to-kur-tuk-tai—Central Montana Museum, Lewistown.

Old Woman Place—Aoki, p. 980.

Oro Fino—Wikoff, p. 7; Peopeo Tholekt/Sam Lott, p. 10.

Place Like Split Rock—Greene, *Beyond Bear's Paw,* p. 228.

Rawhide Place—Aoki, p. 551.

Ripple Place—Aoki, p. 459.

The SAYAK STARS—Aoki, p. 628.
Simí-nekem and Snake River—Baird, Mallickan and Swagerty, p. xvii.
Snake River—Gulick, p. 23 ("Ki-moo-e-nim"); McWhorter, *Yellow Wolf*, final glossary.
Soaring Up Like Birds—Relander, p. 306.
Split Rock—McWhorter, *Yellow Wolf*, pp. 41, 52; *Hear Me*, p. 176.
Sunflower Place—Aoki, p. 510.
Sweat Lodge Place—Aoki, p. 988.
Three Sisters—Aoki, p. 451.
Tipsusleimah—McWhorter, *Hear Me*, p. 196.
Tongue Water—McWhorter, *Yellow Wolf*, p. 26.
Wallowa: Words of Governor Grover—Murray, p. 314.
Wallula—Relander, pp. 287, 290.
Weippe—McWhorter, *Yellow Wolf*, p. 320; Howard et al., p. 245 (McDonald).
White Bird Canyon—Aoki, p. 306; McWhorter, *Yellow Wolf*, p. 50.
White Soil—Wilfong, p. 29.
Yellow Stone River—Linderman, pp. 129–30; McWhorter, *Yellow Wolf*, p. 318.

4. Texts

Forczyk—*Nez Perce 1877*, pp. 9, 37.
Howard, *Nez Perce Joseph*—Aubrey L. Haines, p. viii.
McWhorter, *Hear Me*—Op. cit., pp. 207–8; Aubrey L. Haines, p. ix.
Pearson—*The Nez Perces in the Indian Territory*, p. 32.

5. Calendars, Etc.

Buffalo Calf Season—Aoki, p. 963.
Cous Cake Season—Aoki, p. 973.
Eel Season—Slightly simplified from Spinden, p. 237.
False Flowering Time—Aoki, p. 448.
Indian policy—Wetmore and Grey, p. 284.
Reveille, tattoo and other divisions of army time—After Agnew, p. 140; with various information from Bradley.
River Season—Somewhat after Aoki, p. 537.
Salmon Spawning Season—Somewhat after Aoki, p. 836.
Sapalwit—McWhorter, *Yellow Wolf*, p. 38.

6. General

Áhaha—Aoki, p. 962.
Aparejo—Zimmer, pp. 82–83 (20th [July]).
Barefoot whiskey—Whitman, p. 1168.
Blackfoot rum—Utley, p. 22.
Camas and spatlam—Leighton, p. 39.
Chá-á—Altered from Lewis and Clark, vol. 5, p. 217 (Lewis, Friday September 20th 1805).
Cous—Lewis and Clark, vol. 7, p. 234 (Lewis, Friday May 9th 1806); p. 239 (Saturday May 10th 1806).
Crease—Humfreville, p. 431.
Gangue mineral—Ernest A. Smith, p. 590.
Getting-drunk liquid—Slightly modified from Aoki, p. 581.
German silver—Koch, p. 71.
Í-tsitsitsititsits—Aoki, p. 1007.
Khattát—Aoki, p. 918.
Kinnikinnick—Crow usage: Leforge, p. 161.
Kíw—Aoki, p. 1269.
Kloochman—Washington State University Libraries, Pullman. Holland Library Archives. Cage 3080. Wimpy, Mary Ann Sida Anderson, 1844–1948.
Mokh—Aoki, p. 457.
Pokát—Aoki, p. 555.
Qáw—Aoki, p. 1270.
Qiqaw—Aoki, p. 611.

Qoh—McWhorter, *Yellow Wolf,* p. 55.

Reservation—Wood diary 1878, p. 15; *Executive Orders Relating to Indian Reservations,* p. 147 (ORE-GON, GRANDE RONDE RESERVATION. Executive Office, Washington City, June 30, 1857).

Rocky Mountain fever—Humfreville, p. 412.

Shikèmnúvit—From a display seen at the Tamastlikit Museum, Umatilla reservation, Oregon, August 2009.

Shlap—Aoki, p. 1269.

Sibley tent—Katcher, p. 99.

Side-lining—Humfreville, p. 180.

Silk buffalo robe—Bond ms., p. 4 fn.

Stick game—Lewis and Clark, vol. 5, pp. 137–38.

Taq—Aoki, p. 809.

Tekh—Aoki, p. 814.

Timm—Aoki, p. 815.

Titálin—Aoki, p. 815.

Tiyé-pu—Aoki, p. 776.

"Wakesh nun pakilauitin . . ."—Axtell, Hymn No. 1 (no title).

Wá-wa—Aoki, p. 834.

Wind's tears—Aoki, p. 987.

Wittco Weeon—Larpenteur, vol. 2, p. 397.

Note on English Orthography: "Their the Bravest General of Modder times met his death."—Coleman, p. 21.

Sources

Epigraph: "I think explanations and defenses are bad things."—Quoted in Bellesiles, p. 28.

Erskine Wood's "Pleasunte and Wittie Worke . . ."—Oregon Historical Society. MSS 2445.

Maps (Throughout)

Locator Map of Wallowa—After *Handbook of North American Indians,* vol. 4, p. 172, fig. 5 (Robert Utley, "Indian-United States Military Situation, 1848–1891"), for Fort Shaw.

Military Departments, Western U.S.A./Northeast Corner of Indian Territory—After *Handbook of North American Indians,* loc. cit.; Gulick, map on p. 281 (for Coville); information in Greene, *Nez Perce Summer;* Berthrong, map on pp. 14–15.

Some Places Where the People Lived . . . and How the Bostons Mapped Them—After Aoki's dictionary (most river names, altered by me as described for each in the Glossary of Places); Aoki and Walker, map facing Part I.

The Howards in Leeds, *ca.* 1873—Rough-traced, simplified and embellished from original 1873 map entitled "LEEDS, Scale 2 Inches to the Mile." I purchased this in an antiquarian book and print establishment in Maine. The map is matted and sealed, so that the names, if any, of publisher and printer are obscured.

The Shrinking Reservation—Deward Walker, Jr., *Conflict and Schism in Nez Perce Acculturation: A Study of Religion and Politics* (Moscow: University of Idaho Press, 1985, p. 47); Walker and Aoki, map facing Part I ("The Nez Perce Homeland and Their Neighbors"); Gulick, various maps incl. pp. 110, 150, 1st p. of ch. 27.

Some Indian Languages and Language Families (simplified)—Much simplified indeed, from *Handbook of North American Indians,* vol. 17, back cover pocket map (Ives Goddard, "Native Languages and Native Families of North America").

CAPTIONS

ACKNOWLEDGMENTS

First and foremost I would like to thank my companions on the Nez Perce Trail: my late father, who took me on hair-raising roads and walked a couple of battle-fields with me; my old buddy William Linne, with whom I visited Chief Joseph's grave at Nespelem; my dear friend Katie Peterson, thanks to whom I first saw the route from Lolo to Big Hole to Henry's Lake; and Teresa McFarland, who not only drove me through ever so many Western landscapes and got up before dawn on a number of occasions so that I could write about this or that at such and such a time, but also gave me Hayes's *Historical Atlas of the American West,* made Nez Perce transliterations, simplified Aoki's orthography for the general reader and proofread the first draft of the manuscript. All four of these fine people did an awful lot for my benefit. I think the Trail spoke to each of them in a different way. I could not have written this book without their patient, loving help.

Janis Heple lent me a memoir about Elk City, where her ancestors once lived. Virginia Conte gave me much information about horses.

Joe Williams, owner of The Gun Works in Eugene, Oregon, let me shoot a vintage trapdoor Springfield. His friend David Hascall, an expert hunter and shooter who made this experience possible, fired this rifle with me (and, unlike me, mostly hit the target). David's pretty wife Barbara uprooted stalks of camas from the yard for my edification; one resulting silhouette is reproduced in this book. Thank you all.

My daughter Lisa gave me Davis and Wiley's *Civil War: A Complete Photographic History,* whose photographs I drew on several times, as shown in the Source-Notes.

My friend Tom Robinson, who appears in this book as a character, sent me articles, scanned some old photos and taught me much about the images at the Oregon Historical Society—which is a wonderful institution where I have spent many happy hours over the last decade. Jennifer Kaiser, Scott Daniels, Susan Seyl and several other helpful people went beyond the call of duty for me.

Likewise, I am very grateful to the Holland Library at Washington State University in Pullman. I send my special thanks to Pat Mueller, who gave me the thrill of seeing Peopeo Tholekt's original drawings.

The best single source of General Howard's papers is his old alma mater, Bowdoin College. In the couple of days I was able to spend there, my understanding of the man and his family, friends, enemies and hangers-on was vastly enlarged. It was a moving experience to take into my own hands a consolatory letter to him from none other than Sojourner Truth.

I am also much indebted to the kind people at the Idaho Historical Society (aka the Idaho State Archives and Research Center) in Boise, where I got to read George Shearer's letters and other fascinating documents; to the Public Archives at Butte,

Montana, where I was able to handle the original numbers of *The Butte Miner* and *The New North-West;* the Montana State Historical Society Archives in Helena—a fabulous source of photographs, not to mention James Bradley's letters; the Oregon Secretary of State Archives Division in Salem, the Bozeman Public Library (Montana Room) and (the place I went most often) the Bancroft Library in Berkeley, where wonderful, intelligent people gave me access to Howard's field reports, *Adventures in Geyserland*, and any number of other sources.

I am grateful to my agent, Susan Golomb, and to her two patient assistants, Krista Ingebretson and Soumeya Bendimerad. My appreciations, ladies.

Let me now thank my publisher, Viking, for having borne with me on all the Seven Dreams thus far. My friend and editor, Paul Slovak, has not always had an easy time with this stubborn, uncommercially-minded author. I am sure my next book will be shorter—much shorter, perhaps, if I get fired for having written this one. My copy editor, Maureen Sugden, has once again saved me from myself, overcoming semi-invisible yet nightmarish inconsistencies with brave thrusts of her red pen. Without her, terrible idiocies would have been perpetrated. Maureen, please consider me your grateful friend. Nancy Resnick, my new designer, has done much beautiful, patient work. I am thrilled with the look of the type and its many sweet indentations—whose convolutions required a toilsome coding system, invented by Matt Giarratano and completed by Jane Cavolina. Three proofreaders, Bitite Vinklers, Adam Goldberger, and Roland Ottewell, took the trouble to read this long book against copy, not only for consistency but also for sense, thereby repairing several more inconsistencies. Bruce Giffords, the senior production editor, is a scuba diver who recently swam around in a tank of giant and probably hungry fish. I imagine his descent into this book's dark cold typographical nightmare as having required a great deal of oxygen and maybe some spear-fishing apparatus. Thank you, Bruce.

My father on the Nez Perce trail